THE AMERICANS
A Social History of the United States
1587–1914

Other books by J. C. Furnas

Nonfiction

ANATOMY OF PARADISE
VOYAGE TO WINDWARD
GOODBYE TO UNCLE TOM
THE ROAD TO HARPERS FERRY
THE LIFE AND TIMES OF THE LATE DEMON RUM

Novels

THE PROPHET'S CHAMBER
MANY PEOPLE PRIZE IT
THE DEVIL'S RAINBOW
LIGHTFOOT ISLAND

The Americans

A SOCIAL HISTORY OF THE UNITED STATES

1587–1914

Joseph Chamberlain

by J. C. Furnas, 1905-

G. P. Putnam's Sons   New York

Copyright © 1969 by J. C. Furnas

Library of Congress Catalog Card Number: 69-16082

PRINTED IN THE UNITED STATES OF AMERICA

For her without whom . . .

Acknowledgments

T HIS book is indebted for research facilities first and foremost to the Princeton University Library; then to the New York Public Library and the New York Society Library. Among those helpfully answering specific inquiries have been the Merrimack Valley Textile Museum; Plimoth Plantation; Colonial Williamsburg; Trinity Parish; The International Ladies' Garment Workers' Union; the Chemical Bank-New York Trust Company; the Erie-Lackawanna Railroad Company; the Florida East Coast Railway Company; Stokely-Van Camp, Inc.; the Chamber of Commerce of Pendleton, Oregon; Lafayette University; the National Geographic Society; the American Geographic Society; the U.S. Department of Agriculture; the Texas State Department of Agriculture; the *Christian Advocate/Together*. . . . Individuals kindly supplying requested information include John Ely Burchard, Elizabeth Burton, Abbott L. Cummings, Millia Davenport, Clark Kinnaird, Helen Waite Papashvily, Dorothy Stickney . . . and dozens of others. Marjorie Lawrence Street has given the text the benefit of her skilled eye. Willard Starks' technical prowess in photography has brought out the best in many of the illustrative items. Sandy Huffaker's drawings have made gratifying most of the author's crude snapshots of architectural specimens.

The author is also obliged to Walter Minton of G. P. Putnam's Sons for suggesting this project, which otherwise would never have occurred to him, and to Harvey Ginsberg of the same firm for being so considerate a midwife.

Introduction

THE formula guiding this book was stated a generation ago by G. M. Trevelyan: "History with the politics left out." Completely to leave the politics out of history is, of course, impossible. But deliberately to scamp politics wherever possible allows concentration on people—who Americans were, what they were doing and sometimes why, where they were going and how, what they ate, drank, wore, hoped. . . . And on things—covered bridges and flasks of whiskey, canalboats and the Morgan horse. The writer plans informally to explore what lay behind the United States of America into which he was born in the days when Theodore Roosevelt was President and boys wore knickerbockers and high-laced shoes.

The accounting begins, as it must, with men from the Old World trying to effect useful lodgment on the coast of North America in the 1500's. It ends in 1914 when World War I was foisting worldwide significance on a nation reluctant to assume worldwide responsibility. The sharp break with the past that occurred then was more political than cultural. But in themselves the cultural consequences made up a striking watershed. Thenceforward quite another story was to be told. We know how the first one came out. We are still living in the second.

Nobody is really qualified to write such a book. The writer's inadequate preparation has consisted of being a reader-observer-reporter in many contexts, learning in order to write and writing to clarify what was learned, handling assignments for more than thirty-five years in all but five of the fifty states and in several farther parts of the world, sometimes handling at book length crucial aspects of America's past. He has a conviction that in addition to many years in libraries and among other sources of data, what he has seen and learned in Europe, Africa, the South Seas and Down Under, the West Indies and elsewhere has helped him greatly—if indirectly and sometimes indefinably—in this account of his countrymen's national past.

9

Those well versed in Americana will recognize that this text frequently uses, in addition to customary kinds of source material, cultural data drawn from novels, short stories and plays. Historical novels are, however, largely eschewed. There is invaluable actuality in background used by writers of fiction set in their own times, accepted between writer and reader as immediately familiar and appropriate. Thus, when you read in *Swallow Barn* that the fields of Tidewater, Virginia, *c.* 1850 had "worm-fences of shrunken chestnut" and the local crossroads store sold "queens-ware, rattraps, tin kettles, hats, fiddles, shoes, calicoes, cheese, sugar, all-spice, jack-knives and jewsharps," you have unimpeachable testimony. But no matter how earnest the historical novelist's research, his references and stage props are not evidence; he wasn't there.

No such book as this can be intelligible without making broad statements. The reader will please do the writer the favor mentally to interpolate, every third line or so, phrases like *by and large, on the whole, with predictable exceptions.* Those and others are already occasionally in place as reminders or where particularly necessary. Were they included wherever at all indicated, the book would be half again its present length.

Footnotes are largely, though not altogether, confined to definitions. The reference numbers throughout the body text will be found to identify the sources of quotations, massed at the back of the book, section by section. Illustrations are, with a very few exceptions, pretty much contemporary with the data illustrated.

Contents

Prologue

IN the 1930's a small theater on Union Square, New York City, specialized in Russian propaganda movies. Outside, a striking barker, a swarthy-ruddy man with lank black hair, exhorted passersby to step right in and view the glories of the October Revolution. I asked about him.

"Full-blooded American Indian," the manager said. "When they give him that 'Why don't you go back where you came from?' routine, he has the right answer."

Right indeed, but only relatively so. Historically even that Communist Indian had somewhere he came from. Quite as much as the white Americans of whom Franklin D. Roosevelt spoke so woundingly to the Daughters of the American Revolution, Indians are "all descended from immigrants." Certain thousands of years ago some of their ancestors crossing from Asia into Alaska by the Bering Strait (or an isthmus once there) must have found themselves immigrants—interlopers regarded most unfavorably by other proto-Indians already in possession. The mingled progeny of such successive waves of Asian pioneers are thought to have fanned out generation after generation to create those showy cultures in Central and South America and (after a fashion) to populate the extremes of the continent in Labrador, Florida and Patagonia. This book touches on Indians, however, only as their things, deeds and ways-of-doing —most notably their victuals—affected the later white interlopers from eastward. Though consistently exerting influences, like the westerly winds and the hot summers, Indians were only one of many New World forces shaping the progeny of the Old World invaders of America.

America in this book usually means the sum of persons, ways-of-doing, things, and terrain that became the United States in 1787 and then developed, in some respects degenerated, in others matured, into the nation of our recent past. The name is a notoriously poor fit. Amerigo Vespucci, whom it honors, was an able navigator, but his voyages examining South America hardly entitle him to a hemispherical memorial. *The United*

13

States of America is discourteous to the United States of Mexico and the United States of Brazil, which acquired that style by early, ill-advised imitation of our newborn Federal Constitution. The alternative of saying only *the* United States is even worse. Had our Founding Fathers been tactful and accurate, they would have fallen on something like Immigrantia or Outlandersland or, more functionally, Land of Try Again. At least those would have embodied the context in which the ancestors of Americans* arrived at the dignity of being such.

That word *ancestor* has a flavor of coziness, a sense of belonging far away and long ago, of security and venerable memories shared. Actually, the more remote the ancestor, the less sense in that particular nostalgia. To us the first settlers from the Old World would have seemed outlandish indeed. Three and a half centuries have effected great changes in what Western man expects of himself. A sardonic antiquarian of Knickerbocker descent once told a historical association that most of the early Dutch settlers around Esopus (now Kingston, New York), "could neither read nor write . . . a wild, uncouth, rough and most of the time a drunken crowd . . . dressed in skins . . . not far removed from the wild Indians about them. If [they] this moment were to enter this room every man here present who boasts of his Dutch descent . . . would make a wild dash for the door . . . squawking in terror." [1]

Some of that came of the general uncouthness of the postmedieval Europe that reared them. Some of it probably reflected the particular personal vicissitudes that had sent these individual specimens of Western man and not others to the New World. The rest was the result of immersing such transplanted persons in a strange environment that necessarily led to some rapid and some delayed reactions. The same considerations would apply, in the different terms appropriate to each, to every other cluster of early settlers from Maine to Georgia. Barring the language—and even there you would encounter dismaying changes in pronunciation and vocabulary—you would have felt hardly more at home in Jamestown in 1608 than in an Indian pueblo in A.D. 1400. John Smith's men, or some of them, may have been among your ancestors, but they were not your people.

To establish that does not, however, imply the other extreme of vital alienation from them. They were not your people, yet in terms of their own day they were people, and when you pricked them, they did bleed. Many wore knee breeches, as we do not. But their reasons for doing so were the same as ours in donning trousers, and like all men, they got into them one leg at a time.

* In this book Americans will mean persons of Old World origin coming to North America's original Thirteen Colonies and considering themselves committed to them; or the resident descendants of those and later Old World immigrants.

I

The Big Water and the Big Woods

JOHN SMITH'S AMERICA

I

LAND HO! The New World!

The sea-weary lookout who raised the cry of "Land ho!" as prelude to founding any given Colony* was probably a stubby little fellow. The size of his armor, the height of his doorways, make it clear that the postmedieval European who manned early vessels America-bound—Spanish, French, English, Dutch or Swedish—was almost dwarfish by our notions. If he sailed before the mast, he was probably illiterate. Inevitably he was undernourished, for the ship's provisions of the time, scanty at best, had necessarily deteriorated during a voyage of some months and in any case reflected utter ignorance of the still-unborn science of nutrition.

The blur on the horizon that caused him to sing out was probably as ambiguous as most landfalls. As it gained definition, what he and his shipmates saw might be a rocky headland or, farther south, lowland behind long beaches. Headlands and beaches, however infested with summer resorts, are still there. The great woods growing thick to the margins of coves and rivers are gone. Yet 300 years ago Governors Island, now in the shadow of the skyscrapers of downtown New York City, was so dominated by great walnuts and hickories that the Dutch called it Nut Island.

Those imposing trees were basic shapers of America. For 1,000 miles north to south and westward over an area as large as Roman Europe, they made up a majestic "climax forest" that looked as if it would cumber the earth forever. Its shade was ponderously gloomy, its sun-drenched tops made an undulating ocean of leaves and twigs 70 to 80 feet above ground level. They said a squirrel could travel tree to tree from the Ohio River to Lake Erie by overarching boughs enabling him to disregard streams. By choosing his route well, he could have done the same from the Hudson to Niagara Falls and from Harpers Ferry to Muscle Shoals.

* Colony thus capitalized will mean any or all of the Thirteen at any stage up to 1783. Colonist will mean anybody considering himself settled in any Colony up to that date.

17

Hardwoods prevailed here, conifers there, depending on soil and climate. Underfoot was hardwood duff or fallen needles or standing swamp water. Even the brackish Hackensack Meadows of New Jersey, now a mere desert of reeds in areas where industry is still absent, once had a stand of white cedar. Where the hardwood gentry—oak, hickory, sugar maple, walnut, chestnut, tulip poplar, basswood, cherry—grew tallest, the settler knew the land was richest and lusted after its fertility while dreading the drudgery of clearing it. In its time southern Ohio had myriads of white oaks measuring more than 14 feet around and 70-odd to the nearest branch; there is authentic record of one such forest-grown patriarch 34 feet around the butt. Cottonwoods along the Ohio and Mississippi supplied logs for dugout canoes of 4-foot beam and 60-foot length. Many a great sycamore—largest deciduous tree of the American forest—so flourished that after age and decay had hollowed it, a shelter-needy pioneer family could spend the night therein, after ousting the resident black bear. One such in Ross County, Ohio, was used as a two-horse stable; nearby was a wild grapevine, 16 feet around near the ground, that had three branches each 8 feet in girth and cut up into eight cords of firewood when finally destroyed.

Few such primeval giants have survived fire, ax and disease. One striking fragment remains in Mettler's Woods, in New Jersey, 30 miles from the Empire State Building. There, among power lines, munitions depots and the effluvia of chemical plants, white oaks mast-tall and hogshead-thick still cluster together. They were probably there when Verrazano ventured into the nearby estuary of the Hudson and so got the world's longest suspension bridge named after him. They were as much our Founding Fathers as anybody in knee breeches with a quill pen in his hand. They are also more august than any man, even George Washington, who knew their likes well along the upper Ohio, could possibly manage to be.

Yet the great forest was not continuous. There were scrubby or grassy barrens in upcountry North Carolina and Maryland and in central Long Island; the English taking over from the Dutch in the 1660's utilized part of the last, now the site of Garden City, for what seems to have been the first horse race ever held in America. The summits of the White Mountains and the Great Smokies, well above timberline, were bare. The farther one went beyond the Appalachians, the more frequent and wider the prairies (the French explorers' word, of course): "beautiful natural Meadows, covered with wild Rye, blue Grass, and Clover, [abounding] with Turkeys, Deer, Elks, and . . . particularly Buffaloes," [1] such as Christopher Gist, first articulate observer of the Ohio country, reported in the mid-1700's. A large prairie was too wide to see across. In the "oak openings" of southern Michigan, mighty burr oaks stood ranged as if in a nobleman's park with so little underbrush that wagons could be driven among them through lush grass four feet high.

Gist thought the unforested stretches "natural." No doubt some were: The open mucklands of Ohio and Michigan, for instance, may have been dwindling relics of the drying up of old lake bottoms. But the relative tree-lessness of most barrens, prairies, meadows—whatever the local term—came of the destructiveness of mammals, four- or two-legged. Thus beaver building more and more dams to leave more standing water to kill more trees—and incidentally favor swamp grasses—created the marshy prairies around where Detroit now stands. The lack of underbrush in the oak openings reflected the Indians' custom of firing the woods either to round up game for mass slaughter or to keep visibility good for hunters. Where such deliberate fires killed the trees the consequent open prairie attracted grazing and browsing animals, notably deer and buffalo, that nibbled and trampled down trees trying to get started again. North Carolinians noted that once the local buffalo were killed off for pelts and tongues, the open spaces, previously all cane and wild pea, drifted back to forest. In Kentucky, oak and hickory vigorously took over when the local barrens were spared fire for a few years. Alliance of man and beast kept treeless for long periods the cornfields that the Indians cleared around their semipermanent villages and then abandoned as fertility slacked off. East of the mountains such old fields readily reforested because buffalo had not yet penetrated the Atlantic slope north of the James. But the persistence of prairies in the Ohio Basin warned the forest that Four Legs and Two Legs in inadvertent cahoots were foes to watch. The inadequate weapons of fire and stone tools had enabled red men to make great scars in the woods. Now came white men with metal tools.

The westerly winds that dominate the upper North Atlantic usually afforded sailing ships good passages from America to Europe. They made the reverse passage, east to west, correspondingly arduous—a problem never solved till steam arrived. The Cabots, who had some sort of look at northeastern North America in 1498, probably crossed in the high latitudes of Labrador—which implies bucking the westerlies for some 1,500 miles—and came southward down the coast helped by the Arctic Current. Verrazano followed Columbus' lead: southward from Europe to the verge of the tropics to catch the northeast trade winds across to the West Indies; then up the northeastward-trending American coast helped by the Gulf Stream and westerly breezes; then home in the high latitudes on the westerlies. That loosely circular route follows the great intercontinental eddy of winds and currents of which the Gulf Stream is the mainspring and the Sargasso Sea the sluggish center and which for too many weeks each year swirls the steamy climate of the Caribbean up along the Atlantic seaboard into New England.

Verrazano's way was far longer than the Cabots' in miles but not necessarily so in days. The original *Mayflower* took sixty-six days on the upper North Atlantic course. *Mayflower II*, the replica that crossed under sail some years ago, took only fifty-odd on the Verrazano route. The Colony-founders used both, depending on time of year, destination and

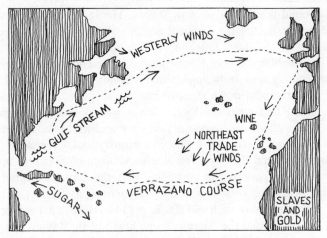

The great eddy of winds and currents that did so much to shape American culture.

personal judgment. By and large in early times the longer way was preferred because it minimized the ordeal (hard on ships, harder on men) of endless beating to windward. John Winthrop's *Arbella* had fair luck with a modified version of straight across in 1630. A generation later the Swedes were still running down to the Canaries, over to the West Indies, up to the Capes of the Delaware.

Such matters of wind and course are not merely technical. They left marks on America. Why did the Founding Fathers drink so much Madeira wine? Because they liked it, no doubt; but also because Madeira belonged to Portugal, England's politico-economic ally, and lay just where her wines made handy cargo for America-bound ships. Why did Negro slavery bulk larger in the Southern Colonies? Because, for one reason among a possible several, ships using Verrazano's route made Southern ports sooner than they did Northern ones. Why was mortality so hideously high among immigrants to America in the 1600's? Partly because of callous negligence, but also because neither route was a reasonably expeditious way to cross from Europe. Anything under a month was thought very good. Seven to ten weeks was practical expectation.

The arriving newcomers usually found good harbors. From the St. Johns River in Florida to Halifax in Nova Scotia the eastern seaboard, more hospitable than the western, offers a noble choice of natural havens, mostly estuaries of large rivers, now the sites of Jacksonville, Savannah, Charleston, Wilmington (North Carolina), Norfolk, Baltimore, Wilmington (Delaware), Philadelphia, New York City, Newport, Providence (though Narragansett Bay has been strangely neglected of late), Boston, Portsmouth, Portland. To keep them fit for modern deep-draft ships takes dredging. But in the 1600's drafts were shallow, for ships were small— relatively even smaller than the men who sailed them, as the replicas now

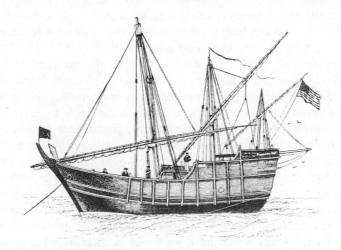

Many of the ships in which seventeenth-century emigrants came to America were no larger than this full-scale reconstruction of Columbus' Nina shown at the Chicago Columbian Exposition in 1893.

at Jamestown show. A diagram at Roanoke Island demonstrates that the typical Elizabethan pinnace that often crossed the Atlantic as consort of Colony-founding vessels could fit into a modern 50-foot lifeboat. The *Sparrowhawk*, fetching several score to Virginia in 1623, when she was wrecked on Cape Cod and left her bones for archeologists to pick, was only 28 feet in the keel, with a 12-foot beam.

* * *

The New World visible over the bulwarks of these decked-over walnut shells was neither actually nor potentially the same as the Old Country. Even now that the great woods are gone there is little European about it, to the dismay of certain kinds of foreigners—and Miniver Cheevy. Men landing north of the Chesapeake found winters colder than at home. Everywhere summers were much hotter. Wise men have suggested that this wide range of temperatures was what made Americans restless and so sharp at business. It sounds good until one reflects that at that rate North Dakotans would be sharper than Marylanders, which hardly holds water.

Colonists arriving in warm weather found many novelties. Fresh from the fetid towns of Europe, they brought their own flies, lice, fleas, bedbugs, mice and rats. But nothing at home prepared them for the quasi-tropical profusion of American insect life—the onslaughts of mosquitoes, blackflies and chiggers; the deafening evening shouting match among locusts, crickets and, as fall approached, katydids. "From the slight chirping of a few grasshoppers or crickets in England," wrote a British visitor in 1819, "no one can have a conception of the noise of a summer night here . . . very unpleasant to ears unaccustomed to it." [2] The katydids' yelps, proverbially predicting six weeks to frost, also presaged the implausibly vivid colors of the northeastern deciduous autumnal forest, likewise far louder than anything Europe had in its line. Among the unfamiliar hazards were skunks, feelingly named *enfants du diable* by early Frenchmen; the dismaying astringency of underripe persimmons, which, as John Smith warned, "drawe a man's mouth awrye with much torment";[3] and the peculiar dangers of such unfamiliar snakes as rattlers. Since they had not yet had time to work up a sensitivity, few can have been bothered by poison ivy at first. But Jimsonweed was rife in Tidewater Virginia, and heedless newcomers who boiled and ate the young shoots for greens were turned into "natural Fools . . . for several days" by its narcotic poison, stramonium; "[they] would have wallowed in their own Excrements, if they had not been prevented."[4]

Maybe the hardest lesson was that though Peruvian bark (quinine) would relieve the prevalent malaria of those who could afford it, none of the New World's newfound wonder drugs, not even sarsaparilla (though considered specific for syphilis), would cure homesickness. Only time did that. Fortunately time was then as plentiful as the wild pigeons and the salmon and shad and sturgeon in the great rivers. As America developed, all those and many other things, including the Indians and the mosquitoes, would grow much scarcer.

Unaware that it would ever be a nation needing a name, America began as a string of isolated settlements gradually gnawing into the woods lining the coast.* But what were those settlers doing there at all?—a question particularly good because actually so few Europeans came to settle in Colony-founding times and those who did were seldom more than small, often eccentric segments of the stay-at-home Old Country population.

That had not been true of the great migrations that broke up the Roman Empire and fermented into the medieval world that discovered America. Teutones and Helvetii, Visigoths and Vandals, set out *en masse* after group decisions and left only small minorities behind. For a Lombard family not to go along when the Lombards felt their hour had struck was passive secession from the mother culture, a stationary emigration. But nowhere in Europe (Ulster in the 1700's might be an exception) was self-exile to America ever a matter of majority movement or even of a prevalent impulse. Hence Mr. Roosevelt's truism means: "We are all descended from one or another kind of come-outers—personal or social misfits, those who couldn't or wouldn't endure what most persons in the Old Country could or would." Those categories do not include all our forebears, of course, but quite enough of them to make it clear that deviants dominated our cultural and genetic backgrounds.

Just what had split a given America-bound forebear away from the stay-at-home majority must have varied with time, place and his particular temperament. Consider that no unassisted individual stirrings of whatever sort could have arranged overseas opportunity for him. For colonizing—settling Western man in the New World—required ships, human raw material, outfits of food, clothing and tools to keep the scheme alive until it took root. "Planting," a gardener's term, was the word in John Smith's time. The settlements were "plantations"—"Rhode Island and Providence Plantations" is still the formal name of the smallest state in the Union. Such enterprise cost money—the very thing that most deviant or unlucky individuals are unlikely to have much of. So sponsorship and funds had to come from moneyed men serving their own interests—kings, noblemen or merchants persuaded that to sink hard cash in colonies would entail gain, economic and sometimes strategic.

England's Muscovy Company trading into Russia via the White Sea and the Dutch East India Company exploiting the Spice Islands had shown what profit nationally chartered corporations could fetch from distant lands. In the 1600's they were imitated by England's Plymouth and London companies (twin arms of the Virginia Company); the Company of New France; the Dutch West India Company—all financed by gentry and merchants sowing seed in order to reap and encouraged by governments hoping to promote national ends. Their business judgment proved bad.

* Scandinavian settlement in America in medieval times was real enough but too temporary to leave cultural effects, so this book omits it.

No such early company made the anticipated profits in America. By the time the Colonies were going concerns worth milking, their backers had already cut their losses and withdrawn. But their mistakes had nevertheless given the nation-to-be a crucial leg up. Without their taste for enterprise, however crass, nobody would ever have heard of Virginia Dare, Myles Standish, Evangeline, Manon Lescaut or Diedrich Knickerbocker. And the ominous Colonial yearning for self-government drew its early sustenance from the transmutation into a semi-independent state of the Massachusetts Bay Company, originally set up as a Muscovy-style commercial corporation.

Few bones were made about the profit motive. Clauses in charters about taking Christ to the heathen, though treated seriously by Catholic Spain and France, were observed largely in the breach by the Protestant founders of the Thirteen Colonies. The English promoters' promises of relief for their presumably overpopulated island were largely bait for royal favor. And even though Columbus' backers do seem to have been eager to convert the Indians, the primary purpose of Castile and León was to gain access to the spice-rich Orient. It spoiled that hope of wealth when their man ran into the 12,000-mile barrier of the Americas, of which neither he nor they had had an inkling. All was retrieved when floods of Mexican and Peruvian gold and silver—which, unlike spices, do not smell, says the Roman proverb—rewarded their poor guess in geography. The notion of procuring spices by voyaging westward without taking Magellan's stormy route around South America remained tempting, however. For centuries the stay-at-homes who planned and paid for the exploration and early settlement of America kept up two quests suggested by Spain's experience. New settlements were to be bases, first, for search for gold and silver, and, second and almost equally important, for finding a navigable passage through the barrier of the New World and across the Pacific (then thought to be much narrower than it is) for trade with the Spice Islands and Cathay.

Englishmen on Roanoke Island in the 1580's pestered the Indians with questions about streams rising in wide waters that might lead to the South Sea (Pacific) and dutifully prospected the mainland for gold. Archeologists working the site recently found a pathetic trace of these hopes—a fragment of an assayer's crucible for testing gold ores. The Virginia Company brusquely told Christopher Newport (after whom Newport News is named) not to return from a supply voyage to early Jamestown "without a lumpe of gold [or] a certainty of the South Sea. . . ."[5] Years after Jamestown, New Netherland and Plymouth were well established, propaganda to lure European immigrants still assumed that the Pacific was not far west of the Blue Ridge and spoke of trade with Cathay as a practical attraction of the new country.

Such will-o'-the-wisps sired by company orders led early explorers far up the garden path through the straitlike estuaries of American rivers. Jacques Cartier sailed hundreds of miles up the majestic St. Lawrence before the savage rapids above the present site of Montreal told him the worst. Twice John Smith tried to make one of the stately rivers entering Chesapeake Bay into the much-sought passage. But both Potomac and Susquehanna soon developed frustrating rapids, and all he had to show for months of small-boat work under a blistering sun was an arm badly swollen from an encounter with a stingray. Until toward the site of Troy, New York, it shoaled to seven feet Henry Hudson had the same hopes for the lordly, salty stream named after him. Yet the notion of possible contact with Asians upcountry was still so lively in the late 1630's that a French backwoodsman sent to explore the area around Green Bay took along a ceremonial robe of embroidered Chinese damask to dress up in when paying his respects to Oriental dignitaries.

As disappointments multiplied, however, the Old Country holders of purse strings grudgingly turned to other schemes based on actual experience of the New World. Questing and settling up both the St. Lawrence and the Hudson, the French brought home many beaver-, deer- and bearskins secured from the Indians by barter at a cost in trade goods absurd in European terms. The English were set the same lesson in the 1580's, when Thomas Harriot's list of "Merchantable commodities" procurable from the Roanoke colony included "Furres . . . great store of Otters . . . Deer skinnes dressed after the manner of Chamoes. . . ." Other items were "Pitch, Tarre, Rosen and Turpentine. There are those kinds of trees which yeeld them abundantly. . . . Fish, plenty of Sturgeons . . . Herings . . . an herbe called by the inhabitants Uppowoc . . . the Spaniards generally call it Tobacco." [6] Though he went on to chatter fatuously about copper mines, Harriot there showed himself farsighted. Fish, trees, skins and tobacco were to be the economic occasions, the basic cultural ancestors, of the permanent settlement of America.

When a courtier interceding for the Pilgrims sought leave from James I for them to settle in America, the king asked, "What profit might arise from those parts?" and was told, "Fishing." "So God have my Soule!" quoth James, " 'twas the Apostles' owne calling!" [7] The Pilgrims surely knew that, too. Probably more on their minds was the rhapsody about American fishing that they had read in John Smith's *A Description of New England:*

What pleasure can there be more than [for settlers] . . . to recreate themselves before their own doores in their own Boats upon the Sea, where man, woman and childe, with a small hooke and line, by angling, may take divers sorts of excellent Fish at their pleasures; and is it not pretty sport to pull up two pence, six pence, and twelve pence, as fast as you can hale and vere a line . . . if a man worke but three days in seven, he may get more than hee can spend . . . and what sport doth yeeld a more pleasing content . . . than angling with a hooke, and crossing the sweet aire from Ile to Ile, over the silent streams of a calme Sea. . . .[8]

Actually the Pilgrims proved to be inept fishermen. But that mattered only to them, for long since, fishing had already founded the tenuous first settlements in northeastern North America. The Cabots were hardly back from their glances at the New World before fishermen from Europe were exploiting the wealth of cod in the shallow-cold waters off Nova Scotia and Newfoundland. Their vessels were often smaller than the explorers'; the hardships entailed were severe, though hardly worse than what they were already used to off Iceland; and Catholic Europe needed Friday fish that would carry inland and keep in all seasons. So also did the Protestant England of Elizabeth I, where, strange as it now sounds, no-meat-on-Friday remained customary to encourage seagoing and reduce demand for the national meat supply. Thus Winthrop's Puritans, retaining that venerable taboo in spite of their hatred of Popery, hove to en route to New England in 1630 to catch cod off the Banks "very seasonably, for our salt fish were spent, and we were taking care for victuals this day (being a fish day). . . ."[9]

By then for more than a century hardy men named Jean, Juan, João and presently John were well at home on the stern and rockbound northern end of the nation-to-be where they landed to salt and dry their catches on jerry-built flakes before taking them home to Normandy, Brittany, the Basque coasts, Portugal or Devonshire. They sometimes came in double crews, the second left ashore in rough shelters to process fish while the first sailed the catch to Europe and returned to begin again. Well before the Pilgrims sighted Cape Cod, such fishermen had created a scatter of flimsy shore stations northward of Cape Ann. The profits of such activities were part of the bait used by Sir John Popham, Chief Justice of England, to attract investors to back his ill-fated colony sent to the Kennebec River in 1607.

Thus in one sense the first Americans may have been fishermen of several national origins. In their inevitable squabbles over who fished where, the melting pot first began to steam. And most apropos, it must have been in their polyglot get-togethers ashore that, between fights, the proto-Yankee fisherman learned *chowder*—the first distinctive American word of many that would eventually plague English lexicographers—for the fish or clam stew that his French rivals made in large pots called *chaudières*. Those chowders lacked milk, for there were no cows within 2,000 miles, and potatoes, for that tuber had not yet triangled to North America via Europe from South America. But ship's biscuit, salt pork and onions doubtless were available. Since fishermen brought no women along, the melting pot was not yet biological. It was nevertheless important —the first quiver of a mighty and still imperfect process.

Fishing also helped keep Europe mindful of the otherwise disappointing lands north of Spain's loot-rich holdings. For 115 years after Columbus, planting schemes had been few and futile in the 1,500 miles between tiny Spanish St. Augustine and the puny French toeholds beyond the St. Croix River. A Spanish Colonial judge, Lucas Vásquez de Ayllón, hoping to exploit a reputedly rich land, settled 500 Spanish men, women and children and a few Negro slaves at the mouth of some southeastern river in 1526. He and many of his company paid for their optimism by dying of local diseases. The rest abandoned the site so thoroughly that scholars are still unsure what river it was: Santee? Pedee? Guesses range 500 miles from the James to the Savannah. Again in 1570 a Spanish Jesuit mission spent a winter on some river in Tidewater Virginia but were massacred in the spring by Indians instigated by a young chief whom they had educated in Spain and brought back to his people to help establish Christianity among them. In this same century of fumbling the Huguenots (French Protestant Calvinists) tried twice: once on Parris Island on the water-logged shore of South Carolina-to-be, now site of the U.S. Marines' boot camp; once again on the St. Johns River in Florida. The first petered out. The second was bloodily wiped out by Catholic Spain.

"Spain" and "Catholic" are both significant. Under papal-inspired treaties of 1493 Spain still claimed all the New World except Brazil. As French the Huguenots were intruders; as heretics they were outlaws. For this was the time of the dog-eat-dog religious wars that both distracted Europe from America and prompted England to plant permanent bases on the American seaboard whence English ships could raid Spanish treasure fleets. That purpose (plus the usual dreams of gold and silver and passage to Cathay) underlay the colony that Sir Walter Raleigh sponsored on Roanoke Island among the North Carolina Banks in 1587. It does not explain what happened to the settlement, soon dismally famous as the Lost Colony. It was having no more than the usual difficulties when John White, its leader, sailed home to England for supplies and reinforcements, leaving behind, among others, his daughter, her husband and a new grandchild, Virginia Dare, first child born of English parents in America. This was the year of the Armada, so sizable vessels could not be spared for such minor missions as colony-supply. When he finally got back in 1590, the settlers were gone. It had been arranged that if they had to leave during his absence, they would record conspicuously the name of the place they were going to, adding a cross if they had left in distress. The presence of a log fort built after White had sailed hinted at some sort of danger. But there was no cross, only a name CROATAN carved on a gatepost. Trenches nearby contained some of the settlers' possessions in a condition indicating they had been buried and dug up again in haste. By whom? The settlers themselves in a panic? Or Indians turned hostile who took the survivors away prisoners? Or Spanish raiders treating this colony of English heretics as they had the Huguenots in Florida?

Croatan may have been the Indian name of an island much farther down the coast, of which White was aware. His alleged reason for failing to go there was a storm that blew his ship far to sea. His lackadaisical decision not to try to return is the more curious because the missing Dare family were his own flesh and blood. That only adds to the puzzle. Until it is solved—and by now solution is unlikely—it remains conceivable that Virginia Dare survived as the first of many Colonial women forced into new lives as captives among the Indians.

The 1600's brought the turn of the second biological marvel of neglected America—not fish this time, but the forest. In England wood products were gaining importance. The great staple export had long been wool in finished cloth as well as in sacks as raw material for Europe's looms. Before spinning, wool must be scoured free of its natural grease, which takes much soap. When woven into cloth, it needs fulling—pounding in soapy water, which takes still more soap. The alkalies needed to make soap of waste fats were then derived from potash, a somewhat refined form of wood ashes. The consequent growing demand for wood ash put a new load on England's wood supply, already committed to uses as fuel and building material. Deforestation was threatening neighborhoods where wool was processed. Other threats came in the simultaneous expansion of iron-smelting and glass-making, both relying on the intense heat of charcoal made from wood, for coal was as yet little used. The situation was the more acute because existing forests could not be fully exploited. Remote ones might still contain plenty of wood, but primitive transport made it uneconomical to get it to where it was needed.

In any case England was newly deep-sea-minded and greedy for masts, spars and the naval stores (pitch, tar, turpentine) used to calk seams and preserve cordage. For all that, she depended precariously on the forests of "the eastern nations"—Scandinavia and the Baltic lands. It was hoped in high places that colonies in America would not only provide bases for harassing Spanish shipping but also supply timber and naval stores from the great New World forests; create populous new markets for English goods, particularly woolens; and siphon off and put to use the Mother Country's surplus population. There were also reports (well founded this time)* of iron ore in "Virginia," the loose term for everything between Mount Desert and the Savannah River, and of abundant sand of glass-making quality. Why not an ample supply of potash for English soap boilers and charcoal-fueled iron and glass industries meeting the Mother Country's growing needs? Almost immediately the interlocking directorates of noblemen, gentry and merchants who held the royal monopolies on planting Virginia sent to Jamestown Dutch and Polish potash burners and Italian glassmakers to set up proper facilities, the first American manufactures. The presence of wild mulberry trees suggested a silk industry, and French silk artisans too were recruited. Thirty years later a sanguine Marylander was still predicting that in spite of previous failures, "Tobacco will [soon] be laid by; and we shall wholly fall to making of Silks . . . which will require little Labour." [10] (Two hundred years later Southern Californians had the same notion, equally in vain.) Poles, Italians, Dutchmen, Frenchmen—the melting pot again anticipated. It was a good omen when in 1624 the House of Burgesses of Virginia—the New World's first representative assembly—granted Colonial citizenship to those non-English potash experts who had managed to survive. And since Jamestown was acquiring a few women, biological mixture may now possibly have begun.

The long, costly sea trip "home" † from America kept New World potash from competing with the Baltic product. But the flora of America did well by the plantations all the same. Naval stores soon gained and retain today a solid place in the economy of the pine belt of the Southeastern seaboard. The first homeward-bound cargo out of Jamestown consisted of clapboard riven from American logs for wood-hungry England and of the pungent wood or roots of the sassafras tree, then highly valued in medicine on the old principle that whatever smells queer (if seldom as pleasantly as sassafras) is probably good for what ails you. The English called it ague tree because the Spaniards thought it good for malaria. Michael Drayton's

---

* Nor was the notion of gold in the Southern Colonies altogether absurd. Some gold has been found off and on in western Virginia. Northwestern Georgia has had several minor gold rushes. One of them led to the shameful expulsion of the Civilized Tribes in Andrew Jackson's time.

† *Home* is the generic English-speaking colonial's way of referring to the Mother Country. It implies marked colonial-mindedness; its disappearance is a symptom marking a colony's emotional readiness for independence. In the 1930's I once heard an Australian lady reproach a Canadian lady for replying, "Why, I *am* home," to the question "Have you been home lately?"

verses (1607) on Virginia's promise mention "The cedar reaching high /
To kiss the sky, / The cypress, pine / And useful sassafras" [11] as equally
estimable. But though its leaves still give the fall woods their gaudiest
colors and constitute the gumbo filé of New Orleans, sassafras has now
lost most of its renown. Outside the South one seldom sees the red
roots sold to make sassafras tea as spring tonic. Nor does the Indianapolis
News annually reprint, as it once did, the "Ode to Sassafras" of James B.
Elmore, the Bard of Alamo:

> In the spring of the year,
>   When the blood is too thick,
> There is nothing so rare
>   As the sassafras stick.
> It cleans up the liver,
>   It strengthens the heart,
> And to the whole system
>   New life doth impart.
> Sassafras, oh, sassafras!
>   Thou are the stuff for me!
> And in the spring I love to sing
>   Sweet sassafras! of thee.[12]

And only in archeological centers like Old Salem, North Carolina, can one
still see the diffidently pretty pink that its use as dye imparts to wool.

A standing cause of friction between Yankee and Briton—hence of
growing resentment of British rule—was the settler's unwillingness to
respect the broad arrow mark of the Royal Navy's timber cruisers reserv-
ing white pines over a certain girth for man-of-war masts. However clearly
marked, such trees were often found to have vanished when looked for,
yet nobody knew who had felled them or what had become of the timber.
More than 2 feet thick and toward 100 feet to the nearest limb, they had
to be hauled to waterside by from 16 to 100 yoke of oxen—an operation
easy to conceal only from people bent on looking the other way. The Pilgrims' first shipment home of marketable commodities to apply on their
debt to their backers consisted of clapboard—and "2 hogshedds of beaver
and other skins" which were essentially as much of a forest product as
wood, for beaver and bear dwindled in numbers as human population
grew and the woods shrank away from the settlements.

Indeed the relation between Colonist and forest was almost termitelike
in intimacy. He did not eat wood, true. But the ship he came in was of
wood. So was the first dwelling that he built and probably the next and
the next. Visitors from a later Europe, where medieval wooden buildings
had burned down or fallen apart and been replaced by brick or stone, often

wondered at the prevalent woodenness of American dwellings. Most tools and gadgets that would now be of metal, ceramic or plastic were then of wood, cleverly and often subtly carved, split, sawn or bent into the required shape: rakes, hayforks, shovels, pails, ladles, troughs; drums for storage and transport of liquids and solids; trenchers, bowls, spoons for table use, as well as cooking; washboards, tubs, door latches, sifters; even the treenails, the wooden spikes that held together the timbers of ships and house because metal was scarce and that type of construction was sounder anyway if there were time and materials for it. Metal was usually reserved for cooking in contact with fire, cutting tools and such lighting devices as lamps and lanterns. Even in that field the hickory-bark torch and the pine knot, rich in resin and turpentine, were widely used indoors and out.

Colonial heating and cooking devoured huge quantities of wood. Even in warmish Virginia the twenty-eight fires kept going in winter at Nomini Hall, "King" Carter's great mansion, demanded four three-yoke oxcartloads of wood daily. Certain industries had the same effect on the incumbent forest. The case of shipbuilding is obvious. The making of maple syrup and sugar called for masses of wood, for the sap carries merely 2 to 4 percent of solid sweetening, and to produce even a quart of syrup means boiling down eight gallons. Indirectly fisheries, too, were destructive. To cure cod for export demanded salt. Much came from the Portuguese islands and the West Indies, but local supply was obviously preferable. Evaporation of seawater West Indian-style was impractical under the fickle New England sun. But wood fires under iron pans created a brisk salt-boiling industry on Cape Cod that lasted as long as firewood was available nearby. How much was needed can be gauged from the saltworks of Salina (now Syracuse), New York, in the late 1790's, when it took a cord of wood to make eleven bushels of salt from a brine far stronger than seawater.

Cape Cod's short-lived glass industry of the early 1800's, which turned out the collector's Sandwich glass, further depleted local forests by demanding not only charcoal to melt the sand but also pearl ash (a refinement of potash) to alkalinize the mix. Many a pioneer found a handy cash crop in burning trees—elm, basswood, sugar maple and beech were best —into ashes for potash for the local ashery to refine into pearl ash. Only after the mid-1700's did American coal even begin to take the load off charcoal, hence off the forest. Until then coal, sent from Britain as paying ballast in ships, appeared as room-heating fuel only in the fireplace grates of the well-off in port towns. Robert Beverley, first comprehensive writer on Virginia, explained in 1705 that though the Colony had "very good Pit-coal . . . no Man has yet thought it worth his while to make use of it, having Wood in plenty. . . . In all new Grounds, [wood] is such an incumbrance that they are forced to burn great heaps of it . . . [and] grows at every Man's door so fast, that after it has been cut down, it will in Seven Years time, grow up again . . . to substantial Fire-Wood." [13]

Iron-smelting was notably wood-hungry. Deposits of iron, usually bog ore, left in swamps by iron-rich waters, were exploited in Virginia by 1619. Practically every Colony eventually put such minerals to use. Transport was too cumbrous to justify moving ore from small deposits to central smelters. Instead, the smelter ("furnace" they said then) was built as near the ore body as other considerations allowed. Helen Furnace, Mary Ann Furnace, Clarissa Furnace—Colonial ironmasters liked to name the works after their womenfolk—persist on the map in obscure neighborhoods to recall these ancient operations. On the same maps Old Forge, Valley Forge, Union Forge and so on recall the complementary installation, at the same spot or separate, where the pig iron was battered by water-powered hammers into wrought iron of innumerable uses. Far off the road in scrubby woods one still finds the ruins of the old stone furnaces, crumbling truncated cones like crosses between windmills and church towers, cold and neglected these many years. Those at Saugus, Massachusetts, Batsto, New Jersey, Hopewell Village, Pennsylvania, and a few other places have been painstakingly restored.

Small as such workings now look, they were numerous, and the total of bar and pig iron that the Colonies annually produced by 1775 exceeded

A representative small iron-smelting plant of the charcoal period with its attached settlement for workers.

that of England and Wales together and constituted a seventh of world supply. They needed only waterpower to run the trip-hammer of the forge and the huge bellows providing air blast for the smelter; a handy supply of limestone (oyster shells would do) for the flux that carried off impurities; and labor to cut wood to burn (that is, undergo destructive distillation in a sod-covered heap) into the charcoal to keep the works going. A large furnace used about an acre of forest a day. The crude bloomery method that bypassed the furnace needed as much or more charcoal per pound of usable iron.

Woodcutting on that scale required labor concentrated on the spot. So the Puritans' ironworks at Saugus, Massachusetts, fostered by John Winthrop, Jr., first successful Colonial project of the sort, became a small community by itself. By the 1700's most other Colonies had such largely self-contained iron plantations off in the woods. The Hopewell layout for instance, in Pennsylvania, had fifty-odd men workers, plus the families of the married ones. The owner-manager lived in an impressively tall Georgian house of stone. Nearby were charcoal storage; blast furnace and foundry; barns for horses, oxen and cows; schoolhouse for the children of the owner and the upper-echelon employees; company store selling against wages the supplies of rum, linen, gunpowder, tobacco, salt, boots and other items not produced on the plantation; farther away a cluster of crude tenant houses and single men's barracks—altogether a striking anticipation of the company town of the 1800's. The woodcutters' and charcoal burners' womenfolk not only performed their own household chores but also spun and wove the wool of the local flock of sheep for store credit. That was taken for granted. Well into the 1800's the employees of the great bog-ore ironworks at Allaire, New Jersey, were paid in scrip good only at the company store, but at that it was the largest one for miles.

From such workings packhorses took the pigs and bars to market or to a convenient waterside where boats tied up. Saugus had its own landing within 100 yards. The Durham boats that took freight up and down the Delaware above the fall line—and ferried Washington's men across to attack Trenton—were developed for the ironworks at Durham, Pennsylvania, carrying 15 tons of iron and drawing only 20 inches of water. Saugus is now a frowsy suburb. Second-growth timber has reclothed the hills around Durham and Hopewell. But salt, glass, iron and the beginnings of lead and copper mining in New Jersey and Appalachia have still left scars in those areas in the Eastern states, long since stripped of trees and now scrubbily desolate, that make one wonder why anybody bothered to clear them in the first place. Around all too many sites Beverley's glib promise of healing growth has gone most dismally unfulfilled.

The settler's baleful influence on the forest, wider than that of industry, came of his seeing it as clog and hindrance to be got rid of as soon as possible. He was, as is often said, land-hungry. But it was hunger for plow-land and pasture, not temperate-zone jungles of sun-thwarting foliage borne aloft on huge boles draped with grapevines as thick as your leg and interspersed with the rotting remains of fallen predecessors. Sometimes, as at early Plymouth, he took over fields already cleared by Indians, who maintained fertility by putting a fish or two into each hill of corn, a trick that the Pilgrims adopted. To keep their dogs from digging up the fish, which ruined the planting, one forepaw was tied to the neck for forty days after seed was in the ground. Usually, however, major forest was the problem—and the Indian had a solution for that too, well described by Beverley: "[They] chopped a Notch round the Trees quite through the bark with their Stone Hatchets . . . that deaden'd the Trees, so that they sprouted no more . . . the Ground . . . would produce immediately upon the withering . . ." [14] because once the leaves were dead and fallen, the sunlight got through to the corn planted between. Underbrush was grubbed up, smaller trees felled, all to be piled around the bases of the large trees and burned, the fire gnawing into them and weakening them so

Stumps, rail fence and mud dominated the pioneer's landscape, here drawn c. 1830 by Captain Basil Hall, RN.

that eventually, between char and rot, they fell where they stood. Then, as occasion served, the trunks were chopped into lengths, rolled into heaps and burned.

The lethal notching, usually called girdling or deadening, was also used to improve grazing for stock run in the woods. The resulting masses of dead timber had, as a visiting Briton of Revolutionary times noted, "a very singular and dreadful appearance." [15] Well into the 1800's as this method of land clearing spread from the Atlantic to the Missouri, alien travelers deplored having to ride for miles through such desolation—there a chestnut still standing like a barkless gray ghost; a great maple broken halfway up; a tulip poplar propped against it at a despairing angle; both sides of the road showing vista after vista of rotting destruction, gaunt and blackened. Such witnesses' accounts of America's shortcomings were often exaggerated, but not in this case. I saw that when, in Australia in the 1930's, I met forests thus girdled to improve grazing. Occasionally a girdled tree had its revenge when it fell in a heavy thunderstorm and ruined part of the settler's laboriously planted corn patch or when a high, decayed bough broke off and stunned a human being far below. The Seneca Indians, great corn planters, hence assiduous tree girdlers, had a special prayer that branches falling from the dead trees in winter might not injure their children in the cornfields. It is all a conservationist's nightmare. But, as a New York State pioneer's grandson once pointed out, the settler cannot be censured for his fanatic arboricide: "The woodland must go before the plow could come. . . . he who removed a tree was . . . a public benefactor. It took a long time to unlearn this. . . ." [16]

In a new girdled clearing the natural accumulation of rich humus on the former forest floor nourished corn well for the first season or two. After that, the ashes of burned trash kept fertility high a few seasons longer. And at the end, as the roots of the burned stumps decayed or were backbreakingly grubbed up, the settler had a cleared area fit for the deeper-searching plow, the sort of cornfield familiar today. It was all even more arduous than it sounds. But immediate felling with axes and removal of the timber would have been far more so. It was only the stubborn and tireless Pennsylvania Dutch who scorned girdling and cleared the land clean, even to stump pulling, the first season.

As tobacco replaced corn as mainstay of Virginia and Maryland, the forest had another enemy. This was the doing of John Rolfe, best known now as Pocahontas' husband, then as father of the American tobacco economy, who almost single-handedly diverted the Chesapeake Bay Colonies from the tree industry that the London Company had had in mind. The local Indians' tobacco grew thriftily, but its coarse flavor kept it from competing in the growing world market with Spain's West Indian leaf. Rolfe imported West Indian seed, bred improved strains—and Virginia became a synonym for tobacco. Too late for investors in the company he had what they sought—a staple cash export—and a basis for steady growth of population and a sort of stability. Other Colonies learned to raise sotweed, as detractors called it. The crop persists in most seaboard states but is a major resource only in parts of the upper South.

Wherever tried, it soon exhausts soils. Today's tobacco farmer relies on artificial fertilizing. The Colonist, with a whole continent at his back, preferred to abandon the land he had cleared as soon as the crop began to dwindle ominously and start anew, felling and burning more trees on virgin soil. The old fields were left to lose what topsoil remained by erosion and grow up in weeds and eventually a scatter of old-field pine, the tree likely first to establish itself on such ruined land. As late as 1773, when some were already introducing less ruinous methods, an outsider characterized farming in the Northern Neck as "slovenly, without any regard to future Crops—They plant large quantities of Land, without any Manure . . . and when the Crop comes off they . . . inclose another piece . . . for the next years Tillage and leave this a common to be destroyed." [17]

Such mining of soil and then neglecting it suited large landowners best.* The smallholder soon ran out of virgin woods and in any case lacked the labor resources needed for clearing at such a rate. Further, tobacco is exacting stuff which must be started in seedbeds; transplanted into carefully prepared fields; weeded; suckered; wormed; harvested; cured; packed in hogsheads—all demanding much labor in a society where labor was chronically scarce. The early Colonist meaning to make more out of tobacco than a frantic livelihood punctuated by successive removals upcountry had to turn to imported forced labor. At first that meant indentured servants (white); then Negro slaves and extensive landholdings. Thereby the effort to make the most of tobacco tainted the South with much that has ailed the region since: a tradition of the big plantation as ideal; a caste of ill-established, hand-to-mouth poor whites; and the cancer of racist feeling born of Negro slavery.

Some histories of America scamp the importance of what is misleadingly called the fur trade. Europe wanted all those beaverskins not so much for luxurious wraps as for fur felt for hats; *beaver* was slang for hat in the 1600's. And the other heavy European demand on the fauna of the New World was not for fur at all but for dressed deerskins. The fashion of buckskin riding breeches lasted long, still surviving in the dress uniforms of ceremonial cavalry. Many Colonists' everyday clothes were of deerskin below export quality but still worth fetching into the settlements. So buckskins became the units of exchange in the Pennsylvania backcountry just as beaverskins did in the Hudson Valley and New England. The origin of a bit of modern slang is clear in the complaint of a trader in 1735 about a

* "Slash-and-burn" agriculture—the technical name for this practice—is common today among preliterate tropical cultures and was widespread in Europe in medieval times.

rascally employee who had "sold only eight bucks worth of goods" [18] to the Indians before absconding.*

Better substitute *peltry trade* for *fur trade*. Packtrains from Shamokin or Bedford in the Pennsylvania hills carried little else than half-dressed deerskins, 100 to the 250-pound load. From 1699 to 1715 South Carolina alone sent to England an average of 54,000 deerskins a year; 160,000 in the peak year of 1748. Southern peltry traders were specially committed to deerskin since, presumably because of warmer winters, Southern beaver were too hairy and not furry enough. Verner W. Crane, expert on the Southern frontier, likens the massacre of the Southeastern deer herd to "the great wastage, by a later generation, of the buffalo of the Great Plains." [19] The bundle that the Indian laid on the trader's counter (with the whiskey jug ready at one end) often also contained bear, otter or marten. The salary of John Sevier as president of the evanescent state of Franklin in the pioneer Old Southwest was set at 200 minkskins a year. But all by themselves beaver and buckskin could have made the trade what it was—the leading edge of the frontier as the white adventurer loaded a canoe or a string of packhorses with bad liquor, unsafe firearms, shoddy textiles and cheap hardware and sought Indian customers out back of beyond where wildlife was still copious and the red man less sophisticated, easier to swindle.

Early Colonies usually forbade trading guns and ammunition to Indians. But neither law nor considerations of public safety could keep most peltry traders from doing whatever was profitable. The Indian traded his gun from B if not from A. John Winthrop, deep in the peltry trade himself, complained that the Dutch and French on New England's frontiers got the bulk of the Indians' beaver by offering guns and powder in spite of formal renunciation of such trade. The Pequots carried off two white girls from a Connecticut settlement in 1637 not, it appeared after they were rescued, to do them violence, but in the mistaken belief that they could teach their captors how to make gunpowder. Some Colonists thought it clever to make the Indian dependent on firearms since he could not manufacture them himself and it increased the peltry trader's hold on him; never mind the incidental danger to white settlers. "Before [whites] came among you," an agent of South Carolina told the Creek Indians in 1725, "there was no other weapon but Bows and Arrows to hunt with, you could Hunt a whole day and bring nothing Home at Night, you had no other Hoes or Axes than Stones. . . ." [20]

---

* The *Dictionary of Americanisms on Historical Principles* merely suggests this derivation, apparently because its editors could find no example of use of *buck* for *dollar* earlier than 1856. To the nonexpert there is a good case in their citation from the Indian agent Conrad Weiser in 1748: "Every cask of whiskey shall be sold to you for 5 bucks in your own town." (Weiser, *Journal . . . Ohio,* 41.)

Certainly the iron hoe that the Indian got for his skins was an improvement. It enabled his squaws to plant and cultivate larger acreage, which, as the Pilgrims saw, led to better supply in the wigwam and greater surplus of corn to trade with. The white men's red or blue blankets and matchcoats of half-thicks or strouds were also an improvement over the Indian's customary winter wear. But no such minor rise in the standard of living could make up for the vicious effects of the peltry trade on the red man. As William B. Weeden truly wrote of the New England phase of it, it inevitably "debauched the Indian [by] . . . revelling in the vices of its customers." [21] Particularly it enabled him to secure hard liquor, to which he had small physical and less moral resistance. The effect is classically described in a report from William Henry Harrison in 1801, when he was governor of Indiana Territory, on the Indians visiting Vincennes:

> . . . dayly . . . in considerable numbers . . . frequently intoxicated to the number of thirty or forty at once . . . drawing their knives and stabbing everyone they meet with, breaking open the houses of the citizens. . . . But in all their frolicks they generally suffer most severely themselves . . . kill each other without mercy. Some years ago as many as four were found dead in the morning. . . . I do not believe that there are more than six Hundred Warriors upon [the Wabash] River, and yet the quantity of whiskey brought here annually for their use is said to amount to at least six thousand Gallons. This poisonous Liquor . . . leads to the most atrocious crimes . . . a Wea chief of note well known to me was not long since murdered by his own son. . . . Little Fox, another chief who was always a friend of the white people, was murdered at mid day in the streets of his town by one of his own nation. . . . I can at once tell by looking at an Indian . . . whether he belongs to a Neighbouring or a more distant Tribe. The latter is generally well Clothed, healthy and vigorous, the former half naked, filthy and enfeebled with Intoxication. . . .[22]

The peltry traders also inevitably took into areas far upcountry the germs of exotic diseases to which the Indians had no resistance. Intrigues with French peltry-trading agencies frequently set them at odds with the Colonists. In the ensuing fighting the Indian probably did far more damage than he received over the years. The score in the frontier wars of the 1750-60's is thought to have varied between 3 dead whites to 1 dead Indian and 50 to 1. But the red man worked from a dwindling population while fresh whites were pouring in all the time. He had reason for his sad superstition that "as many Indians must die each year as the number of Europeans that yearly arrive." [23] Finding a swarm of bees in a hollow tree warned him that his people would soon have to move westward again, for honeybees, like horses, gunpowder and smallpox, were a white man's importation, and these "English flies" usually spread 100 miles in advance of the actual frontier. White clover, also landed with the white man and spreading in pace with the frontier, the Indian called "white man's foot" and considered it a sure token of his people's extirpation.

Thanks to the peltry trade, the whites with whom the Indians first had contact were usually the scaliest specimens of all. One peltry trader on the Pennsylvania frontier in the 1720's was named Jonathan Swindell. The Indians might have used that surname to symbolize all his kind, as they used Onas (Iroquois for *feather=pen=Penn*) for the proprietary government of Pennsylvania under William Penn and his heirs.* There could be marked respectability among the port-town merchants and politicians (often identical) from whom the actual field trader secured on credit goods that the Indians wanted. While the supplier took the risk of the trader's never returning, he also made fat profits that justified the risk. John Winthrop was such a supplier-trader; so were the Pembertons, high among the Quaker oligarchs of Philadelphia, and William Byrd II, first citizen of Virginia, and a number of Albany Dutchmen whose names sound like a *Social Register* of 1900: Gansevoort, Bleecker, Beekman, Schuyler, Van Rensselaer, De Peyster. But few of the men in charge of the packtrains and the log trading post at the forks of the Big Freshwater failed to deserve Benjamin Franklin's description of them as "the most vicious and abandoned wretches of our nation." [24]

Franklin took a dim view of frontiersmen generally. In 1760 he called them "the refuse of both [French and English] nations, often of the worst morals and the least discretion." [25] Even when trying very hard to be fair, Charles A. Hanna, a modern authority, had to characterize the peltry traders as, though brave and canny, also "mercenary, dissolute . . . disloyal, cruel. . . ." [26] South Carolina officially deplored their "Barbarous . . . Imorall and unjust way of Liveing and Deeling [and] Lewdness and wickedness. . . ." [27] ". . . persons that trade among the Indians," said the Colony's statute of 1707, ". . . do generally lead loose, vicious lives . . . and . . . oppress the people among whom they live by their unjust and illegal actions." [28] The Indians were often urged to take trade goods on credit and repay in skins next spring. Since they were usually honest, this spurred them into energetic hunting and trapping in order to get out of debt. But too commonly unscrupulous traders would waylay them on the

---

* Similarly the Iroquois symbolized themselves as the Long House; the Colonial government of Virginia as Assirigoa (Big Knife), their name for Lord Howard, once governor; the French regime in Canada as Onontio. This is much the same as the traditional diplomatic use of the Sublime Porte (Lofty Gate) in referring to the government of the Turkish sultans.

way to settle up, fuddle them with rum, trade them blind for their load of skins, and leave them none to cover the obligation to their original suppliers. North Carolina observers blamed that trick for many of the quarrels that led to killings and inflamed relations all along the frontier. A touch-and-go Indian war almost wiped out the traders in South Carolina in 1715. But plenty more of "the restless and the indigent . . . and servants whose terms of indenture had expired" [29] were ready to try their luck. The ethical standards of such recruits were unlikely to raise those of the trade. "Indeed," says James Thomas Flexner in his biography of Sir William Johnson, "many of the white men who fled to the danger and squalor of the further forests were misfits in civilization, psychopaths, such men as are found today in prisons, alcoholic wards, and the skid rows of big cities." [30]

For a while peltry, however deplorable its context, rivaled tobacco as the liveliest economic reason for developing the Colonies. The Plymouth Pilgrims found it, as acquired from the "salvages," a quick, high-value export to meet their debts with. William Penn sought earnestly to get the boundaries of his Pennsylvania so drawn as to give easy access to the rich peltry trade of the Iroquois. By William Byrd II's time (c. 1720) an Indian caravan from Tidewater Virginia to the Catawba tribes in the Carolina backcountry would include a dozen men and up to 100 loaded packhorses. If forage were plentiful along their well-established trading path, they made 20 miles a day with their shrewdly selected brass kettles, rum, red lead (for face paint), axes, gunpowder, laced hats for chiefs and small mirrors for young bucks to hang around their necks on rawhide lanyards.

The traders' sole virtue—courage—was undeniable. Out ahead of any support but their own nerve, in advance of treaties and blockhouses, they pushed ever deeper into the woods like evil missionaries risking their lives among cannibals. Within two generations Pennsylvania's traders were far across the Appalachians swindling the tribes along the Wabash River 500 miles from salt water. Their counterparts from South Carolina, flowing southward of the terminal massif of the mountains, were competing sharply with French traders working inland from Mobile. In this aspect their legacy to posterity was more than merely the human debris of debauched Indians and half-breeds. It was true of them, as well as of the French *coureurs de bois,* whose exploits they rivaled, that they did more than official expeditions to probe the geography of America. Sometimes also their squalid headquarter posts took root, changed their tone, and imposed some civilization on the traders themselves, or at least on their progeny. Consider Springfield, Massachusetts, founded because the Connecticut River was navigable for boats far upcountry, and thus "fitly seated for a Bever trade with the Indians, till the [traders] encreased so many, that [the peltry trade] became little worth, by reason of their outbuying one another, which hath caused them to live upon husbandry." [31] Two generations from furs to farming. Many an upriver settlement from Augusta, Georgia, to Augusta, Maine (a Plymouth trading colony), had seen some such story enacted.

As Colonials got the hang of other resources, peltry lost relative importance. In the 1720's naval stores, lumber and rice had excelled its export value for the Colonies as a whole; tobacco was ahead of them all. This diversification may have given England a crucial advantage in her up-and-down struggle with other powers that finally left eastern America in English hands. For the glossy promise of peltry had fatally cajoled the French and Dutch into making it the main basis of their American Colonies.

The French came in early by the St. Lawrence and the Great Lakes westward—the finest waterway into America for the eight ice-free months of the year. Another, much later penetration founded New Orleans and came northward up the Mississippi. Yet fifty years later, in spite of the advantages of its site and the fertility of its environs, Lord Adam Gordon, a semiofficial British observer, reported of New Orleans that "Its principle Staple is the trade for Furrs and Skins from the Illinois," [32] and neither indigo nor sugar had yet come to much. Most of the rest of French settlement in a vast semicircle hooking up with Canada was far from the seaboard Colonies and consisted of tiny fortified posts and a few sluggish farming villages. Until after 1700 the ministers of Louis XIV had intermittently discouraged French enterprise in that wide, remote country south and west of the Great Lakes where gold and silver refused to be found by Frenchmen primarily interested in furs and the saving of Indian souls. This New France, nominally an empire as large as Charlemagne's and potentially richer, was little more than a vast, dilute sphere of commercial and missionary influence among diverse Indian tribes.

The French got on better with the Indians than did the British or Dutch, intermarried with them rather freely, learned and more readily adopted their ways. But their trade goods were reputed of inferior quality—they must have been shoddy indeed—and they had the bad luck soon to make lasting enemies of the Iroquois, the best organized and most powerful of all Eastern Indians, masters of the strategic area now called upper New York State. Lasting French influence remained only in the Frenchmen's widely separated port-of-entry areas—French Canada and southern Louisiana. The latter had special support from the nearby French sugar islands; hence its marked West Indian flavor of sugar planting, gang slavery, intermediate caste of mulattoes and a dash of voodoo. All that now survives elsewhere is a few widely distributed words—*prairie, portage,*

cache, flume, parlay—a scatter of wildly mispronounced place-names—
D'*Moyn,* Prairie d'*Sheen,* Vin*senz,* St. *Lew*is, Press*kyle*—and the white
man's designations for the Sioux and Nez Percé Indians.

The Dutch not only trusted in peltry till too late but made the further
error of planting too close to self-righteously aggressive New England.
Soon after Jamestown came into being, Dutch traders had followed up
Hudson's discoveries and settled insecurely on what they called the North
River—as New Yorkers still call the Hudson. It gave them a superb harbor leading into a 150-mile waterway deep enough for the small ships of
the time to penetrate far into the interior. There they were in close touch
with the Iroquois, not only active trappers on their own accounts but soon
able middlemen-traders between the Dutch and the Indians farther west.
Naturally in that peltry-minded era the first Dutch settlement was not on
Manhattan Island but on the site of an abandoned French trading post just
below where Albany now is. A later planting in the estuary of the Delaware—the Dutchman's "South River"—brushed away some Swedes settled there and secured another river avenue (though lacking deep water
higher up) into the Iroquois country. A tiny third project put the Dutch
also well up the Connecticut River on the present site of Hartford just before Puritans from Massachusetts Bay came to settle the same area. In
time Dutchmen also worked up the Raritan River into the heart of New
Jersey-to-be.

All that shows a sense of location worthy of the Netherlands of the early
1600's—then the world's most stirring naval and trading nation. Soon the
Dutch West India Company was in charge of sugar development in Dutch
holdings in tropical America and, rather incidentally, of the peltry trade of
"New Netherland." Another of its concerns was the complementary trade
in West African slaves. All those spheres of interest lay handily to port of
ships taking the Verrazano route. Vessels went from Amsterdam to the
Gold Coast with trade goods; Gold Coast to West Indies with slaves;
West Indies to Europe with bulky sugar and molasses up the North
American coast and putting in at New Amsterdam for a supplementary
high-value, low-bulk consignment of peltry. In that light it makes sense
that Peter Stuyvesant, the peg-legged last governor of New Netherland who
now lies among the pigeons and Bowery bums in St. Mark's churchyard,
was at the same time governor of Curaçao, 2,000 miles away in the West
Indies. Had not the Portuguese recently taken Brazil back from the Dutch,
he might well have found himself governor there also.

Thus to fuse West Indian and American affairs sounds queer to our
America-centered minds, even when the navigational patterns are understood. All transatlantic Mother Countries did it, however, and the consequences were weighty. For sugar and slaves were now replacing gold and

silver and peltry as commodities most attracting the economic fancy of Europeans. Hence a drift toward stepchild status for New France, New England, New Netherland. Only Virginia and Maryland, kept on England's mind by the importance of tobacco in world trade, escaped some loss in relative importance at home. True, the Puritans' settlements continued somewhat to matter as a source of spars and a minor outlet for manufactures. But from across the Atlantic, New England was mainly the tail to the West Indian dog—mere supplier of the timber, salt fish and horses that enabled the masters and slaves of Barbados, St. Kitts and Jamaica to keep turning out sugar. That was one of several things widening the rift, originally largely religious, between Old and New England. By the late 1600's Pennsylvania too was shipping pipe staves (to make molasses casks), flour, barreled salt beef and salt pork to the West Indies and getting back rum, sugar, molasses, slaves, salt and hard money in useful quantities. The relation was so close that when Benjamin Franklin sent out into the world the young printers whom he trained in Philadelphia, as many went to the West Indies as stayed on the mainland. A similar connection existed between the islands and Charleston.

Since there was no question which was the more profitable area, the Mother Country understandably modulated her solicitude to match. Between Cromwell's time and George III's a prime issue in all negotiations for still another peace among England, France, Spain (and, in early days, the Netherlands) would always be who got which West Indian sugar islands and West African slave depots. In the bargaining, mainland American colonies such as Acadia (Nova Scotia), New Netherland and New Orleans were rather woundingly treated as mere counters to sweeten deals with. In the 1670's the Dutch recaptured New York from England but readily let it go on condition that England hand back sugar-rich Surinam in South America. Diplomats now regard with amazement the eagerness of the beaten French to let England keep captured Canada in 1763 on condition that she return the fat sugar island of Guadeloupe. It was a mainland Colonial, Benjamin Franklin, who persuaded the British government that on the whole Canada might prove the better long-term possession. And the only way to perceive the shuttling back and forth of troops and men-of-war between the mainland and the West Indies during the American Revolution is to understand that West Indian issues and situations were the prime concern of both France and England at the time.

Most of the masts of the ships that failed to relieve Cornwallis at Yorktown came from New England forests. Maybe they shared rebel feelings and did not have their hearts in their work. For first and last, from bare beginnings to independence, it was the great woods, as spars and fuel and peltry farm, that shaped the destiny of the Colonies.

II

Outlandersland

WILLIAM PENN'S AMERICA

II

EMMA LAZARUS, whose rich Sephardic Jewish father had been a founding member of New York City's Knickerbocker Club, was accurate if blunt in her famous sonnet of 1886 urging the new Statue of Liberty to welcome the Old World's "huddled masses yearning to breathe free . . . wretched refuse . . . ." She had in mind the Southern and Eastern Europeans then filling the westbound steerages. But her compassion would have applied just as well to the flow of Northern Europeans then still continuing. Robert Louis Stevenson, who got on well with a steerageful of Scottish, Irish and English emigrants in 1879, was struck by the prevalence of "drink, idleness and incompetency" among them. He had expected "the hopeful and adventurous . . . in an impetuous and conquering sally." Instead, he felt like Marmion: ". . . in the lost battle borne down by the flying." [1] Wider knowledge of American history would have prepared him better. At least a majority of the emigrant ancestors of pre-Revolutionary Americans had been refuse in one sense or another, seldom flattering, and if they weren't wretched on leaving home, they were probably so before debarking. The chief difference between Miss Lazarus' and Stevenson's emigrants and those of 200 years earlier was that faster, cleaner ships and better diet on board had greatly heightened chances of surviving the voyage.

For the conditions under which most early Colonists crossed the ocean made "huddled masses yearning to breathe free" no mere rhetoric. The quarters assigned ordinary passengers in the *Mayflower* in 1620 averaged horizontal space of 7 by 2½ feet—and no deck privileges. A hundred years later British law required 6 by 1½ feet per adult emigrant; no allowance at all for children. No wonder that in his *Colonists in Bondage* Abbot Emerson Smith estimates 15 percent as probable average mortality before landing. Thus of 3,000-odd German Palatines shipped from England to New York City in 1710 in ten ships, 470 died on the voyage—say, 16 percent—and 250 more soon after landing. For a hideous extreme, of

200 English Separatists (religious comrades of the Pilgrim Fathers) sailing from Amsterdam in 1618 to take up land in Virginia, 150 died en route. The causes were, of course, diseases brought on by months at sea on a vitamin-poor diet, plus infections gone epidemic in vilely cramped living

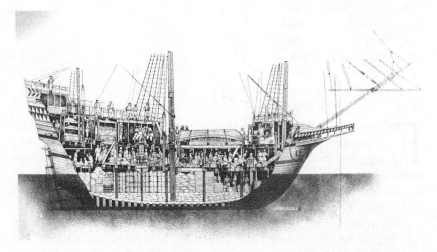

Cross section of the Mayflower *showing the ordinary passengers crammed into the 'tweendecks.*

Courtesy of Plimoth Plantation

conditions, since smallpox, ship fever (louse-transmitted typhus) and various enteric troubles often took passage, too.

Much of such mortality was unnecessary. The Puritans sailing for Massachusetts Bay insisted on decent conditions and adequate diet according to the imperfect standards of the day and brought over shipload after shipload of recruits in the 1630's with small loss. The *Lyon*, which spent years in that trade, once landed 123 passengers, including 50 children, with no loss at all. One reason for that is hinted at in her master's always shipping lemon juice, which was even then suspected of being a specific for the scurvy that was a principal menace at sea; Edward Winslow had already been advising persons destined for the Plymouth colony to bring plenty of beer and "juice of lemons and take it fasting." [2] In time government tried to enforce regulations on diet and number of passengers permissible. But an insane system of reckoning by group units per ton, not by heads—*souls* in the parlance of the day—allowed nasty overcrowding to persist. In any case any rules laid down would have been evaded by owners or captains who, as John Smith warned, "[provided] they can get fraught enough, care not whether the passengers live or die . . . especially a poore passenger." [3] Into Revolutionary times the consequent horrors were comparable to those of the Middle Passage for Negro slaves that so justly stank in the world's nostrils. Henry Laurens of South Carolina, a great merchant familiar with all types of commerce and shipping, said of Irish immigrants coming to Charleston in the 1760's: "[I] never saw an Instance of Cruelty in Ten or Twelve years [of experience of the slave trade] equal to the cruelty exercised upon these poor Irish." [4] Consider also that the crank, high-built ships of that time were often wrecked and the passenger's chances of survival were far lower than in our period of lifeboats and radio. A potential Colonist's chance of surviving to see the New World that he had sailed for, voluntarily or by request, was no better than 4 to 1.

Colonizing, like other enterprises, needs plans based on experience. English merchants forming American plantation schemes had had no colonizing experience, so their early bunglings led to a distressing waste of energy, resources and human lives.

The expedition founding Jamestown in 1607 included too many whose names were tagged *Gent.*—a social label meant to imply gentle birth (that is, of a family entitled to coat armor) but by Elizabeth I's time accorded pretty much anybody with a clean shirt and money in his purse that he had not earned with his own hands; as defined at the time: "Whosoever . . . can live without manual labour, and . . . will bear the port, charge and countenance of a gentleman, he shall be called 'master' . . . and be reputed a gentleman ever after." [5] William Byrd II, a great Virginia gentleman of a century later, described most of the Colony's founders as "Reprobates of good family," [6] which probably flattered some. Not that all were poor stuff. Some accepted ax and spade, overcame lack of familiarity with sweat and blisters, and, once they had the hang of toil, outdid their social inferiors. But the surprise caused by such exceptions indirectly confirms the bad judgment in recruiting that John Smith decried in agonized letters home to his superiors:

"When you sende againe I intreat you rather send but thirty Carpenters, husbandmen, Gardiners, fishermen, blacksmiths . . . than a thousand such as we haue." Again, apropos of the Colony's second year: ". . . those [rated] as laborers were for the most part footmen . . . that never did knowe what a dayes work was." Again, counseling the Puritans planning their colony: ". . . one hundred good labourers [are] better than a thousand such Gallants as were sent to me in [Jamestown], that would do nothing but complaine, curse, and despaire, when they saw . . . all things clean contrary to the report in England." [7]

Exasperation with such poor personnel is understandable. Yet the undeniable fact that things were "clean contrary to the report in England" was justifiable ground for complaint, if not despair, and Smith himself was by no means blameless in the matter. He was conspicuous among those spreading overblown accounts of Virginia in terms likely to attract the foolish and shiftless, following the lead of "that lovable press agent of adventure," the Reverend Richard Hakluyt, who averred that "heaven and earth never agreed better to frame a place for mans habitation." [8] To C. M. Andrews, a great modern expert on the Colonies, Roanoke Island, sandy and ill-watered, was "no fit place for a colony or even for continuous habitation." [9] But to Ralph Lane, head of the first English settlement there, it was "the goodliest and most pleasing territorie in the world." [10] Parsons praised Jamestown from the pulpit with equal unction. The Reverend Daniel Price, preaching at St. Paul's Cross, London, in 1609, promised that that hapless settlement would equal "Arabia for spices, Spain for silks, Babylon for corn. . . ." [11] Thomas Heywood's comedy *Eastward Ho*, representing the Virginian Indians as having solid gold cooking pans and precious stones underfoot, probably moved some ne'er-do-wells among the groundlings to enlist for this new Tom Tiddler's ground. Men more literate but just as rash may have been taken in by Drayton's verses (already quoted in reference to sassafras) recommending the Jamestown scheme:

> VIRGINIA,
> Earth's onely Paradise.
>
> Where Nature hath in store
> Fowle, Venison, and Fish,
>   And the Fruitfull'st Soyle,
>   Without your Toyle,
> Three Haruests more,
> All greater than you Wish. . . .
> To whose, the golden Age
> Still Nature's laws doth giue,
> No other Cares that tend,
> But them to defend
> From Winter's Rage
> That long there doth not live. . . .[12]

Which were more censurable, the Draytons and Hakluyts, who wrote such stuff without ever having visited Virginia, or the Lanes, Harriots and Smiths, who had? In any case "without your Toyle" doubtless sounded just the thing for unsettled sons of small squires and their seedy hangers-on. Projectors of other Colonies were also unscrupulous. Those backing the Popham colony in Maine imported a few Penobscot Indians and taught them to hold forth in English on "how good that country [was] for people to go and inhabit it." [13] But memory of Drayton's verses must have been particularly bitter to a Jamestowner dying of the flux complicated by malnutrition in a mosquito-ridden bark hut with an August thunderstorm pouring rain through its cracks. True, much of the Jamestowners' plight came of their own incapacity. Their "starving time" might never have come had enough of the right sort been sent out to begin with. But true also, the wrong sort had joined up in such disastrous proportions because they had been shamelessly lied to.

In his indignation John Smith could also have recalled that the reasons for planting in America drawn up by Hakluyt, Sir Humphrey Gilbert and others usually mentioned the advantage of thus ridding England of her

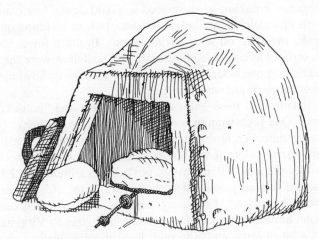

Jamestown baked its bread in squatty clay ovens like this.

superfluity of idle and worthless persons—the kind least likely to be useful in colony founding. That view of colonies as rugs to sweep the undesirable under persisted for centuries and seriously handicapped white settlement all over the world. Supposing substance in the theory that to some extent mental capacity and stable character run in families in a rough and as yet ill-understood way, Jamestown was a bad start for a new nation. It may have been cruelly fortunate that disease and hunger killed so many before women arrived, which kept the victims from reproducing their own genetic shortcomings.

Virginia's first white women were a Mistress Forrest, "gentlewoman"—that is, commanding some means of her own—and her maidservant Anne Burrowes. They remain shadowy except that Anne soon married one John Laydon, carpenter, in the first instance of the Colonists' long-notorious willingness to marry fresh-landed women. There, as in so many other respects, Jamestown set a pattern that subsequent Colonies followed for the same basic reasons. It must be kept in mind that our forebears in the Old World and then in the Colonies looked on marriage less dewy-eyedly than we do. Among gentry and the upper levels of bourgeoisie and yeomanry a marriageable daughter was basically an economic entity expected, other things being equal, to barter her favors-*cum*-dowry for the social dignity of wife and mother. The interviews between Samuel Sewall (one of the most civilized men produced by early New England) and the successive Boston ladies to whom he proposed marriage in the late 1600's sound like negotiations for a merger of two small-town banks. Forty years later Benjamin Franklin, when refused a £100 dowry to sweeten a marriage to his Philadelphia landlady's daughter (whom he found quite attractive), broke the affair off with recriminations. In much lower social strata the girl's services as combined housewife and bedfellow were the economic consideration on one side; the man's contribution as breadwinner and social anchor to windward was the other.

Little is known of these earliest wives, mothers and "housekeepers" in Jamestown. One poor woman is secure of a place in the books because in the starving time her husband killed her, "powdered [salted] her, and [ate] part of her before it was knowne; for which he was executed . . . now whether she was better roasted, boyled, or carbonado'd, I know not; but of such a dish as powdered wife, I neuer heard of," [14] commented a Jamestown chronicler.* For hasty contrast a certain Mistress Pearce, whom John Smith met in London c. 1629, had gone to Virginia in 1610, acquired a bit of land, and, she said, lived there as well as she could in London on £400 a year—then a handsome income. Not until 1619 did the company deliberately send over ninety potential wives. Company tenants could have their pick free of charge; others had to pay in tobacco to reimburse the shipowner for the lady's passage. Even though their virtue

---

* The gamier part of this was denied by Sir Thomas Gates, who reached the Colony soon afterward. His version was that the man's motive was anger, not hunger; that he cut her up to make the body easier to conceal and, when she was found, accused himself of cannibalism as excuse. Discovery of "a good quantity of meat, oatmeal, peas and beans" in his quarters, Gates averred, spoiled that story and got him condemned and burned for murder only. (William Strachey, cited in Louis B. Wright, *A Voyage to Virginia in 1609*, 98, Charlottesville, University Press of Virginia, n.d.) Anyway the poor soul was most foully slain and probably cared little whether or not she was eaten afterward.

and that of a subsequent shipment were officially vouched for, William Byrd II had his doubts. ". . . the Indian women," he wrote while deploring the Jamestowners' failure to intermarry freely with the natives, "would have made altogether as honest wives for the first planters, as the Damsels they used to purchase from aboard the Ships." [15] One way or another they are likely to have come from the bottom of the hymeneal barrel, at best pauper spinsters despairing of marriage at home. It makes one wince to think of the situation of those shy and doubtless self-consciously plain Marys and Barbaras lined up on deck to be looked over by the men of that ramshackle village of quarreling leaders and droopy rank and file. Most of them did not have to put up with the place long. Four out of five were dead within five years.

The principal significance of Jamestown until tobacco proved to be its *raison d'être* was to show subsequent Colony founders how not to do it. That it flubbed the woman problem did not mean, however, that an unimpeachable solution existed. The early Spanish colonists farther south, who also seldom brought their women, cohabited very freely with the Indians. A recent historian calls this "a most profound original difference between Latin and Anglo-Saxon America," going on to point out how in consequence Latin America also has its "racial and other tensions that the lapse of centuries still finds unresolved." [16] In the early 1700's, however, William Byrd II felt strongly that the Jamestowners should have followed John Rolfe's example by espousing Indians on the theory, very liberal for a great Virginian slaveholder, that:

> All Nations of men have the same Natural Dignity and we all know that very bright Talents may be lodged under a very dark Skin. The principal Difference between one people and another proceeds only from the Different Opportunities of Improvement. The Indians by no means want understanding . . . are . . . healthy & Strong, with Constitutions untainted by Lewdness, and not enfeebled by Luxury. . . . Morals and all considered, I can't think the Indians were much greater Heathens than the first [Jamestown] Adventurers. . . .[17]

Apparently no social problem involving sex is simple. The *Mayflower* Pilgrims had another set of difficulties when, taking the third possible course (like the Lost Colony), they brought ready-made wives and families along instead of waiting Jamestown-fashion for things ashore to shape up before sending for them. There is much to be said for and against this method. The issue was probably not, however, well threshed out, for the more one knows of the Pilgrims, the clearer it is that most of the things they did were disaster-courting improvisations.

They began with faulty geography, relying on John Smith's unjustifiably glowing account of the country that he named New England—the seaboard between New York Bay and central Maine. To promote settlement, he wrote of rich offshore islands manifesting their fertility and healthfulness in flourishing "Gardens and Corne fields . . . [and] goodly, strong and well proportioned [natives]." Assuming as others then did that latitude closely governs climate, he pointed out that this region lies as far south as Provence, Lombardy and other Old World countries noted for fruitfulness. (A Dutch contemporary made more sense: ". . . it is a good deal colder there . . . than it ought to be according to the latitude . . . freezes and snows severely." [18]) ". . . of all the four partes of the world I haue seen not inhabited," Smith went on, ". . . I would rather liue here than anywhere." [19] That and more to the same purpose determined the Pilgrims to settle around the Hudson estuary at the southern and presumably more temperate lower limit of this alluring country.

Things began at once to go badly. Tedious dickerings with governments and financial backers delayed the Pilgrims till late in the year. They let their original group of like-minded, industrious, long-acquainted zealots be diluted with many recruits (including women and children, as well as men) of the sort available in London for so risky a venture. Though doubtless of better quality than Jamestown's rank and file, they too were likely to be unstable or gullible, and few can have shared the Pilgrims' truth-seeking devoutness. So that, for every dedicated Pilgrim Father, Mother or Child seasoned by exile in Holland and bound by group loyalty to Separatist doctrine and rather ascetic ideals, there were two hired or bound strangers with no such preparation and of no such promise. There were sturdy exceptions: Myles Standish, soldier; John Alden, cooper, recruited for their skills. But some of the Pilgrims' troubles might not have occurred had the voyagers been more of a piece.

Then the *Speedwell*, the ship they bought as consort for the chartered *Mayflower* and eventual tender for fishing boats, proved unsound (or overrigged) and had to be left behind after two false starts. They made their American landfall far north of their objective, at the wrist of Cape Cod instead of at Sandy Hook. Menacing shoals deterred them from going farther south. Instead, they dithered up and down Cape Cod Bay for weeks, provisions dwindling and weather worsening all the time. Finally, in mid-December, maybe swayed by reluctance to return deep in debt to their backers, they chose a likely spot that Smith's map called Plymouth and set about making the most of a country colder and more sterile than they had hoped for—and not even in the jurisdiction of the London Company, their nominal sponsor. "At least it was the best they could find," wrote Governor William Bradford, their ablest leader, "and the season and their . . . necessities made them glad to accept of it" though it was "a hideous and desolate wilderness full of wild beasts and wild men. . . . For summer being done, all things [had] a weatherbeaten face . . . a wild and savage hue." [20]

Thus to persist was brave. It also showed great trust in a God who, they assumed, tenderly guided them. For all His care, that first winter was ghastly with famine and disease. The chief killer was probably scurvy, scourge of sailors on long voyages, the tooth-loosening, tissue-damaging result of deficiency of vitamin C. It had troubled neither passengers nor crew during the voyage, doubtless because the ship's supply of the usual minor sources of C among her stores—possibly cabbage; probably onions; certainly the unpasteurized beer of the day, a reputed scurvy preventer—had held out. But the beer and onions are known to have run short soon after the final landing. As yet the newcomers had no Indian friends to show them the trick of drinking an infusion of evergreen needles to check scurvy, as the Canadian Indians had done for Jacques Cartier's men in the 1540's. Subsisting on salt meat and ship's biscuit—and precious little of either—they died like flies, the women even worse hit than the men, the ship's crew pretty badly off, too.

Had the Indians attacked, defense would have been impossible. Fortunately for both the Pilgrims and those now proud of descending from them, a plague (still unidentified) had almost wiped out the local Indians three years before. Skulls and bones still lay where their villages had been —"a very sad spectacle" but also betokening a great divine boon: ". . . about the year 1618," wrote an early Puritan chronicler, ". . . befell a great mortality among [the Indians], the greatest that ever the memory of Father to Sonne took notice of, chiefly desolating those places where the English afterwards planted . . . by this meanes Christ (whose great and glorious workes the Earth throughout are altogether for the benefit of his Churches and chosen) not onley made room for his people to plant but also tamed the hard and cruell hearts of these barbarous Indians." [21] Actually it was probably the accidental work of profane Old World fishermen bringing in an exotic disease to which, as happened so calamitously often, the Indians had no immunity. The Colonists' attitude was inhumane, but after all, the ancient Hebrews would have said the same of a plague wiping out the Philistines, and the Pilgrims were great Bible readers. For that matter the English of 1600 would have taken such an epidemic in Ireland as also providential.

One of the few Indian survivors—he had escaped the epidemic by being kidnapped by English seamen and sold as a slave in Spain—had returned and came into Plymouth in early spring, speaking workable English and eager to help. He taught the Pilgrims the Indian ways of eeling and corn planting. Relations with outlying Indians whom disease had not mauled so badly were chancy. Their sulkiness came of previous brushes with rascally whites; the Pilgrims' touchiness was heightened by their belief that these "salvages" were devil worshipers. Unrighteous hired help further aggravated the problems of improvising the means of life. But after four precarious, plucky years Plymouth became a going concern in sharp contrast with what Jamestown had been after the same probation. In June, 1625, Bradford wrote home that the Colony "never felt the sweetness of the country till this year"; and a little later: "it pleased the Lord to give the plantation peace . . . and so to bless their labours as they had corn sufficient, and some to spare to others." [22]

Some of that improvement he laid to revision of the plan of all working for community account on equal rations of food, shelter and other necessities. Now each family was assigned land proportionate to size: "This . . . made all hands very industrious . . . much more corn was planted than otherwise would have been. The women now went more willingly into the field, and took their little ones with them to [plant] corn; which before . . . to have compelled would have been thought great tyranny and oppression." [23] Jamestown, too, had had to abandon such a "common-stock" economy and turn to individual workings. "When our people were fed out of the common store and laboured jointly together," an observer of Virginia wrote in 1614, "glad was he [who] could slip from his labour, or slumber ouer his taskes, he cared not how, nay the most honest . . . would hardly take so much true paines in a weeke, as now for themselves they will doe in a day . . . so that we reaped not so much Corne from the labour of thirtie as now three or foure do provide for themselves." [24] Less under control from the Old Country, Plymouth could make the change sooner, and its results showed soon because her leaders knew more than Jamestown's about dogged industry. Bradford was a weaver; William Brewster a yeoman turned printer in Holland; Isaac Allerton a tailor—and these small craftsmen and responsible rustics had been further integrated by contact with Dutch high standards of industry and skill. Such men would not only slog ably themselves but make sure that the ungodly among them turned to.

It is interesting to note how far back America's taste for private enterprise does go. Governor Bradford rejoiced at the failure of the quasi-communism of the Plymouth community, describing it as Platonic, though it was more likely the ill-advised scheme of the Pilgrims' merchant backers. Note also the American woman edging toward a freedom in the New World that it might never have occurred to her to expect in the Old. And even more significant was the precedent that the Pilgrims had set in leaving the Old World as a come-outer group, self-selected in two steps.

Soon after 1600 this deviant-minded group of Separatists (seceders from the Church of England, forerunners of Congregationalists) had left their rural English homes for Holland, where they could follow their religious ideals in a less authoritarian, less liturgical fashion than the Church of England required. In Holland they remained group-minded and were anxious lest their children blend into the more worldly culture of the Dutch. Hope that a second self-exile would check that drift stood high among the motives behind the voyage of the *Mayflower*. Yet only a minority was moved strongly enough to go. Of 500-odd of these prim English accumulated in Leiden by 1619, fewer than a third chose to try New England, and only 41 actually landed there. Later efforts to bring over more came to little. Those crossing the ocean may have been those taking their ministers' precepts particularly seriously, or maybe they were temperamentally more restless. In either case here was a striking reselection, a second sifting of the faithful like Gideon's. No doubt it implies a higher average of integrity in those so self-chosen. The Colonies usually owed their best human raw material to such self-recruited comrades migrating voluntarily because they deeply believed in things that were unpopular, illegal or impractical in the Old Country.

Pilgrims, Puritans, English Catholics, Quakers, Huguenots, sectarian Rhinelanders, Moravians—all were minority come-outers, seceders from accepted religions who preferred self-uprooting to conformity. Mark, however, that within their own groups they were not nonconformists. That distinguished them from the run of Jamestown-style deviants or misfits enticed by exploiters. Outside their own circle, true, the Pilgrims had been scorned at home in England as smug eccentrics, which probably stiffened their cliquishness. But within that little band of self-qualified saints—which in America became a tiny religious polity on its own—conformity was necessarily high. Doubtless that had much to do with their success. It enabled the ablest of these rather simple people, weak in experience but strong in self-righteousness, to meet the needs of colonizing, to bloom into responsible figures filling the leader niches in a miniature basic society. Much the same thing happened to less likely material after Brigham Young isolated the Mormons in Utah.

The Pilgrims' title to having created America's first *land of steady habits* (a phrase coined for Connecticut but fitting New England generally) is clear. Early Jamestown was dissolute and feckless. Early New Netherland was no YMCA camp. Early Plymouth was sober-paced in spite of some vicious capers among the ungodly lower orders. Otherwise the place lacked distinction. Scale of commitment and prestige of sponsorship came to New England only in 1630 with a great second wave of migration into Massachusetts Bay consisting of some 1,000 Puritans (dissidents hoping to purify the Church of England of anomalous practices) taking over recently settled Salem and founding Boston.

Most of its leaders, unlike the Pilgrims' craftsmen-sages, were minor gentry, prevalently from East Anglia, hotbed of Puritanism—John Winthrop, squire of Groton in Suffolk; Thomas Dudley, steward (that is, business manager) of the Earl of Lincoln; Edward Johnson, the earl's son-in-law; and some Cambridge-trained clergy. Men of affairs in a small way, they organized well. They went to John Smith for advice on what not to do, in which he was ruefully expert. Their advance party founding Salem had had trouble with religious quarrels and unrighteous recruits among the labor force; so Winthrop and Company concentrated on enlisting Puritan-minded, straitlaced men with the skills needed in a well-rounded community. For instance, the settlers receiving town lots at the founding of Newbury, Massachusetts, in 1635 included two parsons; only eight "gentlemen"; two or three merchants; one maltster; one physician; one schoolmaster; one sea captain; one dyer; one glover; three or four tanners; seven or eight shoemakers; two wheelwrights; two blacksmiths; two linen weavers; two woolen weavers; one cooper; one saddler; one sawyer; two or three carpenters. That roster amounts to a community self-supporting within itself, barring agriculture—which the handful of yeomen also listed could handle as supervisors of the thirty-odd unskilled hands also indicated.

It had been clever of Winthrop and Company to secure a royal charter for an ostensibly commercial Massachusetts Bay Company with the usual wide powers and then take the actual piece of signed and sealed parchment with them overseas. That gave the new Colony an unprecedentedly free hand 3,000 miles from the potentially meddlesome Crown. The measure presaged the Colonial mistrust of the Mother Country that would steadily reshape American ideas and ways-of-doing. C. M. Andrews, established authority on things Colonial, explains that to the leaders of the Bay Colony, "thus to rid themselves of all outside earthly authority was fundamental to the success of the Lord's mission . . . final control should not be exercised arbitrarily from England either by company or king." [25] On that implicit basis—set up with a cunning that honors the Puritans' acumen more than their candor—between 1630 and 1650 some 20,000 Puritans flocked to America, principally New England. That number is not impressive now. Then it greatly exceeded the scale of previous settlement and would not be again approached until the great migrations of Palatines and Scotch-Irish generations later.

Massachusetts Bay's community planning wisely followed Plymouth's —adaptation of the medieval manor village to Colonial needs with security and solidarity in view. This worked out to a village-green nucleus dominated by the meetinghouse and surrounded by the dwellings of the constituent families each on a small private lot. For cropping, wood supply and so on, each family also had a much larger allotment of land beyond the village; the settler, having no permanent lodging there, trudged back and forth daily to plant, harvest or cut wood. That wasted time and energy, but the resulting compactness kept all adults in close touch for defense and disciplinary guidance from the leaders and gave the settlement a ready-made social structure. Thus the founders of Lancaster, Massachusetts, explained that in assigning land they had not distinguished between the more and the less affluent "Partly to keep the Towne from scattering too farr, and partly out of Charitie [meaning benevolence] and Respect to men of meaner Estate." [26] Very decent: only that "Charitie" did not keep these tight little oligarchies from what now sounds like marked high-handedness. They carried to strange extremes the settled postmedieval English notion that prolonged entertainment of outsiders was a pernicious drain on resources and threat to solidarity. In 1671 Dorchester, Massachusetts, actually fined a man for letting his own daughter stay with him though it was inadvisable for her to try to return to her distant home and husband in heavy winter weather. When the resources of one Francis Bale struck the town fathers as too slim for his large family, they "advised him to dispose of* two of his children. His wife was not willing, and they p'swaded him to p'swade his wife to it." [27]

The compact village admirably suited subcolonizing ventures and served the Bay Colony well as her people spread westward into Connecticut and south- and westward into Long Island. Indeed her only mistake was choice of Massachusetts Bay to settle on. As Plymouth already knew, the area was colder than "home" in winter; rain was scantier and less well distributed; soil thin over rock; terrain cut up by bleak hills; and neither Boston nor Salem Harbor was better than several other as yet unexploited deepwater havens in milder climates. The wealth of potential waterpower provided by the rugged topography lacked much economic significance until after the first struggles were over. This country was a dismal contrast with the East Anglia whence many of the Puritans came—wide, level,

---

* *Dispose of* did not mean *do away with*. The intent probably was for Bale to bind out the children to a well-to-do householder under whom they would earn their keep and not remain potentially a public burden.

wet distances being drained to become rich farms with some gently rolling higher lands upcountry. Nowhere there does one see the telltale New England stone walls backbreakingly laid up by men picking stones out of the way of the plow and then finding in a few years that the land was no longer worth plowing. Their pastures eventually occasioned bitter jokes about the special sharpness of nose in Yankee sheep produced by grazing between stones. To view the fat East Anglian countryside today from the site of John Winthrop's Groton manor house is to make one wonder what possessed natives of this smiling region to settle in the ruggedest corner of America. Call it another instance of the bad judgment worsened by poor information that had already set others wasting time and lives on Roanoke Island and at Jamestown.

Fortunately East Anglia was and is amphibious, adept in shipbuilding and fishing, as well as farming. Presently New England's well-organized pioneers were not only feeding themselves with arduously raised farm crops but also vigorously exploiting the sea as both fishpond and trade highway. The fish went to Spain and Portugal, as well as to England, and to Virginia to swap for tobacco for reexport. The local forest was shipped overseas in the shape of spars, clapboard, staves for cooperage and shingles, and of New England-built deep-sea vessels not only carrying local goods but themselves often sold in foreign ports, where sound design and construction brought good prices. W. B. Weeden describes this expedient of the early 1700's as "a fleet selling itself every second year." [28] Through that crucial industry the great forest was once more shaping America, founding a tradition of ingenious shrewdness indispensable in the nation's future.

Not all Puritan emigrants chose New England. Some did well in Bermuda; others had bad luck in the Caribbean. For a while it looked as if an early lump of them would be a permanent and necessarily influential part of Virginia. Several of that Colony's clergy, including the Reverend Alexander Whitaker, who married Pocahontas to Rolfe, had Puritan leanings; so did some of the merchant leaders of the founding London Company. Indeed the country south of the James River was filling up with Puritans before the Massachusetts Bay Colony existed. But as England's religious quarrels hardened, religious pressures in Virginia increased. In the 1640's Virginia's Puritans found it advisable to shift up the Chesapeake to form their own isolated Zion at the mouth of the Severn River in the new, Catholic-founded and tolerance-minded Colony of Maryland. They called their township Providence; since 1694 it has been Annapolis. There the godly flourished and in 1655 won a hot little war with the Catholic- and Anglican-flavored forces of the Calvert family's proprietary rule.

They signalized their victory by hanging some prominent prisoners, expelling the local Jesuits, and reversing the Colony's trend toward toleration by passing anti-Catholic laws.

Most of the Colonies had some such knot of Puritans to profit by and cope with. Jersey got some as a secondary swarm from Connecticut settling Newark and below; others were fetched far enough southward to create a shore-whaling station at Cape May. In the late 1600's struggling South Carolina invited a body of them from Dorchester, Massachusetts, to build a pilot demonstration of the New England-style compact, self-protecting settlement. On a grant a few miles upcountry from Charleston they duly founded Dorchester, South Carolina, with quarter-acre house lots around a green and large family plots out in the pinewoods just as in Concord, Massachusetts, and Windsor, Connecticut—only here the water in the streams was black-swampy and the trees dripped with lugubrious Spanish moss. Two generations later most of the population moved on to found yet another Dorchester in Georgia, where the land was said to be better. In the Revolution the British captured the South Carolina Dorchester's strong little fort and burned much of the village. There remains now only the practically indestructible ramparts of the tabby* fort and the tall ruined tower of an old brick church. Long since, these Carolina Yankees, like the Maryland Yankees of Annapolis, have blended into the background and learned local notions of righteousness. Only in New England did the Puritan genius for authoritarian theocracy† flourish as thriftily as pure Puritanism found seemly.

Fond trust in God's providence and governance—strange in people otherwise so responsible and foresighted—may explain the Massachusetts Bay Colony's poor choice of site. God had caused Plymouth to flourish in New England under great difficulties. Might that not mean that thereabouts was His Promised Land for His people generally? The marrow of Massachusetts Bay was even more heaven-irradiated than Plymouth's. Its settlers sought not merely to avoid the rising storm of Stuart persecution while retaining their Englishness. They believed that God was about to

---

* A concrete of oyster shells much used in the Southern Colonies on or near the seacoast—grim-looking and formidably durable.

† Charles M. Andrews (*Colonial Period,* I, 448) denies that the Bay Colony was properly a theocracy: ". . . the influence of the clergy was entirely unofficial and without the sanction of law. They never did more than offer opinions and present recommendations." True—but Puritan governments always craved ministers' advice so strongly that the net effect was just about what a theocracy of priestly rulers could have brought about. Says Andrews: ". . . the clergy were called upon, as a matter of course . . . in affairs of a purely secular nature . . . to offer advice, draw up rules and regulations and make recommendations . . . [and] consulted that they might 'enforme us of the mind of God herein.' "

punish England for her stubbornly evil ways, wielding plague, flood, earthquake, maybe several of those combined, as in Moses' Egypt. In any case,
in that cataclysmic day the righteous would be safer far, far away. Seeking
recruits for the migration of 1630, Winthrop's group assured the prospects
that England's "sinnes, for which the Lord beginnes already to frowne
upon us . . . doe threaten evil times . . . who knowes, but that God
hath provided [New England] to be a refuge for many whome He means
to save out of the generall calamity, & seeinge the Church hath no place
to flie but into the wildernesse, what better worke can there be, than to
goe and provide tabernacles and foode for her against she comes
thether. . . ." [29] In more workaday terms, Henry Cabot Lodge suggested, England's Puritans soon began also to think of New England as
a redeployment base in case they lost the prospective fight with the Crown.

Members of such a New World Zion considered themselves able to
count on God's special favor in this world, as well as the next, provided
they observed His rules as laid down in the Bible and interpreted by His
ministers. That vision of holy prosperity appealed to godly tradesmen and
craftsmen whose gains were eroding under rural hard times and to squires
(like Winthrop) whose lands were yielding less income of late. The idea
of land of one's own certainly lured the pious tenant farmer. Such economic motives were real and present but may have been overplayed by historians of the last generation. Says Henry Bamford Parkes shrewdly:
". . . an English Puritan considering whether God wished him to move
across the Atlantic, would regard poverty or inability to exercise his talents
as a clear indication of God's will that he should move." [30] Make no mistake, the main drive behind the Bay Colony was loyalty to God's will and
to one's own eternal welfare. There is some evidence, by the way, that
Oliver Cromwell was one of those seriously considering going to New
England in the turbulent and frustrating 1630's. Had he done so, bringing
his immense energy and single-mindedness to the Colony's problems . . .
There is a really tempting germ of history as it might have been; almost
as tempting as the story, about as well vouched for, that young Napoleone
Buonaparte had a notion to go with the emigrants from France who
founded Gallipolis, Ohio, in 1790, but was dissuaded by his mother.

For years historians have tried to correct both our forebears' hero worship of early New England and the debunking that followed it. Such wide
swings of emphasis make an intelligible balance hard to strike. For instance, in spite of wishful admirers, these proto-Yankees were not equalitarian-minded. One approached the minister hat in hand. The magistrate
with his gilt-headed walking stick was Master So-and-so, his wife
was Madam, whereas the blacksmith was Goodman Such-and-such and

his wife Goodwife or Goody—a term applied to the bedmakers in Harvard dormitories well into the 1900's. Such titles usefully marked the line between social classes, which was as sharp as in Jacobean England, where, though the clever and lucky might go up the ladder a rung or two (like John Winthrop's clothier grandfather or Shakespeare using London-made money to prop up his family's uncertain social standing), the rungs were distinct and far apart. Massachusetts Bay's lawcourts made no bones of going by class distinctions. Convicted of theft, a gentleman was merely fined and deprived of the title Master; his servants, convicted as accessories, were heavily flogged. Convicted of bearing a bastard, a Boston spinster had her fine sharply reduced because her father was an eminent citizen. Nor was a gentleman as likely as a man of the lower orders to be summoned to court if a girl laid her child to him.

Assignment of pews in the meetinghouse went by social standing, gingerly worked out by a committee sensitive to learning, worldly goods and family connections as gauges of prestige. In early New Haven those below the status of Goodman-Goodwife were assigned no seats at all. As late as 1759 Boston considered that a man's grandfather having been a bricklayer disqualified him from sitting as justice of the peace. After all, however at odds with those at home about religious matters, these were Jacobean Englishmen, who did not become Americans with yeasty ideas about one-man-as-good-as-another merely by crossing the sea. They brought ashore with them the ideas of the 1600's about respecting the condition (that is, social stratum) in which God had seen fit to place you. Early Virginia was much the same for the same reasons. Consider the York County tailor who was fined for matching his horse against another for 2,000 pounds of tobacco, "it being contrary to Law for a Labourer to make a race, being a sport for Gentlemen." [31] To ascribe to the first few generations of New Englanders a taste for the democratic notions of later Americans only distracts notice from the genuine virtues that they showed in their own time—the industry, gumption and pride that made them such capable Colony founders. They did, however, have the foresight—or luck—to avoid the feudal-flavored English institution of primogeniture entail, by which under certain preconditions the eldest son inherited a large estate, whereas in Virginia this device persisted as a prop of the plutocratic stratum until the Revolution. (New England indeed verged toward the reverse system, for there elder sons, as they grew up, were likely to take up new lands of their own and rear families independent of the home-farm, while the youngest was expected to stay home, look after the parents as they aged and take over the old place when they died.) There were other hints that in certain respects the New World was not altogether like the Old. Governor Joseph Dudley of Massachusetts and his son drew their swords to chastise the drivers of some carts that had not got out of the way of their coach quickly enough; one carter told the governor: "I am as good flesh and blood as you," [32] closed with him and broke his sword, and when the governor had him arrested and arraigned, he was discharged without penalty. It sounds like nothing startling now, but then such an outcome would have been pretty much unthinkable in an Old World country of that time.

"What sought they thus afar?" asked rhyming Mrs. Felicia Hemans in a conspicuous contribution to the Puritan-Pilgrim legend:

> . . . Bright jewels of the mine?
> The wealth of seas, the spoils of war?
> They sought a faith's pure shrine. . . .
>
> They have left unstained what there they found—
> Freedom to worship God.

That well-meant British distortion of the Pilgrims' purpose long clogged acknowledgment of New England's built-in intolerance. Neither Pilgrims nor Puritans, of course, sought religious freedom in any recognizable sense. For the good of their faith—the only true faith, hence the only one that they could afford to permit—they wanted an isolation in which they could be just as hidebound as God required. A Puritan of the 1630 landings described his comrades as undergoing "with much cheerfulnesse . . . the laborious breaking up of bushy ground, with the continued toyl of erecting houses . . . in this howling desert . . . that they might enjoy Christ and his Ordinances in their primitive purity." [33] The Reverend Richard Mather, founder of America's first intellectual dynasty, reasoned that "if the discipline which we [early Puritans] practice be (as we are persuaded of it) the same which Christ hath appointed and therefore unalterable, we see not how another can be lawful." [34] His son, the Reverend Increase Mather, deplored "hideous clamors for liberty of conscience." The Reverend John Norton had already described toleration as "liberty to blaspheme, to seduce others from the living God . . . to tell lies in the name of the Lord." The Reverend Urian Oakes considered any toleration of clashing religious opinions the "first born of all abominations." [35]

And so on and on from pulpit after pulpit. It was not wholly priestly arrogance but somewhat analogous to the anger of a responsible physician denouncing cancer quacks or the exasperation of a public-health official when apathy and ignorance clog measures to stamp out a typhoid epidemic. What good had it done to cross the sea to escape God's wrath against wicked doctrines if preachers of error were allowed to reinfect the innocent new Zion? So the Puritans were obliged to hang a few Quakers who forced their way through the quarantine with talk about the Inner Light. On Christendom's holy days the same sense of preventive duty banned the merriment that aped pagans and Papists. Christmas was forbidden not because the birth of Christ lacked weight in Puritan theology but because the carryings-on traditional at Yuletide distracted the soul from its best interests and smelled of ancient heathen festivals, even of "a deference to the Pope of Rome." As for May Day, it was shamelessly secular and tainted with pagan lewdness. John Endicott can have had no qualms about ordering the Maypole of Merry Mount cut down, thereby inspiring Hawthorne with the stereotype of the black-garbed, lank-haired Puritan killjoy. Besides, the Merrymounters had hampered the Lord's Chosen, outdoing them in the peltry trade, treating the Indians more tactfully—and selling them firearms.

Nor would technically political democracy have suited the rearing and circumstances of the early New Englanders any better than social equalitarianism or religious tolerance. One-man-one-vote never entered their heads. At the widest their town meetings, though easygoing in the tone of the proceedings, excluded many variously disqualified by lack of property or of religious credentials. The freemen* of Massachusetts Bay who elected the governor and the General Court (legislature) were a close oligarchy of church members. The Reverend John Cotton, a chief religious sponsor of the Bay Colony, could not "conceyve that ever God did ordeyn [democracy] as a fitt government eyther for churche or commonwealth. If the people be governors. who shall be governed?" Participation in Colonywide elections was also only for church members, and it was the ministers who determined who deserved membership.

The clergy's principal part in this society was taken for granted to a degree difficult for us now to envisage. It was not only fitting but, in the eyes of the congregation, proper that the minister should tell government and people what God wished done. How else could they know? The cubical meetinghouse on the village green housed both Sabbath worship of God and the town meeting that carried out His wishes. (Use of the church building as courtroom or schoolhouse often occurred elsewhere, for instance in Virginia in the 1600's and in Missouri in the early 1800's, but usually only until the community could erect a separate secular building.

---

* *Freeman,* as used in the Bay Colony, had nothing to do with the distinction between bondsman or indentured servant and a free man with no such legal shackles. Instead, it meant a man possessing "the freedom of the company," which usually but not always implied ownership of a share, in any case having the right to participate in its corporate proceedings.

It took longer for a typical New England township to get around to a town hall.) It might also be used casually to store township property— the train-band's gunpowder or hay taken as taxes. But that implies no casualness on the Sabbath. The tithingmen kept the drowsy awake by tickling the nose of an adult with a foxtail or feather on one end of a pole and rapping the pate of a child with a knob on the other.

They also kept the presence of theocracy lively in people's minds by seeking out scandalous behavior, such as swimming or traveling on Sunday, and kept the town's list of habitual drunkards to whom drink was not to be sold. But then it was everybody's duty, and the pleasure of some, to denounce others' sins to the minister for reproof and discipline by public acts of repentance. Virginia, Maryland, South Carolina, even the slack Dutch in New Netherland (notably in Stuyvesant's time), did or tried to do things that now sound outrageous about Sunday observance, dress, fornication, and religious dissent. That was the way of Britain and Europe of the 1600's, and the early Colonists, necessarily children of their time, reflected it. This "holy enterprise of minding other people's business" was, however, particularly "a folkway of New England" [36]—thanks to an energetically theocratic climate, it developed farthest and lasted longest there. Another symptom of religiosity was the wide use of tags of religious cant as names for one's children. Puritans thought it nothing out of the way to name girls Deliverance Legg and Fear Brewster; boys had Preserved, Wrestling, Increase inflicted on them, a thing largely unknown in other Colonies. The only parallel to it that I know of is the Italian anarchist father of not so long ago who named his three daughters Hunger, Poverty and Revolution; the leaden zeal is the same.

New England cannot, of course, be regarded as all of a cultural piece. Roger Williams, exiled from the Bay Colony for contumaciously thinking out loud in the pulpit, developed the notion of government by consent of the governed and nudged toward religious toleration in Rhode Island. Plymouth—the Old Colony—was never as theocratic as her larger neighbor, maybe because Dutch liberality had rubbed off on her leaders while they lived in Holland. The swarmings from Massachusetts that ousted the Dutch around Hartford also showed twitches of liberal impulse. But New Haven, the other element in Connecticut-to-be, renounced trial by jury because the Bible mentions no such thing, and in some respects its celebrated Blue Laws restricted personal behavior more grimly than those of the Bay Colony. That came of eager carrying out of the Puritan's belief that it is a sin not to do all one can, including legal compulsion, to keep one's brother from sinning.

How much sin of other kinds the theocracy had to cope with cannot now be determined. According to its leaders, the amount was formidable even among God's Chosen, for, as Puritans read the Bible and John Calvin, all human beings were born soaked in original sin and few indeed were ever redeemed from it. The Reverend Thomas Shepard, eminent successor of the great Thomas Hooker in the meetinghouse pulpit at Cambridge, was specific, not merely speculative, about spiritual transgressions: "Every natural man is born full of sin, as full as a toad is of poison, as full as ever his skin can hold; mind, will, eyes, mouth, every limb of his body, and every piece of his soul, is full of sin . . . thy heart is a foul sink of all atheism, sodomy, blasphemy, murder, whoredom, adultery, witchcraft, buggery; so that if thou hast any good thing in thee, it is but as a drop of rose-water in a bowl of poison . . . thou feelest not all these things stirring within thee at one time . . . but they are in thee, like a nest of snakes in an old hedge." [37] And there, incidentally, speaks the boy reared in the Old Country; New England planted few hedges and certainly had no old ones.

Four of the eight sins catalogued above are erotic, for the Puritans deserved their name for severity in such matters. They really did affix the scarlet letter to the adulterous, though that was less severe than the death penalty imposed at least twice in the early Bay Colony and was no Puritan invention but an old institution from the Merrie England of medieval times. The lash punished simple fornication. Even couples marrying each other later were not exempt. A Dutchman visiting early Hartford was amazed to see a man and wife who had anticipated the parson getting a whipping apiece and a penitential six weeks' enforced separation. Birth of a first child indecorously soon and too mature sent many a married couple to the pillory or the stocks, and after that secular ordeal they still had to stand up in meeting next Sabbath and make prolonged and fervent protestations of guilt and contrition. Such holy prudery was also common among non-Puritan Colonists, again transplanting an Old Country institution. In England in 1634, for instance, the Bishop of Salisbury's ecclesiastical court tried numerous cases of bastardy, fornication and incontinency before marriage. It would later be conspicuous among Methodists and Quakers. But to judge from Winthrop's account of the self-humiliation that Captain John Underhill staged to purge himself of adultery, the Bay Colony version of such exhibitions must have been particularly crawly.

Some historians suspect that the non-Puritan minority of hired or indentured hewers of wood and drawers of water, maybe 20 percent of the population in early New England, contributed more than their share of sin. Probable enough; but the surmise must be modified by the likelihood that upper-class transgressions would get hushed up and never appear in surviving records. For an exception, the Reverend John Cotton, son of the Bay Colony's most eminent minister, a noted foe of Sabbathbreaking and light-mindedness among women, was dismissed for notorious breaches of the Seventh Commandment and, as further penalty, assigned to a Puritan congregation in Charleston, South Carolina—presumably a place where parsons' morals mattered less. The Reverend Stephen Batchellor of Hampton, New Hampshire, husband of "a lusty comely woman" and eighty years old to boot, nevertheless "did solicit the chastity of his neighbor's wife";[38] she told her husband, saving him from at least actual adultery. They barred the old gentleman from his pulpit for two years and then reinstated him, possibly on the ground that by then he was old enough to know better. As the 1700's came in this leniency filtered downward to some extent. Premarital relations between couples likely to marry seem to have grown so common that some congregations took no notice unless the interval between nuptials and childbed was less than six months.

Strange severities persisted alongside common sense, however. New Englanders believed that children born on Sunday had to have been conceived on Sunday, and since lying with one's wife on Sunday was heinous profanation, some ministers refused to baptize Sunday-born babies. Inevitably the odds tripped up one such parson by bringing his wife to bed with twins on a Sunday. Less comical was the plight of Abigail Muxon of the Buzzards Bay country whose light conduct with a man not her husband had earned her a formal censure in her flighty youth. Thirty years later— no statute of limitations on sin—a harsh new minister dug up the old story and arraigned her for it all over again. New witnesses testified to things that they swore they still remembered. The elderly culprit, doubtless exasperated beyond discretion, swore they lied—and was thrown out of the church.

Much grotesquerie came of the Puritans' following the folkways that God laid down for the early Jews. They deplored gambling not because it flaws the sense of economic responsibility but because, as Cotton Mather explained, the Old Testament recommends the casting of lots to ascertain God's will, so it should not be made part of common games. From the same authority came that early Bay Colony statute making adultery a capital offense; the particular occasion was a case of a Colonist's "soliciting an Indian squaw to incontinency." [39] Thomas Granger of Duxbury, indentured servant in his late teens, confessed to having carnally abused (at various times) a mare, a cow, two goats, five sheep, two calves and a turkey; the Old Colony duly hanged him after killing each of the defiled animals before his eyes as the Bible prescribes. "At New Haven," John Winthrop recorded, ". . . a sow . . . among other pigs had one without hair, and some other human resemblances . . . also one eye blemished, just like one eye of a loose fellow in the town, which occasioning him to be suspected, he confessed . . . for which . . . they put him to death" [40]—with Winthrop's approval formally given on request. The New England Sabbath, Saturday dusk to Sunday dusk, banning all recreation and all but absolutely necessary nonreligious activity, was grotesque for all but the most spiritual-minded. And recall that it was because the Puritans of Salem took seriously the Bible's "Thou shalt not suffer a witch to live" that they made such grisly spectacles of themselves for all posterity.

Posterity has probably made too much of that. In view of how witch-minded the 1600's were throughout the Western world there is no reason to see in Salem a particular mass reaction to Puritan repressions. Both England and non-Puritan Europe were still hunting witches well into the 1700's, after Salem had given it up. The blame for her antics probably lies on the self-intoxicated Puritan ministers—that ordained calamity Cotton Mather conspicuous among them—who had been trumpeting the menacing reality of black magic and miracles in what may have been a frantic effort to shore up their fading importance as spiritual chieftains. In view of their prestige and the hysterical use they made of it, the wonder is that Boston and New Haven did not join in. Charlestown, Massachusetts, had hanged a witch in 1656. In 1680 a Dutch visitor to Boston found the town humming with what struck him as morbid prattle about witchcraft, and when he left, a woman was under sentence of death for practicing black magic on her husband. He could not know that after a series of hesitant reprieves she would eventually be freed scatheless. Until the theocracy had begun its supernal screaming about miracles, witches and portents, common sense had been undermining superstition most gratifyingly. Occasionally New England magistrates interposed between witch and jury and let her off with a promise to leave town or, like Josiah Winslow, heard out a Plymouth man accusing his neighbor of witchcraft and then slapped on him a heavy fine for malicious slander.

Bible-mindedness left another mark on the nation-to-be in New England's cult of christening children after obscure Old Testament figures—Eliphalet, Zephaniah, Ozias, Ithiel, Elkanah and so on—for no better reason than that the context was holy. That can be forgiven because the same Bible-mindedness also created the precocious and enriching Yankee cult of education. Virginia had set aside lands to support some sort of college in 1619, before the Pilgrims saw Cape Cod. But Indian troubles forced abandonment of the scheme; it was seventy years before its revival founded William and Mary. A generation after New Netherland was born it had schools in only (modern town names used) Albany, New Castle, Delaware, and New York City. The Quakers in Pennsylvania, though valuing literacy, mistrusted higher education as worldly, so it took long to rouse even the germ of a university there, and then its parents were mainly Anglicans, Presbyterians and a few half agnostics. But Harvard was founded within seven years of the birth of the Massachusetts Bay Colony. The purpose, like that of Virginia's aborted plan, was religious—to train youths in theology to succeed the English divines who came out with the first settlers. But the eventuality was an institution greatly fostering secular culture.

Likewise, the lower schools that Puritans required townships to set up were meant to train laymen to read the Bible and such ancillary works as Foxe's *Book of Martyrs*. In 1785 the *New England Primer*, basic textbook for Yankee boys and girls, was still singing:

> The Praises of my Tongue
> I offer to the LORD,
> That I was taught and learnt so young
> To read his [sic] holy Word . . .[41]

and its content was still largely religious, even the alphabet from "In Adam's fall / We sinned all . . ." to "Zaccheus he / Did climb the tree / His Lord to see." There also persisted such edifying thoughts for children as

> I in the burying place may see
> Graves shorter far than I;
> From Death's arrest no age is free,
> To read his [sic] holy Word . . .[41]

Here again, however, a thing often thought of as Puritanical religiosity was no Yankee innovation. Elizabethan England had combined religious instruction with the alphabet. But arriving at literacy through soul-improving materials was especially needful among Separatists and Puritans because they eschewed the storytelling frescoes, carvings and painted windows that the medieval church used to give the laity some acquaintance with Bible lore and theology. Those devices led to image worship and unfitting association of holy things with the delight of the eye. Better go direct to God's written Word for knowledge of the Last Supper, Noah's Flood and the wrath to come. Generations later, such assumptions, modified by secular notions about social equality, led to the American public school system—and the doctrine that literacy is a basic right.

The frequency with which Puritan ways-of-doing had such analogues in the Mother Country shows again that New Englanders were as much recently transplanted Englishmen as members of a growingly distinct new culture. Not even their daily family worship and use of pious cant in mundane affairs were singular. Many a non-Puritan gentlewoman or London merchant's wife was then teaching her maidservants the catechism or rejoicing mawkishly in her small son's precocious prayerfulness. Well into the 1700's bills of lading signed by anything but pious shipmasters and consignors in England, as well as in all Colonies, might read: "Shipped by the grace of God . . . upon the good ship called the [*Venture*] wherein so is master under God in this present voyage [John Tarpaulin] . . . and by God's grace bound for . . ." [42] Leghorn or Lisbon. And in spite of their alleged mistrust of the good things of life, Puritans shared their Old Country cousins' liberal use of drink, downing beer and cider not only because water was thought unwholesome but also because these were enjoyable "good creatures of God" as the Bible said. Their special touch begins to appear, however, in the Bay Colony's law passed at Winthrop's behest banning health drinking as "inducement to drunkenness, occasion of quarrelling and bloodshed [and] much waste of wine and beer and vexing to masters and mistresses of the feast . . . forced thereby to drink more oft than they would." [43] In New Haven self-indulgent "tipling" was a crime, and it was taken as clear evidence of this offense that twenty people had downed a gallon of rum among them. "These English live soberly," wrote a Dutchman visiting early Hartford with a surprise natural in a man fresh from New Amsterdam, "drink only three times at a meal, and whoever drinks himself drunk they tie to a post and whip him, as they do thieves in Holland." [44]

He also noted his hosts' habit of invidious comparisons between themselves and outsiders, saying that "they are Israelites . . . [Dutchmen] are Egyptians . . . the English in Virginia are also Egyptians" [44]—the implied metaphor from *Exodus* being obvious. From the beginning New England had borrowed Biblical terms in which to state that she was God's precious remnant reserved from apocalyptic destruction like Lot from Sodom, the apple of His eye, the leaven of the world, and that New Englanders were His new Chosen People. That self-esteem not only fed itself, deepening differences by its very emphasis, but proved appallingly durable. A mere 170 years after the first settlers of Hartford had entertained their Dutchman, George Cabot, eminent seaman-merchant of Boston, was calmly stating his unprejudiced conclusion that "there is more wisdom and virtue [in New England] than in any other part of the United States." [45] Even now some non-Yankees suspect that some of that feeling lingers on Beacon Hill.

Whenever the proto-Yankee sounds as harsh as some of his first parsons, recall, however, that, as J. F. Jameson has pointed out, the rigidities of "intolerance and persecution in the seventeenth century . . . bred solidarity and public spirit in the eighteenth and nineteenth" [46] and that mass common sense did get the better of New England's melodramatic Calvinism in the long run. The same Bay Colony that hanged adulterers made one of the first laws against cruelty to animals, maybe because the Bible told the merciful man to be merciful unto his beast, but it was couched in wider terms: "No man shall exercise any Tiranny or Cruelty toward any bruite Creatures . . . usually kept for man's use . . ." [47] and there were convictions under it. Somehow out of the organized taboos of the seed of Abraham and the black-minded theology of Calvin came a massive integrity that (if it only could have been done gracefully) had reason to admire itself. At their best the emergent Yankees were exhilarating people.

Samuel Sewall had the misfortune to be an *ad hoc* judge in some of the Salem witch trials. Soon afterward his baby daughter died. A consoling friend asked to read from the Bible struck on Matthew 12:7: "But if ye had known what this meaneth . . . ye would not have condemned the guiltless." Sewall, the pattern Puritan, was all conscience, all superstition about Scripture texts, all certainty that God concerned Himself with the fall of sparrows and the ominous deaths of beloved children. This chance text, it seemed to his conscience, maybe already uneasy about the goings-on at Salem, could mean only that the verdicts had been mistaken. As soon as possible he was standing up in meeting and bowing in corroboration as the minister read out: "Samuel Sewall, sensible of the reiterated strokes of God upon himself . . . as to the Guilt contracted [in the Salem trials] . . . desires to take the Blame and Shame of it, asking pardon of men, and especially desiring prayers that God . . . pardon that sin. . . ." [48]

Consider also the public whipper of New Haven, who, ordered to flog an erring sister in 1699, suddenly decided he would do no such thing; he'd rather pay a fine for refusing. Nobody else would take the job, so the lady went unflogged, and thenceforth the good old custom of discouraging whoring with the lash gradually disappeared throughout Zion. And Abraham Davenport of the Connecticut legislature on that awesome dark day of 1780, when "though there were neither clouds nor smoke in the atmosphere, the sun did not appear all day . . . and people were out wringing their hands and howling, 'The day of Judgment is come,' . . ." [49] Davenport rose in his place and said it might well be the day of doom, but that was the Lord's affair; his own was to do his best by public affairs until divine intent was clear, so let them fetch candles and go on with the lawmaking. Candles were forthcoming, and business proceeded, though all members, Davenport as concerned as any, were shaking in their buckled shoes. Or for an involuntary symbol: The Reverend Ebenezer Gay, minister for seventy years of the still-surviving Old Ship meetinghouse in Hingham, Massachusetts, was still active after his ninetieth birthday. One Sabbath morning he failed to emerge from the nearby parsonage to march to meeting as usual when the bell began to ring. It rang to the end of its stint—still no sign of the minister. They went and found him seated in his chair, duly wearing gown and bands, a scroll of sermon in his lifeless hand, ready to rise when the bell would warn that it was time to go do his duty by the Lord and His Chosen People.

By the time of Davenport and the Reverend Mr. Gay the Dutch had ceased troubling Zion for five generations. At every point their procedures —and results—had differed widely and disastrously from New England's. Too late and too little had Dutchmen been encouraged to emigrate, take up American lands and fetch over breeding families. Further, though these were the most literate people in Europe, the Dutch West India Company had been slack about schools for New Netherland. Complaints about that and other neglect of the Colony got small heed from its officers absorbed in such more pressing matters as the price of slaves on the Gold Coast and what Spanish ships the company's privateers had gutted. Between 1620 and 1650 some 50,000 people landed to build up New England. In the same period New Netherland got only some 8,000, mostly men, probably of poor quality. It was charged that whereas the Dutch *East* India Company sent out to its trading posts in the Spice Islands only carefully chosen and long-trained officials, the sister West India Company thought dull inexperience good enough for New Amsterdam and that the better recruits for rank and file went to the rich operations in Africa and the Sugar Islands. Actually the reputation of the Dutch trading garrisons in West Africa, though no worse than that of other nations there, was pretty foul; one wonders what the discards sent to America can have been like.

At least Dutch logistics were good enough to spare New Netherland a starving time, and the wage-earning craftsmen and indentured servants sent—though "Most of them . . . very ignorant in regard to true religion," wrote a Dutch parson in 1645, "and very much given to drink" [50] —were never quite as deplorable as their lamentable opposite numbers in Jamestown. But the compliment is feeble. The best of the lot may have been the peasants half-forced by their landlords to adventure overseas, often so countrified that they still lacked surnames. When the same roster included two men named Jan Jans (John, son of John), they were distinguished by the names of their native villages as Jan Jans van Aalst and Jan Jans van Eysden, say, so their modern American descendants have Knickerbocker names implying a "dignity in the New World never enjoyed in the Old." [51] To this day Old World writers tend to name their wealthy American characters Van Something-or-other; Françoise Sagan is a recent example.

Dixon Ryan Fox, considering the puniness of New Netherland and the bristling success of New England, dwelt on the relative levels of civilization in their respective Mother Countries. In the early 1600's the Dutch already enjoyed wide freedom of religion; much freedom of expression; high employment; wide disparities in wealth, true, but the taste to avoid tactless display. So most Dutchmen lacked the emigrating impulse that made sense for many East Anglian or West Country Puritans. In this wry view "the success of New England and the failure of its rival were caused by the superiority of the Netherlands over 'merrie' England as a place to enjoy life." [52] It bolsters this theory to learn that the Dutch were almost outnumbered in their own Colony. Of the first 300 persons married in the official Reformed church in New Amsterdam, only 163 were Dutch. Governor Willem Kieft told a Jesuit French missionary in the 1640's that he ruled men with eighteen different languages; counting the Indians hanging around, he probably did. The first settlers, though under Dutch auspices, were French-speaking Walloons from what is now Belgium. Danes, other Scandinavians, refugee Portuguese Jews from Brazil, refugee Huguenots mostly from the west and south of France, infiltrating Yankees— New York was a melting pot long before the metaphor was coined.

Well before England ousted the Dutch in 1664, Long Island as far as Oyster Bay was conceded to Yankees swarming across the Sound. Still nearer—Hempstead, Gravesend, Eastchester—were Yankee settlements. There was something almost engaging about the ease with which New Netherlanders (including incumbent Governor Stuyvesant, who stayed quietly on his Manhattan farm the rest of his life) took the change to British sovereignty. Already peevish about being the West India Company's stepchildren, they may have sensed that British rule would mean less bickering and better times—as eventually it did. Their language, however, was more durable than the Walloons' and Huguenots' French. It blended with English in a predominantly Dutch pidgin persisting into the 1800's in backwaters, leaving in today's American speech several solid, homely words: *cruller, cookie, boss, scow, sleigh, coleslaw, boodle, snoop, stoop* (for doorsteps). It is possible, though highly debatable, that the term *Yankee** for those sharp-elbowed New Englanders was a contraction

---

* This book will use *Yankee* strictly to designate New Englanders—that is, people whose Americanism originates in the New England Colonies or states. It will not use it in the Southern sense of non-Southerner, particularly from north of the Ohio River-Mason and Dixon Line, or in the British usage as meaning American generally.

of Jan Kees (John Cheese), a contemptuous nickname that the Dutch applied to them in the early days of wrangling about Long Island. In any case, architects and philologists would agree with James Truslow Adams that the Dutch mark on America has been wider and deeper than their small numbers and short formal hold on the land would seem to call for.

Dutch acceptance of British rule without much lost-cause agitation was not so noteworthy then as it would be now. Before the French Revolution and Napoleon's wars invented the nation-in-arms, before the Romantics invented chauvinism, men slipped with less sense of national treason from one culture-plus-loyalty to another. In West Africa in the 1600's the English, Dutch or Danish slave depot often saw its white employees desert to enlist with the competing nationality down the beach. When New France cracked down on unlicensed fur traders from French Canada, numbers of them went over to the Colonies and apparently thought little of it; so did the dauntless explorer Pierre Radisson; so did Father Louis Hennepin, missionary of equal courage, though lower reputation. The French Crown, following medieval precedent, had Swiss guards; the Netherlands had the Scots-Dutch regiments. Indeed it was cosmopolites who discovered America. Italian Columbus offered his scheme to Portugal, England, Spain; had France also in mind; and would have sailed for Henry VII or Charles VIII as happily as for Ferdinand and Isabella. The Italian Cabots did sail for England; Italian Verrazano for France; English Hudson for the Dutch. The Reverend John Robinson, pastor of the Pilgrims-to-be, seriously considered a Dutch suggestion that he settle them in New Netherland, though it was clear that this entailed renouncing English allegiance. Consider Peter Minuit, Walloon refugee to the Rhineland; then governor of New Netherland for the Dutch; then losing that job only to pop up soon in charge of the Swedes' new Colony on the lower Delaware.

From all that, one cannot, however, argue a generalized tolerance in our forebears. The emotional chasm between Protestant and Catholic was too seldom crossed. In the early Colonists' Europe, society's aggressive feelings preferred to come out in religious hatreds of great intensity and often highly destructive impact. Those Europeans' loyalties to Rome or Luther or Calvin could carry higher charges than what they felt about King Charles or King Louis or Their High Mightinesses the Lords the States-General of the United Netherlands. Even the Stuarts' hold on the English Jacobites owed much of its strength to Catholic vs. heretic and to bishop vs. Dissenter. Such religious affinities across the bounds of throne-centered nationalities had the same feel as modern supranational affinities among members of Communist parties.

South Carolina exemplified this in her different handlings of two successive bodies of French. In the late 1600's she had an influx of Huguenots

(French Calvinist Protestants). Frictions did arise: The rival Anglican and English-Dissenter factions in local politics, uneasy lest the newcomers become an embarrassing third party holding the balance of power, tried to deny them full civic standing. All were Protestants together, however, and fairly soon accommodations were made, and Charleston's prevalent English, Scotch-Irish and Welsh were getting on not only with the Huguenots but also with Germans, Dutch and sprinklings of Swiss, Quakers and Yankee Puritans. Yet in the 1750's the same Colony, grown stabler and more populous, reacted nastily when England landed there a body of the hapless Acadians, Catholic French peasants evicted from Nova Scotia—the *Evangeline* people. Their tactless religion caused suspicion that they might stir up the Indians and Negro slaves; nor did apprehension lessen when the exiles claimed to be prisoners of war entitled to treatment as such and exempt from schemes to farm them out as civilian public charges. Some 10 percent of the poor devils solved their problem by dying. More escaped or were shipped away. The question of what to do with the residue was taken care of—to the satisfaction of the Colony, if not the Acadians—by turning them over as forced labor to the Huguenot settlers, descendants of their traditional and extremely bitter religious foes.

The Huguenots whom South Carolina so successfully absorbed were a notably self-selected group analogous to the Yankee Puritans in their virtues and lacking some of their less endearing qualities. The relative ease with which they settled down in America (and elsewhere) must greatly have surprised the King of France's ministers, for these very same tough sectarians had been for more than 100 years the despair of royal authority. In France's religious civil wars of the 1500's, the leather-clad Huguenot troopers had anticipated Cromwell's New Model Army with their combination of psalm-singing zeal and hard-charging discipline. They had forced the Catholic French Crown to recognize them as a virtual state within the state with special religious privileges and fortified cities of refuge in the west and south of France, in which they soberly prospered in trade and manufactures. The great Cardinal Richelieu, acting for Louis XIII, set himself to break them down. After a famous siege he captured their nucleus fortress of La Rochelle—still a very "proud city of the waters," its castles still guarding the old port as in the Three Musketeers' day—in an unmistakable beginning of the end. By families or small groups, thousands of Huguenots left France for good. Far more remained. After forty years of steady gnawing at their position, the government of Louis XIV revoked the famous Edict of Nantes in 1685, withdrawing the last vestige of toleration. The ensuing emigration has been estimated as high as half a million men, women and children, including a critical proportion of France's craftsmen, businessmen, scholars and so many seamen that French shipping did not recover for generations.

France's loss was the Protestant world's gain. Already aware of Huguenot quality through the previous trickle of exiles, England, Holland, Denmark, Sweden and the German Protestant states offered subsidized transport here, tax exemptions there to attract such valuable citizens and—also important then—fellow foes of Rome. Wherever they settled, they founded new industries, refined established ones, stiffened armies and navies, and left anomalous French names (Bosanquet in England, LeBleu in Holland and so on) as memorials in today's telephone directories. In this Diaspora some went directly to America, landing all up and down the seaboard: New England, New York, Pennsylvania, Virginia, the Carolinas. Others, such as the Bayards, who were so prominent in New York, and Andrew Doz, manager of William Penn's wine-growing experiments in Pennsylvania, did so after a stay in England or Holland. Beverley's *The History and Present State of Virginia* (1705), the first synoptic account of the Old Dominion, may well have been written to attract Huguenots, for of its first six editions, four were in French.

The Huguenots did quite as well for America as for any Old World foster home. John Fiske worked it out that the forebears of three Presidents of the Continental Congress (John Jay of New York, Henry Laurens of South Carolina, Elias Boudinot of New Jersey) all had come from within 10 miles of one another in the country outside La Rochelle. Jacob Leisler, creator of proto-Revolutionary turbulence in New York, was German-born of Huguenot stock. As a boy Anthony Benezet had fled with his Huguenot parents from France to England, turned Quaker there, migrated again to Philadelphia, and became an indispensable pioneer in the movements to get rid of slavery, curb the Demon Rum and treat Indians better. Maybe because they came in small groups to settlements already under way, they could blend their common sense and skills into the New World with a lack of friction that was almost diffident. In New York for a while they and their Walloon fellow Calvinists had a separate French-speaking temple; in Charleston a similar one is commemorated in the pseudo-Gothic Huguenot church (now a museum) by an annual service conducted in French by a Philadelphian Presbyterian minister with a Scottish name. But sooner than among the Dutch the English tongue took over, and most of the Huguenots' descendants turned to either Anglicanism—in most Colonies the faith of the topmost strata—or the Yankee-, Scottish- or Dutch-style versions of Calvinism. In Charleston the Hugers gave in to being called Yewjee; the Legarés, in becoming Legree, inadvertently supplied a name for the most notorious villain ever created by an American writer. Boston made Bowdoin (pronounced Boad'n) out of Baudouin. In Virginia, D'Aubigny turned into Dabney. In time few thought *Huguenot* at all when the Manigaults of Charleston became the richest family in the Colonies; or Peter Faneuil, no pauper either, gave Boston its public hall; or "Nolichucky Jack" Sevier led the over-the-mountains settlements in creating a sovereign state called Franklin.

Such names can be overselected. Also among the Huguenots' descendants were the husband of Mrs. Lydia Huntley Sigourney, who weakly let his wife become the overfertile queen bee of American female poets in the mid-1850's, and Charles Guiteau, the paranoid petty swindler who assassinated President Garfield. It is very clear, however, that early immigrant for early immigrant, the Huguenots' contributions of energy, integrity and skill were outstanding and the more useful for being widely distributed. As recruiter of the kind of people that America-to-be needed, Louis XIV was quite as helpful as anybody who went about it deliberately.

The Sun King's contemporary and pensioner, Charles II of England, also did well in that line, however. He granted a tract of almost virgin wilderness west of the Delaware River to William Penn in informal settlement of repudiated Crown obligations to Penn's late father, an admiral high in the confidence of the Stuarts. They often carved off kingdom-size pieces of America—Maryland, the Carolinas, East Jersey—for individual proprietors, the Earl of This or Sir Somebody That, periwigged worldlings with handles to their names and friends at court. Such men's jerky efforts to get revenue and prestige out of their grants by archaic patterns of landholding did neither them nor their settlers much good. Admiral Penn would probably have fumbled as much as anybody. But his son was several kinds of rarity: an amateur statesman whose schemes took root; a Quaker convert of upper-class rearing; a winning manipulator of ideas and writer of religious tracts. Of all his good sides, maybe the best came out when, as proprietor of Pennsylvania, he was sitting as magistrate and a Swedish woman was haled before him for witchcraft. "Art thou a witch?" Penn asked. "Hast thou ridden through the air on a broomstick?" and when the addled wretch said yes, he said that was her privilege; he knew of no law against it; then on his recommendation the jury found her guilty of only "the common fame of being a witch," [53] not of actually being one, and turned her loose. Thanks to Penn and the social courage of his fellow Quakers, Pennsylvania—a name that Charles II coined to honor the old admiral—promised for a while to be the most civilized place in the Western world. Partly through certain early mistakes, partly through attrition from outside, it has greatly changed. Penn, standing broad-brimmed and knee-breeched on the pinnacle of Philadelphia's City Hall, may be as sad as anybody about that.

In the beginning his Quaker settlers must have sounded like unpromising material. Their Religious Society of Friends, sprung up among restless souls in the raw north of England, then infiltrating Wales and (in a smaller way) Ireland, taught a semimystical relation between God and the individual that, in terms of this world, led to a holy anarchy. Their meetings in house or field were deliberately nonformal, mere flockings together to deepen religious feeling. Anybody present was free to rise and express in prayer or rhapsody anything coming into his head—or her head, for, though Quakers seated the sexes separately (as did the early Yankees), they deemed women equal to men as potential vessels of the Spirit and edifiers of the righteous. In their first enthusiasm they exhibited the usual clichés of religious fervor—trances, speaking in tongues and so on. And as usual, such goings-on got them frowned upon by the less spiritual, whom they called the world's people or the worldly.

That was inevitable anyway, for to foster unworldliness among themselves, Friends denied the secular authority of others and eschewed soul-confusing vanities of dress and ornament. Some might dispense with dress altogether, running naked through villages crying out against steeples on churches and man's alienation from God. All cut themselves off from the world by resisting taxes supporting the Church of England; refusing to take part in war; substituting affirmation for the witness' oath on the Bible; keeping their hats on* in court and before their social betters; renouncing buttons on their clothes because fancy buttons were part of contemporary finery; using the folksy *thee is* for the Frenchified new *you are* for all but intimates. In that intolerant time their eccentric theology alone guaranteed them trouble. Add their militancy in their new, artificial folkways, and the wonder is not that England threw them in jail but that they were not there all the time. As for New England, when a man Quaker burst into meeting at Cambridge, crashed two bottles together, and shouted, "Thus will the Lord break you in pieces!" [54] and a woman Quaker came to meeting at Newbury stark naked in order, she said, "to show the people the nakedness of their rulers," [54] it is even more of a wonder that so few were hanged. Note that Virginia, too, had anti-Quaker laws almost as severe as Massachusetts', culminating with the death penalty for a second return from forced exile, and Thomas Jefferson confessed that he

---

* Hence what Arthur Pound (*The Penns*, 177-78) calls "the stock Penn anecdote" of how Friend William did not doff his hat when entering the presence of Charles II. The king promptly doffed his own, and Penn said, "Friend Charles, why dost thou not keep on thy hat?" "Because," said Charles, who had a warm, if ironic, regard for him, "it is the custom of this place for only one person to remain covered at a time."

could not account for Virginia's failure to hang any, since it could certainly not be attributed to "the moderation of the church, or spirit of the legislature." [55]

Penn planned to give his fellow zealots, under shelter of himself as proprietor, a widely tolerant refuge that would also show the world how near an unworldly society could come to God's way. The aim was akin to New England's, though less shrill and apocalyptic. Fortunately the second generation of Quakers coming up in the 1680's were losing the hysterical tone of George Fox's time, simmering down into a serenity of plain living and plain thinking. Outstanding honesty, industry and reliability were combining to produce a new kind of Quaker. Soon the worldly found him notable for sleek prosperity, as well as the plain language. His hat, though still kept on his head, was of the best beaver; his coat, though still buttonless, was of the finest gray broadcloth. Without some such change Penn's recruits might not have been the admirable Colonists they proved to be. Peaceable among themselves and amenable to a Quaker-dominated government fostering the good of the unworldly, they had no distractions from hard work. Such temporary hardships as living in half cellars dug into the bank of the Delaware could be of spiritual benefit, yet as prosperity and comfortable brick dwellings overtook them, they saw no reason to repine. And being unusually equality-minded for their time, they sympathized with Penn's radical leanings toward wide suffrage and unqualified religious toleration.

Penn-backed Quakers had already settled capably across the Delaware in West Jersey. The vestiges of the Dutch and Swedes along the lower river were readily absorbed. Hence few external pressures warped Pennsylvania's crucial early decades. She even lacked early trouble with Indians because Penn made honest treaties of land purchase with them and— what was even more unusual—kept faith. And peaceable relations came more easily because within a generation the redoubtable Iroquois were to break the spirit of the local Delaware tribes by forcing them to admit themselves no longer warriors but women unfit to fight.

Penn's preplanned principal town, Philadelphia, influenced subsequent American settlements coast to coast. Its gridiron pattern of streets, reminiscent of Roman camps and medieval bastides, represented the best thought of military and civilian planners of the Renaissance, even though 200 years later Henry Cabot Lodge did call it an "imbecile checkerboard pattern now almost universal in the United States." [56] Such multiplied rectangles of private lots interspersed with rectangular parks were staked out on sites even where, as in hill-confused Winston-Salem and San Francisco, they make no sense. The original scheme set each house in the middle of a large lot to be intensively planted "so that it may be a greene country towne which may never be burnt." [57] That arrangement went glimmering as private interest sold off the large lots bit by bit for house sites cheek by jowl. But the householders did follow orders to plant "shady and wholesome trees" [57] along the streets, a pleasant custom also followed elsewhere so that until the automobile came to pollute the air and widen thoroughfares, many American cities were gratifyingly shady in the torrid American summer. The motif was gracefully emphasized from the beginning when Penn overruled his planner's scheme to name the streets after eminent people and substituted the names of conspicuous local trees: Chestnut, Walnut, Locust and so on. That too struck public fancy and was adopted coast to coast by city fathers and real estate development-promoters.

From this orderly port capital between the Delaware and the Schuylkill flour, pork and timber shipped in locally built bottoms were soon competing with Yankee produce in the West Indies. Within ninety years of its founding, Philadelphia would be the second largest city under the British Crown and the cultural focus of Colonial gropings, faint but definite, toward nationhood. The original basis of that prosperity was the immediate backcountry, now masked by suburbs but then smilingly responsive to Quaker husbandry. How well it responded is clear in a letter of 1725 from an Irish Quaker urging his sister in Ireland to join him: He called Pennsylvania "the best country for working folk & tradesmen [skilled craftsmen] in the world. . . . There is . . . 2 markets weekly in Philadelphia, also 2 fairs yearly in Chester & likewise in new castle . . . here all young men and women that wants wives or husbands may be Supplyed. . . . Unkle James Lindly & Family is well & Thrives Exceedingly he has 11 children & Reaped last harvest about 800 bushels of wheat, he is a thriving man . . . has a thousand acres of land. A fine Estate." Clothes, shoes and so on are costly in Irish terms ". . . & yet a man will Sooner Earn a suit of Cloths here than in Ireland, by Reason workman's Labour is so Dear." [58] That sort of letter, whether the date was 1725 or 1825, whether the addressee was Irish, Norwegian, Bavarian, Lithuanian, Italian or Levantine, had much to do with keeping transatlantic immigration flowing.

Quakers acquired other footholds in the more tolerant of the other Colonies, notably the Carolinas, Maryland, New York and Rhode Island. They dominated whaling out of Nantucket and bulked large in the growing prosperity of Providence and Newport in general trade, which often came to include two un-Quakerish branches, slaving and privateering. There is much essential Quaker in a deposition made by Joseph Wanton, master mariner and merchant of Newport, eventually governor of Rhode Island, before an Admiralty court in 1750: "I, Joseph Wanton, being one of the people called Quakers, and conscientiously scrupulous about taking an oath, upon solemn affirmation say that . . ." [59] on such-and-such a date, he had been on a slaving voyage to Africa in the *King of Prussia* and got captured with fifty-four slaves on board by a French privateer. Two other Newport Wantons have been called "among the ablest and most distinguished privateersmen . . . that ever stood upon a quarter-deck to command a ship." [60] One way or another the Quakers often flourished. The daughter of Dean Berkeley, the great idealist philosopher who spent some benevolent years in Rhode Island, had a tale about her father and herself taking tea with a local Quaker using a solid gold teapot. Their host asked had they ever seen such a thing before, and "being told that silver ones were much in use in England but . . . never . . . a gold one, Ebenezer replied 'Aye—that was the thing. I was resolved to have something finer than anybody else. They say that the Queen has not got one.' " [61] Doubtless he had made sure that a very modest, simple design had been used in converting his half joes and moidores and other gold coins into that pot.

However subtle Quaker consciences, any Colony getting a nip of their special quality usually found it salutary. In West Jersey and Pennsylvania the ashes of zeal stayed just warm enough to hatch out certain fertile innovations: something close to manhood suffrage; the widest liberty of conscience in the Colonies; and, though it was long emerging from the shell, women's rights. Not that on landing in America the Quakers pulled a complete Bill of Rights out of William Penn's broadbrim. Pennsylvania made it hot for the pioneer printer William Bradford when he published materials making Friends uncomfortable. It was in New York City, not Philadelphia, that liberty of the press won its first great American victory, a greater one than had yet been known in England. But note that the lawyer who won it, appealing to the jury on grounds of constitutional and human rights, was a leader of the Philadelphia bar, Andrew Hamilton. On the whole, Philadelphia was a Cradle of Liberty long before Jefferson ever saw the Georgian provincial capitol now called Independence Hall.

Discord, too, came of Pennsylvania's civil liberties—specifically from liberty of conscience. Without that lure the Pennsylvania Dutch and the Scotch-Irish might not have come in such numbers. And though both peoples proved invaluable to the nation-to-be, each did much to jar the Quakers' homespun Eden out of plumb.

The case of the Pennsylvania Dutch brings up Louis XIV again. Between 1661 and 1715 the Sun King's ambitions kept fierce armies rampaging up and down Germany, each licking up new stores of food and fodder, driving off livestock, looting and burning, offhandedly killing and raping. In a region still struggling to recover from the horrors of the Thirty Years' War (1618-48) these new calamities may have seemed almost normal; anyway it did not occur to most Germans that a practical remedy, such as emigration, was possible. In the Rhineland, however, and upriver in Switzerland, sporadic religious ferments suggested hope of better things. Several eccentric German sects rather resembled Quakers, being against worldliness, war and anything associated with it, governments included. Penn described the Labadists, for instance, as "near to Friends, as to silence in meeting, preaching by the spirit, plainness in garb and furniture in their houses." [62] Firsthand observation of war may well have sharpened such zealots' hostility to their rulers' ways. Certainly there was chronic hatred of the local despot princes who were always snatching young men from the cow barn to go soldiering somewhere, somehow, and never come back. A cognate hatred of conscription was what sent many Central Europeans to America in the 1800's. Though these stirrings affected some upper-class leaders, they naturally counted most among the village artisans and peasants who were the elements most easily pushed around.

In the 1670's Penn made religious tours of Holland and the Rhineland with his plans for a "Holy Experiment" colony already forming. He was probably struck by the sympathetic tone of these German fellow seekers. To people his Pennsylvania grant, he turned to this ready-made source of godly, useful emigrants. Within a year a consignment of Mennonites and Pietists (Quaker-like German sectarians) had landed to establish outside Philadelphia what was to be known as Germantown. The next year Penn wrote, and published in Dutch and German translations, propaganda pamphlets distributed by paid agents among pious rustics and—more to the point—their preacher leaders. They painted a striking vision of a God-permeated colony flowing with milk and honey, free from close neighbors given to arson and rapine, offering renunciation of war, free scope for religious deviancy and land almost for the asking. That last was always heady talk. In landlord-ridden Europe land of one's own for the man with the hoe was rare. A Dutch baker in Germantown was quoted as an alluring example: By plying his trade and dealing with the Indians, he had already acquired a Negro slave, a cow, "a horse . . . my pigs increase rapidly . . . chickens and geese, and a garden . . . and . . . next year . . . an orchard . . . and I have no rent or excise to pay" [63]—a simple statement loud as thunder in the ears of any European peasant hearkening.

Tidings so dazzling naturally spread not only to Penn's immediate targets, the fringe sects, but also among German Calvinists and Lutherans, who, though on top in German Protestantism, had small reason to think their faith secure in a chaotic empire given to political splinterism, dynastic upheavals and bitter religious hatreds. Even some Rhineland Catholics, presumably also war-sick and uneasy about their militant Protestant neighbors, turned emigration-minded. One way or another, in the early 1700's western Germany held thousands of families, mostly lower class, quivering on the verge of self-exile like the elements of a potential landslide. And when they shifted to the New World, every element of that frame of mind went with them. They landed and remained land-hungry, mistrusted anything called government, looked to religion for social cohesion, as well as salvation, and hated the sight of soldiers. Of a preliminary party Penn wrote gleefully to his staff: "Here come [seventy families] of Palatines . . . a sober people . . . and will neither swear nor fight." [64]

The best of it from a Colony-founder's point of view was that the bulk of such Palatines (so called because the Rhenish Palatinate was the core of the area they came from) frequently represented the most useful economic strata. In 1708 an official British count of some 6,500 of them seeking refuge in England showed 1,063 farmers and vine dressers; 13 wheelwrights; 46 smiths; 66 weavers; 90 carpenters; 32 bakers; 48 masons; 40 shoemakers; 27 millers; 7 saddlers; 6 brickmakers; 3 surgeons (presumably barber-surgeons); 2 locksmiths; 4 bricklayers; 2 glaziers; 3 hatters; 10 schoolmasters. John Smith would have sold his soul to have landed so well balanced a variety of skills in Jamestown.

That particular lot had been dislocated by the War of the Spanish Succession, the overblown final act of the struggle with Louis XIV. England sent many of them to New York to settle up the Hudson and produce naval stores—a scheme that bitterly disappointed all concerned. But it did increase population upriver and, when the disgusted Palatines went even farther into the wilderness west of Albany, firmly advanced the frontier in a strategic area. Governor Alexander Spotswood of Virginia founded his successful ironworks on the upper Rappahannock River with a party of refugee German ironworkers, who, out of money and stranded in England, came to America under passage indentures—a system to be described later. The "German Flats" in New York State's Mohawk Valley and Germanna in Virginia still reflect these sturdy peoples. Whatever set it off—historians are still unsure about that, since the underlying strains were of long standing—the main rush, thanks to Penn's propaganda, was to Pennsylvania. Suddenly, all along the Rhine and its upper tributaries, downbound craft were filled with families who had sold everything nonportable and packed the rest in chests and bundles. Dutch ports in the Rhine Delta bulged with people named Schmidt and Braun who had never before been 20 miles from home but were now voyaging 3,000 miles to the New World, often at the urging of touts called Newlanders.

Many had hoped that the proceeds of selling the cattle and the crops would pay the way overseas. But money went fast during the unanticipated delays of the downriver trip. Boats had to lie up and go through thirty-six separate customs points in the 300 miles between Heilbronn, say, and the Dutch border. It might take six or seven weeks, during which provisions and cash dwindled sadly, and the victims' opinions of governments sank lower than ever. Many learned too late at dockside that what they had left would never cover passage and shipboard supplies for the whole family. They could not return home, for bridges were burned and upstream travel costly. The solution was one form of a migrate-now-and-pay-later system indispensable in populating America, though nobody but shipowners really liked it. Like this: Bewildered Caspar Müller, late of Jagsthausen, became *a redemptioner,* using his remaining cash to apply on passages for his family and binding himself to the ship's captain to pay off the balance by working after he reached Pennsylvania. The captain would sell this obligation (along with Caspar as a temporary quasi-slave) to some shore employer willing to put out a few pounds in cash* for Caspar's services for two or three years. That gave the shipowner a profit and alleviated the usually short labor supply in a growing Colony. The law saw to it that Caspar gave his purchaser a good money's worth and sometimes made some effort to see that he was not too badly treated. Due release when his time was out usually occurred. Provided he could survive "seasoning" diseases ashore, he stood a good chance of eventually settling with his family upcountry on all the acreage that he could hope to handle in a neighborhood of his fellow sectarians supplying advice, example and moral support in the new life. Artisans might be purchased by townsmen and put to their trades; thus a New York City man of 1751 advertised that he had recently bought to "set up in the Potter's Business . . . a Family of Germans . . . supposed to be the most ingenious in that Trade that ever arrived in America. . . ." [65]

Coming of a terrace- and fertilizer-minded people—remember Mark Twain's romance of the Black Forest that hinged on dowries consisting of cow dung—Caspar knew more about caring for the soil than most Colonists, who paid little heed to such matters. So the thousands like him made the limestone lands between the Schuylkill and the Blue Ridge and up into the Lehigh Valley the fat, green, still-distinct and still-fertile empire of the

* For a late sample of the cost of redemptioners' passage in sterling: In 1774 a group of Highlanders paid £3/10 each per adult, children half fare, provisions for all included. The leader of the party had a cabin passage at £6 and supplied his own provisions. (Duane Meyer, *Highland Scots,* 57.) Trying to give modern equivalents for Colonial moneys in purchasing power is futile because the various inflationary policies of the separate Colonies complicate the task too much. Take it that the employers' payments for the time of redemptioners were more or less equal to going wages for the period of servitude minus the cost of food, clothing and lodging during that time.

Pennsylvania Dutch, the long-standing misnomer* for these descendants of Germans and German Swiss. Ever since Benjamin Franklin called them "excellent husbandmen" [66]—and be sure the compliment was deserved, for Franklin disapproved of them in most other respects—they have been and are now the nation's best dirt farmers. Soon after they arrived in force, their pork, beef and grain were principally what fostered the economic health of the City of Brotherly Love. As market and shipping point for their produce, that booming town was correspondingly indispensable to Pennsylvania Dutchdom. But that did not mean cordial relations. To these refugees from organized barbarism, Penn's city and its environs were otherwise only a land of bondage for redemptioners and the seat of a government that, though preferable to that of His Serene Highness back home, was still a government, hence an object of grave misgivings. Besides, it spoke English, and Caspar saw no reason to learn such alien gibberish beyond what he needed for huckstering green stuff from a wagon. As for Pennsylvania's representative government and relatively wide franchise, nothing in his despot-ridden past had prepared him for such outlandish institutions. On the principle that any kind of government was best left alone, for his first several decades in the New World he relegated politics to the Quakers and the Penn family's proprietary while he built up flocks and herds and barns.

Those he knew about. The Pennsylvania Dutch country still has his kind of barn—vast, often stone-ended, stately with elaborate ventilators on the roof ridge, set sidewise into a slope; animals stabled in a semibasement with an overhang on the downslope side; the main story (for hay) as spacious as a sizable church. Its occasional presence well into western Ohio betokens penetration by Caspar's people. In the Old Country his forebears had probably had their living quarters in one end of the barn, sharing space, warmth and smells with the cattle as people still do in Franconia and the Black Forest. In Pennsylvania something moved Caspar to go in for a small separate dwelling drawing a sharper line between man and beast. Peasant immigrants from Scotland, accustomed to keep the cattle with them in their hovel cottages all winter, similarly abandoned the practice in America. For the Scot that usually portended emergence from peas-

---

* When Caspar landed from Rotterdam ships calling himself *Deutsch*, the confusion was inevitable. But it might well have occurred anyway. In the 1600's and long afterward *Dutch* was the English-speaking common man's designation for most Germans, as well as for natives of the Netherlands. A German-owned saloon in a Midwestern town in 1900 would be known as the Dutchman's. Persistence of this broad usage has made necessary that otherwise puzzling American redundancy *Holland Dutch* to distinguish the Hollander from the Pennsylvania Dutchman and the immigrant German.

antry. On Caspar the change seemed to signify less. New World or not, land of his own or not, he and his tended pretty much to stay peasants—the only sizable mass of peasantry that America knew until she annexed outlying parts of Mexico—the first large, self-encapsulating ethnic enclave anticipating those of the industrial cities of the latter 1800's.

The glorious Pennsylvania Dutch barn.

Uneasy about things nonrural; feeling safest within the family; grudging about education beyond basic literacy; reluctant to look beyond a near horizon even though grandfather had crossed an ocean; consistently setting women to field work, whereas in the Colonies generally, wife or daughter went into the field only in emergencies—not for nothing did Maud Muller, "raking the meadow sweet with hay" have that German surname—all those were Pennsylvania-Dutch traits. The language barrier, of course, strengthened their indrawingness. "Few of their children . . . know English," Franklin complained in 1753. "They import many books from Germany . . . of the six printing-houses in the province, two are entirely German . . . but two entirely English. They have one German newspaper and one half-German. . . . The signs in our streets have inscriptions in both languages . . . in some places only German . . . they will soon so outnumber us, that all the advantages we have, will . . . be not able to preserve our language, and even our government will become precarious . . . indeed in the last war [King George's War, the American phase of the War of the Austrian Succession] the Germans, excepting a very few . . . refusing to engage in it, giving out, one amongst another, and even in print, that, if they were quiet, the French, should they take the country, would not molest them. . . ." [67]

Official Pennsylvania's efforts to wean them from the German that their Rhineland-born pastors preached in made little headway, especially among the eccentric sects—the Dunkards, Amish (a split-away from the Mennonites) and other groups of *plain* as opposed to *gay* (Lutheran and Calvinist, hence more worldly) Pennsylvania Dutch. A side result was the elaborate pidgin, including stray and often misapplied English, that now amuses outsiders. "The butter is all" and "The milk is yet" are traditional Pennsylvania Dutchisms, and most of them are pretty strongly German.* The plain sects are still today focuses of nonassimilation. Because use of the internal-combustion engine is sinful, black-curtained buggies still slide along the roads of Berks County, and the motive power of the plow is still a team of powerful, short-coupled horses. Schoolgirls in black bonnets and long black skirts like mother's and schoolboys in flat black hats and long loose trousers like father's still trudge to school in the roadside dust. On Saturday in Hamburg, Pennsylvania, here comes a silky-bearded young husband in that black uniform with his bonneted wife walking dutifully two paces behind—peasantry not much diluted, and their faces are instantly familiar as those in Dürer engravings.

The handy analogue—to the Canadian French, who also persist in peasantry and their own patois derived from a Continental tongue—must be used with care. That basic aloofness also goes back to the postmedieval peasant, true. But history greatly stiffened it 200 years ago, when French Canada was conquered by the English, who, for all their light hand on the bridle, not only spoke another language but were of a traditionally hostile religion. In contrast these Germans had changed sovereigns of their own accord; their chosen refuge was tolerant of their eccentric elements; they prospered to a degree that French Canada did not approach. And apropos, note the difference, whatever it may mean, between these trans-

---

* For instance, "Bis marriya free iss olles weck" means "By morning it will all be gone." Here is a stanza of Pennsylvania Dutch verse written by a Reformed parson late in the last century, subject: "Das alte Schulhaus an der Krick":

> Heit is's 'xäctly zwanzig Johr,
> Dasz ich bin owwe naus;
> Nau bin ich widder lewig z'rick
> Un Schteh am Schulhaus an d'r Krick,
> Juscht neekscht an's Dady's Haus. . . .

Roughly: "Today it's exactly twenty years that I've been away; now I've come back again and am standing by the schoolhouse on the creek just next to my father's house. . . ." (Albert B. Faust, *German Element,* II, 340-41.)

planted Germans and those other Protestant mass refugees from war and persecution in the same general context—the Huguenots.

A fair number of the new-landed stayed in or near Philadelphia, instead of pushing on westward into the German-dominated counties and blended in well, else such names as Rittenhouse and Wister would not have been

In Amish country these funereal carriages still serve the "plain" Pennsylvania Dutch.

eminent so soon. Another kind of assimilation was furthered by the fact that those counties lay across the most deeply trodden ways West. Hence Pennsylvania Dutch were rife among those taking the opportunity to step into the mainstream of America as movers crossing the Susquehanna at Harris' ferry or Columbia and tortuously surmounting the Appalachian ridges to Pittsburgh, vestibule of the Old Northwest. In view of the marked indrawingness of the later generations in Pennsylvania I suggest that self-selection may have occurred here, too. Other things being equal, those remaining in Pennsylvania Dutchdom were the culturally and tempera-mentally sluggish, likely to train their children to mistrust other people's ways. Those cutting away singly or by families to take up lands in, say, Ohio or Indiana would include many boys preferring fiddling to hymn singing and many married men irked by the old folks' stagnant assump-tions and expectations. (They were aside from the many colony-swarms sent out to create Pennsylvania Dutchdoms on a smaller scale down the Great Valley and over the mountains.) The children of these livelier seceders, reared among former Carolinians, York Staters and Pennsylva-nian Scotch-Irish, would grow up talking not German pidgin but the pungent, eclectic new tongue that passed for English beyond the mountains. Soon little of the Rhineland was left but the family name, and that might be well disguised. Richart, Braun and Jungblut readily became Richards, Brown and Youngblood. It could be only one generation from peasant to backwoods farmer—raising better crops than most, however, because he had been reared in Pennsylvania Dutch traditions of how to handle land.

Some of these thousands of piecemeal deserters from Pennsylvania Dutchdom cut wide swaths, like Lewis Wetzel, one of the toughest of the frontier's Indian fighters, and Ebenezer Zane, highway surveyor in the new country. Immigrant German and Swiss gunsmiths, refining Old Country models, made the so-called Kentucky rifle, as crucial in the winning of the West as the C-47 was to V-J Day. The flatboat that floated so many westering pioneers and their plunder to new homes or Southern markets was probably first used by a Pennsylvania Dutchman on the Monongahela River. The wammus, a flannel roundabout jacket, usually red, prevalent among Old Northwesterners—the word still survived in my own boyhood—was introduced by Caspar Müller's descendants. Maybe still more important, if there is such a thing as American cooking, much of it reflects what the over-the-mountains country developed from Pennsylvania Dutch precedents—what transplanted Rhineland peasant wives had concocted from the lavish comestibles of the New World for hard-working menfolks. Butter-dented mashed potatoes, shallow dried-apple pie, cream coleslaw, that sort of thing also went West to fan out beyond the Mississippi along with rifles and suspicion of governments and king-instigated wars.

Scrapple, the Pennsylvania Dutch blend of Colonial cornmeal with German headcheese, became the traditional Philadelphia breakfast. In subtler ways the German immigrant probably had a coarsening effect on Penn's Quakers. The process, being unobtrusive, seems not to have troubled them. The social numbness of this upcountry peasantry enabled Friends to prosper as exporting middlemen while drifting into political sharp practices—notably a legislative system that, with Pennsylvania Dutch acquiescence, kept power in the hands of Philadelphia and its satellite Quaker counties. The pacific bent of the Pennsylvania Dutch also minimized frictions between the Colony and its Indian friends. As years passed, though the red men's respect for Onas persisted, the traders' rum and knavery and the nudgings of the French sometimes stirred them into making trouble on the frontier. But those scalped corpses and burned cabins were far from Chestnut Street, and in between lay that phlegmatic Germanic buffer zone, a sort of populated no-man's-land. That made it easier for the proprietary government and the Quaker-dominated legislature to neglect measures to man outlying posts and skirmish with the Indians. Even during actual war with the French, the Quakers reluctantly authorized only gifts of money, use unspecified, to the Crown or allotted funds for public purchase of "wheat or other grains" [68]—tacitly understood to include grains of gunpowder. Edmund Burke, pondering what he could learn of Pennsylvania from afar in the 1760's, deemed it a great "error to have placed so great a part of the government in the hands of men [Quakers] who hold principles directly opposite to its end and design . . . as a peaceable, industrious, honest people, the Quakers cannot be too much cherished; but surely they cannot themselves complain, that when, by their opinions, they make themselves sheep, they should not be entrusted with office, since they have not the nature of dogs." [69]

Influx of worldly persons and wealth was gradually eroding the Quakers' hegemony. It had already been badly shaken by the Scotch-Irish, a formidable people thronging into Pennsylvania soon after the Germans. In the 1600's the device of colonization was sometimes applied nearer home than the New World. In the same decade as the founding of Jamestown, England, making another wrongheaded effort to cope with Ireland, settled thousands of Lowland Scots Presbyterians in the turbulent northern counties (collectively Ulster) to replace the natives. They did well at it. Three generations later they were a teeming yeoman-craftsman caste still hot Presbyterian (that is, Scots Calvinist) and with Scots tongues in their heads, practicing intensive farming mixed with cottage industry. They lived basically on potatoes and cow's milk while raising sheep for wool and flax for linen, both spun and woven into textiles for export to England. They despised and hated the local laboring-servant caste of original Irish, partly because of their Catholic religion, partly because the process of taking over had meant prolonged and bitter conflict. They also bitterly resented their gentry landlords, mostly of English stock transplanted earlier, usually staunch for the alien Church of England, which insisted on tithes (ecclesiastical taxes) from the Scotch-Irish and Catholic Irish both of which groups considered its doctrines anathema and its presence tyrannical. Such coincidence of religious conflicts with socio-ethnic castes can be relied on to inflame tempers on all sides.

The mercantilist economic theories of the late 1600's gave English weavers a case against their competition from Ulster. England took action heedless of what it would do to the Scotch-Irish, whom she had sent to Ireland not for their but for her own benefit. They were, after all, only a pack of psalm-singing Dissenters and Scots to boot, the same breed that had made trouble for the Stuarts and Cromwell alike. During the next forty years successive measures to prohibit or discourage Ulster's textiles gradually smothered the Scotch-Irishman's basic livelihood. He was also barred from public office on religious grounds, and then came sharply raised rents—a carnival of shortsightedness exacerbated by crop failures in the 1720's. Small wonder that the generalized Scottish distaste for Englishmen became in Ulster savage hatred of a nation that had encouraged, used, and then betrayed them. As the Scotch-Irish necessarily saw it, they and their Presbyterianism had every man's hand against them.

Then they heard that certain Colonies in America wanted population and provided new settlers with what in Ulster's cramped terms were vast tracts of land, and some even offered freedom from religious discrimination. It appealed mightily to thousands on thousands of disgruntled men for whom memory of their recent forebears' transplantation made emigration easier to contemplate than it was for most Old Worldlings. Since Northern Ireland still has plenty of Scotch-Irish Presbyterians, it follows that not all migrated; hence that Ulster, too, underwent that familiar automatic self-selection as those of come-outer temperament left the mass of stay-at-homes. But for a while it looked like creeping depopulation. Between 1730 and 1770, it is estimated, half of Ulster sailed for the New World. When revolution came, a seventh of the Colonists were Scotch-Irish.

Some tried Calvinist New England, which channeled them upcountry as a buffer against the Indians—hence Londonderry, New Hampshire. Those trying the Carolinas also went to the frontier or near it, which suited their own standoffishness, as well as the Colonies' need for a frontier shield. The bulk of them, however, maybe especially mindful of the Quakers' view of religious freedom, poured into Pennsylvania at a rate rising to 10,000 in a single year. By 1720 James Logan, shrewd and scholarly adviser to the Penns, wrote of how "a considerable number of good, sober people came in from Ireland . . . we were under some apprehension from the Northern Indians. . . . I therefore thought it might be prudent to plant a settlement of such men as . . . had so bravely defended Londonderry. . . . These people . . . if kindly used, will, I believe . . . be orderly . . . and easily dealt with." [70] Meaning that Pennsylvania, also applying the buffer principle, channeled the Scotch-Irish into lands beyond Pennsylvania Dutchdom, up and down the Susquehanna, and beyond that lovely river into the narrow but often fertile valleys between the Appalachian ridges.

It was too clever by half. These hardy and self-reliant newcomers soon got the hang of the backwoods, maybe better than any other immigrant group. But they were incapable of the Quakers' blandness toward the Indians, whom they took to be inconvenient and dangerous vermin. Freely they acquired and exercised the red men's own skills in bushfighting, their taste for scalps and so on. Thus, just as in Ulster, they found themselves entangled with a body of indigenous heathen at the instance (only half-acknowledged this time) of a distant, alien government. When they needed countenance and men, munitions, and provisions for their implied mission to curb and, with luck, gradually to eradicate the Indians, little was forthcoming from the Quaker-clogged Colonial authorities. When they complained to the legislature, they found the Quakers disinclined to listen to or make room for worldly troublemakers of any stripe.

Their anger mounted over the years to the climax of the Paxton Boys' march on Philadelphia in 1764, an emergency that moved many Quakers to abandon scruples against bearing arms. As the Colonies had spread away from the seaboard, most of them had seen squabbles arise between the middleman-minded port towns (and the governments resident therein) and the sulky upcountry caught between Indians to westward and creditors to eastward. ". . . Boston, Philadelphia, and Charleston," says C. M. Andrews, "had little liking for the immigrant Germans and Scotch-Irish . . . looked upon them throughout the colonial period as inferior types." [71] Not even the Revolution eased these strains, as Shays' Rebellion in Massachusetts and the Whiskey Rebellion in Pennsylvania showed. But Pennsylvania's versions of them were least edifying—and in the Colony presumably founded on serene harmony!

That irony may owe something to the Quakers' misconception of what the Scotch-Irish might consider being "kindly used," but probably more to the Scotch-Irish talent for black exasperation. One result was further migration. The mountain valleys trended southwestward into western Virginia, the Carolina highlands and eastern Tennessee. A stream of the more restless (or worse exasperated) Scotch-Irish went trickling steadily along those valleys with no by-your-leave to the Colonial governments seated hundreds of miles downslope to eastward. Thus was settled most of what today's planners call Appalachia. The typical participant was probably much like the hale old gentleman of seventy-six years whom a Scottish traveler met at Harrisburg in 1807. He had "accompanied his parents from the county Antrim in Ireland when only six years old, had resided thirty-six years at Paxton [near the present Harrisburg], had afterwards removed to a part of Virginia about two hundred miles distant, where he had a large farm and distillery. He insisted on treating me, as . . . he liked to encourage the consumption of whiskey . . ." [72] and boasted freely of having been one of that Paxton gang of frontier toughs who, during the frontier troubles of 1763, massacred twenty peaceable and defenseless Indians.

Carried southwestward with the Scotch-Irish also came that strong minority of less stick-in-the-mud Pennsylvania Dutch. That same mingled stream, occasionally intermarrying as it flowed, washed over the ridges as the first substantial waves in the arduous and unscrupulous movement that rid the Old Northwest* of Indians. The names of settlers around Fort Pitt (now Pittsburgh) in 1760 are clearly more than half Scotch-Irish or Scottish with a sizable admixture of Germans. In the Revolution the Scotch-Irish were usually pro-Patriot except in certain special situations in the Carolinas. That is, for their own historic reasons, they were hot anti-British on principle and more than likely to share the upcountry's general resentment of Crown efforts to protect the peltry trade by forbidding further penetration west of the mountains after the French and Indian War. For to judge from the names that Verner W. Crane lists—Campbell, Gillespie, McGillivray, McKinney, McIntosh, and so on—by the mid-1770's Scotch-Irish and Scots dominated the Carolina trade.

Wherever the Scotch-Irish went, they took along the pot still, a Scottish institution as rife in Ulster as in Ayrshire, indispensable in the New World for turning the crop of rye (and later corn) into a salable product easily transported by packhorse. Scotch-Irish permeation of Appalachia and the Old Northwest was the reason why whiskey replaced the seaboard's rum and peach brandy as standard cure for the great American thirst. Let that symbolize the dominant Scotch-Irish flavor of the frontier after 1750. It was fitting that the first Colonial settlement west of the Allegheny divide —on a stream the water of which flowed to the Gulf of Mexico—at Draper's Meadows near the present Blacksburg, Virginia, was made by a party of Pennsylvania Scotch-Irish in 1748.

West of the Susquehanna, where the nearest peace officer was probably two days' hard travel away, such men had naturally run fairly wild, creating a catch-as-catch-can substitute for law out of family feuds—a medieval survival still lively in their Scottish background—and out of the impromptu collective discipline that would later be known as the vigilante organization. However Judge Lynch got his name—scholars are unsure— he was morally and spiritually Scotch-Irish. His people make up much of the background that produced the later bigotries of Carry Nation and William Jennings Bryan; most of the tunes that the Old Northwest danced to at its frolics; and the long-boned, shovel-chinned, steel-trap-mouthed, stiff-maned ancestors who look out of the daguerreotypes of the Ulstermen's great-grandsons. Whoever says "Irish potato" to distinguish it from sweet does so because most of the Colonies first knew the white potato as the Scotch-Irishman's staple food brought in with him 250 years ago. Not until the white potato could marry salt cod could the noble New Eng-

---

* The reader must already understand that this means the area above the Ohio between Appalachia and the Mississippi ceded to the Colonies in 1783. *Midwest* won't do, for much of today's Midwest did not come under American sway until the Louisiana Purchase of 1803.

land fish cake come into being. In parallel the Yankee's classic version of the Indian's baked beans waited until the hog was available (for salt pork) and trade had brought the West Indies' molasses northward.

The ethnic roster goes on. After recovering Brazil from the Dutch in 1654, the Portuguese exiled the small local group of Jews. Some took refuge in New Netherland, where, once orders from home forced Stuyvesant to let them alone, they took root as the nucleus of the upper-class and well-to-do Sephardic Jewish colony of New York City; Myer Myers, for instance, was president of the local Silversmiths' Society. Others did much to build up Newport, Rhode Island, and Charleston, South Carolina. According to the Reverend Ezra Stiles' eulogy of Isaac Lopez, great merchant of Newport and partner of a Gentile, he was "the most universally beloved by an extensive Acquaintance of any man I ever knew . . . always carried about with him a Sweetness of Behaviour, a calm Urbanity, and an agreeable and unaffected politeness of Manners." [73] A few got into the peltry trade—Levy Solomon of New York and Levey A. Levey of Pennsylvania were among the traders killed near Fort Pitt in Pontiac's Rebellion in 1763. A Mr. Levy of Newbury, Massachusetts, beat the Yankees in ingenuity by forming Merrimack Valley logs into shiplike rafts to be sailed across the Atlantic to the British timber market. Several of these "Jew's rafts," as the trade called them, actually got there, one in twenty-six days.

Lowland Scots appeared in most Colonies, particularly as merchants in New Jersey and the Chesapeake ports. Those reared in Norfolk, Virginia, still say "hoose" and "aboot." Quakers in Pennsylvania and South Carolina included many Welsh. Others came in among English immigrants as the high incidence today of such names as Morgan, Powell, Jones, Williams and so on shows. Scots Highlanders displaced by the socio-economic turmoil which followed the opening up of the Highlands after the Jacobite rising of 1745 chose upcountry North Carolina. They long spoke Gaelic so consistently that even their Negro slaves occasionally used it to the astonishment of visitors, and in the late 1830's it was still advisable for post office clerks in Fayetteville, North Carolina, to have some knowledge of it. Though it was the House of Hanover they had risen against in the Forty-Five, they turned out with their traditional claymores, targets and pipes to fight for Hanoverian George III at Moore's Creek in 1776. Patriot General Schuyler had to send a force to disarm a similar body of Loyalist Highlanders long settled in upstate New York. Highlander emigrants whose voyage to America was interrupted by the Revolution were enlisted in a Royal Highland Regiment, one battalion of which saw action under Clinton and Cornwallis against the Americans. Their uniforms were duly

Scottish except that, to show their American provenance, the sporrans (furred pouches) dangling before their kilts were made not of the traditional badger fur but of racoon.

Maybe the most civilizing of the coherent immigrant groups—and one of the latest and smallest—was the Moravians, the United Brethren whose religious fellowship goes back to John Huss, Czech father of Protestantism in the early 1400's. Kept underground by centuries of persecution, some finally took refuge with a pious nobleman in southeastern Germany, where they set up a theocratic community based on the renunciation of war and violence, skilled crafts, sacred music, and a rigid separation of the sexes until marriage. Soon they sent out small swarms of skilled, devout families to take the Gospel to the heathen in Greenland, South Africa—and America. One such party, settled in Georgia in the 1730's, came to fear involvement in a threatened war with Spain. They shifted to pacifist-minded Pennsylvania and founded on the frontier model communities named Bethlehem and Nazareth, where the Indians were to be brought to God and civilization. On invitation from a lord proprietor with huge land grants and a good opinion of the Moravians as colonizers, a secondary swarm went to the Carolina upcountry in the 1750's, creating what is now Winston-Salem. Another was already proselytizing the Indians persisting between the Hudson and the New York-Connecticut border. Still another followed the first push across the mountains into what is now central Ohio, where Scotch-Irish militants made the Gnadenhutten massacre of 100-odd unresisting Indian men, women and children an outstanding horror in 1782.

The Moravians' work with the Indians, though rather effective, like that of the comparable Spanish missions in Florida and the Southwest in the same era, came apart in the same way under the strains of national expansion and frontier hatreds. But their influence on their raw white neighbors was valuable and lasting. Their solid, graceful buildings, their serene skills in silversmithing, cabinetry and textiles, their insistence on education—for both sexes within reason—were revelations to the backwoodsmen among whom they settled. George Washington and Elkanah Watson were among those amazed by their municipal water systems of wooden conduits—the first such engineering in the Colonies. And their music, whether choral or instrumental, was, with the possible exceptions of John Singleton Copley's portraits and some of the silver- and cabinetwork in the Colonial port towns, the most cultivated phenomenon in the America of that day. At the Moravians' Bethlehem in 1756 Benjamin Franklin heard "good Musick, the Organ being accompanied with Violins, Hautboys, Flutes, Clarinets, etc." [74] They first brought the trombone to America and also exploited the bassoon, harp, harpsichord, and clavichord. Their Johann Friedrich Peter, composer of adept string quartets, is called the Father of Chamber Music in America. Music was part of their folk tradition, drums and flutes went with the reapers into the harvest field, and a new house was topped off with fanfares of trumpets.

So much attention to the kind of immigrant group created by mutual sympathy gives colonizing all too orderly an air and overstresses its heterogeneity. Once any lot of newcomers was ashore, the way of a man with a maid led to much mingling on the fringes of any group, however compact its intentions. The Quakers read out of meeting those marrying non-Quakers, but such marriages often occurred anyway. The Scotch-Irish and Pennsylvania Dutch despised each other, but the girl whom William Dean Howells' Welsh father married had a Scotch-Irish father and a Pennsylvania Dutch mother all the same. However askance Yankees looked on the Scotch-Irish landing in Boston, they soon blended into New England, learning readily to drink too much cider instead of too much poteen. And to concentrate on self-selected groups distracts notice from the throng of our pre-Revolutionary forebears—probably exceeding in numbers all other groups together—who came over as individuals. Among those hundreds of thousands were persons of sage enterprise taking advantage of transatlantic opportunity. But the bulk of them had entrusted their destinies to others for the presumed benefit of both parties. Some were gullible. Some had been unlucky. Some were being got rid of for their country's good.

That is, what we saw develop at Jamestown and among the ill-financed Palatine immigrants was characteristic of the process all along. Actually the indentured-servant device that primarily populated the Colonies was born at Jamestown. It derived from the medieval apprenticeship that legally bound youngsters to work for master craftsmen—tanner, wheelwright, tailor—for so many years in return for board, lodging, clothing and training in their masters' trades. Its function in America was to alleviate the shortage of hirable labor that plagued all Colonies from Jamestown on. Historically in Virginia it was the halfway house between paid company personnel and Negro slavery. The method was to persuade a man down on his luck to accept a passage to the New World to be paid off by a set term of years of work (say, three to five) for whomsoever his promise to work might be sold to when he landed. The spirit of such transactions is clear in the consequent advertisements of ships' cargoes: "A choice Parcel of Ten Servants and one Woman to be sold, on Board of the Ship Lovely, now lying at the Wharf of the Widow Allen . . . also very good Gloucester Cheese, at Eightpence a pound." [75] The chief difference between the emigrant's indenture and that of the Old Country craft apprentice was that at the end of his time the Colonial servant got not only a basic outfit to begin life with—tools, clothing and such—but in many cases a grant of land. In New World terms his outfit reflected expectation that one new ax, one grubbing hoe, one weeding hoe and sometimes a barrel of corn would support him while he shook down.

Maybe because such servants often proved fractious in the early Old and Bay Colonies, New England relied on them less than did Colonies farther south. It had been awkward in new-founded Salem in 1630 when lack of supplies forced the Puritan command to turn loose to fend for themselves many such servants who had cost £20 each to recruit—an inhumanity for which it seems never to have occurred to anybody to apologize. Indeed Thomas Dudley's account of it to the Countess of Lincoln bewailed only the extreme loss to the Colony. From the Hudson to the Altamaha, however, the indentured white servant was the nascent Colony's basic raw material—and often very raw. England was then shifting from the rigid medieval to the more flexible modern world. Uprooted hundreds of thousands became masterless men (and families) with no niche in the culture-to-be, picking up a livelihood as best they could on the roads and in the growing town slums—the "beggars coming to town" at whom the dogs barked, "some in rags and some in tags. . . ." They were so many and the causes dislocating them so obscure that their misery was widely laid to overpopulation. Hence a standing argument for colonization: It would drain off to the New World men and women useless and often dangerous at home. Only after the 1630's did sentiment even begin to change toward keeping the king's subjects at home, with an equivalent loss of momentum in colonizing projects.

The stomachs of the 1600's were stout enough to take the barbarities consequent on indentures. It was taken for granted that the average level of stability, sobriety and ability among these servants would be low. With admirable candor Beverley's account of Virginia written at a time when many Virginians' fathers had been early Colonists allowed that "this [Colony] was for the most part at first peopled by Persons of low Circumstances . . . for 'tis not likely that any Man of a plentiful Estate, should voluntarily abandon a happy Certainty, to roam after imaginary Advantages in a New World." [76] The availability of recruits meant that when social earthquakes jar a society, as Tudor and Stuart England was jarred, those most readily shaken loose are the least qualified to get on well. That same shaking loose, reducing self-respect, corroding any existing work habits and breaking personal ties, gradually leaves the ill adjusted worse qualified for living than ever. And such strains often damage likelier specimens caught in earthquakes through no fault of their own. Before the field of colonizing emigration opened up, the surplus population of England had had at least two generations of such traumatizing distress and dislocation. Awareness of that underlies Abbot Emerson Smith's summary: "[The Colonies] were a haven for the godly, a refuge for the oppressed, a challenge to the adventurous [but] particularly [in regard to] indentured servants . . . also the last resort of scoundrels . . . men and women who were dirty and lazy, rough, ignorant, lewd, and often criminal." [77] But in the Chesapeake region, fields needed clearing and tobacco pampering, and the Colonist eager for a stake in the new country was ruthless enough to be confident of getting work out of virtual ragtag and bobtail—and willing to pay for having such people brought overseas.

For just as the tingle of profit underlay the first colonizing, the key to the indenture system was that it made money for shipowners. The main use of their little ships was, of course, to fetch bulky sugar, molasses and tobacco eastbound from the West Indies and the Chesapeake. Their westward ladings of hardware, textiles and such Old World manufactures were small in bulk, leaving much cubage unused. So, as William Bradford explained early in the game, to fill that cubage with several score individuals of whatever quality enabled the westbound voyage too to show a profit: ". . . some began to make a trade of it, to transport passengers and their goods and hired ships to that end. And they, to make up their freight and advance their profit, cared not who the persons were, so they had money to pay them. And by this means the country became pestered with unworthy persons. . . ." [78] Those were paying their own way. But say it cost £5—a serious outlay when a shilling a day was going wages—to recruit, victual and transport a down-and-out prospective servant to Virginia. Add the one-in-six chance that he would die at sea, literally a dead loss, yet the tobacco-mad Colonists would pay some £8 to £10 for him alive. The odds were quite good enough to make shipping him a worthwhile speculation.

To persuade him to ship often called for cajolery escalating into swindling; sometimes violence was used on the dejected and delinquent. Just as the transatlantic shipping lines of the later 1800's advertised lavishly in Europe because it paid them to transport the steerage-class emigrants that American employers wanted to attract through that golden door, so did the servant trade of the 1600's put out enticing broadsides and pamphlets. But since most of the potential prospects could not read or seldom bothered to do so, the two-legged advertisement—the professional recruiter—was the main recourse. The slang of the day called him a spirit —hence the surviving idiom *to spirit away;* that is, to cause to vanish under suspicious circumstances. His methods were partly waterside crimp, partly recruiting sergeant. At fairs and markets his paid pipes and drummers wove through the crowd alternating music with short bursts of ballyhoo about sailing free of charge to the plantations where land of one's own rewarded a few years of light and diverting work with women of the same description readily available. At low taverns he treated the tawdry town idlers and the slack-jawed hobbledehoys from the country, harping on the glories of emigration until, half-fuddled, half-dazzled, they signed up. Then they were locked up, lest they run away after a change of heart, in an obscure lodging with free food and drink, such as it was, and free tobacco. Among the very down-and-out the promise of immediate board and room might be a reason for signing. It usually made a mixed bag: A mayor of Bristol in the 1660's listed "husbands that have forsaken their wives . . . wives who had abandoned their husbands . . . children and apprentices run away from their parents and masters . . . unwary and credulous persons . . . many . . . pursued by hue-and-cry for robberies, burglaries, or breaking prison. . . ." [79] Add the unlucky shopkeeper in danger of debtor's prison and the at least nominally skilled craftsman in personal or financial difficulties. Runaway indentured servants listed in the press of Charleston, South Carolina, in the early 1700's included men of a couple of dozen trades, the expected ones plus fencing master, wigmaker, painter, chimney sweep . . .

Spiriting could be an active profession. One zealous practitioner turned in an average of some 500 souls a year. Indentures were legally binding, so if the victim's relatives made trouble, the spirit was likely to be on the right side of the law. In all but outrageous cases magistrates may have looked the other way, welcoming the opportunity to slough off the bouquets of human roses whom the spirit had collected in that upper room in Pig Lane. Outrageous cases were common, however. The temptation toward actual kidnapping—the word itself (kid-nabbing) originated in the servant trade—was strong. Thus in the late 1740's a boy named Archibald Lamont was enticed on board a ship lying off Coleraine in Ulster; up came the anchor, and sail was made, and when he begged to be set ashore, they told him: "It will be many a long day, my lad, before you will see . . . home again." [80] He was sold to a Long Island man and some years later, when he was out of his time, his mother and brothers came to join him. That was the strain of Lamonts producing Thomas S. Lamont, the eminent partner in J. P. Morgan & Company. Those were sturdy people. When such a thing could happen to them, it is easier to understand that the dull teen-age boy big for his years, the drunk in the gutter, the odd son or brother whose family preferred to be rid of him, might well come to in the tween decks of the James Merchant of Bristol America-bound with no more idea how he got there than if he had been a shanghaied seaman. But if *how* was unclear, *why* was not. He represented a pound or so each for the spirit and the shipowner, and his chance of effective protest from the other side of the Atlantic was low enough to make the risk of the law worth taking. Even if he did find friends to protest for him, proceedings initiated 3,000 miles away might be cut short by his death during "seasoning"— physical adjustment to Colonial conditions, including malaria and dawn-to-dusk field work. That often killed more servants than did the voyage.

Labor-hungry planters bought many servants directly from the ship captains. Others were sold in job lots to soul-drivers—speculators who hawked them "through the country like a parcel of sheep, until they can sell them to advantage." [81] Colonial social controls being primitively loose, it followed that runaway servants were a chronic problem. One purpose of the New England Confederation of 1643 (Massachusetts Bay, Plymouth, Connecticut and New Haven) was inter-Colony cooperation in return of runaways. The terms in which they were advertised for and punished on recapture were significantly like those which, applied to runaway Negro slaves, made devastating abolitionist propaganda in the 1800's. No wonder that as the Revolution impended, the Reverend Jonathan Boucher, a Loyalist long resident in Virginia and Maryland, strongly counseled the Crown to enlist servants to fight the Colonials because they not only had got through seasoning, as imported troops would not have, but also "will bring with them an ill Humour and Prejudice against the Country, which will not be unuseful." [82]

It all sounds like Hogarth illustrating Defoe. An early Dutch adventurer named De Vries, for instance, set up a private colony of Dutch and a few English on the coast of Guiana. His colonists managed to capture a small Spanish vessel, and the English persuaded the rest to abandon the colony with crops halfway to maturity and sail off to better themselves in the English West Indies—where the English ringleaders sold all the Dutchmen into indenture quasi-slavery. "The English," De Vries wrote bitterly, "are a villainous people and would sell their own fathers for servants in the Islands." [83]

Early Colonial planters needed women for cooking, washing, cleaning, sewing and sleeping with, and when the workload was heavy, they saw no reason why women should not do field work; so though the bulk of servants shipped out was male, consignments of the other sex were also acceptable. The usual source was the Old Country's workhouses and other legal receptacles, some penal, that social dislocations had filled to squalid overflowing. A satirist who knew early Maryland had one tobacco planter's wife twitting another with having been "late a Four-Years Slave" and drawing the retort:

> The Captain Kiss'd you for his Freight . . .
> And how you walk'd the Streets by night
> You'd blush (if you could blush) for Shame,
> Who from Bridewell or Newgate came. . . .[84]

After discount for ill nature in such talk, it remains likely that a sizable proportion of these Founding Mothers had awkward pasts. Of twenty-one Irish spinsters shipped for Barbados in an English vessel in 1636, a pre-sailing check showed at least three pregnant and one syphilitic. A Huguenot sailing for Virginia in 1686 in an English ship reported that of sixty passengers, fifteen were young male rascals, and twelve were prostitutes who freely committed "abominations" with the sailors and some others. Such public problems' consent to emigrate was frequently the work of bullying magistrates aware that local authorities would welcome their departure. Often it must have been the next thing to forced exile as penalty for minor delinquencies—or for the mere bad luck of being a resourceless woman at the wrong time and place.

The eventual consequences of such emigrations were not necessarily all bad. Such women's chances of marriage were crudely good. ". . . any Maid or single Woman," wrote a promoter of the Carolinas in 1708, ". . . will think themselves in the Golden Age, when Men paid a Dowry for their Wives; for if they be but Civil, and under 50 years of age, some honest Man or other, will purchase them for their Wives." [85] A similar description of Maryland represented that even "loose persons seldom live long unmarried if free," [86] though a flagrant reputation might put off all but poor sorts of husbands. The situation was exactly that, with a minor shift in destination, outlined by Macheath in *The Beggar's Opera*: "My dear Lucy—my dear Polly. . . . If you are fond of marrying again, the best advice I can give you, is to ship yourselves off to the West-Indies, where you'll have a fair chance of getting a husband a-piece. . . ." And even when marriage failed to come to pass, household and bed chores on a pretty crude plantation were preferable to oakum-picking in the stinking, overcrowded jails of England. Some seem to have found pretty fair treatment; now and again a planter's will left a legacy, sometimes substantial, to a woman servant to set her up in life when her time was out.

Recruiting of women from workhouses was paralleled by the sending to the Colonies of male rogues and vagabonds. Again this emigration was nominally voluntary. But when the squire, formidable in full-bottomed wig and beaver hat, leaned over the bench to give a vagrant tinker the choice between agreeing to go to the plantations or being whipped till the blood ran to give him a taste for jail, the American nation usually acquired another obscure ancestor. Similarly in conquered Ireland in the 1650's Cromwell's men seized as nominal vagabonds hundreds of hapless Irish who had done nothing but be visible at the wrong time and sent them to the New World to save the trouble of riding herd on them at home. The West Indies got most of them; hence presumably the trace of brogue in the Negroes' speech in some islands. But America got some, and the brogue certainly entered into American ways of speech to judge from the phonetically spelled letters of George Croghan, Dublin-born peltryman and Indian agent: "The Ingans will think a great dail of a little powder and lead . . . it will be a mains of drawing them . . . escuse both writing and peper and guess at my maining. . . ." [87]

Battlefield prisoners, too, suffered punitive exile. The Colonies got many of the tough Scots taken in Cromwell's victories of Preston, Worcester and Dunbar. John Winthrop, Jr., bought some for his ironworks at Saugus, where now a touching plaque set up by a descendant who prospered recalls their memory. Elsewhere, too, Scottish prisoners from the Jacobite risings of 1715 and 1745 proved better buys than the run of voluntary servants; thus Francis Hume, supervisor of Governor Spotswood's ironworks in Virginia, was an exile victim of the failure of the Fifteen. But former fightingmen could be dangerous, too. It was "several mutinous and rebellious *Oliverian* Soldiers . . . sent thither as Servants" [88] who headed a conspiracy of underlings against the planters of Virginia in the mid-1600's.

Humane feelings may have stirred in the sending out to Jamestown of some hundreds of orphans under the age of fourteen to be bound out to settlers and grow up with the Colony. Dutch orphans turned out well in New Netherland. Humaneness certainly inspired General James Oglethorpe's scheme of the 1720's for a Colony (Georgia) to rehabilitate the human debris swamping England's debtors' prisons—and incidentally to buffer the Carolinas against the Spanish in Florida. Few criminals as such were included. But the notion of emptying the Mother Country's jails of offenders against criminal law and favoring the Colonies with their otherwise wasted services had already been popular for a century.

Spain and France had tried it even earlier on a small scale. Most European nations have tried it since. It particularly answered England's needs in the 1600's and 1700's because ill-advised efforts to cope with increasing crime—another token of widespread dislocation—had set the death penalty not only on such serious crimes as treason, murder, piracy and rape but on many offenses in the middle range—theft down to the value of a shilling, for instance. As usual, overharshness led to alleviating evasion. In practice judges twisted the medieval right of benefit of clergy so cleverly that most minor criminals got off with penalties far milder than death, many with a mere scare that made the law look silly. After that loophole was filled, absurdly wide resort to pardons came in. Those convicted of less than the heaviest crimes were pardoned by the Crown, provided they went to the Colonies as purchasable labor for seven years (fourteen in some later contexts) on pain of hanging if they came back too soon. A case of 1618 shows the thing in action: "Stephen Rogers: for killing George Watkins. . . . He puts himself guilty, to be hung, reprieved after judgment at the instance of Sir Thomas Smith, Knt. [a leader in the Virginia Company] for Virginia, because he is of the carpenter's art." [89] Doubtless the killing of George had a touch of self-defense or accident in it. The great Dr. John Donne endorsed this budding system in a sermon of 1622, using analogies to contemporary notions of human physiology:

> It shall redeeme many a wretch from the Jawes of death, from the hands of the Executioner, upon whom, perchance a small fault, or perchance a first fault, or perhaps a fault heartily and sincerely repented, perchance no fault, but malice, had otherwise cast a present and ignominious death. It shall sweepe your streets, and washe your doores, from idle persons . . . and imploy them; and truly if [Virginia] were such a Bridwell, to force idle persons to work, it had a good use. But it is already, not only a *Spleene,* to drain the ill humours of the body, but a *Liver,* to breed good blood; already the imployment breeds Marriners, already the place gives . . . Marchantable commodities. . . .[90]

In Scotland, where forced exile was legal—in England it was not—an arraigned felon could tell the court that however his trial came out, he could not "after being Accused of such Crimes think of passing the remainder of his life in this Country . . . [therefore] to save the trouble of a trial" [91] please banish him to the plantations—a request usually granted. After 1688 the flow of convicts from England to America slackened because for the next two decades able-bodied criminals were also useful as cannon fodder in the English armies fighting Louis XIV and so could secure pardons by enlisting.

Government usually left means of transport to the pardoned felon. If he had money he could go as cabin passenger to Jamaica or Virginia. Most, however, relied on the same arrangements as those of the servant trade, setting the price they would fetch on landing against the cost of passage. The shipowners seem to have had no misgivings. It gives a lurid notion of the emigrant trade of the day that the same skipper who had been carrying regularly indentured servants thought nothing of putting to sea with the usual crew of 12 or so to handle 100 assorted smugglers, forgers, arsonists, pickpockets and poachers. A few mutinies occurred but that risk was lower here than in the African slave trade. Conditions belowdecks seem to have been on the same level of hideousness. A witness of the mid-1700's visiting a shipment of felons for Maryland said: ". . . all the states of horror I ever had an idea of are much short of what I saw . . . this poor man . . . chained to a board in a hole not much above sixteen feet long, more than fifty with him; a collar and padlock around his neck, and chained to five of the most dreadful creatures I ever looked on." [92] In a ship "with convicts for Maryland . . . driven into Antigua by stress of weather [in 1768] . . . eleven had perished for want, and the survivors had eaten their shoes, etc. to sustain life." [93]

Eager as the Colonists were for forced labor, this influx of hard cases roused uneasiness. Maryland and Virginia, where Negro slaves were replacing white in tobacco culture, passed laws restricting the landing of jailbirds and forbidding ship's captains to sell any such without disclosing their pasts, for, as was inevitable in so rascally a trade, they were often palmed off as normal indentured servants. By 1700, with help from the manpower needs of European wars, the two Colonies had much reduced the trade in spite of protests from shipping interests. But the close of the War of the Spanish Succession in 1713 reduced demand for felon soldiers, and the Crown disallowed the Colonies' restrictive laws. Between then and 1775 some 30,000 convicts, maybe a third women—anyway one twenty-fifth of all immigrants coming to America between 1607 and 1775—were landed, mostly in the Chesapeake area. Where population was still so scanty, it was awkward to digest so many delinquents, plus many new-landed indentured servants of the sort that left home one jump ahead of the law. Among unavailing protests was Benjamin Franklin's suggestion that the Colonies should requite Mother Country's generous gifts of jailbait by return shipments of rattlesnakes. He also cited an unidentified protest calling the English way of "emptying their jails into our settlements . . . an insult . . . [that] would not be equalled even by emptying their jakes [privies] on our tables." [94] Yet for all this commotion, convicts continued to find buyers among planters making a start with white labor till they could afford the heavier investment entailed in replacing it with Negro slaves for life at much more per head.

Any work that convicts did was doubtless all to the good from the callously practical point of view of the Colonies, as well as that of the Mother Country. But it may not have been worth the ensuing extra bad feeling between the two. This cut both ways. Stable Colonists, like Franklin, resented such abuse of the Colonial relationship. And Britons aware of jail deliveries sending convicts overseas naturally associated America with felons. Add books such as *Moll Flanders* and the play by Mrs. Aphra Behn portraying two members of the governor's council in Virginia:

> *Madam Flirt:* . . . they say your Honour was but a broken Excise-man, who spent the King's money to buy your Wife fine Petticoats. . . .

Dullman: Hang 'em, Scoundrels . . . they say too, that I was a Tinker . . . and robb'd a Gentleman's House, was put into *Newgate,* for a Reprieve after Condemnation, and was transported hither—and that you, *Boozer,* was a common Pickpocket, and being often flogg'd at the Cart's-Tale, afterwards turned [King's] Evidence, and when the Times grew honest, was fain to flie. . . .[95]

Dr. Samuel Johnson scrupled not to call the Revolutionary Colonists "a race of convicts [who] ought to be thankful for anything we allow them short of hanging." [96] The Colonies and their Mother Country could work up frictions enough without this further occasion for backbiting. And not even the Revolution taught England better. Soon after peace was signed, here came a shipload of convicts for sale. Only after the new nation passed laws forbidding such enterprise did England develop Australia as a new depository for those not quite qualifying for the noose.

To ease the sting of having to count convicts among our forebears, it is customary to cite the vile poverty of England's submerged classes in Stuart and Hanoverian times; to deplore the barbarity of making it a hanging matter for a mother to steal a blanket to keep her baby alive; and to imply that most of the felons sent to the Colonies were rather harmless victims of man's inhumanity to man. (Australians make a similar case.) Certainly some such shameful hardships occurred, for English justice was then far harsher and more hit-and-miss than now. But Abbot Emerson Smith's delvings into actual court records show that "Petty thieves [such as that hypothetical mother] . . . were generally pardoned, without any condition of transportation," [97] so it is unlikely that there were relatively many of her in the Colonies-bound ships. The data hint at a high incidence of personalities that, whether or not friable to begin with, had been so damaged by squalor, forced drifting or some other social trauma as to be chronic bad risks—like Ann Tuffen, lady arsonist transported to the Carolinas who kept on setting fires in her new context and was sold, by order of court, to the Bahamas to exercise her talents there.

Mother Country maintained that it was decent to give transgressors another chance under stimulatingly new conditions, nor was hope that they might straighten up absurd. A Marylander defending the system in the 1760's said: ". . . a young country cannot be settled and improved without people . . . it is much better for the country to receive convicts than slaves. . . . The wicked and bad . . . mostly run away to the northward, mix with other people and pass for honest men; whilst those . . . who come over for very light offenses, serve out their time . . . behave well, and become useful. . . ." [98] Yet something more than mere prejudice against the unlucky is hinted at in the generalized complaints that too many went right on thieving. Franklin was most emphatic about "the instances of transported thieves advancing their fortunes in the colonies [being] extremely rare . . . but of their being advanced there to the gallows the instances are plenty. Might they not as well have been hanged at home?" [99]

The facts lie somewhere between those extremes but are hard to come by. These were mostly obscure persons and understandably shy of high visibility, so surviving records are fragmentary. A few stand out: Sarah Wilson, maid to one of the court ladies of George II's queen, was transported for jewel theft; ran away from the Marylander who bought her time, and, exploiting her knowledge of aristocratic ways, cut a wide swath from Philadelphia to Charleston as Princess Susanna Carolina Matilda, Marchioness of Waldegrave and cousin of the queen. That hardly implies reformation. But consider further Anthony Lamb, apprentice of a London instrument maker, who got involved with Jack Sheppard, the famous English highwayman. Transported to Virginia, Lamb behaved himself, went north when his time was out, and not only prospered selling navigational instruments in Philadelphia but also taught navigation and business mathematics, much to the town's benefit. His son John became a somewhat turbulent general in the Continental Army. David Benefield of Oxford, somehow qualified to call himself a physician, was lagged for poaching, transported, resumed practice in America, and was presently writing home to his former jailor in England that he was making £100 a year. And it seems well established that south of New England, education in the Colonies owed a good deal to the upper stratum of transported convicts, for even teachers with a cloud on them were better than none. Franklin gave it as an advantage of his proposed Pennsylvania Academy that it would qualify "a Number of the poorer sort . . . to act as Schoolmasters. . . . The Country suffering very much at present for want of good Schoolmasters, and oblig'd frequently to employ . . . vicious imported Servants, or concealed Papists, who by their bad Examples . . . often deprave the Morals . . . of the Children. . . ." [100] The Reverend Jonathan Boucher estimated that two-thirds of the schooling in Virginia came from "INDENTED SERVANTS or TRANSPORTED FELONS. Not a ship arrives . . . with . . . convicts, in which schoolmasters are not as regularly advertised for sale as weavers, tailors, or any other trade. . . ." [101]

A striking case in point was Charles Peale, an English country parson's son sent to Cambridge to prepare for holy orders but leaving without a degree for an appointment in the post office. Soon in debt, he embezzled £900 (then a large sum), was convicted, and, pardoned on the usual basis, went to Maryland. There he served the Colony well as a boys'

schoolmaster. He kept hoping that the influence of his former superiors
—who, it may be, owed him something for having kept quiet about irregularities of theirs—would get him a government post; he also had
hopes of a handsome legacy from a rich uncle named Charles Willson.
In both he was disappointed. But before uncle died, a tender indiscretion
of nephew's had had consequences. He had met a charming young widow
and expressed his admiration so fervently that she became pregnant and,
six months after they married, bore a son wishfully named for uncle:
Charles Willson Peale. Uncle never knew how honored he was. The boy
became a versatile, self-made paragon—one of America's most interesting
professional painters and father of a whole brood of the same profession;
a pioneer scientific collector; and predecessor of P. T. Barnum in that
lively branch of show business, the paid-admission museum.

Among indentured servants, too, a general resemblance to Falstaff's
army did not rule out exceptions. Some might be able but discouraged
craftsmen or educated younger sons of the rising English middle class
escaping from some personal difficulty. Either kind was a boon to the
shipowner, for a carpenter or blacksmith or scapegrace able to tutor a
planter's sons and keep his books might bring £30 sold on deck at Norfolk or Wilmington. Numbers of the less skilled doggedly served out their
time, got their allotments of land, worked them capably, married a steady-
paced former servant woman (few questions asked), and reared a brood
of steady-paced children—a good enough way to build up a new country.
Certain of the first Yankees' indentured servants pulled their weight and
to spare—such as John Howland, *Mayflower* Pilgrim who rose high in
the Colony government; the Lincoln in the Bay Colony who was direct
forebear of President Lincoln; and the father of John Wise of Ipswich,
Massachusetts, the parson who first sowed the germs of equalitarianism
in New England. Of thirty members of the House of Burgesses of Virginia
in 1663, thirteen are known to have landed with their passages paid by
others, hence were presumably time-expired servants. That was how
Adam Throughgood, founder of Norfolk, began his New World career.
Daniel Dulany, former student at Trinity College, Dublin, took the indentured route to America, was bought by a prosperous Maryland magnate who needed a clerk in his law office, rose to acquire land of his own,
become attorney general of the Colony, marry a prominent planter's
daughter, send his son home to Eton and Cambridge. Charles Lynch was
similarly bought by a Virginian magnate in 1725, married his master's
daughter when his time was out, acquired great holdings as a tobacco
planter, and fathered the pioneer in the Shenandoah Valley after whom
the custom of lynching may be named. Nowadays, says Hulbert Footner of the Eastern Shore of Maryland, "Some of the first families . . .

trace their origins back to an indentured servant, and are proud of it—
after he has receded far enough into the background." [102] Horatio Alger
did not invent the American strive-and-succeed story*—he only warped
it into absurdity.

But for every servant thus doing well or leaving offspring who did so,
another probably went adrift again either by running away or by failing
to make a springboard of his freedom dues of land and tools. It was easy
for the feckless to sell the land claim and squander the meager proceeds.
Anyway a few years of tobacco culture—the only kind that servants
learned in the Chesapeake area—exhausted the soil. Too many such
small tobacco farmers moved upslope with the frontier to "squat" on lands
not yet in use, living hand-to-mouth on game, pork and corn. Thus began
the vitamin-shy, fever-ridden, "poor white" subculture that still plagues the
southeastern quadrant of the nation. Since it would usually be the less
capable and energetic former servants who drifted into these degenerative
circumstances, here was another automatic selection of raw material to
be made up into a persistent social fact. Doubtless many freed convicts
—or runaways—followed this upcountry drift, happy to be rid of their
recorded histories among new-forming folkways that, for understandable
reasons, tabooed asking what you or your father had been back yonder.

Miniature clusters of such unfortunates were tucked away in most of
the Colonies. The best known, probably because nearest to civilization,
have been the Jackson Whites of the Ramapo Mountains, where, forty
years ago, illiterate moonshiners could sit on the doorstep of a log shanty
and see the Chrysler Building stretching upward on the eastern horizon.
(They made the best applejack I ever drank.) Their forebears are said to
have been deserters from the Hessian troops of the Revolution; runaway
Negro slaves and white servants from the Hudson Valley; some of the
white prostitutes brought to serve the British garrison of New York City
by a contractor named Jackson; and other waifs and strays of the late
1700's, doubtless including some convicts needing seclusion. But no sizable caste of poor whites developed north of the Ohio River-Mason and
Dixon Line. Relative lack of Negro slavery may be one reason for that.
It can hardly be coincidence, however, that such a caste, however unsatis-
factorily defined, did develop in the Southern Colonies, which had been

* In 1727 a Highlander indentured servant in Maryland sent home a letter eloquent of this, also presenting a fine phonetic-spelling puzzle rich with Highland
accent: "Mi nano mestir kam til de quintry a sarfant and well i wot hi's nou wort
mony a susan pount . . . [another] kam out a sarfant fe klesgou an has peen he
nane man twa yeirs an has sax plockimors wurkin til him alrety. . . ." (Roughly:
"My own master came to this country a servant and well I know he's now worth
many a thousand pounds . . . another came out a servant from Glasgow and has
been his own man two years and has six blackamoors working for him already. . . ."
(Maclean, *Scotch Highlanders in America,* Appendix.)

the principal recipients of all those indentured servants with a considerable admixture of convicts.*

As if trying to make up for the influx of convicts and unpromising servants, the tobacco Colonies soon began to found a homemade gentry on tobacco prosperity. When Cromwell's victory in England did not carry with it control of Virginia at first, a few Royalist squires went there for refuge. Men named Randolph or Washington brought with them clothes and manners better than those of pristine Virginia—and money from the sale of their home manors to buy tobacco land with. Gradually around them and their progeny spread a stratum of planter families commanding wide acreage and learning to relish the fine horses, imported wines, finery and furniture, even books sometimes, for which the newly transplanted Cavaliers—as their venerating descendants call them in a tone of voice implying that they wore their plumed hats even in bed—naturally sent home.

Their values were, of course, nostalgic and imitative. But within the limits of material things they were civilizing, as in their own ways were also Quaker tolerance, Moravian cultivation and Yankee zeal for learning. "The inferior and middling sort of people [of the Chesapeake area]," says Carl Bridenbaugh, "generally found the owner of the big estate courteous, kind, and a fair and understanding judge on the quorum, ready to extend a helping hand before his aid was sought . . . the leading planters were imbued with the belief that they constituted a class whose

---

* The causal relation between the influx of servants and convicts and the South's poor whites has been overstated and taken as evidence of generalized degeneracy, social or genetic or both, among such immigrants. The text has made it clear that in many cases servants and, in some, convicts, did well by themselves and the new country. Overcorrection is illustrated in Den Hollander's "The Tradition of 'Poor Whites'" (in Couch, *Culture in the South*): "The general run of these emigrants was fairly representative of English working classes at large with a sprinkling of small middle class people." In that case why did so many "representative" working people take the deviant or eccentric step of leaving home? He also makes the point that though "The first settlers of . . . Australia were of a much more unfavorable type than the plurality of the Southern redemptioners [that is, were almost altogether convicts] . . . no distinct 'poor-white' class has originated in Australia." This ignores the differing conditions of Australian colonization. The drier, game-poor Australian backcountry offered no such opportunity as did the American for a hand-to-mouth existence in the backwoods. The original scheme to make "a small land-holding peasantry" out of the time-expired convicts was almost immediately wrecked by the rise of large-holding rancher employers who had come out as officers of the guard troops and thenceforward dominated Australian land policy. Few time-expired convicts ever saw the chance to acquire lands of their own as a temptation to turn independent backwoodsmen. From the beginning port-town settlement flourished in Australia, as it did not in the Southern Colonies. Consequently the Australian equivalent of the Southern poor white was the vicious, shiftless Sydney larrikin.

obligations to serve and to govern well must be fulfilled in return for the privileges which were their birthright." [103] Further polish came to Virginia with Williamsburg, the miniature capital set up in the late 1600's, where royal governors (no longer overseas managers for a commercial company but directly under the Crown) and their suites fresh from home set influential examples of how gentry behaved. In our terms much of it was pretty coarse, but it must have been a great refinement on early Jamestown. Between governors and Cavaliers evolved that caste of FFV's that, before spinsterish genealogy took it over, contributed much to the dignity and stamina of the Revolution and to the hegemony of the Old Dominion in the new nation. It was not basically Cavalier in origin, however; the original Byrd, Carter, Page were distinctly self-made men of humble beginnings.

Other Colonies also developed such gentry castes, for nobody yet knew that America was to be democratic in government and equalitarian in ideals and sometimes practice. New England's upper crust—the Winthrops, the Dudleys, the Saltonstalls—came of the same minor English gentry as the Cavaliers and oftener included august, gently born clergymen. In due time it also admitted the cream of self-made businessmen like John Hull, son of a blacksmith, himself a craftsman in gold and silver and thus, by an association then common, something of a banker. New Netherland's equivalent was founded on huge grants of upriver lands to Rensselaers, Schuylers and so on and (after England took over) to Livingstons, Morrises and the like. Pennsylvania's oligarchy consisted originally of leading Quakers whose franchise was protected by property qualifications. In the Carolinas little came of a queer scheme, which had a less than halfhearted trial, of a Colonial peerage of barons, margraves and caciques (the aboriginal West Indians' name for headmen) holding swamp-and-pinewoods fiefs under the lords proprietors. But as peltry and rice made South Carolina a going concern, a gentry sprouted among the large planters and the waterfront merchants to whom they cannily married their sons and daughters. The great Manigault Mansion, now within Charleston, once betokened these interwoven interests. The view from the front was of the city within easy distance for social purposes; that from the rear was of the rice fields that paid for its splendors.

Colonial governors had wide and widely exploited powers to grant lands and other economic favors. That combined with the Colonial grandees' snobbery to make government a prime stiffener of these Colonial upper crusts. Thomas Hutchinson, Boston-born gentleman governing Massachusetts as the Revolution began, headed a whole clan of officeholders, including his brother-in-law as lieutenant governor, his brother and son as high judges and his daughter's father-in-law as chief justice.

Such family solidarity was taken for granted "at home" and naturally flourished in the Colonies, too. Rising Virginians such as the Washingtons owed most of their buoyancy to the favor of governors incumbent in Williamsburg. Hutchinson stayed loyal to the Crown; so did most of these landowners-*cum*-officials-*cum*-merchants, and they usually suffered ruin and exile for it. But a willful minority named Laurens, Washington, Jefferson, Carroll, Stockton, Morris, Schuyler, men of much the same stripe, threw in with the Colonies—else the cause might have been smothered outside Pennsylvania and New England.

Oligarchy, aristocracy, plutocracy, gentry—those terms all fit to some extent but, being borrowed from European contexts, do not precisely suit the new-minted America. Fortunately the Colonies had borrowed from Stuart England a term that, soon obsolete at home, persisted as a useful Americanism: the Quality. "Bakers' bread, what the quality eat," said Huckleberry Finn. "None of your lowdown cornpone." "All America is divided into two classes—the quality and the equality, . . ." [104] wrote Owen Wister. Its loose rightness up to 1914—where this book will end—makes it a fine technical term. From here on: the Quality.

In Wister's time most of the Quality believed that one of the things distinguishing their group was a vaguely conceived but real superiority in genetically transmitted intelligence and integrity. "Good blood" they called it in a wildly inaccurate metaphor still used by the ill informed trying to be wise about silk purses and sows' ears. Genetic forces necessarily shaped our emigrant ancestors. Environmental forces shaped them further. *Nature* and *nurture* would have been the Quality's terms. It is advisable to consider how far the genetic approach is valid. To what extent did those emigrants' genetic heritage bend them toward turning into poor whites or merchant princes and modify what environment did to them—and vice versa—once they landed?

The physical aspect is easier to make sense of. Physical stamina—vigor, resistance to hardship, longevity—is to a considerable extent heritable, else life insurance offices wouldn't ask at what ages your parents died. It follows, however callous it sounds, that the horrible mortality among our ancestors first at sea and then during seasoning ashore had a good side. Very crudely it tended to weed out many genetic strains of low stamina. As the Colonists seeped westward into the hardships of the frontier, that grisly process continued, doubtless with further long-run benefits to posterity.

The issue of temperament—of individual variations in enterprise, social adaptability, emotional stability and so on, so important in the relations between man and his surrounding culture—is knottier. The good blood faction—*eugenist* has been the word since the late 1800's—would have deplored on genetic grounds the notion of building a society at Jamestown by sifting the slums of London for persons gullible or guilty enough to consent to emigrate. Eugenists would have approved, however, of the later stiffening of a ruling caste for Virginia from among stubbornly loyal families of the English elite, alias Cavaliers. Those overemphasizing nurture and minimizing genetic influences on behavior might come to the same conclusions on their own extremely different grounds. The short-comings of poor whites, for instance, would be seen as resulting from the degrading, stultifying ordeal to which England had subjected potential emigrants, creating in them antisocial habits of thinking, feeling and doing handed down from parent to offspring in the Colonies, as well as at home. As for the good effect of Cavalier leadership, the nurture-minded would point out that the tradition of *noblesse oblige* that went with the status of English rural gentry, also transmitted from parent to offspring by precept and unconscious example, could account for it without dragging in possible genetic factors.

Such issues were more important in the past than now—which is lucky because it cannot yet be determined which side exaggerated worse. We do know, however, what early eugenists did not: that in any given mating the genetic dice combine at random, so that two silk purses can readily produce a sow's ear now and again, and vice versa. The dullest American politician I ever met bears legitimately one of the greatest of Colonial Quality names, whereas though Abraham Lincoln's family tree can never be completely traced, the circumstances of his birth make it odds-on that it included many indentured servants and a sprinkling of con-victs. But in any case, after fourteen or fifteen generations of American restlessness the genetic strains that landed up to the time of the Revolu-tion have been so higgledy-piggledy mingled that most of whatever sig-nificance they may have had is lost. Possible exceptions to that generality may persist in such special situations as that of the plain Pennsylvania Dutch and the more isolated enclaves of the South.

Speculation about the temperaments of our Founding Forebears is pos-sible, however, on condition of great caution. Like Stevenson, we hope that a dynamic courage characterized the generic emigrant-pioneer-founder. Did it not take grit and high resolution thus to pack off over-seas, renouncing the familiar old hovel and the ring of familiar voices? Did not the formidable odds of dying en route or soon after landing lend the decision an air of either desperation or gallantry?

Actually the circumstances of most early emigrants hint strongly that desperation did not bulk too large. Those emigrating in self-selected groups had the advantages of sympathetic comradeship and, in most cases, a sustaining sense of divine support. And it was probably some form of hope, however dim-witted, that set most indentured volunteers stepping out as individuals from the mass of the dislocated and downtrodden. As for gallantry, was it a fine impatience with the humdrum homeland, a taste for the bright eyes of danger that enlisted young men with George Popham or John Smith or Sir John Yeamans? There is small evidence of it. In the 1600's that kind of romantic impulse was seldom consciously felt, still less expressed. Suppose such temperaments then existed; they had inarticulately to work off their restlessness in religious heresy or in special susceptibility to tales of Carolina Indian towns roofed with gold. Risk taking is an adjunct of bravery, of course. But it is doubtful whether, in the early days anyway, either organized or individual emigrants knew how high the risks were. The culture they came from afforded little opportunity to learn what faced them. They had no newspapers. Primitive communication clogged the spread of word-of-mouth warnings. Many of them had probably never even seen the sea before being herded on board ship. Practically all they knew of Virginia or the plantations had come from those seeking profit by shipping them.

James Truslow Adams, a bracingly astringent historian, once suggested that those staying in the Old Country were actually the brave ones, that the emigrant volunteer showed "a certain lack of courage when he decided that things had got too much for him at home. . . . Puritan leaders . . . preferred the physical discomforts, but political and religious simplifications of the wilderness to their native land and its insistent problems . . . it may be questioned whether those who remained in England, faced the conditions, including possible martyrdom, and fought the Stuart tyranny to a successful finish, were not the stronger. . . ." [105]

That overplays a minor, though piquant, point and ignores the Puritan's belief that God would soon treat England as He had Sodom—which makes stay-at-home Puritans seem to have lacked either the courage of their convictions or imagination. Imagination—that quality, often a part of mental or emotional restlessness, may be the significant word. It may have been what supplied the crucial extra impulse that self-selected most of the Pilgrims from the mass of their brethren in Leiden; what distinguished most of the Scotch-Irish emigrants from the stay-at-home ancestors of today's Ulstermen; what determined which Loyalist squires would uproot themselves and go to Virginia instead of risking harassment or worse from Cromwell. Since imagination does not necessarily imply intelligence, some low-grade form of it may have helped a particular scapegrace apprentice or cast-off servingman succumb to the blandishments of a spirit, thus setting him apart from thousands of others like him stodgily staying put. It is possible—this ice is very thin—that a crude self-selection of emigrant temperaments on some such basis may underlie the American bent for mechanical invention, which was by no means confined to New England. It may have put a peculiar sting into the American preacher's sense of hellfire, the American reformer's zeal to *do something,* the American speculator's conviction that the wilderness could be populated, and the American slaveholder's dread of slave risings.

The Negro slaves—a most influential set of Colonial immigrants—had done the least self-selecting—in fact, none whatever. A very few were kidnapped directly by the crews of slave ships, though by the 1600's most "European" (West Africa's term for all whites) slavers frowned on that as causing the trade lasting damage. Many were war captives from intertribal raids staged to supply aggressive Negro kings with stocks-in-trade of slaves for barter for rum, gunpowder, textiles and hardware. Eminent captives were likelier than ordinary villagers to be ransomed, so fewer kings and chiefs than legend supposes were shipped overseas. But once the captives were roped together, small further distinction was made. Hence a typical cargo of slaves was likelier to be representative of West Africa than the typical lot of white servants was of contemporary England. Indeed it is probable enough that—assuming the average genetic intellectual potential of Europeans and Negroes to be much the same, as is likely—the black slaves were, on the whole, superior human raw material. Few can have had much idea where the ship was taking them. The exceptions would be those who, before capture, had themselves taken part in the slave trade, hence had learned from white traders or employers a little about why more and more "black ivory" was wanted far away to westward of the setting sun.

As proto-Americans the Negroes were ahead of the Pilgrims, who were still seeking ways and means of migrating when, in 1619, a Dutch privateer with loot from a cruise against the Spaniards put into Jamestown and sold the Colonists "twenty negars." [106] They seem to have been treated more or less like purchased white servants, with eventual freedom assumed.* But the position of Negroes landed later gradually degenerated for reasons eloquent of the coarseness of human relations. They knew little or no English, so were temptingly helpless against imposition. In any case, they arrived under no form of agreement with those who sold them, so had no contractual rights to appeal to and were not presumptively

---

* This account of the development of Negro slavery in the Colonies is necessarily synoptic and neglects the subtleties of detail. Oscar Handlin (*Race and Nationality,* Chapter I) offers an ingenious evolutionary history of the matter based on the attitudes of the day.

entitled, like white servants, to such safeguards as "the custom of the country"—the protective phrase in indentures. At first some were taught enough about Christianity to justify baptism. But thus making them Christians might be taken to imply full community rights, hence eventual freedom of person. Since a perpetual slavery made Negroes especially useful, such proselyting came to be frowned on, even to be prohibited by laws, though the spirit of them was often evaded.

The slave for life was thought to be more docile because he had no consciousness of freedom on the way such as might make white servants restless. He was more productive over the years because he did not disappear into freedom after learning how to tend tobacco. Negro women slaves not only could be put to field work, to which they were well used back in Africa, but by childbearing also built up the available pool of slave labor. Physiologically Negroes were also slightly better suited than whites to dawn-to-dusk toil (with a long noontime layoff) in the muggy, blazing summers of the Atlantic seaboard. White planters trying to justify slavery smugly exaggerated that, but recent responsible studies do show that Negroes' vasomotor system handles hard labor at humid high temperatures somewhat better. Many Negroes also apparently inherit somewhat higher resistance than whites show to the malaria that came to the New World with the discoverers and crippled so many settlements. In the long run, however, neither of these minor racial traits is of high importance.

Basically it was the special convenience of slavery that led to the replacement of temporary-slave whites by permanent-slave Negroes in the rice and tobacco fields—and so to the institutionalization of black slavery in America. Or say that it was the racial trait of his ineradicable skin color denying him the social mobility possible to whites. The white servant, whether he ran away or waited out his time, could disappear into the shifting mass of Colonial whites, or his offspring could. The Negro could not. High visibility was and has remained his inveterate enemy. By association, black began to mean menial by definition, congenital "hewers of wood and drawers of water," as the Bible says of the seed of Ham's son Canaan. Eventually it was taught—with no textual justification at all—that the Canaanites, doomed by the Lord to servitude, had been black, a doctrine still lively in Southern diehard racist circles. Our forebears of Jacobean times already had some color prejudice—see *Othello* and elsewhere—and now it was well worth cultivating as a pretext for lifetime slavery for Negroes. As that cultivation, doubtless unconscious, proceeded, chattel slavery as the status taken for granted for Negroes became deeply entrenched. Laws deliberately widened the gap between the races, making a slave mother's child a slave to her owner even if it had a free white father, banning mixed marriages. As the Negro's presumed sta-

tus became that of slave for life, animal-fashion, the white servant forced
to work alongside him felt a resentment that soured into hatred of Negroes
in general—hence, probably, the specially bitter anti-Negro feeling among
Southern poor whites. A very vicious circle: To protect itself, a slaveholding society built the race barrier high on many social levels. Once thus
embedded in all white attitudes from childhood up, it came to seem normal, which made slavery seem right and inevitable. Bad logic, worse morality, eventual results calamitous.

The equation dark-skinned race = slave also enslaved the Indian. One
thinks of Indian slaves only in Latin America, where, though the Arawaks
of the West Indies died off in slavery and their Carib cousins were too
tough to handle, Indian forced labor was the backbone of Spanish exploitation of Central and much of South America. Yet the tribes of eastern
North America also suffered from the economic consequences of the implication that the color of their skin meant they were imperfectly human.
Efforts to Christianize them, though known in most Colonies, were few
and feeble. The usual attitude shows clearly in John Winthrop's recording
a great wind that "lifted up [the] meeting house at Newbury, the people
being in it . . . yet through God's mercy it did no hurt; only killed one
Indian with the fall of a tree." [107] (When Huckleberry Finn told Aunt
Sally of a steamboat explosion, she said: "Good gracious! Anybody hurt?"
"No'm," Huck said. "Killed a nigger.") This sense of separateness was
heightened by the belief general among Colonists that the Indians' religious rites, which struck most whites as dauntingly grotesque, were homage
to the Devil or maybe a whole pantheon of devils. After their bloody victory over the Pequots in 1637 the Bay Colonists felt no compunction
about keeping the surviving women and children for slaves and selling
some of the men to their fellow Puritans in Bermuda. To the end of the
1600's New England had Indian slaves-for-life. There were only a few in
Massachusetts and on eastern Long Island, but in Rhode Island a sizable
number worked alongside Negro slaves in the stock pastures of the Narragansett planters.

The Carolinas, however, saw the most extensive Indian slavery. In
1704 Colonel James Moore, reporting on his devastating raid on Spain's
Indian missions in the Apalachee country, wrote: "I . . . have killed
and taken as slaves 325 men, and have taken slaves 4000 women and
children." [108] Four years later South Carolina counted 2,400 adult
whites, 2,900 Negro slaves, and 1,100 adult Indian slaves, some 17 percent of the population. The Southeastern Indians were neither as well
organized nor as hardheaded as the Northeastern Iroquois who so stubbornly maintained themselves as middlemen between the whites and the

peltry-rich Great Lakes country. Wars with nearby tribes had taught Charleston that the West Indies would buy Indian captives. As the traders' packtrains followed the old war trails beyond the Carolinas' effective frontiers, taking cloth, rum, hardware to ever more remote tribes, those Indians of the interior learned that the whites would swap their fascinating goods for human beings, as well as for deerskins. The best way to procure human beings was to raid adjacent tribes still underequipped with firearms or just less tough. Going on the warpath was a seasonal collective sport anyway, important in intramural politics and status systems. Now it had economic importance. And Indians had no scruples about slavery as such. It was one of their own minor institutions, and in time the upcountry tribes of the South came to hold numbers of Negro slaves. So the traders directly and indirectly fomented crass, racially suicidal little man-grabbing wars among the Southeastern Indians. It was West Africa all over again—the native's yearning for white man's things combined with lack of racial solidarity to destroy him. Indeed, as a way of wiping out Indians, slaving was almost as good as disease, much better than rum.

Some Indians thus acquired became *burdeners,* packing bundles of deerskins on their backs to Charleston or (later) Augusta, Georgia, where pirogues took them downriver to tidewater at Savannah. Others learned to be horse tenders for the four-footed packtrains of traders who could afford animals that, though more costly and delicate, carried more than men could. A few Indians were sold northward as slaves. But most of those exported went to the man-devouring sugar islands of the West Indies. The presence of this ready market seems to contradict the general impression among Colonists that red men were unprofitable as field labor. The explanation involves an aspect of slavery often relied on by slavers, including the blackbirders of the South Seas in the 1800's. A man hard to break to forced labor in his own country often knuckles under and earns his keep when taken out of it. The male Indian probably earned his reputation for inefficiency at field labor in America. By and large, hunting and fishing were the only work that the Mohican or Delaware or Susquehannock brave knew. Fuel supply, crop tilling and so on were for women, who, as an early Bay Colonist noted, "are generally very laborious at planting time, and the Men extraordinarily idle. . . ." [109] A Pequot slave set to what he considered woman's work was likely to abscond into the woods, where he was much more at home than his white owner. When the Indian chief who captured John Stark in 1752 ordered him to hoe the corn patch—just what whites did to Indians—Stark threw the hoe in the river, saying it was "the business of squaws and not warriors to hoe corn." [110] The chief concluded that he was a fine fellow who knew his own dignity and treated him well thenceforth. Exceptions confirm all this:

Roger Williams noted of the Narragansetts that "sometimes the man . . . either out of love for his wife or care for his children, or being an old man, will help the woman, which by the custome of the country they are not bound to do." [111] The relative willingness of Indian slaves to tend horses and cows in Rhode Island meant merely that Indian culture had no livestock; hence that sort of thing had never got classified as the unworthy business of women.

Similarly Indian men slaves made adequate horse wranglers in Carolina packtrains. Chances of docility and diligence were best, however, when they were shipped to St. Kitts, where climate, plants and animals all were unfamiliar; where lack of family and familiar ways kept normal emotions dull; where life was permeated with a low-grade fear of an overwhelming mass of outlandish things. The mere exotic look of the country would damp the urge to run away in all but the boldest. And precisely those same values underlay the Colonist's preferring African Negroes to Indian slaves, for to a West African, Virginia was as alien as Barbados was to a Catawba brave.

The morality of keeping any slaves, Negro or Indian, was first questioned in America by certain deviant Quakers in Pennsylvania. By 1700 in New England Samuel Sewall, the penitent witch-trial judge whose conscience was often ahead of his time, wrote of his uneasiness about slavery and sought to get some humaneness into Massachusetts' laws degrading nonwhites. It distressed him to see "Indians and Negroes being rated [as taxable assets] with Horses and Hogs." Of a bill forbidding miscegenation, whether in or out of wedlock, he said: "I fear 'twill be an Oppression provoking to God." [112] Meanwhile, slavery as at least a supplement to white labor had infected all the Colonies to some degree. The heaviest concentrations above the Chesapeake were in New Jersey-New York (where the Dutch had introduced Negroes in the 1620's) and Rhode Island. By 1770, however, the rest of New England had some 11,000 Negro slaves primarily in prospering households, driving the coach, mending clothes, minding children, typically called Pompey, Caesar, Psyche, Dutchess in the nastily patronizing fashion of seriocomic slave naming common also in the British and French West Indies. Treatment of them probably varied by place and individual owners. One of the few authentic glimpses comes from Madam Sarah Knight, Boston schoolmistress, who called Connecticut farmers of 1704 "too indulgent . . . to their slaves . . . permitting y^m to sit at Table and eat with them, (as they say to save time,) and into the dish goes the black hoof as freely as the white hand." [113]

Slavery in all Colonies did not, however, mean equal expansion in all.

By 1775 the number of slaves below Mason and Dixon's Line exceeded 450,000. Above it, though the total populations of the two halves were much the same, it was some 60,000. Historians trying to account for this discrepancy usually say something like: "Gradually it was found that different climatic, social and economic conditions made slavery imprac- tical in the Northern Colonies. . . ." Just what social and economic con- ditions are meant is often vague. And did climate really matter much?

No doubt it should have. The Negro's biological fitness for steaming West Africa, though useful in American summers, should have been poor preparation for northern American winters. There is reason to believe that north of latitude 40° (that of Philadelphia) Negroes' dark skins do not absorb enough sunlight for self-supply of vitamin D, lack of which causes rickets in children; hence deformed pelvises in girls; hence high incidence of death in childbed, as well as generally poor physical condi- tions. So the farther north the Colony, the higher the incidence of prema- ture deaths, notably among women of childbearing age; the lower the birthrate; and the less reason to maintain slavery. The point is sound as far as it goes but hardly compelling, for Negro slavery flourished in a strikingly Southern fashion in Rhode Island,* well above latitude 40° and in a climate only slightly milder than that of southern Connecticut, where, in the same latitude, slavery was much rarer.

So climate cannot have been a major factor. What about a liberal dis- taste for slavery in the Northern Colonies? This, too, is dubious. Rhode Island was the most liberal of the New England Colonies, and yet her Quakers, a liberalizing leaven there as elsewhere, were notably active in the New England-West Africa-West Indies slave trade. Could sharp social stratification in the South have predisposed the planter to segrega- tion of field labor by color, as well as by status? Well, Massachusetts was originally about as sharply stratified as Virginia. Could the cause have been economic—a chicken-and-egg relation between the South's con- centration on exporting single cash crops (tobacco, rice) demanding large landholdings and gang labor and Negro chattel slavery in a chronically labor-short situation? That sounds better—but then one reflects that on the same basis Pennsylvania should have developed large slave-worked farms to produce the cereals and pork that she exported so copiously.

* Rhode Island's "Narragansett planters" would today be called ranchers and dairymen. On holdings of two or three square miles, using Negro and Indian slave labor in proportions of about 3 to 2, they ran sheep, cattle and the famous Nar- ragansett pacers, the first distinctively American breed of horseflesh. Some worked up to forty slaves. The largest dairy milked 100 cows and annually made 13,000 pounds of a famous Rhode Island version of Cheshire cheese, as well as much butter. The typical pattern of Big House, elegantly dressed wife, cellar full of Madeira, lavish hospitality, slave servants, horse-mindedness was very close to that of the tobacco-raising Chesapeake Quality. (Cf. Channing, "The Narragansett Planters.")

These flaws in successive theories lead the mind back to a notion mentioned earlier. If it was not climate or social attitude or economics, might it have been geography—a side effect of that vast circular course sailed by ships trading to the New World? It took them from Northern Europe close to West Africa, then close to the West Indies—one the great source of slaves, the other the greatest market for them—then homeward along the North American coast. Slaves were a perishable cargo. Every day they were kept on board increased the risk of profit-marring deaths among them. Hence, other things being equal, a slaver captain preferred to dispose of his unwilling passengers at the first available market—the West Indian sugar islands, usually needing fresh Negroes because the sugar industry killed them off faster than natural breeding replaced them.

By and large, only exceptional circumstances took a cargo of slaves to Charleston or Norfolk. The mainland segment of the trade was always distinctly secondary to the West Indian. Then it took so much longer to get Negroes fresh from Africa still farther up the coast, to Philadelphia, New York or the New England ports, that practically no slave ship of standard dimensions ever tried it. Slave supply north of the Chesapeake remained largely a matter of a few Negroes brought North from the West Indies, not directly from Africa, in the numerous Colonial vessels in either the West African triangular or the direct West Indies trade. That is, the opportunity to stock up amply with slaves at economically worthwhile initial cost came most readily to the West Indies; less readily, though not infrequently, to the rice and tobacco Colonies; and least readily to the Northern cereal, livestock, lumber and fish Colonies. That corresponds precisely to the relative density of slave population in those three regions. It is a curious thought that if steamships, faster than sailing vessels and able to have taken slaves as quickly to New York as to Jamaica, had existed in the 1700's, American slavery might have been on the same scale in all states and the Civil War might never have been fought.

Single, all-explaining causes for historical phenomena are now deservedly mistrusted. Someday, when the whole set of reasons why the South was worse infested with slavery is identified, this winds-and-currents theory may be among them. Anyway, one result of Colonial slavery was to add to the long list of grievances against the Mother Country. The increasing number of Negroes from natural increase supplemented by fresh imports eventually alarmed the Southern Colonies much as the influx of felons had. They passed laws restricting or even banning the further landing of chattel slaves. The Crown disallowed the heavier restrictions because the slave trade was still thought of as worth encouraging. The stepchild mainland Colonies were not to be allowed to stifle the minor but handy slave markets in the rice and tobacco country. Then Jamaica began to have lurid, chronic trouble with runaway (Maroon) Negro slaves colonized in the interior hills and practically impossible to get back under control. That put a really keen edge on Virginia's uneasiness. Hear William Byrd II, a most articulate and knowledgeable Colonist, telling the tale to an influential English friend of his in 1736; the occasion was the decision to bar slavery from the new Colony of Georgia:

> I wish my Lord we could be blessed with the same Prohibition. They import so many Negros hither, that . . . this Colony will some time or other be confirmed by the name of New Guinea. . . . [Negroes] . . . ruin the Industry of our White People, who seeing a Rank of poor creatures below them, detest work for fear it should make them look like Slaves. . . . Another unhappy effect of Many Negros is the necessity of being severe. Numbers make them insolent, and then foul Means must do what fair will not. We have however nothing like the Inhumanity here that is practiced in the Islands, and God forbid we ever should. . . . Yet even this is terrible to a good natured Man, who must . . . be either a Fool or a Fury.
>
> But these private mischiefs are as nothing if compared to the publick danger. We have already [in Virginia] at least 10,000 Men of these descendants of Ham fit to bear Arms . . . should there arise a man of desperate courage amongst [them]. . . . It were therefore worth . . . consideration . . . to put an end to this un-Christian traffick of makeing Merchandise of our Fellow Creatures. At least . . . further Importation . . . should be prohibited. We have mountains in Virginia too to which they may retire and do mischief . . . as in Jamaica. . . . I wonder [England] will indulge a few ravenous Traders to the danger of the Publick Safety, and such Traders as would freely sell their Fathers, their Elder Brothers, and even the Wives of their Bosomes, if they could black their faces and get anything for them. . . .[114]

Jefferson's next-to-last draft of the Declaration of Independence cited England's callous support of slave traders as one of the excellent reasons why the Colonies withdrew their allegiance. But that clause was not in the final draft. Delegates from the Deep South had killed it. Solicitude for the trade can hardly have been the main reason. To check it might raise the value of the Negroes that these Southern statesmen already owned, and as for future supply, experience in past wars that had cut off importation of fresh slaves had shown that natural increase would take care of foreseeable needs. Apparently the "peculiar institution" was already a sacred cow. It made Southern Quality uneasy to think of having even the worst of its unsavory aspects reprehended in public.

The Negro's revenge was already effective. In his bowels and blood-stream came African diseases that did America more damage than all the slave revolts ever occurring. Yellow fever was already an endemic scourge in South America and the West Indies. As contacts increased in the 1790's it struck along the Atlantic coast from Savannah to Philadelphia in terrifying epidemics. Worse still was hookworm, fostered by bare feet, sandy soil and casual defecation—the cryptic parasite that probably did as much as poor genes, poor diet and social neglect together to keep the South's poor whites shiftless. The more virulent kinds of malaria may also be on this grisly list.

The slave too contracted these ailments. But generations of exposure had given him resistances reducing the ill effects. That was not true of the white man vomiting black in the griping throes of yellow jack or leaning fecklessly on a rotting fence while the tiny, hook-mouthed worm bred hungrily in his gut and teemed in the polluted soil. What a pity that in the slave's day biology was so backward that he never knew how much misery for white men was of his inadvertent doing!

III

At Home Abroad

WILLIAM BYRD II'S AMERICA

III

ONLY political history can hope for chronological neatness. The Declaration of Independence, the firing on Fort Sumter, really are trusty points of reference—day-dated events with their very definiteness shaping the future and symbolizing the strains and growings that brought them to pass. For example, the Revolution handily marks the end of the political aspect of Colonial America. But cultural colonialism persisted for generations after 1775 and in some respects is still with us. Likewise the Gilded Age flowed so deviously into the Age of Muckraking that no scholarly hindsights about the Closing of the Frontier can account for all the forces involved or put Father Time's shaky finger on the watershed.

All that having been granted, choice of the decade 1731-40 as the end of America's first phase has ample chronological backing. This decade saw the founding of the last Colony—Georgia in 1733. In 1740 it saw the first permanent settlement of the Moravians, the last influential body of organized emigrants. By then, too, the bulk of the Scotch-Irish and Pennsylvania Dutch was ashore. Their countrymen continued to follow in numbers; so did English, Scots, Welsh and Irish. But most of that was less deliberately organized and added no new ingredient. By 1740 the ethnic hand was dealt for the next few generations. All the elements that would brew up into an independent something called America had been stirred into the vat.

Note, too, that the next decade (1741-50) saw premonitory data of new content. A religious Great Awakening originating with Colonial-born and -trained preachers (though spurred on by outsiders) began to form religious techniques specially well adapted to American conditions. Colonials under a Colonial commander captured, with more luck than judgment, the French fortress of Louisburg in Nova Scotia, which unmistakably introduced a new factor in the struggle for North America. It was in 1748 that the westward-setting tide of settlement—not mere prowling

127

after peltry—first spilled over the Allegheny Divide into the Western Waters. In the reverse direction Colony-born persons began to leave marks on the Old World. Benjamin Franklin set about the experiments in electricity that brought him European fame; Jonathan Edwards attracted attention from European theologians aware of a major speculative thinker crying out in the wilderness of western Massachusetts.

In the opinion of C. M. Andrews, the end of the wars with Louis XIV (1713) marked the beginning of "a state of colonial society sufficiently at rest to admit of satisfactory review." [1] Carl Bridenbaugh, equally expert, made 1742 the end of his first study of Colonial urbanism. The intervening three decades do feel like a plateau between the higgledy-piggledy pasts of the nascent Colonies and their accelerating, converging futures. Those years saw the deaths of William Penn, Samuel Sewall and William Byrd II; the births of George Washington, John Adams and Daniel Boone. Between the progeny of immigrants and the generation succeeding them the Colonial population was now prevalently Colonial-born. What were the circumstances that they encountered and created for themselves?

First, some of the problems that the Colonies had in common: how to handle the Indians, for instance, which usually came to mean how to get rid of the Indians. Creating exports to pay for the imported means of Old Country-style living: tools, wines, finery. Keeping peace between port town and upcountry. And the always irksome juggling of the media of internal exchange: deerskins in the Carolinas, beaver in New York, pounds of tobacco in Virginia. Most such makeshifts were eked out in terms of corn or strings of wampum—the Indians' medium of ceremonial exchange that the Colonists took over as a sort of serious play-money. All that reflected a chronic, severe shortage of gold and silver in circulation. The Colonies' trade with the West Indies was so crucial because New England's lumber and refuse codfish, Pennsylvania's flour and Virginia's pork brought home thence, particularly from non-British islands, a small, steady influx of hard money. A cogent cause of the Revolution was fear lest taxation of the Colonies, requiring gold and silver in payment, drain off to the Mother Country the indispensable minimum of hard money in circulation. "Money is at present a scarce Commodity," wrote a semiofficial British visitor in Stamp Act times, "all goes to England, and I am much at a loss how they will find Specie, to pay the Duties last imposed on them by Parliament." [2]

Little of it was English coinage. The gold was mostly Spanish and Portuguese: moidores, pistoles, joes and half joes (the Portuguese gold joannes), most of them much reduced in value by wear and drastic clipping. The silver was mostly Spanish-Mexican pieces of eight—the Colonies' Spanish dollars—and smaller pieces of the same origin down to reals at eight to the dollar. When coined reals were scarce, the Colonists cut the dollar into eight piece-of-pie-shaped bits. Even now in certain parts of America two bits means twenty-five cents, four bits fifty and so on. A fip was half a bit, the sixteenth of a dollar. Merchants paying duties and settling overseas balances, however, had to keep their books in the official money of account—pounds, shillings and pence. So each coin was first tediously weighed to determine its exact bullion value and then translated into English coinage as modified by the local inflation. Merely to know how much was in the till at a given time required prodigies of arithmetic.

Wide discrepancies among the individual Colonies' paper currencies led to further confusion. As economies expanded and commerce grew complex without matching increase in the supply of hard money, all Colonies issued notes reading *dollars* or *shillings* on the face. But since no two Colonies' fiscal policies were coordinated, no two currencies had the same purchasing power. A paper pound from South Carolina might be worth only a few shillings in relatively solvent Pennsylvania. A striking minor benefit from the Constitution of 1787 was its ban on state coinage and currency, making all that a federal monopoly, and the ensuing standardization of a federal dollar of equal value throughout the nation. Yet so strong is verbal habit that, according to that most reliable historian Samuel Eliot Morison, country people in Maine were still saying "shillin" for a sixth of a dollar in 1897.

Within a given Colony these anomalies usually meant that barter—called "country pay" or "truck"—dominated the economy. Parishioners might pay the minister's salary in firewood and onions. Farmers procured axes and molasses from the store with barreled cider this trip, Goodwife Homespun's cheese the next. When Mary Jackson of Boston advertised pots and pans for sale "for cash or truck that will answer," [3] she meant that, depending on her and the customer's situations and skills in dickering, she would accept maybe turnips from A, a supply of yarn for winter knitting from B, and firewood for her cooking and heating from C. As late as 1800 the accounts of a shoemaker in Wareham, Massachusetts, show him receiving over the years from one family for making its footwear items including salt hay, mutton, molasses, corn, tallow, wool, horse-hire, a goose, candles, wheat. In 1687 John Winthrop, Jr., buying a house in New Haven, paid for it in £100 worth of goats from his ranch on Fishers Island. Hence, says Albert H. Marckwardt's *American English,* the special American use of "to trade" meaning "to shop" clearly developed out of the prevalence of bartering in a frontier society.[4] "I generally trade at the Red Front," [5] Cousin Egbert Floud told Ruggles of Red Gap.

Most Colonists came from much the same range of social strata in their respective Old Countries. So even allowing for difference in origin and in climates (meteorological, as well as theological), one Colony of the early 1700's should strongly have resembled another. It often worked out so, in dress, for instance. The Colonists wore Old Country garb at first because that was what they landed in; in replacing it, they followed familiar patterns; and soon they were trying, nostalgically or snobbishly, to imitate new Old Country fashions as they developed. Knee breeches were pretty much the rule in all Colonies because they were the rule at home. With the 1600's men's trunk hose (the short bloomers familiar in Elizabethan portraits) were lengthening—but only to just below the knee, where they stuck for generations. Young William Penn's pantaloons had caused remark in London in the 1660's. But they were a false dawn. Pantaloons (which evolved into long trousers) had to come diffidently up from among the lower orders as a workaday style that did not really gain a place among their betters until the 1800's. America may have seen them first in rural Pennsylvania, where an Irish Quaker writing home explained that "Trousers . . . are breeches and stockings all in one made of Linnen . . . fine Cool wear in Sumer." [6] In Mexican War times very old American patricians—Nicholas Brown, merchant prince of Rhode Island; Stephen Van Wyck's grandfather; Herman Melville's grandfather —still wore knee breeches, silk stockings and buckled pumps.

The clothes of the Colonial leaders who met at Albany in 1754 to discuss inter-Colonial cooperation were probably not only much the same whichever Colony they hailed from, but they differed from that of their great-grandfathers only in fullness of coat skirts and length of waistcoat. Otherwise a loose, full-sleeved shirt was still tucked into smallclothes with knit woolen stockings—silk for best—and, unless riding boots were needed, low-buckled shoes. Though the silk stockings sound luxurious and were, the effect was inelegant in our terms, for they had no effective gartering, rubber being unavailable. In even the most impressive portraits the stockings of Governor This and Colonel That are usually shown as dismally wrinkled.

Men's underwear consisted of shirttails nearly as ample as those of the archaic nightshirt arranged into a rough equivalent of underdrawers. Colonial women lacked even that. In early New Netherland women of the lower orders wore literally nothing but a neck-to-heels coverall serving as gown and shift. Even the starchiest Puritan spinster had nothing below the waist but the lower edge of her stays (forerunner of the corset), stockings with tightly tied cloth garters, a knee-length linen shift and many petticoats. (The career of John Churchill, eventually Duke of Marlborough and ancestor of Sir Winston, involved this airy fashion; he owed his first footing at court to his sister Arabella, who, though no great beauty in the face, happened to fall off a horse just as the Duke of York, afterward James II, was looking that way.) A close-fitting "body" (sleeved bodice) usually served above the waist. A "short gown" falling to the knee over the petticoat came to supersede that for working wear, and in most weathers women of the lower orders might wear little else for everyday. Striking innovations in fashion at home were sure to be picked up by Quality ladies and often deplored by the conservative. The clergy had been so severe about the voluminous hoopskirts of the early 1700's, so insistent that the Lord would visit calamities on a society so frivolous, that when an earthquake visited the Bay Colony, women took it as an "awful Providence" and "generally laid aside their Hoop Petticoats." [7]

The high-crowned, broad-brimmed felt hats that the early Colonists of both sexes wore were so valuable that they were used till they fell apart or passed on to a favorite heir by specific legacy; one is known to have been worn for fifty-six years. Toward the 1700's, crowns lowered and men began to cock the broad brims into a three-cornered effect; hence the triangular hatboxes sometimes seen in museums. This made the brims useless as eyeshades but contributed to the jaunty air so valued by the dandies of the day. The lower orders' headgear was caps of wool or leather because hats were both expensive and inappropriate for the likes of them. For the same reasons they eschewed the wigs that came in in late Stuart times. The vogue of wig wearing so disturbed the Reverend John Eliot, otherwise deservedly famous as a conscientious Puritan missionary to the Indians, that he blamed it for bringing down on New England the Lord's judgment in the shape of the Indian wars of the 1670's. Wigs had other drawbacks; they were costly, hard to maintain and hot to wear much of the year. On the other hand, they entailed head shaving, which diminished that kind of infestation, to which Colonial ways were all too favorable, that calls for regular use of a fine-tooth comb. It was no mere concern for how their hair looked that led the wife of a Philadelphia schoolmaster of 1765 to assure parents that the smaller boys were mustered twice a week to have their heads combed.

The distinction between right and left was seldom observed in making footgear. The cordwainer (shoemaker) used the same whittled-out wooden last for both. The wearer expected nothing more refined and was aware that alternation every time he donned his boots or shoes minimized wear on soles and run-over heels. The forked bootjack, to hold the heel while the wearer struggled out of the boot, was as much a household necessity as the door latch. Women had low shoes, of fancy materials for show, of course, with pattens (high-platformed overshoe clogs) for muddy going, of which the Colonies usually had plenty. For daily wear cowhide was good enough for most, and many a backwoods wife thought nothing of going barefoot a good part of the year.

Those Thanksgiving calendars showing the Puritans in black breeches and jerkins malign them. For a festival they would have donned their best, which, to judge by the old inventories, was gayer than their male descendants wear now. Coats and breeches of purple, green, scarlet; red and blue petticoats; aprons of green or tawny; red stockings. This was Stuart England transplanted without much change except less display of lace and plumes. William Bradford of Plymouth must have been a fine sight in his violet cloak over a turkey-red silk suit. Silk, finely watered, often heavily embroidered, was the Quality's dress-up finery; wool, imported from home if possible, their everyday wear. The lower orders' homespuns could also be gay. Native dyes—sassafras root, sumach berries, goldenrod—made pretty pinks and yellows. Sober hues came from black walnut and butternut hulls; the real blues from imported indigo. The linen of shirts and shifts was also imported when possible, for Colonial linen, as it came available from locally grown flax, included many of the shorter, coarser—and itchier—fibers. The skilled and ubiquitous Colonial home weaver often blended flax and wool into the harsh, mediumweight linsey-woolsey that frequently clothed both sexes and most ages. The Colonial world was full of the "monotonous rise and fall of the [wool spinning wheel's] tune, now buzzing gently, then louder and louder till its whirr could be heard a furlong, then slacking, then stopping abruptly, then rising to a new climax . . ." [8] as the woman spinner ran back and forth holding the lengthening thread high. When Huckleberry Finn neared the Phelps' cabin, he "heard the dim hum of a spinning-wheel wailing up along and sinking along down again; and then I knowed for certain I wished I was dead—for that *is* the lonesomest sound in the whole world."

Colonial portraits give an exaggerated notion of the luxury of Colonial dress because, for one thing, only the Quality were likely to get painted; for another, sitters usually wore their very best; whereas inventories of the estates of quite eminent persons in the first few generations show only one or two outfits of finery per testator. The merchant's or planter's silk suit and feathered hat were the economic equivalent of a modern banker's wife's mink coat. They were worn only for best foot forward. Effective dry cleaning did not yet exist, so a stain from a spilled dish or a fall in the mud might force discard of a fine taffeta petticoat with replacement ruinously expensive. The purpose of fine clothes was not to look picturesque

The huge, stand-up wool-spinning wheel and the smaller, sit-down flax-spinning wheel made sure that the Colonial housewife and her daughters always had something to do.
Courtesy of Erwin H. Austin

to posterity but, on proper occasion, to keep the cleavages between classes distinct. All Colonies had, and to some extent enforced, sumptuary laws forbidding the lower orders to "take upon them the garb of gentlemen . . . or to walk in great boots, or women of the same rank to wear taffeta hoods . . . although allowable to persons of greater estate or more liberal education." [9] The wife of John Hutchins of Newbury, Massachusetts, arraigned in 1633 for wearing a silken hood, was discharged "upon testimony of her being brought up above the ordinary rank" [10]—further evidence of the early Yankees' stiffly stratified social system. William Penn's wife and daughter, being the proprietor's womenfolk, could sport white satin petticoats and gold chains that flouted Quaker principles. But that does not mean they did so daily or that laced waistcoat and grogram breeches adorned Nathaniel Bacon when he rode over his tobacco plantations.

For all ranks the Colonial wardrobe strikes modern expectations as meager. A rising merchant owned, say, six shirts; one pair of silk stockings; half a dozen pairs of worsted; one hat; two pairs of shoes; one pair of boots. His lady might have two silk petticoats; seven handkerchiefs; several bodies and neckerchiefs to lend variety; two silk gowns or suits. Outdoors both sexes bundled up in cloaks of various materials. Even in the Carolinas and Georgia, they must have been chilly much of the year except in those parts of the Middle Colonies where heating stoves were used. It makes the bones ache to read the lists of clothing recommended for servants sent out to the brisk winters of the Chesapeake area, beginning with two suits (that is, coat, waistcoat and drawers, meaning loose, open-kneed breeches) of *canvas,* which cannot have been warm even if tarred seaman-fashion. Thus a German servant runaway in Pennsylvania in 1749 was advertised as wearing linen trousers and linen stockings in late November. Again, of course, expectations were different then. These people came of medieval Northern Europeans who had lived and died inured to absurdly scanty winter clothing. The furred gown was for his lordship. Late medieval pictures show huntsmen, as well as peasants, wearing only hood, jerkin and woolen hose in the dead of winter, whereas it would mean mutiny today to send even convicts out to winter labor in only long johns and leather jackets.

Apropos, much of what Colonial farmers, travelers and craftsmen did wear was of leather—shirts and coats, as well as shoes, leggings, breeches and aprons. A Williamsburg advertisement of the early 1700's offers not only buckskin breeches for the Quality but also "Bever-skin Breeches . . . very strong and serviceable, fit for Servants and Slaves . . . very cheap," [11] doubtless because they represented the skins left after the beaver fur had been shaved off to make fur felt for hats. By the end of the 1600's wide use of leather had so reduced supply that Massachusetts banned export of ox-, buck-, doe- or fawnhide. Though leather when dry is fair insulation, when wet it is the coldest of integuments and then dries out into an unpleasantness all its own—a thing specially true of deerskin:

". . . the cold and clammy buckskin, saturated with water, clung fast to our limbs," Francis Parkman wrote about being caught in overnight rain on the Great Plains. "The light wind and sunshine soon dried it . . . and then we were all encased in armor of intolerable stiffness." [12]

Leather had been fairly common wear among the European lower orders from whom most Colonists derived. But as they edged toward the frontier, they became dependent on deerhide for the same reason Indians wore it—availability. *Buckskins* was soon a mocking epithet for upcountry settlers in early Virginia. The backwoods dandy developed a dashing exaggeration of the Indian's scanty rig-out—moccasins heavily decorated with colored quills, thigh-high deerskin leggings with fringed outer seams; long loose deerskin hunting shirt dyed black with fringe at sleeves and bottom; cap made of a whole coonskin with the tail dangling behind. For brushy going the leggings made sense. The hair was grown long and braided Indian-fashion to make haircutting needless. Otherwise the ensemble, sweaty in warm weather, chilly in cold, had only one virtue. It so set off a tall, rangy person that the girls back at the settlement on the North Fork couldn't help looking twice. For the same reason vestiges of it survive in the fantastic fancy-leather trousseaux of show-business Western stars.

The thermal shortcomings of leather troubled the Colonist less because he was sluggish about adapting clothes to climate. Negro slaves might be allowed to strip close to naked for field work in the dog days. But it was noted well into the 1700's that the country members of the Pennsylvania legislature sat through stifling July sessions in heavy cloth coats, leather breeches and woolen stockings. Except on the frontier dress long remained an approximation, however sweat-stained, of what the Old Country found advisable or available.

Colonial house heating was on the whole ineffective. It consisted typically of a wood fire in a fireplace with a hearth and a chimney leading straight up in the center—or a sidewall—of the house. (Certain large stone houses surviving on the west bank of the Hudson have a medieval variant of the sidewall design; the fireplace is all hearth with no flanking jambs; the fire burns against the inner face of the wall exposed on three sides; the chimney flue opens in the ceiling directly above. The effect is alarming, but the room probably got more heat than a jamb fireplace with better draft would supply.) The lordliest Colonial fireplaces of my acquaintance are in the Eleazer Arnold House (1687) at Lincoln, Rhode Island; twinned side by side in Rhode Island style, they have a common chimney forming practically the whole house wall. Each is 10 feet wide, 6 feet floor to lintel. There are hundreds only slightly smaller, however, from Maine to Georgia, impressive now for scale and quaintness, memorable then to axmen for the bulk of wood that they consumed. The backstick was as long as the fireplace was wide and as thick as could be dragged through the door and rolled into place. A more slender forestick lay on

In Rhode Island twinned huge fireplaces meant practically all one wall was chimney.

the andirons; the space between was loosely filled with smaller stuff. Set alight and skillfully fed, this arrangement burned as fiercely and persistently as the pit of Tophet. But the fine draft that kept it so vigorous also took heat right up the wide-throated chimney. Much of what efficiency the thing had came of the thick bed of ashes exuding warmth into the room.

Basically, of course, this was a kitchen arrangement. The fire heated pots and kettles hung in or near it, the ashes heated pans and baking devices, and the culinary purpose was as important as that of keeping the room habitable. Many a simple Colonial dwelling had only the single kitchen fireplace. The other two or three rooms, if present, were used for little but sleeping most of the year. Not only cooking and eating but all family activity—drinking, courting, yarn spinning (both literal and figurative) and probably sleeping, too, in at least one bed—went on in the kitchen because, chilly as its remoter reaches might be, it was warmer than anywhere else. In houses with center chimneys—a plan frequent in New England—the other ground-floor room probably also had a fireplace back to back with the kitchen's, but the amenities of a fire in this "settin' room" or "keepin' room" were reduced by the extra labor implied in its voracious appetite for wood.

As bedroom fireplaces came in with easier times, they were likely to be in one corner of an 18-by-20-foot apartment, which left the bed farthest from the fire—and the room usually held several beds—in pretty chilly circumstances. By and large a night in the upper story of many a Colonial dwelling was much like sleeping outdoors. In the New England house in which John Greenleaf Whittier was reared, probably a better one than his grandfather had known as a boy

> . . . awhile we heard
> The wind that round the gables roared
> With now and then a ruder shock
> Which made our very bedsteads rock.
> We heard the loosened clapboards tost,
> The board-nails snapping in the frost,
> And on us, through the unplastered wall,
> Felt the light sifted snow-flakes fall.

In the next generation in Ohio in the Howells' log cabin, elderly but not yet in bad repair: "We sat up late before the big fire at night, our faces burning in the glow, and our backs and feet freezing in the draught that swept in from the imperfectly closing door, and then we boys climbed to our bed in the loft. . . . There were cracks in the shingles through which we could see the stars . . . and which, when the first snow came, let the flakes sift in upon the floor." [13]

The Howells boys' bed probably deserved the name. But in Colonial days bed meant anything to sleep on and was typically a mere palette of blankets in a corner or, as a step upward, a tick filled with corn shucks, straw or wood shavings. A real bedstead with rope netting tautened by a special tool as foundation for the tick was a mark of distinction for master and mistress. The four-poster version had surrounding curtains, not so much for privacy—that mattered little to our forebears—as to fend off icy drafts coming through the lattice windows. Consider the import of the vast number of brass warming pans surviving in museums and antique shops. From New York southward feather beds promoted a stuffy warmth. In Colonies under Dutch influence beds were built even more stuffily into the walls. But in most places the indentured servants deep in the straw in a barnful of large, warm animals were probably better off than master in the first-floor bedroom.

For once winter set in, the walls of no fireplace-heated dwelling in a Northern Colony can ever have been warmed through as comfort in severe cold requires. Yankee diarists complained about the ink freezing as they wrote sitting as near the fire as they dared. The Reverend Cotton Mather recorded a night so bitter that "the Juices forced out of the end of the [firewood] by the heat of the Flame . . . yett froze into Ice on their coming out." [14] He was no reliable witness, so that may have been long-bowmanship, but he must have been very cold indeed to be tempted even to imagine that. An old-timer reared on eastern Long Island in the earliest 1800's recalled one winter morning so chilly even in the kitchen that they hung blankets on clotheslines, tent-fashion, around the fire and all huddled within on the hearth. The Northern custom of "bundling"—a courting couple lying clothed under the coverlid of a bed sometimes with a "bundling board" set on edge between as precaution—betokens the need to keep even a warmly affectionate pair from freezing as they sparked in the keeping room.

As iron grew commoner, the cast-iron fireback, a large plate set behind the fire, was installed to reflect a little more heat out into the room. The heating virtues of hot iron were better exploited, however, by the Pennsylvania Dutch, who introduced America to their German-derived stoves in the early 1700's. The six-plate type was a complete box of rectangular

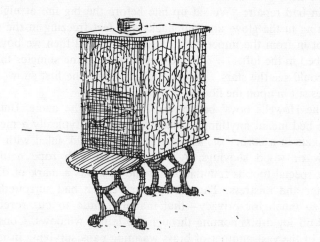

*The six-plate Pennsylvania Dutch stove had its own style
and considerable efficiency.*

iron plates containing the fire; a draft control let in air; the smoke went out of a hole in the top plate into the chimney via a flue; the whole stood on legs away from the wall, so air circulated around it in three dimensions. Once the plates were hot, this warmed a room better than its size promised. In the antique one-room schoolhouse in Old Sturbridge Village, Massachusetts, a small stove of this type raises the temperature at the teacher's desk from 24° F to 70° F in three hours. The five-plate type—the rear plate left out—enabled one fire to heat two rooms. The open side was built into the room wall to tap the fireplace of the adjoining room, and hot coals, shoveled from the fireplace into the stove, heated the room it stood in. This was an adaptation from the arrangement in postmedieval German palaces enabling servants to stoke and clean out the bedroom stoves without entering the room itself. In Germany the corridor doors of the stoves often carried elegantly cast designs of flowers or armorial bearings or patron saints. Pennsylvania Dutch attempts at such ornamental work on stove plates, often Biblical in subject matter, as suited so religious-minded a group, are now, however crude in comparison, eagerly sought collectors' items.

So cozy-making a device as the box stove should have swept the Colonies as the log cabin did. But outside the Middle Colonies the British tradition was strong, and, as Osbert Lancaster said in describing medieval life, "the British think 'if a thing is unpleasant it is automatically good for you.' " [15] Manufacture and use of such stoves were largely confined to Pennsylvania, New Jersey, the Shenandoah Valley—and by no means common there. Yankee ironmasters of the mid-1600's had experimented successfully with casting such stoves as the Pilgrims had known in Holland, but New England pretty much stuck to the fireplace. Not until well into the 1700's were Holland stoves advertised for sale in Boston by Grafton Feveryeare at the sign of the Black Wigg, and there is no knowing how many were sold. For a century or so, meetinghouses had no heating at all. Charles Francis Adams, Jr., called the premises in which his forebears worshiped "far less comfortable than a modern barn." [16] The congregation might bring foot warmers containing hot coals or heated soapstones; and between morning and evening services children, as well as adults, thawed out with hot flip (rum, beer, sugar and nutmeg brought near a boil by being stirred with an iron heated in the coals).

Consider, too, that use of rugs to keep feet from cold floors was unknown. Those able to afford carpets used them for show as table covers or hangings. Noting that before 1820 no house in Quincy, Massachusetts, a very respectable place, had a bathroom, Adams attributed our ancestors' distaste for ablutions to the psychological truth that "When the temperature of a bed-room ranges below the freezing-point, there is no inducement . . . to waste any unnecessary time in washing." [17] By the mid-1700's some of the elaborate estates of the Philadelphia Quality had bathhouses. But by and large, Colonial bathing, whether in New England or in milder climates 1,000 miles farther south, came to little more than occasional dips in pond or stream, hence largely confined to boys and light-minded young men. The heroine of Anya Seton's *The Winthrop Woman* who strips to sport in the sea and then takes a sunbath might as well have been shown listening to a portable radio. A more typical Colonial woman was Elizabeth Drinker, wife of a highly placed Philadelphia Quaker who had a shower bath put up in the backyard for therapeutic use in 1799; Elizabeth tried it out and told her diary that "I bore it better than I expected, not having been wett all over at once, for 28 years past." [18]

Such hydrophobia was not particularly American, of course, just another European way-of-doing coming over along with gunpowder and the alphabet. Recall the surprise of Samuel Pepys, a well-placed Londoner of the late 1600's, when his wife not only took a bath but said she might do it again soon. Not until the 1800's did Americans get from Europe the notion of regular bathing—and not for cleanliness then but as part of a quack hygiene. Meanwhile, ladies and gentlemen of high morality and august standing could ignore the way everybody smelled because, since everybody did, it made no given individual objectionable. No wonder that ringworm and scabies—known to Colonials as scald head and the itch—infested all classes and offered a fertile field for quacks and old wives' cures. When a French visitor to Philadelphia complained that he had got the itch from holding hands with the "housekeeper" of Stephen Girard, eccentric plutocrat of the latter 1700's, she said that was nonsense since "everybody has it in Philadelphia." [19]

Charles Francis Adams, Jr., one of the first historians to look at the Colonial world without deferentially blurring his vision, concluded that "the earliest times in New England were not pleasant . . . the earlier generations were not pleasant to live with. One accustomed to the variety, luxury and refinement of modern life [this was in 1890, *before* general use of electric light, automobiles, telephones and so on] would, if carried back suddenly into the admired existence of the past . . . experience an acute and lasting attack of homesickness and disgust." [20] Bedbugs were rife in all but the best inns. Excretion was taken care of at first in the woods surrounding settlements. Since the close-stool (forerunner of the water closet) was rare in middle-class houses "at home," it was no part of the basic cultural package of the Colonies. For our first 200 years the chief reliance for those unable or unwilling to seek the outdoors was the chamber pot, often disguised among Quality by the *chaise percée* or *commode* made by local craftsmen—the Heyward House in Charleston, South Carolina, has a noble one from the great Thomas Elfe. The use of the pot was not always understood in simpler strata; in pioneer Illinois in the early 1800's a settler's wife bought several from the new stock of the local store for kitchen and table use. The privy, the other solution for the problem, had slow but permanent acceptance outward from towns. "A Citizen here," William Byrd II wrote of nascent Edenton, North Carolina, "is counted Extravagant, if he . . . aspire to a Brick-chimney. . . . Nothing is dear but Law, Physick, and Strong Drink . . . all bad in their kind. . . . Their Vanity generally lies not so much in having a handsome Dining-Room, as a Handsome House of Office [privy]; in this kind of structure they are really extravagant." [21] "Necessary house" was the other name.

Archeologists have been commendably conscientious about reproducing such facilities in, for instance, the restoration of the Tryon Palace at New Bern, North Carolina, though the stench and flies are omitted. Wood ashes were often used as chemical reagent in them. Well into the 1840's even luxurious New York houses still had backyard privies tastefully connected by wooden colonnades. Alien travelers of the time were bitter about such cultural lags when they could bring themselves to mention them at all. Not for several generations would Babbitt's plumbing-mindedness cause a new crop of visitors to be just as scathing in reverse. Meanwhile, there had been only minor improvements over the situation deplored by the town meeting of Newport, Rhode Island, in 1707 when denouncing "several Privy Houses sett against ye Streete which empty themselves upon ye cosways or pavements when people pass . . . spoiling people's apparill should they happen to be neare when ye filth comes out. . . . Especially in ye Night when people cannot see to shun them." [22] To be fair, however, other things helped keep Colonial towns noisome. In both the Old World and America garbage and trash were thrown haphazardly into the street in spite of sporadic municipal effort at discipline. In the Colonies hogs roaming at large were the chief scavengers, sometimes supplemented by buzzards in the South. Horned cattle at large added their droppings to those of horses; the charming watercolor of 1797 that shows what the Governor's House on New York City's Bowling Green looked like has two cows lying contentedly in the driveway.

The family privy and the local well were likely to be too close together. An early advertisement offering a well-reputed Boston tavern for sale listed as all in the same yard stable, pump, five pigsties and one house of office. That had little to do, however, with the Colonist's dislike of water as a beverage, as well as cleansing agent. The Old World, whence the settlers came, still took medieval medicine seriously enough to consider water riskily chilling, weakening and generally deleterious by analogy to its cooling, diluting and solvent properties. On the other hand, fermented drinks—beer for the lower orders, beer and wine for their betters—and distilled strong waters (brandy or gin at first, then rum or whiskey), which were just coming into general use in the 1600's, seemed to warm and strengthen the drinker. And since even the smallest beer cost more than water, to have only water to drink set one down as a pauper reduced to animal provender like the Prodigal with the swine's husks.

Add that few of the servants and transported felons can have set much store by sobriety, and it is understandable that another trait common among the Colonies was thorough-paced drinking. A typical man of the time started the day with a prebreakfast dram of straight rum, whiskey or peach brandy, depending on his Colony. The abstemious, like President-to-be John Adams, confined themselves to a mug or two of hard cider to get the blood stirring. With every meal practically all, including women, children and clergymen, drank beer, cider or spirits and water mixed rather stiff to be sure of counteracting the ill effects of water. An eight-year-old girl from Barbados at school in Boston in 1719 wrote to her father complaining that her grandmother, who was boarding her, made her drink water, and father, duly annoyed, insisted that she get beer or wine as befitted her social station. Apprentices and journeymen in forge, mill or shipyard expected grog at the master's expense midmorning and mid-evening. Farmhands harvesting hay or grain laid down the scythe every other round to have another pull at the jug of rum and molasses in the fence corner. The notion that alcohol at odd times of day was good prophylaxis against the malaria that plagued the Colonies furthered dram drinking. Presently this seems to have steadied down to the institution of the preprandial snort, a forerunner of the cocktail ritual. Before midday dinner in the family of Colonel William Daingerfield of Fredericksburg, Virginia, indentured tutor John Harrower always got "as much good rum toddie as I chuse to drink" as well as "good strong beer" [23] with the meal.

The affinity between fruit and alcohol much influenced the Colonial landscape. Pelt-hunting parties building temporary stations in Kentucky in the late 1700's planted two things in the surrounding clearing: corn, for nourishment, and peach pits, hoping to stock the country with the materials of peach brandy. Josiah Quincy, Jr., riding through Virginia in the early 1770's was charmed by the beauty of the thronging peach orchards planted for the same purpose. The apple orchards that appeared soon after settlement a little farther north had several purposes. Dried apples, for instance, were a large item in the Colonial kitchen particularly when the auspices were Pennsylvania Dutch; so was apple butter. But the main point of every apple tree north of the Carolinas was the hard cider that was replacing beer down the American gullet. A Yankee village of forty families is known to have made 3,000 barrels of cider in the year

1721. No doubt much of it was sold, but the rate of home consumption is clear in Horace Greeley's estimate that among his folks in New Hampshire in the early 1800's a barrel of cider hardly lasted a week in a family of six to eight. Virginia's special crab-apple cider—"pale and clear . . . of most exquisite flavor" [24]—struck young Quincy as favorably as did the peach blossoms. There was also perry (made cider-fashion from pears); metheglin (made of honey and herbs, like mead); persimmon beer; maple-sugar beer.

Rum made from imported molasses was soon a mainstay of trade between the colonies and the West Indies. The Scotch-Irish discovered that corn was as likely raw material for their pot stills as barley or rye. Even the old Gaelic name had crossed the ocean with the pot still, for Samuel Keimer, Benjamin Franklin's first employer in Philadelphia, advertised "right good rich Usquebaugh" for sale among miscellaneous items. The governor of North Carolina praised his upcountry Germans for getting potable spirits out of not only peaches, corn and rye but also potatoes. Only toward the end of Colonial times did the insidious Temperance movement, which would make decent women regard drink as essentially sinful and saddle the nation with still-extant guilt feelings, begin to stir in the minds of Anthony Benezet, Dr. Benjamin Rush and the sternest Methodists. Strange as it now sounds, the straitlaced Moravians of Old Salem, North Carolina, operated their own brewery and distillery; at one point the inventory of their church-owned tavern showed 924 gallons of whiskey; 455 of apple and peach brandy; 137 of rum; 30 of "coniac"; 8 barrels of cider; 60 gallons of Madeira; but no other wine.

The Colonies were strangely sluggish about winemaking. The wealth of palatable wild grapes in Virginia was a prime point in the early explorers' talk about earthly paradises. Those grapes were eligible for winemaking; indeed domesticated varieties developed from them have long been the basis of the wine industries of modern New York State, Ohio and Ontario. Time and again French or German newcomers, urged on by such patrons as William Penn and Governor Alexander Spotswood of Virginia, tried to transplant the Old World wine tradition. Sometimes they seemed to be near success. When Spotswood and his friends, whom he called the Knights of the Golden Horseshoe, rode junketing to the Blue Ridge in 1716, they took along casks of Virginia-made wine to celebrate with. But no lasting results ensued. Wine remained an expensive import for the prosperous. In the days of knee breeches America's contributions to the art of drinking were corn whiskey and the mixed-drink appetizer in the shape of the mint julep—created first with that ubiquitous peach brandy, though now, of course, principally with bourbon.

* * *

In transportation, too, the Colonies resembled one another—unfortunately. Shallops of a few tons' burden sailed on open water; Indian-style canoes for minor streams leading upcountry—those were long the best means to get anything heavier than a packhorse load from here to there. And in early times horses were much too scarce for pack use even where they would otherwise have been handy. For years the best communication between Plymouth and the waters leading into Long Island Sound demanded canoeing up one stream to a portage of a mile and a half, then down another stream flowing into Buzzards Bay. Early Bostonians visiting Watertown or Salem on business or duty—it was too much of an undertaking to allow other motives—used sailing boats to avoid shorter but rough land routes and much fording of streams. In the 1680's the roads between William Penn's countryseat and Philadelphia were so bad for wheels that, though the family had a calash (a two-wheeled passenger cart with hooded top), Penn's wife usually made the trip on horseback, riding pillion behind a groom. Penn preferred his six-oared barge on the Delaware: "I love my barge," he wrote while away from home. "I hope no one uses it on any account and that she is kept dry and dark," [25] to prevent rot and warping. This was not all Colonial primitiveness, however. The Londoner of that day usually preferred a waterman's wherry on the Thames to the mire-heavy streets between the City and Westminster.

This dominance of waterways was clearly economic. In 1689 it cost a shilling to cart from Northampton, Massachusetts, to Windsor, Connecticut, the same load of wheat that would continue thence around by river and sea to Boston—say seven times farther—for eightpence. Water carriage drew the whole pattern of Colonial settlement. Typically the port town dominated the Colony from the mouth of its principal river within a bay (Boston, New York City, Norfolk, Charleston, South Carolina). Along the shores of the bay and also up the river smaller settlements were sustained by water carriage (Newtown [now Cambridge], Massachusetts; Esopus [now Kingston], New York; Chester, Pennsylvania) with outlying farmsteads alongshore. Farther upriver, where rocky rapids or falls made portaging necessary, secondary nuclei of settlement grew up (Albany-Troy, New York; Hartford-Windsor, Connecticut; Richmond, Virginia). There the packtrains and canoes from beyond the falls unloaded their bales of skins and went back into the wilderness with textiles, gimcracks and rum. The skins were boated downriver to the port warehouses for sorting and packing for shipment overseas.

At the same "fall-line" settlements, "movers," headed for upcountry settlement, completed their outfits of tools, provisions and ox-drawn wagons, readily turned into sledges in season; winter was a popular time for moving because snow and runners made it easier for bulky loads in rough backwoods going. There, too, Colonial dignitaries and leaders of the out-lying Indian tribes met to adjust the chronic strains between red men and white. After the Revolution sectional rivalries within a new state might locate the new state capital on the fall-line (sometimes under pretext of central accessibility) to the bewilderment of Europeans unable to see why the seat of government should be in Albany instead of New York City. The most striking example was location of the new national capital just below where the falls separate the upper from the tidal Potomac River.

Water as source of power also shaped Colonial affairs. Only in eastern New England and Dutch-flavored New York was much done with the Old Country windmill, though it was also known in Tidewater Virginia and North Carolina. It took long for the Colonist to learn the massive engineer-ing necessary to harness large streams at the fall-line. But wherever a small stream afforded a good damsite, he put the force of gravity to work with a waterwheel, overshot or undershot depending on situation. Up and down the minor tributaries of the Connecticut, the Hudson, the Delaware, such wheels turned the cumbrous machinery of wood and iron—mostly wood—that ground the Colonist's grain, sawed his planks, pounded his textiles into shape, squeezed the bellows of his blast furnace and forged his pig iron. The same water was put to work over and over in a stream with a good fall. A five-mile stretch of a "crick" in Schoharie County, New York, had ten milldams powering five kinds of mills. The millwright was the aristocrat of Colonial skill. And other things being equal, a mill, particularly a gristmill, much frequented by those bringing their grain to be ground in return for the miller's keeping the traditional tenth, was likely to become the nucleus of a crossroads settlement. The standing joke of the Old Northwestern land speculator was the tale of the man who bought a projected town plot in the wilds of Michigan on the assurance that it already offered not only a good millstream but a mill in operation and then, having come West to see it, wrote home to his partner that he had found a dam by a millsite but no mill by a damn sight.

The preference for floating things from here to there whenever pos-sible caused many travelers from New York City to Philadelphia in the 1700's to use merchant sloops sailing all the way down the Jersey coast and back up the Delaware—say, 300 miles by water to avoid 80-odd by land. Fickle winds and cramped quarters kept the sea trip from being anything one did for pleasure. But it was better than picking one's way on foot or horseback along rough trails through the woods between scattered settlements afflicted with primitive inns. Bridges were few. Some of the wider streams were crossed by unreliable ferries under oar and sail; otherwise, one tried ill-marked fords and swam the horse when necessary. The record of a trip through the Middle Colonies of a pair of Dutch Labadists in 1680 by foot and horseback sounds like Darkest Africa without the convenience of a string of bearers. A generation later between Boston and New York City things were little better for a schoolmistress, Madam Sarah Knight—her terse journal is all missed paths, squalid lodgings and revolting meals. Twenty years later young Benjamin Franklin, a former pupil of hers, combined land and water to get from Boston to Philadelphia, and regretted it. Boston to New York City by sea was tolerable. But he came near to drowning on the boat voyage from New York to Perth Amboy, was almost arrested as a runaway servant during his 50-mile walk overland to Burlington, and between Burlington and Philadelphia got stranded ashore overnight in the open, huddled over a fire of fence rails. He made his first return trip from Philadelphia to Boston some years later by sea. It took two weeks.

Below Pennsylvania travel was even more amphibious. On both shores of the Chesapeake Bay tidal rivers and creeks floated seagoing ships well inland. Virginia's rivers, wrote Robert Beverley of his native land, "are of such Convenience, that, for almost every Half Dozen Miles of their Extent, ther's a commodious and safe Road for a whole Fleet; which gives Opportunity to the Masters of Ships, to lie up and down . . . riding before the Gentleman's Door where they find the best Reception, or where 'tis most suitable for their Business." [26] The tobacco plantation usually had its own wharf where the agent's ship from Bristol unloaded the bales of osnaburgs (coarse cloth for slave clothing), the pipes of Madeira and the trousseau in the latest style for the elder daughter—all ordered on credit the last voyage—and then loaded a return cargo of tobacco to pay for it and, it was hoped (usually in vain), slightly to reduce the heavy balance in the agent's favor. Tobacco might also be traded in defiance of the Navigation Acts to the Yankees, whose tiny ketches were soon wafting up the Chesapeake with salt, wickerwork, tinware—floating precursors of the ubiquitous Yankee peddlers of the 1800's. This direct trade between plantation and supplier bypassed middlemen's warehouses, so the tobacco country developed no sizable ports, and the Quality of Virginia and Maryland were tied particularly intimately to the Old Country. They did not try to supply as many as possible of their own wants.

Internally, says Wertenbaker, streams were to early Virginia what "hard-surface roads are to the farmer of today . . . [used] to visit neighbors, to attend church services, to join the throng at the county court." [27] As tobacco fields pushed upcountry away from deepwater landings, tobacco hogsheads were fitted with temporary shafts and pulled by horse or mule along narrow tobacco roads, but that cumbrous method was used only to reach the nearest stream that would float a sizable boat;

there water took over again. In the mid-1700's on the James River above the falls they decked over two large dugout canoes side by side, making a sort of catamaran on which several hogsheads were lashed to be floated down to the transshipment point. That trick, sired by a clever local clergy-man, shows again that the Yankees had no monopoly on inventive in-genuity.

The Carolina shore is most intricately cut up by estuaries, sounds and creeks. Some of the resulting offshore islands were to be famous for Sea Island cotton, introduced from the West Indies, which supplied England with raw material for fine textiles, lace and thread. For island plantations water transport was as necessary as it was for the stock ranches that Yan-kees set up on the islands in Boston Harbor and for the riverside rice plan-tations that clung near the South Carolina and Georgia coasts, partly be-cause of hostile Spaniards to southward, partly because the elaborate waterworks needed in rice culture depended on tidal action. (Those sluices, dikes, reservoirs and subtle exploitation of tide levels were further examples of early Southern ingenuity.) Great "periaugers" (a corruption of the French *pirogue*) paddled by slaves floated the rice crop downriver for export and fetched supplies back from the Charleston stores or, well scrubbed out, took the planter and his elegant family to and from Charles-ton as the fashionable seasons—based on the avoidance of seasonal ma-laria—shifted from plantation Big House to the town house on Meeting Street. As the South Carolina Quality prospered, they inevitably went in for blood horses, race meets and fine carriages rolling through the pines on sand roads. But their only genuine economic need for horses was in peltry packtrains and for overseers of slave-gangs.

Being all shallows and tortuous channels and awkward bars, the water-ways of the rice country confined seagoing ships to the seaport on the bay. So South Carolina developed a real port city, a small Southern counter-part of Philadelphia—a cultivated (as Colonial cultivation went), brick-built community of merchants skimming the cream off both an upcountry peltry trade and the produce of a fertile hinterland. For a while rice and cotton were supplemented by the raising of indigo. For lack of boat trans-port far inland, South Carolina's peltrymen packed their hides overland all the way to Charleston. The packtrain-drivers' behavior during their yearly descent on town did not suit its increasingly refined atmosphere but was tolerated for cogent economic reasons.

The cabin of horizontal logs that so handily turned the forest into a dwelling is traditionally thought of as the early Colonist's home. It was unknown at first, however, and is a rank anachronism in "historical" paint-ings of the Pilgrim Fathers. The first shelters at Plymouth and Jamestown were like the Indians' wigwam—a booth of saplings bent U shape with both ends in the ground like croquet wickets and covered with thatch, slabs of bark or both. Smoke from the fire within had "no other Vent but at the Door," William Byrd II noted in an Indian village, "and so keeps the whole Family warm, at the expense of both their Eyes and Complexion." [28] It also repelled mosquitoes and did not burn the flooring, for there was none, only beaten earth. The first Philadelphians were no better off in half cellars dug into the riverbank and roofed with poles and turf; nor was printer Samuel Green, who, landing at Salem with Winthrop's party in 1630, had to take up quarters in an empty hogshead, Diogenes-style, for lack of better housing. The log houses mentioned in early Colonial documents seem to have been of rude framing sheathed with logs split lengthwise and set upright calked in between with clay; insulation might be improved by shingling the outside or plastering the inside. East Jersey, too, had such houses "rude in architecture . . . of trees split and stood on end." [29] Salem, Massachusetts, didn't bother to split the logs but just set them in trenches in the round.

The crisscross-corner log cabin, classic symbol of homespun America, had to wait until 1638, when Swedes, settling on the lower Delaware, brought ashore the pertinent skills and traditions. With amazing ease their axmen felled trees of uniform size, cut them to uniform length, notched the ends, and piled them into an interlocked, wall-high rectangle needing no framing to brace it and no metal to hold it together. Calked with what came to be called chinking (chips, sticks or moss forced into the cracks between the logs) and daubing (clay or mud completing the seal), this was a Northern European design known among Swedish and Norwegian Vikings as far back as A.D. 800.* The roof was of poles covered with thatch or bark. Refinements began when the roof acquired a ridgepole, leaving room for a second-story sleeping loft with a pole floor reached by a notched log as ladder. Shakes (huge shingles) might replace cruder roofing. Windows were cut ad lib; seldom many or large, they were filled with lattice (a late medieval device that let in much cold air, as well as some light), or skins worked thin for translucency, or, as outside supplies appeared, greased paper that on bright days admitted quite a little light. In America the chimney was probably of "cat and clay"—heavy sticks set in clay for the heat of the fire to bake hard; it might be finished off by an old barrel open at both ends. The door was a leather curtain, later of

* Jared Van Wagenen, Jr. (*Golden Age of Homespun*, 50), shrewd and knowledgeable about Colonial crafts, doubted that Scandinavia was the source of log cabin design exclusively, advancing the possibility that it evolved out of necessity in at least some of the areas where it appeared. This is possible, but the case made in Harold R. Shurtleff's *The Log Cabin Myth* is good enough to make the alternative unnecessary.

The basic log cabin drawn in upcountry Georgia
c. 1830 by Captain Basil Hall, RN.

broad battens, even a single plank from a gigantic tree hung on ingeniously whittled pintles. For great elegance, puncheons—split logs laid flat side up—covered the earth floor. The final refinement was a cleverly whittled-out door latch worked from without by a deerskin thong through a hole. To say "The latchstring is hanging out" meant "You'll be welcome"; to pull it in meant to refuse hospitality since that locked the door from outside.

The whole required only ax, knife and auger to bore the holes for the wooden pegs (treenails) of the roof structure, or in a pinch its timbers could be lashed together with rawhide. It suited pioneers' needs so well that it eventually fanned out all along the frontier, as popular in the New Hampshire mountains as in the Maryland backwoods, where in 1780 the migrating Moravians found "Virginia cabins, built of unhewn logs and without windows. . . . The chimney is built at the gable end . . . or . . . omitted altogether." [30] The adaptable Cherokee and Creek Indians of the Southeastern hills learned to build excellent log houses with loopholed walls, clay daubing and roofs of shingles, none of which they could have managed without the white man's iron tools. These homely log cabins were what made the American settler a great axman. Clearing could be accomplished Indian-style with hatchet and fire. But to build a cabin, he had to be able to swing an ax with accuracy dependent on exact eye measure. Such accuracy also meant more efficient felling. In the 1750's Benjamin Franklin timed a pair of Pennsylvania frontiersmen building a

*A pioneer blockhouse (note overhang) drawn in Ohio in 1846.
Note the primitive type of steamboat in background.*

*A two-pens-and-a-passage log house serving as wayfarers' inn
in pioneer Ohio.*

*Stump fences looked like a frozen witches' Sabbath
but were highly useful in their time.*

stockade; in six minutes they brought a 14-inch pine to the ground. Kentuckian frontiersmen thought nothing of felling a tree to get at the wild grapes on the vines festooning it or to harvest its nuts. One of the Old Northwest's court day sports was throwing axes at targets as Indians threw tomahawks. Indeed the pioneer grew so ax-happy, said backwoods legend, that he might put a special edge on it and use it for his Sunday shave.

The Pennsylvania Dutch, also in the Northern European tradition, brought with them a style of log house with the logs squared and deeply notched to give a flush wall. That entailed much more work with adz or broadax but also gave consistently thick insulation and had the advantage, important to pioneers, of being pretty much bulletproof. After almost 300 years the Old Witch House on Cape Ann, built, probably for defense, with no daubing at all, its eight-inch logs so nicely squared that no knife-point can get between them, is still proof against anything this side of artillery. On the same principle the logs of the two-story blockhouses* at the corners of the log-palisaded refuge stockades of wilderness settlements were often squared.

It was easy to expand either type of rectangular crib cabin. As a family grew and energy and time allowed, the settler built a second room-and-loft cabin aligned with the first and roofed the gap between to create the two-pens-and-a-passage or dogtrot phase. To enclose the passage and cut secondary doorways made a two-room-and-hallway house. Dormer windows in both lofts made them habitable rooms. Or the settler might raze

---

* In some parts of the Colonies *blockhouse* was the term distinguishing the squared-log style from the cruder crib-of-logs-left-in-the-round (Shurtleff, *Log Cabin Myth,* 11-12). But it was also used much more widely for the kind of fortification spoken of above, sometimes standing by itself as an isolated strongpoint.

the lofts and pile a log second story on the first-floor cribs. To keep wind and rain from nibbling away the daubing, he might nail on weatherboarding of clapboard, shingles, shakes or slabs (the bark-bearing outside pieces split or sawed from logs being squared). Thus a relatively commodious basic American house evolved organically, though from European ideas, symbolizing what America would be: the issue of marriage between the American forest and modified Old Country ways-of-doing. The drive for progressive improvement is also notable. M. L. E. Moreau de St.-Méry, a pretentious but observant Frenchman, described in the Delaware Valley in the 1790's a process several generations old: "First [the American farmer] makes a small hut . . . of logs . . . his sole dwelling. If he prospers he builds a second house of clapboards at least twice as large as the first, which becomes his kitchen. Finally he builds a third, even taller and larger, often of stone. Then the second becomes the kitchen, and the first a cowbarn. . . ." [31] The Frenchman, raised in a country where peasants lived in the same kind of dwelling century in and century out, was impressed.

The Colonist's simplest fencing consisted of tree stumps dragged out of the ground by oxen and upended in a row with their broken-off, fang-like roots uppermost. Such a stump fence was even more weirdly hideous than girdled forest, as the tourist can now see in a fine specimen set up in the Shelburne (Vermont) Museum. If made of durable oak or chestnut, it would last for a generation or so, but the pattern was rather hit-or-miss as a barrier for livestock, and the labor involved immense not only for the oxen but also for the men who dug around and chopped at the roots. The great majority of settlers left stumps in the fields and began, at some early but no longer identifiable time, to rely on another American symbol almost as potent as the log cabin—the rail or Virginia or worm or snake fence.

This was not the Yankee's stone wall laid up as much to get the stones out of the way of hoe and plow as to confine pastured stock, or the tidy Old Country post-and-rail affair that had to have rail ends tapered, posts slotted and postholes dug. The land-exhausting pioneer, particularly the Chesapeake area's tobacco planter, needed a fence that could be readily moved from a worn-out field to a freshly cleared one. So he split long rails a few inches thick and laid them overlapping at the ends in a zigzag some eight rails high that made a practical barrier, needed no below-ground bracing, and was readily laid aside to afford entrance to the field without a gate. No posts set in damp earth meant no invisible rotting. The stake-and-rider variation braced each panel with two additional rails set X fashion. Either version took less time and energy to build than any other fence. The rails were always handy for prying wagons out of China-deep mud. The solid, projecting corners made admirable upping blocks for women mounting horses. Put a spare rail across the angle of a zigzag, upend a washtub on the resulting triangle, and you had a speaker's rostrum higher and wider than the traditional tree stump. For an impromptu pillory, pry the rails apart toward the top; insert culprit's head to the shoulders; let the rails down just far enough. . . .

The rail-splitter's preferred timbers were black walnut and hackberry, but most species grown straight and clear-grained in the big woods would answer. The nooks within the zigzags wasted land, but that mattered little in land-rich country, and they were fine havens for birds and small four-footed creatures. From a distance a rail fence climbing a slope even has a certain decorative quality, though it is easy to agree with Captain Basil Hall of the Royal Navy who called the snake fences of upper New York State in the 1820's "the most ungraceful-looking things I ever saw." [32]

The stake-and-rider version of the omnipresent rail fence.

At the reconstructed Appomattox Court House I recently saw a fresh-split and -laid example still unweathered and curiously handsome—"curiously" because, though I was reared among such fences, I had never before seen a new one. By my time all were waiting for disintegration and replacement by wire and, no matter how often inspected and relaid, always had a neglected air. That was no concern of settlers needing fencing, however. Because the rail fence was the best way to bridle the wilderness, maul and wedges for splitting rails went into the basic outfit of tools along with knife, ax, auger and bullet mold. In no time children were making play fences and play pigpens (which grown-ups made of rails) out of corncobs. A toy rail fence of corncobs is about as American as anything can be. For the rail fence was the American's first original adaptation to the New World, the first American thing developed without at least a solid hint from the Indian or some immigrant group. But the only places where one can now see it in serious use are in the back parts of the upper South, particularly in the hills of Kentucky and Tennessee.

Wherever they could, the Colonists aped the Old Country in architecture, as well as in clothes. That is, of course, no reproach. The generic immigrant—whether ancient Greek taking the Doric order to Sicily or Dutchman taking stepped gables to Manhattan—seeks to reproduce in the new land the buildings among which he was reared. To the first Colonists the wigwams and dugouts into which conditions forced them were deplorable makeshifts, as well as uncomfortable eyesores. As soon as they could, they used the tools they had fetched along—saws to rip log into plank; adzes and broadaxes to shape timbers; frows to split clapboard and shingles—to turn out Old Country-style building materials. Some brick, though probably not as much as the antiquarian-minded hope, came over as ballast in supply ships. Anyway proper clay was often handy, and somebody in the new settlement usually had a notion of brickmaking. Not only was brick a respectable material, but it also meant chimneys less likely to catch fire than the "catted" chimneys of the first huts. As timbers, plank and brick came available, the Colonial port villages, hoping to turn into towns, could soon show splinter-new buildings with architectural clichés of genuine postmedieval flavor—reassuringly like home and a far cry from the simple cabins being rolled up upcountry.

Usually, not always, the results were handsome in the abstract, and since America was to be an important part of the Europe-dominated Western world, her buildings had every right to follow the Western conventions of the day. The difficulty was that in America not all Old Country notions made sense—thatch, for instance. In damp England and the damper parts of Europe, bunched grass, straw or reeds laid on rafters to shed rain were practical, as well as picturesque. Early New England thatched its roofs unaware that local summers, so much hotter and drier than those at home, would bake sun-drenched thatch into tinder. One spark from the central chimney meant blazing ruin. The first few fires must have made the lesson cracklingly clear. Yet so strong was the force of custom that it took Boston forty-nine years to get around to banning thatch, and Peter Stuyvesant, last governor of New Netherland, was the first with the common sense to do so. It persisted for generations on the barns of some Virginia planters and Pennsylvania Dutch farmers presumably because lack of fireplaces in barns lessened the risk.

Because the medieval pointed arch still prevailed in the churches of England in the early 1600's, the first brick churches in Virginia—St.

*The Virginians' early churches were brick approximations
of medieval prototypes from "home."*

Luke's near Smithfield is a reverend example—clung to stubby pointed arches and vestigial buttresses. Because competition for canal frontage had led to long, narrow house lots in densely populated Amsterdam, early New Amsterdam, with different needs and problems, was laid out in long, narrow lots. Because timber had long been scarce in many parts of Britain and the Continent, builders used half-timbering—stout framing diagonally braced for structural strength with the wall area between filled with plaster or brick nogging to insulate the living space within. The principle was that of the skyscraper: a self-supporting skeleton (of steel nowadays) with the walls mere curtains to keep weather out and heat in. Timber-rich America had no need for such construction. Yet in their earliest settlements Yankees, Pennsylvania Dutch and probably Virginians used it anyway because at home that was the proper way to build. It still survives in the Eleazer Arnold House near Providence, Rhode Island, and in the old tavern at York, Pennsylvania. As late as the 1740's the Moravians, fresh from Saxony, were half-timbering buildings in both Pennsylvania and North Carolina.

The English of East Anglia, finding that beating rain gradually washed away the plastering in half-timbering, shielded it with downward-lapping *clapboard*. The same device protected the mortar in bricks used as nogging. America, where clapboards were plentiful, also used them to sheathe lath and plaster. Hence the Norman Rockwell New England village with the clapboarded saltboxes gleaming white and pale yellow among the elms. Yankees had no monopoly on that charming effect. Certain venerable streets in Princess Anne, Maryland, New Bern, North Carolina, and Charleston, South Carolina, show clusters of the same general style of white, amply shuttered, decorously proportioned Colonial dwelling boxes. They mean not that Yankees built them but that the same factors—weather, available materials, provincial regard for dilute fashion—often led to the same results all up and down the Colonial littoral.

When first built, however, and often for some time afterward, such houses lacked some of their present charm, for the white paint was missing. The first few generations of New Englanders used house paint only occasionally on the carved bargeboards under the eaves that softened the outer grimness of their high-gabled wooden mansions. Otherwise, clapboard- and shingle-sheathed houses were left to weather into dinginess. Sound archeology restores them so today and gives valuable glimpses of how very gloomy it must have been when the whole village looked like that. Inside, too, they were depressing. The few small windows of heavily leaded, diamond-shaped panes let in little enough daylight. What did get in was largely absorbed by the darkish wood of unpainted ceiling boards and high wainscot or by the dark paints that prevailed on walls and chimney breasts. Reds were favored—some of brick dust or red ocher mixed with skim milk, an anticipation of modern casein paints. Exterior white may have come in earliest in the Chesapeake area where lime whitewash counteracted mildew on house sheathing brought on by the damp hot summers. When paint did come in farther north, as in Rhode Island toward the end of the 1700's, white by no means dominated; red, yellow and gray-blue had equal acceptance.

Many New England houses of the 1600's had a second-story overhang set off by wooden teardrop pendants. Wild surmise has explained that feature as intended to keep rain off the first-story walls, or to enable the family to shoot down on attacking Indians—hence the modern commercial builder imitating the style calls it Garrison Colonial—or to keep the structure from canting sidewise, or to stiffen the second-story joists. Actually it originated in cramped medieval towns as a device to increase usable floor space in a house on a small plot. Soon become traditional, it also appeared in isolated houses in the country in both Europe and America—a use that Abbott L. Cummings of the Society for the Preservation of New England Antiquities frankly calls "purely vestigial." [33] Here, as in half-timber construction, is another example of a borrowing faithful but point-less—except that it enabled the Yankee builder to make a Puritan gran-dee's house closely resemble what the Quality had been used to in the Old Country. Overhangs appear in the Buttolph-Williams house in Wethersfield, Connecticut (1692), even in the Cupola House in New Bern, North Carolina (*c.* 1712).

The Dutch Colonial story-and-a-half cottage with dormer windows and the forward edge of the gambrel roof often sheltering a long, narrow veranda came to New Netherland from the Low Countries. But it is actually a generalized style also found in East Anglia and along the upper Rhine and made itself at home in America all along the coast into South Carolina. There are splendid examples in brick or stone as well as wood. I have even seen the style in the Dutch West Indies. To come on it in deep-tropical Curaçao, looking as if strayed from Long Island, shows again how little heed the early Colonists paid to climate when borrowing styles of houses or clothes. This Dutch Colonial sort of thing cannot pos-sibly belong in both climatic regions; in fact, it suits neither. Similarly the Northern Colonial builders sometimes neglected to leave adequate garret space to insulate bedrooms from sun-tortured roofs—for such considerations did not apply in Haarlem or King's Lynn. They were shut-ter-minded but in the North had little notion of deep galleries to keep a fierce sun off walls.

Not that they altogether ignored climate. The Yankee learned to spare himself the chore of wading through heavy snows by connecting the wood-shed with the main house, then the harness room with the woodshed, then the barn with the harness room—with variations that might eventuate in a lordly chain of buildings 60 or 70 yards long. Summer kitchens to keep the great cooking fireplaces from increasing the swelter in the main house sometimes appeared as far north as New England and were the rule in Big Houses from Maryland southward. Philadelphians rigged awnings to keep the worst of the summer sun off the brick sidewalks. Most such mod-ifications, however, like the raised verandas around the French settlers' cottages in the Illinois country, were borrowings from the British or French West Indies, where year-round heat had forced drastic alteration of Old World ideas. "I was much struck," wrote a British traveler in 1809, "with the similarity of Natchez to many of the smaller West India towns, particularly St. Johns Antigua, though not near so large. . . . The houses all with balconies and piazzas. . . ." [34]

Actually the most original Colonial buildings—the architectural fellows of rail fence—were the Puritan and Quaker meetinghouses. The reason may have been lack of models to imitate. England allowed neither Puri-tan nor Quaker freedom of worship, let alone special buildings to perform

*The New Englander's overhang dwelling at its simplest—
and most impressive.*

it in. All churches were reserved for the Church of England and planned
with elaborate liturgy in mind. The Puritans' emphasis on preaching
and the Quakers' notions about equal fellowship implied new kinds of
worship-edifices once they were free to build their own in America. In
any case conventional church arrangement—nave, sanctuary, steeple
and so on—was associated with prayer books, persecution and all such
abominations. Whatever the inner cause, the New England meetinghouse
was soon a new and standardized affair: foursquare and of cubical elevation, a forthright piece of engineering in timber as striking as a ship or a
covered bridge, the steep-pitched roof crowned with a platform and often
a cupola for lookout and bell mount. Every beam, plank and shingle in it
were there to provide necessary minimum shelter for a large number of
people obliged intimately to hear every word the preacher said, but all
just as well adapted to the other function of the building as scene of town
meetings. (The design may have owed something to the Pilgrims' first
meetinghouse at Plymouth, a square block with a flat roof that doubled
as artillery platform.) Quaker meetinghouses were even less showy—
peak-roofed, single-room austere affairs of frame, brick or stone.*
Twinned entrance doors emphasized the separation of the sexes in seat-

* A queer old painting in the Cooper House in Burlington, New Jersey, shows the
first Friends' meetinghouse there as hexagonal with a steeply tapering hexagonal
roof with a cupola. It looks like a cross between a New England meetinghouse and
the quadrilateral, low-walled, but exaggeratedly high-roofed and central-spired
churches that the Dutch built in their early phase in America. Whatever the significance of this design in Burlington, I know of no case where it was reproduced.

ing. The lack of painted windows, pulpit or other focus of attention signified the Quaker revulsion from worldly barriers between God and man. For the next two centuries many one-room country schoolhouses, whether in Quaker neighborhoods or not, were built on this model.

As classic Puritanism lost some of its savor after 1700, modified Baroque spires such as Sir Christopher Wren had made modish in England were allowed to rear their non-austere gracefulness in New England—another importation of a thing grown fashionable at home. The advantage of such borrowings was that being in various national idioms, they kept early Colonial port towns from looking too much alike. In the late 1680's, when all Boston houses were of "thin, small cedar shingles, nailed against frames, and then filled in with brick and other stuff; and so are the churches," [35] the rapidly growing town must have been strikingly somber. No steeples yet; against the hills and waters beyond the Back Bay the massed silhouette was hump-shouldered with hip roofs and clustered steep gables. New York was a compact jumble of "very stately and high houses" with Dutch-style stepped or squirmy-Baroque gables facing the waterways and twisting streets. Madam Knight thought the brickwork of "Divers Coullers and laid in Checkers, being glazed . . . very agreeable," and the interiors "neat to admiration."[36] She was also charmed by the gay effect of the sleighs darting swiftly over the snow. Philadelphia, founded after brick and stone had supplanted medievalish wooden construction at home, was staidly multiplying well-built, square-toed houses of brick laid in the contrasting black and red of Flemish bond. Style and size were so uniform that visitors complained of it.

The Dutch Colonial house was generically Northwestern European
—and often of elegant proportions.

The basically cubical meetinghouse developed by England's Puritans was almost as austere as the Quakers' equivalent. Note separate doors for the sexes.

Williamsburg, having troubles usual to new artificial capitals, was a strip village exploding at one end into the cupolaed brick elegance of the Capitol and at the other into the lofty brick elegance of William and Mary College, both following the London style that led into the Georgian of the next few generations. At the time those buildings were, as Beverley wrote with pride, "the most magnificent of any in America," [37] indeed the only ones that a European would have found distinguished. Such

A Quaker meetinghouse in early Ohio.

rivals as what is now Independence Hall and the economic mistake of the Tryon Palace in New Bern, North Carolina, did not appear until the midcentury. The imposingness of Williamsburg's twin marvels was then marred, however, by their walls being shingled over, presumably to protect the mortar between the bricks. Yet even so they probably inspired the elegant brick country mansions that were soon ornamenting the banks of the James River. Until then the Quality's dwellings would have struck their modern FFV descendants as dismayingly simple. The finest surviving specimen, Bacon's Castle, was elegant in Jacobean terms, but originally only a three-bedroom affair. In New England at the same time the typical prospering Puritan's house was four rooms (kitchen included) clustered around a central chimney. Yankees in the next stratum down, though still in better-than-average circumstances, probably had only two rooms—kitchen-living room and chamber—with a garret, where the children slept, and maybe a lean-to (pronounced *leanter*) in the rear for storage and laundry.

In all such dwellings from Maine to Georgia the level of comfort was rising but by our standards still had far to go. Living in the best of them must have been like staying in a wilderness vacation camp 365 days a year without any conveniences invented since John Bunyan's day. Shortcomings in heating, clothing and sanitation have been sketched. Consider

The Wren-inspired spires of Yankee churches were sometimes disproportionate but always impressive.

what else the Colonial household of 1700 to 1740 necessarily did without even in the growing port towns:

Running water: Water for cooking, cleaning, laundry and what washing of the person was done had to be fetched from stream, spring or well in clumsy wooden or leathern buckets, sometimes with a shoulder yoke.

Well-sweeps slightly lightened the task of drawing water from the pre-handpump well.

Passable lighting: The Betty lamp, a step up from the pine knot, was a small covered pan with a hole through which a wick soaked up grease. It often hung from the mantelpiece. The smell was nearest tolerable when the grease was lard; worse when it was rancid tallow; worst when it was fish oil. The rushlight was a length of dried rush soaked in grease, held in a special iron clamp stand, and lighted at one end. It smelled no better. To counter the stench, sweet herbs might be toasted in iron pans over the lamp. With immense trouble enough grease to make pleasantly aromatic candles could be got by boiling bayberries. Few could afford enough of any candles to dispel the gloom. But they were indispensable in lanterns of perforated metal to take along on outdoor errands.

Cookstove: Baking, roasting, frying, boiling, broiling, toasting all were done over, in or near the kitchen fire with a mighty array of spits, gridirons, reflectors, pots, kettles, spiders, Dutch ovens, trivets, griddles, waffle irons and toasters handled with the aid of tongs, peels, trammels, pothooks, cranes and a clairvoyant's sense of just where the ashes had the right heat. The Colonial blacksmith might ingeniously refine the clumpy Old World models of these devices; toasters in particular seem to have brought out the best in him. Many fireplaces had a bread oven set into the chimney on one side and heated by building a separate fire in it, then raking out the coals and ashes. Letting the main fire go out was a social crime, penance for which was the tedious task of rekindling with sparks from a flint-and-steel device or going to a neighbor's with the special metal fire-fetching box. Since there were no matches to light pipes with and paper for spills was scarce, one used a live coal picked up with a special pair of tongs; rugged folks with calloused fingers did it without the tongs.

Refrigeration: Milk and what butter was made were kept downcellar, where it was some degrees cooler, or hung down the well, or stored in a nearby springhouse, in which cool running water from a stream trickled under or between shelved pans and crocks. Even so milk and cream soon soured (leading to the joys of hot biscuits made with sour cream and pearl ash), for pasteurization was unknown. Since neither the cows' rear ends nor the milker's hands got proper cleaning, the bacterial content of all Colonial dairy products would probably have frightened a modern public-health laboratory into fits. People either developed early immunity to such microorganisms or died young of "summer complaint."

Screens: Another catastrophic lack, for it was mosquitoes that spread the massively endemic malaria. The Reverend Jonathan Boucher said in the 1760's, with unwitting truth, that nothing would tempt him to visit certain parts of Maryland in summer because "the Mosquitoes . . . w'd kill me." [38] The mosquito nets of the West Indies had reached Charleston by the mid-1750's but seem to have been little known elsewhere; an Annapolis paper of 1759 advertised "Just imported—Green muskito netting for Bed Curtains . . . ," [39] but as a scholarly physician has noted, there is no mention of such things in Elizabeth Drinker's Philadelphia journal into the early 1800's. Lack of them and of screening on windows left one at the mercy of the flies swarming out of nearby stables, hogpens and privies. As refinement grew, a slave child or the bound girl servant might be set to fanning flies away from the dishes with a leafy branch or, among Quality, a bunch of peacock feathers. In Deep Southern houses a version of the East Indian punkah was pulled from outside by a string swung back and forth over the table as much to disturb the flies as to create a cooling breeze. Common folks had a harsher antifly device: "Two boards, an inch or so apart, baited with honey on their inner faces, hanging overhead where the women could conveniently clap them together . . . whereby a myriad of flies had been sacrificed . . ." [40]—hence, unquestionably, that old-time incivility: "Oh, shut your flytrap!"

Privacy: Few houses had corridors or anything else allowing access to bedroom B without going through bedroom A. Overhead the unceiled floorboards of the lofts where older children and sometimes servants slept usually had wide cracks between, which let sound pass freely but also allowed some heat from the ground-floor fireplace to leak upward. Most rooms upstairs or down, whether kitchen or keeping room, contained beds planned to accommodate at least two persons. The formally designated bedroom was a several-bed dormitory. Trundle beds pulled out from underneath accommodated still more sleepers, typically the smaller children who must have become early acquainted with the facts of life as their parents demonstrated them on squeaky frameworks of wood and rope.

Little of this was peculiar to pioneering or colonizing, however. "Privacy was a luxury undreamed of . . . ," writes Esther Forbes. "It was not a matter of social position. . . . Louis XV at Versailles . . . had no more conception of privacy as a desirable thing than . . . of electricity, and did not miss either." [41]

Clothes closets: In simpler households pegs on the wall served for spare garments, if any. The Quality folded theirs away into the impressive chests and chests of drawers which, whether imported from the Old Country, all carving and panels, or imitated by local craftsmen, were the token of prospering respectability.

Clocks were not altogether lacking even in the beginning, but were long confined to high-level families. The parson timed each of his two-hour Sunday sermons with a half-hour sandglass. Farmers in the fields judged by the height of the sun. The goodwife at home probably had a sun mark on a window sill as crude sundial. It is thought that the Colonial watchmaker's custom of putting a clock in the window was protection against the standing nuisance of passersby coming in to ask the time of day.

Practically all the above was the accepted thing "at home," as well as in America. Indeed in many respects, once the stage of out-and-out pioneering was past, most Colonials were better off than their stay-at-home cousins in Yorkshire, Friesland or the Black Forest. The Scotch-Irishman's backwoods log cabin, for instance, was a vast improvement on the rural housing in Ulster that Francis Hopkinson saw in the mid-1700's: "the most miserable Huts you can imagine, of Mud and Straw, much worse than Indian Wig Wams. . . ." [42] Immigrants surviving to get their feet under them usually had more and often better food, certainly more and better fuel, and the stimulating chance of rising circumstances to come, a thing rare in the Old Country. True, they might have to work as hard as exploited European peasants. But virgin soil gave high returns per foot-pound of energy expended, and what was most important, they were toiling at their own instance and on their own account. Those novelties gradually made America a new kind of society in spite of the Colonists' often misguided insistence on doing things the familiar Old Country way if possible.

*   *   *

Fittingly this nascent society relied from the beginning on a food new to Western man, the Indians' great staple, "maize," as Europeans still call it. The Colonists soon called it corn—the Mother Country's term for a dominant cereal. It was only one, of course, of the vegetable riches that Columbus' discovery added to the world's resources: tobacco, quinine, coca, chocolate, potatoes, manioc (alias cassava or tapioca), tomatoes, most basic types of beans, papaya, pineapple, sweet potato, both the Sea Island and the short-staple kinds of cotton, avocado, sunflower, the squash-pumpkin family of gourds. Recent thought ascribes the runaway growth in Western population that began in the 1700's to the consequent rapid increase in potential food supply per farming man-hour, particularly in potatoes. Exploitation of that list began gingerly, for most peoples are conservative about what they eat. Potatoes did not really catch on in most of Europe and America till well after 1700. Tomatoes required still another century. Those two and most of the above items came from Central or South America, hence were not awaiting the Jamestowners and Pilgrims when they landed. It was ironical that the sunflower, the seeds of which are economically important in Eastern Europe and the Near East, the only item originating in North America, was the one that the Colonists pretty much ignored. But corn—that domesticated overgrown grass spread up through Central America into most of North America—was indispensable. It was thrifty in most climates, easily grown among dead trees and stumps, and without it our country might well never have become a going concern. Certainly it would not much have resembled what, for better or worse, it is now.

The queer bitter-nutty flavor of corn, most marked in the mature grain, doubtless took getting used to. But scarcity of supplies from home soon cured that. Avidly the hunger-gnawed Colonists traded for surplus corn from the Indians and, when that ran out, forcibly seized what the Indians had reserved for themselves. From them, too, they learned how to fertilize a corn crop with fish. At Plymouth the formula was two alewives to the hill; at Jamestown two fish heads, species unspecified. By 1619 the Jamestowners' crop was large enough to permit rent payments in barreled corn. From the beginning the Colonists imported seed for wheat and rye as essential to civilization. But both were unhandy to sow and reap in stump-cluttered fields, hence usually waited until better-cleared land was available. Meanwhile, corn took firm hold on the American economy and to an important extent on the American palate in forms suggested by the Indians' traditional uses.

It was more versatile than wheat and rice, the world's other chief cereals, which must mature to be utilized, whereas corn in the immature milky stage roasted in the succulent green husk—hence the term *roasting ear*

—or boiled is a seasonal delicacy that has always conquered even the most supercilious alien visitor. The modern seedsmen's special sweet corn varieties for such use are thought to have been developed from strains specially cultivated by the Iroquois Indians and their near neighbors. Cut from the cob at the milky stage and stewed with beans (and

Pounding corn into meal was an Indian technique used by settlers lacking hand-grinding or water-mills.

often bits of dogmeat for flavor), it made the Indians a noble dish called succotash.* Dried in the sun or over a fire, the grains hardened for winter keeping; boiled in milk, such dried corn was a voluptuously flavored novelty maybe suggested by the Old Country's frumenty of whole wheat in milk. Pickled in light brine, it developed still another subtle flavor as of some eerie, tenuous cheese. But for the true corn addict the finest form is whole hominy,† made by soaking the flint-hard mature grains of the staple dent varieties (modern field corn, what used to be horse corn) in a dilute lye of water and wood ash to loosen the hulls and soften and preserve the

* The Pilgrims seem to have substituted salt beef for the dog and expanded what they called *soccotash* by adding salt pork and chicken, diced turnips and other oddments. The recipe (in Willison, *Saints and Strangers,* 482-83) certainly sounds nourishing.

† The basic use of the Indians' term *hominy.* Much of the South uses it for hominy grits—the coarse residue from the bolting of cornmeal that has its own great virtues when boiled into a stiff mush.

inner pulp. Properly washed and boiled, this gives the essential soul of the corn flavor.

Cornmeal was, however, the form in which both Indian and Colonial most used this cereal bounty. The Indian—or rather his squaw—arrived at it by pounding the grain in a log mortar or hollow in a rock, just as West Africans pound rice today. The Colonist's trick was worth two of that—revolving millstones powered by hand or a waterwheel. Boiled with water, the resulting meal made the mush (or hasty pudding or samp or supawn or loblolly depending on local usage) that dominated America's local diet. It was particularly nourishing eaten warm with milk. Whittier's "The Corn Song" says:

> Give me the bowl of samp and milk
> By homespun beauty poured!

Or allowed to cool solid, cut in slices, and fried crisp, it was eaten with the maple syrup that the Colonists also owed to the Indians and the New World forest. New England baked a mixture of cornmeal, butter, eggs, spices and imported molasses into a delightful Indian pudding. The Shakers—a religious sect renowned almost as much for cooking as for honesty, celibacy and other eccentricities—substituted indigenous maple syrup for the molasses.

Various mixtures of salt, cornmeal, water, fat and eggs and varied ways of baking in hot ashes or on stone or metal provided hoecake, johnny-cake,* pone, dodgers, and, as leavening was tried, corn breads incorporating wheat flour that ranged from coarse heartiness to great delicacy. A satirist of early Maryland lampooned:

> . . . Pon[e] and Milk, with Mush well stoar'd,
> In wooden dishes graced the Board;
>   With Homine and Syder-pap,
>   (Which scarce a hungry Dog would lap)
> Well stuffed with Fat, from Bacon Fry'd,
> Or with Molassus dulcify'd. . . .[43]

Madam Knight detested the bread made of part corn, part pumpkin that was about all she got to eat at the inn at Stratford, Connecticut. But if what Thomas Hutchinson told George III in 1774 can be relied on, Yankees came to prefer their standard corn and rye ("rye'n-Injun") bread to wheaten. It is doubtful, however, whether corn bread of any kind ever acquired the prestige of wheaten anywhere, for the latter was associated

---

* Sometimes said to be a corruption of *journeycake* since in this form corn bread kept well as rations for travelers.

with the tables of the Old Country Quality. The priests following De Soto through the American Southeast in the 1540's finally decided that corn bread was too outlandish to celebrate mass with. Eventually the hot wheaten biscuit, probably a Colonial version of the Scottish scone, became queen of most Southern tables. In the North wheaten light bread shared that rank. But a good housewife also took pride in her corn bread, and in the rarefied forms of spoon bread and cornmeal griddle cakes, it went further and fared very well indeed. Mature corn parched—to mix it

Young Winslow Homer draws for Harper's Weekly *just before the Civil War a buoyant depiction of a New England cornhusking bee.*

with hot sand was one method—and then powdered was the standard iron ration for the Indian warrior and his backwoods imitator.

No wonder that corn permeated Colonial folkways. Families around the fire found popcorn the most entertaining treat since the four-and-twenty blackbirds. The old grain-harvest customs did not cross the ocean along with the seeds of rye and wheat. Instead, arose the cornhusking bee at which a man finding a red ear in the heap claimed a kiss from any girl in the crowd—apparently a modification of a much less decorous Iroquois custom. Southward and westward the liquor in the jug that urged on jollifying at cornhuskings and elsewhere was probably corn whiskey, and the stopper in the jug was half a corncob. Cross-section slices of cob, half left white, half blackened, were the "men" on the checkerboard of the crossroads store. Cobs often replaced worn-out knife handles. They were otherwise useful and became traditional as supplementary fuel, as a source of smoke to cure meats, as bowls for tobacco pipes; as sanitary supplies in the privy. The Shakers made mats and rugs of braided cornhusks. The stalks, still with the dry leaves, stacked against the cow stable were good insulation in winter and handy provender for the cows.

Inevitably corn became embedded in the settler's emotions as deeply as intolerance for trees. Much hardship in the trans-Missouri settlements of the late 1800's, says James C. Malin's authoritative essay on the region, came of the newcomers' long-standing conviction that corn and farming were inseparable, which delayed their trying the hard wheats that eventually proved to be their salvation.

Men cannot, however, live by corn bread alone. Four- and two-legged sources of high-grade protein—meat, milk, eggs—were sent to the Colonies from the Old World very early in the 1600's. For some time these exotics had to find most of their own provender, as had the deer that they were replacing. New England's intentionally compact settlements long persisted in pasturing livestock under communal guard of neatherd, swineherd or shepherd. Elsewhere, however, settlement being more diffuse and manpower just as short, only milk cows continued to be so pampered. Other cattle, hogs, the few sheep brought over early and goats (favored at first, maybe because they were not quite so vulnerable to predators) were branded or earmarked to show ownership and turned loose in forest or swamp. (A surviving registry of earmarks in Wareham, Massachusetts, gives them clearly in spite of wild spelling: "Joshua Briggs . . . a Scware Crop in ye under side of ye Right ear. . . . Thomas Whittens . . . a mackerels tales in Both Ears. . . ." [44]) They usually flourished in spite of bears, wolves and Indians, whose taste for pork soon undermined the theory, advanced by William Penn among others, that they were relics of the lost tribes of Israel. That began the first time Indians and swine met as the Chickasaws stole hogs from the herd that De Soto's men drove along as a self-transporting commissary.

Fortunately these first-landed animals were mostly the runty beasts of postmedieval times inured to seasonal half starvation and with high survival bred in, hence able to pick up a living untended in alien wilds. Jamestown's free-ranging hogs, ancestors of the razorbacks, so flourished on pine seed, acorns and other New World mast that they committed the

Southern table to pork in all forms from glorious Smithfield hams* to fat-back—and to the disastrous tradition of frying everything in lard. William Byrd II professed to believe that so much pork in the diet made the sluggish North Carolinians of the 1720's "extremely Hoggish in their Temper . . . [and] prone to Grunt rather than speak. . . ." [45] It has been too much hog and hominy in the South ever since. Beverley, Byrd's contemporary, wrote that in Virginia "Hogs swarme like Vermine upon the Earth, and are often accounted such . . . when an Inventory of any considerable Man's Estate is taken . . . the Hogs are left out . . . [they] run where they list, and find their own support in the woods . . ." [46] and could be savage enough seriously to endanger the safety of solitary travelers.

To obtain better pasture for cattle, settlers sometimes followed the Indians' measure of burning the woods seasonally. Even in denser cover cow beasts early did so well that their half-wild presence in the woods betokened that the frontier was just ahead. Advancing on the heels of the peltry trader, ahead of or along with the cabin-building farmer-hunter of the first wave of settlement, the cattleman did much to open up successive margins of new country. It sounds strange now that many first settlers of Newtown (now Cambridge), Massachusetts, migrated to the upper valley of the Connecticut River because it was said to be good cattleland and grazing along the Charles had become scarce. Horned cattle did as well as buffalo to keep old Indian fields from going back to brush and then woods. Most of them would have made Texas longhorns look sleek and refined. Their meat was almost a secondary consideration, though those able to chew it ate a fair amount of it fresh, salted or dried. It was primarily hides, indispensable for boots, clothing, tools, saddles and harness, that made cattle valued on the frontier. The tanner appeared in the frontier settlement almost as soon as the blacksmith, the saddler and the miller. Beef tallow was both lubricant and lamp oil. When the boys were shooting for the hide at a frontier frolic, the best shot got the hide, the next best the fat, the meat going to the also-rans.† And as stoneboats, sledges, plows and finally wheels came in, scrawny oxen from such stock were far better than none.

Colonial cattlemen had dubious reputations—hence the term *cowboys* applied to marauding Tories in New York during the Revolution.

---

* John Bernard (*Retrospections,* 170) called Virginia's hams c. 1790 "the finest I have ever eaten" and attributed their virtues to the great numbers of snakes that the hogs ate in the wilds.

† This is Crockett's formula. It is interesting to note that in describing a somewhat later state of culture—or maybe better chance of good beef animals—R. C. Buley (*Old Northwest,* I, 320) rates the hindquarters as first prize, forequarters as second, hide and tallow third.

It was at Cowpens that upcountry Carolina militia beat a British force in 1781. Such cowpens were backwoods stockyards, or call them corrals, where Colonial ranchers held roundups to choose out animals for the long drive to market. Some owners had their brands or earmarks on 2,000 head. Davy Crockett began his footloose life with an outfit taking such beef on the hoof from eastern Tennessee down the Shenandoah Valley to the open fattening pastures of Pennsylvania, just like later times on the Chisholm Trail, only this range was not wide-open spaces. Soon half-wild cattle were joined by wholly wild horses, ancestors of today's wild ponies on Chincoteague Island and the Outer Banks. Putting out salt for them weekly was about as far as domestication ever went. By the late 1600's they were, Beverley said, "as shy as any Savage Creature" and often "so sullen, that they can't be tam'd" [47] even when captured. Horsey Virginians hunted them for fun. At much the same time the spread of wild horses up from Mexico and Texas was giving the Plains Indians a whole new way of life. Somebody should have warned them that this northward infiltration was as sinister an omen of eventual white intrusion as the appearance of honeybees in the Eastern forests.

Game supplemented the Colonist's corn while his livestock were establishing themselves. Venison was so plentiful at first that men tired of it and yearned for mutton, an attitude curious in those whose peasant ancestors had so hankered after the king's deer. Bear meat, too, was often available. It had a "good relish," said William Byrd II, "very savory and inclining to that of pork . . . our Chaplain lov'd it so passionately that he would growl like a Wild-Cat over a Squirrel." [48] Bear fat, which dandies of the 1800's put on their hair under the illusion that it would foster growth, was thought a palatable substitute for olive oil by the Moravians of North Carolina and the French of New Orleans. In a pinch the Indians could show one how to cook wildcat, which could be "very good eating." [49] So were moose nose and beaver tail. Surveyors in Ohio in the late 1700's who tired of salt meat learned that the loathsomely thick and alarmingly long rattlesnakes with which the country abounded made a nice change. Periodically here came the wild pigeons so numerous and gregarious that their flights darkened the sky and broke down the limbs of square miles of forest when they roosted. People salted them for winter use, as they also did salmon and sturgeon teeming seasonally in the as yet unpolluted rivers.

It was a fat land. Even Jaspar Dankers and Peter Sluyter, hypercritical Dutch missionaries, admired the fare at a Dutch village on Long Island in 1679: "a full pail of Gowanus oysters . . . best in the country . . . as good as those of England [thrown on the fire to roast] . . . some not

less than a foot long. . . . We had for supper a roasted haunch of venison . . . which weighed thirty pounds . . . exceedingly good and tender, also quite fat [with] a slightly spicy flavor . . . turkey . . . fat
and of a good flavor; and a wild goose, but that was rather dry." [50] Well
into the 1800's the commonest favorable note among Europeans writing
about America was that for all its crudities in other respects, America
had in shad, terrapin and canvasback duck three major delicacies—and
even knew how to cook them. The Earl of Rosebery maintained that the
American national bird should have been not the bald eagle but the canvasback. Yet in the early days large shad sold for a halfpenny apiece up
the Connecticut River. A glut of caviar is, after all, a glut of caviar.

Once the frontier phase passed, however, this natural plenty began to
pinch out, dwindling with the woods and barrens that fostered wild meat.
In the late 1600's killing of deer yarded up in deep snow was forbidden
around Buzzards Bay not from sporting motives but to conserve a food
supply. Soon the Puritan settlements on Long Island regulated deer
hunting for the same reason. New York imposed a closed season on the
now-extinct heath hen in 1708. Changing ecology, as well as overshooting,
discouraged some creatures, as when the settlers' eagerness to dig ginseng
for export to the Chinese drug market wiped out the supply of ginseng
berries, a favorite food of wild turkeys. Conversely the open conditions
that forest clearing brought about meant more ruffed grouse, squirrels,
groundhogs, cottontails and quail—and notably more singing birds. Raccoon and possum hunting began to shape up as American institutions "perform'd a Foot, with small dogs in the Night . . . by the light of the Moon
or Stars." [51] But serious provisioning shifted to commercially caught fish
smoked or salted and to home-raised meats.

Basically that meant pork, in the North too. Hog-killing after the first
frost was a seasonal folk festival with the neighbors gathering to finish the
whole process in one day. Under deft knives and cleavers the scalded
carcasses disappeared magically. The fat was rendered down into lard in
great black kettles, and then the bits of connective tissue were squeezed
dry to make the cracklings that children gnawed as they played underfoot. Some odd parts—loins, ribs, feet—might be eaten fresh. Heads and
stray bits went into storage as sausage and pickled headcheese. The bulky
portions—hams, shoulders, sides of bacon—were salted or smoked, often
the latter. The smokehouse, high-shouldered and small without, gloriously odorous within, was as necessary a country outbuilding as the privy.
Hickory, sassafras, hard maple, corncobs—each area had a favorite fuel
for pork smoking.

Salted beef also had a place, particularly in bits cooked along with
hasty pudding and as centerpiece of the Yankee boiled dinner in combina-

tion with such winter-stored vegetables as cabbages, turnips and pars-nips. Thinning woods meant fewer wolves and bobcats, hence more sheep could be run for wool and meat; it is possible that rabies brought in by the Colonists' dogs and hitting the wolves as hard as smallpox did the Indians had something to do with their disappearance. Similar falling off of smaller predators took pressure off poultry at the same time that higher production of corn allowed some grain feeding of plumper geese, ducks, chickens and turkeys—not wild, by the way, but domesticated breeds developed in the Old World from American stock and fetched back again to the ancestral home. As the sentimental propaganda of *Godey's Lady's Book* spread the Pilgrims' Thanksgiving nationwide in the mid-1800's, the barnyard turkey became the symbol of the American harvest home. Fried chicken, a particularly splendid good accruing to the nation from the South's fixation on lard and the skillet, is as much the great American dish, when properly cooked, as planked shad or stewed terrapin. It seems to have been already well established by 1720, when William Byrd II, Colonel Ludwell and Frank Lightfoot dined off it at Green Springs, Virginia.*

Dairying was transplanted vigorously to the New World—by both Dutch and German settlers. Among other early Americans, however, there was little evidence of the modern cult of milk. Mother's supply usually took care of the Colonial baby. Fluid milk from the cow merely supplemented mush or was cooked into chowders. Little butter was made; clabber and cheese had more of a place on the table.

Come spring, the systemic longing for fresh green stuff put on the table the young shoots of what would be considered weeds later in the year—dock, pokeweed, purslane, milkweed, the dandelions that had come over the ocean and flourished—and ramps (wild bellflower, the early leaves cooked as greens) and the fiddle-necks of young shoots of ferns. Soon the seeds of lettuce, cucumbers, beets (grown principally for the tops cooked as greens) and so on were duly imported from home. The lighter vegetables were thought of merely as garnish for more substantial dishes; just

---

* Nowadays classic fried chicken is unavailable in restaurants and rare at family tables. In too many cookbooks the low repute of lard has encouraged substitution of butter for chicken frying—a well-meant but grievous mistake. In any case the chickens are usually too small, virtually broilers. They should be plumply near the far margin of adolescence, which explains what our elders meant when appreciatively describing a girl as about frying size. Nor should chicken ever be deep fried or coated with an egg batter. Unless applied very sparingly, flour leaves a pasty stickiness. Cornmeal is much more advisable and lends a delicate touch of its own flavor. The lard should be half an inch deep in a heavy iron skillet, popping hot to brown one side, then the other, after which heat is lowered to cook the chicken pieces through, each being taken out when done since cooking time varies with thickness. Drain thoroughly. Those uneasy about lard may substitute peanut oil, which works out 90 percent as well.

before the Revolution a British-reared lady living in the country outside Boston complained in a letter home about how these Americans neglect garden stuff and call it all indiscriminately "Sause." The Colonist was more interested in items that would store for winter and the kinds of beans and peas that dried well. Probably his ideal vegetable was the pumpkin he inherited from the Indians. It could be dried in rings on sticks; the expressed juice, boiled down, made fair molasses or fermented into potable beer; and presently pumpkin pie was born.

Watermelons, strawberries and plums and pears, as well as apples and peaches, took kindly to the New World. Some Virginians planted peach

Sap buckets in the maple grove meant spring was only
a few weeks away.

orchards "purposely for their Hogs" [52] over and above the brandy supply. New York's peach trees bore so heavily that the branches broke down; Dankers and Sluyter came on a road in what is now the Bronx "entirely covered with peaches. . . . We asked the boy why they did not let the hogs eat them. He answered . . . there are so many; the hogs . . . will not eat any more." [53] In one sense all that making of cider, applejack and peach brandy was a way to salvage the nutrient carbohydrates of these gluts of fruit, for sugar cost too much to permit modern preserving techniques. The great conical loaf of sugar was kept in a locked box to discourage pilfering servants and children. In the North the Colonists' early sweetening was maple syrup and sugar boiled down from the sap that the approach of spring set flowing; the whites' iron kettles and buckets with handles enabled them to do this more efficiently than the Indians could. "Sugaring-off" became a folk festival with an exclusively New World flavor. All hands thronged into the still-snowy woods to collect sap buckets, feed the roaring fire under the kettles, and throw ladlefuls of syrup on the snow to cool into the wax that was so luscious. All Colonies also soon had honey from imported bees in hives and in the eagerly sought bee trees, in the hollows of which escaped swarms had established themselves. With the honey came beeswax, a lively trade item for both the beekeeping settler and the frontier Indian.

Peaches, strawberries and blackberries were mashed and dried into a chewy and tasty "leather." Drying of pared apple quarters was sometimes done on trays in the sun, or the quarters were strung on coarse string with a big needle and hung near the fireplace. Well-dried apples kept almost indefinitely and had a wild flavor of their own when boiled up and made into pie filling or cooked into stews Pennsylvania Dutch-style. Nutting in the fall was for children, who made play of it, shaking the pelting showers of shiny brown chestnuts down from the great trees, scrambling in the fallen leaves to see who gathered most, taking home sack after sack. Removing the aromatic hulls of black walnuts so stained the hands that not even harsh, homemade soap could cope, but the kernels in those gnarly shells carried one of the subtlest known flavors, unique to the New World as that of Glenlivet is to Scotland. (It took getting used to when one expected its less emphatic European cousin. A Frenchman in the Illinois country in 1723 mentioned "walnut trees, which bear nuts, but of a very bad taste." [54] Virginia-born Beverley said: ". . . very rank, and oily, having a thick, hard, foul Shell, and come not clear of the Husk, as the walnut in France doth." [55]) Shagbark hickory nuts were also hard to crack and pick, but their wild richness was also worth the trouble. Children equipped with flat stones and large pebbles for hammers were greedy about cracking and nibbling, while on the hearth before them, as Whittier remembered, "the mug of cider simmered slow / The apples sputtered in a row. . . ."

The upper classes of postmedieval Northern Europe, particularly in England, got a good deal of meat and fish. But the English lower orders lived largely on bread supplemented by cheese and root vegetables; the Scots chiefly on oatmeal and occasional milk; the Scotch-Irish on potatoes and milk. In view of the relative plenty of the Colonial table, it is no wonder that in spite of malaria, bitter cold, blazing heat and homesickness, the word sent home was often glowingly favorable and put emigration into the heads of more and more landlord-ridden men from Antrim, Galway, the Lothians, the North Country and Pembrokeshire. Note, however, that our forebears signally lacked our chief sources of vitamin C, the scurvy preventer—citrus fruit, tomatoes, green peppers—and in the early days they also lacked potatoes, some of the C of which survives cooking. Why didn't they all die of scurvy every winter as the Pilgrims came so near doing?

The answer probably is that once they had traditional European vegetables going, they could store over winter the minor sources of C that the Pilgrims lacked after the ship's supplies ran out. Onions, parsnips, turnips, cabbages, all conspicuous in Colonial gardens and cookery, retain enough C even after boiling to make a crucial difference if eaten regularly. Stored apples eaten raw doubtless helped, and those many barrels of unpasteurized cider downcellar, and possibly also those many other barrels of unpasteurized home-brewed beer. The German and Dutch settlers' overwinter sauerkraut was a fine preventive. The margin of nutritional safety was often narrow. Boston's first known doctor was a quack fined in 1630 for "taking upon him to cure the scurvy by a water of no worth or value." [56] Dr. Alexander Hamilton (not the one Burr killed) noted that the people of Albany, New York, in 1744 were "subject to rotten teeth and scorbutic gums, which I suppose, is caused by the cold air, and their constant diet of salt provisions." [57] In these circumstances resistance to infectious diseases must have been hazardously low. But marginally, Old World vegetables saved the day.

How it all tasted can only be conjectured. Early cookbooks came from abroad or were cribbed from Old Country ones, so nobody knows just how nascent Maryland cooked terrapin. Madam Knight relished a dish of fried venison. Dankers and Sluyter smacked their lips over smoked striped bass but did not record how it was cooked—and anyway, how gauge their gastronomic standards? Scarcity of butter discouraged supplementary richening except as fried meats were served swimming in lard from the skillet. Surviving reflectors and spits (sometimes turned by dogs gravely working small treadmills) imply much roasting, as well as frying and boiling, at least in Quality houses, but roasts from those scrubby sheep and cattle were probably tough even when overdone, as they likely were. The number of iron griddles happily implies a prevalence of tender, fragrant-brown griddle cakes of wheat or corn or the buckwheat that became an important Colonial food crop and source of honey nectar.

Subtlety of preparation was probably rare, for it was no elegant age. Table forks, just coming in, were finicky luxuries. Eating with the knife was as common as with the fingers—hence the quantities of table napkins in old inventories. Most families ate out of a common wooden dish. Bowls and individual trenchers were also of wood and, however attractive they now look, clumsy to use. The head of the house might have an armchair at table, but to judge from surviving specimens, it was more honor than comfort to sit in. Until toward 1700 the others used benches or backless joint stools. Yet hard seats and simple cooking do not necessarily imply dull food. Classic cod or clam chowder, roast wild turkey stuffed with chestnuts, add the fish and game and variations on corn listed above, and it is unlikely that if the women sweating over the fire took reasonable pains, the Colonist had much difficulty in choking down his victuals.

IV

Thirteen Prosper

BENJAMIN FRANKLIN'S AMERICA

IV

A YOUNG forester reared and trained in New Hampshire was showing me around his district in a Southern hill county. He had been
there long enough for the easygoing local talk to have diluted his
Yankee tongue. But when he said that the local people "nevah think to
pick up the doe-yodd," New England was still speaking clearly.

Some of his New Hampshire forebears may well have been Scotch-
Irish, like those of the hill Southerners around him. Yet their modes of
speech and notions of outdoor housekeeping differed widely. Such contrasts among Americans of like ethnic origin go far back. The Colonists
dressed and drank much alike, but in other aspects regional cultures were
soon drifting apart. That happens when groups from the same general
culture settle far apart with little subsequent contact.

As the 1700's passed the halfway mark and tides set toward the Seven
Years' War—the results of which primed and cocked the Revolution—
the Colonies were still isolated enough one from another to foster divergences. Inter-Colonial trade was growing; New Hampshire, for instance,
was sending fish and lumber to Pennsylvania and the Chesapeake country
in exchange for corn and wheat flour. But only the small crews of the
coasting vessels partook in consequent extramural contacts. Stage wagons,
still few and fumbly even within individual Colonies, had barely begun to
connect New York City and Philadelphia or Boston and Providence. Until
exile brought them together in England or Canada, surprisingly few Colonial Loyalist (or say frankly *Tory*) leaders, however important at home,
had ever met. It would have been the same with Patriot leaders had not
successive Continental Congresses gathered them in the same halls. And
when the Revolution thus brought parochial politicians and amateur soldiers into contact, the frictions were almost as hot as though they separated Colonists and Old Countrymen. A young officer of the Maryland
line, with "The Softest voice, never pronounces the *R* at all," [1] pleased
Sally Wister of Philadelphia in 1777. But there was no cordiality about the

181

Yankee officer who, alerted to expect a body of Southern troops, growled that he did not like men with one eye—referring to the nasty Southern custom of eye gouging in fights. Well after the Revolution a traveler into the new country in Kentucky, where the settlers were mostly Virginians, complained that "in Philadelphia it is imagined that one quarter of the Virginians have lost their eyes by gouging, and that, with many persons in Pennsylvania, it is sufficient to overturn the credit of any measure . . . to say that it originated in Virginia." [2]

Nor were such distinctions necessarily North-South. St. George Tucker of Bermuda and Virginia, visiting the Carolinas in 1774, had noted with finicky surprise that the local gentlewomen talked like Negroes, which implies already developed differences in speech between two parts of Dixie-to-be. North Carolina was already reputed a Rogues' Harbor because its lord proprietors, hoping to attract settlers, had outlawed suits for debt contracted before entering the Colony—an open invitation to Virginia's defaulters. The expedition that founded South Carolina had picked up at Barbados on the way numerous recruits, presumably from among those squeezed out by the shift from small-holding tobacco culture to large-holding sugar culture. The connection thus begun brought so many more Barbadians that Thomas Jefferson Wertenbaker described early Charleston as virtually a West Indian town. Today's Charlestonians' turn of speech, little resembling the general *hush-ma-mouf* Southern slur, may still recall this connection.

The widest cleavage, however, early marked and soon widening, was that between the Yankee and the other Colonists. Private Joseph Plumb Martin of the Connecticut line heard a Pennsylvania woman say that her little girl had been so fractious that she had threatened to give her to the Yankees. "Take care how you speak of the Yankees," said Martin's wagonmate. "I have one of them here." "La!" said the woman. "Is he a Yankee? . . . I don't see any difference between him and other people." [3] In Philadelphia a few years earlier Josiah Quincy, Jr., had found the Quakers' still-lively memories of Yankee persecution of their people causing "general disliking, not to say antipathy . . . against N England." [4] In the Carolinas he had already met strong anti-Yankee feeling, probably reflecting local dislike of the sharp-set coastal traders from New England. As the Revolution took shape, Loyalist and Patriot alike (outside New England) feared lest the crisis end in Yankee cunning dominating the other Colonies. One such viewer-with-alarm, Loyalist Joseph Galloway of Philadelphia, actually predicted that if independence came, North and South would quarrel over the empty West and a Yankee-led North would conquer a South weakened by the morbid effects of Negro slavery. Yankees, wrote Samuel Seabury of New York, think "God . . .

made Boston for himself and all the rest of the world for Boston." [5] In those days few New Yorkers, Philadelphians, FFV's or Charlestonians made the wearisome sea trip or the arduous land trip to see the Yankee at his best under his own vine and fig tree. Nor does it follow that if they had, they would have come to like his dry, laconic ways.

Young Quincy made his trip to Charleston by sea for the good of his lungs, seasick but gamely sprinkling his diary with tags from Vergil, Horace and Sterne. On his long ride homeward from Charleston by land he sensed many moral divergences that had Yankees and Southerners scowling at each other long before the issue of slavery set irritations afire. In South Carolina, "Cards, dice and the bottle and horses engross prodigious proportions of the time. . . . The Sabbath is a day of visiting and mirth with the rich, of license, pastime and folly with the negroes . . . quarreling round the doors of the Churches in Service-time," while their masters in the pews withindoors chatted sociably during the sermon perfunctorily preached from the pulpit. He preferred the simpler gentlemen of North Carolina to the sword-wearing plutocrats of Charleston. Moving northward, he marked steady, if slight, improvement day by day in farming methods, even though the Tarheel and Virginian small farmers were "a vastly more ignorant and illiterate kind than with us [New Englanders]." North of the James, wheat was encroaching on tobacco with obvious economic benefit. But local talk about the "depravity and abominable wickedness" of the local Anglican clergy was so lurid that some later hand tore out the two diary pages following Quincy's mention of parsons neglecting their parishes to run taverns and gamble.

"Williamsburg was inferior much to my expectation. . . . Nothing of the . . . magnificence and splendor" that Charleston showed in some public buildings and Miles Brewton's new Georgian mansion. The William and Mary College Building, imposing from the front, was falling apart behind. Only the well-chosen law library in the Capitol met with the young Puritan lawyer's approval. Annapolis made "a very contemptible appearance" and local "young men of fortune" proved to be "gamblers and cock-fighters, hound-breeders and horse-jockies. . . ." [6] One cannot tell now how much of that was accurate observation and how much parochialism. Fourteen years earlier the Reverend Andrew Burnaby, observing Williamsburg from Old Country standards, had thought it "Far from being a place of any consequence . . . [with] few public edifices that deserve to be taken notice of . . . far from being magnificent. . . . The streets are not paved . . . consequently very dusty." [7] Yet a little after Burnaby, Lord Adam Gordon, an Old Country visitor certainly accustomed to Britain's best, said that Williamsburg "much resembles a good Country Town in England," its people were "well bred, polite, and extremely civil to strangers," the college was "very large and handsome" and the palace "handsome and commodious." [8] The one thing unmistakable in this conflict of opinion is Quincy's note of contempt. Eighty years later that contempt would attain full expression in the fulminations of Yankee Miss Ophelia against the slovenly slackness of Southern housekeeping in *Uncle Tom's Cabin* and the sense of regional alienation that underlay the Civil War.

The ominous sense of foreignness between North and South was particularly clear in the divergent functions of religion. In New England the social focus was primarily the meetinghouse, whereas in most of the South the church had a great rival in the courthouse and, as Quincy remarked, the flavor of Sunday was rather secular. Bradford and the Puritans had kept Yankee settlements compact not merely for "defense against the Indians," says Samuel Eliot Morison, "but to enable everyone to attend divine service, to maintain a vigorous community life, and to keep a strict watch over sinners." [9] Southern dwellings, whether brick Big Houses overlooking a river landing at the foot of a lawn or log shacks in clearings on upcountry creeks, were usually so scattered that to attend church at the ford or the crossroads was a great effort. Law and public opinion soon ceased to make any great thing of whether any given person was there.

"The Gentlemen go to Church to be sure," wrote Philip Fithian, New Jerseyman tutor in the family of "King" Carter of Virginia, "but they make that itself a matter of convenience, & account the Church a useful weekly resort to do Business . . . giving and receiving letters . . . reading advertisements, consulting about the price of Tobacco, Grain, &c., & settling . . . the lineage, age or qualities of favorite Horses. After Service is over three quarters of an hour [are] spent strolling round . . . you will be invited by several different Gentlemen with them to dinner." [10] The man occupying the pulpit in the interval was likely to be a dreary misfit come to the Colonies for lack of future at home, at best the glib, superficial sort whom Quincy deplored in Charleston. The parson of whom Fithian saw most confined himself to "pray'rs read over in Haste, a sermon seldom . . . over twenty minutes . . ." [10] and was presently sick in bed because he had been "up three nights successively drinking and playing at Cards, so that the liquor and want of sleep quite put him out of his Senses— A rare tale this to relate of a man of God!" [10] "The Parson is drunk and can't perform the duties of his office" [11] was several times recorded of another man of God in Virginia. Sifting through old records, Henry Cabot Lodge found "One reverend gentleman . . . [who] commemorated his church and office by fighting a duel in the graveyard. . . . One married a wealthy widow, although he had a wife living in England.

. . ." [12] Parsons scandalously given over to drink and horses were not uncommon in the England of that day, and the worst of them were sometimes sent to America as good riddance. The Reverend Jonathan Boucher called many of his Anglican colleagues in Maryland "of a despicable class . . . shabby Christians . . ." [13] and seriously suggested that friends of Popery in the Colonial government deliberately imported such poor specimens to discredit Protestantism. A visiting divine wrote home to the Bishop of London in 1753 that "It would really, my lord, make the ears of a sober heathen tingle to hear the stories . . . told me by many serious persons of several clergymen in the neighborhood [in Maryland] where I visit." [14] Even supposing the quality of incumbents to have been higher, all Virginia in 1761 had only 60-odd clergymen to minister to maybe 250,000 persons—an absurd ratio of 1 parson per 4,000 population.

In diametric contrast the Yankee minister was the most august figure in the township, well if narrowly trained, wielding authority as majestically as he did his long, gold-headed walking stick. In severe weather the Virginian parson might not turn up at all on Sunday, leaving the faithful who had struggled forth to read to themselves out of the prayer book and go home, whereas, no matter how it rained or snowed, the Yankee minister, living within yards of the meetinghouse, was always there in that gaunt, freezing receptacle for holiness and decorum. And since they, too, were domiciled within five minutes' walk, the congregation had no excuse for absence. Their dutifulness procured them up to two hours of morning sermon on doctrinal subtleties often gingered up with hellfire but in any case interesting the amateur theologians among them, and in the afternoon another sermon just as weighty. The interval was sociable, though not frivolous, devoted to cold dinner prepared the day before to avoid the sacrilege of work on the Sabbath. In good weather the young folks might wander off by themselves. On Thursday evening came lecture, forerunner of prayer meeting, for informal education of the laity—another opportunity for boys and girls to pair off as they came and went.

As the pristine compactness of settlement relaxed in the 1700's, the New England meetinghouse took on even greater importance as focus. Distant-dwelling families looked forward all week to the trip to meeting, Goodwife Candace riding pillion behind Goodman Waitstill, the others trudging behind, carrying their shoes to save wear and putting them on just before entering. Alongside the meetinghouse prosperous families might build horse sheds, their Sabbath Day or "noon houses," more or less weatherproof shacks wherein to eat their cold dinner and get warm at the fire in the small fireplace. Meeting was a spiritual thing and valued as such. But even without that it would have been indispensable, for otherwise, as William B. Weeden said of early New England, "social life was bare and spiritless beyond the possibility of description . . . opportunities for pleasure [in Samuel Sewall's Boston of 1700] . . . would hardly satisfy the common laborer of two centuries later." [15]

Similar religious Sundays, regularly and well attended, served the same social ends among the Pennsylvania Dutch and Scotch-Irish as those peoples of austere beliefs settled the upcountry. The Scotch-Irish taking up land in central Georgia just before the Revolution turned out many "pretty girls . . . in striped and checked cotton cloth, spun and woven by their own hands . . . their sweethearts [wore] sumach and walnut-dyed stuffs made by their mothers. Courting was done riding [horseback] to meeting on Sunday, and walking to the spring when there. . . ." [16] But not until Methodists and Baptists swept in with demandingly personal kinds of religion did the South as a whole reorient its social life around the jerry-built little church in the pines. Until then court day was an equivalent though not as frequent an institution.

Amelia Court House, Charlotte Court House, Guilford Court House, King and Queen Courthouse—old names in the *Postal Guide* still recall the origins of these specialized hamlets in a South that, unlike New England, had small need for even villages. The usual layout was well described in John P. Kennedy's *Swallow Barn*: a low, square brick courthouse surrounded stragglingly by a small brick office for county records; a miniature jail; a disused pillory; long stretches of hitching rack for litigants' and others' horses; two taverns, "one formerly a house of some pretensions";[17] three or four odd dwellings. Within eyeshot also may have been a ferryman's shack by the riverbank; a gristmill above it; in the distance a tumbledown old-field school. Hither came judge and clerk at specified intervals and local lawyers and clients to sue and be sued, testify in one another's suits, sit on juries, gossip, chew tobacco, stage dog-, cock- and manfights, make stump speeches, swap horses and dirty sto.ies, auction off livestock and Negroes, pay debts and incur new ones in impromptu horse races, gambling and land transactions. With this crossroads festival often came dancing and dining at the local Quality's Big Houses, where young and old came by dozens and scores to stay a week at a time, put up dormitory-style on cots and pallets. On a few holidays cruder frolics included the lower orders. Here is the program of the doings on St. Andrew's Day in Hanover County, Virginia, "at the Old Field, near Captain John Bickerton's": a hat worth twenty shillings to be cudgeled for; the violin to be played for by twenty fiddlers, each to bring his own, and "After the prize is won . . . all to play together, and each a different tune, and be treated by the company"; twelve boys twelve years old to run 112 yards for a hat worth twelve shillings; a pair of silver buckles to be wrestled for by "a number of brisk young men"; a pair of silk stockings worth one pistole given to "the handsomest young country maid that appears in the field. . . ." [18] The management promised to fly a flag on a 30-foot pole and provide incidental music from drums, trumpets, hautboys, etc.

In these diffuse Southern communities weddings and funerals also supplied what anthropologists call interaction. But it was the utterly secular court day that set the tone. Its rowdy masculinity was actually close to that of New England's training day when able-bodied men mustered with firearms and sketchy accouterments to try to imitate soldiers, always with much drinking of rum, barking of dogs, expenditure of blank ammunition and strutting of officers well known as Captain or Major in their taverns. Neither court nor training day was notably edifying. And the South, as Quincy and Fithian saw with pain, had no weekly concentration on sober and nonworldly values to counteract the lust of the eye and the things of this world. Southern religion of the mid-1700's was too private for much social value, though it could be real enough; the small libraries sometimes found in Quality houses contained relatively high proportions of sermons and religious morality. It was probably at its best in the numerous households holding daily family worship, whether of Calvinist tenor upcountry or Anglican near tidewater, and at its quaintest in that pagan by nature William Byrd II, who so often had occasion to write in his diary: "Said my prayers . . . committed uncleanness with her, for which God forgive me." [19]

If relative isolation of the Colonies one from another necessarily heightened differences, in one way it heightened resemblances as the Quality of each Colony imitated the Mother Country's ways with self-conscious zeal. For lack of communication between Virginia and Massachusetts indirectly encouraged attachment to England's upper-class leading strings. Say a prospering Carolinian of 1730 wanted higher education for his son and disapproved of tutors or failed to find good ones. He could send him to Harvard or Yale. But they were largely theological in tone, and the voyage thither was almost halfway to Britain where the Inns of Court (for prospective lawyers), Scottish universities (for prospective doctors) and Oxford and Cambridge offered learning higher in prestige and quality than anything then available in the Colonies. Of the two considerations prestige probably weighed more. Pennsylvanian and New Yorker fathers eventually had less reason thus to transplant their sons, yet they did so almost as freely. By the mid-1700's half of Philadelphia's lawyers had attended the Inns of Court. Even in New England, where mistrust of the Old Country was strong and colleges convenient, the overseas solution was popular. A large, if not always primary, motive must have been hope of acquiring "home"-style manners and attitudes along with professional training for bar, bedside or pulpit. When Henry Laurens, eminent Charlestonian, twitted South Carolina for failure to found an equivalent of Harvard, a candid local snob replied that the Carolina Quality needn't contemplate an institution that "might deprive their sons of the only advantage of being distinguished among their Countrymen" [20]—that is, the cachet of overseas schooling and social experience.

These young temporary expatriates—coming home to America for vacations was impractical—eventually returned elegantly garbed and knowing enough more than they previously had to impress stay-at-homes, as well as themselves. Thomas Jefferson considered that such polishing in Europe gave the young fellow "a contempt for the simplicity of his own country . . . a spirit for female intrigue destructive of his own and others' happiness, or a passion for whores destructive of his health . . . [he] learns to consider fidelity to the marriage bed as an ungentlemanly practice . . . returns to his own country, a foreigner . . . speaking and writing his native tongue as a foreigner. . . ." [21] One sees something of that in Benjamin Franklin's son William, home from his studies in the Inns of Court, accompanying his father on "a little excursion in the Jerseys" including the Passaic Falls and patronizingly averring that he had not had "the least idea that views so agreeably enchanting were to be met with in America." [22]

In the twenty years before the Revolution scores on scores of young Philadelphians sailed for Italy to admire the "Dying Gladiator," take a standard grand tour through France to England, and stay there for some years of learning from books—and from the well-placed Britons to whom they carried letters of introduction. The result of such interchange in Boston in the early 1700's was, as a British visitor noted, that "In . . . their Dress, Tables, and Conversation, they affect to be as much English as possible." [23] John Harrower, indentured Scottish tutor for the Daingerfields of Fredericksburg, Virginia, wrote home in 1774 that he was "obliged to talk english the best I can for [Mrs.] Daingerfield speaks nothing but high english, and the Colonel made his Education in England." [24] Yet snobbish as such men might be, they sound better than the West Indian planters' sons whose ideal was to settle permanently in England and buy an elaborate countryseat. Certain young Americans could have afforded that. Instead they gave their birthplace the benefits of their hard-won polish. Few (like William Franklin, who became the Crown's governor of New Jersey and a Tory in the Revolution) made a career of Anglophilia. Their sires were usually able men deep in local affairs, and these new-polished sons often proved valuable, if somewhat sniffish, Americans —for example, William Byrd II, educated at the Middle Temple, active

Colonial politician and governor-baiter, founder of Richmond, Virginia, creator of the finest early Colonial library.

The connection with England was always strong because thence came so many of the materials of good living. Virginian planters, like isolated ranchers ordering from mail-order houses, did most of their shopping through the masters of the ships that tied up at their plantations. In 1687 a Huguenot immigrant was puzzled by the reliance of the Virginia Quality on the Mother Country for furniture, hats, boots, and linen when "they have fine woods . . . could raise wool, have plenty of beaver at hand for hats, leather for boots, etc. . . ." [25] and as for linen, he said, though he had seen fine flax grown, it was left to spoil because there wasn't a single woman in the Colony who knew how to spin it. Thanks to this sluggishness, it remained true for generations that Virginia's nearest source of supply of those items, plus paper, cutlery, books and medicines, was Philadelphia, weeks distant by water, many onerous days distant by packhorse over unspeakable roads and unbridged rivers. It really did seem simpler and cheaper, as well as vanity-gratifying, to procure such things where one's fashions and one's religious doctrines also came from—England. Even Irish beef and butter (both salted for export) could compete with local supply in the Colonies.

Presently, of course, industrial enterprise in the Northern Colonies and growing inter-Colonial trade began to supply most requirements of foodstuffs and crude manufactures. But the prestige of the transatlantic article persisted in luxury items and whatever required much skill. That was unfair to the growing number of fine Colonial craftsmen, but inevitable. The account books of Peter Faneuil show that Boston merchants, as well as FFV planters, sent overseas for such things. At one time or another he thus ordered silk stockings for his own use and white thread stockings for his sisters'; table silver and candlesticks engraved with his arms; razors, spectacles, cookbooks, a backgammon table with counters and dice; bits for his coach horses—several of which items he could certainly have procured in Boston, and of fine workmanship too. Then here goes his watch to be cleaned by an English expert and a silk suit of sister Mary Ann's to be dyed, watered and sent back—a round trip of at least 5,000 miles and three months.

As Colonial economies expanded and gave the Quality more leisure, genteel means to Old Country-style entertainment appeared. By 1700 coffeehouses in the port capitals were imitating those that served as focuses of men's social and business doings in England. That run by Mary Ballard in Boston assured gentlemen that they would be served "at any time of Day, after the manner of [coffeehouses] in London." [26] Except among

Puritans and Quakers the Colonists had always danced, in however rugged a fashion, whenever a special occasion brought a fiddler, drink and elbowroom into conjunction. Now Old Country dancing masters, often French, sometimes landing on indentures that made ransoming them a good investment, were polishing up Colonial caperings and making it worth a tavernkeeper's while to install a second-story ballroom with fancy-painted walls and candle sconces with tin reflectors.

Horse racing had begun in the 1660's on the Long Island barrens sponsored by Governor Richard Nicolls, who seems to have been the first to cite improvement of the breed as pretext for the sport of kings. Meets as near Old Country-style as possible soon sprang up in the Southern and Middle Colonies. Purses posted by the Jockey Club of Fredericksburg, Virginia, ran to 100 guineas, then a most substantial sum. In 1766 Philadelphians with country places near Gloucester, New Jersey, formed a club to promote the yoicks kind of fox hunting, which must have puzzled local coons and skunks, as well as local foxes. To secure authenticity, they imported English red foxes—a futile measure, for these bushy-tailed immigrants, less snobbish than their sponsors, interbred with their American cousins and blended indistinguishably into their new environment. It pleases me to think that the fine red fox who sometimes does ballet leaps across the far end of my lawn in New Jersey probably has, like me, certain English ancestors sent to the New World very much against their will.*

In 1743 Benjamin Franklin advised his fellow Colonists that "The first Drudgery of Settling new Colonies, which confines the Attention of People to mere Necessaries, is now pretty well over; and there are many in every Province in Circumstances that set them at Ease, and afford leisure to cultivate the finer Arts. . . ." [27] In spite of the Puritans, who considered the stage sinful, and the Quakers who thought it morbidly worldly, the finer art of the theater had already cropped up, albeit raggedly and on a small scale. In Williamsburg in 1716 a married pair of dancing teachers, with the countenance of patrons including such august names as Harrison, Lee, Nelson and Randolph, imported a troupe of English actors to perform "comedies, drolls, and other kinds of stage plays." [28] They were professional enough for William Byrd II, whose standards were metropolitan, to say that they acted tolerably well. In Boston the minor officers of British regiments posted there amused themselves and eked out

* America also had plenty of gray foxes, but, I am told, that species is less satisfactory to hunt with horse and hounds because it often breaks the scent by climbing trees or running along the tops of fences, whereas red foxes, less acrobatic, are likelier to stay on the ground, thereby leaving a continuous scent. It would be interesting to know what gray foxes thought of the advent of zigzag rail fences.

their low pay by staging occasional plays until in 1750 Massachusetts awoke to the danger and banned any such palterings with the Devil. In the mid-1700's an English troupe of provincial caliber headed by Lewis Hallam and his wife came to the West Indies and the non-Yankee Colonies with Shakespeare, Otway, Rowe, Cibber—the standard repertory of the day. Charleston, Philadelphia and New York saw much of them in the next few years. Their doubtless deserved success led to the building of a permanent theater—in Philadelphia just outside the town limits to evade a Quaker-inspired municipal ban on theaters. So far as I am aware, it was this company that invented the subterfuge, much resorted to in the 1800's, of billing a play as a moral spectacle or dialogue or lecture to stay inside the law against theatricals. In Newport, Rhode Island, in 1761 the company found it necessary to advertise *Othello* as "Moral Dialogues in Five Parts, Depicting the evil effects of jealousy . . . and proving that happiness can only spring from the pursuit of virtue." [29]

It was all imported, of course—actors, plays and the tastes to which they appealed. The only serious play by an American ever staged before the Revolution—*The Prince of Parthia,* a bit of Otway-and-water by Thomas Godfrey, a versifying Philadelphian—never saw footlights again. The one performer known to have been native was stagestruck Nancy George, who ran away from Philadelphia to New York City with a strolling troupe in 1749. Also usually imported were the animals exhibited by traveling showmen on village greens—"an Ourangogang (or Man of the Wood)," [30] or a lion, or a camel, or a German horse understanding several languages. Native-bred exceptions might be a hog weighing 900 pounds, or a porcupine, or an alligator, or a black moose. Punch and Judy, also imported, began to crop up on street corners. Strolling stunt artists picked up a livelihood by dancing the tightrope with their feet chained. The ugliest entertainment utilizing animals was also very popular in at least Tidewater Virginia and New York City—bullbaiting, the bull tied to a stake to be assailed by powerful dogs specially bred for savagery and tenacity, very much an Old World institution.

Carl Bridenbaugh inclines to credit the appearance of the Hallam acting company with importantly stimulating secular music in the cities where it played, particularly in Philadelphia. This is likely enough. The theater of the 1700's relied on music more consistently than ours does. In addition to the fiddlers in the orchestra pit, the songs interpolated in the stage action and the between-acts duet or dance to music were important aspects of the entertainment. In America these might well be the first professional renditions of formal secular music that the customer had ever heard. But there was a foundation to build on. Musical instruments, particularly fiddles and flutes, had come over with many consignments of immigrants, of course, along with folk ballads, dance tunes and, more solemnly, the basic hymn tunes of the various Protestant psalmodies. In the 1730's-1740's travelers were reporting little groups of ardent amateurs giving occasional "consorts" with violin, flute, hautboy and harpsichord in the port cities. Charleston imported a French music master in 1762 and paid him an annual salary to develop her new St. Cecilia Society of local amateurs and their admiring listeners. In Philadelphia, Francis Hopkinson, an able amateur on several instruments, as well as a composer and lyricist, organized a noted group, part professional—it included Governor John Penn and James Bremner, an outstanding local music teacher[30]— that sounds like an ensemble of genuine quality. Their music—Handel, Pergolesi, Scarlatti, Vivaldi, Arne, Purcell—was typical of what immigrant teachers trained Colonial aspirants to value. All up and down the seaboard Scottish, German or Italian musicians sought a livelihood by acting as badly needed musical missionaries, giving lessons, organizing concerts, setting up stores to sell sheet music and instruments. By and large this, too, was all exotic, like the theater. But it depended on a culturally healthy participation to an extent impossible today. No records, no tapes, no radio-TV—if you wanted to hear a given melody of Purcell, you played or sang it yourself, as did "King" Carter and Thomas Jefferson, great gentlemen of Virginia. And Carter's family tutor, Fithian, remarked that "any young Gentlemen travelling through [Virginia] is presum'd to be acquainted with Dancing, Boxing, playing the Fiddle, & Smallsword, & Cards." [31]

That small-sword was a far less innocent and more snobbish importation than the fiddle. It implied the formal duel, a custom seriously infesting the Colonies of Fithian's time. Earlier, fists and cudgels had been the resorts of the quarrelsome even among Southern Quality. One reason may have been that early Colonial authorities had allowed little leeway to the seconds and protocol sort of thing in any social stratum. Plymouth's first and last duel occurred between two indentured servants fighting with cutlasses and knives, who were punished by being tied together neck and heels. A nephew of Governor Thomas Dongan of New York who killed his man in a duel in the 1680's was promptly convicted of manslaughter. The grand jury stepped in when the incumbent of Philadelphia's Anglican parish—those Colonial parsons!—challenged one Peter Evans for slandering a lady. This is further evidence of the middle-class tone of the Colonies. In the Old Countries a ruling oligarchy tending to aristocracy was inconceivable without the duello. Merchants' and yeomen's sons, however, had no need to pay such sharp-edged heed to the point of honor. What now naturalized the duel in New World ways-of-doing—which led to shamefully much civic damage in the next few generations—was the sophomoric admiration of young American Quality for the fire-eating ways of Captain Spontoon and Ensign Spatterdash of His Majesty's *n*th Regiment of Foot stationed in the Colonies during the French and Indian War.

Over the years, however, dueling probably killed fewer than the watering places aping those of fashionable Britain. Settlement had hardly begun when the Colonists learned, usually through the Indians, of the new country's springs of mineral-impregnated waters. Most of these mixtures from nature's pharmacy tasted or smelled foul enough to convince both Indians and whites, whose scientific criteria were much the same 300 years ago, that they were good for what ails you. Many of them would, when ingested, produce what an early Pennsylvanian recommended as "purging . . . both by Siege and by Urine, all but as good as Epsom" [32] —the renowned English watering place that gave the name to the Epsom salts with which our forebears corrected constipation. Often they were also naturally hot and soaking in them made arthritics feel better. Almost from the beginning minor mineral springs at Lynn, Massachusetts, and in the outskirts of Philadelphia were thus resorted to. But not until the latter half of the 1700's did the Colonial cult of soaking and sipping among fashionable company, as Old Country great folks did at Bath and Spa, get into its stride. For only then was the Colonist's yearning to imitate whatever good society did at home encouraged by roads navigable enough to get him—and more to the point, his wife—to the springs without practically prohibitive hardship.

Typically, for sound geological reasons, such springs were up in the hills well away from town. Sir William Johnson, self-made great man of the Mohawk Valley and an adept frontiersman, could make his way into a wilderness to assuage his aches and pains in what is now Saratoga Springs. George Washington, also a veteran of the frontier, noted the potential value of Berkeley Springs in the foothills of the Alleghenies in 1748; in 1756 Lord Fairfax gave them to Virginia "that these healing waters might be forever free to the publick, for the welfare of suffering humanity." [33] But it took the slightly better roads of the 1760's to bring it about that more than a very few visitors from Tidewater came to Berkeley—eventually renamed Bath after England's famous watering place. At the same time slightly improved vehicles and roads at least recognizable as such were developing use of the springs on New Jersey's Schooleys Mountain in the rough highlands that would furnish so much iron for the Patriot cause. Yellow Springs, outside Philadelphia, could not become a fashionable Quaker resort until a public road thither was opened in 1750; thirteen years later it was so popular that the stage wagon made thrice-weekly trips. And the rise of Bristol, Pennsylvania, to the status of

smartest watering place in the Colonies was due not so much to the griping
purges that its waters induced as to its location on the main stage route to
New York City.

Such a spa was usually crude at first. At Warm Springs, Pennsylvania,
in 1775, for instance, those taking the waters lived in cabins and did
their own cooking at a common fire. As the fad grew and transport improved, however, genteel boardinghouses and pump- and dancing-rooms
came in. The eminent doctor who sponsored Bristol as a watering place
persuaded the town to drain the adjacent mosquito-rich swamps and enlarge the church to keep pious visitors happy. Dr. Benjamin Rush, a
physician of high professional repute, as well as of versatile social and
civic interests, made a survey of Pennsylvania's therapeutic springs, listing their various uses with an occasional dash of common sense rare in
the medicine of his day. But he had the bad luck to include a well, recently
dug by a Philadelphian in his backyard at Sixth and Chestnut streets, the
water of which tasted so horrible that the whole town flocked to it for all
kinds of ailments. Rush was only one of thousands dismayed when the
overpumped well went dry and efforts to renew the flow showed a direct
communication with the owner's privy—hence the powerful flavor.

The high cost of board at well-known Colonial spas limited the clientele to the Quality of Pennsylvania and Virginia and soon to their social
counterparts from New York and Maryland, even the West Indies. They
brought their finest clothes and manners, for they meant to dance as well
as defecate, to break hearts as well as cure the itch. This blend of latrine
and ballroom seems anomalous to modern Americans, but it is the basic
tradition of the European spa and is still as strong as ever in modern Germany. Francis Asbury, the great apostle of Methodism in America, deplored the carryings-on at Berkeley soon after the Revolution: "When I
behold the conduct of the people who attended the springs, particularly
the gentry, I . . . thank God that I was not born to riches . . . I cannot
partake of pleasure with sinners." But he noted fairly that "The water was
[so] powerful in operation [that] my studies are interrupted." [34] Actually the frivolous worldliness that troubled him was important, as Carl
Bridenbaugh's monograph on Colonial spas points out, because it provided
"a powerful solvent of provincialism" [35] just when the Colonies were
about to need to make common cause. Newport, Rhode Island, made the
same kind of contribution as the Carolinian and Georgian Quality came
each summer by coasting sloop to enjoy the famous cool breezes of
Narragansett Bay. The summer-shore industry was also stirring at Cape
May, New Jersey, and Gravesend Bay, New York, where visitors toyed
with the new English notion that cold seawater was good for you whether
applied externally by surf bathing or swallowed by the pint. But all that

was embryonic. The spa, much nearer maturity, was what gave the Colonial grandee the most gratifying illusion of genteel life "at home." Almost as gratifying was the parading of the mace, the Speaker's wig and gown and the other details by which the South Carolina House of Assembly and other Colonial legislatures gravely aped His Majesty's High Court of Parliament at Westminster.

Emulation of England in religion, too, had the side effect of somewhat reducing the cleavage between Colonial South and Colonial North. Until the 1700's approached, Anglicanism—the Colonial form of the Church of England technically under the wing of the Bishop of London—was largely confined to the tobacco country and southward. The first efforts to propagate it elsewhere, which followed a wide administrative revision of Colonial governments, were much hampered by Calvinists' and Quakers' chronic dread of prayer books and bishops. As lurid memories dimmed, however, and Anglophilia grew, many prosperous Bostonians, New Yorkers and Philadelphians of the second or third generation found reason (maybe sometimes spiritual) to abandon their fathers' tenets. Christ Church in Philadelphia joined King's Chapel in Boston and Trinity Church in New York City as brick-and-mortar evidence that Dissent was not to have it all its own crude way in the Northern Colonies. (According to legend, an eminent Rhode Island Quaker wishing to marry a Presbyterian and finding the meeting that he attended inexorably disapproving, said to the lady: "I will give up my religion and thee shall thine, and we will go over to the Church of England, and go to the Devil together." [36]) Such Anglican penetration of local plutocracy had made Quakers a distinct minority in Penn's own Philadelphia well before the Revolution, and there was serious talk of weaning American Anglicanism from the diocese of London and creating special Colonial dioceses and bishops. One end in view was to spare Colonists aspiring to the Anglican ministry a trip to England to be ordained. Doubtless another was to strengthen the resemblance between how things were done at home and among Colonial wearers of silk stockings.

British governors and their suites had their own effect on manners. Corrupt Lord Cornbury, a cousin of Queen Anne's, being both a transvestite and a poor governor of New York, was a doubtful recommendation of Old Country ways. But able governors such as Alexander Spotswood and Robert Dinwiddie (both Scots) in Virginia and William Tryon first in North Carolina and then in New York left marks on Colonial life, as well as on politics and their own personal means; so, quite literally, did Francis Nicholson who personally designed the street plans of two new Colonial capitals, Annapolis and Williamsburg. A governor's impact on his sphere of responsibility did not necessarily have much to do with his relative popularity. The local Quality might squabble with His Excellency over the price at which government took tobacco for taxes, funds for fighting the French, peltry-trade licenses, smuggling and concomitant graft. But for all that, the merchant's or planter's wife narrowly watched His Excellency's lady to see how teacups were now handled, and the merchant's son ably imitated the new oaths imported by the highborn secretary.

Increasingly the Crown strengthened cultural ties between Quality and government by appointing local-born men to the prestige and wide powers of governorship. As the Revolution neared, New Hampshire (John Wentworth), Massachusetts (Thomas Hutchinson) and New Jersey (William Franklin) had such incumbents; two of them had had English schooling. This flattering device gave the Crown the services of knowledgeable Colonists and the support of their local cliques and tended to separate the Colonial Quality from the lower orders in a manner useful as strains increased. As the storm came, all three of these governors clung to the Crown and, along with thousands of Loyalists, mostly from the Quality, suffered exile or worse. In New York a compilation of how leading families took sides shows fifteen Loyalist to only three or four Patriot.

On the frontier—particularly in the Appalachian valleys connecting the several upcountries as the back of a comb holds the separate teeth—American-born settlers were already fusing into hints of a distinct American-to-be. But his emergence was slowed by more than mere lack of inter-Colonial communications in the downslope areas. Where the Scotch-Irish or Pennsylvania Dutch settled in clots, a certain standoffishness persisted, delaying acculturation. On the highway between Charlotte, North Carolina, and Asheboro, North Carolina, one crosses Irish Buffalo Creek and, a few miles farther, Dutch Buffalo Creek, still named as distinctly as the communities created on them two centuries ago. Besides, immigrants from the British Isles kept landing to dilute whatever specifically American ways-of-doing formed in the older settlements. Such newcomers came of widely varying social origins. Lord Fairfax visited Virginia in middle age to look after inherited land grants and soon returned to settle in the Shenandoah Valley as the only English peer resident in America—where he lived out the Revolution supine and unmolested. After service as governor of Virginia, Spotswood stayed on and established an iron industry on his unscrupulously acquired lands. Peter Harrison, a bright young Englishman coming to Rhode Island, became both a successful merchant and America's first notable architect. Captain Charles Cruikshank, a wealthy Scot, bought and settled down on a fine estate on the Schuylkill in 1761. Charles Lee, a flighty soldier of fortune, saw America while in the British

Army in the French and Indian War and soon returned to take up lands in Virginia; when the push came, he joined the Patriots, much to his own and their sorrow. Many lesser figures in British government service threw in their permanent lots with the new country. Other such acquisitions were relatives joining those already established (as did John Paul Jones by way of the West Indies); craftsmen hoping to prosper where competition was slacker; seamen sensing opportunity, like John Barry, Irish merchant skipper who became the Father of the American Navy.

The flow of indentured servants and convicts continued all the while. In this latter phase the relative proportions of stability and ability among them may have been higher. Of seventy-five indentured men landed in Virginia in the ship *Planter* in 1774, for instance, fifty-eight claimed to be of skilled trades; only seventeen called themselves mere husbandmen, grooms and such. As for highly valuable latecomers arriving as free men, what would the Revolution have been had Thomas Paine not tried his luck in America just before it broke out? Or the Constitution without Alexander Hamilton, well into his teens when he came to New York from the Virgin Islands? Eight other Founding Fathers who helped draft it were alien-born.

Philadelphia may have best exemplified Colonial cultivation and the prosperity that it rested on. Jonathan Boucher, English-born and -educated, called it superior "either in size or commerce" to any but five English cities, and likely soon to be "the London of America." [37] For Lord Adam Gordon, several cuts above Boucher socially, it was "one of the wonders of the world if you consider . . . [its] Spacious publick and private buildings, Quays and Docks, the Magnificence and diversity of places of Worship . . . the plenty of Provisions brought to Market . . . the first Town in America . . . [and] bids fair to rival almost any in Europe. It is not an hundred years since the first tree was set where the City now Stands." And note this from this Briton: ". . . the propriety of the Language here surprized me much, the English tongue being spoken by all ranks, in a degree of purity and perfection, surpassing any, but the polite part of London." [38] For Josiah Quincy, Jr., it was a revelation of "numbers, wealth, splendor, luxury, and vice"; of good music; the best bread, "sparrowgrass" (asparagus) and butter he had ever tasted; and of suave refinement in John Dickinson's suburban estate with its gardens, greenhouse, bathhouse, grotto, study, fishpond, "distant prospect of the Delaware . . . paintings, antiques. . . ." [39]

Dickinson was an Inns of Court-trained lawyer-politician who had first done well in his own right and then married a fortune (set at £50,000 to £80,000, equivalent to several million dollars today) with the daughter of Isaac Norris, Quaker plutocrat. An even larger Quaker fortune, based on ninety-odd houses in Philadelphia and an upriver estate, was that of Dickinson's contemporary Samuel Powel. In both cases third-generation money had been shifted from the crude risks of shipping and peltry into urban rentals and mortgages and large landholdings, the same process with which John Jacob Astor created a dynasty in the 1800's. William Allen's case illustrated it in midstream. After elaborate polishing in England at Cambridge as well as at the Inns of Court, he came home, sagaciously employed a tidy legacy from his prosperous Scotch-Irish father in a wide range of projects—shipping, distilling, iron—and reinvested much of the profits in real estate and business loans.

His two daughters were quite as eligible matches as Isaac Norris' girl. One married John Penn, grandson of William, heir to a fourth of the proprietor's interest in the Colony; the other married James De Lancey of New York City, an English-educated, third-generation lawyer-politician and avid sportsman, famous for his fighting cocks and the imported thoroughbreds that earned him the title of Father of the New York Turf. When "King" Carter of Virginia wanted a wife after his two years in England, he chose a sixteen-year-old daughter of the eminent Tasker clan of Maryland. Here is a strong odor of dynasties proliferating and consolidating by marriage. Armorial devices began to appear on the gleaming door panels of the stately, if clumsy, private coaches and chariots that the Quality kept in the port towns. Isaac Norris could not quite bring himself to have a crest on the door of his coach, going no further than gilded initials, but the vehicle itself was as large and shiny as anybody's. In 1770 a Philadelphia printer got out the first work on American genealogy, prophetic of the DAR and implying that the Colonial upper crust meant to become a permanent caste. Abraham Redwood, Jr., son of a West Indian sugar planter, settled in Newport, Rhode Island, united his inherited fortune with that of a local magnate's daughter, and built a fine town house with the warehouse in back on the water and an impressive garden within a brick wall entered by wrought-iron gates ordered specially from England. It all sounds like the similar revolution that filled Elizabethan England with "new men" wangling coat armor for themselves and arrogating to themselves power and prestige based on the profits of trade and the exploitation of newly acquired lands. Only in their case the land had been taken from Catholic monastic houses, not Indians.

Imitation of English great folks' taste for having a countryseat, as well as a town house, naturally followed the cultivation of family trees. John Winthrop's inland farm; Peter Stuyvesant's *bouwerie* outside New Amsterdam; William Penn's elaborate upriver estate—all had shown the way. The town house on Broadway or Society Hill, a sober and (in early terms) opulent three-story affair of brick, stayed in the family. But grandson, who had seen proper use of family money in England, acquired large acreage well out of town—on the far end of Manhattan Island or up the Schuyl-kill—as site for a country mansion as near Mother Country-style as he could manage. The garden plans were usually taken from English hand-books and often carried out by Scottish gardeners attracted to the Colonies by word that these Colonists were mad for gardens and paid high. Dr. Thomas Graeme's place in Bucks County, Pennsylvania, carried faithful copying to the point of including a 300-acre deer park. Colonel John Schuyler's estate near the Passaic Falls in New Jersey was surrounded by five miles of five-rail cedar fence and stocked with English as well as native deer.

Quincy's jottings about Dickinson's place in 1774 are a good summary of how it worked out. The grotto was a current proto-Romantic fad un-mistakably imported from overseas. The "antiques" were either casts or originals of Roman origin bought in Italy by grand-touring young Phila-delphians. The paintings came the same way, more or less professional copies of Raphael, the Carraccis or Guido Reni reverently shipped home to a country still only fumbling at the graphic arts. (About the only can-vases by professionals of good Old Country standing visible in the Colonies were London-painted portraits hanging in the Big Houses of the tobacco country, such as the Byrds' Westover, and a few portraits brought over by the New Amsterdam Dutch.) The style of the country mansion itself, now clear of transplanted medievalisms, was modishly Georgian—our word now, not theirs then. For that was the all-victorious new building fashion whether in town or country, whether in Portsmouth, New Hampshire, or Savannah, Georgia, whether the trees of the new-planted avenue were live oaks in the Carolinas, tulip poplars in Virginia or hemlocks in the Hudson Valley.

Like the formal gardens that went with it, this Georgian style came to America both in homing Colonists' heads and in imported design books published for builders. These showed great English town and country houses, some with mirror-image flanker wings of lower elevation, in any case everything as bisymmetrical as a Rorschach ink spot. Colonial build-ers, their engineering the sounder for a large dash of shipwrights' tradi-tions, ably translated the engraved lines on paper in these books into dwellings of all sizes, churches, town halls and colleges that were, at their best, as handsome as their prototypes in London. Other books supplied precise details for the proper carving of wooden-pedimented doorways, Palladian hall windows, drawing-room paneling and mantelpieces, all in the graceful pseudoclassic motifs dear to admirers of Palladio and Gibbs.

Craftsmen used to handling local pine, black walnut and tulip poplar brilliantly interpreted and often subtly modified these Georgian carving clichés into detail of exquisite quality. As white (or at least pale-tinted) woodwork replaced the old somberness, visibility within the Colonial dwelling improved. It was better still after Europeans skilled in fancy plasterwork arrived to ornament the ceilings with chalk-white wreaths and cherubs. Those unable to afford that hired other artisans to paint the ceiling *trompe l'oeil* to look like molded plaster. Our forebears had no uneasiness about decorative faking. Graining to make a poor wood look like a fine one, marbleizing to make wooden panels look like expensive stone, rustic work to make the outside of a wooden wall resemble cut stone often appeared in the best houses, such as plutocratic Godfrey Malbone's mansion in Newport, Rhode Island, or Sir William Johnson's quasi-feudal manor house, Johnson Hall, in the Mohawk Valley.

At first this wave of building more stately mansions that swept over the Colonial soul, public and private, lacked architects as such. The man who designed Philadelphia's Christ Church, James Porteus, was the only professional in the Colonies in the early 1700's. The planter or vestry wanting new quarters called in a known local builder, studied with him a book of designs, worked out scale and plan, and let him create, without too much fuss about details, a fabric of wood and masonry that served the purpose well and often had an admirable spontaneity. As the thirst for overseas modishness grew, however, professional architects migrated to make careers in America. Robert Smith, a Scottish Quaker, designed for the young College of New Jersey (now Princeton University) Nassau Hall, one of the most original Georgian buildings in the country. John Hawks, brought to North Carolina to carry out his design for the Tryon Palace, was suavely able, if more pedestrian. George Mason, Father of the Bill of Rights, fetched over William Buckland, woodcarver–builder, to glorify the dormered basic design of his new Gunston Hall in the Northern Neck of Virginia. He not only gave Mason a lovely money's worth but also stayed in America (like Hawks) to have the major hand in the Georgian efflorescence of Annapolis. The designer of Miles Brewton's Charleston mansion, the blocky Georgian masterpiece that so impressed young Quincy, which Carl Bridenbaugh calls the handsomest city dwelling surviving from Colonial times, knew the value of being able to advertise himself locally as "House Builder in general, and Carver, from London. . . ."[40]

Such work from immigrant professionals valuably stimulated and refined local practice. Probably, however, though it may be ungracious to say so, the Smiths and Bucklands were not badly needed except to reassure their patrons about getting genuine Mother Country-style design and workmanship. From Portsmouth to Charleston that existing collaboration between builder and patron with book of designs and builder produced an architecture of great virtues—flagrantly derivative, true, but when had Colonial building been anything else? There was little amateurish about the creations of some Colonial magnates acting as, in effect, their own architects. They believed, as did Thomas Jefferson in the next generation, that a well-rounded gentleman should be as much at home with Vitruvius as with Horace and Bacchus. Georgian book designs that had brick primarily in mind were widely translated into Colonial dressed stone. Northern New England did a few in beautifully austere granite. From upper Maryland through eastern Pennsylvania and New Jersey many minor masterpieces in pointed fieldstone survive, often as well-to-do suburbanites' pets, the spotty texture and mellow coloring of the walls setting off the primly painted wood of portico and window trim. Where readily worked stone was scarce, the picture in the book was blithely embodied in wood with small concern for what Palladio or Wren would have said about that. Masonry was visible only in the foundation and the great chimneys at each end which the Georgian canon required instead of the Yankee's central chimney. Faithfulness to the drawing went the length of wooden quoins—the stone blocks forming the corners of many Georgian brick houses.

Here again the availability of wood was shaping America. In general, the horizontal stripings of shadow cast by clapboards painted white or yellow—colors nicely emphasizing the dark-painted, pinned-back shutters—lent a relaxing charm to Georgian proportions. If money ran low, clapboard could be omitted from the back of the house, away from public view, in favor of rough sheathing of shakes painted the old homely beef-red. In churches wood carried out Wren-ish steeples prettily, but a clapboard church of oblong floor plan sometimes had an insipid air, nothing like what dark stone did for Peter Harrison's King's Chapel in Boston. America's wooden Georgian was probably at its best when a railed captain's walk or square cupola was added to the roof, giving the mansion a dash of the trig profile of the old foursquare Yankee meetinghouse. At the other extreme, a Georgian simplified and diluted to its lowest terms, usually in wood but sometimes in grim red brick, always imperturbably bisymmetrical, set rural America's ideal of the prosperous farmhouse for the next three generations. Its use of cubage was too rigid to answer farm needs. The floor plan was ill adapted to northern winters. Nevertheless, it was what Mrs. Farmer wanted as symbol of the family's standing in the community.

How proud she must have been when they moved out of the old clap-boarded double cabin! It is difficult now to realize that such sub-Georgian farmhouses then lacked the venerable overtones of quaintness that please the antique-minded today. The same is true of the mansions of Miles Brewton and William Byrd II as the tourist now sees them. Two centuries ago they were splinter-new, expensive monuments to new money and social climbing. That is why unabashed reproduction—using the original plans to build a vanished building from the foundation up, as in the Tryon Palace—may paradoxically create historical documents nearer truth than the carefully preserved House of the Seven Gables. In the days when His Excellency entertained here among all his fine new furniture from London, the bricks were still in mint condition with sharp edges like those that modern archeologists specified only a few years ago to re-create the old walls. The trees were new-planted and small—like these present replacements. All that clean white plaster and those as yet squeakless floors had that same flourishing sparkle. And conversely, had His Excellency's lady glimpsed the faded, rubbed brocades on sofas now so reverently preserved in the Metropolitan Museum, she would have scolded for ten minutes and sent for the upholsterer.

Withindoors the full-scale Georgian dwelling improved on its semi-medieval predecessor in sometimes so placing stairs and corridors that privacy in bedrooms was possible. Mount Vernon is a good example. Its higher ceilings kept the first floor cooler in summer. Its larger windows and rectangular panes larger than the old diamond-shaped ones gave the interiors more light. Coincidental with Georgian design, a trend toward smaller fireplaces with flared cheeks threw more heat into the room and less up the chimney. Benjamin Franklin's newly invented stove—actually an iron-plate fireplace set out into the room to radiate heat better—was used here and there. But otherwise, comfort and convenience lagged behind elegance. The demands of exterior symmetry put sizable windows where they need not have been. Clothes closets were still almost altogether lacking. For all their wealth and pride the patrician Schuylers in their country mansion near Albany, New York, had to shift for the winter into a smaller attached dwelling, because the large one was hard to keep habitably warm, and to close most of its rooms in summer to keep the swarming flies from fouling the fine furniture with their excreta. That plague went on and on. Thomas Jefferson told with great glee how torture from horseflies biting through silk stockings had had much to do with the speed with which the delegates voted the Declaration of Independence in the summer of 1776. Twenty years later Elizabeth Drinker, the fine flower of self-respecting Philadelphia Quakerism, was writing that, at the family's countryseat, "The flies are so numerous . . . that if I sit still reading or writing for an hour, I find it necessary to wash my face and hands; the reason is obvious." [41]

In some respects, however, civilization was on the way by the time the signers met. For years Philadelphia had had brick sidewalks, much street paving, a kind of streetlight and municipal watchmen patrolling from 10 P.M. to 4 A.M., singing out the hours and the weather Old Country-fashion. Other large port towns were close behind. In most of them public pumps at intervals made water easier to obtain. And as a subtler token of rising refinement the solidifying dynasties of Quality began to embalm their chiefs' dignity in family portraits—and American painting was on its way.

The actual birthplace of American painting was, however, the Colonial tavern. The typical limner (a painter specializing in portraits) of the day had got his start making inn signs. Colonial inns followed the medieval custom of advertising the business within to those without by setting up a tall pole topped by a striking image painted on a board. In the Boston and Philadelphia of the mid-1700's, more literate than any places abroad outside Holland, the device had lost some of its original point, but such signs identifying from afar not only taverns but also the shops of cobblers, glovers, druggists and so on were useful when street signs were few and street numbers nonexistent. So all up and down the Colonial seaboard the Bunch of Grapes, the Blue Anchor, the Ship, the Cross Keys, the White Horse, the Silent Woman (headless, of course), the Indian Queen (also borrowed from England, though she was really Pocahontas come home again) continued to mark out the tavern, inn or ordinary. Vestiges of the old signs remain today in the map names of Red Lion, Pennsylvania, Rising Sun, Maryland, New Jersey's White Horse Pike.

Mere daubing with a steady hand can work out a recognizable blue anchor, ship or bunch of grapes. A red lion or white horse takes higher skill; an Indian queen is even more demanding. There emerged the specialist iconizer able to turn out a combination of high-collared coat, more or less human face and cocked hat to be labeled indifferently the Pitt's Head for the British statesman, or King of Prussia for Frederick II, indispensable ally of England in the Seven Years' War, or the Paoli's Head for the Corsican rebel so popular among the English in the mid-1700's. Then it was a short step—and one often taken after 1700—to putting what was alleged to be the likeness of a pursy Colonial magnate on wood or canvas above the high collar. The consequent portrait usually showed a gentleman in a laced coat or a lady in a low-cut gown with a conical waist, the overall effects so consistently similar that later antiquarians concluded that the painter must have carried around with him made-up can-

vases lacking only the face, painting in the paying patron on the spot.*
While there, the limner might also be knocking off a landscape on the
plaster above the parlor mantelpiece or filling the panels over the dining-
room wainscot with "a grove of trees all looking as uniform . . . as
Quakers at a meeting or soldiers on parade," [42] as Mrs. Sarah Josepha
Hale saw them in her New Hampshire childhood. Before moving on to
the next likely village, he might pay the inn landlord for his lodging and
meals by reverting to his first trade and touching up the fading face and
cocked hat alleged to resemble General Wolfe, the hero of Quebec, on
the creaking sign.

Note that as yet America lacked her own military heroes to name taverns after and that, when they appeared, as in Sir William Pepperell, the
superior prestige of British heroes took priority. Actually Wolfe's nose
was probably of inaccurate shape because early American portrait- as well
as sign-painters usually made that feature pretty much the same in all their
sitters of whatever age, sex or condition of life. Snub or beaked, crooked
or straight, it all came out to a genteel aquilinity or an elegantly tipped
slimness. The same failing can be detected in fashionable Old Country
painters of the same time. The other clichés of costume, composition and
pose beloved by these Colonial limners came from the imported engravings of fashionable painters' depictions of eminent Britons—statesmen,
duchesses, divines and so on—that Colonial booksellers imported along
with the sets of engravings of Hogarth's "Marriage à la Mode" or "The
Rake's Progress" that so often hung on the Colonial Quality's parlor
walls. America had no duchesses and no statesmen of national scope; its
portraits from the best and second-best hands alike were about half of
merchants and their womenfolk, a fourth to a fifth of ministers.

The best Colonial portraits now classed as "primitive" have a posterish,
two-dimensional bite all their own. Sometimes there is a tingle of kinship
with Japanese prints, sometimes an anticipatory whisper of Manet or
Toulouse-Lautrec lacking the genius. Occasionally, as in the portrait
of Mrs. Thaxter in the Old Ordinary at Hingham, Massachusetts, a wonderfully dry dignity of character work appears. The two virtues coincide
in the double portrait by Jessey Grandey of Mr. and Mrs. Barnabas Myrick
in the Sheldon Museum at Middlebury, Vermont. But such successes are
rare among the thousands of surviving examples of the old limners' work. It
would certainly startle them to learn in the other world how seriously collectors of primitives now take their run-of-mine work. The *Larousse Encyclopedia of Modern Art* says dryly that "Naïve painting is perhaps appreciated more in the United States than elsewhere." [43] In a recent set

---

* James T. Flexner (*The Light of Distant Stars*, 210) is impressively firm against
this, but it would be fun if it were true after all.

of catalogue notes for an exhibit of post-1830 American painting, Alfred V. Frankenstein adds a thoughtful note: "We tend . . . to think of primitive painting as a peculiarly American phenomenon, but this is not true; America has simply stressed the primitive more than Europe because America possesses far less art in general to stress." [44]

That sitters willingly paid reasonable sums for such portraits as now clog historical societies and collections of primitives is understandable because they lacked specimens of better portraiture to found higher standards on. Our forebears of the 1700's had sound taste in furniture, silver, Madeira and architecture, but there is no polite way to account for the gap between the elegance of their drawing rooms and the paintings adorning them. It is incredible that anybody should ever have taken seriously the murals of Abraham, Isaac, the ram and other fauna along the stair in the fine Warner Mansion in Portsmouth, New Hampshire. True, they should be carefully preserved and reverently shown, but examined out of context, they would be instantly attributed to the man who used to paint the display posters for the carnival sideshows.

The temper of the leading edge of Colonial painting improved as the 1700's wore on, however, and European artists of some professional status tried their luck overseas. Gustavus Hesselius, a Swedish convert to Moravianism, painted ably in Pennsylvania and had a capable portraitist son. The unpretentiousness of such artists' notions of themselves is clear in their advertisements of willingness to do all kinds of painting "in the Best Manner . . . Coats of Arms drawn on Coaches . . . Landskips, Signs, Showboards, Ship and House Painting . . . Old Pictures clean'd and Mended." [45] Similarly William Williams of New York City, a limner of some repute, "undertakes painting in general, *viz.*, History, portraiture, landskip, sign painting, lettering, gilding . . . cleans, repairs and varnishes . . . and teaches the art of drawing." [46] Among the Pennsylvania Moravians, immigrant John Valentine Haidt turned out half-professional, if lamentable, imitations of Italian Baroque religious paintings to use in teaching Indians the Gospel; one must assume that both the missionaries and the Indians thought them pretty fine. In 1728 John Smibert, a Scot trained in London, accompanied the great Dean Berkeley to New England to teach art in a projected school for Indians. The project aborted, but Smibert married a Boston lady with money and embarked on an influential career of painting eminent Bostonians. His prized copies of Italian masters are thought to have given certain Colonial artists of the next generation their first notion, stimulating though secondhand, of what European painting could be like. In his own right he probably belongs near the top of James T. Flexner's category of Old Country artists working the Colonies because they were "inferior workmen who had been unable to make a good living at home. The product of European provincialism. . . ." [47]

Indeed a pupil of his, Robert Feke of Rhode Island, distinctly outpainted his master. Even more gratifying was the implausible career of John Singleton Copley, stepson of a Boston limner-engraver-schoolmaster associated with Smibert. The boy must have been a natural painter, as Jim Thorpe was a natural athlete. When, in his late teens, he launched into portraiture as necessary livelihood, he can never have seen a canvas from a hand superior to Smibert's or Feke's. Within ten years (1766) a picture of his sent to London got him elected a Fellow of the Society of Artists and the comment from Sir Joshua Reynolds that it was "a wonderful Picture to be sent by a Young Man who was never out of New England and had only some bad copies to study." [48] By 1774, when the impending Revolution sent him to England never to return, he had done numerous portraits as notable for character work, incisive individuality of style and just plain able painting as anything then being done in the Western world. This success made him the first American to show the Mother Country that high esthetic talent could arise in the New World. Writing, painting and building were to be the arts most vigorous in maturing America. It would be generations before any American writer's work had the stature, relative to overseas standards, of Copley's painting.

England had already been deeply impressed by a slightly older Colonial painter, Benjamin West of Philadelphia, who became George III's favorite artist and eventually succeeded Reynolds as president of the Royal Academy. In Pennsylvania he had risen from sign painter to limner of such promise that a group of Philadelphians sent him to Europe to absorb art. That made him the first of thousands—doubtless by now hundreds of thousands—of sometimes talented Americans thenceforth flocking to Rome, later to Paris, Antwerp and Düsseldorf to hone up their sensitivities and geniuses in the correct climate. In Rome in 1760, West struck just the proper tone to please a Europe already sighing after noble savages and expecting a fresh-caught American to know all about them. They showed him the Apollo Belvedere, and he exclaimed, in what language is not clear: "How like a Mohawk warrior!" Such fatuous tactfulness may help account for the ease with which his career caught fire when, all plumped out with newly assimilated art, he reached England in 1763.

Italy had grounded him in the contemporary cult of classic chastity of design, and his grand period dramas on canvas, with everybody frozen in a stage tableau, wearing helmets and tunics or less, are credited with inventing pseudoclassicism for David and other French painters to enlarge on. Presently, however, he produced an anticlassic innovation, painting

British generals in battle scenes clothed not in Roman garb but instead in the scarlet coats, buckskins and top boots that were officers' battle dress in his time. (Not long before, it had been startling for an actor to dress Macbeth as a Scot in plaid and kilt instead of as a contemporary prince in wig and smallclothes.) This daring caught on, eventuating in those shiny pictures of Napoleonic battles and reviews peopled by military tailors' dummies. None of that affects West's professional merits, which, though pedestrian, were not negligible. The best of him, however, was the kindliness with which he welcomed ambitious young Americans to London, not only forming a sort of loose academy of them but going out of his way to use his influence in their behalf with important people. Copley was among those benefiting. Some critics feel that Copley's long career in London was marred by the results of his taking West's rather rhetorical approach to art too seriously. Yet there is stunning work in some of the younger man's grandiloquent historical pieces, and some of his best portraits were done in England. In any case, the Old World's ready adoption of West's innovations is significant because it was the first substantial esthetic repercussion of America overseas. Until then such feedback had been economic and come from below Florida, such as monetary inflation from the influx of Latin-American gold and silver.

Some of that Latin-American silver and a little of the gold, usually as European coinage, trickled northward to constitute the Colonies' chronically scanty circulating medium. Mr. Quality often contributed to that scarcity—of which as businessman he probably complained bitterly—by handing over to a silversmith silver coins with which to make sugar bowls, teapots, porringers, spoons or ladles. Such metal did not altogether lose its economic function. The silversmith, often a kind of banker, as has been noted, would take back his handiwork as collateral for a credit to a client needing ready funds. But most of the time this reshaped metal lacked monetary use. Esthetically it was probably worth the inconvenience. The Colonies' silversmiths were as brilliant as their architect-builders. From Jeremiah Dummer, John Hull's apprentice who also painted the first identifiable American portraits, to Paul Revere, Massachusetts' silver was vigorous and charming. Quaker leaning toward simple design led to high refinements in Philadelphia. Changing English styles, arriving with imported pieces, stimulated and modified the already lively local traditions of Dutch and Huguenot craftsmen. And though the lower orders seldom attained silver, the designs of the Colonial pewterware that served them for show as well as use were happily refined by imitations of the silver on the Quality's sideboards.

By the mid-1700's that sideboard was a worthy setting for elegance— no longer the heavy, angular, coarsely, if strikingly carved, affair of oak of postmedieval look but a silky-finished piece of mahogany with exquisite proportions and dainty imported brass drawer pulls. The dining table, the chairs around it—for by now everybody in Mr. Quality's household had a chair instead of a stool—and the beds, chests of drawers and candlestands upstairs were of equal refinement. The taming of furniture had kept pace with the rise of Georgian design in both the Old Country and the emulous Colonies. Some of the Colonists' best pieces were imports. More often they came from the shops of immigrant cabinetmakers trained to London standards and well able to follow the drawings in their indispensable copies of Chippendale's *Gentleman and Cabinet-Maker's Director.* American boys apprenticed to such masters learned equally high standards of workmanship, but they seldom showed the experimental turn that sometimes gave American houses and silver flavors of their own. Say that in cabinetwork the Colonies came nearest to the Colonial Anglophile's ideal—to approximate Old Country things and ways-of-doing. Their only substantial innovation was the occasional use of American woods, such as tulip poplar and wild cherry.

When Madam Knight, the indomitable schoolmistress, took her rough-and-tumble ride from Boston to New York City in 1704, her escort part of the way was the postrider whose arduous business it was to carry a leather bag of intercolonial mail through all weathers. Sometimes he was a postwalker, plodding through woods and along stream beds, pouch on back, but usually what mails our forebears sent traveled on horseback because hooves were faster than wheels along the primitive but established post roads. Tough as whang leather, the riders spent their lives muddy to the shoulders among ruts, mudholes, freshet-swollen fords and snowdrifts to get one Colonial capital's business letters and presently newspapers to another.

The first such service was set up by Governor Francis Lovelace of New York in 1672 with a monthly horse courier to Boston via Hartford; the rider had a small salary plus pickings from carrying private letters at so much each. He was, Lovelace wrote to Governor John Winthrop, Jr., of Connecticut, as he needed to be, "active, stout and indefatigable,"[49] but he, or anyway the service, lasted only a few months. By 1690, however, renewed efforts had regular service at least nominally established all the way from Portsmouth, New Hampshire, to Philadelphia. Postage was so high as to be out of most persons' reach, so volume was small. When the Revolution began, America had only twenty-eight post offices. But their function was important out of proportion to the scale of operation. The letters that they carried were usually correspondence between magnates about important politics or business. The printed matter—newspapers and pamphlets—was the principal means of spreading secular ideas and also went principally to people who mattered. Thus the postal system—with which Benjamin Franklin was much concerned as the Crown's co-postmaster for all the Colonies after 1753—wove a web of connective tissue among Colonial leaders, gradually tying the separate Colonial polities together across the top.

The miseries of wheeled transport are reflected in the fact that by the time mounted mails were making New York City from Philadelphia in one day, the trip by boat and stage was still taking four. But at least as head-swaying, plodding yokes of oxen gave way to teams of horses, stage wagons were coming into use. In the 1740's travelers could thus cross the narrow waist of New Jersey with more or less regular boat connections at either end, up the bay to New York City, down the Delaware to Philadelphia. These contraptions had no springs; boxlike bodies with cross-benches; canvas tops making them resemble wheeled wigwams; wide-tired wheels to lessen the risk of miring down; and four hapless horses, straining to keep at least nominally in motion over what passed for a road. The horses were much better off in winter snow, when the wheels were replaced by great sled runners called bobs. In bitter weather the passengers, however, seated in so cold and drafty a vehicle, might come uncomfortably close to freezing to death. By 1750 Philadelphians condemned to visit New York City could, if they disliked the saddle so strongly that ordeal by stage seemed preferable, leave "on Mondays from the Sign of the Death of the Fox [an inn] in Strawberry alley . . . [ride] the same day to Trenton Ferry . . . on Tuesday to Brunswick . . . [whence] the wagon of Isaac Fitzrandolph takes them to the New Blazing Star [an inn in what is now Jersey City] the same day, where Robin Fitzrandolph with a boat well suited, will . . . take them to New York that night," [50] making only three days. Memorable ones, though—the wagon benches had no backs, and unless it was raining very hard, it must often have been a relief when the driver had the passengers get out and walk to spare the horses.

A competing service, the Swiftsure, began via Elizabethtown and Trenton in 1761. By 1771 one John Mercereau had the time down to a day and a half in summer, so, without ironical intent, he called his service the Flying Machine. A thirty-shilling fare for insides, twenty for outsides (implying that by then the vehicles were more like the English stagecoach with seats on top) ruled out all but prosperous patrons. But at least such services persisted and encouraged catalytic intercourse, however painful to purse and person, between Colonial towns. Similar services linked Philadelphia with Baltimore, Annapolis and soon upper Virginia over dismally similar roads. A two-wheeled, two-horse affair called a curricle was carrying three passengers per weekly trip from Boston to Portsmouth, New Hampshire, in two days. In 1767 a stage wagon linked Boston to Providence, whence boats went to New York City via Narragansett Bay and Long Island Sound. The Sound remained so much better a highway than anything on land that New York to Boston stages did not appear until 1790. Except for that gap, however, the Colonial traveler just before the Revolution could go in public wheeled conveyances from the Potomac to the Piscataqua—a good half of the seaboard of the nation-to-be.

Private conveyances had a longer history, albeit they were in very limited use. Boston is known to have had a coach in 1679; New York by 1674 for the governor's use. In 1686 the rowdiness of a Boston coaching party scandalized Samuel Sewall "about 9. aclock . . . singing as they come, being inflamed with drink . . . curse, swear, talk profanely and baudily to the great disturbance of the Town and grief of good people." [51] They may have chartered the coach-for-hire known to have been then available in Boston. Gradually the number of private coaches and chaises (one-horse, two-wheeled) increased. So did the quality of roadways and the venturesomeness of drivers. By the 1740's the roads fanning out from town were good enough to make it worthwhile to operate roadhouses to which one drove out for tea and fresh air on nice days. James Birkit, a West Indian visitor to New England in 1750, admired the smooth graveled roads encountered as far north as Exeter, New Hampshire. In 1754 a Harvard tutor named Flynt, having business at Portsmouth, New Hampshire, risked the trip in a chaise with an undergraduate as driver; the boy's heedlessness let them in for a jolt so severe that the Reverend Mr. Flynt was thrown out on his venerable head but with no harm that milk punch at a handy tavern could not assuage. Presently Governor Jonathan Belcher, the cultivated Yankee whom the Crown had sent to govern New Jersey, was boasting that his four spanking trotters could whisk him from Burlington to the Philadelphia ferry, say 17 miles, in two hours—which implies fair road surface. Even in scantily settled Virginia, Lord Adam Gordon found in 1764 that the Quality's six-horse coaches could do 8 or 9 miles an hour for 60-mile stretches: ". . . you may conclude from this that their Roads are extremely good." [52] In relative terms, you may; only the standards of the time, even in England, were incredibly low, and remember that there was nothing all-weather about the best roads. They were tolerable only in summer, unless one's coach, like that of John Hancock's plutocratic father, was designed to go on runners in wintertime.

Not until a private company built the first American turnpike from Philadelphia to Lancaster, Pennsylvania, in the 1790's did American

horses know anything like what we now call a highway. Until then almost all four-wheeled vehicles seen far from town were freight wagons
and the few stages. Restriction of coaches to a radius of a few miles from
the town house mattered less, however, because their chief purpose was
urban display anyway. A late-1700's edition of the *New England Primer*,
moral guide of New England's children, promised that:

> He that ne'er learns his A, B, C,
> For ever will a Blockhead be;
> But he that learns these Letters fair
> Shall have a Coach to take the Air.[53]

When he got it, its panels gleamed with red, blue or green paint, and he
did his best to convince himself that its thoroughbraces—heavy leather
straps where later makers used springs—really did reduce jolting. The
coach was the outward and visible sign of success like a chauffeur-driven
limousine. Just before the Revolution eighty-four Philadelphia families
had one—or the slightly less elaborate chariot that was almost as imposing. "Almost every Gentleman of Condition," Fithian wrote of Virginia
in 1774, "keeps a Chariot and Four; many drive with six horses." [54] But
it caused much comment in Philadelphia when William Allen went to six
horses—matched black ones. The wife of Joseph Galloway, another
wealthy Philadelphian who remained Loyalist, had her carriage seized
and sold by the Patriots and was outraged when "as I was walking in the
Rain, My Own Chariot drove by . . . what wou'd [her daughter] say
to see her Mama walking five squares in the rain at Night like a common
woman . . . all will be right yet & I shall ride when these Harpies walk
as they Use to do." [55]

What kept most Colonial coaches rolling was, of course, the vigorous
economy of the port capitals, the result of our forebears' zeal to exploit the
biological riches of the New World, wild or under cultivation, upcountry
or offshore. Barring iron and the copper of northern New Jersey, the great
day of mineral riches was still to come.

Such Colonial enterprise did not always bear looking into. For all the
elegance of the lady in the coach, a chief prop of her affluence was probably smuggling, directly or indirectly. Basically each Colonial region had
specialty exports: rice, naval stores and indigo from the Carolinas; tobacco from the Chesapeake area; cereals and meats from the Middle
Colonies; fish, rum and timber from New England. But common to all
and usually driven by the same merchants was a broad and lucrative illicit

import and export trade in systematic defiance of the laws meant to keep the Colonies profiting the Mother Country exclusively. From Portsmouth to Savannah dislike of England's Navigation Acts, Molasses Act and so on combined with high, middle and low corruption to make a shrewd lawless-less bulk large in Colonial development.

The Yankees may have been first. By the late 1600's their coasting shallops and ketches trading into the Carolina sounds and the creeks of the Chesapeake were taking tobacco in payment for hardware, wooden-ware and salt, landing the tobacco at home, and reexporting it to Spain, say, in return for Canary wine for thirsty Colonial gentry. A rewarding trade—but unlawful at every step. England required all Colonial tobacco to go to England, and the Colonials were forbidden to trade for wine directly with any nation but Portugal, England's ally. Just as in the peltry trade, however, law was one thing, gain another. Slack enforcement made it easy to land hogsheads of tobacco after dark and reship them as salt fish for Madeira (Portuguese) with no official check on what they really contained; land them in Vigo or the Canaries (Spanish); load up with Spanish wine, then touch at Madeira to pick up a few additional casks of local wine for the customs at Boston to sample as camouflage for the illicit Canary deeper down in the hold. An emissary from Virginia to Massachusetts reported there was plenty of Canary wine in Boston in 1690. Sixty years later at Portsmouth, New Hampshire, James Birkit noted that Canary was the wine most drunk among his hosts.

The many variations on that pattern were clever and usually profitable. As America grew West Indies-minded, the Dutch and French sugar colonies proved as likely customers as British Barbados and Jamaica for fish, salt meats, cereals and lumber, and no mere laws of Parliament's passing deterred Yankees, Philadelphians or the rising Scottish merchants of Norfolk, Virginia, from exploiting that situation. Back from Martinique or Surinam came small but highly welcome sums of silver and gold and illicit molasses, illicit sugar, illicit silks and laces, illicit brandy and Dutch gin. "Some of their Chiefe men," Birkit learned in Philadelphia, ". . . drive on a very large and contraband trade with the French . . . to the great damage of the Honest and Fair trader." [56] Much of the wealth that Peter Faneuil put into the civic hall that still honors his name came from smuggling so extensive that the only proper comparison is with the rum-running of the 1920's—and even that bulked smaller relative to the total economy of the time. The secret compartments so often built into Colonial dwellings of the 1700's, now usually identified by the costumed hostess as hideaways for runaway slaves, were actually all too likely meant for safe storage of low-bulk, high-value smuggled goods.

Such free trade (a jaunty euphemism) flourished even during England's wars with France, Holland or both. This slackness about trafficking with the enemy need surprise nobody. The same thing went on across the English Channel and the North Sea heavily in peacetime, substantially even in wartime. Late in the 1700's William Pitt publicly stated that duty had been paid on less than half the 13,000,000 pounds of tea annually consumed in England. Smuggling, G. M. Trevelyan says, "added to the interest of the people's lives almost as much as poaching, and was regarded as equally innocent." [57] Thomas Amory, eminent merchant of Boston, wrote to a beginner in 1721 that it was easy "to import all sorts of goods from . . . France and Spain, though prohibited . . . [instruct] the Captain not to declare at the Custom House. . . . There are no waiters [customs watchmen] kept aboard [arriving ships]." [58] What few Crown officers were assigned to customs work usually understood well enough that their function was not so much to block illicit imports as to take some 10 percent of the rough value to line their own and their superiors' pockets and look the other way. A reform-minded governor of New York in the early 1700's reported that under his predecessor smuggling had been so extensive that though the port's trade was risen 300 percent, His Majesty's revenues had fallen 50 percent.

Soon all involved, from the merchant in his countinghouse to the foremast hand in his ship, took these arrogated privileges as established rights and were outraged when sporadic enforcement checked the flow of smuggled goods. Thus in 1719 a customsman at Newport, Rhode Island, who had the audacity to seize some hogsheads of illicit French wine was jailed on a trumped-up charge preferred by a Quaker merchant-magistrate while a waterfront mob made off with the evidence and stove it in. It sounds like—and was—a presage of the Boston Tea Party. Indeed not least of the causes of the Revolution was the dismay of the Colonial port towns faced after the Seven Years' War with intensified Crown enforcement of laws theretofore half-disregarded. Doubtless part of what stirred up the Tea Party, for instance, was resentment of Parliament's insistence on its taxing power. But another was fear lest the new situation wipe out the long-standing price advantage that the smugglers' tea enjoyed over that of lawful importers. Minor tea parties in other Colonies showed that Boston smugglers were not the only ones troubled. John Hancock, whose signature on the Declaration of Independence now symbolizes a great life insurance company, was simultaneously and not at all accidentally a Revolutionary leader and an outstanding free trader. Many of the dodges that illicit slave ships used in the 1800's to thwart international measures against the slave trade—such as carrying two sets of papers, both false, and shipping captains of several nationalities to deal with various shore authorities—had been well developed by respectable American merchant smugglers long before the slave trade was outlawed.

Many such Colonial merchants and Crown officers scrupled not to league themselves with pirates. As early as 1647 Major Edward Gibbons, organizer of the Bay Colony militia, though once a member of the peltry-trading gang at Merry Mount, came back from a trading voyage to the West Indies with what was obviously loot acquired from buccaneers—and was allowed to dispose of it profitably, no questions asked. Later the wars against Louis XIV encouraged privateering under several flags. Control of privateers being always lax, the line between them and pirates, seldom clear, practically disappeared; and merchants in Charleston, New York, the Rhode Island ports and Boston eagerly bought prize goods from highly dubious privateers. The shadier it got, the more advisable it was to cut Crown officers in—which increased the already large possibilities of personal gain in an appointment to a Colonial governorship.

Certain notorious pirates, who made no pretense of having privateer commissions, began to prey on the rich shipping of the Indian Ocean and set up a shore depot in Madagascar for convenience in refitting. Supply ships went out to them there under commission from Governor Benjamin Fletcher of New York, who got $100 per crew member in each ship, plus costly presents for himself, wife and daughter, and substantial cuts for the local merchant members of his official council. The owners of the supply ships could afford handsome bribes, for they made almost 3000 percent on rum sent outward and high profits on East Indian loot brought back. (One such owner was James De Lancey, fortune-founding grandfather of that horsey young New Yorker who married one of William Allen's daughters.) When Thomas Tew, head of the pirates' depot on Madagascar, visited New York City, Fletcher entertained him and rode about with him in the official coach. When his superiors remonstrated, he replied that he was treating the fellow well in the hope of curing him of his shocking habit of swearing. Fletcher's successor tried to break up such alliances between New Yorkers and pirates but merely stirred up a hornet's nest of eminent citizens telling him to mind his own business. Relations were just as cordial between the Quality of the Carolinas and Edward Teach, alias "Blackbeard," privateer turned pirate and maybe the most psychotic ruffian in the business. This curious and widespread tolerance disappeared only with the gradual dwindling of piracy. Retired pirates such as Captain Thomas Paine of Newport, Rhode Island, and Captain Giles Shelly of New York lived free-spending lives unmolested to the end of their days.

During the Seven Years' War several Colonial governors made a good thing of taking bribes to grant ship captains permission to visit the enemy's sugar islands ostensibly to exchange prisoners of war—two or three prisoners being a mere pretext for a richly profitable smuggling voyage to Cap-Français or Monte Cristi. The power to make land grants was even more lucrative. Sometimes local magnates were the direct beneficiaries with bribery certain under the table, as when half of 25,000 acres set aside for Scotch-Irish immigrants in upper New York in 1764 wound up in the hands of Oliver De Lancey and Peter Du Bois of the governor's entourage. Sometimes the governor himself was the owner under one or another cloak. He probably owed his appointment to personal connections at home who assumed that to fill his own pockets and take care of his friends was a governor's main purpose. Such behavior in office trained the Colonists in bribery, chicanery and disrespect for law. Not that they needed many lessons. The atmosphere of swindling pervading the peltry trade and land deals with the Indians had already greatly eroded whatever consciences the settlers had brought ashore. In the same year when Major Gibbons was selling buccaneers' loot in Massachusetts, the newish settlement of New Amsterdam was struggling against smuggling and had already developed the speakeasy; a third of the local taverns were illegal, and all, legal ones too, ignored the council's ban on selling drink on Sunday. Nor can this early talent for lawlessness be ascribed to resentment of authority natural among immigrant convicts and indentured refugees from Old Country slums. Land scandals (in New Hampshire), wholesale smuggling (in Massachusetts), cordial dealings with pirates (in Rhode Island) were also quite lively in New England, which got so many fewer convicts and servants.

Yet there were regional differences in moral tone. Massachusetts at least, as Samuel Eliot Morison points out, "never passed through the lawless, gun-toting, frontier-bully stage . . . picturesque but leaving a tradition of lawlessness." [59] Only south of Pennsylvania did backwoods rowdyism include the savage custom of mutilating the loser in a fight by biting off ear or nose, gouging out an eye, occasionally going as far as castration. In the most civilized neighborhood in Virginia in 1773 Fithian described the probable causes of fistfights among "young Fellows. I suppose . . . one has in Jest or reality some way supplanted the other [with a girl]; or has . . . called him a thick-Scull, or a Buckskin, or a Scotchman, perhaps one has mislaid the other's hat, or knocked a Peach out of his Hand, or offered him a dram without wiping the mouth of the Bottle . . . just causes of immediate Quarrels, in which . . . is allowed . . . Kicking, Scratching, Pinching, Biting, Butting, Tripping, Throttling,

Gouging, Cursing, Dismembering. . . ." [60] All these tactics crossed the mountains into the Old Northwest, where the climax of even a "fair holts" fight was likely to be the victor kneeling on the vanquished's belly, thumbs on his eyeballs to be plunged in unless he shouted, "Nuff!" loud and soon. Henry Adams thought that sort of thing reflected the primitive fighting customs of Yorkshire. Others detect a flavor of Scotland. Whatever its cultural ancestry, mark how long and vigorously it persisted wherever Southern-flavored pioneering went, while other Old Country ways of dress, speech, drinking and so on were dwindling away. A population with a high admixture of social misfits might well take most readily to, and cling longest to, so vicious a tradition of personal combat.

But mobbing, which could get very brutally out of hand, was as popular a sport in New England as anywhere else. When a thirty-family group of Scotch-Irish settling at backwoods Worcester, Massachusetts, began to build a Presbyterian church for themselves outside the local Puritan religious frame of reference, their Yankee neighbors, led by respectable men, sawed and chopped it down and burned the pieces. Riding out of town on a rail seems to have first appeared in Boston in 1675, the victim being one John Langworthy who had been working as a ship's carpenter without having served proper apprenticeship. The complementary tar and feathering, an Old Country notion of great age, seems to have been neglected until 1769, when Boston applied it to an alleged informer against smugglers. After that it played a considerable role in Revolutionary disorders. George III, as incapable as most Englishmen of getting Americanisms just right, received exiled Governor Hutchinson of Massachusetts with: "I see they threatened to pitch and feather you." "Tarr and feather, may it please your Majesty," [61] Hutchinson said patiently. "Yankee Doodle" as the British garrison of Boston sang it in 1775 contained:

> Yankee Doodle came to town for to buy a firelock.
> We will tar and feather him and so we will John Hancock! [62]

In Yankee contexts at the right season the victim might be previously stripped and rolled in the snow. Irate neighbors did that to Joseph Smith, the Mormon Prophet, in northern Ohio in the 1830's; twenty years later anti-Drys did it to Temperance zealots in Maine. Such mobs, common in the Old World, proved important in stoking up the Revolution in most Colonies. Local village women sometimes took a hand in the stripping and tarring, as in the case immortalized by Whittier: "Old Floyd Ireson / With his hard heart / Tarred and feathered / And carried in a cart / By the women of Marblehead."

*   *   *

The notion of Yankee housewives, as well as Yankee fishwives, ripping the breeches off objects of community dislike may disconcert those assuming that Colonial—and especially New England—women were as prim as Longfellow's synthetic Priscilla Alden. Consider the crowds of women who welcomed home an unsuccessful Massachusetts military expedition in 1707 by throwing the contents of chamber pots on them, shouting, "Souse, ye cowards!" [63] And the women of Schoharie County, New York, who, when the sheriff came to enforce evictions on some Palatine German squatters, knocked him down, dragged him through the street puddles, rode him on a rail, and sent him home with two ribs broken and an eye missing.

These furies stand out vividly enough, but in general, data on Colonial women is discouragingly meager. Common knowledge goes little farther than Pocahontas (was the Pocahontas who married John Rolfe also the teen-age tomboy of the same name who turned cartwheels naked in Jamestown?); Martha Washington, a sort of shadowy national grandmother; Molly Pitcher, idealizedly vague as legends usually are. What of all the others, all the strapping daughters, many-skilled wives, mothers dead in childbed, devoted old maids, sporadic bluestockings, religious careerwomen, indentured drudges, doughty widows, transported strumpets, witchy old midwives?

The peevish fine lady is quite distinct in the Madam Galloway who took the loss of her chariot so hard. For corrective, there lived in the same 1770's a Mrs. Nott of Connecticut working herself, her two small sons and the family cow, which she put in the plow for lack of better draft animals, very hard indeed to wrest a living for them and her invalid husband out of a stony farm. In midwinter one son wore through his only warm clothes with a finality that ruled out patching. In spring that would have been no crisis. Mrs. Nott was accustomed to shear, spin, weave and tailor the wool from their sheep into clothes for them all. But it was inconceivable to shear a sheep in the dead of winter. She nevertheless sheared one —and wove out of straw from the barn a thick braided overcoat that saw the shivering beast through to warm weather. It must also be eloquent of Mrs. Nott's sterling qualities that though she made her sons walk four miles to church every Sunday, blow high, blow low, neither developed any revulsion against religion; in fact, both became distinguished ministers of the Gospel.

Haddonfield, New Jersey, is properly named for Elizabeth Haddon, a Quaker girl who came to the New World on her own in 1701 to found the town on a 500-acre tract owned by her stay-at-home father, a London merchant. In the process she reencountered and married the Quaker missionary whose account of America in her father's house had inspired her to go there. In the next generation Eliza Lucas Pinckney, English-reared daughter of a British Army officer, managed her father's Colonial interests during his absences on duty and single-handedly founded the indigo culture of South Carolina, which came to rival rice in the Carolina economy. In the 1760's a sensuous-looking young woman named Barbara Heck, born in Ireland of Palatine refugees, caught the new religious enthusiasm called Methodism and raised such a moral storm among her fellow cultists in New York City that she is generally credited with having founded America's first discrete Methodist congregation. A zealous, one-eyed British Army captain named Thomas Webb also had much to do with that pioneer preaching house on John Street. But it was the redoubtable Barbara who drew the plans and, once the men had built it, whitewashed the interior with her own hands.

The postmedieval world from which the Colonists sprang had customarily countenanced women in certain activities other than housewifery. They could, for instance, be midwives, like Anne Hutchinson, whose theological heresies nearly rent the Bay Colony asunder in its early years. Exiled, she contributed her share to the turbulence of early Rhode Island and died with her boots on, so to speak, when the Indians massacred her small colony of heretical true believers settled on what is now Pelham Bay. Women could operate inns and even taverns, as in New York City, where an acceptable provision for a needy new widow was to grant her a free dramshop license. In many striking cases, widows whose husbands left going businesses knew enough about it to step successfully into their shoes. Thus Margaret Hardenbroeck, young relict of a New Amsterdam merchant named De Vries, picked up where he left off, often went supercargo on her own ships and had a nasty name for penny-pinching among the emigrants whom she shipped westbound. After her second marriage to well-off Frederick Philipse, she handled her interests separately from his so well that on her death her estate made him one of the richest men in the Colonies. Mrs. Martha Smith of Long Island carried on the late Smith's shore whaling station. Mrs. Sueton Grant of Newport, Rhode Island, ably managed the small fleet of ships, including several privateers, that Grant left her; once, convinced that her counsel was bungling her lawcase, she rose in court, got the judge's leave to replace him, and won herself a verdict—probably making herself the first woman to practice law in any English-speaking community.

The craftsman's or small tradesman's widow also could take over the shop. When Benjamin Franklin's brother James died in Newport, Rhode Island, where his printshop was issuing the Colony's first newspaper, his widow, Ann, kept the business going. Several Philadelphia printers' widows did the same, and during the Revolution, when William Goddard of Baltimore was too busy to run his printing business and the attached *Maryland Journal,* his sister Mary took over as editor and publisher. John Singleton Copley's mother maintained her dead husband's tobacco shop even after she remarried. One encounters other Colonial widows as retailers of exacting specialties, such as cutlery and optical items, or running small manufactories of coaches, soap, rope, even horseshoeing shops. Not that the lady donned a leather apron and pared hooves; she merely hired competent farriers to keep the shop going. But their willingness to take her orders and supervision shows that the 1700's readily accepted businesswomen.

Maybe some of the resiliency of these managing widows came, for the younger ones anyway, from the lifting of the burden of frequent pregnancy. "I have often thought," Elizabeth Drinker confided to her diary, "that women who live to get over the time of Child-bearing . . . experience more comfort and satisfaction than at any other period of their lives." [64] Sincerely as he was mourned, it remained true that a husband's death greatly heightened a premenopause wife's chances of old age— for childbed was the ailment that, far more than malaria or pulmonary or enteric diseases, filled the graveyards with wives. Only the crudest methods of birth control were known, and few doubted the wisdom of the Bible's advice to "be fruitful and multiply" in an age when scarcity of labor made children an economic asset. Six or seven children in ten years and then a long rest under a slab headstone with a grimacing cherub carved on it were what many a young bride had in store. And young she was; to get beyond the age of twenty-five unmarried was to become an irretrievable old maid; the expectation in upper as well as lower social strata was marriage between sixteen and eighteen. A young groom from a long-lived family background could look forward to two or three successive wives. Captain Hand of Sag Harbor, Long Island, outlived five and buried them all in the same graveyard plot, leaving room in the middle for himself under this equivocal inscription:

> Behold ye living mortals passing by,
> How thick the partners of one husband lie;
> Vast and unsearchable are the ways of God,
> Just but severe his chastening rod.[65]

An especially capable widow was Patience Lovell Wright of Bordentown, New Jersey. Quaker-reared, married to a Quaker much her elder, she was left a widow with three children and small resources. She turned to her long-standing hobby of molding effigies in clay and wax—an art developed in late-medieval Europe for state funerals, then for three-dimensional portraits of literal lifelikeness for living persons. Such a waxworks artist might have a gallery of representations of famous people to show the public with paid admissions—the origin of the Madame Tussaud sort of thing, already known in the Colonies in the early 1700's. By 1771 plucky Mrs. Wright had such a show in New York City with figures of the Reverend George Whitefield, the outstanding evangelist of the day, and John Dickinson, recently noted for his politically potent *Letters from a Farmer in Pennsylvania*. A disastrous fire badly damaged the show, but she supplemented what was left with other figures created by her sister, also a wax sculptor, and took them, herself and her children to London. There, doubtless helped by the introductions that Benjamin Franklin gave her, she prospered exceedingly, about as well and at the same time as Copley. She was noticed by and invited to model the great Earl of Chatham, and by the king and queen, who took a great fancy to her and let her address them Quaker-fashion as George and Charlotte. As the Revolution loomed, she candidly expostulated with George about his mistaken Colonial policy, and the relationship cooled. Nevertheless, her "tall and athletic figure . . . piercing glance . . . simplicity of heart and character" [66] and amusing volubility kept London treating her good-naturedly. She not only stayed in England but managed now and then to smuggle over military and diplomatic information to Benjamin Franklin, who was by then in charge of the new United States' affairs in France.

Too few of her works survive to indicate whatever esthetic qualities they may have shown. If she was an artist, as well as a "Famous Waxwoman" as the *London Magazine* called her, she was a rarity among Colonial-born ladies. The only other Colonial woman portraitist of reputation was probably Irish-born—Henrietta Johnston, wife of an ailing Anglican clergyman of Charleston, first artist in America to use pastels. Her fees for limning Charlestonians and later a few New Yorkers helped keep the household solvent. Watery as they now look, her portraits were a better money's worth than most Colonial-born artists were turning out *c.* 1720, when she flourished.

Also Old Country-born was Anne Bradstreet, America's first lady author. The title page of the volume of her verse printed in England in the mid-1600's dubbed her "The Tenth Muse Lately Sprung Up in America," and since she was of the highest New England Quality—her father had been governor of the Bay Colony—she was endorsed by eminent local clergymen. It is customary for academic criticism to speak respectfully of her verses, but the bulk of them deserve Charles Angoff's remarks about her "jingling, dreadful manner," [67] and if the best of them vanished from libraries tomorrow, it would be a loss to cultural history but not much to literature.* Her pertinence here is that even though her auspices were so august, she still had occasion to complain that:

> I am obnoxious to each carping tongue,
> Who say my hand a needle better fits. . . .

Contemporary reluctance to countenance the bluestocking was well expressed in John Winthrop's account of the sad case of the wife of Governor Edward Hopkins of Connecticut:

> . . . A godly young woman and of special parts . . . fallen into a sad infirmity, the loss of her understanding and reason, which had been growing upon her divers years by occasion of her giving herself wholly to reading and writing, and had written many books. Her husband, being very loving and tender, was loath to grieve her; but he saw his error, when it was too late. For if she had attended to her household affairs . . . and had not gone out of her way and calling to meddle in such things as are proper for men, whose minds are stronger . . . she had kept her wits and might have improved them usefully in the place God had set her.[68]

It was in Philadelphia—center of the Quaker tradition of equal footing for women in matters of mind and soul—that Colonial women first infiltrated letters on any scale. Their leader was Elizabeth Graeme, daughter of that rich physician who set up a deer park. She broke her engagement to William Franklin because of the young fellow's flagrant philanderings and went to England to forget. There she acquired intellectual tastes and social experience and returned to Philadelphia to launch America's first salon for knee-breeched dabblers in arts and letters. Her versifyings under the pseudonym Laura set other local ladies rhyming. So many of the results appeared in local newspapers that a misogynist complained bitterly about the ubiquity and insipidity of a generic "Miss Sappho Hexameter." [69] Actually the best lady poet of Colonial times proved to be an African-born Negro slave girl, Phillis Wheatley, whom her Bostonian

---

* Madam Knight put into her journal bits of verse of much the same caliber, but none of them saw print for 200 years. Madam Bradstreet's best efforts are included in most anthologies of American verse. Since Madam Knight's are not, here is a representative bit, the opening of her verses to the moon lighting her journey:

> Fair Cynthia, all the Homage that I may
> Unto a Creature, unto thee I pay;
> In Lonesome woods to meet so kind a guide,
> To Mee's more worth than all the world beside. . . .

owners, struck by the child's intelligence, encouraged and educated. Her rhymes, mostly in the heroic couplets then fashionable, were well received in both England and America and, though of no great distinction, were as good as much then published in the Mother Country.

Obviously Colonial society, being provincial, lagged behind Europe in giving countenance to feminine intelligence. The Reverend Mr. Burnaby complained of Virginia's ladies in 1760 that they were "seldom accomplished . . . unequal to any interesting or refined conversation . . . immoderately fond of dancing . . . but . . . chiefly spend their time in sewing and taking care of their families; they seldom read . . ." [70] There is confirmation in Thomas Jefferson's advice to his daughter, who was reared in the very generation that Burnaby described, to be sure to learn needlework because in American country life "a woman can [often] have recourse to nothing but her needle for employment. In a dull company and in dull weather for instance. It is ill manners to read; it is ill manners to leave them; no card-playing there among genteel people; that is abandoned to blackguards. . . ." [71]

On the other hand, notions about clinging vines did not reach full tenacity until the Romanticism of the late 1700's had permeated first Europe and then the New World. In any case clinging vines would hardly have thrived in the barefoot, root-hog-or-die atmosphere of hominy-pounding and rawhide with which every Colony began. When a settler came down with the "fevernager," his woman had no choice but to turn her hand to many things that were normally his tasks. *The Plain Dealer* and Defoe's novels make it clear that in later Stuart times the English took for granted the ability of certain women, some respectable, some not, to fend for themselves far more freely than they did in the 1800's. Certainly such redoubtable immigrants as Eliza Pinckney and Barbara Heck—and dozens of others less conspicuous—were the kind so feelingly described in *Ruggles of Red Gap* by Cousin Egbert Floud in speaking of an American lady relative—she could, he said, fight a rattlesnake and give it the first two bites.

Women of the Colonial Quality also lacked several other traits of the high Victorian clinging vine. They drank spirits freely not only at table with water but often in the jolting form of that prebreakfast eye-opener. They not infrequently smoked pipes, a survival from the Colonial 1600's, when an immigrant Frenchman observed with astonishment that in Virginia before entering the church on Sunday, and after leaving it, the entire congregation, minister, women, children of both sexes, as well as men, stood around gossiping and smoking. A hundred years later Elizabeth

Drinker took it as nothing out of the way when she found her good friend, Hannah Pemberton, of the topmost rung of Philadelphia Quality, "smoking her pipe with 2 [British] officers, one of whom is quartered there." [72] They took snuff as frequently as any elegant ladies in the England of the day. In the summer they often had the good sense to go without stays, a breach of European decorum. And they used—or were well accustomed to hearing—profane and obscene terms. The wife of a North Carolinian interested in land grants had no reason to wince when the tract under discussion was spoken of as near Slap-Arse Swamp; the documents had no other name for it. Poultices for rattlesnake bite were made of the irritant leaves of a plant known, for easily imagined reasons, as arsesmart. Piss-oak was the common designation for a species so difficult to dry out that water ran out of its ends when it burned. A visitor happened to mention feminine hysterics to a prominent New York merchant, who, "pretending to discover to me an infallible cure . . . spoke good neat bawdy before his wife, who did not seem much surprised at it." [73] Anne Blair of Williamsburg wrote to her married sister in 1768 a vivacious account of a wind-breaking match between two aristocratic local belles.

Such data hardly imply that a dinner party at a Maryland Big House in 1750 sounded like Mark Twain's *1601*, only that its gay give-and-take might well have dismayed your grandmother. It can be assumed that Philadelphia's Quakerishness made local decorum stricter than, say, Virginia's, yet surviving diaries of some of the most gently reared girls in town show that they had the run of the bawdiness in the novels of Fielding and Smollett. An outspoken culture "at home" meant outspokenness in the Colonies, too.

Whether behavior was equally free is difficult to judge. Evidence on the actual ways of men with maids is necessarily ambiguous. Bundling, that "wicked and base custom of these parts," [74] was as common in the Middle Colonies as in New England, and overstepping doubtless occurred in many cases. A good snow sent New York's Quality youths and maidens off in one-couple sleighs under laprobes, and toll was certainly freely collected at the Kissing Bridge at the upper end of town. The diaries of William Byrd II and Lucinda Lee Dalrymple give the impression that in Virginia after the gentlemen had had their Madeira in a houseful of ladies of assorted ages, there was much slap and tickle about the proceedings. Yet years among the Quality of the Northern Colonies convinced the officers of Rochambeau's French regiments that the incidence of marital fidelity among their hostesses was very high, and they marveled at the grace and skill with which unmarried daughters parried involvements, though allowed "the same degree of liberty which married women [have] in France and which married women here do not like." [75] There, already well developed, is that special romping freedom for girls with which America disquieted European visitors all through the 1800's.*

Outside New England erotic freedom for men was wide; at least known data make Colonial leaders sound fairly free and easy, and there is no reason to suppose the lower orders more straitlaced. Benjamin Franklin owned to at least one and possibly two bastards. The powerful father of Robert Morris, fiscal hero of the Revolution, had two by an established mistress. William Franklin turned a bastard of his over to father Benjamin to rear. The wooden leg of Gouverneur Morris, brilliant Quality politician of New York, was widely attributed to an accident incurred during a gallant episode. In the 1720's Philadelphia's most renowned libertine was a local Anglican parson. At Newport, Rhode Island, a visitor strolling with a local merchant and an eminent local physician encountered "a handsome bona roba in a flaunting dress [who] laughed us full in the face," [76] and the physician confessed to being at least her temporary keeper.

Such professionals were scarce, Rochambeau's officers reported, in smaller settlements. Even in Williamsburg, small but a provincial capital, William Byrd II found whores few. In the fall-line depots for the peltry trade, however, certain women, white or Indian, were accessible, and the largest towns, all seaports, hence with special demand for prostitutes, had no lack of them. Boston was well supplied by the 1670's and seems to have remained so. The riverbank half cellars in which the early Philadelphians lived eventually became brothels. In New York City in the 1740's the Battery was the place to pick up a woman. By the 1770's prostitutes were settled 500 strong—nearly 2 percent of the population—in an area grinningly known as Holy Ground because Trinity Church owned it. The land that Trinity gave as the site for King's College, embryo of Columbia University, abutted on this nest of brothels, which caused comment. In Southern seaports, once slavery was well established, what might be called chattel prostitution—a nasty side effect of slavery—may have discouraged white prostitutes. It was by no means only seamen who kept the girls flourishing in Northern ports. Benjamin Franklin often went to Philadelphia's strange women as a young man. The young rakes with whom Dr.

---

* A hint of lesbianism to match the occasional streak of male homosexuality in Colonial life comes from Moreau de St.-Méry, not a first-class witness: The women of Philadelphia, he wrote, being "without real love and without passions, give themselves up at an early age to the enjoyment of themselves; and . . . are not at all strangers to . . . unnatural pleasures with persons of their own sex." (*American Journey,* 286.) No doubt Philadelphia had such cases in his day, just as Dr. Benjamin Rush had alcoholic women among his patients of all classes. But Moreau was an outstanding example of the inability of so many French writers describing America, right down to Simone de Beauvoir yesterday, to abstain from overweening generalizations.

Hamilton drank at a tavern in New York City in the 1740's talked lovers and ladies genteelly but, as the shank of the evening neared, went awhoring as coarsely as any foremast hand or James Boswell.

Apparently our Colonial forebears were, not surprisingly, men of their time and acted like it. This glance at Colonial gallantry requires the story of Agnes Surriage of Marblehead, Massachusetts. Daughter of a fisherman, though her maternal grandfather had been an English merchant of standing, she was earning a living as a maid of all work at the Fountain Inn in Marblehead in the 1740's. Charles Henry Frankland, collector of HM Customs at Boston, happened to go to Marblehead on business and also happened to come upon Agnes scrubbing a floor and showing, legend says, a good deal of bare foot and ankle and, when she looked up, a very pretty, fine-skinned white face framed in black ringlets. Frankland is said to have begun the acquaintance by giving her a crown piece to buy shoes with, continued it by persuading her parents to let him pay for having her schooled in Boston, and eventually set her up as his mistress. When living with her caused too much outcry in Boston, he moved her to a handsome house that he built on his 480-acre tract at Hopkinton, Massachusetts. Meanwhile, he had become Sir Charles by succeeding to the baronetcy of an uncle who had been a Lord of the Admiralty. In 1754 he went home and fondly took Agnes along. His family looked askance at her, so the couple went to live in Lisbon. There the great earthquake of 1755 caught Frankland and buried him in wreckage. Agnes came desperately looking for him and saved his life, some said by actually tearing away the beams and stones herself. In any case he emerged so grateful to both Providence and Agnes that he married her. Touched by the new Lady Frankland's devotion, his family accepted her. The happy pair returned to Boston, where she became a leader of the Boston Quality, then at the height of its pre-Revolutionary elegance; Frankland died; she went home when the Revolution grew serious, soon married a banker. . . .

Oliver Wendell Holmes personally looked into all the ascertainable facts of the case and then wrote a flimsy narrative poem about Agnes. Otherwise, one would be sure that this was the plot of an unpublished novel by Samuel Richardson.

Charles and Mary Beard maintain in their *A Basic History of the United States* that as the Revolution neared, the Colonies' average literacy exceeded that of any of their Old Countries—England, Scotland, Ireland, France, Holland, Germany—meaning it was highest in the world at the time. Though unverifiable by statistics, that was probably true and a great credit to Calvinist and Quaker insistence on reading as the road to righteousness. It was no ground for boasting, however. By our standards average literacy in Europe was extremely low, and the best that could be said for America was that hers was higher and rising. From any absolute point of view, Colonial education was sporadic, seldom in skillful hands and ill organized.

Of all the aspects of the Colonies that resist generalization, this is stubbornest. Opportunity for the average child to learn to read at least stumblingly ranged from very poor in the South to theoretically good but actually only fair in New England. The scattered nature of Southern settlement discouraged schools. A schoolroom is pointless unless a certain number of potential pupils lives near enough to reach it in most weather; this is why in the early 1800's in upper New York State school districts were calculated to include the homes of children not more than four miles away, the distance a child of school age was assumed to be able to walk twice a day. On the separate large Southern plantations the master's children often had tutors, usually from Britain or a Northern Colony, practically never of local origin—this dearth of Southern-reared tutors is eloquent of the shortcomings of Southern schooling. The tutor might take into his schoolroom—typically the lower story of a small separate building in the loft of which he slept—children from nearby plantations with a small fee for his services. Or—though this could not be counted on—the local Anglican parson might be decent, sober and literate enough to eke out his scanty stipend by an old-field elementary school of logs or plank near the parsonage, supposing it central enough for pupils to come by horseback. Thus Quality children, girls as well as boys, were exposed to reading, writing, elementary ciphering and maybe a smattering of Latin for the boys. Quality of instruction varied with the inborn teaching talent of the given tutor or parson, whose own schooling had probably had more birching than brains in it. The planter himself, like Patrick Henry's father, might teach a promising son Greek and Latin, or a mother or maiden aunt might take sons and daughters through whatever elementary grounding she possessed. Only in a few sizable settlements—Norfolk, Charleston, Annapolis—was it worth a general schoolmaster's while to keep open for tuition-paying offspring of local Quality, as Charles Willson Peale's father did.

Even those sketchy facilities served only a small top layer of society. Below that Southern education hardly existed. The smaller tobacco farmers gradually relinquishing the Piedmont to the big planters; the settlers in the pinewoods clearings and on the bends of the creeks living hand-to-mouth on corn, hogs and game; the peltry traders in and out of the woods; the crossroads craftsmen shoeing horses, repairing wagons, tanning leather, making saddles—not to mention the largely submerged Negro slaves—had mostly had illiterate parents and stayed illiterate. In the high upcountry, where Calvinism and Lutheranism fostered Bible reading among the Germans and Scotch-Irish, the alphabet was likelier to be part of the common man's world. But his lip-moving reading of print did not necessarily imply that he could also write. Too many of him had to mark X on documents.

Snobbery and nostalgia did the Southern Quality a favor in moving them to send their sons home for secondary schooling. Only thus could they maintain the cultivation evident in some planters' sizable private libraries and the skillful writings of Southern Colonial leaders. Eventually —though it took generations—the climate implied in this lettered leadership raised William and Mary from a mere academy offering little beyond penmanship and Latin grammar to something like an institution of higher learning. Some of its alumni, such as Thomas Jefferson and Edmund Randolph, were highly cultivated men who had never seen Old Country universities. Lord Adam Gordon noted in 1764 that "many [Virginian] gentlemen . . . have never been out of their own Province, and yet are as sensible, conversable and accomplished . . . as one could wish." [77] It is clear in the cases of Jefferson, Edmund Pendleton, George Mason, George Wythe, Patrick Henry and so on, however, that most Virginians noted for learning and acumen, as well as integrity, among the Founding Fathers were basically self-educated, owing far less to formal schooling than to their own buying, borrowing and devouring of books. For some temperaments that is a good way to learn, as many Americans have shown since. These amazing Virginians had thus to ripen their minds without access to the rich public libraries that we have long known as the universities of the self-schooled. In 1775 the only two nonprivate libraries south of the Mason and Dixon Line were the good small law library at William and Mary and the subscription general library supported by the Quality of Charleston.

In that and most other respects things were much better north of the Chesapeake. In Philadelphia in 1731 Franklin had founded America's first proper subscription library—as vital to New World culture as his demonstration of the electricity in lightning was to physics. Fruitful imitations sprang up in New York (1754), Boston (1756) and then in other Colonial capitals. This device—essentially the pooling of the book-buying resources of the literate—was particularly needed because of the outrageous dearness (in terms of real wages) of books in the days before power presses and cheap paper had revolutionized publishing. Three dollars a volume for a history of Charles V sounds reasonable until one reflects that this was maybe two days' wages for a skilled journeyman. To amass "King" Carter's library of some 1,500 volumes, second-largest in Virginia, must have cost as much as a 300-ton deep-sea ship.

The South-North contrast was also sharp in higher learning. When the Revolution came, the South had only William and Mary above the secondary level. Each Northern Colony had at least one such institution; New Jersey had two, the College of New Jersey (now Princeton) and Queen's College (now Rutgers). The curricula of all were narrow, but their very existence was of high significance. Private secondary schools in Philadelphia in the mid-1700's were good enough to attract from other Colonies boarding pupils preparing for eventual entrance into Old Country universities. The city's church-sponsored schools (Quaker, German-Lutheran, Presbyterian, Anglican) taught likely boys on a semi-scholarship basis on the same benches as the sons of the Quality. Indeed Carl Bridenbaugh rates the school facilities of not only Philadelphia but also Boston and Newport, Rhode Island, of the early 1700's as better than anything England had outside London—a verdict still impressive after one is reminded that English school systems were also very fragmentary, in fact, not systems at all.

In the port capitals the apprentice system filled in some educational gaps for the sub-Quality boy. The indenture binding him for a set term of years to a shopkeeper or locksmith to earn his keep while learning the trade usually required the master to see that he learned to read and write English and do elementary bookkeeping. Literacy is not exactly essential to craft skills or business profits; witness the fine work of West African goldsmiths and the keen dealings of West African market mammies. But the handiness of figures and the written word in commerce is obvious, and a craftsman-to-be was more useful to his master, as well as to himself, when able to read written instructions, write specifications for materials, and calculate areas and dimensions in laying out work. In the Western world, of course, those same three R's are the basic tools of general learning and cultivation. So Colonial master craftsmen either taught them to the apprentices or paid the many local private teachers to do so. It was after-hours work; Copley's stepfather advertised in Boston "Mr. Pelham's Writing and Arithmetical School . . . open from Candle-Light till nine in the Evening, as usual, for the benefit of those employ'd in Business all the daye." [78] Ambitious journeymen, too, paid fees for instruction in simple accounting, navigation, the key European languages, sometimes in trade-sponsored schools, sometimes to free-lance teachers. It was all a sporadic anticipation of the business college night-school.

At first the Bay Colony had much the most cultivated Colonial population. Except for hired and indentured servants probably all Puritans arriving in 1630 could read and write, and the ratio of university graduates to total population was higher than in any nation then or today. To maintain that was the purpose of the educational system that the Puritans soon put into effect. The town school prepared all children to learn to fear God by reading. The grammar school in the principal village in the neighborhood trained the cream of the boys—a selection usually based on social status, as well as brains—in the languages needed to study the humanities and theology. Then Harvard fitted the likelier grammar school boys for the pulpit or, when vocation to the ministry was weak, secular politics. But within a generation of the first laws requiring towns to provide and support such schools, enforcement began to fray at the edges, as so often happens in America. Universal literacy, the intended end, was often narrowly interpreted to mean mere ability to put up a show of reading. That was easily faked in a system perfunctorily administered, committed to learning by rote, and seldom using texts better than the hornbook—an alphabet and a few short sentences on a piece of paper protected by a sheet of transparent horn—and the meager, religion-fraught *New England Primer*. Enforced attendance was not yet thought of. Parents preferring to teach their own children were allowed to do so with few checkups on results. As the efficacy of the legislative broom wore away, towns began altogether to neglect to provide schools or teachers. When fined for it, they often chose to pay year after year rather than go into the more expensive and bothersome education business. And the longer that went on, the harder it was to find literate, let alone competent, teachers.

In remote places home teaching was the principal resource. Having studied the gnarled spelling and crabbed hands of family records from the Buzzards Bay country of the 1700's, W. R. Bliss says: "The wonder is that [these isolated Yankees] could write at all. When we consider that there were but few schools . . . of short duration, and of low grade, that all laws intended to maintain schools had been, as the legislature declared, 'shamefully neglected,' we must attribute the ability of the farmers to write as well as they did to an education received by the fireside at home." [79] Here may have been reflected the falling off of the old system of settlements compactly clustered around the nucleus-green with schoolhouse as well as meetinghouse and tavern. As Yankees settled on their outlying farms in defiance of authority, literacy seemed less and less pertinent to the daily concerns of woodchopping and corn, apple, cattle and sheep culture. That is, rural New England was sliding toward the fecklessness about learning common elsewhere as one approached the frontier.

Large settlements and conscientious small ones cobbled up a slack system of "dame schools"—a borrowing from England—in which superannuated or single and usually fairly ignorant women taught small fry their letters for small fees often supplemented from town funds, plus more advanced "moving schools," also with some tax support, held in improvised quarters in various parts of the township in succession. Here and there grammar schools survived from the original scheme to be of great value in educational revivals in the 1800's. But meanwhile, many towns had taken the Revolutionary crisis—which damaged New England less than any other Colonial region—as a pretext for dropping even the pretense of providing schools. The Yankee thirst for education was genuine and eventually most healthy for America. But its peaks in the 1600's and the 1800's left a dismal valley between.

Dame schools and moving schools taught both sexes, for Puritans granted that women had souls to save on the same basis as men's. Beyond that low level, Colonial New England did little about further schooling for girls. For ladylike accomplishments—orthography, needlework, dancing, scraps of French, instrumental and vocal music—the belles-to-be of Salem, Boston, Providence, Newport, Hartford and New Haven could attend, at their parents' expense, primitive equivalents of finishing schools usually taught by needy gentlewomen, often recently over from England, in what all concerned hoped was London-style. There were usually a few girls up from the West Indies to get the double benefits of a less enervating climate and lessons in deportment. Yankee girls of bluestocking tastes had to study on their own or under family tutelage. Outside such schools, always small, never numerous, the sole formative influences on the upper-class girl were those of her mother, aunts and acquaintances in the neighborhood. The results could be good—consider that loyal, shrewd, outspoken helpmeet Abigail Adams. The faces of the Boston ladies who sat for Copley assure the beholder that pungent intelligence could survive such vapid educational arrangements. Again Philadelphia, not Boston, led the Colonies toward civilization in first recognizing women's need for more than a genteel literacy. That came to pass fittingly among the Friends, the implicit champions of women's equality with men. Anthony Benezet, Huguenot turned Quaker, defender of the drunken Indian and the Negro slave, pioneer of mild discipline in the classroom, set up an academic-oriented school for girls, to which the Quaker Quality gratefully sent their daughters: Sally Wister, Deborah Norris, Anna Rawle. There, it could be maintained, the New World women's rights movement was born.

Colonial society showed great contrasts. It was a far cry from Benezet's school and Copley's silk-swaddled ladies to the peltry trader's woman wearing only a short gown and maybe moccasins, crouched on the log step of the cabin, smoking her pipe and viewing Beaver Creek through a cloud of mosquitoes, not yet married to her man because no preacher had shown up and by now ceasing to care. Not twice a year did she see a piece of printed paper, and then since she couldn't begin to read it, she probably greased it and used it for a windowpane.

Schools and libraries are not the only means to learning. While classrooms scamped their job in the 1700's the printing press took up some of the slack in the Northern Colonies. That had begun in Cambridge, Massachusetts, in 1639, when newcomer Stephen Day, locksmith by trade but turned printer, pulled the first proof from the press imported by the Reverend Jesse Glover, who had "died on sea hitherward." [80] Day's first item was a form of oath to be taken by freemen (voting members of the oligarchy) of the Bay Colony; the second an almanac. The third, a revision of the Puritan metrical version of the Psalms, redressed the balance toward religiosity.

Thirty years later Governor Sir William Berkeley of Virginia immortalized himself by openly thanking God that his Colony still lacked printing presses and free (that is, open to paying pupils) schools. Their governors did not boast of it, but the Carolinas, Maryland, New York and the Jerseys were still also unsullied by printer's ink. In 1685, however, new-founded Pennsylvania was infected by the advent of William Bradford, apprentice and son-in-law of a Quaker printer of London, recommended by George Fox himself to the Friends creating their "Holy Experiment" in the New World. They soon had reason to doubt George's judgment. Bradford's first print job tactlessly dubbed William Penn Lord Penn, and the ensuing rebuke was only the first of several Quaker interferences that ended with Bradford's shifting his press to New York City. For the moment note that the offending first publication was an almanac and that Bradford, his son Andrew and the apprentices whom they trained into master printers were soon spreading presses and bookselling (a sideline usual with Colonial printers) through the Middle Colonies. Yankee printers expanding Day's beachhead had already got out the first Colonial newspaper—abortive but a momentous precedent—and, in a sort of paper-hatted Diaspora that included James Franklin of Boston and his young brother Benjamin, were infiltrating not only New England but also the Middle Colonies.

On cumbrous, hand-powered, screw-pressure presses with imported type, soon badly worn, these indispensable craftsmen printed government proclamations, laws and license forms; for shipowners their manifests and bills of lading; for wrangling divines and men of ideas their pamphlets and interminably succeeding pamphlets replying to pamphlets replying to previous pamphlets; ballad broadsides for sale by hawkers in town and peddlers in the country; and newspapers, as journalism developed and occasion served. But most consistently, following the lead of Day and Bradford, they compiled and printed almanacs.

The original use of these pamphlet-size publications was superstitious. Most Colonial farmers, following their medieval and prehistoric forebears, observed the phases of the moon and other astrological data in plowing, planting, grafting and so on—like the Old Northwestern farmer in Edward Eggleston's *The End of the World* who had always planted potatoes in the dark of the moon and killed his hogs when it was waxing "lest the meat should all go to gravy." [81] Few Colonial merchants let their ships sail without looking into the astrological omens for the day. Most of them probably took such matters seriously, and those who did not had to conform because captains and crews were believers. Notable ironies might result. The great Godfrey Malbone of Newport, Rhode Island, insisted that his two new-built privateers sail on Friday in a violent snowstorm because their horoscopes unmistakably recommended it. Neither ship was ever heard of again. Stephen Girard, on the other hand, neglected astrology while stubbornly holding to Friday as his lucky sailing day. Such notions were rife in all Colonial social strata along with other superstitions and old saws likewise imported from the Old Country. And an almanac calculated for American longitudes was the best way to keep posted on the astrological data essential to such comforting wisdom.

As they gained more pages, almanacs included tide tables genuinely helpful to fishermen and shipowners and long-range weather predictions that, however inaccurate, sounded impressive. These bound-together printed pages hanging by the shop door or the farmhouse fireplace amounted to a consulting service for farmers and businessmen. Almanacs of the 1960's still carry the astrological data, signs of the zodiac and all. In country places one still hears of planting root crops, turnips or radishes, in the waning moon so the developing root will go properly downward. But the importance of such considerations to the general public has dwindled along with the sale of almanacs per capita. The millions of the astrology-minded of today get their ready-made good advice from newspaper columns. The almanac industry reached its low point in tone, if not in distribution, after the late 1880's as patent-medicine companies distributed free almanacs carrying the usual contents plus propaganda for various compounds of snakeroot, Kickapoo juice and grain alcohol.

That all Colonial printers issuing almanacs believed as firmly as the purchasers in dark-of-the-moonshine is unlikely. Franklin, whose *Poor Richard's Almanac* is now the best remembered of the lot, may have taken little stock in its technical data, and the typical printer of his time already had some of the later newpaperman's skepticism. That did not

mar his liking for an item that needed yearly replacement. Sell a farmer a
Bible or a book of home cures, and it lasted a lifetime; but he had to buy a
new almanac yearly if only to keep track of weeks and months in a culture
lacking the advertising calendar. Soon it was learned that to vary the filler
—the proverbs, Bible verses, and other odd chunks of type that completed columns or pages of almanacs—in succeeding issues gained the
printer a better share of the annual market. The eclipse and tide tables
were necessarily much the same in all. But a profitable name for entertainment value could be created by improving the quantity and quality of the
interpolated jokes, sometimes mildly dirty, medical lore, historical anecdotes and moral advice, not unlike the small bits that the *Reader's Digest*
uses for the same purpose. Poor Richard's wise saws, some original,
some refurbished from folk material, were only the survivors among a
wealth of such squibs mutually plagiarized by the dozens of annual Colonial almanacs stocked in crossroads stores and carried through the country
by peddlers. They gave the authority of print to frugality, caution, foresight, modesty in dress and act—bourgeois virtues, true, but Colonial
societies hoping to settle down stood in need of such advice as: "Keep thy
shop and thy shop will keep thee. . . . Early to bed and early to rise
. . . Brag is a good dog but Holdfast a better. . . ."

As practice texts for children learning to read at home, these salty bits
were far better than the interminable, exotic Bible which was probably the
only other reading matter in the house. Dr. Daniel Drake's pioneering
family in very early Kentucky was by no means illiterate, yet the library
consisted only of "the Bible, Rippon's Collection of Hymns, the almanac,
Dilworth's Spelling Book, and a romance of the age of Chivalry entitled
the 'Famous history of Mentellion.' . . ." [82] So the almanac functioned
as a miniature school reader anticipating the eclectic McGuffey type. The
first piece of secular American literature to circulate widely in the Old
World was Franklin's almanac-flavored *The Way to Wealth,* the homily
of a crossroads sage quoting freely from Poor Richard. Its transatlantic
popularity shows that at least one Colonist could handle the language of
Bunyan and Defoe pithily, that the France of Louis XV and the Germany
of Frederick II took eagerly to what we think of as a peculiarly English-
speaking kind of smugness, and explains why when the French turned an
East Indiaman over to John Paul Jones with which to harass the British
and immortalize himself, it was thought appropriate to the ship and the
French cult of Franklin to rename her *Bonhomme Richard.*

The Colonies had some ten viable newspapers by the 1730's, including two (in Williamsburg and Charleston) even in the relatively unlettered
South. Some were printers' unsupported ventures. Others, like Bradford's
in New York City, were openly or secretly subsidized by governors need-

ing an organ for public notices and official versions of public affairs. To modern eyes these atrociously printed little weeklies—the printers knew their job but operated far from overseas sources of new type and presses —show little else to justify calling them newspapers. Their news consisted of hearsay bits about the current war in Germany; single-line notices of ship movements; one-sentence obituaries of foreign kings or Colonial Quality. Advertisements offered goods, sometimes from prize cargoes, for sale by auction or private dicker; rewards for runaway apprentices, servants or slaves ("homespun jacket, jean breeches; has a down look; speaks with a brogue, given to lewdness with women . . ."). The rest of the sheet was filled with extracts from Old Country periodicals or books, maybe a bit of nominally original doggerel or prose slipped under the printer's door at night or put in his hand at the adjoining tavern by a gentleman of political or literary bent. For through the 1700's the Colonial printer was likely to be editor, publisher and contributor all in one. Reporting as such hardly existed.

These *Postboys, Couriers* and *Gazettes* nevertheless had stimulating effects read aloud on the porch of the crossroads store or picked up in a waterside coffeehouse. And in view of how few native printers had even seen the inside of Colonial secondary schools, their grammar and spelling were amazingly clean. That probably came of the high Old Country standards of the master printers who, like Bradford, came to the New World for opportunity and trained American-born apprentices in the way they should go. Carl Bridenbaugh considered the resulting caste of printers particularly influential in the port capitals where, more than anywhere else, the Revolution was hatched: "The superior education that . . . their profession required made them important members of the growing middle class, and the widening market for their wares . . . brought them material prosperity that often placed them economically at the head of it . . . as their profession depended upon a free press . . . they tended to ally themselves with radical movements and . . . the patriot cause . . . to the best of them printing was not only a trade but a calling." [83]

A former apprentice of William Bradford's, John Peter Zenger, printed in his opposition-backed paper attacks on the governor of New York that set off a momentous criminal libel trial in 1735. It raised the issue whether the truth of a libel was a valid defense and set the precedent of giving the jury the last word in such matters. This "first major victory for the freedom of the press in the American colonies" [84] put the American publisher ahead of his counterpart in England in public privileges—and left him a much freer hand in accustoming the lower orders of Colonial towns to absorbing printed ideas. That enabled the Revolution to base itself on a paper war, enlisting not only certain disgruntled members of the Quality but also many craftsmen and laborers against what their pamphlet press called encroachment by the toploftical, government-suborned Colonial oligarchies. The tactical value of the new journalism so went to Jefferson's head that he wrote soon after the Revolution: ". . . were it left to me to decide whether we should have a government without newspapers or newspapers without a government, I should not hesitate a moment to prefer the latter. But I should mean that every man should receive those papers and be capable of reading them." [85]

Colonial printers could also turn out bound books, a skill of which New England's theologian oligarchs took great advantage. Their thousands of published items were mostly sermons and theological controversy, a literature as professional as a law library and often less readable. Only occasionally did an exceptional divine—the Reverend Roger Williams, heretical founder of Rhode Island, or the Reverend Charles Chauncy—print distinguished prose. Fiction in New England was out of the question. Her Colonial poets, usually clergymen, were no improvement on Anne Bradstreet. Modern scholars find substantial merits in the verse of the Reverend Edward Taylor, English-born and -reared minister of Westfield, Massachusetts, Harvard roommate of Samuel Sewall. He did not publish when living, however, and the great monument of Yankee poetry was *The Day of Doom,* the Reverend Michael Wigglesworth's interminable, if ingenious, string of jingles describing all the details of Calvinist theology, which went through edition after edition. The primary reason why there was no end of making many books in Colonial New England was that the region took its clergymen and their subject matter just as seriously as they did themselves. The stock of a Boston bookseller of 1685 consisted of 391 schoolbooks (almost certainly with a high religious content); 311 volumes on religious subjects; 55 Bibles and Testaments; 50 textbooks on navigation, 36 on law; only 21 items on history, medicine, soldiering or romance.

Yet in this very New England one of the outstanding philosophers of the 1700's, Dean Berkeley, a notable prose stylist himself, grew so sanguine about "The Prospect of Planting Arts and Learning in America" that he depicted the Muse, disgusted with England and Europe,

> . . . In distant lands [waiting] a better time,
> Producing subjects worthy fame. . . .
>
> In happy climes the seat of innocence,
> Where nature guides and virtue rules,
> Where men shall not impose for truth and sense
> The pedantry of courts and schools;

> There shall be sung another golden age,
> The rise of empires and of arts,
> The good and great inspiring epic rage,
> The wisest heads and noblest hearts.
>
> Not such as Europe breeds in her decay;
> Such as she bred when fresh and young,
> When heavenly flame did animate her clay,
> By future poets shall be sung. . . .

That was the sheer optimism of benevolence, for the level of writing would have been even less inspiriting elsewhere in the Colonies. Among writers from the Middle and Southern regions duly treated in the usual *History of American Literature* for the pre-Revolutionary period, only Franklin, John Woolman, the Quaker saint, William Byrd II and dilettante Francis Hopkinson, some of whose heroic couplets and lyrics for his own tunes have style, merit inclusion. Not for another century would the creativeness that Berkeley invoked gain momentum in American writing. In New England the Muse was pulpit-smothered, and as for the Middle and Southern Colonies, consider C. M. Andrews' reason for not saying more about "mental attitudes and opinions" in his *Colonial Folkways:* ". . . the colonists, except those in New England, were not accustomed to disclose their inner thoughts, though it is not at all unlikely that large numbers of them had no inner thoughts to disclose." [86]

V

"The American, This New Man..."

OLIVER EVANS' AMERICA

V

THE REVOLUTION was more than a merely political watershed. It sent into forced or voluntary exile some 200,000 Loyalists, including the bulk of the Quality and a sizable proportion of the lower orders—craftsmen, shopmen, seamen—mistrusting the new situation. For scale this mass migration has been likened by Arthur M. Schlesinger, Sr., a cautious scholar, to the exodus of the Huguenots from France. A bitter affair, for these were no mere transplanted English returning home but mostly American-born. Jonathan Sewell, an eminent Massachusetts *émigré,* wrote sadly from England: ". . . what a regale . . . Shagbarks and Cranberrys would be to us Refugees" and spoke of a fellow exile as able "neither to live nor to die in peace but in Salem, his once happy seat." [1] Many such homesick Loyalists were men of outstanding experience in administration and business. The new nation's compensation for losing them was a better chance of cultural freedom. The exiles were the most Old Country-minded element. America badly needed their social skills. But she also needed a strong sense of root-hog-or-die independence that Loyalist hankerings after the old leading strings would have diluted.

The Patriots' victory also opened up the vast region between the mountains and the Mississippi where, to shield the Indians—and the peltry trade—England's hated proclamation of 1763 had barred settlement. After varying delays the states holding claims to parts of this region modified or abandoned them in favor of the United States as a whole. That commonsense statesmanship endowed the disparate former Colonies with a great joint property for the American as such, distinct from the Yankee or the Pennsylvania Dutchman, to evolve in.

In 1780, before the upshot of the Revolution was evident, a middle-aged Norman, calling himself J. Hector St. John Crèvecoeur, who had spent much of his life in the Middle Colonies and seems to have thought both parties to the war wrongheaded, managed to get to London, where he sold to a publisher a manuscript called *Letters from an American Farmer*. Issued in England in 1781, soon published in France, Holland and Germany, it did much to keep Europeans' eyes on their North American cousins. It suffers from the author's native—and naïve—taste for sweeping statement and tidy analysis and contains strange errors such as: "The heat of the climate . . . is always temperate" [2] in Charleston, South Carolina. Ludwig Lewisohn rightly called it "delightful literature but fanciful sociology." [3] Yet it did pose a famous searching question: "What then is the American, this new man?" [4]

Therein Crèvecoeur, however sententiously, was serving notice on the Old World that as the former Colonies shook down and grew westward, a new national type might come into being. The outcome of the Revolution—the Western world's most jarring political impudence since the Roundheads executed Charles I—gave the book immediate interest. Soon the French Revolution—in some ways a repercussion of the American, though unlike it—sharpened the edge of his theme. The Old World has fretted ever since over a semi-abstract entity called America or the American in a fashion warping both parties to the relationship. The spate of windy comment that Crèvecoeur set gushing had much to do with flooding Northern Europeans into America in the 1800's—a concern to British industrialists and Prussian politicians, as well as to American land speculators. In fact, it began almost at once. The Paris office of the Scioto Company, angling for French purchasers of its new-granted lands in southeastern Ohio, made great play in 1786 with such extracts from Crèvecoeur as: "If a poor, resourceless man with nothing but his hands to support him should ask me, 'Where can I go to settle down and live without care with no need of cattle or horses?' I would reply: 'Go to the banks of one of the streams that fall into the Ohio or the Scioto. All you'll have to do is scratch the soil and put in your wheat, your potatoes, your cabbages, your turnips, your maize, your tobacco, and let Nature do the rest. All that while enjoy fishing and hunting.' " [5]

In 1780 Crèvecoeur's question was premature. It should have been: "What then will the American, this new man, be?" Though Yankee and Buckskin were markedly unlike their immigrant forebears, the ethnocultural mash was still far from analyzable condition. Nevertheless, years of Revolutionary urges had already set tingling a self-conscious Americanism which would in turn brew further change. Well before Crèvecoeur's book saw print, Noah Webster, a young Yale man teaching school in Goshen, New York, was completing a potent symbol of the nation-to-be—Webster's *Spelling Book,* the backbone text of American schooling for the next several generations. It and its subsequent sister works, Webster's school readers and dictionary, laid it down in both theory and practice that, in token of independence, America would insist on a linguistic destiny separate from the Mother Country's—would, if she chose, retain terms or pronunciations out of favor in England; develop her own if she liked; drop the *u* from *honour* as not only useless orthographic clutter but a relic of a Toryish taste for Continental elegance. Such doctrinaire nationalism was rampant at the time.

The issue of pronunciation was especially acute because, as if even language were fostering schism, the speech habits of the English upper classes but not of the Colonists had just been radically changing. "An affected erroneous pronunciation," Webster wrote, ". . . crept into practice about the theatre and court of London . . ." [6] and mentioned with particular contempt the *tyoob* (for *tube*) sort of thing, which he travestied in the phrase *tshumultshuous legislatshures;* the tendency to swallow final *r*'s and say "secretry" for *secretary* was probably also part of it. ". . . our language has suffered more injurious change . . . since the British army landed on our shores [in the Seven Years' War]," he maintained, "than it had suffered before in . . . three centuries." [6] It doubtless greatly widened the transatlantic rift when the dandy young officers of the redcoat regiments came mouthing the new fashions. That growing difference between the speech of the British Establishment and the American combinations of provincial English dialects with Scottish, Welsh, Irish and German speech habits has disturbed Anglo-American amity ever since. Even now it clogs cordiality when, as two men are settling a delicate matter or even merely scraping acquaintance, A sounds to B like an adenoidal oaf and B sounds to A like a twittery ham actor. Worse, many cultivated Britons cannot help shrinking from the presumed vulgarity of anybody whose manner of speech differs from that of English upper-class schooling. In America indigenous accent—Yankee, Southern, Midwestern, more narrowly Bostonian, Texan, Charlestonian—is largely regional in significance. In England it has notoriously been a highly meaningful social label.

The split with the Mother Country was further widened by Americans' divergent views of the French Revolution and the ensuing turmoil. French political theories, notably Montesquieu's, had influenced the Founding Fathers and were marked in the Constitution of 1787. Such Colonial statesmen as Franklin, Jefferson and Gouverneur Morris developed a well-tempered Francophilia from being well treated in France, particularly by Frenchwomen. It was not surprising that Jefferson and Morris labeled dime (old French for *tenth*) the tenth-of-a-dollar coin in the new nation's system of coinage, though they made no effort to tell posterity how to pronounce it. Many on both sides of the water confused the origins and development of the French Revolution with those of its American predecessor, which was mistakenly taken to be a close prototype. That led to much singing of *"Ça ira!"* and toasting of Liberty, Equality and Fraternity in the political clubs set up in American port towns in imitation of the Jacobins —so much indeed that Revolutionary France's first envoy to the United States erroneously assumed that he had the American public and government in his pocket.

Add that the dogged organizer of the wars against militant France was the old red-handed, red-coated enemy, Britain. Not even the undeclared little naval war with France in 1798–1800 or the rise of Napoleon's dictatorship on the ruins of revolutionary idealism could dissuade many Americans from their Francophilia. (The gradual erosion of this group is recorded in American place-names. Napoleon's earliest victories were hailed by at least nine settlements named or renamed Arcola, eight Marengos, six Lodis. Later victories at Austerlitz and Jena appear on today's map at least twice each; Ulm once. There are no Eylaus or Friedlands at all. But an eventual burst of at least twelve Waterloos [1815] contrasts strikingly with a single Trafalgar [1805] in Indiana.) The exotic nature of the issues betokened the new nation's immaturity. But it also gave her a rich new source of stimuli—French ideas, art forms, cultural aspirations—to rival those from the Mother Country, which had previously pretty much dominated America. Here was the beginning of a very gradual orientation of the American toward the Continent. It was braked then, however, and still is now, by a generalized suspicion of all things Old Worldly as enervating and diluting the native vigor of America. In Royall Tyler's comedy *The Contrast*, staged in 1787 in New York City, the first American play of passable merit, the foolish fop tells the stable hero: "Believe me, Colonel . . . when you shall have seen the brilliant exhibitions of Europe, you will learn to despise the amusements of this country as much as I do." "Therefore," says the colonel sternly, "I do not wish to see them; for I can never esteem that knowledge valuable, which tends to give me a distaste for my native country." [7] Or hear Noah Webster tell it to the American schoolroom: "Europe is grown old in folly, corruption, and tyranny . . . laws are perverted, manners are licentious, literature is declining, and human nature is debased. For America in her infancy to adopt the present maxims of the old would be to stamp the wrinkles of decrepit age upon the bloom of youth and to plant the seeds of decay in a vigorous constitution . . . a durable and stately edifice can never be erected upon the moldering pillars of antiquity." [8]

Among minor symptoms of new-fledged Americanism were the post-Revolutionary tavern signs. No more Royal Standard or Rose & Crown or General Wolfe. Elder inns might retain the neutral Bunch of Grapes or

Three Horseshoes. But in newer settlements, westbound visitors noted, hostelries were named for General Montgomery or General Wayne or time and again General Washington. Home from his long sleep, Rip Van Winkle saw with bewilderment that the name on the tavern sign had been changed to Washington under the unaltered "ruby face of King George" and "The red coat . . . changed for one of buff and blue. . . ." Or, more aggressively, the tavern in crude new Terre Haute, Indiana, had for sign the Eagle & Lion, the former picking out the latter's eyes.

Unfortunately many patrons of such rechristened taverns had come to believe that the patriotic American way to use tobacco was to chew it. The juicy cud and the concomitant copious spitting were first observed by Vespucci among the Caribbean Indians. Sailors making the West Indies took up chewing maybe because they could thus enjoy tobacco with both hands occupied; possibly also because it entailed no fire hazard belowdecks. By 1700 it had a solid foothold in the Colonies. Countryfolk near New Haven, Madam Knight noted, "keep Chewing and Spitting as long as their eyes are open." [9] Dr. Alexander Hamilton made a day's stage in Jersey with an old codger who "spoke not one word all the way but coughd and chawd tobacco." [10] In the Walworth Museum at Saratoga Springs, New York, is a combination kneeling-cushion-footstool-cuspidor used by a chewing worshiper in the 1774's.

On the whole, however, chewing in the Colonies had been socially lowclass. At one's ease in home or tavern, one smoked a pipe. "Segars," another West Indian notion, were meeting acceptance. The "stogie" favored by Pennsylvania teamsters was a black, twisty, cheap and strong cigar named after the Conestoga wagons. Snuff taking was strongly associated with the Tory Quality, whence the patriotic chewer's satisfaction in the wide difference between his messy spitting and the dainty pinch of snuff up one nostril and then the other. It was ironical that the dipping of snuff —using the end of a chewed stick to stow it between gum and lip to steep in saliva—presently became a vice of sluttish women that spread to their menfolk. Snuff still sells steadily among the lower strata of the South.

As chewing gained favor among farmers, storekeepers and the upcountry lawyers and printers who led the Jacksonian generation, tobacco juice fouled the national scene to an extent that disgusted not only alien visitors but also all abstaining Americans and the housewives who had to clean up the mess. No single other thing, not even Negro slavery, did so much as the stains on the American eagle's white shirtfront to encourage the supercilious European to label the new nation barbaric. Though folklore made range and accuracy in spitting matters of humorous pride, care consistently to hit the sandbox or cuspidor was considered unnecessary, even rather unmanly. No matter how plentiful such targets in steamboat saloons, hotel lobbies, railroad cars, courtrooms or domestic sitting rooms, the nation's carpets, as well as its floors, were soggy with that "detestable yellow dye which mars everything in this country" [11]—the witness no finicky Britishwoman but a New York-born lady settled in Michigan in the 1830's. The legislative halls of Congress were as bad as any, its great men depicted in Herman Melville's *Mardi* as the chiefs of the Temple of Freedom of Vivenza "turning their heads into mills . . . grinding up leaves and ejecting their juices. . . ." [12] By 1860 nineteen-twentieths of the tobacco processing in Virginia and North Carolina, where the industry centered, was of chewing tobacco. The flood of spittle hardly ebbed until the turn of the century. Indeed spittoons were not removed from all federal buildings until 1945.

Rising self-awareness also created spontaneous American stereotypes, folk creations soon taken up by the popular arts but already well formed in the public mind. The stereotype frontiersman slightly over life size, whether villain or hero, did not triumph in fiction until James Fenimore Cooper, Robert Montgomery Bird and Davy Crockett, each in his own way, exploited him. But the raw stuff of him already existed in the actual frontiersman whose behavior amazed FFV's at upcountry watering places and in Daniel Morgan's riflemen, whom Revolutionary veterans remembered at the siege of Boston. The Yankee as comic countryman, an American version of a stock English stage character, came early to pass in Tyler's *The Contrast*. He persisted in various elaborations for almost 150 years. But the other Yankee stereotype—as swindler, weasel-keen at a trade, all opportunist, pious-spoken—that developed a generation later was spread far and wide by the ingenuity of the Yankee peddler.

The Yankee, of course, had no monopoly on unlovely traits, but he did show the worst of himself outside Yankeedom. Lack of fertile soils early forced New England into small manufactures—woodenware, tinware, other small hardware—and the need of a market for them. As roads improved, restless young fellows, often from Connecticut, went west and south with small portable stocks of such "Yankee notions." As they learned the art of peddling, they added miscellaneous items suitable for a shoulder pack—"kerchiefs, laces, finger and ear-rings, blue, crimson and yellow beads . . . ribbons, tapes, thimbles, silver-washed and shining; hair-combs and brushes; needles . . . buckles, buttons and bodkins." [13] As he prospered, the Yankee peddler might graduate to a packhorse, then to a horse and cart, then to a four-wheeled shop wagon built rather like a roomy hearse filled with Yankee notions and hung around with brooms, chairs, churns.

As specialization arose, the load might comprise chiefly the painted tinware that collectors now prize. To the pioneers' Old Northwest, Edward Eggleston says, New England was "but a land that bred pestilent peripatetic peddlers of tin-ware and wooden clocks. Western rogues would cheat you out of your horse or your farm if a good chance offered, but this vile vender of Yankee tins who called a bucket a 'pail' and said 'noo' for new . . . would work an hour to cheat you out of a 'fipenny bit.' "[14] The clocks had works of hard maple—sometimes mountain laurel or wild cherry, which was best—so accurately cut in many cases that they kept time quite well. Indeed some still do. But quality varied, and folklore abounded with tales of the Yankee clock peddler's virtuosity in swindling. One had the Yankee starting his foray with twenty clocks bought cheap because defective springs enabled them to run only an hour or two; placing nineteen, promising each customer that he would come back again in a week and replace it if it proved unsatisfactory; duly keeping his word by using the twentieth clock—just as defective—as replacement; collecting his money; and then making a point of never coming back to that neighborhood.

Hard money being scarce, the run of Yankee peddlers would swap for beeswax, peltry, wool yarn, maple sugar, butter in tubs, ginseng (the wild root gathered for export to China, where great superstitious value was set on it because of its humanlike shape), wood ash—any backwoodsy product that would sell or swap profitably at the next sizable settlement. Between his keen sense of dickering and his sometimes unreliable goods, the Yankee's reputation was soon as bad as that of his forebears trading to the Chesapeake plantations by sea in the 1600's. Connecticut is ineradicably the Nutmeg State because of the wooden nutmegs and wooden hams and cheeses that he proverbially stocked. Often, like the German Jewish peddler who succeeded him, he would settle down in a likely spot and open a store, hence Davy Crockett's character of Job Snelling, "a gander-shanked Yankee"[15] storekeeper in Tennessee whose father back in Connecticut had invented the wooden nutmeg; his mother, Patience, had made the first white-oak pumpkin seeds; Aunt Prudence had developed those cigars of cornhusks soaked in tobacco water with oak leaves for filling; and Job himself had first thought of selling mahogany sawdust as cayenne pepper. In that idiom the Yankee did for America's picture of New England what pawnbrokers did for immigrant Jews. "A Southern man," J. K. Paulding was already writing to a friend in 1813, "derives most of his knowledge of the men of the East, from the precious specimens . . . sent among them in the persons of . . . Tinmen and Sea Captains who are in general the most tricky & contemptible Knaves in this or any other country." [16] From 1830 on, that was dismally important, for it enabled Southerners to refer Northern opposition to slavery to obscure but probably contemptible Yankee-like motives.

Doubtless non-Yankees were unduly severe on these nasal-spoken missionaries of convenience. They brought needed items to those for whom a trip to the store was a major project. They brought the news, and their wheedling gossip cheered up many a lonesome daughter or mother. And for all this suspicion of them, their acumen and prestige as traveled persons commanded respect. When Judge Thomas Haliburton of Nova Scotia wished to reproach his countrymen with laziness and lack of enterprise, he put his strictures in the mouth of Sam Slick, clock peddler from Connecticut, who found it worthwhile to come hundreds of miles from home to milk the easily bamboozled Bluenoses. Some Sam Slicks were unquestionably men of parts, maybe even sometimes of integrity, though evidence of that is harder to find. Bronson Alcott, a Yankee peddler in his youth, was addicted to ideals, but Transcendental philosophy never modified his remarkable selfishness about his wife and family. Solon Robinson, Connecticut boy peddling into the Old Northwest at the age of eighteen, had a versatile and influential career as an organizer of agricultural societies and a star feature writer for the New York *Tribune*, but his formal publications all too clearly label him crank and weaver of shoddy. Beyond them the profession showed such dubious ornaments as Benedict Arnold, great fighter and traitor; Parley P. Pratt, high-ranking Mormon killed by a suspicious husband; Collis P. Huntington, one of the Big Four who founded the Central and Southern Pacific railroads on elaborate fraud; and Jim Fisk, the roly-poly swindler and womanizer allied with Jay Gould in the shenanigans that ruined the Erie Railroad and U. S. Grant's reputation for common sense.

Retailing on wheels and service by pedestrian kept the country roads of the early 1800's in good use. One hears of two Yankee brothers with a hat factory in the Catskill foothills, one handling production, the other always on the road with a covered van full of hats, equally clever at working off a single item at a farmhouse or selling a gross or two to a storekeeper in a growing town. The tobacco peddler might have "a neat little cart, painted green, with a box of cigars depicted on each side-panel, and an Indian chief, holding a pipe and a golden tobacco-stalk, on the rear." [17] Or he traveled afoot with enough leaf in his pack to enable him to sit down in the kitchen and roll so many dozen cigars on order. In the 1790's pioneering Kentucky was already infiltrated by an occasional traveling tinker mounted on a pony, with his molds and soldering irons in his saddlebags, working his way cabin to cabin to repair the tin cups and pewter basins that were so valuable in the new country far from the manufacturer. The traveling shoemaker carried only his basic tools, for he could count on the employing household's having a shoemaker's bench and lapstone for him to work with as he stitched and pegged new boots and repaired worn ones for the whole household during the week or two he stayed. Hence the multitude of genuine antique shoemaker's benches used as coffee tables in today's houses.

The most American thing that post-Colonial America did was not painting Wayne over Wolfe on the tavern sign or borrowing a nasty habit from the Indians of South America, but spilling turbulently over the mountains into what would be Tennessee, Kentucky, Ohio, Indiana, Michigan, Illinois, Wisconsin. The typical, if not the statistically average, American was becoming, as Crèvecoeur saw, a chronic "mover." As deer and Indians thinned out, the peltry trader went farther west. Into the country he relinquished came the cattlemen building rough sheds and railed pens and maybe girdling a few trees to improve pasture. With them soon blended the first wave of westering subsistence pioneers attacking the forest more widely in order to plant extensive crops. Presently, however, would come talk of a richer valley across the ridge. Many settlers had already shown themselves susceptible to such rumors. Others, who had mortgaged some of their newly acquired land to moneyed men to pay for tools or seed or stock, were already deep enough in debt to wish to move on and try again. So often and often, though the cabin was still too new to leak much, its builder packed up the old woman, the brats and the plunder and was off once more. The interval might be so short that it was still the same yoke of oxen hauling the old wagon, the same hound dog padding alongside, the same cat resignedly asleep in a basket among the load, the same cow towing behind. "Local tales . . . are trampled underfoot by the shifting throng," Washington Irving complained. ". . . ghosts . . . have scarcely time to turn themselves in their graves, before their surviving friends have travelled away from the neighborhood . . . when they turn out at night to walk their rounds, they have no acquaintance left to call on." [18] The new mobility of America after World War II had precedent in our forebears' footlooseness.

Not all in the first wave of corn-planting settlers were so mobile, however. The less sanguine or less restless, the luckier or abler might stay a decade or two before the next move. If they had chosen the best land, hence had special reason to be content, they might stay out their lives. Maybe their sons kept the old place after them. But whenever a new treaty opening up Indian lands or a fresh round of hearsay stirred temptation, plenty of self-chosen movers responded. Thus automatic selection was still sorting out temperaments to keep the leading edge of America flavored with imagination—as well as recklessness, fecklessness, ignorance and opportunism—and a high incidence of courage. Most of these movers were American-born and likely to have a fair notion of the hardships that new country entails. Their decisions to pack up and go probably often came of awareness that pap or grandpap had done the same in his time and come out all right. But it would take doing. As Marcus Lee Hansen has pointed out, pioneering had become "a specialized occupation in which only a few could succeed." [19]

With the frontier shifting ever westward, a standard pattern of waves and phases passed over each area, making the eastern Iowa of the 1840's like southwestern Ohio in 1800, like the lower Shenandoah Valley in 1750. Transportation called the basic tune. At first wheels were lacking. Peltry and the trader's barter supplies moved by boat or canoe (and human backs at portages) or by packtrains of Indians or horses—or by mules as the importation of stud jackasses, of which George Washington had the finest, made them available. Hooved packtrains marching single file turned the Indian war parties' paths, which often followed the easiest grades as if skilled surveyors had plotted them, into broadening ruts twisting up the valleys to the mountain passes. The early mover might deepen this rut further by lashing a small load to a V- or Y-shaped heavy stick to be dragged by a horse—the same travois that the French Canadians got from the Plains Indians, who had invented it for draft dogs.

By 1733, however, wheels and the opening of the Great Philadelphia Wagon Road had tied the Susquehanna backcountry firmly to the Delaware tidewater. Soon it grew southward and westward across Maryland into the Shenandoah Valley, drawing into the Quakers' great port the pork, beef and wheat of that promising area; then, following the Iroquois Great Warriors' Path all the way, it tapped the North Carolina upcountry. Rough as it was, it enabled movers to use wheels. Late in the 1750's axmen widened the over-the-mountains trails for wagon trains supplying troops attacking Fort Duquesne (later Fort Pitt, then Pittsburgh). The ensuing demonstration that wheels could cross the Appalachians with pay loads encouraged private migration and drew Pittsburgh into the seaboard culture, source of its books, finery and religions, as well as the salt, firearms, powder, paper and tools with which to shape wilderness life.

Queen of both wheeled migration and the export of crops was the Conestoga* wagon. Like the Kentucky rifle, it was the work of the Pennsylvania Dutch, who developed it to freight heavy produce—barrels of flour and pork, kegs of lard and butter—to urban markets. Many museums

* Conestoga identified a minor sept of Indians on the lower Susquehanna and a later white settlement there at which this wagon is said to have been perfected; there was a Conestoga strain of draft horses to match. An old Philadelphia tavern had The Conestoga Wagon as sign.

now display its venerable remains: heavy-wheeled, wide-tired for execrable roads; whaleboat-bodied to keep the load from sliding out on steep grades; bonneted with white canvas stretched on bows; painted sky blue with red running gear. Tar to lubricate the axles rode in a bucket hung below; a toolbox on the side held wrench, hatchet, gimlet and so on for the roadside repairs so frequently necessary; from the near (left-hand) side a "lazy board" slid out for the driver to perch on as he steered the lead team with a single rein. If scorning the lazy board, he might ride the near wheelhorse or walk by him,* carrying a Loudoun County-made blacksnake whip as badge of office. Museums cannot reproduce his zest in cracking that whip or his rowdy pride in his job and the broad-chested majesty of his four- or six-horse team. Wearing the finest brassbound harness often festooned with harmonized jingling bells, these compact, deep-muscled beasts were the admiration of loafers and small boys all the way West. Once they were well coordinated, no stranger could drive them; they "did not refuse to do his bidding, they simply ignored his existence," [20] an old-timer recalled.

Most movers could not afford such wagons and horseflesh. They got there just the same with smaller farm wagons and carts, even handcarts sometimes or no wheeled vehicle at all. In 1772 the Reverend David McClure, a missionary in the high backcountry, saw a westering family of "about twelve . . . The man carried an ax and gun . . . the wife, the rim of a spinning-wheel in one hand, and a loaf of bread in the other. Several little boys and girls, each with a bundle, according to their size. Two poor horses, each heavily loaded. . . . On the top of the baggage of one was an infant, rocked to sleep in a kind of wicker cage. . . . A cow formed one of the company . . . a bed-cord . . . wound around her horns, and a bag of meal on her back. . . ." [21] Cow beasts in the shape of oxen were commoner than horses in movers' wagons—cheaper and sturdier, though slower. Early legislators should have put the oxcart, as well as the ax and the plow, in the blazonry of their state seals. A good yoke of oxen, their horns tipped with brass knobs for show, invariably named Buck and Berry, hardly needed the touch of the owner's gad—a length of hardwood sapling with a three-foot leather thong—to haw, gee or start the load; voice alone would steer them if they knew and trusted the man behind it.

The horse-drawn Conestoga was nevertheless the handsomely engineered ideal of the early American highway. Gail Borden, a Founding Father of Texas, tried to carry the metaphor further by rigging masts and

* This Pennsylvanian preference for handling a team from the left, which gives better visibility when the vehicle keeps to the right, may account for the American keep-to-the-right tradition on later highways, a custom persisting after automobiles came in.

sails on it for motive power on the open plains. He was more successful with his process for evaporating and canning milk.

Thanks to John Ford, the West's covered wagon—not the Conestoga, except on the Santa Fe Trail, but the standard, smaller farm wagon with a driver's seat where the heroine can look charming in a sunbonnet—remains immortal. We are not so conscious that once the spill over the mountains jarringly surmounted the Appalachian ridges, wheels usually again yielded to running water, boats and human muscle. The peltry traders had long used the Western Waters—the streams combining to enter the Mississippi—as highways for canoes and skiffs. Those currents happened to go the way the movers were headed, so they took to the water as soon as they could—on the Monongahela or Allegheny, or where the two joined to make the Ohio at Pittsburgh, or at Wheeling, where the Ohio resumes its southwestward course after its great northward bend.

The workhorse of the Ohio before steam was the keelboat—a close cousin of the shallow-draft, double-ended Durham boat of the Delaware River. Some 70 feet long, 10 or 12 in the beam, it made fair time downstream under six pair of oars with a crew of twenty-odd men. By 1794 packet-keelboats were running regularly from Pittsburgh to the riverbank village of Cincinnati. Indians being still troublesome, these craft carried small arms for crew and passengers, were loopholed for 6-pound cannon, and provided a separate cabin for ladies. "The top is boarded and shingled like a house, the sides are tow cloth . . . put up or down at our pleasure," [22] Lydia Bacon, a U.S. Army officer's wife, recorded in 1811. The return trip against the current was arduous, with poles pushed against the bottom on the shoreside, oars on the other, for staying close in kept the boat away from the main force of the stream. On straight reaches the prevailing westerly winds often made it worthwhile to rig a sail. Indeed those winds were often so strong that in times of low water, hence weaker current, keelboats moved upriver almost as fast as down. Their crews were widely considered the drunkenest, most profligate and toughest ruffians on the continent. Out of them came the legendary Mike Fink, a sadistic glorification of a real person, the Western Waters' folk hero. But they also produced Henry Shreve, peltry trader turned keelboatman, who went on to demonstrate the practicality of steamboats in the West and invented the snag boats that helped keep them out of trouble.

Boatbuilders meeting the needs of movers soon created several larger and clumsier craft never meant to come back upstream. Their mover owners broke them up downriver and sold the timber or used it to build their own dwellings. There was the broadhorn, a barge carrying up to 100 tons, so called for its two huge sweeps forward; the flatboat, merely an immense, oblong, watertight open box with room for all the livestock, necessary fodder and wagons of several families floating to a new destiny; and the ark, a flatboat with a bulletproof shack amidships, its resemblance to Noah's craft heightened by the mooing, cackling, whinnying, squealing, bleating and barking often accompanying its ungainly progress downstream. The families on board cooked over a fire on a bed of earth or sand and got fresher air and sounder sleep moored to the bank for the night

The flatboat steered by the man in the stovepipe hat is passing embryonic Cincinnati, Ohio, while another is unloading on the shore.

than they had enjoyed in the land-wheels leg of the trip, sleeping on the floors of taverns where the wagoners put up on the implicit condition of drinking enough whiskey to justify free lodging.

In that day before industrialization the river that thus supplied free motive power was, all observers agreed, lovely. At most seasons its water was clear blue; the glittering long reaches cleaving the forested hills were often lively with whitecaps; the convoluted bends among the higher hills had a Rhine-like style. But the movers' voyages were no supine driftings through sentimental scenery. The Ohio was no tame canal. Their cumbersome craft were so at the mercy of current and breeze that the steering sweeps were in frequent use to work ark or flatboat away from shallows; to keep the wind from forcing her aground at the head of an island; to set her into the swifter-running fork of a divided channel; to get her out into the current after the nightly tie-up—and all done by men who, however handy with ax and rifle, might never have been on water before in anything but a ferry. The inexperienced might tie up in the wrong place, drawing a killing-and-looting visit from Indians wading the shallows after dark or from ruthless white river pirates who had learned the river as keelboatmen. The head of the family must have been much relieved when he had tied up for the last time, yoked Buck and Berry, hauled the wagon lurching ashore, loaded up, and set off for the high ground to see if the country yonder really was, as returning land-lookers had averred, "the prettiest place this side of heaven." [23]

The strongest testimony to the importance of water in settling the over-the-mountains country is the procedure of the party from the Watauga country of eastern Tennessee who founded Nashville, Tennessee. They—and their goods—floated all the way down the Tennessee River and then rowed and poled all the way up the adjacent Cumberland River, doing at least 800 miles by water to avoid some 200 by land. Yet where water was unavailable, land routes were doggedly created and used. Before the Revolution restless men in the Shenandoah Valley and the Carolina upcountry had pushed illegally southwestward into the Tennessee Valley and through the Cumberland Gap into what was soon famous as the Kentucky Bluegrass. Both movements took the usual course: bear and deerskins; then cattle; then rough homesteads around stockade and blockhouse. The Kentuckians' most renowned leader, Daniel Boone—Quaker-born among the Pennsylvania Dutch; teamster, land agent, mighty hunter—became another of the frontier's folk heroes, one more palatable than Mike Fink. These movements met relatively little help from running water and much backbreaking work manhandling wheels over trails unfit for them. The same was true of the heavy drift of Yankees away from their exhausted, stony fields across the Hudson into rich-soiled, lake-embellished western New York and, as the mover tradition and human propagation persisted, still farther west along Lake Erie into southern Michigan and northern Indiana—in time into northern Illinois and then Iowa. New York land speculators such as half-mad Peter Smith and eminently sane John Jacob Astor, whose holdings lay just where these Yankees calculated to settle, were pleased to see them.

A sample New Hampshire family headed for the Black River country between the Adirondacks and Lake Ontario in 1804 presented the usual picture of "women . . . in the wagon . . . [and] in a confused heap as is the custom . . . the children, spinning wheels, chairs, and trunks. Two cows followed. These people travel economically. They feed their children with the milk from the cows." [24] And the sight that wrung Charles Dickens' heart on the Illinois prairies must have been sadly familiar: "a solitary, broken-down wagon, full of some new settler's goods . . . deep in the mire; the axle-tree broken; the wheel lying idly by its side; the man gone miles away to look for assistance; the woman seated among their wandering household gods, with a baby at her breast; a picture of forlorn, dejected patience; the team of oxen crouching down mournfully in the mud, and breathing forth clouds of vapor from their mouths and nostrils. . . ." [25]

The Homestead Act of 1862 that practically gave land free to anybody settling it in good earnest was still to come. In theory and usually in practice the mover paid the government or the holder of a previous grant for the acres he hankered after. The Crown had, for instance, granted to a company in which George Washington's stepbrothers were major figures (and he a minor one) lands around the forks of the Ohio to open by persuading families to settle there and pay the new owners nominal sums per acre. Congress made similar grants to speculative syndicates after the Revolution. One such created the first substantial settlement in Ohio with a colony of New Englanders sent to build Marietta well below Wheeling. Another cajoled numerous gullible and ill-prepared French into buying and settling some of its lands on the river—hence the name of Gallipolis, Ohio. By 1785, however, Uncle Sam was selling directly to settlers, which cost them no more and led to less swindling. The millions of acres thus disposed of were informally called Congress land. Many a settler able to command a few hundred dollars eventually found himself in the solid position of old Jack Means of Edward Eggleston's *The Hoosier Schoolmaster,* whose pipe-smoking hag of a wife accounted for it in pellucidly pure Hoosier:

> . . . this yere bottom land was all Congress land in them there days; and it sold for a dollar and a quarter, and I says to my old man, "Jack," says I, "Jack, do you git a plenty while you're a-gittin'. Git a plenty while you're a-gittin'," says I, "fer 'twon't never be no cheaper'n 'tis now," and it ha'nt been; I know'd 'twouldn't. . . . And Jack he's wuth lots and gobs of money, all made out of Congress land. Jack didn't git rich by hard work. Bless you, no! Not him. That a'n't his way. Hard work a'n't, you know. 'Twas that air six hundred dollars he got along of me, all salted down into Flat Crick bottoms at a dollar an' a quarter a' acre.[26]

Before going on sale, new lands from which the Indians had been ousted, often with some color of legality, were surveyed on a system of east-west base lines—townships 6 miles square; 640-acre, mile-square sections; 160-acre quarter sections—a formula eventually carried well beyond the Missouri. From the air it still dominates the Midwestern land-scape: the straight roads along township lines meeting at neat right angles; the jogs in them where the surveyor periodically corrected for compass variation; the uniformly sized 40-acre fields reflecting great-grandpap's custom of dividing the quarter section into four "forties." Disturbed by dis-orderly stream beds but persisting beyond them, carried over ridges re-gardless, lapsing only where the later subdivider bought an old farm and laid out street patterns, the old lines may be as traceable 2,000 years from now as Roman camps and fields are in England. It worked out better than Virginia's haphazard system of grants in Ohio, in which large parcels of-ten conflicted and the land seeker did his own surveying, which, as R. C. Buley says, led to endless litigation.

Another sort of line still discernible, though not from the air, is the ten-uous boundary between the settlers from the Northeastern and Middle Colonies and those up from Virginia, Kentucky and farther southeast-ward. The old National Road (pretty much present Route 40) more or less marks the division. The differences are those of speech habits, door-yard tidiness and thrift. Often modified by circumstances such as the gen-erally more fertile nature of the Northeasterners' country, vague at best and blending more confusingly each generation, the cleavage neverthe-less remains as real as the hot Copperheadism that reflected it in southern Indiana during the Civil War.

The minority of settlers who paid nothing for over-the-mountains land were of two sorts—war veterans and squatters. Part of the veterans' inducement to enlist had been promises of a postwar land grant; Ken-tucky, Ohio and Indiana saw much of this, though, as might have been foreseen, the newcomer with a land warrant was often not the veteran but the clever man who had bought it from him back in New Jersey. The squatters were individuals or families from the ignorant, depressed seg-ments of upcountry society who had pushed into the wilderness uninvited and gone to clearing, planting and cabin building without legal status. With luck it would be years, even a generation before some rightful owner came with papers showing that his new purchase included that particular piece of creek bottom. Having studied the situation, he might conclude that it was safer to pay the squatter for his improvements—a few acres cleared; fifty rods of worm fence; a cabin already half-tumbledown—than to risk a rifleshot from across the creek some evening.

Such a remonstrance was particularly to be expected when, as was of-ten the case, the squatter was one of the poor whites, "that curious . . . race," as Eggleston describes the Old Northwestern version, ". . . the half gypsies of America, seeking by shiftless removals from one region to another to better their wretched fortunes, or, more likely, to gratify a restless love of change and adventure. . . ." [27] They "entertained a contempt for the law that may have been derived from ancestors transported for petty felonies. It seemed to them something made in the interest of attorneys and men of property. A person mean enough to 'take the law onto' his neighbor was accounted 'triflin' . . . good, whole-souled men settled their troubles with . . . fists, teeth, and finger-nails—and very rarely, when the offense was heinous and capital, with bullets or buckshot. . . . Hanging by lynch-law was reserved for the two great crimes of horse-stealing and murder." [28] Eggleston notes that they practically never used oxen, preferring even "a poor horse when possible." But Meredith Nicholson, describing the species Brown Countyite, envisaged "a rude wagon drawn by oxen. A dusty native walks beside the team, and seated on the floor of the wagon is an old grandmother, smoking." [29] The most frightening representative of this moonshining, whitecapping, snuff-dipping and originally Southern stratum of society is the weasel-like little girl from Six-Cross-Roads in Booth Tarkington's *The Gentleman from Indiana*.

By the time formal settlement reached an area it might contain squatters enough to make it worth a politician's while to take up the cause of securing them proper titles. Or they might organize a "claims association," its members pledged to appear, when lands squatted on went legally on sale, in numbers large enough to discourage other bidders than the squatter from offering to buy—at his own low price. Or it could be a mass settlement, as when Stephen Girard bought 50 square miles up the Schuylkill in 1830 and had to pay a total of $145,000—a handsome fortune then—to quiet the claims of its German squatters holding "color of title by undisputed occupancy for more than twenty years." [30] There was no "poor Mr. Girard" about it, however; he got his money back, and to spare, from lumber and coal. All such legal and sublegal maneuverings contributed to make the surveyor running his beelines across the hills with chain and compass the mainspring of effective settlement and the only basic member of the pioneering community who had to have some education. The parson from Back East setting up the academy that became Indiana University was told by the typical applicant confronted with its classical course of study: "Daddy says he don't see no sort a use in the high larn'd things—he wants me to larn English only, and book-keepin', and surveyin', so as to tend store and run a line." [31]

Clearly, what with litigious squatters, fraudulent purchase of veterans' warrants, conflicting Colonial, federal and state grants and hasty surveys, land-title disputes were as widespread a plague in the new country as malaria—and as unhealthy when settled by private violence. Many others got into the courts, such as they were. The seaboard settlements had inclined at first to class lawyers with rattlesnakes and boasted of how long they had managed without them. Over the mountains, however, the lawyer was very early among the technical specialists joining the mud-clogged, stump-cluttered hamlet called Waynesville or Buckeye Bend, appearing after the surveyor, saddler, blacksmith and miller but in the same year as the tanner, well ahead of the preacher, and very far ahead of the doctor.

What law he had was acquired by reading in the office of a small attorney Back East, nominal reference to which would probably admit him to practice in the new states. Professional standards of the time were low. In 1834 Judge Thomas Lacy of the Superior Court of Arkansas Territory admitted to the bar brash young Albert Pike, later a journalist and then a controversy-haunted Confederate general, who had merely been reading lawbooks on his own, without examination, on the ground that after all, it wasn't like issuing a diploma to practice medicine; he couldn't kill

Stumps in the main street of Columbus, Georgia, in its earliest years as drawn by Captain Basil Hall, RN.

anybody by poor practice of law. The young lawyer come to Buckeye Bend boarded at the tavern—until he married a local girl—and maintained a tiny log office in which to receive clients and entertain cronies with cards and whiskey. But chances of his being in that office on a given day were low. Much of the time he was away on circuit. The population of the new country was scattered, its legal system primitive. To cope with the settlers' litigiousness and witnesses' reluctance to travel far over atrocious roads, the courts—and the bar practicing before it—had to be as migratory as Merovingian kings. From courthouse to courthouse, county by county, judge and lawyers rode horseback pilgrimages together in an organized circuit on a schedule known in advance so that suitors could literally draw near and choose an attorney from the saddlesore talent available.

Here was an ancient English institution transplanted to an Old Northwestern setting that needed it as badly as had Henry VII's kingdom. Both bench and bar rode in the same uniform: "tall black hats, 'tailcoats' . . . and 'biled shirts,' with limp cotton collars rolling over black neckerchiefs tied in single bows," as Joseph Kirkland, the novelist, recalls them. The saddlebags of each contained "his entire wardrobe except what he had on him and . . . Blackstone's Commentaries, the Revised Statutes of Illinois, Jones' Forms of Procedure [and] a travelling flask of whiskey." [32] A Hoosier old-timer remembered some more smartly equipped with portmanteaus behind the saddle and umbrellas—which must have heightened the picturesqueness of the troupe as it splashed through the yellow mud on rainy days. The judges ranged from backwoods great men as well grounded in common sense as in law to the more rugged type of the Iowa justice of the peace who, berated in court by a local rowdy for not ordering meals for the prisoners in jail, did not hold him in contempt but personally clubbed him senseless, for which His Honor had himself duly tried for assault and battery and acquitted. After the day's session this legal traveling circus sat on the "long, low wooden porch of the [county-seat tavern] almost level with the dusty road in front . . . in amiable, anecdotal confab," [33] smoking or likelier chewing with feet up and hair down. This backwoods bar was the great nursery of politicians, some with national destinies, giving Stephen A. Douglas, Lewis Cass and many others besides Abraham Lincoln the feel of their constituents-to-be. And, however windily the eagle spread his wings and screamed at Fourth of July celebrations, it fostered a style of debate that knew the uses of plain talk and close logic.

The store across the way from that tavern porch would have begun as "a double log-building. In one end the proprietor kept for sale powder and lead, a few bonnets, cheap ribbons, and artificial flowers, a small stock of earthenware and cheap crockery, a little homespun cotton cloth, some bolts of jeans and linsey, tobacco for smoking and tobacco for 'chawing,' a little 'store tea'—so called in contradistinction to the sage, sassafras and crop-vine teas in general use—with a plentiful supply of whisky, and some apple-brandy. The other end . . . was a large room, festooned with strings of drying pumpkin, cheered by an enormous fireplace, and lighted by one small window with four lights of glass. In this room, which contained three beds, and in the loft above, Wilkins and his family lived and kept a first-class hotel." [34] But as the settlement developed, the store

would have a building of its own, which became, "after closing-time . . .
a club-room, where, amid characteristic odors of brown sugar, plug tobacco, new calico, vinegar, whisky, molasses, and the dressed leather of
boots and shoes, social intercourse was carried on by a group seated on the
tops of nail-kegs, the protruding ends of shoe-boxes, and the counters.

*The "Entertainment" sign indicates that the settler building this double
log cabin and log barn in the Old Northwest expected to put up travelers
as cash supplement to his income.*

. . ." [35] The group was all men, of course. The women were at home
doing the mending and seeing that the children stayed in bed. What equivalents of club life their sex had occurred in occasional afternoons of quilt-
ing or sewing bees.

Strong resemblances were inevitable between the groundbreakings and
clearings of the Old Northwest and their pre-Revolutionary prototypes
in the upcountry Carolinas, the Pennsylvania valleys and the upper Connecticut Valley. The net results of too many trees, not enough tools, poor
transport and a previous low standard of living are necessarily cognate
wherever found, in Siberia or ancient Gaul. Thus the first dwellings of certain new settlers in Michigan in the 1830's were shanties built "against
a sloping bank, with a fireplace dug in the hillside, and a hole pierced
through the turf by way of chimney. In this den of some twelve feet
square, the whole family had burrowed since April. . . ." [36] At Salem,
Massachusetts, careful archeology has reproduced just such dens as the

first quarters of John Endicott's Puritans in 1628. The dugouts sheltering the first Quakers of Philadelphia must have been similar.

Over the mountains, however, conditions were often aggravated. Squirrels were not just a nuisance to the crops in new-cleared fields; they came every few years in plagues-of-Egypt hordes that swam rivers and left only a few ears of corn per acre. Nests of yellow jackets in the ground in new-plowed fields, half-killing both plow teams and plowmen as they swarmed out when disturbed, were not just an occasional hazard but recurred every few furrows. Sources of supplies and markets for produce were not only farther away in miles, but the intervening mountains made them harder to reach. Mere distance from salt for packing the hog crop, as well as daily table use, seriously slowed settlement. Not until upper New York State, western Pennsylvania and the Kanawha country of West Virginia-to-be began salt boiling could the westward push develop momentum. Instead of a log cabin, the settler family's first quarters were likely to be the more rugged half-face camp—a booth of forked posts joined by a crosspiece, poles slanting to the ground on the north side to support a roof of dirt and brush, the sides of logs, clay and brush, the southern front open to the ever-burning fire built just outside. The family of Thomas and Nancy (Hanks) Lincoln spent a winter on new land in such a well-ventilated structure.

The trees to be coped with ran even larger in the Old Northwest than in the Northeast. In these well-watered lowish latitudes sycamore, tulip and oak had ideal growing conditions, and their outlandish size sorely taxed the usual clearing methods. But the big new land offered compensations. "We cleared land, rolled logs, and burned brush," Sandford C. Cox recalled of the upper Wabash country, "blazed out paths from one neighbor's cabin to another . . . hunted deer, turkies, otter, and raccoons—caught fish, dug ginseng, hunted bees . . . and—lived on the fat of the land." [37] The size of the average holding, much greater than had been usual east of the mountains, was particularly gratifying. "We had most awful times at first," the woman of a new household in Michigan told a neighbor. "Many's the day I've worked from sunrise till dark in the fields gathering brush and burning stumps. But that's all over now; and we've got four times as much land as we ever should have owned in York-State." [38] This lavish scale of land use was also evident in the minor towns soon growing in the new country. The Reverend Henry Ward Beecher's young Yankee wife transplanted with him to raw, new Indiana noted that these people did not build their houses huddled together, as in New England's towns, but with generously wide back and front yards on broad streets lined with shade trees. That tradition lasted a good while west of Pittsburgh, where towns luxuriated in gracious shade until Dutch elm disease and automobile exhausts began to do their worst.

The lady of the Old Northwestern log cabin usually walked behind her husband if the trail was at all narrow and not only was accustomed to seeing him come into supper and sit down in the only chair with his hat on, but was unaware that elsewhere men behaved differently. Having been born and "raised" in a single-room cabin, she often had equally crude ideas of womanly conduct. So far nobody had yet called this horny-handed helpmeet a pioneer mother. And cultivated persons on the seaboard, like Washington Irving, seeing her and her family on the dusty track westward, thought of them not as O Pioneers! but as mostly rootless ne'er-do-wells whom civilization would never miss. The region they were headed for was known then as The Backwoods with heavy connotations, often justified, of ignorance and squalor. Being so far from ships and imported goods, the new settler's establishment was a mass of low-grade makeshifts homely in all senses of the word.

Following unwritten law, the approaching stranger coming in view of the cabin hails from the edge of the clearing: "Hello-o-o-o-o! the House!" and repeats it once or twice as his horse follows the wagon track winding among the stumps and half-burned log piles. Nice stout cabin . . . log corncrib . . . log smokehouse and six or seven hogs asleep in its shade. If the old man—meaning the head of the house regardless of actual age—is away with the oxen and wagon, the only non-homemade item conspicuous is the great iron kettle, the family's least replaceable and most valued possession (except its weapons), used as washboiler, reducing vat for maple sugar, hog scalding—and just now to boil soap in. Not for some years will this establishment rise to the refinement of a rain barrel at the corner of the cabin fed by an eaves trough of hollow log. Until then the hard water from the spring is "broke" by admixture with highly alkaline wood ashes to soften it for laundry use.

The old woman—not yet thirty, but most of her freshness is gone, and if she survives her next two bouts of childbed, she will look like an old woman and no mistake—has left off stirring the slippery brown mess to shade her eyes and try to make out whether she knows the stranger or the horse. The odors of woodsmoke from the fire and of rancid fat bitter with lye from the boiling soap are tinged with carrion from the fresh pelts (coon, muskrat or mink) drying on the cabin wall, for though beaver is losing its market, hatters still want coon fur and Old Country ladies still want fur wraps. Bare-bottom children wearing only tow-linen shirts cluster in timid confusion around the cabin door guarded by a baying creature of the general description hound dog. At one side of the door on a shelf of adzed plank are a basswood basin, a gourd of soft soap and another for dipping drinking and washing water out of the wooden pail below. A bare area among the weeds shows where the harshly alkaline soapy water is thrown. The old lady is barefoot, though it is only April, and wears nothing but a shift and a linsey-woolsey short gown—except the sunbonnet without which she never goes outdoors.

Inside accommodations consist chiefly of a single room with a good fireplace, log walls whitewashed inside, pegs to hang garments on, two large beds each with a trundle bed beneath, a few splint-bottom chairs and a chest of drawers. The pride of the house is the coverlets with fine traditional woven-wool patterns called Pine Bloom, Dogwood Blossom, Tennessee Trouble, Indian War, Cat Trace. Squalor it was, but apropos, consider the cautionary doctrine of John Burchard and Albert Bush-Brown, historians of architecture: "It is possible to live a healthy, perhaps even a happy life, in the woods . . . under physical conditions which would be intolerable in a metropolis. Consequently the rural slum has never been so frightening as its big brother in a city. The frontier was one big rural slum saved only by the fact that the open spaces were not far away. . . ." [39]

Only in the context of the Old Northwest they were not open. All around the clearing stood the wall of forest. Forty years later, clearing would have progressed much further, but as yet over there, by no means as far as the horizon, the great woods loomed like an army beleaguering the settler's heirs—or successors if he had turned mover again. Only slowly did the combination of portable steam sawmills and improved transportation make it worthwhile to go into lumbering at any great distance from streams that would float rafts. Meanwhile, the settler cleared only the cream of his quarter section and, though still proud of owning so much, left the rest as a reservoir of fuel and building material. In William Dean Howells' boyhood in Ohio "half the land was in the shadow of these mighty poplars and hickories, elms and chestnuts, ashes and hemlocks; and the meadows that pastured the red cattle were dotted with stumps as thick as harvest stubble." [40]

Those woods are long gone now, and replacement by second growth has been sporadic. Yet look sharp here and there, and you can still find the old cabin serving as an obscure outbuilding on some out-of-the-way, slovenly farm or almost rotted away in what has become a frowsy pasture. That cabin was certainly seeing better days when its old man of twenty years and his old lady of seventeen had thought it near enough finished to spend their first night within, while the oxen lay outside chewing their cuds and the katydids deafeningly predicted six weeks to frost. These people were no characters from a historical pageant or figures in a self-conscious WPA mural but, as R. C. Buley has said, like their own log houses, "inelegant and crude, but with lasting qualities. . . . In estimating them the contempt of superiority is no less to be guarded against than the idealization which ascribes super-abundance of vision, courage, industry and virtue to them . . . they were just folks, doing their day's work, and caring little for the verdict of history." [41] Only a few would have had the touch of conscious sentiment that led John McNeill, pioneer in Schoharie County, New York, to leave instructions in his will to bury him on the spot where he felled the first tree to make room for his cabin.

Physical security and subsistence were the settlers' first concerns. But within a few years, as corn grew and hogs multiplied, the economics of the cash crop demanded the Western Waters again. No doubt the neighborhood soon had an elementary general store, successor to an Indian trading post, swapping peltry and whiskey, ginseng and beeswax for textiles, ammunition and other such easily transported cultural links with the seaboard. But the store was only a very minor market for corn and pork for area consumption, and by and large, those commodities were too heavy and bulky for profitable shipping across the mountains. True, droves of cattle were driven from the Old Northwest to Baltimore in the early 1800's, and hogs sometimes went the same route in charge of men undaunted by the prospect of having to swim them over the Ohio River at Wheeling. But the risks were unmistakable, and the poor condition of the animals at the other end reinforced the commonsense conclusion that, season in and season out, water transport of already slaughtered and pickled beef and pork got the most value out of a given animal. That made New Orleans, situated where the Western Waters drew together in a single stream to meet salt water, the economic focus of the over-the-mountains region.

The settler built or had built for him a small flatboat on the handiest stream that would float it; loaded it with corn and barreled pork and whiskey and beef, sometimes cattle on the hoof; and, with the spring rise, sent his or a neighbor's sons drifting with boat and cargo down Goose Creek into the Wabash into the Ohio into the Mississippi and down to the Spaniards' French-founded and -flavored port for sale and reshipment of the comestibles to the West Indies or Europe, the flatboat being sold and broken up for local use as timber or firewood. The boys brought home the proceeds by several means, all cumbrous—in a ship from New Orleans to an Eastern port; this cost cash money and meant a long walk home over the mountains; or working their way back upstream on a keelboat, which was no place for a backwoods youngster carrying money; or walking the hundreds of miles of Natchez Trace that angled across into Kentucky and was infested with land pirates and unpredictable Indians. They got through often enough to keep the trade lively long after steamboats came in; Abraham Lincoln was one of thousands making the trip at least once. Stephen Foster's father, associated with a Pittsburgh mercantile firm, made trip after trip downriver on flatboats and brought return merchandise around by sea to Philadelphia, thence by chartered Conestoga wagons over the hump to Pittsburgh again.

This intimate relation between the newest part of the new nation and the Mississippi waterway was dramatized in 1802 when the Yankees of Marietta, Ohio, sent a cargo direct to Jamaica in a seagoing vessel built right there on the Ohio some 600 feet above sea level. Local boatyards experienced with large keel- and flatboats had already sent several bluewater ships down for sale in New Orleans. Soon the Monongahela, even the quite minor Kentucky River, saw such launchings—usually small brigs but now and again a three-master. Maysville, Kentucky, built at least one 400-tonner. In the spring of 1803 a 15-foot rise in the Ohio sent downstream the schooner *Dorcas & Sally* of 70 tons, Wheeling-built and Marietta-rigged. The next day after her came the schooner *Amity* of Pittsburgh, 70 tons, and the ship *Pittsburgh,* 273 tons, taking 1,700 barrels of flour and herself for sale in New Orleans. Between Jefferson's embargo on trade with Europe and the hazards of getting vessels of seagoing draft over the rapids at the Falls of the Ohio that created Louisville, this industry was stifled, not to revive until seagoing patrol craft were built on the Ohio in World War II. But such Western experience in shipyards was already paying off in the new boom in building steamboats and explains how, when Commodore Perry needed cordage, anchors, sails and other such blue-water items for his fighting fleet on Lake Erie in 1813, he was supplied with them from, of all places, far-inland Pittsburgh.

Spain's control of the New Orleans bottleneck of the downriver trade kept up a realistic fear lest the over-the-mountains country be forced under a foreign flag or break away from the new Union as a rashly independent nation occupying New Orleans. Those taking such possibilities seriously included not only opportunists Aaron Burr and James Wilkinson but also George Washington, all assuming that the new settlers cared less about what flag they lived under than about getting their produce to market. Had change of sovereignty actually been tried, no doubt most of the American settlers would soon have regretted it. Remember, however, how new the Stars and Stripes were; how many weary days it took to travel by land from Independence Hall to Dirtyface Creek, Ohio; and how lightly and inadvisedly the Yankees of the Hartford Convention of 1814 were to consider dismembering the Union. For that matter, the Yankees' over-the-mountains segment—Vermont, New Hampshire and northeastern

New York State—defied Jefferson's embargo of 1807 and the nation's belligerency in the War of 1812 by flagrant trading with the enemy in Canada. Northward-flowing Lake Champlain and the streams feeding it were these realists' Western Waters, Montreal their New Orleans, and it took more than federal law or war to keep their rafts loaded with potash, pork and whiskey from reaching what was considered their natural market. In 1814 the British forces menacing Plattsburg, New York, got most of their beef and flour from York State and Vermont farmers eager for good English hard money.

The Champlain branch of the Erie Canal, giving that country the proper cheap water transport over the hump into the Hudson waterway and the American market, took care of this schismatic trend in 1823. In 1803 the Louisiana Purchase of New Orleans—and incidentally the vast region between the Mississippi and the Rockies—had taken care of the Western Waters problem. But not until east-west railroads finished what canals and highways had merely begun—knitting the Old Northwest to the eastern seaboard instead of to the river-rich South—did these waterway-created cleavages lose meaning. Right up to the Civil War observers who had not yet discerned the difference that railroads made kept predicting that America would split in three, West and South allied against Northeast.

The settler's dependence on water transport as part of his choosiness about land made the opening up of the Mississippi Basin pretty hit-or-miss, as James C. Malin has pointed out: "Large areas not served by water were bypassed . . . there was no connected frontier-line. . . . Instead, scattered water-based diffusion centers served the land-mass interior. . . ." [42] Hence, for instance, the narrow strip of early settlement creeping up the Whitewater from the Ohio almost halfway to Lake Erie while the wilderness howled pretty much unbroken for a day's journey to east and west. The modern analogue is the strip development along a highway, and the Old Northwest's equivalent of split levels and shopping center was cabins and the gristmill, sawmill and blacksmith shop at the ford.

The mover from Back East did not at first properly value the prairies that increased in number and size as one pushed westward. True, such miles-wide open stretches, where deer, buffalo, prairie chickens and field mice flourished, were devoid of trees. But that very fact made him wary; where he came from, lack of big trees meant poor land. Besides, to "locate" in the middle of a prairie put him far from the plenty of firewood and building material of the big woods; prairies had few streams for water and transport, and their tall and rank grass meant a sod of roots so tough that breaking it up with the plow, even with three yoke of oxen, was about as arduous as tree-clearing. Hence many early settlers preferred the hill lands along the northern bank of the Ohio, rich in springs and streams, densely forested with huge oaks, hickories, beeches, ashes, tulip poplars, sycamores, all meaning a thick bed of rich humus to grow corn in, and the first three giving plentiful mast for ranging hogs. Now that the humus has washed down the streams to the Gulf of Mexico, those parts of southern Ohio and Indiana are poor, and it is hard to believe that they were once preferred to good prairieland. As erosion took hold, of course, and fertility declined and springs slackened their flow, decreasing returns often set the settler moving again—and by that time the virtues of the prairies were better understood.

Having lived very simply Back East, too, settlers coming West to better themselves usually did so. They had nowhere to go but up—a process well described at firsthand in the novels of Joseph Kirkland. A cut above the average—and rather likelier to do well soon—was the class of settlers on whose wagons rode maybe a genteel chest of drawers with brass pulls and shiny sides, protected by old bedquilts, and in one of its drawers bulbs, roots and slips—peonies and lilacs from the old garden to be planted around the new home. Even more prosperous and cultivated folks might also get movers' fever. Say an uncle or a cousin had been an officer with Wayne or Harrison in the Indian wars and had come back talking buffalo-studded meadows and gigantic timber betokening soil far richer than the run-down family acres in Harford County. "At times," says R. C. Buley, "officers and men seemed more interested in . . . prospective speculation or settlement than in the defeat of the Indians." [43] Or say a grandfather who knew the right people had once acquired title to thousands of Western acres that he had never bothered to inspect, and now that it was a good time to cash in, a younger son and growing family were sent West to settle on the best of it and supervise disposal of the rest to advantage. They would go in good wagons with hired men to drive and care for the teams and tents in case taverns proved too full or too squalid. Virginia Quality leaving exhausted tobacco fields to start again in cotton in Mississippi, as did Thomas Dabney, for instance, marched their slaves along in a troupe led by the overseer in a wagon. Wife and children might stay behind until, after a few years of building and clearing, the new place was worthy to receive them. By then the road might have improved enough for them to travel in the family carriage with young Mr. Landgrant escorting them on a sleek saddle horse. Numbers of such carriage parties were going to Kentucky through Winchester, Virginia, in the spring of 1794—a thing that would have made Daniel Boone stare. But it was not rapid transit. A generation later it would take Andrew Jackson a solid month to travel in his own carriage from Nashville, Tennessee, to Washington.

The house that welcomed Mrs. Landgrant and the children to the new country might still look out on mud, stumps and a distant prospect of deadened trees. But it was itself impressive, usually built of brick burned on the place with a minimum of timber in construction because sawmills were scarcer than deposits of good brick clay. Grouseland, the Georgian mansion that General William Henry Harrison built at Vincennes, Indiana, to match his dignity as governor of Indiana Territory, used brick not only in the 22-inch outer walls but also in the interior partitions; the place has twelve fireplaces, and the wooden trim is mostly black walnut and tulip. On his hermitage island in the middle of the Ohio, Harman Blennerhassett, the cultivated Englishman who knew no better than to get fascinated by Aaron Burr's smelly plans, created an allegedly Persian pavilion two stories high, 60 feet square and with wings attached to the main house by open verandas. Nothing is left to show what a Persian pavilion looked like in the backwoods c. 1800. But the greatest of early Old Northwestern houses does survive near Chillicothe, Ohio—Adena, the creation of Colonel Thomas Worthington, an FFV who freed his slaves in the early 1790's and started life anew in southern Ohio on 5,000 acres of forest. Some say at least the sketch from which the builders worked was the work of B. H. Latrobe, the English architect who had much to do with the U.S. Capitol and engineered Philadelphia's precedent-setting waterworks; it may be confirmation that Adena's powerfully pitched roofs and general style strongly resemble the model penitentiary that Latrobe designed for Virginia at about the same time. In any case, built of tawny local stone with two wings on vaults, it has a medieval simplicity and air of being at home with itself that makes it to my mind the finest house in America. ". . . one of the most tasty houses . . . westward of the mountains" [44] was the less sweeping estimate of an admiring British traveler of Worthington's time. Knowledgeable restorers have painted its interior trim of black walnut in the proper offbeat colors. Our forebears used black walnut for panels not for the beauty of the grain but because the wood works easily.

Most such wilderness showplaces, whether built by Sir William Johnson and Gerrit Smith in New York State or Andrew Jackson in Tennessee, were mansions only relatively. Cabin dwellers regarded them with astonishment and often some resentment, but in our terms they are of only moderate size and splendor. As steamboats supplied better transport, however, modish Empire furniture and hangings lent due elegance to the interior. (Colonel Worthington brought some furniture over the mountains from Philadelphia; craftsmen fetched in for the purpose made some on the spot.) And the dimensions of the exteriors could be fashionably inflated by adding porticoes of allegedly classical columns. For a Classic

Adena, gracious showplace of the Old Northwest.

Revival was sweeping architecture Back East, and the Quality of the over-the-mountains country felt themselves entitled to the latest style.

Classic Revival takes in, for a loose definition, most buildings with conspicuous white columns built in America between the Constitutional Convention (1787) and 1850.* Relatively unaffected by simultaneous imitations of the classical in Europe, the style rewards study. It nicely illustrates certain post-Revolutionary American traits. It was popular because it offered the rising American a striking new way to call attention to his success and its ancillary banks, courthouses and churches. It provided the standard backdrop for the magnolia-mint julep-Miss Cindy Lou myth of the South. And yet for all its ostentation and staginess, its best surviving examples show marked charm and even dignity—which cannot be said of several other borrowed architectures foisted on America later in the 1800's.

Thomas Jefferson is thought to have begun it by midwifing the design of the new commonwealth of Virginia's new Capitol in Richmond in the

* Greek Revival, the usual term, is confusing. Well into the 1800's the inspiration of such buildings was largely Roman in intent at least, not Greek. Greek Revival better fits the second phase, starting in the 1820's, which did use authentic Greek models. All this is clear from any careful reading of Talbot Hamlin's *Greek Revival Architecture in America.*

mid-1780's. The prototype that he suggested to the French architect who drew the actual plans was the famous Maison Carrée at Nîmes in Languedoc, an oblong Roman temple with a narrow Ionic portico on a high basement—a building toward which American tourists would probably be even more respectful were they aware that it is the ancestor of Scarlett O'Hara's Tara.* The working model sent across the ocean had wider proportions, however, and whereas the columns of the original are of stone in the Roman way, the New World version has tall single tree trunks sheathed in brick and plastered over. When finished in 1790, they nevertheless did give the Old Dominion's raw little fall-line capital (vice Williamsburg left to decay down the peninsula) the classical air that Jefferson had had in mind.

At the same time George Washington was doing his share by adding to the riverfront of Mount Vernon a range of square columns the full height of the façade holding up a dormered overhang the full width of it. This has the air of a grandiose expansion of the old Dutch Colonial arrangement—a story-and-a-half cottage shooting up and attenuating like Alice in Wonderland. Whatever its ancestry, here was the white-columned gentleman's residence that interbred with Jefferson's Romanisms so fruitfully. The fusion occurred in 1790, when New York City, providing a Presidential mansion in the belief that the national capital would remain there, set on the site of the present Customs House a tall Georgian brick box with half its façade masked by lofty Ionic columns supplemented by matching pilasters. This applied classic elements to a city dwelling placed high and stately on the most conspicuous spot in town. Fashions are seldom made in a day. The ensuing decades, particularly in large cities, also built many stubbornly Georgian houses with merely pilastered or columned doorways. Charles Bulfinch, English-trained offshoot of Boston Quality, transplanted to Beacon Hill and other parts of New England his own lovely versions of the style of the brothers Adam then so fashionable in London, which combined Georgianism with Greco-Roman detail. But after the War of 1812 the showy, prevalently two-story-high columns proliferated vigorously. It was easy enough—just specify a portico reminiscent of "the Parthenon of Virginia" [45] as novelist-politician John P. Kennedy called that edifice dominating Richmond. Columns were also freely added to existing houses, whence, as at the Schuyler House near the Saratoga battlefield, restorers have since removed them.

* America's Classic Revival is certainly anticipated by the pedimented porticoes of the Redwood Library in Newport, Rhode Island (1748) and the Jumel Mansion in New York City (1765) well ahead of Jefferson's Capitol, as well as the three-sided colonnade of the Eagle Tavern, East Poultney, Vermont, of 1785. There is little evidence, however, that any of the three much affected building styles in their neighborhoods, whereas Jefferson's Roman-mindedness proved highly infectious.

Gradually the full treatment—lofty columns in a wide portico crowned by a proper Roman architrave and sometimes a pediment—spread from Maine to Georgia and far westward into New York State. The architrave was usually a false front. That was harder to detect when, as the fashion gained momentum, the colonnade crept around two more sides so that the viewer had to be in the rear of the house to unmask the guilty secret. Occasionally—as in central Georgia, where Classic Revival arrived just in time to celebrate early new cotton fortunes—it extended around all four sides. White columns of various heights also appeared on the local

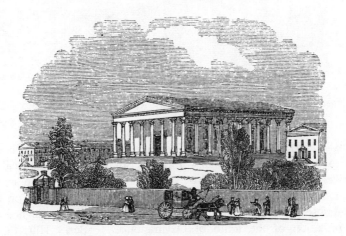

Girard College in Philadelphia was one of the high points of the Classic Revival.

bank, the lawyer's tiny office on the square, the courthouse, the schoolhouse and owner's office flanking the Cotton Belt Big House, even on the wellhead cover as at the Grady House in Athens, Georgia. They gleamed on high far above the sightseers on the Hudson River steamboats in the immense Corinthian colonnade of the famous Catskill Mountain House. I have yet to find a Classic Revival privy, but I don't doubt that one exists somewhere, or once did.

The tide swept on into the county seats of the growing Old Northwest and the cotton boom country of Alabama and Mississippi. By 1836 things had gone so far—in miles as well as emulation—that a newspaper in Chicago, at the far edge of settlement, besought builders to cease "multiplying the abortive temples with which the land groans." [46] Even the Indians were infected—when John Ross, part-white chief of the Cherokees prospering in the Indian Territory, built a classically pillared man-

Classic revival buildings dressing up early Rochester, New York.

sion just outside Tahlequah, the Cherokee head town. People began to associate the style with raw new fortunes. In Kennedy's satirical novel *Quodlibet,* the suddenly wealthy Baltimorean builds a house on a hill "with a Grecian portico in front . . . a Temple of Minerva on top of the ice-house . . ." and had the new quarters of his bank designed as "an exact imitation of the tomb of Ozymandias." [47] Berry Hill, the most fulsomely Doric of Virginia's Big Houses, was built not by an FFV but by

Vermont's State House, drawn here in the 1830's, has the basic features of the nationwide tradition.

James Bruce, a clever merchant from Petersburg, whose nine retail outlets in the Chesapeake region first worked out the principle of the chain store and gave him one of the first large American fortunes. Naturally the most extravagant development occurred among the cotton snobs of Mississippi and upper Louisiana. But it lasted longest—in a fashion owing more to Mount Vernon than to Vitruvius—in the extremely attenuated columns rising four or five stories above the rocking chairs on the verandas of the great wooden resort hotels built between 1840 and 1870 from Saratoga to Cape May.

It also had demure aspects in the white-painted country churches of the Northeast with recessed porticoes of two to four properly proportioned Doric or Ionic columns. In full Greek idiom it answered the needs of Baltimore's Jewish community in the recently restored Lloyd Street Synagogue. When a succession of eminent architects applied it to the U.S. Capitol at Washington and crowned all with a dome, they created a potent prototype for state capitols. The best of the consequences may be those at Raleigh, North Carolina, and Columbus, Ohio, both partly the work of the distinguished Connecticut architect-engineer Ithiel Town; the latter is of such simple and elegant proportions as to be almost Quakerish. The "most fantastically vulgar in its details as in its mass, of any of the typical state capitols," [48] says Talbot Hamlin—justifiably—is that in Indianapolis. Serene or vulgar, however, all capitols of this school helped to create an implicit impression that laws would be invalid unless passed by a legislature sitting in an oblong building with columned porticoes, lots of steps and, if possible, a dome.

Culturally this was Europe's new fad of classicality that had sent Jefferson to look at the Maison Carrée in the first place. It had been set off by the finds at Herculaneum and Pompeii, urged on by paintings like Benjamin West's and Jacques Louis David's and by the obsession of the leaders of the American and French Revolutions with the classical heroes of Plutarch's *Lives*. In Europe it led to colonnaded churches like that of La Madeleine in Paris and to summerhouses in England modeled on the Temple of Vesta in Rome. America's version went all that one better with country residences resembling the Parthenon.

It was a time when the fraternal order organized by former officers of the Revolutionary armed forces could unembarrassedly call itself the Order of the Cincinnati after the Roman farmer-warrior who always gladly returned to the plow after saving his country. (Nobody noticed how few Continental generals had hayseed in their hair: Benjamin Lincoln was a farmer, but John Sullivan was a lawyer; Thomas Mifflin and Thomas Sumter small merchants; Rufus Putnam a surveyor; Anthony Wayne a tanner; James Mercer and Henry Dearborn physicians; Henry

Knox a bookseller; Nathanael Greene an ironmaster.) When Putnam's Ohio Company of Associates founded Marietta, Ohio, they called the muddy track from the river to the stockade the Via Sacra and the area within the stockade the Campus Martius. A promising riverbank village farther down the Ohio was soon named after those self-styled Cincinnati; the unlettered Hoosiers trading there called it Sinsnatty. The names that Jefferson proposed for the new states eventually to be carved out of the Old Northwest were mostly of a clottily classical flavor: Assenisipia, Metropotamia, Polypotamia. Classic-minded land speculators or their surveyors sowed new lands with still persisting, wildly anomalous placenames that stupefy Europeans studying road maps: Georgia has Rome

*An 1880's view of the Ohio State Capitol at Columbus,
serene and elegant.*

and Athens; so has upstate New York, as well as Utica, Marcellus, Brutus, Syracuse, Palmyra, Ithaca, Troy. And in all such settlements the postlog-cabin round of building was thick with white columns. They were the more numerous for America's response to Lord Byron's championing of the Greek rebels against the Turks in the 1820's—hence the names of Navarino, Wisconsin, and Ypsilanti, Michigan, and the second and more carefully Greek-detailed phase of the Classic Revival.

This migration from the banks of the Tiber to those of the Genesee inevitably led to confusion. Choice of capital style leaned toward the ornate

Corinthian and Composite orders, but as pedantry crept in, the chaster Tuscan and Doric asserted themselves. With them the skinniness that came of using dressed tree trunks was unfortunate. Though a very slender Corinthian column is defensible esthetically and historically, drastic attenuation robs the Doric of its virtues. In such instances as the Holmes House at Alfred, Maine, the pine spars are undisguised. But camouflage was usual—either brick-and-plaster sheathing or fluted and curved-section slabs of wood.

Novelist Anthony Trollope, a more reliable observer of America than his scribbling mother but an inept archeologist, deplored the use of pseudo-Greek wooden columns to glorify otherwise humdrum dwellings. It should have occurred to him that the purpose was the same as that in the matured Greek temple—to mask and make imposing the boxy shelter-shrine within. The forerunners of classic Doric columns of stone had been just such upright, undressed logs, only shorter, hence stockier. Further, the classic Doric frieze (triglyph, metope, guttae) is known to have been an approximation in stone of visual details making structural sense only for the wooden beams and pegs of which early Greek temples were built. So the dainty frieze of the Classic Revival church at Harlingen, New Jersey, imitates in wood a Greek imitation in stone of a long-vanished wooden original in preclassic Greece. It is unlikely that, in spite of Trollope, the notion of wooden columns would have grieved the Greeks of 800 B.C. or those of Pericles' Athens, who, never having heard that form follows function, took imitative fakery with ignorant calm. Their cousins in Corinth and Greek Sicily were blithely plastering over columns

The Eagle Tavern's classic colonnade consists of innocent pine spars that the Greeks would have understood.

of local limestone to make them look like marble. They would doubtless also have approved the columns crowned with tobacco leaves and Indian corn instead of acanthus that Latrobe designed for the U.S. Capitol.

The grave sins of the Classic Revival were subtler. Since it usually neglected entasis, the subtle curving of the long lines of column and platform that gave character to the Greeks' greatest buildings, the effect was vaguely insipid. Its carving of capitals, railings and such was often coarse, especially in the South. Indeed, for lack of skilled wood-carvers the acanthus leaves for Corinthian columns were sometimes cast iron, as at the Hermitage. Striving for ostentation raised porticoes too high for their proper purpose—to keep the baking sun off the walls and give shaded sitting places. (The two-story galleries of Charleston, Mobile and New Orleans, borrowed from the West Indies and sensibly imitated by many taverns in the North in the 1850's, served that end better.) The Classic Revivalist was also probably unaware that the Greeks and Romans confined such overweening design largely to public buildings, that the outsides of even some fairly splendid private houses looked like fortified barracks from without. He would doubtless have rejected with horror suggestions that architrave and frieze be painted red and blue as in ancient Greece. For the early 1800's only pale, naked stone was chaste enough to be classical.

The end product was certainly best where it belonged—on public buildings such as the New York Subtreasury and the Charleston Exchange. Never look gift horses too hard in the mouth, however. Get enough greenery around Tara, stand away, blur the eyes, and it still looks mighty fine. Queen Sophie of Greece told Robert Hale Newton that she had long sought a modern style of dwelling to "harmonize with the Peloponnesian landscape and climate. Nothing from Europe or Asia Minor seemed right. Finally, chancing upon photographs of the Greek Revival in America, she found them to be the perfect solution!" [49] and was arranging for Greek architects to go to America to study Cindy Lou's ancestral mansion when World War I intervened.

As the new nation shook down, certain other importations from the Old World did far more than the Classic Revival to knit the thirteen parochial states together—particularly improvements in transportation. One such was the turnpike, not just a locally maintained—or neglected— track from hamlet to hamlet but running purposefully from commercial center to commercial center charging tolls to finance itself. In the Old World construction and maintenance of turnpikes were a public responsibility. In America a private company taking the economic risk in hopes of profit was usually, though not always, the builder-operator. In either case, to cover cost and expenses-plus, users were charged fixed rates at fixed points—so much per two- or four-wheeled vehicle of this or that type or per head of cattle or sheep—horsemen and pedestrians by no means exempt. Many charters allowed only those going "to mill [to have a grist of corn or wheat ground] or meeting [on Sunday]" [50] to pass free.

Turnpike came from the pole (pike) pivoted across the road at the tolltaker's booth, which was usually also his dwelling, to keep the customer from further progress until he paid up. (A similar graduated toll system governed fares at private or public ferries, some well run and equipped, some very poor, that were the intermediate stage between ford and bridge.) Modern superhighways designed for concrete and gasoline still retain the old word, along with the annoyance of successive stops to pay small sums. Whenever he could, the farmer of 1820 bound for market with a load of corn worked out an alternate route, roughly parallel, on the growing network of minor roads, which he called his shunpike. That word too survives; I have seen it on a township road sign south of Madison, New Jersey, and on a minor road entering Route 2 east of Burlington, Vermont.

The turnpike was a late medieval institution in England but failed to reach the New World until well after the Revolution. Its first conspicuous American success was that of the Lancaster Turnpike from Philadelphia into the heart of the Pennsylvania Dutch country opened by private promoters in 1791, an elaborate successor of the old Great Wagon Road. The consequent rapid stage service from Philadelphia to Lancaster over its stump-free, graveled surface covered 70-odd miles in twelve hours. In the next generation turnpikes spread freely into the middle states and New England, radiating spoke-fashion from the port capitals and upcountry commercial centers like Albany, usually privately built but not always. Few paid off as their backers hoped. The advent of canals in the 1820's and of railroads two decades later kept them poor. But they showed the new nation that roads did not have to be quite as bad as those the Colonies had put up with. And those open when the War of 1812 came had a burst of glory as the British naval blockade shut down on the coasting vessels previously taking New England manufactures and middle states wheat south and bringing back rice and cotton. By 1814 20,000 horses and oxen were hauling some 4,000 big freight wagons from as far north as Boston to as far south as Augusta, Georgia, mostly on turnpikes. Amused by this replacement of ship and sailor, the wagoners painted Mud-Clipper or Sailor's Misery or Neptune Metamorphosed on their vehicles. Newspapers printed such doggerel as

Tho' Neptune's trident is laid by,
From north to south our coasters ply.
No sail or rudder need these ships,
Which Freemen drive with wagon whips. . . .[51]

The trips took forever: twenty-six days from Boston to Baltimore; ten days from Baltimore to Richmond. The charges per hundredweight were high to match. But at least interstate commerce was not altogether choked off.

The rise of turnpikes had already set the U.S. Post Office shifting mails from horse and rider to stage wagons. In turn that encouraged the expansion of stage services to get additional revenue by carrying mails. Gradually stages running more or less on schedule in most weathers had criss-crossed the well-settled Northeast—say, from Washington to Portland, Maine—and had ventured gingerly over the mountains beyond Pittsburgh and into the Southeast. Better roads brought better vehicles, but read that with caution—the roads were only relatively better.

Refinements combining lightness and strength eliminated the spring-less, hulking stage wagon, with canvas hood and benches for thirty-odd, and culminated in a peculiarly American vehicle, the Concord coach, so-

*The Concord coach, nine-passengers-inside version,
drawn by Captain Basil Hall, RN, c. 1830.*

called from Concord, New Hampshire, where it was born. High-slung on high, wide-tired wheels, elegantly shaped, it was an offshoot from the private gentleman's carriage crossed with the tallyho type of British coach familiar in Regency prints. It took six, nine or twelve inside passengers, depending on its length, with one seat beside the driver—the place most coveted in good weather—and as business grew, a few more seats appeared on the roof, originally for luggage only. A hooded rack behind held more luggage. In the commonest nine-passenger model, those seated three in the front seat and three in the rear seat were best off. The third three, facing forward on a thwartwise bench, had only a broad leather strap slung behind them to brace against—an exquisitely uncomfortable arrangement. No inside passenger had decent legroom.

To absorb road shocks, which were often practically unremitting, the rocker-bottomed body was hung on thoroughbraces—wide, multi-ply leather straps—better than anything the old stage wagon had, less likely to break than later steel springs, but causing the coach body to respond to each jolt or jostle with a nodding-forward motion "like the violent pitching of a vessel . . . [with] a strong wind ahead" [52] that readily induced dryland seasickness. As compensating advantage, thoroughbraces enabled the horses to start a heavily loaded coach more easily, since their first jerk heaved the body backward and then helpfully forward in reaction to the elastic leather. To reconcile the passengers to discomfort, there were the splendors of sitting on silk plush upholstery in a subtly designed and beautifully made shell of white oak gleaming with paint and varnish and sporting on the door panels genuine oil paintings of mythological allegories. The specimen preserved in Concord, expertly restored by an old gentleman who spent his life decorating Concord coaches, has a scarlet body, yellow running gear picked out with black, and on the panels painted views of the New Hampshire Statehouse.

Such elegance contrasted sharply with what awaited the passenger when this gaudy instrument of torture deposited him for the night at one of the old stagecoach inns. Now the rambling old place has often been restored with unlimited white paint, a gift shop where the barroom used to be, apple pandowdy on the menu and ghastly pink French dressing on the salads. In the turnpike era, though inns varied in quality, the average expectation was, to judge by surviving accounts, low not only by today's standards but by those of the American Quality of the time. The basic layout was a barroom, a dining room and kitchen and so forth on the ground floor; upstairs a large assembly room for dances and meetings with a fiddler's bench on one side; and a clutter of small to middle-sized bedrooms. The bar was also the landlord's office where accommodations were assigned and bills paid, which was awkward for women and prim men shy about tobacco juice and local loafers. The dining room had only one long table, like the Old Country table d'hôte, where the landlord and his wife presided over many platters and tureens containing a great variety of lukewarm items, mostly fried and very greasy.

The bedrooms lacked fireplaces usually, privacy almost always. Two or more beds to the room, two guests to the bed (sexes duly respected) were normal. With luck there was a washstand with bowl and pitcher but seldom water in it. Soap-and-water duties were usually performed out-doors at the pump or the well. None of this, a well-born Polish immigrant observed in 1804, surprised Americans: ". . . they do not travel . . . except on business . . . have very little baggage, elegance in amenities is unknown to them." [53] For one's clothes a few pegs on the wall was all one could hope for. Harriet Martineau, traveling widely in America in 1834, found this true even of many private houses, as well as at inns and hotels: "I believe I had the use of a chest of drawers only two or three times during my travels." [54] As one worked westward, sheets tended to disappear; this was not necessarily a loss because when present, they of-ten showed signs of much previous service. Chances of bedbugs were dauntingly high. A genial Briton of 1819 was willing to give the landlords "a large share of the blame, yet . . . their customers are of so filthy habits that . . . it is extremely difficult in this warm climate to keep free from bedbugs, particularly at inns, as they are constantly carried in the cloaths, luggage, etc." [55] Francisco de Miranda, a Venezuelan patriot exile, who liked American girls in his bed but not male strangers or bugs, made a habit of sleeping on the floor in inns to avoid being gnawed. And this hazard, too, was not uncommon in private houses to judge from a passage in an etiquette book of 1859 warning the reader that it is impolite to drop even a hint to your hostess that you found wildlife in your bed when staying overnight.

This slackness about details, to put it kindly, was just as evident in the roads one traveled over. "As no attention has been paid to forming or draining roadbeds," wrote David Stevenson, engineer uncle of Robert Louis Stevenson, in the 1830's, "it is only for a few months during sum-mer that they . . . are tolerable." He was aghast at the corduroy roads made in backward areas by juxtaposing 12-foot logs across the road, which kept wheels from sinking into soft ground but also forced them to progress "by . . . leaps and starts, particularly trying to those accus-tomed to the comforts of European travelling." [56]

Less temperate comments were frequent from testier visitors. The Reverend Mr. Read of the Congregational Union of Great Britain, touring Ohio in 1834 on the Lord's business, thought the road between Sandusky and Columbus more like a stony ditch than a road; a stagecoach with him as sole passenger took seven hours to go 23 miles. He was even worse off when, below Cincinnati, he was one of three passengers in a fast mail coach the horses of which trotted, keeping him so "jarred and jolted, as to threaten serious mischief . . . my hat was many times thrown from my head, and all my bruises bruised over again. It was really an amusement to see us laboring to keep our places." [57] It was, after all, an American stage driver in Illinois who said that the mud was often so deep on his run that though he had driven a team of mules for months, he did not yet know what color they were—he never saw anything of them but their ears.

Europeans were struck by the lavish use of lumber in the plank roads which, as sawmills proliferated, often succeeded corduroy—mile after mile of heavy plank spiked to parallel stringers, passable enough when new but soon so split, rotten and twisted loose that it was small improvement on the prolonged mudhole that had preceded it. Even on the great new National Road from Cumberland, Maryland, to Wheeling on the Ohio River (eventually crossing the Old Northwest into Illinois), where the English macadam technique of building with crushed stone was used, a certain stage operation was known as the Shake-Gut Line—doubtless with reason. After finishing a camel trip through the same desert that gave Moses' Israelites so much trouble, George Perkins Marsh, geographer and father of the American conservation movement, wrote home philosophically that arduous as it had been, "any forty days of *stage* travelling in the United States would involve more of fatigue, danger and discomfort of all sorts." [58]

The drivers of the four- or six-horse teams harnessed to the shiny coaches were doubtless as fine artists with the ribbons as their roadside admirers believed, but when even the best road was no great thing, an average of 5½ mph was all that regular schedules dared promise from Cumberland to Wheeling; through less hilly New England Boston-to-New York maybe 6 mph. A traveler making the 40 miles from Providence to Boston in fewer than five hours wrote with no sarcastic intent that if anybody wanted to go faster, he could charter a streak of lightning. Even under the favorable conditions necessary to make such time, the shaking up was severe. Those coaches must have been amazingly well made to hold together at all under what speed-minded drivers put them through on roads that would have taxed a Jeep, usually "in so wretched and neglected a condition as hardly to deserve the name of highways . . . quite unfit," Stevenson said, "for any vehicle but an American stage and any pilot but an American driver." [59]

The combination looked its best when the driver pushed his jaded team to a last showoff spurt up to the Sickle & Sheaf at a spanking trot, bits jingling, heads tossing, horn blowing and the local storekeeper returning from his annual buying trip to Philadelphia waving to his family from the box seat. It was at its most impressive when, after the Mexican War and the gold rush turned eyes on California, Uncle Sam needed fast mail and passenger transport between the body of the nation and its new appendages on the West Coast. After much shilly-shally it was decided to subsidize a mail-coach route from Missouri to San Francisco in a sagging, 2,800-mile loop via Fort Smith, Arkansas, El Paso and Los Angeles. That was farther than a route straight across but promised less trouble from snow and in any case better suited the Southern-minded politicians who dominated Washington in the 1850's.

The contract went to John Butterfield, a transport veteran who had begun life driving a stage, come to own stage lines in western New York State, got into canal packets, lake steamboats, plank roads, early railroads, telegraph lines and the express (private mail and parcel service) business, the last eventuating in the birth of the American Express Company. Under him the Overland Mail Company took hold with the calm complexity of a great circus settling down on a new lot. He bought 250 new Concord coaches and, for use in the empty, dry reaches of the far Southwest, a number of light, flat-bedded "celerity wagons" with leather curtains instead of glass windows and seats that unfolded to bed length. He set up 200-odd stage stations, bought 1,800 horses, and hired drivers, conductors—supercargoes in command like railroad conductors—station bosses, blacksmiths, wheelwrights, ostlers, herders to mind the stocks of relay horses and veterinarians to keep them healthy, in all more than 1,000 employees, many of whom loyally made a sort of uniform out of Butterfield's customary dress on field trips—a long yellow linen duster and a wide-awake (wide-brimmed, low-crowned) hat.

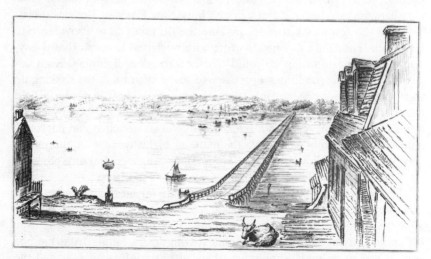

The Long Bridge across Lake Cayuga, always marveled at by Europeans, as drawn by Captain Basil Hall, RN, c. 1830.

The covered bridge was the finest offspring of the American's collaboration with wood.

The contract called for twenty-five days from the Father of Waters to the Golden Gate. The first westbound and eastbound Overland mails, leaving at the same time, both made it in twenty-four. They soon had it down to twenty-two. For three years the Concords rolled as regularly as sunrise and sunset full of passengers at $100 one way—a low rate for a trip that, rugged though it was, had great advantages over the alternative comprising two steamers, the Panama Railroad and the risk of yellow fever. When the mails filled the lower body of the coach, as well as the roof, the passengers lay on the mailbags and reported it a very comfortable way to travel. When the Civil War interrupted service, Butterfield shifted smoothly to the central route via South Pass and Salt Lake City and presently sold out to Ben Holladay, another renowned virtuoso of stagecoaching. Holladay sold in turn to Wells, Fargo and Company, the express and banking house sired by two of Butterfield's former associates that had made California its oyster. Wells, Fargo, too, knew a good thing when it saw it in the Concord coach. Pitching like a whaleboat, dust-covered and durable, it was the connective tissue of the Pacific Coast until the railroads came. On minor runs it remained so for another generation in the hands of such famous California drivers as Hank Monk and "Colonel" Clark Foss.

* * *

Most Concord coaches were used to fording streams and the alternate risks of crude ferries casually navigated. Bridges were not unknown. Even in the 1600's a few were built, for pedestrians first, then widened to take horses, then again to cart width. But what with the awkward breadth of many American streams and the costliness of construction relative to community resources—the same factor that kept roads so bad—they remained few until after 1800. Then, however, the American's woodmindedness coupled with his ingenuity to beget that symbol of rural nostalgia, the covered bridge—a triumph of rule-of-thumb engineering.

Clubs of covered bridge fans now watch solicitously over many of the hundreds of surviving examples in the Northeast and the Old Northwest, where they most prevailed. They also try to correct sightseers' misguided notions of what the covering was for: not to protect loads of hay from sudden rain; not to keep weather in general off travelers as if it were a railroad snowshed; not to give Him and Her in a buggy a fleeting tunnel-of-love privacy as promised in the misapplied term *kissing bridge*.* Only incidentally did it afford a rainy-day play place for boys and sometimes a lurking place for highwaymen. Actually the covering was arrived at in a logical evolution of engineering as gratifying as the patterns of the trusses holding it together.

The Yankees' first bridges were platforms crossing streams on multiple piles. It was a memorable day when a Great Bridge of that type was opened across the Charles in 1662. Then it was found that perpendicular trusses high across the roadbed on either side strengthened such a bridge —until rot and weather weakened the trusses. Plank housings protected them—only in heavy storms wind pressure on the resulting wooden wall distorted the roadbed and piling. Transverse braces took care of that— and, once in place, irresistibly suggested roofing to keep rot-causing rain and snow off the roadway planking. So the roof of a covered bridge is simply a timber-preserving measure so effective that it makes the extra cost worthwhile. To build a bridge thus, like an attenuated barn, is not unique to America. "Covered bridges are found," says H. W. Congdon, a zealous expert, "in all well-forested countries from Norway to China." [60] Those I have seen in the basin of the upper Rhine are very like American ones. The notion may well have entered the Middle Colonies with the Pennsylvania Dutch, like the long rifle and the hewn-log

---

* A kissing bridge was any bridge, not necessarily covered, where local custom required a man and woman driving by themselves on wheels or runners to stop in the middle and kiss. The best known was on Manhattan Island. See Andrew Burnaby's *Travels*, 81: ". . . there is a bridge, about three miles distant from New York, which you always pass over as you return, called the Kissing-bridge; where it is a part of the etiquette to salute the lady who has put herself under your protection."

house. Yet it is also likely that it sprang up spontaneously in New England, where, thanks to shipbuilding, timber engineering was very well understood.

After the early 1800's the square-sectioned frame began to be so strengthened by one or another kind of special truss that it could span minor streams without support from piling or piers. The lattice truss, invented by architect Ithiel Town, was an early instance; then came the Burr truss with a laminated wooden arch—each type with its own admirers and diverse uses. In 1812 Louis Wernwag, a German coming to America in 1786 to escape military service, threw a single-span, all-wooden covered bridge 340 feet across the Schuylkill at Philadelphia. Three years later Theodore Burr, inventor of the aforesaid truss, beat that with a 360-foot single span across the Susquehanna. Michael Chevalier, the French radical economist, complimenting Americans on their skill in constructing wooden bridges, called "those of Switzerland, about which so much has been said . . . clumsy and heavy [in comparison]." [61] Yet for all their lightness, these American bridges were most durably built. The flood that carries away a modern concrete-and-steel bridge as an unusable wreck may merely float an old wooden covered bridge from its abutments and lodge it somewhere downstream, trigly undamaged, to be put back into service at the new site with new approaches—a great tribute to the obscure village experts who, lacking blueprints but long experienced with stresses and timber, shaped and mortised and treenailed it together. Not only bridges but the aqueducts that carried America's canals across large streams were also often covered with the same purpose of structure-preservation.

George Washington was a man of varied concerns. While adding pillars to Mount Vernon in the mid-1780's, he was also projecting canals to make the upper reaches of the Potomac useful. Within a few years Henry Knox, one of his ablest citizen generals, was securing a state charter for a canal from Boston to the upper Connecticut River. Nothing came of that, nor

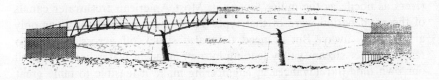

Structure of covered wooden bridge over the Schuylkill at Philadelphia as drawn by David Stevenson, engineer-uncle of the author of Treasure Island, *in the 1830's.*

did Washington's scheme get off the ground for decades. But these and other projects of the day presaged the canal-mindedness that swept America along with the Classic Revival. Whatever affinities the two things had are cryptic indeed. The results of one were showily elegant and often permanent; of the other rowdy and fleeting. One flouted engineering; the other gloried in it. Yet the canal idea came over from Europe at much the same time, and the curve of its rise and fall was roughly identical.

Here, too, a European transplant soon showed a specially American shape. Many of the Old Countries had long used locks and artificial waterways to protect mooring basins from tides, to take barges around obstructions in rivers, to raise them over moderate humps separating the feeders of distinct river systems. Most of that was mere correction of nature's minor negligences while still relying chiefly on river channels to float things up- or downslope. In the mid-1700's, however, the Duke of Bridgewater, a stodgy English peer smarting under personal mishaps, retired to his coal-bearing estates and set about getting more out of them. His method was to create an artificial channel to float coal to Manchester in barges, halving the cost of getting it there. A second canal tapped the Liverpool market. Soon he was making an annual 35 percent on his investment—and England was in a canal boom that did much to quicken the inchoate Industrial Revolution.

Already waterway-minded, the Colonies took note that engineering paid when applied to barge transport. Pennsylvanians were soon talking of improving the navigation of the Schuylkill. Advising them from England in 1772, Benjamin Franklin hit on the essential part of the duke's success: English canal builders, he said, "seldom or never use a River where it can be avoided. . . . Rivers are ungovernable things. . . . Canals are quiet and always manageable." [62] One could use as fairway the valley that a river had cut and tap the river itself for water. To that extent major and minor American streams—Potomac, James, Susquehanna, Delaware, Merrimack and so on—lent aid and often their names to canals. But it eventually proved best in most cases to turn the actual floating of the canalboat from here to there over to man-dug artificial rivers as docile as the mules towing it. Most American freshwater canals of the great period were of that type. They might parallel the river only a few yards away. But at need they also struck off across country to reach another stream valley leading into an adjacent watershed. Not until our own time did advances in engineering make it feasible to tame great natural rivers like the Rhine with power dredges, dams and high-lift locks.

The trauma of the Revolution smothered Pennsylvania's canal-mindedness. Those reviving it afterward neglected Franklin's advice and began to put money and ingenuity into developing the Schuylkill with thirty-four dams and twenty-nine locks in some 100 miles of slack-water engineering. Generally, for the next generation canals were built only to bypass falls or rapids (notably on the Connecticut and on the James above Richmond) or to connect an immediate backcountry with its saltwater port as in South Carolina's Santee Canal (1802) and Massachusetts' Middlesex Canal (1803). The liveliest such half measures were taken along the Mohawk River route from the upper Hudson to the Great Lakes. In spite of natural obstacles, stubborn men had long been poling boats up the Mohawk to the Great Oneida Carrying Place where Rome, New York, now stands—a swampy watershed out of which a stream named Wood Creek led into Oneida Lake, thence down the Oswego River to Lake Ontario. They crossed the portage slung on wheels with the aid of a "horn breeze"—yokes of oxen. At the western end of Lake Ontario where the way into Lake Erie is blocked by Niagara Falls, cargoes were unloaded and oxcarted up the Niagara scarp to Lake Erie and its waiting schooners.

Agitation by an able Yankee, Elkanah Watson, who had personally studied European canals and discussed them with Franklin and Washington, and by others kept New York State reminded of the possibility of improving this route substantially enough to tap the potentially rich trade of the Old Northwest. A minor canal around the Little Falls of the Mohawk, another at the Wood Creek portage, increased the size of boats available and led to a mouth-watering lowering of cost per ton and heightening of volume and business. The hint was not lost on imaginative New Yorkers grouped around Governor De Witt Clinton. They determined to use the Mohawk Valley for an artificial-river type of canal, the longest in the world, from the upper Hudson to Lake Erie right over the Niagara scarp with—for audacious good measure—major branches to Lake Ontario and by way of Lake Champlain into Canada.

Surveys showed that the crucial humps of the Lake Erie and Lake Champlain routes were, though formidable engineering problems, not insurmountable. After vainly seeking help from the federal government and the new states of the Old Northwest, which stood greatly to benefit from the scheme, New York finally went it alone. The engineers principally in charge, James Geddes and Benjamin Wright, two country lawyers who had never seen a real canal but knew land surveying, threw great stone aqueducts across the Mohawk and Genesee rivers and amazed Europeans with their double flight of five contiguous locks cut out of solid stone to get up and down the Niagara scarp. By 1819 the first leg of the great Erie Canal, from Utica to Rome, opened with appropriately elaborate speechifying and brass bands. By 1825 another mass of celebrants, clustered around Governor Clinton, were broaching a keg of Lake Erie water on a barge in New York harbor not to drink, of course—precious little water was drunk on that glorious day!—but to empty into the salt water to symbolize completion of the great artificial waterway from Buffalo to the Hudson.

It really was an occasion. It destined New York City to be out and away the national focus, eclipsing Philadelphia and Boston.* By moving immigrants and manufactures westward more cheaply than wheels did, and by floating eastward cereals and salted meats, wagon transport of which was uneconomic, it expanded the economies and population of the Old Northwest as explosively as it developed the Empire State herself. The infant merchant marine of the Great Lakes, only recently grown large enough to call for building lighthouses, also boomed to serve the canal's western outlets at Oswego and Buffalo. It was much more worthwhile to grow wheat on Illinois prairies when it could go out of Chicago by schooner to Buffalo, where a new milling industry turned it into barreled flour to go down the Erie Canal and the Hudson to feed the Northeast or be transshipped to Europe. Midstate Illinois farmers hauled their grain northward in pairs or groups so the teams could double and triple up to pull through the worst mudholes. The womenfolk had good reason to compete with one another on who supplied the men with the best ham, pie and cold fried chicken to eat en route, for the proceeds of that load of forty bushels at four bits a bushel fetched home barreled salt and dry goods and knickknacks. The opening of the Champlain branch of the Erie Canal in 1823 abruptly swung the trade of the border country away from Canada and diverted the interests of its population of smugglers into the American sphere. Canalboats, sloop-rigged, sailed down the lake to Whitehall, unstepped their masts, left them ashore to be picked up on the return trip, and proceeded on to the Hudson under horse or mule tow on the new canal.

All that came of the temerity of building the world's longest canal through what was still three-quarters wilderness. An understandable canal fever had seized the other states even before the Erie was completed. Among the consequences were shifts in international relations and transatlantic immigration. States embarking on internal improvements—some roads, railroads as time passed, but principally canals—sold large bond issues to finance them. Overseas investors paid small heed to the distinction between bonds of the United States, then brilliantly solvent, and those of the individual state of the Union. When most such state projects failed to prosper and the bonds went to default, British bondholders assumed

* Philadelphia was already slightly handicapped by the lower salt content of the Delaware River at the height of the port, which allowed awkward freeze-ups in the same weather that still left the more saline Hudson ice-free. Baltimore, too, had much of the same trouble. See J. S. Buckingham's *America*, II, 223, and Michael Chevalier's *Society . . . in the United States*, 223.

that the federal government would make good. The storm of protest blowing up when no such thing occurred lasted for decades and added the ugly word *swindling* to tobacco chewing, slaveholding and abuse of the mother tongue as reasons to dislike America. "The mass of your countrymen," Dickens' Martin Chuzzlewit tells Elijah Pogram, the American statesman who bore a tactless resemblance to Daniel Webster, "begin by stubbornly neglecting little social observances, which have nothing to do with gentility, custom, usage, government, or country, but are acts of common, decent, natural politeness. You abet them in this, by resenting all attacks upon their social offences, as if they were a beautiful natural feature. From disregarding small obligations they come in regular course to disregard great ones; and so refuse to pay their debts . . . a part of one great growth, which is rotten at the root." [63] As for immigration, canals required immeasurable pick-and-shovel work in a country chronically short of labor. That brought across the water the first conspicuous swarms of Catholic Irish, harbingers of the even greater mass of Pats and Mikes who would build the railroads east of the Rockies and in due season change the cultural face of Northeastern America.

For ease of hump-surmounting the Erie Canal route was the best approach to the Old Northwest from the seaboard. Unfavorable topography —meaning mountain ridges some 2,000 feet above sea level—severely handicapped the efforts of other states to compete with the Erie for eastbound produce. A generation of intermittent progress got Washington's Potomac scheme, finally known as the Chesapeake and Ohio Canal, no nearer the Ohio than Cumberland, Maryland. Virginia's James River and Kanawha Canal had much the same history, attaining limited usefulness but never linking up with the Western Waters. Pennsylvania's effort to give the Erie a rival, once she remembered Franklin's artificial-river policy, teamed the newfangled railroad up with canals in a scheme as ingenious as it was expensive and futile.

A recent scholar described the working result, opened in 1834, as "a cumbrous mongrel . . . that technological monstrosity, a canal over mountains." [64] From Columbia, Pennsylvania, on the Susquehanna (reached by rail or by the new Schuylkill-Susquehanna Union Canal), canalboats took passengers or freight 172 miles up a canal following the Susquehanna and Juniata rivers into the hills at Hollidaysburg. There the boats were taken apart in sections, hauled by steam winch up an inclined-plane railroad over the Allegheny summit, let down again to Johnstown, Pennsylvania, reassembled and floated 150 miles down another canal to Pittsburgh, triumphantly crossing the Allegheny River into town on a gigantic aqueduct. The whole required no fewer than 174 locks, each entailing time and heavy maintenance and attendance costs, in addition to the uneconomic portage railroad over the worst of the hump. But such disadvantages were blithely discounted when canal fever was high. The Morris Canal across hilly northern New Jersey, surmounting a hump of 924 feet in a crow-flight distance of 60-odd miles between Phillipsburg on the Delaware and Jersey City on tidewater, had 23 inclined planes, as well as 23 locks.

Ohio contracted canal fever early. To connect the Ohio River and Lake Erie and give Ohio produce the advantage of the Erie Canal, she pushed to completion from 1829 to 1833 two separate canals 100 miles apart, giving all-water transport from New York City to New Orleans. An accidental dividend was diminution of malaria in some counties as the canal drained certain swamps. Indiana presently began to build—and almost finished—a grandiose canal along the Wabash and Maumee rivers to tap the Great Lakes at Toledo, Ohio. Illinois pushed another canal of majestic intentions along the Illinois River to La Salle, Illinois, before the lengthening shadow of the railroad halted the scheme. Most Northeastern states had also built minor canals, such as that up the Delaware from Philadelphia to Easton, Pennsylvania, and the Delaware and Raritan across the narrow waist of New Jersey. The latter combined with the already existing Chesapeake and Delaware Canal at sea level across the narrow peninsula of Delaware and with the Great Dismal Canal through the swamp south of Norfolk to provide inland water carriage from the North Carolina sounds to New York Bay. That had been one of the dreams of Albert Gallatin, the brilliant Swiss-born Secretary of the Treasury whose report on internal improvements of 1807 had had much to do with keeping canal-mindedness alive.

The earth moving involved in such projects was ancient Egyptian in scale and nearly so in method. Pick and shovel were supplemented only by horse-drawn scrapers, for the steam-powered monsters that dug the Panama Canal were still far in the future. The Erie and Pennsylvania Main Line canals were originally 40 feet wide at the waterline, 28 at the bottom with a 4-foot depth of water. To dig hundreds of miles of such a ditch without heavy mechanized equipment would have been demanding in favorable country. Much canal construction was done through rocky hills to be blasted apart with no explosive better than black powder or through such swamps as the Montezuma marshes near Syracuse, New York, where the Irish toiled away naked except for shirt and cap among formidable clouds of mosquitoes.

Once the ditch was dug and the heavy-timbered locks built, here came the blunt-bowed canalboats towed by horses or mules abreast or in tandem, two, three, four to the hitch depending on load and the resources of the boat-owner. America's motive power for boats on artificial inland waters was still animal muscle; only now four-legged creatures substituted for two-legged creatures shoving on poles or manipulating oars or paddles. The change meant no refinement. The canalboatman was about as rough as any Irish pick swinger. Indeed they were often identical, for Pat out of work when the digging was finished might well secure a job on the boats flocking to use it. But as Walter D. Edmonds' authoritative stories of the Erie Canal show, the "canawlers" also included plenty of rugged locals named Campbell, Marshall or Schwartzmeister. They soon became a distinct social class deplored by village respectability aware that the red-armed slattern all too visible in the window of the stern cabin as the boat floated past had never yet married any of the successive canawlers with whom she slept as part of the cook's job. The crudity of her unabashed presence matched that of the colors of paint—the gaudiest greens, reds, yellows—lavished on the boat's topsides.

As for other vices, the flimsiest propaganda ever issued by the American Temperance Society was its claim of having got practically all Erie Canal boatmen to sign the pledge. Canawlers prided themselves on special tobacco so strong that only they could smoke it; and on applying to draft animals language that would not be equaled until the mule skinners of the Far West took over. Priority at locks was theoretically a matter of first come, first served. But *first* was often spelled *fist* as one hard-driving bully captain claimed precedence over another. The canawler's shibboleth was "Low bridge!"—the warning that one of the many cross-canal bridges was too low to clear a man standing on deck. Though many, including President James A. Garfield, had been driver boys on the canals before rising to respectability, the general repute of canawlers was so low that they might well prefer not to remember their pasts; hence the bit in *David Harum* about the small-town banker from upstate New York being driven around Newport, Rhode Island, in season, observing the new-fledged millionaires in their elegant turnouts and saying to his host: ". . . I'd like to bet you two dollars to a last year's bird's nest that if . . . some one was suddenly to holler 'LOW BRIDGE!' . . . nineteen out o' twenty'd *duck their heads*." [65] The canals had their stately aspect, however. A cultivated young lady reporter for *Godey's Lady's Book* observing Syracuse, New York, in 1845 "could not help thinking of Venice" because of the "fine bridges . . . [and] wide street built so directly on the grand canal that . . . you may step out from the door into a boat." [66] Understandably she neglected to mention that the boat would be no gondola full of masked musicians but a mule-drawn scow full of wood ashes and barreled salt pork.

Canals were planned with bulk carriage in mind. But the first vessel to traverse the first-opened part of the Erie Canal was a passenger barge carrying celebrant bigwigs. Taking a hint from canal-wise Europe, the American canal system expanded its passenger services on a scale unique to the New World. American roads were still so bad that almost any alternative was preferable. Line boats—the more or less scheduled cargo

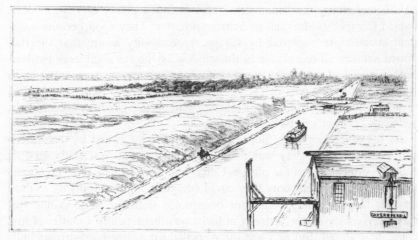

*The western end of the Erie Canal showing horse tow and lock,
drawn by Captain Basil Hall, RN, c. 1830.*

carriers—sold deck passage to those, usually westbound immigrants, willing to bring their own food, risk exposure to bad weather, and put up with "cent-and-a-half-a-mile, mile-and-a-half-an-hour." [67] At least, it was less arduous than walking, if slower. The packets—built for passengers, so called after the fast mail and passenger ships of the day—offered progress at 4 mph, slower than the stagecoach on better-than-average roads but also safer, far smoother and, since the fare included berth and meals, much cheaper. Recalling the *General Sullivan* packet on the Middlesex Canal in his boyhood, Edward Everett Hale thought it "one of the most charming ways of travelling . . . to sit on . . . deck . . . and see the country slide by you, without the slightest jar, without a cinder or a speck of dust, is one of the exquisite luxuries." [68] To prevent erosion of the banks, 4 mph was the usual speed limit. But Hale claimed 5 mph for the *General Sullivan,* as did William Dean Howells for the Dayton to Hamilton (Ohio) packet of the Miami Canal of the 1840's, a craft of:

> . . . such incomparable lightness and grace as no yacht . . . could rival. . . . The water curled away on either side of her sharp prow . . .

and the team came swinging down the towpath at a gallant trot, the driver sitting the hindmost horse of three, and cracking his long-lashed whip with loud explosions . . . suddenly the captain pressed his foot on the spring and released the tow-rope. The driver kept on to the stable with unslackened speed, and the line followed him, swishing and skating over the water, while the steersman put his helm hardaport, and the packet rounded to, and swam slowly and softly up to her moorings. No steamer arrives from Europe nowadays with such thrilling majesty.[69]

That was a daytime trip in summer, midday dinner on board, passengers lounging under the awning or singing to the accompaniment of the foot-pumped harmonium that elegant boats usually shipped. Canal travel at night was another matter. Meals were served on demountable tables in the gentlemen's cabin. After supper all passengers went on deck, whatever the weather, while captain and crew stowed the tables and pulled down three tiers of swing-down bunks—mere shelves hinged to the wall and skimpily padded with straw ticks. Women and children had similar stowage in a curtained-off ladies' cabin. The arrangement grimly recalled the keelboat packets of the Western waters, had also cropped up with few refinements in the early steamboats of the Northeastern rivers, and obviously fathered the Pullman and Wagner sleeping cars of later times.

In merely double-tiered bunks in Pullmans it was never commodious. Its canalboat phase was atrocious. Passengers were assigned to berths in order of arrival on board. When they numbered more than the berths, late arrivals slept on the floor or on the tables. The fattest were assigned to the lowest tier to reduce chance of injury if the supports gave way. David Stevenson, who saw much of canal packets in 1837, sadly recalled the blessed quiet of the handsome canal packets of Belgium in contrast with American cabins 40 by 11 feet containing forty fellow sufferers kept awake by the massed croaking of myriads of bullfrogs infesting the canal. To open the cabin windows in summer meant all-night war with mosquitoes, and in chilly weather the universal dread of night air kept them closed. Few of the men took off their boots, fewer still undressed beyond shedding coats and cravats, and there was nowhere to put clothes anyway except on easily upset stools or on the floor fouled with tobacco chewers' spittle. The bedding, packed in piles by day, was "saturated with the perspiration of every individual who had used [it] since the commencement of the season. . . . The smell of animal effluvia, when [it] was unpacked, was truly horrid," [70] said George Combe, a Scottish traveler less given to complaint than most Britons. The prevalence of raw whiskey—there was always a bar—tobacco smoke and the persisting odors of food fried in rancid lard added to the richness of the atmosphere.

Accounts of the ladies' cabin vary only in some of the smells, since whiskey and tobacco were lacking. Miss Martineau found "the heat and noise, the known vicinity of a compressed crowd, lying like herrings packed in a barrel . . . the appearance of the berths . . . so repulsive, that we were seriously contemplating sitting out all night, when it began to rain so as to leave us no choice." [71]

In the morning, which never came too soon, passengers were again shooed out on deck while the bunks were secured and tables set up for 6 o'clock breakfast. Toilet facilities consisted of one washbasin for each cabin, a common hairbrush and a single towel. The water used was hauled up in rope buckets from the canal, which was pretty stagnant between locks and incessantly fouled by the excreta of draft animals, boatmen and passengers. Dinner was at 11 A.M. Lack of surviving comment on canalboat food may mean not that it was good but that nobody expected anything of it. The place of alcohol as anodyne to one to five days of such travel is implied in the failure of a line of Temperance canalboats set up on the Erie Canal by General Ashbel Riley, businessman and foe of the Demon Rum.

In 1807 Robert Fulton, a brilliant engineer who was also an able promoter and a fair portrait painter, demonstrated the practicality of steamboats on the Hudson. In 1815 the *Enterprise* steamboat took supplies from Pittsburgh to Jackson's men at New Orleans and then struggled all the way back upstream to the falls at Louisville, Kentucky, steam's first uphill trip on the Western Waters, at a speed leaving the tediously poled keelboats nowhere. The resulting boom in two-way steamboats west of the mountains explains why Pennsylvania was so eager to get canalboats over the hump. For Eastern merchants saw that, whereas it cost $5 to $8 per hundredweight to haul hardware, say, over the Appalachians to Wheeling, it cost only $1 by sea to New Orleans and thence up the rivers by steamboat.

Hence the early 1800's were even more the steamboat age than the canal age. Once the clog of an ill-advised franchise monopoly for the Fulton interests was removed after the War of 1812, America showed the Old World what steam could do on freshwater and wrote still another —and much more dashing—chapter in the history of her waterway-mindedness. Some of the success of the Erie Canal itself was due to the use of steam tugs to haul its canalboats down the Hudson without transshipping cargo to river sloops at Albany or the uncertainties of taking the boats themselves down under sail.

Visually the gawky broadhorn and the low-profile canalboat snaking along behind mules were much duller than the high-rise, bellowing,

smoke-belching steamboat bulling her way by indigenous power. So striking an innovation took getting used to, of course. In steam's first years,
passengers on the Hudson were carried in safety barges towed behind
steamboats on hawsers long enough to lessen the risk to life and limb if the
boiler blew up. Advertisements of such craft also promised freedom from
"The noise of the [steamboat's] machinery, the trembling of the boat,
the heat of the furnace. . . . " [72] But as engineers learned their business, the risk of explosion lessened. With the 1830's safety barges
disappeared, and steamboats carrying passengers, as well as high-value
freight, were plying the waters of about every major waterway from the
St. Johns in Florida to Lake Champlain. Even the upper Connecticut
River supported busy miniature stern-wheelers; "quaint little caricatures," [73] George Templeton Strong called them, highly amused by the
way they were juggled through rapids by a single bow steersman using a
paddle. "I am afraid to tell how many feet short this vessel was," Dickens
wrote of the one he encountered, "or how many feet narrow . . . but we
all kept the middle of the deck, lest [it] unexpectedly tip over . . . the
machinery . . . worked between [the deck] and the keel: the whole
forming a warm sandwich, about three feet thick." [74] The James River
was deep enough for seagoing merchant ships to navigate almost to Richmond. But that was tricky under sail, so they stopped at Norfolk and let
their cargoes come downriver to them in steamboats less timid about
wind and tide. Before railroads penetrated the Southeast—and that took
a while—river-type steamboats out of Charleston using the tranquil
channels among the Sea Islands were much the best communication southward to Savannah, Brunswick, and into Florida.

Apart from cheapness and smoothness of water carriage, steamboats
added a speed unattainable for any distance on land until railroads were
well developed. Six mph was fast on major stage runs; steam could knock
off 12 or 15, and the engines were just as fresh as ever after hundreds of
miles. No two steamboats were exactly alike. But they were consistently of
shallow draft and low freeboard, soon reaching at least 300 feet overall,
piled with imposing superstructure for passengers' use topped with a tall
funnel for each of the twinned engines. Their paint gleamed white, their
flags and pennants snapped in the self-created breeze, and their whistles
echoed up and down the river in exhilarating contrast with the blatting of
the canalboatman's tin horn. They often carried a small band or sometimes a calliope (the "steam pianna" still sometimes heard today on carnival lots). Live musicians were considered more refined, but when at 7
A.M. the *Armenia* cast off at Albany, her calliope shrieking "Auld Lang
Syne" and drowning out the hundreds of "Take care yerselves!" impressionable youngsters remembered it the rest of their lives. She was a crack

boat scheduled to spin all the way downriver before dark even though putting in at each sizable town, with more "Auld Lang Syne" at each departure. The attendant scenery, much less vandalized than it is now, was actually handsomer than that of the Rhine, to which the knowing likened it while regretting its lack of ruined castles. More prosaic was the role of

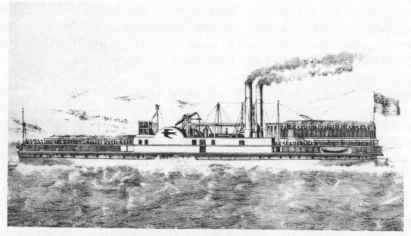

Well-developed Hudson River steamboat of the late 1830's.

the Erie Railroad's steamboats taking thousands of gallons of milk a day to New York City from the line's upriver terminal at Piermont, New York— a great thing, steam-created, for the cow-keeping farmer and the city child.

Accommodations on overnight runs were too like those of canal packets at first; staterooms in adequate numbers seem not to have appeared until the late 1840's. Sexes were segregated; half-fare children slept on cabin benches with pa's carpetbag for pillow. But there was ample cubage in both ladies' and gentlemen's cabins. David Stevenson, who so deplored canalboats, admired the dining saloon-men's cabin of the steamboat *Massachusetts* on the New York-Providence run in 1837: 160 feet long, 12 high, "entirely unbroken by pillars," where 175 passengers could dine, with good service, too. He said that when such saloons were "brilliantly lighted up, and filled with company . . . in small parties at the numerous tables (into which the large tables are converted after dinner) . . . [engaged] in different amusements," they were more like "the coffee-room of some great hotel than the cabin of a floating vessel." [75] Some of these Sound boats had bathrooms. Indeed, in view of the cramped accommodations in oceangoing vessels of the day, it was probably these

American freshwater steamers that set the transatlantic trade the example of providing luxurious public rooms. The large lake steamers were also part of this. The *Western World* of the Buffalo-Detroit service of the 1850's, for instance, sounds fancier even than any Mississippi packet of that decade; she was 364 feet long, had 116 staterooms, was stuffed with pianos, marble tables, enormous mirrors, luxurious sofas and carpets, and one of the public rooms had a stained-glass dome.

Steamboating on the Western waters naturally had its own ways. Individual staterooms began to appear in the 1830's just as on the Eastern rivers. Low-income travelers could buy deck passage with rough bunks undercover, bringing their own food—that cost only a fourth as much as first class and was, said an expert on Western travel, "very undesirable. . . ." [76] Yet that was how the swarms of German immigrants landed from transatlantic ships in New Orleans penetrated far up into the Middle West, and for them quiet waters and fresh air must have been welcome.

Western motive power was usually the high-pressure steam engine developed by Oliver Evans and first installed in a riverboat by William Shreve in 1816. Its advantage was that it needed less room than a low-pressure engine, which allowed more cargo per voyage. Its minor disadvantage was a loud, coughing exhaust that shook the whole jerry-built craft and carried for miles, so that people around the bend knew that a steamboat was coming long before she was in sight. Until one was used to it, high-pressure engines spoiled the passenger's sleep with "the most violent shaking the human frame was ever called upon to support." [77] Its major disadvantage was higher risk of an exploded boiler. This defect, inherent in the primitive boilers of the day, was enhanced by Western steamboatmen's disregard of their own and the passengers' safety in the interests of speed, for fast trips meant prestige and more profit. Disastrous fires were rife among wooden steamers everywhere, but explosions were the regional specialty over the mountains. And a steamboat explosion was a real catastrophe. When the *Oronoko* blew up on the Mississippi in 1838, 130-odd died. On the *Moselle,* famous for several record-breaking trips, 120-odd went the same way. The *Princess,* blown up near Baton Rouge in 1859 trying for a record passage to New Orleans, killed more than 200 and badly injured 100 more out of 400 passengers on board.

Explosions were often the result of racing with a rival boat regardless of safety. The folklore about tying down the safety valve for racing had plenty of basis. In the heat of contest a captain running low on fuel would even reduce the profits of the voyage by feeding the fireboxes fat bacon from the cargo, grease from shipments of soap fats and timbers from the superstructure. Even if the boiler held, there was an excellent chance of fire from the torrents of sparks streaming from the overloaded stacks. Midwest-reared John Hay crammed the whole slapdash scandal into "Jim Bludso of the Prairie Belle," celebrating the engineer of a doomed steamboat racing a newer rival:

> . . . And so she come tearin' along that night—
> The oldest craft on the line—
> With a nigger squat on her safety-valve,
> And her furnace crammed, rosin and pine.
>
> The fire bust out as she clared the bar,
> And burnt a hole in the night,
> And quick as a flash she turned and made
> For that willer-bank on the right.
> There was runnin' and cursin' but Jim yelled out,
> Over all the infernal roar,
> "I'll hold her nozzle agin the bank
> Till the last galoot's ashore." . . .
>
> And sure's you're born they all got off
> Afore the smoke-stacks fell—
> And Bludso's ghost went up alone
> In the smoke of the Prairie Belle. . . .

On an Ohio River boat in 1844 Professor Benjamin Silliman saw how "The furnaces . . . poured out torrents of sparks . . . in contact with the dry warm and unprotected pine boards of the floor above . . . showers of sparks and cinders were falling . . . upon the . . . cotton, paper and other combustibles [stowed on the hurricane deck]. . . ." At Silliman's protest the captain broke out fire buckets and rigged a hose, but apparently if he had kept quiet, no such precautions would have been taken. The astonished founder of the Sheffield Scientific School at Yale also noted that there was only one small boat "to convey 200 to 250 people ashore . . . and should the tiller ropes be burned (the tiller chains ordered by law of Congress are not always provided), it might be impossible to run the steamer ashore. . . ." [78]

Western boatyards were rough-and-ready to match. The only refinement in construction—not decoration—was in underwater lines to add speed to cargo capacity. Steamboats were built to pay for themselves and as much more as possible in an ungodly short expectation of life. Owners usually figured an average of five years before a new boat got snagged (running into a drift tree hidden below the surface) and sunk, or blown up, or burned, or shook herself to bits. Of 413 different boats using the canal around the falls at Louisville in 1836, some 60 were out of service within a year because of accidents, decay, etc., and 104 of the rest were

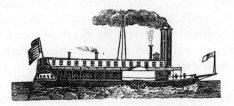

*The early Western Waters steamboat showing marked vestiges
of seagoing design persisting.*

new. As it grew evident that riverwork required only minimum bulwarks
and freeboard, the Western steamboat evolved into something that seamen seeing it for the first time hardly recognized as nautical. Eastern
rivercraft usually retained some of the horizontal, forward-questing air of
a blue-water hull. The vessels lining the levee for miles at Cincinnati and
St. Louis were little more shiplike than the boxy flatboats that had shown
them the way downriver.

Basically here was a sharp-bowed, almost flat barge with a pair of steam
engines forward of midships, each with an exaggeratedly tall stack, and
aft of them a two- to three-story wooden box, warehouse below and verandaed dwelling above. On side-wheelers, the queens of the Western Wa-

The fully developed Western Waters steamboat of the 1870's.

ters, paddle boxes amidships added a swelling cumbrousness on each side. As rising revenues allowed more expense on ostentation, fancy iron-work appeared to crown and brace the stacks, and paddle boxes were graced with gaudy paintings illustrating the boat's name—*Fairy Queen, Sultana, Reindeer*—or exploiting popular emblems such as eagles, rising suns and liberty caps. Gay as it all was, the basic top-heaviness remained. The great thing always looked as if about to turn turtle instead of swiftly wafting several hundred tons of merchandise and hundreds of passengers down the middle of the wide stream. The same ungainly profile accom-panied steamboating up the Missouri, Tennessee and Cumberland rivers and the minor but sizable streams feeding into the Ohio, such as the Big Sandy, the Scioto, the Wabash, the Green. Steamboats even tried tribu-taries of tributaries of tributaries, for instance, up the North Fork of the White River to Indianapolis. But though hopes were high, water seldom was, and Indiana's new capital had to content itself with eventually being the largest city in the United States *not* on navigable water.

Coal as steamboat fuel began to come in on the Hudson and the Great Lakes in the 1840's. But in the West wood long remained the chief source of energy, so the steamboats added another gnawing danger to forests. The first one to ply between New York and Long Island was a failure because shipping enough wood for the trip left too little room for cargo. A typical New York City to Albany steamer would use 40 cords (more than 5,000 cubic feet) each way. The Western river trade created the equivalent of filling stations—riverside woodyards offering 4-foot billets already cut and piled by the cord for the roustabouts to load. The opera-tors were usually secluded among rank forests and swamps from whatever civilization was budding elsewhere on the Big River. The pasts of some of them made isolation advisable. Others were ambitious men carving new plantations out of the woods by selling its trees for fuel and using the pro-ceeds to finance draining and labor. Their woodcutting crew might con-sist of footloose ne'er-do-wells and occasionally included a runaway slave fed and harbored in return for his toil.

There was much such human driftwood. The rankest accumulation was in the fetid eddy of Natchez-under-the-Hill, the riverside slum be-neath the bluff that still stayed foul even after vigilantes worked it over in the late 1820's. Most of the human debris was in sluggish motion, how-ever—shantyboatmen, spiritual and possibly actual descendants of the keelboatmen, living in roofed craft developed from the flatboat model and fishing, hunting and pilfering as chance offered. Raftsmen, also of the keelboatman stripe, handled the sweeps of the great rafts of sawlogs float-ing southward from the lumbering economy of the upper Mississippi, living in shacks on the logs, and raising hell when they got ashore down-

*Early Western Waters steamboat (note lowish stacks and low profile)
wooding up, as drawn c. 1830 by Captain Basil Hall, RN.*

river. There were floating gristmills with undershot wheels, anchoring
where the current was swift for maximum power until no local villager
had any more corn to grind, then drifting on downstream to the next settlement. Peddlers' store boats identified by the yard of cotton print flown as
ensign were floating shelved showrooms offering gewgaws and elementary

*Captain Basil Hall (c. 1830) draws a couple of backwoods types
and (right) a Western Waters steamboat pilot off duty.*

supplies, cash or trade, to lonesome plantations and mud-smothered hamlets. The upper Mississippi knew floating brothels calling themselves dance halls, usually two flatboats lashed together. Marginal entertainers operated showboats towed from one riverside settlement to another for as long a stay as the traffic would bear. In 1853 a daguerreotype artist named Simpson prospered mightily floating down the rivers on a flatboat, staying in a place while business lasted, going on to the next, hunting and fishing when a vacation seemed in order. Most such drifters ranked far below the steamboatmen—captains, pilots and their apprentices, clerks and the assistant mud clerks—who were the aristocracy of the river. William Dean Howells' great-uncles and William Vaughan Moody's father were steamboat captain-owners out of Ohio River ports, and a proud thing it was for both promising boys.

Doubtless those imposing gentlemen were not among the steamboat captains who took a percentage of gamblers' earnings to look the other way. Actor Frank Chanfrau, with his perennial tours in the 1870's in *The Arkansas Traveler,* was perhaps first to depict the Western steamboat as a paradise of slim-fingered gamblers, lovely octoroons fleeing to freedom, drawling colonels and close-harmony deck gangs. Steamboats did harbor gamblers in much the same numbers as did the shiny new hotels in New Orleans, Memphis and St. Louis that afforded the same opportunity to rub elbows with potential suckers. The steamboat not only made money out of passengers when railroads were scarce and wheels or horseback cumbrous, but also acted as social club in which river-town Quality could scrape acquaintance and cement personal alliances, economic or marital. But its real significance was in the corn and pork fetched South to feed King Cotton's and Queen Sugar's slaves; in the cotton itself headed for transshipment to Liverpool or Boston; in the shoes and textiles coming upriver from New Orleans and Mobile, plus all the other large and small items from the North and Europe that the South did not supply herself—steam pumps, pianos, flour, needles, knives. . . .

However graceless, the steamboats were as imposing within as without —full of Brussels carpets, fringed curtains, dingly chandeliers and rosewood paneling. They certainly had a stimulating effect on the small riverbank settlements where they put in to land three barrels of molasses and a case of chewing tobacco—for competition was stiff, and all but the largest and fastest accepted small shipments. To the barefooted locals this grandiose contraption was an occasional glimpse of another world. It showed more fresh paint than the whole village had seen since it was founded. It teemed with people whose everyday garb outshone even what Mr. Bob and Miss Selina of the Big House wore Sundays. It glistened inside with cut glass, mirrors and polished silver, actually served ice in the dog days, reeked with the smoke of real segars from a place called Cuba, had slaves with white aprons bowing and scraping wherever you looked— a different order of reality from the muddy-hocked mules and one-gallus values of Bricksville. In this respect Bricksville was better off than the cognate small settlements situated away from navigable water in the red hills of Georgia and the prairielands of the Old Northwest, where such gaudy but catalytic visions never came.

It would be handy if all this layered neatly into the Stagecoach Era, the Canal Era, the Steamboat Era, the Railroad Era. Overlappings and survivals always flaw neat patterns. A generation after steamboats were hundreds strong on the Western Waters, keelboats and farm-built flatboats made of huge tulip-poplar planks were still going downriver with the farmers' pork, lard, corn, sometimes horses and cattle; others took coal to New Orleans from Pittsburgh. The feckless, drifting presence of these craft was a great trial to steamboat pilots navigating in thick weather. The post-steamboat future was simultaneously beginning to take shape in the introduction of steam towboats shipping their cargo not on their own decks but in separate barges—a device that would make highly important use of the Father of Waters and the Ohio long after steamboating was as dead as dueling. Many years after steamboating was established on the Hudson, the famous Hudson River sailing sloops were surviving so well that no pre-Civil War painting of "View from West Point" or "Prospect of the Hudson from Hyde Park" was complete without showing several at once. For all their 90-foot masts and great spread of canvas to make the most of light airs, they were noted for tedious and uncertain voyages, with four days the average run from New York to Albany. But their hulls were capacious, their crews small, and they could afford to put into places steamboats scorned. Well into the 1900's they were still bringing the bricks of the Haverstraw yards to New York City. Within a 20-mile radius of Philadelphia in the 1840's, when railroads were taking on well, steamboats still connected the Camden and Amboy with the city and dominated the resort trip to Cape May. Canal packets and stages were still taking passengers upriver to Easton, Pennsylvania, and other stages fanned out northward and southeastward where rail lines were still lacking.

In fact, the age of steam that fatefully shifted the burden of providing motive power away from human and animal muscle was long in taking orderly shape. It had come to the Colonies in 1755 with a primitive Newcomen engine used to drain a copper mine at Belleville, New Jersey. It ran a trial steamboat for John Fitch on the Delaware in the 1790's and by 1800 was helping pump the water of the Schuylkill into Philadelphia's precedent-setting municipal waterworks. In 1805 on the road around that

pumping station—where the mansard-tortured City Hall now stands—
Oliver Evans, one of the finest of America's self-trained inventive geniuses, demonstrated his steam-propelled monster on wheels that anticipated the railroad locomotive and the farm tractor. But seven years after
Fulton had persuaded steam to conquer the Hudson, the most suitable

*Oliver Evans' steam dredge had road wheels as well as paddle
wheel to show that steam could also propel a land vehicle.*

motive power that one Moses Rogers could think of to improve service
on the New-York–Brooklyn ferry was eight horses walking in a circle on
deck to turn a capstan geared to a paddle wheel; the craft was naturally
called a team boat. It was not significant, but several really fateful inventions of that extraordinarily fruitful time did not originally depend on
steam and would still be doing well without it today if James Watt's
mother had never owned a teapot.

Soon after the Revolution, Evans had set up his wonderful gristmill
on a stream near Wilmington, Delaware. Until then the power of water-
wheels had merely turned millstones. Evans used it also to hoist the grain
to the top of the mill in an endless chain of buckets—previously the work
of men hauling up tubs with rope and pulley—and then to take over the
laborious sifting and spreading operations necessary after grinding. Millers
were sluggish about taking it up, but eventually this early example of
automation sharply increased the gristmill's output per man-hour. It was
adaptable to steam when the time came but did not need it to achieve its
ends. The same applies to Eli Whitney's cotton gin, which, though eventually often steam-powered, would have encouraged the planting of up-

land cotton and perpetuated slavery almost as effectively had it remained altogether mule-powered, and to Whitney's other and even more portentous invention—the making of firearms with interchangeable parts, the germ of the modern assembly line.

It was also waterpower that turned the new muscle- and timesaving machines in the English textile mills. And it was New England's tradition of waterpower that brought such machinery to America—in a queer cloak-and-dagger fashion. England, understandably hoping to keep the world-wide advantages of her new techniques, forbade not only export of textile machinery or drawings of it but even the emigration of people familiar with it. To breach this embargo, various American interests offered sizable rewards for the smuggling out of the machines or designs for making them. This came to the ears of Samuel Slater, a sharp young Briton who had learned much as apprentice of a partner of Richard Arkwright, the great man of spinning machines. Slater's indentures specifically pledged him, like other apprentices, not to betray his master's secrets. Nevertheless, having crammed his head with the full range of the new English textile inventions, he told his mother that he was off to visit London, assumed the role of an emigrating farmhand, and got out of England unhindered. He landed in New York City but was soon in touch with Moses Brown, eminent and canny Rhode Island Quaker, who had been trying to develop spinning machinery to match the fine waterpower at Pawtucket, R.I. By 1790 the firm of Almy & Brown, made up of Moses' relatives, had a new partner named Slater who, in a triumph of memory and mechanical skill, created at Pawtucket an Arkwright type of spinning mill. It did well. So did Slater. He married into a local textile family and eventually owned a versatile range of textile enterprises. It should be added—and in terms of the time was commendable—that once the new mill was operating, he set up a Sunday School to teach the three R's to the children, aged seven to twelve, who worked long hours in it six days a week.

Alexander Hamilton's premature attempt to create an industrial city at the fine waterpower of the falls of the Passaic in northern New Jersey failed at about the same time that Slater's second mill was built. But the next few decades saw ample justification of Hamilton's hopes for waterpower. As Yankees learned from Slater and experience, they exploited the dynamic potentialities of the Merrimack River to create Lawrence, Lowell and several other such textile towns in Massachusetts and New Hampshire. The Colonists had long known that in clever hands a small head of water meant better living for the neighborhood and prosperity for the miller. Now much heavier investment in large dams and waterworks on sizable streams began to mean cash dividends for risk capital, labor flocking in from the country to cluster around the mill, heightened incentives for immigration from Europe, and a dozen other problems, all new. The only precedents for the handling of these accumulations of labor were the paternalistic-dictatorial mining plantations, and following them proved to be a traumatic dead end. Another difficulty was the inability of water-power to provide the year-round operation necessary if heavy investment were to make the most of each dollar sunk in machinery. In Northeastern winters ice often interfered. Many a morning Slater had to break ice off the mill wheel before the day's production could begin. Eli Whitney's musket factory at New Haven was continually plagued by failing supply of iron because "the Streams on which most of the Forges stand [are] nearly dry through the Summer and until late in Autumn." [79] Here was steam's opportunity. But steam needs ample fuel, and the neighborhood of most mill towns was already short of wood for heating and cooking, let alone industrial power. Not until canals—the Delaware and Hudson, the Morris, and the Delaware and Raritan—began to float Pennsylvania's anthracite across New Jersey in barges could heat begin to take over from falling water in New England's mills.

In faraway Pittsburgh, which had seams of bituminous coal practically in town, the Industrial Revolution had a different history. Foundries, saw-mills and glassworks flourished with smoke-rich scenic effects. ". . . the whole town presents a smoky appearance," a British visitor wrote in 1818, welcoming this token of its destiny as "the Birmingham of America," [80] which is exactly what it turned out to be. Farther west at Charleston (now in West Virginia) another touring Englishman was "delighted . . . to see the smoke of the coals ascending from the glass-works . . . This smoke it is that must enrich America; she might save almost all her [money paid for imports] if she would but bring her black diamonds into service." [81] Attitudes toward coal smoke have changed.

Note that technological ferment in post-Revolutionary America centers in the Middle States and, in spite of Eli Whitney, Slater, et al., has surprisingly little to do with New England, the accepted center of American ingenuity, cradle of Darius Green and his Flying Machine. The first steamboat on the Western Waters, for instance, was built by a Manhattanite whose principal interests lay in New Jersey; its engine was of a type created by a Philadelphian. The group of brilliant experimenters who gave America the lead in making steamboats practical—John Fitch of Windsor, Connecticut, James Rumsey of Maryland, Oliver Evans of Philadelphia, John Stevens of New Jersey, Robert Fulton of Philadelphia—had only one Yankee among them, and his principal trials were conducted on the Delaware. We have seen that the Kentucky rifle, the Conestoga wagon and the flatboat of the Western Waters all were born among the Pennsylvania Dutch. Again it was Middle States men who developed railroad locomotives of native design. The first American steam-hauled train worthy of the name was assembled in the South—on South Carolina's Charleston and Hamburg. The first vessel using steam to cross the Atlantic was built in and sailed from Savannah, Georgia. The clipper ship was born in Baltimore.* Nobody is sure just where that great, unquestionably American invention, the rocking chair, first appeared, but available evidence points to Philadelphia. Always excepting Whitney, the large credit entries under New England in the technological ledger before 1840 are the cradle scythe for grain, the Concord coach, the first Bridgewater kind of American canal (the Middlesex) and Samuel Colt's revolving-breech firearms. A notable list but not critically essential to our grandfathers' times.

Such comparisons are always overemphatic, of course. This one is made here partly to correct a widespread misapprehension of the locus of American inventiveness; partly to show how the technological, as well as cultural (in the narrow sense), center of gravity of America has tended to rest in the central transverse strip of the country ever since the Quakers founded their chief settlements.

As seaman and pioneer of foreign trade and whaling, however, the Yankee really did show the nation the way. The men of New York City, Philadelphia, Baltimore, Norfolk, Charleston and New Orleans were also clever in countinghouses and able on quarter decks and before the mast. Though Yankees built more shipping relative to population, New York and Baltimore shipyards held their own or better in the subtlety of lines and strength of hull that made American sailing vessels the world's best. The swift sailing packets that New York put into the transatlantic trade after the War of 1812, bowling along under a press of sail that made the masters of Old World rivals gulp, were unmatched in that service. J. S. Buckingham, a widely experienced British traveler, called them "as beautiful specimens of naval architecture as ever came from the hands of the builder . . . elegant maritime hotels . . . each one launched, is superior to all her predecessors. . . ." [82] The first American ship to trade at Canton (1784) was either New York's *Empress of China* or a rerigged 80-ton Hudson River sloop, the *Experiment,* that had no business on such a voyage but made it in excellent time without losing a man of her crew of fifteen. But by and large it was usually a Yankee ship that first showed the

---

* The belief that the schooner rig, vastly important in world shipping as well as to America, was invented in Gloucester, Massachusetts, in 1721 was seriously questioned by Thoreau, and according to the editor of a recent edition of his *Cape Cod* (Dudley Lunt, W. W. Norton, 1951, 192-93 and n.), recent studies of ship design bear out his skepticism.

new gridiron flag of stars and stripes in any outlandish harbor that afforded high-value cargoes or water and fresh provisions for whaling crews. For nobody outdid the Yankee in combining businessman and seaman. There had probably been nothing like it since the Phoenician skipper-merchants' tiny craft first cleared the Strait of Gibraltar to trade with Northern Europe for tin and amber.

This was particularly Massachusetts' glory based on Boston and Salem. Some ships from most New England ports followed the Bay State's lead. But it was the descendants of John Endicott's and John Winthrop's Colonists who so frequented the far-flung ends of the earth that the natives of many Pacific and Indian Ocean islands thought that Salem or Boston was the name of the country that all Americans hailed from. In 1784 Elias Hasket ("King") Derby of Salem, already rich from privateering, sent his *Grand Turk*, recently a crack privateer, to the Cape of Good Hope. The voyage paid. Next year he sent her farther, to the French colony of the Île de France in the Indian Ocean and on to China. Within four years Boston's *Columbia* was in the peltry trade between China and the Pacific Northwest, discovered the great river that would be named for her, and came home as the first ship to carry the new American flag around the world. From Boston also, the brig *Hope,* not much larger than the *Experiment*, rediscovered the Marquesas Islands in the South Pacific on her way to the Northwest and China, and the ship *Massachusetts,* 600 tons, largest merchantman yet built in America, made Macao, the Portuguese trading foothold in China. When, in 1789, the first Congress under the new Constitution gave American ships a customs duty advantage over foreign bottoms, a sort of explosion of shipping enterprise scattered Massachusetts ships all over the routes to California, India, the Philippines, China, the Dutch East Indies, Madagascar, Arabia—even into forbidden Japan, under charter to Dutch interests admitted to trade there.

These vessels were never as large as the majestic East Indiamen plying between England and Bombay. But wherever they put in, they drew professional admiration of their sailing qualities and their crews, who were like nothing seen before or since. For one thing officers as well as hands ran strangely young. The *Benjamin* of Salem went to the Cape and India in 1792 with a captain of nineteen and chief mate of twenty, both already widely experienced in long voyages. Barring the captain (a Methuselah in his forties), the average age of the officers of the *Hercules* of Salem off to the East Indies next year was twenty-three; that of the able seamen six months less. Nor were they the kind of foremast hand committed to life at sea because they were misfits ashore. Many were keen youngsters signed on to learn seamanship in order eventually to walk the quarter deck themselves. The *George* of Salem, built as a privateer but turned merchantman when peace intervened, made her maiden voyage with a crew most of whom had already studied navigation—an exacting branch of practical mathematics—and all of whom could read and write. Here was a striking version of the new man, the American. The super-cargo of Derby's *Astrea* on a voyage to Manila in 1797 was Nathaniel Bowditch, soon world-famous as creator of the handbook of navigation most depended on by ships' officers. Under his tutelage the whole ship's company of twelve came home qualified navigators, and every man Jack of them lived to be a mate or captain. Thanks to his indispensable book, which is still used, Bowditch is the Yankee name most renowned in the world at large, as eminent as Hoyle in the field of games. He deserved every word of the eulogy that his death in 1838 drew from his fellow master mariners of Salem: ". . . as long as ships shall sail, the needle point to the north, and the stars go through their appointed courses in the Heavens, the name of Dr. Bowditch will be revered as one who helped his fellowmen in time of need, who was and is to them a guide over the pathless ocean, and of one who forwarded the great interest of man-kind." [83]

Those who, like Bowditch's seagoing pupils, qualified for command of Yankee ships had an opening toward prosperity that later merchant skippers lacked. They were allowed to ship substantial ventures of their own—trade goods or cash to be laid out in foreign goods brought home for profit. The hands were allowed smaller ventures. A few lucky voyages might set a young officer well on the way to buying an interest of his own in a ship. For these voyages often paid handsomely. The ideal was the case of Captain Jonathan Carnes of Salem who heard in a Sumatran port of a distant coast abounding in unexploited white pepper. He returned to Salem, built a fast schooner with backing from a local merchant, manned her with a closemouthed crew, and sailed for an unspecified destination. Eighteen months later she was back with so much pepper got almost for the asking that the voyage paid seven times the cost of ship and expenses. The *Franklin* of Boston once returned from Java with the officers quar-tered in a temporary deckhouse because the cargo of coffee and spices had overflowed the holds and filled the after cabins.

Unless the market had gone far down while the ship was away—which sometimes caused long faces ashore—such a lading meant riches. Derby died in 1799 worth more than $1,000,000, possibly the greatest American fortune of his day. His fine mansion, all chimneys, pilasters and lofty cupola, was capsheaf of a school of merchant-built houses that made Salem a principal architectural glory of the nation. George Crownin-shield, one of five seagoing brothers whose success in Salem's heyday made their name as eminent as Derby's, used part of his wealth to build a seagoing private yacht, the first such rich man's toy in America, the *Cleopatra's Barge*. She was as like Cleopatra's craft as seaworthiness and speed allowed—chock-full of costly upholstery, silver and gold table services and good drinking and eating—and for general gaiety her hull was painted as many colors as Joseph's coat, in a herringbone pattern on one side, in horizontal stripes on the other. Though built for pleasure, even she could not stay out of the Pacific trade. After her owner's death she was sent to Hawaii to dazzle King Liholiho, who swapped for her a whole shipload of sandalwood (highly prized by the Chinese) and presently piled her up on a mid-Pacific reef to sail no more.

Some voyages merely took coined silver to the Far East and brought back tea and silks. But the shrewdest management made every leg of the trip pay. Say Captain Beacon of Beacon, Bay and Company has small vessels in the West Indies trade, which keeps the firm long on sugar. As a young merchant captain he is well aware of the heavy Far Eastern demand for the iron, hemp and canvas of the Baltic Sea countries. So he may send a couple of the firm's brigs up the Baltic with sugar sold at a profit to pay for and bring back to Boston Baltic goods with which to freight a large East Indies-bound ship. Off she goes to India, sells the Baltic stuff at a profit, invests the proceeds in Indian cotton, takes that to China, sells it at a profit, invests the proceeds in tea, silk, chinaware, which will mean another profit home in Boston. Or a ship might go out with New England rum and salt meat to West Africa, pick up palm oil, round the Cape to Arabia Felix for coffee. Winthrop Marvin's *The American Merchant Marine* lists as items also often imported in Massachusetts ships hemp from the Philippines; tallow from Madagascar; dried fruit from the Mediterranean; rubber, hides and wool from South America—most of it smelly but all of it usually profitable on top of several profits already made en route. Such trade was no Yankee monopoly. Philadelphia's Stephen Girard, for instance, also knew how to make a fortune by such enterprise as voyaging to the Far East for coffee, pepper and sugar, selling them in Europe, putting the proceeds into a mixed cargo of wines, soap, butter, hats and glassware, and taking that for sale to the French colonies in the Indian Ocean. His four large ships named after philosophers of the Enlightenment (Girard himself was the least enlightened of men), *Voltaire, Helvetius, Rousseau, Montesquieu,* were as familiar sights in Canton as any New England vessel. But the primary flavor of it all was of Salem and Boston.

An owner might ship a supercargo to handle the buying and selling. Usually, however, that was up to the captain, who thus had to be not only seaman enough to bring the ship home in good time from distant, unlighted oceans and uncivilized, unmarked harbors, but also a canny diplomat-trader bargaining in strange tongues with capricious Oriental dignitaries. Once his ship left soundings, he had no way to check with the home office, so his instructions were of the loosest. Depending on what he heard or surmised en route, he could alter the ship's destination and the nature of her return cargo, charter her to alien governments or merchants, even sell her and dispatch the accumulated cargo home in other bottoms. It follows that there was as much buy and sell as yo heave ho in the training of these versatile skippers. A lively youngster whose family knew the right people in Salem or Boston or in New York City or Philadelphia spent a couple of years in his patron's countinghouse before shipping out, maybe as captain's clerk, to learn seamanship and exotic commerce firsthand. With such a career in mind his schooling had included some navigation, ship's husbandry and a foreign language or two, as well as what well-to-do parents' boys usually learned. The results were so marked that by the 1830's the British themselves were officially acknowledging that American officers and crews as well as ships were "vastly superior" [84] to their own.

For the ablest American skippers, however, the eventual objective was not a rewarding life at sea but a rapid rise via the captain's cabin to life ashore as a merchant shipowner making shrewd judgments with knowledge acquired abroad. It was workaday economic ambition, not love of fresh air and adventure, that enabled these men so imperturbably and sagaciously to take the hazards of pirates, savages, storms and uncharted reefs. In the newly cotton-mad South of their day the way for a likely youth to get to the top of the tree was to buy a few thousand acres of Mississippi swamp to clear and plant to cotton, as Jefferson Davis did. In the port towns of Massachusetts the upward path led to Zanzibar, Callao, Kronstadt, or to the Cannibal Islands, where the ship fried for months while her Yankee crew gutted and dried a full cargo of the disgusting sea slugs called *bêches-de-mer* to trade to the Chinese, who highly valued their alleged aphrodisiac qualities. Anything, however arduous or risky, to secure that serene wooden house on Chestnut Street and the gratification of being an important, Madeira-drinking man of far-flung affairs.

Outbound cargoes usually consisted of wares from elsewhere than New England. A fantastic exception appeared when, soon after 1800, two Bostonian brothers named Tudor, of a well-considered shipping family, decided to make money by exporting New England's winter crop of ice to warm climates. ("Lord" Timothy Dexter of Newburyport, Massachusetts, according to legend, had already gone them one better by founding his fortune on profits from a consignment of woolen mittens and warming pans sold in the West Indies.) Their first cargo made Martinique in the

French West Indies with enough ice unmelted to prove their point. By 1821 Frederic Tudor, the brother who stayed with the scheme, was shipping ice regularly to Havana and New Orleans. In 1833 he startled the world and his imitative competitors by landing a profitable cargo of ice in India. It had taken bitter years of trial and error to work out proper methods of storing and draining for long voyages in the hottest latitudes; this was Tudor's contribution. The specialized machinery, tools and storage to get the ice to shipside at low cost were the work of a mechanical-minded associate named Wyeth. Within twenty years ice—in effect the New England climate used as an export asset—was also going to China, the Philippines and Australia, the whole trade coming to 140,000 to 150,000 tons a year.

Even stranger than this, however, were New England's whaling and sealing, again concentrated in Massachusetts. American whaling seems to have been born in Long Island Sound, where early settlers of Connecticut saw the local Indians putting off in flimsy canoes with the implausible purpose of using stone weapons to take not only porpoises but right whales. The Quakers of Nantucket Island off the triceps muscle of Cape Cod made whaling a specialty. By 1700 their principal support came from the sale of whale oil (for lamps) and whalebone (for stays) got by pursuing the great creatures in small ships that launched highly seaworthy rowing boats made double-ended like the Indians' canoes. Indians from local colonies of tamed survivors usually made up part of a whaler's crew and remained invaluable subalterns, particularly as harpooners, down through the history of Yankee whaling. Other Yankees manned a whaling colony set up at Cape May, New Jersey, by Dr. Daniel Coxe, for a while an enterprising proprietor of West Jersey.

The Gulf of St. Lawrence and the waters between Virginia and the Azores were soon thoroughly whaled. A Nantucketer was operating profitably off Brazil by 1774. In his famous speech on the Colonies Edmund Burke paid cogent tribute to these intrepid saltwater butchers who were so eager—because it paid—to go rowing in mid-ocean with only a half-inch plank between them and an enraged mammal the size of several elephants. The officers took the same risks as the men, and combat morale in whaling seems usually to have been high. When "Blo-o-o-ows! She blows!" from the masthead lookout announced several whales at once, only two low-ranking shipkeepers stayed on board. The rest of the ship's company, always the mates, often the captain, too, were out there in the flimsy boats, all as described in *Moby Dick*. The whaleman's trade joke was the Nantucket sleigh ride—the tortured whale trying to get rid of the harpoon by towing the boat at outboard-motor speed until his tiring enabled its occupants to close in and finish him off. If he fought, the risk of drowning or other sudden death was grave—and all for only a few dollars per man. Whalers, like Yankee fishermen, worked on lays—proportionate shares of the profit down to one seventy-fifth for each able seaman.

After the Revolution whaling expanded as strikingly as merchant shipping. Within a generation four-fifths of the world's whaling was in American, mostly Yankee, hands. Whalers from Nantucket, New Bedford —which presently had the largest whaling fleet—and odd ports on Long Island Sound and Massachusetts Bay had gone all over the Pacific and Indian oceans, soon also up beyond the Bering Strait into the Arctic Ocean. The voyages were notoriously long. A lucky ship might fill all its casks with whale oil in a mere eighteen months; but three years was the average expectation, and if it took four to make a full ship, four it was. Such ordeals by calendar naturally made seamen reluctant to ship, so in its greatest days whaling was a seagoing stepchild looked down on by mariners aware that few who could get anything better would consider such berths. Toward the end—major American whaling did not survive the depredations of Confederate raiders and the great freeze-up of the Arctic fleet a few years later—the forecastles contained mostly recent Portuguese immigrants, South Sea Islanders eager to go sailoring white man-fashion and occasional Yankee farmboys callowly eager to go to sea. At least they saw strange corners of the world. Whalers went wherever whales were, and their captains preferred to recruit—lay up to overhaul the rigging, lay in fresh provisions, and give the crew some liberty—in spots remote enough to lessen the risk of desertion. Maui in the Hawaiian group and the Bay of Islands at the northern tip of New Zealand were best known among these accumulations of ship chandlers' sheds, big-footed local women and bad rum. Such impromptu settlements were sordid enough, but at that better than the slums where seamen accumulated in the world's great ports.

Sealers were a sort of furtive variety of whaler. Their work was safer, if just as bloody, for there was no risk to invading a colony of seals and clubbing them to death for skinning. But it did mean going where the quarry was concentrated, often to the bleak fringes of the Arctic or Antarctic. Since the odd places that sealers poked into made shallow draft and nippy handling advisable, their vessels were smaller than the roomy, bluff-bowed whalers. In several instances government exploring ships were about to land a party to take formal possession of a presumably unknown island when around a headland came a sealer sloop from Stonington, Connecticut, that had worked the place for some years and kept quiet about it to prevent competition.

Sumatra, Callao, Arabia Felix, Patagonia—Yankee merchantmen and whalers and sealers took their men far from the indrawing Puritan parochialism of their forebears. Hence the wealth of lovely Chinese ceramics in the old houses of Salem, Boston and Providence and the great collections of South Sea artifacts in Salem and Boston. Local matrons preparing to restore a fine old house in Woodstock, Vermont, recently found a strange weapon up attic. Nobody in town knew what it was. But many a whaler, including the one who originally brought it so far upcountry when he left the sea, could have told them it was a shark's-tooth spear from Micronesia. Those stimulating contacts dwindled as Yankee shipping petered out, with the rest of the American merchant marine, in the latter 1800's. The retired sea captain of *The Country of the Pointed Firs,* the shipbuilding and seagoing coast of Maine, deplored the way "a community narrows down and grows dreadful ignorant when it is shut up in its own affairs. . . . In the old days, a good part o' the best men here knew a hundred ports and something of the way folks lived in them. They saw the world for themselves, and like's not their wives and children saw it with them . . . they got some sense of proportion. Yes, they lived more dignified, and their houses were better within and without. Shipping's a terrible loss to this part of New England from a social point of view, ma'am."[85] For Massachusetts it was probably even more important.

That Sunday School of Samuel Slater's was said to have come about when some of his millboys were debating how to spend their only day off, and Slater, happening on them, inquired what was under discussion. One had proposed raiding an orchard; another had demurred. Slater said: "You boys come to my house and I will give you all the apples you can eat, and I will keep a Sunday School." [86]

That anecdote has a richly Victorian flavor. It could come from any pious book for children of 1840. But the year was 1793, which illustrates how traits that we think of as Victorian often far antedate the queen whom the term recalls. Well before she was born, let alone conspicuous on her throne in 1837, that waxy anxiousness of moral tone that underlies Victorianism had been widely propagated on both sides of the water by the skillful writings of redoubtable British ladies—Hannah More, Maria Edgeworth, Anna Letitia Barbauld—who, like their countryman Slater, had begun to flourish while the 1700's were still unrolling. They were anomalous in the same setting as the three-bottle men and gambling fever of pre-Regency and Regency times. But they outstayed vice and became major instruments in persuading the English-speaking world to accept all that *Victorian* now means to us. That is, Slater's Sunday School, like so many other vigorous American institutions-to-be, had its roots in the Old Country's recent past.

Specifically it came of the numerous schools for underprivileged children set up in England in the 1780's, usually under the auspices of the various Dissenting sects, well represented in America too, that rejected the established Church of England. Tireless Francis Asbury was already fostering the idea in the underschooled parts of Virginia where Methodism most flourished. In Philadelphia Dr. Benjamin Rush was persuading even the Episcopalians, successors to the standoffish Colonial Anglicans, to support an interdenominational Sunday School. It retained a strongly Puritan cast, however. Its purpose, like that of New England's nominal school system, was to give young souls access to Christianity through ability to read the Bible and pious tracts. But in a day when real public school systems were lacking, early Sunday Schools also reduced the general lack of learning skills that society was doing too little about.

Certainly the new nation was neglecting some of its marginal segments. Not only on the frontier but in the ramshackle back streets of the port towns, the wings of the Gospel, widely held to be the birthright of every soul, seldom brushed the threshold. In the secular field, the idea of free, universal elementary education, now taken for granted among us, was only forming in a few imaginations like Thomas Jefferson's. More effectively, the practical need for the three R's was becoming keenly appreciated in towns growingly committed to commerce and skilled trades. The higher a family's income, the better it could afford to hire its sons instruction from private or semisubsidized teachers of youth or to pay the premium of an apprenticeship that taught the boy or got him taught. But it was an obvious loss to the business world, as well as to God, that the potentialities of so many likely poor boys went untapped because their illiterate parents, however ambitious for them, could not pay for schooling. That was one reason why staid Philadelphians, whether especially Gospel-minded or not, helped Rush's Sunday School. They may also have hoped that the heavy doses of the Decalogue and the Proverbs that went with Sunday School lessons in reading and writing might help check the lower orders' drift toward rowdiness and Frenchified leveling notions.

For no sooner was the Revolution over than the remaining Patriot Quality began to glance uneasily at their less affluent fellow Patriots. It was suspected that they resented the Federalists' snug seat in the saddles that the Tories had vacated. It was disquieting to recall how active and ugly these people had been as anti-Tory mobs. All too promptly their dislike of the money power that the seaboard Quality held over upcountry debtors had shown itself in the organized mob actions of Shays' Rebellion. They also took seriously that word *equal* in the Declaration of Independence and had insisted on a Bill of Rights in the Constitution. Under the extended franchises of the new state constitutions—which sound appallingly illiberal to us now—too many of them had acquired the right to vote. In 1800 they had actually voted the Federalists out of power, never to return. In 1818 came the catastrophe of cutting off tax support from the Congregational Church of Connecticut. The Reverend Dr. Lyman Beecher, outstanding American theologian of his time, called the Jeffersonians who accomplished this "Sabbath-breakers, rum-selling, tippling folks, infidels and ruff-scuff generally." [87] Behind such epithets lay what Jeannette Mirsky and Allan Nevins shrewdly describe in *The World of Eli Whitney* as the new "respectability . . . a word called into being for the industrial society that was emerging." As they translate former Puritan-Dissenter attitudes into successor terms:

> [Respectability] equated sober deportment with strict probity, it transferred its mistrust from "enthusiasm" to "impulsiveness," and the general term "sinner" splintered into . . . "debtor," "drunkard," "beggar," "wastrel," "laggard"—indicating kinds and degrees of asocial behavior. The terms, still carrying the same full emotional charge of guilt, are an indication of the way society shifted its attention from the godly life to the business life.[88]

That climate meant heavy support from the Quality for the early wave of reform, of which Sunday Schools were part. In other fields it meant Quality-financed organizations to distribute Bibles where they would do the most good; to supplement them with pious tracts, little stories or homilies pointing morals and prescribing religion in what was meant to be a popular tone; to set up savings banks where workingmen could safely hive up funds and so acquire a sense of having a stake in the country; to supply poor neighborhoods with preaching and hovel-to-hovel visiting, as well as to found frankly named Societies for the Suppression of Vice or the Prevention of Pauperism to keep families from morally destructive penury.

True, America was supposed not to have pauperism. "You never see a beggar on the street," was a common report from Old World visitors, hostile or friendly, struck by this contrast between the great towns of Europe and New York City or Philadelphia. Actually, as Henry Cabot Lodge long since noted, by the time of the Revolution large towns had sizable amounts of destitution. In the hard times of 1819 so new a town as Cincinnati was collecting shoes and clothes for resourceless families. One of J. K. Paulding's stories of the same period contains a pompous man of property in New York City who "If he happened to encounter a beggar woman at the door . . . sent her about her business, with a most edifying lecture on idleness, unthrift and intemperance . . ." and scolded the city government "for not taking up the beggars," [89] which certainly implies that in spite of what alien sightseers on Broadway wrote home, beggars were a problem. The matter of the women who did not beg is all too clear.

The high ratio of prostitution from the mid-1700's on means much urban poverty. As the elder streets slid into slumminess, they housed growing aggregations of the unlucky and feckless, some native, others recently arrived to find the New World not all it had been painted.

Since our forebears had so much alcohol around, it can be assumed that their underprivileged strata heavily abused the amazingly cheap liquors available. In many cases, as Paulding's Pharisee hinted, drink could have been the cause of poverty. Anyway the association of the misbehavior of the lower orders with alcohol was strong and persuaded the reform-minded Quality that to discourage drink would help better the social climate. War on spirits was one of the earliest American reforms. Like many other important things, it appeared first in Philadelphia, where in the 1760's the Quakers, again paced by Benezet, were decrying hard liquor as wasteful and eroding to the soul. Dr. Benjamin Rush agreed on medical as well as moral grounds, recommending the cause to his nationwide acquaintance on the partisan Federalist plea that spirits were "antifederal . . . [encouraging] all those vices . . . calculated to dishonor and enslave our country." [90] In his view other vices included demanding wider suffrage, supporting revolutionary France and advocating soft paper money to ease the payment of debts. All through the later Temperance and prohibition movements this condescending affinity between the haves and the drys persisted. Eventually the concept *Republican* often had a dry halo, while north of the Mason and Dixon Line *Democrat* carried a strong smell of booze.

The fate of the post-Revolutionary pauper-ne'er-do-well-unlucky person was harsh. New England's sense of collective responsibility was strong but grudging. The township that had on its hands persons unable to cope was likely to auction them off to the lowest bidder—that is, those willing to clothe, feed and shelter them in return for what use there was in their forced labor, plus cash from the township, bid lower and lower until the most penurious proffer was reached. The system did not lead to pauper-pampering. It was notably ill suited to the needs of the superannuated, the disabled and the psychotic, to all of whom it was often applied. As numbers of such people grew, they might be collected into workhouses or almshouses, following Old Country precedents intended to combine some self-supporting work with wholesale savings in costs of maintenance. Pauper children were usually "bound out" without money as consideration to adults willing to support them in return for their minor services in dwelling and field. The agreement might stipulate that the bound boy have a horse and saddle to start life with when his time was out at the age of twenty-one. A bound girl might get a bedding of clothes—sheets and blankets for a bed, which seems equivocal but was meant to qualify her for marriage to a man of her own station. Windsor, Connecticut, once solicitously required the employer of a bound boy to "use his best efforts to get his scurf head cured" [91]—apparently ringworm was among the lad's troubles. A decent family taking a bound-out child—"Little Orphan Annie's come to our house to stay"—was one thing. The crass or brutal or just callously regardless household would be quite another. The basic flavor of the whole thing is clear in the requirement of certain New Jersey jurisdictions that the publicly supported pauper must wear on his clothes a large blue or red letter *P* to convince others of the advisability of working hard to avoid such disgrace.

Historically America's first clustered efforts at reform derived from the Mother Country's Society for the Reformation of Manners of the early 1700's, which had deplored and prosecuted profanity, public indecency, drunkenness, Sunday trading and other such disruptive breaches of decorum, and from the associated Society for Promoting Christian Knowledge, which, in addition to propagating the Anglican Church in America, had fostered charity schools for poor English children and distributed Bibles to the underprivileged. Reformism very definitely landed in America in the early 1730's, when the well-meaning founders of Georgia, hoping to create a moral climate to turn the victims of debtors' prisons into sound pioneers, barred from the new Colony both slavery and strong drink. Within a few years the Colonists had got both bans rescinded—certainly to their detriment in the first case. Otherwise "Temperance," as it came to be called—erroneously—was largely of New World origin, hence unique among the reforms that bulked so large in Western intellectual and moral life between 1760 and 1914. In most other instances a given reform was born in European, usually English, imaginations; consolidated for a decade or two; attracted Americans aware of cognate problems in their own backyards; and was then imported lock, stock and barrel for as much of an American career as zeal could create for it.

Such borrowings were merely the American phase of the urgency about doing something about others' distresses that came over thoughtful Westerners in the mid-1700's. Agitation for better treatment of debtors, convicts, the insane, women, animals, prostitutes, sailors and paupers; for the conversion of the heathen; against tobacco, slavery, Sabbath-breaking and lotteries, as well as spirits, was contemporary with or born soon after the Sunday school, Bible-and-tract and savings-bank movements. Each such emulation of Mother Country led to closer ties that helped socially to make up for the political breach of the Revolution. And in most cases—the exceptions were foreign missions, Sabbath observance and Temperance—the effects were civilizing.

As reforms gathered momentum among the Quality hoping to do the lower orders good, regional or statewide organizations also set up valuable ties across state boundaries. It must greatly have widened the acquaintance of Theodore Freylinghuysen of New Jersey, for instance, to be at the same time high up in the American Tract Society, the American Bible Society, the American Temperance Union, the Sunday School Union and the Home Missionary Society. All such institutions had annual national meetings, usually in "May week" in a large Northeastern city, gathering the do-good eagles from all over to bolster one another's zeal. Another such eminent joiner was Charles Marsh of Woodstock, Vermont, early an officer of the American Bible Society, the American Board of Foreign Missions, the American Education Society, the American Colonization Society and the American Society for the Promotion of Temperance. Sometimes women were equally versatile on the subnational level. The young FFV lady of *Swallow Barn* whom Kennedy described as "too inveterately charitable" certainly derived a stimulatingly wide outlook from her involvement in "three Sunday schools, a colonization society . . . a tract association . . . and the cause of temperance." [92] But even so, in view of the toploftical tone of the whole reform tradition, she probably thus busied herself in much the same spirit in which Virginia gentlewomen had always looked after and dosed the ailing slaves in the quarters because they were by definition incapable of looking out for themselves.

That "colonization society" as one of that serious young lady's concerns was evidence of rising uneasiness about the eventual fate of the American Negro. Remember the excision from the Declaration of Independence of Jefferson's testy comments on the Crown's encouragement of the slave trade. Eight years later the Congress of the new nation refused to vote, as part of the plan to organize the over-the-mountains country, that "after the year 1800 . . . there shall be neither slavery nor involuntary servitude in any . . . states" created out there. It was the narrowest of squeaks, "lost by an individual vote only," [93] Jefferson wrote bitterly.

As it was, states below the Mason and Dixon Line had thwarted the first effort of those above it to set a national limit on the spread of slavery. This made the outline of the sacred cow beneath the veil a touch clearer. Since many farsighted Southerners had been deploring slavery before and after the Revolution, it is often assumed that had Whitney's cotton gin not foisted a cotton economy on the South, slavery would have dwindled away there, as it was already doing in the Northern states. Chronology makes this look dubious. That ominous vote on the ban on slavery over-the-mountains was taken nine years before the Whitney gin cleaned its first pound of cotton. Maryland, which would never be a cotton state, and Virginia, which never grew much cotton of any kind, were among those voting no. And it was still two years before Whitney ever saw a cotton field when in 1790 North Carolina, ceding her claims in the Southwest Territory below the Ohio River to the United States, made it a condition that a clause forbidding slavery be dropped from the act creating it.

For the South already thought Negro labor indispensable to producing corn, wheat, tobacco, naval stores, rice, indigo and iron. Those all were reasons to value slavery regardless of cotton. How much of that made economic sense—slaves did adapt pretty well to work in such commodities —and how much was disingenuous clinging to a social situation aggrandizing white men in their own eyes cannot be distinguished. It seems clear, however, that when the impact of the cotton gin came, so many important Southerners were already slavery-minded that the accession of King Cotton may merely have consummated, not foreordained, the death of human freedom in the South. The distinction created from 1787 to 1790 between legal slavery below the Ohio and a ban on it above somewhat sharpened matters since Southerners strongly disliking slavery left the South to get away from it. One of the most valuable elements settling the Old Northwest consisted of antislavery Quakers leaving the Carolinas for the more breathable air of free territory. Another consisted of Quality slaveholders, mostly Virginians, selling their lands, freeing their slaves and starting fresh in the new country of which Mr. Washington and Mr. Jefferson, both open decriers of slavery, thought so highly. One such was the Colonel Thomas Worthington who built Adena. Another was Edward Coles, slaveowning Virginia planter and former secretary to President Madison, who freed his slaves in 1819, took them along into Illinois, settled each family of them on 160 acres of land—and in the 1820's was a crucial leader in the close political struggle that kept Illinois free soil. James Townsend, come West from Maryland to help found Morgantown, Kentucky, developed a distaste for slavery and freed all his own, giving those wishing to stay in Kentucky $50 each, taking along into Indiana those wishing to make a fresh start with him, each to have a cabin built for his family. Each such individual departure lowered the level of opposition to slavery in the South—still another example of culture-shaping automatic selection of personalities.

The Colonization movement was a well-meaning half measure appealing to uneasy consciences both North and South. Its particular occasion was the accumulation of freed or born-free Negroes in both regions as court action or laws imposing gradual emancipation operated in the North and Southern slaveowners freed individuals or abetted them in earning and buying their freedom. The proportionate number was highest in the Chesapeake area. By 1815 such nonslave Negroes in the whole nation probably numbered some 200,000. The organizers of colonization were ensnared by a fallacy that still attracts wishful minds, white and Negro— that because American Negroes' ancestors came from West Africa, they would be better off resettled there away from the strains and indignities of their lives in white-dominated America. This homeland notion neglects the wide differences between Baltimore's slums and West African villages. It would have been little more absurd to suggest resettling the Christianized Indians of Martha's Vineyard in Outer Mongolia because their ancestors had come from Asia. Yet Colonization had been taking shape ever since the Revolution. Persuasively formulated by the Reverend Robert Finley, a Presbyterian parson from New Jersey, it created an American Colonization Society under such august sponsors as Bushrod Washington, nephew of the national hero and an Associate Justice of the U.S. Supreme Court; Henry Clay, already a chief power in the West; Francis Scott Key, not only author of "The Star-Spangled Banner" but also a leader of the Maryland bar; the Reverend Dr. Lyman Beecher, outstanding Presbyterian theologian and reformer; ex-President Madison; incumbent President Monroe . . .

Borrowing promotional methods from the reform forces of Britain, the society soon had its own propaganda journal, the *African Repository,* as well as annual conventions and component state societies raising funds, enlisting members and recruiting free Negroes for shipment. The elder slave states—Maryland, Virginia, Kentucky—were most active, but New York, Ohio, Mississippi also saw much Colonization stir. Quietly the program was widened to encourage slaveowners to free Negroes—usually by will—on condition that the Society send them out of the country. As haven for them a free Negro state called Liberia was founded in 1822 on the steamy, frowsy Grain Coast of West Africa. Informal support from the benignly interested federal government made it in effect Uncle Sam's first overseas colony, its chief village named Monrovia after the President, its flag a simplified Stars and Stripes. At best its climate and diseases would have staggered American-reared Negroes. They also had to cope with hostile local Negro tribes who felt no solidarity with these interlopers from another world, with outlaw slavers preying on natives and Liberians alike, and with European powers resenting Yankee intrusion into their shabby spheres of influence. Early Liberia was held together only by a trickle of supervisors and supplies sent by the Society and the occasional appearance at Monrovia of a U.S. Navy ship on antislaver patrol.

Growth would have been feeble anyway. Few free Negroes cared to give up the homelike squalor in which most of them supported themselves for the dubious risks of a distant Africa. For recruits the Society came to rely on slaves freed specifically for emigration, and as law, as well as public opinion, began to frown on this, supply was uncertain. People of goodwill sometimes put their weight into it. But whereas Clay had estimated that the Society could ship the nation's annual increase of 6,000 free Negroes and 46,000 slaves—a total that, as he said, was no more than the number yearly landed in Cuba by illegal slavers—actually only a few hundred ever sailed in a given year. By 1860 the total from the beginning was only 11,000-odd.

At first most antislavery elements in America approved of or at least did not oppose Colonization. But the growth of the Negro population, slave and free, made the scale of the Society's project look ever more absurd. It was not even beginning to export the annual increase of free Negroes alone. In attacks led by William Lloyd Garrison, eventually the archhero of abolitionism, who made more sense on Colonization than on most subjects, antislavery forces broke with the back-to-Africa notion. It was pointed out that though Colonization was obviously futile, its mere conspicuous existence and the prestige of its leaders allowed conscientious men the illusion that something effective was being done for Negroes. It was strongly—and justly—suspected that part of the appeal of Colonization to the Southern Quality lay in its promise to dispose of free Negroes, whose anomalous presence was considered unsettling to slaves. The scarcely masked assumption that, as the Grimké sisters, South Carolina Quality turned abolitionist, indignantly wrote, the Negro "cannot rise in his native America to a level with his white brother," that he "must go to Africa to enjoy the blessings of liberty and equality," [94] embarrassed liberal minds. Such sound reproaches from the Negro's self-avowed friends crippled Colonization after the mid-1830's. Most antislavery leaders, such as Gerrit Smith, the nation's greatest landowner, and James G. Birney, eventually nominee for President of the Liberty (antislavery) Party, turned against it. It kept its colony afloat with Uncle Sam's spasmodic help. Mrs. Stowe still took it seriously in the early 1850's, sending George Harris, the heroic mulatto of *Uncle Tom's Cabin,* to a promising new life in Liberia. Even after Appomattox Abraham Lincoln was recommending Colonization to Negro leaders. But such illusions gave the corpse only a false semblance of life.

With the collapse of hopes for Colonization perished the last concerted effort of slaveholding Quality to try goodwill on the Negro problem. In the same few years the local antislavery organizations that had proliferated among churchgoing farmers as well as Quality in the South ominously dried up and blew away. All that was connected—though probably not as closely as was asserted at the time—with Garrison's rise as shrillest screamer among antislaveryites and with the slave rising of 1831 led by psychotic Nat Turner in the country below Norfolk, Virginia. To us, gifted with 20-20 hindsight, the bitter debate preceding the Missouri Compromise of 1820, which struck Jefferson as a fire bell in the night, had already left small doubt that the South would never consent to see the expansion of slavery completely hemmed in.

The failure of Colonization also coincided with a shift in the North away from the improve-the-lower-orders approach to reform. It persisted in many do-good activities, of course, particularly those close to church-going. But Ralph Waldo Emerson's "men with beards" were now conspicuous in reform circles as never before. Garrison, though smooth-shaven, was a portent. Condescension in broadcloth, Dr. Rush-fashion, had not been enough. The cranks were eager and able to take over.

The cultural dependence on the Mother Country implied in early reform was also marked in the field of letters during the decades after independence. Portrait painting was keeping its head sturdily above water in the work, however British-flavored, of Trumbull, Peale and his family and, gloriously, in that of Gilbert Stuart. The Federal refinements of American Georgian architecture and the Romanistic Classic Revival were making this at least a silver age of building. But writing of distinction hardly existed outside political controversy, most notably in *The Federalist* papers of the late 1780's by Alexander Hamilton, John Jay and James Madison. None of them, note again, was a New Englander. New England was groping prolixly after belles lettres in the persons of the Hartford Wits, a mutual admiration society of educated men of ability in other fields—but ill advised to have invaded literature. The American reading public was expanding at least in step with the population, as the growth of libraries and publishing showed. But the nontechnical shelves of libraries and bookshops were dominated by the fiction and verse, not of Joel Barlow (author of *The Columbiad*, an epic of the discovery of America) or Philadelphia's Charles Brockden Brown (author of twitchy, murky melodramatic novels), but of Fielding, Sterne, Smollett, Fanny Burney, Hannah More and Mrs. Radcliffe. As the talents of Thomas Campbell, Thomas Moore, Sir Walter Scott and Maria Edgeworth developed in Britain, the former Colonies followed the fashion of admiring them.

Of two causes of this failure to patronize home writers, the major one was that *The Mysteries of Udolpho* and *The Lay of the Last Minstrel* were more readable than the works of Brown, Barlow, *et al.* The minor one was probably cultural colonialism. An economic factor might be added. Lack of international copyright allowed the American printer-publisher to pirate for newspaper, magazine or book use any British writers that he fancied, standard or brand-new, without paying the author a single dime. This unfair competition—equally unfair vice versa, of course, but that was not the point when there were twenty professional British writers to one American—persisted until Congress reformed matters in 1891. For instance, the first seven years (post-1830) of *Godey's Lady's Book*, the dominant woman's magazine of its time, were practically solid piracy of British authors.

How much this damaged a possibly budding American literature is uncertain. James K. Paulding, much more successful than most American writers in developing readers among his countrymen, thought it a healthy safeguard against Americans' being tempted to write for the larger and more cultivated British market. *C.* 1800, say, there was as yet no body of American professional writers committed to living by writing plays, verse or novels. The American playwrights of the early 1800's were either stagestruck Quality, some of pleasant talents, or actors and managers occasionally cobbling up actable scripts without being primarily dependent on writing for the stage. The ablest post-Revolutionary poet, Philip Freneau, earned his basic living as a partisan editor-journalist with intervals of commanding coasting vessels. The Hartford Wits had other professions, such as law, or independent means. This situation, too, had a curiously long future. The first American writer of anything like stature primarily to depend on writing books—not journalism collected between hard covers afterward—was Harriet Beecher Stowe, and she was forty years old when her amateur pin-money scribbling bloomed into *Uncle Tom's Cabin* and sudden professional status in 1851. The first man of stature to do so was Henry James.

Granted, one can be a professional writer without making books one's sole support. Attitude and degree of talent also count; were Fielding the magistrate and Richardson the bookseller amateurs? In his active years Washington Irving was variously law student, editor, businessman, and on the national payroll as diplomat in Spain and England. But few would contest the statement that the anonymous publication of his *Knickerbocker's History of New York* in 1809 qualified him as the first important American writer as such. The difference between him and his predecessors in print is indefinable but real, of the same order as that identifying big league caliber in a baseball player. If such comparisons make sense, which is doubtful, one must say that Irving did not write as well as Copley had painted. But his success in the Mother Country was of cognate warmth, which, in view of John Bull's chronic sulkiness about the Colonies, was a compliment to both the writer and British discernment.

This hint that an American literature—at least a body of professionally competent writings from American hands—might be brewing up was repeated after 1812 in the successive *John Bull* items of Paulding, Irving's ally in youthful satirizings of New York City, and in the tales and novels about old days up the Hudson that he dashed off in the intervals of Jacksonian politics. Still another hint came when young William Cullen Bryant, a cultivated Yankee lawyer, published a markedly professional set of verses about death. (The magazine that printed them, the *North American Review*, the new nation's first viable periodical, was founded by that brother of Frederic Tudor's who helped him create the ice-export trade.) The year 1821 saw not only Irving's the *Sketch Book,* which embedded Ichabod Crane and Rip Van Winkle in American folklore, but also James Fenimore Cooper's *The Spy* and the first novel of the first tolerable American-born lady novelist, Massachusetts' Catherine Sedgwick. In 1824 Boston's William Austin added his astringent fantasy about *Peter Rugg, the Missing Man.*

Most of those works have been long blighted by the curse of the school reading list. All derived from Old Country models, no less so than the drearinesses of Brown and Barlow. But suddenly here were derivative writings with their own inner stirrings. It is stimulating, not irritating, to discern how joyfully and fruitfully Paulding had soaked himself in Swift, Sterne and Rabelais. Even Cooper, for all the rhetorical sins that Mark Twain justly censured him for, had something of the gait, stance and limberness of statement that mark the born writer. Note further the New Yorkishness of the development. Irving and Paulding were Manhattanites. Cooper did his growing up on the family lands upstate. Bryant made his career as editor of the New York *Evening Post.* These men's Southern imitators—Kennedy in Maryland, William Gilmore Simms in South Carolina—were imitating New Yorkers. In that same year of 1821 the first section of the Erie Canal opened. In the arts, as well as in economics, New York City was supplanting Philadelphia as the focus of the nation.

In religion, too, America expanded broad hints from the Old World into specifically American results as widespread as and deeper in significance than the white columns of the Greek Revival. Religious matters are awkward to discuss nowadays because most readers are less familiar than their forebears were with basic theological issues. But what to do about God had been a shaping ingredient of some Colonies and was to play a weighty part in developments over the mountains.

The newborn Colony of Georgia, conceived in righteousness, early attracted support from the English clergymen brothers, John and Charles Wesley, who had been trying to bring Christian promises of personal salvation home to sinful Britons—a struggle that ended in their followers' reluctant secession from the Church of England and the rise of the Dis-

senting sect called Methodists in America. In the Wesleys' wake came
eloquent George Whitefield, to devote much of his life to preaching his
Calvinist version of their ideas from Georgia to Massachusetts. His emo-
tion-rich sermons drew crowds relatively comparable to Billy Sunday's
fifty years ago or Billy Graham's today and produced many equally emotional conversions to loud hopes of salvation. One of his sermons moved
Benjamin Franklin, the thrifty skeptic, to empty his pockets into the
collection plate. Visitors to Philadelphia, aware of its reputation for easygoing worldliness, were dismayed to find few dances and bibulous dinners
since Mr. Whitefield had passed through.

More important his harpings on man's precarious relation to a God of
both wrath and love had stirred up many hearers in a fashion that few of
their regular preachers had ever cared to attempt; had heartened certain
American religious zealots, such as Gilbert Tennent in New Jersey and
Jonathan Edwards in Massachusetts, who were already groping toward a
closer impact of Calvinism on the individual; and had outraged both the
American branch of the Church of England that was official in the Southern Colonies and the conservative wings of the Presbyterian, Congregationalist and Reformed Calvinisms that bulked so large in the Middle Colonies and New England. When Whitefield died while evangelizing Newburyport, Massachusetts, in 1770, he had long been the most pervasive
and persuasive figure in the Great Awakening—a yeasty movement using
mass harangues of overwrought hearers to sharpen their sense of the
immediacy of God in their lives and in their ministers' growingly emotional
theology. By then many ministers who had originally welcomed the zeal
that went with this quickening had had second thoughts and were as dismayed as if, said Barrett Wendell, "half the respectable classes [nowa-
days] . . . should fervently abandon their earthly affairs, and, enrolling
themselves under the banners of the Salvation Army, . . . proceed to
camp-meetings of the most enthusiastic disorder. . . . The Great Awakening which expressed itself in mad shoutings and tearings off of garments
was more like what the earlier Puritans had deemed the diabolical excesses of the Quakers." [95]

Indirectly Whitefield had also furthered inter-Colonial solidarity by
fostering a sense of brotherly feeling among his followers across Colony
boundaries, by weaning flexible Colonial minds away from churchly ties
with the Mother Country, and by sensitizing the American conscience to
man's right to suit himself among theologies—all of which is thought to
have increased the Colonists' taste for equalitarian notions and dislike
of overseas leading-strings. A born schismatic, Whitefield had broken
with the Wesleys. Within a year of his death, however, they reaped where
he had harrowed by sending to America in 1771 Francis Asbury, another

ardent soul and even more durable. Afoot or on horseback in all weathers, he was soon exhorting and exploring all over the Colonies. Thus learning them at strenuous firsthand, he seems gradually to have sensed the strength of the Revolution and hoped for a specifically American-based Methodism to match. After independence he was the new nation's outstanding Wesleyan and a valued friend of the eminent physician-patriot-reformer Dr. Benjamin Rush. Asbury's chief service to his Lord, however, was to organize a body of hard-riding fellow evangelists, who sowed Methodism hot from their burning hearts all through the inflammable backwoods, as well as up and down the seaboard.

Each had a specific territory to ransom from sin by periodic preachings at points where hearers could readily meet. Their regular tours of such fords, courthouses and crossroads gave the legal-flavored name *circuit* to their routes and made them *circuit riders*—a term soon as much a part of American speech as *lynch law* or *pieplant*. Mud to the horse's girths; even deeper floods to swim; malaria; abuse from backwoods rowdies; dog days or blizzard, the circuit riders kept at the Lord's work. Even in that rugged age they stood out for grit and stamina. Much of their pluck probably came of knowing that Bishop Asbury had done as much and more before them and still yearly outstayed most of them in the saddle.

Methodism being strongest among the lower orders of the elder settlements and the backwoods, these preachers raised from the ranks of converts were seldom learned men. But that did not keep them from spreading their message. It was an arresting one. Anybody could attain eternal bliss beyond the grave—and conversely avoid the white-hot horrors of hell—if he could bring off the spiritual rebirth of handing his soul back to God who made it. The Ten Commandments were shown to be God's taboo discipline for the redeemed, essential in daily life and perverted into soul poison by neglect, so all this gouging and lallygagging had better stop. And let scorners understand that a man of God needed no Latin or Greek, that with Christ in his heart and just enough education to read the Bible, a preacher was all the better midwife of souls for lacking academic sophistication. The Apostle Paul, such a preacher told Bloomington, Indiana, in the raw 1830's, "never rubbed his back agin a college, nor toted about no sheepskins . . . you'da perished in your sins if the fust preachers had a stay'd till they'd got sheepskins! . . . I don't depend on no larnin' whatsoever, but . . . on the sperit. . . ." [96] Hence Methodism was the last major American sect to found colleges; only in the 1830's were Randolph-Macon, Connecticut Wesleyan and Asbury (now De-Pauw) born.

Salvation potential for all sounded good to Calvinists taught that only an elect few inscrutably chosen by God would escape eternal fires. And plain folk, whether Calvinist-reared or not, loved to see Greek and Hebrew taken down a peg along with the broadcloth wearers associated with schooling. Methodism as circuit riding embodied it was a muddy-booted, everybody-good-as-anybody religion close to the backwoodsman's prejudices and sharply contrasting with the conventional sects. In any case those sects had neglected the backwoods, particularly from Maryland southward. In previously churchless neighborhoods, where cutting notches in a stick was the best way to tell one day from the next, the circuit rider's periodical visit and galvanic rantings about the terrors of hell and the infinite mercy of Christ were something to look forward to even among those not highly religious-minded. He also made marriage available for couples preferring not to live in sin and have bastard children and said fitting words—spontaneously too, not just gabble out of a printed book— over the new graves that grew so numerous what with milk sickness, consumption and childbed. As local conversions multiplied, a particular preacher might be settled at Muddy Run to preach weekly in the schoolhouse, if there was one, or standing in the doorway of a member's cabin so the overflow outside could hear.

Or a Baptist preacher might thus provide regular worship for a new settlement. Long endemic in Rhode Island and the Middle Colonies, the Baptists had gained momentum from the Great Awakening and made the most of it, notably in the newer parts of the South. In upcountry Virginia, Philip Fithian noted in 1774, they were "growing very numerous . . . quite destroying pleasure in the Country; for they encourage ardent Pray'r; strong & constant faith, & an intire banishment of Gaming Dancing, & Sabbath-Day Diversions. . . . Parson Gibbern has preached several Sermons in . . . which he has labour'd to convince his People . . . that what they say are only whimsical Fancies or at most Religion grown to Wildness and Enthusiasm." [97] Their teachings were not quite as comforting as the Methodists'. But they were gratifyingly stiff on sin and Sabbath keeping, and their reliance on amateur preachers—farmers or workmen handling plow handles or lapstone six days a week and letting zeal make up for learning in the pulpit on the seventh—went Methodism one better in appeal to equalitarianism. "Some of the settlers here [out from Pittsburgh in 1772] had not heard a sermon in fourteen years," wrote the Reverend David McClure, Presbyterian missionary. ". . . A few illiterate preachers of the Baptist persuasion have preached about, zealous to make converts." [98] Their insistence on adult baptism by total immersion—no token drops on the brow but a good sousing over head and ears—was also effective. The scene was usually a beach or running stream; the preacher prayed waist-deep as they led out to him the neophyte garbed in symbolic white; the congregation sang appropriate hymns.

One arm back of the shoulders, the other hand on the chest, lay him back, down, well under the surface—and a newly ransomed soul came up gasping, streaming and morally impressed with itself and the ritual; the colder the water, the better.

Methodism countered with a system of dividing congregations into classes of ten or so, each in charge of a notably righteous lay member to look out for its components' spiritual welfare and combat backsliding by prayer and vigilance—an expansion of the job of the Puritan tithingman. Such a class leader acquired prestige among the pious, as well as the gratifying duty not to mind his own business. Soon the less rigid among Presbyterians, aided by the strong bent of the Scotch-Irish settlers toward their own version of Calvinism and church organization, made a third in this competition for converts in the new country. But the tide was against them. The more equalitarian Baptists and Methodists so overran the South and the Old Northwest that (counting their schismatic splinters) they have ever since been the most numerous Protestant sects in America.

Thus they could and did do much to tone down the barbarities of the new settlements. Where these faiths took hold, they had more than secular law to do with gradual diminution of mayhem and abuse of strong drink. For John Wesley had set himself against not only drunkenness but against practically all beverage alcohol. Bishop Asbury, soon fanatic about it, caused his circuit riders to denounce dram drinking and the Devil in the same breath. The Baptists, equally aware of the same antialcohol texts in the same Bible, did the same. To this the prohibitionists of the late 1800's owed much of their strength in the South, as well as in the Midwest. To the conviction that spiritual leaders needed only the unvarnished Word of God, the fear lest learning be a screen between man and raw salvation, the South also owed its Fundamentalist mistrust of new ideas that explains the deliberate grotesqueries of the Scopes trial. And by developing the spectacular camp meeting for saving souls wholesale, these explosive evangelistic sects gave America one of its typical institutions.

The general phenomenon was old. Leaders of the Great Awakening had known how to rake a mass of hearers over the coals of hell so earnestly that they infected one another with apprehensive hysteria and eventual joy as "the victory" succeeded "conviction of sin." The pre-Christian cults of the Near East had shown the same symptoms. But it was backwoods Kentucky of 1801 that put the tradition into its classic American shape at a memorable camp meeting under mixed Presbyterian, Methodist and Baptist auspices at a place called Cane Ridge. The time was August, the height of sultry summer when haying is long past and corn has been "laid by"—had its last cultivation. In a large clearing a tent sheltered the platform for preachers. Around it were smaller tents and wagon room for the thousands of the soul-hungry and curious, bringing food and bedding for a stay of several days and even more important nights. Gastronomic rivalry was intense as each family produced and shared around its versions of all possible frontier delicacies. "Indeed," wrote an observer, "a camp-meeting is the most mammoth picnic possible; and it is one's own fault, saint or sinner, if he gets not . . . the best the land affords." [99] But food for the soul was the chief end in view. Experienced preachers working in relays screamed damnation and eternal love from stumps and wagon beds, as well as the platform, dashing down in the crowd to assail waverers, tearing themselves ragged with contagious emotion, alternating verbal onslaughts with mass singing of popular hymns couched in lurid metaphors of blood and love and ransom and war.

Lit by bonfires and torches, this rhythmic, raucous atmosphere led to striking excesses. As the power gripped these workaday men and women and their sunburned sons and rough-handed daughters, they were expected to and usually did give way to violent physical antics as standardized as those of voodoo in Haiti. After an agonized struggle with sin under the lash of the exhorter the convert would suddenly be struck down writhing and slobbering as if by a stunning blow. Or he would get the jerks—a twitching so severe that a woman victim's long hair might snap like a whip —or the jumps—superhumanly high leaps persisted in for hours—or the barks—yapping like a dog while on all-fours—or the flops—violent quasi-epileptic convulsions. Such seizures were often as arduous as the feats performed by those under hypnosis. Straw was spread thick on the ground to keep the spiritually newborn from injuring themselves. Some spoke in tongues, babbling raptly in what was hopefully taken to be holy tongues like those of the Apostles at Pentecost; this has now reappeared in some staid Protestant sects. Anybody witnessing modern survivals of these acrobatic goings-on, still lively among certain Fundamentalist sects, has little doubt that in some terms or other they are genuine—certainly not conscious affectations. Beyond that, attitudes vary widely. Edward Eggleston, who had been a Methodist preacher before he turned writer and who knew the early Old Northwest intimately, retained a wondering sympathy for it all while acknowledging the superficial grotesquerie. Sam Clemens, equally familiar with the data, maintained that "the Methodist camp meetings and Campbellite [offshoot of the Baptists, now the Disciples of Christ] revivals used to stock the asylums with religious lunatics" and called them contemptuously "wildcat religions." [100]

The most dynamic camp meetings thus overcame only a minority of those present. The confused reports of Cane Ridge—which certainly did as well as any—had 1,000 to 3,000 "brought to the ground" among an attendance of 10,000 to 20,000. There and at subsequent such occasions "the power" and the bonfires eventually flickered out, the tents were struck, and the teams hitched up for the 10, 20, 30, 50 miles back to normal life from house to barn to cornfield to hogpen. The sequelae among the participants naturally varied. The preachers usually came away exhausted but exultantly counting up souls. The saved, whether or not aware of the capers they had cut under the "power," must often have taken away with them an abiding sense of having transcended ordinary limitations and got nearer to a greater something that the preacher said was God. The majority, though failing to feel it all, had nevertheless been impressed by its repercussions. Even those scoffing or deploring such patently unspiritual doings—of whom there were always many—had at least seen a show as absorbing as a childbirth staged like a three-ring circus. Apropos, the next spring unlucky girls had "camp-meeting babies" because under stress of hymns and shrieking exhortations young folks often strayed off into the summer night beyond range of the torches and resolved their tensions in ways that their elders had not intended.

The eventual net effect on the morals and Christian charity of the saved was usually small. Such considerations did not keep many recurrent camp meetings from developing permanent quarters such as those of the Methodists of the 1830's on Deal Island on the Eastern Shore of Maryland with permanent, sand-covered wooden platforms as "fire-stands" and five ranks of clapboard and shingle huts. Such permanence and periodicity, as of a festival, betray the probably most valuable (if unacknowledged) role of camp meetings in backwoods life and in later areas where backwoods habits of mind persisted. They were religion-sanctioned, annual emotional debauches cognate to Carnival or Saturnalia (if the analogy is not pushed too far), after which folks could better endure having to be steady-paced the rest of the year.

Such blowings off of steam at a convenient season when they did no economic harm were especially useful in a society that had few small and still fewer large-scale entertainments. Joseph Kirkland's novels described early Illinois as "a society without holidays and almost without amusements." Since corn shucking was done in the fields—the consequent cold-numbed hands and split thumbs were a memorable misery—husking bees did not exist. "Sociable christenings . . . none. A marriage [was] more often a visit to the preacher or to the justice . . . on Sunday social visiting [was] sacrilegious." [101] Among those well tinged by righteousness the hoedown dances were immoral. (A subterfuge so transparent as to be almost innocent could be found from upper New York State well into the South in the play-party—skipping and running games called

Wink-'Em-Slyly, Copenhagen and so on which involved a great deal of catching and kissing the girls and were distinguished from dancing only because the music was confined to the participants' own singing, fiddles and all other instruments being sinful.) Apple-peelings were known, but spelling bees, amazingly important in Old Northwestern society, had to wait for schools to take root. Thanksgiving had not yet reached the nation outside New England, and it took long for the savor of paganism to lift from Christmas and New Year's. County fairs had not yet come into being.

The permanent campgrounds tacitly admitted their social uses when, after the Civil War, evangelical sects set up actual summer resorts where the righteous could imitate sinners' mountain or seashore vacations while still soaking up Gospel as pious pretext. Flimsy wooden cottages smelling of hot resin were built for the saved to buy or rent around the great revival hall, with Sunday services and midweek prayer meetings and periodical revivals conducted by visiting experts. Intoxicating drink was always barred. Of such resorts now surviving, Ocean Grove, New Jersey, and Pacific Grove, California, may be the most notable. Robert Louis Stevenson, observing Pacific Grove out of season in 1879, sensed "a life of teetotalism, religion and flirtation, which I am willing to think blameless and agreeable." [102] The tone was different in sterner times in Kirkland's Illinois where failure of acceptance by the crossroads church was a passive ostracism, particularly for women. When "a public, spasmodic regeneration was looked upon as necessary to individual salvation" and revivalism retained much iron and gall, it was most advisable to get conspicuously "convicted o' sin [at camp meeting] 'n' made a child o' grace by a change o' heart." [103] In that climate even rural balladry could reflect the lurid lights cast by the flames of hell:

> A story I will now relate
> 'Twas of a gal named Polly Bates;
> She'd dress up fine and curl her hair,
> When others was engaged in prayer.

> She'd go to balls, she'd dance and play
> In spite of all her friends could say:
> "I'll turn to God when I grow old
> And then he will receive my soul."

> One Friday morning she fell sick,
> Her stubborn heart begun to prick,
> She now was sorry she done wrong
> But had put off the day too long.

She called her father to her bed.
Her eyes was rolling in her head.
"O father, father, fare you well
While wretched Polly groans in hell.

"O mother, mother, you I leave.
For wretched Polly do not grieve.
As I am now you soon shall be.
Prepare for death and follow me."

Her face grew black, her hands grew cold,
Her spirit left her earthly mould.
Now all young friends a warning take,
And quit your sins for Polly's sake.[104]

The terms are no subtler than those of the *New England Primer*. Nevertheless, the evangelizing of Western Americans gave them a valuable means to an intellectual life. It made many care responsibly how and on what terms God had set them in the universe. And those hungry for mental stimulus and able to read their Bibles eagerly listened to controversial sermons and acquired skill in theological disputation. After a while they could draw as glibly as the preacher on the appropriate texts from *Romans* or *II Corinthians*. The cleavage between the Old Light Presbyterians, who opposed the loosening-up effects of the Great Awakening, and their New Light rivals; the resistance of Methodism to limitations on the scope of that salvation that Christ's Atonement implied; the aptitude of the Baptists for schism, which created not only the Two-Seed-in-the-Spirit Baptists but also the Primitive (or Hard-shell, grimly Calvinistic) Baptists and the Campbellites, out of whom rather indirectly came the Mormons—all set off unending but, for the participants, rousing discussions among amateurs of one or another heresy or orthodoxy. Violent personal quarrels might ensue. The Montague-Capulet consideration that a young couple wishing to marry came of different kinds of Baptists might break it off. But on the intellectual level it was, on balance, gain. For all its love of obscurity, theology has always been a fine mental gymnasium for those interested. So the crossroads theological tournament was added to the circuit court as an exercise ground for backwoods brains. In 1840 a Universalist missionary named McGwen challenged a Methodist circuit rider to debate at Knightstown, Indiana, a settlement on the National Road, on the question: "Will all men be holy and happy in the future state?" Though the neighborhood had no particular reputation for piety, it flocked to hear in such numbers that no local church would hold them, and the debate was adjourned to a nearby grove with room for all. They spoke alternately for three days, the audience with them every step of the way.

Crude as backwoods courts, lynchings, camp meetings and divinity were, it remained true that on the whole, justice and the soul were better looked after than bodies or minds. That could also apply to the seaboard settlements. Indeed it was a good thing that law and theology bulked unduly large because without them people would have had very little to sharpen their intellects and tastes on.

Not that they did not use their brains, often most capably. Common sense, judgment and imagination had wide scope among large and small farmers given to horse trading and land speculation; moneylending merchants; rising industrialists; inventors; and the keen minds that produced *The Federalist* and Albert Gallatin's *Report on . . . Public Roads and Canals.* But in all that, the manipulative overshadowed the contemplative. This could hardly be avoided among a generation for whom books were at best scarce and expensive and journalism was primitive and often puerile. No universities to offer evening courses for hungry adult minds. No graduate schools to foster scholarship. Only theology and its ancillary dead languages were intensively studied. Mathematics usually appeared as instruction in navigation or surveying. The sciences, now absorbing so much of society's available intelligence, were largely confined to a few zealous individuals groping into ill-explored fields and pathetically eager to hear of others with the same interests.

Medicine alone among the scientific callings had followed the lead of law and theology in setting up professional schools—first in Philadelphia, then in New England, then within a generation of settlement in Kentucky and the Old Northwest. Even so, for some generations apprenticeship to a practicing physician was the usual gate into the profession outside the largest towns. Today's medical student, versed in chemistry, biology and psychology, has been steeped in exacting and mind-stirring sciences and techniques. But there was little mental stimulus in what was taught in those few medical schools or in old Dr. Lancet's office either. Medicine was still handcuffed by arbitrary theories inherited from the ancient and medieval worlds based on the principle that disease comes of imbalance among the humors (basic body elements), and the physician's task was to restore balance by dosage with violent drugs, bleedings and so on. Hence the probably needless death of George Washington in 1797. Still vigorous at the age of sixty-seven, he caught cold and had doctors in. Conscientiously they weakened him by prolonged bleeding, then by calomel to purge his bowels and tartar emetic to make him vomit, then applied blistering poultices. Forty years later the doctors whose ministrations

Sam Clemens' Missouri neighbors sometimes survived were still persisting in such therapy and in "Good measure. . . . Only the largest persons could hold a whole dose. Castor oil . . . half a dipperful . . . The next standby was calomel. . . . Then they bled the patient and put mustard plasters on him. . . ." [105]

Some gleams of light had appeared since the day when John Winthrop, Jr., had been a Fellow of the Royal Society, the most renowned physician in the Colonies—and simultaneously an ardent alchemist. In 1707 the Reverend Cotton Mather acquired an African slave who told him of the West African trick of inoculation with smallpox matter to give the subject a mild, immunizing case of the disease. When next that periodically calamitous scourge of the eighteenth century threatened Boston, Mather, making great sense for once, advised local physicians to try inoculation. The only one with the independence of mind to take it up was Dr. Zabdiel Boylston, who inoculated his own son (he himself had had the disease previously) and recommended the process to his patients. His house and Mather's were mobbed by a populace, egged on by the newspaper published by Benjamin Franklin's brother James, who saw in this a wanton risk of spreading the infection. But Boylston stuck to it and had the eventual satisfaction of showing that of 286 Bostonians thus deliberately infected in hopes of light cases, only 2 percent died, whereas of 5,779 contracting smallpox in the natural way 14 percent died. Nevertheless, in Charleston, South Carolina, in 1738 fear of inoculation was still so strong that a well-considered local physician sponsoring the practice was driven out of the Colony.

The new century brought from England the much less dangerous technique of vaccination against smallpox—a fine new weapon against one of the new nation's worst killers. As counterweight a new epidemic terror had recently arrived—yellow fever up from the West Indies in the bloodstreams of infected persons to find waiting in America the right species of mosquito to incubate and spread it. Its onslaught gave Philadelphia in 1793 the air of London during the Great Plague. Two men were the heroes of the emergency: Stephen Girard, the wealthy French-born curmudgeon, who, instead of fleeing out of town like most, denied that the disease was contagious and actually volunteered to manage the pesthouse set up for its victims; and Dr. Benjamin Rush, whose keen sense of duty kept him doctoring practically day and night, week after week, bedside to bedside, rich or poor, throughout the whole grisly ordeal. It does not detract from his fine self-dedication that for yellow fever he recommended and administered bleedings and purgings so severe as even to alarm his colleagues. Heaven knows how many whom his well-meant stubbornness killed might otherwise have pulled through.

Alexander Hamilton, whose less august doctor prescribed only opium, quinine and sponge baths, survived yellow jack. So did Mrs. Charles Willson Peale, whose eccentric painter-husband had his own notions about medicine and hygiene and gave her nothing but solicitous nursing. Since nobody had yet shown the relation between mosquitoes and yellow fever, neither MD nor layman could make sense about it. Girard tried hard, not only practically proving in his own person that it was not contagious, but also preaching that clearing the filth from Philadelphia's garbage- and ordure-laden streets would prevent recurrence—which, by eliminating many of the mosquitoes' breeding places, it might have done. As it was, the disease came again and again, and to New York City, Boston and elsewhere. But this insistence on cleaning up did lead indirectly to the building of Philadelphia's municipal waterworks, the first such project in a large American town.

All the while from Maine to Georgia our forebears' energies and resistances were sapped by malaria, alias fevernager, the shakes. The virulence of its several varieties ranged from strong risk of fever-racked death to periodic disability predisposing the victim to succumb to other diseases. Malaria had probably followed the same course as yellow fever to the West Indies, thence up the Atlantic seaboard with Negro slaves and ships' companies, and had the same luck in finding already well established the species of mosquito that it required. Only this invasion had come much earlier, well back in the 1600's, and had greater success in establishing numerous permanent focuses of infection, as common talk soon recognized. "Sickly country" meant a region with enough wetlands to make malaria a local institution—which fits most areas actively penetrated by settlers up to the Civil War. "The sickly season," when the Quality fled from the low-lying seaboard, was from midsummer to mid-October, when frost suppressed the mosquitoes until the next year. And the violent shaking that went with the recurrent chills was as basic to frontier humor as gouging, snakes in the boots and tall tales about marksmanship.

For inevitably in their own bloodstreams the pioneers took malaria over the mountains along with the fiddle and grandpa's Bible. Malaria was already rampant in 1810 on the Wabash at Busro Creek, where the Shakers—doughty colonizers, hard to discourage because God was on their side—settled on rich lands. By 1827 they had to confess defeat and abandon the graves of their dead and the site of years of wasted toil. In 1825 in the Sangamon country of Illinois, where Abraham Lincoln came from, Henry Schoolcraft, the early explorer-ethnologist, thought the hazard of malaria so high that "I [run] as great a risk every season which I spend here as in an ordinary battle." [106] During Howells' boyhood in southwestern Ohio "there were few houses where [malaria] was not a familiar guest. . . . If the family was large, there was usually a chill every day; one had it one day and another the next . . . accepted as something quite in the course of nature, and [they] duly broke it up with quinine. Some of the boys had chills at school; and sometimes, after they had been in swimming, they would sit round on the bank till a fellow had had his chill out, and then . . . all go off together and forget about it." [107] The formidable Kentucky-born old lady in Meredith Nicholson's *A Hoosier Chronicle, c.* 1890, was still preaching that "Sassafras [tea] in the spring, and a few doses of quinine in the fall, to eliminate the summer's possible accumulation of malaria, were all the medicine that any good Hoosier needed." [108] But it had not been that simple 100 years earlier, when swamps were extensive and quinine even harder to come by than it was expensive.

The association between swamps and malaria was widely known. But medicine, unaware that the mosquito was the indispensable link, thought of the disease as somehow caused by bad air (in Italian *malaria*) created by vegetable matter rotting in damp places. On that faulty basis the best doctor could only prescribe quinine (a genuine specific for suppressing the debilitating symptoms) and wait for the advance of farming to drain swamps and clogged river bottoms. To such enterprise the settlers inadvertently and unconsciously owed the gradual retreat of the malaria hazard. But sometimes progress worked the other way. New England's milldams created new patches of mosquito-harboring wetland, and the spread of canalboats and steamboats increased the traveler's exposure to mosquitoes. Many a pioneer lived out his life assuming with grim good reason that he would come down with the shakes yearly in spite of talk about one's eventually becoming acclimatized, meaning malaria-proof. The story was that when somebody asked General David R. Atchison of Missouri, patron saint of the Border Ruffians of the 1850's, had he got acclimatized, he answered: "I've been here twenty-five years and God damn my soul to hell if I haven't entertained twenty-five separate and distinct earthquakes, one a year." [109]

Necessary ignorance of germs also saw to it that tuberculosis was mishandled. It was not even known that the same sort of organism caused scrofula (a once common and often deforming infection of the lymph nodes) and consumption of the lungs. For the latter, Dr. Rush and others sharing his sure instinct for the wrong thing recommended vigorous exercise, particularly horseback riding, since it was thought that horse smell was good for weak lungs. The standard children's diseases did their share to keep infantile mortality high. In summer, typhoid fever passed on by infected streams and wells was certainly rife under the various names of bilious fever, the flux and so on. Hookworm, another disease of filth and microorganisms, remained a major—and utterly unrecognized—problem principally in the South, where bare feet were commoner than up North and average temperatures ran higher. But the over-the-mountains country was compensatingly handicapped by a mysterious "milk sickness," otherwise called the trembles, the slows, the puking fever, the tires, that often killed and at best left the victim burdened for months with the symptoms indicated by the above names. It was known to be associated with drinking milk or eating beef. Not till the 1920's was the cause identified as a powerful poison, tremetol, in a weed called white snakeroot that infested the rough pioneer pastures and was eaten by livestock. The one good thing about it was that the raw whiskey that our forebears took as remedy for so many ailments really was good for this one—alcohol tends to neutralize the poison, which is a cousin alcohol.

The early American medical schools knew and taught much more about surgery than about physiology. In apprentice training the average doctor's assistant was likely to learn a good deal of rough-and-ready surgery as his time progressed. Nobody had any notion of asepsis, of course, and infection of incisions was taken for granted—there was much wise talk about the relative beneficence of various types of pus and inflammation. Anesthesia consisted at best of horse doses of brandy or rum. The patient was strapped to a table usually with assistants each holding his head or a limb. But it is a great credit to the skill of these knee-breeched surgeons and to their knowledge of anatomy that so many of their subjects survived amputations of limbs and excisions of kidney stones and superficial cancers. Amputations were frequent because that was the only hopeful way to handle a compound fracture; reducing and splinting it practically guaranteed death from infection. Hence the high incidence of one-armed and peg-legged men 150 years ago. Since no surgeon, however clever, dared go into the main body cavities, appendicitis and gallbladder trouble and so on were not operable. Such major work had to wait until 1819, when Kentucky-born Dr. Ephraim McDowell, home to practice surgery after study at Edinburgh, got around to reporting his successes in removing diseased ovaries from backwoodswomen—the first major contribution to medicine made by an American.

It remains true nowadays, of course, that by and large the surgeon knows more about what he is doing than the internist often can. Scorn for these old-time physicians must be further tempered by the realization that nowhere else in the world was medicine then better, that the skills and traditions that hundreds of American doctors of the 1700's brought home from Edinburgh or Paris as basis for founding medical schools and training apprentices were on much the same level of competence—10 percent knowledge, 40 percent pseudoscientific surmise, 50 percent bedside manner—as that of their august preceptors across the water. Their position was well defined by Dean Cecil Drinker of the Harvard School of Public Health: "With little knowledge of the structural changes produced by disease and none at all of the chemical and functional alterations resulting from illness, the physicians of 1800 were unable to visualize what was happening to the patient. But when Adam Kuhn or Benjamin Rush was called . . . he had to tell the . . . family what was wrong with the patient. . . . Diagnosis in the hands of these shrewd and experienced men was no doubt good . . . [but] when it came to deciding what would probably happen and . . . what to do in the way of treatment, they had no knowledge on which to build." [110] So, as James T. Flexner says of Dr. Rush: ". . . the patients wanted doctors . . . sure of themselves, and the doctors needed for their own happiness to believe that their prescriptions helped. . . . A Svengali who would hypnotize himself, his patients and above all his colleagues into believing he was right was certain to be regarded as a great scientist." [111] And he steered his clinical course pretty much by dead (no pun intended) reckoning. There is a great deal of long-outmoded medical history in a Winthrop Chandler "primitive" painting in the Campus Martius Museum at Marietta, Ohio, showing a certain Dr. Gleason, very solemn with his long walking stick and boots, taking a lady patient's pulse *through the bed-curtains* to spare her modesty.

That professional climate necessarily led to much unconscious and some conscious quackery. In 1796 Dr. Elisha Perkins of Connecticut, a reputable enough physician, made a great medical stir with his Metallic Tractors, spikelike bits of brass and iron that cured rheumatism, other inflammations and certain kinds of tumors when a skilled hand drew them lightly over the affected areas. He promoted use—and sale—of the tractors far and wide, and after his death his son cut a wide swath with them in Denmark and England, founding in London a Perkinean Institute and coming home in 1816 with profits of $50,000 in his pocket, then a fortune. There began the Old Country's susceptibility to American crank cults and ideas, which would be more amusing if only over the years the balance of trade had not been so heavy in the other direction.

Plenty of folk medicine was available to Americans skeptical about formal medicine as certain shrewd Romans were about the claims of the official augurs; those unable to afford its fees, which were very high in terms of the time, or living in areas still lacking doctors; and those emotionally attached to Old Country rustic ways—all those categories together probably included nine-tenths of the post-Revolutionary population. Old wives' formulas and the herbs they called for, some tinged with white magic, came overseas with each lot of Palatine peasants, Highland crofters and East Anglian yeomen. The Indians had an elaborate pharmacopoeia of wild herbs, roots, barks and so on capable of combining into potions tasting quite as impressively bad as anything white men had. Here, as in woodcraft and farming, the settlers freely adopted Indian practices and let them interbreed with those of medieval Europe. The early suspicion that Indians had truck with the Devil may have been reinforced by the gnarly gestures and mutterings with which Indian wise men stewed up their astringent messes. So such native items as butternut bark (effective only when peeled upward), slippery elm, bloodroot, Jimsonweed, poke-berry (the last two highly toxic, hence doubtless having striking effects) rubbed elbows with the Old World's saffron, pennyroyal, tansy (which escaped and became a weed), garlic, scrapings from brass spoons, flaxseed and sorrel in the prescriptions handed down from great-grandma or gravely printed in newspapers, almanacs and the backs of books on how to keep house. With Negro slavery, tinges of West African herb lore also became discernible.

The consequent fantasies strung together by backwoods Galens and their female competitors sometimes showed a grisly imagination. There was some sense in treating cholera morbus (a seldom-fatal enteric trouble not now too closely identifiable) with a combination of French brandy, lime juice, sugar and a little hot water, for a stiff hot punch is likely to make one feel better, no matter what the ailment. Five or six wineglasses a day of the best rye whiskey flavored with boneset and blue vervain for the shakes followed the same theory, though the taste was probably not as good. But the shakes were also treated with soot from inside a chimney —useless if from a stovepipe—taken in boiling water three times a day with sugar and cream; this was also good for typhoid fever. It took only fifteen days or so to cure even the most violent cancer with the expressed juice of the woolly-headed thistle, as recommended in Prudence Smith's *Modern American Cookery* of 1831, but it could be done in four days by a rival recipe book's mixture of white oak ashes mixed with calomel, saltpeter and pulverized centipede applied with a piece of new soft leather. It is difficult to imagine the mind to which it occurred to treat bedwetting with fried-mouse pie; maybe this was one of Macbeth's witches in a maternal mood. Thence it is a ready transition to the Pennsylvania Dutch powwow doctor, whose title reflected the prestige of the Algonquin Indians' powwow (medicine man) but whose practice was largely Euro-pean white magic using incantations and ritual gestures to blow the fire from burns, stanch hemorrhages, remove warts, cure erysipelas. Powwow-ing still goes on up the back roads of Lancaster County, I understand. The lore and the power pass from older man to younger woman and vice versa. Preceptor and disciple cannot be of the same sex.

Apparently the average American family's procedure 150 years ago was to try everything that oldwifery suggested at the onset of an illness, and in case of recovery, credit pumpkin-seed tea or cow-dung poultices. Only in chronic cases refusing to improve under folk therapy did they seek out an orthodox doctor—by which time the patient's poor condition allowed Dr. Leech to make the best of both worlds. If the case died, he had been called too late; if he lived, he had saved him. It was irksome, however, when a family of Quality and ability to pay went over to the enemy in despair. In the same Philadelphia where America's first hospital had flourished for 50 years, an eminent household might nevertheless send a stubborn face cancer to "Sam^L Wilson, a black man . . . a Cancer doctor" to see if his outlandish practices would help—which caused the family physician to deplore the bad judgment of discarding him "for Indians and witchcraft—pow-wow doctors." [112] With most other complaints, however, the sufferer may well have been better off with the wise old woman down the road in a cabin crammed with pots of salve and bunches of "yarbs." She was probably Dr. Leech's equal in reassuring the patient, bolstering the indicated faith in eventual recovery—always important in therapy—and though her strange teas and amulet bags and rubbings with goose grease can hardly have done more than psychological good, they were preferable to the doctor's bleedings in that they did far less physical harm. Most physicians of Rush's day were probably as devoted as he was. The backwoods doctor undergoing much the same ordeals as the circuit rider, only with a basic pharmacy, lancet and tooth puller in his saddlebags instead of the Bible, usually deserved the great respect in which he was held. Nevertheless, if all the orthodox doctors practicing in America in 1800 had been massacred, their own practices thus stifled and no further doctors trained or imported, demand for gravestones would probably have greatly slackened for the next 50 years.

Dentistry was a branch of doctoring, consisting largely of extractions. Ingested alcohol was the only anesthetic available. Attempts at false teeth, usually of animal ivory, were crude and seldom satisfactory. Tooth brushing was considered merely a cosmetic measure which the very finicky supplemented by use of special whitening powders procurable from druggists.

VI

Ideas and the Almighty Dollar

ABRAHAM LINCOLN'S AMERICA

VI

THOREAU'S hermitage cabin in the woods by Walden Pond was only 500 yards from the railroad between Boston and Fitchburg, Massachusetts. The clatter and rush of passing trains set him considering what was in 1847 still a new kind of transport. It had brisked people up, he thought: "The startings and arrivals of the cars are now the epochs of the village day. They come and go with such regularity and precision, and their whistles can be heard so far, that the farmers set their clocks by them, and thus one well-conducted institution regulates a whole country. Have not men improved in punctuality since the railroad was invented? Do they not talk and think faster in the depot than they did in the stage-office? . . . To do things 'railroad-fashion' is now the by-word." He liked "the steady and cheerful valour of the men who inhabit the snow-plough. . . . On this morning of the Great Snow . . . I hear the muffled tone of the engine bell . . . which announces that the cars *are coming* . . . notwithstanding the veto of a New England northeast snow-storm." [1]

This relative regularity of service in spite of snow and ice, mud, high or low water made steam railroads the core of American transportation within a generation of their first trials. Already in the late 1830's they were supplementing canal and steamboat as symbols of American go-ahead. "What . . . 'fetters' the heels of a young country?" Sam Slick, the Yankee clock peddler, asked the Nova Scotians. "The high price of labor. . . . What's a railroad? The substitution of mechanical for human and animal labor. To [Americans] it is river, bridge, road, and canal, all in one." [2] And with it came major and minor changes: political as the rails tied the interests of the Old Northwest to those of the Northeastern and Atlantic states in time to save the Union in the Civil War; economic as they opened up areas lacking waterways and gave the farmer distant new markets for perishables such as milk and garden truck; social as they made possible freer visitings among widely distributed relatives, colleagues and

343

friends and created the commuting suburb far from the noisy, smoky city, yet only "forty-five minutes from Broadway"; civic as they ran a zone of disfigurement through and sometimes around each municipality they served, hence the sour connotations of *the wrong side of the tracks.*

To all that, steam was essential. The original railroads were short wooden or iron-shod tramways over which horse carts moved coal or stone more efficiently than was possible over conventional roads. A conspicuous example was Massachusetts' Granite Railway, 3 miles long, built in 1826 to move the granite blocks for Bunker Hill Monument from the quarry to barges at tidewater. Horses were also the original motive power of the Baltimore and Ohio, hauling its first passengers in 1830. But the striking success of George Stephenson's steam locomotive in England in the late 1820's was soon emulated in America. Charlestonians throwing a railroad across South Carolina to the Savannah River planned on steam to begin with. Early in 1831 their primitive locomotive with a vertical, wood-fired boiler puffed out of Charleston hauling first a flatcar carrying a cannon and gun crew firing salutes, then two passenger cars full of ladies and gentlemen. They were celebrating an indubitably great occasion—the first run of an American steam-propelled, several-car train—but doubtless were relieved when the panting monster reached the end of its 6 miles of track without mishap. In five months came the first serious accident—the boiler blew up when a fireman held down the safety valve to stop its irksome hissing. But by 1834 the line had reached the river 165 miles away, completing what was then the world's longest railroad. Within five years it averaged 600 passengers a week on a route for which one stagecoach thrice weekly had sufficed before the rails set people eagerly traveling.

Passengers bulked as large in early railroading as they do now in aviation. The Mohawk and Hudson, New York State's first railroad, was laid from Albany to Schenectady in 1831 to compete with the stages that saved travelers the easternmost leg of the Erie Canal trip. Just when steamboats, stages and canal packets were prospering as rivals and mutual supplements in passenger hauling, here came the rails taking the cream of it from all three. For people wanted to travel year round if possible. Ice and uncertain water supply closed canals several months of the year north of latitude 38 degrees—the very region where they were concentrated. Seasonal ice shut off steamboating on the Hudson; on the Great Lakes; in the northern Mississippi Basin. Low water often laid up Ohio River steamboats even in warm seasons. Stages advertised year-round service, but fall rains, winter ice and snow, and spring thaws often put maintaining schedules out of the question. Once engineers had adapted track ballast and metal rails to American conditions, however, the American iron horse—a tall, rangy breed with two coupled drive wheels on a side—offered something much nearer all-weather usefulness. His sand-box tamed wet or icy tracks. Armed with a snowplow he could, as Thoreau observed, conquer most snowstorms.

Stages survived marginally until automobiles came in but only as feeders for railroads and steamboats. Most canals—enticed into untimely

Currier & Ives' celebration of the American railroad locomotive.

being by the glittering success of the Erie Canal when railroads already impended—never paid for themselves and within a generation fell on evil days even as freight haulers. Only the Erie, the Illinois and Michigan and the canals floating Pennsylvania's anthracite coal to market kept their health past the 1850's. After the Civil War the railroads easily smothered what canal competition remained. The Delaware and Hudson built a coal-hauling steam railroad along its own canal and eventually abandoned water transport. The Pennsylvania Railroad acquired the Camden and Amboy in 1871 and encouraged the Delaware and Raritan Canal, its sister operation, to go to seed. The Chesapeake and Ohio Railroad made a right-of-way of the towpath of the James River and Kanawha Canal. The Pennsylvania and Ohio Canal connecting Lake Erie with the Allegheny River fell into gradual dilapidation after coming under control of the Cleveland and Mahoning Railroad, and the seal of the state of Ohio no longer showed the canalboat that once shared it with hills, a rising sun, a sheaf of wheat and a bundle of arrows. The ruins of the canals had many destinies: as crumbling eyesores; as good places to fish or canoe. A few have been restored as mementos of a very slow-and-easy kind of transportation.

The advantages of railroads over other means of transport were not as clear to all as to Sam Slick. In the 1830's Pennsylvania, Illinois and Indiana tried to combine canal and railroad. Nor was it yet certain that the new device was best operated by private enterprise. By analogy with public building and operation of highways, Pennsylvania, North Carolina, Georgia and Indiana ran their own pioneer steam railroads for a while. Georgia and the city of Cincinnati still own and lease out important trackage. The possibility that state railroads might flourish—which might have altered America's future—was marred by the states' mistaken efforts to run them as if they were canals or toll highways with steam merely supplementing horsepower. Anybody conforming to certain standards and paying so much a mile could put his own horse-drawn cars on the track. As rival drivers vied for the right-of-way, ensuing confusion soon taught that, as in the old story, this was "a hell of a way to run a railroad," that management had to confine use of the line to its own rolling stock and take over all control of its movements. In the political climate of a day when a movement to turn the postal system over to private hands could gain wide support, the next step was to hand over state-owned lines, usually by sale, to private enterprise under state charter. The shadow of state enterprise survived only in a few provisions that after twenty or thirty years the state could buy the line back—options never exercised.

To encourage building, the states granted the private railroad companies eminent domain—the right to take over private land without the owner's consent—and sometimes lent them part of their construction costs. Virginia bought and still holds a block of stock in the Richmond, Fredericksburg and Potomac. From the 1850's on, huge grants of state and Federal land were made as construction subsidy. The purpose of all this, public or private, was to bring the state and its citizens the general blessings of railroad-induced economic growth and sometimes to give the state's principal seaport an edge over rival ports in other states. Colonel John Stevens, eminent inventor-promoter of steamboats and railroads, secured Pennsylvania's first railroad charter in 1823 (for a line from Philadelphia to the Susquehanna) on the plea that "when this great improvement . . . shall have been extended to Pittsburgh, thence into the heart of the extensive and fertile state of Ohio, and also the great western lakes, Philadelphia may then become the grand emporium of the western country." [3] As enthusiasm grew, the same sort of appeal enabled promoters to sell stock piecemeal to farmers, merchants, banks and others likely to profit from the iron horse's magic touch on trade.

Whatever state enterprise might have done, in private hands railroad construction boomed until at mid-century 9,000 miles of line were open. It was not yet a continuous system. To go from New York City to New Orleans using rails as much as possible would still require using steamboats here, stages there. Ambitious little lines fanning out of Cincinnati or St. Louis did not necessarily hook up with others out of Chicago or Fort Wayne. But Boston already had a continuous line over the mountains to tap the Erie Canal at Troy, New York, and funnel the trade of western Massachusetts and Vermont-New Hampshire into Boston. New York City, Philadelphia and Baltimore all were pushing private-enterprise trunk lines to tap the rich trade of the Old Northwest. In 1851 and 1852 all three projects holed through, so to speak. The Erie Railroad reached Lake Erie below Buffalo. The Pennsylvania Railroad, private successor to the state's rail-inclined plane-canal hybrid, reached Pittsburgh. The Baltimore and Ohio finally made it to the Ohio River at Wheeling well below Pittsburgh. A year later consolidation of the little lines between Albany and Buffalo created the mighty New York Central.

Culturally—if railroads can be tied to their origins—the B & O was half Southern, but its economic aims were the same as the Pennsylvania's. Though the South had been ahead of the nation in practical railroading, by the time the Civil War began Dixie had only one railroad line through the Appalachians into the Ohio Basin. The presence of the North's four iron ligaments into the area beyond the mountains erased the last bit of meaning from Europeans' hopes that the ungainly Union would eventually split into several jostling nations. By 1861 the rail traveler, supposing he made a few changes of cars on some routes, could breathe smoke and cinders all the way between any principal Northern seaboard city and Chicago, Cincinnati, or St. Louis.

Early railroads necessarily floundered at first, and their passengers suffered to match. Engineers had to work out the kinds of rail, tie and ballast that would keep tracks parallel and more or less on the same level. Management had to learn what the bunty little engines could and could not do. A Baltimore newspaper explaining in 1835 why the New York mails were late showed how unreliable things still were on the Camden and Amboy two years after steam had replaced its horses: It had taken an extra ninety minutes to load on the cars the freight landed by the connecting steamer at Perth Amboy, New Jersey. Then the train proved too overloaded to make the grade outside town. Trying again with a lightened load, she lost the track in sand washed over it by a heavy rain. Then a freight car went off the rails. Until Morse's electric telegraph solved the problem, train dispatching was subprimitive; that was first worked out in good style by the Erie Railroad using Ezra Cornell's new telegraph line paralleling its tracks. Delays and vexations were inevitable with the multiplicity of short connecting lines—ten between Albany and Buffalo, for example—often with different gauges (span between rails) so that through cars could not be handled. Almost from the beginning, however, what the rails offered was on the whole much better than what the stages could. A Briton touring the states in the 1830's wrote fervently of the contrast between a "wretched vehicle called the Hartford stage . . . five hours in going . . . 27 miles and . . . the swift and well warmed cars" [4] between Boston and Springfield, Massachusetts. By 1832 the federal postal system was beginning to take the mails from the stages and entrust them to the still-sketchy railroads—a virtual subsidy that in itself greatly encouraged railroad building.

Whether the mails rode comfortably did not matter; if it had, many an early railroad would have lost its contract. But stage travel was usually so disastrously miserable that railroad accommodations, however poor we would have thought them, were preferable. The first passenger cars were essentially a fusion of several coaches—as the European compartment car still is. Soon, however, radical redesigning among Pennsylvanian and Maryland carbuilders evolved an American type of car—long and heavy on two sets of four-wheeled trucks, entrances at each end, aisle down the middle, two-person seats on each side as in modern buses and planes. The seats were hard, and the floor was usually slippery with tobacco juice. Through Civil War times the best that could be said for that nuisance was that it was slighter northeast of Philadelphia than southwest of Washington, D.C., where people complained of yellow splashes not only on the floor but also on the seats and window shades. Practically everywhere, according to one dismayed British visitor, one hesitated to pick up a dropped coin unless wearing an old glove. And once upholstered seats were installed, bedbugs became a widely deplored hazard.

At first such cars had no facilities for excreting or washing; after all, neither had stagecoaches, and the trains stopped frequently. In warm weather the air rushing in at open doors and windows smelled of the rancid beef or mutton tallow that lubricated the axles and carried in dust from the roadbed mixed with fumes, cinders and soot from the wood-burning engine. The accompanying sparks were a nuisance to passengers and a standing menace to woodlands near the track. In winter the windows were shut, and a red-hot wood stove in the middle of the car distilled essence of unbathed traveler from those sitting near it. Those far away almost froze. Experienced passengers rushed for the seats in between, where alone one could be reasonably comfortable.

Dining cars were long merely talked of; hence mealtime was the one detail in which stages bested the railroad. Instead of drawing up at a tavern with a commodious bar and time to patronize it as well as the dining room —granted that the quality of food was problematical—the rail passenger had as little as ten minutes at a trackside "one-story erection of pine boards and a counter inside covered with pea coffee and putty pies," [5] as George Templeton Strong recorded arrangements on the railroad between Rochester, New York, and Buffalo in 1844. The very early conductors might hold the train for passengers wandering off to a nearby tavern and failing to return promptly. But as schedule time grew important, the rule of ten minutes for refreshments was rigidly enforced. Thirty years ago this system persisted in Australia; I can testify to the inadequacy of ten minutes. Your forebears of 1845 did not mind haste as you would, however. They were gobblers, gulpers and bolters anyway even when there was plenty of time at the hotel or steamboat table. Alien travelers agreed on that as unanimously as they did on the menace of tobacco juice. As typical witness, take Nikolaus Lenau, a poetic German trying farm life in Ohio in the 1830's, about a typical hotel "long table, fifty chairs on either side . . . food, mostly meats, covers the whole. . . . The dinner-bell resounds, and a hundred Americans plunge in; no one looks at another, no one says a word, each one plunges upon his own plate, devours what he can with great speed, then jumps up . . . and hastens away to earn dollars." [6]

The aisle of the passenger car was the place of business of hawkers boarding at each stop to sell newspapers, fruit, candy, nuts, tobacco and patent medicines before the train started again. Soon these fast workers fused into the institution of the train newsboy or "peanut butcher" with headquarters in the smoking car and a stock including cheap reading matter, perfume and toys. He went repeatedly through the train tossing into laps, according to age and sex, paperback books, cigars, apples, whistles, returning to retrieve what was refused and collect money for what was kept, counting, of course, on boredom to sell novels and smokes and on parents' inability to persuade a small boy to give up the nice apple so shiny from having just been polished up with spit. Among youngsters who filled that job were Thomas A. Edison; Tom Taggart, the Irish-born Hoosier who flourished as U.S. Senator from Indiana and owner of the great spa-hotel-gambling hell at French Lick, Indiana, home of Pluto Water ("If nature won't, Pluto will"); and William A. Brady, fight promoter and theatrical producer, who once told me that on Western trains he usually sold $400 worth a week at 20 percent commission.

Some found the intrusive newsboy a nuisance. Most put up with him as an accepted part of travel, like grimy hands, and an occasional performer of needed services. The one on Robert Louis Stevenson's Central Pacific emigrant train of 1878 was a valued source of advice, information and had "a kind countenance. He told us where and when we should have our meals, and how long the train would stop; kept seats at table for those . . . delayed, and watched that we should be neither left behind nor unnecessarily hurried." [7] He was the better liked because, unless available data sorely belie them, most American conductors and trainmen were surly Jacks-in-office niggardly with information, and in stations it was nobody's special business to tell the public anything but the price of a ticket to Middletown.

A Philadelphia merchant said of early railroads that they would be "the perfection of traveling . . . if one could stop when one wanted . . . were not locked up with 50 or 60 tobacco-chewers; and the engine . . . did not burn holes in one's clothes . . . and the smoke . . . did not poison one . . . and [one] were not in danger of being blown sky-high or knocked off the rails." [8] He omitted the hazard of the snakehead —a by-product of the early rails consisting of timber topped with spiked-down strap iron. When the strain of a passing train worked the spikes loose, the iron, suddenly released, curled up and stabbed through the floor of the car, bringing everything to a smashing halt and sometimes impaling a passenger. The sudden appearance of a snakehead through the seat that he had just been occupying led Professor Benjamin Silliman, a veteran traveler, to call crossing the Atlantic in a sailing packet safer than railroading at home.

Use of solid-iron rail of the familiar T-section put an end to snake-heads. The spark menace was reduced by the spark-catching diamond or beehive smokestack that persisted on certain lines into the 1900's. But for fifty years—until steam heat from the engine came in—it was assumed that in a winter wreck the red-hot stoves would probably set the cars ablaze. Livestock straying on the line often caused derailments. The first steam-powered train on the Camden and Amboy came to grief on a hog. Appropriately it was that line's chief mechanic who made the first cow-catcher—the iron scoop to keep trespassing animals from under the wheels. Like the spark-suppressing stack, this was only a large, not a complete, improvement, and loss of livestock remained a sore issue between farmer and railroad. The refusal of the new-built Michigan Central to pay the full value of such impromptu fresh meat led to serious sabotage. Rails were greased, journal boxes filled with sand, passengers cars showered with stones and buckshot.

Farmers also hated the surveyors who ran railroad lines across fields or farms diagonally, leaving triangular parcels of land irksome because short furrows lose the plowman time in frequent turnarounds. Urban damage came of laying tracks through the middle of towns—a thing that amazed Old World visitors. In Troy, New York, for instance, one had "an excellent opportunity of seeing the streets as the railway passes directly through them, and passengers are conveniently dropped at the door of their hotels." [9] Well into the 1900's the New York Central took up much of the main street of Syracuse, New York, and the New Haven still does so in Providence, Rhode Island. Before the Civil War people did not grasp the stupidity of thus condemning the most frequented part of town to noise and smoke. The railroad was a splendid new economic fad and welcome to take over the lakefront if it liked. Only later did it become clear that this would eventually blight the potentially most pleasant sections. Those railroad-smothered lakefronts became frowsy, grimy, noisy wildernesses of tracks, water tanks and warehouses.

Outside town the railroad was less of an eyesore. The geometric formality of a well-maintained double track is good counterpoint for softly informal farming landscape. It was advertisements aimed at the passenger that did the damage here. As the practice grew, an Englishman noted in dismay in the late 1870's: "Wherever there is a bit of fence, a conspicuous gable end or a surface of wood, stone or brick that can be seen from the railroad and converted into a sign, there [the American manufacturer] will advertise himself and where there is no coign of vantage he will create one [with] a sign fifteen or twenty yards long in the middle of the next field. . . . Rising Sun Stove Polish haunts you by every railway side on the continent." [10] (Steamboat passengers, too, could be thus afflicted: In 1867 Francis Parkman found that the great Indian monsters that Marquette saw painted on the bluff above Alton, Illinois, had been obliterated to make room for a huge advertisement of Plantation Bitters.) The destructive effect of railroads on forests left still other marks on the landscape. It was not only that sparks set woods afire in dry seasons, but that in any case the iron horse's appetite for wood was as sharp as a steamboat's, and there were a great many iron horses to feed as the track-laying boom of the 1850's brought America's railroad total up to 30,000 miles.

All that while the basic passenger train of locomotive, tender, baggage car and several coaches (one a smoker) had changed little. The locomotive had gained power. Track was stabler. Average speeds had risen from, say, 15 mph to 25-30 mph, the severity of accidents increasing to match. But for years the only new amenities had been washrooms and drinking water from a common tumbler not yet known to carry germs and fancy woodwork inside the car supplemented without by garish paint, usually yellow with contrasting trim. Crude attempts at dining cars had got little further than installing a buffet, rather like the free lunch of a saloon, in the smoking car. The first sleeping cars sound like today's bunk cars for section gangs; ladies never went near them. But during and just after the Civil War several kinds of specialized rolling stock bloomed: The mail car came into service. Sleeping cars decent and handsome enough for a decorous clientele—George M. Pullman's version was first used on the Chicago and Alton in 1865—were close behind. The design of his and his rival Wagner's palace cars owed too much to the tiered bunks of the canal packet of evil memory but excelled it in cleanliness, sanitary facilities, privacy and quality of bedding. By 1867 Pullman had a hotel car combin-

A pre-Civil War three-tier sleeping car. The artist has made it look twice as wide as it conceivably can have been.

ing fold-up passenger berths with a galley and crew able to cook edible food in minimum elbowroom. That led to Pullman's separate dining cars of the familiar design and eliminated refreshment stops on the new long runs furthered by consolidations and interline agreements.

The palace car tradition also led to fancy, extra-fare parlor cars for daytime runs, often with special rear platforms to make them observation cars—the brass-railed setting in which generations of whistle-stopping Presidential candidates would be photographed. By 1870 George Westinghouse's air brake was solving the problem of controlling long high-speed trains, and coal, less bulky than wood per BTU and now easier to come by in most regions, had usually replaced wood in the tender. These improvements made possible the distinctive American version of the luxurious limited train: a hulking coal-fired locomotive followed by mail car, sleeping cars, dining car sandwiched among them, and last the observation car whisking past and dwindling away down the interminable track. Within a decade the fanciest limiteds had electric light, replacing dangerous gas and kerosene, and barber, maid and stenographer (male) for the passenger's convenience. The gleaming exteriors of such rolling stock led workaday railroaders handling switch engines and slow freights to call the limited a "string of varnish."

Its insides might have been called a string of plush, for nowhere did the tortuously carved, high-polished, thick-tasseled, sullen-colored, deep-carpeted, fancy-mirrored, brass-cuspidored taste of the Gilded Age reach greater heights than in the first generation of Pullmans and diners. Consider, for example, a new diner put into service on the Pennsylvania's Jersey City-Chicago run in 1882: It had stained-glass clerestory windows, "large double silver chandeliers . . . an exquisite silver adorned sideboard of carved mahogany, plate glass and dark velvet plush . . . everywhere mahogany . . . quaintly carved. . . . The curtains that run upon silver rods above the windows are of carmine and golden-olive velvet plush, relieved by rich salmon-covered cloth, stiff in patterns of gold bullion. . . . The seats . . . are upholstered in deep carmine and golden-olive velvet plush. . . ." [11] All that deep pile and complicated carving in a service committed to grit, grime and dust were especially absurd in a day that knew not vacuum cleaners. But Pullman's deft, deferential Negro porters, apparently able to go a lifetime on only a few hours of catnapping a night, kept these outrageous dust catchers cleaner than most lady passengers could hope for from their servants at home.

As varnish expanded, here at last was an equivalent of the gussied-up steamboat to dazzle the upcountry mill village and the prairie junction where the limited stopped for water. Theodore Dreiser's first meal in a dining car (on the Wabash Railroad eastward from St. Louis) seemed to him "the acme of elegance and grandeur. Could life offer more than . . . riding about the world in these mobile palaces?" particularly when, while breakfasting on broiled chicken, one saw "poor-looking farmer boys in jeans and 'galluses' and wrinkled hats [looking] up at me with interest." [12] Twenty years later Merton Gill, not yet the movie star but still clerking in a general store at Simsbury, Illinois, worshiped such a train during an unscheduled stop at the depot: "beautiful sleepers . . . an observation-car, its rear platform guarded by a brass-topped railing behind which the privileged lolled at ease . . . a wonderful dining-car . . . flitting white-clad waiters, the glitter of silver and crystal and damask, and

favored beings feasting . . . [he] used to fancy that these people might
detect him to be out of place . . . take him to be an alien city man awaiting a similar proud train going the other way. . . ." [13]

The Pennsylvania Railroad put the first of the limiteds into service in
1876, as the nation celebrated its hundredth birthday. By a grim coincidence these strings of plutocratic varnish were thus born just in time for
scarring and scorching in the savage railroad strikes of 1877, the nation's
first major labor troubles.

Railroads carry things, as well as people. Indeed freight had literally
preceded passengers when the pioneer Charleston and Hamburg, nervous after that first boiler explosion, set a flatcar piled high with bales of
cotton between engine and coaches. Freight had even preceded the locomotive: In 1832 the Camden and Amboy's first freight service had consisted of three cars of 3½-ton capacity, each drawn by a single horse,
seven or eight times the load per horse expected in wagoneering. As ship-
pers and consignees learned the beauties of speed in transit and reasonably prompt arrival, the canalboats found themselves carrying only the
heaviest, bulkiest—and lowest revenue—cargoes such as grain, coal and
brick. Areas lacking waterways began to find that a few men in a train
crew on rails could move from here to there what would have been too
costly to transport in 100 wagons driven by 100 teamsters. Instead of hauling their corn and wheat all the way to Chicago to load on lake vessels,
Illinois farmers of the mid-century had to drive no farther than the
nearest siding of the Burlington or Illinois Central. At 10 miles per hour,
rails took cattle and hogs to the packinghouse or Eastern feedlot faster,
and with far less manpower per head required, than when they were
driven in herds on their own four feet. For the same reasons the wagons,
steamboats and canalboats lost much of the Northeast's miscellaneous
westbound manufactures—calico, cutlery, boots, hats, window glass,
crockery, salt mackerel, patent medicines and gimcracks. The boxcars in
which all that rolled over the mountains returned eastward with the Old
Northwest's whiskey, peltry, wool and beeswax. The wagoners understandably resented it all:

> Come all ye bold wag'ners, turn out man by man
>> That's opposed to the railroad or any such a plan
> 'Tis once I made money by driving my team
>> But the goods are now hauled on the railroad by steam. . . .
>
> It ruins wheelwrights, blacksmiths and every other trade,
>> So damned be all the railroads that ever was made.
> It ruins our mechanics, what think you of it, then?
>> And it fills our country full of just a lot of great rich men.[14]

In due course a wide range of specialized freight cars—box, stock, coal, gondola and so on—and cabooses to shelter the train crews came into use. They were mere boxes of timber and plank set on wheels, utterly functional but nonetheless ugly. It was a decorating age, however, and some lines sought to brighten any eye resting on its boxcars. There were two-color jobs, say yellow and blue; at one stage the New York Central adorned its pale-gray freight cars with huge portraits of the governors of various states on red backgrounds.

For more than a century the freight dollar has bulked ever larger in railroad thinking. As locomotives gained power, freight trains lengthened and the tie-up of traffic at grade crossings as long freights shunted back and forth became an American institution—much more frequent in our fore-bears' time, when practically all crossings were at grade and municipal regulations, if any, about maximum blocking time were ill enforced. The lengthening of trains to about all the engine could get into motion had a memorable side effect for wakeful urban children in pre-Diesel times. Many houses were within earshot of one or another freightyard where the long consists were made up. Late in the quiet night the big locomotives would couple up and struggle to get the night's work moving. The snort-ings of their tortured exhausts would come right into the bedroom with an accelerating and then suddenly frustrated authority as compelling as jun-gle drums:

CHUFF . . . CHUFF . . . CHUFF . . . and the drive wheels would slip and the exhaust race frantically chuffchuffchuffchuffchuff, maybe moving a little. CHUFF . . . CHUFF . . . CHUFF . . . moving a little for sure, but she slips chuffchuffchuffchuff. Try still again: CHUFF . . . CHUFF . . . CHUFF . . . CHUFF . . . CHUFF, and off she goes slow as molasses in winter but imperceptibly gaining speed, snakes creaking and squealing out of the yards and presently whistles for the first grade crossing: Lon-n-n-n-ng! Long! Short! Shor-rt!

No American over forty years old reared within sound of a railroad will ever forgive the Diesel for depriving the world of the American steam lo-comotive's whistle, that most exhilarating and yet saddest of sounds, so unlike the womanish scream of European locomotives. From those exhaust rhythms and such whistles the Lomaxes, outstanding authorities on American folk music, derive "the blues . . . the stomps . . . boo-gie-woogie . . . hot jazz with its steady beat. . . . What you hear back of the notes is the drive and thrust and moan of a locomotive. Of course there's the African influence, the French influence in New Orleans, the Spanish influence from Cuba . . . but in our estimation the distinctive feeling of American hot music comes from the railroads." [15] In quite an-other context the travail of a heavy freight engine slipping at the start, so familiar to urban high school pupils, became the basis of the locomotive school yell.

A hundred years ago that formidable whistle had not yet been standardized. Some engineers had their own multi-toned whistles, like elementary calliopes, and played tunes on them as they thundered through the night or used signature signals like Casey Jones' imitation of a whippoorwill:

> The switchmen could tell by the engine's moans
> That the man at the throttle was Casey Jones. . . .

Assigned to a new engine, such a musicianly engineer unshipped and transferred his whistle. In the informal days of railroading, engines, too, were allowed personalities. Like ships, they were named for company magnates or mythological figures or scenic features illustrated by pictures painted on the flanks of the tender. The Old Colony Line's *Pilgrim* had the landing from the *Mayflower* depicted in fine detail. The Denver and Rio Grande's *Spanish Peaks, Royal Gorge, Mt. Holy Cross* and so on carried scenic views to match. Drive wheels were picked out in red and yellow; brass lace edged fittings and cabs; the panels of the boxy, oil-burning headlights had multihued curlicues; and an engineer duly proud of his *Susquehanna* or *Roderick Dhu* (probably christened by the poetry-struck daughter of the superintendent) saw to it that the fireman kept the brass bright, the colors clean. That was easier when the fuel was wood, giving more sparks but less smudge. As coal took over, decoration gave way to sober black. Names, too, disappeared in favor of numbers as operations over long distances came in. It was too cumbrous to write orders for the involved duties of dozens of locomotives individualized as *Winnipesaukee, Flying Dutchman, Titan,* not to mention the time saved when telegraphers could just hammer out a few arbitrary numbers.

That was a weighty issue because by the 1860's telegraphy, which had been trying to live up to its possibilities since the 1840's, was as intimately necessary to railroading as the nervous system is to an animal. The focus of the wide-eaved, stove-overheated wooden depot at Podunk Junction was not the ticket window or the baggage room but the desk in the bay window with a view of the tracks where the operator sat pounding his key and then writing down its cryptic tickings and clackings to hand to the conductor as Number 23 rumbled past. Only thus could management deploy fleets of engines and swarms of rolling stock in the necessary imperial fashion. At Cincinnati's celebration of the completion of the Ohio and Mississippi Railroad through to St. Louis in 1857, Salmon P. Chase, first Republican governor of Ohio (later Secretary of the Treasury and then Chief Justice of the United States), ranked Morse's distance-killing gadget with the Iron Horse itself as a shaper of continental destiny: ". . . the Railroad, the Locomotive and the Telegraph—iron, steam and lightning —these three mighty genii of modern civilization . . . will know no lasting pause until the whole vast line of railway shall be completed from the Atlantic to the Pacific." [16]

There in Cincinnati Chase was far from salt water, else he would probably have included the steamship among "mighty genii of civilization." For at the time he spoke, steam had had its sea legs for twenty years and since 1848 had outdone both sailing vessels around the Horn and Butterfield's continental stages in keeping the nation in touch with its new segment on the Pacific Coast. Maybe Chase scamped the point because its salient aspect—the transatlantic steamship—was primarily John Bull's pidgin. The little *Savannah's* first steam crossing of the Atlantic in 1819 had been ambiguous. Her engine, merely auxiliary to sail, was used in only a minor part of the voyage; anyway no other steam-equipped vessel tried it again for fourteen years. And not until 1838 did two rival British steamers, with sail now auxiliary, make maiden crossings from Old World to New, badly beating average time for the crack New York sailing packets that then dominated the run. The *Great Western*, faster of the two, did in two weeks what usually took the Black Ball or Swallowtail packets at least three.

Soon, as official action goes, Her Majesty's government gave a fat subsidy in the form of mail contracts to Samuel Cunard, an astute Nova Scotian, who had sent a primitive steamer tactfully named *Royal William* (for Victoria's seagoing uncle, William IV) from Canada to England in 1833. Now he launched four British-built steamers for a transatlantic mail-and-passenger shuttle, founding a British domination of such services that lasted until airplanes gnawed it away. The ships were ungainly, built along sailing-vessel lines but swollen by paddle boxes amidships and further disfigured by a skinny, tall funnel between fore- and mainmast belching coal smoke to choke the hands laying out on the yards to make sail. Their top speed—8-10 knots—was exceeded by the handsome sailing packets, given the right wind. But that could not be counted on, whereas steam slogged alone in greater disregard of weather on courses requiring a minimum of sea-miles and was likely to make port well ahead of sail, hare and tortoise-fashion. Presently the screw propeller created by the great Swedish engineer John Ericsson, later of *Monitor* fame, proved itself on the transatlantic run to be more efficient, as well as less clumsy, than paddle wheels. Yet conservative builders kept paddle wheels on important ships up to the Civil War. And elementary sparring for sail did not disappear from the most advanced liners until the 1890's—just as wagon types of wheels and dashboards long remained on early automobiles as vestigial reminders of carriages.

The early Cunarders made Boston their American terminus, which spared the New York sailing packets the full weight of this newfangled competition. In 1847, however, Cunard began sending every other sailing to New York. In the 1850's the federal government granted subsidies resulting in an American competing service, the Collins Line, founded by a veteran of sailing packets. While they lasted, its four paddle-wheel, wooden liners, largest afloat in their day at toward 3,000 tons, wrested both prestige and crossing records from Cunard. Frustratingly soon two of the four met horrible disaster. The *Arctic,* rammed by a French steamer

The ill-fated Arctic, *one of the finest transatlantic paddle-wheelers.*

in a fog, sank with a loss of 200-odd lives, including Collins' family and every last woman on board. In 1856 the *Pacific* sailed from Liverpool and was never heard of again, a thing grimly possible in pre-radio times. Collins' rebuilding program was damped by reductions in the mail subsidy caused, it was thought, by Southern reluctance to support so Northern-flavored and North-favoring an industry as shipping. The *Adriatic,* the new wooden Collins liner that, at 4,100 tons, was the finest steamer afloat, was sold to English interests in 1858. In token of Britannia's determination to rule the mail-and-passenger waves, 1860 saw the maiden crossing of the British *Great Eastern,* an iron monster of 18,000 tons with quarters and decorations anticipating the luxury liners of the early 1900's. Only in sail, as the shipyards of Massachusetts and New York refined and enlarged their crack packet ships into the famous clippers, the most beautiful things that ever floated, did the American merchant marine continue to show the world the way.

The clippers' swift beauty was Chesapeake-born as Baltimore shipbuilders developed from the local type of pilot boat a schooner with uncannily speedy underwater lines. The principal midwife was French-born Joseph Despeaux, a refugee from the lurid slave risings of the French West Indies in the 1790's. His square-rigged clipper privateer *Alexander,* eighteen guns, launched in 1810, made great profits for Benjamin Crowninshield of Salem, Massachusetts, which presumably called the attention of Northern shipbuilders to the virtues of the type. When steam invaded the North Atlantic, the American sailing packet lines needed still faster ships to compete, and clipper-style lines and the jaunty name itself began to infiltrate design. The development centered on Donald McKay, a young genius of a shipbuilder, Nova Scotia-reared, trained as shipwright in New York City, soon building his own ships in Newburyport, Massachusetts, and then in Boston. In the 1840's his and others' long, narrow-hulled, lofty-sparred speed queens gained fame all over the world of shipping as the Yankee Clippers. McKay's *Sovereign of the Seas* once logged an average of 15 knots for twenty-four hours at a time when the fastest steamer could hardly make 13. The clipper *Natchez* once ran from Canton to New York City in seven weeks—eleven was considered fast. Even the names of many of these ships were shapely and dashing: *Flying Fish, Flying Cloud, Shooting Star, Westward Ho, Sweepstakes, Sea Serpent.*

But speed and beauty alone would not account for their existence, of course. The boom in clipper building was response to a particular situation. Developed first to meet the dogged challenge of steam on the Atlantic, the type was thus available when the California gold rush gave it a special function. The steamer-Isthmus of Panama-steamer route to California was prohibitively expensive for bulky cargo, dauntingly so for passengers. For food supplies, hardware, household goods and such and for the less affluent gold seekers, it made much more sense to utilize the sleek clippers all the way around the Horn, and once in the Pacific, such ships could take a hand in the Far Eastern trade, bringing high-value cargoes much more quickly than conventional competitors could. Steamers could not yet handle the Cape Horn passage in regular voyages because coaling facilities were not yet available along the far reaches of South America. Between East and West Coasts foreign-flag sailing vessels were ruled out of competition with American clippers because of Uncle Sam's rules against goods going from one American port to another in foreign bottoms.

Culturally it mattered little whether Britain's red rag ensign or the Stars and Stripes flew over the transatlantic steamers that gradually got the bet-

The classic clipper, pure beauty.

ter of even the clipper packets. The contribution of seagoing steam was supranational—to set mails flowing reliably and speedily between Old World and New. That greatly stimulated business, literature, the press and technology. And now for the first time prosperous Americans could travel to the Old Countries with something approaching modern scheduling, as well as comfort. The finest sailing packets, neat and lavishly decorated as their cramped quarters were, jovial as their skippers and few dozen passengers might be, were chancily uncertain of arrival and relatively rugged for the socially ambitious womenfolk of American bankers, grain brokers and real estate operators. The first-class quarters of the *Atlantic,* however, or even her Cunarder rivals had a reassuring air of being part of a luxury hotel and carried sufficient passengers of one's own affluent stratum to make the trip fashionably plausible. Thus it was the steamer that created the American woman encountering Europe, who, often accompanied by her man paying her way, so fascinated Henry James. And even more important these coal-burning monsters of wood and iron with names ending in *ic* and *ia* wove between the opposite shores of the Atlantic economic, personal and esthetic ties heavier and wider than were conceivable when sail was the only way to conquer great waters. It was not least important that as competition among fast steamers brought steerage-class rates down, the emigrant coming by steam to the New World was likelier to go home again after ten years of saving money either for a visit or to retire.

Steam had got into the American coasting trade by the early 1830's. First in river types of vessels up and down Chesapeake Bay; up Long Island Sound from New York City to the Narragansett ports and rail connections with Boston; along the sounds and creeks behind the Sea Islands of the Carolina-Georgia coast. Then they acquired higher free-board and ventured out on the high seas to connect Boston with Down East and New York City with Southern ports. Gradually these snorting side-wheelers took the cream of passengers and cargo from the traditional schooners and brigs not only along their own shores, where the law gave them a monopoly, but also on the runs to Havana and Mexico. They had their teeth well into the job when in 1848 steamship men were suddenly called on for mail service to newly acquired California via the Isthmus of Panama. One line of steamers took mails, high-value freight and passengers from New York City to the Isthmus, where they crossed by muleback and canoe and boarded the steamers of a Pacific-based line running up the Coast to San Francisco. The gold rush coincided with the first Panama to Golden Gate voyage of the first ship on this Pacific end of the service, the *California* of 1,000 tons. Within a few years the ships on these runs, merged into a single line, the Pacific Mail, were thrice her size and yet crammed with cases of California fever westbound and California gold and convalescents eastbound. In the wreck of the eastbound *Central America* on the shoals of Cape Hatteras in 1857 some $2,000,000 in gold and 400-odd lives, mostly of passengers, were lost.

By 1855 the transit of the Isthmus was made on the new Panama Railroad; a second pair of steamer services were using a rival transit across Nicaragua via the San Juan River and the magnificent lake that it drains; a third, shorter still, was planned, and eventually got into service, across the Isthmus of Tehuantepec in Mexico. In due time the transcontinental railroad undercut them all, and the Pacific Mail turned to the run between California and the Orient. (Extravagant visions of a sea-rail connection monopolizing the shipment of goods to and from the Far East disappeared when the Suez Canal tactlessly opened in 1869.) The coastal steamers survived amazingly well on shorter runs. Within my own time one could steam out of New York City in an engagingly old-timey ship with tiny staterooms and thumping engines for Yarmouth, Portland, Boston, Norfolk, Charleston, Savannah, Jacksonville, even New Orleans. By now all that remains of them is that number in *Porgy and Bess* about the boat that's leavin' for New York.

To reach California—culmination of the American extrusion westward—had always been a special problem. Wagons, steamboats and canalboats had effective settlement of the Old Northwest well under way before the railroads came in. Wagons and steamboats without canals had done it in the Old Southwest and the lower end of the Louisiana Purchase. But even such large streams as the Red River and the Arkansas grew unfriendly to steamboats as they approached the higher plains. Once the land definitely rose toward the faraway Rockies, hooves and wheels were the only resources. Pack animals, draft animals and wagon wheels. And just in time to make good for America on Berkeley's "Westward the course of empire," smaller wheels on railroad iron. The good bishop had probably thought of the movement as a steady welling westward like a creeping flood. Actually, thanks to restlessness and opportunism, it was more like a cross between an end run and hopscotch with the transcontinental rails eventually hooking the pieces together.

Practically every year of the early 1800's had seen new, energetic American gestures westward usually made by private enterprise. In 1811, for instance, the Western Waters' first steamboat was launched, and John Jacob Astor's American Fur Company built at the mouth of the Columbia River, on the far margin of the continent, a trading post that, though it soon aborted, was the first American settlement on the Pacific Coast. Both occasions were deliberate and entailed the hoisting of flags—and of drinks. Less formal in the same year, yet maybe as momentous, was an inconspicuous symptom in "Tejas"—an outlying adjunct of Spain's Mexico, where a Spanish priest named Miguel Hidalgo y Costilla was leading a revolt against the Mother Country. Mexican residents of Texas taking up arms to support him found themselves joined by a number of *American* residents strayed far from wherever they had once called home—extreme examples of American footlooseness. The new United States had already bitten off more than even young jaws could chew for another forty years in acquiring the immense Louisiana Purchase. Yet here were irresponsible Americans already pushing uninvited into a far country under a foreign flag—and meddling in local family quarrels as if by right.

What had brought them was, as usual, peltry—horsehides this time, from slaughter of the wild herds proliferating in the scrubby woods of East

Texas, the same galloping epidemic of horses that so delighted the Plains Indians. In an organized follow-up Moses Austin, Yankee-born pioneer in lead mining in early Missouri, bankrupt in the hard times of 1819, persuaded the Mexican government to let him settle 300 American families in the country north of San Antonio. Thenceforward the slaveholding segment of the log-cabin frontier seeped steadily into the fertile Texas lands then supporting only a few Indians and Mexicans. This creeping migration had a flavor not of Creole Louisiana next door but of one-gallus Arkansas. Two thousand miles westward, at Monterey in California—another loose adjunct of Spanish America—a Kentuckian peltry trader named James Ohio Pattie was well enough established by 1825 to take a hand in quelling a mutiny among the Mexican garrison. The next year white Americans led a party of trappers across the Sierra Nevada and the Mojave Desert to the San Gabriel Mission, only a day's ride from the Pacific; their arrival in what is now Los Angeles County startled their missionary hosts as if they had risen out of the ground. Sometimes such adventurers remained, married into Spanish-Mexican ranchero families, set up housekeeping, and prospered.

A dismaying proportion of this trickle of overland interlopers had left home for urgent reasons and gave both Texas and California good starts on traditions of lawlessness. As early as 1836 it was necessary for a promotional tract extolling Texas to deny that it was, as the scorners maintained, "the great penitentiary of America, where outlaws, murderers, thieves, and vagabonds resort. . . ." [17] At least that wasn't as true as it had been, the lady writer said, and cited gratifying instances of ex-convicts straightening up and prospering. In the sea California, however, had a second avenue of gringo infiltration—of a somewhat higher average of integrity. It brought Yankee ships buying cowhides—soon called California banknotes—for the shoe factories of Massachusetts. There was also a triangular trade, Peru-Hawaii-California, presently expanded into systematic smuggling by Americans based in Hawaii. Each of the tiny chief settlements of California—San Diego, Los Angeles, Santa Barbara, Monterey, San Francisco—was slipping under the influence of English-speaking opportunists, usually American, some British, former ships' captains or supercargoes or even foremast hands who scented the potentialities of the country and stayed ashore to exploit them. For instance, Thomas Larkin, Massachusetts-born trader, became U.S. consul in Monterey and a canny intriguer for annexation; Benjamin Foxen, sailor from the British ship *Courier,* married into a Spanish family in Santa Barbara, was rechristened William Domingo and did well, though he had the bad luck actually to be sentenced to four years' imprisonment for killing a man in 1848. Such aliens' marriages into the local Quality gave them flying starts, and the concomitant necessity of turning Catholic seems to have set lightly on such bridegrooms. Conspicuous among them was a footloose Yankee drifted up from Mexico who became a weighty merchant-politician in Los Angeles under the anomalous designation of Don Abel Stearns. His connections were so good that when extensive smuggling got him into hot water, his method of cooling things off was to pull wires and get himself appointed collector of customs.

Other Americans of the same or sometimes better quality had also been seeping into the Oregon country up the coast comprising the basin of the magnificent Columbia River. Astor's peltry post at its mouth had withered into the hands of the energetic, Canada-based, Scotch-flavored Hudson's Bay Company. Neither Britain nor the United States had a solid claim to the region, but for what each case was worth, a man from Mars would probably have said that geography and extent of occupancy were both on Britain's side. American adventurers kept nibbling at its peltry supply, however, and by 1829 there was formed in Massachusetts a bustling Society for Encouraging the [American, of course] Settlement of Oregon Territory. It accomplished nothing—except to keep Oregon in the public mind and prompt the sending of missionaries to the Indians there. They went overland—a really heroic trip in the mid-1830's— showing that what was soon known as the Oregon Trail was practical for ordinary people, not just hardened trappers and explorers, and sending back word about the fertile, temperate and well-watered lands between the Cascade Range and the Pacific Coast. In the 1840's, while the British and American governments were snarling over legal title to the area in the-54°40′-or-fight controversy, a trickle of restless or imaginative Back East farmers with families were braving the Oregon Trail and effectively settling the country and the cultural question of whether it would be British or American.

The cultural gulf between British Canada and America had always been narrow. Had the scales tipped the other way, the Americans reaching the Willamette Valley in the early 1840's might well have become as good subjects of Queen Victoria as did the Midwestern farmers who migrated into the Canadian wheat country later in the 1800's. But California and the rest of the Southwest were another matter. There mixed and too often curdled the New World white man's two principal cultural heritages: one Northern European, largely Protestant, dominantly British; the other Iberian, Catholic, dominantly Spanish but diluted by the Indian to an extent inconceivable among gringos. Though the two had shared North America for centuries, previous contacts had been sterile. During the early 1700's Spain had held Florida and the eastern Gulf Coast and reacted spasmodically to British pressures from northward. But no stimulating acculturation had occurred, only the ruin of a string of Spanish missions with two purposes: avowedly—and sincerely—to infect the Southeastern Indians with civilization and Christianity, and incidentally—but importantly—to provision and otherwise support the Spanish garrison at St. Augustine guarding the Bahama Channel, the main eastbound communication between Spanish America and the Old Country.

Such missions were the great tool of Spanish-Mexican expansion into several parts of what is now the United States. Since they remain salient in today's traditions of our Southwest, they need explanation. If left alone, Spain might never have pushed her colonial ventures north of Mexico. Her plucky early explorers failed to find gold and silver above the Rio Grande, bringing back only a conviction that the region was too remote and too dry to bother about. It was not a stupid verdict. Later gringos too applied to much of the great West a bluecoat general's description of the Dakota Badlands: "Hell with the fire gone out." [18] Even had her explorers' findings been less dismal, Spain of the 1600's was going downhill, and Mexico, left half-autonomous by the Mother Country's debility, had been weakened late in the 1500's by exotic diseases that killed off most of her Indians. A salient beyond the Rio Grande to found Santa Fe was the extent of penetration northward, and late in the 1600's resentful Indians wiped that out. Encroaching rival nations, however, presently brought reaction. France was nibbling at the Gulf Coast of Texas. Britain seized the Spanish missions in the Southeast and deliberately founded Georgia to threaten Spain's surviving hold in Florida. Russia, having followed the peltry trade across Asia, was reaching out for sea otter and by the mid-1700's threatened to encroach on California. Spain's claims to all the New World (except the snout of South America that the Pope had awarded to Portugal) had never died. To counter these successive insolent intrusions, Spanish America made expansionist gestures—to reestablish herself in New Mexico and Texas and to do something about virgin California.

Her method, seasoned by trial in Mexico and Florida, differed from that of Protestant colonizing powers in its serious regard for the interests of the incumbent Indians. For the loyally Catholic and devout Spanish Crown, the highest interest of Indians or any other human beings was the welfare of their souls. So, though earthly considerations were also present—"We came here to serve God and the king, and also to get rich," [19] said Bernal Díaz del Castillo, chronicler of the conquistadors—the nucleus of a typical Spanish colonizing scheme was Catholic missionaries, Jesuit, Dominican or Franciscan. Thus the task force founding what is now San Antonio, Texas, in the 1720's consisted of Jesuits supported by a handful of the tough, leather-jacketed soldiers who did the fighting and garrison duty for the viceroy of Mexico; a few officials representing his civil government; and some settler families from the Canary Islands, long-colonized Atlantic possessions of Spain. Raised to the rank of hidalgo (roughly *gentleman*) as reward for volunteering to emigrate, they were soon complaining as bitterly as if they had still been plebeians about the hardships of pioneering in Texas. Catholic France's colonizing had shown a similar structure, including marked solicitude about the Indians. But the missionaries brigaded with soldiers and settlers in New France, though always important, never secured the dominant power that their Spanish counterparts won in the American Southwest—and in some parts of South America—wherever the Indians proved to be the right sort of raw material.

That was important. The Jesuits of San Antonio had small luck with the neighboring Apaches, and not for lack of trying either. One of the strangest pictures in American history is that of the Jesuit fathers dancing hand in hand with Apache chiefs around a hole dug in the middle of the plaza in which, for reasons of heathen ritual, a horse was then buried alive. But the immediately local Indians were more susceptible spiritually, or more readily awed by soldiers, or more eager for beads and blankets as rewards for sitting still during sermons—anyway they soon let the missionaries recast their lives for them. The chief features of the landscape were the great dilute-Baroque towers of the several mission churches that docile Indians built for the greater glory of God. For contrast: In 1778 the secular governor of San Antonio lived in the jail because it was the best dwelling in town.

A chain of such towers marked the penetration of California begun in 1769, two years after Daniel Boone first saw Kentucky. Soldiers, officials and friars (Franciscans, for the Jesuits and the Spanish Crown had fallen out) came from Mexico by sea to found San Diego. Father Junípero Serra, presently in charge, had already distinguished himself in creating missions in inhospitable Lower California. Now his ability and zeal—both formidable—built another skein of spiritual blockhouses from San Diego to San Francisco Bay, which Spanish explorers had only recently discovered. By the early 1800's a score or so of such missions, more or less a day's journey apart, had brought to California such exotic arts as irrigation, stock raising, weaving, singing from notes and the cultivation of the conscience. Very likely Father Serra had thus saved California from the Russians so the gringos could have it. Certainly he had done its eventual tourist industry a service with those Spanish place-names invoking sonorous saints: the secularities of Palo Alto and Monterey are smothered by San Luis Rey de Francia, San Luis Obispo, San Juan Capistrano,

*San Luis Rey may be the most successful translation
of Spanish Baroque into Californian terms.*

San Miguel Arcángel and El Pueblo de Nuestra Señora la Reina de los Angeles.

From afar the mission towers showed up better than the extensive walled quadrangles attached. One purpose of these was to protect livestock in case of attack, as in the blockhoused stockades of the Old Northwest. Room enough for that meant a perimeter overextended for defense, as the Texans found when they holed up in the Alamo, a former mission; besides, the walls were usually too low and the fortified gateways too few. But defense mattered less as the Indians came to heel. The function of the quadrangle changed—no longer to keep enemies out but converts in. For to save souls, these Spanish missions, from Florida to California, had to become sanctified concentration camps.

A Catholic scholar recently defined their intent as "to convert the [Indians] to Christianity and then lead them out of savagery. . . ." [20] Soon, however, these well-meaning followers of St. Dominic, St. Francis or St. Ignatius of Loyola had discovered what Puritan missionaries would learn later in Hawaii: that they had to think the other way around. Unless pagan ways-of-doing were broken down and Western ones came in, little Christian doctrine, whether the Decalogue or the subtler Beatitudes, could be got into Indian (or Hawaiian) heads. Revised tactics were called for. The task force would seek out a given group of the relatively undeveloped and docile Indians of Southern California; use tact and gifts of tobacco and gaudy textiles to persuade them to help friars and soldiers build a rudimentary mission of chapel, dormitory and barracks; then concentrate on culture, as well as soul, forcing the puzzled Indians to work hard at Western-style tasks and attend mass twice daily. Fear and blarney turned these oddly feckless people who had never known herding or cropping into shepherds, cowhands and gang farm labor. Their women learned weaving, spinning, washing—till the mission taught them better, they had worn too few clothes to have laundry problems—and Mexican-style cookery of the corn, wheat, meat, beans, onions and peppers that the men raised under strict supervision. Their hyperdocility was crucial. The less malleable Indians of the lower Colorado River put up with missionaries' notions just so long and then massacred friars, soldiers and all, as the New Mexican Indians had done in the 1680's.

A typical quadrangle enclosed ample expanse of courtyard lined with adobe (mud-brick) one- or two-room dwellings, each for a single, newly monogamous family continually under the missionary eye. In the center

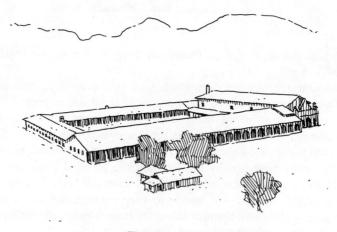

A typical mission quadrangle in California,
keeping Indians in and sin out.

the communal well; here and there the pottery, the carpentry-shop, the two-man saw frame, the weaving shed, the winepress, all manned by Indians working for the common supply distributed on a basis of need modified by the relative prestige of Indians and whites. This pious communism, nearer Marx than Russia has yet come, was a more secure life than the Indians had known. But inevitably it palled on some. The shirker, man or woman, was put in the stocks or flogged for the good of the soul and the edification of others. Any clearing the wall to take to the hills was pursued by soldiers led by a friar, who, on catching him, pleaded with him to return peaceably. If that failed, he was tied up and lugged back to the mission, where admonition, prayer and the lash recalled him to his duty to his soul. The likeness to slavery was even stronger when the missions rented out their Indians to secular rancheros. The friars were unmistakably sincere, as well as zealous. Yet the usual result, whether in Paraguay or California, was that few of the Indians learned much about Christianity and that, as discouragement grew, the missionaries regarded them as "wayward, if lovable, children to be kept in permanent bondage." [21]

Legally the wide lands that the missions exploited were the property of the Crown lent them for holy ends, and the vast stocks of food and herds of cattle and sheep were the Indians' common property managed for them by the missions. The friars chose the most promising tracts and were able boss farmers. As production outstripped need, surplus cereals, cowhides, coarse textiles, pottery and wine were sold not only to the tiny local civilian markets but also to trading craft from Mexico and foreign parts—England, America, Russia. That was illegal (as well as taboo to Franciscans), but Yankees were not the only pious early Americans smuggling in defiance of a Mother Country's commercial laws. From the beginning the missions dominated the Golden State-to-be. They had the most and best livestock, the most reliable labor, and since they afforded wayfarers lodging, were virtual innkeepers taking their pay in contributions. As overseas contacts grew, the traveler guest often found imported wines and liquors available. It is easy to grin at what would have dismayed St. Francis. It is also easy to see how, what with the Indians' shortcomings, the zealot's impulse to do neophytes good regardless, and the able manager's urge to do a job better and better, this evolution into commercialization came to pass. And at least, so far as is known, the friars relaxed their ascetic vows only at table. It suggests chilblains and arthritis merely to enter one of the surviving thick-walled, sunless cells, like root cellars aboveground, where, scantily clothed and practically without bedding, they slept on beds of hide and rope.

The successful Mexican rebellion against Spain led to the ruin of the missions and their Indian wards. In the 1830's Mexico, more secular-minded than the Mother Country, withdrew the missions' land privileges and began to grant the tracts thus freed to friends of the government. The friars went back sorrowing to Spain or Mexico, leaving the Indians adrift. They now lacked their forefathers' experience in living off the country; besides, the lands, the wild produce of which had supported grandfather, now mostly belonged to strong-armed rancheros. They could work for these secular masters at the old tasks, hoeing and herding, but it was bewildering to steer one's own life in the white man's world without the discipline to which the missions had accustomed them. Many took to drink

—as ruinous for them as earthquakes proved to the neglected mission churches. Some local officials connived with the rancheros in various systems of quasi-forced labor to keep the unruly in a position to earn their bread—much as the defeated South tried to do with the freed slaves after the Civil War. Others stagnated as Don José Ranchero's meek serfs.

Uncle Sam eventually redressed Mexico's harshness—only nominally since no lands were returned—by handing the titles to California's ruined mission churches back to their monastic founders. Many are now restored as sanctuary museums, attracting tourists in flocks as regular as those of the swallows of San Juan Capistrano. In a few, as at San Xavier del Bac near Tucson, Arizona, local Indians still make up the congregation. There and elsewhere restoration has concentrated on the chewing-gum ornateness of portal and reredos rather than the handsome geometric designs that once ornamented the nave walls and tower exteriors. The old padres might prefer it so. Like other transplanted colonists, they too sought to build churches as near as possible like those back home, and their day in Mexico and Spain was that of Baroque gone Rococo. In only a few instances could they import to remote California the fanciful carvings that God's house deserved. Sometimes they had only *trompe l'oeil*—itself then a fashionable device, however—made by sketching on the wall back of the altar stately pillars, niches and swags for the Indians to paint with local pigments like children with a gigantic coloring book. The designs, necessarily done from memory, were watery in spirit and then more so after being blurred with paint. But peeling traces remain to testify that here long ago squat Indians balancing on scaffolding did their best, for reasons that most of them had no way of grasping, to make a plastered wall resemble Fra Tomaso's recollections of a church in Rome 7,000 miles away.

While the Indians decayed, the new owners of the mission lands took over as the core of the miniature economy. Sequestering the missions' livestock, as well as the acres they grazed, they raised and sold tallow, cowhides, cereals and lumber in usually illicit trade and took in payment not only the salt, gunpowder and hardware that they could not produce but also the contraband silks, laces, perfumes and gewgaws that the ship captains knew Doña María and her several daughters coveted. Don José Ranchero, too, dressed expensively in tight jacket and breeches of smuggled silk or broadcloth and rode abroad on a silver-rich, high-pommeled saddle worth more than any horse in his corral. His one-story ranch house of adobe might look like an ammunition bunker or was at best, as Albert Pike described the governor's palace at Santa Fe in the 1830's, "a mudbuilding . . . with a mud-covered portico supported by rough pine pillars." [22] It was about as thick-walled and dark as a mission dormitory; its floor was beaten earth. But in that chronically sunny climate it was a cool refuge from dust and glare, and its farther reaches were lively with the doings of the dozens of Indian retainers—mostly women and their progeny but also some unusually steady males—who saw after the poultry, horses and garden, did the cooking, cleaning and laundry, and waited on the numerous Ranchero family hand and foot.

The small scale of this mushroom-new oligarchy now sounds strange in Southern California, land of the supercolossal, whether movies or olives. Spain's expansionism had been so slack and the logistic obstacles so clogging that by 1821 Texas and California had little more than 4,000 Spanish-Mexicans each. As Earl Pomeroy's *The Pacific Slope* points out, "There are more Basque sheepherders in . . . Nevada and eastern Oregon today than there ever were Spaniards in all of Spanish California." [23] The rancheros' rule was as stultifying as that of their friar predecessors and far less concerned with responsibilities. That was bad for Indians and masters, too. Few of the gay *caballeros,* let alone their tiny-footed, demure-eyed sisters, could sign their names. At fiestas both sexes joined their Indian serfs in enjoying fights to the death between a bull and a grizzly bear; the bull's foreleg was chained to the bear's hind leg to make it an even, hence horribly prolonged match. The indolence of all classes was so pervasive that gringos called it California fever and noted ruefully how it also infected the children of Yankees gone Spanish.

Yet this tiny subculture had pleasant manners and an openhandedness common in master-and-serf polities. On those traits the descendants of the American intruders eventually based glorification of the ranchero era into a Southwestern counterpart of the South's magnolias-*cum*-Cindy Lou. In 1877 a lady writer for *Harper's Magazine* "surrounded by . . . open galleries with the stars overhead" in the courtyard of Menger's Hotel in San Antonio already felt "in the heart of Old Spain." [24] (Menger's was actually built by newly arrived Germans and included part of their first *Turnhalle.*) In Robert Louis Stevenson's account of Monterey in 1879 a budding cult of nostalgic Hispanicism is evident. Helen Hunt Jackson's *Ramona*, though meant to lend dignity to the California Indians, left millions of readers sighing after the Castilian-hidalgo elegance of the rancheros. Gertrude Atherton, San Francisco novelist who played this tune most glibly, called their California "the one Arcadia the modern world has ever known" and bewailed "the dashing caballeros and the lovely donas who once called Monterey their own and made it a living picture-book." [25]

A recent elegy by R. L. Duffus, changing the flavor, calls Mrs. Atherton's Arcadia "a manner of life that never was what it seemed and has as much to do with life in California today as have the relics of the Stone

Age." [26] But that is hindsight in 1968. David Starr Jordan, liberal educationist and first president of Stanford University, had long since foisted Spanish names on new streets in Palo Alto, and Charles F. Lummis, booster editor of the *Land of Sunshine* magazine, had people restoring the old missions and lining suburban streets with houses like pastel-tinted sugar cubes. It all culminated in the red-tiled glories of the Southern Pacific Station in Los Angeles and the hyper-Mexican Baroque of the San Diego's Panama-California International Exposition in 1915.

Current architectural fashion in California derives from other nostalgias, but what was once called Mission style, now modified as Southwest Provincial, still dominates new building in Arizona. In ironic fact, the strongest genuine reminder of pre-gringo times in the Southwest is the millions of Mexicans—many American-born citizens, many more having immigrated formally or informally—who do so much of the essential daily or seasonal work in the land between Houston and the Pacific beaches. In New Mexico, where white settlement antedates the Lost Colony, they have long held political power and still look down on gringos as crude newcomers. The gringo, of course, has always been scornful of them—which is graceless, for he was already borrowing from the Mexican *vaquero* the trappings and techniques basic to the folklore of the great West.

Stock-minded newcomers named Smith and Jones knew about corrals and branding from Back East traditions. But they soon borrowed from the Mexican the deep-seat, straight-leg saddle; the *reata* and the complementary high-heeled boots; the chaps to protect legs from spiny brush; the burro without which the prospector would seldom have located paying minerals; the multiple uses of the mesquite trees that furnished fuel, timber for fence posts and light construction, and large bean pods for cattle feed. Indeed they learned as much from the Mexican as the Colonial settler had from the Indian of the eastern seaboard. And simultaneously the *vaquero* was playing tutor in still another environment. The Hawaiian cattle industry still calls its cowhands paniolos because their originals learned cattle handling in the early 1800's from imported Mexicans calling themselves Españolos.

Non-Spanish names, implying gringo infiltration, were in the majority among important landowners around Los Angeles by the 1840's. In the northern, even less developed end of California the authorities had encouraged a flighty German-Swiss adventurer named Sutter to set up an ambitious colony, half ranch, half trading post. Originally manned by European and Hawaiian drifters, it attracted other such by sea and land, mostly American, very few Mexican in origin. It often does look as though history has stacked the deck. Here she was flagrantly preparing the scene for American expansionism—Manifest Destiny. Next she arranged to have James Marshall (a native of New Jersey) discover gold on Sutter's land, which would flood the newly acquired territory with American adventurers and change California's economic center of gravity and cultural complexion—eventually the nation's, too, for that matter. To clinch the charge of deck stacking, consider that the fateful gold find of 1848 was not California's first. In 1842, with the Mexican War still some years away, a Southern Californian ranch hand dug up a clump of wild onion in the hills northeast of Los Angeles and saw gold in the dirt they grew in. In the next three years some $8,000 in gold was washed out of local soil; 20 ounces of it were sent around the Horn to the Philadelphia Mint, the first California gold seen Back East. It caused strangely little stir, whereas Sutter's gold struck fire all over the Western world. The reason must have been that the man who dug the onions was named Francisco López—and history preferred to postpone the gold rush until it could occur under gringo auspices.

The first gold rushers of '49 were those nearby when the news came out: the former trappers, ship jumpers and recent wagon-party arrivals who gave the miniature settlements of Northern California their marked American flavor. The crews and sometimes the officers of ships happening to be on the coast joined the rush to the mines. Even U.S. Navy ships found themselves critically shorthanded. Then the dazzling strikes that some firstcomers made along the streams flowing down the western slope of the Sierra Nevada set off a massive second wave from outside—principally footloose young men ready to bet the risks of a trip to California on the chance of a quick fortune.

The specific risk associated with the two-steamers-and-Isthmus way was that of contracting yellow fever in one or another Central American swamp. Thus died, among many luckless others, Theodore D. Judah, foresighted engineer of railroads whose favorite project, the transcontinental railroad, would obviate the danger of yellow jack. The safest way, though ungodly long and cramped, was around tempest-harried Cape Horn by sailing ship. The third, of course, was to cross the 3,000-mile-wide continent by dry land—much of it far too dry. The risks there were starvation, Indians, sometimes cholera, in a few lurid cases cannibalism. None of that kept young men and their parasites and suppliers from coming by tens of thousands. Within a year the tenuous village of San Francisco had exploded into a population of more than 40,000.

This first mass of men trying their luck in California must have been America's prime example of a self-selecting, temperamentally homogeneous migration. Neither the *Mayflower* Pilgrims (even aside from their admixture of strangers) nor Penn's Quakers can have been so consistent.

374   THE AMERICANS

Those groups brought families, and even under strict intrafamily discipline children often fail to resemble their parents in basic reactions. Most
of the gold rushers were either bachelors or left wives and children behind
to await their return. Few seem to have planned to settle on the coast.
Make your pile and go home to enjoy it was the typical plan.

Typically the forty-niner was from the Northeastern and Middle Atlantic states, making the trip by sea. To judge from the home states mentioned on the epitaphs of those dying on the overland route in 1849, it
was preferred by gold seekers from west of the Appalachians, a disproportionate number from Missouri. The forty-niner's lack of women and obvious rashness bring the Jamestowners to mind, which may be unfair.
Though he often came from upper social strata—a sizable minority had
attended college—he was not afraid of hard work, usually persisting
doughtily in the fortune hunt even after learning that it entailed such arduous tasks as shoveling gravel, digging shafts and building flumes in the
Sierra foothills. The norm was probably a high-spirited youngster willing
to let gold tempt him away from the shadow of the meetinghouse steeple
and the gloom of the lantern-lit cow barn, or the smell of the calf binding
of lawbooks, or the droning drawl of the loafers drying their boots on the
store stove. Jamestown's corrupt fecklessness was probably lacking even
when the forty-niner was enjoying himself most dissipatedly. Within that
norm, however, probably lurked a good deal of latent instability. In many
cases those who actually made their lucky and got home with it found
home unrewarding and returned to the unbuttoned land of Eldorado.
Some of that inadvertently peeps out of Sam Clemens' enthusiasm for
the adventurers. His experience in the Nevada silverfields of the 1860's
persuaded him that the forty-niners must have been "the *only* population
of the kind that the world has even seen . . . two hundred thousand
young men—not simpering, dainty, kid-gloved weaklings, but stalwart,
muscular, dauntless young braves . . . the very pick and choice of the
world's glorious ones. No women, no children, no gray and stooping veterans . . . all the slow, sleepy, sluggish-brained sloths stayed at
home. . . ."[27]

Supermen or not, stable or unstable, between 1849 and 1853 their devotion dug and washed into circulation more than $200,000,000 in gold
—a major addition to the gold supply of the United States and the world,
reflected in a brisk inflationary boom in the 1850's. That effect implies
correctly that little of it stayed on the coast. It promptly went Back East or
to Europe to pay for the canned goods, picks and shovels, red flannel
shirts, slouch hats, high boots, firearms, hard liquors, fine wines and fancy
women imported to outfit a man for the diggings and see that whatever
gold he came back with procured him a good time. Knockdown houses

complete with carved brackets, printing presses and paper for them to print, mirrors for barrooms and pianos for brothels arrived in the clippers that vied for fast passage around the Horn. Gold rush San Francisco really was, as folklore tells, the kind of place where men paid lavishly to have their dirty shirts sent 2,000 miles by schooner to Hawaii for washing. Thanks to that background, the place remained for decades a sort of financial and commercial three-ring circus. Wild glut interspersed with wild shortage led to price fluctuations that made Californian retailing as chancy as looking for pockets of gold along the American River. One cool head, seeing cases of oversupplied tobacco and hardware used as crossing-walks in the muddy streets of San Francisco, bought the hardware for a song, hauled it upcountry and sold the scythes it included for $25 apiece. In early Sacramento Collis P. Huntington, soon one of the Big Four of the Central Pacific-Southern Pacific empire, gave $20 a ton for a distress lot of iron bars and within a few days was selling them at $1 a pound.

It has been maintained that, however rich a fair number of gay young gods struck it, that collective bag of $200,000,000 by no means covered their common investment in transport, supplies and man-hours—that is, on the whole, gold seeking was not a paying proposition. The losers were probably a majority. Those who did not trickle back home stayed to take jobs with the hauling or express companies that handled traffic into the diggings; or in the retail stores, warehouses, saloons and hotels that filled miners' needs in the booming settlements; or in the building trades stimulated by their frantic growth. All such livelihoods, though precarious in themselves, were parasitical on the miner, who was taking still greater risks to win the gold that was virtually the new country's only marketable commodity in outside terms. Not for another twenty years would wheat, lumber and to some extent fruit (including wine) give Northern California an intelligible economy.

Some clearheaded hangers-on soon saw that the way to wealth was not to go digging but to provide goods and services for those who did. A logical end product was the Wells, Fargo express company, outlasting all competitors for the privilege of supplying the miner with mail and stage transportation, running his errands, and looking after his gold—all at a neat percentage off the top. In colonial situations the middleman-trader-forwarder-banker-factor, with his unrelenting commissions, is usually eventually king of the trough. For instance, storekeeping in Sacramento, principal jumping-off place for the miners, was what gave the Big Four their start toward dominating the whole Golden State.

They made a significant and consistent group: all active in the newborn Republican Party; all young except Mark Hopkins, who was a doddering thirty-five years old when he came West. Charles Crocker, Collis P. Huntington and Leland Stanford were twenty-eight. Crocker was the only Midwesterner; Stanford and Hopkins were from upper New York State; Huntington was from Connecticut. Crocker alone knew anything of mining; he had been a country blacksmith working an iron deposit in northern Indiana when he got California fever in 1850, and in California he soon gave up digging and took to retailing dry goods. Stanford had left home to practice law in the backwoods of Wisconsin; his brothers' accounts of their profits from keeping store in California led him to move again (leaving his young wife still farther behind in Albany, New York) to prosper in wholesale groceries in Sacramento. Huntington had risen from Yankee peddler and collector of dubious notes of hand to store-owning in a small town. Hopkins had clerked in such a store, then turned commission merchant in New York City. The last two came West in 1849, the holy year, and went into the hardware business together. Stanford and Huntington eventually fetched their wives West; the others married Back East girls. As the gold boom went aground in the mid-1850's, all four had the resources to stay afloat, and when the Civil War set the transcontinental railroad abuilding, at last committed to the latitude of San Francisco, they clubbed together to exploit its Western segment. Hence their great fortunes surviving, as vanished glaciers leave terminal moraines, in Stanford University; the Huntington Art Gallery and Library; and the Top of the Mark anomalously commemorating a most abstemious millionaire.

Sacramento also saw the prosperings of Darius Ogden Mills, young banker from New York State, arriving in 1850, and of two agile young lawyers from Kentucky, James Ben Ali Haggin (aged twenty-three on arrival in 1850) and Lloyd Tevis (twenty-five when he got there in 1849), who joined forces, moved to San Francisco, where the decisions were made and the bodies buried, and handled themselves so cleverly that when they both died rich, they had between them strong grips on railroads, stage lines, express companies, steamships, telegraphs, mines, irrigated lands, ice . . . Consider also the unprepossessing group of four Irish adventurers—John W. Mackay, James G. Fair, James C. Flood and William S. O'Brien—whose pooled luck and various kinds of staying power made them plutocratic kings of silver-mad Nevada, economically a colony of San Francisco in the 1860's. Three were real forty-niners; Mackay arrived in 1851. All were men of their hands. Back East Mackay had been a shipwright, Flood a carriage craftsman, O'Brien a grocery clerk, Fair an Illinois farmboy with a passion for machinery. Mackay and Fair had years of catch-as-catch-can mining; Flood a touch of it. When they opened their great game of buying into opportunities created by others in the new, highly industrialized, chemistry-based silver mining of the Comstock Lode Mackay was digging and timbering shafts on contract; Fair was a mildly successful gold seeker putting his small capital into Nevada on strong hunches; and Flood and O'Brien, after success with a one-bit (second-class) saloon near the San Francisco Mining Exchange, had gone partners in a stockbroking firm.

Barkeeps, lawyers, retailers, bankers, shipowners thus stood out among the beneficiaries of forty-nining. For a few gaudy years Providence also gave the rancheros of Southern California a share in the milking of the red-shirted miner. The gold rushers' need for nourishment in a signally un-developed region had boomed demand for beef from the cattle herds of the missions' former empire. A steer that might once have netted Don José $12 to $15 for hide and tallow (the meat used locally or left to rot) now sold for $75 when driven northward as beef on the hoof. So while the gringos scattered gold dust among the faro dealers, whores and flimsy doggeries of San Francisco, the smooth-shaven, olive-skinned Quality of Santa Barbara and Los Angeles were spending the proceeds of their cattle on solid silver bits for their horses, silk finery for their wives and daughters and costly rugs from France laid, to the astonishment of visitors, on the beaten earth floors of their *salas*.

Presently a several years' drought devastated their pastures. By the time rain and grass returned, the gold boom had dwindled. Lacking tide-over resources, many rancheros failed and were bought out by gringo op-portunists—and Southern California reverted to sluggishness irregularly relieved by a notable lawlessness. It had always had horse stealing and cattle rustling. Smuggling had been the core of local enterprise, such as it was. Murder for private reasons was as much a local institution as the fandango. But violence took on a new dimension as unsavory characters came south to get away from San Francisco's Vigilance Committee and the less formal groups that periodically cleaned up smaller settlements as in Bret Harte's "The Outcasts of Poker Flat." Then, as the native Mexi-cans understandably came to resent the gringos' take-over, the region south of the Tehachapis went in for killing and highway robbery on a scale mak-ing the early gold rush country northward, now thought of as so rugged, look bloodlessly refined. In one period of fifteen months alone Los Ange-les County, containing only 8,000 persons, had 44 homicides, and the one man tried for murder in this period had been acquitted. One of a party of Eastern surveyors visiting Los Angeles in 1860 reported that local people were puzzled—and somewhat apologetic—"because there have been no violent deaths during the two weeks that we have been here." [28]

Toughness is hard to assess statistically. Maybe the most striking record of homicides in the great West was that of Wasatch, Utah, the early ceme-tery of which showed 24 graves, 23 of men who had died with their boots on, the twenty-fourth of a prostitute who had poisoned herself. In the decade after the Civil War places now obscure, like Bodie, California, and Newton, Kansas (in the great cattle-drive days), were also famous for wholesale manslaughter. But such traditional fast-gun settlements as Tombstone and Deadwood were never such a Bloody Gulch as Los Angeles had been a generation before them. Southern California's trigger-happy drifters and road agents with Mexican names and motives can be safely credited with bringing Los Angeles her first superlative—she was the toughest place in California that ever amounted to anything permanently. There, in fact, first shaped up the stock characters, scenery and props of the movie Western. Horses ridden at the run. Cattle milling in the old corral as the rustlers close in. Long, low ranch houses. Mexican villains. Revolvers. Stagecoaches. Tenderfoot from Back East . . . In 1860 that ugly reality was beginning to fade. By 1920 it had returned to set up movie lots and locations where the old genuine ranchos had been, reenacting the sordid past as prettified, puerile, galvanic fantasy.

Unpredictable side effects, often a nuisance in drugs, can be salutary in other fields. Thus the telegraph made possible newspaper beats on distant events, which led directly to the founding of what became the Associated Press. Growing need for telegraph operators opened a new field of employment for women in the early 1850's. Telegrams for ordering goods and railroads for shipping them soon revolutionized dealings between big-city wholesalers and over-the-mountains retailers, who no longer had to make annual trips to Philadelphia or New York City to order a complete year's stock from a single all-purpose supplier. Now they counted on delivery of reorders in a short time, which allowed more flexible inventories. Market quotations telegraphed to country newspapers reduced the guesswork in farmers' and small-town dealers' marketings of pork, grain and so on. The tight schedules that telegraphy gradually imposed on railroads finally forced the creation of standard time zones; until then cities had used their own sun times and great confusion was inevitable.

A highly oblique side effect of the railroad was the birth of the express industry as private competition and hairshirt yardstick for the federal postal service. That in turn had its own side effects on the growth of the Far West and the rise of the mail-order industry, cultural catalyst of the jay town. Historically all this came of the Colonial's dim view of the infrequent and cruelly expensive pre-Revolutionary mails. By law the movement of parcels and letters along any route that His Majesty's Post Office designated a post road was a Crown monopoly. The Colonists' talent for ignoring irksome laws, however, suggested that a letter would get from New York City to Boston, say, faster and, even more to the purpose, cheaper if a business acquaintance riding thither took it along and gave it to the addressee or left it at the tavern that he frequented. Captains of coasting vessels made a small good thing out of charging less than postage to do the same. Utterly illegal, the system was nevertheless so well established by the early 1770's that Yankees warned a Crown postal inspector that anybody protesting or informing against it would never escape tar and feathers.

Apparently the post-Revolutionary shift of the mails to stages soon supplemented by steamboats improved service enough for the new federal Post Office to make headway. But as transport expanded and people grew used to more frequent intercity and -regional contact, nobody remodeled the Post Office to match. Until 1845 its charges were stiflingly high: 10 cents for 30-80 miles; 18¾ cents for 150-400 miles; more than 400 miles 25 cents—a scale that meant, as Edward Eggleston wrote of early Ohio, that "for poor people correspondence was not to be thought of except on the occasion of a death or a wedding." [29] In cities, home delivery, where available, cost extra. Even those able to afford such charges and the underlings to send daily to the post office had plenty to complain about, however, for clumsy sorting and distribution systems had interregional mails slowed down to a walk.

In 1844 Morse's telegraph began somewhat to relieve the clogging of national communications—and eventually, of course, to take crucial revenue away from the federal Post Office. The next year Congress lowered postal rates and, in 1851, went to a 3-cent lick-and-stick stamp nationwide, a clever mail-stimulating innovation borrowed from England. Long since, however, private enterprise had taken over the potentially profitable fraction of the vacuum left by Uncle Sam's fumbling. In 1839 an astute young Yankee, William F. Harnden, revived the old Colonial dodge, making regular train trips to and from Boston and New York City taking letters and parcels in his carpetbag at fees well below Post Office rates. That allied the speed and reliability of railroads—used by the Post Office, too, but only in a clumsy way—with the attraction of at-the-door delivery. Very soon Harnden had so far outgrown carpetbags that he needed special railroad cars. The success of his express* service brought nimble-witted competitors swarming in. Within four years twenty eager imitators, including the soon-renowned Adams Express Company, were operating out of Boston, and the idea was spreading all over like measles. In 1845

* The word seems to have been borrowed from British usage, as in the express messenger sent with a single important message in haste. It had come into use for the express train, first meaning what we call a special train, then applied to a scheduled train dedicated to speed and few stops. Messenger long remained the term for the man in charge of an express company car of mail, packages and valuables.

Pomeroy & Company's express of Buffalo, New York, had the impudence —or enterprise, depending on the point of view—to sell its own postage stamps to prepay letters in its own letter boxes and to advertise a 6-cent rate from Buffalo to New York City for the letter that Uncle Sam charged 25 cents for. In California large and small express services, usually with their own mail drops and agents, were in business well ahead of the U.S. Post Office and remained tactlessly more efficient for years to come. And at one time Adams Express let it be known that it would like nothing better than to take over the entire postal system, paying Uncle Sam 1 cent per letter, a proposition that received much support from the nation's press.

Uncle Sam's appeals to the sovereign's monopoly of the postal function as hinted at in the Constitution were as futile as if the sovereign were still George III. Equally futile were dismally well-founded complaints that the expressmen were taking the cream of the business, the short distances and thickly settled areas, leaving the government only the unprofitable parts of it—the same thing that, by capturing so much high-revenue freight, trucks and planes would do to the railroads in the mid-1900's. It must have been especially irksome to see in large cities the local express companies' bright-colored letter boxes more numerous and more handily placed than Uncle Sam's—and with faster delivery. When the Post Office cleverly went in for money orders, which cut into express revenues from the safe transport of cash, American Express invented the modern type of money order with a tear-off margin to indicate amount and outdid Uncle Sam by selling them in drugstores and railroad stations, whereas the government's were procurable only at post offices.

The Post Office's first success in getting some of its own back came in the 1860's with railroad mail cars in which eyeshaded gnomes in shirt sleeves sorted the mails as they howled through the night as part of limited trains, presently in special all-mail-car consists scheduled at better than limited speeds. That, combined with the 3-cent nationwide letter rate, wrested first-class mail away from private handling. Since the Post Office lacked a proper parcel-post system, however, that huge segment of its potential business was left to the large express companies developing through dog-swallow-dog competition on a roughly regional basis; American Express, Southern Express and so on, sometimes branching into banking, always highly collusive in interarea arrangements, and collectively growing much too big for their breeches as the decades went by. When the federal government denied the noisome Louisiana Lottery the use of the mails in 1890 and the racket moved to Honduras, it was the express companies that enabled it to service its American customers until well past the turn of the century.

Well might A. M. Simons' *Social Forces in American History* (1911) call the express industry "peculiarly American. In all other countries [its] functions are divided between the freight departments of the railroads and the postoffice. This would undoubtedly have been the case [in America] had . . . not . . . the demand for this service [come] at a time when . . . individual initiative ruled industrial and political life." [30] Not until the reformist days of 1911-13 did Uncle Sam set up a competing parcel post that, in effect heavily subsidized, could wean America from the express habit. For two generations kerosene lamps and corsets from Sears, Roebuck and gallon jugs of whiskey crossing the boundaries of dry states to relieve unregenerate thirsts, as well as small-bulk shipments of manufactures from axes to zephyr yarn, traveled to the customer in the elegantly varnished and maintained express wagon. Miniature versions of it were the pride of small boys. Ellis Parker Butler's *Pigs Is Pigs,* the most popular bit of humor of the pre-Sarajevo decade (possibly excepting Thomas J. Jackson's *On a Slow Train Through Arkansas*), centered on an express depot coping with a catastrophically prolific shipment of guinea pigs.

The protagonist of *Pigs Is Pigs* was a stubborn, hot-tempered, brogue-ridden Irishman named Mike. An outstanding contemporary success among Sunday newspaper funnies was Rudolph Dirks' Hans und Fritz characters playing pranks in an imported German tradition of slapstick graphic humor. Such peaks in the popular entertainment of grandfather's boyhood betoken the diversities of the great waves of immigration of the 1800's. As the century rolled on, many other ethnic ingredients appeared —the Norwegians, for instance, well before the Civil War, and, after it, other Scandinavians, the Italians, Poles and various Baltic, Balkan and Levantine peoples. But since the Irish and Germans had led the post-Revolution influx, they had had the most extended opportunity to create popular awareness of them. The shows grandfather saw and the songs he heard were full of shamrocks and shillelaghs, lager beer and tasseled smoking caps. Time had not yet fully developed the stereotypes expressed in Where-do-you-worka-John and the late Chico Marx's comic Italian.

A New World that had ejected vested authority and was now vaunting new-fledged freedoms and opportunities naturally exerted strong gravitational pull on Old Countrymen given to Crèvecoeur's sort of romanticized half-truths. Simultaneously economic hardships continued to suggest emigration to craftsmen of restless temperament, and for a while the hard-up could still arrange indentured passages. In the decade or so after actual independence in 1783 came many yeasty newcomers particularly from Britain, including Joseph Priestley, pioneer chemist and religious radical; William Cobbett, for a while a stormy petrel of American politics and journalism; Thomas Cooper, humanitarian radical whose long life in America as physician-scientist-lawyer-politician-heretic led him somehow into stout intellectual defense of slavery. But the wars set off by the French Revolution gradually stifled the merchant shipping that westbound migrants needed and also kept many underprivileged Europeans at home in uniform. Only after Waterloo could the mass shift of population that had created America regain momentum. In the 1820's some 150,000 souls made the passage. The 1830's quadrupled that; the 1840's tripled that— a twelvefold rise in the rate of immigration that far outstripped the rate of growth of America's native population, slaves and all.

The languages of the bulk of newcomers between 1783 and the Civil War were familiar, but the people speaking them were not just the same as before. There were, for instance, numerous French refugees from the guillotine, from the slave risings in the West Indies, from the Bourbon restoration after Napoleon fell—but few of them can have had the austere flavor of the Huguenots of a century earlier. These were Catholic-reared, and besides, many of them had experienced the Enlightenment and Robespierre topped off with Napoleon. The masses of Germans entering America from the 1820's averaged lower than the Pennsylvania Dutch in piety and peasant-mindedness. In Revolutionary America *Irish* had loosely covered both the Scotch-Irish of the major influx and the scattering of south-of-Ireland Catholic immigrants. After 1800 these proportions were reversed. Millions of Catholic Irish jostling the Germans in the scramble to the New World were the first to insist on the wide cultural gulf between themselves and the dour Presbyterian Ulstermen of the frontier. Because America continued to sound better than Ulster, some Scotch-Irish kept coming, and the flaxseed trade between Pennsylvania and Ireland meant ships were highly available. One cause of the turbulence that gave the Irish canal diggers a bad name was the chronic hatred between the two kinds of Irish on the same job. Indiana had to call out the militia to prevent a pitched battle on the anniversary of the Battle of the Boyne, at which Protestant England Ulster broke Catholic Ireland's heart in 1690. Federal troops had had to be similarly used in 1834 to cool off quarreling Irishmen digging the Chesapeake and Ohio Canal. Irish labor on the National Road had already made itself unpopular by a trick of blocking the fairway with felled trees and forcing travelers to pay to have them removed.

The visibility of these new Irish and Germans was heightened by their tendency to settle in town in enclaves in contrast with the Irish and "Dutch" immigrants of the 1700's, who soon went upcountry voluntarily or under pressure from government and settled far over the town dweller's horizon. Some of the new Germans reaching the Old Northwest by steamboat up the Western Waters or along the Great Lakes turned to farming, but many others set up large German communities within St. Louis, Cincinnati, Chicago and Milwaukee. This urban-mindedness was not inevitable. The Scandinavians, a cognate new group also coming in from the

Emigrants coming ashore in New York City in the 1850's.

1830's onward, embraced life on the land as eagerly as the Pennsylvania Dutch ever had, making Minnesota and the Dakotas the granary of the New World. True, Ole Hanson had been a hardscrabble peasant at home and was stubbornly land-minded. But so were Terence O'Reilly and his father and grandfather before him, rural victims of political and religious vendettas, stupid landlords and an economy coaxed into overpopulation by the ease of potato culture. Yet whereas Ole couldn't wait to get a plow into prairie sod, Terence seemed to think it one of the best things about emigrating that it broke his commitment to husbandry. Even when work on a canal or railroad sent him over the mountains and he stayed West when it was finished, he seldom dwelt more than a stone's throw from some booming main street. Indeed an Irish canal diggers' temporary shantytown became the nucleus of Akron, Ohio.

Any change must have been an improvement if the original was like the railroad builders' village that Dickens saw in upstate New York in

1841: "clumsy, rough and wretched . . . hovels. . . . The best were poor protection . . . the worst let in the wind and rain through wide breaches in the roofs of sodden grass . . . some had neither door nor window; some . . . were imperfectly propped up by stakes and poles; all were very . . . filthy. Hideously ugly old women and very buxom young ones, pigs, dogs, men, children, babies . . . dunghills, vile refuse, rank straw, and standing water, all wallowing together in an inseparable heap, composed the furniture of every dark and dirty hut." [31] That was out in the country. The 100-odd cabins of "The Acre" in Lowell, Massachusetts, sound little better calculated to give the Irish a good name. But for single men untroubled about the risks of malaria, railroad and canal making had attractions. Chevalier, the careful French economist, reported in wonder that a railroad gang he investigated got up to 75 cents a day, plus rough barracks lodging and three meals, each including bread, butter, meat, coffee and six to eight drams of whiskey depending on the weather, whereas in France such work brought 24 cents a day and feed yourself. He picked up an eloquent anecdote of the Irish pick swinger having a letter written for him telling the family back in Ireland how well he was doing on rations with meat three times a week. The letter writer asks why say that when he knew very well it was three times a day? "Because," said Pat, "if I told them that, they'd never believe me." [32]

Popular history has it that the disastrous potato famines of the 1840's, actually starving thousands in Ireland, were what sent the Irish streaming overseas. America was well aware of that catastrophe and sent emergency food generously. One cargo of grain went in a three-mast ship specially built for the purpose in Marietta, Ohio, in a temporary revival of bluewater shipbuilding. Another of food and clothing contributed by Bostonians went in the USS *Jamestown* lent by the Navy. Actually the proportion of Irish among immigrants to America in the five years after the famine—44 percent—was no higher than it had been in the five years preceding. The potato blight had only rendered impossible a situation already intolerable. Thousands of descendants of St. Patrick's converts to a religion that had proved a sociopolitical millstone around their necks had already left bitterly or resignedly.

At first they had flooded into England and Scotland, where their wild poverty, primitive habits and association with the least desirable jobs deepened the Protestant, English-speaking world's traditional contempt for them. Conditions in the ships taking them to America were little better than those of the noisome 1700's—five, six, even eight adults in a berth calculated as minimum for a married couple with a child or two. But they were little worse than those in a Liverpool slum, and even that had been preferable to a hovel back in Roscommon. The Irish exodus seems to have been already sizable by the 1790's, when they dominated the Five Points district of New York City. In the War of 1812 a unit of New York City militia known as the Irish Greens was sent to the Niagara frontier. The Irish were so well established in New York City in 1817 that they felt it worthwhile to march on Tammany Hall protesting against lack of their countrymen among political nominees and demanding that their resident hero, Thomas Addis Emmet, be nominated for Congress. In the next year or two a temporary revival of the redemptioner business sent recruiters into all parts of Ireland, putting emigration into heads that otherwise might never have thought of it. Hard times in 1819 caused the recruiters stuck with unsalable "servants" to turn them loose ashore, and penniless Irish were so rife in Philadelphia that the well-meaning urged Congress to rescue them with a special land grant in Illinois.

Had the measure passed, some might have welcomed it, for the Irish distaste for the land was not universal. As part of the effort to plump out the newly independent Republic of Texas in the 1830's, certain promoters named McMullin and McGloin settled a colony fresh from Ireland in a tract on the Gulf Coast around a hamlet duly named San Patrick, since regularized into San Patricio. But these ill-equipped and usually illiterate refugees mostly landed in large port cities and mostly stuck in the urban slums that their predecessors were spreading, if not creating. However fetid, such neighborhoods were reassuringly full of fellow Irish. For the same reason, says Wayne G. Broehl, Jr., in explaining the Molly Maguires of the Pennsylvania coalfields, the Irish took to the small coal villages because they "gave the sense of close-knit community so desired by the Irish . . . one of the main reasons why . . . [though] eighty per cent had farming backgrounds, only about six per cent settled on farms . . . with only the marginal farming experience of growing potatoes, they were used to the communal life of [the] cotter system and were fearful of the isolation and loneliness of Western farming." [33]

In the Pennsylvania coal industry it was also too like Ireland. The actual miners, holding the jobs with prestige and better pay, were imported English and Welsh with the Irish relegated to lowlier work—driving mules, doing chores for the miners, picking over the mined coal. At home the symptoms of their despair had included individual and mass riot and hard drinking. In America, where as yet their miseries had lifted only partly and the habit of despair was still strong, they went on fighting and drinking as if eager to confirm the worst things traditionally laid to their charge. Ole Rynning, the Norwegian parson-schoolmaster whose memorandum on America moved thousands of his countrymen to emigrate, noted in 1837 that "From Ireland there comes yearly a great rabble who, because of their tendency to drunkenness, their fighting and their knavery, make themselves commonly hated. A respectable Irishman hardly dares acknowledge his nationality." [34]

It seems to have occurred to few that America's boasted canals and railroads would have been long abuilding, if ever finished at all, without these reprehended Irish, who also were essential to its burgeoning cities' needs for pick swinging, hod carrying, dray loading and so on. A little less drawing aside of the skirt of the garment would have been becoming. Instead, between the Quality's disdain and the abjectly low standards of sanitation and interaction that the Irish brought from Ireland's rural slums to America's urban slums, their group reputation was deplorable. The analogy to the recent situation of Puerto Ricans in American cities is striking. The Irish were probably worse off then, however, because bad conscience about ethnic stereotypes hardly existed. In all social strata, stage, press and gossip were free to make *drunkenIrishman* as much a single word as *damyankee* would be. It struck the whole nation as all too appropriate that the greatest pledge-signing Temperance crusader in the world should be Father Theobald Mathew of Cork, come to America particularly to bring his emigrant fellow Irishmen the mass teetotalism that he had imposed on millions at home on the Ould Sod. There really were signs saying NO IRISH NEED APPLY and clichés about potato mouths and "They kept the pig in the parlor." Girlish Lucy Larcom, snugly reared in Beverly, Massachusetts, and wondering what her English-written books meant when talking about beggar children, had her "childish desire to see a real beggar . . . gratified" when her family moved to Lowell in the 1840's: "Straggling petitioners for 'cold victuals' hung around our back yard, always of Hibernian extraction. . . ." [35]

Nor could the Germans escape stereotyping. They became, as Albert B. Faust complained in *The German Element in the United States*, "inseparable from lager beer, Limburger Cheese, Sauerkraut and a string of sausages . . . a red nose, a tipsy gait, and a fund of good nature." [36] But as those items hint, they stood higher than the Irish in public esteem. Some of the reasons may have been that their habits were less violent; their persons were cleaner; their religion was usually Protestant; and their average of literacy was higher.

In that last respect, improvement continued with each decade. The bulk of the first small wave seems to have been, as with the Pennsylvania Dutch, peasants and craftsmen hoping to better their lot in a rich New World that, as particular inducement, lacked effective forced military service. At the same time a quarter million or so Germans were moving eastward to settle in Russian-controlled Poland at the invitation of the czar, and Brazil was trying to entice others to the southern half of the New World, with only minor success. The small man wanting economic elbow-room and willing to go overseas for it probably dominated German emigration, whether to America or elsewhere, until World War I. But during the 1820's it also became clear that many of the reactionary governments of post-Napoleonic Germany seriously contemplated wiping out the traces of French *liberté, égalité, fraternité,* and livelier-minded scholars, students, lawyers, physicians, journalists, urban craftsmen with some schooling, even some shopkeepers, found the air growingly oppressive. Again popular history errs in attributing the movement of cultivated Germans to America to the single emergency of the revolutions of 1848. Many such did come then. But since the early 1820's Germans of goodwill and ideas had been leaving their fragmented *Vaterland*—object of a romantic veneration well expressed in 1840 in *"Die Wacht am Rhein"* but born in the nationalist uprisings against the French thirty years earlier—by ones and twos, some to avoid real hazard of arrest, some in general precaution, some out of distaste for the odor of political bullying.

These voluntary exiles settled in precarious clumps in London (like Karl Marx) or Paris (like Heine), where the authorities were not quite so nervous about jarring ideas couched in German, or followed Priestley, Cooper, *et al.* to America as a *soi-disant* home of good intentions and liberty. Among those landing here in the 1820's were young, liberal scholars named Karl Beck, Karl Follen and Franz Lieber, who Anglicized their first names and richened the thinning culture of Massachusetts with the contemporary German cults of swimming and gymnastics, protoprogressive education and hero worship of the new German scholarship. Follen became a pillar of Garrisonian abolitionism; Lieber was the founding editor of the *Encyclopedia Americana* and eventually a great professor of law. An opportunistic Viennese, Franz Josef Grund, who also began his American career at Boston in those times, eventually distinguished himself as creator for the Philadelphia *Public Ledger* of the first inside-stuff column from Washington. Gustav Körner made his career in the German colonies of Illinois, got into politics, became a close friend of Abraham Lincoln's and a very usefully able U.S. minister to Spain in the touch-and-go diplomacy of the Civil War period. In all urban colonies of Germans—in St. Louis, Milwaukee, Cincinnati's Over-the-Rhine beyond the Ohio and Miami Canal—articulate alumni of Bonn, Leipzig or Jena talking Hegel or Proudhon over their beer were probably the best-educated persons in town and, as the language barrier lowered, might become valuable cultural stimuli. Here is a pathetic footnote to the movement: Among the trade goods that John Sutter, of gold rush fame, took to Santa Fe in the 1830's were several German university students' fancy uniform jackets bought from St. Louis pawnshops to attract Indians with their gilt braid and bright colors.

Germans tended to concentrate in the Mississippi Valley because the flow of cotton out of New Orleans to European ports meant that west-bound shipping was always available at low cost from Havre to the Gulf ports. Further impetus came in 1824 from a book, *Account of a Journey to the Western States of North America* by Gottfried Duden, a young German physician-lawyer who had bought some Congress land in north-ern Missouri. Sutter was only one of thousands of Germans whose im-pulse to emigrate was crystallized by Duden's Crèvecoeur-ish account of (this is Marcus Lee Hansen's summary) "bountiful harvests . . . pas-times in the forest and on the river, the glory of sunsets and moonlight nights, the absence of overbearing soldiers, haughty clergymen and in-quisitive tax collectors." [37] Read aloud by the most literate denizen of a tax-ridden village in Westphalia or Hanover, it roused malcontents to leave home, as William Penn's pamphlets had stirred the Palatine 100 years earlier, as Rynning's pamphlet would stir the Norse in the 1830's. Also susceptible were many better-educated "counts and barons, scholars, preachers, gentlemen-farmers, officers, merchants and students . . . pos-sessing some means and therefore unaccustomed and not willing to do the work of laborers" [38] who also decided to buy land near Duden's and live happily ever after. Too few of these made good pioneers; the peasants among their fellow settlers called them Latin farmers, meaning overedu-cated. But they did implant better than peasant manners in the German settlements along the Missouri, and the peasants themselves, farmers as able though not as crankish as the Pennsylvania Dutch, made the land pay almost as well as Duden had promised.

This concentrated Germanness in central Missouri was not entirely spontaneous. Early in the movement two young Germans named Münch and Follenius, identifying the good life and advanced ideas with the archetypal *Vaterland*, planned to found "a new and free Germany in the great North American Republic . . . an essentially German state . . . for all those to whom, as to ourselves, conditions at home have become unbearable . . . a model state in the great republic." [39] Note that word *model;* Germany was to show America how to build civili-zation. Arkansas was their first choice of site for manifesting German virtues. Actually little came of this *Giessener Auswanderungsgesellschaft* (that is, Emigration Society of Giessen, the town associated with it), but its intentions were symptomatic. Organizations of Germans al-ready in America were already asking Congress to allot especially favor-able lands for new German immigrants to Wisconsin. Failing, they chan-

neled individual newcomers thither in hope of creating a new Germany
west of Lake Michigan. "Europeans," Faust explains, "[then] generally
considered the United States a complex whose component parts might
at any moment disjoin and form separate sovereign principalities . . .
by concentrating their immigration . . . such Germanized states might
in time separate from the Union if they did not get what they wanted." [40]

Such schemes usually professed to envisage the nominal suzerainty
of Washington. In the 1830's the new independence of Texas and its thin
population suggested to certain fanciful German noblemen the idea of
settling in the likely country between Austin and San Antonio enough
Germans to bring about eventual control. Britain, hoping to reduce
Uncle Sam's leverage on Texas, approved. So also did the Republic of
Texas, which must mean that it had no inkling of the Germans' long-run
purpose. The largest such scheme landed 150 families under the slipshod management of Prince Karl von Solms-Braunfels, who, though assigned the best log shack in the settlement, went home after one year.
His plebeian charges remained perforce, and their flourishing economy of
moderate-size farms was soon showing the South that slavery was not
essential to prospering in a slave state. True to pattern, they developed
a lively movement to separate western Texas from the cotton- and slave-
dominated part; desire for German control seems to have been as important as dislike of slavery in the scheme, which faded under pressure
from non-German Texans in the 1850's. Their chief town, New Braunfels,
still talks a somewhat American-tinged German in some families, supported a German newspaper until the late 1930's, and has left a
markedly Teutonic flavor in that end of Texas. In 1870, thanks to persistent emigration from the *Vaterland,* San Antonio had more Germans
and Alsatians than Americans, English and Irish combined. The new
street on which the town's Gilded Age crop of plutocrats built their
mansarded mansions was—and still is—called King William Street in
honor of Wilhelm I, King of Prussia.

Certain groups of Germans organized to emigrate after 1800 had
religious motives, such as those of the Rappites, who founded three successive experiments in holy communal living at Harmony, Pennsylvania,
New Harmony, Indiana, and then back to Economy, Pennsylvania, everywhere setting their backwoods neighbors fine examples of thrift, cleanliness, skill and integrity. Even without religious stiffening the secular
German colonies in Missouri were probably standoffish. Yet it is only fair
to mention the analogy between the Bay Colony Puritan, quitting an evil,
corrupt and tyrannous homeland to set up an ideal, sanctified and yet
bristlingly English state in the New World, and the German patriot-
intellectual, leaving a corrupt, repressive situation to go overseas to create

an ideal, freedom-committed and yet bristlingly German state such as the *Vaterland* should have been.

The early 1800's saw minor parallels in non-German contexts. Soon after Waterloo, Morris Birkbeck and George Flower, middle-class Britons, enlisted some of their countrymen for colonies in Illinois meant to be British-flavored right down to ditched hedges and cold boiled beef for breakfast. The alarm that these men's pro-migration propaganda created among England's labor-employing landlords was probably one reason for the flood of unfavorable accounts of America published in England at the time. There were colonies of Welsh in upstate New York in which "one may travel for miles and hear nothing but . . . Welsh . . . They have their newspapers and magazines in their native tongue, and support many churches wherein their language alone is preached," [41] wrote a traveler in 1848. Here again it was a book, the Reverend B. W. Chidlow's *The American,* that determined so many to emigrate. So far as I know, however, the German colonists of the 1820-30's were the only group so tenacious of their ethnic heritage that they dreamed of a national state within the United States. A group that did try something like that and met disaster was native—Joseph Smith's Mormons.

Then, just as this narcissistic Germanism had had time to wear thin, Europe exploded into the antireactionary revolutions of the late 1840's. Those in Germany were suppressed, some pretty brutally. The militant young intellectuals who had plunged in faced either prison or lifetimes of moral suffocation. They were the self-exiled forty-eighters, successors to the Follens and Liebers of the 1820's and, since more of them came at the same time, strongly affected the Germans already in America. They settled mostly in the urban German enclaves; naturally used their status as heroes—which many of them actually were—to recommend themselves; and set up German newspapers so energetically that by 1860 America had 27 *daily* German newspapers in fifteen cities and 250-odd other publications in that language—far more than any other immigrant group supported. During long, garrulous evenings in the *Bier-stube* the Greens, as the established Germans called the newcomers, reproached their predecessors, the Grays, with having lost that zest for the Germanness that should be reshaping America. Some raised funds to support the dwindling revolutionists in Europe, which led to appeals to *Vaterland*-ish feeling as hot as those of a Fenian of the 1860's wringing contributions from Irish-Americans.

Their relaxed ideas about what one did on Sunday further alienated them from the communities in which they settled. People named Smith and Jones became frowningly aware that the Dutch beer gardens did their best business on Sundays purveying to whole families, children

included, beer and white wine with seltzer, music and dancing. By association with Sabbath-breaking, their lager beer, the secret of which
these outlanders brought with them, took on an odor of raffishness—
which did not, however, prevent its taking firm hold on American drinking habits. Worse, Germans from the river towns ventured out into the
country to set up saloons in smaller places where dry sentiment was
steadily growing, so that *German* and *local gin mill* tended to become
synonymous. A country girl named Smith wishing to marry a man named
Schmidt might find her parents unwilling to see her throw herself away
on a stumble-tongued and doubtless Sabbath-breaking Dutchman.

Despite mutual clumsinesses and prejudices, the genial urban Germans had a genuinely civilizing effect on Midwestern crudities. Howells,
for instance, recalled from his boyhood in Dayton, Ohio, "the kindly
German printer-folk . . . the smoke of their pipes and the warmth
of their stove" [42] and the nephews of the German jeweler in Columbus,
Ohio, who taught him to fence and lent him Goethe on elective affinities.
The jeweler, who had a bullet in his leg as souvenir of the barricades of
Berlin, became the doughty German radical of *A Hazard of New Fortunes*. At the other end of the spectrum of cultivation, credit the Germans with naturalizing the Christmas tree in America, also the hot dog,
not yet called that, of course, not even yet known to youngsters as the
weenie (short for *Wienerwurst* as of 1900) but already sold hot on the
streets of Cincinnati by Germans wearing aprons and high hats. (Not
until 1867, it appears, did a Coney Island hawker add the long, soft roll
indispensable today.) The explosions of 1848 also inspired the Prussian consul in New York City to buy and fetch to America for safekeeping a large number of German paintings of the Düsseldorf school.
Displayed by successive owners for thirteen years at a special Düsseldorf
Gallery, they were a great popular success, a significantly deleterious
influence on American art—and source of what was probably the first
American joke about art: the fashionable young lady who wondered
"how Mr. Düsseldorf found the time and patience to do them all so
well." [43]

Almost solidly antislavery, the immigrant Germans enlisted in great
numbers on the Union side of the Civil War and were a principal cause
of Missouri's staying out of the Confederacy. Many forty-eighters had
seen fighting at home, some of it serious, and made good, if seldom brilliant, officers of the many prevalently German regiments. Franz Sigel
and Carl Schurz, both thick in the troubles of '48, had important Union
commands. Schurz later became an elder statesman of the mugwump
wing of the Republican Party. In our eyes it is curious that Josef Wey-
demyer and August Willich, able field commanders in blue, had both

THE WIENER WURST MAN.

One of the German street vendors who first introduced the ancestor of the hot dog to America.

been close to Marx and Engels in the days when Marxism was aborning. As yet, to most Americans, Communist meant merely crank-founded communities holding all things in common and often addicted to cracked wheat. The association was the readier since Germans were conspicuous in the new health cults of homeopathy, phrenology and the water cure. In the long run, certain other legacies were more durable: the following of German models in education and learning; the cult of physical exercise; the acclimatization of professional standards of music; and the importation of the radicalisms—anarchism and realistic Socialism—that Germans of the Weydemyer-Willich type identified with human destiny. For long, however, that was, as Stow Persons has said, "narrowly confined to German-speaking circles. It would be difficult to say whether [for certain Germans] Marxism functioned primarily as an expression of their aspirations for the working class or as a means of sustaining their ethnic and cultural identity in an alien world." 44

The German Jews who left home at much the same time and often for the same reasons as Lieber or Schurz were a rich extra dividend. Until after Waterloo America had only some 3,000 Jews, mostly Sephardic (out of the Iberian Peninsula) and long settled in Colonial seaports. Among them had been Haym Salomon of Philadelphia, who died poor after straining to shore up the shaky finances of the Revolutionary government; Moses Levy of Philadelphia, first Jew admitted to the Pennsylvania bar and counsel for Dr. Benjamin Rush in a libel suit sending William Cobbett back to England; Mordecai Noah of Philadelphia, newspaper editor, flag-waving playwright and proto-Zionist founder of an abortive Jewish colony on an island in the Niagara River; Abraham Mordecai of the Alabama frontier, who built the first cotton gin in the area and, having married a squaw, spent his declining years living Indian-fashion among her people. . . .

After 1815 the sizable Jewish population in Germany had had to face not only general reactionaryism but also widespread revivals of the medieval laws specifically against Jews that had been neglected under the French. Some 15,000 of them had come to America by 1840. The typical case landed with just enough money to buy a stock of peddler's goods—if he hadn't enough, Mordecai Noah was likely to stake him—and took to the road, pack on back like his Yankee competitor. He often went through the same history of graduating first to horse and wagon, then to a permanent store in a likely new town. That was the story of, for instance, Adam Gimbel, Bavarian Jew landing in 1835, whose general store in Vincennes, Indiana, led to the present Gimbel's chain of department stores. Letters home about the new country—such letters as Irish, Germans and Norwegians were sending—brought relatives and friends until the post-Civil War census showed 250,000 Jews, largely of German origin. Cincinnati, cultural and numerical focus of America's Germans, was naturally the same for the compatriot Jews with their own press and theological school.

Anti-Semitism had not been unknown in America. In 1737 the election of a Quality candidate to the New York Colonial Assembly had been successfully challenged on grounds that some of the votes for him had come from Jews. The rabble of New York City occasionally made derisive gestures toward the well-established local Jewish families, particularly when they mobbed a Jewish funeral in 1740. Judge William Cooper, paternalistic land speculator and father of the novelist, reported some nasty snarls in a letter to him from an upstate politician about an election contest between "a gentleman and consequently a federalist, and a dirty stinking anti-federal Jew tavern-keeper." [45] But on the whole, it is surprising that there was not more of it in view of our forebears' inevitably strong feelings about a completely non-Christian religion in their midst. Whatever the reason, anti-Jewish feeling in post-Revolutionary America, particularly in the Old Northwest, was nothing like that in the Old World. A Quaker lady in Ohio, moved by a Bible reader's curiosity, went to Cincinnati when Jews first appeared there, said to the first one she could find: "Is thee a Jew? Thee is one of God's Chosen People. Will thee let me examine thee?," turned him around a few times, and said in innocent ruefulness: "Well! Thee is no different from other people!" [46] In one small town in Indiana the immigrant Jewish storekeeper's wife was so popular that the new high school was named after her.

It was particularly fitting because schooling and Jews are inextricably associated. Their folk passion for learning unquestionably gave America a massive injection of brains—a thing no nation ever had too much of. That would hold good even without the recent surmises of some geneticists that intelligence (so far as it is measurable) averages a bit higher among Jews than among other Caucasoid ethnic groups.

A few German Jews plied their commercial skills in the Southern ports and upcountry, where slaveowners sometimes accused them of illicit traffic with the slaves in drink and pilfered oddments. A good many Germans landing in New Orleans from Havre or Hamburg got no farther up the river. Some Irish were fetched South to build railroads not because Negro slaves could not do the work but because it was man-killing work and slaves cost $1,000 each, whereas a dead Irishman was a loss only to himself. By and large, however, the post-1800 immigrants seldom tried their luck in the big-plantation South. During the 1700's Huguenots, Moravians, Scotch-Irish, Highlanders and Swiss had readily entrusted their futures to that part of the world. What put the new immigrants off was clear. Most of the South had come down with Whitney's Disease. The able Yankee's fateful gadget had given upland cotton a brilliant future, and for oblique reasons the South preferred to exploit it when possible on large plantations worked by gangs of slaves. That greatly narrowed opportunity for white men committed to work with their hands. In the South Negroes, usually slaves, did most of what the Irish did in the North. Many Germans showed no categorical objection to settling where slavery was legal; else Baltimore, New Orleans, St. Louis and much farmland in Texas and Missouri would not have seen so much of them. But apparently it looked to them as if cotton (and rice and sugar) and free men did not mix.*

* In his recent *American Immigration* (Chicago, University of Chicago Press, 1960, 188), Maldwyn Allen Jones says that the failure of the South's efforts to attract immigrants after the Civil War means that slavery had little to do with lack of them there before the war, that the real reason was not slavery but "lack of free land and—until the twentieth century—of large-scale industry." That may have something in it as of 1860. By then the South had little worthwhile land free in the sense of being available at costs immigrants could contemplate, and few cities

Actually in those days when only plow, hoe and mule were needed to make a crop, gang culture of cotton was not essential. (Today the efficient cotton grower's tractors, mechanical pickers and weed burners require large operations to justify heavy investment.) Before as well as after 1863 many small-holding Southern farmers raised cotton as a cash crop with the help of only a few Negroes on what Huckleberry Finn called "one of those little one-horse cotton plantations and they all look alike. A rail-fence round a two-acre yard . . . big double loghouse for the white folks . . . round-log kitchen . . . three little log nigger-cabins in a row t'other side the smoke-house . . . then the cotton-fields begin, and after the fields the woods." At certain times the owner might work alongside his slaves. In some instances the labor was all white—his own folks, for only a minority of Southern families had slaves. Such family farms, making a few bales a year, were a substantial part of the cotton plague that spread westward through Alabama and Mississippi and then crossed the Big River into Texas and Arkansas.

The Dixie* type of operation with gang slave labor was no more necessary to King Cotton than to Queen Corn in the Old Northwest. It prevailed only because past involvement with rice and (to some extent) sugar, both of which required wide acres and many hands, had suggested to Dixie's Quality and would-be Quality that cotton, too, demanded that method. They were readily persuaded because many acres, many slaves and the associated lavishly genteel way of life best glorified the planter in his own and others' eyes. When Kentucky-born Jefferson Davis, as yet no aristocrat, went into cotton on virgin land in Mississippi, he began with wide holdings and numerous slaves to clear and plant, as his already prospering brother Joseph had done before him. N. B. Forrest, another strive-and-succeed Southerner on whom fate had an eye, did the

sizable enough to offer the kinds of work that, in the North, gave livelihood to immigrants who did not have settling on the land in mind. But in the 1820's, say, little of that obtained. The North's industries were relatively small. The canal boom was only begun, the railroad boom was still to begin. There was free land in much of the over-the-mountains South, as well as in the Old Northwest. Yet the bulk of a fairly sizable immigration landing from Baltimore northward stayed north of the Ohio River-Mason and Dixon Line. Most of the Germans landing in New Orleans went to the trouble and expense of going hundreds of miles upriver to settle in Missouri—a slave state but well out from under the shadow of the big-plantation crops; that is, rice, sugar and cotton. The cultural repercussions of slavery, particularly the big-plantation type, did not vanish immediately after emancipation, as Jones' position assumes. And it was probably they, rather than the legal fact of slavery, that had made the Irish, Germans and Norwegians fight shy of the economy that made slavery look worst.

* Henceforward Dixie means the South that was tied emotionally and to some extent economically to large-plantation slavery, the South that insisted on the Civil War, the Deep South of today, or close to it. Up to 1820 and the ugly quarrels over the Missouri Compromise no such special label was necessary.

same. So did Thomas Dabney, FFV, leaving his exhausted ancestral holdings in Virginia to shift his force of slaves into the new world of cotton.

Thus extravagant acreage and slaves to match—the emotional logic may have been reversed—became Dixie's outward and visible sign of being somebody, even more significant than a Manhattan merchant's country place or the silver gorget, gift of a general or governor, worn by a whiskey-sodden Indian chief. To come of folks who had always held slaves was best. To come of folks owning many was acceptable. To have at least a few meant discernible standing. But to know one came of folks who never had any at all was wounding. The term *cotton snob*

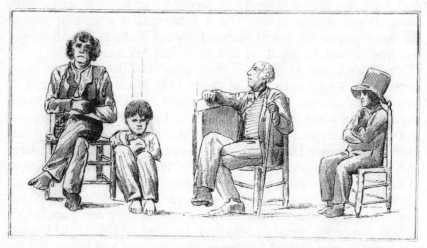

Several members of a backwoods family in Georgia
drawn by Captain Basil Hall, RN, c. 1830.

was applied only to the flashiest cases of sudden acres and slaves, not to Forrest or Scarlett O'Hara's father. It is distressingly likely that the slavery-perpetuating aspect of Whitney's Disease came of emotional, not economic values. For over the years cotton paid the large slave owner well only in a few special contexts—on newly opened land for a while or in the stubbornly fertile delta country of Mississippi. In most others soil depletion aided the sloppiness of gang labor in running things downhill. This emotional commitment to the large, many-slave operation is basic to understanding how slavery could so darken the Dixie organism, encapsulate the South, and widen the rift that Josiah Quincy, Jr., already sensed in 1774.

The fecklessness of the typical big cotton plantation did not imply, however, that slavery might not pay in other uses. Virginia's coal and iron mines depended heavily on slaves; so did her mechanized manufacture of chewing tobacco and the sizable Tredegar Iron Works in Richmond. On most large plantations the blacksmiths, carpenters and such who kept the place going were slaves of skill. Many a plantation owner boasted of a certain picked slave who ran the cotton gin or the sugar mill. His overseer probably relied on Negro drivers to get satisfactory work out of the hoe gang.

Such slaves' ability hints that Dixie's weak industry—even the steamboats vital to her economy were built on the free side of the Ohio—came less of the blight of slavery than of the Southerner's failure to see Negroes as anything other than field hands, plus sluggishness about exploiting the region's fuel and raw materials. Not until after the Civil War did Southern textile magnate Daniel Pratt—a Yankee born and bred but well adjusted to the South—set his son-in-law to creating Birmingham, Alabama, out of a previously neglected wealth of coal and iron. Suppose somebody had done so *before* the nation outlawed slavery. Suppose it had been found that slave labor did as well in the consequent new smelting and forging operations as it did at Tredegar—Dixie might have had a major industrial economy based on ownership of the employees as well as of the buildings and tools. This is by no means inconceivable. It worked in ancient Rome in simple manufacture. It would have brought actually to pass what Marx mistakenly thought capitalist industry would become—an economy affording its human tools just enough of the proceeds of their labor to keep them alive and working. Only the Southern system would have paid in kind—rations, shelter, clothes, brogans— not money.

A monstrous thought not improved by the consideration that Dixie's agricultural slavery was already monstrous enough. By definition the slave could never be well off in any context. Nobody in prison is ever well off. F. L. Olmsted, keen observer of slavery in the 1850's, as well as a great landscape architect, best epitomized the South's "peculiar institution" when likening the slave's situation to that of a convict at forced labor. He might have added that the sentence was the penalty for skin of the wrong color, almost invariably ran for life, and had begun the moment the plantation midwife slapped the congenital convict into uttering a protesting wail. Still there are prisons and prisons. This one had the unusual advantage that the convicts were of both sexes and unstinted in erotic privileges; indeed since natural increase made slaveholding more profitable, copulation ad lib was, other things being equal, in the owner's interest. The other good thing about American slavery was that on the whole it was not as brutal as that of the British and French West Indies of the 1700's; this may be why those colonies could never rely on natural increase but always had to import fresh slaves from Africa to make up the labor deficit. And Dixie's masters and mistresses were mostly better than abolitionists allowed—though not as kind as magnolia merchants have since represented—and in any case, since all penal systems show special strata, some slaves were a good deal better off than others.

The equivalent of the trusty, for instance, was Uncle Plato entering between the white columns with a mint julep for the colonel while an offstage chorus of field hands softly renders "Nobody Knows De Trouble Ah Seen." Compared to members of the hoe gang, the principal house servant had better clothes, usually handed down from Massa; maybe rather better quarters in the loft over the detached kitchen; and less arduous work, though it was also more exacting from sunup till Massa went to bed. His daughter Mandy, trained from childhood as maid for Ole Missus, slept on a pallet across the lady's bedroom door for instant availability. Plato's wife—kindly owners might have had them "married" by the local slave preacher, though marriage of slaves had no standing in law—was probably the cook, assuring him and their offspring a diet of leftovers superior to the field hand's ration of corn and fat pork supplemented by what fish and game he could come by and what vegetables he and his raised in a small allotted patch. Best of the slave trusty's privileges was that of contact with what Massa and Missus and their guests said and did. Parochial and ill informed, as all but Dixie's top Quality were likely to be, their frame of reference was stimulatingly wider than anything among the shacks of the slave quarter. When Massa had gone to the springs in his younger days and taken his young body servant with him, Plato had sharpened his wits on an even finer and more headily complex world of strange Quality and other slaves from far places, even cities.

Certain other convicts were on a sort of parole except that it did not contemplate preparation for freedom. Owning a slave did not oblige one to work him or her oneself. Say a husband left an estate including numerous slaves. His widow might sell the land and move to Savannah or Mobile, deriving income from hiring the slaves to others at so much a week as if they were livery-stable horses. The hirer took over lodging, food and clothing as if he owned the slave. Or if the estate included skilled specialist slaves, she could let them "hire their time"—ply their trade around town or up and down the countryside for as much as they could earn, paying Missus so much a month for the privilege. Workers in metals or wood, nurses, seamstresses, laundresses, stevedores, barbers, draymen, prostitutes . . . Those with a bent for buy-and-sell trade—a strong tradition among their West African women forebears—were street vendors with their wares on head trays. The streets of Charleston, South Carolina, were famous for the musical cries of such Negro hawkers, some free, some hiring their time, offering fish, fruit, pastries and such.

An ambitious slave with a kindly owner might himself suggest his hiring out with a view to saving enough to buy himself free. To amass the $1,200 to $1,500 that such a probably superior Negro might be worth, while also paying a stipulated $20 to $25 a month meant poor food and worse lodging; but the end in view made years of such struggle seem worthwhile. (The Spanish slaveholding colonies had a less exacting system. Slaves customarily got one free day a week, those who cared to work that day received money credit against eventual self-purchase.) Except that they could not change residence at will, these time-hirers behaved pretty much as if already free, joining with the growing number of free Negroes somehow earning a living in towns to form a subculture of their own with its churches, burial societies, Sunday afternoon strolls and visits. Particularly after a free Haitian Negro, Denmark Vesey, was hanged in Charleston, South Carolina, for an insurrectionary conspiracy, local authorities had recurring spasms of mistrust of these clusters of the socially despised under slipshod control—seldom more than lackadaisical patrols and a sort of curfew. There seems to have been surprisingly little need for such nervousness. In spite of zealous compilations of small, often apocryphal incidents hoping to make the American slave sound militantly restless, it is evident that he very seldom tried collective physical rebellion. Even after the flaming example set by the slave risings in the French West Indies in the 1790's—of which all town and many rural American slaves were certainly aware—the South saw only three substantial Negro risings: Vesey's; Gabriel's in the country outside Richmond, Virginia; and in 1831 the lurid flare-up in the Virginia Tidewater led by Nat Turner. The next thirty years saw no serious incidents at all.

Note also that Dixie's Negroes seldom left the land of slavery even when they were free to do so. Nothing prevented the free Negroes from going North; indeed, as the colonization movement had shown, the community would have been glad to see them go. The time hirers had unusual opportunities to arrange running away to freedom beyond the Ohio River-Mason and Dixon Line. Yet relatively few in either group took advantage of their situations. Such passivity hardly implies reconciliation to the inferior status that the South imposed on all labeled *Negro*—usually defined as anybody with a known dash of Negro ancestry, however light the skin, bond or free. The delights of knowing your place are largely the invention of the class at the top. That so many free or time-hiring Negroes, many doubtless people of unusual enterprise, stayed in Baltimore, Richmond and Charleston may have come of parochial ignorance and consequent uncertainty as to what awaited the black new-comer to the distant free states. It was even possible that, ironical as it may be, some had a born-and-raised-there fondness for the slack little cities that tolerated them, provided they stayed in line. In New Orleans, heavily marked by the West Indian three-caste system, certain light-skinned social organizations actually offered to fight on the Confederate side in 1861.

An understandable error of the abolitionists was to assume that the born slave or the Negro born free in a slavery-ridden culture necessarily felt about slavery as a born-free white would if suddenly enslaved. Hence John Brown's disastrous hope that the slaves near Harpers Ferry would take up the arms he offered them, as they distinctly did not. Even in parts of Dixie where slaves outnumbered whites and, as local white men went to the Civil War, their numerical advantage heightened, not a single slave rising occurred. Think what might have happened in Ireland under such circumstances! This lack of militancy cannot be glibly accounted for. It was not innate cowardice. Negro troops had already acquitted themselves well in the Revolution, would do so again in the Civil War, and have done so in every one of our wars since. Maybe the roots of it lay in the utter familiarity of slavery in the Southern Negro's universe. His African forebears had been both slaves and slaveholders and -traders, taking it all for granted. In the South before federal troops burst in, few Negroes aware that a world without slavery existed knew it vividly enough to struggle to bring it about for themselves.

Even the daily sight of free soil moved only a few to try their luck. For some 1,200 miles slavery and freedom faced each other across an unfenced boundary, much of it in wild country, or rivers that, though wide, were crossable on a log any dark summer night. Thousands of slaves lived in riverside farms, villages and towns on the slaveholding bank. Thanks to the shadowy volunteers of the Underground Railroad, odds of recapturing a slave on free soil were hearteningly low. Yet the number crossing was strangely small. Probably the most reliable data are those adduced by spokesmen for Dixie trying to stiffen fugitive slave laws, for while exaggeration would be a reproach to slavery, yet the problem had to sound substantial. Senator John A. Quitman of Mississippi, a rabid proslaveryite, put it no higher than loss of 100,000 slaves in the forty years from 1810 to 1850—an average of 2,500 a year. In 1860 a New Orleans newspaper lowered that to 1,500 a year. Splitting the difference gives 2,000—which agrees with an estimate made from other data by John Bach McMaster, the great historian. That is only one two-thousandth, say, .05 percent, of the South's slave population at the beginning of the Civil War.

No figure implying so much human hardship can be negligible. But had indignant unrest among slaves been widespread, that ratio would certainly have been much higher. Almost invariably they ran away by ones or twos. Their motives, as stated in 600-odd interviews with a Negro Underground Railroader in Philadelphia, were, in descending order: need to get away from a threat of being sold South as punishment or to settle an estate or debt; need to get away from an eccentric or cruel owner; generalized dislike of being a slave with no complaints about master or working conditions. That last and least category probably included the especially imaginative individuals goaded into acting by awareness that freedom lay just across the river or only a few score miles toward the North Star. Though it stirred so few into motion, that factor of proximity had weight. The great majority of runaways reaching the hands of Levi Coffin, wily Quaker "president" of the UGRR in eastern Indiana, came from less than 100 miles below the Ohio. Those helped by the Philadelphia division of the line came from no farther south of the Mason and Dixon Line.

None of the country they came from was the classic Dixie of gang-slavery plantations on which, other things being equal, slaves were treated even more stultifyingly than on family farms and in and near towns. In the Deep South too a notably harsh overseer might mean runaways. But the typical case was less a striking-out for freedom than a sort of truancy, the culprit sooner or later coming back for his whipping and the possibility of being sold off the place as a poor risk. This lack of enterprise probably reflected both the high stultification and the lack of the stimulus of being aware that free soil was nearby. Dixie's few serious runaways might hole up in a large swamp, of which the region had many, to eke out a savage living. If pursuit with dogs failed, one of them might hold out for years, even life, the situation on which Mrs. Stowe, attempting another well-meaning best seller to follow *Uncle Tom's Cabin,* based the prolix claptrap of *Dred: A Tale of the Great Dismal Swamp.*

Free Southern Negroes, time-hiring slaves, runaway slaves were small minorities in that descending order. The bulk of slaves lived the lives of anthropoid vegetables as the crews, unskilled, semiskilled and skilled, of the farming operations, large and small, of their owners, callous or conscientious. A cultivated Polish visitor to Mount Vernon in 1797 felt reverence and liking for its august proprietor, but his account of the slaves' lives reads curiously in view of Washington's high-mindedness and sincere dislike of slavery. The huts, he said, were "more miserable than the most miserable cottages of our peasants. The husband and wife sleep on a mean pallet, the children on the ground; a very bad fireplace, some utensils for cooking. . . . A very small garden with vegetables . . . with 5 or 6 hens, each one leading ten to fifteen chickens . . . the only comfort . . . permitted . . . they may not keep either ducks, geese or pigs. They sell the poultry in Alexandria, and procure themselves a few amenities." [47] Rations were a peck of corn a week per adult, half that per child, and twenty salt herring a month; at harvest time the field hands got some salt meat; clothes—a homespun jacket and pair of breeches yearly. This was a showplace. Whitney's Disease and the convict system were at their most characteristic on the typical cotton plantation of Dixie, say, 1,000 acres still mostly in woods but being gradually cleared for fresh fertility as the first-exploited acres wore out.

Maybe no Big House, for Massa lives on the white-columned Old Place in the next county, coming here to look around only every few weeks. In charge is the white overseer, sometimes a Northerner come South to acquire a stake of his own in this temptingly shiftless country. He works on salary plus bonus for every bale of cotton over a quota— which does not lead to squeamishness in the way he works the hands. He and his family (if he has one) live in a weatherboarded dwelling of no pretensions at the head of a double file of slave shacks on each side of a strip of bare mud or dust, depending on weather. House and shacks alike are on low stilts; under them children, dogs and hogs scuffle among odd refuse. Shack walls are of logs with neglected chinking or of planks from the nearby steam sawmill sun-warped so that cracks show between. Cracks also flaw the floors. During the few long cold months the wide-throated clay chimneys hardly begin to warm such rooms. In them dwell 100 or so slaves of both sexes and all ages; at a given time nobody, not even the overseer, is sure how many. The work force comes to some 40 hands, comprising 2 or 3 rough craftsmen and maybe 20 full hands (able-bodied field labor); 10 half hands (boys well enough grown for field work); and the other theoretical 10 filled in by strapping women hoe hands as strong as their men and quarter hands (larger children and the partially disabled still fit for cotton picking and light chores). Only the overseer can read in any proper sense of the word. But there may also be a woolly-pated slave patriarch who is allowed to preach on Sunday and can spell out some of the most familiar verses in the Bible that he treasures wrapped in a handkerchief on a rafter.

All above the age of ten work. The overseer seldom physically sets his hand to anything, of course, but as harried superintendent he is on the go all the time, usually in the saddle. The hands are turned to at sunup and work till sundown six days a week. Some owners think it well to give them Saturday afternoon for their own gardening, washing, mending, fishing and so on. Old women past useful age ride herd on the scampering huddle of everybody's small children. In the field their elders are sluggish but steady, perfunctorily compliant like convict labor the world over. In the growing season they plow, plant, hoe and pick cotton —or corn for basic rations. The rest of the year they dig ditches, clear new land, cut firewood, and, if there is nothing else to keep them safely busy, mend the deplorably rutted tracks locally called roads. Two Negro drivers, slaves themselves, carry long cowhide whips as badges

Two Negro slave drivers and a rifle-toting backwoodsman
as drawn by Captain Basil Hall, RN, c. 1830.

of office in the field. They are occasionally used to blister the back and shoulders of a delinquent, usually male, sometimes female, who gives way to a fit of the sulks. The hands are encouraged to sing at their work. It gets more out of them per day, and nobody minds if the words of the songs, set or improvised by some natural chorister among them, are sometimes disrespectful of white authority.

The nearest settlement—a store, a cotton gin, a gaunt Baptist church for whites, a few slatternly dwellings—is at a crossroads three miles away. A slave may visit it only with a written pass from the overseer to show when the "paterollers"—local whites taking turns as a police force associated with the militia—stop him for questioning. They are empowered to whip him on the spot if pass or answers are unsatisfactory. Otherwise he sees nothing of the outside world from birth to burial but the steamboat that sometimes comes coughing along the distant river but never puts in at the plantation because the near bank is swampy; cotton for shipment is hauled to the landing on firm ground beyond the settlement. Sex; superstitions watered down from African and European originals; a few Saturday nights of fiddling and dancing when the overseer permits; furtive talk in a slurry English of minimum vocabulary about the runaway known to be lurking in the swamp and how Big Henry kicked Sukey out of the cabin—those are about the only activities distinguishing them from the mules whose ears they sight through as they guide the plow.

Their situation compares unfavorably with that of the most woebegone village in West Africa, for normal human responsibility has been leached out of it. Since their transplanted forebears spoke so many mutually incomprehensible tongues, they have adopted the white man's as lingua franca and forgotten their own except for a few such surviving terms as *goober* (peanut). The original dislocation was drastic, and with Massa suspiciously discouraging religion, sabotaging marriage when it gets in the way, and frowning on interplantation contacts, a healthy new culture among the field hand category of slaves cannot get started. It was there on the big plantation that the numbing, warping, retarding convict system left the most damaging legacy not only to modern Dixie but to the black ghettos of today's North, clogged with the culturally crippled fresh up from away down South in the land of cotton.

Not all gang-worked plantations were quite so dehumanized. Housing might be better. In spite of misgivings and even laws against inculcating religion, some owners actually encouraged Christianity among their hands. Laws against teaching slaves to read and write—lest they write forged passes, communicate between plantations, and maybe even learn something of the free world—were also sporadically evaded. Yet a good many plantations, particularly in sugar and rice, probably sound worse than the above sketch. Everywhere overseers were deplored evils, probably deservedly so in spite of the owners' tendency to lay all the sins of slavery on overseers and take to themselves the credit for occasional decencies and kindnesses. Chances of tolerable owner-slave relations were better on the small cotton farms or on the middle-size to smallish diversified operations of the cotton-free Border States (Missouri, Kentucky, Maryland) which—and this is hardly accidental—never seceded. Everywhere, however, the owner's individual temperament was too important. Some of the most outrageous abuses of slaves that made burning ammunition for abolitionism occurred outside Dixie. In one respect closer relations between Negro and white on smaller farms and in town were worse because white men thus had wider opportunity to impose themselves with cynical grossness on Negro women.

That abuse appeared in all situations, of course. The overseer was seldom called to account (except maybe by a shrill wife) when a succession of nubile black girls in his charge bore saddle-colored babies. Randy white youths dwelling near a plantation thought the same girls fair game with no recourse but to lie down in the fence corner. Yet considerations of relative numbers and situations make it probable that fewer interracial couplings occurred thus than where the owner's sons reached puberty only a few yards from the slave quarters or where Massa daily encountered the handsome young laundress attached to the Big House. Semiformal keeping of crossbred mistresses was largely, though not completely, confined to the Gulf Coast. But unless Southern gentlewomen's privately recorded misgivings were fantastically exaggerated, most Southern men of all strata in slaveowning areas—the isolated mountain regions had very few Negroes—from Quality to white trash regarded Negro women as fair game with no rights. Some abolitionists held that the Southern man's liking for an institution that kept Negro women so accessible was a chief reason for the South's shrill defense of slavery. That probably makes no more sense than psychiatrists' suggestions that the South's resistance to desegregation comes of white jealousy of Negroes' alleged sexual prowess. But the accessibility was as real as it was discreditable to the white man.

His pleasure in it left an ineradicable monument in the light skin color of so many among what America still chooses to call her Negro caste. That is best realized by visiting West Africa and perceiving that one has never before seen a largely unadulterated Negro population. Practically all are as black as America's blackest.* A less striking, indeed ob-

* Most of this book had been drafted before the recent shift from "Negro" to "black" to designate Americans with discernibly West African genetic traits. Many Northern politicians and most of the communications industry have adopted the term. I have, of course, considered making the change throughout this book. Several reasons have deterred me. For instance, there is no reliable way to learn how acceptable the term "black" may be to the many million Americans most directly affected. It has been used contemptuously for centuries, particularly by the British. Then the change seems pointless as a matter of logic. "Negro" is simply Spanish-Portuguese for "black." Neither term accurately describes either the skin pigmentation or (if "Negro" is used as anthropologists sometimes use it) the genetic makeup of most of the Americans to whom it is applied. Either word could apply to the many Melanesians who are very distantly if at all related to the West Africans from whom American Negroes descend. So "black" is no improvement if intelligibility is the test. There is good reason to believe that the actual motivation, maybe often unconscious, of the current sponsors of "black," or the militant,

scure, corollary is the probably very high number of white Americans who, thanks to the ease with which light-skinned offspring of technically Negro parents can pass in a society as fluid as ours, have at least one Negro ancestor back three or four to a dozen generations. In 1955 I made a calculation based on minimum conceivable passings before 1805 which, after severe commonsense reduction, made it inescapable that that must hold good of 10,000,000 to 20,000,000 Americans now technically white. Analysis of the U.S. Census shows that thirty years ago at least 2,500 annual passings occurred, many presumably further contributing Negro genes to family lines. Odds that one is so endowed rise, of course, in direct proportion to the number of one's ancestors from the South.

The length of time one's ancestors have been American is also involved. All the genetic materials in me, for instance (assuming no lapses from virtue among my women forebears), are known to have been established in America before the Revolution; a sizable minority was Southern; none was Yankee. That makes it statistically very likely indeed that during those 200 years my family tree acquired not just one but several touches of the tarbrush. So from the racist point of view there are risks in being a WASP or what genealogy-minded ladies used to call Old American. A Polish-American, say, established for only a couple of generations in the relative insulation of the Polish enclave of Buffalo can be far more confident of lacking such admixture.

The effect of a forcibly submerged caste of racial convicts was not limited to genetics. Thomas Jefferson—an FFV witness reared in intimacy with slavery—told a correspondent in the 1780's: "The whole commerce between masters and slaves is a perpetual exercise of the most boisterous passions, the most unremitting despotism on the one part, and degrading submissions on the other . . . the child looks on . . . puts on the same airs in the circle of smaller slaves . . . and thus . . . duly exercised in tyranny, cannot but be stamped by it with odious peculiarities. The man must be a prodigy who can retain his manners and morals undepraved by such circumstances." [48] The point can be overstressed. Robert E. Lee and Jefferson Davis, otherwise different kinds

---

separatist-minded leaders among them, is to express alienation from all whites, even their most earnest well-wishers, instead of an effort toward higher accuracy of group-definition. Were I to make the shift in this book, I might well find within a year or two that a new token of alienation, maybe "Afro-American," had succeeded "black." In the mid-1950's, when I was working on *Goodbye to Uncle Tom*, "Negro" was recommended to me by Negro leaders as better than the gingerly, meaningless euphemism "colored." I shall continue to follow this advice.

of man, were among numerous prodigies who managed to combine slave-owning with decency. But Southern Quality often told foreign visitors between 1820 and 1861 of their persisting uneasiness about what slavery did to their own children.

Another social lesion came as the poor white's hatred of Negroes, created when his forebears wormed tobacco alongside new-landed Africans, widened to include the Quality, whose power was built on slavery and whose house slaves seldom hid their contempt for poverty in a white man. The poor white, mind, not the yeoman type of cotton farmer who could hope that his boys might rise to planterhood if the price of cotton stayed up and the cotton kingdom kept stretching westward. Few such hopes came to the hookworm-riddled, malaria-shaky, traditionally shiftless whites, living hand-to-mouth where nobody else would among the sandhills or up yonder in the knob country. The yeomen made up the backbone of the Confederate Army. One reason why they fought so devotedly was that they resented Yankees as "nigger-lovers" trying to undermine the system that sometimes made big slave-holders out of little ones. They were Dixie-minded secessionists like the North Carolina infantryman in tattered butternut who, Avery Craven tells, said to the man next him at the moment of surrender at Appomattox: "Well, damn me if I ever love another country!" [49] The poor white's byword was "This is a rich man's war and a poor man's fight," and his performance often consisted of resisting conscription by becoming an expert deserter. What kept the slavery-free hillmen of East Tennessee so lukewarm toward the Confederacy was probably as much sourness toward the Quality leaders of Dixie as love of the Union.

Jefferson's account of the vicious effects of slavery on whites could still end optimistically in the 1780's: "The spirit of the master is abating, that of the slave rising . . . his condition I hope preparing . . . for a total emancipation . . . with the consent of the masters, rather than by their extirpation." [50] He doubtless had in mind the strong antislavery feeling that he shared with most of his august Virginia contemporaries —the sort of thing that sired the Colonization movement and looked vaguely promising for another thirty years. During his last years, however, wishful minds, even in Virginia, were shaping what came to be known as the "positive good" theory of slavery in counterattack on its detractors. The early leader was an able casuist, Thomas Roderick Dew, precocious president of William and Mary. His disciples included many anxious about the health of King Cotton, not least those Virginians and Marylanders whose surplus slaves were sold to Dixie's planters. Some of the alleged positive goods about slavery were that it relieved the Negro from having to look after himself, for which he was unfit; that it freed white men from drudgery so they could pursue higher things; that it carried out God's will as shown in His condemning Noah's grandson Canaan (presumably black, though the Bible fails to say so) and his seed to slavery forever and ever. Yet antislavery sentiment remained strong in Virginia, notably in her less slave-committed half, west of the Blue Ridge. As a showdown with the positive good forces began in the 1830's, it was still conceivable that she would be the first state below the Mason and Dixon Line gradually to free slaves as had her Northern sisters, each in her own good time.

Then in August, 1831, Nat Turner, paranoid slave preacher and cunjer man, led his superstition-fuddled followers to kill fifty-five whites of all sexes and ages in an aimless terrorizing of Southampton County in the southeastern corner of Virginia. The poor twisted creature could hardly have found a worse time to sharpen Southern fears of slave rising. For on the preceding New Year's Day William Lloyd Garrison, a young Yankee of smug good intentions and a genius for vituperation, had launched in Boston his presently famous abolitionist paper, *The Liberator*. Its early subscribers were mostly Northern free Negroes; at first even the antislavery segment of Northern white opinion paid it little attention. But copies of it had got into the South and convinced Southern editors that this newly inflammatory voice in the abolitionist press, which had often been severe but nothing like Garrison in full scream, was meant to stir up the slaves. After August many such editors, being as irresponsible and almost as shrill as Garrison, shouted that Nat Turner's rising was the first fruit of such Yankee incendiarism. It was highly unlikely. There is no reason to believe that Turner or any of his disciples ever saw the paper. But slaveholders were in no mood for common sense. Their anger against what they took to be Northern criminal irresponsibility flared up at the right time for what was coming to be known as the Slave Power—meaning the exact opposite of power for the slave, of course.

It is sadly probable that this accidental conjunction of Garrison and Turner made the difference when, that touch-and-go winter, the Virginia legislature voted down by a narrow margin a bill for gradual extinction of slavery. The vote was significantly solid Aye west of the Blue Ridge; almost solid No east of it. Agitation for gradual slave freeing did not completely cease. Stirrings surfaced in the southern Ohio Basin into the 1850's. But the antislavery momentum that the Missouri Compromise of 1820 had merely checked was now reversed in the South. Henceforth the issue was dead in Dixie. Whatever the private regrets of Colonel X of South Carolina or Senator Y of Arkansas, for purposes of public discussion slavery had utterly become a sacred cow, and the star of positive good kept rising. The local antislavery societies, once so numerous in the South, shriveled like plants when the climate changes. Southern abolitionists such as James G. Birney of Kentucky and Alabama had to shift across the Ohio or keep silent. The militant statesmanship that soon brought Texas into the Union at the cost of war with Mexico was born of this newly aggressive proslaveryism aware of the high suitability of eastern Texas for cotton culture. That adventure worked out so well, presently adding the whole Southwest to America, that positive good, drunk on Manifest Destiny, began to covet Cuba and Central America. The filibustering parties concerned were usually based on New Orleans and led and financed by Southerners hoping to expand the scope of the American slavery system. The same blend of crass freebooting with picturesqueness clung to the plans of Dixie's hotheads, notably C. A. L. Lamar of Georgia, close relative of a founding father of Texas, to revive the overseas slave trade in the 1850's. One of Lamar's ships was the yacht *Wanderer*, pride of the New York Yacht Club's squadron, still under the club burgee in the early part of her first slave-smuggling voyage.

For the South—maybe to distract herself from the grisly reality of her situation—was fond of decorating her penitentiary culture with romantic flummery. Ever since publication of Scott's early romances her editors and orators often called their readers and hearers Southrons. This late medieval Scotticism distinguishing Scots from Englishmen was felt somehow to clarify the difference between Dixie's chivalrous Quality, spiritual kinsmen of Roderick Dhu and Ivanhoe, and the note-shaving, psalm-singing, milk-and-watery hypocrites of the North. With calamitous results on history Scott's writings were probably even more popular among literate Southerners than anywhere else in the world. Mark Twain called attention in 1883 to Scott's having run Southerners "mad, a couple of generations ago . . . [with] . . . his grotesque 'chivalry' doings and romantic juvenilities." [51] W. F. Guess' recent wryly affectionate book about South Carolina cites the complaint of a local statesman of the 1830's about his grandson's spending all his time either in outdoor sport or reading the *Waverly* novels. The editor of the Richmond, Virginia, *Examiner,* protesting against the mildness with which Lee's cavalry treated Chambersburg, Pennsylvania, in 1863, advised the South "to abandon those polite notions of war which she got from the Waverly Novels." [52] By the 1850's Northerners were jeeringly referring to the Southern Quality as the Chivalry. It was pertinent enough. When a Virginian doctor founded a secret order of amateur conspirators to bring northern Mexico into the orbit of American slavery, he called it the Knights of the Golden Circle; its branches were to be castles; and the Golden Circle was the rim of the Gulf of Mexico-Caribbean Basin that these midget megalomaniacs hoped eventually to take over. The plume in the hat of General J. E. B. Stuart, the Confederacy's most conspicuous cavalry leader, was—and was intended to be—as potent a symbol as the white plume of Navarre.

The knights motif was not confined to the South. Scott was read throughout the nation and widely imitated by the sham medievalism of hack writers in cheap story papers. A new mutual benefit lodge or labor union was like as not to call itself the Knights of This or That. But only in the South did self-dubbed knights actually saddle up and play chivalry in "tournaments" that spread from Maryland into the Carolinas and Kentucky in the 1840's and became embedded in local folkways. The contestants were not quite prepared for genuine medieval tourney-ing involving men in full armor charging one another on horseback with heavy spears and then trying earnestly to disable one another with broad-swords. But they did revive the medieval "riding at the ring"—spearing bracelet-size rings with one's mount at a dead run, which calls for fine horsemanship and a steady hand. Costumed in bright silks, the young bloods of the vicinity on their best mounts entered as Knight of the Ever-glades, Knight of the Black Lance, Knight of the Rappahannock, Knight of Hiawatha or some other such vapid conceit. The one with the luck and skill to carry off most rings was privileged to crown his best girl, hopefully dressed in fluffy elegance, Queen of Love and Beauty. As a youth on the family farm in Maryland, John Wilkes Booth spent much time with horse and lance practicing for such derring-do. The Chesa-peake Bay states staged such a tournament at the Philadelphia Centennial in 1876. The Philadelphia *Times* noted that "the like of it had never been seen in Philadelphia before," [53] but it seems to have been well received; the Queen of Love and Beauty was a Miss Perkins of Bucking-ham County, Virginia. County fairs in Kentucky had tournaments, and they are still kept up as nostalgic tourist bait at Mount Solon in the Shen-andoah Valley.

Though they sound like Penrod and Sam, antebellum tournaments were not just young folks' frolics. They had overtones. President Dew —the pioneer of the positive good theory of slavery—presided over an early one at which Judge Beverley Tucker, eminent professor of law and champion of slavery and states' rights, supplied the knights' pre-contest instructions in blank verse. The outstanding contender in Vir-ginia's tournaments was Turner Ashby (alias Knight of the Black Prince), so superb a rider that, to give others a chance, he often competed with-out saddle or bridle—and won anyway. He died in the War Between the States but not before his plumed hat and prowess had made him a cavalry legend second only to Stuart. For all the pretentiousness of tournament and Southron, mind, these men with feathered headgear on craniums full of romantic yeast were as brave as any who ever forked a horse. The trouble was that their book-born, narcissistic values betrayed them into illusions about an aristocratic monopoly on devotion and courage. A chief reason for the South's disastrous readiness for war was a windy belief that one Southron could lick four Yankees. The sequel again demonstrated that it can be fatal—a mistake made by John Brown and Adolf Hitler—to believe one's own delusions to the point of acting on them—in this case babble about Cavaliers and mudsills of society, as Judge James Henry Hammond of South Carolina called Negroes, and about how Cotton Is King of the world economy, hence the world would never allow the South to lose a war.

The steady widening of the North-South split was not a walling off. In some ways interregional economic ties and personal relations were closer than they had been in Colonial times. The shoes and cane knives issued to slaves on Louisiana sugar plantations came from New England. The cotton and hemp that New England made into calico and cordage came from the South; so did the molasses in Boston's baked beans. The corn and pork that fed the slaves of the Yazoo bottoms came downriver from the Old Northwest. As Dixie expanded westward, ambitious Northerners streamed South to seize the attendant opportunities. Some not only prospered but turned Southerners of a notably hell-snorting kind like John A. Quitman of Rhinebeck, New York, later of Natchez, Mississippi, Mexican war hero, flagrant filibuster and raucous Congressman. John Slidell of New York City became an eminent lawyer-politician in New Orleans, then a spokesman for Dixie and one of the Confederate diplomats whose seizure by the USS *San Jacinto* badly strained American relations with Britain early in the Civil War. David Bradford of Pennsylvania, a militia general who preferred to leave home after the Whiskey Rebellion failed, flourished in Louisiana as his Big House, The Myrtles near St. Francisville, still stands to demonstrate. The same point is made by the mansion that General-to-be Albert Pike, Boston-born lawyer and friend of the right people, built outside Little Rock, Arkansas, with white columns 35 feet tall. One of the few prejudices that Dixie lacked was that against outsiders helping maintain the hegemony of King Cotton and his concomitant Slave Power. Those were carpetbaggers on the right side.

When Mrs. Stowe sent Miss Ophelia, the Yankee martinet spinster, to her cousins in New Orleans, the slaveholding, soft-living St. Clares, she hit on a real and not unimportant thing—the often close family connections between North and South. The Butlers of Philadelphia had large rice interests in the Sea Islands and consequent close ties with Georgia and South Carolina. S. F. B. Morse's parson father made most of his career and all his reputation as geographer in New England but had Quality relatives in South Carolina very useful to his artist son when he went there on a portrait-painting foray. The family trees of many Northeastern Quality names—Roosevelt, Astor, Brevoort—show charming Southern girls, typically from Virginia or South Carolina, embarking on interregional unions as in Colonial times. Such marriages often originated in summertime at the ever more elaborate Northern watering places, such as Saratoga, whither, when cotton was high, Colonel Bighouse might take the girls and their mother as a change from the same old annual stay at the springs in the Virginia hills.

The nuptials of Sally Bighouse and Roger Brownstone of the Stuyvesant Square Brownstones were useful ballast for the storm-tossed

The promenade veranda of a great resort hotel of the 1830's.

Union since both families swung weight in their respective contexts. The effect paralleled the countenance that was given to anti-abolitionist riots by merchants of Boston and Cincinnati whose close business relations with Dixie made them solicitous of the welfare of the Slave Power. But trouble, as well as interregional solidarity, could come of personal relations. The colonel naturally fetched along to Northern spas his own slave body servant and a slave maid for the ladies. Just as naturally he was vexed when abolitionists encountered en route tried to persuade Plato and Mandy to strike for freedom now that they were on free soil.

Every time the guests at fashionable Congress Hall glimpsed Plato on an errand for the colonel, it reminded them that this genial gentleman had virtual life-or-death power over some hundreds of fellow human beings—just as that woman's book described—else he couldn't afford Saratoga.

His son, Roderick Dhu Bighouse, sat a horse splendidly and had charming manners when calm but was more quarrelsome among his male peers than was usual in Philadelphia or Hartford, and the knife in his inside breast pocket—no great "Arkansas toothpick" of course, but a neat dirk with a jeweled handle more suitable for social occasions—caused comment. The extent to which Southerners carried lethal weapons, pistols sometimes, but mostly fighting-style knives, as habitually as cravats or small change—in court, in legislative chambers, in their offices, in barrooms, wherever they might meet anybody in a disputative frame of mind—deserves notice as showing the emotional disparities between North and South c. 1850. In few other parts of the Western world in 1860 could it have happened that the Reverend J. H. Ingraham, minister of Holly Springs, Mississippi, author of an early religious-historical novel of high repute, *The Prince of the House of David,* could die of a gunshot wound from accidental explosion of the pistol in the pocket of the coat he was taking off in his own vestry.

The differences in way of talking were also pervasive and hard to blot out of consciousness. One has the impression, however, that the divergence has widened since Sally Wister noted the blurred *r*'s in the Maryland captain's pretty speeches. A Southerner at the University of Virginia could distinguish among the Charlestonian accent, the up-country South Carolina accent, the Alabaman accent. Vestiges of those variations are lively now. But to those reared north of the latitude of Philadelphia, whether the speaker comes from Tallahassee or Memphis, there is an identifying rough kinship of missing *r*'s, skewed vowels and a lyrical spacing of syllables, usually slow but characteristic even when hurried, as striking to the ear as a black skin to the eye. Differences in vocabulary also existed, but too few to matter.

It is not clear to what extent the Negroes' groping toward their owners' language underlay this general style of speech. In 1774 Bermuda-reared St. George Tucker observed with pain that the Quality ladies of South Carolina talked like Negroes. Presently Lady Nugent, wife of the governor of Jamaica, said the same of the planters' ladies coming to Government House. The curious and confusing thing is, however, that the speech of British West Indian Negroes differs widely from that of their American kinsmen. British West Indian slaves came from the same parts of Africa as did those of the mainland Colonies, and the emigrant forebears of the

British West Indian whites from the same strata of British society as those of the Southern Colonial whites. Yet for reasons so far inscrutable, the same ethnic backgrounds and mixtures produced markedly different talk. It can only be said that some Negro contribution to the generalized Southern accent—an entity that does exist in spite of local variations—must be assumed, else the boundaries of its use would not so nearly coincide with those of quondam slavery.

Moreau de St.-Méry, the often captious French colonial, liked the version of it that he found in Norfolk, Virginia, in the 1790's: "[Virginian] women have the sweetest of voices; . . . the English language, ordinarily far from sweet, becomes something quite different on their seductive lips." [54] When not too nasal, such speech in a woman's voice is still an ornament of American life. From a man beyond his twenties, however, it sounds somewhat babyish to non-Southern ears, which is necessarily alienating. Take it for granted that it heightened the sense of mutual foreignness as the drawling Tennessee slaveowner chatted on the veranda of the Saratoga hotel with the textile magnate from Holyoke, Massachusetts, who said "idear" through his nose and believed in free schooling for the children of the low-paid spinners and weavers in his mills.

Between them they represented the two most self-satisfied subcultures in America. Their differences lay not in degree of smugness but, for one thing, in the Yankee's being inquisitive as well as acquisitive, versatile as well as opportunistic. Where the South of 1850 could muster, say, two great technical innovators—Matthew F. Maury, creator of modern oceanography, and Cyrus H. McCormick, finally doing well with his reaping machine, both Virginians—New England and New York State could show a dozen. Whereas the Virginians of the late 1700's had shown their embryonic nation the way in political innovation, Virginian leaders of the 1850's did little but concoct increasingly absurd defenses of slavery. Such contrasts made it difficult then—as also in the 1930's, when the Southern Agrarians revived the attitude—to accept the Southerner's arrogation of virtue to his way of life, or rather to the way of life that parochialism and Scott had led him to believe he led. The point was made by Broadus Mitchell, a Southern scholar, with a harshness that no Yankee could have dared in decrying the nostalgic Southerner's belief that, however the Old South lacked literacy, economic skills and so on, it had to be admitted that "we developed culture. . . . If we did," Mitchell wrote, "it was so elusive that the observer today cannot find it. It did not take form in music, poetry, prose, buildings, works of engineering, jurisprudence, science or theology, let alone the infinitely more difficult matter of decent human comfort and independence for the average man. A staple agriculture with slave labor gave us only exploitation—cunning, suave, inveterate . . . every principle gave way before the support of this interest; every contrivance was at its service." [55]

The contrasts between the Southerner's soft voice and the revolver in his pocket, between his silky deference to ladies and his habits with Negro wenches, were most damagingly used by the abolitionism that had soon become rather more anti-Southern than it was pro-slave. George Templeton Strong showed the consequences in his diary in 1856: "We at the North are a busy money-making democracy, comparatively law-abiding and peace-loving, with the faults (among others) attributable to traders and workers. A rich Southern aristocrat who happens to be of fine nature . . . strikes us . . . as something different . . . more ornamental and in some respects better. He has the polish of a highly civilized society, with the qualities that belong to a ruler of serfs. Thus a notion has got footing here [i.e., New York City] that 'Southern gentlemen' are a high-bred chivalric aristocracy. . . . I believe they are, in fact, a race of lazy, ignorant, coarse, sensual, swaggering, sordid, beggarly barbarians, bullying white men and breeding little niggers for sale." [56] A good many Northerners had come around to that way of thinking, partly through observation of the Bighouse family, partly through propaganda. R. L. Duffus saw in this a significant aspect of the Civil War: "Vermonters . . . did not like to be trifled with by the arrogant and overweening. . . . I think this, rather than any abstract doctrine [was] responsible for the massive ferocity with which the male Vermonters of the 1860's, not one of whom ever had to be drafted, rose to help Mr. Lincoln put the slave owners of the South in their places." [57]

Mark Twain's scorn of the South's pseudochivalry extended to her sham-medieval buildings such as the battlemented State Capitol of Louisiana at Baton Rouge. That was unjust. In the mid-1800's the North was guiltier than the South of romantic fakery in bricks, mortar and millwork. North or South, all this followed from the archaic-mindedness that already had banks looking like pagan temples. Inevitably it went beyond the Greco-Roman world into other Old World architectures—or at least their cliché-details. Soon genuine medieval houses built by Puritans of the 1600's were left to decay in New England's seaports while American architects emulated medieval crenellations and pointed windows in designing new buildings public and private. Nathaniel Hawthorne innocently summed up this attitude describing "my native place" as "covered chiefly with wooden houses, few or none of which pretend to architectural beauty." [58] His native place was Salem, Massachusetts, then even more glorious than now with masterpieces of New England Georgian and dwellings contemporary with the House of the Seven Gables. Or hear James Fenimore Cooper, a traveled man of Quality and literary reputation in 1852, about "the want of ancient edifices in America. Two centuries and a half ago are no very remote antiquity; but we should regard buildings of . . . a much less age, with greater interest did the country possess them. But nothing was constructed a century ago [say, before 1750] . . . worth preserving on account of its intrinsic merits." [59] Writing when he did, Cooper was careless of the hundreds of seventeenth-century buildings now so religiously and commendably preserved in a fiercely antique-minded America that would consider his point of view barbaric.

Americans were not primarily responsible for the imitative eclecticism that ruled their buildings for the next few generations. Here, as often before and after, they followed the lead of Britain and Northern Europe —collectively the cradle and stronghold of the backward-yearning romanticism of Scott and Hugo. But America succumbed eagerly to this transatlantic fashion for English pinnacled towers, Italian belvederes and Swiss balconies—generally what a clever tongue, which I wish I could properly identify, summed up as "the pointed ironic" style. Our new nation may have especially craved archaic spires, turrets and mullions because it had been settled too late to show a proper complement of castles, minsters and fortified manor houses. And fashion was stern. Only twenty-eight years after Bulfinch's Boston State House was completed, Alexander Jackson Davis,* a keen young architectural draftsman fated to be a great prophet of eclectic building, called it "by no means remarkable for its beauty," merely "distinguished by its character and location." [60]

Overlapping the Greek-minded second phase of the Classic Revival was a minor burst of Egyptianism. The occasion was gradual publication over two decades of descriptions of ancient Eygpt made by archeologists attached to Napoleon's foray into Egypt from 1798 to 1800 and the ensuing travel to and popular books and lectures about the mysterious Land of the Nile. Hence those Egyptian place-names—Memphis, Cairo, Luxor, Thebes and Karnak—still on the map of America.

For a wonder the only effect on dwellings was occasional use of lotus-bud or papyrus capitals on the skinny columns of the portico. But the massiveness of the pharaohs' taste in design was thought suited to public structures of austere purpose such as prisons, libraries, court-

* Not to be confused with the previously mentioned Andrew Jackson Downing; this was Ithiel Town's protégé and early partner. To make things even more confusing, there was also Andrew Jackson Davis, a spiritualist conspicuous at the time.

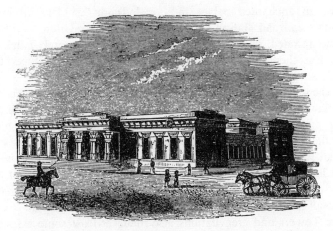

New York City's "The Tombs" prison was most frowningly Egyptian.

houses. Ithiel Town put an Egyptian tollgate on a bridge on the National Road. The blocky grimness of the Egyptianate gate of Mount Auburn Cemetery in Cambridge, Massachusetts, set a lively fashion. So did the lotus-columned portico and inslanting walls of New York City's Hall of Justice and House of Detention—a conscientious name for a combined courthouse and jail that popular usage immediately dubbed "The Tombs," described by Dickens as a "dismal-fronted pile of bastard Egyp-

So (one with a Baroquelike wiggle) were a number of the tombs in the cemeteries of the day.

tian, like an enchanted palace in a melodrama." [61] The inside of an Egyptianate railroad station or lodge hall had no relation to the palace or temple imitated, of course. The desired style was merely stuck on the outside. But there was ample precedent for that in the superficialities of the Classic Revival—and the Parthenon.

Just then American innovations in penology and consequently in prison planning were attracting worldwide notice. Liberal though the underlying purpose was, the resulting buildings often imitated medieval castles, their battlemented silhouettes dressing up the outskirts of town with what looked like the backdrop for a dramatization of *Ivanhoe*. This was not impractical. The same architectural features once meant to keep enemies out—high walls of massive masonry, elaborately barred gateways, small windows far aboveground—also served nicely to keep prisoners in. Towers and crenellations also made at least some associational sense for military schools (West Point, The Citadel at Charleston, South Carolina), police stations, arsenals and armories for militia, but very little when applied, as they also were, to girls' schools, libraries and country mansions. Such objections miss the point, however. Nobody was trying to make sense of any kind. Those frowning keeps—like as not built of wood—were just another symptom of the cult of archaic building styles already so strong on the other side of the Atlantic.

The spurious Gothic gaining prestige in England in the late 1700's had not crossed the ocean until after Waterloo. Then, however, new American churches followed the look, if not the engineering, of English Gothic because that was the picturesque, hence fashionable, way to build a house of worship. The style of the new Trinity Church at the head of Wall Street designed by an expatriate English architect suited the needs of Episcopalian ritual—not those of a good many other sects, but they built Gothic anyway. The busy complications of the gigantic Cathedral of Milan came to rival English Gothic as the model for small Calvinist churches in brand-new towns with Red Indian names. Since construction in wood cost 30 to 40 percent less than the same design in stone, wood began to imitate Gothic details as blithely as it had those of the Greek Revival. A Gothic wooden church near my home has hollow tower buttresses faked up in horizontal clapboarding. Even after a century of fires and demolitions most sizable American towns retain specimens of carpenter-Gothic dwellings with carved bargeboards under the eaves of steep gables and perpendicular sheathing giving a high-pockets look. At White Sulphur Springs, Virginia's ranking spa, the 1830's saw a row of story-and-a-half Gothic cottages rise to face the previous row of Greek Revival cottages across the lawn.

Secular buildings—banks, warehouses, railroad stations—began to

*The Erie & Kalamazoo Railroad, first to be built in Michigan,
had an elegant passenger car of Gothic design. Each of its three
compartments carried eight passengers.*

show pointed tops on window frames, sharply peaked gables and crock-
eted pinnacles. In wood or stone the fashion imposed itself on everything—on Oak Hall, Boston's first large men's ready-to-wear store of the
1840's, all battlements and pointed arches; on a now-elderly covered

*Architect Gervase Wheeler's elegant version
of the Carpenter Gothic cottage.*

bridge in New Hampshire with a Gothic ogival arch over the footway; on a story-and-a-half passenger car built for an early railroad in Michigan. A new Gothic bookcase among objects abandoned was found along the trail to California in 1849 by a party of forty-niners who broke it up for fuel to boil the coffeepot with.

Today people trick out surviving "Carpenter Gothic" cottages in nursery-bright colors, white or yellow with green or scarlet trim, which give a deceptively cheery effect. It would have distressed the architects of 1840. They deplored the white paint dear to Greek Revival as glaring in sunshine and too prominent in a landscape: ". . . all positive colors, such as white, yellow, red, blue, black, should always be avoided," was the law laid down by Andrew Jackson Downing, eminent creator of elaborate country places for the wealthy; instead, use "Fawn, grey, drab, brown" [62] with the trim in a darker version of same and the shutters darker still. That would have depressed us, but Downing and his compeers thought it properly picturesque. "Effective building of a country house wants a picture-maker as much as an architect," [63] advised Donald Mitchell (Ik Marvel) in his widely influential *Rural Studies*. This attitude made some uneasy. Theodore Winthrop, a peevish but promising novelist killed early in the Civil War, said of New York University's Gothic building on Washington Square that by daylight it was "so unreal and incongruous, that I should not have been surprised to see a squad of scene-shifters at work sliding it off and rolling it up. . . ." [64] But the architects', and apparently the clients', ideal remained just that—the stage set—and they were almost eager to arrange for materials to masquerade as something else. A great Gothic country house designed by Alexander Jackson Davis in 1834 to overlook the Hudson above Tarrytown called for "stone or brick, stuccoed in imitation of stone . . . the bay windows . . . of wood, painted and dusted with pulverized marble or grained in imitation of oak. . . . The battlements and gable . . . of wood, painted to match the stone. . . ." [65]

The cult of the picturesque explains the vogue not only of the Gothic but also of the Swiss chalet, a type of dwelling much on the Western world's mind then because the Swiss tourist business was having its first great boom. It was conceded that the Swiss custom of housing the livestock in the lower story and the human beings in one end of the upper one would never do in America. But the prototype chalets, which Mark Twain so admired in Switzerland, were built of wood throughout, which prevented the anomaly of imitating stone construction in wood, and it certainly made for picturesqueness to borrow those wide gables, broad eaves, multiple balconies and exterior stairs all gimcracked up with quaint carving till the architect's rendering for the client looked like

*The pseudo-Gothic dominated the college campus long before
the building of the Harkness Quadrangle.*

the cuckoo clock that Uncle Elihu brought home from his trip abroad.
Unfortunately Swiss practice was to leave the wood unpainted—"red-
dish brown in tint, a very pleasing color," [66] Mark Twain said—
or merely stained, which encouraged the fashionable somberness. And
the relative smallness of windows in both the Gothic and the Swiss

*A Carpenter Gothic church and a Classic Revival city hall
in upstate New York in the 1830's.*

*In Antrim, New Hampshire, a still extant mansion almost succeeds
in combining Classic Revival, Gothic and Mansard-French.*

idioms combined with the taste for dark walls and carpets to create interior gloom that not even occasional bay windows could relieve.

In such respects America did better with a third imported style—the Italian villa. "People had always been told that the house . . . was an Italian villa," says Edith Wharton's *The Age of Innocence.* "Those who had never been to Italy believed it; so did some who had." [67] After the American architect had modified the British architect's modification of the tall Italian country house, about all that remained was wide eaves, emphasis on window-frame moldings, maybe an emphatic gable over the principal door, often a grandiloquent square tower high above the main block. Baroque-curly brackets apparently supporting the eaves were almost invariable. In larger specimens a porte cochere might help tie the lofty mass to the ground. In the flush times of the early 1850's this was the house that the banker built after making his pile, and it was no bad money's worth. Massive walls, high ceilings and central stairwell meant coolness in summer; sometimes vertical ducts and vents circulated cool air from the cellar into the rooms. Tall windows lighted the rooms graciously. The slim-pillared loggia that often informalized the façade contributed to the evolution of that American institution, the front porch. In this context it was called a veranda, sometimes a piazza (as in Herman Melville's *Piazza Tales*), a use of the term that doubtless puzzled Italians but did not keep the thing itself from being a fine place to sit on summer evenings and watch the fireflies, provided too many mosquitoes did not come with them. An elaborate Italianate

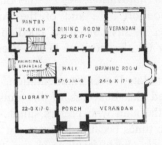

PLAN OF PRINCIPAL FLOOR   PLAN OF PRINCIPAL FLOOR

Twin Italianate villas designed for the American carriage trade by Calvert Vaux, English-trained but practicing in America and colleague of F. L. Olmsted in designing New York City's Central Park.

villa might have two or three piazzas and some second-story balconies to match. At the same time many an older house of Georgian blockiness was having a pillared one-story porch built all the way across the front or at one side.

Wood soon seduced the Italianate villa, too. Its adaptability being so much higher than that of brick or stone, it tempted designers into breaking up the cube into an asymmetry charming when the proportions were judicious and at least striking when they were not and going extravagant with balconies and pinnacles owing much to the Swiss influence. Curious as the effect sometimes was outside, such elaboration allowed something close to design from the inside, the shapes and relations of rooms determined not by considerations of exterior symmetry but by those of the needs of the family. The result was some of the most habitable dwellings yet seen in America. European observers of later times noted this flexibility as a stimulating American innovation: ". . . the outgrowth of both the [American] urge for comfort . . . and of the American tendency to tackle problems directly," [68] says Siegfried Giedion, pointing out that it made straight the way for the work of H. H. Richardson and Frank Lloyd Wright.

The disadvantage was that it stimulated overornamentation, already too lively a trend. Downing defended this busyness of the outsides of houses by a toplofty comparison of the man who prefers simple-looking houses to the man who prefers simple tunes because he wots not of symphonic music. Withindoors the relatively chaste fashions in furniture and decoration crossing to America from the Regency and Empire traditions were, as the mid-1800's neared, encroached on by imitations of Jacobean and Rococo work. It was not yet the age of clutter, inside or out, but the seeds were sprouting. Philip Hone was aghast at William Paulding's new country mansion in Dutchess County "of white or gray marble, resembling a baronial castle . . . with towers, turrets, and trellises; minarets, mosaics, and mouseholes; archways, armories, and airholes; peaked windows and pinnacled roofs . . . the whole . . . an edifice of gigantic size with no room in it; great cost and little comfort. . . ." [69] Within a few years P. T. Barnum could find a reputable architect to build him in that exotic Oriental country called Shoreline Connecticut a great wooden wedding cake of a Persian palace complete with three onion-shaped domes. And the bracketed style—born of the Italianate villa's under-eaves pseudosupports, at its best when applied to high-cube houses with central cupola gazebos and many verandas— was taking the bit in its curlicued teeth and pointing the way to the General Grant-Queen Anne mode of the post-Civil War architectural debauch.

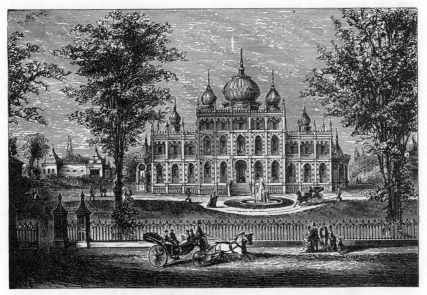

P. T. Barnum's pseudo-Oriental mansion, Iranistan,
was the sight of Bridgeport, Connecticut.

In Eastern cities clutter was temporarily forestalled when the Italianate was applied to row dwellings. Habitability was also lacking, however. Such construction with party walls on narrow lots meant too much of the available cubage devoted to stairs and corridors and confined windows to the narrow ends of the building, the rear ones looking out on well-like backyards. New York City's high stoops, in which some see vestiges of Dutch precaution against floods, also made for stuffily dark basement kitchens. The ranges of street windows were a miniature travesty of the Italian palaces inspiring the original designers. Repetition of such façades with only minor variations for block after block of new-built streets was depressing enough in the red brick used in Baltimore. In New York City and Boston the usual facing was brownstone—the reddish-brown sandstone that for no intelligible reason* became stylish in the mid-1800's and "coated New York like a cold chocolate sauce," [70] as Edith Wharton said. Frederick Van Wyck spoke feelingly of "those rows of gloomy dark houses so much alike that the streets

* Lewis Mumford (*Sticks and Stones,* 94-95, New York, Dover Publications, 1955) has suggested that brownstone was so widely used because its color minimized the grime from coal smoke in New York City. But New York then, as for many years later, used mostly anthracite, relatively smokeless coal.

426   THE AMERICANS

gave the impression of tunnels, and you were lucky if you could pick out your own doorway after dark." [71]

Business firms, too, took to brownstone with elaborate carving to express respectability and ample resources; but the street-front roof line, usually corniced and bracketed on private houses, often bloomed into a false pediment of Baroque intentions inscribed with the date of building and the firm name. We now think of the false front only in connection

A false front in a small town in Delaware as prototype of Wild West architecture.

with the TV-and-movie West, but the effete East had used it long before Bloody Gulch was ever built, as John Maass has pointed out. The oldest clear example that I know of is the imposing paneled parapet of a Greek Revival wooden bank building, thought to be the design of Ithiel Town in 1835, now preserved at Old Sturbridge, Massachusetts. A surviving drawing of Chicago's levee in 1833 shows on most of the frame-and-weatherboarding buildings the classic high, square mask rising above the second-story windows, proving that the Old Northwest knew all about false fronts. But then the device has an august history—something very like it was a favorite device of the Baroque architects of the 1600's for making an old church look fashionable.

The stuffy kitchens of New York City's brownstones were typically equipped with cast-iron cookstoves with smoke pipes leading into chimney flues. Long hinted at by the baking ovens attached to Pennsylvania

Dutch six-plate stoves, these newfangled improvements over the wood-burning fireplace had come in soon after the War of 1812—squattily ugly to begin with, more so as the founders tried rashly to ornament them. They concentrated heat where it would do the most good, under skillets and soup kettles instead of wasting so much up the chimney. Adjustable drafts gave the cook's judgment a new tool and got more cooking done per cubic foot of wood—a serious consideration as the forests shrank farther from town and growing cost of transportation kept the delivered cost of fuel rising. In 1850 enough firewood to cook one scanty meal cost poor folks in New York City a dime—and when a dollar was a day's wages.

Adaptation to coal soon made cookstoves more efficient still. Actually they were just one aspect of the revolution in the application of fire to human purposes that steamboats had begun in the new century. Here, for a change—as also in freedom of the press and the anti-Rum movement—America showed the Old World the way. The James cookstove, patented in Troy, New York, in 1815 was to be standard equipment for the next generation. And a few miles to westward a momentous series of heating stoves came of the inventiveness of the Reverend Dr. Eliphalet Nott, president of both Union College at Schenectady, New York, and Rensselaer Polytechnic Institute at Troy—a notable man whom we last met as son of the doughty Yankee housewife who sheared that sheep in midwinter. During his ninety-three versatile years he was also a noted theologian, an eloquent pleader against slavery, an influential friend of public schools—and a naïve crusader for temperance. In a day when students at Harvard still staved off dormitory chill with open fireplaces, Union's young gentlemen had Dr. Nott's stoves; wood supply was their own responsibility, which probably also helped keep them warm. Nott's patents on heating devices, particularly that on the first efficient base burner for anthracite coal, paid him well as their virtues gained popularity. Yet in some areas acceptance of stoves was as slow as that of the automobile would be after 1900. In the Boston of Edward Everett Hale's boyhood (say, through 1840) open-fire cooking remained the rule, and only schools and offices were likely to have heating stoves.

Much of that was probably old-foginess. The things were mixed blessings, however. "Redhot stoves in close rooms are among the abominations of the age," [72] said Horace Greeley's New York *Tribune* in 1860. "A chimney fireplace," an advice to housewives book said in 1857, "is preferable to a stove which is apt to give the air a close or disagreeable smell and produce headache. . . ." [73] Foreigners often complained bitterly. Not only Britons but young Salomon de Rothschild, well used to heating-stoves in Europe, found American winter air pure and invigorating, but "inside the house one [is] suffocated by hot-air stoves. . . ." [74] Yet in large, drafty rooms the complaint might run the other way. Howells shiveringly recalled the failure of two huge stoves, one on each side of the orchestra, to heat the theater in Columbus, Ohio —hard on the audience, even harder on the flimsily costumed performers —and the type froze solid in the water it was washed with in his father's stove-heated printshop. For all such drawbacks, stoves conquered fireplaces and in various shapes and sizes dominated cold-weather life everywhere—in steamboats, canalboats, coasters, railroad cars and stations, churches, country stores, where the smell of wet cowhide boots propped on the rail of the potbelly stove and the sizzle of tobacco juice on its roasting surface were standard phenomena.

Howells first met and admired central heating in the beautiful new Ohio State Capitol of the 1850's, but the notion was already twenty years along in the New World. By 1826 the Rappites, manifesting the heating-mindedness of the Teutonic American, were warming their workshops at Economy, Pennsylvania, by pipes from the steam engine. Presently a New York City theater and the public rooms of certain hotels in Boston and New York had primitive steam-heating arrangements. In the 1830's at least one private house—Shirley, a James River mansion—had wood-fired hot air welling up through handsome brass registers to the first floor. Among the hot-air-heated Quality of New York City in the 1840's, "the moment the ladies rose [from dinner] they went into the parlors and stood over the registers." [75] Such installations were crude and even more difficult than stoves to modulate. With reason the hygienic-minded pointed out that both stoves and basement furnaces deleteriously dehydrated the air in the rooms. The pan of water on the stove and the passing of furnace-heated air over water to restore humidity are devices as old as Morse's telegraph. But the hygienic-minded overreacted and ascribed to central heating (and sometimes stoves) all the ills that winter brings. Such unprepossessing temperatures as 60° F maintained by open fires were solemnly recommended. Downing implied that if builders only knew how to design chimneys that wouldn't smoke—they had only to read his books—stoves would tend to disappear and that passage of air through any but the best-designed furnace robbed it of oxygen and loaded it with poisonous by-products from cast iron. Catharine Beecher, a glib adviser to women, overimpressed by current knowledge of the role of oxygen in metabolism and the inadvisability of too much carbon dioxide, shrieked that "since the invention of air-tight stoves, thousands have died of slow poison"; that, on the authority of a French physician, "one of the results of unventilated rooms is scrofula"; and that if little Jimmy wakes up fractious in the morning, it is probably because, "having slept in a close box of a room" with the former fireplace sealed up, "his brain [has been] all night fed by poison, and he is in a mild state of moral insanity." [76]

In spite of such alarmists, central heating became a permanent American institution, and its abuse continues to cause grave dissension between men and women and unnecessary fattening of the national fuel bill. By heating rooms more evenly than fireplaces could, it and the stove also created another American institution—"the great table in the middle of the [sitting] room, with its books and work [waiting] only for the lighting of the evening lamp," [77] as Ik Marvel, laureate of American sentimentality, recalled it. Around that focus of light gathered the whole family, just as the lithographs and whole-family portraits show them—father reading the paper with a statesmanlike air; mother at her sewing; sister stitching at her work (meaning embroidery or tatting of ornamental intent); the younger children doing their lessons or playing a table game; the dog snoozing at father's feet; the cat playing with a stray spool of thread. In their grandfather's time the middle of the room would have been too chilly in winter, nor could grandfather's candles or dim lamp have served so many for close work. For lighting had improved almost as much as heating, particularly with the astral lamp that cut out downward shadows. The best light came from camphine, a mixture of alcohol and turpentine; but it was ungodly likely to explode, so until kerosene came in around 1860, hogs and whales continued reluctantly to oblige. The exacting chore of keeping the sitting-room lamp clean and its wick properly trimmed might exceed the skill of the hired help, so mother took it over herself. Its marked superiority had soon relegated candles of various degrees of costliness—wax, spermaceti (another product of the long-suffering whale), stinking tallow —to kitchens and occasional use in dining and bedroom.

Cost of installation seems to have slowed down acceptance of coal gas to light dwellings. Baltimore had given this English innovation its first American trial in 1819. Following decades put it to use in theaters, streetlighting, showy restaurants, hotel public rooms, but only sporadically in private houses. Indeed gas was firmly associated with goings-on more gaudy than godly. The phrase *the glare of gaslight* went with the cold bottle, the hot bird and the sinfulness of song and dance. Doubtless the explosiveness of the stuff and its lethal habits even without combustion also made it sound like an uncomfortable housemate. Our forebears were less used than we are to living intimately with things as wild as coal gas, gasoline and electricity. Readily as they took to cookstoves, the possibility of firing them with gas was little exploited until after the Civil War. And in any case this derivative of coal could develop only in step with the gradual, though steady, growth of coal mining as water and rail transport changed it from the local specialty of a few states to a chief pillar of the national economy.

Thanks to American wood-mindedness, *sluggish* might be the word rather than *gradual*. Britain had mined coal since medieval times. On the New World side of the water Nova Scotia exploited coal long before the Colonies did. The likelihood of "Good Coales" in Pennsylvania was known in 1698, when an immigrant Welshman noted that "The Runs of Water have the same Colour as that which proceeds from the Coal-Mines in Wales." [78] (Early settlers along the Ohio preferred relatively muddy river water to that from local springs "issuing through fissures in the hills, which are only masses of coal . . . so impregnated with bituminous and sulphureous particles as to be . . . nauseous . . . and prejudicial to the health." [79] Coal mining has increased but obviously did not originate this natural pollution.) Actually Virginia saw the first exploitation in the mid-1700's. Robert Beverley had mentioned Virginia's very good coal, but nobody bothered with it, he explained, because wood was so plentiful. Only after the mid-century was it economic to substitute it for charcoal in iron smelting. When the Revolution interrupted normal shipment of English and Nova Scotian coal to Northeastern ports, the handiness of Virginia's coal near tidewater on the James River encouraged shipping it by water to Philadelphia—a new market that persisted in a small way. By 1800 the nascent industries of Pittsburgh were smoking up the neighborhood with bituminous coal from local seams. But Pittsburgh housewives insisted that wood would always be a better cooking fuel. The product of Kentucky's first coal mines, boated down the Kentucky River to Frankfort, was used only by blacksmiths and—a strange bit of pampering—to warm the state penitentiary.

Eastern Pennsylvania's anthracite coal, rock-hard and difficult to kindle, was accepted even more slowly than bituminous was. During early efforts to market it, in fact, many refused to believe it would burn at all. Advertisements in Philadelphia in 1819 still had to challenge skeptics to come to the coalyard and see with their own eyes. The first anthracite mining in the mountains around Mauch Chunk, Pennsylvania, on the Lehigh River (a tributary of the Delaware) had hard sledding. Prospects brightened when the Royal Navy's harassment of coastal shipping in the War of 1812 shut Virginia's bituminous off from Philadelphia. As the end of the war revived that trade, the high cost of getting anthracite down the tricky Lehigh discouraged the future of peacock-tail coal, as it was called, from the iridescence of its fractures. But in 1817 a stubborn and ingenious Quaker, Josiah White, built horse railways to haul it from mine to riverbank and then reformed the Lehigh with "bear-trap" dams that raised the water level without obstructing barge movement.

Within a few years demand for anthracite was creating those equally ingenious canals, the Morris and the Delaware and Hudson, to connect the anthracite country with the New York and New England markets. Dr. Nott did his share by solving the problem of anthracite in heating stoves. All this not only made Pennsylvania doubly important in the industrial development of the new nation but also kept the cities of the Northeast relatively free of the acrid grime from bituminous coal that would soon foul up such Old Northwestern cities as Pittsburgh, Cincinnati and St. Louis. The relative smokelessness of anthracite was so marked that the Delaware, Lackawanna and Western Railroad, built to haul it to Buffalo and New York City, made a national figure of Phoebe Snow, an elegant, if mythical young lady who rode the Lackawanna in snow-white clothes with no fear of smudging because all the line's locomotives burned anthracite:

> When Phoebe Snow sets out to go
> From New York City to Buffalo,
>   She travels white,
>   Arrives clean and bright,
> On the Road of Anthracite.
>
> Her laundry bill for fluff and frill
> Miss Phoebe finds is nearly nil.
> It's always light though gowns of white
> Are worn on the Road of Anthracite.[80]

Coal had already made possible extended steamship voyages that the bulk of wood fuel would have made economically absurd. By the 1840's Long Island Sound, Hudson River and Great Lakes steamboats were using both kinds of coal. During the Civil War the Pennsylvania Railroad adapted all its locomotive fireboxes to the bituminous coal prevalent in its sphere of influence. Other lines did so as scarcity of wood appeared in their areas, and conversely certain Southern railroads, notably the Florida East Coast until 1900, far from coal and running through forests profiting from long growing seasons, stayed with wood and beehive stacks longer than any others. Generally coal-burning engines hauling long trains of loaded coal cars westward and eastward, northward and southward, and coal-burning towboats shoving multiple tows of loaded coal barges up and down both Eastern and Western rivers enabled industry to abandon the unreliable waterwheel and thankfully install the coal pile and the shovel-wielding stoker. Along the upper tributaries of the Ohio, coal enabled ironworking rapidly to outstrip salt boiling, glass and pottery making as ranking industry. Well before the Civil War iron was taking over from wood in the hulls of ships and the structure of warehouses and office buildings, jobs that steel would eventually do better, true, but usurpation by metal was the significant thing. America was losing her dependence on the upward-growing, self-renewing wood of the forest and committing herself to the irreplaceable ores and fuels procurable beneath the surface.

Our forebears perversely took it into their heads to wear more clothes just shortly before stoves and central heating came along to overheat the nation. Underdrawers, for instance, began to supplement women's stays and shifts early in the 1800's, among the Quality first, of course. How this came about is not clear. Apparently such things had been sporadic among Italian and French women for a couple of centuries. Samuel Pepys' French wife is one instance; Casanova disapproved of them. But it may have been the diaphanous gowns of Empire times that actually established bifurcated underthings among English-speaking women. Those thin muslin balldresses were chilly wearing, and the court ladies in drafty palaces took to fine woolen, knee-length, flesh-colored, close-fitted breeches that they hoped were undetectable to the eye. It was at first thought immodest for a woman thus to wear something like a man's smallclothes. But even though dresses soon grew more substantial, the notion persisted, and drawers, more loosely cut in light fabrics such as the linen of shifts, were soon requisite to self-respect in most urban contexts—and by the usual transatlantic infection invaded America. Within a generation they were on public view as pantalets beneath the shortish skirts of small girls rolling hoops.

What put underdrawers on American men is even less clear. There are hints of such articles of linen toward the close of the 1700's. Stephen Girard's laundry, for instance, included a dozen pairs that were probably underwear, though the issue is clouded by the use in his day of *drawers* to mean loose breeches for warm weather wear. Certainly by the 1830's Dr. Daniel Drake, inquisitive medical pioneer, was noting with gratification that flannel as well as linen drawers were extensively worn in the Old Northwest, which must mean they were even commoner in the Northeast. Flannel wearing as an alleged health measure had come in with the other crank notions of the time. Catharine Beecher explained knowingly that:

> . . . flannel protects the body from sudden chills when in a state of perspiration . . . produces a kind of friction on the skin . . . while its

texture, being loose, enables it to retain much matter thrown off by the body, which would otherwise accumulate on its surface . . . young children should wear flannel next the skin . . . laboring men should thus wear flannels . . . as preservatives from infection, in unhealthy atmospheres. They give a healthy action to the skin, and thus enable it to resist . . . unhealthy miasmas . . . caused by excessive vegetable decomposition. . . . But those who thus wear flannel, during the day, ought to take it off, at night, when it is not needed. It should be hung so that it can be well aired, during the night.[81]

Apparently now that they had underwear, Americans had already taken to sleeping in it. The lady's failure to mention laundering does not imply that flannels were not occasionally washed, certainly seasonally. Their redly flapping presence on the clothesline enrichened American culture with jokes about "the short and simple flannels of the poor" and the legend of the origin of pink lemonade at the circus—a concessionaire's wife washed her husband's flannels by mistake in an unusually watery batch of lemonade and the dye proved not quite fast. Red flannels were thought to have particularly benign therapeutic influence, as Thoreau found among Maine lumberjacks. Parents ill versed in the need for laundering often sewed up their children in their red or gray flannels for the winter, with consequences that led experienced schoolteachers to seat them well away from the stove.

As the cult spread, flannel petticoats of hygienic intent were common on women and girls. Note that boys were much less widely beflanneled. For a long time their cold-weather clothing was strangely skimped. In cold weather the Yankee farm boy had a homespun jacket and trousers, a wool hat, knit mittens, a long woolen scarf-comforter, cowhide boots over wool stockings and no underwear of flannel or anything else. In southwestern Ohio in Howells' boyhood the sons of even prosperous parents had neither overcoat nor underwear: "When a boy had buttoned up his roundabout [jacket] and put on his mittens, and tied his comforter round his neck and over his ears, he was warmly dressed." [82] In Howells' view the only virtue of those cowhide boots was that their stiffness in cold weather helped to support a skater's ankles. They soaked up melting snow so readily that the wearer could count on painful chilblains all winter: "At night they were so wet that you could not get them off without a bootjack . . . sometimes you got your brother to help . . . and then he pulled you all around the room. In the morning they were dry, but . . . hard as stone, and you had to soap the heel of your woolen sock . . . before you could get your foot in." [82]

Men, too, had abandoned the buckled low shoes of the 1700's and gone into boots, previously used principally for riding. Of cowhide for countrymen and the lower orders, of elegant leathers for the Quality and cut tight to make the foot look genteelly slim, they were almost hidden under the long tubular pantaloons that had succeeded knee breeches. Americans had made this change sooner and more completely than Britons. By the 1830's few except some Quakers and a few elderly parsons showed the calf of the leg. That is, paradoxically, as footgear had risen toward the knee, breeches had lengthened toward the instep, often with a strap under the boot to hold them snug, like ski pants. Tension would not spoil the crease, for the crease was anathema, taken to mean that the pantaloons had lain on a shelf to be sold ready-made instead of being tailored to measure. Tucking the bottoms of the pantaloons into the boots was associated with professional rowdies or backwoodsmen—those who kept a fighting knife in the boot top and wanted nothing hindering when they made a quick snatch for it.

Hats had lost most of the brim, and the crown had heightened into the stovepipe shape that gave lawyers, businessmen and others an equivalent of today's briefcase to carry papers in. But they were worn just as tall by keelboatmen and Bowery boys as by bankers. Men's dress-up finery was losing the gay colors of the 1700's. For Sunday Mr. Brownstone had a blue or black broadcloth cut, depending on the fashion, in frock or tail (vulgarly called claw-hammer) style, in any case with tail pockets for his large silk handkerchief. To temper this severity, his double- or single-breasted waistcoat was of light-colored satin and probably embroidered, and out from the V of its cinched-up embrace burst the frills of his fine linen shirt graced by a heavy gold brooch and culminating in the starched points of an attached turned-up collar sheathing his jowls. They were held in place by the multiple folds of a white neckcloth or a black silk cravat wrapped so firm and high that turning the head was difficult. Yet there could be a good deal of color in the rig-out. David Harum recalled the small-town rich man's son on circus day with "a blue broadcloth claw-hammer coat with flat gilt buttons an' a double-breasted plaid velvet vest, an' pearl-gray pants, strapped down over his boots, which was of shiny leather, an' a high pointed collar an' blue stock with a pin in it . . . an' a yellow-white plug beaver hat." [83]

With the mid-1800's shirt frills were giving place to the board-stiff boiled shirt, still surviving for white-tie wear. This completed the oppressive confiningness of an outfit that must have made the wearer feel like a bird trussed for the oven. The notion that one's best clothes could be comfortable, as well as becoming—as these were to a strong-featured man—was still to come. Mr. Brownstone's only free-and-

Little Rollo's father is majestic in the stovepipe hat and cloak of the 1840's.

easy garment was the tartan-lined cloak swinging from his shoulders as he paced down the street, knobbed walking stick in hand. His wife was even worse off in waist-pinching stays, tight-gartered stockings, chin-cramping bonnet strings and whatever version of voluminous skirt was in style that year adding to the weight of her flannel and taffeta petticoats. The most extravagant was the hoopskirt of the late 1850's—a fantastic nuisance in carriages, buses and narrow doors that had an indecorous way of tilting up behind to expose a lady's calves and at best, as a contemporary wit wrote, made "a damsel, slender as a reed" look like "St. Peter's dome with a small child stuck in it." Particularly in warm weather Mrs. Brownstone might well have envied—but probably did not—her backwoods counterpart, whose workaday costume consisted of nothing at all but an unwaisted, ankle-length sack of coarse linen or linsey-woolsey with a poncho type of hole for the head secured by a drawstring at the neck.

Even on hot Sundays Mr. Brownstone dutifully donned ceremonial broadcloth. In large towns he might wear a heavy coat in summer as well as winter. But even there, as the thermometer neared 90° F all but the most pompous merchants might be seen downtown in white ducks or at least with jackets of brown or white linen or gingham or seersucker imitated from East Indian example. The high hat might also give way to a leghorn straw such as the artist wears in Asher Brown Durand's engaging painting of William Cullen Bryant and Thomas Cole, the painter, in the Catskills. But note that for all the warm weather

Recurring examples of the bell-shaped contour.
From pp. 14–16 *Recurring Cycles of Fashion* by Agnes Brooks
Young. Copyright 1937 by Harper & Row, Publishers, Incorporated.
By permission of the publishers.

and the bucolic situation, both subjects are still swaddled to the chin in cravat and shirt collar and are certainly wearing waistcoats. In downtown business offices only clerks were privileged to work in shirt sleeves with their cravats off in the dog days. The man-dog-and-crony sporting prints of Currier & Ives usually show the jolly outdoorsmen roughing it in waistcoat and cravat. Their informality is conveyed by the wide-awake hat*—a low-crowned broadbrim. Only country children, particularly boys, had comfortable summers. From April to October a farm boy wore nothing but a straw hat, a shirt, attenuated trousers of cotton jean held up by a single knit gallus, and shoes only when bullied into them to go to Sunday school. American boys of the Lincoln-Mark Twain-Howells background limped most of the time—from chilblains in winter and stone bruises in summer.

Their summers were also lightened by their privilege of cooling off naked as jaybirds in that social as well as sanitary institution, the Ole Swimmin' Hole celebrated by Howells and Mark Twain as well as James Whitcomb Riley. It was as old as the Boston of Benjamin Franklin, whose swimming-mindedness fostered the art around Philadelphia and made local young fellows for several months in the year probably the only urban Americans whom we would think tolerably clean in person. Franklin had read a book about how to swim. The art was usually learned by trial and error. Bronson Alcott's boy acquaintances at Wolcott, Connecticut, used the millpond. Of three swimming holes on White River in early Indianapolis, the boys preferred the one at the National Road ferry landing, where the adjacent high bank of slippery clay made a fine slide into the water. Doubtless ladies in stagecoaches crossing the ferry looked the other way. A more formal sort of swimming came in with the lessons given to Bostonians by the young German refugees of the 1820's. The cleanliness arrived at was still, however, the least of their motives. Swimming was part of the cult of physical training, also including stiff gymnastics performed by the numbers on parallel and horizontal bars and so on, associated with the intellectualized and yet militaristic German nationalism.

The cult of sea bathing creeping along the beaches since the Revolution had little to do with the fun of splashing in the surf but much with the crankish belief of certain eminent British doctors that salt water invigorated the ailing organism, particularly in cases of scrofula. Recall how Miss Beecher and Dr. Drake thought the insulation against chill of flannel next to the skin was only incidental; in their view its chief purpose

---

* The *Universal Oxford Dictionary* derives this from its being a hat with *no nap* —a notable pun, as of 1837. Alvin F. Harlow (*Old Bowery Days,* 303, New York, D. Appleton and Company, 1931) associates it with "white felt hats of peculiar shape" worn by the nativist Order of the American Star, whose slogan was "Wide awake! Wide awake!" Republican paraders in the campaigns of 1856 and 1860 also wore wide-awakes.

The persisting weight of multiple petticoats in the 1850's moved Mrs. M. M. Jones to invent suspenders for ladies. The long drawers were flannel.

was to prevent malaria and ventilate the skin—that is, flannel was worn for its absorbency and itchiness, not its warmth. One of the most original architectural ideas of pre-Civil War America was the octagonal building* designed and publicized by Orson S. Fowler in the 1850's. This version of the high cubical villa, though posing awkward problems of floor plan, made engineering sense by clustering chimney, plumbing and gas system all in a central core. That was secondary, however, to Fowler's faith in the spiritual virtues of the eight-sided shape. Several hundred such houses, mostly large, survive in the Northeastern quadrant of America to show how seriously many of his well-to-do contemporaries took his advice. Merely incidentally Fowler's enthusiasm for concrete as building material was far ahead of his time. The octagonal house inadvertently exemplifies the great frequency with which our pre-Civil War forebears gained improvement—in what they wore, ate, drank, lived in, dosed themselves with, played at, smelled like—from cranks preaching new gospels for reasons mostly wrongheaded and irresponsible and often innocently ignorant.

*   *   *

* Octagonal buildings—barns, churches and so on, as well as dwellings—had been tried earlier in America. Fowler was first to detect in that shape the semimystical virtues suggesting his cult of it—or vice versa.

Indeed cranks bulked so large and so damaged America four or five generations ago that it is well first to describe the benefits that occasionally resulted. A good place to begin is with Sylvester Graham, self-constituted expert on diet as the cause of most human woes, whose name survives in graham flour and graham crackers. His craving to advise man for his own good took him into the Presbyterian ministry in New Jersey, then into the wider field of Temperance lecturing. Pondering the Demon Rum, he surmised that the craving for drink might come of unhealthy food and poor eating habits. Such notions were then rife; eating red meat was thought to heighten libido; the strength of heavy beers lent athletes endurance. Graham observed, as many foreign visitors already had, that the typical American bolted his food; ate more meat than most Europeans, much of it fried; had a sallow skin and chronic dyspepsia; and drank too often. Though necessarily ignorant of dietetics—no such science yet existed—he worked out a didactic vegetarianism meant not only to prevent alcoholism but also to foster physical and spiritual health. Its base was unbolted wheat flour baked into bread or crackers not to be eaten till slightly stale and then elaborately chewed to promote digestion and maximum nutritive powers. Such flour was certainly better than the bleached stuff that commercial millers sold, and the bran that the baking trade removed so the flour would keep well contained valuable vitamins. Only, of course, Graham died much too soon to have known of vitamins. He was going on opinionated guesswork, plus a vague impression—a crotchet of his day still strong among us—that the nearer "natural" a thing is, the more virtuous.

The "naturalness" of eating meat and fish did not, however, keep

O. S. Fowler's octagonal mansion at Fishkill,
New York, now long vanished.

Graham from tabooing them as inhumane and also coarsening to the spirit. He endorsed most vegetables, fruit and pure cold water—alcoholic drinks, result of the "unnatural" process of fermentation, were anathema—and recommended not only leisurely eating but also cheerfulness at table. Much of that too was sound advice for a culture in which green salads were scarce and vegetables in general considered mere "sass" or garnish for meats and invariably followed by plenty of lard-shortened pie. (The "sauce room" in the plan of Fowler's ideal octagonal house was not where he kept the Worcestershire, but the vegetable storage.) Cheerfulness at meals was another sound corrective, for unless most alien travelers lied, few Americans then conversed at meals, just gobbled in silence and stalked away, still chewing the last mouthful. Graham's lectures and books expounding all this profitably attracted hypochondriacs hoping for panaceas, genuine sufferers from constipation and indigestion, and those eager to hear that virtue can come of chewing the right things and eschewing the wrong. Many of his adherents were intelligent and conspicuous. The refectory of Brook Farm, the high-toned cooperative ideal colony a few miles from Boston, naturally had a Graham table. There were Grahamite boardinghouses for the sanguine-minded, one of which was intermittently patronized by Horace Greeley, an easy mark for crankisms. Bakers and butchers, of course, hotly denounced Graham.

He had not invented vegetarianism, that hardy perennial as old as classic Greece and always attracting the crypto-ascetic. Other Americans too were playing the game of table reform. John Burrill, a New York City dentist, taught that foods should never be eaten chilled or hot, always at room temperature; that those bent on higher things should cook up their victuals a week's worth at a time, dishing out the cold cornmeal mush and cold boiled carrots meal by meal—all unseasoned, mind, for seasonings and condiments pervert natural flavor, the only moral kind. (This consideration handily reinforced abolitionists' boycotts of the products of slave labor, since most spices and molasses came from slave-holding regions.) William Alcott, physician cousin of the Transcendentalist, champion of physical culture and better schools, kneaded such notions into his influential writings about the good life. They were carefully followed by, among others, the household of Theodore Weld, ablest of the abolitionists. His wife and her sister had been reared among the Quality of Charleston, South Carolina, before turning Quaker and antislavery, but seem never to have regretted the elaborate cuisine they left behind them.

Catharine Beecher carried doctrinaire dining to the point of advising serving only one dish at a meal and making it the moral duty of house-wives "to avoid a variety of tempting dishes." [84] Even more refined was the vegetarianism with which Charles Lane, an English radical educator who thought exploitation of animals immoral as well as inhumane, infected Bronson Alcott. Their good life community of Fruitlands at Harvard, Massachusetts, abjured not only meat but also dairy products, animal fertilizers and use of draft animals. Fruitlands broke up before they could work out a substitute for leather in footgear. One might think the theory could be carried no further, but that was done by Junius Brutus Booth, the erratic English actor settled in America, father of Edwin and John Wilkes Booth, who so zealously adopted what he thought to be the ideas of Pythagoras that he forbade not only eating animals but also flower picking and tree felling on his farm in Maryland.

Public interest in Graham's theme of you-are-what-you-eat led him to expand his repertory with other ideas borrowed from other amateur hygienists: regular light exercise; frequent bathing; open bedroom windows; looser clothing, which usually included dress reform, aimed chiefly at women, whose stays were a serious orthopedic scandal and prime target of the rights-for-women crusaders. (With great symbolic fitness general use of the heavy-boned corset finally went out with the triumph of votes for women at the time of World War I.) That all four notions were commendable was again rather accidental. The cranks' reason for recommending bathing was not so much cleanliness as keeping the pores open; for open windows an alleged but probably nonexistent shortage of oxygen in closed rooms. In spite of these misconceptions, however, the noisy zeal of such as Graham left beneficial residues in the daily habits of influential people whose examples affected the literate strata of American society to their great betterment.

Americans' acceptance of bathing—that is, exposure of the whole body to water above 32° F—involved quack cults other than Graham's; for instance, the steam doctoring that swept the country after 1800. This apotheosized the old wives' cult of herbal medicine, often combining the Indians' steam baths with magic-tinged dosings that persisted wherever the frontier had passed through. From a backwoods rearing in New Hampshire, one Samuel Thomson, founder of what he called botanic medicine, acquired a good opinion of folk medicine and a correspondingly poor one of what his followers called "calomel doctors." He taught that heat being inseparable from life, absence of it leads to obstruction of the glands, with consequent sickness and death. So patients with cancer, ringworm, rheumatism, consumption, scrofula and almost any other complaint were steamed over hot stones doused with water or vinegar and generously dosed with one or more of six master herbs, use of which Thomson had learned from the local wise woman back home, liberally laced with cayenne pepper to keep the heat rising. He prescribed these basic herbs by number, 1 to 6, supplementing them with such esoteric botanicals as puccoon, cohosh, unicorn root, goldenseal and preparations called liquid flames and bread of heaven. As proof of the efficacy of it all, the patients often survived. One died in Newburyport, Massachusetts, and Thomson was had up for murder. His acquittal enabled him to spend the rest of his long life benefiting his fellowman, largely by proxy as sponsor of a great army of licensed Thomsonian followers.

Some were itinerant; some traveled only till they found a promising place to settle down and take patients away from the regulars, as conventional MD's were known. Such a steam doctor's qualifications consisted of having paid $20 for a copy of Thomson's combined textbook-autobiography and filling out the diploma-license sold with it. Reading it was not required, though many Thomsonians certainly did so and took the system seriously. Theoretically the herb supply could come from the woods, but authenticity and purity were best assured when one ordered from the botanical pharmacies that Thomson licensed in large cities. By 1835 the regulars of fast-settling Ohio admitted that a third of the state's people were entrusting themselves to Thomsonians. One Ohio practitioner was William Rockefeller of Cleveland, father of John D. and the Standard Oil Company, who had become a botanic physician after a long and mysterious career as wandering cancer quack and hawker of miraculous bottled elixirs. Eventually schisms among Thomsonians and the rise of homeopathy as refuge for those mistrusting conventional medicine took the steam out of the movement, so to speak. It sank into a bedraggled quackery calling itself eclectic medicine that a generation ago was still running diploma mills in a few backward states. As of 1830, however, in view of how little the regulars knew and how much of what they did was potential homicide, who is to say that all those early Ohioans were not better off with steam doctoring? At least it taught them it was possible to survive getting wet and warm all over.

A generation after Thomson's indigenous discoveries the future of American bathing was further expanded by an exotic therapeutic cult called "hydropathy" formally, "the water cure" informally. It too was created by a folk-based amateur, a Silesian peasant named Vincenz Priessnitz, who, aware of medical use of cold compresses, tried them on his own broken ribs and finger and was pleased with the results. Further success when he treated others led him to conclude in his artless peasant way that cold water was good for almost everything. The system that he developed, including walking barefoot through morning dew for some ills, brought him such renown that the Austrian government built him a great hydropathic hospital. There he installed a battery of water-exploiting devices, some of which are still used: sponge baths, sitz, plunge and steam baths; the notion of playing high-pressure hoses on patients, of wrapping them in sheets wrung out in cold water. He had some combination of soppy tortures for any sufferer. As his fame spread, England had a propagandist Hydropathic Society and many sanitarium resorts called hydros where the ailing reveled in arduous regimes, gooseflesh guaranteed. Simultaneously England was being invaded by the shower bath from India and the Turkish bath from the Near East—for systemic stimulus rather than cleanlinesss, of course. The bath cult of fashionable young men about London created a wide impression that elaborate and frequent messings about in water were elegant as well as healthy— hence a whole school of "balneotherapy" that helped hydropathy break down resistance to bathing.

Philadelphia had a hydro by 1847. Of the many subsequent water cures, the best known were the Brattleboro, Vermont, Water Cure House and Dr. Joel Shew's establishment at Lebanon Springs, New York, but Dr. James Caleb Jackson's at Dansville, New York, and Dr. R. T. Trall's in New York City also came into high favor, particularly among intellectual reformers. When a Temperance convention in New York City in 1853 refused to seat women delegates, including such portentous feminists as Lucy Stone and Susan B. Anthony, Dr. Trall welcomed their indignation meeting, including their men allies, to his hydro premises, a fitting refuge for a group already preaching cold water. Hydropathy, too, was moribund within a generation. But it left its mark on the plumbing industry. The hygienic aura that it cast about its specialized hardware led to those elaborate bathrooms in post-Civil War mansions stiff with sitz baths, steam cabinets and shower installations with as many nozzles and valves as the engine room of a cruiser. A family thus equipped would unquestionably be the cleaner for such fascinating gadgets evolved for bathing —for the wrong reasons.

The Germans' "homeopathy" was another example of long-term benefit from misbegotten science—and of an imported hair shirt for calomel doctors. Its father was Samuel Hahnemann, a trained physician as training then went. Imaginative, if erroneous, observation led him to new theories of drug therapy that, published c. 1810, gradually gained currency in Europe and a generation later flooded the English-speaking world. Illness, he taught, is best treated with drugs that artificially induce in the patient the symptoms of his disease. That is, the observation that quinine makes the healthy run fevers accounts for its effectiveness against malaria, a feverish disease. Hence the term *homeopathy* (similarity of feeling) and the basic maxim of the cult: *Similia similibus curantur* ("Like cures like"). He added a conviction that the drugs and treatments of conventional medicine, which he called allopathy, were ill chosen and too strong and developed a new pharmacopoeia based on traditional herb remedies and administered in minute doses drowned in water.

The first postulate was just arbitrary crankishness. The second was an indirect but eventually sweeping blessing. The homeopathic doctor's patient got everything that a "regular" doctor could do for him. He was kept in bed, visited as often and as reassuringly, and had to pay bills for just as impressive amounts. And yet he was also spared the risk of being weakened halfway to death's door by heroic bleedings and horse doses of calomel or antimony. Instead he was copiously flushed out with quantities of water flavored with lobelia or gelsemium or whatever Hahnemann's books prescribed for his ailment. The flood did him little or no good, of course, but at least—here was homeopathy's unadmitted long suit—it did him no harm, imposed no unnecessary handicaps on his natural stamina and the as yet unexplored biochemical efforts of his system to effect recovery. So by and large the homeopath's patients got well oftener than those of the regulars, and with less puking and purging. In the manipulative skills—surgery, obstetrics, orthopedics—where Hahnemann's ideas had little bearing one way or another, homeopaths studying the same anatomy came to be as canny and deft as their rivals.

Brought to America in 1825 by Hans Burch Gram, a disciple of Hahnemann's, homeopathy opened its first medical school in Allentown, Pennsylvania, in 1836. Soon there were homeopathic hospitals—the most august, in Philadelphia, was named for Hahnemann—and a veterinary branch to give mules with the heaves and victims of hog cholera the benefit of his ideas. The regulars fought back condescendingly and enjoyed exposing the flaws of homeopathic teaching—such as the theory that high dilution actually *increases* the potency of homeopathic drugs. The cult lost momentum as the invasion of medical research by something nearer genuine science gave the regulars unfair advantages. But meanwhile, the inadvertent common sense of its practices was having an effect. Bleeding lost standing. The homeopath's strange pharmacopoeia made little headway, but numerous regular drugs, notably violent purges and emetics, were more cautiously handled. As the backbiting died away, Dr. Oliver Wendell Holmes, a great physician and philosopher of medicine, as well as man of letters, credited homeopathy, for all its absurdities, with doing much to break up "the system of over-drugging and over-dosing which had been one of the standard reproaches of medical practice." [85]

Conspicuous and vulnerable as homeopathy and hydropathy were, when Dr. Holmes needed a specimen pseudoscience to dissect in *The Professor at the Breakfast Table,* he chose phrenology—and wisely because its connotations and implications were wider. This, too, left important residues. The source was again German—by a striking coincidence, Vienna. In the late 1700's Franz Josef Gall, a Viennese physician whose early work on brain structure had value, took up human behavior. He analyzed it into forty-six component abstract qualities—Benevolence, Amativeness, Combativeness, Veneration, Acquisitiveness, Philoprogenitiveness and so on—then divided the surface of the brain into areas, in each of which he located one such quality; then sought in the irregularities of the outside of the skull, detectable by measurement or the skilled hand, indications of the under- or over- or normal development of the brain area beneath. That gave a gauge to the strength of the corresponding quality in the subject's behavior. Thus a man with a large bump of Amativeness was likely to run after women, but an equally marked bump of Conscientiousness might enable him to keep himself under control.

Dr. Johann Kaspar Spurzheim, a disciple of Gall's, brought the new cult to Boston in the 1820's by way of England. He seems to have been winningly persuasive in person and impressive in performance. While examining convicts in the Charlestown, Massachusetts, penitentiary, he singled out a man and expressed surprise at his being there, since his skull showed no criminal bent, and sure enough, new evidence establishing his innocence soon came up. Spurzheim died after some years of marked success in lecturing and proselyting. His replacement in the American field was George Combe, a soberly enthusiastic Scot whose inevitable book about his extensive travels while phrenologizing in America is one of the best such items of the period. He too examined criminals, usually finding their bumps of morality deficient and those of their animal passions overlarge, and drew for his audiences the then relatively novel conclusion that such men were "incapable of resisting the temptation to crime . . . are moral patients and should not be punished but restrained . . . with as much liberty as they can enjoy without abusing it." [86] He also applied phrenology to mental disease and studied the inmates of insane asylums. In Portland, Maine, was a woman deranged by grief for the death of a son and bent on suicide. A phrenology-minded doctor examined her skull, found the area of Philoprogenitiveness warmer than the rest, bled the area, poulticed it—and she was cured!

Scoffing was not confined to Dr. Holmes. John Quincy Adams, paraphrasing Cicero about the Roman augurs, said he did not see how two phrenologists could look each other in the face without laughing. J. K. Paulding turned out a masterpiece of Swiftian drollery in his account of Drs. Gallgotha (a brilliant pun) and Spurrem in his *Merry Tales of the Three Wise Men of Gotham*. Anatomists peevishly pointed out that nowhere does the brain touch the skull bones, nor does the structure of one reflect details of the other. Hack humorists welcomed the whole thing as an easily ridiculed "bumpology." For generations now it has been clear that phrenology has no validity whatever, not even such few marginal wisps of sense as cling to astrology and alchemy. Yet there was no denying the integrity and (barring phrenology) acumen of such men as Combe, and this latitudinarian teaching was influentially popular among thousands of serious-minded Americans drawn to anything calling itself science and emotionally inclined toward moral tolerance.

One of Combe's eminent Yankee converts, for instance, was Horace Mann, chief creator of the American public school system, who named his second son George Combe Mann. Among others of marked ability or anyway eminence to take phrenology as seriously as their modern counterparts now probably take the Oedipus situation were Henry Ward Beecher, popular preacher and moral leader; Dr. Charles Caldwell, founder of medical education over-the-mountains; Dr. Samuel Gridley Howe, pioneer in education of the blind; Allan Pinkerton, chief of federal intelligence in the Civil War and founder of the still conspicuous Pinkerton detective agency. General George B. McClellan's staff relied on phrenology to screen women to spy for the Army of the Potomac. A Philadelphia clergyman published *Phrenology in the Family* to guide parents in the educating of their children's feelings. For though there was a good deal of determinism in the "science," it also taught that awareness of phrenological truths and their use in diagnosing temperaments enabled the believer to develop moral at the expense of immoral qualities.

Though Britain and the Continent also saw active phrenologizing, America was the scene of its widest acceptance and strongest influence —another analogue to the history of Freudianism. Much of that was due to a pair of native American enthusiasts, O. S. Fowler, whose sideline invention of the octagonal house has been mentioned, and his brother, L. N. Fowler. The latter's wife, *née* Lydia Folger of a renowned family of Nantucket whalers, was the second American woman to receive an MD and applied her scientific standing effectively in lectures on phrenology in America and, after 1860, in England. The family publishing house, Fowlers & Wells of New York City, prospered not only with O. S.'s popular expositions of phrenology but also with the wall charts and casts of skulls that traveling minor lecturers needed in their act. For this was a tempting opportunity for footloose people with the gift of gab and willingness to believe what so many august persons endorsed. The second qualification was not essential, but it probably helped and doubtless most of the itinerant phrenologists of the 1830-60's managed it.

Following the trails blazed by the Yankee and Jewish peddlers, the steam doctors and circuit riders, they took bumps and Philoprogenitiveness wherever they could gather an audience in tavern or schoolhouse. Headlined THE PROPER STUDY OF MANKIND IS MAN, their printed handbills promised both a lecture series (the first one usually free as bait) and private consultations. The lectures combined the magic of a "science" bristling with new long words and the fascinating implication that what people do isn't their fault—it's how they're made and reared. Long and hard these spellbinders worked the old trick of enticing volunteers out of the audience to have their bumps felt and their dispositions described in terms so glibly general and amusing that a good time was had by all. The next morning individual applicants at four bits or a dollar a head received what amounted to a piquant new kind of fortune-telling. This was basically a branch of show business. One such lecturer did well in the Old Northwest in the late 1830's traveling with a dwarf and a seven-foot four-inch giant as phrenological exhibits. He called himself Doctor and probably stayed with his scientific career as long as it paid. A former petty storekeeper who had read a few books and turned phrenologist told Combe that he usually made $200 to $300 out of a week's stay in a town of 1,500 population.

Besides the publishing and supply business, the Fowlers maintained phrenological rooms in Boston, Philadelphia and New York City, where experts, often styled Professor, gave private readings for $3—a thumping sum then, but it bought several pages of personality analysis and clotty advice on conduct. The premises also offered busts of notables of phrenological interest, such as Aaron Burr, Horace Mann, William Cullen Bryant, Greeley, Napoleon and Laura Bridgman, the Helen Keller of the time. Under an assumed name young Mark Twain once had $3 worth from L. N. Fowler himself and came away unimpressed; the expert had found that the bumps of the author of the already famous Celebrated Jumping Frog indicated that he completely lacked a sense of humor. In the late 1880's, however, when the novelty had long worn off phrenology, Frances Willard, the Joan of Arc of the Women's Christian Temperance Union, the most formidable woman in America, still took phrenological readings seriously. In the same year (1900) were published Freud's *The Interpretation of Dreams* and the *Fables in Slang* of George Ade, satirizer of the day's foibles in Chicago, showing "The Learned Phrenologist . . . in his Office surrounded by his Whiskers. Now and then he put a Forefinger to his Brow and glanced at the Mirror to make sure that he still resembled William Cullen Bryant. . . ." [87]

The backhanded modernity of phrenology appears clearly in what has always been my favorite case of L. N. Fowler's: A married client complains of pains in the back and crown of his head. Fowler studies his skull and ascribes them to jealousy of his wife, which has set up a primary inflammation in the organ of Amativeness (toward the base of the skull) and a secondary one in that of Self-Esteem (in the top of the skull). He then ascertains that the client's wife's organ of Amativeness is subnormal in size, hence the coldness that made her husband suspect her, and once all that is explained, the husband's pains disappear. More generally phrenology prepared society for some of the postulates of modern sociology, which assumes that social misbehavior comes primarily from society's failure to do right by the individual. Or say that misbehavior is his reaction to having to get along in a situation incompatible with his emotional makeup. True, phrenology considered that makeup largely innate, whereas current sociology and psychiatry tend to assume that the individual's emotional patterns are imposed after birth (or maybe after conception) and would have been different under different environmental circumstances. But the Spurzheims, Combes and Fowlers did not altogether rule out the possibility of reshaping a warped temperament and in any case did much to divert emphasis from free will as determinant of behavior and to fix attention on interaction between society and a socio-psychological automaton with rather rigid traits, whether innate or acquired.

That is, since phrenology tinged our thinking, we are readier to believe that what A does, however regrettable sometimes, is not his fault. The fault lies with the gross conformation of his brain, or with the society that took him when he was a sort of amorphous emotional putty and shaped him into what he is today, or—this is on the upbeat now— with the array of genes that he was conceived with. We now know that the first is nonsense. To what extent the latter two are valid may long remain debatable. But to act on any of the three is to exempt the individual from blame for what he does and lay it on society. Society should have recognized A's bump of Acquisitiveness and not put him in a job that would betray him into felony, or should have determined that he probably carries the genes associated with schizophrenia and protected him from the emotional strains that would bring it to the surface, or should have perceived that it was his slum childhood that twisted him into criminality and sought to make amends not only by retraining his emotions but also by wiping out slums to prevent more such cases in future. The benefit from the last is that, correct or not, it helps get slums cleared, which they probably would not be on any other theory.

The other point is that all three assumptions erode the strive-and-succeed legend already lively in the America of the mid-1800's—the belief that since now and again a slum urchin managed to become a great and useful citizen, any given slum urchin could have done so had he tried as hard.

Materials on phrenology were by no means the only publications of Fowlers & Wells. Their flourishing list appealed to all the crankisms so far described and some not yet approached. Mail order or over the counter they also sold works entitled *Vegetable Diet: as Sanctioned by Medical Men and by Experience in All Ages,* by Dr. William Alcott; *Tobacco: Three Prize Essays* by Drs. Shew, Trall and Baldwin; *Home Treatment for Sexual Abuses,* by R. T. Trall, MD; *Parents' Guide for the Transmission of the Desired Qualities to Offspring,* by Mrs. Hester Pendleton; *The New Hydropathic Cook Book,* by R. T. Trall, MD; *Water-Cure Applied to Every Known Disease,* translated from the German of J. H. Ranssee; *The Phonographic* [Shorthand] *Teacher* by E. Webster; *The Complete Gymnasium . . . Calisthenic, Kinesipathic, and Vocal Exercises for the Development of Body and Mind,* by R. T. Trall, MD; *How to Live . . . or Domestic Economy Illustrated . . .* by Solon Robinson, a staffer on Greeley's *Tribune* who once reproached mothers for allowing their daughters to be plied with ice cream loaded with "passion-exciting vanilla"; and in summary a book by Greeley himself, *Hints Toward Reforms.* "Uncle Horace" 's New York *Tribune* promoted not only most of these reforms but also temperance, dress reform and the antislavery movement.

Those clusters of at least allegedly good causes were like those of the previous generation—only ingredients and personnel had largely changed. The initiative had passed from those carrying gold-headed canes to those of lower economic and emotional stability. Under staid encouragement Sunday School and savings bank went on growing in scope. But after 1830, say, the number of causes seeking public support multiplied, usually through importation from overseas, and included many that now look dubious. Rehabilitation of the blind, yes; more humane prisons, more room for the insane, yes; protection of seamen, yes; manual labor colleges—that is, schools combining study with subsistence labor in field and workshop—yes. Narrow or sweeping, all those, it is now clear, promised well for the community. Women's rights, including removal of legal liabilities as well as votes for women, made undeniable sense. The antislavery movement, however stupid some of its tactics, was rooted in decency and a realistic view of the nation's long-run welfare. But there was far less to be said for the already shrilly intemperate Temperance and antitobacco crusades, for diet reform as preached without modification by common sense, and very little for spiritualism, phrenology and agitation against the movement of people and mails on Sunday. Yet the more volatile among our forebears often ignored what now seems to us glaring discrepancies in quality and undiscerningly swallowed a wide variety of those things all at once.

Garrison, for instance, went in for spiritualism, Temperance, women's rights and the fight against tobacco, as well as that against slavery. Dr. Dio Lewis, a homeopath, whose lectures set off the great Women's Crusade against Rum in the early 1870's, was as active in the calisthenics cult as in Temperance and diet reform. Discrimination was not altogether absent. Horace Greeley and Catharine Beecher boggled at women's rights. The stable minds of Charles Francis Adams and certain Quakers managed pretty well to concentrate on antislaveryism; R. H. Dana stuck to that and seamen's rights. But many conspicuous reformers betrayed their subliminal impulses by nibbling at everything on the menu. Their discernment was often blurred by religious considerations; Sunday observance and humane treatment of convicts, for instance, both widened the opportunity of salvation for the erring soul—and all too often opened the way for wishful credulity and self-dramatization. Too often it looks as if a need to feel especially sensitive and righteous underlay their crusading. Just which cause to use to scratch that itch was of minor importance sometimes. This is innocently clear when one sees Susan B. Anthony in one generation and Frances Willard in the next each sitting down early in life to choose deliberately a righteous cause to identify with. Miss Anthony chose women's rights; Miss Willard, Temperance. But it is unmistakable in their life stories that the first purpose of each was to bestow on the world the benefit of her keen mind and moral sensitivity, that the choice of field to work in could just as well have gone the other way, and that each retained a high-minded hankering to dabble in other good causes, some pretty crankish.

*   *   *

In our 1900's the classic reform syndrome has included sympathy with labor of the sort manifested in the categorical refusal of many otherwise uninvolved persons ever to pass any picket line. Barring scattered exceptions, such as Fanny Wright and Wendell Phillips, the pre-Civil War reformer had little concern for the labor movement. It was not Garrison or any Beecher but the rather conservative George Templeton Strong who wrote in his diary in 1860 after the collapse of a jerry-built textile mill in Lawrence, Massachusetts, crushed or burned alive some 200 employees: "It becomes us to prate about the horrors of slavery? What Southern capitalist trifles with the lives of his operatives as do our philanthropes of the North?" [88] In that day the social-minded intellectual often had his hopes so concentrated on the good life of cracked wheat and cooperation and his sympathy so absorbed in the plight of the slave or the convict that he paid little heed to the periodically precarious situation of the industrial worker.

Tunnel vision was not the whole story, however. Labor as an entity had low visibility. The word was not yet the label on the newspaper cartoonist's stereotype of a brawny character in a square paper cap. Class distinctions among a given generation c. 1830 were peevish when made between "ruff-scuff" and carriers of gold-headed canes, but less so when between those who worked with their hands and those who did not have to. For at any given time many prospering merchants, lawyers, politicians and parsons were half-proudly, half-diffidently aware that they themselves had risen from among hornyhanded farmers and small-town artisans. The loudest voices denouncing industrial employers as a class for tyrannizing over their hands with company stores and ruthless discharges in hard times came not from liberals demanding change but from Southern apologists for slavery, such as George Fitzhugh of Virginia, contrasting the security of the slave with the unstable situation of the Northern proletarian. And whereas lager beer swept the country within a few years of arrival, that far more stimulating other German import, the Marxist doctrine of the explicit class struggle, had hardly begun to affect workingmen's thinking before the Civil War.

As the 1800's came in, skilled artisans had been organizing along craft lines benevolent associations for sickness and burial insurance. In New York City, Baltimore and Philadelphia their leaders began to use these ready-made groups to put pressure for higher wages on employers (who were often formally or informally allied) and, inevitably, to stage strikes to show they meant business. Tailors and cordwainers (shoemakers) led the way. New York City's cordwainers even achieved that chronic apple of discord, the closed shop. The beauty of strikes in highly skilled trades is, of course, that strikebreaking is difficult; tailors and shoemakers cannot be trained overnight. The successes of these early unions led employers to seek help from the courts. There was an English common law doctrine, applicable in America (except Louisiana) in the absence of specific statutes, that for workmen to organize for militant ends amounted to the crime of conspiracy. Application of this to striking unions temporarily took the steam out of labor organizing in America.

In the 1820's hard times led to the formation of local Workingmen's Parties calling in political terms for free, ubiquitous public schools to give the rising generation better opportunity; abolition of imprisonment for debt, which weighed heavily on wage earners in hard luck; mechanics' lien laws giving the workingman priority over other creditors when an employer went insolvent; and soon for the ten-hour day—sunup to sundown was still the prevalent custom—and free land in the West as economic recourse for workingmen preferring to bow out of the competition for jobs. The movement had its own press, and its objectives were so sound that most of them came to pass within thirty years. With it unionism revived, particularly among the skilled trades. By 1836, Allan Nevins estimates, two-thirds of New York City's workingmen were unionized. The Philadelphia area saw strikes of bakers, canalboatmen in the coal trade on the Schuylkill and even the notoriously sweated seamstresses. The carpenters set fire to houses the builders of which defied the unions. There were impressive processions of demonstrators and emotion-charged mass meetings. The throng of workingmen in New York City's City Hall Park protesting in 1836 against the conviction for conspiracy of leaders of the striking tailors' unions was said to be the largest crowd ever seen in town. William Cullen Bryant's *Evening Post* vehemently took up the unions' cause. In 1835 Mathew Carey, outstanding book publisher of the day, once a hot young revolutionary in his native Ireland, had presided over the Philadelphia seamstresses' mass meeting with a local clergyman lending him countenance on either side.

Yet support from the eminent outside labor's ranks was still rare. The typical attitude of the upper strata was that of ex-Mayor Philip Hone who called the striking New York City longshoremen "malcontents . . . Irish and other foreigners, instigated by the mischievous counsels of the trade-unions and other combinations of discontented men. . . ." [89] Already recent immigrants were so rife among the labor supply of the large American towns from Baltimore northward—skilled Germans and Britons, as well as pick-and-shovel Irish—that those alarmed by labor's gropings toward power were always thenceforth tempted to blame sinister aliens. That motif would be a standard factor in the persisting reactionary politics of nativism long since foreshadowed by the Federalists' exasperation with their alien-born critics in the 1790's.

Then and later the charge was not without color of plausibility. The radical leading edge of the Workingmen's Parties, for instance, consisted largely of Fanny Wright; Robert Dale Owen, son of the socialist-minded founder of New Harmony; and George Henry Evans, outstanding editor of the labor press—all three Britons. The underground Molly Maguire organization in the Pennsylvania coalfields during and after the Civil War was clearly a transplantation to American labor problems of the terrorism epidemic in the misery-racked Ireland from which its members mostly came. The new nation had always relied on being strengthened by immigrant craftsmen bringing Old World skills to the well-paying New World market; indeed well into the 1900's American industry relied heavily on importation of such men and remained precariously parasitical on European traditions of craft training. Many of these exotic Welsh and Cornish miners, German engravers, piano-makers, tailors, printers and wood-carvers, English textile mechanics and machinists were likely to be, by one or another of those familiar self-selecting processes, fond of their own ideas and prone to turn up among leaders in the New American unions. But there was no reason specifically to blame them for fomenting militancy. Nobody needed to teach the sons and grandsons of the American working-class mobs of Revolutionary days how to run mass meetings or riots as occasion indicated.

Labor's response to the gold-headed canes' disapproval naturally verged toward hints at overt class hatred. A handbill distributed at the great New York City protest meeting had a tone that Hone called "most diabolical and inflammatory." "The freemen of the North," it said, "are now on a level with the slaves of the South! . . . Judge Edwards has established the precedent that . . . the rich are the only judges of the wants of the poor man." [90] Watching a parade of unions in Boston in 1834, Horace Mann, a fairly typical reformer, observed with acumen though small sympathy that "The bond of association among these men is mutual support and defence against what they denominate aristocratic institutions and manners. This principle is rapidly extending itself . . . if something is not done to check it, the advantages of possessing wealth will find what to me would be more than counterpoise in the envy and dissocial feelings which it will occasion." [91] Had the courts maintained pressure on the unions, militancy might have built up dangerously to match. But in the early 1840's, most notably in Massachusetts in a famous decision from that same Chief Justice Lemuel Shaw who first laid down the separate but equal doctrine for public schools, the law pretty well abandoned the conspiracy weapon. The way was open for union *organizing,* though the thorny thickets of strikebreaking, closed shops and injunctions still lay ahead. In the 1850's the prosperity inflation following the influx of California gold saw the germ of nationwide craft unions sprout among printers, cigar makers, machinists and some others. But Chief Justice Shaw had done nothing to reconcile employers to the union as a thing to learn to live with. In the seats of the mighty, union busting would long be the ideal, and industry's labor policy would usually consist of getting as near that as possible.

Though hygiene had so much oblique help from cranks, it took its time about qualifying among American habits. Dr. Drake's report on such matters as of 1854 described bathing as far from being general in the Old Northwest. The region's sizable cities had commercial bathhouses, but only the very prosperous used them. The Northeast had had them since the 1790's, but it was another fifty years before bathrooms in city hotels or even elaborate new dwellings were widely expected. A youth entering Yale in 1858 noted it as gratifying that his boardinghouse had a bathroom in which even warm baths were available if one heated one's own water. The rules of Vassar College, opened in 1865, required the girls to bathe—twice weekly.

Some of this lag came of the long-standing suspicion that bathing was a health hazard. In 1835 the Common Council of Philadelphia almost banned wintertime bathing; in 1845 Boston forbade it except on specific medical advice. Poor water supply was also probably involved. A bathtub that has to be filled and emptied with hand pump and pail represents a chore too onerous for a culture chronically complaining of lack of domestic help. When the weather obliged, cisterns containing rainwater from the roof, particularly when above second-story level, filled the tub by gravity, making bathing more practical in the town or country dwellings of the prosperous. But many cisterns were belowground and required arduous hand pumping. (The situation cried out for the European bidet, which gives the most cleanliness for the least water, but, so far as I know, America of the mid-1800's used it only in French-influenced Louisiana. Abortive attempts to naturalize it seem not to have begun until after the Civil War, when so many more women of the Quality got to Europe.) In spite of the example set early by the Moravians' wooden conduits, large-scale waterworks were long in coming to most Americans. When Philadelphia built the first, it was for a mstaken purpose—to prevent yellow fever by supplanting the city's polluted wells; nobody yet knew that the disease was passed on by mosquito bites, not filth. The opening of the system in 1801 was celebrated as resoundingly, however, as if the epidemiology had been sound. That ample supply of water from the Schuylkill became at once a prime boast of civic pride. Presently Cincinnati and then Pittsburgh followed the example. It was forty years before New York City and Boston did; by then the opening celebrations were cluttered up with Temperance organizations, to whom cold water had become a sort of fetish. The first municipal sewer system, Boston's, waited until 1823. Meanwhile, the limitations of pumps, buckets and stairs persisted. Philip Hone wrote peevishly in 1841 of Gadsby's Hotel in Washington, D.C., best in the nation's capital, as "that caravansery of long cold galleries . . . negligent servants, small pillows, and scanty supply of water." [92] An observant Scot, inclined to like America, complained in 1832 that in one of New York City's two best hotels "even water [is] not so plentiful as is requisite, most of all in a warm climate—neither hot nor cold baths . . . nor proper accommodations of a . . . still more necessary description. The waiter shrugged his shoulders on pointing out . . . a row of temples alternately for males or females. . . ." [93]

George Combe was indignant in the early 1840's because even in water-minded Philadelphia there were "sad deficiencies [as to water closets] even in genteel houses. The most refined and sensitive individuals of both sexes suffer great inconvenience rather than travel from twenty to fifty yards in the open air, when the thermometer is at zero . . . physicians of great experience [lament] the extent of suffering that may be traced to this cause." [94] That spells out what was meant when Calvert Vaux, English architect who worked with Olmsted in creating New York City's Central Park, denounced the away-from-the-house privy of American country life as "troublesome, unhealthy, indelicate" as well as "ugly." [95] He tried to correct the last by designing little Gothic structures combining a summerhouse with a view of the garden on one side and a two- or four-holer on the other; stenches were reduced by tall vent pipes and periodic flushings. But the only sound solution was to persuade the client to let him draw a cistern-flushed WC or two into the floor plan. Horace Mann, building Massachusetts' insane asylum at Worcester, the state's first, was very proud of its system of garret cisterns and water closets, accommodations for excretion far superior to what any New England hotel then had.

Advanced as America was with steamboats and manhood suffrage, its sanitary practices looked medieval to alien eyes. London's butchers still clogged the streets on occasion with droves of sheep and cattle. But in New York City of the 1840's Britons were amazed to see thousands of unchaperoned hogs ranging all over town as freely as their ancestors had in the Colonial woods. "We are going to cross here [on downtown Broadway]," Dickens wrote. "Take care of the pigs. Two portly sows

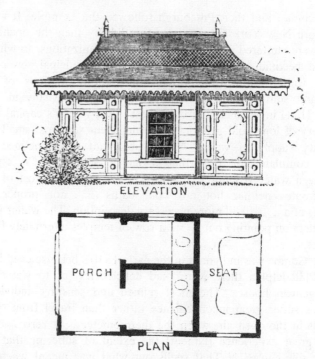

ELEVATION

PORCH   SEAT

PLAN

Design for a combined summerhouse and privy for a gentleman's estate worked out by Calvert Vaux, English-trained architect eminent in America in the mid-1800's.

are trotting up behind this carriage, and a select party of half a dozen gentlemen hogs have just now turned the corner. . . . Ugly brutes. . . ." [96] That they could pick up enough to eat to make it worth their owners' while in pork to house them at night indicates how much garbage and ordure were still being thrown into the streets, much of which even the hogs refused, so that it persisted and corrupted. Pork on the hoof was just as common a sight in other places. Cincinnati allowed it long after New York City had got rid of it, having roundups of hogs whenever they grew too flagrantly numerous and selling them to the local pork packers at auction, proceeds to the municipal treasury. In the intervals anybody who wished to could run down and kill a stray hog for his own use. Not for nothing was the town called Porkopolis.

A problem, the worse for being insoluble, was the accumulation of horse droppings as the number of omnibuses, carriages, private or for hire, and carts and drays grew to match population and rising standards of comfort. It is difficult for those reared after the automobile ousted the horse to realize how excrement thus pervaded the outdoors of the nineteenth-century city, making it a sort of equine latrine. Cobblestone pavement kept sweeping up hopeless even when tried. The English sparrows imported in 1850 to eat caterpillars flourished on the stuff, but even their population explosion made no headway against the problem. It dried in the summer sun to become high-flavored dust blowing into mouth and lungs. In wet weather it incorporated into the mud that was tracked everywhere, fouling the bottoms of women pedestrians' long skirts, gradually impregnating the straw on the floor of the omnibus until the passengers might as well have sat with their feet in a horse stall needing cleaning. ". . . the city is pestilential," George Templeton Strong said in August, 1852, of New York City. "The streets smell like a solution of bad eggs in [ammonia]." [97] In Howells' ideal country, Altruria, electric vehicles had eliminated the horse, which made the cities "as clean and quiet and healthful as the country." [98] Writing in 1893, he was unaware that the rival internal-combustion engine, elbowing electricity aside, would liberate the horse only to set up a worse pollution.

In extensive use of ice, however, the Brownstone culture was well ahead of the Old World. The upper South began it amazingly early—a tribute to the New World's sizzling summers. In the ruins of Jamestown, necessarily dating back into the 1600's, archeologists have found special pits unmistakably for storing ice—a tradition as old as the Roman occupation of Britain. The Jamestowners probably used them for chilling wine and for delaying spoilage in meats and butter. The FFV plantation of the 1700's might have its icehouse annually filled from pond or river, for ice and julep were early soul mates, and a layer of ice safeguarded the table butter in July. So far, however, these were gastronomic, not sanitary, measures. A Frenchman in Baltimore in 1794 reported ice in the drinking water in summer—an early use of that American bugbear ice water for Britons to deplore as frightfully-unhealthy-isn't-it? In the same decade visitors to New York City learned with pleasure that it was customary to ice the local rum punch. Much of the ice came from the Collect Pond, a body of water already on its way to become the site of the Five Points, foulest slum in America; meanwhile, its shrinking margins were the dump for inconveniently large dead animals. Our forebears were casual about that sort of thing. In 1835 it was shown in a libel case tried in Albany, New York, that the largest local brewery, famous for the rich flavor of its beer and ale, drew its water from a pond into which drained the sweepings from a slaughterhouse and a glue-works, the effluvia of several privies—and the gradual disintegrations of cats and hogs found dead in the streets.

The Shakers, a religious sect with gastronomic leanings, brought from the Northeast to the Old Northwest their expert icehouse design: heavy-timbered double walls with sawdust between; triple roofs similarly insulated; stone floors covered with straw and then sawdust. Applied to ships, these insulating principles were what had enabled the Yankees to create the ice-export trade through the torrid zone. The beautiful swift American sailing packets on the Liverpool run had ice compartments in the 1840's. Fowler's palatial octagonal house at Fishkill, New York, built to demonstrate all the advantages of his theory, had a two-story ice storage, the lower part a walk-in refrigerator for meats, butter, eggs and such. On the urban Brownstones' level an insulated refrigerator was served daily by the ice wagon—the first appearance of an American institution that disappeared only in the 1920's as the gas or electric refrigerator came in. Here and there the simple ice pit persisted—a large hole with an insulated roof. But even with all this ice-mindedness, responsible application of cold to comestibles was a long way from universal to judge by the numerous household hints as to how to refresh tainted meat and by the consistent alarm of foreign visitors over the saw-edged flavor of the butter so copiously poured over American vegetables.

The Shakers' fondness for ice may have given them the honor of inventing an American specialty that shook the British even worse than ice water and bad butter—iced tea.* It certainly was not first known, as incautious legend says, at St. Louis' Louisiana Purchase Exposition in 1904. In 1860 Solon Robinson was recommending it; in 1894 it refreshed Owen Wister in the Can Can Saloon in Benson, Arizona, just about as far from the pious peace of a Shaker village as a drink could get. Ice cream was known in pre-Revolutionary Maryland, but it seems to have been French refugees who established this Italian invention in the Atlantic port cities. Moreau de St. Méry thought Philadelphia's ice cream equal to that of Paris. It must have carried light-minded connotations, for old Elizabeth Drinker, a great lady among Philadelphia Quakers, shook her head when "William and Mary went this evening out to eat Ice'd cream; the eating ice'd cream or going to the ice'd cream house, are two acts neither of which I admire or approve." [99] Served in glasses (so it could be conveniently carried around in a crowd?), it was a sort of door prize at the Vauxhall Gardens evening resort in Man-

* There was some British precedent for taking tea cold: One ingredient of West Indian rum punches in the old days might be cold tea.

hattan soon after 1800 and was otherwise soon inseparable from warm-
weather goings-on. On the Fourth of July, 1836, R. H. Dana, homeward-
bound from California but still in bleak Antarctic waters, wistfully recalled what would be going on in Boston: ". . . the ladies . . . walking
the streets with parasols over their heads, and the dandies in their white
pantaloons. . . . What quantities of ice-cream have been eaten!" [100]

Soda water, the other part of America's most original refreshment
(except the cocktail), arrived soon after 1800 with a flavor of science
added to the sticky syrups mixed with it. It came of the discovery by
Joseph Priestley, the English pioneer in chemistry and Unitarian theology, who later took refuge in America, that the bubbly water of a
famous English spa was just ordinary water with carbon dioxide gas
dissolved in it. A Philadelphian named Nooth worked out an apparatus
for making it. Young Benjamin Silliman, later so eminent in scientific
education in America, bought one of Nooth's outfits. Its product proved
so popular in New Haven, Connecticut, that he went into the bottling
business as a sideline to his professorship at Yale, and once he found
bottles that would stand the pressure, it prospered. How many of his
customers were undergraduates aware of Lord Byron's hint about "Sermons and soda-water the day after" does not appear. But the stuff was
thought of as good for hangovers, and the deplorable American drinking
habits of the day may appear in the observation of a British visitor to
Philadelphia in 1819 that "the first thing every American who can afford
five cents . . . takes, on rising in the morning, is a glass of soda
water." [101]

The torrid summers also had much to do with the rapid spread of
soda fountains beyond large cities into the growing backcountry towns.
Dr. Daniel Drake installed Cincinnati's first soda fountain in his drugstore
there. Soda dispensing continued to be associated with persons calling
themselves Doctor, sometimes properly, and the drugstores over which
they presided. Hence the otherwise anomalous institution of the corner
drugstore soda fountain that, though fading like the phrase *drugstore
cowboy,* still lingers here and there. There may even have been a hark-
ing back to Priestley's discovery in Boston's quondam habit of calling a
soda fountain a spa. The first ice-cream sodas that I can get word of
were served in the American exhibit at the Paris Universal Exposition of
1867 and were, one of the U.S. commissioners in charge reported, the
only successful American gastronomical item. To have been thus included
among typical Americana must mean it was already popular at home.
There is a rumor that it was first developed in a German confectionery
store in San Antonio, Texas.

*   *   *

Pumpkin pies had also been conspicuous, though not popular, in that Paris display of things American. We are unaware nowadays how large the sweet pie, usually of fruit, bulked in American nutrition for most of the 1800's. The British fondness for meat pies—veal and ham, steak and kidney and so forth—took firm hold on the New World only in chicken pie; for our mince pies are more fruit than meat. As wheat flour changed from luxury to staple, however, America's glut of fruit put pie on the typical American table twice a day and in New England thrice, not as mere alternative to pudding or other sweets but as a major part of a man's fuel intake. Hence *pie book* for the book of meal tickets good at local eating houses issued to railroad employees. The IWW's "Pie in the Sky By and By" parody of the revivalists' "In the Sweet By and By" naturally cited pie as an accepted symbol of good living. On special occasions such as company or Sunday dinner self-respect required several kinds, and a guest had to eat at least a small segment of each—which was no hardship in a household presided over by the right women-folk. Depending on region and season, the choice lay among apple, peach, pear, plum, cherry, raspberry, blackberry, strawberry, blueberry (in New England), cranberry, gooseberry, grape, green grape, red currant, green currant, rhubarb (widely known as pieplant), wild grape, elderberry, dried apple, dried peach, prune, raisin, squash, pumpkin, sweet potato—and for fancy work outside the vegetable kingdom cream, custard, lemon. Dried fruit were likely to turn up in fried pies—thin-filled, folded-over half-moons fried tingling brown on each side.

The pie explosion waited until well into the century, however, probably because classic American pies need much sweetening, hence depend on the retail price of sugar. Molasses was cheap, but its pungency swamps other flavors. Maple sugar had the latter disadvantage; moreover, the time and energy needed to process it made it expensive. Cane sugar, sold in cone-shaped chunks—hence Sugarloaf as the name of a conical peak—weighing several pounds and so hard that it took special pliers to crack off bits, was so dear that it was kept in special lockboxes to thwart pilfering children and servants. Understandably it was reserved for tea and coffee and for judicious use in juleps, punch and other mixed drinks. What changed all that was a sugar boom in Louisiana after Uncle Sam took over. Larger plantations and better processing machinery greatly lowered costs of production. The newly available steamboats took this cheaper raw sugar up the river to final refining plants in St. Louis, Louisville and Cincinnati—supply centers for what presently became the Pie Belt, as sugar appeared at a practical price in the city grocery and then the crossroads store. To a lesser degree Northeastern refineries, fed by ship from New Orleans and Cuba—where a comparable sugar boom was viciously expanding the slave-smuggling business—enabled pie also mightily to flourish in New England and the Middle Atlantic states. In a manner of speaking America's prevalent dyspepsia c. 1850, associated with gobbling heavily shortened piecrust, was an automatic penalty, inadequate but irksome, for the stifling hardships of the Negro slave cutting cane—one of the world's least enjoyable jobs—in Iberville Parish.

Britain's fruit tart, ancestor of American pie, is usually deep-dish. New England's pie retained some of that high-rise effect; the over-the-mountains version evolved toward an elegant shallowness. The filling of a classic Old Northwestern cherry pie is well under half an inch in depth, making for a slight candying together of the cherries. To vent steam during baking, a palm-leaf design of small holes is pricked with a fork in the upper crust. And that is the only time a fork need touch it, for its shortening of lard in proper proportion enables its crust to be flaky and tender and yet firm enough to be lifted and eaten by hand—the first bite from the apex, the last a final segment of crunchy brown edge-crust with some filling attached. The bottom crust should have the same consistency and delicate browning as the top—a thing difficult to manage. Indeed good American pie is not easy to create, and there lay some of the dyspeptics' trouble. Pie in quantity they had to have, being Americans. Too much of what appeared on their own tables or commercially was soggy-baked or overshortened—hence all too durable when ingested. But they gobbled it down anyway.

The same drawbacks attended hot biscuits. Too often in vain cooks sought to strike a proper balance between varying qualities of saleratus —a crude potassium alkaline—and the varying acidities of the buttermilk, sour milk or sour cream reacting with it to generate the gases to raise biscuit dough during baking. One of the few things on which regular, homeopathic and botanic doctors agreed was that the national habit of bolting heavily buttered hot biscuits ominously yellow with imperfectly neutralized saleratus was deplorable. The element of chance could not vanish from even the ablest cook's hot biscuits until accurately formulated baking powder, combining acid and base in dry form, arrived in the 1850's. A particular benefactor in this respect was Professor Eben Norton Horsford, a clever analytical chemist, whose highly successful baking powder enabled him to retire young and make a hobby of the Viking settlements in North America, proving to his own satisfaction that, forming a semimythical polity called Norumbega, they had settled the estuary of the Charles River.

Yeast for leaven had come to the New World with the first Colonists, of course. The resulting wheaten light bread varied in quality with the baker's skill, for the application of heat to food was even less scientific then than now. The accepted way to test the heat of an oven was to thrust in the hand and count seconds till one had to pull it out with a faint scream. Twelve meant hot, twenty-four moderate . . . The corner cutting of commercial bakers was soon causing trouble. Stephen Girard, French-reared on the world's best bread, despaired of ever getting an eligible loaf in Philadelphia. It would probably have killed him had he ever tried the salt-rising bread evolved, maybe around his time, by some backwoods housewife possessed of wheat flour but no yeast. Its rising comes not of the reproduction of yeast, or from a chemical reaction as in baking powder, but of the corruption of a mixture of milk and cornmeal tempered with salt. The wild organisms involved can never be quite the same twice, but the smells consequent on the baking vary little in intensity. Harsh things have been said about them. In the 1930's the fumes from a bakery in New York City supplying salt-rising bread for a few addicts so annoyed the neighborhood that its manufacture was suppressed as a public nuisance. How far back it goes I cannot determine. In the 1830's a cultivated lady in pioneer Michigan wrote of it as a menace to society. But then the equally cultivated Kate Milner Rabb of Indianapolis had the hero of her learned fiction about early Indiana call it "most delicious. . . ." [102] Indeed it is, when at its best—as if a delicately reared, unsweetened plain cake had had an affair with a Pont l'Évêque cheese.

This bread was said to be good for dyspepsia. Always that harping on dyspepsia—they said the same to recommend tomatoes, which came on the American gastronomic scene at about the same time as steamboats appeared on American rivers. The Old World at first had the notion that these juicy red orbs of Latin-American origin were poisonous, to be grown only for show. But the French refugees in New York City in the 1790's brought in the custom of eating them, maybe from the West Indies, and an Italian Catholic priest settled in Newport, Rhode Island, c. 1800, introduced them there. They may have been sold for eating in New Orleans soon after the Louisiana Purchase, maybe spreading up the rivers as cheap sugar did. Within a generation, anyway, Dr. Drake found them accepted from the Gulf to the Great Lakes and extravagantly endorsed by a Western Reserve physician as remedy for not only dyspepsia but also diarrhea and liver-trouble, for keeping open the pores and warding off cholera. The rising patent-medicine industry was soon in the field with Dr. Miles' Compound Extract of Tomato, tomato pills and so on. Since nobody yet knew that tomatoes are rich in the antiscurvy vitamin C, doctors presuming on their own ignorance had again done patients a favor by accident. With the taboo thus resolved, it was quickly learned that tomatoes were delicious raw or cooked. And soon they were overused. Ever since tomato ketchup, homemade or "boughten," crowded its way to the table as a fixture toward the end of the 1800's, too many Americans have vied with Southern Italians in cherishing the illusion that almost anything—even clam chowder—tastes better with tomato flavor in it.

That our forebears ate too much is evident without the deplorings of diet-minded doctors and omniscient spinsters' books of advice. Sunday dinner at ex-President John Adams' in Quincy, Massachusetts—a household simpler than those of most Boston merchants in 1817—began with Indian pudding, a curious appetizer, and went on to three meats and four hearty winter vegetables; the wine was Madeira in the good old-fashioned heavy tradition. In the 1840's the Van Wycks of New York City, Quality in comfortable circumstances but no plutocrats, went through six or seven courses, with wines, every weekday at 5 P.M. Sunday breakfast was "Beefsteaks or chops, coffee, potatoes, hot rolls, griddle cakes with syrup, hot corn bread or muffins, and eggs. . . ." After Sunday dinner at 1 P.M. rather heavier than the weekday groaning board, there was at 6:30 P.M. "a hearty supper of hot biscuits, cold meat, game, salad and sweets" [103] with tea. It was just as well that Mr. Van Wyck usually walked from his house on Twelfth Street to his office on Vesey Street and back for dinner in midafternoon.

Fashionable evening parties had elaborate buffets dominated by oysters stewed in cream, fried in heavy batter, baked in rich sauces. All along the coast from the Carolinas to Cape Cod American oysters were not only far more plentiful than now, hence cheaper, but much larger. Thackeray said that eating his first was like swallowing a baby. Oyster cellars and oyster parlors were as widespread as soda fountains as far inland as railroads and careful packing could get a barrel of oysters without spoilage. The flavors varied with origin, but none, though all were pleasantly delicate, had the marked zest of Northern European oysters. That may account for America's proliferation of fancy ways to cook them. There was a simple majesty about the gumbo filé that General Winfield Scott, hero of Chapultepec and a renowned gourmet, too, brought to New York City: Fry a cut-up chicken; boil it to rags; add thirty or forty oysters with their accompanying liquor; after ten minutes add twenty-three spoonfuls of powdered sassafras leaves, and more, if necessary, to make the liquid drain thready off a spoon; serve in soup plates on plain rice.

At a prominent hotel, whether in a large city, at the shore or at the springs, one was confronted with bills of fare that took as long to read as the Declaration of Independence. The Commerical Hotel in Memphis, Tennessee, for instance, listed on March 20, 1854, oyster soup, redfish, seventeen entrées, nine boiled meats, nine roasts (including Muscovy duck and bear), twenty-two vegetables and twenty sweet desserts, of which nine were pies. Each vegetable was probably served in its little separate "saucedish" like the water dish of a birdcage. The inevitable fleet of such clustering around the plate always annoyed British visitors, none more than Anthony Trollope in the early 1860's: "How I did learn to hate those little dishes and their greasy contents! . . . horrid little oval dishes. . . . Those horrid little dishes! . . . how could they have been made to contain Christian food?" [104] "American plan" prevailed, and the reflection that it was all included in the rate did not blunt appetites already geared to gluttony. Most of the viands came on table in cold dishes well ahead of the gong announcing dinner and were at best lukewarm by the time they were on the diner's plate—which also was cold. Nor did a plethora of items guarantee availability. F. L. Olmsted, the traveler who preserved that Memphis bill of fare for posterity, reached the table a few minutes late, and the first five things he asked for were already all gone.

Again it is difficult to gauge the quality of all this quantity. Packing in ice probably enabled saltwater fish to get well inland in edible condition seven or eight months of the year. Certain freshwater fish, such as the Great Lakes' whitefish, were admirable. American meats, however, still lacked the full benefit of the improved bloodlines and highly organized finishing feeding of our day. Local specialties such as New England's molasses-baked beans, fish cakes and chowders could well have been savory then. But the cook, as always, was the crucial factor. A famous New York City hotel disguised in a novel by Theodore Winthrop as the Hotel Chuzzlewit had for breakfast "fried beefsteak, hard eggs, *café au delay*, soggy toast, flannel cakes, blanket cakes, and washleather cakes"; for dinner "beef in the raw or in the chip, watery vegetables, quoit pies, and . . . your choice at two dollars a bottle of twelve kinds of wine, all mixed in the same cellar and labelled in the same shop." [105] ". . . if my French palate," wrote Michael Chevalier, a good-natured visitor of the 1830's, "had to decide between the dinner of a great [American] city-hotel (excepting those of Boston, New York, Philadelphia, and Baltimore) and a country inn where I should sit by the side of the blacksmith . . . I . . . should really choose the latter." [106]

Jefferson had tried hard to add French suavity and imagination to New World cooking; so had the French refugee immigrants of the 1790's. Words like *filet, bisque* and *salmi* began to appear on bills of fare particularly after Boston's Tremont House, a pacesetter for American hotels in several ways, went heavily Francophile—at least in print. (New York

City's Astor House countered with a scornful but futile policy of using French for a dish only when there was no sound English translation.) Doubtless French notions of sauces, seasonings and gentle handling had a salutary effect on a nation that mingled plain roast and boiled with a passion for the sound of lard popping in the skillet. But the spelling confronting the customer was often ominous. As late as 1855 the United States Hotel at Saratoga, peer of any resort in the country, was stammering about: "Filet of Veal a la Gardinere . . . Tenderloin of Mutton a la Maire d'Hote . . . Currie of Veal en Bordured de Riz . . ." [107] One wonders how much Frenchness had actually rubbed off on the *chef de cuisine* making out that *carte du jour* or on the one in Memphis listing "Giblets volivon" and "Blamonge." The Gulf Coast's Creole cooking, centered in New Orleans, was as much Spanish-Colonial as French West Indian, and neither implied close kinship with that of the Trois Frères Provençaux in Paris. The real significance of the cult of *à la* may have lain in its heightening of the nation's gradual orientation toward the Continent—as opposed to Britain—already begun in the popularity of the French Revolution and, rather indirectly, of the German crank therapeutic cults.

As sharply competing bars multiplied in towns, their rival generosities with free lunch further encouraged stuffing oneself. Anybody buying a beer or two at a typical corner saloon for clerks and skilled workmen had the run gratis of several cheeses, baked beans, hard-boiled eggs, salt herring, crackers, bread, pickles, maybe a stew or a heavy soup. With beer at five cents a young fellow on a low beginner's salary could have a considerable midday meal at very little cost. The more glittering establishments, whose habitués wore brocaded vests and pointed boots, threw in with the brandy smashes and sherry cobblers oyster stew, Welsh rabbit, cold game, Smithfield ham. Farmers ate even more than city fellows, of course, though with better reason. Indeed the cultural basis of all this stuffing was rural, a carry-over into town of eating habits justified, if at all, by sweating-hard work twelve hours a day, six days a week.

Champagne soon so dominated expensive festivities based on gaslight and oysters that the concoction of counterfeit fizz, wired cork, straw basket, customs marks and all became a minor industry in New Jersey. But the French tradition of still table wines took root only among the upper layers of the Quality. On a crack resort-country steamboat on Lake Champlain in the 1850's, for instance, the wine list carried five champagnes, four sherries, only one claret, no other table wine. Philip Hone, though something of a parvenu, yet knew and dined with a great many of New York City's Quality; in 1836 his extraordinarily ample

*Nicholas Longworth's vineyards near Cincinnati overlooked
appropriately Rhine-like scenery.*

private cellar contained nothing but 2,688 quarts of Madeira and sherry.
Those fortified wines also retained considerable favor among fast young
men because they were almost as expensive as champagne and higher
in alcohol content.

Nicholas Longworth, a canny New Jersey lawyer settled in Cincinnati
and prospering in land speculations, did all he could to popularize white
wines from cultivated strains of native grapes in his Ohio vineyards.
Foreigners and high-chinned Quality from the East alike were impressed
by both his still wines and his sparkling Catawba. The German vine-
dressers whom he imported for his vineyards described them as equal to
those at home, and the German colony in Cincinnati bought them with
alacrity. To most Americans, however, wine remained, as it still does, a
rather alien affair with toploftical connotations. Until California vineyards, mostly under German and German-Swiss auspices, got their feet
under them after the Civil War, American winemaking remained a
stunted struggle for foothold in northwestern Ohio and upper New
York State, plus rural puttering with scuppernong grapes (in the Carolinas), mustang grapes (in Texas), elderberries, blackberries and
dandelions. Grandma might be locally known for some such bucolic
tipple, but it was not drunk with meals. For that purpose, as temperance
and change of usage eliminated cider and spirits and water, America
was turning—much to the consternation of Frenchmen—to washing
down three meals a day with sweetened coffee rich with cream.

The Frenchman was often further troubled by the size of the American breakfast and some of its dishes, such as the buckwheat griddle cakes that foreigners often compared to disks of warm flannel. This New World delicacy—if that is the word for a thing so hearty—represented not an item of indigenous flora or fauna that America was lucky to have, such as shad or terrapin, but imaginative adaptation to human use of a cereal that Western Europe had largely relegated to poultry and cattle. The ancestor may have been the Scottish pikelet, but size and texture had greatly altered. A batter of buckwheat flour duly "riz" overnight in a warm kitchen after infection with the remains of yesterday's organism-rich batter, baked on a hot griddle kissed with a bacon rind, eaten with butter and maple syrup, so suited New World taste that neither the lumber camp nor the shiniest hotel could get along without it. C. 1850 New York State alone was growing nearly 4,000,000 bushels of buckwheat a year, largely for human consumption.

Early FFV planters trying anything for a profit sometimes baked ship's biscuit—much like the soldier's despised hardtack—to sell to sea captains as ship's stores. The beaten biscuit of the Chesapeake area, a traditional adjunct of Smithfield ham, may be a refinement of this prosaic item. In parts of Polynesia ship's biscuit is still considered a delicacy.

Cracked-wheat prophets of the early 1800's often scolded Americans for neglecting exercise. The charge was pointless for most of the population. They were still on the farm or otherwise laboring so hard for such long hours that hygienic exertion was unnecessary. Whether woods-clearing settler or established farmer, pa kept himself, ma and their sons and daughters above the age of six busy with the thronging chores of field, woodpile, orchard, kitchen, smokehouse, dairy, laundry, soap kettle, ash heap, loom. The teamster who walked almost as far as the team needed no further rhythmic muscle use and stirring up of the lymphatic system. Sunup to sundown the lumberjack swung his ax; the railroad construction gang carried rail, drilled rock for explosives, shoveled ballast; the miner wielded pick and shovel. But towns becoming cities needed more and more pen-pushers and machine tenders, minor and major administrators, whose work was either wholly sedentary or consisted of standing behind a counter, or before a steam- or water-powered machine, or at bars consummating deals over drinks. The walk to and from work in Mr. Van Wyck's fashion languished as distance between job and home lengthened. The most well-to-do substituted carriage wheels. The next several lower strata crowded the public omnibuses now bowling along, often at a trot to save precious time for the passengers and collect more fares per day for the owners. In winter they were put on runners or replaced by great "man-of-war sleighs" holding up to 100, standees included.

To fill the consequent exercise gap, Mr. Brownstone and his clerks had little notion of deliberate athletics. Horseback riding carried prestige and was deemed healthful, but keeping a horse was expensive. As a medical man Dr. Holmes recommended riding but also spoke feelingly of the offhandedness with which horses chewed up dollar bills, as well as hay. Skating was fashionable but seasonal and even in season at the mercy of fickle weather. Athletic clubs hardly existed, for the German cult of the gymnasium had not yet spread far, and not even New York City's august Racquet Club antedates 1846. Baseball, just struggling to birth, affords little exercise anyway. Football was primitive and sporadic; golf, brought in by the Dutch in embryo, long forgotten; tennis, tank swimming, basketball not yet born. Boxing, foot racing, rowing were largely for the lower orders, particularly from the British and Irish lower classes who had a background of such sports. A given stock clerk in the Tappan brothers' silk warehouse in New York City doubtless had had a farmer grandfather who could shoulder a bushel of wheat with each hand. His town-reared grandson was pasty-faced, spindly and easily run out of breath because his muscles had had little to do. His puniness was so striking that alien visitors seeing thousands of him recalled the talk of Buffon and other naturalists of the 1700's about the New World's dooming imported domestic flora and fauna to degenerate.

Such forebodings of degeneracy were strengthened by observation of the New World townsman's womenfolk. Young Mrs. Benjamin Brownstone's grandmother had devoted to wool spinning whatever time was left from the day's chores. It was done on that perpendicular wheel as high as a girl's sleek head—now standing insufficiently explained in the local old-mill museum—with its swift revolutions drawing her to and fro in a half-dancing run, the thread held high in a charmingly graceful gesture that made men's hearts skip a beat and gave her the habitual carriage of a blooded filly. Carrying books on the head at a fashionable academy had given granddaughter no such style. And since she and young Brownstone lived in a genteel boardinghouse for their first married years—a bedroom-and-full-meals arrangement also available at hotels at varying price scales—she had precisely nothing to do. High rents and inability to find servants at reasonable wages were the reasons usually given for the prevalence of this fashionable makeshift among well-off couples above the Mason and Dixon Line. It might even turn permanent; children were reared in boardinghouses as if in ocean liners never making port.

The bedrooms of even expensive hotels were small and niggardly furnished, so while husband was breadwinning downtown, his spouse killed time in the large and lavishly tricked-out public rooms belowstairs. Foreigners wondered at their listless lives "in wonderfully rich and gay dresses, reclining on damask-covered sofas, or lounging in the universal rocking-chairs—a few reading or playing the piano, but the majority passing a *dolce far niente* kind of existence, which would be insupportable to the thrifty and domestic English wife." [108] In these feckless women's terms an hour's ride into the country in a carriage—barouche, brougham or sleigh according to season—was exercise. On a slightly lower economic level the equivalent was a trip downtown in an omnibus and a stroll for a few blocks of dawdly shopping in one's most elaborately overtrimmed bonnet. The American's dislike of using the legs was already apparent in 1832, when a Scot at fashionable Saratoga found that whenever he and his party went for a bracing walk, people in passing carriages always pulled up to "very civilly offer us a ride . . . and hardly believe us serious when, in declining, . . . we tell them that we prefer to walk. . . . It absolutely seems disgraceful to be seen walking." In a nearby village "No one, who does not live in the village, walks to church on foot. All have conveyances of some sort . . . and come in them . . . a human being walking anywhere on the public road is rarely seen. The earnings of the laborers enable them to travel in the stages." [109] That contrasts strongly with the old days of Goody Perkins riding pillion behind Perkins and the rest of the family following barefoot, shoes in hand. It was an even greater contrast with Scotland of the 1830's —another good rough index of the relative standards of living that made emigrants urge stay-at-home relatives to cross the sea.

It was the wrong time of year for that observant Scot to see the one exception—for schoolchildren. Americans had escaped from the compact Yankee village. The district schoolhouse was a good way from the dwellings of most of its pupils scattered each on 100 acres or so, and neither the condition of the roads in winter nor the township budget admitted attempts at a school bus. Whatever the weather, children came —or did not come—to school on foot, often a matter of several miles each way five days a week. This may offer one explanation of the Americans' pedephobia. He, and she too, had often had an early bellyful of walking, whereas Old World rustics' children, with no school to attend, had had less plodding through icy mud on chilblained feet. In some states a second factor may have been the Negro's scorn of a white man too poor to own a horse—what West Indian slaves called a walkfoot buckra. A third was the horse-mindedness of a rural culture where distances were long, feed and pasture cheap, and it was unusually likely that a country boy could acquire a horse, a good horse, and find occasion frequently to show it off before folks. This strong smell of horse was crucial because, though the westward-creeping nation was heavily committed to waterways and oxen, the saddle was the chief tool of backwoods communications and interactions.

Mails, such as they were, moved by postrider on most routes. Two settlers bound from here to there, yet able to command only one horse "rode and tied." This Old Country device had A ride the animal for a given distance, then tie it to a roadside tree and walk on; B to walk until he reaches the tethered horse, ride it the same distance, passing A en route, then dismount in turn and tie it up . . . Thus each rode part of the journey, making better average time than he could have afoot, and frequent rests kept the horse in better shape than if he had been ridden steadily. Other wayfarers tempted by the sight of the mount awaiting A or B were salutarily aware that in backwoods justice horse stealing was worse than manslaughter and a frequent occasion of lynching. To call a man a horse thief was the ultimate insult. As a new settlement stabilized, it often formed a Horse-Thief Detection Association—an institution probably originating in New England after the Revolution and spreading over the Northeast—to run down such enemies of mankind—and incidentally any other local perpetrators of crime. Some such organizations had enviable records of getting their men. With dues, officers and regular meetings, they were a sort of farmers' equivalent of the Ladies Aid and persisted in many places until the appearance of state police forces forty and fifty years ago rendered them superfluous.

In his *Notes on the State of Virginia* Thomas Jefferson denied Buffon's theory of the biological degeneracy of America. Actually he had only to point out the sturdy new breeds of horses developed there. The Narragansett pacer, the Colonies' first definite strain, appeared before wheels were of much use, hence was a saddle breed. But as the Pennsylvania Dutch turned to wheels and wagon roads, they bred a Conestoga strain of draft horses—chunky, powerful complements to the Conestoga wagon and also most impressive at plowing. As improved roads encouraged the use of one- or two-passenger light carts, like the deacon's "wonderful one-hoss shay" (the Yankee's corruption of *chaise,* analogous to a wheeled chair) or the calash or the sulky, doctors and clergymen needed a horse to draw in harness and also stand up under saddle where roads still forbade wheels. In 1789 Justin Morgan, a Vermont singing teacher, took in on a debt a dark-bay stallion colt, a genetic freak from Springfield, Massachusetts, whose get filled that need with the great Morgan strain of three-purpose horses—saddle, harness, plow.

The one-hoss shay, indispensable to Yankee doctors and parsons.

His ancestry was never cleared up. Gossip said that his sire, who must have had some Arabian in him, was stolen in the Revolution from the commander of a troop of Tory partisans—one of the De Lanceys of New York City, always a horsey family. Named for his new owner, the original Morgan sire had several owners during the thirty-three years he lived. By his fecundity and emphatic genes Justin Morgan the horse gave Justin Morgan the man immortality. Nothing that an American horse trader could say about an animal in the shafts of a buggy carried more weight than "a touch of the Morgan strain there."

This compact patriarch weighed just under 1,000 pounds—small for a horse. His neck was powerfully thick at the base; his eyes were "very dark and prominent with a spirited but pleasant expression . . . muzzle small . . . muscles . . . remarkably large for a horse of his size. . . . His hair . . . at almost all seasons short and glossy . . . a very fast walker. In trotting his gait was slow and smooth, and his step short and nervous. Although he raised his feet but little he never stumbled. His proud, bold and fearless style of movement . . . [has], perhaps, never been surpassed . . . perfectly gentle and kind to handle . . . taken out with bridle or halter he was in constant motion and very playful. . . ." And lest he sound like a horse angel, he had two crotchets recalling the late W. C. Fields. He disliked children and, if loose, would chase out of sight any dog that came near. In harness he was "an eager and nimble traveler, but patient in bad spots"—ideal for American roads. In farmwork "whatever he was hitched to generally had to come the first time. . . ." [110] Under saddle he was great at quarter racing—the horse-age's equivalent of drag racing, a straightaway quarter-mile dash leading to the present special breed of quarter horses. And the beauty of it was that he and his progeny handed down generation to generation with a consistency rare in genetics that whole complex of nerve, temperament and muscle to thousands on thousands of Morgans and part Morgans.

These doughty Yankee horses specialized in hauling the Yankee-made Concord coaches in wet or dry, steep or level, snow or thunderstorm.

Foreigners commented on how gentle the otherwise cross-grained stage driver was with his four-footed, prick-eared colleagues, never touching them with the whip, only "smacked it in the air and talked to [them] as though . . . they understood every word . . . the horses themselves are more docile and tractable than [in Britain] . . . no vicious or refractory horses in any . . . teams." [111] Hitched single or double to the farmer's Dearborn wagon—a light covered affair with side curtains, sometimes equipped with wooden springs, sometimes with passenger seats, used for a multitude of chores by the American of the early 1800's—the Morgans were an equivalent of the Model T Ford. They drew New York City's newfangled horsecars in the 1850's. In the Civil War they made fine cavalry mounts. For the first half of the 1800's they dominated the harness racing in sulkies that became essential to all county and state fairs and that has been a major American contribution to international sport.

The "carryall," a modification of the farmer's Dearborn wagon,
was the family standby in the mid-1800's.

Not until after Appomattox did the Standardbred horse, based on the Hambletonian strain, take over trotting and pacing and, by incorporating some of the best Morgan strains, almost annihilate the rival breed. In the mid-century the glossiest token of worldly success was a fine pair of trotters, usually Morgans, able to make those of a rival new millionaire eat dust in an impromptu brush on the open road. And virtuosity in horse trading, usually of harness horses, was a trait of the folk ideal.

The Morgan's magnetism persists. When extinction was almost complete sixty years ago, Uncle Sam, with cavalry remounts in mind, set about rebuilding the breed on a farm in Vermont, later taken over by the University of Vermont. Now the great stud there, a striking tribute to the strain's genius for breeding true, attracts 30,000 horse-minded visitors a year.

A much less dashing sort of beast had also been helping discredit Buffon. Until 1800 he could have cited the American sheep as proof that Old

World vertebrates pined and dwindled in the New World. The bewildered creature that Dr. Nott's mother dared to shear to clothe her son was probably a sorry specimen, like all the others on whom the Colonists relied for everyday clothes and minor meat supply.* Napoleon inadvertently changed that. The finest wool in the world then came from Spain's Merino sheep, and the Spanish Crown had always cannily banned export of breeding stock. But the First Consul's wars in Spain and Portugal so shattered those already friable nations that the ban on sheep export went by the board along with a great many other things, c. 1801-2. British and American diplomats on the spot began to buy from the best flocks and send home hundreds of regally pedigreed and richly fleeced ewes and rams.

Some went to Australia to found the wool industry that became that turbulent convict colony's first valid reason for being. Others came to New England from the U.S. minister to Portugal, David Humphreys, former aide and intimate of George Washington and a member of the Hartford Wits. In the New World his Merinos and those of William Jarvis of Boston, U.S. minister in Madrid, proved fine investments as others recognized in them a Godsent means to profit from New England's stony hills. Eli Whitney paid $300 for a ram and ewe, "dirty looking animals, but I have [already] been offered four hundred for the pair . . . the demand is much greater than can be supplied." [112] A thousand for a single ram was reached after Jefferson's embargo on trade with overseas belligerents cut off importation of fine British textiles, for Merino wool was the only fiber with which American looms could hope to supply homemade equivalents. The boom broke when British goods reappeared in the American market at the end of the War of 1812. But meanwhile, salutary Merino genes were permeating and expanding American sheepdom. By 1840 some 2,000,000 sheep, profitable wool producers now, were nibbling on the slopes of Vermont and New Hampshire. The wool craze did a good deal to start the great emigration from New England westward as outsiders came buying hill farms and the previous owners used the cash to resettle themselves in New York State and the upper parts of the Old Northwest. They filled the rolling hills of eastern Ohio with wool on the hoof marketed through opportunistic dealers; John Brown of Harpers Ferry, who considered himself primarily a sheepman, came to grief trying to buck these sharp customers. And many an Old Northwesterner learned from already

* It is often suggested (see Jameson, *American Revolution,* 50-61) that the inferior nutritive quality of the native American grasses may have had something to do with this. Certainly introduction of European grasses, such as bluegrass, was important. On the other hand, American horses flourished on native pasture.

experienced Yankee newcomers that sheep, which will browse practically anything, are even better than cattle to keep the adjacent forest from creeping out into laboriously cleared fields.

That service was the worse needed because among the most vigorous emigrants from the Old World had been weeds previously unknown in the New and soon flourishing in a manner further to discomfit Buffon. Prewhite America had not been weedless. Among indigenous items still plaguing farmer and gardeners were ragweed, curse of the allergic; the extravagantly rank and tropically gorgeous (though poisonous) pokeweed; Jimsonweed (a corruption of "Jamestown weed"), cousin of the deadly nightshade with psychedelic powers valued by the Indians. But relative lack of what ecologists call open-soil habitat—meaning prevalence of tilth and turf—had kept them from showing what they could do. They wanted bared soil to seed in and plenty of sunshine—exactly what was supplied by the pioneer's cleared field and then by the graded road, the canal embankment, the railroad right-of-way. Indigenous weeds traveled westward along the growing American railroad system almost as fast as the early trains steamed.

Along with them traveled interloping weeds from Europe. They had made the Atlantic crossing as seeds polluting seed wheat, rye and so on; in dirt on stones brought as ballast by ships with light cargoes; in hay and straw used as packing for imported china and glassware. A Briton in New England in 1675 already saw on the roadsides old friends from home—exotics here—such as dandelion, shepherd's purse, plantain, mullein. Traditional English herbs such as tansy, deliberately imported to plant in gardens for their alleged medicinal virtues, escaped and were thoroughly at home in the liberating atmosphere of the New World. Purslane, now widely established here, may have come as a garden vegetable. Morning glory, barberry, spearmint, are other exotics deliberately introduced and escaping to explosive effect. The mint was welcomed by all but teetotalers and sheep; but morning glory is a pest, and barberry harbors a black rust that heavily damages wheat. This world of plant immigrants was, in fact, like that of the human ones. Some of those chosen as likely acquisitions for a new country proved disappointing. Many came without responsible auspices. And by and large the weeds (human, as well as vegetable) did as well or better than anybody had a right to expect.

The Merinos also had a hoof in creating a great American institution, the country fair. Elkanah Watson, the energetic Yankee so eager to see navigation improved between the Hudson and the Great Lakes, had retired to an estate in Massachusetts' Berkshire Hills and during the Merino boom acquired a breeding pair. When he showed them on the common at

Pittsfield, the attention they attracted gave him the notion of organizing annual shows of livestock and farm produce during which smart farmers could swap experiences and buy and trade seeds and sires. The first blooming of the scheme in 1808 sounds already well matured. There was a band, the committee members wore badges of wheat in their hats, and the feature of the parade was a team of sixty-nine oxen—New England's draft oxen were the backbone of lumbering in the North, and breeding them was important business—drawing a plow held by the oldest inhabit-ant of Berkshire County. Watson, a born missionary, persuaded Coopers-town, New York—of which James Fenimore Cooper, not yet a novelist, was the leading magnate—to try such a Farmer's Holiday, as he called the Berkshire doings. It was a great success, with the governor sending a sack of special Mediterranean seed wheat of which each guest at the banquet got a half-pint to try. By 1820 Watson's zeal, plus the intrinsic merits of the notion, had practically every farming county in New England holding an annual fair. The movement slackened in the 1830's but accelerated again in the 1840's and has ever since been as salient a detail of American farm life as red paint for barns.

Gradually these fairs became means not only to widen acceptance of better seeds and sires but also to urge the American farmer to farm bet-ter—a thing of which, except among the Pennsylvania Dutch, he stood sadly in need. Historians usually attribute his stubborn fecklessness before the important mechanization that began in the mid-1860's to two factors: the New World's chronic shortage of labor, which encouraged lick-and-a-promise methods; and the long-persisting plenty of new land to exploit. Even if he knew the tricks of soil and fertility conservation—and nobody had ever introduced him to them—why devote precious man-hours to such purposes when, as this farm wore out, another was to be had virgin-fertile for a few dollars an acre a few hundred miles farther west? In the most elementary part of good farming, visitors from Europe, where cow and horse dung were properly valued, were astonished by the New World's neglect of its use, even on large operations under important and responsible owners. The huge stock barn on General Philip Schuyler's estate on the Hudson was so built that the animal droppings fell through the floor to the ground below, where spring rains washed them into the river, for, they told Mrs. Grant of Laggan in the mid-1700's, "the soil in its original state [does not require] the aid of manure." [113] Sixty years later at Governor Thomas Worthington's great estate of Adena near Chillicothe, Ohio, dung merely accumulated in a great barn with no effort to get it on the land, and all through that fine new Scioto River coun-try all animal manures were consistently "flung into the river," wrote an astonished Briton, "I dare say that the Inn we put up in does not tumble into the water less than 300 loads of horse-dung every year." [114] An able English farmer going west to settle in Illinois in 1821 saw nothing intelligent done with dung until he reached the lower Shenandoah Valley, where Pennsylvania Dutch influence was heavy.

Some notion of crop rotation was beginning to seep into the agricultural mind in long-settled regions, thanks partly to the introduction of clover by the Reverend Jared Eliot of Connecticut in the mid-1700's and of alfalfa by "American Farmer" Crèvecoeur in the 1790's—a boon in gratitude for which his adopted country should forgive him his foolish writings about her. Jefferson was a great man for crop rotation, too, and for the contour plowing that would slow down erosion, which was much more of a problem in America than in moisture-sodden Northern Europe. But even minor acceptance of that was rare until other Southern prophets of soil conservation took it up again in the 1850's, anticipating the educational campaigns of the 1930's. Tile drainage, a long-standing European device, did not begin its American career until the 1840's, as the preachments of the budding agricultural press finally began to take hold.

As steam came in, note-taking Britons planning books about America often landed in Boston from a Cunarder and decided that in some respects it was like a British town—an opinion that made Boston purr when it read their books. Then they began a well-established round of scenery and sociology: the Hudson Valley seen from the steamboat; the same seen from the colonnaded Catskill House; Niagara Falls and its rival at Trenton, New York (long since blotted out by hydroelectric dams); New York State's and Pennsylvania's model prisons; Congress in session, spittoons and boot soles conspicuous. Before leaving Boston they usually made a side trip to see the girl textileworkers of nearby Lowell, Massachusetts—a sociological wonder in their day, last heard of in Rodgers and Hammerstein's *Carousel*.

Francis Cabot Lowell, a wellborn Bostonian, had deserved well of the commonwealth by bringing back from England in his clever head the design of the power loom—a technological feat comparable to Slater's in mentally smuggling in the design of the spinning machine. Until then handweaving had sadly clogged American textile making. Now at Waltham, Massachusetts, Lowell and his backers built a momentous plant in which waterpower took cotton from bale to spindle to loom all under one roof. By 1822 the system was applied to further such facilities at the 30-foot fall of the Merrimack River at Chelmsford, Massachusetts—a locality soon renamed Lowell and pregnant with economic significance.

The visiting Briton probably knew about textile labor at home. It consisted of rootless families struggling to keep body and soul together by working children, as well as both parents—the classic proletariat of the Industrial Revolution. The same pattern developed in New England in spinning mills built at scattered waterpowers. These Yankee proletarians usually lived in company housing and, like the employees of the typical ironworks, were more or less tied to company stores, but at least these mill villages were new and as yet less dismal than the sooty, overgrown industrial cities of England's Midlands. What made the visitor to Lowell goggle, however, was the system of labor supply there perfected by imaginative capitalists. The hands prevalent in these red-brick, many-windowed fortresses of efficiency, each topped by a toylike white belfry, were respectable and self-respecting, relatively well paid and well fed, unmarried country girls buying where and what they liked once room and board were paid for.

The streets of English textile towns were regularly filled with grubby slatterns of various ages shuffling to and from work of such grim hopelessness that they often sought relief in drink and fornication (the latter sometimes to eke out the wages and secure the former). In Lowell an English visitor of 1828 looking out the hotel window when the 6 A.M. bell called the payroll to duty, saw the town "speckled over with girls . . . glittering with bright shawls and showy-coloured gowns, all streaming along . . . with . . . an elasticity of step implying an obvious desire to get to their work." [115] The contrast lasted long. Fourteen years later in a cold season Dickens was amazed to see these girls' successors well decked out in "serviceable bonnets, good warm cloaks and shawls . . . healthy in appearance, many of them remarkably so . . . the manners and deportment of young women, not of degraded brutes." [116] Twelve years later still another brisk young Briton called "The difference between a Manchester factory girl and a Lowell 'young lady' . . . great indeed. The latter is generally good-looking, often pretty, dresses fashionably . . . takes delight in flowers, which gives a gay appearance to the factory rooms." [117] No posies in England's "dark Satanic mills."

The secret was that these several thousand young ladies were not from among the squalidly necessitous but daughters of independent upcountry farmers and artisans and came to Lowell not to face a monotonous lifetime of machine tending but to devote only a few years to acquiring money for personal advancement, their own or another's. During the average four or five years' stay a careful Lowell girl might pile up $300 to $400 in the local savings bank. On reaching this predetermined goal she quit work, bought the linen and furniture needed for a proper young-married start in life, and went home to espouse the nice young fellow who had been waiting for her. Or a weekly dollar or two sent home enabled her brother to get through college and become a minister or her father to reduce the mortgage on the old place. Or she was paying her way through a girls' academy by alternating academic years with years of millwork fitting herself to teach school at home or as a missionary of the three R's in the teacher-hungry Old Northwest. ". . . none of us had the least idea of continuing at [mill jobs] permanently," [118] wrote Lucy Larcom, a Lowell girl off and on who finally went West to teach and became a wellknown lady versifier with a park in Lowell named in her memory.

Employers did not discourage such off-and-on employment. If Amanda Brewster took some months off for a visit home or to teach a district school for the summer, that was her affair, and she was welcome to return when she liked. Such smart and reliable girls were as interchangeable as the parts in Eli Whitney's firearms, and the more cordial they felt toward the mills, the likelier they were to keep up the labor pool by recommending millwork to their younger sisters and cousins. The system sounds like an extension of the Yankee custom of the marriageable daughter of a family in decent but limited circumstances going as help to a well-to-do local household (of which, like as not, husband or wife was a distant cousin) to earn and save small wages for a trousseau. Even though she did so much cooking and washing, she was on a fairly even footing, eating with the family, introduced to guests, on first-name terms with the daughters of the house. And her lady employer, Miss Larcom said, "if her nature were at all generous . . . added to [wages] her friendship, her gratitude and esteem." [119]

For the Lowell millowner, to spin about such girls a sense of neighborly-cousinly solicitude was a local social duty, as well as sound personnel policy—for, unlike the English woman hand, the Lowell girl usually had a livelihood-basis back home to retire to if she felt put-upon. To prevent parental uneasiness about her being far away among strangers, she was encouraged to live in an approved—and sometimes partly subsidized—boardinghouse, the rooms, table and landlady of which were so diligently inspected that it amounted to a proto-YWCA. The girls slept two to four in a room—just as in the farmhouse back home—and paid some $6 a month for bed, meals and laundry. The run of meals was *breakfast:* hot biscuit or toast, pie, butter, coffee or tea; *dinner:* meat and potatoes, vegetables, bread, butter, coffee or tea; *supper:* hot biscuit or bread "with some kind of sauce," probably meaning a vegetable, or maybe applesauce or preserves, cake, pie and tea. The fare back home was probably about the same. The week's pay of $3 to $3.50 left a good residue for the savings bank, less each girl's share in the cost of the newspapers and magazines and maybe the piano for after-hours recreation in the dining room —and also the cost of the pretty clothes. They caused comment when they went home to Perkins Center "with new silk dresses and Navarino bonnets, trimmed with flowers, and lace veils and gauze handker-chiefs," [120] and the sight moved many a country mouse to try her wings as a Lowell girl. Some thought that too much went into finery. If so, it meant only that Hiram had to wait a little longer for his bride.

The employers required regular attendance at some church. Most of the girls might well have gone voluntarily; many devoted another hour or two of their only free day to Sunday Schools. They often subscribed to a lending library, and the cleverest of them published under the auspices of local parsons a literary magazine, *The Lowell Offering,* that struck for-eigners as the most amazing detail in the whole picture. It included topical references to phrenology and sometimes astringent comment on some as-pects of the mills. The very best of it was capable and the average hardly more insipid than the typical gift annual of the day. A volume of selections that Harriet Martineau published in England under the title of *Mind Among the Spindles* elicited suspicion that the sponsoring ministers or somebody had rewritten or heavily edited the contributions. The mistake was natural. England had no counterparts of the independent-minded, knowledge-hungry girls whom New Hampshire farms produced along with apples, maple sugar and stone walls.

Working hours—six days a week, twelve hours a day in summer, a shorter sunup to sundown at other seasons—were undeniably long; but permission for time off for shopping and other personal needs was not difficult to secure and the year-round average day was around ten and a half hours—certainly no longer than the girls' mothers worked back home. Nor was millwork heavy. Most assignments afforded slack time enough to tempt them to bring in books to read. Forbidden to do so, they still smuggled in pocket Bibles as least heinous. The pay was good in terms of the time. Chevalier, an economist as impressed as anybody, con-trasted this margin after board of some $2 a week with the fact that "few women in Europe [in the 1830's] outside some of the great cities can earn more than . . . $1.00 a week [gross]" [121] and pointed out that in Europe food also cost more than in America. Yet it would be false to draw the picture all roses. The employers' blacklists barred reemployment of girls showing improper spirit by light conduct such as neglect to go to church at a cost of $6 a year—three weeks' average savings—for pew space. In 1836, as hard times loomed, the employers cut wages and dis-continued the 25-cent weekly subsidy of the individual's board bill. The girls, maybe aware of the contemporary strikes of the Philadelphia seam-stresses, struck. Three thousand walked out to hold an indignation meet-ing in a park, one of the first strikes among textileworkers in American history. The speeches of their leader, a young woman using one of the town pumps as rostrum, were also the first local instances of a woman addressing a public meeting, which, said a Lowell girl witness, caused consternation among her audience. In consequence of the witness' adherence to the cause, her mother was dismissed as an accredited boardinghouse keeper.

The bosses won; the cut stuck. But the memory lingered even after employee relations had sweetened up again. In the boardinghouses the girls continued occasionally to sing, partly in nostalgic fun, the rallying song of the abortive strike, to the tune of a bit of anti-Catholic propaganda about the sad fate of nuns:

> Oh! isn't it a pity such a pretty girl as I
> Should be sent to the factory to pine away and die? . . .

In 1845 a Lowell girl named Sarah Bagley led some of her sister hands in forming the Female Labor Reform Association that played a part in the New England Workingmen's Association's agitation for union recognition and the ten-hour day. As editor of the association's paper, *The Voice of Industry,* she also helped bring about the Massachusetts legislature's first investigation of working conditions in the textile industry, which were by no means up to Lowell standards generally. But the day of the sweetly superior Lowell girl was gradually passing, and Miss Bagley retired, apparently in disillusion, in 1848.

This deterioration was accelerated by the panic of 1857, a reaction to the inflation associated with California gold, which jarred most Lowell owners into selling off their stocks of cotton and either ceasing or curtailing operations. That broke the already weakening chain of labor supply from upcountry farms. When Lowell's cotton-textile industry resumed full speed ahead after the end of the Civil War had renewed cotton supply, it was largely manned—and womaned and childrened—by immigrant Irish of less stable habits and by the first French Canadians coming over the border hungry for wage livelihood in towns. The Lowell girls, those "fair, unveiled Nuns of Industry, Sisters of Thrift," [122] as Whittier had called them, were no more; indeed Prince Jerome Napoleon, visiting Lowell in 1861, had already reproachfully reported as much to Chevalier. Yet they had left progeny—in a most respectable way.

Their basic situation—temporary employment for youth of nonproletarian status needing money to prepare for supra-proletarian futures—stimulated the embryonic American tradition of working your way through college, particularly in the field of summer hotels. Further, the Lowell girls showed the nation that a nice girl could stay nice, even though working for men managers out in the great world far from home. It is often thought that self-reliant employment for women had to wait until the typewriter was invented. Actually the lady telegrapher and the girl typesetter were well broken in before the Civil War. By the 1850's the Cheney Brothers' silk mills in Massachusetts had women as clerical help in the office, as well as in the spinning department, and Mrs. Sarah Josepha Hale, who often combined a sense of realistic social reform with being editor of *Godey's Lady's Book,* had got A. T. Stewart, New York City's most conspicuous dry goods magnate, to replace some of the male sales help in his fine new store with girls. Since 1848 Philadelphia's School of Design for Women had been training them in mechanical drawing for a livelihood. All that—minor but premonitory of so much opportunity to come—was several cuts above the kind of work available for the woman trying desperately to keep herself and her dependents afloat in a slum environment. The best she could hope for was desperately sweated take-home sewing.

If single, she could have got better quarters and adequate meals and a dollar or two a week by domestic service. But for the American-born that was practically unthinkable except in the Yankee-rural context mentioned above. Nine-tenths of the sweated sewing women of the mid-1800's, according to Emerson David Fite's authoritative estimate, "preferred to stick to the needle and starve" rather than "put themselves on a plane of equality with the negroes and the Irish" [123] in better paying household work. Word usage reflected this. The farm girl who had decided to "live out a spell" because "her folks have been sick and [she wants] a little money to pay the doctor" [124] considered herself "help" or a "hired girl." Refer to her as a servant in her hearing, and she was gone, with a flounce of skirts and a very red face. Employment agencies' signs in cities offered not servants but "Male and Female Help," a term still surviving in the classified pages of newspapers. The scanty supply of domestics thus offered was mostly Irish immigrants well inured to the term *servant* where they came from, but American sensitivity quickly penetrated to them, though for lack of training to do anything else, they were still willing to take such work in the new country.

In earliest Pennsylvania it had already been noted that newly married women ". . . are for the most part a little uneasie, and make their husbands so too, till they procure them a Maid Servant to bear the burden of Work, as also in some measure to wait on them." [125] That was a readily attainable mark of status when indentured girls were coming ashore from the Old Country with every ship. But 150 years later the wife of a rising young man in Albany, Harrisburg or Cleveland, with a house and children to tend, needing a servant or two not only for prestige but for help in cooking and cleaning, well able to pay for them, was much worse off. About all she could get was an Irish girl fresh out of the bogs, usually willing to turn her hand to things, but imperfectly aware of the uses of soap and with no notion of how to cook anything but potatoes or oatmeal. Demand for even such girls, implying as they did the prospect of months of vexatious training, was so high that well-to-do New York City women patrolled outside Castle Garden, the landing place for immigrants, for first pick of the newcomers. Women now bewail the good old days when servants were readily obtainable. Relatively they were more so then; but Fredrika Bremer, the Swedish novelist, found servantless households rather usual in New England in the mid-century largely "from the difficulty there is in getting good servants . . . the family waits upon itself . . . a thing to be esteemed but not to be loved, and I am not comfortable with it." [126]

Men immigrants, also usually Irish, had pretty much the same psychological monopoly of the menial-flavored jobs of driving and caring for the horses and carriages of the affluent and waiting on hotel or restaurant tables. Their chief rivals for such work were Negroes—which further embittered relations between Irish and Negroes and kept the status of domestic service low. Here, too, in good times the supply of even potentially capable help was thin. That simple American ingenuity, the heavy iron hitching weight to tether a horse to where posts were lacking, was attributed by a British observer of 1854 to lack of grooms to hold one's horse. A. J. Downing recommended to intending housebuilders dumbwaiters and speaking tubes because "In a country like ours, where . . . civil rights [are] equal and wages good, good servants . . . are comparatively rare and not likely to retain their places for a long time." [127]

The bad odor of *servant* extended to *master*. Many a British visitor was taken aback by the fiery reaction elicited by asking a coachman, housemaid or industrial workman: "May I speak to your master?" It amused James Fenimore Cooper that around New York City *boss* had become the acceptable substitute in many situations, yet the old Dutch word meant precisely the same thing. One can readily surmise how this taboo on *servant/master* came about. In the growing Colonies *servant* had retained much of the Biblical sense, meaning bondsman or -woman—at worst the exiled and sold convict serving out his time, at best the voluntary redemptioner too poor to enable him to pay his way overseas. It would have been taken for granted that the "Maid Servant" for whom the early Pennsylvania bride yearned was under some kind of indenture. And *master-mistress* meant the person who had one way or the other bought your time and owned you twenty-four hours a day for so many years. Worse, *servant* had naturally extended to Negro bondsmen gradually drifting downward into chattel slavery, and as the Negro-hating Irish lower orders were well aware, Colonel Bighouse usually called his human chattels servants rather than slaves. There has probably never been a time when people in comfortable circumstances did not complain about the difficulty of securing good domestic help of either sex. But there probably has never been any Old World society in which the emotional values of economic and social ambition, equalitarianism and race hatred have so conspired to keep those complaints justified.

The high priority that note-taking visitors gave to American penitentiaries as well as to the Lowell girls came of the new nation's world leadership in prison reform. Here again the relative civilization of Quaker-flavored Philadelphia was seminal. In the 1780's, at the same time when Dr. Rush was introducing some decency into the treatment of the insane—a great work carried through the next two generations by Dorothea Dix and Dr. Samuel G. Howe—the Philadelphia Society for Alleviating the Miseries of Public Prisons was born. By 1797 a young Polish nobleman, companion in exile of Thaddeus Kosciusko, was amazed at the contrast between what he had experienced as a political prisoner in Europe and what he saw in Philadelphia's new stone penitentiary. The inmates, mostly minor felons, were hard at assigned manufacturing tasks meant to pay most of the cost of their support while teaching them honest trades— weaving, shoemaking, various kinds of woodworking—to keep them out of mischief after release. Earnings above their bare expenses were saved up for them as nest eggs to help in starting new lives. They slept not in cells but in clean mass dormitories, and cleanliness in jail was a novelty in a decade when Samuel Thomson's cellmate in the lockup of the self-respecting town of Newburyport, Massachusetts, could observe that their quarters had enough lice to shingle a meetinghouse. That was one reason why the popular term for typhus was jail fever. The most severe punishment for misbehavior in this Philadelphia prison was not irons or flogging but solitary confinement for the few days usually leading to a promise to obey the rules. "The warden who conducted us," the young Pole wrote wonderingly, ". . . spoke to [the prisoners] softly. . . . They carry in their faces and dress more the air of workmen than of condemned criminals . . . no rattle of chains. . . ." [128]

That system included several of the penal devices with which society seeks today to rehabilitate convicts. Presently, however, Pennsylvania turned solitary confinement from special punishment into the chief rehabilitating device in its new Eastern State Penitentiary near Philadelphia. The theory was that practically complete isolation would break down the criminal's spirit for spontaneous reconstruction on sounder foundations. Forger, pickpocket, arsonist—on admission each was hooded as if for the gallows, and the next thing he saw was the inside of the solitary quarters that he would never leave until his time was served out. For all those years the only faces he saw were those of the inspecting warden, the chaplain and the keeper who fetched food and water. All he knew of his fellow convicts was what he could work out with furtive code tappings. The small interior cell, one of many lining corridors radiating from a central guard-house, opened into a small, unscalably high-walled yard for air, exercise and, if he wished, gardening. His work—shoemaking, weaving or what-ever—was paid for. A Bible in each cell presumably encouraged a search for salvation with a chaplain's occasional help. The women's division had the same regime.

This Solitary System made a great noise overseas. Its proponents could soon point to many allegedly successful reformations. Chevalier called it an "excellent penitentiary where everything was neat, quiet and com-fortable (if that word may be applied to a prison)," whereas French pris-ons were "noisy, filthy, unhealthy. . . ." [129] It was nominally humane—a great point in a society sprouting a bad conscience about the traditional brutalities of prisons—and certain robust temperaments may have come out of this enforced monasticism nearer emotional health than when they went in. It solved the otherwise defiant problem of homosexuality. It still relieved the taxpayer of much of the cost of incarceration. But that ends the list of its virtues. For most convicts it must have been subtle tor-ture no less acute for being well meant. A good look at it in 1842 so ap-palled Dickens, an imaginative and highly gregarious man, that he de-voted some 6,000 words of his *American Notes* to:

> . . . this dreadful punishment . . . this slow and daily tampering with the brain. . . . On the haggard face of every man among these prisoners, the same expression . . . that strained attention which we see upon the faces of the blind and deaf, mingled with a kind of horror, as though they had all been secretly terrified. . . . Parade before my eyes a hundred men, with one among them newly released from this solitary suffering, and I would point him out.[130]

The sister rival of the Solitary System—and preferred by most ob-servers, Dickens included—was the Silent System of the New York State penitentiary at Auburn, New York, and later at the model penitentiary at Sing Sing. It, too, had the convict pay most of his own way by industrial labor—sometimes by quarrying stone to build other silent system peni-tentiaries—and was generally a more restrictive version of the original Philadelphia plan. The inmates slept in separate one-man cells built in easily supervised tiers; were forbidden to speak to one another, except for necessary shoptalk; went to meals in lockstep; and in some versions brought their rations back to eat alone in the cell. Strict enforcement of the noncommunication rule was, of course, impossible. But arduous supervision kept violation at workable levels, and the individual cells were, from authority's point of view, a great, if costly, improvement on the former dormitories which, under sloppy control, could be about as near a lackadaisical hell as anything usually encountered this side of the grave. Solitary, core of the Pennsylvania system, was reserved for chronic rule breakers. Massachusetts' adaptation of the silent system worked so well that wardens boasted of letting the keepers go unarmed. Here the women convicts' work was making cheap, coarse garments for the Deep South trade. That was a grave weakness in both these schemes. The better the convicts learned their trades, the more profitable the prison industries, the more the taxpayer was relieved, the larger the start-life-over-again hoard waiting at the end of the sentence, the likelier private enterprise and its labor force were to shout "Unfair, slave competition!" in tones that legislatures always heard and all too often heeded.

As the impetus of prison reform slacked off, the champions of solitude and silence nevertheless continued to belabor each other with pamphlets and speeches and legislative reports bristling with contradictory claims of so many reformed per hundred and reciprocal accusations of inhumanity inherent in the other system. Men of the stature of Horace Mann and Dr. Samuel G. Howe were militant on the side of solitude. Silence, gradually diluted, not to say modified and emasculated, drew ahead and forms the ancestry of much of today's penal procedure. Solitude shriveled away but did persist, in modified form, in Pennsylvania long enough to appear in Dreiser's *The Financier* in a context of the late 1800's. The historical point of the rival panaceas is not so much that either held much hope of solving the problem of the criminal, as that the model penitentiaries set up to prove one of the rival points greatly influenced the lagging penologies of the Old World. Here was a curiously ironical feedback. In the 1600's and 1700's the Old Countries, unable to do anything decently positive about their felons, had dumped them overseas to sink or swim by themselves. Now these outcasts' descendants—or anyway cousins or countrymen—were showing the Old Countries how to apply intelligence and imagination, though sometimes wrongheadedly, to the kind of social refuse that they had sulkily swept under the rug. As striking evidence that civilization really was coming to pass over there among the gin slings and Indians, this was better than the writings of Washington Irving.

The number of such ideas flowing both eastward and westward would continue to increase. It was as well, for instance, that the Lowell girls *et al.* were showing the American woman that it was possible for her to be independent. For new cultural pressures from over the water were simultaneously eroding the well-to-do wife's integrity. As living standards had risen, the leisure once confined to the nobleman's and rich merchant's wife had infected the strata immediately below—country gentry and minor merchants and manufacturers—a thing soon reflected in the New World as it aped the Old World cousins. The Pawtucket girl whom Samuel Slater married in the 1790's came of a textile family and knew the business well enough to invent a new way to double-twist cotton thread that made her people's fortune. In the 1830's the typical shipowner's or silversmith's wife was much less familiar with the family business than her grandmother had been. The shop or countinghouse was no longer on the property but downtown, whither husband daily repaired early, not returning until midafternoon dinner. Meanwhile, the wife's day had consisted of chivying unsatisfactory servants, whose presence made it theoretically unnecessary for her to turn her hand over in kitchen or bedroom; dressing one way and then another to suit the clock; paying calls on other women equally idle; shopping for items of which she already had equivalents; dipping into a watery novel showing a heroine given to fainting and the interesting pallor that went with wasp-waistedness; but probably only scantily practicing the accomplishments (drawing, painting, playing the piano, singing) that she had brought home from that young ladies' seminary. It was small loss, for her skills in such arts were seldom high, and the rest of it embodied well enough the ladylike pattern of behavior that showed that she was too valuable and delicate for anything more exacting and that her husband desired her presence because he was trained to believe her fragilely precious and was proud of being able to finance her stagnation. Childbearing and -rearing, the one intrusion of reality, flawed the pattern. But parturition often led to chronic ailments, sometimes genuine, in any case to inactivity. And though nursemaids as such were rare, much of the routine of dressing, feeding and airing a small child could be relegated to hired help.

This confusion of leisure with prestige had mattered little when it afflicted only a few thousand women in the Old Countries. It induced social anemia on both sides of the water when throngs of the socially aspiring took it up. Theoretically each brownstone house was presided over by this clinging vine kind of lady, a thing we associate with the Victorian era though it was in full bloom—or rather, full wilt—before Victoria acceded. Fortunately it did not completely take over among the affluent. Except in a few small cities such as Charleston, South Carolina, the typical wife of a white-pillared planter was pretty active as manageress of the plantation's usually sloppy but complicated housekeeping. And outside Dixie a minority of well-to-do urban wives lacking the temperament for stagnation found socially approved activity in good works: visiting the poor; sewing flannels for the poor; teaching the children of the poor—*deserving poor,* of course, but the very visits and interviews necessary to separate sheep from goats were interesting. In net effect, benefits probably did accrue to a number of individuals down on their luck. J. S. Buckingham, well acquainted with the Old World's benevolences, said that in the 1830's New York City had "ten times the number of women in good society [undertaking] . . . moral objects and benevolent institutions, than . . . any city of the same population in Europe . . . while the husbands are busily engaged in their . . . avocations, a good part of the wealth they acquire is directed by . . . their wives into useful and charitable channels." [131] In the 1850's George Templeton Strong, in a position to know about such matters, felt that in his time New York City women's "personal labors for the very poor . . . and personal intercourse with them had greatly increased." [132]

This picture of Man keeping his nose to the grindstone while Woman sensitively succored the needy and promoted morality unfortunately encouraged a view of the sexes already too prevalent in the circles that set the articulate tone of the time. It was becoming part of the lady myth that woman was not just more fragile but also more refined, spiritual and decorous than man; that the coarser sex, as well as the poor, was a proper object of her missionary work. ". . . the wife," Catharine Beecher wrote in 1846, "sways the heart [of the husband] whose energies may turn for good or evil the destinies of a nation. Let the women of a country be made virtuous and intelligent and the men will certainly be the same . . . to American women, more than to any other on earth, is committed the exalted privilege of extending over the world those blessed influences which are to renovate degraded man."[133] The Reverend Dr. Nott advised Woman to cajole Man into teetotalism by "that soft, persuasive, colloquial eloquence which, in some hallowed retirement . . . exerts such controlling influence over a husband's, a brother's, a son's heart . . . [women] have a heaven-appointed armour, as well as a heaven-appointed theatre of action." [134] That is, the fashionable cant of the day was casting Woman as the princess yoked to the barbarian chieftain.

Man's neglect of cultivation enhanced this sense of superiority. Business left him little time to read much but the *Journal of Commerce,* or so he said. As early as the 1830's Franz Josef Grund, an opportunistic Austrian liberal immigrant, summed up the cultural dichotomy between the sexes in America by having the narrator of his *Aristocracy in America* ask why, if its men were so crassly buried in business, Boston was called the Athens of America, and being answered: "That . . . refers to our women, not to our gentlemen. Our ladies read a great deal. . . . What else have they to do?" [135] As custodian of the family's leisure, Woman was patroness of the sticky melodrama of *The Last Days of Pompeii* and the garrulous, weepy pieties of *The Wide, Wide World* and the women's magazines packed with advice on how to be simultaneously a good house-keeper and a person. She was also the one familiar with music, whether torturing her piano at odd moments or dutifully staying awake during the Italian opera. In further contrast Man's work kept him out in the world, rubbing elbows with all sorts and conditions of men, exposed to their crudities and vices and consequent temptations not always resisted, whereas Woman mingled with her social peers or superiors only, all presumably as virtuous as herself. The one exception, her dealings with the poor, was so *de haut en bas* that it emphasized the gulf between their knowing squalor and her immaculate, gracious innocence. "When woman shall once awake to the great vital truth that she is God's vice-gerent upon earth," Mrs. M. M. Jones, matron of Dr. Trall's hydro, told a World's Health Convention in 1864, ". . . she will hold the Archimedean lever that shall reform the world." [136]

Such overweening talk was, of course, largely symptomatic, flattering to listen to and read, but not likely actually to affect the relations between most harkening wives and husbands with the dominant temperaments that many possessed. Unworthy members of the immaculate princess caste sometimes fouled the image by getting tiddly in public or being taken in adultery so conspicuously that it could not be hushed up in the papers. But Man seldom took advantage of such derelictions to dispute Woman's arrogation to herself of the moral and esthetic upper hand. If she liked it so much on a pedestal, he would admit that in the abstract she looked mighty unsullied and queenly up there. The deference that he accorded her in steamboats and stagecoaches startled visiting Frenchmen and Germans and even the English, though, having a touch of the same habits at home, they were rather better prepared. What most struck Continental observers was the system, to which at least lip service was universally paid, of marrying without dowry, he proposing and she accepting on a basis of mutual inclination and hope of compatibility. The consequences were usually sound, it stands to reason, among the rank and file of hopeful young couples. But boardinghouse or hotel life followed by the listless leisure of the brownstone boudoir among the well-to-do might often spoil a promising young wife. In the fashionable climate thus brewed, Old Worldlings often noted a thing still strong in America six or seven generations later. American women called the tune in practically everything but politics, business and sport. Theirs were the controls in social life, gastronomy, good works, literature and the arts and, as the woman teacher came in after the 1830's, elementary education.

A tiny minority among serious-minded women mistrusted Man's solicitude, however. They came to feel that neither taking Christmas baskets to the poor nor giving oyster-and-champagne evenings completely filled their potential roles in society and parthenogenetically brought forth the American movement for women's rights. The time was ripe. As incidence of women in business had fallen off, so had vestigial examples of the right to vote among women whose property holdings qualified them for the franchise. Until 1776 Worcester, Massachusetts, still listed women's names among voters. Until 1807 lack of statutory restriction on sex and color at least theoretically allowed certain women to vote in New Jersey. After that there was no question of their doing any such thing. In other respects their position had long been smotheringly narrow because English common law, applying in America in the absence of modifying statutes, gave husbands control of wives' persons, beatings included, control also of their children and all of a wife's property at marriage unless in a previously created trust, and assumed her to be incapable of standing suit in court as if she were a minor child or mentally incapable. Divorce—always of special concern to women where the double standard prevails—was so cumbrous, so limited in grounds and necessarily so scandalous in content that it very seldom occurred. And once such issues were raised, doubts of the indefensible double standard itself naturally crept in.

The groundbreaking hints before 1800 had been British, notably the *Vindication of the Rights of Women* by Mary Wollstonecraft, the iconoclastic lady free lance so sensitive to the ferments of the Enlightenment that she behaved and thought as if anticipating the heroine of an H. G. Wells novel. Presently Elizabeth Drinker was writing in her diary that she had read Mrs. Wollstonecraft and that "In very many of her sentiments she speaks my mind; in some others I do not altogether coincide. . . ."[137] This response in good Quaker language from a woman Quaker of the Philadelphia Quality reminds hindsight that, contrary to St. Paul's explicit teaching,* the Friends allowed women to preach and, certainly not by coincidence, several prominent women's righters of the next generation or two—Lucretia Mott, Susan B. Anthony, Abby Kelley Foster, the Grimké sisters—were born or "convinced" Quakers.

America first saw feminism rampant in the 1820's, however, in the person of Frances Wright, a tall young Scotswoman of independent

---

* "Let your women keep silence in the churches: for it is not permitted unto them to speak."

means and behavior. In her bookish teens she became infatuated with America and at the age of twenty-three took the then extraordinary step of visiting it accompanied only by a younger sister. Americans were cordial. She wrote a tragedy and, by knowing the right people, got it produced and went home to annoy conservative Britons with a book praising the States. Five years later Lafayette made an old-age tour of the nation to which he had given his young manhood, and conspicuous in his entourage was all five feet ten—a towering height for a woman in that undernourished time—of Fanny Wright; she had attached herself to him during a politics-minded sojourn in France. Their relation seems to have been warm but filially-parentally innocent. She stayed in America to haunt Robert Owen's cooperative colony at New Harmony, Indiana; to show America how to solve the slave problem by enabling slaves to earn freedom; and to instill into Americans, who struck her as on the whole a promising people, her ideas about women's rights and the evils of formal religion.

To spread them, she lectured in the Ohio Valley towns, then in the seaboard cities. After years of harping on both topics she left them pretty much where they had been, though her rising interest in labor problems had an influence on early American labor organization. Philip Hone heard her in New York City in 1828, called her a female Tom Paine—which was unfair since her personal behavior was that of a perfect lady—and resented her using the best theater in town when he would have preferred to see plays in it. She could fill such large houses partly because her subject matter was explosive in a period dominated by men, pulpits and employers, but chiefly because, had she touched nothing more controversial than the joys of spring, the very notion of a woman hiring a hall, putting out handbills, mounting a platform and speaking her mind to all comers on whatever subject was startlingly unprecedented. Her mere getting away with it, in spite of jeers from the press and denunciations from the pulpit, did wonders for women's rights in America. Rawboned and humorless, but somehow disarming with her steady gray eyes and short fair curls, she secured not conviction, except among already sympathetic minorities, but a certain tolerance of herself personally. That was important for others who soon emulated her daring. Broken ice is usually difficult to put back together, and in any case fragmentation furthers melting.

The next into the breach were quite as unmistakably gentlewomen as Fanny Wright—the Grimké sisters, whom we last saw sedulously serving cold boiled carrots. Their Oxford-educated father, a justice of the Supreme Court of South Carolina, was of Huguenot Quality stock. Sarah, the elder sister, had rebelled against the Episcopalianism imposed by a cultivated, stern mother and against the emptiness of Charleston's renowned social life—and turned Quaker. Sister Angelina followed her in all that and in developing antislavery feelings under the tutelage of the Quakers among whom the pair settled in Philadelphia. Here the privilege of speaking out in meeting on the same footing as men gave them confidence in woman's ability to stand up and sound off. With the distant encouragement of William Lloyd Garrison, Angelina ventured into abolitionist journalism. When Theodore Weld (who was to marry Angelina) came recruiting and training antislavery agitators, the sisters volunteered to make speaking tours of women's antislavery meetings. As ladies from Dixie with first-hand inside knowledge of slavery, they were great acquisitions for the cause. On the platforms of closed, for-women-only meetings where decorum did not forbid their speaking, both became effective talkers, Angelina especially so, maybe because she was fair-haired, blue-eyed and the less hard-favored of the pair. Her eloquent appeals for the slaves she had known made so much talk among her lady hearers in Massachusetts that abolitionist men began to listen at open windows, then sneak in by ones and twos, then fours and fives, until, quite unintentionally, the Grimkés were as flagrant as Fanny Wright, shamelessly standing up there and holding forth before *mixed audiences.*

None of Miss Wright's ice breaking had occurred in New England, so the sensation was particularly marked. Many abolitionist leaders paternally took the Grimkés to task. The General Association of the Congregational Ministers of Massachusetts had read from pulpits a pastoral letter warning of "the dangers . . . [threatening] the female character . . . [risked by] those who encourage females to bear an obtrusive and ostentatious part in measures of reform, and countenance any of that sex who so far forget themselves as to itinerate in the character of public lecturers." [138] More crisply a parson in Groton, Connecticut, said he would as soon rob a henroost as go hear the Grimkés speak. An eminent theologian mentioned the Quaker women of the 1600's who had scandalized New England by going naked in public and added: "Miss Grimké had not been known to make such an exhibition of herself—yet!" When a friend of Angelina's remonstrated, he growled: "Should I have said she did?" [138] But the sisters persisted, confident that they were helping the slaves and (it was growingly likely) their fellow-women, and their patent gentility took the edge off their impudence. By 1838 Angelina was winningly lecturing before the Massachusetts legislature—an all-male audience!

The effect of thus inadvertently exerting and then asserting rights for which Quakerism had prepared them was to make them ardent feminists in advance of a formal feminist movement. In writing and speaking for the equality of the sexes, they had Garrison's always vociferous support, which helped create an unfortunate public association of women's rights and antislaveryism with Temperance and assorted crankisms. That greatly hampered the first two causes. Once the Grimkés had given woman a toe-hold on the platform, individual women were soon exploiting it in other reform movements. Abby Kelley, a Yankee Quaker read out of meeting for public lecturing for abolitionism, went on to become a fiery termagant as an early feminist. Apple-cheeked little Lucy Stone, Oberlin 1847—the college had graduated its first three women students in 1844—ignored her Alma Mater's teaching that women should not speak in public and plunged into tireless lecturing—slavery tonight, Temperance tomorrow night, women's rights the night after, on all such topics demonstrating that the only sound reason for keeping women off platforms was that they might outsmart the men. By the early 1850's Lucy's college friend, Antoinette Brown, was not only an experienced lecturer but also a Congregationalist minister, first in that persuasion. Soon after becoming ordained, she invited Lucy to address her flock. To Lucy's fears lest her ideas and costume—she wore the famous Bloomer garb—get the new pastor into trouble, she replied: "You are the greatest goose and granny-fuss that ever I did see. . . . They . . . know that you wear Bloomers. . . . Any congregation that I may preach to will not be scared overmuch by anything you say." [139]

The Bloomer costume was then giving the young women's righters a symbolic uniform. It went back at least as far as the Owenites of New Harmony, whose women wore a knee-length tunic over loose trousers gathered harem-style at the ankle. Fanny Wright had a portrait drawn wearing it while holding a horse; maybe she used it as a riding habit, but so far as I know, she never appeared in it otherwise in public. In the 1840's it was assumed by Mrs. Elizabeth Smith Miller, feminist daughter of Gerrit Smith of Peterboro, New York, the great landowner and unstable friend of practically all reforms. She considered it more sensible than the traipsing skirts and multiple petticoats of the day and also a symbol of emancipation from the bonds that man's society imposed on woman. John Humphrey Noyes, founder of the Perfectionist Oneida Community, further pointed out that "The present dress of women . . . is immodest. It makes the distinction between the sexes vastly more prominent and obtrusive than nature makes it. In a state of nature, the difference . . . could hardly be distinguished at a difference of five hundred yards, but as men and women dress, their sex is telegraphed as far as they can be seen. Women's dress . . . proclaims that she is not a two-legged animal, but something like a churn, standing on castors." [140] Among those soon imitating Mrs. Miller were Elizabeth Cady Stanton, Susan B. Anthony, the Grimkés—the cream of the early feminists. The name came from their colleague, Mrs. Amelia Bloomer, editor of *The Lily,* a feminist paper endorsing such recognition of bifurcation.

Under the attrition of public gawking and worse, the lady wearers' zeal waned in a few years. Mrs. M. M. Jones, the matron of Dr. Trall's hydro, explained why she gave up wearing Bloomer garb out of doors: ". . . however modestly . . . you may pass about your business, base rowdies congregated round street corners, hotel steps, and lager beer saloons will look at you . . . in a manner that will cause every drop of blood to run cold within your veins. . . . Lost women, pointing . . . their polluted fingers, will follow you . . . [children] hooting, and shouting, and yelling . . . today pelting you with snow-balls, and tomorrow with apple-cores. . . ." [141] More chattily Lucy Stone confided to "Dear Susan [Anthony]" how irksome it was when fellow passengers in trains recognized her ideas by her clothes and sat down beside her to "bore me all day with the stupidest stuff in the world . . . the blowing up of the wind is so provoking . . . people stare and laugh. . . ." In Louisville a Negro woman had demanded: "Is you one of them theater women?" [142]—and for Lucy's kind the theater and those gracing it were both anathema. Nor was sympathy with women's rights a guarantee of approval. In Philadelphia Lucretia Mott's daughters were woundingly ashamed when Grace Greenwood, the lady author, called when Lucy was there and fruitlessly besought her to give up Bloomer dress. Horace Mann's wife, finding the Grimkés still thus attired in 1856 at the Fourierite colony at Eagleswood, New Jersey, thought that "with their gray hair and attenuated forms," it made them "look ridiculously . . . but they . . . seem to think it is the only way in which they can assert their personal liberty." [143] But only a few years previously Fredrika Bremer, no zealous feminist, had seen the same costume on the same ladies and thought it "very becoming . . . [and] well calculated for walking through the woods." [144]

When Mrs. Stanton gave up the trousers but hoped to preserve the freedom of the knee-length skirt, "She cannot do so," Susan wrote to "Dear Lucy." "It will only be said that the Bloomers have doffed their pants the better to display their legs." [142] Mrs. Miller stayed with the ship longest largely because her earnest father thought that "a principle was involved . . . and . . . to make the costume acceptable it must be seen." Mrs. Miller had a fine figure and wore it to better advantage than anybody else, Lucy admitted, but also noted that "little by little her skirts lengthened until they were no longer noticeably different from those of any other women." A pity, she thought, thus to abandon "a dress at once comfortable and useful, in which you could walk upstairs and not step on your clothes . . . still clean after the longest walk in mud and slush. . . ." [142] It had been just a hope. Bloomers survived only among the lady Perfectionists in Noyes' community and as special dress for ladies' gymnastics and surf bathing. At fashionable Nahant, Massachusetts, in 1854 a young Briton thought this "Bloomer kind of costume" charming, "of the gayest colours . . . the upper part contrasts strongly with the lower. The head [is] surmounted by a quaintly-shaped white cap . . . a strange scene [that] does not abate in interest when the ladies emerge from the water, exhibiting trousers of all colors, and countless pairs of little white feet, twinkling on the sand." [145]

Now the name of the lady editor of *The Lily* means only an obsolete

The Bloomer costume lasted longest at the Perfectionist colony of the Oneida Community. Here lady and gentlemen Perfectionists play the new game of croquet.

undergarment. Downright trousers for women with no masking skirt appeared only on Dr. Mary Walker, Syracuse Medical College 1855, who wore them as a nurse in the Union Army and in 1864 was commissioned assistant surgeon—a landmark that should have been more important for feminism than, thanks to her waspish disposition, it actually proved to be. Feminist principles could still be manifested, however. When Lucy Stone married a brisk abolitionist (brother of Dr. Elizabeth Blackwell, first woman to take an American medical degree), she wore a long gown of rose-colored silk and looked very sweet. But she never used her husband's name, staying Lucy Stone to the end of a long life, and Blackwell signed with her and gave to the press a rousing denunciation of the barbarous legal clogs still imposed on married women in many states.

Yet there had been progress in that field. The case for fair property rights for women was so good that by 1850 Mississippi, New York, Indiana, Pennsylvania, California and Wisconsin had taken remedial steps. A regional women's rights meeting at Seneca Falls, New York, in 1848 had already included votes for women among its goals; in 1850 a nationwide successor reaffirmed this. But now the movement was unluckily tangled in quarrels over Man's reluctance to give Woman equal standing in the Temperance and abolitionist crusades. In both, pomposity moved men leaders to deny full participation to some of the ablest and most devoted women agitators America ever saw. When, in 1840, Garrison coupled feminism with his other concerns, the broad-based American Anti-Slavery Association split into backbiting segments, of which only the Garrisonian wing had women in council, as well as at the fund-raising bazaar. When Mrs. Mott, Mrs. Stanton and a few other leading women's righters bustled off to London as delegates to a World's Anti-Slavery Convention, they found their credentials rejected and their rightful places denied because it was unprecedented for Woman thus to put herself forward—and only the Garrisonians among the American delegates rose in their defense.

In the 1840's strong-minded women in Pennsylvania and New York State (including Mrs. Stanton, Miss Anthony, Miss Brown, *et al.*) had declared war on the Demon Rum as a principal occasion of Man's oppression of Woman. They sought admission to the Sons of Temperance, then the outstanding anti-Demon agency. Like the abolitionists, the Sons split on the issue, and the dissenting splinter that broke away and admitted women was a puny affair. In the early 1850's the same New York women tried again with a Daughters of Temperance organization that came close to recognition. But in 1852 the Sons' state convention snubbed Miss Anthony as a delegate from the Daughters. She and her smarting colleagues withdrew to form a separate Women's State Temperance Association. The next year she was again denied a seat on the platform of a World's Temperance Convention in New York City because, said the crucial resolution, the common uses of society denied women such notice. The police had to be called to quell the consequent clamor. Small wonder that Miss Anthony and Mrs. Stanton soon renounced active Temperance work in order to concentrate on votes for women as a great thing in itself and, once obtained, as a fine anti-Demon weapon usable whether the oppressor Man liked it or not.

Hopes of revising relations between the sexes were strong in the days of stovepipe hats. Take it in a physical sense in the case of Robert Dale Owen, son of the Scottish industrialist founder of New Harmony, whose American career included politics, spiritualism and a book recommending birth control by coitus interruptus in spite of the Bible's frowning on the practice. Also in that of John Humphrey Noyes, who taught his blandly respectable (though polyandrous-polygynous) flock to build the good life on reserved ejaculation; the boys were instructed in the technique by women past the menopause, hence beyond risk in case of impulsive errors. At much the same time the Mormons were persuaded by the strong appetites of their Prophet leader into Old Testament-style polygyny—a form of marriage ill suited to newly settled regions, where women are always chronically scarce. On the face of it the Shakers were still less logical in imposing celibacy on men and women dwelling in the same lay-mo-

Seeing the Shakers perform their shuffling holy dances was a principal feature of travelers' visits to their settlements.

nastic buildings. Obviously, had everybody turned Shaker, as the soul's good required, lack of new births would gradually have destroyed the human race. But they were so sure that the end of the world was imminent that they saw no need to provide for perpetuating a mortal human species. The same confidence led into celibacy the Rappites, the sturdy colony of German religious zealots.

Religion-based industry and self-respect—plus brilliant ingenuity—made the Shakers the most valuable of all the eccentric groups trying their wings in America after the Revolution. Their founder was an English blacksmith's daughter, Ann Lee, so rapt by an extravagant side cult of Quakerism that she came to consider herself a female incarnation of Christ. (To that extent the Shakers showed a dash of feminism, and though men converts dominated their polity in later years, women had more weight among them than was usual elsewhere.) In 1774 Mother Ann and a few of her devotees came to America and settled on a tract of new land northwest of Albany, New York. The name came of their trembling during religious seizures. Their mass dances—close-order drills of separate bodies of each sex marching, jumping, hand clapping and singing—interested outsiders most, though their celibacy, of course, created prurient speculation. Mother Ann, who had been married and had abandoned her man, made her fear and hatred of sexual intercourse violently clear. A consummated marriage was "a covenant with death and an agreement with hell" [146]—the same lurid bit from the Bible that Garrison later used to describe the United States Constitution. Any carnal congress, connubial or otherwise, was "filthy gratification," [146] and in the hell she depicted those guilty of it were tied up and tortured in the genitals. Out of her foulmouthed, twitchy ministry, however, came orderly, celibate, authoritarian, communistic settlements known for meekness, honesty, and agricultural and mechanical achievements of a high order. Just when the Old World was projecting high-minded communist societies, the success of the Shaker "families"—an ironic term—swarming like bees into New England and the Ohio Basin seemed to show that such polities were practical.

Disappointing many who had discounted her denials that she was immortal, Mother Ann died in 1784. With her violent eccentricities out of the way, her followers went stolidly on creating the low-pressure little Shaker communisms that so appealed to the idealistic intellectual. Though standoffish, they tolerated visitors and—another attraction for the intellectuals —remained near enough to the world to be touched by the crank cults of the day. They had a vegetarian interval. They decried regular medicine and espoused steam doctoring and herbs. They adopted Temperance principles and used pasteurization to check fermentation in their famous cider made not from wormy windfalls but from perfect fruit. Gradually they developed a notably puerile kind of spiritualism as an adjunct to their faith. But they had no scruples against hiring outsiders to work on their fat farms. And their buildings, tools, livestock and orderly methods were the wonders of a rural America that badly needed examples of improvement in such respects.

The flatheaded broom that we still use, far more efficient than its clumsy, cylindrical predecessor, was a Shaker invention appropriate for so tidy a people. So were the split wooden clothespin, the one-horse farm wagon and Shaker versions, some widely adopted (and never patented) of the screw propeller, the turbine waterwheel, the hand-powered washing machine, the threshing machine, and so on and on. They were the only American group of so many trying over several hundred years to make a going thing of silk culture. They crossed the half-wild, rangy backwoods hog with the white Big China breed and produced the Poland China strain that would be the mainstay of pork raising for generations. Retail sale of garden seeds in small, labeled paper packets was a Shaker innovation; so was the clever machine that filled them accurately. Shaker honesty kept the quality so high that they long dominated the field. Their woodenware, textiles, yarns, dried and preserved fruit were also famous. Shaker wagon peddlers made lucrative rounds with such items in the neighborhood of each colony; storekeepers also gladly stocked them on consignment. The botanical departments of drugstores displayed Shaker herbs of special prestige. As the patent-medicine industry came to bloom, the Shakers' bottled remedies more than held their own.

Their herb-lore had much to do with the famed savoriness of Shaker cooking. At table their ascetic leanings, like those of California's Franciscans, failed them. They were known for luscious pies, gravies flavorsome because they used the water the vegetables were cooked in, elegant breads. Before the day's work in cooper shop or gristmill—for to prevent monotony, the Shakers rotated trades; every man or woman was trained in several skills, each of which was exerted for a month or two at a stretch —the body was fortified by a six o'clock breakfast of oatmeal, stewed fruit, hash, eggs, coffee, pie and doughnuts. Zestful eating was one of the many salutary ways of glorifying God—only no waste! A Shaker had to eat every morsel he saw fit to take on his plate, and "Shaker your plate!" was a disciplinary byword well known to dawdling children in the neighborhood of Old Northwestern Shaker colonies.

All that is barely in the past tense. Vestigial remains of a few Shaker colonies hung on into the 1960's. The last few of Mother Ann's faithful now huddle together, clear-eyed and calm, at Sabbathday Lake in Maine. Their buildings survive here and there gauntly but nobly proportioned with a strength and grasp of engineering principles worthy of ancient Rome. Their purely designed furniture, spare and strong as a ship's top-hamper, are the marvels of museums and collectors' prizes. Yet it was a wan sort of existence. The Shakers' picturesqueness cannot obscure that. Dickens was understandably put off by a brief look at the Shakers of Lebanon Springs, New York, particularly by the "grim old Shaker [in charge] with eyes as hard and dull, and cold, as the great round metal buttons on his coat and waistcoat; a sort of calm goblin," [147] while giving them all due credit for the integrity and skills with which he found them universally credited. Fredrika Bremer had much the same reaction, more staidly stated.

Their passion for neatness—each room had a row of pegs so no broad-brimmed Shaker hat or demure Shaker bonnet was ever untidily laid anywhere else—was part of the wry complaint of an elderly Shaker that the life was "like boarding school with no vacations . . . no ending of the term." [148] The flagrant childishness of their hymns goes with "Shaker your plate!" and the holy games like those in kindergartens. Clapping and skipping, everybody sing:

> I mean to be obedient,
>   And cross my ugly nature,
> And share the blessings that are sent
>   To ev'ry honest creature;
> With ev'ry gift I will unite
>   And join in sweet devotion—
> To worship God is my delight
>   With hands and feet in motion. . . .[149]

or again:

> I'll learn to walk in wisdom's ways,
> And in her path I'll spend my days;
> I'll learn to do what Mother says
>   And follow her example.
> All pride and lust this will subdue,
> And every hateful passion too;
> This will destroy Satan's crew
>   That's seated in the temple. . . .[149]

This effect as of extremely skillful but slightly retarded children is probably what caused Colonel T. W. Higginson, a man rather given to crankisms and righteousness, to write of "the pallid joylessness" [150] of the Shaker doings that he witnessed. The cult owed its spiritualistic bent to the allegedly occult experiences of the girl children being reared in the Niskayuna Shaker colony. Symbolically Shakerism drew what viability it had from the practice of adopting orphan children who might otherwise be public charges and bringing them up on the principle of the bent twig. They were doing what they thought right. But it is difficult to forgive the local authorities thus saving the township money and trouble by exposing defenseless children to a world of emotional anemia.

Jamestown and Plymouth saw fit to abandon the original communistic features of their polities. But after the Shakers showed the way, deliberate, self-consciously communistic schemes proliferated in America. (A better word, in view of what Communism with a capital C has come to mean, will be used from here on: *communitarian.*) The moral climate emanating from the French Revolution encouraged hope that a perfectly righteous (or equitable) world could be created from the model of a synthetic pilot plant properly based on correct social or religious theory. Projectors considered America an as yet uncorrupted environment, hence hospitable to virtue, hence a likely place for such tryouts. Several highly disciplined groups of eccentrically religious Germans followed the Rappites to the new nation, took up land in the Middle West, set up more or less all-in-common economies to bridge over early difficulties, found they

The orphans whom the Shakers adopted were dressed the same
as their ascetic guardians.

worked and retained them, and, since they avoided the mistake of celibacy, flourished. The Mormons, following the fads of the day, just as they had in taking to botanicals and wildcat banking, went through a common-property phase. On the secular side were the conspicuous but fragile Owenite experiment at New Harmony and several efforts to make a start on the communitarian ideal society formulated by Charles Fourier, a Frenchman with a hopeful view of human beings' potentialities. His outstanding missionary in the New World was Albert Brisbane, who paid Horace Greeley to let him run a Fourierite column in the New York *Tribune,* persuaded the famous Good Life colony of Brook Farm, offshoot of the Transcendentalist movement, to become a Fourierist phalanx, and, after zealous support of a "free love" Progressive Union movement, fathered Arthur Brisbane, most conspicuous of William Randolph Hearst's henchmen.

Brook Farm's new "phalanstery" building burned down on completion in 1846, and the scheme did not survive the blow. Other American attempts at a viable phalanx succumbed to other traumas. But the Mormons prospered mightily after Brigham Young got them to the Far West, where the gold rush and the building of the Union Pacific brought them transfusions from the hated Gentiles' economy. Noyes' able management of his Oneida Community led to handsome profits particularly from the manufacture of silver-plated tableware and steel traps—a cruel product for idealists. Perfectionism ended in a business corporation of high solvency. (One of the nonresident Perfectionists was cashier of the Second National Bank of Freeport, Illinois, and father of Charles Guiteau, the young petty swindler who assassinated President James A. Garfield in 1881; the Guiteaus' family grace before meat was: "I confess Christ for this food and I thank the Lord for John H. Noyes and the Oneida Community . . ." [151] Young Guiteau spent several long periods at the community.) Among the Germans of the Amana Community in Iowa religious zeal had a similar result; a reputable line of electric refrigerators now keeps the name Amana alive in the national consciousness. Communitarian arrangements seem to have done best under authoritarian control, usually one man, with religious sanctions. Mother Ann, Joseph Smith, John Humphrey Noyes, and Christian Metz and Barbara Heynemann (the captains of Amana's soul) would have disagreed about the place of sex in the cosmos, but they all had in common megalomanic self-confidence and inability to brook insubordination. Maybe that is why their fantasies left substantial, if incongruous, residues, whereas New Harmony, Brook Farm and the Icarian colonies under French auspices in Texas and Illinois, all of which lacked salutary despotism, have long been one with Nineveh and Tyre.

Salt Lake City and Shaker furniture as legacies from fanaticism are the more notable because as America was increasingly given to that sort of thing, most of it proved sterile, as well as lurid. The example of Mother Ann seems to have worked powerfully on a certain Jemima Wilkinson, the handsome sister of a well-established Rhode Island ironmaster. She said she had died and gone to heaven, leaving her body active, zombie-style, as vehicle of a Spirit of Life, a Universal Friend sent by God to warn mankind of the imminent wrath to come. Soon she was preaching celibacy and leading her flock to set up a holy backwoods colony in that paradise of paranoia, upper New York State. About the same time in Vermont appeared a nameless Canadian hinting at being the True Christ, forbidding marriage and recommending unlimited promiscuity; he also boasted of not having changed his clothes for seven years. He required men converts to eat standing, women to do their praying prone. In 1815 they all straggled westward in a lemmingish sort of way and, according to John Bach McMaster, vanished, wagons and all, somewhere on the prairies of Missouri.

Somewhat later the trouble with William Miller's followers was that they failed to vanish. An upstate farmer converted from amateur agnosticism to the Baptist faith, he determined by calculation based on Biblical data that the end of the world would come at 3 A.M. on March 21, 1843. (Noyes could have told him better: The end of the world had already come, not long after the Crucifixion, which explains how mortal man can be perfect here and now.) Miller's preachings, aided by a paper called the *Midnight Cry,* persuaded some 50,000 persons, mostly in the Northeast, and drew disrespectful attention from all over the nation. The faithful were to gather on hilltops for convenient ascension to heaven. Gerrit Smith, the wealthy reformer, was among those taking Miller's program dead seriously; he wrote to his wife, who happened to be away from home when the *Midnight Cry* published final confirmation of day and time: "My dearly Beloved:—We have just had family worship—perhaps for the last time. . . . I know not, my dear Nancy, that we shall meet in the air. . . ."[152] To assuage the disappointment arising when the end failed to materialize, Miller set another date for 1844. That failed, too. Many of his followers nevertheless retained their faith in his general teachings, a psychological feat resulting in the presence today of some 400,000 Adventists of several varieties still at least nominally confident that the end of the world is somehow near.

Religion of the Swedenborgian variety was associated with the half-legendary activities of John Chapman ("Johnny Appleseed"), the young Yankee who determined to make the new country over-the-mountains white with apple blossoms if he had to do it single-handed. At cider presses in the fall he would collect myriads of seeds and rove the country planting them in half-acre clearings, roughly fenced to discourage browsing deer and cattle, and as the seedlings gained size, settlers were free to come and take what planting stock they liked. His first headquarters area was around Pittsburgh; in later years around Mansfield, Ohio. From youth he had been a rather innocently dreamy sort, and after he was kicked in the head by a horse the first winter of his apple scheme, he was queerer than ever. Long-haired and wildly bearded, ragged and barefoot, for he could never resist the impulse to give away to the needy any clothes or boots that well-wishers bestowed on him, he was as well known in the Old Northwest as "Old Tippecanoe" Harrison himself. His own nursery plantings and orchards, numerous and widely scattered, never came to much in fruit, for he would have nothing to do with grafting superior scions on them; the right way to grow fruit trees was strictly from seed, as God had intended. But the birds and deer doubtless appreciated his trees, and he made no antigrafting stipulation when selling planting stock, for which he would take money if it was offered. Countless barrels of cider, gallons of applejack and dried-apple pies caused the early settlers to bless Johnny Appleseed's choice of a queer way to live.

Then, to show that the religious spur was not indispensable to make an American mind rear and plunge, there was John Cleves Symmes, nephew and namesake of the New Jersey land speculator who founded Cincinnati,

Monument in Hamilton, Ohio, to John Cleves Symmes, Jr., who made it his lifework to persuade mankind that the earth is hollow and we live inside it.

announcing in 1818 that the earth is hollow and "habitable within; open at the poles for the admission of light . . . containing within itself half a dozen concentric hollow spheres. . . ." [153] He asked the federal government to send an expedition to confirm his findings. Rebuffed, he turned to wealthy Stephen Girard, who made no reply at all. The residue of this one-man cult is not large but poignant. Symmes' grave monument at Hamilton, Ohio, is topped by a stone globe whose poles are duly carved open.

There was utopianism—belief that the right formula will create the Good Life—even in the Temperance movement that left so bitter a residue after Prohibition. To certain minds the evil of drink and its associated crimes and sins suggested that it was the pin that held most of the world's troubles together. On the face of it poverty, prostitution, fornication-*cum*-bastardy, homicide, insanity, malnutrition, political corruption, damnation —for drunkenness erodes integrity, and St. Paul listed drunkards with murderers and sodomites as ineligible for salvation—all were intimates of the Demon Rum. Remove him, and the whole basket of snakes might untwine and dwindle away, sparing society most of the cost of jails, asylums, poorhouses and hospitals—and giving individual souls a better chance of heaven. Hence the affinity between organized religion and Temperance in America. Further, many churchgoers were tinged with a vague uneasiness lest the Millerites and their predecessors and successors in millennialism be right, the end of the world was not far away; hence soul-saving reforms as likely as Temperance should be pushed while there was yet time. Such mundane gospels as phrenology and Grahamism lacked this direct appeal. It accounts for the enlistment against Rum of whole battalions of ministers, merchants and bankers who would never have put up with a Grahamite dinner and usually passed by on the other side when the plight of the Negro was brought to their attention.

Weighty men in broadcloth could back early Temperance agitation the more readily because it made a socially reassuring distinction between distilled and merely fermented liquor. Not alcohol as such but the distilled concentrations of it—whiskey, gin, brandy and as generic folk symbol of the viciousness of all hard liquor, Rum!—were what the pulpit and the early Temperance press deplored as poison to body and soul. Before the Revolution hard stuff, culturally a newcomer among English-speaking drinkers, had been attacked by John Wesley, founder of Methodism, and by Anthony Benezet, the Quakers' versatile and well-meaning spokesman for reforms. In 1784 Dr. Benjamin Rush, close to leaders in both sects, produced an *Inquiry into the Effect of Spirituous Liquors upon the Human Body and Mind,* the basic document of early Temperance. It warned primarily against "the habitual use of ardent spirits," * for Rush and the class of readers he addressed associated spirits particularly with the lower orders. While traveling, the Quality might take some concoction of rum or brandy, say, or maybe even on a bitter cold evening at home; but there was a presumption that their characteristic drink was Madeira and that one thing wrong with the lower orders was a coarse overfondness for spirits. Certain Yankee ministers thought this a tactical opportunity. Wean all decent persons from spirits, leaving them wine and, where that was too costly, cider or beer; then ragtag and bobtail, sticking to rum because incapable of heeding warnings, would purge society of undesirable elements by drinking themselves to death. In pursuit of that

* Data in this section are from my *The Life and Times of the Late Demon Rum.*

policy Elkanah Watson, father of the county fair, set the Berkshire (Agricultural) Association encouraging farmer members to plant more apple trees and hopvines.

So far the catchword *Temperance* had not been too ironical. Its approaching perversion was implicit, however, in what is usually taken as its practical birth in 1808. A country doctor, Billy James Clark, practicing near Saratoga, New York—a fateful area—read Rush's *Inquiry* and burst in on the local parson announcing: "We shall all become a community of drunkards in this town unless something is done to arrest the progress of intemperance." The pioneer Temperance society, then and there founded, pledged its members wholly to abstain from hard liquor but allowed wine at public dinners, as a sort of social duty. That went farther than what Rush had had in mind. It gaspingly assumed that at least a large majority of persons exposing themselves to hard liquor are doomed to be degenerating drunkards.

The actual odds are nothing like so high, of course, even among daily drinkers. That was clear all through American life at the time. It was the British visitor's standard observation that though most Americans were steady tipplers, disabling inebriety was seldom seen. ". . . many of them," said a witness in 1818, "drink [spirits] almost the moment after they get out of bed, and also at frequent intervals during the day; but . . . excessive drinking is rare." In 1828 Captain Basil Hall marveled that this "universal practice of sipping a little at a time, but frequently . . . [every] half an hour to a couple of hours, during the whole day" produced so little overt drunkenness. But commonsense fact seldom meant much to the kinds of parsons and pamphleteers then urging on the Temperance movement. Their craving for viewing with alarm led them to most intemperate statements. In 1811 the Reverend Nathaniel Prime of Long Island maintained that "drunkenness and lewdness go hand in hand . . . few who have drunk a gill [four ounces] of ardent spirits can be exposed to . . . small temptation without becoming adulterous in the sight of God." The Reverend Dr. Heman Humphrey, mainstay of Amherst College, warned that "All who embark on this flood [of spirits drinking] are in danger of hell fire." By 1821 the Reverend Dr. Lyman Beecher, never a man to keep his oar out, was lending his prestige to the contention that ". . . no man can use [spirits] prudently or without mocking God can pray . . . 'lead us not into temptation.'"

That substituted a nursery-style Mustn't Touch for mature self-control in the use of spirits. On that crude basis was created the vigorous national American Temperance Society modeled, like so many American reforms, on the propaganda machines that had moved Britain to outlaw first the overseas slave trade and then slavery in the West Indies. This array of foes of Rum, many also deep in other reforms, claimed 8,000-odd local branches set up in all but two states, more than 1,500,000 members pledged to eschew spirits and 4,000 distilleries put out of business— not an absurd figure, for the small local distillery was often as much a part of a new settlement as the tannery. And the official meaning of Temperance had been unscrupulously established as: "the moderate and proper use of things beneficial; and abstinence from things hurtful. Ardent spirits being . . . poison . . . and . . . the grand means of intoxication, [we pledge to] abstain from the drinking and . . . furnishing of [spirits] and [to try] to induce the whole community to do the same." That is, temperance, a discretionary virtue of deservedly high repute, was now lending its prestige to Temperance, a self-righteous taboo.

Temporarily the righteous had forgotten that the old children of Israel knew not distilling and that, according to their Bibles, it was wine, not spirits, that led Noah and Lot to behave so scandalously. The omission was to plague them sore. Not only were lower-class drunkards not disappearing—another generation of them stepped gamely up to replace their Rum-killed elders—but it was soon plain that to identify hard stuff as prime villain was to ignore the shattered cider-drunk, a standard object in the rural landscape, and the overconvivial Quality always demonstrating that one can get falling-down drunk on fine old Madeira. Temperance leaders on the local level began to use a New Pledge binding the taker to total abstinence from anything detectably alcoholic—that is, from wine, cider, beer . . . "Taste not, touch not, handle not" was the slogan of this extension of the taboo so sweeping that it came to apply even to the use of wines and brandy to flavor cooking. To justify the New Pledge, one now had to exaggerate the risks of degenerate alcoholism lurking in any acquaintance with alcohol. T. S. Arthur, author of *Ten Nights in a Barroom,* which, as novel and then stage play, did for Temperance what *Uncle Tom's Cabin* did for abolitionism, wrote that "for every [moderate drinker] who restrains himself, ten will rush on to ruin." A Methodist circuit rider's sermons wandered still farther from sense in "I never knew a man . . . in the habit of drinking regularly that did not become a drunkard."

The persistence of millions of regular drinkers who did not exemplify Temperance propaganda by becoming drunkards was exasperating. This led the zealot to denounce the genuine moderate drinker as savagely as if he had been a distiller or a barkeep. Thomas S. Grimké, intellectual reformer and elder brother of the famous sisters, laid it down that "Temperate drinkers are the parents of all the drunkards who dishonor and afflict our country." Gerrit Smith, as hot against Rum as he was against slavery and for Bloomers, told the U.S. House of Representatives: "I would that no person were able to drink intoxicating liquors without immediately becoming a drunkard." Such extreme doctrine troubled many staider members of the American Temperance Society and its broad successor, the American Temperance Union. In 1836 it adopted the New Pledge but only after a divisive fight. This dissension, coupled with others over divorcing Temperance from antislaveryism and over whether to enlist law against Rum, cost the movement much momentum. And after the panic of 1837 men in broadcloth were disinclined to dig deep into their pockets for the cost of Temperance's printing and propaganda agents.

Actually Temperance, like abolitionism a few years earlier, was about to shift base. Initiative was now to come not from the top down but from the bottom up—from the gutter, in fact. So far the purpose had been largely what Dr. Clark had envisaged—to keep normal persons from becoming drunkards. Drunkards themselves were either denounced as loathsomely hopeless or patronized as horrible examples. Now, filling the partial vacuum left by loss of zeal among the Quality, alcoholics among the lower orders seized the stage in a sort of Drunkards-of-the-World-Unite! frame of mind, proclaiming a new gospel of self-rehabilitation. It began in the 1830's as drink-bedeviled wageworkers in Boston, New York City, Philadelphia and Baltimore got together to take the New Pledge and—much more important—help one another keep it while persuading other alcoholics to come and do likewise. The Boston group's grasp of the issues was sounder than Rush's or Clark's. "FRIENDS," read their manifesto, "you are wretched. . . . You can have no peace here, and no peace hereafter . . . we were once drunkards. . . . We are now happy, our wives are comfortable; our children are provided for; we are in better health . . . we now drink . . . no kind of intoxicating liquor. There is no safety for you nor for us, but in giving it up entirely. Come then, ye drunkards . . . cast off the fetters of intemperance, and forever determine to be free." This contention that many abject alcoholics could be salvaged by total abstinence was new among Temperance men. So was this spontaneity independent of leadership from their social superiors.

By 1840 these stirrings had flowered into the Washingtonian movement that swept the nation. Its founders were craftsmen—a tailor, a carpenter, two blacksmiths, a silversmith and a coachmaker—who all drank too much too often in a Baltimore tavern. In fun they sent two of their number to a Temperance lecture. They returned uneasily impressed, and the upshot was the Washington Temperance Society, a mutual-support teetotalers' club based on the new pledge. At weekly meetings they rose to tell outsider guests, potential members threatened by alcoholism, how far down drink had dragged them before they won free and how much better their and their families' lives were now that the Demon had been sent packing. As the six founders developed skill as down-to-earth platform missionaries, the number of their newly vitalized members grew toward 1,000. The analogy to today's Alcoholics Anonymous is strong. So is that to the "experience" sessions at the camp meetings of the time, where the saved described their past sins and present happiness to attract the waverers. But the early Washingtonians, unlike AA, renounced prayer and other religious props for staunchness. They also declined to follow the conventional Temperance zeal in denouncing saloonkeepers as callous tools of the Devil, pointing out instead that no law forced anybody into a saloon in the first place.

The Washingtonians originally limited their membership to those with gnawing drink problems. As their numbers grew, however, attracting wide attention, they began to admit well-meaning admirers and tended to become a pledge-signing society of the old kind. This was encouraged by the brilliant platform performances of an early recruit, English-born John H. W. Hawkins, a drink-shattered hatter, who was soon making a career of spreading the Washingtonian good word in the Northeastern states. Membership spread from Maryland to Maine and westward to the Mississippi. Abraham Lincoln, hardly a drinker at all, was one of hundreds of thousands joining as a morally healthy gesture. There was a ladies' auxiliary, the Martha Washingtons. There were Washingtonian parades stiff with transparencies and floats extolling the virtues of pure cold water and dramatizing the perils of Rum in symbols such as snakes and devils. It was showy, but it meant dilution of the steely zeal of the original self-rescued band of brothers keeping their eyes firmly on the realities of alcoholism. Presently Hawkins was calling for resort to law ("Moral suasion for the unfortunate drunkard, and legal suasion for the drunkard-MAKER") and abusing barkeeps ("You might as well talk about a pious devil, a virtuous prostitute, or an honest thief as to talk about a rumseller . . . having 'a good moral character.' ") He also took up religion, even obtaining ordination as a Methodist minister.

Thus spreading itself too thin, Washingtonianism frayed and came apart. But it had handed Temperance over to the people, and out of its ruins came another popular movement in the shape of solemnly teetotaling fraternal orders. Veterans of the Washingtonian wars organized the first outstanding one, the Order of the Sons of Temperance, which added to teetotaling the lodge-style features of sickness and death benefits. By 1850 the Sons had enrolled some 200,000 members—a success imitated by the Order of Templars of Honor and Temperance, the National Temple of Honor, the Society of Good Samaritans, the Independent Order of Good Templars . . . The last eventually outstripped the Sons and even spread to Europe. All had secret meetings under guard, grips, passwords, officers' titles of the Most Worshipful and Worthy Potentate sort. Few civic parades were complete without the Sons or the Good Templars or both marching sweatily under their gaudily embroidered trappings of mystic meaning, the band playing some such Temperance war song as "Away the Bowl!" or:

> No matter what anyone says, no matter what anyone thinks,
> If you want to be happy the rest of your life
> Don't marry a man if he drinks!

After them probably marched the local children's Cold Water Army piping something similar under charge of solicitous Sunday-school teachers of both sexes. For as the Civil War approached, Temperance's presumptions and propaganda sprayed over most American institutions. Squibs and bits of verse denouncing Rum had long been tucked into the ubiquitous almanacs. Succeeding editions of the blue-backed *Webster's Speller* had taken to occasional anti-Rum essays about the cost of tippling and its physical effects. There were Temperance novels by the score, Temperance newspapers and song recitals. Temperance plays infiltrated the basically wicked stage. Acceptance by repertory companies came not only to *Ten Nights* but also to its predecessor, *The Drunkard,* and to *The Bottle,* an imported adaptation to the stage of the material in the temperance engravings of George Cruikshank, the highly popular English illustrator.

There were Temperance hotels—mostly bad, as even Temperance men admitted—Temperance steamboats and canal packets, Temperance merchant ships much approved of by underwriters. The U.S. armed forces severally abolished or commuted the morning ration of spirits. There were two successive Congressional Temperance societies—badly needed, too, for the heavy perfume wafting up from the legislative chambers was a good third Old Monongahela rye, the other two ingredients being chewing tobacco and unbathed statesman. One of the noisiest I-was-a-drunkard-but-no-longer-thank-God Temperance spellbinders trouping the land was Thomas F. Marshall, Congressman from Kentucky, never more eloquent against Rum than when stumbling drunk. The most striking example cited *in terrorem* was Edward A. Hannegan, Congressman from Indiana, who wound up an alcoholic career by the drunken murder of his brother-in-law.

Thus early Temperance was a well-pushed home attack beginning a simpleminded campaign. In the mid-1800's all social action, however, leaned on oversimple notions of motivation and psychological sanctions. The effect was to embed in American folk feeling a sense of defilement about potable alcohol probably unique among non-Moslems. However many went on drinking, some destructively, many not, the taboo was traumatically, elastically alive. When frolicsome friends threatened to force a slug of whiskey down the virgin throat of young Clement Vallandigham, later Congressman from Ohio and spearhead of Copperheadism, he said in all dead seriousness that he'd kill anybody who tried. Rum had become generically THE UNCLEAN THING. It surprised no Temperance zealot when, as biology developed, alcohol was found to be a by-product, literally the excrement, of the microorganisms of fermentation. What a propaganda stroke!

Early Temperance, uneasy lest the good cause be entangled in politics, renounced "any appeal to legislators . . . for the aid of authority in changing the habits of . . . their fellow citizens."* The Washingtonians also refused to appeal to law, holding that what to do about Rum was a matter between the individual and his own backbone. In the Bible, however, law and taboo were two faces of the same coin. Probably there had first been a body of long-standing taboos of inscrutable origin; then formal laws represented as coming via Moses from the God who imposed the taboos codified the penalties that infringers had to expect. The shift from Temperance to prohibition followed that same course and was carried farthest in New England, the most Old Testament-minded part of America. At the time it was called reenforcement of moral suasion (creating individual teetotalers) by legal suasion (to keep Rum from creating new drinkers among the new generation and to deny it to recalcitrants and backsliders). New England was also the American home of the Puritan notion that it is sin not to do everything one can to keep one's brother from sin. It was, said Dr. John Jewett, eminent Temperance agent, a duty for "every Christian to wage a constant and uncompromising war on every demoralizing and destructive habit, custom or institution. . . . We share the guilt with every wicked system . . . within . . . our influence . . . which we do not study and perseveringly labor to annihilate." It followed that not to enlist law in the war on the soul-smothering sin of drunkenness was itself a sin of omission of great gravity.

Through applying the licensing power to taverns, law had got its foot in the door in Colonial times. The obvious fact that most Colonial villages drank too much suggested to the selectmen or chosen freeholders or whatever the local authorities were called that it would be well to reduce the number of tempting tippling places. One way was to revoke or fail to renew a certain ratio of outstanding licenses. The suppressed taverns often went underground as prototypes of the speakeasy—in New Amsterdam in the 1650's, for instance. In 1673 a Boston parson upholding the need

* Data in this section are from my *The Life and Times of the Late Demon Rum.*

for taverns also deplored "those private, dark Houses, where wicked Persons sell Drink and Destroy Souls to get a little Money. . . ." As ideas about Rum hardened, as the connotations of taboo made alcohol the unclean thing, municipalities turned to the device of "no-license"—extending the licensing power into refusal to renew any Rum license at all. It was still legal to drink Rum; but no longer to do so in the sociable atmosphere of a barroom or to buy it at the grocery, which probably also sold it by the drink at the far end of the counter. In 1833 the nationwide Temperance movement endorsed the no-license approach as an orthodox weapon. When the U.S. Supreme Court upheld it some years later, the map was already peppered with no-license townships or counties.

The flaw was enforcement, of course. The thirsty in a no-license county abutting on a normal county had only to cross the line to find taverns to booze in and groceries to buy liquor from. After the first burst of righteous zeal the community often grudged the vigilance and expense required to suppress its own speakeasies.* Some communities, tired of the burden of enforcement and the absurdities consequent on slackness, restored licensing. Local Temperance men usually argued, however, that the proper remedy was to persuade the next township to dry itself up—and the next and the next until sources of supply became impractically distant and a piecemeal statewide victory for no-license was imminent. Better still, suppose the whole state went no-license by act of legislature . . . Enter statewide prohibition full-fledged.

The first statewide use of law to cripple Rum was Massachusetts' fifteen-gallon act of 1838, a measure more ingenious than ingenuous. It banned sale of spirits in quantities less than 15 gallons and required the buyer to take it all off the selling premises at once. Its framers are thought to have had in mind the old distinction between social strata, for the lower orders would seldom have enough money to buy so much at once, whereas men in broadcloth could keep their cellars well supplied. Subterfuge and lax enforcement kept the scheme from showing what it could do. One might, for instance, buy 15 gallons plus 1 gill, drink the gill on the spot, and return the 15 gallons for refund.

Refusing to learn, however—the Demon's enemies have never been good at learning—the Temperance forces of Maine put through in 1841 a law banning the sale of alcohol categorically. After a stiffening revision in 1846 this Maine Law became the glittering ideal for Temperance workers everywhere. "This thing is of God!" old Lyman Beecher told his con-

* Blind pig and blind tiger as synonyms for speakeasy probably originated in a Yankee subterfuge. The customer paid a ten-cent entrance fee to see a blind tiger, say, and was given a free drink—for giving Rum away was not illegal—while being shown a stuffed striped cat wearing a blindfold; or a pig ditto.

gregation. ". . . God's work every step of the way . . . the powers of hell are in dismay. That glorious Maine Law was a square and grand blow right between the horns of the Devil. . . . I seem to see him falling back . . . and the consecrated host of God's elect press close upon him . . . and send him back to Hell." Meaning, in terms familiar to religious people at the time, that this victory for Temperance was an unmistakable sign of the times as harbinger of the impending millennium, maybe tomorrow, maybe next year, that was so often salient in the thinking of pious reformers.

The human personification of God's new law was Neal Dow, a cocky little Washingtonian (distinctly of the sort with no history of alcoholism), athlete, businessman and politician, who, as several-times mayor of Portland, Maine, made a career of trying to show that prohibition could be enforced in a statewide context. Whatever he did—and he was clever and tireless—only produced brief intervals of semidryness between long intervals during which a man wanting a drink in Portland could find upward of 300 places to buy it in. Liquor smuggling into Maine became an industry worthy of the eighteenth-century ancestors of the participants. Subterfuge was greatly favored by the law's allowing municipalities to sell liquor for medical and industrial uses. Doctors made tidy extra incomes by prescribing for victims of drought. A town putting the right man in charge of its liquor sales and then asking few questions could cover much of the municipal budget with the profit. In effect the state was winking at bootlegging on condition that the proceeds be applied to public ends. Presently federal courts held that the state could not hinder inbound shipments of liquor to individuals, provided the original package was intact. Express companies operating in New England in the 1850's were glad to flood theoretically dry Maine with mail-order Rum in original package pints, quarts and demijohns.

Well-to-do persons willing to do their drinking at home and take some trouble about filing mail orders can have had small inconvenience from the famous Maine Law. For others it doubtless made drinking inconvenient and expensive in inverse proportion to the size of the community. In some places it led to rudimentary anti-Rum vigilantism; in towns it embittered relations, already strained enough, between the established and the foreign-born populations, largely Irish; and it made Neal Dow a national figure. Not an impressive accomplishment on the whole; but it took sabotage a few years to get into motion, and meanwhile, Temperance zealots were telling audiences outside Maine that the experiment was a brilliant success. By 1855 thirteen states, including all New England, New York, New Jersey and several over the mountains, had adopted versions of Dr. Dow's Sovereign Remedy for Woe, Sorrow and the Sin of Noah. In

1854 Governor Horatio Seymour (Democratic nominee for President in 1868) had vetoed New York's first attempt as unconstitutional. It cost him the next election and even a cultivated non-teetotaler like George Templeton Strong was saying: "I've no sort of sympathy with the temperance fanatics. . . . But . . . it would be better for mankind if alcohol were extinguished and annihilated." [154] Seymour's hot-temperance successor rejoiced to sign a new version winningly entitled "An Act for the Prevention of Intemperance, Pauperism and Crime"—which the state courts threw out.

That saved New York the usual disillusioning experiences with enforcement. Within a few years state-level prohibition had been eliminated by repeal or court action in most of the thirteen trying it. Even in Maine things got so grotesque that the law was modified to permit hotels to serve by the drink and individuals to buy for home use, and Dow went off to England to tell Britons how well prohibition had worked. Only Massachusetts and Vermont stood firm; in 1858 Maine reverted to illusions and re-enacted prohibition. It was a game but futile gesture. Outside New England experience with Maine Laws had discredited prohibition for the next generation. And in any case attention was diverted to the other reform of nationwide mass interest. The cause of antislaveryism was coming up for resolution by blood, not ballots.

All reforms of whatever merit were hampered by the perversity of the persons promoting them reacting on the sulkiness of the vested interests affected. Antislaveryism floundered worst of all because it created the most thwarting strains.

To begin with, the outlawry of the overseas slave trade, effected in 1808, was about all it could expect from Uncle Sam. Even the most wishful abolitionist understood that the federal government had no power over slavery in states where it already existed. Nor could propagandists hope to soften slaveholding states into trying the emancipatory programs that had wiped out Northern slavery by the mid-1830's. For by then the Slave Power had pretty well suppressed the possibility of antislavery agitation in its domain. Southern antislavery societies, once numerous, died without attempting to go underground. Threats backed by occasional informal whippings and formal prison terms kept Northern propagandists out. Southern postmasters, nominally free of state pressure but actually political puppets of the dominant slaveowners, neglected to deliver antislavery publications. So the abolitionists—our term henceforth for zealous antislaveryites agreeing that, as sin against God and crime against man, slavery should be abolished—were unable to reach the only person who could remove slavery, the slaveowner who dominated the Southern state governments. They could only abuse him from a distance.

Their frustration was reflected in the epithets they used—woman flogger, manstealer, baby seller—terms the more exasperating because there was much truth in most of them. The slaveowner's reply was correspondingly corrosive and deepened the abolitionist's bitterness about him. For Benezet in the 1770's a chief concern had been Christian solicitude for the welfare of one's brother the slave in this world and the next. That was now dwarfed by the emotional luxury of hating. As early as 1829 Fanny Wright told an audience in slaveholding Wilmington, Delaware, that she considered organized abolitionism marred by "much zeal, little knowledge. . . . Hatred of the planter seemed oftentimes to be a stronger feeling than interest in the slave." [155] By the late 1840's this change had gone so far that Theodore Weld, ablest abolitionist organizer, withdrew from the movement for which he had done so much.

For abolitionists, being human, were also prone to emotional and intellectual crudeness. It accomplished more with wavering Northern audiences to tempt them to hate Colonel Bighouse than to suggest they take a responsible interest in the future of the Negro in America—the only alternative to the demonstrated failure of Colonization. Northerners of reasonable goodwill also responded well to the melodramatic phenomenon of runaway slaves—shivering creatures, hunted and forlorn but long on pluck, who were better antislavery propaganda than any white abolitionist had ever concocted. But there again, the emotional end product was too likely to be mainly hatred of the owners they were running away from. Anyway such fugitives were few and necessarily furtive. Most Northerners coming into actual contact with them were from a special group already deep in the cause. And unfortunately there prevailed among Northern whites generally an erroneous but deep impression that they knew about Negroes—and what they knew lent little hope of freedom's doing much for them.

The North had had a Negro population since early New Netherland. By Revolutionary times it had reached 50,000-odd, mostly slaves. In the memory of many still alive in the heyday of abolitionism (1831-59) Northern slavery had been variously extinguished. As the Civil War approached, the North had some 200,000 free Negroes concentrated in towns and cities, where their high visibility made the most of itself. That was unlucky because circumstances—poverty, lack of foresight, certain cultural lags and pseudoscience—had been keeping Northern free Negroes from putting their best feet foremost.

They had had a largely passive part in their own emancipation. The first effective step came of white Puritan conscientiousness in Massachusetts. Her state constitution evolved in the Revolutionary climate of 1780 had gone the Declaration of Independence one better by adding "free" to "equal." It was noted that this might well mean freedom for Negroes held as slaves. The courts agreed, and that was that. Elsewhere the process was less simple, to reduce economic loss, and took longer. But even so, public conscience made uneasy by antislavery agitation probably had much to do with it. Usually white legislators representing white, property-holding constituents passed a law providing that after a certain date children born to slave mothers were free at birth (or on reaching a certain age) while their elders remained slaves till death. So slavery for some was a long time dying out while at the same time a growing class of free Negroes gradually came into being. Even where, as in New York City and New Jersey, slave populations were relatively high, such schemes proved practical. How they would have fared below the Mason and Dixon-Ohio River Line nobody knows. In the Border States occasional proposals of this sort never cleared the barrier of the legislature, and so far as I know, no such were ever even proposed in Dixie proper. Indeed the last thirty years of slavery saw most Southern states barring or discouraging even private manumission of slaves.

Would the North's interracial relations have been better had the slaves' freedom come suddenly, strikingly, instead of piecemeal? During the ensuing decades Massachusetts, where that happened, treated Negroes a trifle better than did her sister states. In any case, the results of creeping, half-unnoticed, negligently prepared-for emancipation were as poor as might have been predicted. The functions of Northern slaves had ranged, as in the South, from field labor through household service to skilled trades; but most of them knew little beyond menial chores when freedom overtook them. It set them adrift on the world no longer able to count on free lodging, food and clothes—such as they were—and often with no better prospect than catch-as-catch-can employment in the lowest job strata. Inevitably this created a Negro proletariat in festering Negro ghettos on the edges of towns, prototypes of Harlem-to-be, composed of ruinous impromptu shacks and called something like Nigger Hill or Little Africa. The only whites willing to share such neighborhoods, as in New York City's appalling Five Points, were the vicious underprivileged likely to teach the Negroes their own self-destructive ways. So the representative Northern Negro freedman lived too many in a leaky room, lowered property values by his presence, was last hired and first fired, and made up a disproportionate part of the population of the local jail. Former slaves of exceptional integrity, overcoming lags and pressures by heroic pulling on their own bootstraps, came to the surface as trusted coachmen, cooks, waiters; some developed their own businesses in catering, livery-stable keeping, dressmaking. These tended to keep clean and stay sober, support their own churches and mutual benefit societies, seek earnestly to create for the dark-skinned a miniature culture paralleling what white example recommended. But the limitation implying lower caste was always lurking. In whaling, for instance, a white able seaman expected the one-seventy-fifth lay when profits were divided; his Negro messmate, equally able to hand, reef and steer, could get only the one-ninetieth.

Even the exceptional Northern Negro's struggle toward middle-class virtues told against him when whites sneered at a "dressed-up nigger" preaching or being polite to the other sex in imitation of his fair-skinned "betters." The notion that there was something essentially comic about the Negro had been born in British books about the West Indies, some of them widely read in America, and spread by the nationwide success of the Jim Crow vaudeville turn originated in Louisville in 1828 by actor Thomas D. "Daddy" Rice. In street-beggar rags, blacked up with burnt cork, he came on skipping and swooping in a grotesque, shuffling dance to his own hoarse singing of a bit of fugitive street music: "I jump jis' so / An'ev'y time I turn about I jump Jim Crow. . . ." This not only added an ill-omened term to the language, but put blackface into the stage comic's kit of tools and led to the minstrel show.

Born in the 1840's, all over the nation in the 1850's, this was an expansion of the act of the strolling entertainer, making his way from county seat to county seat with songs and dances of a quality marginal for city audiences but more than good enough for entertainment-starved yokels. When engagements were scarce, legitimate actors of some prominence, like John Bernard, might thus go trouping by twos and threes to keep their ribs from growing too prominent until times improved. Such tuneful vagrants found that blackface vastly amused village audiences and presently that urban music hall audiences shared the taste. The scale of the act grew until here was a full evening of entertainment staged by a half dozen to a dozen "nigger" minstrels consisting of white song-and-dance men and knockabout comedians in blackface. Their popularity vastly disgusted the leader of a small German orchestra unprofitably touring America in 1852: ". . . the so-called minstrels have all the best business here. . . . They paint their faces black, sing negro songs, dance and jump about as if possessed, change their costumes three or four times each evening, beat each other to the great delight of the art appreciating public." [156]

Announcing themselves by a musical parade through town on arrival, minstrel troupes became an institution like corner saloons and county fairs. They wore exaggeratedly sharp-cut, often wildly colored tailcoats with great burlesque shirt collars framing blacked-up faces set off by a smeary red travesty of the Negro's everted lips. The program of sentimental and comic songs thick with references to watermelon, chicken stealing and "yalla gals" was steered by the interlocutor, the only performer not in blackface, dressed instead like a yokel's idea of an elegant gentleman to serve as combined straight man and master of ceremonies. Dialogue was the principal concern of a character named Bones seated at one end of the line of chairs across the stage and of another named Tambourine at the other. "How is you tonight, Brer Bones? . . . How is you feelin', Brer Tambourine? How's yo's symptoms seem to segashuate dis ebenin'?" [157] and then on into specialty acts culminating in a strutting mass promenade, the walk-around. "Dixie" was written by a famous minstrel, Dan Emmett, as a walk-around in 1859. He had already contributed "Old Dan Tucker," and Stephen Foster had written most of his best-known numbers for minstrels' use. But those pages in the songbook hardly compensate for the social damage from such intensifying of the Negro stereotype. The stage always showed the dignified white interlocutor patronizingly diverted by the caperings of blacks playing the fool and coward and getting tripped up by the big words and anomalous fine manners of the superior race. The same taint was on the contemporary colored caricatures of Negro life taking black skin and Negroid features as sure cues for laughter.

It was fitting that the equalitarian language of Massachusetts' Revolutionary constitution was construed to free her slaves. It was most unfitting but deplorably true that in the decades after the War of 1812— known in politics as the Era of Good Feeling—a second round of new state constitutions took the franchise from most Northern free Negroes in the interests of the Jacksonian or common white man. The typical process was: The public grows restive under requirements that the voter must show a certain amount of taxable property, which limits the franchise to the relatively prosperous, including some few Negroes able to qualify. A convention to improve the state constitution proposes the statewide manhood suffrage that the democratic-equalitarian sentiment of the day considers the just due of the common man. Both the white common man and the Quality object that this will give the vote to the Negro common man—known for ignorance, irresponsibility and petty crime—a highly undesirable voter. The point is strengthened by the long-standing practice of informally excluding Negroes from jury lists and rejecting Negroes' testimony in legal cases involving whites. After due deliberation the convention satisfies everybody but the free Negroes by revising the proposed clause to read "*white* manhood suffrage" or, as in New York State, imposing on Negroes property qualifications not required of whites.

That illiberality aligns the Northern white lower orders, however equalitarian on their own behalf, with the Southern poor white in categorical hatred of black skins. (In the North it probably also owed something to uneasiness about the Negro as competitor for jobs in hard times.) The emotional values are those in the diatribe of Huckleberry Finn's Pap encountering a free Negro: "He had the whitest shirt on you ever see . . . and the shiniest hat . . . there ain't a man in town that's got as fine clothes . . . he had a gold watch and chain, and a silver-headed cane. . . . And that ain't the wust. They said he could *vote* when he was at home. Well, that let me out. Thinks I, what is the country a coming to? It was 'lection day and I was just about to go vote myself if I warn't too drunk to get there; but when they told me there was a State in this country where they'd let that nigger vote . . . I says I'll never vote agin. Them's the very words I said; they all heard me; and the country may rot for all of me. . . . And to see the cool way of that nigger— why, he wouldn't a give me the road if I hadn't shoved him out of the way. . . ." New states admitted to the Union from the Old Northwest, in the lower part of which Southern ways were strong, usually denied Negroes the franchise from the beginning. By 1840, says Leon F. Litwack's authoritative *North of Slavery,** 93 percent of Northern Negroes lived in states barring them from the polls wholly or for all practical purposes.

Upcoming widespread establishment of genuine, statewide public school systems in the North was another victory for equalitarianism that bypassed the Negro. All he usually got from this educational revolution was a separate system of segregated schools held in inferior buildings and taught by teachers paid less out of a separate budget with much less money per pupil—the same swindle that the South installed after Reconstruction. A test case against school segregation brought in Boston in 1845 drew from the chief justice of the commonwealth's Supreme Court, Lemuel Shaw (who was also Herman Melville's father-in-law), the first expression of the separate but equal doctrine with which the U.S. Supreme Court confirmed Southern segregation in 1896. Biracial secondary schools fared no better in New England. In 1835 an attempt to teach white and Negro boys in the same classrooms in an abolitionist-minded academy at Canaan, New Hampshire, stirred up a mob that dragged the schoolhouse off its foundations with oxen the way large logs were snaked out of the woods. In 1832 a Quaker teacher, Prudence

* To which this section is greatly indebted for both its exhaustive research and its able organization.

Crandall, had tried schooling white and Negro girls together in Canterbury, Connecticut, been harassed into giving it up, then tried a boarding school for Negro girls only—and drew down on herself a special act of the legislature forbidding the education of Negroes from outside the state. In the ensuing litigation the chief justice of Connecticut, David Daggett, clearly anticipated the Dred Scott decision with his doctrine that Negroes could not be citizens.

Even so New England was readier than the rest of the country to attempt civilized race relations. Several smaller cities in Massachusetts had already abandoned school segregation when Justice Shaw handed down his decision, and in 1855 the legislature barred segregation throughout the state. The northernmost New England states (Massachusetts, Maine, New Hampshire, Vermont) had the grace never formally to revoke the Negroes' right to vote; granted, these were the states with the least Negro population per capita. Massachusetts also had the honor of being first to abolish Jim Crow cars on railroads and in 1843 repealed her laws against interracial marriage. The first colleges to admit Negro students were Dartmouth and the Yankee-founded Oberlin and Western Reserve in Ohio. President Edward Everett of Harvard, no hot abolitionist either, made it known in 1848 that any Negro youth applying for admission would be accepted, if qualified scholastically, and if the white students chose to withdraw, all the income of the college would be devoted to the Negro's education. Much of the credit for these scattered decencies goes to the Garrisonian wing of abolitionism, strong in New England, which worked hard to get disabilities lifted from Negroes to give them a better opportunity to show that they could use freedom responsibly. The purpose was not quite as hopeless as their stubborn efforts to scold Simon Legree into striking the shackles from Uncle Tom.

Those alleviations, minor and largely confined to one region, only slightly flawed the accuracy of the summary of Northern Americans' attitude toward Negroes given by Charles Mackay, a Scottish observer of the late 1850's: "We shall not make the black man a slave . . . buy him or sell him; but we shall not associate with him. He shall be free to live and to thrive, if he can . . . pay taxes . . . but . . . not . . . to dine and drink at our board—to share with us . . . the jury box . . . to plead in our courts—to represent us in the Legislature—to attend us at the bed of sickness and pain—to mingle with us in the concert-room, the lecture-room, the theatre, or the church, or to marry with our daughters. We are of another race, and he is inferior. Let him know his place—and keep it." [158] By itself the senseless but historically understandable equation *black skin = slave = menial destiny = permanently degraded caste* accounts for (without excusing) much of what is there set forth. But phrenology and physiognomy (the pseudo-science of reading character by the face) were now also encouraging windy nonsense from the learned about the lower mental powers implied by real or supposititious Negro physical traits such as thickness of skull bones, small cranial capacity, prognathous jaw. The gist of it was that the Negro was, if not of a wholly different species from the whites, a distinct variety nearer the animal. Such "scientific" prattle emanating typically, though not always, from eminent Southern physicians such as Dr. Josiah C. Nott of Mobile, Alabama, and Dr. Samuel A. Cartwright of New Orleans, Louisiana, was welcomed as corroboration of the Bible's alleged derogation of Noah's allegedly black grandson.

Circumstances peculiar to the North also enabled the monster of race prejudice to sprout reinforcing tentacles. Thus communities urged to treat Negroes better might resist on the candid ground that to do so would attract Negroes from less enlightened places—and did New Haven or Boston want more of them than it already had? "Once open this door [to education of Negroes]," said the town fathers of Canterbury stating their "unqualified disapprobation" of Prudence Crandall, "and New-England will become the Liberia of America." [159] Rapid rise in Ohio's Negro population in the 1820's brought on the first serious enforcement of the state's Black Code requiring immigrant Negroes to show court certificates of their freedom and post $250 bond against good behavior. The flurry died out, but meanwhile, 1,000-odd well-established local Negroes had left for Upper Canada (now Ontario), the governor of which extended them a warm welcome. Cincinnati, where enforcement had been most earnestly sought, was then worse off than ever. She had lost the "sober, honest, industrious, and useful portion of the colored population" who had previously exerted a certain "moral restraint . . . on the idle and indolent [Negroes] as well as the profligate." [160]

Then the Northern ports into which Irish immigrants crowded from the 1820's on were the same Philadelphia, New York City and Boston where the free Negro depended for his marginal-or-worse living on the most arduous and least attractive jobs. Precisely those same jobs were needed by the dislocated Irish, whose cultural standards—if that is the word—of sobriety, literacy, sanitation and respect for law were hardly better than those of the neglected Negroes. Competition for these pick-swinging, filth-handling employments was good for neither group. It made the Irishman particularly hate his "naygur" rival. It taught the Negro that even the stinking cellar of the economy was no refuge, for these strange, turbulent whites now came crowding in to take from him who had nothing even that which he had. The preference of both groups for city life, however slummy, because of its ethnic coziness, kept this friction hot. It had much to do with the ease with which urban pro-Dixie forces could raise antiabolitionist mobs to break up meetings and burn halls, and with the great violence of the Draft Riots in New York City in 1863.

That special bitterness gradually relaxed over the years, of course, as the abler or luckier Irish rose from the shanty-Irish status to and far beyond the lace-curtain stage. Gradually the social function of Negro-hating Northern-style has devolved on later immigrants such as the Poles and other Slavic groups. Who will in turn succeed them in this social niche is not yet clear. But so far the Negro has been the favorite target of white newcomers beginning at the bottom—where his high-visibility skin color tends to keep him. Its connotations are not inevitable but historically persistent and powerful and were all too easily absorbed by newcomers who had never laid eyes on a Negro before landing at Castle Garden or Ellis Island. It is a pointless but nagging thought that if everybody had been born blind, America's race problem would be reduced some 99 percent.

In the 1840's a runaway slave from Maryland or Kentucky risking so much merely to find his skin color assigning him to some noisome Niggertown in a free state might well have wondered whether it had been worth the effort. The answer to the question may be to point out that he seldom tried to correct the mistake. Only a few went on northward into Canada even after the harsh Fugitive Slave Law alarmed the black ghettos in 1850. The number known to have gone back into the shadow of slavery is fantastically small. For foul as Northern attitudes were, those who had won freedom after being slaves seem firmly to have grasped the abstract proposition that come what might, skin color or not, it was better to own oneself.

Boston was hardly at its sober best when an antiabolitionist mob hauled William Lloyd Garrison through the street with a rope around his waist and much bluster about shifting it to his neck. Even less edifying were the mob-kindled fire that destroyed the brand-new hall in which abolitionists held a convention in Philadelphia, and the mobs in Cincinnati, smiled on by local businessmen with large dealings in Dixie, who at various times broke up an abolitionist's printing press and burned Negroes' dwellings. Unedifying, not surprising. These major and many minor incidents on free soil showed that neither nationhood nor the slow spread of schooling had marred America's talent for mass violence —an unfortunate legacy from the Mother Country too zealously developed.

It can have been little comfort to Elijah Lovejoy, the stubborn abolitionist printer who became the movement's most clean-cut martyr when killed by a mob in Alton, Illinois, that the same lawlessness often struck at other kinds of target. School pupils, even in New England, often "turned out the teacher." That might mean mere mischief—barring doors and windows, blocking the chimney to smoke him out—but it could work up the older boys, several larger and tougher than he, into beating him severely and throwing him out on his head. In the Old Northwest the marriage of an old maid or a too-recent widower or a local Wife of Bath, arousing amusement or disapproval, might be shivareed (cf. the French charivari), which meant mobbing the house where the couple spent the wedding night. It was largely noise produced by baskets full of cowbells, drumming on washtubs, clashing of tin pans, grinding of skillet lids, operation of a "gigantic watchman's rattle . . . called in the West a horse-fiddle . . . [and] a dumb-bull"—that is, a keg strung like a gigantic Halloween ticktack to create a "hideous bellowing," [161] as Edward Eggleston recalled such festivities in southern Indiana. In rural New England among the lower orders most newlyweds were so treated, and the groom was ducked or ridden on a rail if the drinkables and eatables that the mob expected were not plentiful.

A cognate spirit underlay Massachusetts' rough handling of the Shakers—houses broken into, leaders flogged—because their neighbors believed the prurient gossip that their strange practices occasioned. Threats of tar, feathers and worse drove Noyes' Perfectionists from Putney, Vermont. Noyes had already jumped bail after indictment for adultery, the crude interpretation that Putney put on his theory of holy communion of body as well as spirit. It was not the Mormons' doctrine of polygyny, however, that moved mobs to drive them from Ohio and then from successive settlements in Missouri. If they had plural wives so early, no outsider knew of it. Public dislike of them came rather from their aggressive tactlessness in always telling the local Gentiles how God would take over this neighborhood lock, stock and barrel, and give it to the Mormons as their Promised Land. Note that once the Shakers and the Perfectionists became going concerns minding their own business, both enjoyed good to cordial relations with their immediate neighbors, whereas the Mormons' rising prosperity at Nauvoo, Illinois, after their exodus from Missouri, set off the third round of mobbing that lynched their Prophet and drove most of them to Utah. By then, of course, their marital deviancy was coming to light; but the Illinoisans' principal motive for behaving so crudely seems to have been resentment of the state within a state of which the theocratic dictator was General Joseph Smith of the private army called the Nauvoo Legion.

The Masonry-flavored secrecy of the Mormons' initiatory ceremony may have contributed to the Gentiles' barbaric violence. In the 1840's many Americans still looked nervously askance at fraternal orders with a religious tinge of which Masonry was the prototype and prime target of suspicion. First brought to America in the mid-1700's, the craft spread widely after the Revolution and became inadvisedly conspicuous. In any given community the local leaders of the Quality probably belonged, and the Masonic lodge in full mystic regalia was an accepted feature of the Fourth of July parade or the proceedings welcoming a national dignitary. George Washington had given the craft quasi-official standing by using a Masonic Bible at his first inauguration and a Masonic trowel to lay the cornerstone of the U.S. Capitol. The cornerstone ceremonies for the Boston State House were dominated by the Grand Lodge of Massachusetts, headed by Paul Revere. During Lafayette's tour of America in 1824 his membership in Masonry was much emphasized. A mounting impression that Masonry and Masons were a touch overweening exploded into serious hostility in 1826, when an upstate New Yorker, William Morgan, who was about to publish a book on the secrets of Masonry, vanished under circumstances very strongly suggesting organized foul play.

The ensuing anti-Masonic hysteria was egged on by men like the Reverend Lebbeus Armstrong—the same who abetted Dr. Clark in founding the Temperance movement—who, speaking as an apostate Mason, went about telling audiences that "the whole system of Masonry belongs to the powers of darkness . . . its tendency is to subvert the moral government of God. . . . Freemasonry, unmasked and exposed to the glare of the world, is incontestably proved to be the Man of Sin." [162] A national Anti-Masonic Party—a sort of rehearsal for the Know-Nothings of the 1850's—attracted hard-bitten professional politicians like Thurlow Weed, editor of the Albany (New York) *Evening Journal,* and Thaddeus Stevens of Pennsylvania, bitter foe of slavery and Dixie. After only a few years these stalwarts went on to greener pastures. There was only one good thing to say for the whole mare's nest —a congregation in Oneida County, New York, ousted their young minister, John D. Pierce, for being a Mason; he turned to home-mission work in pioneer Michigan and there bloomed into brilliance as father of a great state educational system.

Those Know-Nothings for whom anti-Masonry showed the way were a late phase of an ailment endemic among Americans, periodically reaching epidemic scale—a clot of paranoid-flavored feelings collectively known as "nativism" but with a supplementary skew toward religious bigotry. Its favorite target has often been the Catholics because the

Pope was allegedly scheming to turn America into a medieval Spain, Inquisition and all. But it has also frequently slopped over on immigrants because, as in the new waves of Irish after 1820, they were Catholics; or because they spoke lame English or none—both counts applicable to many from Southern Germany—or because they had strange and sometimes indecorous ways-of-doing such as the Germans' merrymakings on Sunday; or just because they were markedly different and flocked together. The Irish, as is common among uprooted, ignorant people with a tradition of violence, fell foul of the law in conspicuous numbers. Hence such protests—not wholly baseless either—as that of Mrs. Lydia H. Sigourney, queen of American she-poets, when visiting the pentitentiary at Auburn, New York: "A great proportion of the [inmates] are foreigners. . . . To furnish a poor-house for the decrepit of other realms might be accomplished in our broad land of plenty; but to be a Botany Bay [the Australian convict colony] for their criminals, is a more revolting and perilous office." [163]

This usually soft-spoken lady's shrillness need surprise nobody. Harriet Beecher Stowe, Hartford's other lady literary star, was almost as severe about the immigrant mill hands of New England. Philip Hone, former mayor of New York City, complained in 1836 that "all Europe is coming . . . all that part at least who cannot make a living at home . . . not one in twenty is competent to keep himself." Seventeen years later he was lumping German immigrants with Irish as "filthy, intemperate, unused to the comforts of life and regardless of its proprieties." [164] For the uneasiness on which nativism floated was not confined to the lower orders. Nativist mobs might be led by such unsavory characters as J. S. Orr, a bearded street preacher, who, calling himself the Angel Gabriel, tooted a horn before launching on his anti-Catholic tirades; and Ned Buntline (E. Z. C. Judson), author of cheap fictions, once a turbulent midshipman in the U.S. Navy (resigned); dishonorably discharged from the Union Army in 1864; once lynched in Nashville, Tennessee, surviving only because somebody with poor judgment cut him down in the nick of time. But others conspicuous in nativistic activity were S. F. B. Morse, respected painter, as well as inventor of the telegraph; James Harper of the four brothers whose publishing firm bulked even larger in the 1840's than it does now; George Perkins Marsh, scholar and father of American conservationism; and, naturally, Lyman Beecher, a man of reliably wrongheaded instincts, who added an intemperate anti-Catholicism to his skill in theology and fervor against vice.

Among English-speaking Protestants c. 1830 dread of Catholicism was pretty much taken for granted. It was a heritage from centuries of exposure of Britons and Colonists to politically useful—but not always absurd—antipapal feeling occasioned by England's post-Reformation scuffles with Spain and France, both militantly Catholic and persecutors of Protestants as heretics. Men of progressive stamp, as well as henchmen of church and king, indulged in public Pope-hating. The Reverend Jonathan Mayhew, a Puritan divine notable for liberal views in Massachusetts in the early mid-1700's, scrupled not to call the Church of Rome "a filthy prostitute . . . mother of harlots. . . ." [165] Such clerical billingsgate often came to parsons' tongues when Rome was mentioned. For that equalitarian Patriot Sam Adams, a possible growth of Popery in America was even worse than the Stamp Act; in fact, he saw the hated stamps as somehow opening wedges for a Catholic installation of Satan in America. At one time or another all the Colonies, even liberal Rhode Island and Catholic-founded Maryland, disenfranchised Catholics. Yankee Puritans were shy of celebrating England's Guy Fawkes Day because the James I whom Fawkes had been prevented from blowing up was almost as anti-Puritan as his son whom the Puritans beheaded. But they could transfer the tradition of noisy parades and burnings in effigy to a Pope Day insulting a trio of their own abominations—the Pope, the Devil and the Pretender (the Catholic Stuart candidate for the English throne backed by France and Spain). In 1775 Washington, hoping that the sturdily Catholic French Canadians would help the Colonies against Britain, had sternly to suppress tactless Pope Day doings among the Yankee regiments around Boston.

In that naïvely anti-Catholic climate were reared those who, like Beecher, considered themselves qualified to steer America in the 1830's. During his pastorate in Boston in the late 1820's he kept his sermons spicy with denunciations of the Pope. Stirred by warnings from Presbyterian home missionaries—preachers taking formal religion to the neglected frontier—he shouted about an allegedly formidable conspiracy to make the Old Northwest a fief of Rome. That was what the hypersuspicious made of the vestiges of French Catholicism along the Western Waters and of the minority of Catholics among those German immigrants coming upriver from New Orleans. There was talk of 600-odd Catholic priests from Portugal's suppressed monasteries fanning out over the Mississippi Basin. "Catholics and infidels have got the start of us," [166] Beecher told his family and worked so hard to raise funds for a Presbyterian seminary in the Old Northwest as base for a counterattack on the Pope that he was chosen to head it. Lane Seminary in Cincinnati, the result, accomplished little against a foe who wasn't there but partook indirectly in a war on another enemy. The leader of its early students, Theodore Weld, acquired at Lane much that later made him the St. Paul of abolitionism, and among the family whom Beecher moved to Cincinnati was daughter Harriet, who, during her stay, was greatly moved by the sight of runaway slaves and once crossed the Ohio into Kentucky a few miles, where she had her first and only—but how fateful!—firsthand glimpse of slavery.

The present point about Beecher is the eagerness of so prominent and learned a man to take the Popish menace seriously. Dread of Papists among his contemporaries climbed to explosive pressures in the early 1830's. *The Protestant,* a nationally circulated paper, stoked the fires. By 1831 New York City had inflammatory public lectures about the Pope sponsored by a Protestant Association—a name ominously identical with that of Lord George Gordon's British anti-Catholic society that burned down seventy houses and four jails in London in 1780. Americans first used arson to deter Catholicism in Charlestown, Massachusetts, across the river from Boston, where a boarding school in charge of the Ursuline order of nuns had long been under suspicion because most of its pupils came from Protestant families. In 1834 the temporary aberration of one of its lay teachers set off rumors obviously based on cheap anti-Catholic novels about excessive penances, dungeons for rebellious novices and so on. A mob, barely giving the nuns time to evacuate the pupils, gutted and burned the place. Public feeling on the mob's side was so strong that no attempt was made to arrest even the ringleaders. Twenty years later the legislature was still refusing to pay damages and housewives were whispering about how Irish servant girls were treacherously sneaking their employers' Protestant babies off for secret baptism into the Roman faith.

More lurid were several ghost-written accounts of alleged tyrannies and lecheries in convent life, chief among them *The Awful Disclosures of Maria Monk . . . During a Residence . . . in the Hotel Dieu Nunnery at Montreal.* Non-Catholic investigation exposed its ridiculous charges about, among others, burying in the cellar more priest-sired babies than the place's population of nuns could possibly have conceived in the time given. The book nevertheless sold and sold—fine ammunition for anti-Catholic screaming in the pulpit, in print and on street corners. It was soon supplemented by an at least apparently more sober work, *Foreign Conspiracy Against the Liberties of the United States,* from S. F. B. Morse. Son of an eminent Congregationalist minister, he had been rabidly anti-Catholic ever since, while a student of painting, he had seen a mass irreverently served in Dijon, where he had stopped over because of conscientious scruples against travel on Sunday. The targets of his book were the Jesuits and the post-Waterloo reactionaries of Europe; otherwise the title is self-explanatory. Its forged quotations attributed to Schlegel, the eminent German philosopher, are harder to explain. Presently Morse was sponsoring the anonymous *Confessions of a French Catholic Priest* and running for mayor of New York City on a nativist ticket. His blend of inventive cleverness with hypersuspicion reminds one of the late Henry Ford, though Morse, reasonably well cultivated for his time, lacked Ford's implicit excuse of meager education.

"Hurrah for the Natives!" [167] wrote George Templeton Strong when James Harper was elected mayor of New York City on a nativist ticket. But he was aghast three months later when Philadelphia's nativists raided Catholic churches and burned a Catholic schoolhouse and scores of dwellings in Irish neighborhoods. "I shan't be caught voting a 'Native' ticket again in a hurry," [167] he promised his diary. That experienced politician-author James K. Paulding was writing to Andrew Jackson that this "new Faction . . . called the Native American Party . . . [is] with the exception of the Abolitionists . . . one of the most mischievous . . . that ever reared its Gorgon head among us. Its object is to create a bitter, unrelenting prejudice . . . [against] Foreign Emigrants, who will of course return the compliment . . . and we shall have among us two races . . . both white . . . each animated by bitter . . . hostility, and ready to proceed to the same, or greater extremities, than those lately witnessed in that Pattern of all cities, Philadelphia." [168] But too many of his compatriots had pathological emotional drives deep enough to enable them to stomach that sort of thing. A nationwide plague of immigrant- and Catholic-hating riots did not keep the Know-Nothing Party of the 1850's from attracting overt or crypto-xenophobes in numbers that badly shook traditional politics and even today have a certain bearing on what can happen here.

This high tide of nineteenth-century nativism owed something to the same proselyting device that the Sons of Temperance were using—the claptrap oaths and passwords and grandiloquent titles of the fraternal order. The Order of United Americans founded in New York City in 1844 —Harper was a member—may have been the first effort to organize xenophobia into a superpatriotic lodge. In 1849 New York's nativists tried again with an Order of the Star-Spangled Banner that pledged members to oppose Catholics wherever found; to vote only for native-born candidates for government office; to work to get the requirement for naturalization of aliens raised to twenty-one years' residence; and never under any circumstances to admit knowing of any such thing as the order. To all inquiries a member was to reply: "I know nothing." Hence the nickname that they adopted informally themselves, even after creating for political campaigning a nationwide American Party, the existence of which had to be freely acknowledged. A member wishing to learn the time and place of the next lodge meeting asked another: "Have you seen Sam?" Bits of colored paper of various shapes conveyed other kinds of information.

The Know-Nothings' rise may also have been aided by the coincident lecture career of a renegade Italian priest, Alessandro Gavazzi, come to America in the early 1850's after triumphs among English anti-Catholics. At its peak, *c.* 1854, the party had three national publications: *The Wide-Awake and Spirit of Washington; The Know-Nothing and American Crusader* (motto "God and our country! Deeds not words!"; emblem "a youth extending his right hand to a star and trampling the Papal tiara underfoot"); and *The Mystery,* "published nowhere, sold everywhere, edited by Nobody and Know-Nothing." All were "full of low and coarse invective," said a British observer of the time who feared lest "the Americans have breathed life into a Frankenstein that will cause much trouble." [169] Fortunately the Know-Nothing structure came apart under the strains of the slavery issue and disappeared during the distractions of the Civil War. Vestiges of its methods may be discernible in the Ku Klux Klan of the late 1860's; they were very much so in the American Protective Association of the 1880's and 1890's.

One of those who investigated Maria Monk's memories of high times in the convent was William L. Stone, editor of the New York *Commercial Advertiser.* The contemporary editor of the New York *Evening Post* was William Cullen Bryant. On a spring morning in 1831 Philip Hone, the invaluable diarist, glanced out his bedroom window while shaving and saw the two editors meet on the sidewalk opposite; whereupon Bryant produced a whip and began to lash Stone about the head with it. It seems that they had had some sort of personal difficulty at a recent convivial dinner.

Stone is now long forgotten, but Bryant is firm in his niche as a majestically bearded, kindly-looking old gentleman who wrote some of the first American verses that were unquestionably poetry. The contrast between that image and this glimpse over Hone's shoulder is startling today. Then, however, though Hone called it disgraceful, it represented a recognizable way for eminent citizens to behave. A certain incidence of horsewhippings and duels was normal among the upper strata in America, as well as in the Old Countries. The cultivated William Austin, creator of *Peter Rugg, the Missing Man,* not only fought a duel with a militia officer but, after the two stipulated exchanges of fire got him a bullet in the leg, demanded and got a third—and a bullet in the neck that finally persuaded him that honor was satisfied. Benjamin Franklin, not a fire-eating type, recommended that full liberty of the press be modified not by the courts but by "the liberty of the cudgel . . . *pari passu.*" [170]

The amazing vilification that Americans permitted themselves, particularly in the press, may have been encouraged by the Hamiltonian doctrine, recognized by the courts of most states, that the truth of a libel could be adduced in defending it. Basically, however, these vestiges of medieval values had crossed the ocean along with the mass violence that besmirched America. They fitted well with the frontiersman with a knife in his boot top for impromptu vindication of his prestige—the type cited in Charles M. Andrews' *The Colonial Background of the American Revolution* as disgusted when arrested for manslaughter because "Nowadays you can't put an inch or so of knife into a fellow . . . but law, law, law is the word. . . . I mean to go to Texas; where a man can have some peace and not be interfered with in his private concerns." [171] Several social rungs higher were the two doctors of Hannibal, Missouri, whom the boy Sam Clemens saw fighting in the street with sword canes. The mere notion of habitually carrying sword canes is eloquent. The two idioms blended in 1846 in a duel at Richmond, Virginia, between two armed-to-the-teeth editors, which began with the conventional pistols but went on into a freestyle hacking match with bowie knives, tomahawks and broadswords. One died shockingly mangled. Brought to trial, the other was quickly let off by a right-thinking jury.

A Southern flavor is strong there—and in American personal homicide as a whole. I know of no incidents in the Northern academic world comparable to that of the student at the University of Virginia who shot and killed a member of the faculty in 1842 or the drunken student at Oakland College in Mississippi who stabbed and killed the president during a discussion of the Compromise of 1850. Only the South had traditional dueling grounds—under the Dueling Oaks at New Orleans; at Bladensburg, Maryland, outside the District of Columbia. Young Horace Mann thought of the South as particularly the region where "they have an idle habit of making small holes thro' a man at the distance of ten paces." [172]

The new state of Illinois had grimly set that sort of matter straight in 1819 by trying and hanging one Timothy Bennett of Belleville, who had quarreled with a neighbor over trespasses committed by a horse and killed him in a rifle duel at twenty-five paces. But the North's hands were by no means clean. In Wisconsin a member of an early legislature, defied and struck at by a fellow member on a point of veracity, drew a pistol and shot him dead on the floor of the house. About the same time in Burlington, Iowa, two local citizens settled a family quarrel with revolvers on the street so cleanly that both died on the spot. New York

State-born James Watson Webb, editor of the New York *Courier & Enquirer,* was as notorious a duelist as any Creole dandy in Louisiana; one of his sons was named William Seward Webb in gratitude to Governor William H. Seward of New York for having pardoned the child's sire after conviction for dueling with Tom Marshall, the fiery Congressman and Temperance lecturer. Among Manhattanites fighting duels in the pre-Civil War era were an international banker and several members of good clubs. One pair, eager to exchange shots because of a difference of opinion over the place of Garibaldi's birth, went all the way to North Carolina to avoid interference from the law. Others found Maryland handier and just as unlikely to make trouble afterward.

F. Opper's idea of Kentucky politics, c. 1900.

The challenged party seldom chose the sword. Fencing was no part of the American's world outside the armed forces. The choice might be grotesque—harpoons, for instance—but pistols were the rule. The likeliest exception was rifles, and at ghastly short range. A Yankee Congressman, Jonathan Cilley of Maine, accepted a challenge from a Kentucky colleague in 1838—Webb was at the bottom of it—and was killed in a rifle duel. By the standards of the time Preston Brooks, the Congressman from South Carolina who beat Senator Charles Sumner half to death on the floor of the U.S. Senate in 1856, was well within his social rights in challenging Anson Burlingame, Congressman from Massachusetts, because of his comments on the incident. Burlingame chose rifles and Navy Island in the Niagara River as the place. Brooks backed out on the ground that, the North being so inflamed against him, he could not travel there safely, but gossip said that he had learned that Burlingame, reared in the Old Northwest, was a crack rifle shot. Early California being what it was, there was nothing far out of the way about the duel in which the chief justice of the State Supreme Court shot and killed a U.S. Senator. But one remains struck by the eminence on the national scene of men from other areas who found it necessary to resort to the field of honor: not only Andrew Jackson, Aaron Burr, Alexander Hamilton, highly placed U.S. Navy officers like Stephen Decatur and James Barron, but also Henry Clay, John Randolph, Thomas H. Benton, Henry A. Wise.

So far as I know, America's last formal duel was an exchange of pistol shots on the Delaware-Maryland border in 1877 between James Gordon Bennett, Jr., son of the publisher of the sensational New York *Herald,* and the brother of a nice girl of a prominent Baltimore family whom Bennett was thought to be courting. The occasion was an unidentified insult that Bennett offered her when he was drunk on New Year's Day; brother horsewhipped him for it in front of the fashionable Union Club; and challenge and duel ensued. Neither was hit; Bennett immediately went to Europe and spent practically all the rest of his life there. Some years later young Theodore Roosevelt, ranching in the West, became aware that the French marquis who owned the adjacent ranch was about to challenge him over a boundary dispute. He decided to make it rifles at twelve paces, "each to shoot and advance until the other was satisfied." [173] But first he wrote an olive-branch letter, which the marquis found so firm and gentlemanly that he asked the young man in spectacles to dinner—and there went the nation's last whiff of coffee and gunpowder at dawn. In the South after the Civil War, Willard Thorpe has observed, the formal frills of the duel withered away in favor of shooting on sight the man who affronted one. This regression to the frontier's preference for informal homicide came to its height in the bullet-ridden politics of Kentucky in the late 1800's. Or maybe in what is now called the walkdown in Westerns.

The tradition of violence even got into so innocent an activity as fire fighting. Until after the Civil War all American firemen were volunteer amateurs. Quite early, as in Benjamin Franklin's Philadelphia, citizens appalled by frequent heavy losses from fire mutually pledged to drop everything when the alarm bell rang from town hall or meeting-house and go to work on an organized basis with axes, ladders and long lines of men passing leather buckets of water hand to hand. Soon they imported from England primitive fire engines supplying hoses with water under pressure worked up by hand pumping. These wheeled contraptions were got to the scene by firemen hauling on hand ropes, then working at the pump handles, half a dozen to a side, on the spot. It was a civic duty usually more exciting than effective. The most powerful handpumper in New York City in the 1850's, for instance, the famous Big Six, could throw a stream only 30 feet in the air, and few rivals could approach that. Discipline and quality of tactics depended

The heroic fireman was all the more admired for being an amateur and a volunteer.

largely on the personality of the foreman or captain, who was no less an amateur than his men. As expanding cities developed numbers of such companies, coordination was weak, little more than mutual agreement roughly assigning each to a specified area.

Yet the system was better than nothing, and the volunteer fireman was a national institution with heavy social overtones. Membership was by invitation; the members chose their captain by vote as much for his personal popularity or prestige as for his fire-fighting skill; the building

where the engine and hose carts were stowed became an informal clubhouse as enjoyable to hang out in as the livery stable or the back room
of the tavern. Except that they are better equipped and trained, all this
remains true of the volunteer fire companies that still provide fire protection in many small American communities. In staid places the cores of
the organization are men of substance, as they were generations ago in
Cambridge, Massachusetts, for instance, where Winslow Homer's father,
a solid hardware dealer, and the boy's employer, owner of a lithography
business, were pillars of the fire company.

By then in larger towns politics and ethnic origins, however, were already flavoring fire fighting. The captain was likely to be the precinct
leader or a close associate of his. The members were often the ward
heelers active on election day in getting out the vote, distributing tickets
and exerting the cryptic or overt pressures that kept the other side's
voters away. As the Irish naturally tended to recruit Irish for what
amounted to a politico-social club and the Germans to recruit Germans
and the Ulstermen to recruit Ulstermen . . . Rivalries between fire companies had been too lively to begin with. Which reached the scene first;
whose engine had what location; whose hose went on what hydrant or
tapped a particular pond; which company had won the last contest in
ladder climbing—it hardly needed the Irish jeering at the Germans to set
off battles of fists and stones. The threatened warehouse or hotel might
burn down before its nominal rescuers had beaten the other outfit to a
pulp and got back to business.

Thoreau described a serious public problem when writing of "the
rowdy world of the large cities . . . vermin [clubbing] together in
alleys and drinking-saloons, its highest accomplishments . . . to run
beside a fire-engine and throw brickbats." [174] William Marcy Tweed,
the archetypal rotten political boss, got his start in politics running ahead
of the Big Six shouting orders at his henchmen through a silver-mounted
speaking trumpet. "The better class had either neglected the companies
to which they belonged," wrote an old-timer in Cincinnati, "or had been
shouldered out by the worse element. . . . The Mose of New York
[the stage fireman created by Frank Chanfrau], the brazen-cheeked,
red-shirted ruffian, was duplicated in every municipality." [175] As the
cult of the plug-ugly kind of fireman grew, Mose took on Paul Bun-
yanesque proportions as the city's peer of the rivermen's Mike Fink—he
was eight feet tall with arms so long he could scratch his kneecaps without bending his knees; carried a keg of beer at his belt in summer;
fought with a wagon tongue in one hand and a flagstone in the other.

Strange as it sounds, the supersession of Mose by a professional
salaried fire department did not begin until 1865, when New York

City got rid of him. In other cities the volunteers' resistance was fierce even when the new department offered to hire the abler amateurs. They resented demobilization itself and also the new steam-powered, horse-drawn pumpers, development of which combined with the spread of proper municipal water systems to encourage the change. When Cincinnati bought such a steam engine, it was taken for granted that to turn it over to a volunteer company would mean its swift destruction. A local iron founder, a rough-and-ready hero of the volunteers, was persuaded to recruit a paid company to handle it. But even he, personally driving it to his first fire, thought it necessary to augment his force by the toughest of his own foundrymen and a battalion of 250 heavy-fisted Irish borrowed from a local ward heeler to protect the operation—and

sure enough this small army barely sufficed to best the mob of volunteers bent on riot and sabotage.

Steam pumpers gave American cities one of their most exhilarating spectacles—the great gray or white horses, manes flying and hooves thundering, followed by the smoke-belching engine all scarlet paint and gleaming brass and festooned with fireman in insouciant attitudes. But then for small boys it had been almost as showy in Mose's day when the long double line of red-shirted heroes came sprinting along with their graceful pet engines so bedizened that nothing in a professional firehouse ever held a candle to them. It was not mere brass and glitter. Many well-established artists had once made eating money by painting elaborate allegories or mythological or historical personages in all the colors of the rainbow on the panels of fire engines. Salomon de Rothschild, son of the great European banking house, accustomed to lavishness, was amazed at the extravagance of the parade of 6,000 volunteer firemen of New York City honoring the visiting Prince of Wales in 1860.

Each carried a torch in one hand and with the other grasping a rope hauling along "Engines [of] all shapes . . . [and] colossal size . . . a foreman spends everything he can to decorate [them] with jewels, paintings,
and gold and silver ornaments. . . ." [176] When the end came, instead
of letting the old machine rot and rust away, one of the superseded
New York volunteer companies, violent to the last, made one final run
and wheeled her to a watery death in the river.

Down South, for all the local liking for violence, the hulking eldest
boys seldom threw teacher out of elementary district schoolhouses—because the South had few of them. That was not Thomas Jefferson's fault.
In 1779 when drawing up for the new commonwealth of Virginia a
complete school system, ABC's through university, he had dreamed
most enticingly of beginning with three years of elementary school gratis
for every free child, with scholarships for the most promising boys all
the way to the top. His purpose, unlike the religious one of New England's zeal for education, was secular—that "of rendering the people
the safe, as they are the ultimate, guardians of their own liberty. . . .
Every government degenerates when trusted to the rulers of the people
alone. The people themselves are its only safe depositories. And to
render even them safe, their minds must be improved to a certain degree." [177] Nothing came of this lovingly worked out scheme but the
founding of the University of Virginia without the state-created infra-
structure that he had stipulated. This did give him the satisfaction of designing the complex of heavily Palladian buildings that many regard
as his masterpiece, and "Father of the University of Virginia" was one of
the three achievements that he wished carved on his tombstone.
But free elementary education for all comers in public schools had to
wait in the South until Reconstruction and in the North until awareness
of European advances jarred the public conscience of New England and
the Old Northwest into action after 1830.
      It was high time. Decades of neglect had not improved New Eng-
land's old system of township-created, though not altogether tuition-
free, schools plus local academies. Whittier's roadside schoolhouse like
"a ragged beggar sunning" was conceivably still in use. Connecticut
had applied to schools the money from land sales in her Western Reserve of Ohio and was accustomed to considering her schools the best
in the nation. True, Lyman Beecher's brood and Bronson and William
Alcott, Theodore Weld and P. T. Barnum had attended Connecticut's
district schools, but the schoolhouses were, says an authoritative summary, "for the most part less comfortable, less sanitary and less decent
than even the prisons of the day . . . on the average twenty feet long,

eight feet wide and seven feet high [less cubage than the standard rail-road boxcar]. . . . Less than half of the fifteen hundred [in use], most of which were situated on the public highway, were equipped with 'places of retirement' for either sex." [178] They were unevenly heated by fireplaces, later by box stoves. Walls and floors were seldom weatherproof; roofs often leaked; window placement had no regard to where pupils would need light. Where part of the pupils' fees was paid in firewood, the worst wood, green or of poor kinds, naturally found its way to the school woodpile, and a child whose father was behindhand with his quota was kept away from the fire. Desks were often of the same size for

The "little red" type of schoolhouse.

gangling adolescents and small fry. Blackboards and maps were almost unknown. Pupils usually supplied their own textbooks with little effort at standardization; it was a fortunate school the younger children of which each had some edition of *Webster's Speller*. (The ubiquity of that valuable but limited work goes far to account for the belief of the backwoods family that "eddication" consisted largely of ability to spell gnarly words. The spelling bee maintained now as a nostalgic stunt was then a cultural occasion as important as a cornhusking or a shivaree.) The pupils' copybooks were usually homemade, with teacher setting the copy at top of the page. Arithmetic problems (usually known as ciphering), compositions and such were written on the pupil's slate—a rectangle of a better quality of slate than that used in roofing set in a wooden frame—with a slate pencil, a pointed thin rod of consolidated slate powder, the letters or figures wiped off readily with a damp sponge. This primitive device persisted for an amazingly long time. Mark Sullivan's investigations found that 25,000,000 slates were produced in America between 1895 and 1900, the peak years, with 6,000,000 still needed in 1913.

Since there was no formal teacher training, standards of recruiting, loose at best, were crudely applied by school committees hampered by ignorance, nepotism or charitable intent. An old-timer in New Hampshire recalled that it was "the custom to employ those for teachers who were in the most need of support; if they could read a chapter in the Testament, teach the Shorter [Calvinist] Catechism, and whip the boys, they were sufficiently qualified." [179] The best were young men earning their way through academies by alternating a year or two of teaching with a year or two of learning. Thence quality graded down to somebody's nephew who wasn't good for much but had learned a little of each of the three R's. Slack as the system was, by sheer weight of probability its teachers sometimes had natural ability and integrity gratefully remembered by their charges after they had turned into important men. Such was Mentor Graham, the happily named teacher who greatly influenced Abraham Lincoln. But there was equal probability of the sort of thing inspiring these verses found on an Old Northwestern schoolhouse wall at the end of the term:

> Lord of love, look down from above
> And pity the poor scholars.
> They hired a fool to teach this school
> And paid him fifty dollars.[180]

Where children were put to farm chores as soon as they could perform useful work, the occasional summer term could be attended by small fry only. A woman could manage them, so somebody's niece took charge at six bits a week and boarded around among the pupils' families. In winter, however, the large boys reappeared in school after their summer and fall in the fields, and few women could cope. By no means all men could. Discipline for all sizes of pupil was based on blows—from the ferule (a flat ruler for whacking the palms of the hands or other parts of the body for minor offenses) to the birch rod or hickory switch for flogging behinds or shoulders. The nautical rope's end is also occasionally mentioned. Merely to glance up from one's book earned a touch of ferule. There was too much of the spirit of the woman teacher in upstate New York who habitually moved about whacking pupils on the thighs at random and, if she saw one flinch at her approach, administered extra whacks because that showed consciousness of guilt about something. To promise to flog the boys generously was often the best way for an applicant for a teaching post to win the committee's favor. Conversely, when Dio Lewis, a picker-up of new ideas later conspicuous in several reforms, renounced corporal punishment as a teen-age teacher in the Mohawk country in the 1840's, the neighborhood thought him out of his mind.

It troubled nobody that on occasion the male teacher beat the big girls, too. No other means of major discipline was recognized, and these schools were necessarily coeducational. A separate teacher and ramshackle building for each sex would have been wildly beyond the community's

The classic log schoolhouse, essentially a basic log cabin. Young James A. Garfield, later President, taught in this one.

resources. One of the few noncorporal punishments for misbehaving boys was to make them sit on the girls' side. In many early schoolhouses the entrance doors, as well as the seating, separated the sexes as among Quakers; hence it was economy, not ideas about equal footing for the sexes, that taught boys and girls together. But when coeducation came along as a forward-looking idea in secondary schools and colleges— at radical Oberlin, for instance, in the 1830's—it was doubtless easier for the public to accept because Americans, unlike Europeans, had long been used to seeing males and females in the same classroom.

The chief difference between New England's elementary schooling and the Old Northwest's was that the latter was even worse and less available. The leaders of early Ohio and Indiana had had a Jeffersonian regard for popular education and expressed good intentions in early legislation. But pioneering conditions so clogged performance that by 1836, of almost

500,000 young Ohioans between the ages of six and twenty-one, less than 30 percent had been in school at all that year. The needs of genuine mass education were so ill understood that many citizens actually hoped that the rise of Sunday Schools—a lively part of home-missionary activity—might cover the problem of the three R's and save the community the pain of levying school taxes. A member of the Ohio legislature described what some, probably most, of available schooling was then like:

> The old Irish school master holds forth three months in the year in a poor cabin with greased-paper window panes. . . . The children begin at a-b, ab and get over as far [in the *Speller*] as b-oo-b-y, when school gives out and they take up their spring work on the farm. The next winter, when school takes up, if it takes up so soon again, having forgotten all they had been taught previously . . . they begin again at a-b, ab, but year after year never get any farther than b-oo-b-y, booby.[181]

The "poor cabin" had often been taken over for school use after some settler had abandoned it for better quarters. Its equipment was "one split-bottom chair for the teacher . . . rude benches . . . of slabs or puncheons for the pupils . . . broom, water bucket, and tin cup or gourd." [182] No desks; writing was done with the slate on the knee. And teacher selection and teaching hazards were, again, like those in the Northeastern backwoods, only more so. "Want to be a schoolmaster, do you?" says the head of the school committee to the hero of *The Hoosier Schoolmaster,* which reflects the author's highly firsthand experience in southern Indiana. "You? Well, what would *you* do in Flat Crick destrick, *I'd* like to know? Why, the boys have driv off the last two, and licked the one afore them. . . . You might teach a summer school when nothin' but children come. But . . . They'd pitch you out of doors, sonny, neck and heels, afore Christmas." [183]

The partial vacuum left by such poor public education was filled by hit-or-miss private or anyway nongovernmental enterprise. Many raw settlements had a subscription school taught by a migrant Easterner who crammed into one room boys and girls of all ages whose parents would pay, say, $2 per quarter each. Not much actual cash was expected; in early Kentucky the schoolmaster might agree to take 75 percent in trade—jerked venison, furs, bar iron, linsey, young cattle, pork, corn or whiskey, probably also young. If he made a go of it, he became a permanent part of the community; if drink, incapacity, the local boys—or the local girls—proved too much for him, he departed to try again farther toward the frontier. Along the seaboard, teachers relying on monetary tuition fees and tending to be stabler types had long been intrenched in teaching all comers things by which one might profit economically, socially or spiritually. After the Revolution many literate men—and some women—came from the Old Countries to set up in American cities private classes in the practical kinds of mathematics, bookkeeping, languages, grammar, polite accomplishments such as dancing and music.

In New England the tradition of the publicly supported but fee-charging local academy, of which Boston Latin School was the outstanding example, turned wholly private in the founding of the Phillips Exeter and Phillips Andover academies before the dust of the Revolution had settled. There followed a boom in academies into the Old Northwest from Yankeedom and Pennsylvania. A typical growing upcountry town in the North was pretty sure to sprout a high-shouldered brick building, maybe financed by a dozen or so local Quality, to house day and boarding boys taught by a recent graduate of the University of Pennsylvania or Yale and an assistant or two of lower academic attainments. Still girlish Mrs. Sheepskin and a couple of hired help handled the bed-and-board department. Sheepskin might be ordained and so could maintain a religious sponsorship, usually Presbyterian, that encouraged parents to entrust their sons to him. The curriculum might vary depending on the boy's planned future; say, four years for those intended for college, three for potential businessmen, as much time as was practical for those meaning to teach. For a typical curriculum here is what $3 a term secured in the academy at Oswego, New York, attended by John D. Rockefeller: reading, writing, orthography, elocution, mental algebra, geography and the use of the globes; $5 added Latin, Greek, Hebrew, French, moral science, political economy, botany, mineralogy, geology —only not all at once and only as occasion served. There was a good deal of window dressing about the farther reaches of academies' catalogues. But it could be relied on that ferule and birch went with the daily lessons and that prayers were never omitted.

Presently the desire of the local Quality to have ladylike daughters, as well as literate sons, led to a similar building across the square —the Plaintown Female Seminary for boarding and indigenous young misses in cloaks and bonnets. The courses detailed in this prospectus were often laid on even thicker. An Englishwoman opening such a school in Lexington, Kentucky, in 1808 asked $200 a year to board a girl and teach her "Reading, spelling, writing, arithmetick, grammar, epistolary correspondence, elocution, and rhetorick; geography, with the use of maps, globes, and the armillary sphere; astronomy with the advantages of an orrery; ancient and modern history; chronology, mythology, and natural history; natural and moral philosophy; musick, vocal and instrumental; drawing; painting, and embroidery of all kinds; artificial flowers, and any other fashionable fancy-work. . . ." [184] In presumably less gullible New Haven in 1825 the pretensions were almost as elaborate. The daughter of Ithiel Town, the eminent architect, was graduated from the New Haven Female Seminary with alleged proficiency in "Moral Philosophy, Evidences of Christianity, Natural Theology, Astronomy, Logic, Philosophy of the Mind, Dictionary . . . Elocution . . . Latin, French and Greek . . . Fine Needlework, Perspective Drawing, Landscape, Figure, Flower, and Velvet Paintings, and Music." [185]

One wonders whether her "Perspective Drawing" was up to her father's elegant standards. But doubtless Miss Etha Town came out of that whirlpool of mental varnish able to write a pretty hand, recite a pretty set of verses, paint a pretty piece of china, and even conjugate *amo* effectively. For many of the women who taught in and sometimes directed these institutions had had solid, if narrow, preparation—for instance, Catharine Beecher, whose seminary in Milwaukee was famous, and Mrs. Lydia Huntley Sigourney, the conspicuous poetess, who had a well-known one in Hartford, Connecticut, before she married. Consider also Bethania Crocker of Massachusetts, whose Congregationalist minister father had grounded her well in Hebrew, as well as Greek and Latin. In 1839 at the age of sixteen she went to Oxford, Ohio, to preside over a new female seminary founded on $10,000 subscribed locally and smiled on by the faculty of Miami University in the same village. Within four years she not only had the school going so well that it became the Oxford College for Women but had married the son of the president of the university. There was indeed a beckoning light for Lowell girls earning to get enough learning to go teach in the West.

Particularly successful boys' academies too might prove to be the germs of degree-granting colleges. That was the story at Amherst, Washington and Jefferson, Hampton-Sydney, Hamilton and numerous others. The upgrading was simplified by the still modest curricular demands of the American college, which, as Nicholas Murray Butler wrote, was "Up to the close of the Civil War . . . mainly an institution of secondary education, with some anticipation of university studies toward the end of the course." [186] Correspondingly low standards among the academies made it necessary for most newly established colleges to set up preparatory departments where applicants could put in a year or two learning enough to enter. When Horace Mann opened Antioch College in 1852, a coeducational experiment presumably drawing particularly keen applicants, he imposed something like Harvard College standards of admission and found that only 8 of 212 could qualify for the freshman class; the rest, including a number of ministers already ordained, were put into preparatory work.

The same lack of conventional preparation might turn up among college faculty. When, in 1801, Yale contemplated setting up a chair of chemistry and natural history—its first venture into exact science—the appointment went to a young alumnus, Benjamin Silliman, who, though most promising, knew nothing of either chemistry or natural history. To take care of that, the college paid his way to attend scientific lectures for two years at the conspicuous Medical School in Philadelphia and then for a year in England. This curious process worked out well. The germs of responsible science that Silliman planted and ably fostered at Yale grew into the Sheffield Scientific School. When Bowdoin College installed a chair of modern languages and chose a promising young alumnus, Henry Wadsworth Longfellow, to fill it, he knew little more of modern languages than Silliman had of chemistry, so he was sent to Europe to study them for three years. Soon called to Harvard where, writing his own textbooks for lack of others and gracefully inspiring in his students his own reverence for German scholarship and the glories of the Romance tongues, he left admirable footprints on the sands of American learning. (The University of Virginia, finally opening in 1825, took the other way, importing half its original faculty from England.) Jonathan Baldwin Turner was in the middle of his senior year at Yale when appointed professor of Greek and Latin at a new college founded by Yale Divinity School students in pioneer Illinois. Yale sent him West with a hasty blessing and fired his diploma after him months later. His subsequent career had less and less to do with classical tongues and more and more with the virtues of Osage orange hedges, the creation of a common school system in Illinois and the founding of the University of Illinois.

The sound excuse for such reliance on unprepared (by our standards) youngsters is that teaching and scholarship, like many other things, have to begin by beginning. Judge Tapping Reeve's famous law school at Litchfield, Connecticut, set up in 1784, eventually had as faculty two men—Reeve and a colleague, James Gould—neither of whom had ever attended a law school. In their youth the only one in America was at William and Mary hundreds of miles away in Virginia. Apprenticeship—reading law and copying documents—in an established lawyer's office was otherwise the only way to qualify for the bar.

It was the time of Jackson and the common man. In spite of recurring hard times, standards of living were rising except among Negro slaves.

But standards of education were rising only among the relatively affluent. While elementary schools based on taxes or land grants lagged, pay-for-what-you-get schools were flourishing on all academic levels. This vexed the equalitarian-minded and, for different reasons, the gold-headed canes. Jefferson had desired an even start for all to develop the group responsibility and sound group judgment that the health of democracy needed. Many Americans, particularly in New England, still assumed that right thinking and right doing (in terms by then less Bible-ridden than those of the 1600's) were the prime ends of education and viewed with alarm a system that gave the poorest schooling to the lower orders, which presumably most needed moral shaping. Further, such a two-ply arrangement not only deepened caste divisions, but also troubled the Benjamin Franklin kind of mind by reducing society's chances of making the most of potentially bright but poor youngsters among the lower orders. Further it prevented the spontaneous contacts in classroom and playground between children from upper and lower strata that would stimulate and civilize both better than was possible among schoolmates of their exclusive stripe. That last point was a psychologically fertile importation from certain Old Country educationists whose theories and radical practices had much to do with creating what became the American public school system of today.

Britain contributed only the abortive Lancastrian scheme of an English Quaker, Joseph Lancaster, who was bringing literacy to the masses by a sort of academic perpetual motion. One began by teaching the three R's to x number of likely poor children; at a certain stage they were set, under supervision of their original teachers, to passing on what they had learned to a new lot of illiterates while continuing themselves to learn; in due time the second echelon too became part-time amateur teachers of a third echelon of illiterates. The Lancastrians claimed that as x became x^2 and x^2 became x^3, one adult teacher could handle some 1,000 learners. Wonderfully cheap per pupil, it did fairly well among the abjectly ignorant English urban proletariat and attracted warm support from Dissenters and the Church of England too. In 1818 Lancaster brought it across the ocean to Baltimore and New York City; it also had some success in a few towns in Ohio. But it failed to flourish in America partly because it necessarily overemphasized reading and memorizing —a fault already marked in the schools of the day—and also possibly because it failed to counteract stratification. For it had come to fame as primarily schooling for paupers, and American parents able to pay at least a little tuition disliked that flavor. Indeed had it got embedded in the tax-created schools, it would have deepened the caste split.

The continent of Europe was more helpful. Part of the intellectual yeastiness in the wake of Rousseau, Montesquieu, Diderot, *et al.,* had been radical educational theories leading in directions that we now call progressive. The chief figures were, like Rousseau, Swiss, though from the German side of Swissness: Johann Heinrich Pestalozzi, whose experimental school omitting corporal punishment and stressing positive emotion and learning by doing was famous in the early 1800's; and Philipp Emanuel von Fellenberg, who hoped for a universal educational system of Pestalozzian ideas organized on Jeffersonian lines to give children of all social strata and caste destinies the fertile experience of common mind training and physical labor. The Prussian government, apparently liking this monolithic scheme, put Fellenberg's notions to use in conjunction with the gymnastic-hygienic tradition of the Prussian nationalist movement. Americans studying in Germany as German philosophy and scholarly methods became fashionable brought home these stimulating heresies. Joseph Cogswell and George Bancroft (later the renowned historian of the United States), two such returned Germanophiles, installed them in their forward-looking new school for boys near Northampton, Massachusetts. William Maclure, an immigrant Scot otherwise noted in America as geologist, diplomat and underwriter of Owen's New Harmony colony, had already visited Pestalozzi in Switzerland and brought back a Pestalozzi-trained teacher to put theory into practice in Philadelphia. Presently Maclure imported another such, William Phiquepal d'Arusmont (who later had the disastrous courage to marry Fanny Wright), to do so at New Harmony. In 1836 the Reverend Dr. Calvin Ellis Stowe, just married to Harriet Beecher, went to Europe for firsthand knowledge of such matters to guide Ohio in school improvement. It was just such a series of multiple cultural forays as that naturalizing Freud in America in the decade before World War I.

An immediate result was the founding of a number of Fellenberg-inspired manual-training schools and colleges, where resourceless young men could earn at least part of their way by pitching hay and cleaning out stables on the attached farm that fed faculty and students. Surviving colleges that originally had the manual-labor feature in some form are Mercer, Davidson, Randolph-Macon, Oberlin. The drawbacks proved to be uncertain markets for what the students produced when their work extended beyond staple foodstuffs, and besides, as an alumnus of such an institution said years afterward, he and his classmates were going to college "to study, not to make brooms and barrels for the salvation of their souls." [187] More lasting in results was a series of appointments by certain Northern states (Michigan in 1836; Ohio and Massachusetts in

1837; Connecticut in 1838) of state superintendents of education who hoped to use some of these new ideas to improve schooling.

Their zeal was heightened by memories of their own schooling. Michigan's Reverend John D. Pierce, for instance, had had scanty, bleak grounding in hardscrabble country schools of New Hampshire; had begun to teach himself Greek and Latin at the age of twenty in order to enter Brown University; and after admission had put himself through by alternate years of teaching in the very kind of school he hoped to wipe out. It is understandable that in Michigan he laid out a comprehensive scheme for state-backed, tuition-free elementary schools all the way to the present University of Michigan—the only part that came to pass in his lifetime. At the age of thirteen Connecticut's Henry Barnard had been so disgusted with the miserable elementary school he attended that he was planning to run away to sea when his father offered him the opportunity to change to a select academy with a little more to offer. Massachusetts' Horace Mann got into Brown after a dismal and meager elementary schooling largely by doggedly poring over the 116 books (of which 40 were on theology) with which Benjamin Franklin had set up a public library in the boy's home township of Franklin, Massachusetts. It is a pity that the self-made and often open-minded Franklin could not know what his gift accomplished. For Horace Mann had as much or more than any other single figure to do with America's acquiring free elementary education and the normal school system that revolutionized—and feminized—American elementary teaching.

His first career had been as able lawyer and legislator making and keeping influential acquaintances by what is said to have been marked personal charm. A reformer from his undergraduate days, he was hot for abolition and Temperance, and his zeal for phrenology sadly confused the theoretical aspects of his writings. One of his sisters-in-law was Elizabeth Peabody, collaborator in Bronson Alcott's early experiments in radical education and later a principal missionary of the kindergarten in America. In a climate of windy ideas Mann nevertheless managed a gratifyingly sporting and practical approach to school reform. He aimed not to handicap or ban private schools, even though he considered them damagingly anti-equalitarian. His purpose was to make free public schools so good that even affluent parents would entrust their children to them. The massive amount of private education in New England today indicates that he did not altogether succeed. But the effort effected solid improvements on many fronts.

To begin with, along with Henry Barnard, he denounced tumbledown schoolhouses and demanded reasonable provision for heating, ventilation, sanitation, lighting and seating. (The minimum response in rural areas was the little red schoolhouse* of great folk prestige.) Mann insisted that singing, as well as geography and history, should be added to the three R's in the crankish but constructive belief that music would do as much as the other two to make good moral citizens—always his prime objective. He deplored corporal punishment as at best an uncivilized last resort. He told townships that unless most of their school taxes were to be wasted in the long run, they would have to build and maintain good public libraries as long-lasting supplements. He disregarded the college-university level, alias higher education, until late in life, when he was put in charge of the new and experimental Antioch College as its first president. But Barnard and he (following Prussian and French precedents deriving from Pestalozzi and Company) succeeded in attaching to American education the government-run normal school on a sort of high-academy level to train teachers for the new dispensation in *how* as well as *what* to teach—a notion new to American school boards. Opening the first such institution at Lexington, Massachusetts, in 1839, with a handful of students, the new principal found them so poorly prepared that he had to take them back through spelling and simple arithmetic before going on into educational theory and its practice in the demonstration elementary school attached. The notion of normal schools spread swiftly, however, and the term became part of the American language; several post offices are named Normal after the teacher's colleges situated in town.

Like his fellow Temperance crusaders, Mann had a panacea mind. Enough of the right kind of schooling would largely wipe out crime, poverty and vice. Looking back after the Civil War, Edward Everett Hale wrote that it would be hard to convey "How much was then expected from reforms in education. . . . If we only knew enough, it was thought, we should be wise enough to keep out of the fire." [188] But that was the intellectual vice of Mann's time. In spite of such misconceptions, he laid sound foundations for democratic education by shaming the nation into providing decent schoolrooms, new subjects and teaching that called for more than skillful use of the rod and regurgitation of formulas.

Mann, Pierce, Barnard and colleagues can hardly have anticipated some of the eventual side effects. By now normal schools and the ancillary departments of education have done rather too good a job of getting recognition for teaching as a profession requiring exacting special training. *How* overshadows *what;* the shoe is on the other foot. Even before

---

* Until the mid-1800's there were few red schoolhouses of any size because they were so seldom painted; those of logs could not be, of course. The first mention of the LRS I know of is in Artemus Ward, "The Showman's Courtship" (*c.* 1860): ". . . blushin as red as the Baldinsville skool house when it was fust painted."

World War I my teachers in the best elementary public school in a Mid-western city noted for its good educational system knew far more about teaching than they did about what they taught. And they all were women. And in the city's best high school the relatively few men teachers were concentrated in science and mathematics.

In the seventy years since that normal school at Lexington had opened, teaching on the elementary and secondary levels had become largely women's work. The way to full-time careers for spinsters in the coeducational classroom had begun to clear when moral began to replace physical discipline. It widened enticingly when coeducational policy, prevalent in the new normal schools, gave women the same training facilities as those accorded men. Here was a fine opening for nice girls wanting a decorous livelihood, the same kind who, as Lowell girls, had been relying on academies to qualify them to teach. By Civil War times to "go to the normal" in one's late teens and then to teach school until marriage—which might not occur at all in regions losing population to the West—made up a typical pattern. It certainly raised the average respectability of the elementary teacher. With bright, decent young women available, there was less need to hire the kind once described by an historian of early Ohio as "a well educated but rather dissipated man of Quaker parentage." [189] But this ripening association between copybooks and women kept the prestige of the newly recognized profession from rising to match its growth in numbers. When teaching became women's work, men were less likely to go into it. This deprived the American educational system of many potentially fine talents and probably did the schools as much damage as the normal schools' emphasis on method rather than knowledge.

The teacher in the state systems of the Old Countries where Pestalozzi rose and Fellenberg sprung seems to have seen no such social devolution. The European teacher is very often a man. G. Stanley Hall, one of the most influential psychologist-educationists of the turn of the century, greatly admired the wholesome heroine of the sticky tale of Swiss village life in which Pestalozzi embodied much of his doctrine. It was most American of Hall thus to describe her: "Gertrude is the Good Teacher, by whom alone the world is to be saved . . . regeneration is not to be effected by endowments, legislation, or by new methods . . . but . . . by the love and devotion of noble women . . . the good Gertrudes of all stations of life, the born educators of the race, whose work . . . we men-pedagogues must ponder well." [190]

The same years (1836-38) that saw Mann and colleagues set about rebuilding the common schools also produced the first of the famous

McGuffey Eclectic Readers—a new cultural fuel, so to speak, for the new educational engine. William Holmes McGuffey was another strive-and-succeed educationist who had hard-earned knowledge of the shortcomings of American schools. As a boy in the Pennsylvania hills just before the War of 1812 he had only sporadic backwoods schooling, yet by the age of thirteen he was teaching a school in backwoods Ohio. From raw new academies and then an academy nominally turned college he scraped together enough further learning to teach classical languages at Miami University, soon became president of Cincinnati College and a leader in movements to improve Ohio's schools, and spent his last thirty years as professor of mental and moral philosophy at the University of Virginia. A creditable career, but so far twenty other men in education in the Old Northwest had deserved equally well of the Republic. What made McGuffey a household word among millions who had never heard of Horace Mann or Jonathan Turner of Illinois or Caleb Mills of Indiana, peers of McGuffey in their own states, was a series of six graded readers, plus a speller and a volume of selections for declamation compiled by himself with the occasional help of his much younger brother Alexander.

These books were to the Northern generation reared in time for the Civil War—the one that read *Uncle Tom's Cabin* and saw the railroads' trunk lines cross the Mississippi—what *Webster's Speller* had been to their fathers. In both cases the preeminent work had plenty of rivals. Then, as now, the textbook business was a good one, and many other spellers and readers were published and flourished regionally. But it was the McGuffey line that dominated the field, selling some 100,000,-000 copies up to World War I as successive editions fell apart. As Henry Steele Commager has so ably described, they gave those of our great-grandfathers who had their schooling in America a "common body of allusion and a common frame of reference" [191] vastly important to cultural cohesion. Just as Yankee children of 1727 had in common the warning in the alphabet of the *New England Primer* that "Xerxes the great did die / And so must you & I," just as most American children who saw the inside of a schoolhouse in 1827 had in common the *Webster's Speller*'s "Fable I: Of the Boy That Stole Apples" and got stoned down out of the tree, so did their children of 1857 and their grandchildren of 1887 have in common from *McGuffey's Fifth* Daniel Webster's: "Sink or swim, live or die, survive or perish, I give my hand and my heart to this vote!" The only comparable stores of stock attitudes and tag lines were the King James Bible, always read in church and Sunday School and often in family worship, and the hymns sung over and over in those places and by mother and sister over their housework. Those two sources also are dried up today or going dry. The "common body of allusion" today depends not on books but on advertising and comic strips, on popular songs, not hymns. A few years ago a faculty member of an eminent women's college warned an English woman scholar embarking on some exchange lectures in literature: "The only reading that you can count on to be familiar to all your freshmen is . . . *The Catcher in the Rye.*"

Reactionaries seeking to discredit the modern educationist have created around the *McGuffey Readers* a cult that overstates their virtues. The materials selected did, for instance, plunge the pupil stimulatingly into contact with new words and ideas originally set down by adults for adults, instead of flabbily limiting vocabulary and ideas to things already familiar. But the moral attitudes inculcated, as was the fashion then, were, as Commager says, inclined to crudity of the Benjamin Franklin school. And few of these moral-heavy bits had the taut style that keeps Franklin, and England's Maria Edgeworth and Letitia Barbauld, still worth reading. In that respect children dependent on McGuffey were best off with his selections from the Bible and Shakespeare. Commager properly commends the lack of literary chauvinism that, contrary to the spirit of Noah Webster, included much material from British writers. The roll of writers included is, however, top-heavy with New Englanders. The final editions of the *Fifth* and *Sixth Readers* (1879) between them contain seventy selections from New England writers, as opposed to fifty-eight from the rest of the nation—fourteen from the South; forty-four from the rest of the North. That would be understandable in school texts prepared in New England primarily for that regional market, as many were. But the McGuffey line was founded by non-Yankees, published in the non-Yankee end of Ohio, and intended for a national market.

The reason was that New England's talent for taking schooling seriously had led to something like literary and intellectual domination of America. It had begun with the Ichabod Crane kind of youth going West to teach school and the high incidence of Yankee tutors employed by the Southern Quality. In the mid-1800's the tidy, literate Yankee teacher girls flocking westward established the New England twang as the voice of the eternal schoolmarm, and by the banks of the rivers of Iowa and Michigan they naturally caused their pupils to commit to memory the songs of their Zion about wrecked schooners, breaking waves dashing high, sandpipers on beaches and "Massachusetts—there she stands!" Except in Ohio the innovator fathers of the new-forming public schools had usually been Yankees—some, like Mann, reshaping their home states; others, like Stowe, Turner, Pierce and Mills, self-chosen missionaries carrying the right to learn to the benighted West. North of the National Road, where immigration from New England and upstate New York had been consistently heavy, their fitness to do so was seldom questioned. In the wake of such men's work, always with a savor of codfish about it, Yankee suzerainty over things of the mind was taken more and more for granted, just as New England-style white houses with green shutters spread through northern Ohio into the Great Lakes states. Those Yankee schoolmarms would have seen nothing extravagant in Horace Mann's regional Pharisaism:

"In surveying our vast country," he wrote in 1846, "the rich savannahs of the South, and the almost interminable prairies of the West . . . where . . . all the nations of Europe . . . could find ample substance—the ejaculation involuntarily bursts forth, WHY WERE THEY NOT COLONIZED BY MEN LIKE THE PILGRIM FATHERS? . . . how different would have been the fortunes of this nation had those States . . . been founded by men of high, heroic Puritan mould;— how different in the eyes of righteous Heaven, how different in the estimation of the wise and good. . . ." [192] Narcissism so ripe and thorough can carry conviction by sheer effrontery.

Literacy and literature are intimately related, though neither necessarily implies the other. So New England's hegemony was directly reflected in the canon roughed out by the McGuffeys and ramified and refined in the literary texts used in most American schools for generations after the Civil War. Around 1900 it struck Booth Tarkington that in at least one room of most American elementary schools, over the front blackboard back of the teacher's desk, hung four photo portraits in various shades of bilious brown "of great and good men, kind men, men who loved children. Their faces were noble and benevolent. . . . Long day after long day, interminable week in and interminable week out, vast month on vast month, the pupils sat with those four portraits beaming down on them. . . . Never, while the children of that schoolroom lived, would they be able to forget one detail . . . the hand of Longfellow was fixed, for them, forever, in his beard. And by a simple and unconscious association, Penrod Schofield was accumulating an antipathy for the gentle Longfellow and for James Russell Lowell and for Oliver Wendell Holmes and for John Greenleaf Whittier that would never permit him to peruse a work of one of those great New Englanders without a feeling of personal resentment. . . ." [193] There they were, a fixed symbolic group like the four Evangelists, all alike in being vehicles of the gospel that Boston State House was (as Holmes had sardonically said) the Hub of the Universe.

How well Longfellow, Lowell, Whittier and Holmes show the vicissitudes of fashion in literature as well as whiskers! Modern criticism neglects them in favor of Melville, Whitman, Poe, Thoreau, Hawthorne and Emerson, of whom, as it happens, only three were of New England rearing. As prophets—in a nonliterary function highly valued by modern criticism and sometimes coincident—the men on that schoolroom wall had felt no call to rival *Walden, Leaves of Grass* or the most portentous of Emerson's Transcendentalist poems. But never mind these distinctions. Lump all ten writers together, add Dana's *Two Years Before the Mast* and the best of Abraham Lincoln's speeches, and you have a literature of scale, versatility and some originality. Americans in general might be still chewing tobacco and countenancing the grotesqueries of camp meetings, but their nation's writing had come of age.

In confirmation the Old Countries perceived as much. In 1820 the Reverend Sydney Smith, great English wit, had uttered his famous taunt: ". . . who reads an American book, or goes to an American play, or looks at an American picture or statue?" [194] Within a generation Longfellow was outselling Tennyson in England; French critics were so taken with Poe that they thought they had discovered him—all of which had more bearing on the rise of American letters than the callow delight the Old World took in Cooper's cardboard characters. It further firmed up this change in attitude when a striking group of historians, Yankees and Harvard graduates all, demonstrated that several Americans could turn out works that for acumen, scholarship and handsome manipulation of the language no cultivated Briton could afford to miss.

George Bancroft's gravely rhetorical *History of the United States,* beginning to appear in 1834 as the first of these contributions, had least appeal overseas. Its attitude was spread-eagle, its style full-blown in a vein even then going out of usage except on platforms. But William H. Prescott, struggling against a blindness almost as sad as Milton's; Francis Parkman, who went beyond the Missouri as an ailing young lawyer to consort with hunters and Indians for his health and came back a brilliant historian; and the somewhat dandified John Lothrop Motley were successively recognized as peers of the Old World's guild of historians and throughout the ups and downs of historiographic fashion have pretty well kept their position in academic esteem. Overseas acceptance was the readier, true, because their subject matter was sometimes European, as in Motley's work on the Netherlands and Prescott's on Spain, or often peripheral to the United States, as in Prescott's masterpieces on Mexico and Peru and Parkman's on New France. True also, most of them had studied in Europe, as was already not unusual after college. But anybody who thinks of the Harvard of the Monroe-Adams era as long on social prestige and short on mind training (as some later alumni did) should recall that there these four had acquired their grounding and—a consideration when discussing literature—the inclination to be cordially readable that made Prescott, Parkman and Motley stylists as elegant as they were individual.

Yet do not envisage a vigorous young nation glorying in and eagerly supporting new-blown historians, poets, novelists and thinkers. There was much exultant palaver; but actually, of those writers still in critical favor, the American reading public *c.* 1850 accepted only Poe, Hawthorne and Emerson with much generosity, and Emerson owed more to the lecture platform than to the bookshop. After the first travelogue-minded interest in his lush accounts of Polynesia, Melville's work, even *Moby Dick,* was little heeded; his later livelihood came from daily stagnation as a customs inspector. The pre-Civil War versions of *Leaves of Grass* had little more than a *succès de scandale* consequent on its blurred references to hetero- and homosexuality. Fowlers & Wells, which took over the first edition of the book, finally had to give away the copies left on its hands. The ease with which the Old World writers' works were pirated still kept American readers of any cultivation dominated by Dickens, Bulwer-Lytton, Thackeray, Ainsworth, the Brontës, Tennyson, Carlyle, Macaulay, Mrs. Hemans, Dumas, Victor Hugo, even after some publishers began indirectly to observe foreign writers' rights by paying sizable fees for advance proofs from which to set pirated editions. The occasional American-written best seller, such as Susan Warner's massive bouquet of deathbed scenes *The Wide, Wide World,* was in some respects encouraging but could not redress the imbalance.

European dominance was also marked in children's reading. America had some indigenous juveniles, such as those of Peter Parley (Samuel G. Goodrich, one of whose hack writers was Hawthorne) and the Reverend Jacob Abbott whose innumerable little *Rollo* books acquainted hundreds of thousands of children in roundabouts or pantalets with Rollo's Cousin Lucy and Rollo's magisterial father and Rollo's wheelbarrow and Rollo's indispensable mentor Jonas, the hired man who knew how to do everything and also everything Rollo should not do and why. But imported British-written texts were the rule in the Sunday School libraries that were undermining the literary taste of the rising generation. Juveniles of secular origin also were, as Lucy Larcom recalled, "nearly all English reprints." She liked the moral tales of Mrs. Sherwood and Miss

Edgeworth: "Primroses and cowslips and daisies bloomed in these pleas-ant story-books . . . we went a-maying there, with our transatlantic playmates. I think we sometimes started out with our baskets, expecting to find these English flowers in our own fields. . . ." [195] Thus, in spite of Noah Webster and young Mr. Jefferson Brick of the New York *Rowdy Journal,* England's apron strings were still strong long after independence.

The insipid verses illustrating the engravings of the annual "keepsake" giftbook of the day—Philadelphia's *Atlantic Souvenir* and *The Gift,*

Title page of the Rollo *series.*

Boston's *The Token,* New York City's *The Talisman*—though mostly American-written, preferred such exotic flora as primroses and wall-flowers and British fauna, too, in the shape of nightingales and skylarks. Bryant's verses about bobolinks and Whittier's about blackberry stains—both McGuffey selections—were getting away from this dependency on the poetical stage props of an elder world. Still the absurdity dwindles when one reflects that in leaning on ancient Greece, the Shakespeare of *Venus and Adonis,* the Keats of "Endymion" and the Tennyson of "The Lotos-Eaters" had done much the same sort of thing.

Longfellow carried water from the Pierian spring on both shoulders and with graceful effect. He clung to Old World materials—Scandinavian, Spanish, German—with a fondness understandable in a scholar. But he also added much to the national gallery of wholly or partly synthetic American folk figures that already included Poor Richard, Rip Van Winkle, Peter Stuyvesant, Leatherstocking and the Noble Red Man. Evangeline never existed, but in the bayou country of Louisiana descendants of her Acadian fellow exiles show you the live oak under which her lover slept as she passed unheedingly by. John Alden and Priscilla Mullens did exist, but since nobody knows what they were like personally, Longfellow was free to mold them to his heart's desire for the waxworks. Its management also owed him Hiawatha, who had had a shadowy existence among the Iroquois, and Paul Revere, as real and almost as versatile a person as Benjamin Franklin but now doomed jinglingly to gallop forever past every Middlesex village and farm. Holmes made clever use of the next pair:

> All through the conflict, up and down
> Marched Uncle Tom and Old John Brown—
> One ghost, one form ideal.
> And which was false and which was true,
> And which was mightier of the two,
> The wisest sybil never knew,
> For both alike were real.

John Wilkes Booth contributed the tall figure in the corner. Davy Crockett was largely self-created out of his own publications rather than out of what he did. The later 1800's added Huckleberry Finn and Tom Sawyer. A new country with no medieval past had no opportunity to build up its Robin Hoods and Fair Rosamonds drop by drop as if they were cultural stalagmites. It must cherish the deliberate creations of poet, novelist and biographer—and presently they are satisfactory enough.

Yet there was another Longfellow—the treadling versifier who stood on the bridge at midnight and declined to be told that life was but an empty dream. The work of this one was far closer to the vast body of verse cobbled up in his time by the banker's daughter, or sometimes his narrow-chested son, that ran riot in the corners of newspapers headed "The Muses' Bower" or "The Castalian Fount," and were sometimes collected in slender volumes with a wispy engraving of the versifier as frontispiece. Mature men shared this guilt, but all too often the way was shown by the more sensitive sex. In the 1830's, for instance, though Mrs. Sarah T. Bolton was not yet nationally famous for her inspirational poem

"Paddle Your Own Canoe," she was already rhyming away for the local papers. Of her apostrophe to Indiana in the Indianapolis *Gazette,* two stanzas may suffice:

> Home of my heart, thy shining sand,
>   Thy forests and thy streams,
> Are beautiful as fairyland
>   Displayed in fancy's dreams.
>
> Home of a thousand happy hearts,
>   Gem of the far wild West,
> Ere long thy sciences and arts
>   Will gild the Union's crest. . . .[196]

The admiring brother of such a poetess described her method to Huckleberry Finn: ". . . she could rattle off poetry like nothing . . . she would slap down a line and if she couldn't find anything to rhyme with it she would just scratch it out and slap down another one, and go ahead. She warn't particular." To read Mrs. Sigourney and the other seventy-eight clustered around her in *The Female Poets of America* chosen by Thomas Buchanan Read (himself a brisk versifier) in 1852 shows how popular the method was. Note that both in this selection and in its predecessor of the same title edited by Rufus Griswold poetesses from New England far outnumber those from any other section, with Yankee-permeated New York State second. Of them all, only Alice and Phoebe Cary, sisters from Cincinnati who developed one of New York City's earliest literary salons, were ever close enough to Pegasus to know what color he was. (Another salon was that of Mrs. Anne Charlotte Lynch Botta, editress of a widely successful *Handbook of Universal Literature,* whose verses were atrocious but did not frighten from her hospitable doors such habitués as Emerson, Julia Ward Howe, William Cullen Bryant.) A fair sample of what the mid-1800's welcomed from such ladies may be taken from Miss Lavinia Stoddard:

> And not from me the sportive jest,
>   The mirthful jibe, the gay reflection,
> These social bubbles fly the breast
>   That owns the sway of pale Dejection. . . .[197]

Lest misogyny be suspected, it should be said that the verses of such contemporary male songsters of reputation as Nathaniel P. Willis were little better. Or take Albert Pike, Yankee ornament of the Arkansas bar and Confederate general, celebrated as author of "The Widowed Heart":

Thou art lost to me forever!—I have lost thee, Isadore!
Thy head will never rest upon my loyal bosom more;
Thy tender eyes will never more look fondly into mine,
Nor thine arms me lovingly and trustingly entwine,—
Thou art lost to me forever, Isadore. . . .[198]

It was obliging of the newspaper editor to print these local bards' out-pourings. (The same thing was going on in the English provincial papers of the day.) Besides, he had to fill the columns of his four-page paper. It had improved little since Franklin's time. Income was somewhat better supplemented by advertising wholesale and retail; and from operators of steamboats, stage lines, theaters (if the town were large enough), hotels and boardinghouses; and from owners of strayed animals. There were long letters from local political zealots and public legal notices if the editor's politics were right. The rest was local produce prices and, in seaports, shipping movements; accounts of three-headed calves, high winds, epidemics and lurid crimes clipped from the exchanges—the free mail copies of other papers with which distant editors favored one another to facilitate just such mutual cannibalizing. The same sources supplied occasional bits of foreign news. There might be a letter from Washington, where political reporting was beginning to stir, or from the editor's politician-patron's nephew traveling in Europe; possibly a serialization of a pirated novel; but only a few dabs of local news.

In the largest towns, however, beginning in Philadelphia in 1783, six-days-a-week publication had begun, and the staff reporter appeared to relieve the editor (who might still be doubling as boss printer) of part of the burden of covering produce markets, keeping a political ear to the ground, and turning out copy. Not that much of what we now think of as reporting was done until well in the 1800's. The typical end product was well summarized in the complaint of Franz Josef Grund, soon to turn newspaperman himself, that "An American paper . . . is said to be edited with great talent when it contains in each number from half a column to a column of original matter; the rest consists of extracts [from other papers] and advertisements." [199]

Primarily such papers were organs of local factions of national political parties. The tone of their "original matter" consequently was often almost as violent as anything with which Philip Freneau and William Cobbett had favored their fellow partisans in the free-swinging Philadelphia of the 1790's. Russel Nye has noted that what now seems to us the indecent harshness of William Lloyd Garrison's attacks on slaveholders was only the accepted journalistic idiom of the day—a sound point if one allows for the special genius, possibly psychotic, that put extra sting into Garrison's billingsgate. The familiarity of the American editor with horsewhips and challenges to duels, though partly custom, also came of A's understandable exasperation when Editor B of the Prairieville *Clarion* put it in print that he was a swindling scoundrel with the habits of a degenerate ape and a six-inch yellow stripe up the backbone.

Rowdy as it was, this was at least a free press. The meaning of the phrase then was, as it should still be to avoid confusions, freedom from governmental interference in the shape of crippling taxation or prosecution for speaking out of turn. And as the 1830's proceeded, Franklin's protégé began to grow up—at least to take on some aspects of today's newspaper. Much of this came from improved technics—the steam-powered press imported from England speeded up printing and lowered cost per copy. Soon printing from cylinders instead of flat forms added further efficiency. Now larger circulation became practical—until 1833 no American newspaper had reached the 5,000 mark—with a matching reduction in price to the reader well below the accepted six cents. In large towns one-cent dailies attracted wide man-in-the-street readership that made possible some lessening of control from politicians and merchants. Conversely the concomitant necessary appeal to the concerns of lower-stratum readers forced wider coverage of news originating in court-rooms, places of amusement, hotel lobbies and churches, as well as produce exchanges and shipping offices. James Gordon Bennett's New York *Herald,* which had much to do with this trend, changed the daily paper from being "dull, stilted, unenterprising, and dependent on political cliques" to being "democratic and sleeplessly active," [200] a summing-up from Allan Nevins and Milton Halsey Thomas. In the 1840's Morse's telegraph enabled legwork reporting to replace hearsay in covering distant events. That led not only, as already noted, to news-exchanging press associations but also to larger amounts of out-of-town news in a given paper. And with the wire-fed penny press relying on single-copy sales as well as subscription came the American newsboy, ragged, barefooted, precociously knowing urban rival of the straw-hatted farm urchin as stock hero of the rags-to-riches success story, and with him the extra edition with bulletins of battles or catastrophes hawked in the streets with echoing shouts of "Weeee-uxtry! Papuh! Read all about it!"—a street cry that vanished when radio took over the extra's function.

The Mexican War of 1846-48 roused the newspapers of New Orleans, the largest American city near the fighting, to unusual enterprise that created modern-style war correspondence. Large type for display headlines and advertising flash was still to come, as were modern techniques for reproducing illustrations. But challenged by the mass appeal of the sprouting new papers, advertisers and compositors made ingenious play with white space and patterns of repetition—P. T. Barnum, the archetypal showman, was notably clever with such tricks—and the relative importance of fresh news in keeping circulation rising began to force advertising and literary matter off the front page. By 1841 Horace Greeley's New York *Tribune* was showing that, for all its fondness for cranks and their crotchets, a mass-circulation paper could be decent as well as quick on its feet and interesting without having to be foulmouthed. Its weekly

"HOT CORN! HERE'S YOUR NICE HOT CORN!"

The barefoot girl-child selling hot boiled sweet corn
on street corners was the female equivalent of the
newsboy in New York City in the 1860's.

edition, a sort of news comment and literary magazine in newspaper format, eventually had a circulation of 200,000, largely outside the South. It became America's first nationally significant paper in a sense never applicable to Hezekiah Niles' *Weekly Register* out of Washington, widely read though it was by editors and politicians. And his *Tribune* made Greeley more of a national figure than any of his journalist contemporaries. He was anticipating the national renown-to-be of sectional newspaper heroes such as Murat Halstead and Fremont Older and the nationwide gestures of Pulitzer, Hearst and Scripps, and he did his share in the concentration of the national attention on New York City as the source of ideas.

The growing dependence of this large-circulation press on advertisers had noxious aspects—some general, obvious and even more serious in our time than they were when beginning; and some noisomely specific. The New York *Herald,* penny-press creation of Scottish James Gordon Bennett, developed its own national fame for welcoming the thinly veiled or quite candid advertisements of prostitutes, houses of assignation, abortionists and pretty much any other facilities the Prodigal Son—or Daughter —might need. Many other papers were so carefree about the advertisements of quack remedies for "Women's Complaints" and venereal disease that in 1852 a visiting Briton declared them "unfit to be introduced into private families." [201] Almost all papers—Bryant's *Evening Post* was an honorable exception—unblinkingly accepted unbridled claims for less indecorous cure-alls. Many country papers depended for their very existence on printing for pay any advertisement of Elixir of Snakeroot or Hippocratic Balm that Dr. Ananias Nostrum submitted.

Indigenous magazines also existed: New England's staid *North American Review* modeled on the British *Quarterly* and *Edinburgh* reviews, the prestige of which had American publishers pirating their contents as soon as the new issues came ashore; New York City's *Knickerbocker Magazine* and Philadelphia's *Graham's,* to both of which the Longfellow-Lowell-Bryant stratum of writers and the leading vapid poetesses contributed; Richmond's *Southern Literary Messenger.* Philadelphia, still abreast of New York City as a center of publishing, also got out for Mrs. Brownstone and her fragile friends *Godey's Lady's Book* and *Peterson's Magazine,* both combining easy reading with rapt reverence for fashion—a formula still paying today. Their colored engravings of the latest Parisian styles worn by doe-eyed countesses blessed with implausibly tiny children became the favorite motifs of lampshade makers in the 1920's. But all the above were upper-stratum affairs. In the late 1850's Frank Leslie, a Scot as enterprising as Bennett, and the Harpers' firm began to put out imitations of the new English weeklies lavishly illustrated with woodcuts showing news events in great detail. These appealed to all strata, and though they carried fiction and odd verse, were two-thirds newspaper. The only non-newspaper periodical reaching what we would call mass readership was the *New York Ledger,* turned from a commercial sheet into a story paper by Robert Bonner, a Scotch-Irish lad from Londonderry, who, apprenticed to the printing trade in Hartford, Connecticut, became one of the fastest typesetters in the United States. Paying writers very well for that time, he bought from the Lowells and Bryants, but his standbys were the slambang melodramatics of Sylvanus Cobb, Jr., and presently the implausible tearjerkers of Mrs. E. D. E. N. Southworth. Note how much the Old Country had to do with creating the popular American periodicals: Bennett, Leslie, Bonner—none American-born.

Note also that the fashions in *Godey's* and *Peterson's* were French; indeed the actual engravings were often imported from France. Parisian modes had conquered dressmaking in America as they had in England, a development accelerating after the steamship made it likelier that Mrs. Brownstone would visit Paris in person. Headway against that had barely begun in the late 1850's with the designing department set up in New York City in the dress-pattern and dressmaking establishment of "Mme." Ellen Demorest. Even she closely followed French trends and, though born in Saratoga, New York, had that Gallic *Mme.* in all the advertising to match her husband's old Huguenot name. For Mrs. Brownstone's husband English tailoring remained the ideal. But the handlebar mustache and absurd Imperial chin tuft of their young son-about-town in the 1850's imitated the new-risen Louis Napoleon. France's wars in North Africa and Italy had drawn attention to her picturesque Zouave light infantry wearing Moslem-style uniforms and trained in open-order drill carried out at the double. Because it was dashing and French, American militia had taken to Zouavism, clothes and all—which explains the otherwise strange fact that early in the Civil War thousands of troops, mostly Northerners, had their baptism of fire wearing fezzes, bolero jackets and baggy red trousers. As further token of the cultural gravitation of the Second Empire, the mansard roofs and Renaissance pavilions of Napoleon the Little's architectural taste were elbowing aside the Gothic and the Italianate. Up to the 1850's most French influences had reached America by way of Britain. Henceforth they would be increasingly direct.

In Abraham Lincoln's time thousands of American fathers were given to reading aloud to their dear ones around the lamp on the center table. Thus by way of the paternal voice were Dickens, Scott, Cooper and Irving and Longfellow's verse narratives embedded in children's consciousness. As Rollo and Lucy grew up and married, they were likely to maintain this admirable custom; it lasted well past 1900. The local lawyer in the 1840's also read the newly arrived President's message to the boys whittling on the store porch; the preacher lived by impressively uttered words; so did the legislator stumping his district or making his eagle scream on the Fourth of July; colleges and law and medical schools depended heavily on lectures in the absence of adequate libraries; the medicine-show doctor extolled Kickapoo Snake Oil from the tailgate of his torch-lighted wagon—all keeping the human voice well employed and the American well accustomed to being edified, instructed or entertained by standing or sitting among a number of fellow listeners and concentrating on a single articulate person. This reliance on the spoken word fell off with the rise of elaborate newspapers but revived with the telephone, radio and television.

In the 1830's it bloomed into the lyceum system, a thing soon economically important to writers, crusaders and thinkers and intellectually important to all seeking self-improvement. The first lyceum began in Millbury, Massachusetts, in 1826 as an innovation of Josiah Holbrook, friend and collaborator of Horace Mann and early projector of manual-labor and normal schools. After a long discipleship absorbing Silliman's early lectures on science at Yale, he had written a widely used textbook on geometry, made a business of supplying schools with teaching collections of scientific materials, and by popular lecturing in person had learned how eager the literate public was to know more of science and of many other things.

For that demand a lyceum organized paid-in-advance lectures at regular intervals, usually with a different speaker on a different topic each week. Ideally it also offered subscribers a library and reading room, but the core of it was a sponsoring committee of local pillars of society, an amateur secretary to handle details and book speakers, and the use of a hall, a speakers' stand and a pitcher and tumbler. This week "The Character of Napoleon"; "Phrenology" next; "The Moral Beauty of Woman's Sphere," "Missionary Life in Godless Burma," "The Wonders of Chemistry" (with demonstrations involving blue flames and curious smells) . . . As the lyceum gained momentum, entertainment slipped in only slightly disguised. The Hutchinson Family of Singers, for instance, mingled comic skits with their moral repertory of sacred and, where local sentiment permitted, Temperance or abolitionist songs. By the mid-1830's there were some 3,000 such lyceums, mostly in the North. Booking lecturers had become a bustling little industry, and a nationwide lyceum association had led to what would become the National Educational Association. Other eventual offspring included mechanics' institutes—an English notion turning into lyceums for self-improving workingmen, one of which became New York's conspicuous Cooper Union—the chautauqua circuit shows of the early 1900's, and the whole lecture business right down to our time.

In a necessarily watery way lyceums probably effected a certain amount of adult education. Their real point, however, was social. In a town lacking movies, television and the automobile and mistrusting the theater (where it was available), this was somewhere to go on a weeknight besides regular Thursday prayer meeting. A modern young man would hardly ask a girl to sit on a hard chair for an hour and a half to hear Dio Lewis on homeopathy; but his great-great-grandfather did, and the girl let him hold her hand as they walked home in the dark. Curiosity, too, was gratified. One might have read one of flashy young Henry Ward Beecher's sermons and studied his noble brow and meek low collar in the steel-engraved frontispiece of the book, but how much better to see him in the flesh 30 feet away and get the full gurgle of that famous voice! Visiting British lions—among them Sir Charles Lyell, the geologist; J. S. Buckingham, the philanthropist; George Combe; Thackeray—lectured their way around the country often under lyceum auspices, and in smaller places their very foreignness and fame, never mind what they talked about, enabled them to do very much better than pay expenses.

Fees naturally varied with the lion's eminence. For Emerson and Holmes, each of whom seems to have put on an excellent show in his own way, and many other notable figures—Bronson Alcott, Theodore Parker, Horace Mann, Benjamin Silliman, for instance—lectures were a major source of livelihood. It was often money hard earned. Today's one-night-stand lecturer finds his career exhausting; think what it was when airplanes and taxis were unknown and it meant constant changes at strange times of day from unreliable stagecoach to engine-racked steamboat to over-heated train to verminous tavern. Again the strong flavor of New England about cast and setting is significant. The lyceum was born there, its organizers were largely New Englanders, and the emissaries of knowledge, wisdom and morality whom it sent trouping the nation were likelier than not New England's current cultural heroes, who thus further strengthened New England's hold on the nation's mind.

In American towns above the crossroads level after the War of 1812 professional show business, mobile or fixed, occasionally or regularly relieved the dearth of formal amusement. It might be a pair or trio of song, dance, and comedy artists. John B. Gough, the glib little Englishman who came up from alcoholism to become the greatest of Temperance spell-binders, once trouped, for instance, with two strolling accordionists who squeezed out marches and quicksteps through the small towns of the Northeast in alternation with his comic songs, dialect monologues and snatches of ventriloquism. Or a traveling waxworks combined with animals, some stuffed, some live, featuring an elephant or lion. Artemus Ward (Charles Farrar Browne), Abraham Lincoln's favorite humorist, first struck public fancy with newspaper humor about such a show: ". . . three moral Bares, a Kangaroo (a amoozin little Raskal . . .), wax figgers of G. Washington Gen. Tayler John Bunyan Capt Kidd and Dr Webster in the act of killing Dr Parkman . . . my snaiks is as harmliss as the new born Babe. . . . All for 15 cents . . ." [202] Plodding through dust and mud in a couple of wagons, such outfits broke trail for the one-ring circuses under canvas that, drawing on British talent and tradition, toured the settled parts of America from the 1830's on, having begun as strolling equestrian shows. For a sample, take the Great National Circus consisting of a ringmaster, a clown, a comic rider, a tumbler, a trick rider, the Whitby Family's combination of singing and dancing on the slack wire, a four-pony act, a pair of comedy mules and Mr. Valentine Denzer's trapeze work followed by his spinning a globe with his feet while lying on the back of a galloping horse. That sort of thing made Circus Day rival the Fourth of July in the small boy's calendar long before Barnum and Bailey.

When the Artemus Ward kind of showman prospered, he might fatten up the collection and house it in a fixed museum in a sizable town. The one that Buckingham visited in Syracuse, New York, in 1840 had two live anacondas as a major attraction. The waxwork figures of national heroes were so much alike that only the names on the labels distinguished Stephen Decatur from Oliver Hazard Perry; in a tableau with Samuel and King Saul, the Witch of Endor wore a wasp-waisted black bombazine gown and the traditional pointed hat to confirm her witchiness. Performances were heralded by "a wretched violin, a hurdy-gurdy and a long drum" playing in a street balcony. Such places turned at night into "a sort of provincial theatre" [203] with farces, songs and dances. In marked contrast the museum lovingly developed in Philadelphia by Charles Willson Peale, painter and early paleontologist, was rich with animal and mineral specimens arranged with an imagination that anticipated modern museum methods. It almost filled Independence Hall and, though Peale by no means disdained showmanship, was important in interesting the general public in natural history. His most conspicuous painter son, Rembrandt Peale, carried it on for a while so responsibly that when Commodore Charles Wilkes' expedition came back from the South Seas with a wealth of biological and ethnological material, the U.S. Navy turned it over to Peale's Museum for temporary safekeeping. But eventually Peale's own collections were swallowed up by P. T. Barnum's gaudily ballyhooed museum on Broadway in New York City. There directly opposite St. Paul's Chapel, most refined of New York's churches, Barnum's balcony band played "Free Music for the Million" off and on all day and all evening, and his banners proclaiming THE FEEJEE MERMAID and LIVING SEA SERPENTS drew huge crowds to his live menagerie and the "moral exhibitions" in the museum's sizable theater.

The term *moral* there and in Artemus Ward's "Moral Bears" was the showman's subterfuge still very lively after several generations. Not long after the Revolution Boston's frowsy old New Exhibition Room was offering moral lectures and dialogues consisting chiefly of songs and dances and acrobatics. By then the device can have deceived few and was intended to enable the law gracefully to look the other way. With diminishing reason the museum as cover for playhouse persisted into the 1870's. In the long vestibule of the Boston Museum, long since an out-and-out theater, one still saw the dusty old "paintings, and plaster casts, and rows of birds and animals in glass cases . . . the mummied mermaid under a glass bell . . . the stuffed elephant . . . Cleopatra applying the asp . . ." [204] All that was the half of Peale's Museum that Barnum had sent to Boston thirty years previously.

Those devices betokened a cultural climate that greatly minimized the impact of the stage in even large cities before the Civil War. For the intimacy between footlights and unrighteousness was still notorious. In the upper strata only worldly-minded men, only the distinctly so among women went to theatrical performances. ". . . the most opulent and the most religious members of the community," Buckingham saw in New York City in 1840, "do not . . . approve of theatrical exhibitions"; he ascribed the large houses drawn by dollar-hungry English stars to "foreigners and persons who do not belong to either of the classes before enumerated." [205] Harriet Beecher Stowe had never entered a theater until the late 1850's, when curiosity drew her to a stage version of *Uncle Tom's Cabin*. When George Templeton Strong saw the Keans in *Richard III* in 1846 at the age of twenty-five, it was this cultivated and well-received young lawyer's first visit to a playhouse since he had seen a child prodigy do Shylock fifteen years earlier. In the country places among the church-minded, even the circus was taboo. "A man in that time might be a miser," Eggleston wrote of southeastern Indiana, ". . . dishonest in a mild way . . . censorious and a backbiter . . . he might put the biggest apples on the top of the barrel . . . and the church could not reach him. But let him once see a man ride on two bare-back horses, and jump through a hoop!" [206]

Much of that came of Dissenters' frowning on playhouses and players in the Mother Country of the 1600's. Actually it went back even before Dissent to the Elizabethan laws treating actors as vagabonds by definition, exempt from prosecution only if formally sponsored by some great nobleman. The Reverend Dr. Timothy Dwight, "Pope Dwight," expresident of Yale and open-minded on some topics—he had a hand in encouraging coeducation and the presence of scientific courses in college—still called actors "a nuisance in the earth, the very offal of society" [207] in the early 1800's. A generation later the Reverend Dr. Theodore Cuyler of Brooklyn, another eminent Presbyterian with a large following, described the theater as "a chandeliered and ornamented hell—a yawning maelstrom of perdition—whose dark foundations rest on the murdered souls of hundreds." [208] But not all that was mere gratuitous bluenosery. In even the best-conducted theaters respectable women with escorts could patronize only the dress circle tier, for the floor of the house was for men —and occasionally a certain kind of women—while the upper boxes and the gallery were the acknowledged haunts of either street rowdies or whores and men seeking temptation. It followed that shy or timid women tended to stay away altogether. Further, each theater was clustered among tough billiard parlors, saloons "and other resorts for the profligate and idle," said New York City's *Broadway Journal* in 1845. "We see no necessity for making a theater a drinking house, a gambling house, and a something else house, as well as a play house, but . . . the theatre is just as dissolute now as it was in the days of Charles the Second." [209]

The content of the show might also put off women—and men of prim inclination. The traditional bill added to the main attraction—usually five acts of tragedy or melodrama—one-act fore- and afterpieces often gingered up with breeches parts for women and licentiousness and buffoonery that caused Dr. Daniel Drake to cite them as one reason why moral people stayed away from theaters in the Old Northwest of the 1840's. The 1960's would not wish to see *Death of a Salesman* prefaced by Red Skelton and followed by a scene from *Hello, Dolly!;* but the equivalent did not strike our forebears as incongruous. The actress who had been playing the dying heroine's confidante was likely to turn up singing a flirtatious ballad before the curtain between the acts. Not until the 1850's, when the extraordinary length and popularity of the stage versions of *Uncle Tom's Cabin* forced a change, did management begin to understand that a successful main production could stand on its own feet.

The advent of the Italo-French ballet particularly disconcerted the staider American Quality. Young Benjamin Silliman at London's Sadler's Wells Theater thought "very indecent" the capers of young ladies who had "laid aside the petticoat and appeared in loose muslin pantaloons . . . modesty seems not to be a necessary qualification in an actress." [210] When a French ballerina, Mme. Hutin, appearing at New York City's Bowery Theater in 1827 in a *pas seul* as an afterpiece to *Much Ado About Nothing* came skipping on in a scanty costume, all the ladies in the dress circle left the house in a body, and in a letter to the press S. F. B. Morse appealed to American womanhood to get the theater abolished lest such a thing happen again: "let an institution [the stage] that has dared to insult you, be forever proscribed." [211]

In many other respects theatrical matters of that time differed from those of ours. In the largest towns some theaters had gained great size, seating 3,000 and more. But the box set (simulating a room with the side toward the audience missing), an innovation of 1841, was seldom used.

For indoor as well as the main outdoor scenes the crude old flats and side scenes persisted, and the actors often worked on the apron well in front of the proscenium, as Thomas Betterton and Mrs. Bracegirdle had in Restoration London. Gas-lighting was more flexible and brighter than oil lamps and probably safer, but you and I, used to electric lighting, would have found proceedings dismally dim. We might object even more to the frequent intrusions of show-stopping applause in dramatic productions, not at the ends of acts or even scenes but in the middle of the action. An eminent actor with a zealous following—say, Edward Forrest—played something like histrionic golf. His ripping off of a famous passage in *The Gladiator* would set the house cheering so madly that he and the cast had to freeze and wait till they could be heard again and the play go on toward another anticipated high spot and another exhilarating outbreak. Mark Twain, first meeting the Germans' way of delaying applause until the end of the act, persisted in thinking the old way better as likely to keep the actors more stirred up.[212]

The school of acting that he had in mind would have struck us as atrocious. At best it was expertly paced, sweeping, clearly shouted scenery chewing such as few now alive have ever seen seriously tried, as extravagant as the plumed, spangled, furbelowed costumes for both sexes without which the audience of a tragedy would have felt cheated—a tradition direct from Shakespeare's stage. Most of the original proponents of such acting in America had been British professionals of less than first rank finding it more profitable to tear passions to tatters overseas than at home. Among such sanguine immigrants in the 1790's had been John Hodgkinson, "an actor from Bath, who preferred trying the New World to further toil in the [English] provinces," [213] said John Bernard, suave London comedian doing the same thing; hot-tempered and handsome Thomas Abthorpe Cooper, leading man and lessee of New York City's Park Theater; Thomas Placide, French tightrope dancer who flourished as impresario in America; and in the next generation Samuel Drake, who took the first company of professionals into the Ohio Basin, and the Chapmans, leaders of the showboat industry. Indirect consequences included Edgar Allan Poe, son of a charming English actress for whom a Boston law student abandoned law and went trouping as her husband, and Thomas Sully, conspicuous painter of portraits of the American Quality, whose actor parents landed him in Charleston at the age of nine.

After peace with Britain in 1815 the certified great also rose to the lure of dollars: Edmund Kean, sultriest of tragedians in 1820, and then his new-risen rival, Junius Brutus Booth, intermittently psychotic, whose actor sons had their own part in American history. Edwin became king of the serious American stage; John Wilkes, also a conspicuous leading man, found another road to notoriety. In 1830 came Charles Kemble, gentle-manly comedian and able tragedian, younger brother of John Kemble and Sarah Kemble Siddons, the acknowledged royalty of the British stage, among the first to break the social barrier between green room and drawing room. In this foray to pay debts consequent on ill-fated manage-rial ventures, he brought along his daughter Frances Anne, new and glow-ing ingenue queen of London, who was equally triumphant in America. For a while, however, her luck in the New World soured. She married an elegant young Philadelphian, Pierce Butler. Rashly she published a book of her experiences in America showing that she was very young, as well as very clever, and that America was still hypersensitive to alien com-ment. Though Butler had edited the manuscript before it went to the printer, its reception set off frictions in the marriage, which, heightened by Fanny's articulate disgust with what she saw of slavery on the Butler es-tates in Georgia, led to divorce. Presently she turned bluestocking and had an Olympian career of what were by all accounts memorable one-woman readings of Shakespeare. Her reason for quitting the stage, which had treated her so well, in favor of a lamp and reading desk on a bare plat-form was—both an eternal truth and a comment on the theater of her day—that Shakespeare was too good to be mauled about on tawdry stage sets by a troupe composed mostly of second- and third-raters.

Gradually arose a generation of indigenous actors. By the late 1840's a large majority of those making up to go on any given evening in Amer-ica were American-born. At the top were Edwin Forrest, billed as "The American Tragedian," specializing in blood-and-thunder roles written by American playwrights who never got a fair share of the profits, and Charlotte Cushman, a genteel, rawboned Boston girl, who, losing her voice early in what had promised to be a singing career, took to acting and became the leading American-born actress, specializing in male char-acters in Shakespeare. There were American playwrights: William Dun-lap, painter, producer, author of journeyman comedies and melodramas; John Howard Payne, boy prodigy as an actor, creator of "Home Sweet Home" and (with Washington Irving) of a really amusing farce about Charles II; Dr. Robert Montgomery Bird of Philadelphia, physician with a pen-and-ink talent who gave Forrest durable vehicles in *The Gladiator* (about Spartacus) and *The Broker of Bogota*. There was a strong feeling that the American stage should achieve independence. In seeking publica-tion of plays with American settings written by himself and his son, J. K. Paulding called for "an American Drama . . . [not] so entirely in-debted to Foreigners for Plays neither referring to national manners, or national feeling." [214] This desire for theatrical independence had some-thing—though not as much as rank nativism—to do with the incredible

Astor Place riot, in which partisans of Forrest mobbed the British tragedian W. C. Macready in 1849 and got so far out of hand that the militia
had to fire on them, killing twenty.

But it was mostly ambition, little substance. James Nelson Barker of
Philadelphia had made competent efforts to use American themes, particularly in a play about Pocahontas and another, *Superstition,* about the
Salem witchcraft troubles, Indian wars and refugee regicides; he wrote
dramatic blank verse better than most English playwrights of his time. So
did another Philadelphian of the next generation, George Henry Boker,
whose *Francesca da Rimini,* lackadaisically received in 1855, was successfully revived by Otis Skinner and Lawrence Barrett late in the
1800's. But through the 1850's minor troupes working the Middle
Atlantic states and the Old Northwest, a week here, three nights there,
stuck to traditional roles almost solidly British: *Macbeth* with its violence
and juicy supernatural doings; *Othello* for raw emotion; *Richard III,* most
actorish of Shakespeare's villains; James Sheridan Knowles' *Virginius* and
The Wife, now about as thoroughly forgotten as the Reverend Henry
Hart Milman's *Fazio*—which gave Fanny Kemble one of her most becoming roles—and almost always the English version of the German
August Friedrich Ferdinand von Kotzebue's *The Stranger,* farthest-
fetched triumph of sentimentality. The farces and short musical pieces
used before and after were also usually British standbys like *Miss in Her
Teens, The Padlock, All That Glitters Is Not Gold, Black-Eyed Susan.*

British example was also followed in the development of the star
system, thus defined by a dramatic critic of the 1860's: ". . . a Star is an
actor who belongs to no one theatre, but travels from each to all, playing
a few weeks at a time . . . sustained in his chief character by the regular
or stock actors [of the local theater]. A stock actor is a good actor and a
poor fool. A Star is an advertisement in tights, who grows rich and cor-
rupts the public taste." [215] Everybody in the local company knew the
lines and usual stage business for anything the visiting celebrity was likely
to have in his repertory, so elaborate rehearsal was hardly necessary, and
the audience in Erie, Pennsylvania, or Richmond, Virginia, came not to
see a new-fledged play fresh from a successful Broadway run, but to com-
pare James Murdoch's performance of Joseph Surface with that of the last
visiting star to do *The School for Scandal.* Grand opera still retains many
of these values. At the time their emphasis on the performer, not the vehicle, was poor sprouting ground for dramatists. Even in the mid-1800's
the outstanding manufacturer of new plays for American production was
Dion Boucicault, an Irish actor-producer-writer doing well in London before he ever saw America. And *Our American Cousin,* the bill at Ford's
Theater on the night when Booth shot Lincoln, the vehicle in which the

great Joseph Jefferson III glorified the stage Yankee and which gave the American audience its first adequate silly-ass Englishman, was written by a British journeyman playwright, Tom Taylor.

Throughout the century London saw many fewer American scripts and actors than New York City saw British scripts and actors. It took the creation of a new entertainment medium—the movies—to strike a balance. Except for the blackface minstrel show, the only native innovations on the American stage until well past the Civil War were dynasties of New World-based stock characters: the Yankee, whether villain or simplehearted righter of wrongs, written into every other script to give the company's specialist in such roles his due opportunity; the frontier eccentric, all comic honesty, wildcat-skin cap and patter about being half horse, half alligator, probably first seen on the stage as Nimrod Wildfire, in J. K. Paulding's prizewinning farce *The Lion of the West,* based so closely on the Davy Crockett figure that the author felt it advisable to assure Crockett, who was no man to trifle with, that nothing personal was meant; the lofty-minded stage Indian, most conspicuous in the title role of *Metamora,* another of Forrest's indigenous successes; and, for urban appeal, Mose, the tough New York City volunteer fireman and Bowery hero, plug hat on the side of his head, pants in his boots, shiny soap locks trained forward of his ears, in *A Glance at New York,* a crude role that gave years of lucrative success to a New York-born actor, Frank Chanfrau. Full of street brawls and fire-fighting scenes to set off Chanfrau's version of the thug with the heart of gold, it drew extremely well in lesser cities and towns inquisitive about Gotham, which was rapidly assuming its permanent rank as focus of national attention. Note further that the creator of Nimrod Wildfire, James H. Hackett, took him to England and did well in the 1830's and that Chanfrau did likewise with Mose—both signal confirmations of the Mother Country's already strong conviction that American and barbarian were synonymous terms.

By 1859 Artemus Ward's enlarging show offered not only waxworks, snakes and kangaroos but also "komic songs" and "a Grand Movin Diarea of the War in the Crymear." [216] Moving diorama (to edit the showman's version) was the current phrase glorifying the earlier panorama—a strip of canvas, say, 10 feet wide and some thousands of feet long patiently painted to represent a series of related scenic subjects. Set upright on tall spindles to roll past the spectator under lights and supplemented by a lecturer with an adequate gift of gab, it was the next best thing then available to an actual trip on a boat down the Hudson or on a magic carpet over the Rockies. The Mississippi was a favorite subject. Longfellow relied on a moving diorama of the Father of Waters for the river scenery in *Evangeline*. A much less pretentious such depiction of the Battle of Bunker Hill, with sound effects, brought John B. Gough to grief in his strolling days; he was fired because he was seldom sober enough to keep the crank turning and the firecrackers going off to match the cues in the proprietor's spiel. The quality of art possible in such painting was necessarily as slapdash as in a scenic backdrop for a second-rate theater. The device itself derived from the theatrical arrangement that enabled a character to walk along a road, say, without going offstage. There was nothing too anomalous about that. There was a curiously marked flavor of showmanship about the fine arts in America in the early 1850's.

It was certainly strong in those pseudo-Greek and -Gothic buildings. And paintings or statues as paid-admission attractions appealing to curiosity, patriotism, religious feeling or pruriency—in no case was the esthetic emotion assumed to be primary—had long been part of the museum-style show on the same footing as waxworks and stuffed animals. Copley himself had gathered this. In his London phase he exhibited his "The Death of Chatham" (a mass portrait of the British Parliament that combined the appeals of patriotism and curiosity) not at the Royal Academy, as was expected, but privately at so much a head admission—which netted him some £5,000, then a neat fortune. A similar exploitation of religious interest drew £2,500 to Benjamin West's imposingly large "Christ Healing the Sick." Presently Rembrandt Peale toured American towns with his large allegorical painting of "The Court of Death," taking in an average of $1,000 a month. The formula was not infallible. S. F. B. Morse was sadly disappointed in cash returns from exhibiting a huge multiple portrait of the U.S. Congress in session; again, in 1832, an immense canvas of a gallery wall in the Louvre hung with miniature copies of several dozen famous paintings let him down badly.

A likelier vein was worked by John Vanderlyn, protégé of Aaron Burr, who sent him abroad to develop his manifest talent by study first under Gilbert Stuart and then in Paris. He painted and brought home with him in 1815 a mythological subject, Ariadne sorrowing supine in a woodland glade wearing merely a wisp of something transparent across her pudenda,* a canvas that James T. Flexner calls "the first impressive nude in American art." [217] She attracted many admission fees. Vanderlyn secured from New York City a free site for a rotunda gallery in which to exhibit his huge illusionistic painting of the gardens of Versailles, a work on which he had greatly counted, but its vegetable charms did not draw as "Ariadne's" did. The same sort of values applied in the next gener-

---

* The collection of Vanderlyns in the Senate House Museum in Kingston, New York (the painter's birthplace), includes a small oil sketch of exactly the same abandoned lady wearing considerably more drapery.

ation to the popular renown of the several marble copies of "The Greek Slave"—"a naked and almost boneless woman," [218] comments a recent critic—done by Hiram Powers, American sculptor expatriate in Florence, that were shown around America in the 1840's and 1850's. (Powers' first modelings were waxworks for a Chamber of Horrors in his native Cincinnati—show business again.)

Female nakedness for art's sake seems to have first landed in America in 1763, when James Hamilton, son of the great lawyer who defended John Peter Zenger, brought to Philadelphia several of Benjamin West's copies of famous paintings, including a naked "Venus" of Titian's. How she fared in society I do not know, but in 1784 an immigrant British portraitist, Robert Pine, had in the same city a cast of the equally naked

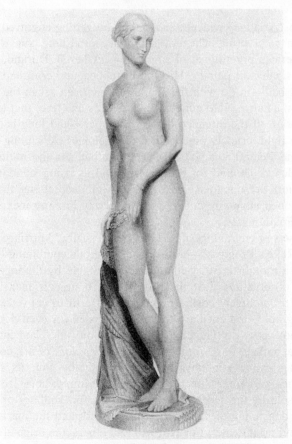

Contemporary engraving of Hiram Powers'
momentously naked "Greek Slave."

"Medici Venus" that so disturbed local ladies that he dared show her only in private to selected friends. In 1816, a year after "Ariadne" landed, the new Philadelphia Academy of the Fine Arts included in an exhibit the fifty casts of statues, many naked, imported from France for students to draw from, since drawing from a naked living model was still in the future. Protest was quelled by excluding the squeamish sex except one day a week when the casts were draped for the occasion. That sort of thing was unconscionably long adying. The barroom nude encouraged several generations in the notion that FOR MEN ONLY was the basic connotation of all pictures of naked women. Such art was what caused saloon-smashing Carry Nation to tell a barkeep in Kansas *c.* 1900 that he was insulting his own mother by showing a woman stripped naked in a place where it wasn't decent for a woman to be to begin with.

In time "Ariadne" widened her public by getting engraved for popular circulation as a print. The craftsman accomplishing this was then the finest American practitioner of engraving—Asher B. Durand, presently to be also a significant painter. His and his colleagues' craft had much—and most of it bad—to do with the shape of American art in the 1800's. Engraving—the cutting into a metal plate of dots and lines that take printer's ink and print off the intended design on paper—had long been a fine art in its own right, crudely practiced in the Colonies by, among others, Paul Revere and Peter Pelham, Copley's stepfather. As the multiplication of books widened demand for illustrations and as rising standards of living allowed more persons to aspire to elegant wall decorations, the Old World had developed engraving into a profitable way to copy inexpensively the content of paintings.

Those sets of engravings after Hogarth—usually "Marriage à la Mode" or "The Rake's Progress"—were taken from oils combining brilliant execution with moralistic storytelling made palatable by the ingenious detail of social observation. Just the thing for a bourgeois mansion—only it would be prohibitively costly to get Mr. Hogarth to copy the series, and the photography and ancillary techniques needed for even poor reproduction did not yet exist. The engraver could, however, plant himself before the original and cut into his metal plate another work of art, copying so far as black-and-white stipplings and fine scratching can, its composition, color values and three-dimensional illusion. Impressions from the plate could be sold by the score or hundreds for a few shillings or a pound or two each, depending on the quality of the work and the market judgment of artist and print dealer. For Hogarth and others, the original painting became a mere first step toward the prints that were the artist's main economic objective—as in the relation between the author's manuscript and the published book. Hence the thousands of British and French engravings, some fine, some deplorable, mostly mediocre, of portraits of the eminent, battles, cities, palaces and great estates, allegories and anecdotal groups shipped across the Atlantic for sale in the Colonial and post-Revolutionary seaboard towns. The usual outlet was a bookshop or the shop where the local limner stocked colors, brushes, drawing paper and such for local amateurs. Then, in 1805, Jacob Perkins of Newburyport, Massachusetts, developed engraving on steel. His purpose was to achieve engraved designs so fine that those trying to counterfeit banknotes would give up in despair. He did revolutionize banknote printing. And maybe even more important, the technique of steel engraving thus developed enabled the commercial art world to get many more good impressions per plate than had previously been possible from copper. The esthetic effect of the harder metal was harsher, but it greatly lowered cost per salable print, hence greatly widened the market.

Until the 1820's, however, American engraving was not up to the best European standards. The American painter seeking the print market—which he particularly needed since America afforded little outlet for original painting other than those portraits at modest fees—could get proper plates made only overseas. It was a great day for the American artist's pocket when John Trumbull, eminent specialist in depicting Revolutionary scenes and battles—and fair enough, for he had served awhile on Washington's staff—employed young Durand to engrave his mass portrait of the signing of the Declaration of Independence and the work proved up to the Old World's best. Now the American artist-showman with a grandiloquent or piquant picture not only could troupe it from town to town to collect admission fees, but could also sell to many of his viewers a fine reminiscent engraving of it to put on the parlor wall at home. It further affected the development of American art that now engraving could be both craft training and livelihood for young artists. Until then youngsters destined to success in painting had usually learned the rudiments in the workshops painting tradesmen's signs, coach panels and such.

As the number of skilled engravers grew by immigration, as well as local training, American publishers could embark on homegrown keepsake souvenir books with numerous full-page plates and fancy initials and vignettes scattered through, just as sticky-sickly in subject matter as their Old Country prototypes. As governmental fiscal policies encouraged the founding of hundreds of wildcat banks, their demand for banknotes provided further work for first-class engravers. Durand's exquisitely worked out banknote engravings are credited with inventing the bare-breasted female abstractions of vaguely classical air still familiar on stock certificates and murals of the pre-PWA school. Others showed "Archimedes on a cloud, lifting the world with a lever, its fulcrum . . . a supposed American mountain peak, with a canal lock"; "Franklin, seated on a chair, in relief against clouds streaked with lightning"; "a graceful female figure holding a flagon and cup, quenching the thirst of the American eagle." [219] Scenes of hayfields and apple pickings were also numerous, along with steamboats and railroad trains. Some banknotes reproduced famous paintings.

A particularly influential by-product of the boom in engraving was, however, the "art union," a notion combining an esthetic lottery with some aspects of the modern book club that came in from Germany in 1839. Thus the American Art Union bought pictures and sculptures from American artists on the recommendation of a jury of businessmen amateurs. Candidates for purchase were exhibited in its gallery in New York City as bait for subscribers. For $5 a year they got a monthly art magazine, one large and four small steel engravings of the union's best-considered acquisitions—and a lottery-drawn chance to win one of the original paintings. Before New York State's antilottery law suppressed the scheme in 1853, its membership had exceeded 16,000—meaning distribution of 80,000-odd engravings a year—and lucky members had won some 2,400 paintings. Smaller regional art unions in Cincinnati, Philadelphia and Boston contributed to the flood of engravings. By buying only the work of artists either born in or resident in America, these institutions greatly fostered American painting, particularly in landscape and genre, then the fields toward which juries leaned. And by inaugurating free admission to its gallery, the American Art Union attracted an annual 250,000 visitors—in itself a great stirring up of a taste for painting among Americans, for there were as yet no great free or nominal-admission museum collections such as are so widely available today.

Yet under the circumstances of the time those visiting an art union gallery at least once in a lifetime remained a small minority of the population. The genuine mass influence came from those hundreds of thousands of engravings distributed not only by art unions but also by individual purchases of imported as well as American popular items. Inescapably hung in parlor and dining room, lawyer's and doctor's offices, hotel corridors, barbershops and restaurants, these black-and-white versions of pretentious paintings became as familiar to American eyes as the design of the Stars and Stripes. Edith Wharton wrote feelingly in the late 1800's of the kinds of "cousins who inhabited dingy houses with engravings from Cole's Voyage of Life on the drawing-room walls." [220] She might have made it "Columbus Before Ferdinand and Isabella," "Washington Crossing the Delaware," "Shakespeare and His Friends" or "The Stag at Bay" (the popular designation of Landseer's "The Challenge").

As pieces of craftsmanship many of these were of unquestionable quality whether the engraver was American or an Old Countryman. The esthetic rub was that in very few cases could even the finest engraver convey the peculiar merits—supposing some such present—of the painting that he copied after, and the change was usually for the worse. The translation of the painted composition into a second medium through the hands of another artist led to a pervasive insipidity. (Photographs of paintings produced parallel, though different, damage in a later generation.) Francis Steegmuller has recently complained of how even the fine copper engravings illustrating James Jackson Jarves' *Art Studies* of 1861 "in their very exquisiteness falsify the pictures. . . ." [221] John Canaday recently deplored in the New York *Times* the way even the original Robert Havell engravings of J. J. Audubon's famous bird paintings—the form in which they are usually seen—sacrifice some of the beauties of the work of the artist's own hands. To see one of the original paintings of Hogarth's "Marriage à la Mode" series after familiarity with only the fine engravings of it that our forebears bought is like a sudden burst of light in a cobwebby-dim room.

It was also difficult to surmount the temptation, inevitable once the sale of engravings became important, to keep the engraver and the printshop's public consciously or unconsciously in mind when choosing subject and way to handle it. The result was often as calamitous as when a novelist keeps too hungry an eye on Hollywood. The mawkishness of a specious original painting would be squared and cubed by the platemaking process. So the result was to immerse any potential American awareness of art in a morass of perverted, sickly grays a world away from the wonders of engraving created by such as Dürer and Callot. This was no peculiarly American plague. For the same cultural reasons flabby steel engravings also infested the parlors and publications of Britain, France and Germany. But damage to the American eye may have been more pervasive because relatively few Americans had the opportunity to see better graphic art as an antidote. They might try to sound deceptively knowing. When Whittier described the tints of the fall woods as "richer and deeper than those which Claude or Poussin" used; when Meriwether Lewis, co-explorer of the way to the Pacific Northwest, "wished for the pencil of Salvator Rosa" [222] at the falls of the Missouri, each sounded as much the connoisseur as if he really had been overseas and seen Poussins and Rosas. Actually that was just a fashionable way of writing. In America it was 100 to 1 that the occasional canvas alleged by a sanguine owner or dealer to be the work of some such traditional master was a forgery, a poor-to-fair copy or an extremely wishful misattribution. Not until 1860, when Jarves fetched home his collection of early Italian works, did the New World see a sizable number of authentic fair to good European paintings. And then, being mostly pre-Raphael, they were difficult for the taste of the time to appreciate.

The climate in which the American eye was trained worsened further after the 1820's, when two brothers named Pendleton established in Boston the newish, German-invented process of lithography and took an apprentice named Nathaniel Currier. Roughly speaking, lithography prints off impressions of drawings done on flat stones with a special greasy crayon. The results are readily colored by hand. Soon operating on his own in New York City, eventually abetted by an artist technician, James Merritt Ives, Currier covered with inexpensive to cheap colored lithographs those areas of American walls not already devoted to steel engravings. The firm had many lively competitors in Boston and Philadelphia, as well as in New York City, but always showed them the way and outlasted them all.

Its first successes (1835-40) were in effect newspaper pictures, representations of disastrous fires by land or sea published on the heels of the event. For the next generation Currier & Ives maintained this tradition of picturing things people would be inquisitive about, whether an explosion or a candidate for the Presidency, thus fulfilling a great need in the days before photography and halftones. Continuing topics of debate, such as Temperance and fast horses, were consistently represented. Timeliness cuts both ways, however. Politicians' faces and the year-before-last's steamboat disaster tended to disappear in favor of newer subjects. Likelier to hang year after year in places not quite up to the elegance of steel engravings were the firm's many, many timeless subjects: "American Homestead—Spring" with pa and the oxen plowing the field back of the story-and-a-half house; ma fetching water from the well; the children playing in the lane; ewes and new lambs lying fluffily under the blossoming apple trees. For a more ambitious kind of customer "The Four Seasons of Life" showed Quality folks in a bracketed country mansion with a view of the Hudson. There were railroad trains all headlight and beehive stack; the U.S. Capitol; clipper ships and whaling scenes for the saltwater-minded; hunting and fishing episodes; and always and forever half-lengths of languishing ladies with oversize eyes and undersize hands as conventionalized as Persian miniatures.

They sold for between 20 cents and $4, depending on size and attractiveness of subject, by mail order from a catalogue, or from the local store, or from the print peddler—still another of America's itinerant purveyors of everything from corn cure to soul cure—rapping at the door to show the steamboats and scenes from Longfellow's poems in the pack on his back. He might knock a little off the price if the whole series of four called "American Country Life" were taken and might pay for a night's lodging with a gaudy "GOD BLESS OUR HOME" or a "Noah's Ark" for the children. For forty years collectors have vied for Currier & Ives prints (and cognates from their competitors) as entertaining and nostalgic Americana, which they certainly are. The best way to understand how attractive that banker's Italianate villa looked to his less affluent contemporaries is to see it as Currier & Ives depicted it. Why boys ran away to sea in the 1850's is very clear in this vision of the clipper *Nightingale* sleeking past Castle Garden outward-bound under topsails. But, as James T. Flexner has pointed out, the cultural shapes cast by these prints are not as purely American as zealots assume. Most of the artists painting the originals for lithographic reproduction or drawing direct on the stone were from the Old Country. So were most of the women who did the coloring at wages so low that the cost came to less than a cent a print. The original of that jolly "Maple Sugaring" scene was painted by a Briton. "The Pioneer's Home on the Western Frontier" done in 1867 by a German has such anomalies as putting the door of the log cabin in the gable end; a fine crop of shocked wheat in a field completely cleared of trees; and a marked air of Black Forestry about the pioneers depicted. The New England "Way-side Inn" in the series from Longfellow, painted by an English gentle-woman who is said to have long supported a drunken husband by artistic chores for Currier & Ives, is a Tudor mansion with mullioned windows.

The publishers, rather than she, are to blame for allowing that. Yet even where Mrs. Fanny Palmer drew from firsthand material, as in her series on Mississippi steamboats, she shared the lack of esthetic virtue in these mid-century lithographs. Except in the best sporting items about horses, hunting and fishing, composition and draftsmanship are usually banal to clumsy. Most of the coloring is at the same time dilute, harsh and queasy as might be expected from the factory methods that applied it. In comparison the typical art union engraving was a stimulating masterpiece. Yet these tinted lithographs, often with attractively entertaining subjects, far outnumbered the engravings and had far greater opportunity to corrupt the eye. The parallel effect now would be to paper the nation's walls with Sunday-paper colored comic strips. Worse, the teacher of drawing in seminary or academy might set a vapid engraving of a genre subject or a sentimental Currier & Ives lithograph as an example for the pupil to copy. Or an ambitious boy or girl might copy it on his own. The resulting bungling imitations of "Mama's Precious with Her Doggie" or "Washington at

Yorktown" often show up in museums among the primitives that curators value so highly. It is a queer way for a Currier & Ives hack to have got there, but doubtless half an arrival is better than none.

At least mass distribution of prints did help support American artists. Engraving gave Durand's career a solid start, and George H. Durrie's engaging paintings of rural Connecticut were exactly what the lithographers needed. More, and on the whole more stimulating, patronage came from a few prospering collectors, largely in New York City, who took a man-in-the-street interest in original American art handling subjects of ready appeal. One way or another artists of vigor began to emerge from the ruck of sign painters, illustrators, engravers and emulous amateurs. Yet their generation never matched the brilliance of old Gilbert Stuart, finally home from long and turbulent success in England to spend his last twenty-odd years immortalizing eminent Americans and their handsome ladies in a suavely incisive style all his own. Even when nearing seventy and partly paralyzed, he still insisted on painting an irresistible young matron and turned out a late-blooming masterpiece, his portrait of Mrs. Thomas C. Upham (now at Bowdoin College). Stuart had got close to being as much a self-priming genius as Copley had been in his younger phase. His successor as limner of choice among eminent Americans, though in a less masterful idiom, was Thomas Sully, developed by study in London after encouragement from Stuart. He had a marked skill in making ladies look prettier than life, though still recognizable. Indeed his attitude toward customers was so euphoric that he could make even Andrew Jackson look sunny.

Durand and Vanderlyn ably portrayed paying clients and artistic friends. S. F. B. Morse's best painted reports on his fellowman show a cogent firmness inconsistent with his conviction, shared by most of his contemporaries, that portraiture was a bread-and-butter concession to Mammon that degraded fine talents. (This notion may have played a part in his share in establishing in America the daguerreotype, thence the photograph—a thing that, by relieving graphic art of the obligation to represent, greatly altered it in subsequent years.) Morse had come down with this toploftical virus while studying with Benjamin West—a genial and benevolent person but ideologically a sort of Typhoid Mary—and had written home: ". . . had I no higher thoughts than being a first-rate portrait-painter, I would have chosen a far different profession. My ambition is to be among those who shall rival . . . the genius of a Raphael, a Michael Angelo, Titian. . . ." [223] A great painter, West and many of his Old World contemporaries maintained, should concentrate mainly on ideal subjects—historical, mythological, allegorical, religious—in other words, on sublime illustration.

This imported passion for grandiloquence proved almost as unfortunate for American painters as imported malaria had been for Americans generally. It suited engravers, whose customers liked the inspirational, the melodramatic and the sanctimonious. But it eroded artistic values. It had a hand in tearing down what may well have been a great talent in Washington Allston, South Carolina aristocrat, pupil of West, friend of S. T. Coleridge. It is still actively painful to read how Allston toiled and toiled at and then let alone and then obsessively returned to a gigantic masterpiece-to-be showing "Belshazzar's Feast," then died suddenly with much of it rubbed out for another fresh—and probably fruitless—attempt at revision. Such thirst for the lofty fouled up the work of Thomas Cole, British-born youngster who rose from making printing blocks for his father's wallpaper factory to show America how to base creativeness on specifically American topography. His originally energetic painting of Catskill wilderness and Connecticut River vistas might have been the core of a fruitful life. But it did not immunize him against the derivative need to spend years in Rome painting allegorically "The Course of Empire" and "The Voyage of Life" in a vein that bedeviled as well as bedazzled him.

The virus even touched his friend Durand but not strongly enough to keep him from becoming chief of the indigenous Hudson River school of landscape, which was to a healthy extent a declaration of independence from Old World clichés of topography and composition. In the 1850's a rising Hudson River man, Frederick Church, had an opportunity to exert his gathering powers on South American scenery and treated America—as well as Europe, where they also attracted fascinated attention—to large, glowing canvases that amounted to disturbing and yet satisfactory fireworks. The exactness of their detail lent an odor of the lecture-accompanied travelogue-panorama, however. It was strengthened by Church's collecting hundreds of dollars a day in admission fees to see, for instance, his "The Heart of the Andes" displayed majestically alone under a theatrical kind of lighting. Indeed several of his best-known canvases could have been entitled "Stage Scenery for the End of the World."

Some of the most straightforward work of the time had been done by William Sidney Mount, a country boy from an artistically ambitious sign-painting family on the Sound side of Long Island. He dabbled callowly in scriptural subjects reflecting an admiration of West, but grew out of it. At the age of forty he tried to get Goupil & Company, New York City art dealers who had an International Art Union promoting European paintings and contributing to American art students' study abroad, to finance a trip to Europe for him, but fortunately he had no luck. What he did do was spend a lifetime painting the people and country around Setauket, where he was born—farmers, farm boys, Negro farmhands, farm buildings and farm vistas. His work sold on its charm, which is often the greater for his skills being largely self-developed. When necessary, he fell back on portraits for livelihood. Some of his genre pictures now most widely known are rather too candy-box plump for their own good. But his famous "Spearing Eels at Setauket" and his painted homage to a certain workaday group of gray Long Island farm buildings are worth whole galleries of windy depictions of "Faith Seeking the Upward Path" or "Marius amid the Ruins of Carthage."

Among others who, like Church and Mount, learned to paint with quality (albeit occasional crudity or clumsiness) without visiting the Old Countries to be shown how were John Quidor, slashingly macabre illustrator of Irving's fantasies; George Caleb Bingham, observer of river and village life in the Midwest;* George Catlin, who got the Plains Indians down on canvas most ably of the several who tried; and Edward Hicks, a fanatic Quaker whose numerous versions of "The Peaceable Kingdom" of Noah's Ark animals behaving as nicely as the Bible says they will sometime now appeal greatly to our generation reared with Henri Rousseau and Gauguin.† Hicks, Quidor and Bingham all began as sign painters. Catlin drew for lithographers. Out of the body of American graphic craftsmanship was springing native ability creating its own idioms.

Note, too, how both the good and the bad of it centered in New York. Morse, Cole, Durand and Church came from other states but gravitated, as if naturally, to New York City, the center of the engraving and lithographing industries, as well as of the site of the only art union of national scope. It was in New York City that Goupil & Company chose to set up their paint-and-canvas bridge between Old World and New. There, too, the Düsseldorf Gallery's mass of German genre was exhibited for years with considerable success in persuading Americans that good pictures should look as if intended to make entertaining jigsaw puzzles. Jarves' collection of early Italians was first seen in the same gallery in New York City. The central strip of the nation was assuming preponderance in art, as it already had in invention, distribution and pre-McGuffey literature.

* Bingham eventually studied in Germany and got less than no good from it. I omit Audubon, whose bird paintings are certainly works of art, because he was reared altogether outside the United States, studied under David in France as a youngster, and throughout his career maintained rather close connections with Europe.

† From a point of view which I personally share, Hicks' works are more curiosities than significantly vigorous works of art. Nevertheless, they are superlative examples of the attraction that indigenous primitives exert over the picture-seeing public of our day, which qualifies Hicks for inclusion in any intelligible account of American art. This might not be true fifty years from now.

About American sculpture before the Civil War one should say no more than that certain Americans—one a Yankee tomboy, Harriet Hosmer—tried the art professionally with a contemporary success and prestige that are now difficult to understand. Like Horatio Greenough, their prototype, they usually set up shop with a great air of genius-at-work in Rome or Florence, an expatriation that suggested Hawthorne's *The Marble Faun*. Their imitations of classic statuary diluted by Canova and Thorvaldsen were at least no worse than those created by Old World sculptors in adjoining studios. Powers' perennial "The Greek Slave" was highly acclaimed in London in the 1850's. The Prince of Wales (later Edward VII) bought a version of Harriet Hosmer's "Puck," which enabled her to sell thirty copies to those—Americans, as well as Britons—agreeing with HRH's taste. The attitude of the time among cultivated persons is clear in the comments of Charles Mackay in the late 1850's: ". . . in sculpture . . . the artistic genius of America is seen to the best advantage," and after admiringly mentioning Powers, Harriet Hosmer, Thomas Crawford, he picks out for symbol of this genius a work of E. H. Baily, "a Puritan girl . . . stripped and tied to the stake, preparatory to her cremation by savages; a figure in which innocence, modesty, beauty, supplication, and horror are inextricably blended . . . a joy and a sorrow for ever." [224]

Recent search for in-the-round equivalents of primitive painting has stocked our museums with ship's figureheads, cigar-store Indians, over-the-door eagles, weather vanes and hitching-post effigies all great fun to look at whether or not their esthetic virtues are as great as the curators claim. Otherwise nature's masterpiece, the Old Man of the Mountain, about which Hawthorne wrote a better story, "The Great Stone Face," long remained the high point of American sculpture. The most valuable contribution from any of its participants was not carved in marble but printed on paper—Horatio Greenough's clearly stated ideas about the need for an uncluttery architecture that would express function as delightfully as the lines and rigging of a fine sailing vessel. In the 1850's, when he published them, they were so completely ignored that when other men said the same things later, people thought they were brand-new.

Andrew Jackson Downing, arbiter of architectural taste in the 1840's, once equated Powers statues with Beethoven symphonies. Cultivated and laudatory—but pointless for most Americans, for such music was hard to come by in a day lacking not only phonographs, radios and tape recorders but even symphony orchestras outside large cities. In the course of a normal year, as late as 1850, only Boston, New York City and Phil-

OUR
SECAR
CANT
BE BEAT

E. W. Kemble draws the typical cigar-store Indian, now highly valued by collectors, on wheels for convenient taking-in at night.

adelphia heard many such compositions or saw operas requiring sizable instrumental ensembles. For secular professional music the rest of the country depended on the oompah-crash of the band of the occasional circus and the tweedle-eedle-boom that pointed up the acting and paced the skippings about on the local stage. Local militia corps seldom had more than fife and drum for parade music.

Yet the amateur musician had had a creditable great deal to do with keeping instrumental tunefulness alive. The Colonial idea—except in highly Puritantical or Quakerish circles—that it was becoming to make one's own music and applaud what one's friends made persisted not only in cities but among the cultivated—and soon crossed over the mountains. Though Pittsburgh in 1807 was still a rough-and-ready jumping-off place for the frontier, a British visitor found there an Apollonian Society of twelve amateurs recognizably performing chamber music from Bach, Haydn and Mozart. In a less august context the Golden Fleece Tavern in Salem, Ohio, was musical nucleus of the neighborhood. The owner's sons with clarinet and fiddle plus two convivial neighbors with flutes accompanied the singing of the two daughters of the house. On special evenings the fiddling son sat himself on a chair on a table in the barroom and enlisted his brother in the traditional skit of *The Arkansas Traveler*—a chuckleheaded backwoodsman home from his first trip to New Orleans trying in vain to reproduce a jig tune he heard there. His reiterated efforts to work it out supply the obbligato for give-and-take with the other brother in the role of passing stranger:

> *Fiddler:* How did your potatoes turn out last year?
> *Stranger:* They didn't turn out at all; we dug 'em out. . . .
> *Stranger:* How far is it to the next tavern?
> *Fiddler:* I reckon it's upwards of some distance.
> *Stranger* (testily): Why don't you play the rest of that tune? . . .[225]

and so on and on, strung out for half an hour with the company in the barroom just as delighted as if they didn't know exactly what line was coming next and that at the end the stranger will whip out a fiddle and lead the backwoodsman through to the last rasping notes in a triumphant duet.

Apparently there were almost as many flutes as fiddles in country places. Many a schoolteacher had one, and many a young fellow reading law with the local judge fluted dulcetly to entertain his girl when he went sparking. But it was the fiddle that ruled the occasional dances in free-and-easy communities where, as an Old Northwesterner recalled, "the girls' eyes shone with fun and whiskey"[226] and rival bullies fought out their respective pecking levels in the yard to the tune of "Money Musk" and "Skip to My Lou" from within the house. Instrumental music had the less place in recently settled country because churches largely did without it. Through the 1700's organs—mostly short-winded and squeaky but impressively costly—had been associated with Church of England-Episcopalian services in cities. In New England the typical congregation had continued to sing, unaccompanied, their gnarly metrical versions of the Psalms "lined out" to them by precentors so unskilled in music that the traditional tunes were often unrecognizable. Suggestions that instrumental accompaniment might prevent such devaluation of "Old Hundred" were spurned as profane. It seems to have been the bass viol that first surmounted this barrier among Congregationalists and Baptists, possibly because, until jazz corrupted it, of all musical instruments it makes the least frivolous noise. Even so it had rough going. The town meeting of Wareham, Massachusetts, for instance, instructed the informal meeting-house choir not to use the bass viol "unless they give Capt. Joshua Gibbs . . . previous notice,"[227] so he could stay away that Sunday. Probably he felt like the elderly citizen of Quincy, Massachusetts, who, when the groans of a bass viol first filled the Sabbath air, got up and walked out of the meetinghouse, saying he would never "come to God's house to hear a great fiddle."[228]

New England's special contribution to American sacred music consisted of influential hymns that may well have affected the American ear as damagingly as engravings and lithographs did the American eye. Yankee hymnwrights of the late 1700's did not altogether deserve that reproach. All were amateurs hoping to enable noises made before the Lord to be more joyful. The fuguing tunes of William Billings, tanner of Boston, backed up by his insistence on using a pitch pipe to set accurate keynotes, helped wean congregations away from the old fumbly ways. His music is long out of use. But Oliver Holden, carpenter of Charlestown, Massachusetts, struck out one tune that survives as its surging dignity demands—"Coronation," usually sung as "All Hail the Power of Jesus' Name"—and earned the tablet to his memory in his birthplace, Shirley, Massachusetts. In the next generation, however, the fateful figure of professional Lowell Mason began a devolution, involving his disciples and emulators, that reached bottom late in the 1800's. As founder of musical education in public schools, Mason was most important. But he also supplied the air for "Mary Had a Little Lamb."

During and after the War of 1812 he was one of those Yankees gone South for economic opportunity, specifically in the dry goods business and then into a bank in Savannah, Georgia. Come of a musical family—his father played the cello in the church at Medfield, Massachusetts—and as a boy an avid experimenter with any musical instrument he could lay hands on, he played the organ in Savannah's Independent Presbyterian Church, led the choir, organized a singing school Yankee-fashion, and was superintendent of an interdenominational Sunday School. After half-serious study of composition with an immigrant German musician, he used his choirmaster's experience with pleasing and suitable numbers to compile a collection of hymns, some of his own make, published in Boston in 1822 by Boston's Handel and Haydn Society, the nucleus of musical activity in New England. He kept his name off the title page because "I was then a bank officer in Savannah, and . . . had not the least thought of ever making music a profession." [229] The thing sold so well, however, that it led to second thoughts. In 1826 Mason took a permanent place in Boston's musical world in charge of several church choirs and then, while earning a basic livelihood as a bank teller, became director of music for Lyman Beecher's church, soon as famous for the quality of its singing as for its minister's rabidly anti-Catholic and anti-Unitarian sermons. Soon Mason was also president of the Handel and Haydn. Thenceforward he dominated American church music, composing hymns, collaborating with satellite composers, editing and publishing widely popular hymnals, mostly for adults, some for Sunday School children. Of twenty-three hymns in *Songs the Whole World Sings,* a standard collection of numbers deeply embedded in American memory, four are his—a proportion higher than that of any other composer: "Nearer, My God, to Thee"; "My Faith Looks Up to Thee"; "There Is a Happy Land"; and "Work, for the Night Is Coming."

The first two exemplify the workmanlike sogginess of Mason's musical bent; the latter two his trend toward dance rhythms. "Happy Land" is a good hoedown and "Work" a nice soft-shoe number. His "From Greenland's Icy Mountains" was nearer dignity. Even nearer was the "Toplady" tune, long familiar as "Rock of Ages," from his associate, Thomas Hastings. But usually Mason's disciples took their tone from his less admirable work. George James Webb, British organist who had an influential career in Boston, wrote the music usually sung to "Stand Up, Stand Up for Jesus." Yankee William B. Bradbury was guilty of "Just as I Am Without One Plea," "He Leadeth Me," "Sweet Hour of Prayer." In fairness to these well-meaning men it must be said that they seldom actually composed the stanzas that went with their tunes, which were usually stickier than the vehicle melody. Words and music blended readily, however, and there is no reason to believe that the composers or the congregations who sang the results felt any incompatibility. As chief of the school Mason showed a master's eye for the dross usually available in any reputable poet's works when choosing Cowper's "There Is a Fountain Filled with Blood" for one of his most rousing tunes.

Anybody who has ever heard that hymn soaring out the open windows of a Methodist church on a hot Sunday morning knows the worst and the best that this chin-bearded businessman with an ear did to the musical destiny of Americans. For to millions of them after 1830, particularly among the straitlaced and well placed, who eschewed tavern dances and stage shows, such hymns were about the only consistently available music—a further token of how the trappings of religion pervaded the nation. The dominant Protestant population, herded through the hymn-ridden Sunday Schools into weekly churchgoing, had these harmonious banalities just as deep in their viscera as the *McGuffey Readers.* Women sang them weekdays at their housework in the hearing of young children. Evening choir practice, much attended by courting couples, inextricably intertwined "Blest Be the Tie That Binds" with young love. Southern Negroes allowed to go to church learned such tunes, took them back to "Niggertown" and the quarters, and—the one good thing to the credit of this musical tradition—stretched, debanalized and transmuted them into the spirituals that rank with the Negro's jazz as the New World's important contributions to the sum of music. Suppose an angel had revealed to those Presbyterians in Savannah that that bright young Yankee from the bank was working on something that, all inadvertently, would stir their slaves to collective creativeness. And not altogether non-apropos, it was an obscure Methodist hymn of this school that provided the dynamic tune for first "John Brown's Body" and then "The Battle Hymn of the Republic."

The name Mason was carved into American music in another fashion when Lowell's son Henry went successfully into manufacturing parlor organs and then pianos. Mason & Hamlin still persists in the American piano industry. Disciple Bradbury, too, prospered at piano making. Prosperity had already attended Jonas Chickering of Boston, first to build grand pianos with full iron frames to withstand the enormous tension of taut wires. In the 1850's particular prestige, as well as prosperity, came quickly to the Steinways (originally Steinweg), economic refugees from Germany's troubles of the 1840's, who brought to America the best European standards of piano making. For the piano market was booming. From the 1830's on, the foreign visitor was often struck by the presence of these bulky, shiny and expensive things—of the square type at first, which eventually gave way to the richer-toned upright—in the parlors of persons whose counterparts in Europe would never have dreamed of such cultural privilege.

This "prodigious frequency of pianos," J. F. Jameson once remarked, ". . . might easily deceive unwary travellers into the unwarranted belief that we were a musical people." [230] Disillusionment came with performance. The daughter of the house, whether in Baltimore or Buffalo, was disastrously likely to favor visitors with Kotzwara's "The Battle of Prague," a then-popular fancy piece imitating artillery fire, the thunder of hooves, the shrieks of the dying, that left scars on the souls of two such disparate auditors as Mark Twain and Charles Eastlake, the didactic English esthete. Possession of a piano was the token of the arrival at ladyhood of the ringleted and ambitious young woman, even though she lived on the Grangerfords' half-backwoods plantation where Huckleberry Finn heard and admired "The Battle of Prague." Heaven knows what most of those far-distributed pianos sounded like for lack of tuning. But that did not keep them from being great focuses of social activity as the young local Quality gathered around to sing "Believe Me, If All Those Endearing Young Charms."

Lighter to transport and less likely to get out of tune were the foot-pumped, keyboard wind instruments known in various forms as melodions, harmoniums, parlor organs, all grumblings and shrill sweetnesses. Their pedals pumping the air were covered with carpeting, the moving parts were almost entirely of accurately machined hardwood, as in the wooden works of Yankee-made clocks. The cases lent themselves to gingerbread-and-jigsaw ornamentation and, since they took up no more room and cost less, often graced the parlors of families who could not quite afford a piano. Frances Willard, redheaded chieftainess of the Women's Christian Temperance Union, had poignant memories of the parlor organ that her father bought for the Wisconsin farmhouse c. 1850; later, as they prospered, he came home one evening with a shiny new piano in the wagon. When Frances, already strong-minded, still preferred her dulcetly groaning old friend, pa had it thrown out of the house so the piano could reign supreme. Much at home as those reed organs were in parlors, however, their typical use was to accompany hymns in country churches unable to afford pipe organs. Though in sympathetic hands they can play anything from Bach to boogie-woogie, they became the instrument of choice for and inextricably associated with the Mason-Bradbury school of hymns—for which indeed the Salvation Army still uses them.

A young lady with a new piano in the parlor who had not learned the rudiments of music reading and fingering at a seminary might turn to the local piano teacher, usually an immigrant German like Mason's preceptor in Savannah, making a livelihood in the new country by instructing in several instruments—flute, violin, piano. The young folks singing around her piano after she had the hang of it reflected our forebears' healthy obligation to make their own music if they were to have any. They may have got their rudiments from the early singing school, whose itinerant teacher was usually a Yankee missionarying music through the country as other Yankee young men did the three R's. Equipped with a pitch pipe and a stock of songbooks using primitive but easily grasped notations, he signed up young persons of both sexes for courses of so many evenings of mass lessons developing from unison into part-singing. A typical such school observed with wonder by the Venezuelan traveler Francisco de Miranda in the 1790's, consisted of some thirty girls and double as many young men come from miles around, each bringing his own singing book and a candle to peer at it by. They enjoyed both the singing and one another's society. Indeed Dr. Nott once told his senior class at Union College that "singing schools, where the sweet strains arouse the tender emotions and lead to early marriages" [231] were a prime cause of the rapid growth of population in New England. When the course was finished, the teacher moved on to another raw, new community to do it all over again. Crude as his training and methods were, he was badly needed because music was no part of the American school system—until Lowell Mason, a Yankee building on the Yankee tradition, made it so.

No such achievement is ever single-handed, of course. Mason's crucial ally was a fellow Yankee, a Congregationalist parson, William C. Woodbridge. An ardent Pestalozzian, he had admired the imaginative ease with which European schools of that persuasion taught children to sing.

Though never able to learn to read music himself, he lectured around New England in the late 1820's on "Vocal Music as a Branch of Common Education" and organized a children's choir on Pestalozzian lines. Presently he met Mason, whose pious interest in Sunday schools had already resulted in *The Juvenile Psalmist,* half hymns for children, half elementary textbook in music. Woodbridge converted Mason to Pestalozzian approaches. The result was the Boston Academy of Music, basically a pilot-plant demonstration of free mass singing classes for children whose parents would sign them up for a full term. Then Horace Mann, just entered on his crusade for effective common schools, grew interested—not so much because music was a richening human experience as because he assumed that lusty song led to more vigorous use of the lungs, hence better purification of the blood and fewer deaths from tuberculosis.

Mason's approach was less clinical, but for him, too, the esthetic aspects were secondary. For him the "highest and best" thing about music was its "moral influence." [232] That attitude, also infesting painting and literature, was as much a part of the time as the phrenology that so appealed to Mann. Here at least it proved useful as palatable pretext for music in the schools. Mann, Mason and Woodbridge were a formidable team. In due course the school authorities of Boston formally approved of singing in the classroom. When appropriations to match failed to appear, Mason paid out of his own pocket for the required songbooks and other materials and contributed his teaching time gratis. From one point of view it was sprats to catch whales, for he was to reap a tidy fortune from nation-wide adoption of his ideas, which boomed the sale of his textbooks. By 1852 singing classes were part of schooling in not only Boston—which came up with the money next year—but also Buffalo, Cleveland, Cincinnati, Chicago, Pittsburgh, Bangor, New Orleans, Louisville, Providence, St. Louis. Mason also invented the musical convention of schoolteachers gathered from outlying communities into a given city to learn basic musical values. Yet there is no reason to see his business sense as primary in his becoming what a recent biographer called "the father of singing among children." [233] His moral and religious tenets; his love of music; his fondness for children, so evident in his great skill in teaching them; his general goodwill, equally evident in his standing eagerness to help promising talents—each of these probably outweighed dollars and cents. It is nevertheless pleasant to be able to state that unlike many a pioneer in cultural good causes, he was full of this world's goods as well as honors when he died at the age of eighty in a fine suburban mansion in Llewellyn Park, an exclusive plutocrats' ghetto in New Jersey's Oranges.

It was further gratifying that one of his sons, William Mason, became an important pianist and piano teacher and colleague of violinist Theodore Thomas in bringing good chamber music to New York City in the 1850's. Thomas was later to be a titanic force in transplanting the greatest symphonic musical traditions of his native Germany to America. Most of the professional musicians who, for political, personal or economic reasons, sowed music in this undercultivated environment were Germans. The others were French or Italian, seldom English. Europeans similarly dominated the opera companies that, beginning in the 1820's, sought to enlarge footholds in the Northeastern cities. By 1833 New York City had a fussily elaborate opera house with boxes with gilded panels and light-blue hangings leased to pretentious families at $6,000 each. The box-holders' womenfolk already understood that such a showcase was synonymous with cosmopolitan prestige, even though former Mayor Philip Hone found it tiresome to have to sit so long listening to languages that he did not understand. The association thus woven between opera and diamonds still persists among us. In time every other red-brick theater newly built in growing towns for the use of stock-and-star companies and minstrel shows carried on its carved Italianate gable: "Grand Opera House." But partly because of sustained competition from the continuing immigration of well-trained European musicians, partly because of American slackness about taking music really seriously, a sizable class of professional American instrumentalists and singers was slow to develop. Except for the folk and amateur levels, music retained exotic, usually German or Italian, connotations. Even American street music consisted largely of the seedy German band of a drummer and a few tooters on brass, and the ragged Italian's hurdy-gurdy.

One of Mason's associates had learned early that his original hymns were much more widely accepted when attributed to "Kl—f" or "Zol—ffer" than to plain Thomas Hastings. He would have found nothing remarkable about the twentieth-century custom of sending a girl named Jane Smith to study in Milan and bringing her back to triumph in her native country as Angelina Toffanetti. The first workmanlike American grand opera, *Leonora,* done by a pair of Philadelphian brothers named Fry, ran for twelve nights in 1845, but its libretto was adapted from an Englishman's play with a French setting (*The Lady of Lyons*), its musical models were plainly Italian, and its only revival in the rest of the 1800's was produced in New York City in 1856 by an Italian troupe that had translated the libretto into Italian. Arthur M. Schlesinger, Sr., once pointed out that "Home, Sweet Home," the most widely known "American" song, had only its lyric from American John Howard Payne, a good deal of an expatriate anyway. His words were "set to a Sicilian tune by an English musician and first sung in an operatic drama in London." [234] In 1930 John Tasker Howard, a historian of music challenging himself to identify music peculiarly American in flavor, could cite only "Yankee · Doodle," "Dixie," "The Arkansas Traveler" and "Sucking Cider Through a Straw."

It is hardly inexplicable then that in American culture the sort of music that the Old World takes most seriously retained almost down to our own day a position analogous to that of table wines—expensive, assumed to be better when imported, carrying prestige, not unpleasant after one gets used to them. None of that applied, of course, to a Beacon Hill Brahmin, who really relished and bought good Hock or Burgundy, or to George Templeton Strong of the Manhattan Quality, who owned and played a fine pipe organ, maintained it in the family residence as solicitously as if it were a mistress, and all his life promoted good music, sacred or secular, as earnestly as he would the cause of a client of his law firm.

The opera snob, the women's magazine . . . Hindsight scanning the, fourth and fifth decades of the 1800's sees many such signs that a world that we can think of as non-archaic was shaping up. By 1820 Boston had built its elegant new Tremont House, which doomed the old roadside tavern kind of hotel by taking the room clerk's and cashier's functions out of the barroom and actually providing some single-occupancy rooms for those preferring not to share with strangers. Within a generation the ensuing elaboration of hotels was so extravagant that a British actor staying at New York City's St. Nicholas Hotel said that he daren't put his boots out for cleaning lest they come back gilded. Not only the seaboard cities but those as new as Cincinnati and Memphis were investing in hotels with rooms by the hundred, public ladies' parlors, lobbies as well as bars, and dining rooms as splendidly gussied up as the steamboats that brought the customers. The states were hinting at economic coming-of-age by banning the lotteries with which our knee-breeched forebears often built churches, college halls, canals, turnpikes and orphanages. When banks were few and savings banks unknown, the lottery had a valid function as a way to amass otherwise inaccessible small sums from many persons into totals large enough to finance large projects. But now banking was there to stay and reformers had come to feel that the lower orders' fascination with the wheel of chance was a serious moral and economic drain on them and the community. The latter point was soon unmistakable. After becoming illegal, the lotteries left flourishing bastard offspring in cities in the shape of illicit "policy rackets"—the poor man's few-cents-a-chance lottery. America has been trying and failing to do something about policy (or "numbers") ever since.

In 1839 several Americans, including the versatile S. F. B. Morse, were just as clearly anticipating modern times by experiments with the French-invented daguerreotype, forerunner of photography. Used principally for portraits, the process, which left a sunlight-imposed likeness on a chemically coated copper plate, spread all over the nation within a few years. Itinerant daguerreotypists had the same sort of careers as steam doctors and singing teachers, immortalizing the citizens of a given town at two bits apiece as long as business held up, then moving on to the next one down the river or along the canal. Some moved in "Daguerrean cars"— like gypsy vans fitted up to double as studio and darkroom. There survives a daguerreotype taken somewhere upcountry in gold rush California showing Batchelder's Daguerrean Saloon parked on its own four wheels ready for the miners' business with Batchelder himself standing in the doorway in the wide-awake hat and bandanna neckerchief of the region. The portraits were often unduly hard-favored. Human beings' faces tended to show the strain of having to sit frozen-still for about a minute of time-exposure; it is a comfort to know that your great-great-grandfather probably did not look quite that grim. But the best daguerreotype portraits, such as those of Mathew Brady, later the chief photographer of the Civil War, are breathtaking. Nobody with the most refined modern cameras and lights ever did better. By the 1850's the actual photograph utilizing a negative from which prints could be duplicated was coming in.

But the parallel with today that one expects least of the America of turned-up shirt collars is the slack permissiveness about children reported with more or less disapproval by the majority of alien visitors. When small Henry Adams refused to go to school, his august grandfather, John Quincy Adams, silently took his hand and irresistibly led him to his duty in a fashion that left grandson still impressed sixty years later. That was not the picture that outsiders saw. In the late 1790's Julian Ursyn Niemcewicz, the young Pole who liked Americans very much, described the five-year-old daughter of General Anthony White of New Brunswick, New Jersey, as "a spoiled child, as are most American children. One hears her sometimes say to her mother, 'You damn'd bitch.' The least inconvenience that she encounters makes unhappiness for the whole household." [235] An unfriendly British witness of 1818 noted that "The children are rarely forbidden or punished for wrong doing . . . only kindly solicited to do right," and ascribed to this "the prominent boldness and forwardness of American children . . . never to be slighted or affronted with impunity." [236] Any adept in the hundreds of Old Worldlings' books about America before the Civil War could cite dozens and scores of such comments from observers of all degrees of accuracy and responsibility. They agree on the point almost as unanimously as on the shortcomings of American roads.

Though this permissiveness may have been strong only among the upper strata, it nevertheless contradicted what most articulate Americans thought about discipline and respect for one's elders long *after,* as well as before, Pestalozzi's romantic teachings on such matters were imported. It is inconsistent with the almost universal resort to frequent corporal punishment in the schools these reprehended children attended. The alien travelers' disapproval would have nowhere met with more sympathy than from Rollo's father and mother, archetypal prosperous parents *c.* 1840. The evidence is too strong to ignore, however. Something in American air must encourage permissiveness. That millionaire's spoiled brat whom Kipling drew with such ecstatic loathing in *Captains Courageous* in 1897 had a long-standing ancestry.

VII

A Chromo Civilization

HORATIO ALGER'S AMERICA

VII

The Civil War gave the courthouse square its prevalent sculptured monument—the standing infantryman. In Dixie he wears a slouch hat; in the North a slant-topped forage cap. His pedestal carries the names of the local citizen soldiers who never came back. A strange thing about the North's Civil War—not the South's, maybe because the Chivalry were closer-knit—was the number of young men destined to distinction whose names had no opportunity to be carved there. In four bloody years the North put nearly 2,000,000 men into blue uniforms. But thirty or forty years later a roll call of those eminent in the arts, finance and ideas who had been of fighting age in the early 1860's showed an immense number who had not gone to war.

For instance, William James (brother Henry was physically unfit); W. G. Sumner, redoubtable early sociologist; H. H. Richardson and Richard Morris Hunt, eminent architects; James A. McN. Whistler, conspicuous expatriate painter, all were abroad, mostly studying, during much of the fighting; none enlisted. Charles W. Eliot, a great president-to-be of Harvard, lost his appointment there in late 1862 and was offered a lieutenant colonelcy by Governor John Andrew of Massachusetts; he cited family financial reverses and his own weak eyesight as his reasons for going abroad to study instead. Thomas Eakins was studying art in Philadelphia. William Dean Howells was U.S. consul in Venice; among the rising young lawyers and newspapermen with whom he had boarded in Columbus, Ohio, he later recalled, only two or three enlisted. Edwin Booth and Joseph Jefferson, America's finest young actors, went on acting. Mark Twain and Bret Harte were journalists on the West Coast; the first saw some weeks of irregular Confederate service before washing his hands of the war and going West to take a political job under his brother. Clarence King, father of the U.S. Geological Survey, was in California as topographical engineer. Earl Pomeroy's *The Pacific Slope* calls it common knowledge that the mining camps were full of men of military age. At one juncture the governor of Iowa issued a proclamation forbidding men to leave the state until after the state's draft quota was completed. Artemus Ward, the nation's leading funnyman; John Burroughs, eminent naturalist; Ignatius Donnelly and Henry George, exponents of important radicalisms; James Fisk and Jay Gould, predatory wonder boys of postwar finance; Peter A. B. Widener and Charles T. Yerkes, builders of streetcar empires and corrupters of aldermen; John D. Rockefeller, great economic innovator of his day; John Wanamaker, inventor of the department store; Joseph H. Choate and Chauncey M. Depew, kings among corporation lawyers; Grover Cleveland . . .

Some young men with conspicuous futures outside politics did go to war: Oliver Wendell Holmes, Jr., the great Supreme Court Justice; Charles Francis Adams, Jr., railroad expert and historian; T. W. Higginson, the fighting parson radical, abettor of John Brown and postwar literary man; Lester Ward, a chief catalyst of American sociology; the Reverend Russell H. Conwell, the author of *Acres of Diamonds,* inspirational best-selling lecture tract; Ambrose Bierce, the atrabilious author-journalist who alone in his time anticipated the pattern that we now expect of young-man-goes-to-war-comes-back-bitter-and-writes-about-it. John W. De Forest had the same kind of experiences and wrote about them better and less bitterly. Winslow Homer smelled some powder as civilian artist for *Harper's Weekly.* A few others did some things with a trace of the war effort. Henry Adams was a secretary for his father in the crucial post of U.S. minister to Britain; John Hay was one of President Lincoln's secretaries; Andrew Carnegie was a mainstay of the Pennsylvania Railroad and organizer of the invaluable military telegraph service; Walt Whitman nursed the wounded. But expanding this latter list much further is difficult. The national elite, however defined, did not rush to war. Among both graduates and young undergraduates at Yale and Harvard, a bare 25 percent did so.

That is no particular reproach to the upper strata, however. Lincoln's calls for volunteers in 1861 were responded to by 700,000 men. But by mid-1862 it was clear that, as Eugene Converse Murdock, a student of Civil War recruiting, says, that represented "the full, hard core of patriotic citizenry . . . the limits of patriotism [had] been reached within the volunteer system," [1] and conscription was necessary. The form it took, allowing the better-off to pay substitutes to take their places, cast what now seems to us another ugly crosslight on the values of the time. That was one of the frictions—the several others were less defensible—behind the predominantly Irish-immigrant riots against the draft in New York City in mid-1863. American equalitarianism was apparently not yet mature enough to require at least nominal equality of sacrifice among all strata of a true nation in arms. In later life Howells was the only prominent laggard who, to my knowledge, showed marked signs of self-reproach. Yet the above is not intended to make William James or Clarence King or Thomas Eakins, all unquestionably civilized and responsible persons, look bad. It is mere warning that though it already had baseball, oil wells and doctrinaire apostles of free love, the America that so dismayed Henry Adams when he returned to it in 1868 would in many respects have seemed to us a foreign country. Foreign and still somewhat barbarous.

Yet it also showed premonitory paradoxes. In those same war years, for instance, civilians of both sexes were acknowledging the social burden of war as no nation had ever done before by creating the U.S. Sanitary Commission to alleviate its minor strains and hardships. This originated in the grass roots as the womenfolk of men mustered into local units banded together to send after them amenities that armies neglect: homemade edibles, for generals had not yet admitted the possibility of improving Army chow; extra socks and flannels; such home remedies as goose grease and mustard plasters. Dr. Elizabeth Blackwell, first woman to receive an American medical degree, coordinated these informal groups in New York City into a Women's Central Relief Committee. The government in Washington, mindful of the importance of a British Sanitary Commission organizing volunteer services in the recently concluded Crimean War, encouraged a nationwide American counterpart spreading such agencies as Dr. Blackwell's into many kinds of civilian support for military morale and health. Here was a precursor of today's wartime Red Cross not only procuring and distributing small comforts for the men, but making, buying and shipping supplementary hospital supplies; looking after soldiers' families in trouble; expediting travel for those on furlough or coming home discharged; holding numerous Sanitary Fairs of minor and major size to raise funds, a technique already well known to women agitating against slavery and Rum. Mining towns in the West were full of husky young patriots a long way from the fighting but eager to shell out new-mined silver and gold at Sanitary Fairs.

The Easterners in charge at the top were male, eminent and able, such as the Reverend Henry W. Bellows, cultivated young minister of New York City; Dr. Samuel G. Howe of Boston, effective crusader for better care of the deaf, blind and insane and the husband of Julia Ward Howe, the beautiful and witty bluestocking who wrote "The Battle Hymn of the Republic"; Frederick L. Olmsted, crucial reporter on slavery and, as landscape architect, a principal inspirer of America's municipal park systems. But the rank and file in cities and county seats, particularly in the Old Northwest, were women organizing, coordinating, reporting, many learning for the first time that picked members of their sex could do such things as well as men. The whole northwestern area of the commission, including 4,000-odd branches, was directed by Yankee-born Mrs. Mary A. Livermore of Chicago. Mrs. Annie Wittenberg of Keokuk, Iowa, went nonchalantly under fire at the siege of Vicksburg and managed her diet kitchens for the wounded so well that Grant incorporated them and her directly into his command. The great Dorothea Dix, battler for decent care of the insane, and Clara Barton, who later brought the American arm of the Red Cross into being, recruited women nurses for Army hospitals and improved the flow of hospital supplies. It was understandable that after the war Mmes. Livermore, Wittenberg, *et al.*, disinclined to return to stagnant domesticity, became spearheads of the great women's movements against Rum and for women's rights.

First, however, their Sanitary Fairs had had an inadvertent side effect, drastically revising American notions of the nation's past and of elegance in the home. Or say that a strange by-product of the Civil War was the American cult of antiques, of Colonial artifacts, of New World ancestor worship. In early 1864 Poughkeepsie, New York, staged a Sanitary Fair, whose most popular feature, says a surviving account, was a "Dutchess County Room One Hundred Years Ago . . . ten cents admission . . . fifty cents for a 'tea' in the rural style of a hundred years ago." Visitors entered by a Dutch door with a genuine wrought-iron knocker of *c*. 1740. ". . . a pretty waiting-maid . . . in ancient petticoat and short gown" showed them into a carefully authentic room with "a low ceiling with huge projecting beams . . . a huge fireplace with old Dutch tiles. . . . Over the mantelshelf . . . silhouette likenesses . . . antique candle-sticks . . . an Old English clock in tall mahogany case, and a delicate ebony candle-stand . . . a sofa brought into Dutchess County from Holland in 1690 . . . a . . . dining-table of solid mahogany [of similar date]. . . ." The lady attendants were "members of the oldest families on the Hudson . . . in the costumes of their . . . great-grandmothers . . . the genuine dresses. . . . One . . . spinning merrily on the great wool-wheel; another making thread with an ancient flax-wheel. . . ." [2] The infection spread downriver. A few months later the great Sanitary Fair on New York City's Union Square had a Knickerbocker Kitchen with a similar cast and props: a mirror said to have been Peter Stuyvesant's, a Beekman family cradle of 1754, a corner cupboard from the Hasbroucks of Kingston, New York, 150 years old . . .

The same bacillus seems to have been stirring in New England. In 1861 the Essex Institute of Salem, Massachusetts, had moved to its grounds for restoration and veneration a small building of the 1600's thought to have been the town's first meetinghouse. In 1875 Salem marked the centennial of Massachusetts' ousting of the British with a sizable display of Colonial artifacts. Local names of weight—Loring, Pickering, Saltonstall, Derby, Lee—were attached to these chairs and tables, satin petticoats, jewelry, swords and muskets, silver porringers, portraits and so on. At the national celebration of the one hundredth anniversary of independence in Philadelphia in 1876, certain New England exhibits dwelt with influential emphasis on the motif of Colonial ways-and-things. Massachusetts' official building was modeled on "the style of houses common to Colonial times" [3]—not too authentically, to judge from pictures and descriptions of it as painted brown with green trim. Connecticut probably did better with an archaic-flavored edifice (designed by Ik Marvel, the bucolic essayist of *Dream Life*) of pine "stained to give it the dark look of age," [3] the narrow-windowed interior graced by a spinning wheel, an antique sideboard, a tall wooden-works clock with an applewood case. The strongest influence, however, probably came from the very popular New England Log House said to be an "exact imitation of the country dwellings of a hundred years ago." [4] From its low-beamed ceiling hung ears of corn and strings of dried apples and peppers. Its reverend artifacts included John Stark's spurs, John Alden's desk, a chair of John Endicott's and the cradle in which was rocked Peregrine White, the baby born on the *Mayflower*. Daily from noon to 3 P.M. twenty ladies in costumes of the mid-1750's served old-time Yankee baked beans, brown bread and boiled dinner and explained the fireplace-style cooking utensils, "whose very simplicity made them incomprehensible to the victim of modern improvements," [4] says one historian of the Centennial Exposition, to whom that meant gaslight, cookstoves and running water in kitchen sinks.

I cannot identify the person who had that original inspiration in Poughkeepsie. Whoever it was, she or he had much to answer for: Williamsburg, the antique shops of Bucks County, Pennsylvania, and the sizable industry, aboveboard as well as underground, of manufacturing reproductions of archaic originals for the American furnishings market. There had long been collecting of antique silver, china, coins, gem seals, of course. This, however, was collecting not so much of things as of connotations. Emulation of those Saltonstalls and Beekmans was what created the cult of antiques. From these reverend exhibits thousands of socially ambitious women learned that the most august families in New York and New England carefully retained as honored heirlooms and symbols of their hereditary importance hardware and furniture that had been out of fashion for generations. It was eagerly noted that much of what was so respectfully displayed looked like stuff relegated to the garret back home. Hopeful young matrons wrapped up their heads against dust and cobwebs and mounted the uppermost flight of stairs in search of rickety candlestands and cradles. When found, they were furbished up, established in the parlor in curious contrast with the tortured walnut-and-horsehair sofa that had been Uncle Elmo's wedding present, and accounted for to callers as being full of Colonial charm—a phrase that spread the disease as effectively as sneezing spreads the common cold. "When household antiquities became fashionable," Sarah Orne Jewett wrote of small-town New England Quality only a few years after the centennial set all this going, "the ladies remarked upon a surprising interest in their corner cupboard and best chairs, and some distant relatives revived their almost forgotten custom of paying a summer visit. . . . One . . . prowled from garret to cellar . . . but . . . was not asked to accept even the dislocated cherry-wood footstool that she had discovered in a far corner of the parsonage pew." [5]

Those who had either thrown out grandma's old samplers and pewter or lacked grandmothers of the kind who left durable possessions sensibly determined that if one lacked heirlooms of one's own, the best thing to do was to buy other people's. This was the advice proffered by Clarence Cook, astringent critic of art and architecture in the 1870's:

> . . . everybody can't have things that came over in the Mayflower . . . those of us who have not drawn these prizes . . . must . . . scour out backcountry where perhaps we may light upon . . . owners who cannot conceal their wonder at people . . . willing to pay hard cash for chairs and tables . . . that seem to them not worth taking as a gift. . . . In Boston a polite internecine war has for some time raged between rival searchers . . . young couples in chaises on the trail of old sideboards and brass andirons . . . the best places in which to look . . . are . . . the henyards, the closets and drawers having for years been given over to the fowls. Several handsome oak cupboards that now adorn pretty Boston drawing-rooms had to be feathered and singed . . . this . . . is one of the best signs of returning good taste . . . long victim to the whims and impositions of foreign fashions . . . much more sensible than it seems to those who look upon it as only another phase of the "centennial mania" . . . there is [also] . . . the pleasant knowledge that . . . all of [such furniture] was made for Americans or bought by them; and . . . in saving it from dishonor and putting it in safekeeping, we are bringing ourselves a little nearer in spirit to the old time.[6]

Possession of somebody else's ancestors' candlesticks suggested to the new owners that it would also be near in spirit to the old time to burn candles in them. John Adams or Benjamin Franklin would have doubted the sanity of anybody's dining by candlelight once gas or kerosene was available. But it was discovered or alleged that ladies looked better under such illumination—or lack of it—hence the eventual affinity between candlelight and the creamed-chicken-and-waffles sort of restaurant. (The *reductio ad absurdum* is the pitch-black cocktail bar

A disappearing bedstead of the 1870's marvelously camouflaged by the prevalent carved ornamentation.

still surviving from the 1930's.) Maybe the most striking anomaly occurred, however, when the antique-minded found in garrets or second-hand stores stiff old portraits lacking all identification of subject or artist and bought them not as esthetically significant primitives—that came later—but because no matter whose ancestors they were, they went with the Windsor chairs that, Cook warned, were "bought up at once wherever they were offered for sale." [7]

His soundest point involved taste. By and large these exhumed relics had better lines and proportions and often sounder workmanship than the overornamented, factory-made stuff filling most parlors and bedrooms of the centennial era merely because carvings, fringe, horsehair and red satin were fashionable. The Silas Laphams' drawing room in South Boston (then not quite yet taken over by the Irish) gives a glimpse of the consequences among the well-to-do:

> . . . the chandelier was of massive imitation bronze; the mirror over the mantel rested on a fringed mantel cover of green reps, and heavy curtains of that stuff hung from gilt lambrequin frames at the window. . . . In front of the long windows were statues . . . which . . . represented . . . Faith and Hope to people without. A white marble group . . . an Italian conception of Lincoln Freeing the Slaves—a Latin Negro and his wife—occupied one corner, and balanced the whatnot of an earlier period. . . . These phantasms added their chill . . . to the violence of the contrast when the chandelier was lighted up full glare, and the heat of the whole furnace welled up from the registers into the quivering atmosphere.[8]

Cook's liking for antique-minded "good taste" smells faintly of snobbery. Consider his observation that this "revival of old simplicity . . . has been working its way down from a circle of rich, cultivated people to a wider circle." [9] That has now culminated in the reproductions and approximations of Colonial fire irons, lamps and floor mats offered by gifte shoppes. But at least children reared among the chairs and tables of 1750, whether or not their parents had an hereditary right to them, did not get their eyes perverted by pseudo-rococo writhings as their ears were by Sunday School hymns. The same applies to the effect on later children of the more or less careful reproductions of traditional Colonial highboys and side chairs—the most careful were forgeries for sale as genuine— soon on the market.

What happened when fashion steered away from the Laphams' ideas without regressing into the Colonial is sadly clear in Henry Adams' account of how the charming and cultivated widow heroine of his novel *Democracy* refurbished a conventional town house in Washington in the late 1870's: "A new era . . . had dawned upon that benighted and heathen residence. The wealth of Syria and Persia was poured out upon the melancholy Wilton carpets; embroidered comets and woven gold from Japan and Teheran depended from [the curtains]; a strange medley of sketches, paintings, laces, embroideries, and porcelain was hung, nailed, pinned or stuck against the wall; finally that domestic altar-piece, the mystical Corot landscape, was hoisted to its place over the parlour fire, and . . . peace reigned in that redeemed house, and in the heart of its mistress." [10] Granted that the separate ingredients were probably of better quality than the Laphams' things, the whole must nevertheless have looked just about as much like flood tide in an auction room.

*The thoroughly gussied-up parlor of the high General Grant era
complete with center-table kerosene lamp and base-burner coal
stove. And note cuspidor.*

Charles Eastlake, a most influential arbiter of English—and to a large
extent American—taste predicted in 1865 that "fifty years hence all the
contents of our modern [furniture] shops will have fallen into useless
lumber, only fit to be burnt for firewood" with maybe some pieces in
the South Kensington Museum "in some Chamber of Horrors . . . to
. . . illustrate . . . bad taste in this century." [11] That makes him
sound like a harbinger of better things—falsely, however, because what
he and Cook and some others of their day meant when recommending
simple lines, severely conceived ornament, sense of structural elements
in design—all of which they talked about with twentieth-century glib-
ness—is all too clear when one turns the page and sees the drawing of
the tortured sideboard that exemplifies their doctrines, to our eyes about
as calamitous as anything from early Grand Rapids. How risky in any case
to prognosticate on matters of fad and fancy! The General Grant pieces
now in museums—and antique shops with unblushing price tags on
them—are prized not as horrors but as pieces of vigorous Victorian design
in imitation of the imitation Rococo of Louis Philippe's France or the
imitation Renaissance of the Second Empire. A recent New York *Times*
was even speaking respectfully of the freshness of design in the mass-

produced furniture from Grand Rapids of the 1880's, a place and time until now, of course, synonymous with misguided garishness. In the antique trade the gap between rejection and resurrection seems to run forty or fifty years. Early in the 1950's the dealers' spotlights picked out the Art Nouveau of *c.* 1900 with a particular eye to Tiffany glass, lampshades and all. In 1968 one hears of a lively new interest in the fumed-oak Mission furniture, all slabs, squared-off sticks and obtrusive corners, that went with the cult of things Californian *c.* 1910.

Temporary mock-ups such as the Knickerbocker Kitchen led to permanent restoration of actual houses of the 1700's with appropriate furniture and hardware. Genteel visitors to Saratoga in the 1880's, for instance, made excursions to the old Schuyler place thus solicitously worked up by atavistic local ladies. Plymouth, Massachusetts, and Mount Vernon saw other such cults of quill pen and corner cupboard take shape. The architectural historians of Newport, Rhode Island, suggest that the cult of the Colonial was fostered by "the general rise of summer resorts . . . after the Civil War . . . [in New England's old ports, such as Newburyport and Gloucester, where] a considerable amount of Colonial architecture, in various stages of picturesque dilapidation, was still standing . . . associated with the cleaner and more simple dream world which the vacationing refugees were seeking." [12] For some such reason people did begin to act on the principle that even though one had no ancestral homestead to cherish, one could buy and cherish another's; or build a reasonable facsimile of a Colonial mansion albeit with better plumbing and heating. Even in Davenport, Iowa, *c.* 1890, according to Octave Thanet (Alice French), local magnates indulged wives in new houses "after the old colonial pattern as modern architects see it." [13]

Yet at the same time the creation of genealogy-minded societies of patriotic flavor was barring intruders from the inner arcana of the cult of knee-breeched Colonial forebears. Hereditary privilege was invoked to control that. Between 1875 and 1894, the same period in which antique worship developed, were founded the Sons of the Revolution, the Sons of the American Revolution, the Daughters of the American Revolution, the Colonial Dames of America, the Society of Mayflower Descendants. Like the major general in *The Pirates of Penzance,* the parvenu could still buy a chapelful of somebody else's ancestors and play they were his own—that is, the American could buy a Colonial grandee's fieldstone mansion and furbish it up as if rehabilitating the old line. But unless his wife could prove descent from an ancestor fighting redcoats as the original owner had, no DAR badge for her. That requirement founded a cult of genealogy that created a still-lively small in-

dustry of expert researchers. So far as I know, nobody has tried to form
a Daughters of the American Loyalists able to prove descent from one
of the many thousands of American-born who fought for George III
against his rebellious subjects, though the proportion of Colonial Quality
among them was probably much higher than among Washington's men.
The DAR sort of thing, however, has entailed some incidental good.
The demand for documentation of qualifying data has greatly furthered
the discovery and preservation of Colonial archives.

The nationalistic implications of these ancestor-worshiping societies
might imply a significant weakening of the persisting ties between Britain
and her strayed Colonies. Every decade after 1783 should have meant
cumulative attenuation as the new nation grew into her own and felt her
cultural strength broadening with size and richening with fresh opportunity. Actually no such thing was occurring. For that, technological
advances were partly to blame. The natural process of growing apart
was more than counteracted by devices making it faster, safer, more
convenient—and often more profitable—to multiply and strengthen the
old ties that had begun as those between Old Country and Colony. Every
new steamer on the transatlantic run meant that things and attitudes
newly in vogue in London or Paris traveled westward sooner and more
weightily and reached more Americans, that more American students
could go earn their scholastic wings in German universities and come
back imbued with German notions of knowledge and how to acquire
it, that more fledgling American artists could attend the Atelier Julian
and return convinced that no still life was worth looking at unless it included a wine bottle and a Brie cheese. When America's celebration of
the completion of the Atlantic cable in 1858 was succeeded by a break
that frustrated the project for eight years, the amused sneers from the
British press struck George Templeton Strong as "ungracious" and
wounding because "What we exulted over so absurdly was the prospect
of closer communication . . . with England." [14]
None of that was bad in itself. A gradual loss of contact with the
Mother Countries would have deprived America of her birthright as part
of the great Western tradition—a thing that cultural chauvinists like Noah
Webster tend to undervalue. But 100 years ago the interchange was
more lopsided than it is now. The Goncourt brothers, visiting the Universal Exposition in Paris in 1867, deplored much of it as "the final
blow levelled at the past, the Americanization of France, industry
lording it over art, the steam thresher displacing the painting. . . ." [15]
They were crying out before they were hurt. Serious cultural feedback
would not begin until Hollywood became center of the world's movie

industry. In the Goncourts' day not only was young Mrs. Brownstone filling the new house on Murray Hill with Second Empire furniture and bedeviling her dressmaker with fashionplates copied from Parisian ones and her cook with books of à la recipes, but young Mr. Brownstone was likely to be deep—much deeper than he is today—in a comparable Anglophilia.

It was not new. The Anglophilia of the Colonial plutocracy had passed pretty much intact to their Federalist successors in power, thence to the beneficiaries of second- and third-generation wealth in Boston, New York City and Philadelphia. Only ten years after the British burned the White House, J. K. Paulding noted sardonically how young Jonathan still "had a bad habit of imitating Squire Bull [his father]. . . . It was enough for him that John Bull did this, and said that . . . dressed after such and such a fashion, and held such and such opinions. . . ." 16 In earlier times a club had been a group of political or social cronies who met weekly, say, at a certain tavern to tipple and talk and maybe plan. Franklin's Junto is the best-known example; Boston's Saturday Club of prominent and cultivated men who took one another seriously (Holmes' beloved "mutual admiration society") was a late one. By the 1840's, however, the large Northeastern cities were forming Pall Mall-style—it was hoped—gentlemen's clubs for daily frequenting and the fostering of back-scratching prestige. Some clubhouses were specially built for splendor; others were taken over ready-made after bankruptcy struck down the maker of a quick fortune who had built a mansion not wisely but too well. George Templeton Strong was well aware of the Anglophilia of such "mere Institutions for the Doing of Nothing—systematically; places where a parcel of boys [he was all of twenty-five himself] have larger facilities than elsewhere for lounging and loafing . . . [trying] to look like Pelhams and Vivian Grays [elegant heroes of Disraeli's so-British novels]." 17 Within a year of writing that, he himself belonged to both the Quality-heavy Union Club and the cultivated Century Association.

When the Prince of Wales visited America in 1860, the public dinners, receptions and extravagant balls that marked the progress of this stubby and chinless stripling through Detroit, Chicago, St. Louis, Cincinnati, Washington, Philadelphia, New York City, Boston and Portland, Maine, outdid what had been accorded the aging Lafayette in 1824. Five thousand people massed outside his hotel in Chicago on the chance of seeing his shadow on the window blinds of his suite. Governor William F. Packer of Pennsylvania showed him the Colonial portraits in the State Capitol at Harrisburg and boasted cordially, if scandalously, that Americans "cannot follow our ancestry more than a few generations back without tracing the line to a British redcoat." [18] It was thought gratifying that the prince actually shook hands with two Irish farmhands in Illinois and exchanged autographs with the only survivor of Bunker Hill. And the nation's pleasure in its own snobbish hospitality was complete when, in acknowledgment, the boy's royal father, Prince Albert, arranged that the next year's subject for an annual poetry prize at Cambridge University should be: "The Prince of Wales at the Tomb of Washington."

Opportunity for the Gilded Age's gilded youth to acquire English ways and clothes was widened not only by improved steamer service but also by the undiscriminating tendency of the English upper classes to think all Americans pretty much alike—all equally curious but to be asked once to dinner if the suggestion came from somebody important whose elbow had been jogged by a diplomat or a banker with American connections. Callow travelers thus favored brought home a good try at the proper accent and the requisite disdain of all things American and left their measurements with a proper London tailor for regular replenishing of their sleek new wardrobes. Edgar Fawcett, a minor novelist who pattered along certain paths later to be honored by Edith Wharton's tread, described young Gansevoort of the Metropolitan Club who "walked, talked, sat down, smoked his cigar and carried his umbrella precisely like an Englishman, and yet . . . it was all spurious . . . and not unconscious habit." [19] To judge from the dialogue Mrs. Wharton set down some decades later, such blatant Anglicism was essential in the brandied-Wall-Street-and-Newport set: "I say, you know— you'll please remember he's a blooming bounder," says one. "Deuced bold thing to show herself in that get-up," [20] says one of his elders. Doubtless the prep-school version of the Anglophile accent went with those lines. It lingers today in the topmost social strata of the Northeastern states and among elderly actors; whereas, of course, the finest American speech is the farthest from British flavor, as in that of A. Philip Randolph, founder of the Brotherhood of Sleeping Car Porters and elder statesman among American Negroes. Habitually he makes the English tongue sound like a spontaneous American compliment to the human race.

In 1876, centenary of independence, James Gordon Bennett, Jr., brought polo to America and trained novice rider-players in an armory before displaying the game for respectful and expensive racing crowds at New York City's Jerome Park. Other rich poseurs brought over drags—costly private versions of the obsolete British stagecoach—and, imitating elegant Britons, prided themselves on the skill with which they drove them four-in-hand loaded inside and out with fashionable men and women. In Brookline, suave suburb of Boston, Howells noted how "the stone cottages, with here and there a patch of determined ivy on their northern walls, did what they could to look English amid the glare of the autumn foliage." [21] "The bad taste," he added elsewhere, "is in the wish to imitate Europe at all; but with the abundance of money, the imitation is simply inevitable." [22] Certain Anglophiles had the candor to shift permanently to England: Whistler in the 1850's; Henry James in 1876; the wealthy mystico-religious reformist Robert Pearsall Smiths of Philadelphia in the mid-1880's; William Waldorf Astor, first American to become a peer of England, in 1890; Edgar Fawcett in 1897. Some wives of self-made rich men made no bones of leaving their husbands in America and living lavish lives in Paris, notably Mrs. James Gordon Bennett, Sr., and Mrs. John Mackay, whose Dublin-born husband was the least unimpressive of the kings of the Comstock Lode. But what most such neo-Colonials wanted was to be exemplary missionaries of Old Worldliness among their benighted countrymen.

The effects were often striking. In the early 1890's a well-meaning group of Anglophiles called the American Acclimatization Society thought it would be charming if the American fauna included all the birds mentioned in Shakespeare. Their imported thrushes, chaffinches, nightingales and skylarks died out. Their starlings did not—hence the losing battle of many of today's cities against the noise and corrosive feces of flocks of millions of starlings and the near wiping out of several species of native birds whose nesting places starlings take over. A few years earlier the Reverend Endicott Peabody, whose strongly Yankee name belied his education in England, had founded in a Massachusetts township (once wiped out by King Philip's Indians) the famous Groton School patterned as closely as his zeal could manage on the aristocratic public schools of England, cold baths and all. He had recently been ministering to the heathen of Tombstone, Arizona, in its most carefree phase. Even so the reaction seems excessive and had anomalous consequences on his manly young pupils' habits of speech and, because of Groton's instant high prestige, on the atmosphere of the most fashionable Northeastern private preparatory schools for boys. That sort of tutelage was limited, of course, to the few whose parents could afford—and whose social status justified admission to—such privileges. Almost immediately, however, the scope of Anglicization was immensely widened by the publication in St. Nicholas Magazine (already solidly acknowledged the proper reading for the Quality's children) and then in book form of Little Lord Fauntleroy.

This was the most widely sold work of a popular English woman writer resident in America since girlhood, Mrs. Frances Hodgson Burnett. It tells of the sturdy small son of a charming, hard-up American widow, whose late husband, son and heir of a real English earl, had been disowned by his crusty father for marrying her. Increasing age moves his lordship, now gouty and crustier than ever, to fetch sturdy, golden-haired Ceddie (for Cedric) back to be educated in England as befits the prospective heir, courtesy title Lord Fauntleroy. The boy's sturdily sweet disposition wins his lordship around to the point of reconciliation with mama, and everything is awfully hands-across-the-sea. The nub of the story is the success of the boy in making the English feel, in spite of his early Yankee rearing, his innate patrician qualities. The point is probably all the more lovingly made because Mrs. Burnett's rearing had been that of a petty shopkeeper's daughter in the English Midlands.

The worst of it was that little Lord Fauntleroy wore his golden hair in long curls, and the illustrations by Reginald Birch, a mainstay of *St. Nicholas,* showed him sturdily facing grandfather in a knee-breeched,

Reginald Birch's drawings of Little Lord Fauntleroy had as much to do as Frances Hodgson Burnett's text with inflicting his image on the American mother—and too often her son.

black velvet suit with a broad white collar. Many American mothers above a certain income level not only took him to their hearts but socially crucified their boy children by putting them into black velvet and never allowing their hair to be cut. For good or ill other immigrant Britons left traces on America between the Civil and the Spanish-American wars: James Redpath, first efficiently to organize the lecture branch of American show business; Alexander Graham Bell; Edward Weston, second only to Edison as father of the electric industry . . . But only Mrs. Burnett could claim so deeply to have affected the emotional health of so many American boys.

The grown-up counterpart of Little Lord Fauntleroy was the Anglophile cult of hands across the sea. Its catchword was *Anglo-Saxon*. Certain English historians had been dwelling on the sturdy virtues of the days of King Alfred. One result was the fashion, soon spreading to America, of Anglo-Saxon names for the children of the next generation: Edith, Edna, Alfred, Harold . . . Another was the notion that since the founding Colonists had been mostly English (= Anglo-Saxon), the common heritage of Anglo-Saxon blood (as that pre-Mendelian time spoke of inherent traits), as well as of the Mother Country's culture, implied an eventual common future. Indeed the motto of the cult came from the explanation given by Commodore Josiah Tattnall, USN (later CSN), of why he had ordered his command to join a British squadron in bombarding Korean shore batteries in 1859: "Blood," he said, "is thicker than water."

The earliest proponents of gradual rapprochement of the Anglo-Saxon nations into marriage healing the divorce of 1776 were mostly British. An early symptom was the set of verses read by Charles Mackay, the Scottish minor poet, at a dinner in his honor at the best restaurant in Washington, D.C., in 1858, in which "Said brother Jonathan to John [Bull]"

> Our Anglo-Saxon name and fame,
>   Our Anglo-Saxon speech,
> Received their mission straight from Heaven
>   To civilize and teach.
> So here's my hand, I stretch it forth,
>   Ye meaner lands, look on!
> From this day hence there's friendship firm
>   'Twixt Jonathan and John! . . .[23]

But within a few years the strains of British sulkiness during the Civil War intervened. Not until 1887 did John Bright, MP, great free trader and friend of the Union in the Civil War, write to the Committee for the

Celebration of the Centennial of the American Constitution: ". . . in the second century of your national life, may we not ask that our two nations may become one people?" [24] In 1893 Goldwin Smith, the liberal Oxford scholar who made himself a second career after the Civil War teaching at the new Cornell University, recommended in a history of America for Britons' use a voluntary union of the United States and Canada under British sponsorship as token of the overriding cultural importance of blood ties. Ten years later radical H. G. Wells was broadly hinting at a reunion. This flattering courtship was causing many well-placed Americans to purr voluptuously and strike Anglo-Saxon attitudes. A few years previously Henry James was writing to William: "I can't look at the English-American world . . . save as a big Anglo-Saxon total, destined to such an amount of melting together that an insistence on their differences becomes more and more idle and pedantic." [25] (As a recent critic has pointed out, of course, had that observation been correct, Henry James, of all people, would have found precious little to write novels about.) Such receptiveness often had a feel of DAR defensiveness, of new uneasiness over the New Emigration, of the perpetual right of Americans of the allegedly Anglo-Saxon stripe to call the tune and rule the roost. In 1890 an American scholar's *A Short History of Anglo-Saxon Freedom* was candid about it:

> We have been so over-hospitable in receiving all comers that we are in some danger of losing our character as an Anglo-Saxon land. The Thirteen Colonies were a fairly homogeneous body, with Celtic and Teutonic admixtures too small to affect appreciably the mass about them. . . . [Now] One in every six of us is of foreign birth while one in every three has both parents of foreign birth . . . it is natural for thoughtful men of the original stock to feel somewhat insecure . . . an important reason for a brotherly drawing toward those who, in spite of superficial differences, are yet substantially one with ourselves. Every Anglo-Saxon should hold the leadership of his race to be something which is bound up with the welfare of the world.[26]

This brushing aside of the good third of pre-Revolutionary population of German, Dutch, Swedish, Scottish, Scotch-Irish, other Irish and French origin was only half the absurdity, of course, in that time. None relished it more than Finley Peter Dunne, whose saloonkeeping Irish sage, Martin Dooley of the West Side of Chicago, began his career in the nation's newspapers in the early 1890's, in time to zero in on the full bloom of Anglo-Saxonism:

"You an' me, Hinnissy, has got to bring on this here Anglo-Saxon 'lieance. An Anglo-Saxon, Hinnissy, is a German that's forgot who was his parents. . . . [President McKinley] is an Anglo-Saxon. His folks come fr'm th' County Armagh [in Ulster]. . . . An' Dooley has been th' proudest Anglo-Saxon name in th' County Roscommon f'r many years. Schwartzmeister is an Anglo-Saxon, but he doesn't know it. . . . Pether Bowbeen down be th' Frinch church is formin' th' Circle Francaize Anglo-Saxon Club." [27] Soon the siren song of the English advocate of hands across the sea is epitomized across the bar: "Foolish an' frivolous people, cheap but thrue-hearted an' insincere cousins. . . . Ye love th' dollar betther thin ye love anything but two dollars. . . . Ye have desthroyed our language. . . . Ye'er morals are loose, ye'er drinks are enervatin' but pleasant, an' ye talk through ye'er noses. . . . Ye annoy us so much ye must be mimbers of our own fam'ly. . . . We have th' same lithrachoor. Ye r'read our Shakespere so we can't undherstand it an' we r'read ye'er aspiring authors, Poe an' Lowell an' Ol' Sleuth th' Detictive. Ye'er ambassadures have always been kindly received . . . whether they taught us to draw to a busted flush . . . or recited original pothry to us, we had a brotherly feeling f'r thim that made us say, 'Poor fellows, they're doin' th' best they can.' So . . . come to our ar-rms, and together we'll go out an' conquer th' wurruld. . . . We feel like a long-lost brother that's been settin' outside in th' cold f'r a week an' is now ast in to supper—an' sarched at th' dure f'r deadly weepins." [28]

Maybe the most striking aspect of Anglo-Saxonism as pretext for Anglophilia in the late 1800's was the rise of an explicit American imperialism to imitate Britain's. The position was that only by creating a large navy, acquiring colonies and ruling dark-skinned peoples could the American branch of Anglo-Saxonism live up to its family heritage. Henry Cabot Lodge, Theodore Roosevelt, John La Farge, John Hay and Captain A. T. Mahan, USN—whose *The Influence of Sea Power upon History, 1660-1783* (1890) much affected British and German as well as American navy-minded imperialists—were among the leaders of this sincere flattery of Britain. In 1885, however, it had been most eloquently popularized by a prominent Congregational parson, the Reverend Dr. Josiah Strong of Cincinnati, who, asked to rework a pamphlet promoting home missions, turned it into a book called *Our Country* that became a momentous best seller by blatantly exhorting America to take up the white man's burden (a phrase that Kipling had yet to coin). Strong tended toward the peevishly arbitrary anyway. He was anti-Catholic, anti-Mormon, anti-immigrant,* anti-Rum and anti-Socialist, as well as pro-Anglo-

* The absurdities and extravagances of nativism need not altogether obscure the intelligible cultural case against unrestricted immigration. In their *Beyond the Melting Pot* (1963) Nathan Glazer and Daniel Patrick Moynihan, one "the son of a

Saxon. He considered the Anglo-Saxon uniquely gifted in the cultivation of civil liberties and "spiritual Christianity," the two ingredients of "the highest Christian civilization." Therefore, "to the English and American people we must look for the evangelization of the world. . . . The Anglo-Saxon . . . is divinely commissioned to be . . . his brother's keeper. . . . God, with infinite wisdom and skill, is training the Anglo-Saxon race for an hour sure to come . . . this powerful race will move down upon Mexico . . . and South America, out upon the islands of the sea. . . . God . . . is . . . preparing in our civilization the die with which to stamp the nations . . . [and] preparing mankind to receive our impress." By 1900 he was writing a conspicuous sequel maintaining that the notion "that there can be no rightful government of a people without their consent, was formed when world conditions were radically different, and people could live separate lives."[29]

Only a few years later the yearning American Quality were also relishing "An Habitation Enforced" by Rudyard Kipling—whom Mr. Dooley explicitly had in mind as a professional Anglo-Saxon following the example of God in chastening whom He loves. It is a story of how a wealthy American, worn out by his soul-destroying career on Wall Street, buys a lovely old English farm and gradually discovers to the immense delectation of Anglo-Saxonry that it is the ancestral homestead of his long-ago forebears. It must be said of it that it is far better than *Little Lord Fauntleroy.*

The immense buildings that housed the Centennial Exposition of 1876 were mostly taken down when it was over. Highly permanent, however, was another huge structure that also much impressed visitors to Philadelphia that memorable and influential summer—the towered and towering bulk of the new City Hall nearing completion in the square in the middle of town, where seventy years earlier Oliver Evans' wheeled steam monster had been demonstrated. Even in those days of low prices the building cost some $10,000,000. It covers ground enough for almost six football fields and, counting in the 20-foot figure of William Penn on the central tower, rises 450 feet above street level. An admiring journalist defined its purpose as "to express American ideas and develop American genius." Actually John McArthur, Jr., its architect, following the fashion of the day for public buildings, made it, as the same writer had already acknowledged, "a rich example of the spirit of French art

working-class immigrant, the other, the grandson," say: ". . . we would not know how to argue with someone who maintained that something was lost when an original American population was overwhelmed in the central cities by vast numbers of immigrants of different culture, religion, language, and race" (22).

. . . bold and effective . . . [in] outline . . . with highly ornate columns, pilasters, pediments, cornices, enriched windows and other appropriate adornments." [30]

This was a gigantic example—another was the even more massive post office (now demolished) in New York City's City Hall Park—of American adoption of the style in which Napoleon III built his additions to the Louvre, all pavilions, heavily framed windows and smug-faced mansard top stories. The official name was French Renaissance, but it reflected rather the pinchbeck glories of the Second Empire than those of the Valois dynasty. It is the General Grant style of every other Midwestern county courthouse and a principal reason for many Americans' sense of anticlimax when seeing Paris for the first time—so much of it looks like the insane asylum and Public School Number Eight back home. The reliably identifying feature, the mansard roof line or tower top, attained its most implausible monumental use on the towers of the otherwise undiluted Gothic of the Mormon Temple at Manti, Utah. Its many horizontally jutting elements make it the favorite latrine-nesting scaffold of pigeons. And its imposingness naturally led American architects to apply it to all sizes of private buildings in wood, as well as brick or stone. Thus imitated in wood, the pavilions of the Louvre replaced the Italianate villa as the standard local magnate's mansion. Broken by skittish dormer windows, often topped by iron filigree like the lace at a lady's throat, the mansard story still outnumbers the peaked roof in the elder parts of many towns. I have even seen a wooden cottage consisting entirely of a single mansard story set on a basement as if sliced off the top of somebody's General Grant house.

These many tributes to the taste of Napoleon the Little did not, however, monopolize the Gilded Age. America's eclecticism, energetically keeping up the picturesque-mindedness that had imported the Gothic, the Italianate and the Oriental for the previous generation, now had several new strings to its bow. So the post-Civil War decades became a Laocoön-like tangle of architectural elaborations—not to say aberrations —still dominating the look, and an amazing one it is, of American small towns. The German-Americans' breweries, as well as their halls for *Turnverein* and *Sängerbund,* often insisted on looking German, not unimpressively. As German learning, science and art attracted Americans, American buildings without specific German association nevertheless reflected the impact on students of architecture of the late medieval German builders: steep-roofed, overhanging gables; towers round in section and extravagantly profiled; fanciful brickwork; variegated slates on the roof— the best of it survives in Memorial Hall at Harvard and Jefferson Market Courthouse in New York City. Both illustrate T. H. White's comment

*The monument to assassinated President James A. Garfield
was a masterpiece of German pseudo-Gothic.*

on this school that "Its ugliest extravagances have a *succès de scandale*." [31] A less explosive success was scored in the Germanophile elements of the massive, precedent-setting Dakota apartment house on
Central Park West.

Or the designer of a new college dormitory in Pennsylvania or a new
patent-medicine factory in Ohio might fancy the stepped gables and
baroque detail of the Low Countries. Or he had the enthusiast's indigestion
that so often followed reading Ruskin—a man with immense leverage
in America, as well as England—on the moral beautles of *The Stones
of Venice* and drew up something squattily arcaded, clottily carved and
so striped by horizontal courses of white masonry that it looked like a
petrified polychrome layer cake. This sort of thing spread even into
places like Selma, Alabama, the principal hotel of which, a local lady

recently told me, was "copied from Venus, Italy." All these styles were, of course, used on churches, which had to be as fashionable, as well as on dwellings or railroad stations. The wooden church with a mansard steeple took on a curious jauntiness when, abandoning the dim color schemes of the 1870's, later congregations had it painted white.

Further to confuse the grave discussions of America already proliferating in the late 1800's came the Queen Anne style of "the era from President Garfield to President Cleveland . . . with its pressed brick and fancy shingles, pressed tin cornices and ceilings, its spindling lathework and amusing attempts at Elizabethan half-timber . . ." [32]—which

In Selma, Alabama, the Hotel Albert brought "Venus"
à la Ruskin to the Black Belt.

is Robert Hale Newton's plucky attempt to define the indefinable. This, too, was in part a legacy from the Centennial Exposition, where the British Government Building was an agglomeration of Jacobean high chimneys and gables and neoclassic detail withindoors that, for no ascertainable reason, England had recently been calling Queen Anne. When American designers got into it, the result was something that, though not looking particularly English, certainly looked like nothing else. The town house of brick or stone with clumpily columned and balustraded doorway and steep-gabled front was labeled Queen Anne. So was the suburban villa of wood with multiple gables and whimsical verandas and balconies all sticks and fretwork. Sometimes such elements were applied to elder houses to bring them up to date, which created a stand-

*Admiring neighbors probably called these houses "Queen Anne"
for lack of any more definite designation.*

*P. T. Barnum's second Bridgeport mansion, Waldemere,
was an imperial version of Queen Anne.*

Xenia, Ohio, drawn in 1846.

Xenia, Ohio, drawn from a photograph taken in 1886,
after eclectic architecture has swamped the town.

ing joke about "a Queen Anne front and a Mary Ann back." Even the interiors of Pullman sleepers of special elegance had bosses, frettings and groovings alleged to be Queen Anne. But in spite of the difficulty in knowing what it meant, the term retained prestige. Well after 1900 Perkins of Portland, the frenetic promoter created by funnyman Ellis Parker Butler, was saying that he hoped to make his real estate development near Chicago "a refined and aristocratic suburb . . . high-toned and exclusive, with Queen Anne villas, and no fences." [33]

This "anarchy of amateur fancies" [34] (as G. M. Trevelyan describes the parallel architectural spasms in England) mingled with the fantasies on themes stated by Ruskin and Baron Haussmann to make new streets in affluent American neighborhoods exhilarating or dizzying, depending on the point of view. It must not be assumed that the fashionableness of such extravagances prevented dissent at the time. Howells deplored the newer part of Fifth Avenue as "a delirium of lines and colors." [35] Clarence Cook denounced in 1880 "architects [who] cannot design a house or a church but they must carve every stone . . . break up every straight line . . . plow every edge into moldings . . . refuse to give us a square foot of wall to rest the tired eye." [36] Montgomery Schuyler, a wittier critic of the day, said that the new houses in the neighborhood of Fifth Avenue and Sixty-Seventh Street required "the intervention of an architectural police. They are cases of disorderly conduct done in brick and brownstone," and that the Queen Anne movement had taken on "rather the character of an explosion than of an evolution." [37] He doubtless had in mind the way candlesnuffer towers from medieval French castles were appearing on the corners of multi-verandaed wooden dwellings with stained glass in the windows lighting their wide stair landings and wooden curtains of rod-and-spool work setting the entrance hall pointlessly apart from the front parlor.

Eventually this exuberance went airborne into antics impossible to blame on any style in the eclectic range. The mansion that Booth Tarkington's Major Amberson built on Amberson Boulevard was definable only as "Faced with stone as far back as the dining-room windows . . . a house of arches and turrets and girdling stone porches [with] the first porte-cochère seen in that town . . . a central 'front hall' with a great black walnut staircase, and open to a green glass skylight called 'the dome,' three stories above. . . . 'Sixty thousand dollars for the woodwork *alone!* Yes sir, and hardwood floors all over. . . .' " [38] We all know that house or did until they tore it down—at great expense, for it was built like a powder magazine—to put a supermarket and parking lot on its three-acre site, or maybe an undertaker is exploiting the funereal elegancies of that black walnut.

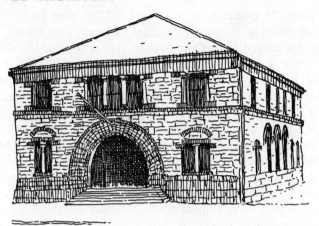

*Richardson's post office in North Easton, Massachusetts,
epitomizes the glumness of his basic style.*

This orgy of eclectic showiness began after the Civil War but went on
with hardly a pause, rather inexplicably, through the hard times of the
late 1870's. ". . . much building and little architecture" [39] was S. E.
Morrison's summary. A knowledgeable lady guide in Charleston, South
Carolina, once explained to me that the one good thing about Charleston's poverty after Appomattox was that it had spared her the gingerbread horrors built in more affluent cities. A major exception to it all
was the work of Henry Hobson Richardson, Louisiana-born, Harvard-bred
descendant of Joseph Priestley, the freethinking English scientist exile.
He combined prestige as an architects' architect with widely influential
economic success. But even this gratifying case takes careful qualification.

Paris-trained in fashionable eclectic idioms and flatteringly urged to
make his career in France, Richardson came home in his late twenties
and within a few years was turning out both dwellings and public buildings of marked originality and power. His basis was the round-arched,
squat-columned, masonry-exalting Romanesque. Professionals revere his
sense of meaningful proportion in handling and ornamenting heavy
masses of stone. Something about his work also pleased lay clients not
only around Boston, his headquarters for most of his career, but also in
the nothing-is-too-good-for-our-town cities of the Old Northwest. Experts naming his best work are likely to include the Marshall Field
Building in Chicago; the Cincinnati Chamber of Commerce; the jail-
cum-courthouse in Pittsburgh. His full set of public buildings—community hall, library, post office and station in North Easton, Massachusetts

—was a commission from the Ames family, much of whose wealth came from a shovel factory there. His series of railroad stations for the Boston and Albany heavily influenced design of that kind of building for the next generation.

He sometimes used brick, as in Sever Hall at Harvard, or shingle sheathing in a manner that critics have much admired. But his great love was stone, which was both strength and weakness. His middle-period buildings look as if they should be somewhere in the bleak Hebrides with waves breaking at their bases; for all the skillful vigor of their decorative

The Cincinnati Chamber of Commerce Building was widely considered one of H. H. Richardson's masterpieces.

touches and the drama of their irregular masses, they are depressing to look at day in and day out. The style was admirable for prisons, banks, maybe libraries; less so for other assignments that he undertook, such as lecture halls and private houses. Schuyler said of an early Richardson house in Chicago that, noble as it was as an edifice, "considered as a dwelling . . . [it] ceases to be defensible, except, indeed, in a military sense." [40] For though his interior planning was often able, Richardson's emphasis of masonry by use of deep, low openings neglected the human need of light and air—in a day when neither electric lighting nor forced ventilation was yet generally available to correct his foibles.

Sometimes his stone-mindedness led to walls not of dressed granite or sandstone but of naturally water-rounded cobblestones which, even in his severe handling, gave an effect as of peanut candy for giants. In this medium, imitators built some really hideous structures, such as the Grove Park Inn near Asheville, North Carolina. It was little better when applied only to the exposed chimneys or veranda columns of otherwise tolerable houses. That, from the point of view of the nation's cultural welfare, was the other drawback to Richardson—he had imitators, many and ill advised. In his last few years he had begun to reach out for a protomodern treatment of windows and surfaces, particularly in office buildings, but the parasites had not lifted their eyes to match. The Carnegie Library here, the post office there, the high school on the right side of the tracks, the lugubrious, stone-heavy, low-arched railroad stations all along the Seaboard and Western often still survive as misbegotten tokens of how fashionable clichés derived from his middle period became. Suzanne La Follette thought that "Richardson's solid and frowning Romanesque . . . symbolized the sinister power of the entrenched monopolists" [41] of his time. It must at least be said that anyway all the pseudo-Richardsonian work has been a morbid and unnecessary drain on the American psyche. Toward the end of a wet, chilly winter day the only appropriate things to issue from those cavernous portals would be suicides' funerals.

So it may have been as well that Richardson was an architectural dead end except so far as he showed that an American architect could think for himself. The promising factors in American building after the mid-1800's came from engineers and technologists, some well before the Civil War. For instance, the builder's shift to the balloon frame —an innovation springing from the gradual development of cheap machine production of nails. When cut and shaped by hand, nails were expensive, and most American buildings depended for structural strength on either solidly laid-up walls of stone or brick—the thicker the stronger,

as in Richardson's civilian fortifications—or on framing of heavy timbers tied together by dovetail or mortise and tenon that had to fit with
excruciating accuracy. Neither method used much metal. Both called for
much time and high skill. When nails got down to a few cents a pound in
the 1840's, however, a Yankee, Augustine Taylor, settled in Chicago—
from its birth a source of architectural innovations—showed that sound
structure could be achieved with multiple sticks of skinny lumber properly
spaced and braced and fastened together by liberal use of nails. The
first demonstration of the theory, a wooden church, was supposed to fall
down but refused to. It even survived being dismantled and rebuilt
on two successive new sites, showing how well it was engineered—
and how restless early Chicago was. For the last 100 years that is the
way most American dwellings have been built.

The term *balloon* was unkindly meant as implying fragility, but such
construction is actually extremely strong. *Birdcage* would have better
fitted this cubical framework of many perpendiculars, necessary horizontals and diagonal braces enabling two-by-fours to do what required oak
timbers 10 inches square in section in the traditional barn. Weather is kept
out by sheathing or stucco over lath and plaster and any insulation that the
builder's fancy chooses. In some ways this combination of many-element
structure and non-weight-bearing wall reverted to the old half-timber tradition and anticipated the steel-frame skyscraper. There were esthetic
hazards. The technique encouraged the cubical box with garret and front
porch so wearingly familiar in small towns and on farms after 1890, say,
and worse still, those flat-roofed box tenements with a flimsy gallery
marking each story, usually painted dirty gray-blue, in the industrial suburbs of Chicago and New England. But the good part was that the balloon
frame facilitated the flexible, often eccentric interior layouts that made so
many Renaissance and Queen Anne houses eminently habitable. As critic
John Maass has pointed out, the "historicizing flummery . . . covered a
very sound body . . . planned from the inside out." [42]

While iron nails were thus showing what their new availability could
do, the same metal was learning to take over structural functions once reserved for wood. In the 1830's Pennsylvania's ironmasters finally learned
how to use anthracite coal instead of charcoal for smelting, and national
production of iron rose smartly. Some of the consequences were
frivolous, such as the fashion for floral-patterned strips of ironwork
on verandas and porticoes. We think of this as a Creole thing in Savannah
and New Orleans; actually such Southern ironwork was mostly prefabri-
cated in the North for shipment to Dixie and widely used in the Northeast, too. Presently iron had a sort of fashion boom as material for
curlicued white-painted seats on cemetery plots, for gates and balconies

and fountains, for the statuary—iron dogs, deer, and lions as well as half-naked nymphs—that ornamented the lawn of the General Grant house. In serious uses the esthetic effect was better and the importance to architecture greater when around 1850 James Bogardus, inventor of ingenious things like gas meters and sugar grinders, began casting iron into solid columns and lintels to frame buildings with. There he had a balloon-birdcage building only with the structural members all metal. Presently he was suggesting that New York City's imitation of London's Crystal Palace Exhibition of 1851 be housed in an iron-framed, glass-lighted sort of circus tent with a sheet-iron roof hung on cables, the frame to be dismantled afterward and sold for building purposes. The practicality of that was never tried. But his iron-frame warehouses —one of the first still stands in Lower Manhattan—were such a success that soon hundreds of similar structures for office as well as storage use were going up from Boston to New Orleans and from St. Louis to Baltimore.

Builders usually wanted the columns cast to look pseudoclassically Tuscan or Corinthian and the horizontal elements to be elegant with Renaissance detail—the esthetic model being the many-windowed Italian palace. Supplementary sheathing might be brownstone or marble. But for all the archaism here were significant beginnings. Not only was the skeleton all metal, but the windows gradually tended to expand to fill the whole space between columns, a move toward the mostly-glass wall. The necessity for frequent painting to prevent rust was the minor shortcoming. The major one was a lamentable tendency of cast iron to weaken under great heat and let buildings collapse in major fires, as Chicago and Boston found to their cost in the 1870's. Substitution of steel for iron later in the century took care of that. Add the elevator—as New York City's iron-front Haughwout Building, talk of the town, did in 1857—and nothing was lacking to make up something like a proto-skyscraper.

The passenger elevator was offspring of the hoists used by the mining industry to bring up the iron ore and the coal to smelt it. The notion took on practicality when Vermont-born Elisha Graves Otis, more safety-minded than most men of his day, bossing a construction job in Yonkers, New York, worked out an automatic stop to go into action when the cable of a hoist broke or the winch failed. The first elevators worked by steam, then by hydraulic power that was smoother and allowed faster hoisting. One of the most talked of things in that new Philadelphia City Hall was the luxury of four elevators, one in each corner of the lofty building. By 1880 the Dakota apartment house overlooking Central Park had elevators large and powerful enough to hoist the carriage six or seven floors to load Mr. and Mrs. Tenant, then lower them and it to the courtyard, where the horses were put to. The Dakota was only the grandest of a number of apartment houses sprung up after the Civil War to elaborate in America the French notion of several family establishments sharing a common building. The notion took getting used to in the American mind partly because, being French, it was probably immoral; partly because multi-family dwellings were associated with Irish or Negro squalor in noisome slums made up of houses that had seen better days. But it was pretty well accepted by the late 1880's, when the protagonists of Howells' *A Hazard of New Fortunes* wondered at the number of such buildings in New York City and at the implausible names carved on their elegant façades. The Stuyvesant, Manhattan's very first French flats, was the property of a genuine Stuyvesant. But what lay behind the Wagram, the Esmeralda, the Jacinth? To this day the answer to such questions lies shrouded in the mysteries of the real estate mind. The problem makes the 1880's sound so modern.

The Civil War, the Sanitary Commission, the Centennial Exposition are bound to keep recurring in these contexts. Thus one of the most attention-catching exhibits at the Centennial consisted of twenty-nine table-size, anecdotal sculpture groups in plaster by one John Rogers. The attending public already knew most of them. Exemplars of them stood in parlors all over the country, typically on a special stand in the light of the bay window between the long, dust-catching draperies. A good half of them showed scenes from the Civil War, then only eleven years past. Indeed it was the war that had set Rogers on his way to a nationwide recognition comparable in scope to that of Norman Rockwell in our time. He had first come to extensive notice when his "Checker Players"—a bit of hayseed-flavored genre in three dimensions notable for carefully literal detail and straightforward folksiness—was shown at the Sanitary Commission's Cosmopolitan Bazaar in Chicago. A previous group, "The Slave Auction," had mightily pleased the abolitionists a few years earlier; indeed somebody called it "Uncle Tom's Cabin in Plaster." Now Rogers was to become, as Vrest Orton, a collector of Rogers groups has pointed out, "the only man in the long history of [sculpture] . . . able to place a piece in the average home," [43] a feat that brought him a well-earned prosperity.

Of straight Yankee stock—his ancestor namesake had been a president of Harvard; his mother was a Derby from Salem—he was prevented by eye trouble from practicing the engineering for which he had trained. But his clever hands enabled him to do well as a boss mechanic and took him into clay modeling as a hobby. Presently he went to

Rome for a few months' study under an English professional sculptor. Presumably it was his eyes that kept him out of Union uniform—a bit of luck for the Union, for while he would probably have been a plucky enough young officer, his contributions to home-front morale were important. Most of his wartime output showed soldiering. There were straightforward illustrations: "The Sharpshooters," "The Picket Guard" of dashing Zouaves. There were some acknowledgments of hazard: "Wounded to the Rear," "The Wounded Scout" being ministered to by a Negro slave who is about to be bitten by a copperhead (symbol!). But the run of them were laid behind the lines: "Mail Day," the soldier writing home; "The Camp Fire or Making Friends with the Cook," in such high detail that even the bubbles in the soup in the kettle are there; "The Returned Volunteer, or, How the Fort Was Taken," the young veteran telling the blacksmith and his cronies all about it.

Most sales were made through a mail-order catalogue. As public liking was further buoyed up by Rogers' early civilian subjects—"The Farmer's Home," "The Village Schoolmaster" and so on—he became a small industry with twenty-five helper craftsmen in his shop in New York City. In the next thirty years some 100,000 groups showing some eighty subjects were sold for from $5 to $50, depending on size and elaborateness. There were also appropriate tables and pedestals at reasonable prices. Newspapers would mention the debut of a new group as if it were a work by an eminent writer. A few child subjects—a little girl playing hide-and-seek; a little boy (the model is said to have been young Henry L. Stimson) enjoying the game—were life size. But most were in the 18 to 24 inch range, sometimes, as in "The Fugitive's Story" (Garrison, Whittier and Beecher, all highly recognizable portraits, listening to a runaway slave with a baby), involving four or five figures. As the war grew remote, Rogers turned almost wholly to folksiness, the titles helpfully incised on the base: "Coming to the Parson"; "The Favorite Scholar" (the young schoolmaster mightily smitten by the pretty girl student); "Going for the Cows" (including farm boys, a Morgan horse and a dog frantically digging for a woodchuck); "Weighing the Baby" on the country store's scales.

A few portrayed actors in their best-known roles—Booth as Othello, Jefferson as Bob Acres—or set up idealized scenes from Shakespeare or Boucicault's plays, or Irving or Longfellow. Wholesome young folks making their own fun staged posed tableaux representing well-known Rogers groups, maybe "The Tap on the Window" with the local banker's daughter as the charming girl coyly reacting to a suitor embodied in the town's risingest young lawyer. The theatrical touch belongs here. In one aspect the groups are ingratiatingly stagy illustrations of the homey

America of self-respecting farm and small-town "setting" rooms that Rogers' contemporaries had been reared in and were now getting self-consciously nostalgic about. The appeal was very much the same as that of Denman Thompson's perennial play *The Old Homestead,* a character actor's staging of what he seemed to remember things had been like in Swanzey, New Hampshire, the heart of the covered-bridge country, in his young manhood.

Lloyd Morris has credited Rogers with rather more than the traffic

One of John Rogers' most popular statuary groups
as represented in the catalogue from which thousands
of his works were ordered by customers.

may bear in calling him "a daring innovator . . . [who] applied a forthright realism to recording ordinary, everyday American life . . . a faithful transcript of the manners . . . amusements, interests, costumes and furnishings of the day . . . with sentiment, often with humor, sometimes with pathos. . . . In . . . 'The Foundling' and 'The Charity Patient' he vigorously indicted social injustice. . . ." [44] Viewed as sculpture, too, some of the groups are by no means ineffective, limberly molded and preserving conviction extremely well in view of the reduced scale. But the special values are as nonplastic as the literary allusion in the one of "Why Don't You Speak for Yourself, John?" The soundness of detail, the engagingness of these one-third-size forebears of ours make the American studying them in 1968 feel as if he had just attended—and enjoyed—a taffy pull at the Little Women's house. No wonder that, after a term of neglect, the Rogers groups became collectors' items of high dollar value about the same time as Currier & Ives prints —to which, in all candor, they are vastly superior both as works of art and as emotional record.

Lithographed pictures had been upgraded in the 1860's by the development of the chromolithograph, which used a separate stone for each color, anticipating modern color reproductions of paintings. Its great man was Louis Prang of Boston, a German self-exile learning wood engraving and lithography in America and then bringing this new process in from Germany in 1864. It was an improvement on the crude hand tinting of the Currier & Ives school. "All our chromos," said Prang's catalogue in 1876, "are fac-similes of oil or water-color pictures by the best artists in most cases equal to the originals." [45] But by the standards of today's color reproduction (still imperfect, of course), it distorted color schemes and in any case usually imposed the hand of the copying lithographer between the artist's and the beholder, transmitting only the general composition and structural detail of the subject with a rough stab at the colors. Artists of high repute, such as Albert Bierstadt and Eastman Johnson, drew doubtless welcome revenues from Prang chromos of a few of their canvases. Winslow Homer did Adirondack scenes for Prang that, maybe because Homer was an old lithographer himself, are, considering the drawbacks of the medium, startlingly good. Catharine Beecher, still exuding advice at the age of sixty-nine, said that to hang five or six chromos of the quality of Bierstadt's "Sunset in the Yosemite" ($12 each) would ornament a house better than building on it a skinny, jigsawed side porch costing twice as much. But most of Prang's artists were mediocre or worse, and in any case a chromo of a fine picture was like the unmistakable opening of the *Unfinished Symphony* played on a barrel organ.

Far wider impact came from the cheaper (50 cents to $3, say) and far cruder chromos produced to decorate the American wall with garish fancy mottoes, sticky family scenes, impossibly pneumatic little girls and darling little boys, doggies, kitties and flowers and birdies, and travelogue scenery often of California. The mere titles indicate the tone: "Maiden's Prayer," "After the Storm," "The Captive Child," "The Love Token," "Little Prudy." Such visual confectioneries were heavily promoted among the premiums that women's magazines gave to amateur subscription seekers turning in ten or twenty new names, which implied wide distribution. What the Connecticut Yankee, the well-paid mechanic foreman, said he most missed at King Arthur's court was "chromos . . . It made me homesick to look around over this proud and gaudy but heartless barrenness and remember that in our house in East Hartford, all unpretending as it was, you couldn't go into a room but you would find an insurance chromo, or at least a three-color God-Bless-Our-Home over the door; and in the parlor we had nine."

The insurance chromo signified that advertisers had quickly exploited this color-rich new process to make their appeals more striking. The label on the patent-medicine bottle and the display card on the drugstore wall showing the patient "Before" and "After," the large historic depiction of "Custer's Last Stand" advertising beer, and the comic railroad restaurant scene advertising The Great Atlantic and Pacific Tea Company blazed with color of a poignancy also attracting those selling sewing thread, tobacco, farm wagons, cheap railroad fares to the West and the chewing gum that had come in by the 1870's. The theater and the circus took it up even more flamboyantly. In the previous generation management bringing out a melodrama could only print and post up elaborate handbills of pretty solid type prolixly describing the action. Now one-sheets, three-sheets and even larger bills posted up all over town could show in glaring color and graphic action the thrilling moment when the lightning express bore down on the heroine lashed to the track and the grand ball scene from which she eloped with the villain through the French doors upstage center. The lithographed promise of the gaudy clothes shown on the minstrels in the cakewalk number greatly supplemented the customary parade through town on the morning of the performance. Soon the drummer driving his hired livery-stable horse and buggy in the country around the county seat got the impression that all that held together the roadside barns and wagon sheds was the great lithographed twenty-four-sheets of beautiful bareback riders mingled with roaring lions and polka-dotted clowns pasted up on their weather-boarded sides to make sure nobody missed the great news that the show would electrify Springville on July 29.

Of the theatrical "paper," particularly it must be said that no more deplorable art ever infested a culture. The colors were at the same time harsh and sickly, the drawing slickly awkward, the composition not even banal. The complaint is pointless, true, for the aim was to sell tickets, not to educate the eye. It is nevertheless easy to understand why, when E. L. Godkin, editor of the *Nation* and then the New York *Evening Post,* wanted to express his disapproval of the most garish and least mellow aspects of the Gilded Age, he called it "a chromo-civilization." [46]

The list of American painters represented in the art exhibit of the Philadelphia Centennial takes up three pages of type. Among the names of

A three-sheet lithographed poster of the 1890's.

those so honored who were alive and active at the time, only a few are now familiar to anybody but the specialists who, in the last decade or two, have ransacked American painting for artists to revive—and profit by. Here are Thomas Moran, Eastman Johnson, Albert Bierstadt, Louis C. Tiffany, John La Farge—and Winslow Homer, represented by his early "Snap the Whip," showing barefoot country schoolboys working off their energies at recess. The two other indubitably important painters of the day, Thomas Eakins and Albert Pinkham Ryder, both already well into their strongest work, Eakins born in Philadelphia and working there, were omitted. How fitting in a chromo civilization!

Americans had long been given to the picturesque notion that whatever talent a youngster might show, it could never be really fulfilled without training at the European fountainheads of art. Rome, London, Antwerp, Düsseldorf, Paris—over the years the focus changed, but the eastward yearning did not, nor yet the cultural cringe that went with it. (The thing was not exclusively American—Britons, Scandinavians, Germans also flocked first to Rome and then to Paris for art's sake.) The tradition had met marked American exceptions, beginning with the tactless case of John Singleton Copley. But had he never lived, Winslow Homer would have sufficed. "By contrast with his contemporaries, who were looking more and more to France for leadership," says Lloyd Goodrich, "[Homer] spoke in accents strongly original and strongly American. . . . If any artist of modern times can be called self-made, it is he . . . his art was a long step in the direction that America had to follow to reach artistic maturity—by growth from within more than influence from without." [47]

Whatever power created Homer might almost be accused, in fact, of deliberately flouting that image of the artist popularized in the 1840's by the sugared-over pictures in Henri Murger's *Scènes de la Vie de Bohème* and emulated by succeeding generations throughout the Western world. Early hackwork should have spoiled the youthful Homer's talent but did not. Buoyantly it survived an apprenticeship in a Boston lithographing establishment and then some ten years of journalistic drawing for the new method of wood engraving that pictures-and-text magazines were exploiting just before the Civil War. He was twenty-seven years old before

Young Winslow Homer draws for Harper's Weekly *the you-splash-me goings-on at Newport just before the Civil War.*

he ever tried painting. He never married; except for hints of a blighted conventional engagement, nothing about his love life is known. To the distress of acquaintances aware of what artists should look like, his only striking feature was a sweeping red mustache left over from his days as an artist-war correspondent—and in those days everybody had at least a mustache. He had the air of "a successful stockbroker . . . black cutaway coat, faultless linen . . . symmetrical necktie, stiff derby hat." [48] He practically never talked art, even with fellow painters of stature, and the studio of his early days in New York City was not, as the canon required, cavernous and awash with costumed lay figures, exotic weapons, imposingly carved armchairs, rich hangings, draped easels, but only a smallish bare room with a good light.

Homer really did enjoy painting and the outdoor life that went with doing so in the Adirondacks, on the Maine coast and in the semitropics. But he often professed to paint primarily for eating money and in his later years "thought a lot about money. His letters were full of it. . . . From what he said, art was a business. . . . There was no humbug in him about art being its own reward; he believed that pictures were made to be sold. . . . [Yet] he never painted merely to sell, but primarily to please himself. . . . And he painted only as many [pictures] as he felt like, even when his work was most in demand." [49] He founded no school; he had no pupils and allowed only children to watch him at work. He fits into no pseudo-evolutionary, lecture-platform scheme of the history of Western art. Not that he was adrift from his time. He showed traces of the early Pre-Raphaelites; probably found stimulus at a crucial stage in his one trip to Paris, where he doubtless saw something of what the French, particularly Manet, were up to in the late 1860's; probably assimilated most fruitfully into his own bent the Japanese prints that were in such high repute with artists after the 1850's. But on the whole he went his own way without overt, diversionary enthusiasms.

His paintings, most with an anecdotal tinge, some not, whether of light-drenched schoolrooms or women at the seaside or cornfields in the fall or men hunting in the big woods or codfishers in lonely dories or the Atlantic Ocean in awesome rage—which sometimes took him close to abstractionism—or the clear glories of shape and color in his watercolors of the West Indies and Florida, were mostly good, some stunning. Late in his life but in plenty of time to spoil him, he was renowned and bemedaled, but he never played lion. Really, by sentimental standards his life included only two artistlike touches: In his latter decades he was much of a recluse in a small shack overlooking the sea-battered coast of Maine, and once he had the hang of brush and pigment, he painted rousingly well.

His independence of the fashions of his day brings Robert Frost to mind. More broadly, however, particularly in his trust in the spontaneous rightness of his own grasp, he was, as Albert Ten Eyck Gardner has noted, a touch like another loner Yankee, Thoreau. "The life that I have chosen [in Maine]," he wrote to a brother in 1895, "gives me my full hours of enjoyment for the balance of my life. The Sun will not rise, or set, without my notice and thanks." [50] The words have Thoreau's rueful but arrogant irony right enough. Homer lacked Thoreau's cracked-wheat crankishness, however; the merely cantankerous was his style as he got "sot" in his ways.

Gardner suggests that the relative ease with which he found buyers came partly of his subjects, that the factual soundness of his portrayals of hunting, fishing, ships and so on meant as much to the cultivated but hearty Boston and New York City men who bought them as did the painter's esthetic integrity. That does not mean, of course, that the buyers were insensitive to the latter. Certainly that was untrue of Thomas B. Clarke, the dealer-connoisseur whose acquisitions of Homer's works after the late 1880's did most to consolidate his position. Clarke was also a great admirer of the works of George Inness, who painted in frenzies of inspiration landscapes that he hoped would express a Swedenborgian sense of God; and even took his keen flair for quality among American artists so far as to buy a few of the strange canvases of Albert Pinkham Ryder, who personally and in his art—except in being a loner and founding no school —was the antithesis of Homer.

A strange eye ailment kept Ryder indoors by day in his 10- by 12-foot studio on Washington Square. There he incessantly painted and repainted and recast and rethought and revised and enriched his pictures, usually smaller than a book page like this one, of moonlit sea visions and curious figures doing things that were still ambiguous after the title explained that the subject was "Jonah" or "The Flying Dutchman" or "Toilers of the Sea." They brought him little money, but he needed very little, and he retained such a sense of identification with his works that long after making a sale, he would sometimes take a picture back from the owner for a few improving touches. Often dim but never vague, small but not at all cramped, as well integrated as a metope from the Parthenon, prolongedly and repeatedly revised into a most deceptively simple pattern of intense emotion, a good Ryder shows him to have been the most original American of his time, more so than Walt Whitman, a sort of country cousin William Blake.

One is tempted to ascribe the integrity of his work to lack of dilution with Old World values, for Ryder had had only a couple of years of formal art training in New York City and never visited Europe. That notion does not survive the simultaneous appearance of Thomas Eakins. After such art study as Philadelphia afforded during the Civil War, this promising youngster dutifully went abroad, studied sculpture as well as painting in well-thought-of ateliers in Paris and traveled in Spain, then the focus of a reviving interest in Velázquez and Goya. Repatriating himself in the early 1870's, he took to studying anatomy, not in the usual art-academy context but among the cadavers in the Jefferson Medical College, while he set about practicing what the Old World had taught him. He did numerous portraits, for which rather too often he was not paid because the sitters disliked being shown to look like that. Their difficulty was not distortion, as it might have been today, but the reverse—a disconcerting accuracy of detail and a dry sense of character as finely selective as a chemist's re-agents. The privilege of being the subject of great portraiture was not adequately valued partly, of course, because few yet saw Eakins as what he was, the greatest American portraitist since Stuart.

It took his whole lifetime and some years beyond for him to be ac-knowledged as, in Lewis Mumford's still-proper estimate of forty years ago, "one of the two or three American artists to rank with the best paint-ers of his period in Europe, in solid achievement, if not in the power of innovation." [51] Maybe responding particularly to the Frenchness of his training, the Larousse Encyclopedia of Modern Art makes him "perhaps the greatest American painter of the century." [52] As a sideline he liked to paint the stripped-down athletes rowing single or double sculls on the Schuylkill. Each of the resulting canvases shows a lean, glistening, super-alive world of three familiar, yet strangely vivified dimensions that makes you jump when you come upon it around the corner of an eclectic exhi-bition. The layman needs no expert guide to tell him how superb this is technically or to relate it to this or that trend in Eakins' youth as a student. The superbness was in Eakins, even though Europe had given him a kit of tools that he used with all the skill they deserved, whereas Ryder and Homer, Yankees both, pretty much shaped their own as the job taught them what was wanted.

As if to emphasize the potentialities of American painting betokened by those three men, the New World also contributed to the Old certain substantial talents whose ethnic sense was weaker or their rearing more cosmopolitan. It remains baffling but true that Whistler's West Pointer engineer father entered him as one of the corps of cadets in the sincere belief that he might make a soldier. The cultivated and quintessentially Philadelphia-Quality spinster Mary Cassatt went to study art in Paris, and became an honored disciple of Degas and a remarkable painter, prin-cipally of mothers with small children as if in lieu of actual motherhood for herself. But neither her nor Whistler's significance was any more American than T. S. Eliot's. All such people were merely problems for

Henry James to pick at without resolving. Such feedback of capable persons preferring the Mother Countries for one or another reason had been going on since the late 1700's. There was Lindley Murray, Quaker merchant of Pennsylvania, who made a fortune in trade during the Revolution, settled down on it in England, and presently wrote an English grammar that was standard for some generations. There was Benjamin Thompson, ambitious young Tory refugee from Massachusetts, making himself so useful to the Elector of Bavaria that he was created Count Rumford (of the Holy Roman Empire) and presently showing the British, already lagging in such matters, the advantages of the drip coffeepot and the kitchen range.

John La Farge exemplified a subtler, or anyway less forthright, kind of expatriation. Through his French *émigré* father he had well-placed French connections. Youthful studies in France gave him a basic leaning toward sententious murals and the necessarily conventionalized values of stained glass. As a craftsman innovator in the revival of glass already in progress in his day, he sought to get beyond mere imitation of medieval work in a fashion requiring respect, though the colored windows that he devised are often insipid enough. Actually Ryder, quite inadvertently, did better than La Farge in getting the concentrated impact of a fine glass-window design into a small compass—only the medium happened to be thick paint on canvas. La Farge's inability to handle reality directly is most notable, however, in the paintings that he did while traveling with Henry Adams in the South Pacific. Most of them look like sketches for murals of abstractions like Pagan Joy or Primeval Innocence, and the colors are thinly charming, as in spring in France. Apparently he had irreversibly trained himself to be—and for all his choosing to live and work in America, remained—an artsy-craftsy cosmopolite almost as rootless as an air plant. Albert Ten Eyck Gardner sums him up as "a writer and craftsman, an art critic and a decorator . . . his work, accomplished as some of it may be, always retains the tentative mark of the dilettante . . . his paintings never rise to the professional degree of mastery that is evident in all of Homer's paintings." [53]

Two buildings at the great Centennial Exposition of 1876 were devoted exclusively to selling popcorn to the festive-minded crowd. Soda-water stands scattered through the main building were of white or colored marble with silver mountings. An amazing new device, the telephone, just patented by Alexander Graham Bell, a young Scottish teacher of phonetics, was on display. There was a colossal steam engine of the type invented by George Henry Corliss, maker of power plants for textile mills. Its twin vertical cylinders, as imposing as the pylons of an Egyptian gate-

The Corliss engine, mechanical marvel
of the Philadelphia Centennial.

way, ran all the massive industrial machinery on display in the whole building. People went home talking about it as obsessively as Henry Adams did about the dynamos at international exhibitions of twenty years later. Steam was already two generations in use, however. Significance seekers saw other omens in the presence on the grounds of an impressive building housing only women and their concerns.

It covered almost 30,000 square feet, nearly football-field size. That was a hard-times year. The drag of the panic of 1873 was still heavy on the economy, as the railroad strikes of 1877 would show. Working conditions for female operatives were no longer those of Lowell's great days; indeed in most mill towns they never had been. A novel of Elizabeth Stuart Phelps' about a textile community up the Merrimack c. 1870 described what one heard on the streets on Saturday night as "fragments of murderous Irish threats; of shattered bits of sweet Scotch songs; of half-broken English brogue; of German guttural thick with lager; only now and then the shrewd, dry Yankee twang." [54] Yet with either brazenness or innocence—probably the latter, for 100 years ago management had little sense of public relations—the textile industry had taken much space in this Women's Building to show shiny new machinery tended by neat and primly efficient women. On the esthetic side were paintings by women and sculptures in marble by women. But the creative triumph was a high-relief bust of a beautiful girl done in butter by Mrs. C. Brooks of Arkansas, kept on ice to preserve its subtleties during the blazing Philadelphia summer. Toward the end of the doings Mrs. Brooks visited the building and gave a demonstration with a "shapeless, golden mass" of what was doubtless the best butter. Using only "paddles, cedar sticks, broom straws and camels' hair [brushes]," she transformed it into "a relief bust of another sleeping beauty" in "an hour and a quarter." [55]

It also caused remark that the 60-horsepower steam engine running all the machinery in the building was in charge of Miss Emma Allison of Grimsby, Iowa, a girl "highly educated . . . in theoretical as well as practical engineering [who] offered an example . . . to the engineers of the male sex in the neatness of her dress and . . . the cleanliness exhibited in both engine and engine-room." [56] This sporadic raid of housewifely standards into the realm of coal scoops and oily waste should have reminded men visiting the Women's Building that only two years earlier Woman had stormed another of Man's presumed refuges—the saloon. Indeed the earthshaking tramp of Midwestern ladies joining the Women's Crusade of 1873-74 against Rum was probably one of the reasons why Woman had a building all her own at Philadelphia. Far more clearly than butter sculpture or loom tending that movement had shown that the lesson of the Sanitary Commission was not lost, that Woman would go on forging ahead as a militant and highly opinionated fraction of the population arrogating to herself a large hand in things like centennials—and morally entitled to show men how to abate public nuisances like saloons and how to keep engine rooms clean too. Men viewing that engine room with alarm could not, however, go have a drink and think it over. Thanks to Woman's imperative wiles, sale of alcoholic beverages was barred from the grounds.

The Women's Crusade had had several disturbing aspects. For instance, it had brought into American social agitation the device of civil

The Women's Building at the Philadelphia Centennial.

disobedience-nonresistance. The first crusaders included a strong minority of women Quakers, which may account for these tactics. But the core of their method was to exploit the notion, by then well established, that womanhood had a special moral superiority, a right to say unhand-me-sir under any and all circumstances, and that for some reason of sentimental magic the tears and prayers of a mother had special power.

Actually the movement had had premonitory twitches before the Civil War.* In sporadic instances Midwestern housewives understandably overwrought because bartenders persisted in selling drink to their alcoholic

CENTENNIAL ROLLING-CHAIR.

In spite of summer heat this gentlemanly sightseer at the Philadelphia Centennial of 1876 wears a smotheringly full rig-out.

husbands took the law into their own hands and sometimes alone, sometimes backed by a few like-minded lady neighbors, stormed and smashed up the offending premises. (Late in the century Carry A. Nation made a psychotic career of the same approach.) But the great crusade of the mid-1870's was serenely nonviolent. Its godfather was Dr. Dio Lewis, the eminent apostle of Temperance, righteous diet and calisthenics, one of whose repertory of lectures was "The Influence of Christian Women in the Temperance Cause." Much of it consisted of the story of his dear old mother in New York State, cursed with an alcoholic spouse, who had summoned the godliest women of the local church and led them, praying and

* From here on this section is a compression of Chapter X of my *The Life and Times of the Demon Rum.*

singing hymns, into the local saloon to bid the startled owner in God's name to close down, which, after a doomed struggle against their tireless spiritual ministrations, he consented to do, Glory hallelujah! and on into a rhapsody on what women got together with God's blessing could accomplish.

As Lewis lectured his way through the land late in 1873, he got warm hearings for his mother's prowess. Finally in Fredonia, New York, in the far western tip of the state, his plea to the women in his audience to follow the late Mrs. Lewis' example brought 100 of them to their feet with their husbands pledging support, and the next morning, led by a judge's wife and a minister's wife, "revered matrons as well as young ladies," they poured into the local hotel barroom. Denying that he ever drank himself, the terrified principal partner promised to stop selling drink if the ladies would make the druggist across the street do the same. By nightfall they had brought the druggist to his knees. Lewis went to spread the flames to Jamestown, the county seat; there 50 women were soon on the prowl and bar after bar was closing. In southwestern Ohio, where his bookings next took him, they kindled such a blaze that it spread spontaneously. In Hillsboro, seat of a county founded by high-chinned Virginians accustomed to setting influential local examples, the lady leader was the wife of a judge and daughter of an early governor of the state. "Let us proceed to our sacred mission trusting in the God of Jacob!" were the words with which she mustered her storming party of lady Methodists, Baptists, Presbyterians and Quakers—Episcopalians and Catholics were usually less zealous about the war on Rum—and led them against saloonkeepers and druggists.

The tone was sweetly imperious. The first saloonkeeper to resist was told: "We have come not to threaten, not even to upbraid; but in the name of our Heavenly Friend and Saviour and in His spirit to forgive and to commend you to His pardon if you will abandon a business . . . so damaging to our hearts and homes. . . . Let us pray!" When a recusant locked the barroom door to prevent a sort of kneel-in, the second most august matron in town knelt on the top doorstep and prayed at him through the keyhole until he knuckled under. In December slush and snow the ladies knelt around saloon doors in an immobile picketing that forced the customers to be prayed at on their way in, which often spoiled the flavor of the drinks inside. "Passers-by uncovered their heads," wrote an eyewitness for the religious press. ". . . not a man who saw them kneeling there but felt that if he were entering heaven's gate and if one of these women were to approach, he would . . . let her enter first." As the weather worsened, the ladies' menfolk provided a roofed, three-sided shelter with a small stove in which they could in comparative comfort beleaguer John Barleycorn. When a Rum seller surrendered and went out of business, the ladies saw to it that he got fair value at the sale of his fixtures, glassware and so on, often bid on things themselves, in fact, to be long preserved as mementos of when mother was a heroine. The silver-mounted gavel with which Francis Willard kept conventions of the Women's Christian Temperance Union in order is said to have been a bung starter thus acquired from a Hillsboro bar.

Eastward into Pennsylvania, northwestward into Illinois and Michigan, scores of sizable towns now saw what the newspapers were calling the

*This picture of a Women's Crusade raid on a saloon
in New Vienna, Ohio, was drawn from a tintype
photograph taken on the spot.*

Women's Crusade. Only in the large cities—Cincinnati, Cleveland, Pitts-burgh—did the authorities do much to discourage it, in spite of the dictum of an Indiana judge that "Mob law enforced by women is no better than mob law enforced by men." For in smaller places the authorities were well aware that the embattled ladies were egged on or at least not frowned on by the powers behind the scenes in the community. Their menfolk were usually the local bankers, ministers, merchants, large property own-ers. The saloonkeeper recognizing among the crowd of bonnet-and-shawled self-righteousness in his barroom the wife of the banker who held his mortgage, the wife of the lumber and coal dealer to whom he owed $653, the mother of the county attorney and the daughter of his family doctor was unlikely too roughly to resist their holy bullying. Only a small minority of the assailed threw water on the ladies or put pepper on the hot stove to make them sneeze. Besides, there was the American taboo on shoving a lady, which the crusaders exploited with the aplomb of skilled blackmailers. They had always known in their bones that they were the morally superior sex, endowed by their Creator with privileges to match. See how these brutal, hulking barkeeps quailed before pure womanhood while the male lords of creation merely stood on the other side of the street admiring their women for doing what men could never have done without provoking violence and the law—even had they had the spunk and imagination to try.

Within months the blaze died out, of course, and the saloons—or successors—were back in business. But the lasting implications were not lost on some. The New York *Tribune* had predicted in 1869 that the next war in America would be between "women and whiskey, and . . . rum will flow freely in the gutter." The Women's Christian Temperance Union, one of two organizations largely responsible for eventual prohibition, was a direct and almost immediate outgrowth of the Women's Crusade. Women's success in closing down local bars, said the Fredonia paper, would be "a great educator for women. By the time that band has tramped a week . . . not many women will say: 'I have all the rights I want. Don't ask me to vote.' " Like the early women's righters, many women felt instinctively that the two causes were complementary. Through the years to World War I suffrage and prohibition would be Woman's twin principal concerns, inseparable in emotional charge, though some of her leaders tried to keep them apart in tactics and strategy. But even more important is the wider point. In the 1870's many Western nations had feminists; some had Temperance movements. In no other than America, however, is it conceivable that either husbands or police would have let local matrons, however high-minded, however well connected, defy decorum and public order as these did. The legalistic and economic details would still be long ironing out. But it was, after all, an American versifier, William Ross Wallace, amateur poet and friend of Edgar Allan Poe, who wrote that "The hand that rocks the cradle is the hand that rules the world."

One reason for the delay before the hand that rocked the cradle could drop a ballot in the box was the insistence of certain exuberant leaders of womens' rights on associating votes-for-women with tawdry or ridiculous public figures and extraneous or hampering side issues. Part of the carryover of women's militancy had consisted of an American Equal Rights Association, including not only able women but certain abolitionists demanding both votes-for-women and votes-for-Negroes, whose exact political status since emancipation was yet to be settled. That was unquestionably a good cause, but it was also likely to hamper its sister cause and vice versa, as was soon painfully evident. Better tactical judgment was shown by the separate New England Women's Suffrage Association led by Mrs. Livermore (the executive genius of the western Sanitary Commission), Julia Ward Howe, Lucy Stone, *et al.*, who carefully confined themselves to the single issue.

As if to show just what not to do, Elizabeth Cady Stanton and Susan B. Anthony of the Equal Rights organization, battling for equal rights laws in Kansas, saw fit to accept the financial and oratorical help of the increasingly strange and most conspicuous George Francis Train. In the 1850's this young Yankee had been a dashing figure in shipping and railroads and a highly articulate leader in a vague movement of the time known as Young America, which sought to mingle the Manifest Destiny kind of amateur imperialism with the economics of free trade. Always ebullient, making speeches whenever he encountered a platform, stump or empty hall, he developed a sort of manic versatility after the Civil War. He espoused the Irish nationalist Fenian movement that sought to use America as a base for ejecting the English from Ireland. He plunged into the revolutionary Paris of the Communards and got himself expelled from France. He went around the world in eighty days, which gave Jules Verne the suggestion for his famous story. That was the ally whom the ladies displayed to the voters of Kansas. Votes-for-women and votes-for-Negroes alike met disastrous defeat in the referendum. Mrs. Stanton and Miss Anthony persisted in valuing Train, however—and doubtless also the money that he gave the cause—and went touring all over the North with him, they demanding women's rights from the same platforms that he used to recommend himself for President. Then they collaborated with him on a propaganda newspaper combining their schemes for women with his about paper money and keeping European goods out of American markets.

In a protest to Miss Anthony, William Lloyd Garrison, who understandably disliked Train's eagerness to sneer at "niggers" to please Irish audiences, deplored such linking of equal rights with a "crack-brained harlequin and lunatic . . . ranting egotist and low blackguard." It was also beginning to look as if votes-for-Negroes would come to pass on its own, as it soon did, at least nominally, and leave votes-for-women uncompromised. The result was a several-stage split that went twenty years unhealed. A majority of equal righters, led by Mmes. Livermore, Howe and Stone, abetted by Wendell Phillips, the Reverend Henry Ward Beecher, the Reverend Colonel T. W. Higginson and others with unimpeachable abolitionist pasts, expanded the New England Women's Suffrage Association into a nationwide American Women's Suffrage Association. A sizable, militant minority, led by Mrs. Stanton, Miss Anthony and Theodore Tilton, a winsomely handsome young religious journalist and disciple of Beecher's, formed the National Women's Suffrage Association.

Votes-for-women was bound to arouse jeers and horrified opposition among the stodgy-minded. After all, even though the end of the Civil War saw some 300 women doctors in practice, the hand of tradition was still so heavy in America that the Pennsylvania State Medical Society forbade its members to consult with lady colleagues. But the NWSA ladies saw to it that their admirable cause had ten times as much trouble as necessary. In addition to the persisting association with Train, Mrs. Stanton kept shouting ever louder for relaxation of divorce laws—a highly sensitive topic that the staider leaders of the American organization had wisely let roll to the outfield. And then, to make sure that the public would invariably identify the suffrage cause with rabid attacks on social stability, the National Association warmly welcomed the support of a striking blue-eyed eccentric, Victoria Claflin Woodhull, who did them more damage than a dozen Trains could have. That was a pity, for on its own merits the case for suffrage was close to undebatable.

The compromising capers of La Woodhull manifested several significant aspects of the Gilded Age, just as those of James J. Walker meant a good deal about the Jazz Age. Victoria and her sister Tennessee, also attractive in a more pussycat fashion, came of a family of pathologically turbulent poor whites drifting around the Middle West as the girls' activities in spiritualism, faith healing, cancer quackery, blackmail and (very probably) prostitution met various vicissitudes. In 1868 the whole Claflin clan—parents, siblings and parasites—came to New York City where father secured for Tennessee (sometimes spelled Tennie C.) an audience with old Cornelius Vanderbilt. The commodore's senility was complicated by hypochondria preyed on by any quack able convincingly to promise help. Whatever therapy Tennie applied, the old gentleman continued so grateful that he set the two sisters up as the world's first lady stockbrokers, Woodhull and Claflin, supplying not only capital but also the speculative tips of which, as king of the New York Central, he had many.

The ensuing gossip, private and in the press, roused Victoria's latent genius for publicity. Among the family parasites were two half-cultivated personages, Colonel James Blood, a handsome and more or less informal successor to Victoria's husband (who still hung around, however), and Stephen P. Andrews, a vastly bearded Yankee who had once been a crusader for shorthand in the schools, then a principal in a free love cult with headquarters at the expensive end of Broadway in the 1850's. At this Progressive Union Club unlimited passional attraction was encouraged among its several hundred members of both sexes on the theory that emotion alone, without regard to law, should govern erotic relations. Another of its leaders was Albert Brisbane, foremost exponent of Fourier's good life colonies and soon to be father (by the duly espoused Mrs. Brisbane) of Arthur Brisbane, chief henchman of the Hearst newspaper empire. Ten years later, when Andrews swam into Victoria's ken, he was promulgating a windy, semimystical anarchy called pantarchy. Contact with him and his multiple ideas set her writing deep-thinking pieces for the newspapers—or anyway submitting them under her name. In one of them she announced her candidacy for the Presidency in the next election, thus joining Train and the Mormon Prophet Joseph Smith in making the ultimate American gesture. Soon a convention of the Equal Rights Party nominated her. Frederick Douglass, the escaped slave best representing Negro ability among abolitionists, had the poor judgment to let himself be put on her ticket for Vice President. At the same time Tennie C. was accepting the honorary colonelcy of a battalion of Negro militia.

All that caused more talk and aligned the Claflins with the cause of the Negro, as well as of women's rights. Now they were to espouse another kind of freedom. Andrews and Blood had discovered common belief in free love, a doctrine probably already familiar to the Claflins. They were also familiar with the grimier aspects of the semireligious cult of spiritualism founded in the 1850's by the skilled fakings of the Fox sisters of Rochester, New York. And Spiritualists often stirred free love in among the great truths that the spirits of the departed taught from the Other Side where, as the Bible averred, there was neither marriage nor giving in marriage. (In any case the practice of something like that was not new to the sisters.) For Victoria the notion may have been not only carnally but also intellectually welcome. For she was going intellectual. She claimed to have had the tutelage of the spirit of Demosthenes in guiding her career. Now under that of her living henchmen, Andrews and Blood, she gleamed with forward-looking soul and mind, which enabled her to nestle up to the National Women's Suffrage Association. Once there, her good looks, conquering charm and never-flinching, pure-brass effrontery soon had her speaking at NWSA conventions; testifying for women's rights in Washington with a single rose at her throat; and electrifying her lady colleagues in public lectures coming out flatfooted for free love at its freest, shouting back to hecklers that certainly she practiced what she preached and would take a different bedfellow every night if she wished. While the rival AWSA moaned in despair, Mrs. Stanton and some of her strongest-minded allies pluckily if ill-advisedly refused to censure Victoria; indeed Mrs. Stanton went as far as to say that she would welcome to the feminist movement even out-and-out-prostitutes who saw the light and cared to volunteer. Victoria might have resented that but did not.

This was heady stuff for all, the Claflin girls included. They sought other exhilaration from publishing a racily radical paper, *Woodhull and Claflin's Weekly,* front page full of the advertising of Wall Street houses and some savings banks, editorial content probably written mostly by Andrews and Blood. It assailed prostitution, the politicians and policemen who preyed on it and the men who patronized it; it preached women's rights in clottily forthright language; denounced Wall Street manipulators; hinted darkly at the paper's having highly damaging data about kings of finance and other eminent men. In all those fields the sisters doubtless knew something of what they were talking about. They knew nothing of the international labor movement then gaining militancy, but they espoused it anyway. Their *Weekly* was first to publish Marx's *Communist Manifesto* in America. When the New York City units of the International Workingmen's Association, the American wing of Marxism, formally mourned the leaders of the Paris Commune shot late in 1872, the banner of Section 12 was carried by Victoria and Tennie with Andrews and Theodore Tilton right behind. Section 12 of the association had become a Claflin fief preaching suffrage, free love and Andrews' private brand of anarchy, as well as labor's rights. Expelled for such antics, it kept on as a splinter party.

Tilton, though married to a cozy young wife, frequently helped Victoria practice free love, or so she said, probably truly. His infatuation also led him to father a glowing biography of her relying with no misgivings on her own account of her past. His punishment was disproportionate to his folly. Late in 1872 the *Weekly* ran a story about the alleged deflowering of two young girls by a minor Wall Streeter, an admirer of Tennie's, with details that led Anthony Comstock, already America's protector against vice, to have the sisters arrested under a new federal statute against obscene matter in the mails. (Comstock's notoriety would reach its height in 1913, when he feuded with a New York City art dealer about displaying a prizewinning French painting of a pretty, naked girl entitled "September Morning." All he accomplished was to make sale of reproductions of it extremely profitable. Indeed, as Margaret Leech and Heywood Broun said in their biography of him (1927), much as reporters and jokesmiths built him up in the intervening forty years, "The scope of his censorship has grown vastly in the telling . . . his actual interference with books, plays and paintings of sincere intent was slight." [57]) The sensation about the lustful broker was dwarfed, however, by the feature of the issue—an account of Henry Ward Beecher's adulteries with the wife of his disciple, Tilton.

The only thing lacking was a mushroom-shaped cloud. Beecher had long been the most conspicuous parson in America—a self-confessed hero of both abolition and the Union cause; a champion of liberalism in religious and secular matters, including ardent support of careers for women in medicine and the pulpit. His sisters, Catharine and Harriet, had both been publicly deploring Victoria and her ideas; Harriet had condescendingly satirized her as Audacia Dangyereyes, a character in a novel serialized in the *Christian Union*. But his half sister, Isabella Beecher Hooker, had been among her militant feminist supporters. Though several exhaustive books have been written about both Victoria and the Beecher-Tilton scandal, just why she detonated her bomb is lost in the convolutions of her jangled psyche. Beecher denied it all. Tilton sued for alienation of affections. After sixteen weeks of the most widely publicized trial America had ever known, during which all the principals were shown to have acted like emotional imbeciles, the jury disagreed, and the leaders of Beecher's church in Brooklyn were strangely willing to take that as exoneration. He went on with his unctuously successful career. Tilton eventually left the country, burned out. Soon Victoria and Tennie visited England, where both married Englishmen of wealthy, upper-middle-class prestige and spent the rest of their long lives doing good according to the respectable ideas with which change of air and cushioned security had imbued them.

It was unfortunate that so many well-meaning and personally decent persons—which does not include the principals in the famous trial—mistook Victoria's self-aggrandizing antics for courage or acumen or inspiration or imagination. Lasting damage to the cause of suffrage resulted—directly by identifying free love with it in the public mind, indirectly by warping the judgment of some of its ablest leaders. In 1869 Wyoming Territory had enfranchised women, but not until the 1890's, after the American and National factions had kissed and made up, did any state do so. Defeat of a suffrage-granting bill in the Michigan legislature was directly attributed to the Beecher-Tilton affair. And in 1876, the next year, the management of the highly significant Women's Building at the Centennial allowed suffrage only an obscure corner for its propaganda.

The other excuse for thus summarizing the Claflins' goings-on—some of the gamiest are omitted as impertinent—is that during their liveliest years, which happened to fall in the post-Civil War decade, their nose for society's soft spots led them to dabble in so many of the morbidities of the day. At that time the problem of what to do with the Negroes, free or lately freed, was being guiltily swept back under the rug. A new mordancy—partly native, reflecting the embittering strains of industrialization; partly imported as immigrants brought in New World habits of thinking and feeling about class relations—was showing itself among labor. The idyllic values implicit in Pestalozzi, phrenology and Fourier's and Robert Owen's genteel notions of the Good Life were giving way to the crudities of spiritualism and the cultural degenerations of anarchism and free love. And for the first time Wall Street plungers had seized the nation's imagination, replacing the forty-niner in the daydreams of cupidity.

The astute banker in William Dean Howells' *A Traveler from Altruria* explained in 1893—the year of a financial panic and of the invention of that trust-midwife's forceps the "holding company"—that the politician-publicist-statesman had once been the nation's cynosure, that formerly such literary figures as Longfellow could compete even with triumphant generals for public notice, but that since the Civil War "In any average assembly of Americans, the great millionaire would take the eyes of all from the greatest statesman, the greatest poet, or the greatest soldier." [58] It was true enough; only the shift had begun before the Civil War. *The almighty dollar,* the catchphrase so popular among supercilious European visitors, was coined by Washington Irving in 1854 to designate the "great object of universal devotion throughout our land." [59] And a generation earlier the majesty of massed dollars, no matter how amassed, seemed unduly to exhilarate the popular mind when Stephen Girard, that close-fisted, astringent character out of Balzac, died the richest man in America. Trained as a sharp-dealing officer in merchantmen out of Bordeaux, he had settled in Philadelphia, where overseas trade and shipping, banking and timberlands all answered well to his manipulations. Presently John Jacob Astor, the immigrant German who dominated the American peltry trade for forty years, caused awed talk by selling out for $20,000,000— which he reinvested largely in New York real estate, thereby creating an even greater fortune for his heirs. In the 1850's Northeastern steamboats and railroads became infested by Daniel Drew, a horse trader and cattle drover who had first driven beef on the hoof over the Appalachians to seaboard markets. His adaptation of horse-trading standards to Wall Street gave the nation its classic—and widely suggestive—examples of how to outsmart everybody but yourself. In the end he did that, too, but meanwhile, the brilliant success of his methods of dollar breeding had elicited many chuckles of grudging admiration and put ideas in many clever heads.

Neither Girard nor Astor nor Drew would have set well with the toploftical merchants, mostly Tories, who had been the richest men in the Colonies, nor yet with such stately nabobs of Federalist days as Elias

Haskett Derby of Salem or Thomas Handasyd Perkins of Boston. These new plutocrats had nasty manners and their business methods would have made even John Hancock blush. Yet there was one thing to be said for them. They did not, like their immediate successors in plutocracy, bedizen their women and bedazzle the public with ostentatious luxury. Their most lavish gestures had some social value. Before dying broke, Drew had given sizable sums to institutions of learning—narrowly Methodist to glorify the faith of his boyhood, but for all that affording the rising generation a certain amount of education. Most of Girard's estate went to set up a great school for orphan white boys, notorious in our time through integrationists' attacks on the founder's terms of admission, but again, over the last century it supported and taught many needy youngsters. The $400,000 with which Astor's will set up the Astor Library has been the principal nucleus of the great New York Public Library, probably the most fertile center of self-education in the country. It was the haughty ostentation of his heirs that gave rise to proverbs about Mrs. Astor's plush horse and the absurdities of Ward McAllister's list of the exclusively eligible Four Hundred.

Gaudiness among millionaires may be said to have burst the chrysalis in 1853, when Cornelius Vanderbilt, already great in shipping though not yet in railroads, wishing to visit Europe in a manner befitting his new importance, had built for the trip the first great American steam yacht, *North Star,* a side-wheeler nearly as large as the transatlantic liners of the period —270 feet long, 3,500 tons—costing half a million dollars. Her main saloon was all satin and rosewood, her staterooms all lace curtains and silken hangings, her steam-heating system camouflaged by bronze trellis-work.* The owner showed no architectural megalomania, however, living and dying—and receiving the ministrations of Tennie C. Claflin—in his merely very roomy brick house on a side street off Washington Square. The millionaire's mansion that was the talk of the town in the 1850's, the prototype of so much extravagant house pride to come, was on Fifth Avenue—the marble palace of A. T. Stewart, once a youngster from Ulster who had preferred a merchant's career in America to training for the Pres-

---

* *Cleopatra's Barge,* built for George Crowninshield of the eminent family of that name in Salem, Massachusetts, fifty years earlier, was a large private yacht fitted out pretty luxuriously in terms of her time, as is shown by her owner's quarters preserved at the Peabody Museum in Salem. But her owner was a widely experienced master mariner, as well as merchant entitled to a busman's holiday on a costly toy that he could well afford, whereas Vanderbilt's only claim to being an old salt was his start in life sailing a sloop fetching vegetables from the truck gardens of Staten Island to the New York City market. The other previously conspicuous American yacht was the *America,* designed by George Steers, which won the famous America's Cup in 1851 by challenging the English Royal Yacht Squadron and outsailing all its entries.

byterian ministry at home and was now in the middle of making a fortune of some $50,000,000.

Those were the boom times set off by the buoyant effects of fresh gold from California. After a severe slump in the late 1850's the next boom times came from fresh blood shed in Virginia. To the inflation consequent on financing a war partly with fiat paper money as well as bonds—in 1864 the greenback paper currency touched bottom at 34 cents gold—was added that of the vigorous new oil industry. Even honest war contractors made money in wads. The dishonest reaped a triple harvest by various fraudulent dodges that the public summed up in the term *shoddy,* the designation of the sleazy reprocessed stuff often substituted for genuine woolen cloth in the manufacture of uniforms. Fifth Avenue on a mild afternoon in late March, 1865, before Lee had yet surrendered, was, noted George Templeton Strong, "absolutely thronged with costly new equipages . . . a broad torrent of vehicular gentility, wherein profits of shoddy and of petroleum were largely represented. Not a few of the ladies in the most sumptuous turnouts, with liveried servants, looked as if they might have been cooks or chambermaids a few years ago." [60] The oil boom had already produced a cluster of lively legends about "Coal Oil* Johnny" Steele, the oilfields teamster who had unexpectedly inherited a rich oil-property and blew his new wealth in spectacular spendings; for instance, the story went, when a hotel clerk in Pittsburgh refused him a room because of his grimy teamster's rig-out, he bought the place and evicted everybody but himself. And in quite another economic idiom, John D. Rockefeller was already building in Cleveland an oil refinery with the soon-to-be-momentous name Standard attached to it.

By then Vanderbilt was deep in railroads. So were Drew and Jay Gould, the cold, black-bearded little store clerk from upstate, and flabby-fat, fair-haired and randy James Fisk, who had learned the rudiments of slick dealing as a tin peddler. The war of manipulations, bribery of legislators and stock watering between Vanderbilt and the latter three in cahoots for control of the Erie Railroad in the late 1860's was Wall Street's greatest up to then. Presently Gould and Fisk topped it for effrontery and excitement with an almost successful effort to corner gold that smirched even the White House. It was eloquent of the Gilded Age—in this aspect so clearly the right setting for the Claflins—that Fisk's showiness made him a popular hero. For $850,000 he bought the new Grand Opera House, New York City's most sumptuous theater, not only for stage spectacles but

* *Coal oil* was first applied to lamp fuel distilled from oil shale in Canada and imported into the United States; it originated in previous distillation of such fuel from coal. From the first *kerosene* was used for lamp fuel derived from petroleum. The term *coal oil* persisted in many areas, however, the two fuels being practically identical in use.

also to house in its upper stories the Erie's offices and himself in a sultanic suite of rooms. As colonel of a militia regiment he himself sported gorgeous uniforms and paid for flashy ones for the rank and file. In an equally gaudy seagoing uniform he often personally presided over the sailings of the Long Island steamboats that he controlled. He was openhanded with beggars and hangers-on, enjoyed driving in an open carriage with an expensive trollop by his side, and when a rival for the esteem of a particularly juicy one shot and killed him, the appropriate segments of the public mourned him as a sort of tallowy Robin Hood. "Jim Fisk he was called, and his money he gave," ran the song they sang:

> To the outcast, the poor and forlorn,
> We all knew he loved both women and wine,
> But his heart it was right, I am sure,
> Though he lived like a prince in his palace so fine,
> Yet he never went back on the poor.

There were other forms of conspicuous consumption. Jay Cooke, the Philadelphia banker who managed the wartime bond issues, bought a whole island in Lake Erie on which he built a grandiloquent castellated summer palace wherein he entertained relays of low-salaried preachers chosen from among the Methodists, Episcopalians, Baptists, Presbyterians and Lutherans as deserving objects of two weeks each in cool luxury. In spite of all the merit thus presumably acquired, overcommitment to the Northern Pacific scheme to build a transcontinental line to Puget Sound sent Jay Cooke and Company crashing in 1873 and set off the worst financial panic of the century.

Note the manipulative origin of most of these eye-catching fortunes. Previous American plutocrats had been typically merchants buying cheap and selling dear but also getting goods to where they were wanted and extending credit to expedite the process; or manufacturing innovators like Lowell and his associates, installing more economical ways of producing goods; or land speculators like Peter Smith and his reform-minded son Gerrit, obtaining unexploited tracts by hook or crook, often the latter, but at least doing all they could to encourage buyers, which put more of the country into productive use. Many combined all three as occasion served. The Yankees so deep in getting railroads built west of the mountains—John Murray Forbes and the Ames brothers, midwives of the Michigan Central, the Chicago, Burlington and Quincy, the Union Pacific and so on—were channeling capital into building up the country albeit to their own profit. Eli Whitney, S. F. B. Morse, Elias Howe and

Isaac Singer (the two chief developers of practical sewing machines) derived from important inventions financial rewards ranging from very comfortable to lavish. Even Vanderbilt made a real, if ramshackle, contribution with his shipping lines to California. But he had had nothing to do with building the railroads with which he and such as Fisk and Gould played their titanic games of beggar-my-neighbor. The lines already existed when the manipulators moved in. Their prolonged bout of pull-devil-pull-baker left the Erie a financial cripple, and later promoters so diligently imitated their cynical device of stock watering—a term said to derive from the cattle drover's trick of causing steers to drink heavily just before the purchaser weighed them—that our railroad economy still shows the ill effects.

What enabled them to stack and second-deal the cards so nimbly was the rise of the private corporation—a legal entity akin to the chartered companies of the early Colonies but assuming new forms in the 1840's to meet the new financial needs of industry, railroads particularly. Chartered by a state to build and operate a canal, say, or make and sell plows, the corporation came to be regarded by the courts much as if it were a person. It can contract debts, sue debtors, buy and sell. Investors may buy pieces of it—like promoters taking pieces of a prizefighter—called shares that afford proportionate dividends from profits and proportionate voting power in electing a board of directors responsible for management. The president or principal manager is usually chosen from among the directors. Shareholders usually give him successive proxies entitling him to vote their shares at directors' meetings. In larger corporations shares may be sold at prices reflecting investors' estimates of the company's prospects—hence the appearance of such securities on the open market of stock exchanges. An advantage for the investor is that whereas in partnerships each partner, however small his interest, is liable for the debts of the whole, the corporation has limited liability, confining creditors to levying only on the assets of the corporation as such, not those of the shareholders as individuals. Another is that shares traded on exchanges can be readily turned into cash at widely acknowledged, impersonally arrived at values. To arrange easy contact between offer to sell and offer to buy and vice versa, stock speculators soon had such devices as short selling, put-and-take options and specialist dealers.

One advantage for the organizers of corporations is that by taking subscriptions for stock from many minor investors, a large accumulation of otherwise unavailable cash can be got together. Thus the corporation supplemented the growing banking system in taking over the economic function of the lottery. As individuals the directors of a corporation, who usually held large blocks of its stock, long had the further advantage of inside knowledge of its affairs, cueing them to buy and sell shares for speculative gain in advance of stock-market fluctuations. As corporations grew in size, capital involved and number of shares—the latter often ballooned by stock watering—all but the largest stockholders virtually gave up efforts to influence company policy. Only their willingness to buy or eagerness to sell remained the index of public judgment on that score. Their motive for buying was fined down to nothing beyond direct evaluation of the prospect of either sustained dividends or a rise in market value per share, whereas shares in early turnpikes, canals and railroads had often been sold to local merchants and farmers on the less direct ground that in addition to the possibility of dividends, the scheme would build up the neighborhood and make new customers and new markets available to wide-awake persons.

This legal corporate person is a highly impersonal form of economic enterprise. The shares, while not losing their original function of raising, maintaining and increasing needed capital, became impersonal counters in a game called stock exchange played worldwide—for the same things developed simultaneously in the Old World—for keeps and lending itself to clever rascality as readily as horse racing. The disapproving speak of Wall Street gambling. The Wall Street speculator can make a good case for himself as highly necessary lubricator of the capital market—and then falls into the telltale habit of calling consistently high-value stocks blue chips. As the game grew conspicuous after the Civil War, the villager's oblique respect for the smart horse trader, the tinhorn sport's admiration of the frozen-faced professional gambler, and the street loafer's worship of the gaudiness of yachts, marble-and-gilt houses and fancy women all fused to give the manipulative millionaire of Wall Street precedence over other breeds of hero. Edgar Fawcett, the semi-expatriate novelist who put a lightweight finger on many things ailing his native country, thought it was the wild fluctuations of the price of gold in greenbacks in the 1860's and 1870's that did the most emotional damage to the public: "Brokers' offices were crowded . . . the clerk invested his precious salary; the old man staked his slender annuity; the widow risked her all. . . ." [61] But the street boys' gossip in the New York City of 1866 in Horatio Alger, Jr.'s first book is all about the Erie shares that were also a glittering lure. Anyway, in the late 1870's Fawcett went on: "These calamitous days [of gold-speculation] are now past . . . but Wall Street still remains a prodigious fact . . . a constant intoxicating temptation to many of our best minds . . . the love for this sort of gaming grows with what it feeds on." [61]

Boston, Philadelphia and Chicago also had securities exchanges. San Francisco's, specializing in volatile mining shares, offered action dizzying enough for the gamest player. As the techniques of speculation grew more widely appreciated in the late 1800's, the amateur public also acquired the habit of singeing its wings in Chicago's commodity exchanges, buying and selling futures in wheat, barreled salt pork, corn and so on. But Wall Street stocks outshone all other fields. And that meant another concentration of the national attention on New York City. Fifty years earlier it had seemed natural for the Bank of the United States, fiscal focus of the nation, to be in Philadelphia. But with the Civil War, the crucial gold exchange, index of the fluctuations of Uncle Sam's prospects militarily and economically, settled significantly in Wall Street. And after the smashup of Philadelphia's Jay Cooke, there remained little doubt of the permanent hegemony of the lower tip of Manhattan Island as financial capital. The money changers were following the lead of the largest ocean liners and the most conspicuous actors. Wall Street joined the Bowery, Broadway and Fifth Avenue—and maybe Pennsylvania Avenue—as the only streets that practically everybody in the country had heard of.

The relative numbers of self-made men among the plutocrats of the Gilded Age were notable even for America. Earlier times had occasionally seen an able son improve on a heritage from a well-established father —Robert Morris and John Hancock, for instance; then Francis Cabot Lowell and Gerrit Smith. Among the far wider opportunities after the Civil War that would also be the story of John Pierpont Morgan and William H. Vanderbilt, but there were few other such instances. Henry Clay had coined *self-made man* to distinguish the less ruggedly reared men of the seaboard from the cowhide-booted, self-tutored Westerner reaching eminence in spite of a downright backwoods rearing. But by now, true to Howells' complaint, money, crude and powerful, was equivalent to eminence in that equation. Nor, except for Jay Cooke and a few others, were these dollar-breeding self-makers likely to come from over the mountains. Little places in New York State contributed a striking number: Gould, Drew, Rockefeller, Russell Sage, Philip Armour. So did the back parts of Pennsylvania: J. Edgar Thomson, organizer of the Pennsylvania Railroad, and Tom Scott, his ruthless, brilliant junior. John Wanamaker, risen from errand boy to creator of the modern department store, was a product of Philadelphia; so was Peter A. B. Widener, from butcher boy to traction king. Andrew Carnegie, Scottish-born, began to learn his way through life as bobbin boy in a textile mill. Not until the next generation did the self-made Westerners come East to weigh in with fortunes made in merchandising, meat, machinery, mining and the manipulation of the wheat and pork markets. And when they did, it was odds-on that, like Marshall Field, Armour, California's Big Four and the Bonanza Kings of the Comstock Lode, they had been born in the Northeastern states or the Old Country.

Jim Fisk might be the pattern hero of the cheap hedonist, but staid people's ideals of the self-made man were fulfilled by, say, Wanamaker—chronic Sunday School teacher, first paid secretary ever employed by a Young Men's Christian Association, model family man, developing his original economic schemes with prayer as well as business genius and a jeweler's eye for administrative detail. John D. Rockefeller was another such. That affinity between copybook virtues and self-made wealth became proverbial when, most timely in 1867, just as the Gilded Age hit its full stride, a Harvard-educated clergyman, Horatio Alger, Jr., published a book for boys, *Ragged Dick: or Street Life in New York*. Ragged indeed but staying honest in spite of a sordid environment, Dick eventually happens to be on hand to save from drowning the small son of a properly grateful rich man—and so to affluence. In the next thirty years Alger wrote that story or something very like it scores of times. *Jed the Poorhouse Boy* and *Luke Larkin's Luck* and *Struggling Upward* and the rest sold among them more than 200,000,000 copies. Most of the royalties went to the Newsboys' Lodging House in New York City, where the author, a man of sincere concern, if simple views, about vice and poverty, lived most of his life studying and sympathizing with the bootblack-newsboy-street hawker stratum of young America. When the plight of the Italian boy musicians brought to America to be kept in brutal peonage came to his attention, he showed real courage and enterprise not only writing *Phil, the Fiddler* to rouse public sympathy for the victims, but also stirring up the police, addressing mass meetings and otherwise agitating so ably that the annoyed *padrones,* the boys' slave masters who had bought them from their parents back in Italy for export and mass exploitation, came around one night to beat him up and had made a good start when accidentally frightened away.

Other agitations of the day eventually combined with Alger's to create the nation's first Society for the Prevention of Cruelty to Children in 1875 —a great thing for Phil the Fiddler, a fine monument for Alger and allies. Far more conspicuous, however, was the astonishing readership that put "the Alger hero" in the national waxworks. Horatio Alger Awards are now made annually to ten Americans considered outstanding cases of rising to eminence from lowly starts. These lamely written, episodic books valuable only for a perfunctory familiarity with the everyday detail of New York City, the usual setting, must have affected American attitudes as intimately, though maybe less massively, as the *McGuffey Readers* and *Webster's Speller.*

What they inculcated deserves a closer look. The success that they envisage is quite crass—straight-out silk-hatted wealth. And the process implied was more of a lottery than is usually understood by those using the Alger hero cliché. It ignored the Wanamaker-Rockefeller pattern of gradually creating a great enterprise from small beginnings by vigilance, acumen and imaginative organization. As the late Russel Crouse once pointed out, Alger's young hopefuls usually spend most of the book getting into and out of dangers and difficulties, often the result of gratuitous malice, but making small progress toward any meaningful career until—presto!—here is a burning house containing a plutocrat's baby daughter to be rescued—and papa's lavish gratitude does the rest. All that courage and virtue do for the Alger hero is to keep his nose clean so that when he sees a runaway horse bearing down on the bank president's wife, he will be an eligible subject for patronage. This prominent aleatory element smells more of Wall Street or a gold rush than of strive-and-succeed. However disillusioning, that does make the Alger hero a child of his time. After all, it was by rescuing a plutocrat from certain aspects of senility that the Claflin girls got their start. But it is highly significant of the basic set of American assumptions that in the form in which it became proverbial, the Alger story was erroneously thought to consist of strive-and-succeed.

Benjamin Franklin's proverbs and the striking cases of so many Singers and Carnegies had a great deal to do with that. Heavy reinforcement came when the same decade that started Alger scribbling for gain saw publication of Herbert Spencer's early and most momentous applications to society of the new theory of biological evolution. Duly wafting over to America, Spencerism heavily affected ebullient and at least semischolarly John Fiske of Harvard, who became a Spencerian missionary to the New World, and William Graham Sumner of Yale, the erudite former parson who was to be even more impressive than Fiske not only as preacher of Spencer's gospel but also as a principal founder of American sociology. The principles of free trade and progress by private profit were already as fashionable in American economic thought as in European. What Fiske and Sumner and their and Spencer's other American disciples now did with the notions of natural selection and survival of the fittest made strive-and-succeed sound like a moral duty incumbent on the individual, like the blood-creating marrow of civilization, and interference with laissez-faire competition in the business world like a crime against humanity.

This "social Darwinism," as it came to be called, was particularly welcome among captains of industry and their allies in legislatures because it never pointed out that the protective tariffs under which American industry flourished flagrantly flouted the theory of laissez-faire; and that these devout believers in the healthiness of survival-of-the-fittest competition were smothering it by forming trust after trust. But it could have made even less sense and still been valued among those likely to endow chairs of economics because it would still have made government regulation of private enterprise sound obscene and allowed self-made men to feel that their power and affluence marked them as important elements in and evidence of the cosmic process.

The Civil War also gave America its national game, or at least made it national. Baseball originated obscurely in the Northeastern states out of several bat-and-ball games—town ball, one old cat and so on—and attained recognizable shape in the late 1840's. Around New York City fashionable young men took it up and organized informal teams. Gradually it spread southward as far as Baltimore, westward to Buffalo; by 1860 it had somehow got to the notably inelegant cow town of Los Angeles. At first largely an amusement for the Quality, it gradually became equalitarian as the gentlemen players enlisted from lower social strata men of high athletic aptitude whose skills were useful, never mind their poor grammar. Quick thinking and accurate reflexes proved to be qualities not confined to any single social level.

So far, however, though there was a National Association of Baseball Players, a trend toward charging spectators admission, and some intercity competition, baseball was merely the hobby of a small segment of young men. The guns of Fort Sumter broke up even that modest beginning, for baseball players were the kind likeliest to enlist. Actually it was the best thing that could have happened to the game. This dispersion of baseball players into the Army spread the taste for it throughout the young manhood of the nation. Every large enough piece of flat ground near an encampment saw a baseball game with improvised equipment. There was always a cobbler in the outfit to sew a leather cover on a tight-wound ball of twine, and bats and bases were no problem at all. By the end of the war most returning soldiers had taken baseball in at the pores, and within a few years the same was true of all small boys.

Men's colleges took it up. In 1869 the first professional team, the Cincinnati Red Stockings, trouped the country taking on local clubs and showing off the new style of uniform that their name implied—knickerbockers and the short-sleeved blouse, vestiges of which cling to today's clubs. In 1876—fittingly the centenary year—a National League of eight big-city professional clubs was formed to coordinate schedules, to standardize rules—and to combat the bribery-betting complex of corruption already developing. And Yankee game though it was, it soon spread so widely in Dixie that in spite of lack of major-league clubs there until after World War II, Southern players with unlikely names—the standard was something like Cletie Flitch—were for generations the backbone of professional baseball.

In the earliest stages the game had archaic features. For years pitching was underhand, the number of innings ran into dozens, the batter had privileges that he now lacks, and the scores were high. But its snowballing popularity may have reflected its almost unique peculiarity—that though it maintains a high potential of excitement, since any minute practically anything can happen, baseball is remarkably unstrenuous. Half the time most of one team are sitting down while most of the other team are just standing out there, tensely waiting for an emergency to come their way— if it does. So gratifying a blend of outdoor sport with inaction was never again attained until the electric cart came along to spare golfers the trouble of walking. Much the same could be said of the Englishman's cricket, of course. Theoretically it, too, should have flourished in America. For a while it seemed likely to with intercity matches played not only in the Old World-minded Northeast but in the Middle West of the 1860's and 1870's. One of the most striking lyrics of the Sweet Singer of Michigan (Mrs. Julia A. Moore) describes what seems to have been a curiously hazardous match between the cricketers of Grand Rapids, Michigan, and those of Milwaukee:

> From Milwaukee their club did come,
>   With thoughts of skill at play,
> But beat they was and then went home—
>   Had nothing more to say.
> Grand Rapids club that cricket play,
>   Will soon be known afar,
> Much prouder do the members stand,
>   Like many a noble star. . . .
>
> . . . Mr. Follet is very brave,
>   A lighter player than the rest,
> He got struck severe at the fair ground
>   For which he took a rest.
> When Mr. Dennis does well play,
>   His courage is full great,
> And accidents to him occur,
>   But not much, though, of late.
>
> This ball play is a dangerous game,
>   Brave knights to play it though;
> These boys would be the nation's pride,
>   If they to war would go. . . .[62]

In the end, however, American cricket persisted only among nostalgic British immigrants. More vigorous team sports were arising as responsible doctors like Holmes joined cranks and German exiles in preaching the virtues of exercise. Rowing clubs appeared in imitation of those of the English universities, both in the oldest colleges and among hearty young businessmen. A loose, primitive form of soccer come down from Colonial times was sometimes played on college campuses where the authorities tolerated the accompanying noise, fistfights and loss of study time. In the 1860's this venerable game interbred with imported rugby, and by the time the Red Stockings were on their first tour, four rugby-minded colleges—Rutgers, Columbia, Princeton and Yale—had codified the rules on which the present American football grew. Both rowing and football are strenuous, and their acceptance in such high-prestige colleges probably went far toward breaking down the physical sluggishness of the Quality's young men. It took a curiously long time, however, for football to expand from the campus into the more turbulent world of the vacant lots, whereas the readiness with which baseball went pandemic may hint that it would soon have done so without the help of the Civil War camps.

That is, its moral aspects may have coincided with those of the developing Gilded Age. Few other team sports so openly assume that any player in his right mind will consistently take all possible unfair advantage and break any rule when there is a chance of impunity. The pitcher uses illegal and potentially lethal beanballs as tactical tools. A clever catcher shifts his mitt to make a ball look like a strike. He knows he is deceiving nobody, least of all the plate umpire, but the hoary old trick is permanently imbedded in the game like the runner's ever-present threat of spiking the baseman and the manager's fit of rage over a close but obviously correct call at the plate. The atmosphere of a baseball game accepts the stacking of all decks—pretty much the atmosphere of Wall Street c. 1870—and of that other American-grown diversion, poker, based on deadpanned deception. The pattern baseball player of all time, Ty Cobb, combined the split-second reflexes of "Gentleman Jim" Corbett with the snarling aggressiveness of a pit terrier. The most renowned of all baseball managers, John J. McGraw, was highly admired for his sulky ruthlessness. Given the necessary reflexes, Jay Gould would have been a weasel-fast shortstop famous for aggressive baserunning and John D. Rockefeller a manager as calmly and primly masterful as Connie Mack.

As baseball drew growing crowds and college football became an autumnal folk rite among the Quality, the joys of mass excitement in a huge spectator-sport crowd were no longer confined to the racecourse. Abler heads than mine must explain why cultures so different as those of Latin America and Japan proved so hospitable to baseball. At least it has been a much less brutalizing force than the professional pugilism that was simultaneously pervading the sporting world. Already in 1842 Philip Hone called prizefighting a "disgrace formerly confined to England . . . [now] one of the fashionable abominations of our loafer-ridden [New York City] . . . [with] tens of thousands of degraded amateurs of this noble science" sneaking away to attend bouts staged in Staten Island or Westchester to avoid city laws against them.[63] The rules were not to-day's but the London Prize Ring version that allowed certain wrestling holds and several punches now barred, let a round run till one man fell or was knocked or thrown down, and put no limit on the number of rounds. The bout ended only when one man's second literally threw up the sponge or he proved unable to come up to scratch—a mark in the middle of the ring—to square off to begin the new round.

The rugged young men who survived such ordeals did their share to give the Irish a bad name by being usually either Irish or of second-generation Irish stock. Of the three best known in the 1860's, "Yankee" Sullivan went to California after an active ring career in the Northeast and had to commit suicide to avoid being hanged by the San Francisco Vigilance Committee for various criminal capers. John C. Heenan, who learned to slug in California as the Benicia Boy, won fame in a notably savage drawn fight with Tom Sayers, champion of England, and for marrying Adah Isaacs Menken, the beautiful Gypsy Rose Lee of her day. John Morrissey, who had licked both Sullivan and Heenan in his time, made a small fortune following market tips from Commodore Vanderbilt and went on to serve two terms in the U.S. House of Representatives before becoming the gambling king of Saratoga Springs. (The commodore liked his protégés high-flavored—like the times.) Bearbaiting, popular in Colonial times, had disappeared; but cockfighting still attracted all strata, and the vicious English cults of rat-killing terriers and matched fighting dogs came across the water along with prizefighting. At the age of seventeen Frederick Van Wyck saw his first stag show in a livery stable on Eighth Street in Greenwich Village; it offered a dogfight, a cockfight, a rat-killing session, a butting match between two billygoats and a boxing match between two women naked except for trunks. In most large cities certain saloonkeepers specialized in arranging such festivals.

Even in the august field of formal music, even in staid New England, the ferments of the Gilded Age produced strange extravagances. The Civil War was still going on, Gettysburg was only three months past, when Boston dedicated in her new Music Hall the greatest pipe organ in the New World, one of the two or three largest anywhere. Its elaborate musical insides were the work of German experts who shipped them over for assembly; it was asserted with awe that the bore of the largest pipes was so great that a man could crawl into them. Its inaugural program ranged from the overture to *William Tell* to Bach's Toccata and Fugue in D Minor. The dedicatory ode, written by the wife of the editor of the *Atlantic Monthly* and recited by Boston's own Charlotte Cushman, the great expatriate American actress, went down well. But it was the look of the thing that most impressed, as well it might. Sixty feet high with towered, domed clusters of pipes soaring over an arched recess for the organist, the whole

The great organ of Boston's Music Hall.

thing resembled the façade of a church gone mad. Most of what was visible consisted of black walnut carved by New York City's Herter Brothers, German immigrant leaders in the new style of decoration, into a welter of masks, muscle-bound Atlantid figures, cherubs, trophies of musical instruments from violins to sleigh bells, busts of Bach and Beethoven, a statue of St. Cecilia clutching a lyre. As a slowly descending curtain revealed this grand example of the passion with which black walnut shook the Victorian craftsman, the audience rose "positively enraptured" with "a tumult of applause" [64] and, once the program concluded with the "Hallelujah Chorus" from *The Messiah,* stormed the stage for a closer look. A New York paper said despairingly that that organ case "has been minutely described, but not adequately; it never can be . . . it was like a vision." The correspondent of another confessed that "I hardly thought of its being real." [64] Insides and all, including a battery of brass trumpets kept polished though the audience never saw them, the whole grandiloquent contraption weighed more than 60 tons.

Between wise use of immigrant talent, largely German, and the work of Lowell Mason and other devoted music men, Boston then had a better right than New York City or Philadelphia to be called musical capital of the nation. Pride in that may have contributed to the seizure of musical megalomania manifested in Boston's Peace Jubilees of 1869 and 1872. The specific irritant producing the spasms, however, was Patrick Sarsfield Gilmore, Irish as his name. As a boy in County Westmeath he had idolized the bandmaster of a British regiment stationed there, learned the cornet and the rudiments of composition, and, when the regiment was sent to Canada, gone along. Soon crossing the border—as did a great many of New England's immigrant Irish from all walks of life—he had Gilmore's Band well known in Boston when the Civil War came. At the age of twenty-one he was off to war as bandmaster of the 24th Massachusetts; then presently in charge of all Union military bands in the Department of Louisiana and author of "When Johnny Comes Marching Home Again." His first spell of musical gigantism led to a monster concert in New Orleans at which an orchestra of 500 pieces accompanied a chorus of 5,000 adults and children. Returned to Boston after the war, he agitated for an appropriately large expression of the nation's thankfulness for peace—a project eventually translated into a music festival of such proportions that it hardly mattered that by the time it came to pass peace had been around for more than four years.

The wooden auditorium for the Peace Jubilee held 50,000 spectators confronted by a chorus of 10,000 men and women seated in a facing amphitheater. Between was an orchestra of 1,000 pieces with a bass drum eight feet in diameter. Leader of the first violins was Ole Bull, one of a dozen musical celebrities taking part, mostly Old Worldlings, of course, but that was to be expected. On opening day chorus and orchestra managed to stay pretty well together on *"Ein feste Burg ist unser Gott,"* the overture to *Tannhäuser* and the "Gloria" from Mozart's Twelfth Mass. Enthusiasm was to say the least of it unbounded when "The Star-Spangled Banner" was rendered by all hands augmented by a fresh military band, an extra drum corps and real cannon fire set off by electricity. It doesn't sound like Boston, but it must have sounded like many other things all at once. Presently the crowd was again ravished by the "Anvil Chorus" hammered out on 100 anvils in flawless rhythm by 100 volunteer firemen in black trousers, red shirts and white caps. The second day had

President Grant as guest of honor of a similar program. He was, as General Sherman told an aide, unable to tell "Yankee Doodle" from "Old Zip Coon," but he found the artillery well handled. The Reverend Edward Everett Hale, Dr. Oliver Wendell Holmes (who wrote an ode for opening day) and both Senators from Massachusetts were distributed through the proceedings. Lowell Mason was often on the platform. Whatever he thought of the music, it must have gratified him to see that huge chorus made up of the singing societies that his work had fostered and to reflect that forty years earlier, when he had put his shoulder to the wheel in Boston, not even press-gangs could have rounded up 1,000 fairly competent instrumentalists in the vicinity.

So fine a time was had by all that three years later Gilmore could persuade Boston to mount another such musical corroboree, a World's Peace Jubilee and International Music Festival vaguely celebrating the recent end of the Franco-Prussian War. After all, the pre-1873 good times were still spinning. This time he doubled everything: The chorus numbered 20,000 from 165 singing societies, mostly Yankee; the orchestra of 2,000 included 28 American bands, the British Grenadier Guards band, a quartet of cornet virtuosos sent by the new Emperor Wilhelm I of Germany, and most notably an orchestra imported by Johann Strauss, whose "The Blue Danube" and "Tales from the Vienna Woods" were then all the more charming for being new. Strauss was paid $100,000 to take part, particularly to lead the massed orchestras in "The Blue Danube." To do so, he stood on a high podium with deputy conductors posted among the 2,000 musicians to watch through opera glasses and relay his beat. A cannon shot was to signal his first downbeat. The cannon went off prematurely, and neither Strauss nor many others ever forgot the ensuing musical chaos. Even so Gilmore's second orgy attracted hundreds of thousands to its seventeen performances—more than twice the draw of the 1869 effort—and doubtless left a residue of benefit by giving many their first hint that music could surpass Sunday School hymns and secular "compositions made up of sugary successions of thirds and sixths." [65] It was a poor way to learn that, but for the susceptible better than none.

The eccentricities of the Gilded Age were stuffy, often stultifying, usually vulgar. But to concentrate on them, real as they were, is to distort. In the same year as Gilmore's gaudy jubilees George Templeton Strong, returning home from successive rehearsals of the New York Philharmonic and the Church Music Association, told his diary: "I've seldom heard so much great music in the course of one day. . . . It's pleasant to think how much better off in this respect [my sons] are than I was as a child . . . and how fully they appreciate their privileges." [66] In that same time the tireless German missionary of sober music Theodore

Thomas was recruiting competent orchestras and touring them far and wide between the seaboard and the Mississippi, taking the Old World's standards to places where only sixty years earlier Indians had been eating boiled dog. The music he brought was exotic, but the programs were calculated with loving cunning gradually to cajole those whose idea of a fine orchestral number was "The Battle of Prague" into holding still for Beethoven. His musicians were practically all German, but a nation so backward musically was lucky to have so many aliens up to Thomas' unrelenting standards. Charles Edward Russell, who knew Thomas in his later phase in Chicago and wrote of him with reverence, saw in him the principal cause of the establishment of the early great American symphony orchestras, in boisterous Chicago as well as in the elder Northeast, and of the existence in 1926, a generation after Thomas died, of "fifty-one grand orchestras giving regular and competent seasons . . . that but for his sowing and the produce thereof would have been impossible." [67]

Another achievement, also musical, was the Fisk University Singers, a small group of Negro students whose recital tours singing spirituals all over the United States and Britain raised the money that made a going concern of their new Alma Mater in Nashville, Tennessee. Almost overnight they added a new idiom to the world's music with "Swing Low, Sweet Chariot" and "Steal Away to Jesus." Soon the fancier Tom-shows—touring dramatizations of *Uncle Tom's Cabin* fast degenerating into slapstick and spectacle—interpolated spirituals sung by Negro choruses wearing theatrical rags. This gave a few Negroes their first taste of the professional stage. But no paid chorus doing what the stage manager thought indicated could sing like the devoted Fisk students just sitting there on a platform, opening their mouths—and penetrating the marrow and viscera of their audiences. Grave, conventionally dressed, devout, they were a fine antidote for the capering, grinning minstrels' travesty of the Negro. The large, staid audiences that they drew—Fisk being a project of the American Missionary Association—became aware, most of them for the first time, that Negroes could have dignity and that out of the whites' sticky hymns they had made the first music with a right to call itself American.

White Americans' religious music was also distinguishing itself at the same time—by getting even stickier. Organized evangelism was partly to blame. Among Yankees seeking their fortunes in the feverishly booming Chicago of the 1850's had been a lay religious zealot from Massachusetts, Dwight Lyman Moody, a retail shoe clerk. Immersing himself in Chicago's churchly stratum, he brilliantly organized a Sunday School of 1,000-odd eager souls and during the Civil War distinguished himself in the U.S. Christian Commission, which sought to do for soldiers in religious terms what the U.S. Sanitary Commission did in more mundane matters. After the war there was no question of any more shoe business. He went to work for the newly developing Young Men's Christian Association as chief religious officer and built in Chicago a great supradenominational tabernacle for mass saving of city folks' souls through eloquent exhortation and stirring music—an urbanization of the backwoods camp meeting. At a YMCA convention in 1870 he met a religiously musical Pennsylvanian of his own age, Ira D. Sankey, and recruited him to manage the musical department of these colossal gospel meetings.

Within a few years MoodyandSankey had fused into one name like GilbertandSullivan. They made evangelism into the elaborately organized industry now at its peak in the career of Billy Graham. Moody and a devoted staff skillfully handled advance publicity for a season of gospel warfare in a given large city, lining up support from the local clergy and businessmen, hiring the largest hall in town, or building one if nothing large enough was available, arranging mass choirs, sending special agents to stir up local women—for a short time Frances Willard was in charge of Moody's women's meetings.

After the show opened, night after night Moody and assistants thundered and pleaded and denounced sin, and hundreds and thousands "gained the victory," professing the conversion that would save them from hellfire. Music of the right soul-saving quality was essential, probably the prime agency for many, in bringing these emotional spasms about. Sankey not only provided plenty of the right sort, but consistently led the necessary hurricanes of human voices himself and wrote numerous hymn tunes that his experience taught him would be particularly singable and soul-rousing. "The Ninety and Nine" may be the best known today, but "There'll Be No Dark Valley" and "Under His Wings" also conspicuously mingled the good word of the Gospel with head-tossing rhythms. The typical Sankey hymn sounds like "Goodby, My Lover, Goodby" marinated in the Swanee River, but falls short of both.

Sankey's chief lieutenant was a handsome baritone, P. P. Bliss, who contributed to his principal's hymnbooks hymns that added a sort of rapt sententiousness to the prevalent bounciness. When 5,000 persons warmed up by one of Moody's sermons got their teeth into Bliss' "Let the Lower Lights Be Burning," they were grain white for the harvest. And Bliss' almost inebriate gurgle was carried even farther by William G. Fischer, a Philadelphia bookkeeper, amateur musician and author of "I Love to Tell the Story" and "Whiter Than Snow." But maybe the apogee of this sacred Tin Pan Alley was attained by another amateur, W. H. Doane, a manufacturer of woodworking machinery who created "Tell Me the Old, Old Story," "Rescue the Perishing" and that flabbily buoyant masterpiece in waltz time "Near the Cross." In the last, as often elsewhere, Doane had the help of words from the nation's richest source of hymn lyrics, Frances Jane Crosby—a figure to hurry over because she so dismayingly combined pathos and bathos. She was accidentally blinded as a baby. In New York City's famous Institution for the Blind she learned quickly and showed a knack of rhyming which, a visiting phrenologist said, implied high poetic talent. As a teacher at the institution she turned out jingly verses, no worse than the usual poetessery of the day, some of which became popular set to music. In middle age she had married a blind organist, one of her former pupils—a gratifying story of handicap pluckily overcome with her little books of verse giving a special sense of accomplishment. But in 1864 she wrote a hymn that went well set to music. Its success sent her into a creative frenzy. She could and did turn out six or seven hymns a day. In fact, her output was so extravagantly large and yet so well suited to the purpose that publishers disguised its thousands of items under 200-odd pseudonyms that still conceal her single-handed dominance of the usual revivalist's hymnal.

When George Templeton Strong was congratulating his sons on their musical advantages, he might have gone on to mention improvements in several other aspects of their lives. For instance, they were, if they preferred, let off from shaving. The taste of their times for beards has often been ascribed to the soldiers' reluctance to shave in cold water under field conditions during the Civil War. Actually this fashion began with British imitation of the Europeans visiting London's Great Exhibition of 1850 wearing not merely the mustache and goatee of the cult of Louis Napoleon but in many cases full beards. The Crimean War of 1854–56 may have fostered this fashion. America was certainly taking to it well before the Civil War. By 1851 William Cullen Bryant was luxuriantly fringed; Lincoln's short beard appeared in 1860. The next two generations moved readily from soup-strainer mustaches to elaborate whiskers. Smooth-shaven Emerson could no longer have used "men with beards" to sum up a wide spectrum of cranks and eccentrics. The variations included clean lip over long beard, a style favored by small-town bankers and Brigham Young; pendulous "dundreary" side-whiskers, with jaw and chin shaven, so called after the comic Englishman in *Our American Cousin;* a short version was "sideburns" after the Union's General Ambrose Burnside. All those called for regular shaving round the edges, however. Even General Grant's full beard, kept short, had to be clipped, whereas there was maximum convenience in the majestic full growth of S. F. B. Morse and Henry Wadsworth Longfellow.

At the same time Britons, incidentally setting styles for their American cousins, questioned the need for high boots under long trousers and went into lace-up or buttoned or, soon, elastic-sided footgear rising little above the anklebone. The buttoned boot required that obsolete tool now puzzling browsers in old garrets, the buttonhook. The same daring innovators also turned their shirt collars down over lighter cravats so that it was ac-

Button-shoes, now so long forgotten.

tually possible to turn the head freely. That led to the detachable, stiff-starched collar anchored fore and aft to a neckband shirt. The advantage was a saving in laundry, for a daily change of collar allowed one shirt to go two days, more in emergencies, particularly after the advent of detachable cuffs. The disadvantage was the daily struggle with the collar button, which besides, like the buttonhook, was always getting lost.

Ill-advised persons did their best to defeat the purpose by bringing in the cylindrical stand-up detachable collar almost as hampering as grandfather's shirt collar-*cum*-neckcloth. Even the turnover style was much less easy than today's collar-attached affair. There was also the problem of daily supply of collars properly starched, a thing difficult for many laundresses. One solution was paper collars—an early instance of today's cult of the dispensable—costing little and thrown away after use. By 1870 seventy-odd companies were making them, packed ten a box. On the other tack were collars never needing starch that could be sponged clean and never wilted under summertime sweat—made of celluloid, the first widely used plastic. They were a fire hazard to smokers, however, and in any case both paper and celluloid collars were considered low. So was the rustic custom of donning a starched collar for church but failing to add a necktie to mask the glow of the brass collar button. Lower still was the workingman going about in a neckband shirt collarless. Everybody grasped the connotations of the popular song, an apostrophe to his girl from a hesitant suitor:

> I don't think your Uncle John
> Ever had a collar on.
> You're a perfect lady but when I get hitched for life,
> *I want an orphan!*

The knee-cramping trouser strap under the boot disappeared. The absurd tailcoat was replaced (except for formal evenings) by the cylindrical frock coat of various lengths—the longest was a Prince Albert—or for unceremonious wear a single-breasted, loose jacket.

Changes in women's fashions were not so benign. Bonnets were giving way to hats. Soon the bonnet would persist only as religious insigne of the Quakers and Shakers and in the sunbonnets of gingham over cardboard with which farm women shielded their complexions during outdoor chores —much better for the purpose than the garden or picture hat in which elegant ladies did their posy gathering. Corsets stayed stiff and deforming, skirts long and numerous. The bizarre successor of the hoop was the bus-

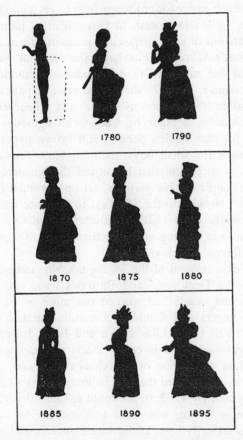

Recurring examples of the back-fullness contour.

From pp. 14–16 *Recurring Cycles of Fashion* by Agnes Brooks Young. Copyright 1937 by Harper & Row, Publishers, Incorporated. By permission of the publishers.

tle—a horsehair pad or wire frame tied on behind under the dress to make a lady's rear look like the rear view of a horse and rider. This not only gave the illusion of a really monstrous steatopygia but also prevented sitting comfortably on anything but a stool. In that era of jigsawed verandas and rococo hatstands, fashionable gowns were naturally more elaborate than they have ever been before or since—amazing complexes of overskirts, capes, flounces, trains, ruchings, jabots, cravats, frogs, pointless buttons, lace insertions—often in dark, heavy-rich materials dragging in the dirt unless the wearer confined herself to house and carriage.

As yet all dresses were cut out and stitched up singly at home whether by hired dressmakers or mother and the girls. The development of standardized paper patterns in graduated sizes, an American invention of the 1850's, made it much easier for any seamstress to get a good fit along modish lines. "Mme." Ellen Demorest, first to sell dress patterns to a mass market, made hers out of tissue paper and promoted them most profitably in *Mme. Demorest's Mirror of Fashions*. She also put out an elaborate pattern catalogue for mail orders and had some hundreds of agents throughout the country. By 1873 the annual sales of patterns had topped 2,000,000. Close in the Demorests' wake was Ebenezer Butterick of Sterling, Massachusetts, a tailor by trade, who figured out a range of graded patterns for men's shirts done in stiff brown paper; then another for homemade suits for small boys; then for basic dresses for women, which last grew so successful that he moved the business to New York City and, with a couple of able partners, set up a women's magazine, the *Delineator* (which lasted into the 1930's), to promote fashions and patterns to match. In the early 1870's E. Butterick and Company's pattern plant in Brooklyn was sending out more than 6,000,000 patterns a year; the business still flourishes today.

Simultaneous development of the sewing-machine industry had a great deal to do with the Demorests' and Butterick's success. In the 1840's several Yankees and others had worked out more or less practical devices to replace fingers and thimbles. A certain number were sold, the most successful rivals being Elias Howe and Isaac Singer. For a lively decade they fought each other in court, finally pooling interests and patents in 1856. Mass production of interchangeable parts, a principle already well understood, enabled the new industry to sell 130,000 machines in the next four years. By 1863 Singer could sell his 40 percent interest in the pool for a large fortune and retire to Europe. (An illegitimate son, Paris Singer, was an early lover of Isadora Duncan's and an associate of Addison Mizner in making Palm Beach so intemperately pseudo-Spanish.) Howe stayed home to watch his millions pile up. By 1870 the nation was buying half a million sewing machines a year, and the nagging whir

*Brigham Young, patriarch of the Mormons, greets a touring party
of journalists and their wives all diked out in the latest fashions
of the 1870's.*

of flywheel and jigging needle had replaced the eerie wail of the spinning
wheel as the characteristic sound of a properly managed American household. Glib salesmen sold them door to door with a demonstration model
in the back of a spring wagon and painless-sounding arrangements for
easy payments. One could even buy a combined sewing machine and parlor melodion, this pedal for music, that one for sewing a fine seam. Elaborate improvements and extra gadgets so multiplied models and brands that
at the Philadelphia Centennial Howells found a full half mile of sewing-
machine exhibits an oppressive sight.

The industry's second market, equally well exploited, consisted of petty
manufacturers of ready-made clothing, soon a thriving sequel industry.

For some while hole-and-corner dealers had hired poverty-stricken women at sweated rates to hand-sew ready-cut shirts and cheap slops— frocks, trousers, roundabout jackets as work clothes for sailors and laborers; shirts and pants for Southern slaves. In Cincinnati and St. Louis, as well as the Northeastern seaports, production of such marginal attire from cotton and dubious woolens persisted by virtue of a steady basic demand and low labor costs. By 1854 sewing machines were revolutionizing the business in Cincinnati, where German Jews employing largely German immigrant women had concentrated the Western clothing trade in establishments averaging 100 cutters and sewers, some working in the shop, some at home. These machines making in an hour and a quarter a man's shirt that took a needle-wielding hand some fourteen hours came just in time to turn out the millions of uniforms needed in the Civil War. Brooks Brothers in New York City had already been making important advances in the art of subtilizing standardized sizes to bypass most of the tedious and costly fittings that custom tailoring requires. By the end of the war military contracts had taught many firms how to use batteries of machines to turn out fairly wearable jackets and trousers. Suits in standardized measurements could now be advertised for mail-order sale at $10 for men, $5 for boys. Those able to afford to patronize tailors made jokes about reach-me-downs—that is, garments got down from a shop shelf (coat hangers were still in the future) instead of being made to measure. But in time the principle of size modulation and methods of alteration were so refined that the best American ready-made jacket now usually fits 95 percent as well as if tailor-made. That is an indigenous American art that the rest of the world has still to learn in its farther arcana.

The shoe trade was also revolutionized by sewing machines when they were adapted to stitching soles to uppers—again just in time to keep the Union armies shod. Gordon McKay, the Yankee who bought the patent on and refined the original sole-stitching version, was soon drawing $750,000 a year in royalties. The versatility of patterns and the convenience of the home sewing machine combined to slow down a parallel revolution in women's wear. For a good while, mass production was applied chiefly to relatively undemanding garments such as cloaks and separate skirts.

Between the shipping of those first sewing machines to Cincinnati—a wonderful alliance between Yankee gadgetry and the Old World Jewish flair for the customer's needs—and the efficiencies and incisive stylings of today's Seventh Avenue lay a noisome morass of sweated ghettos and savage trial and error. At least here, however, the Gilded Age created an eventually constructive aspect of America. Thanks to imaginative use of the Howe-Singer invention, sartorial class differences began to fade sooner in America than elsewhere. "Human dignity owes much to the Hebrew reorganizers of the garment trades, who wiped out class distinctions in dress," [68] says Samuel Eliot Morison. The nearer ready-mades resembled tailor-mades in style, fabric and cut, the nearer Americans were to looking as if created equal—nearer than Jefferson had had a right to expect. And the human mind being so simple, looking equal actually helps people feel equal.

Mr. Strong's sons also had much improved light to study by. The Indians had known the "rock oil," sometimes more learnedly called "petroleum," polluting the surface of some streams in northwestern Pennsylvania and western New York State. They had naturally taken its uninviting odor and appearance to betoken strong medicinal properties and lackadaisically collected it. The whites adopted both theory and practice. In small vials as "Seneca oil" the stuff was a stock item for the traveling medicine showman. In the 1850's Canada had begun to ship into the States the whitish, keen-smelling lamp oil called "coal oil" that was actually distilled from oil-bearing shale. At the same time that John Brown was laying his first plans for a slave rising, distillation of petroleum was leading to "kerosene," a less expensive rival to coal oil and, like it, a vast improvement on the whale oil then generally used in lamps. With slight modification of the existing wick-and-chimney lamp, kerosene gave the American sitting room a really fine, clear, strong light.

A sizable supply of oil to distill was the problem. The methods of the day—such as laying blankets on the surface of oil-covered water and wringing out the soaked-up oil from them—were woefully inadequate. Pennsylvanians had already used derrick drilling to tap underground salt water for boiling down. Oil was known to be down there, too. In fact, it often made itself a nuisance by coming up along with the salt water. In 1859 drilling brought in oil in striking quantity near Titusville, Pennsylvania, starting the first oil boom in the familiar pattern—the rush for leases, the frantic wildcatting, the overproduction and wars among refiners, the disastrous fires, and over and over again the "Coal Oil Johnny" story. It was the first convulsion of the economic scramble that would supply oil for the lamps of China, cause shockheaded black men speaking the Beach-la-Mar pidgin of the far Melanesian Islands to call the moon "kerosene-lamp-belong-Jesus-Christ," and greatly relieve the minds of the world's whale population. With a nice sense of timing fate arranged for much of the American whaling fleet—a substantial part of the economy in pre-Civil War days—to be destroyed partly by Confederate cruisers, partly by loss of many ships in the ice beyond the Bering Strait. Whaling persisted in steamers out of San Francisco using the bomb harpoon that so greatly reduced its hazards. But when whale oil lost its function as luminant, the great days of New Bedford and Nantucket had gone. Yankee farm boys no longer had much opportunity to ship as landsmen on whalers and come back cured of restlessness or turned into seagoing tramps for life.

The special point of the kerosene lamp was that it gave country and small-town folks as good or better light than city folks' gas. R. L. Duffus, mellowest of newspapermen, country-reared in Vermont long enough ago, recently wrote: "I still believe the well-tended kerosene lamp gave as good light as any luminant in history." [69] It was certainly superior to that of gas burned in the crude fishtail type of burner, though presently the European-invented Welsbach mantle of gauze impregnated with chemicals lent new brilliance to both rivals. Incidentally, kerosene supplied a safer and brighter political tool in replacing the torches that enthusiastic partisans carried in torchlight processions. "I hev no politics," Artemus Ward asserted. ". . . If I [had], I spose I should holler versiffrusly in the streets at night, and go home to Betsy Jane smellen of coal ile and gin in the mornin." [70] It is curious that so much of the Western world thus had to wait into the second half of the 1800's for a reading light as good as its transportation.

Duffus was also candid about "What was wrong with kerosene lamps . . . the wicks had to be carefully tended . . . sometimes smoked . . . it was necessary to wash the glass chimneys every day or so." [69] Some also objected to the inevitable tinge of kerosene in the air. But outside the house, too, the kerosene lantern was a vast improvement on the old candle-fitted affair for the before-dawn and after-dark chores. Kerosene carriage lamps with reflectors gave the first hope of knowing where the horse was taking one after dark over unlighted roads. The new fuel also increased the range of locomotive headlights. The consequent rush to use kerosene accounts for the striking fact that the great fortune with which John D. Rockefeller of Standard Oil retired in 1893—something well toward $200,000,000—was only one of several that his company created out of the American oil industry even before the automobile's thirst for hydrocarbons enlarged its market. One side of Standard Oil was ruthless monopoly building in the name of efficiency but probably also reflecting a taste for power among its chieftains. Another, as John T. Flynn maintains in his biography of Rockefeller, was wide distribution of a scrupulously high-quality product serving a great need. It was just as well that there was something scrupulous about Standard Oil—at least one thing.

The light of the kerosene lantern also often glanced back from the gaily painted metal of one or another newfangled farm machine that—

like the sewing machine—was at the same time revolutionizing a major part of the economy and making a fortune for the man who created it. The reaping machine of Cyrus McCormick, solid and tireless Scotch-Irishman from the Shenandoah Valley, came out of a huge factory crucial to the amazing growth of Chicago in the 1850's. It has been contended that the productive prowess of these machines, enabling two persons to do the work of twenty with hand-swung cradle scythes, sending floods of American grain to Europe throughout the Civil War, was a specific factor in the Union's victory. In fact, the reaper enabled women to fill in for men away in the Army. Home missionaries in Iowa reported seeing not only farmwives but children of ten and twelve, girls included, driving these great horse-drawn contraptions as if born to it.

Just in time to supplement the reaper, the threshing machines of Jerome I. Case and others came on the market. Sophisticated metallurgy enabled John Deere and James Oliver to design plowshares to meet the special requirements of prairie farming. Those and some minor innovations turned the American farmer from a clumsy and backward miner of the fertility of the land, as we have so far seen him, into a fairly efficient operator. As yet, however, he was limited to muscle power, largely of animals, not the mechanical steam power that was coming in elsewhere. The steam plow was a disappointment. Reapers continued to depend on multiple hitches of horses to haul them through the grain and power the machinery. The threshing machines gradually took to steam power as Case and others worked out the wheeled, self-propelled steam engine that looked like a small, badly designed locomotive unaware it had left the track, to haul the thresher to the job and run it on the job with a power takeoff. In wood-poor prairie country it burned the straw from the threshing; in the South it ginned cotton. A snorting, clanking, puffing steam traction engine hauling a huge, red-painted threshing machine along a country road was one of the finest seasonal sights of long ago, though horses encountered along the way often disagreed and bolted disastrously. Henry Ford once said that what first interested him in automotive transportation was a boyhood glimpse of this majestic manifestation of self-propulsion.

Note that the factories making these devices—plus the famous Studebaker farm wagons—were situated in Chicago, Racine, Wisconsin, Moline, Illinois (in the complex of towns at the Rock Island crossing of the Mississippi), and South Bend, Indiana. It was Cyrus McCormick who had first seen the advantage of manufacturing farm machinery in the middle of its potential prime market instead of on its eastern edge. Now around that nucleus would grow an immense industrial complex based on the iron and copper of Minnesota and Michigan, the coal of southern Illinois and Indiana, the steamships of the Great Lakes and the north-south, east-west and diagonal railroads that by 1860 made a railroad map of the Old Northwest look like several superimposed games of ticktacktoe.

Those railroads, still building new branch lines into promising areas, were the more important because country roads were neglected. In 1869 Harvard's great president-to-be, Charles W. Eliot, a responsible witness fresh from Europe, wrote that the whole United States had "hardly twenty miles of good road, in the European sense." [71] What the farmer hauled his crops to market on was usually perfunctorily scraped gravel slackly maintained by a semimedieval system of labor and equipment supplied by local taxpayers. Side roads might never see even gravel. In public transport the era of metal and steam was doing much better for city people. In New York City, for instance, Strong's sons had seen the principle of wheel on metal rail widely applied to move people from dwelling to job or shop. The first rails laid in the street were so deeply slotted, hence such a nuisance to other vehicles, that the notion languished. In the 1850's, however, an improved rail allowing a fairly flush surface appeared in Philadelphia, and for the next generation—until electric propulsion came in—horse-drawn streetcars dominated urban transport. In 1900 some 28,000 cars drawn by 105,000 mules or horses were clanging along 6,600 miles of track.

Rails were far easier on the horses, for though the much larger car took two or three times as many passengers as the stage or bus that it replaced, reduced friction compensated for the heavier load. For two-legged crea-

The basic horsecar. The team might be mules.

tures the improvement was not without flaws. Smoother, yes; faster if traffic permitted; permitting lines to reach farther—but one's feet were still cold in winter in spite of all the fetid straw. The Strong boys' father much deplored "those foul, overcrowded, mephitic Third Avenue [horsecars]." [72] At morning and evening rush hours, when all seats were full, standees clung to overhead straps, and others hung to the steps outside. W. D. Howells' reaction to the Cambridge-Boston horsecars of 1870 is prophetic of today's big-city subway: ". . . the people who are thus indecorously huddled together, without regard to age or sex, otherwise lead lives of at least comfort . . . wherein furnaces make a summer heat . . . light is created by the turning of a key [on the gas jet]. . . . Yet . . . when they ride to or from business or church, [they] fail to assert rights that the benighted Cockney, who never heard of our plumbing . . . or even the oppressed Parisian, who is believed not to change his linen from one revolution to another, having paid for, enjoys." [73] Nor in his experience were horsecars any better in Philadelphia, Baltimore or St. Louis, let alone New York City.

Indecent congestion reflected both indifference to public comfort and growing inability of horse and rail to handle the increasing tides of humanity daily sweeping into and ebbing out from the city center. That led to civic constipation. A thoughtful physician, Dr. Rufus Henry Gilbert, aware of the unhealthiness of New York City's mounting slumminess, proposed enlisting steam to whisk people out to settle the upper reaches of Manhattan Island, where fresh air and decent elbowroom were still available. Let horsecars handle local passengers, but run swift locomotives high above on elevated tracks, stopping only every third of a mile or so. After a false start the scheme worked. Several of the city's north-south avenues were presently smothered by hulking iron pillars and light-stifling superstructures along which rattled and screeched smoke-belching little monsters hauling all comers to any point along the route at five cents a head. Dr. Gilbert not only got no return from his promotion of the El system—which greatly raised the value of speculatively held real estate in Harlem—but lived long enough to see its cars just as congested at rush hours as any horsecars had ever been.

Along the El-smothered avenues, besides, the noise and dirt of the trains made uninhabitable for anybody who could conceivably afford anything better the four- and five-story brownstone and brick houses already there. Soon the El-created blight meant linear slums reaching all the way up the island—a side effect negating much of what the doctor had had in mind. For their first decade or so, however, the Els had the prestige attached to being fast and modern. They even went in for "palace cars" charging double fare for more room, plush upholstery and fancy woodwork. The system fascinated the young matron of Howells' *A Hazard of New Fortunes*: ". . . the most ideal way of getting about . . . the fleeting intimacy . . . with people in second and third floor interiors . . . the coming and going of the trains marking the stations with vivider or fainter plumes of flame-shot steam . . . the superb spectacle, which in a city full of painters nightly works its unrecorded miracles." [74] Long after squalor had overtaken the El, its first glories were recalled by the design of those stations—stylish little extravaganzas of jigsaw-Swiss and wedding-cake Gothic, all eaves and skinny columns and unexpected red-and-white stained glass, when you could see it for the grime.

Those El lines in New York City were the first American urban rapid transit. Brooklyn, Chicago and Boston also built such systems; only the last two had the good sense to wait until electricity could replace the calamitous coal-burning locomotives. Much sooner San Francisco, spurred to ingenuity by hills too steep for horsecars, had an alternative way that also kept the power plant from being a trackside nuisance. An English engineer, Andrew Hallidie, experienced in building suspension bridges with wire rope, maybe taking a hint from an abortive experiment on New York City's first El, invented the cable car, still maintained in San Francisco as a civic pet and tourist attraction. An endless steel cable ran in a protected slot between the car tracks. Steam engines at one end of the track, which might be miles long, kept the cable crawling along. With a clawlike "grip" the car driver took hold of the cable when he wanted forward motion, let go when he wanted to stop. An implausible device, but it conquered Nob Hill among others, making it practical for the wealthy to build on its summit such a concentration of palaces that Robert Louis Stevenson called the area "itself a kind of slum . . . the habitat of the mere millionaire." [75] Impressed, New York City replaced horse with cable cars on two lines. The sharp curve on the Broadway line at Union Square was soon known as Dead Man's Curve because it often caused the grip to loose hold on the cable, throwing the speeding car out of control. Howells considered the cable cars' "silent speed . . . even more dangerous than the tumultuous rush on the avenues . . . the foot-passenger has to look well . . . lest in avoiding one car another roll him under its wheels." [76]

He also deplored the outrageous bribery and corruption often underlying the franchises under which private corporations thus used the city streets for highly profitable and often flagrantly overcapitalized Els and horsecar lines. The great fortunes of such as Peter A. B. Widener of Philadelphia and Charles Yerkes of Philadelphia and Chicago were founded thus on the rotting consciences of aldermen, mayors and judges. In a fragmentary way some of the loot eventually came back to the public, of course, in such things as the University of Chicago's Yerkes Observatory and Harvard's Widener Memorial Library. But the preceding process had been noisomely unedifying, and the wrath of men like Howells, already strong in the 1880's, shows how widely this civic disgrace was recognized well before the days of muckraking. Nor was such wrath the weaker for the sloppy maintenance, stupid scheduling, inadequate traffic control and insolent employees that were particularly likely to go with transport monopoly in that day of no regulation of public utilities—a tradition still kept up in public transportation in several large American cities.

Steam on rails had already created the American commuter keeping his economic foot in the city and his domestic foot in what was extra-urban country when he moved there but, thanks to too many of him, was soon suburbs. Steamboats had created some of that sort of thing up the North and East rivers in the 1830's; Theodore Weld, for instance, lived near Nyack but went daily to a New York City office by water. The rail version may well have been invented by F. S. Lathrop, an eminent citizen of Madison, New Jersey, who suggested in 1841 to the Morris and Essex Railroad (now part of the Lackawanna) that they sell him a ticket for a year's unlimited rides to and from Newark, New Jersey, for $100, a heavy discount* for quantity. Soon both businessmen patrons and railroads found this advantageous, and well-off families began to move to the country for the summer with the breadwinner spending an inordinate proportion of his waking life on the train. Then he might buy a permanent country place, then decide to live there year round amid greenery and clean air.

By 1845 the new Old Colony Railroad (now part of the New Haven) had thus made Quincy, Massachusetts, a suburb of Boston. The Main Line (of the Pennsylvania Railroad) westward from Philadelphia had the same effect. Concentration of self-exiles along the Vanderbilt-controlled rail lines into Westchester and Fairfield counties was so heavy by 1865 that P. T. Barnum—himself a suburb-promoter around Bridgeport, Connecticut—made a great name in the Connecticut legislature by denouncing the lines' scheme to raise commuting rates now that the victims were committed by buying property. Llewellyn Park in New Jersey's Oranges, the first real estate development platted and landscaped as a unit for rich men's country mansions, and A. T. Stewart's Garden City for more modest incomes, built on Long Island's Hempstead Plains, where the first formal American horse race had been run 200 years earlier, depended on frequent rail service into New York City. Practically from its beginning commuting consisted mostly of mere solvent-to-prospering white-collar men. The sight of them pouring out of the cars of the Fitchburg Railroad (now part of the Boston and Maine) at North Cambridge, Massachusetts, depressed Howells in 1870: ". . . suburbanly packed and bundled . . . even when empty-handed somehow proclaiming the jaded character of men that hurry their work all day to catch the evening train out . . . and their dreams all night to catch the morning train in." [77] Laurence Gronlund, Danish-born and gingerly Marxist,

* Hence *commute* and so *commuter*. The *Universal Oxford Dictionary* gives one meaning of *commute* as "to change (one kind of payment) into another."

viewing his adopted country with optimistic dismay, thought it had been better when merchants lived over their shops among their customers. "Now they have deserted their posts of social duty . . . only come into town . . . on weekdays . . . a real grievance of the working-classes." [78] Between Mr. Lathrop's keen nose for a discount and Dr. Gilbert's concern about the public health, urban blight has roots much more than a century old.

The railroads and the Civil War filled the end of the social spectrum farthest from the steady-paced commuter by creating the American hobo —a figure potent in our folklore. America had always had social misfits, economically or emotionally deviant, living hit or miss on the economic fringes and readily shaking the dust of a given place from the feet because moving on seemed like a good idea at the time. Huckleberry Finn's Duke and King were immortal instances. The vicissitudes of immigration, the frontier and cyclic depressions continued to send wandering many men less gifted than that precious pair for living by one's wits. War, however, institutionalized all that, as described by Josiah Flynt (Willard), eccentric and sociological-minded nephew of Frances Willard, mother goddess of the WCTU. Jack London himself endorsed the reliability of Flynt's account of the tramp-hobo based on years of deliberate living with them.

The dislocations of war, Flynt said, "left a large class of men so enamored of camp life that they found it impossible to return to quiet living and . . . took to wandering about the country. Occasionally they worked a little . . . but by 1870 they had given up all intention of working." Aimless wandering gradually led them to tramp railroad rights-of-way. Since America had no European-style laws against trespass on railroad property, "the railroad-tramp . . . [gradually learned it was] more comfortable to sit in a box-car and ride. . . . The trainmen thought that many of these trespassers were deserving but penniless out-of-works and . . . made . . . no serious effort to keep the tramp off their trains . . . by 1880 the latter was accepted . . . as an unavoidable nuisance on railroad property." [79] The system was so common that local police might turn a vagrant loose on condition that he take the next train out—*freight* train, no ticket, being understood.

As the nuisance showed signs of permanence, the railroads did try to abate it because risks of pilferage, damage to rolling stock and attacks on employees began to loom too high. Private police were hired to keep these knights of the road out of freightyards as far as was possible when those large and confused areas were so inadequately lighted. Train crews were sternly ordered to get rid of all unauthorized riders found. Though such orders were seldom altogether effective, efforts to enforce them did some-

Tramps riding on the rails.

what divert the nonpaying customers from empty boxcars to other and far
more risky ways of riding: blind baggage (occupying the niche of the false
door on the front of the baggage car); riding the [brake] rods under the
car; trucking it (clinging to the hardware between the wheels of the
trucks). It argues really strong wanderlust or desperation in cases of genuine hard luck to take that sort of risk two or three times a week for years.
Flynt estimated that *c.* 1905, which was not during hard times, every night

Tramps throwing a conductor from a train.

saw some 10,000 professional vagabonds thus outwitting the railroads' henchmen. He put the total of the whole itinerant caste at some 60,000. Nor was outwitting the whole story. A softhearted brakeman finding such a rider might be blarneyed into letting him change into the security of a boxcar. A venal one might be bribed to do it or anyway to let him stay on board. A very stern or vicious one might do his best to dislodge the hobo while the train was at speed, with an odds-on chance of death or serious injury.

Between these riskings of one's life to get from A to B, neither of which places promised much, the "stiffs"—the nearest thing to a generic term including all varieties of chronic parasites of the rails—clubbed together in "jungles." These were waste areas, usually handy to railroad yards, often with a few shacks patched together out of salvage lumber and flattened-out tin cans—improvised slums with a rapidly revolving population and excessive ventilation in winter. They teemed with lice, fleas and bedbugs, but then so did the flophouses, jails and casual-labor bunkhouses that were their world's only alternatives. Pausing in a jungle enabled one to swap yarns and tactical information about the railroad bulls' methods here and the public attitude toward panhandlers there, for local variations were wide. On the railroad water tank at San Marcial, New Mexico, for instance, Jack London once saw a memorandum chalked for his fellows: "Main-drag fair. . . . Bulls not hostile. . . . Roundhouse good for kipping. . . ." [80] Translation: Pickings for beggars were fair on the principal street; the local police were not severe on vagrants; and sleeping in the roundhouse in the railroad yards was allowed. With the jungle as base, one could raid into town to beg for cash or scrounge food at back doors, steal shirts or underwear off clotheslines if the chance offered, maybe acquire marginal meat scraps and vegetables or stolen chickens to stew up into the hobo's catch-as-catch-can "mulligan." But rich mulligans were rare. Malnutrition must have been as rife as scabies except among those especially clever—as Jack London claimed to be—at gulling housewives into asking the poor fellow into the kitchen and cooking him the kind of square meal he said his mother used to make. The handout of cold leftovers was acceptable and helpful but seldom long on vitamins.

The reaction of many another housewife, understandably nervous about morning callers of such dubious repute, was to slam the door in the face of what she called a tramp. That omitted the real, if not rigid, distinctions among the substrata: In hard times—and for a generation after 1873 there were more hard times than good—the out-at-elbows applicant might well be jobless and desperate but pathetically harmless, not yet making vagrancy a hard-nosed career. If persistent hard luck pushed him over the line into the *hobo* class of rootless men, that still usually implied a willingness to take a job when opportunity came. Indeed the itinerant laborer who worked in lumber camps in the winter and hired out for wheat harvest in the Dakotas in late summer, considerably nearer a real niche in the economic system than the *bum,* considered himself a hobo and several cuts above many of the wanderers whom he encountered in jungles as he shifted himself and his bindle (bundle of possessions) from job to job. At certain seasons railroads in some areas made a point of tolerating hoboes because of their function as migrant labor in lumber, harvesting and so on. Even when a hobo began to sink toward the bum, he might still consent to put in a few hours at the woodpile with a bucksaw in return for victuals and permission to sleep in the barn.

In England of the 1600's *tramp* had meant pretty much what *hobo* would in America in 1890. By then, however, American usage had *tramp* synonymous with *bum*—a chronic vagrant seldom or never considering employment, relying on scrounging and begging and so often with a prison record that Flynt said "Tramps proper are discouraged thieves." [81] Drink was what had torn many such loose from society. In others a temperamental instability had been broadened by the unsettling effects of unemployment or soldiering, as Flynt pointed out. And then as times improved, they had lacked the impulse to try to restore themselves to the world that had temporarily rejected them. A *road kid* or *prushun* was a teen-age boy run away and fallen in with stiffs, usually traveling as apprentice captive of a patron tramp (a *jocker*), who taught him to scrounge and panhandle and often exploited him erotically. The steady back-and-forth relation between prison and jungle would have kept homosexuality flourishing even had the jungle itself not been full of it, for women were scarce in this society until the depression of the 1930's.

It was the stiffs' custom to chalk on the local railroad water tank or freight platform not only information useful to his peers but also his moniker (London spells it *monica*)—the nickname by which alone the professional vagrant was known; as "Texas Slim / bound west" or with merely an arrow pointing up or down the line. This kept name and movements alive for friends and acquaintances. Such indications of the recent visits of free spirits like Buffalo Smitty, New Jersey Red, Yellow Dick, Burley Bo, Ohio Fatty, the Monkey Kid and so on inevitably stirred the imaginations of the kind of restless youngster most likely to hang around the yards. While the tramp thus became a crypto-hero of the cornsilk-cigarette set, adults' reactions were mixed. He was mistrusted, even feared, a thing often most inhumanely expressed. The same Mrs. Mary A. Livermore who had worked herself to the bone funneling Sanitary Commission supplies to the sick and wounded wrote in the very hard times year 1878: "Tramps have no claim on human sympathy. When they invade my house and ask for bread, I bid them begone without ceremony. The hand of society must be against these vagrants; and they must die off . . . the sooner they are dead and buried the better. . . ."[82] Not long before, the Chicago *Tribune* had thought it a becoming topical joke to suggest putting "a little strychnine or arsenic in the meat and other supplies furnished a tramp. This . . . puts the coroner in a good humor, and saves one's chickens and other personal property from constant depredation." [83]

Gradually, as the tramp became an institution, he turned into a standard figure of fun, for all his sinister connotations. The ragged, shuffling figure needing a shave, toes sticking out of the boots, hair out of holes in the hat, was a cartoonist's standby, usually running down an alley with a bulldog swinging from the seat of his trousers or trying some wheedling absurdity on the grim lady of the house, broom in hand and jaw set. Everybody knew Nervy Nat, whose vagabond insouciance in some ways anticipated the "little guy" whom Chaplin made so famous. Everybody instantly recognized the interstratum antagonisms in James Whitcomb Riley's small boy's account of how:

> A Old Tramp slep' in our stable wunst,
> An' [the hired man] he caught
> An' roust him up an' chased him off
> Clean out through our back lot!
>
> An' th' old Tramp hollered back an' said,—
> "You're a *purty* man!—*You* air!—
> With a pair o' eyes like two fried eggs,
> An' a nose like a Bartlutt pear!"

The tramp comedian in strangely ill-fitting pants, grotesque shoes and battered hat lewdly outwitting the toploftical and dandified straight man was indispensable in the lower reaches of show business. Some of the jungle's harsh lingo remains in the American language: *handout, moocher, shine, punk* (originally meaning a road kid discarded by his jocker).

The disproportionate visibility of this tiny subculture—maybe only .001 percent of the population—came of wide awareness of tramps panhandling downtown or knocking beseechingly at back doors; of the settled man's uneasiness in the presence of the drifter; and doubtless of what might be called the Huckleberry Finn complex—the puerile impulse common among most of us to get away from the widow and Miss Watson and turn vagabond without soap or obligations. The last has a romantic savor till one understands that the emotional tone of the jungle was laced with glib cynicism, persecution feelings, self-adulation for having seceded from society. Think of it as a blend of the age-old gypsy's Ishmaelitism with the copping-out of the hippie of the 1960's—only messily warped by lack of women. It had only two virtues: strong in-group loyalty, a thing tramps shared with thieves; and relatively little race prejudice. The jungle was one of the very rare situations that freely accepted Frisco Sheeny and the Syracuse Shine.

Another offspring of the railroads and the Civil War was the cowboy of the Old West. The late 1860's saw the Kansas Pacific Railroad (now part of the Union Pacific) building westward toward mining-boomed Colorado; and Texas crammed with 5,000,000 head of cattle raised under Mexican-style conditions of open range, fancy roping and short shrift for the rustler. Their owners, eagerly seeking markets now that the war was over, began to drive them northward to shipping points on the new railroad for loading into cars for the Kansas City and Chicago stockyards. Such a drive sounds formidable now but did not then to Texans who in the 1850's had driven herds to Kansas City direct, even to Chicago, and a few times farther still through worse country to take advantage of the high price of beef in gold rush California. In a few years another vast grazing area became available. The traditional population of the country into which the Kansas Pacific and (farther north) the Union Pacific were pushing consisted of thousands of Indians living off millions of buffalo. Now Uncle Sam was herding the Indians into reservations and appallingly efficient professional buffalo hunters, killing primarily to get hides for sleigh robes for the Eastern market, were wiping out the great lumbering beasts. This left the grass and water of western Kansas free for cattlemen, and it was soon learned that, contrary to previous belief, cattle could winter well enough on the Great Plains unsheltered. Thenceforward, while the steers of a given herd driven up from Texas went eastward for beef, the bulls, cows and calves were sold for breeding stock to experienced Texans and others going into cattle ranching along and beyond the rails. Gradually the cattle country, keeping pace with the diminution of buffalo and Indians, spread into Wyoming and northward beyond the Canadian line. What was once written off as the Great American Desert—a daunting phrase embedded in popular thought by the U.S. Army officer after whom Pikes Peak is named—was becoming the Great American Ranch.

The cattle thus taking over from the buffalo (as their cousins had from the deer of the Eastern forests) were like those of California—rangy long horns descended from stock brought into Mexico by Spaniards three centuries before and noted more for survival power and breadth of horns than for efficient output of beef per acre. Acres were plentiful, however, and profits gratifying on even such meat-poor animals. Besides, the breed could not be improved much while the range stayed open. A rancher going to the expense of bringing in superior bulls also did his neighbor a genetic favor, and it was difficult to keep neighbor's scrub bulls away from his own cows. It took a long time and a revolution in ranching methods to dot the West with the white-faced cattle now producing beef so efficiently there.

The men making the drive to railhead were second-generation Texans whose rawhide-tough sires had taken the country away from Mexico, expert Mexican cowhands working for Texans, and non-Texans from all over who had come to the Lone Star commonwealth out of restlessness or for even more pressing personal reasons, or were demobilized Confederate soldiers drifted southwestward out of distaste for what defeat had done to Dixie. A fair number were Negroes, former slaves trained to cattle, as their racial brothers had been in the Narragansett country of Colonial times, now free and on the payroll. Throughout the growth of the Great American Ranch, Negro cowpunchers bunked and drank in the same rough-and-ready places as white ones, ate on the same footing around the same chuck wagon, and took the same stampedes and snowstorms gamely enough to erase prejudice. Here as in the tramps' jungle, the color line faded—the more strangely in view of the heavy Southern flavor of the cattle kingdom. It was principally drawly Texans who, as cattle spread over the new country, taught tenderfoot and pony the cow-handling techniques that Texas had learned from Mexico, for, as wrote Owen Wister, who knew Arizona, as well as Wyoming, "Let it be remembered that the Mexican was the original cowboy." [84] This northward drift, bringing with it Southern speech and taste for private violence, made the region between the Mexican and Canadian borders a single cultural province, blurring continuation of the line between North and South that had roughly followed the fortieth parallel across the continent from the Delaware to the Missouri.

Horse, hat and revolver are the cowboy's ritual attributes. "How they rode!" Mark Twain wrote of "the Mexicanized Americans" of Nevada. "Leaning just gently forward out of the perpendicular, easy and nonchalant, with broad slouch-hat brim blown square up in front, and long riata swinging. . . ." [85] Westerners were contemptuous of the "silly Miss Nancy fashion of the riding school" which taught rising to the trot. The hat crossed the wide-awake of the 1840's with the Mexican's sombrero—not at all like the style with the brim curled up on each side now favored by TV cowboys and Deep South sheriffs.* To some extent the revolver

* This is clear in photographs of the Great American Ranch in its great days, as well as in Frederic Remington's drawings. The flat four-inch brim sometimes turned up against the head in front. In the Northwest the crown was creased low porkpie-

may have reflected the Southern taste for going armed, but it was undeniably handy against varmints and rustlers, as well as for personal safeguard in town. The large kerchief around the neck pulled over nose and
mouth to keep out the dust of cattle driving. That was one of the cowhand's few hygienic measures. He bathed no oftener than any other country

E. W. Kemble draws the idealized cowboy of the 1890's.
Note the early version of the Western hat.

hired hand and vermin knew about bunkhouses. His diet was principally
beans, grease and tough meat. His work was not only physically grueling
but often nervously exacting, requiring a sixth-sense feel for what cow
critters, which can be collectively as skittish and contrary as two-legged
ones, would do next. What his brutally broken mount would do next also
had to be kept in mind, and unless Emerson Hough has greatly maligned
the cowpuncher, the rider was often as rough with the horse as the horse
would have liked to be with the rider.

As cattle got into the mountain states wherever pasture and water
offered between ridges, mining and beef raising led a tenuous coexist-
ence. A gold strike might strip a ranch of hands—the emergency that
Owen Wister's Virginian so deftly handled. In one year a man might put
a summer season of prospecting between a ranch job in Montana and
another in Texas. Both miners and cowboys frequented some of the bo-

style. Elsewhere it was left high with two dints in front or four as in the old Army
campaign hat—and Smokey the Bear's forest ranger hat now. Hollywood Westerns
of the William S. Hart period show the same style.

nanza towns. The stage holdups, gamblers' feuds, impromptu shootings and whoring of such places mingled inextricably with the cowboy legend —and not anomalously, for the equally raucous railroad shipping points, such as Abilene, Kansas, already had cowboys well versed in such matters. The gambler-gunman of the Wyatt Earp type was as much at home in the cow town of Dodge City as in the silver-mining town of Tombstone, Arizona. A talent for violence had value for the sort of employer—of whom there were many—who expected his outfit to harass and, if necessary, fight it out with nesters (homesteaders taking over and fencing the open range) and sheepmen, whose flocks not only competed with cattle for grass but were thought to damage the range by nibbling too close and packing the earth down.

In the first two great decades vast numbers of steers were shipped eastward to be plumped out with Midwestern pasture and corn, killed in Kansas City or Chicago, sent as dressed beef in the newly perfected refrigerator cars not only to the Eastern states but to Europe, particularly Britain. British interest in the sources of this flood of meat elicited such tales of unlimited grazing and profits that millions of pounds sterling crossed the ocean for investment in Western ranches in Canada, as well as in the States, sometimes with lively young Britons attached as ranch managers. But the winter of 1886–87 was the exception to the rule that cattle could survive Great Plains blizzards. Disastrous freezing and starvation took such toll that the steam went out of the cattle boom, never to revive with such extravagance. That same year America's first practical electric streetcar, which doomed the horsecar, went into operation in Richmond, Virginia, gradually undermining the Great American Ranch's steady market for four-footed motive power at $15 a head unbroken. A new era was arriving anyway. Homesteaders were nibbling away at the cattle kingdom's eastern flank. And with them came a new style of fencing, menace or blessing, depending on whether one was old-style cattleman or nester—barbed wire.

This brilliantly simple device to keep livestock where they belonged —and out of growing crops—came of the lack of fencing timber in Midwestern prairielands. Without economical fencing—always the settler's crying need—the prairie farmer of Illinois, say, could do little against the cattleman who wanted the country kept in open range, giving grazing animals priority over crops. Importing fence rails was much too costly. So were cattleproof ditches. Hedges, Old World-style, might do, and after disappointments with several native and imported shrubs, a solution was found by an able Yankee, Jonathan Baldwin Turner of Illinois College, otherwise distinguished as the promoter of public schools and a state university for Illinois. He had got hold of a thorny small tree native to Arkansas called Osage orange because its baseball-size, globular green masses of seed look like green oranges; the French peltrymen called it *bois d'arc* because the Indians used its tough, springy wood for bows. After years of testing, Turner pronounced it hardy in prairie winters and vigorous enough to make cattle-tight hedging. Then he began to preach Osage orange as devotedly as Johnny Appleseed had planted apple trees, for he saw in it the low-cost fencing that would bring about his ideal "democratization of the prairie." [86] Within limits he was right. The Midwestern open range lost out to enclosure, and the Osage orange spread eastward wherever enterprising farmers were spellbound by salesmen of planting stock. In odd parts of the middle Atlantic states today one finds the neglected remains of the old plantings raggedly persisting as souvenirs of Turner's constructive zeal.

There were disadvantages, however. Osage orange took two clippings a year, a sizable chore, to keep in shape; its far-spread roots stole water and nutrients from crops for some yards on each side, which began to matter as land grew scarce; and an unusually severe winter temporarily stunted it. Galvanized (for rust resistance) fence wire had long been available; indeed the Union had used it for defensive entanglements late in the Civil War. But on hot days it stretched and on very cold ones shortened, which led to sagging, and large beasts like cattle and horses learned to make matters worse by shouldering against it to give them access to the greener grass on the other side. In 1873, the story goes, three ingenious residents of De Kalb County, Illinois, strolling through the county fair, admired a display of wooden fence rail cow-proofed with sharp wire points set at intervals. Six months later each of the three was applying for a patent on a new kind of fence wire: two-ply twisted to take care of the heat-cold problem, barbed to deter animals from pushing against it. Several strands of such wire stapled to a minimum amount of post timber offered many of the good points of Osage orange hedging and none of the bad ones. Within a few years two of the inventors had fused interests in a flourishing Barb Fence Company; presently the third was drawn into what would become first the monopolistic American Steel and Wire Company and then an important component of the U.S. Steel Corporation.

The key to that success was none of the inventors, however, but a free-wheeling young Illinoisan, John W. Gates, sent to sell barbed wire in Texas in 1875. To counter scornful doubt that a few strands of wire could hold Texas' formidable longhorns, he used barbed wire to make the Plaza of San Antonio into a large corral, drove into it a bunch of cattle chosen for size and vigor, and challenged all and sundry to stampede them over, under or through his wire. After a few attempts the cattle could not be got to try again. They merely milled around, staying yards away from this barely visible thing that bit and stung. Their ability to learn fast was the first large stepping-stone in the conspicuous career of "Bet-a-million" Gates, Wall Street plunger and juggler of great corporations. More to the point the repercussions changed the open-range Great American Ranch into a region of large to huge stock farms, the phase in which much of it remains today. Once the arbitrary barbed-wire fences kept cattle put, improvement-breeding became practical; windmill-pumping of water from deep wells replaced reliance on poorly located streams and water holes; and the cowhand became primarily a fence inspector, a pliersman, riding and riding to check and repair wire in the intervals of his numerous other chores.

That was the revolution that led Owen Wister to his elegy of 1902 for "the cow-puncher, the last romantic figure upon our soil" as part of "a vanished world. . . . The mountains are there, far and shining, and the infinite earth, and the air that seems forever the true fountain of youth, —where is the buffalo, and the wild antelope, and the horseman with his pasturing thousands?" [87] All gone, he noted, in the dozen years since he had first written about the West.

Though an Easterner who belonged to the right clubs at Harvard and in his native Philadelphia, he also had a special streak of ginger in him, maybe deriving from his grandmother Fanny Kemble, as brilliant on horseback as she was on stage and platform. Anyway, sent West for his health as a young man (like his good friend Theodore Roosevelt), Wister fell in love with the cattle kingdom, came to know it intimately and wrote of it so well—and in terms of his time so originally—that he is properly credited with having fathered the cowboy as folklore. Before him only dime novelists of the another-redskin-bit-the-dust stripe had made pen fodder of the trans-Missouri West. And even when they showed the hero of their puerilities as a cowboy, he was seldom engaged in his employment, rather in a welter of rustlers, gamblers, road agents, hair-breadth escapes and damsels in distress. The nation knew little more of the area except an occasional magazine or newspaper account of a nester vs. rancher war and the rodeo-style riding in "Buffalo Bill" Cody's Wild West tent show. Wister depicted his cowboys in three dimensions, shown as mostly drifters, some weaklings, some vicious monsters, many quite likable, sleeping with squaws sometimes and whores at others, but respectful toward women who sent them about their business, given to gambling and drinking as available, fools about money but mostly reliable on the pledged word, some with bottom enough eventually to settle down. His major creation, *The Virginian,* was an engaging blend of the cowboy's good points with enough integrity and savvy to win the Quality schoolmarm from Back East and become an important rancher.

He had also killed the villain in the last reel. Obviously this "first and basic Western" has, as Wister's daughter says, "been seen and read under hundreds of titles since." [88] It was not cliché then. It became a great best seller and contributed to the vernacular the Virginian's response at the poker table when the villain calls him a son of a bitch: "When you call me that, *smile!*" It had the advantage of being a real Alger story—not the kind that Alger wrote—and its stray flickers of harsh social attitudes, nature's nobleman contrasted with the feckless many, was no drawback in a time that was mad about Kipling and liked novels pitting tall, handsome young capitalists against bestially cunning labor leaders. Its form was, like the hero's, charmingly loose—lightly linked episodes built around the Virginian, in only a few of which does the schoolmarm figure. The one about the wayfarers in the mountains forced to believe themselves haunted by the ghosts of the rustlers they have left hanging in the cottonwood grove on the plain is admirable. The one about the neurotic hen destroyed by human good intentions is even better.

What froze the book into cliché was a cloyingly successful dramatization in 1903 starring Dustin Farnum, later an outstanding Western movie star. The theater imposed a stagy concern with what happened next to Him and Her and neglected the subsidiary humors and ironies that are the chief virtues of the original. Much the same thing happened in other terms when they staged *Uncle Tom's Cabin,* which also set up in the national waxworks stereotypes and stock situations morally and esthetically inferior to the materials in the book. The several movies made of *The Virginian* progressively heightened the damage into our time*— needlessly, however, for the stereotype cowboy already had plenty of sawdust stuffing. By the late 1890's the "Old Cattleman" stories of Alfred Henry Lewis, a young Kansas City lawyer who had spent several years punching cattle in the Southwest and then turned extremely successful newspaperman, gave the public labored drolleries about gambling and shooting scrapes that had the same kind of popularity that Damon Runyon's chronicles of Broadway had in the 1930's and 1940's. The analogy is the better because internal evidence makes it clear that Runyon leaned heavily on Lewis for both his style of dialogue and his taste in plots. Artists, too, contributed greatly. For some years before Wister and Lewis began to write in 1891, the Western drawings of

---

* A recent *The Virginian* serial on television had nothing but the title in common with Wister's book. Use of the title was merely a backhanded reflection of how long the impact of the book has lasted.

Frederic Remington had grown popular. So had those of Charles M. Russell. Both were vigorous draftsmen who had seen a lot of the Great American Ranch's things, doings and persons at or near their most vigorous. Russell may have been the better reporter, Remington the better artist. Some of his paintings get beyond mere excellent illustration. But both always had the magazine's art editor faithfully in mind, and with unerring instinct their imitators seized on and extended their shortcomings, eventually creating the Hollywood cowboy.

In *The Virginian* the tenderfoot narrator's first meal in the hotel of Medicine Bow, a water-tank hamlet on the Union Pacific, was of beef —corned beef from steers sent all the way to Chicago to be processed and sent back in square cans. The next day a cowhand preparing for a long ride buys canned sardines, canned chicken and, for drinking, canned tomatoes. On the outskirts are "The ramparts of Medicine Bow —thick heaps and fringes of tin cans . . . that civilization had dropped upon Wyoming's virgin soil . . . the wind has blown away the ashes of the [cowboy's] campfires; but the empty sardine box lies rusting over the face of the Western earth." [89] Already in the 1850's a gold rusher's wife had described Rich Bar in the Feather River country as "thickly peppered with empty bottles, oyster cans, sardine boxes. . . ." [90] The "herring boxes" that the forty-niner's Darling Clementine wore instead of Number Nine shoes were the oval tins (*boxes* in a usage persisting in the French *boîte* for tin can) in which herring is still packed. The Irishman's goat eating tin cans from the refuse behind the shanty was a reliable cliché of the Eastern comic artist, and Happy Hooligan of the funny papers *c.* 1910 wore a tin can for hat. Generations before beer was ever canned the tin can was established in folklore and widely disfiguring landscape and roadside.

Preserving sterilized foods in sealed containers was a European invention to meet the needs of Napoleon's commissary. Soon after Waterloo it came to America to flourish even more vigorously than at home. Fish and fruit were first, in glass to begin with, then in soldered tins. In 1847 the assistant steward of Lafayette College at Easton, Pennsylvania, successfully put up tomatoes in small tin pails with soldered lids. Just before the Civil War an astute grocer in Indianapolis, Gilbert Van Camp, once a tinsmith, created another momentous canned staple—pork and beans in tomato sauce. The Union armies, like Napoleon's, needed highly portable nutrients that would keep, and Van Camp's Army contracts made his new venture the nucleus of the present Stokely-Van Camp food empire. Those beans bought in case lots also thriftily supplemented rat cheese, salt herring, crackers and such in keeping the patrons of a gin mill feeling welcome and thirsty. Gradually this tomato sauce version superseded New England's molasses formula as the standard American baked bean. In 1897 Van Camp's rubbed it in by shipping East a whole train of its baked beans—and its equally popular tomato ketchup—with the cars labeled in huge letters: BEANS FOR BOSTON!

Canned tomatoes and canned meats also bulked large among Civil War supplies. By modern standards it was crude canning. The pressure kettle for reliable sterilizing was not used until 1875. The sanitary open-top can allowing clean filling waited until after 1900. But in spite of multiplying jokes about the new bride cooking with a can opener, cans made available to a great many persons the year round nutrients previously out of reach economically or physically or both. All over the world canned condensed milk supplied babies and invalids with bacteria-free cow's milk well before pasteurization was understood—and with the accidental advantage of a broken-down curd that babies could digest better than that of the natural product. As a coffee diluent it grew ubiquitous on the usually milkless Western ranch. The typical cowhand, short of reading matter, could recite from memory all the fine print on the label of Gail Borden's Eagle Brand. Think of those cowhands and miners getting also the rich fat-soluble vitamins of sardines and salmon hundreds of miles from salt water in a form much more convenient than that of salt mackerel packed in kegs. For all the crude packing, those canned tomatoes still supplied vitamin C for soldiers and were worthily conspicuous in the supplementary rations that the U.S. Sanitary Commission sent to military hospitals. Among civilians their use was just as salutary. Canned sweet corn cut off the cob came on the market, sloppy but flavorsome, highly nutritious and achieving good use of surplus from an otherwise seasonal crop. Canning gained such a foothold that guests at the hotels in St. Augustine, Florida, were complaining that down there where game was still plentiful and most cultivated vegetables would grow the year round, they were fed largely on canned stuff, because that was less trouble.

A different advance in nutrition came when John L. Mason of Vineland, New Jersey—for all its jolly name a godly real estate project founded on Dry principles—perfected the mason jar in 1858. Now farmwives—and townwives buying by the bushel at the peak of supply—could put up excess vegetables and fruits, particularly tomatoes and berries, unsuited for storage in a cool, dry place. This added another to the long list of farm women's summer chores, and a hot one, all steam and scalding water. But at the end it was a prideful sight—rank on rank of gleaming glass jars of scarlet tomatoes, peaches and raspberries and pickled green tomatoes and sweet corn relish and cucumber pickles and jams and jellies in glass topped with paraffin wax—a by-product of the kerosene boom. Previously mother and the girls had used tin cans sealed with sealing wax, so in spite of the virtually complete triumph of Mason's glass, they still called this fine-smelling and busy season canning time.

By now the kitchen icebox was adding its bit to improved nutrition. Several types of machines, the soundest a European invention, were supplementing the North's ponds and rivers with artificial ice for hygienic cold. Hence the taming of the frightening flavor of American summer butter and improvement in the taste of fresh vegetables shipped over considerable distances. Meat supply was rationalized by cold storage, inaugurated in 1881, allied with refrigerator cars out of the meat-packing centers of Kansas City and Chicago. But every plus implies a minus somewhere. Mechanical refrigeration also greatly heightened the breweries' capacity to age beer. Ensuing overproduction led to the consolidation of breweries (often with British capital buying into firms dominated by their German founders) into savagely competing giant concerns. Desperate for outlets, they set up chains of captive saloons owned outright or controlled by mortgages on building or fixtures and forced to sell only Brand X beer. Too many saloons per capita in large cities meant lowering what standards of decent operation there were and an increasingly blackened reputation for the enemies of the saloon to exploit. That had much to do with the success of the Anti-Saloon League's strategy of "The Saloon Must Go," which, embarked on in the late 1890's, led to the Eighteenth Amendment.

Unless alien visitors' reports were unwontedly polite, from the mid-1800's on the Frenchified cooking in America's most celebrated metropolitan restaurants, particularly the successive establishments of Swiss-born Lorenzo Delmonico, was nearing high European standards. Delmonico intelligently made a point of not only high-prestige *à la* dishes but also of the special virtues of American game and fish. New Orleans' blend of Colonial Spanish with French West Indian with Deep South notions of cooking was developing an authority all its own. Outside a few great cities, however, few public restaurants reached such heights, and from the bits of evidence available, one dimly discerns a steady descent into hell touching bottom in the railroad hotel dining room, all grease and soggy starch. The conspicuousness of the lard pail on both the grocer's and the housewife's shelves meant all too much. Not until the 1890's did the over-ladylike but hygienically and in some ways gastronomically salutary reforms of the Fanny Farmer-Mrs. (Sarah Tyson) Rorer kind of cooking school and cookbook begin to lighten and widen the range of American eating.

The cuisine thus diluted remained difficult to define since it derived from several cultures and had regional aspects; but negatively anyway lightness was not its basic quality. In 1878 Mark Twain, overexposed to the vapid cooking of European resort hotels, tantalized himself by listing American dishes he would make up with on getting home. He mentioned buckwheat cakes with maple syrup, eight kinds of hot bread, squash, fried chicken, numerous fruit pies and cobblers, several freshwater fish (Sierra Nevada brook trout, for instance, and Mississippi black bass), green corn in two forms, such New World fauna as terrapin, coon, possum, soft-shell crabs, canvas-back duck and wild turkey, other such New World specialties as succotash, chitterlings, hominy, Boston baked beans and sliced tomatoes with sugar and vinegar. Given reasonably good performance in the kitchen, one could arrange some blissful dinners from that roster. The witness' eloquence soared highest when contrasting Europeans' notion of breakfast, including coffee that "resembles the real thing as hypocrisy resembles holiness," with the American tradition of beefsteak for breakfast, "a mighty porterhouse . . . an inch and a half thick, sputtering from the griddle; dusted with fragrant pepper; enriched with little bits of melting butter of the most unimpeachable freshness . . ." with "smoking hot biscuits" [91] and hot buckwheat cakes on the side.

Note that by 1878 the icebox-minded American is implicitly reproaching Europe with overlively butter. Note also the celebration of steak with coffee—a combination almost incomprehensible in Old World terms at any meal—as "the average American's simplest and commonest breakfast." [91] Howells ascribed it to both the Quality and their house servants in a small town in New Hampshire. Frank Norris had the cheap streets of San Francisco c. 1890 odorous with "coffee and frying steaks," [92] probably round steak cut under half an inch thick. For to most Americans of that time, steak, whether for breakfast or for supper when the old man got home on the horsecar, was a thin expanse of beef with flour beaten into it, fried in lard; in certain regions this persists today. The usual sauce was a cream gravy of skillet scrapings with milk and flour, such as is traditional with fried chicken. The result can be a pleasant dish, but the requisite knack is not common. The usual end product is dark chewiness outside, gray chewiness inside and an indefinable flavor as of hot tin.

Yet perspective must be observed. The bare economic possibility of beef more or less daily, however abused in cooking, was the kind of detail in immigrants' letters home that fetched their relatives to America by millions. It illuminated the contrast, present from Colonial beginnings, between the American's and his Old Country cousin's average level of diet. By and large the American had more to eat, often better to eat. The proportion of protein in what he ate was often higher. And now canning enriched that diet with minerals and vitamins previously less available. Anthropologists believe that the eventual somatic results of these and later improvements in nutrition are primarily what makes American men tallest and heaviest of any large ethnic group yet measured. The process, recognized for fifty years, was the final blow to Buffon's notions about the stunting effect of the New World. It is clearest among descendants of recent immigrant groups. Sons of Japanese parents in California, for instance, grow 1.5 inches taller than their cousins born in Japan. Sons of Southern Italian-born parents in Boston run 2.1 inches taller than their fathers. Those changes are too consistent and rapid to be accounted for by mutation or other genetic factors. "Explanations for these striking trends are still not wholly satisfactory," says Carleton S. Coon and Edward E. Hunt's *Anthropology A to Z* (1963), "but nutrition seems to be prominently involved," [93] and the evidence adduced is impressive. Even more striking maybe is the steady lowering of the age at which girls first menstruate which has also accompanied this nutritional advance.

Neither gross size as such nor sexual precocity is an unmixed blessing. Large people require more calories and amino-acids per capita and greater headroom and length of bunk, and the disadvantages of girls' being capable of pregnancy at the age of twelve instead of fifteen to sixteen, as in their grandmothers' day, are both complex and self-evident. But there is no denying the biological good judgment of the potential emigrant attracted by an America where feeding more generous than anything his forebears had ever known was taken for granted.

Immigration too felt buoyant effects from the Civil War. The new farm machinery could fill much of the war-created gap in manpower for the farm. But in mines, factories, railroad maintenance and operation—all under heavy pressure not only from recruiting but also from civilians with new easy money—labor shortages were inevitable. Agents of shipping companies fanned out over Ireland and Germany telling of jobs awaiting people with the good sense to go seek them in a land of opportunity. The payment of large enlistment bounties—the device with which Uncle Sam and local authorities filled Army quotas—was also good bait. Though no official recruiting agents were sent overseas, the shipping agents could make it informally known to Terence Riley and Hans Müller that enlistees received bonuses of several hundred dollars and, under a new law, automatic citizenship on discharge. Recruiting tents flaunting banners and bonus offers were set up only a few yards from the exit from Castle Garden, the immigrant-processing station where New York State strove solicitously to see that the new-landed immigrant was fairly treated. So Terences and Hanses wound up in blue uniforms in such numbers that some zealous Southerners still maintain the North could never have won without them.

Further to attract manpower westward, Congress revived the old redemptioner system, dead for a generation. For prospective emigrants with a little capital, there was also the attraction of the railroad lands that the younger Western railroads had acquired from the government as construction subsidy and were now selling at low prices on easy terms to create settlement—and profits from freight and passengers —along the line. In 1864, for instance, the Illinois Central offered: "1,000,000 Acres Superior Farming Lands situated near Towns, Villages, Schools, and Churches . . . in farms of 40, 80, and 160 acres, on long credit, short credit, and for cash. . . ." [94] The accompanying imaginative work of art showed a stand of corn at least 14 feet high, the cheery farmer taking the day off with dog and gun, and a railroad train puffing along most conveniently in the middle distance. After mid-1862, when the momentous Homestead Act redeemed a Republican platform pledge of 1860, land-hungry Europeans were further dazzled by word of this amazing country where the government actually gave land for nothing, 160 wide acres of it, to anybody willing to settle on and cultivate it for a few years.

By then Germans and Irish were old stories, entering the New World along well-worn grooves and buoyed up by the presence of enclaves of their cultural kinsmen in numerous Over-the-Rhines and Yorkvilles. Differences existed, however. These Germans included fewer men of cultivation and ideas, more peasants and artisans, whose reasons for emigrating—readily available land, better pay, more openings for skill—were purely economic. Through 1890 they came in numbers exceeding those of the Irish. Wisconsin was their most popular goal, not at all accidentally. Already before the Civil War the state had a commissioner of immigration with the good German name of Hermann Härtel advertising its beauties in the German press. In 1867 a new State Board of Immigration asked three immigrant residents in each county for names of friends back in Germany to be officially urged to emigrate. Presently the state joined informally with the Wisconsin Central Railroad to maintain an agent in Basel to persuade woods-minded Swiss and Bavarians to come to Wisconsin.

Though plenty of Germans filtered north from Wisconsin, Minnesota's efforts to attract immigrants apparently had the greatest success in Scandinavia. That migration had seriously begun in the 1840's, when Ole Rynning, laid up with frozen feet in a small Norwegian colony in Illinois, had written and sent home for publication a pamphlet urging Norwegians to consider America. More honest than most such propaganda, it admitted that the winters were cold, that most American dwellings were inferior to Norwegian barns, that in prairie country wood for fencing was awkwardly scarce, and warned that rumors of a sweeping plague leaving land and farmsteads vacant for anybody caring to move in were false. But the rest reverberated with contrasts unfavorable to the Old Country, the sort of thing basic to emigrants' principal motives a century ago:

> It costs nothing to keep hogs in this country. They forage for themselves both summer and winter . . . pork is eaten at almost every meal. . . . With a rifle [one] does not have to buy meat for the first two years . . . the rivers abound with fish . . . every one is free to engage in whatever honorable occupation he wishes, and to go wherever he wishes without having to produce a passport. . . . Servant girls can easily secure work. . . . Women are respected and honored far more than is the case among the common people in Norway. . . .[95]

It was said that wishful poring over Rynning's pamphlet was what taught many a peasant to read. Thousands of such came in the next decade, often by way of the St. Lawrence and the Great Lakes into the new lands north and west of Chicago. After the Civil War, masses of Swedes, Danes and Finns, feeling the strains of economic change, growing population and equalitarian hopes, joined the movement into the northern Plains, urged on by the Homestead Act and propaganda from railroads, steamship lines and states needing manpower. The emotions and hardships involved are powerfully drawn in O. E. Rölvaag's *Giants in the Earth,* written first in Norwegian to make sure the second generation would know what their fathers and mothers were like. Ax- and woods-minded as befitted the fathers of the log cabin, these large-boned newcomers furnished most of the lumberjacks and sawmill hands harvesting Minnesota's and Wisconsin's timber for rafting down the rivers or eastward on Great Lakes schooners. Paul Bunyan's ancestry may have been French Canadian, but the tone of the industry that he symbolized was as Scandinavian as lingonberries.

Particularly hard times in Sweden in the late 1860's coincided with America's post-Civil War boom to put Swedes in the forefront of this benign Scandinavian invasion. Between 1868 and 1890 almost half a million of them left their native farms and timberlands. Primarily their typical motive was, as usual, hope of economic opportunity. But also as usual, it was often sharpened by one or more familiar kinds of secondary consideration. Letters from Swedes already in America told of relative equalitarianism in the New World, where you could go into a store to buy something without having to take off your hat to the bookkeeper. American ways contrasted enticingly with the sharp Swedish social stratification between Quality and peasant and peasant and hired man—or woman. The established Swedish Lutheran Church was harsh about dissenters. Sweden was apprehensively imitating the Continental powers by inaugurating compulsory universal military service. The typical Swedish emigrant was a peasant or subpeasant. Many were farm laborers who had hired out before they were ten years old and, even as grown men, were paid only the equivalent of an American dollar or two a month plus room and board and an annual clothing issue of a pair of boots, two shirts and a pair of mittens. Another heavy element in the emigration was the women farmhands who worked not only in housekeeping and dairying but also in field labor often as arduous as that done by men. As these husky girls heard of America as a land where women did no field work at all, they came flocking across the ocean to take over in the warm, clean jobs afforded by the American town lady of the house. Within a generation Ingrid and Helga were names almost as nearly synonymous with *maid of all work* in the upper Middle West as Bridget and Nora had ever been in the Northeast.

Competition among states hungry for population settled Scandinavians in western New York State, Illinois, the Pacific Northwest. By now names ending in -*quist, -holm* and -*sen* are taken for granted in most American communities like those ending in -*wood* and -*ton*. But the bulk of them came to their opportunity in the region of Minnesota and the Dakotas. The huge snowfalls customary there merely made them feel at home. Knowing a trick better than the Indians' clumsy snowshoes, they used skis in America for practical purposes long before Swiss resorts made them fashionable for fun. In the late 1850's a Scandinavian named John A. Thomson improvised skis to get the mail through a great snowstorm to a mining camp in the Sierra Nevada. Soon the miners were staging the New World's first ski races. On the Great Plains telegraph companies found that Scandinavian linesmen on skis were indispensable in winter maintenance. Particularly in Minnesota the heavy concentrations of Scandinavians encouraged the usual standoffishness accompanied by education and religion persisting in the Old Country language, preacher and teacher hand in hand. These peoples were less aggressively ethnic-minded than the Germans, however, and, also lacking the social handicap of being Catholic, settled in fairly well.

The social onus of having the same religion as Charlemagne and the

Black Prince hung more heavily on the Irish after the Civil War because now even more of their new immigrants came from Catholic Ireland, even fewer from Protestant Ulster. At the same time American Catholicism expanded through an influx of French Canadians attracted away from the archaic poverty of their peasant culture by the cash-wage economy of New England's textile and shoe towns. They and the Irish (with odd knots of Greeks and Portuguese as time went on) were taking over many mills east of the Hudson. The American-Canadian border was and still is so informal that the exact curve of the movement cannot be charted. But by 1890 the U.S. Census showed some 300,000 persons of French-Canadian origin or immediate descent—a far greater pool of Gallic genes, for whatever that is worth, than came with the Huguenots of the late 1600's or with the refugees from the French West Indies in the late 1700's. At first they tended to be over-mobile, going home with their earnings after a thrifty few years or frequently changing jobs or towns. Their Catholicism and alien speech inevitably struck their Yankee employers as grounds for mistrust. Yet as the least restless settled down in Nashua, Biddeford or Pawtucket, they came to command respect for thrift and stability, virtues discerned in them by even that astringent spirit, Senator (then Congressman) Henry Cabot Lodge.

They imported their own clergy from Quebec when possible, however, and, tenacious of their own thick version of the speech of their Norman-Breton forefathers, stayed aloof as clannishly as the Pennsylvania Dutch. It was noted that though naturalization was needed to qualify for voting, the French Canadians were the least likely of any immigrant group in the Northeast to take out first papers. Given the collective temperaments of the two, it was probably inevitable that there would be friction between them and the Irish in spite of a common religion. Howells saw it in North Cambridge, Massachusetts, where French Canadians working in local brickyards c. 1870 boarded in a barracks set in a consistently Irish neighborhood known as Dublin. He thought these strangers good-humored and eligible, but "Mrs. Clanahan . . . who . . . may be considered as moving in the best Dublin society, hints that, though good Catholics, the French are not thought perfectly honest." He relished thus finding Dublin "fearful of the encroachments of the French as we [Protestant bourgeoisie] . . . dread the advance of the Irish."

Apropos he went on to "the spiritual desolation occasioned by the settlement of an Irish family in one of our suburban neighborhoods . . . when the calamitous race . . . appears, a mortal pang strikes to the bottom of every pocket. Values tremble. . . . None but the Irish will build near the Irish . . . fear spreads to the elder Yankee homes about, and the owners prepare to abandon them. . . . Where the Celt sets his foot, there the Yankee . . . rarely, if ever . . . returns." [96] Apparently skin color is not an essential factor in what we now call block busting.

More exotic and standoffish than the French Canadians—and also worse penalized for it—were the Chinese of the West Coast. In the early bustle of the gold rush they had been more or less welcome. In 1851 the leading Californian newspaper called these tough, hardworking newcomers pouring in by thousands a "worthy integer of our population." [97] Since 1849 San Francisco had taken self-conscious pride in the polyglot population consequent on the wide impact of the news of California's gold. It had quickly brought Mexicans and Chileans up from southward; Frenchmen displaced by the bitter consequences of the revolution of 1848; from westward not only Chinese but "Kanakas" from Hawaii, jumping ship like so many others, and footloose Australians, an unfortunate number of whom provided San Francisco with a ready-made professional underworld of transported British criminals. Indeed the first to be hanged by San Francisco's first Vigilance Committee was a ticket-of-leave man from Down Under. By 1852, however, the Americans dominating the goldfields had gone xenophobic, harshly denying these various kinds of foreigners equal rights in the golden future. Informal restrictions on all but American miners varied from place to place but were practically universal and often culminated in categorical expulsion of all but Americans from a given camp. The first to be thus run out and otherwise discriminated against were usually the Chinese. They were permitted only to rewash the tailings of abandoned workings or, renouncing the gold they had come for, to turn for livelihood to the ancillary functions of laundry, cooking, truck raising and construction labor.

More thousands kept coming, however. Even the economic margin in the implicit restrictions of California offered a better living than did overcrowded China. Yellow-skinned, blue-clad, flat-hatted, scrawny but tireless, they pick-and-shoveled the Central Pacific over the Sierras to meet the Union Pacific, one of the great railroad-building feats of all time. The value that the ruling powers of California set on such docile and efficient labor was clear in the Burlingame Treaty of 1868 giving Americans and Chinese reciprocal rights of free entry into their respective countries. For a while the Central Pacific's permanent right-of-way labor force was 60 percent Chinese. But the barriers between them and the white society employing them steadily heightened. They brought in few of their own women except prostitutes, which was rightly taken to mean that they considered themselves mere economic sojourners with no stake in the country—a thing also true of many American gold rushers, but in Chinese it seemed crasser. They even thought burial in New World soil unworthy. The ships that brought fresh live coolies eastward took back to China on the return voyage the coffined corpses of their predecessors who had died. Their picturesque, many-layered China-town was soon one of the sights of San Francisco. Its internal dissensions, fought out in terms imported from China, gave the police much trouble. Its very presence, inscrutable and as slummy in some respects as New York City's Five Points had ever been, made local white lords of creation chronically uneasy.

"John Chinaman" became the favorite butt of San Francisco's raucous humor. His pigtail, his inability to separate *l* and *r,* his alleged taste for rats first came to Americans' attention there by the Golden Gate. As his restaurants gained foothold, they suffered from rumored association with petty crime, leprosy, white slavery. In St. Louis in the early 1890's Dreiser, the experienced newspaperman, regarded the few local Chinese restaurants as "really hangouts for crooks and thieves. . . ." [98] Some-times the stereotype overlapped that of the Negro. In Old San Francisco —in this context a curious description—chicken stealing was the China-man's folk crime when he was not inflicting nameless Oriental cruelties on tong rivals in the opium-scented cellars of Chinatown. For news-paper jokesmiths like Mark Twain, all Chinese stunk. (Robert Louis Stevenson, coming West on an emigrant train in 1879, thought the car in which the Chinese were segregated smelled less offensively than the one reserved for whites.) In Bret Harte's terms Chinese were deplorable gamblers; his Heathen Chinee embodied the disapproval of Oriental chicanery felt by a white San Francisco itself deep in crooked games of chance and manipulation of mining stocks. Yet the Chinese really were gambling-mad. Worse, they could and would put up with wages and working conditions unthinkable among whites and even save money while thus undercutting the race in charge. So when, in the late 1870's, hard times drew San Francisco's white wage earners by thousands to meetings on the sandlots to hear Irish-born teamster Dennis Kearney's harangues on their very real grievances, his spewings and snarlings at the Nob Hill millionaires were only his second-best card. His ace was "The Chinese Must Go!"—a slogan creating the strange spectacle of a scape-goat with a pigtail. Kearney's threats of leading his followers to make public dormitories of the Nob Hill mansions came to nothing. But their delight in beating up the Chinese and burning their laundries and shops elicited a revival of the Vigilance Committees that had cleaned up the town in the 1850's. The mob was ax-handled into behaving, and

Kearney was jailed for inciting to riot, which was pretty much the last of him as a leader.

His Workingmen's Party went on, however, to give the state a new constitution that would have accomplished more had the courts not nullified much of it. An indirect result of his demagoguery was the federal Act of 1882 barring free immigration of Chinese. But plenty of them were already ashore, conspicuously doing things their own way and rousing such ugly-mindedness as that in "Thoroughbred," a Kiplingesque story written by young Frank Norris in the mid-1890's: A bloodthirsty Chinese tong mob, cornering an enemy on the grounds of a Nob Hill mansion, incidentally threatens the beautiful daughter of the house and two of her suitors. The pluckier one boldly confronts them and "recognizing, with a crowd's intuition, a born leader and master of men [the Chinese] felt themselves slipping back into the cowed washmen and opium-drugged half-castes of the previous week. It is so rarely one sees the coolie otherwise than as the meek and cringing menial of the laundry or the kitchen that when he turns and shows his teeth . . . [it] is like getting a rat into a corner. The Hop Sing tong, curs to the marrow, chattered and cowered before him. . . ." [99] Thus California's anxiety about the Yellow Peril, soon spreading nationwide, was not, as is often assumed, the creation of William Randolph Hearst's headlines. It was already ripe and lurid in the yarn that young Rudyard Kipling spun in his *American Notes* about his solo evening in San Francisco's Chinatown the same year that young Hearst first took over his father's newspaper. In some ways this was even less edifying than the Negrophobia in the South. Sinophobia was a color prejudice honed to an especially keen edge against the counter-contempt of the Chinese for whites—for the most numerous people in the world have always been among its most devoted xenophobes.

It was unlucky that Kearney and so many of his followers were Irish, for the Irish had already been getting a bad enough press in the 1860–70's. They had long incurred public disapproval by letting corrupt politicians exploit them in several kinds of political fraud in return for practical assistance and reassurance in learning the ropes in the New World. They were particularly the backbone of New York City's Tammany Hall machine which, reaching particular power in the late 1860's, gave America an unprecedented demonstration of treasury looting on the grand scale. They had been prominent in 1862 in a whiskeyfied mob in the Pennsylvania coalfields that prevented a train carrying Civil War recruits from proceeding to Philadelphia. And they had been heart and soul of the anti-conscription mobs that terrorized New York City for several days in 1863 in the worst riots the nation had yet seen. Though beginning as protest against the glaring inequities of a new draft law—the prosperous could hire substitutes or buy exemption; the poor man had to go if his number was drawn—the violence soon turned into a race riot, with mobs killing Negroes on sight as the economic enemies of the Irish and the occasions of the unpopular war. The clearest evidence of the race aspect lay in the burning down of an orphan asylum for Negroes. By the time the authorities had restored order with militia and federal troops taking over, nearly 1,000 persons were known dead, mostly civilians and their Negro victims.

Among such hotheads were many whose actions sometimes caused doubt whether they really knew they had ever left Ireland. In 1860 the solidly Irish 69th Regiment of New York militia had refused to march in a parade honoring the visiting Prince of Wales. Some Irish enlisting in the Union Army openly proclaimed plans to use their military experience later against tyrannous England. Soon after the war the American arm of the Fenians, Ireland's most militant undercover movement, raised a war chest by sale of bonds to its membership of (reputedly) 250,000 Irish-Americans, and in the next few years sent several armed expeditions well stiffened with Civil War veterans across the border to attack Canada. Many Americans were then particularly inflamed against Britain because of her opportunistic help to the South in the war, a matter kept warm by the continuing dispute over the *Alabama* claims for damages done by Confederate cruisers of English origin. But the Fenians' inflammatory shenanigans could hardly be winked at, and it was irritating to have to send troops to restrain them—particularly when those captured by the Canadians, and others taken landing in Ireland off a ship named *Erin's Hope,* tried to use their new American citizenship as legal shield.

American Fenianism petered out in 1876 and 1877 partly because the Roman Catholic hierarchy opposed it. For a while its only result had been to make federal union of the Canadian provinces seem advisable in view of these recurrent emergencies on the border. But some of the war chest remained and left a mark on history when it was devoted to developing the submarine. To create an underwater torpedo boat with which to destroy the Royal Navy had been the dream of a recently arrived young Fenian, John Philip Holland, a teacher in a parochial school in Paterson, New Jersey. His fellow Fenians financed an experimental model that, tried out in the Passaic River, worked promisingly. They put another $23,000 into the larger *Fenian Ram,* which had many key features of today's submarine. The Fenians never managed to get it into effective service. Holland turned to the U.S. Navy. Only after years of frustrated effort to combine sound theory with the Navy's ideas did he finally break away and build on his own the eminently successful *Holland,* ancestor of all modern submarine fleets. He died in 1914, too soon to appreciate how calamitously well the Germans would use his beloved invention against England, the very enemy he had always had in mind.

The Presbyterian-Ulster fraction of the great Irish emigration also brought its ethnic enmities along to the New World, organized in a fraternal order called the Loyal Orange Institution. The name honored William of Orange (King William III of England), champion of Irish Protestantism. Canada, where both kinds of Irish settled in great numbers, was plagued for generations by the Orange Lodges' insistence on parading on the anniversary of the Battle of the Boyne (1690) wearing orange-colored sashes and singing "Lillibulero," the jaunty, jeering song that was to Ulster what "Dixie" is to the professional Southerner. American cities with large Irish populations had the same problem when the Orangemen thus rubbed the noses of all the Catholic Irish in their historic humiliation. In the mid-1890's Mr. Dooley was disgusted to hear that "th' Orangeys' procission" had marched unscathed: "Jawn, live an' let live is me motto. On'y I say this here, that 'tis a black disgrace f'r to let th' likes iv thim thrapse about the streets with their cheap ol' flags. . . . I mind th' time well whin an Orangey'd as lave go through hell in a celluloid suit as march . . . on th' twilfth of July." [100]

In the early 1870's New York City saw pitched battles involving firearms, as well as clubs, brickbats and fists, because a largely Catholic Irish police force was reluctant to give the Orangemen's parade the protection ordered by the mayor. The annual shindy of 1871 left forty-seven dead. George Templeton Strong shared the indignation of most non-Irish Americans: "If . . . both factions, well armed, could be brought together within . . . the Union race course, and kept there . . . until both parties were exterminated, criminal justice in New York would be administered at a greatly reduced expense next year." This staid Episcopalian lawyer could not even sympathize with the anti-Catholic faction in this family feud among aliens. When police protection proved adequate the next July 12, he called the marching Orangemen "a scurvy gang . . . so enveloped by policemen . . . [they] looked like a procession in custody on its way to the Tombs." [101] And as some of the unacknowledged majority of decent Irish began to prosper and rise toward lace curtains, a few even to affluence, they were savagely lampooned as beggars on horseback—as in the portrait of Mrs. Patrique Oreillé in Mark Twain and Charles Dudley Warner's *The Gilded Age.*

In the same decade Irish immigrants in the anthracite coalfields of

Pennsylvania did their share to strengthen the popular impression of Pat and Mike as violent troublemakers. Imported Welsh, English and German miners and supervisors had the good jobs. The Irish did the poorest-paid and often heaviest work—mule driving, coal sorting, pick-and-shovel chores for the miners—and were further aggrieved by the usual abuses—forced patronage of company stores secured by payment of wages in company scrip and tokens, and company housing so bad that the only thing to be said for it was that the cabin back home in Roscommon had been worse. Ireland had long been shot through with loose, secret anti-authority organizations under mass nicknames—the White Boys, the Threshers and so on—using blackmail and terrorism based on arson, mayhem, stock-slaughter and murder to resist church tithes, evictions and any ensuing criminal proceedings. By suppressing overt union organization the mine-owners had made it clear that anthracite had little but overexploited drudgery to offer Irishmen—who turned to the familiar weapon of terrorism to express their discontent.

Gradually it became common talk that the rising incidence of threatening letters, accidents to unpopular foremen and those testifying against Irishmen, and the occasional unsolved murder were the work of a mysterious group, the Mollie Maguires—a name straight out of Ireland's undercover world. Efforts to cope with rising lawlessness were clogged by the Irishmen's clannish—and under the circumstances cautious—inability to hear, see or mention evil and, as it turned out later, by a widespread delusion among them that there were no legal penalties on perjury in open court, and that the law could touch only the actual triggerman in a conspiracy to commit murder. Certain low taverns run by Irishmen were thought to be the Mollies' hangouts. The Roman Catholic Bishop of Philadelphia was among those convinced that they were actually the militant arm of the Ancient Order of Hibernians, the Catholic Irish equivalent of the Orangemen. That charge was never made to stick. By the mid-1870's, as hard times increased the strains between boss and employee, things were so thick in the coal country that the Pinkerton detective agency was hired to tackle the Mollies. A Pinkerton man posing as a petty criminal worked his way high into the confidence of the disgruntled Irish at a risk extremely real, though it lost nothing in his telling, and in 1876 his testimony got twenty men tried and hanged.

Some students still doubt that a definite, identifiable Mollie Maguire organization actually existed. It was undeniable, however, that hanging so many alleged Mollies did restore something like law and order. So lurid a melodrama naturally became the talk of the nation. Just as naturally the Irishman's reputation was blacker than ever. Actually this was rock bottom. Thenceforward the way was upward as the stage Irishman expanded and worked up goodwill for Pat and Mike and as social suspicion gradually diverted to other targets—labor leaders generally, anarchists particularly, the Jews. But the road would be long and bitterly exasperating, past signs saying "No Irish Need Apply." In 1889 General Horace Porter, a conspicuous after-dinner wit and stalwart Republican, probably thought he was touching on an immutable social datum when joking with a visiting French journalist about the curious place of the syllable *van* in America—the highest social level put it before the name as in Van Rensselaer; the lowest after—as in Sullivan.

Irish, Chinese, Negroes—the Civil War had disbanded the Know-Nothings, but Americans still had a habit of wholesale mistrust, readily becoming contempt, of those unlike themselves. So far, however, the nation had resisted anti-Jewish prejudice pretty well. Men of New York City's long established Sephardic Jewish families had been among the founding members of the city's best clubs. Their daughters sometimes married into august Knickerbocker families. Though his Jewishness was pretty evident—the name had obviously been Schönberg, and he had arrived as the American factotum for the great international banking house of Rothschild—August Belmont had readily Gentilized himself and became a social leader. When Edgar Fawcett and Edith Wharton used him as a basis for fictional characters, they failed to hint at his ethnic background. In Louisiana Salomon de Rothschild, a visitor from France, found it astonishing that acknowledged Jews like Henry M. Hyams and Edwin W. Moise (both born in Charleston, South Carolina) should be in the topmost echelon of state government and that Judah P. Benjamin and David Levy Yulee of Florida (both born in the Virgin Islands) should stand so high in Dixie's regional councils. Young Rothschild failed to secure election to the elegant New York Club but not, according to George Templeton Strong, because he was Jewish; the trouble was his being "immoderately given to lewd talk and nude photographs." [102]

Certain German Jews risen from petty trade in the backcountry to private banking and opulence in New York City preferred to retain deeper Jewishness in a firm social enclave of their own. Yet some of these, too, belonged to elite Gentile clubs. Their group's situation was like that of Gentile German immigrant families come to power and influence in Chicago and St. Louis—rather isolated, true, but as much by their own wish as that of others, with neither side making much of the courteous separation. It strengthens the point that these German Jews valued Germanness. Their own clubs were the San Francisco Verein, the Allemania (in Cincinnati), the Harmonie Gesellschaft (in New York City). They had French chefs, Irish maids and English butlers but German governesses, says Stephen Birmingham in *Our Crowd,* and sent their sons to the university in Berlin or Leipzig.

There had been some latent doubts about Jews. The English novels so much read by the Gentile upper strata—not evanescent trash either, but those of Dickens, Thackeray, George Eliot—took it for granted that Jews were more or less idiosyncratic creatures typically engrossed in despicably predatory livelihoods. When, as in *Our Mutual Friend,* fiction aimed to show a worthy Jew, it only made him seem remote and exotic. Accompanying hints of morbid strangeness were probably sharpened by the popularity of Eugène Sue's *The Wandering Jew* and the unctuous glitter with which Benjamin Disraeli dramatized himself as a world figure. Fawcett depicted the New York Stock Exchange of the 1870's as including "grimy, red-lipped Abraham Isaacs, in whom the usual prudence of his race had been conquered . . . by a longing rapidly to amass millions." [103] But the issue had not sharpened woundingly until 1877, when the fashionable Grand Union Hotel at Saratoga, owned by the estate of A. T. Stewart, rejected Joseph Seligman, head of the country's largest group of Jewish banking interests.

The ensuing squabble gained bitterness as it spread across the nation. Seligman's supporters—many eminent Gentiles included—set up a boycott of the Stewart store that was held at least partly responsible for its being sold to Wanamaker. A more serious consequence was an epidemic of overt decisions to bar Jews from resorts, clubs, college fraternities and such. Birmingham* suggests that by giving latent attitudes a clear lead, this "first publicized case of anti-Semitism in America" [104] actively created or anyway quickened the sentiment. Presently Laurence Gronlund's *The Cooperative Commonwealth,* a highly influential work hoping to combine Marxism with sweetness and light, careful to mention "such noble Jews as Karl Marx and Lassalle," was nevertheless denouncing the 1880's as "the Jewish age" and calling for "battle against this new Jewism . . . that special curse of our age, *Speculation,* the transfer of wealth from others to themselves by chicanery without giving an equivalent." [105]

In the 1880's deepening anti-Jewishness owed much to sudden changes in the quantity and character of Jewish immigration. In 1881 the Russians made the large Jewish population of eastern Russia and Poland the scapegoats for the assassination of Czar Alexander II. The ensuing massacres, first of several waves of pogroms, made the Eastern European Jews the harried successors of the Huguenots and the Pennsylvania Dutch seeking asylum overseas from organized violence. The

* This section relies considerably for both data and interpretations on *Our Crowd* and on Professor Nathan Glazer's *American Judaism* (1957).

urge to migrate was sharpened by increasing restrictions on where Jews lived and what they did for a living. The stated purpose of Russia's extremists was to kill a third of the Jews, drive out another third, and convert the rest. The Eastern European Jews' isolation had long been extreme. "The Jew in Germany felt that he was a German," says Rabbi Lee J. Levinger, ". . . the Jew in Russia was a Jew and not a Russian at all. He had his own courts, his own local community organization. . . . He lived in a Jewish neighborhood of a city, or in a Jewish village, and hardly ever met a gentile except in business, or if the gentiles came to collect taxes or attack the Jewish quarter . . . he never became a Russian and was seldom treated as a friendly alien." [106] And growing poverty enforced by special taxation and clogs on occupation and mobility were making such Jews as ragged and dirty as the Christian peasants who so viciously hated them.

They emigrated by families, sometimes entire villages at once, in numbers approaching those of the Irish of the early 1800's. Between 1881 and World War I some 1,500,000 of the czar's Jewish subjects arrived in America. Another 500,000 came from Rumania and the eastern elements of Austria-Hungary fleeing from lesser but ominous menaces. By the 1920's 7 of 8 Jews in America were of Eastern European birth or immediate descent, and the proportion of Jews to Gentiles had risen from 5 in 1,000 to some 3 in 100, mostly in large Northeastern cities, particularly New York City.

The German Jews' spreading-out to seek economic opportunity had taken many to small towns. These newcomers huddled together in urban enclaves like the Irish and for the same reason—the cultural self-sufficiency, amounting in Russia to a modified extraterritoriality, that had so long been forced on them. They badly needed the emotional support of hearing Yiddish all around them and the familiar group ritual in the synagogue, just as Pat and Mike needed neighbors with Irish tongues in their heads and Father Kelly there behind the confessional curtain. They crowded off the ship into New York City's Lower East Side and mostly stuck there in what Morris Hillquit, who went through it all, rated as "the most congested spot on the face of the globe" [107]—a partly self-created ghetto. For these culturally tortured people, the ghetto was no novelty, however, and verminous, noisome and noisy as it might be, it was better than Russia's Pale of Settlement, where, to take Abraham Cahan's *The Rise of David Levinsky* as authoritative, four families in one cellar room was nothing unusual. The new-landed hero of this novel, looking about him in streets teeming with Jews who had been in America only a few years, saw "far more self-confidence and energy . . . than [among] the crowds of my birthplace . . . these people were better dressed. . . . The poorest-looking man wore a hat . . . a stiff collar and a necktie, and the poorest woman wore a hat or bonnet." [108] Moreover, as the careers of Cahan, Hillquit and many, many others soon began to show, it really was true that America lacked czarist-style legal repressions.

The David Levinskys contrasted sharply with the German Jews, whose standards of living had been higher even at worst, whose experiences with Gentiles had been broader and not so murderously harsh. Having as often been petty craftsmen—tailors, furriers, small mechanics —as traders and hucksters, the Eastern Europeans turned for a living to the needle trades already much in the hands of German-Jewish employers, an industry still heavily sweated in spite of sewing machines. The Jew, German or Eastern, who had got just far enough ahead to have a tiny business of his own made pants for cheap wholesalers on a narrow margin and sweated the later-comers as part of the expected order of things. Within a few years not only was the manufacture of ready-made clothing almost a Jewish monopoly, but its sordid-looking rank and file were practically all Eastern in origin. The Yiddish that they spoke, a deviant form of archaic German, offended the cultivated German Jews, who prided themselves on good German, which many still used in their homes. And the intellectual gap was as wide as the linguistic one. The German Jews were moving toward a Reform Judaism modifying Biblical theology and relaxing many of Moses' laws. The Easterners clung to every last detail of the God of Jacob and His rituals and encompassing safeguards. After all, He and they had been the only reassurance in the czar's medieval world of pogroms and humiliations.

In a good many temperaments those reagents had produced a hot political radicalism sometimes anarchist in tone, oftener proto-Marxist, anyway convinced that no existing governments can have any good in them and the only hope of humanity lies in undermining or smashing them all. By 1888 immigrant Jews of this sort were helping organize strikes in the needle trades, first among pantsmakers, then among cloakmakers and so on, eventually 15,000 strong in militancy. Hard-won success in thus improving pay and hours strengthened the affinity of American Jews of Eastern background with Socialist trends. German Jews, on the other hand, particularly in New York City, which drew to it many who had prospered in the backcountry, were usually conventional in politics and concepts of the economic future. Belmont was high in Democratic councils before and during the Tweed Ring scandals. Joseph Seligman was invited to run for mayor of New York City on the Republican ticket early in the 1870's—a hint of the Jews' relatively high standing in the city.

It cannot be set down to seeking the votes of an ethnic bloc, for in that day the Jewish vote did not exist.

Small wonder that the cultural split between German and Eastern Jews was wide and deep, with vestiges still persisting. The Germans' well-meant efforts to clean up and retrain these uncouth outlanders were often thought of as gratuitous impudence. As their numbers on Manhattan Island made New York the largest Jewish city in history, the Easterners developed a brisk Yiddish-speaking culture with its own literature, press, theater and impeccably kosher cuisine. Immersion among their own people kept many who landed as adults from learning English. The children, however, took in English through the pores, as children do. Their average level of intelligence seems to have been as high as among the German Jews, and their obsessive feeling that learning was almost magically honorable set many of their sons enjoying the new country's unaccountably liberal educational facilities in medicine and law. Painful self-denial among a bright boy's family and frantic hard work on his part often produced striking results. Other youngsters got out of the ghetto by way of show business as managers or performers or into petty retailing, maybe starting with a street pushcart and progressing to a small store as profits permitted.

Sheer numbers spilling out from the Lower East Side would have made them conspicuous in New York City as the German Jews had never been. Add their strange speech; the strange script in their show windows; their strange food taboos; the eccentricities of their pietistic sects with long beards, long curls down the cheeks, long black coats and round black hats; the extreme acumen and energy with which many of them pursued profit or learning. The reaction of the New Yorker, who had never been more imaginatively tolerant than any other American, was an intensified version of his earlier anti-Irishness. The anti-Jewishness revealed by the Seligman affair became an epidemic that rapidly and calamitously infected much of the country. New Yorkers were soon calling the Jews "the Chinese of our retail trade" and Delmonico's "a veritable synagogue at the dinner-hour, for these mongrel Americans are not *personae gratae* at the clubs, and are driven to congregate in restaurants . . . one meets them socially nowhere . . . idle young gentlemen . . . ride in the horse-cars [through a Jewish neighborhood] and make bets as to the percentage of their fellow-passengers who . . . will have straight noses. . . . [The Jews] attempted in the name of the Germans of New York, to foist a statue . . . of Heine upon their good-humored stepbrothers, but this was too severe a test of their influence, and the statue was declined." [109] In show business the Heeb comic, as depicted by David Warfield, began to be differentiated from the Dutch comic, as perfected by Joe Weber and Lew Fields, though Weber was as Jewish as Warfield.

In 1892 Charles W. Eliot, deploring the failure of widespread schooling to civilize populations—a complaint that in itself implies an age more sanguine than ours—cited the acknowledged social fact that "The Jews are ostracized in educated Germany and metropolitan New York." [110] The pushy Jewish drummer had replaced the swindling Yankee peddler as the archetypal sharp dealer. In cultivated magazines casual bits such as those in Owen Wister's stories strengthened this attitude. The vulturish Jew as international banker brooded over *Caesar's Column,* the sociopolitical fantasy by Ignatius Donnelly, semi-Marxist Midwestern radical. A Midwestern German character in Howells' *The Son of Royal Langbrith* denounces the sycophantic Jewish sculptor as "Little Sheeny! . . . He ought to be a puller-in. He could sell you any misfit in the store," [111] and the gentle-minded author seems to take it for granted that on occasion anybody talks like that about Jews. Comic artists readily added the flashy, hook-nosed Jew to the array of stereotype targets already including the potato-mouthed Irishman and the flap-footed Negro. As if resenting their new comrade in proscription, the Negro and the Irishman almost outdid the white Protestant in Jew-despising, for they were likeliest to encounter the oversharp, petty trader of the puller-in type. I wish I had some notion of how the denizens of New York City's Chinatown near the site of the old Five Points felt about their teeming Jewish neighbors.

In 1894 Octave Thanet, a lady novelist, went to Pullman, Illinois, focus of a crucial strike of the American Railway Union, to look into what many feared, and some hoped, was the opening round of a revolution. She decided that the danger was exaggerated, that however turbulent such affairs got, insurrection in industrial contexts would never have dangerous support from the mass of the nation—because that mass was native-born. This affinity between the immigrant and organized working-class militancy had long been taken for granted. Now it became a new form of nativism with a heightened sense of economic threat reinforcing old assumptions.

This impression that the alien-born workman was more of a firebrand than the native-born was not sheer nativism, however. Barely 10 percent of the Workingmen's Party, the American arm of the Marxist First International known as the Socialist Labor Party after 1877, were American-born. Their press was conducted largely in German, and their conventions were as heavily German-flavored as those of the brewery trade. Of ten anarchist leaders arrested as accessories to the sensational Haymarket bombing of 1886 in Chicago, seven were German-, one English-, two American-born. Prohibitionists made much of the intimate relation between anarchists and the beer halls and meeting rooms over German-run saloons where such gestures were talked of. In the Pullman strike it was the pick-and-shovel labor, much of it alien-born, that supported the boycott of Pullman rolling stock, while the railroad brotherhoods—engineers, conductors, firemen—whose members were much likelier to be native-born went out of their way not to cooperate. Indeed the brotherhoods still felt themselves to be insurance-oriented and were gingerly about strikes. Most leaders of the Knights of Labor, a temporarily conspicuous attempt at one big union embracing all industries, were of British or Irish origin. And even some of the relatively few American-born labor leaders had an exotic flavor. The parents of Terence Powderly, wildly mustached, teetotaling chief of the Knights in their great days, were Irish newcomers. Those of Eugene V. Debs, organizer of the American Railway Union that the Pullman strike destroyed, hero of hopeful American radicalism in the pre-World War I era, were semiculti- vated Alsatians. The boy, though born and reared in utterly American Terre Haute, Indiana, was soaked in the European tradition of social bad conscience as manifested in Victor Hugo and Eugène Sue, after whom his parents had named him Eugene Victor Debs.

Such transplanting of Old World habits of mind—or feeling—was only part of it. The alien was not well acquainted with strive-and-succeed, while his American-born rival for a given hourly-wage job may have taken it too seriously for his own economic good. One of Howells' Boston Brahmins cited his industrialist brother-in-law as saying: "The Americans [on his payroll] never make any trouble. They seem to understand that so long as given unlimited opportunity, nobody has a right to complain." [112] Impressive radicals confirm this. Socialist Morris Hillquit, commenting a generation later on times he had known personally, said that though "European wage-workers were . . . 'class-conscious' . . . the American working-men . . . had yet before them the example of too many men who before their eyes rose from the ranks of labor . . . to wealth and power." [113] Friedrich Engels himself, the Reds' Oliver to Marx's Roland, wrote to Henry Demarest Lloyd in 1893 that America's "fatal hour of Capitalism" would have to wait until the American working class was not "composed in its majority by foreign immigration." [114] And Lloyd testified in 1897 for an English audience that "[America's] Socialist Labor Party of German Marxians has never taken hold . . . and never will, for the Americans, whatever their political mistakes, are not so stupid as to make a class movement of an agitation to abolish class." [115]

The clog on class solidarity was, as Hillquit clearly saw, the lively public awareness that Andrew Carnegie really had been a bobbin boy in a textile mill and Isaac Singer, whose name stood out of the curlicued ironwork of the ubiquitous sewing machine, a wandering machinist. Not that strive-and-succeed was exclusively American. In England, and to a lesser extent on the Continent, the Industrial Revolution was also creating self-made men, and in the mercantile field, long before that, the legend of Dick Whittington was the original Alger story. But the incidence of rags-to-riches was far lower in the Old World, and the societies concerned were much less fluid to begin with. So the psychological tingle filtering down to the average worker was less likely to weaken the far more formidable class structure. The Welsh coal miner in the Pennsylvania hills; the German journeyman baker in Chicago; the Irish peasant learning to carry a hod of bricks up a ladder in Boston —all had come to America heavily conditioned to rigid strata.

Well before the flaming railroad strikes of 1877 Charles Nordhoff, sociological journalist, called "Trade-Unions and International [Marxist] Clubs . . . a power almost entirely for evil" since they taught the recruit "to regard himself, and to act toward society, as a hireling for life . . . only demanding better conditions . . . to infuse with this spirit . . . the non-capitalist class . . . would . . . be one of the gravest calamities that could befall us as a nation . . . [arousing] an unreasoning and unreasonable discontent. . . ." So far, he suggested, the availability of good, cheap land had "acted as safety-valve . . . a large proportion of our most energetic and intelligent [workmen] do constantly seek these lands, where . . . at the worst [they] leave their children in an improved condition . . . the knowledge that anyone may do so makes those who do not more contented with their lot." [116] The next two decades saw the supply of good cheap land dwindle toward the famous closing of the frontier in the early 1890's of which historians have made so much—and much of it justified. Certainly the consequent narrowing of economic opportunity must have fostered the rise in militancy among native-born industrial workers toward the end of the century, aligning their habits of feeling more closely with those of the alien-born at the next bench.

Dazzling talk of unhampered opportunity might have been among the things originally attracting those aliens. But even while land was available, they may have been city-oriented and finding the New World full of sharp elbows, as well as opportunity, peevishly prejudiced against

Micks and Dutchmen and (after 1873) short of even the dirtiest and most arduous job openings. They were likely to conclude that the New World felt much like the Old after all—bosses on top, workers on the bottom, and a great gulf fixed between established affluence and the sweaty man in the flannel shirt. And unlike many of the American-born, these were genuine proletarians, having neither reserve resources nor any family on the old farm or in the upcountry village for refuge when times were bad. Among them came their militant countrymen, such as the Irish rebel and the Eastern Jewish radical, chronically hostile to powers that be in general, often experienced in organizing discontent, and preaching it in the immigrants' own language. Their chance came with the calamitous unemployment of the late 1870's—some 3,000,000 out of work, equivalent to 14,000,000 now—with practically none of today's unemployment insurance and state-organized relief to alleviate their situation. And those still with jobs probably had to take—or strike against—drastic wage cuts to match the shrinking volume of business.

A revival of union organization in native terms was already stirring, usually with mutual benefit insurance conspicuous, gradually turning— as had happened to the pre-Civil War unions—toward aggressive bettering of wages, hours and working conditions. After the Civil War Wendell Phillips, co-hero with Garrison of radical abolitionism, had espoused the cause of labor, run for governor on a Labor-*cum*-Prohibition ticket (remember the liberal overtones of the anti-Rum movement then) and received a thumping 14 percent of the vote cast. His advice to workingmen was—organize! "I welcome organization," he told the shoeworkers in 1872, ". . . whether it calls itself Trades-Union . . . International or Commune; anything that masses up the units . . . [into] a united force to face the organization of capital. . . . Claim something together, and at once; let the nation hear a united demand from the laboring voice. . . ." [117] Into the 1930's American labor would be working out that formula, finally more than succeeding in developing the social weight to counterbalance the employers' economic power. The highly mechanized new silver industry in Nevada had inadvertently given birth to the most effective union the nation had yet seen, forcing on employers the eight-hour day and pay scales keeping its members well-off in spite of inflated local prices. In the mass-producing shoe industry created by McKay's sole-sewing machine, the Knights of St. Crispin (patron of cobblers) gained 40,000 to 50,000 members, becoming the largest American union *c.* 1870. Garment cutters in Philadelphia founded the Knights of Labor to organize all workingmen on a nationwide basis, along with ancillary technicians and sympathizers who cared thus to stand up and be counted.

As in the lodges of the Knights of St. Crispin and the brotherhood motif of the railwaymen, the titles of the officers of the Knights of Labor —Venerable Sage, Unknown Knight and such—marked the taste of the day for secret-society rigmarole. (Similar trappings ornamented the Patrons of Husbandry—the Grange—a farmers' insurance and social fraternity, including women, soon putting political and economic pressure on railroads and commodity speculators, and the Pennsylvania oilfield men organizing against Standard Oil's octopoid tactics.) For labor unions, secrecy was not altogether puerile. Employees openly organizing their fellows often lost their jobs and had trouble finding others. Yet secrecy was poor public relations. Secret associations of militant workers made people recall the Mollie Maguires. After the Knights of Labor abandoned secrecy in 1881, their numbers rose in five years from 19,000 to 700,000. And labor organizers already had enough opprobrium to contend with. After the bloody Paris Commune of 1870 which Phillips among others cordially endorsed, though simultaneously advising Americans to try the ballot box first, anti-union employers—and it was hard to find any other kind—hung the alarming epithet *Communist** on aggressive labor. Gestures such as the pro-Commune march of the Workingmen's Party which the Claflin girls joined aided the identification in the prejudiced public mind. Then as the 1880's approached, one segment of immigrant German radicalism was swept off its never too firmly planted feet by a vociferous new cult hot from Europe, notably Germany—anarchism.

Its Old World leaders, preaching brotherly cooperation in economics and social morality lofty enough to dispense with laws and government, had recently been using what they called "propaganda by the deed"— meaning terrorism, particularly assassination of eminent persons single or wholesale, royalty preferred. Their self-chosen apostle to America was Johann Most, fresh from prison terms in the new German Empire and then in England, where he was jailed for publishing an article congratulating the Russian radicals on their success in killing Czar Alexander II—the same gesture that set off the pogroms that drove so many Russian Jews to America. In person Most was, like many anarchists, a mild man and no more wildly bearded than many of the kings and plutocrats

* The proper term, of course, was *Communard,* the designation for all supporters of the Paris Commune regardless of the many varieties of radicalism that they included. Until then Americans had used Communist, often with a small *c,* to mean the visionary Utopist such as the Fourierite. Our current use of it specifically to identify the committed adherent of the Third International, the Bolshevik aspect of Marxism, goes back no farther than 1919. But the reactionary mind is still likely to use it to this day as a pejorative epithet for any thing or person suspected of a Socialist flavor.

whom he thought enemies of mankind. But in America his and his adherents' talk and printed writings, utterly flamboyant and indiscreet, inevitably caused public alarm even though usually couched in German —or Russian or Yiddish or Italian, the last for the inspiration of the developing influx of the poverty-stricken from Southern Italy. Anarchists' notion of the best way to promote the eight-hour day in Indianapolis was to pass out a handbill before a demonstration: "Workingmen to arms! Peace to the cottage and death to luxurious idleness! . . . One pound of dynamite is better than a bushel of bullets. Make your demand for eight hours with weapons in your hands, to meet the capitalistic bloodhounds, police, and militia in proper manner." [118] Dynamite, then rather a novelty, especially drew them. "Stuff several pounds of this sublime stuff into an inch pipe," advised an anarchist paper in Chicago. ". . . plug up both ends, insert a cap with fuse attached, place this in the vicinity of a lot of rich loafers who live by the sweat of other people's brows, and light the fuse. . . ." [119]

The Chicago anarchists' antics culminating in the Haymarket bombing were so stupid that Edward Bellamy, whose Utopist fantasy *Looking Backward* became the bible of the amateur radical of the 1890's, ironically suggested that they must have been "paid by the great monopolies . . . to talk about . . . blowing people up, in order, by alarming the timid, to head off any real reforms." [120] The occasion was mass agitation for the eight-hour day, a cause taken up by many segments of Chicago's labor movement with the anarchists as minor volunteers. Local sentiment was inflamed by several important strikes involving some 50,000 men, in one of which the police had fired on an aggressive mob and killed 3 strikers. The anarchists called a mass meeting of protest and made up for the disappointing turnout—only some 3,000, where 25,000 had been hoped for—by the fervency of their harangues. The mayor of the city had instructed the special force of police stationed nearby that the potential trouble was over; the crowd was dispersing. But the police took it on themselves to break up the dwindling crowd; somebody threw a dynamite bomb that killed a policeman and wounded several; in the ensuing fight more were killed on both sides . . . and after a trial denounced by practically the entire Chicago bar as close to a legal lynching, several of the anarchist leaders were hanged as accessories, several more imprisoned for life.

Who threw the bomb was never known. Protests against the manner of the trial, in which no legal evidence of connection between accused and bomb was shown, were utterly justified. It was also true, however, that the thrower had only done what those on trial had just been exhorting workingmen to do and that their moral responsibility was as real as that of the rabid kind of abolitionist for John Brown's lunacies at Harpers Ferry. The effects of the incident were several, all deplorable: It gave American labor radicalism its first and least worthy martyrs. It killed the eight-hour-day movement for the time being. And it gave employers a fine weapon against restless labor. For a generation after the Haymarket affair the cause of labor carried, however unfairly in most contexts, a flavor of bomb-throwing, foreign-accented, beer-sodden fanaticism.

That was particularly effective when imposed on the already vivid public memory of the rail strikes of 1877, which, says Wayne G. Broehl, Jr., a sober student of economic history, had brought "the country about as close to real revolution as it has ever been." [121] Set off by repeated wage cuts on the Baltimore and Ohio, trouble spread as far north as St. Paul, Minnesota, as far west as Omaha, Nebraska. It took U.S. Army units, as well as state militia, to smother it. The strikers in the always hard-nosed area around Pittsburgh particularly distinguished themselves by burning much of the Pennsylvania Railroad's rolling stock and forcing the humiliating withdrawal of a large unit of militia besieged in a roundhouse. Such violence fitted dismayingly well with the harsh vocabulary of economic warfare, much of it current today, that the press and the strike-rally speaker had been teaching an apprehensive public since the early 1860's. A shop resisting unionization was "foul"; workers refusing to join were "rats," "blacklegs," "black sheep" or "scabs"; some of those terms were also applied to strikebreakers. "Pickets" posted ostensibly to dissuade blacklegs from entering a struck shop readily took to violence as the most effective dissuasion.

Most of those eloquent metaphors were imported from British working-class talk in witness of the importance of militant British immigrants in the American labor movement. Any kind of relation between the employer and an organized body of employees was new to most Americans. The right to strike was no longer challenged in court. But the position of the scab, whether refusing to walk out or hiring in as strikebreaker, held infinite potential bad blood. The plant owner whose father and grandfather had been accustomed to hire mill or section hands in individual bargains failed to see why the employees' unquestioned freedom to quit the job on strike in collusion with others did not leave unimpaired the employer's freedom to hire others for the jobs thus voluntarily abandoned and to use force, if necessary, to keep the factory gate open for the new hands. And as for any such outrageous notion as the closed shop! In many situations Negroes, usually needy and seldom with much reason to feel solidarity with whites, proved readily available strikebreakers. It hardly mollified the rising tempers of a detail of Irish longshoremen pickets to see the despised black man brought in to work the cargo under the protection of hired guards. The white American workingman, native- or foreign-born, was no integrationist.

The most resounding clash of the old and the new points of view came in 1892, when strikers who had taken over the Carnegie Steel Company's key plant at Homestead, Pennsylvania, shot it out with a bargeload of strikebreakers hired from the Pinkertons—the same agency that had broken the Mollie Maguires—and drove them off. (Ironists should note that back in Scotland the families of Andrew Carnegie and Allan Pinkerton, immigrant boys both, had been outspoken radicals.) State militia sent to restore order broke the strike, as expected. The striking union disintegrated, and Henry C. Frick, Carnegie's ruthless and able colleague in charge, became a hero among the less farsighted wearers of silk hats and broadcloth. His popularity rose even higher when a Lithuanian-Jewish anarchist, Alexander Berkman, made a master stroke of propaganda-by-the-deed by trying to assassinate him in his own office. Senator John M. Palmer of Illinois, presently to be the Gold Democrats' candidate for President, had the independence of mind to denounce Frick for hiring a private army and the social foresight to assert that the strikers had a right to be in the premises and "a right to employment there . . . to insist upon the permanency of their employment and . . . on a reasonable compensation." [122] But this uncanny anticipation of the ideas of the 1930's made no sense to the average American, who, belonging no more to the industrial wage-labor stratum than to the Newport-villa crowd, approved of Frick's victory, which set back organization in the steel industry for a generation. Indeed in the very year of the Homestead strike so civilized and open-minded a pundit as Charles W. Eliot, deploring the failure of formal education to "protect . . . from delusions and sophisms," listed as the sort of foolishness he had in mind astrology, theosophy, "strikes . . . boycotts . . . the persecution of Jews . . . the violent exclusion of non-union men from employment." [123]

Well before the railroads' troubles in 1877, long before the Haymarket bomb set industrialists seeing anarchists under beds, public anxiety about labor's rising militancy was cropping out in American novels. Fictional use of such issues may have been suggested by the success in 1870 of Charles Reade's *Put Yourself in His Place,* an adrenalin-rousing depiction of British unions' use of gunpowder, vitriol and arson to maintain domination of the cutlery industry. American writers handled such topics more mildly. The moral of their stories usually was that decent, native-born labor was being misled and the misleaders, as well as their most gullible dupes, were usually immigrants. In any case the organizer, the walking delegate, was almost invariably sinister. T. S. Arthur, of *Ten Nights in a Barroom* fame, was in the vanguard with *The Strike at Tivoli Mills*; its villain is a low Irish saloonkeeper organizing weak-minded workers in an industrial village in Pennsylvania. More cultivated readers were sought in *The Breadwinners* by John Hay. This clever young Hoosier had been a devoted secretary to President Lincoln; this led to marriage with the daughter of a Cleveland railroad magnate, eventual intimacy with the imperialist cabal that included Theodore Roosevelt, Henry Cabot Lodge and portentous Captain A. T. Mahan—and a part-time writing career of some note. The Breadwinners of his novel of 1883 were a secret organization in a lakeside city resembling Cleveland, a sort of urban Mollie Maguires fomenting unrest among workingmen with a violent revolutionary take-over somehow in mind. Its chieftain was native-born, but his name, Andrew Jackson Offitt, was, the eminently Republican author explained, "an unconscious brand . . . [showing] that the person bearing it is the son of illiterate parents, with no family pride or affections, but filled with a bitter and savage partisanship . . . [and] servile worship of the most injurious person in American history." [124] The mayor, a truckler to the mob, falls down on the job. The hero, a second-generation plutocrat with a fine Civil War record, suppresses the Breadwinners with vigilantes recruited from among war veterans.

Hardly a masterpiece, the thing has historical value because Hay was in so good a position to know and so eager to express how labor's new attitudes were regarded in the seats of the mighty and in the press of the day. Howells, whose *A Hazard of New Fortunes* (1890) was one of the few novels then depicting a foreign-born radical as a warm and well-meaning person, got unwontedly bitter about that sort of thing. The narrator of his *Altruria* says:

> I understand [from the papers] that the walking-delegate is an irresponsible tyrant, who . . . from time to time orders a strike in mere rancor . . . and then leaves the workingmen and their families to suffer the consequences, while he . . . rolls in the lap of luxury, careless of the misery he has created. Between his debauches . . . he is employed in poisoning the mind of the workingman against his real interests and real friends. This is perfectly easy, because the American workingman, though singularly shrewd and sensible in other respects, is the victim of an unaccountable obliquity of vision which keeps him from seeing his real interests and his real friends. . . .[125]

That same year Octave Thanet wrote to a magazine editor that the American workingman was losing "all the feeling of duty to his fellow citizens . . . being diverted to the one perilous channel of *class-feeling!* he is a workingman before he is an American—or a man." [126] That was certainly the way the Old World-reared immigrant at the next bench had been urging him to feel, not necessarily because it was true but because that was the way it had been in the Old Country. As industry grew larger, more impersonal, more complex and nearer monolithic, with trusts forming right and left to mock the captain of industry's professions of love of healthy competition, the American—or anyway certain emotional types among Americans—might well have edged toward that notion unaided. But bosses like Frick, the strive-and-succeed farm boy who wouldn't heed Carnegie's canny misgivings about the way he ran things at Homestead, were doing their best to help the Old Worldling Marxist make his point. There was also the gradual clogging of the escape hatches leading from rags to riches. "A class is fixed," wrote a minor observer in 1880, "when nine-tenths of those composing it can never get out of it. . . . Why mock working-men by putting rare exceptions as the general rule?" [127]

The Good Life envisaged for New Harmony and Brook Farm had been an effervescent importation like champagne—heady and insubstantial. In the next generation Marxism and anarchism, though weightier, had been imports further handicapped by swaddlings of language and exotic attitudes. While red flag and black flag drooped uncertainly, however, a pair of unimpeachably American prophets came out of the wilderness of 1880 prophesying in readily understandable terms well calculated to foster national uneasiness. In several ways, some significant, the lives of Henry George and Henry Demarest Lloyd were parallel. Both were born in great seaboard cities: George in Philadelphia in 1839, Lloyd in New York City in 1846. Both had narrow, intensely Protestant-pious rearings. Both went West to work on newspapers and thereby came into contact with the social and economic data underlying their life's work: George to the San Francisco Bay area, Lloyd to Chicago. A rigid mind would be tempted to hint that here again the east-to-west central strip of the nation was calling the American tune.

George was the more theory-minded of the two. California showed him the most striking American examples of smotheringly large land grants—first from the Spanish Crown, then from gringo governments. He also found that the ups and downs of California journalism meant very hard sledding for himself and his young wife and their progeny. That "gave him a burning personal knowledge of poverty, which was reflected in all he afterwards wrote and did." [128] And his experiences as not only journeyman printer but gold seeker and foremast hand and Democratic politician in the try-anything-once Western tradition were stimulatingly broad. Out of them this very serious man, thoughtful as well as sensitive, developed a feeling even stronger than that of traditional economists for land as the fundamental fact of society. In the perversion of land use he saw the key to the gravest economic ills.

The general approach was not new. Mill, Marx, Spencer had shaped it in various forms. But he was unaware of that and earnestly worked it out for himself in a turgid but ingratiating book with the inspired title of *Progress and Poverty*. It told the Western world that what ailed it was landlordism. Underprivileged toilers, in this view, owed their inability to make ends meet to the great landlords—the Southern Pacific, William Waldorf Astor, Trinity Church—who held society to ransom by exacting rents to match increased land values created not by the passively predatory owner but by the growth of the very society thus being bled. The remedy was for the state to recapture by taxes the excess of rent—a sort of veiled confiscation—and unearned increments acquired by selling land risen in value. Thus relieved of unnatural burdens, the economy would know no more cyclical depressions with their shocking symptoms of bankruptcies and unemployment. And since no other taxes would be needed to pay for government's functions, individual consumers and business too would be relieved of the load of conventional taxation—hence the catch phrase *single tax* for the movement of which George became international spearhead.

In the decade that saw the rise of the electric light, the new U.S. Navy that fought Spain in 1898, and the Women's Christian Temperance Union, the single tax was a panacea cult. George's book sold by millions in the Old World as well as the New. Not only wishful wage earners and chronic landlord haters but imaginative industrialists, like Joseph Fels, the soap magnate of Philadelphia, took it up. In 1886 George ran for mayor of New York City on a labor-Socialist ticket and probably would have won if Tammany Hall had not taken the desperate measure of running against him a notably honest man, industrialist Abram Hewitt, instead of one of its own henchmen. Even so he got 32 percent of the vote in a three-cornered contest. That was the high-water mark, though he spent his remaining twelve years much in the public eye with lecture tours and the organization of Land and Labor Clubs to spread his gospel.

One of its shortcomings was pointed out by Laurence Gronlund, whose Cooperative Commonwealth was a competitor in the field of social therapy. *Progress and Poverty,* he said, would be more tactful if addressed to Britain instead of America: "To start the solution of the social problem . . . where as yet the great majority of farmers own the land which they cultivate, with a proposition to divest all landowners of their titles, is to

commence by making a very large proportion of [those] to be bene-
fitted hostile to the change." [129] Maybe because of that threat to the
chronic speculative-mindedness of the American farmer, the single tax
had only sporadic and indirect influence on social action. But it cannot
be dismissed as an evanescent, sterile fad. It was in itself a portentous
omen—the first California-born cult to flow eastward over the Rockies;
there would be so many more. And it did much to make Americans of
certain temperaments wonder whether free enterprise as the great capitalists practiced it did not sometimes mix the bowsprit with the rudder.

Lloyd contributed heavily to that rising uneasiness by becoming, in
Louis M. Hacker's phrase, "the first and finest of the muck-rakers" [130]
a generation before Theodore Roosevelt applied that epithet to Ida M.
Tarbell, Lincoln Steffens, *et al.* As a handsome and articulate undergraduate at Columbia College he had denounced monopoly in his commencement speech. Amateur politics among New York City's Liberal
Republicans (Horace Greeley's following) disillusioned him with high-
minded logrolling. He secured a job with the then flexible Chicago *Tribune,* presently became its financial editor, and learned a great deal
fast about how railroads, land grants, speculative finance and industry
worked. At the time there was no better place in the world to learn such
things. He married the charming daughter of the second largest stockholder in the paper—a step that, one way or another, gave the young
couple a comfortable living for life. Lloyd's campaign for the Haymarket
rioters caused a break with the *Tribune,* though he retained a block of
stock. But he was already launched as viewer-with-alarm. In 1881 he had
written—and Howells had pluckily printed in the *Atlantic*—"The Story
of a Great Monopoly," a stinging history of how the railroads had
abetted Standard Oil in swallowing up the national oil industry.

That article and its several sequels on grain speculation, land grants
and other touchy topics made him one of the most catalytic Americans
of his time. Excitement over the Standard Oil item was so high that the
magazine reprinted the issue seven times. Charles Edward Russell, then
a stripling in a Vermont academy, wrote thirty years later of how reading it gave him "an entirely new . . . conception of the forces at work
in my country. . . . Yet I had been reared in an . . . Abolitionist
family in which opposition to the corporations was held to be the next
great work after the destruction of slavery . . . with [Lloyd's] article
it dawned upon Americans . . . that . . . the Republic could no more
endure an oligarchy of capitalists than an oligarchy of slaveholders." [131]
The mere content of the article would have caused a stir. Its impact
was not lessened by the crackling wit with which Lloyd wrote in this early
part of his career. Standing Terence (*humani nihil a me alienum puto*)

on his head, he wrote to a colleague: " 'Nothing human is foreign to me,' said the ancient lover of men. Nothing foreign is human to me, says the modern American Know-Nothing." [132] After showing the corrupt origin of certain laws favoring Standard Oil's take-over of the oil-refining industry, he went on: "The Standard has done everything with the Pennsylvania legislature except to refine it. . . . America has the proud satisfaction of having furnished the world with the greatest, wisest, and meanest monopoly known to history." [133] An admirer of Lloyd's sent these pieces to Robert Louis Stevenson, wintering in the Adirondacks; that adept of prose skills wrote back that Lloyd "writes the most workmanlike article of any man known to me in America, [barring] Francis Parkman. Not a touch of the amateur; and but [Henry] James, Howells and . . . Parkman, I can't call to mind but one American writer who has not a little taint of it." [134]

Ida M. Tarbell's classic *History of the Standard Oil Company* of 1902 was merely a masterly elaboration along lines that Lloyd had already laid down very crisply. Two of his later books, a study of the coal miners' troubles at Spring Valley, Illinois, in 1890, and a rounded-out analysis of trust monopolies, *Wealth Against Commonwealth* (1894) became widely respected scripture among those trying to bell the capitalist cat. A trip to Europe after his break with the *Tribune* in 1885 had given him the cordial acquaintance of such stimulating radicals as William Morris and Sergei Kravchinski (alias Stepniak), the Russian terrorist who had stabbed to death the chief of the czar's secret police. His attitude toward what society should do about itself underwent a gradual radicalization that culminated in 1903—the year of his death —in formal affiliation with Socialism. His style went off to match, so that sometimes he sounded like just another enthusiast throwing soggy epithets as if they were tomatoes. But he would have made a difficult Socialist, for he retained flashes of his idiosyncrasy and skepticism. In 1898, when he was already a marked man as pleader for anarchists and for the American Railway Union leaders jailed after the disastrous Pullman strike, he still resisted the orthodox Socialist program of the state's taking over all means of production, writing: "I believe private ownership for private gain, and competitive and individual initiative, to be entirely consistent with public and private morality and welfare under certain conditions. Ours is a dual world in the industrial as well as in every other quarter." He went on to say that the state could never have built the American railway system to "its present economic perfection" and that on the whole, great as the sins of private enterprise had been in that field, they did not wipe out the greater good thus accomplished; only by now the state should take over for its own protection.[135]

The outstanding contribution of his last years came of a field trip to the Antipodes which made him zealously preach American adoption of the New Zealand system of compulsory arbitration of labor disputes, and there was a salty refusal to wear any man's collar, even that of organized labor, a force in which he devoutly believed, in his pointing out that there was "no better credential for the idea of arbitration courts than the fact that . . . both sides are vehemently, passionately opposed to it. Enemies in all else, union labour and union capital are friends in their fright at the suggestion that the public shall compel them to adopt rules of order instead of a military code. . . . They are class leaders of class movements seeking class advantage; the public is their prey. . . ." [136] It is a touch disconcerting to learn that this unquestionably sincere champion of the abused masses had his clothes tailored in London and, when he wanted a summer place, built on the farthest headland of Narragansett Bay a seaside mansion that would have been quite at home in plutocratic Newport nearby; his great friend and frequent ally Clarence Darrow was better advised to affect the rumpled country lawyer. But much of his wife's father's money also went to hard-up radicals fighting what Lloyd thought the good fight as well as to Bond Street, and in his very last year, even as a newly avowed Socialist, he could still tell his notebook: "Americans are fond of saying that we have no classes. Delusive as this boast is, it at least shows that the people feel that the spirit of our institutions demands that there should be no class. These Karl Marx sectarians . . . look only at their own class . . . the minority." [137]

One of the radicals to whom Lloyd lent a hand was Gronlund. His accomplishment had been to bridge the gap between Marxism as a gnarly eccentricity of the beer-hall doctrinaire with small pertinence to America and Marxism as universal solvent of social injustice particularly pertinent to America's genius at organizing production and distribution. The Marxism in his *The Cooperative Commonwealth* (1884) was well disguised. In all innocence Eugene Debs told federal questioners in 1894 that he could not be a Socialist since all his ideas came from Gronlund, not Marx. The deception was probably unintentional, for Gronlund's temperament led him to mix more and more religious feeling into his radicalism. He said Marx-flavored things but without the orthodox abusive snarl. A principal concern of his book was to recruit an elite of well-prepared persons of goodwill and acumen to make sure that the inevitable revolution evolved into the good life. Ten thousand such could turn the trick if ready in time, he thought. "Everything is ripe, especially in the United States," he wrote in 1890, "except leaders. I am convinced they will come out from the deeply religious minds. . . . What is needed is to convince them that this coming change is God's will; that the society to be ushered in is not a pig-sty, filled with well-fed hogs, but is, indeed, the Kingdom of Heaven on earth." [138]

Toward his death he was hoping to indoctrinate the new generation by forming an American Socialist Fraternity alongside the Phi Delts and Sigma Chis on college campuses. It came to nothing. But since 1888 a great missionary work for the Good Life had been achieved by another book—*Looking Backward,* a novel spelling out the social paradise potential in public ownership of the means of production as Gronlund conceived it. Edward Bellamy, its author, was a Yankee journalist—frail, rather a recluse, known as the writer of short stories and novels mostly of an occultist cast. *Looking Backward* sold slowly at first. Then, the story is, a Boston department store put a large remainder stock of it into a show window, bargain hunters buying it began to talk, and it skyrocketed into an *Uncle Tom's Cabin* kind of best seller. Hundreds of thousands of copies rolled from the presses in America, Canada, Britain and the Down Under colonies, and (in translation) in Germany, Scandinavia, Russia, Italy, France. The year before Bellamy died he finished an explanatory sequel, *Equality* (1897), which, though no such success in sales, contained a striking economic allegory in pseudo-Biblical language that, as "The Parable of the Water Tank," circulated by millions as a Socialist propaganda tract pretty much all over the world. The Old World, inventor of Socialism, was now taking lessons in it in a New World interpretation.

The sleeping hero of *Looking Backward* shifts ahead in time from plutocratic Boston in 1887 to the Socialist-Good Life Boston in 2000. A piquant feature of this world-to-be is its anticipation of piped-in music and radio as cultural tools. The phonograph and the telephone were already far enough along to give Bellamy the requisite hints. By 2000 America has become a monolithic, industrially and culturally integrated community (with strong resemblances to the Soviet Union, as Heywood Broun noted in the mid-1930's), where all get equal shares of the national product and all must work at what they are best suited to do, both sexes, to the age of forty-five. Profit based on speculation and exploitation has vanished along with money, so man's inhumanity to man has also withered away.

The immense sale of the book must mean that a large proportion of Bellamy's contemporaries were gnawingly hungry for so promising an apocalypse—for its gospel is its only attraction. Charles and Mary Beard, though great historians, disqualified themselves for literary criticism by calling *Looking Backward* a "lively romance." [139] Bellamy's handling of what story it has is unenticingly bald, yet also spinelessly prolix. The characters are voluble constructions of cardboard embodying the author's ideal New England ladies and gentlemen, for in the future everybody is bloodlessly cultivated after the manner of Louisburg Square, the beautiful heroine most girlishly so. William Morris, who had his own notions of the Socialist Good Life in his own British terms, complained justly in a review of *Looking Backward* that Bellamy had no imagination beyond "a great city; his dwelling of man in the future is Boston (U.S.A.) beautified." [140] Yankee parochiality of mind was never more evident. Morris would have been snorting yet had he known that many of the ways in which Bellamy beautified Boston obviously derived from *The Gates Ajar* and *Within the Gates,* popular novels of the time in which the lady author, Elizabeth Stuart Phelps, constructed for herself and her readers an extremely literal heaven. She began with the problem of whether everlasting bliss would afford the saved pianos as well as harps, and, being musical, supplied heaven with a great open concert hall in which the beatified soul of Beethoven conducted a celestial oratorio, the performance being piped all over by a sort of long-lines electronics.

The influence of the Civil War on his scheme also shows Bellamy as child of his place and time. Too young to have fought himself, he had a great liking for his elders' tales of soldiering and in his late teens tried to get into West Point, only to fail the physical examination. So when creating mankind's future, he took the equalitarian implications of the Civil War draft as a moral precedent. He was candid about the inevitable resemblance between monolithic State Socialism and an army gaining recruits by begetting them. Says the inquiring hero: ". . . you have simply applied the principle of military service . . . to the labor question." "Yes," says his tireless informant, "that . . . followed as a matter of course as soon as the nation became the sole capitalist." [141]

In the perfected future the hand of steel is ingeniously padded with options and training programs to align job assignment with liking. Drastic reductions of working hours sweeten irksome or noisome occupations. But the phrase *a national army of industry* is freely used, and soon sanctions are stated and the stockade appears: "A man able to do his duty [that is, work] and persistently refusing, is sentenced to solitary imprisonment on bread and water till he consents." [142] At least Bellamy meets the problem head on, instead of paltering with a "vagabond wage" such as Bertrand Russell once advanced as a reluctant solution. Writings of Bellamy's supplementing *Looking Backward* also mention as penalties for minor "idleness, disobedience of orders, neglect of duty . . . a temporary increase of work hours, or a severer sort of work." [143] His approach to the problem of tramps, then much on the public mind, sounds more like that of a hard-nosed sheriff than of an idealistic planner of sweet reasonableness: ". . . thousands of . . . life-long idlers, paupers, vagabonds . . . will starve, freeze and endure every pang sooner than accept work even when it is offered to them. . . . Nationalism will do with this class . . . what the present order cannot do . . . make them work. Equality of rights means equality of duty, and in undertaking to guarantee the one, the nation will undertake to enforce the other." [144]

Such frankness might have alarmed Americans traditionally leery of military arbitrariness and Europeans whose radical leaders often called conscription a crying evil. But for millions the pull of the good time coming in such glowing contrast with the crass, brutal present smothered possible misgivings. Hoping to consolidate his explosive success, Bellamy turned from a shy scribbler following where social logic led into an amateur juggler of public relations. With his royalties he financed a movement to bring to pass his kind of future and cannily labeled its objective not Socialism but Nationalism. To his wide public in Russia he explained this as emphasizing his basic principle that "industries should be nationalized" [145] instead of, as in some Socialist plans, belonging to the given industry's workers. Actually, it was made clear elsewhere, he avoided the Socialist label to keep his scheme free from association with red flags, sexual license and "abusive tone about God." [146]

That was good tactics, and there surely was a difference between the genteel heroine of *Looking Backward* and the loudmouthed, disreputable Claflin girls waving banners in a procession of avowed and unwashed Marxists. The Nationalist label was a subterfuge as successful as it was transparent for those who, though seeing through it, did not take alarm. By 1894 Bellamy could afford to write an introduction for the *Fabian Essays* of the right wing of British Socialism that went candid again, acknowledging that "Nationalism is the form under which socialism has thus far been brought to the notice of the American people." [147] Well before that, Terence Powderly of the Knights of Labor, Samuel Gompers of the new and likely American Federation of Labor and P. J. McGuire of the Brotherhood of Carpenters and Joiners were supporting the slapdash chain of Nationalist Clubs encouraged by Bellamy's headquarters in Boston. Eugene Debs credited Bellamy's book equally with Gronlund's for having made him a Socialist. Frances Willard, lecturing to Oxford undergraduates, warmly recommended it. Soon Britain too had Nationalist organizations, and Clement Attlee once told Bellamy's son that the British Labour Party was "a child of the Bellamy idea." [148] Gorky classed Bellamy with Henry George and Jack London as American influences important among Russian radicals. In the recent

Edward Bellamy Abroad, Sylvia E. Bowman and collaborators* make a good case for influence of similar weight in most countries of the Western world, even on the theosophical movements out of the Eastern. Another good case could be made for the suggestion that his out-of-character struggle to make the most for mankind out of the success of his book was responsible for Bellamy's death of tuberculosis—an ailment typically associated with emotional strain—at the age of forty-eight after he had overdriven himself to finish *Equality.*

A few voices besides Morris' marred the reception of *Looking Backward* among the world's radicals. Krupskaya, not yet Lenin's wife, thought it "a barren picture . . . dull and tedious" [148] compared to the turbulently stimulating ferments among Russian urban workers. Henry George called it "a castle in the air with clouds for its foundations." [149] But the harassed, mortgage-ridden farmers of the Midwest liked it as well as did most impatient city radicals. Soon the Nationalist movement was blending with—and then drowning in—the Populism of the 1890's, the program of which calling for nationalization of railroads, express companies, banks and so on frightened Wall Street half to death. Forty years later, Heywood Broun reported, many of the movers and shakers riding the radical tide of the 1930's, though good Marxists superficially scornful of *Looking Backward,* would confess that reading it was what had first jarred them to the left. At the same time John Dewey, Charles Beard and Edward Weeks were rating it second only to Marx's *Capital* as the most important book since 1885. Dewey specifically welcomed the prospect —abortive, as it proved—of a new Bellamy Club movement. John Haynes Holmes, most conspicuous radical preacher of the pre-World War II decades, handed down the professional opinion that "As surely as *Progress and Poverty* is the Old Testament of our American social Bible, so surely is *Looking Backward* the New . . . two parts of a completed whole." [150]

Actually the greatest achievement of George and Bellamy and their books had been so politely to disguise their messages that between them they created, right under the noses of a Socialist-despising public, a crypto-Socialism as indigenously American as its creators' backgrounds. *Looking Backward* in particular had made Socialism free of respectable dining tables, and none knew it better than Bellamy. "Until very recently," he wrote in that preface to *Fabian Essays,* ". . . That socialism could never take root in a republic like ours was assumed as an axiom . . . today the most significant and important movement among the American

* This account of Bellamy and his book owes many data to Professor Bowman and the others. None of them, however, would probably agree with my description of the qualities of *Looking Backward.*

people . . . is . . . the growth of socialist sentiment . . . the various
. . . radical social and economic reforms on socialist lines are the most
prominent themes of public discussions, and of private debate." [151] Or,
as Mr. Dooley would soon observe, socialism was "no longer talked to
ye in Platt Doitch, but handed to ye . . . fr'm behind an ivory fan. . . .
It suits me betther . . . thin whin Schultz screened a Schwabian account
iv it through his whiskers." [152]

A strong element in Bellamy's appeal was the goodwill toward men
obvious even in his strictures on tramps and slackers. The same quality,
though sometimes masked by indignation, showed in Lloyd, Gronlund (who almost succeeded in renouncing the emotional luxury of
abusing capitalists) and the early Debs, so cordially celebrated by his
fellow Hoosier and drinking crony James Whitcomb Riley:

> . . . where's a better all-round friend
> Than Eugene Debs?—a man that stands
> And jest holds out in his two hands
> As warm a heart as ever beat
> Betwixt here and the Mercy Seat!

In 1891 the appearance of a novel entitled *Caesar's Column* made it
corrosively plain that goodwill did not necessarily go with the creation
of hypothetical futures. Its author, Ignatius Donnelly, was the Philadel-
phia-born son of a Catholic Irish-born physician. Having failed as a speculative town-founder in the booming Minnesota of the 1850's, he became a prominent Republican orator noted for war-mindedness and
the advocacy of lavish land grants to railroads. When the Republicans
grew shy of him, he shifted base into railroad and trust baiting as a
leader in the Granger-Greenbacker-Populist complex of social rest-
lessnesses. He was also conspicuous as writer of books deadly serious on
fantastic topics: *Atlantis,* developing what is still the most popular
lost continent cult; *Ragnarok,* about the effects of a putative stray comet
on the earth; and *The Great Cryptogram,* carrying further the notion advanced in 1857 by Delia Bacon of Tallmadge, Ohio, that Shakespeare's
plays were written by somebody else.

His *Caesar's Column* is a sort of black mass *Looking Backward.* It
sold very well in America and still has morbid significance. For one
thing it shows how violent paranoid feelings can become in a man and yet
not prevent his coping with daily living. This future that Donnelly
drew so gloatingly is a technological marvel of electricity, aviation
and efficient economic management, yet foul with the power lust of an
omnipotent international trust founded by predatory Jews, based on a
brutalized proletariat in the country as well as in the city. In the

course of the book, it is violently overthrown by a nihilistic but Marxist-thinking "Brotherhood of Destruction." The North American culture falls to ruin. The Jewish member of the brotherhood's triumvirate takes off in an airship for Palestine with $100,000,000 in gold with which to rebuild Solomon's kingdom. The few decent survivors—all Gentiles, of course—flee in another airship to the East African highlands to create a bucolic Utopia. This nasty work, which reads as if the author had been allowed writing materials behind bars in an institution, was praised by Frances Willard, Hawthorne's literary son Julian, and James Cardinal Gibbons, the nation's most eminent Roman Catholic prelate. Worse, it was read on a scale that was appalling in view of what Richard Hofstadter has called its "sadistic and nihilistic spirit." [153] Apparently Donnelly's itchy hatreds felt good to many in the turbulent 1880's. For the next ten years the Populists, many of whom were viewers-with-alarm of more or less goodwill, let him write most of their political platforms.

The wide appeal of Donnelly's coarseness can be seen as cognate to other symptoms of his time, such as the temporary success of the slaveringly anti-Catholic American Protective Association and the public's delight in the printed antics of Peck's Bad Boy. Week after week his creator, George W. Peck of Milwaukee, Wisconsin, turned out first-person tales of how Henry, the bad boy, tricked his father into grievous misadventures with a goat, a swarm of bees, the police, the congregation of his church, a boy in girl's clothes—anything for a wildly impractical practical joke. Printed in Peck's weekly paper, they made him so popular locally that he was elected mayor of Milwaukee in 1890, governor of Wisconsin the same year, and reelected two years later. Collected in book form in 1883, they sold all over the country for the next forty years. The attitude is misanthropic. The groceryman in whom the boy confides is a petty swindler; the boy's mother silly at best, sly and stupidly gullible; his father a bombastic, skirt-chasing hypocrite who claims to have fought in the Civil War but was actually a sutler purveying rotgut whiskey. The modern reader's dismay over the things cannot be altogether set down to changes in styles of humor, for he may very well still be able to laugh with other outstanding humorists of that time, not only Mark Twain but such rough-and-tumble clowns as Petroleum V. Nasby and Bill Nye. This is slapstick without good sight gags, and there was something to mistrust in a public so relishing it that Peck's Bad Boy became a national proverb. Peck is worth reading, however, for the cultural details of grocery store, street corner and back parlor, and for being the first city-flavored jester to be taken to the American heart. Until then American humor had pretty well confined its most successful manifestations to the idiom of the barnyard and the old swimming hole. Population was shifting into town.

It was a cultural landmark when, in 1890, William Morris finished his *News from Nowhere*. This charming carving of a medievalistic Utopian future not only outshone *Looking Backward* as literature, but also enabled Morris to correct what he saw as Bellamy's errors in cultural psychology and esthetics. Here—shades of Sydney Smith!—was an eminent Briton first reading an American book, then making criticism of it the unacknowledged basis of a major work of his own. This signified that literary feedback from the New World to the Old had passed the stage of approving acceptance, as of Longfellow and Poe, and had reached that of influence by stimulation. Britain was taking Walt Whitman more seriously than America yet did as a technical innovator, which he was, and as an authentic voice of America, which in terms of the time he probably was not. After the Civil War sad-eyed Artemus Ward (Charles Farrar Browne, Cleveland newspaperman turned platform entertainer) convulsed England as he had America with lectures on "The Babes in the Woods" and "Life Among the Mormons." In the next decade Mark Twain's early books had even wider success in Britain. Between them these two kings of American drollery—more representative than Whitman—markedly affected subsequent British funnymen, Jerome K. Jerome, for instance.

Note that neither Whitman, Browne nor Mark Twain had ever looked a college registrar between the eyes. In them the Mother Country met no counterparts of the bright young men from "Oxbridge" who dominated British writing, serious or light. America had something like that in Henry Adams and his brothers, John Hay, Owen Wister and Henry and William James. But there was more cultural weight in the first group, alumni of the most influential American university of the 1850's to 1880's —the newspaper and attached printshop, which had already turned out Franklin, Garrison and Greeley. Now it also turned out Howells and Henry George and for peripheral cases Bret Harte, rolling-stone journalist whose flattering reception in England was his downfall; Frank Stockton, a wood engraver before he turned editor on *St. Nicholas* and then a writer of nimble fantasy; and Edward Eggleston, self-educated after backwoods schooling, Methodist preacher, then novelist and pioneer in the formal social history of America. America of the 1920's and 1930's retained part of this tradition in the assumption that those wanting to write did well to start in a city room after college. But many of Howells' fellows started by learning to stick type and pull proofs without the benefit even of high school. Printing, Howells said, was "simply my joy and pride. . . . My first attempt at literature was not written, but put up in type . . . till journalism became my university, the printing-office was mainly my school." [154]

Howells showed this American phenomenon at its best. His self-acquired cultivation was genially wide and so flexible that he readily became a principal advocate for the great Russian novelists in America. As he learned about and adjusted to the great world, it made him the first non-Yankee to edit the *Atlantic Monthly*. In his later phase in New York City he was a sort of big brother of American letters, advising his peers—even when they were nothing of the sort—and helping likely youngsters with spontaneous kindness. But the bitch goddess success did not stifle his growing alarm over the discrepancies between luxury and want, between security and hand-to-mouth penury beneath that great world—the sort of thing that led to sadistic hysteria in Donnelly and artsy-craftsy nostalgia in Morris. It became emotionally needful for Howells to treat labor's side of unions and strikes with respect, and in 1894, the year of the disastrous Pullman strike that shifted Debs into the arms of the Marxists, he published a notable goad to public bad conscience, *A Traveler from Altruria*. In this sustained dialogue set in a New England summer resort a visitor from a decently organized society plays Socrates to representative, well-placed and by no means all stupid Americans trying to explain American society to him. The banker is the pick of the lot because he is in a position to know more of actualities than the others. His hewings to the line show Howells' matured irony at its best:

"I wonder you are not ashamed of filling [the Altrurian] up with that stuff about our honoring some kinds of labor . . . we don't go about openly and explicitly despising any kind of honest toil—people don't do that anywhere now; but we condemn it in terms quite as unmistakable. The workingman acquiesces as completely as anybody else. He does not remain a workingman a moment longer than he can help; and after he gets up, if he is weak enough to be proud of having been one, it is because he feels that his low origin is a proof of his prowess in rising to the top against unusual odds. . . . The American ideal is not to change the conditions for all, but for each to rise above the rest if he can." [155]
Some years earlier Howells' elderly Virginian in *A Hazard of New Fortunes* contended that slavery had had aspects preferable to those of the America of 1890 with "commercialism . . . the poison at the heart of our national life . . . stolen insidiously upon us . . . the infernal impulse of competition [embroiling] us in a perpetual warfare of interests, developing the worst passions of our nature, and teaching us to trick and betray and destroy one another in the strife for money, till

now that impulse had exhausted itself and we found competition gone and the whole economic problem in the hands of the monopolies—the Standard Oil Company, the Sugar Trust, the Rubber Trust . . ." [156] —proto-muckraking and reminder that it was Howells who bought Lloyd's study of Standard Oil for the *Atlantic*.

As a writer he had a surefootedness among words that explains Stevenson's listing him among Americans with no touch of the amateur. He wrote too much and loosely; yet, like Thoreau, he handled the language as if he had invented it. His best novels depicted the Yankees and New Yorkers among whom the small-town boy from Ohio would never be wholly at home—which shows in his work without marring it. Thus exploiting expatriation, he was more like Henry James than like his great friend Mark Twain, who needed the boyhood data to bring out the best in him. What today's critics take as undue primness in his approach to the novelist's materials was merely part of his time like his puffy mustache. After all, Winslow Homer was an admirable painter though he did no voluptuous nudes.

The other writers of the 1880's who had Howells' organic intimacy with the language were both women and Yankees. Sarah Orne Jewett was queen of the local color specialists who were already staking out picturesque provinces of the American scene with varying degrees of success in applying well-worn plots to regional peculiarities. Actually Miss Jewett was *hors-concours*. She knew her native Maine so congenially well and lived so far inside her materials that her meticulous literary artistry seemed of a piece with them. Emily Dickinson lived out her thwarted life in Amherst, Massachusetts, and could personally have been invented by Nathaniel Hawthorne. But there was nothing regional about her posthumous verses that Colonel T. W. Higginson astonished the world with in 1890. Nor was there much specifically American about them. The best of them were as international as starshine and did as much to open up new possibilities for poetry in the English-speaking world as Whitman had done before her or Eliot and Pound would do after her.

The close relations between Howells and Mark Twain make the contrasts between them striking and useful. Nobody admired *Huckleberry Finn* more than Stevenson, but it was probably not oversight that kept Mark Twain off his list of reliably professional American writers. This is a hard saying today. Ever since 1919, when Waldo Frank taught American criticism that "Mark Twain was a man of genius . . . the soul of Mark Twain was great"; that *Huckleberry Finn* is "the voice of American chaos . . . the American hero . . . the American soul," [157] both Mark Twain and his best work have had the life squeezed out of them under mountains of writing and lecturing expanding on Frank's fulsomeness. (In the same years the same happened to Melville and *Moby Dick,* though with more excuse, since the book itself had leanings in that direction.) The result has been to put the writer and his characters into those national waxworks in ritual attitudes as banal as those of mural painting.

Mark Twain the professional entertainer, deliberately conspicuous in white suits and preening himself on his skill in timing lecture-platform laughs, might rather welcome that new opportunity for display. So probably would Tom Sawyer, also a showoff. But Huck Finn hardly deserves to be pawed over and massaged out of shape in the kind of television discussions of the basic American archetypal symbols that he would certainly classify, in his own immortal phrase, as "soul-butter and hogwash." Huck has been sacrificed to the academician's and the scriptwriter's need to generalize impressively about an America that never existed, and so has his creator. If one had to rescue just one American book from the flames of the end of the world for eternal preservation, there would be no hesitation—*Huckleberry Finn* from the time Huck reaches Pap's cabin to his arrival at the Phelps plantation. But that hardly makes Mark Twain whatever "a great soul" may be or in any normal sense "a man of genius" like, say, Leonardo da Vinci. It is just that half-inadvertently—as the feeble beginning and end of the book show—he managed for once to stay out of the way of his own great talent. The result was lamentably shapeless, but it was also the Great American Novel * that his contemporaries speculated about so busily that they failed to recognize it.

Thus to have given birth to a cultural monument of the order of *The Pilgrim's Progress* or Monticello is distinction enough. But to glorify Mark Twain as prophet and prodigy is further hazardous because it overlooks several other Mark Twains in addition to the professional stage showman: There was also the newspaper humorist supplying the entertainer with material, much of it superior to the repertories of his lecture-platform rivals; this was the trainer of the Jumping Frog and the reporter of the personal column in the Camelot *Weekly Hosannah.* Then the amateur businessman self-persuaded that he understood the door-to-door book-publishing industry and the subtleties of typesetting machines and gallantly paying for his presumption by grueling lecture tours and hack writing to reimburse the consequent creditors. Then

* James F. Light, recent biographer of De Forest, says (*John William De Forest,* New York, Twayne Publishers, 1965, 100) that his subject first coined this hopeful phrase in a critical piece in *The Nation,* January 9, 1868.

the brash graduate of what might be called the University of Gutenberg out of his depth in medieval history and trying to be peevishly intelligent about it in *The Prince and the Pauper* and *A Connecticut Yankee.* And the emerging crackerbarrel atheist floundering in black anger because the universe couldn't be bothered to explain itself to him, doomed to keep on trying to express the depths of his despair, but always sounding shallow about it. The sum of all those, including the keen sense of humor and the talent for friendship, is nevertheless no great soul. But it must be said, though with no wish to sound like Waldo Frank, that most of it was indeed highly American.

The Civil War, that versatile phenomenon, had much to do with the boom in publishing books for door-to-door subscription that proved so unlucky for Mark Twain. The many energetic young men whom demobilization set job-seeking enabled subscription-publishers to hire plenty of tireless book agents, and the war supplied rich subject matter appealing to a wide public that, having been through a nation-shaking experience, wanted to mull over and gossip about it. The American Publishing Company of Hartford, Connecticut, flourished with Horace Greeley's *The American Conflict* and Albert D. Richardson's melodramatic work on *The Secret Service.* Mark Twain's eventually ill-fated Webster and Company had a false dawn of immense initial success with General Grant's memoirs, of which more than 300,000 copies sold at $9 to $27 a set, depending on how fancy the binding was. Then, as the supply of boys-in-blue material dwindled, the nation's centenary in 1876 brought on thick popular compilations of the history of America and books on the Centennial Exposition complete with steel engravings of all the buildings to remind those who had been there of what they saw and those who had not of what they missed. By then subscription-publishing was a permanent part of the book world with important cultural effects.

The bookstore system, 200 years in being, could move books. It had brought publishing immortality to such indigenous best sellers as *Uncle Tom's Cabin,* Susan B. Warner's *The Wide, Wide World* and Maria S. Cummins' *The Lamplighter.* But those were fiction, sticky with religion, and in any case aimed at those with the habit of bookreading. Subscription publishers sought the potential customer who seldom entered a bookstore. The bait was largely religious at first. For instance, Hubbard Brothers, of Philadelphia, with six branch offices coast to coast, offered a Complete Domestic Bible "with over 200 highly finished engravings" for $7.50 to $20, depending on binding. The National Publishing Company, also of Philadelphia, had a Bible competing in the $8.50 to $15 range and, to lie beside it on the parlor table, a hack-written *Pathways to the Holy*

Land "with 242 Fine Engravings and Maps" at $3.75 to $6; or one might prefer *The Light in the East,* a prolix life of Christ "with over 200 fine engravings" at the same price. But the Hubbards also dabbled in secular items with the New American Fireside Edition of *Robinson Crusoe* at $2.50 to $6; *Ocean's Story,* about ships, navigation and "Works and Wonders Beneath the Sea . . . 200 Spirited Illustrations" at $4 to $6; and certainly *not* to keep on the parlor table, *The Ladies' Medical Guide,* $2 worth of gynecological-obstetrical advice with lavish illustrations but "of a high moral tone." In 1870 National countered with a 1,065-page sex treatise by O. S. Fowler, the irrepressible phrenologist, *Creative and Sexual Science, or Manhood and Womanhood, and Their Mutual Interrelations,* advising at verbose but seldom specific length on "Perfect Children; Their Generation, Endowment, Paternity, Maternity . . . Sexual Impairments Restored, Male Vigor and Female Health and Beauty Perpetuated and Augmented. . . ." The American Publishing Company, having done extremely well with *The Innocents Abroad* in 1869, went profitably into other popular humor with the works of Josh Billings and Samantha Allen.

Those were steep prices when one could get a suit of hand-me-down clothes for $10 and a recent novel for $1. But the numerous pictures and gilt-paneled bindings gave money's worth beyond the content, and the prospect was warned that "Our Subscription Books Are Not Sold in Book Stores." It was now or never to secure the moral or thrilling or patriotic or rib-tickling experience concentrated in these otherwise inaccessible pages. Householders previously reading little but the Bible and the almanac signed up dazzled by anticipation. Within a few years the book agent whose knock on the door led to such opportunity was a stock figure in American life competing for loose dollars with other canvassers for sewing machines, clocks, windmills and lightning rods.

"AGENTS ARE WANTED!" said the advertisements, "either sex, to sell works of high moral tone, rare literary merit and positive and permanent value . . . which, from their intrinsic and sterling worth, will be welcomed to every home and fireside . . . and be a credit to the canvassers who introduce them. . . . Agents are supplied at a very small advance from original cost (giving them nearly all the profits). . . . Agents for GOOD BOOKS are a lasting benefit in any community, and their calling is a noble one. . . . W. L. Smith of Fayette Co., Tennessee, sold 83 Bibles in eight days. . . . Mrs. H. Vansizer of Ada, Michigan, sold 140 Bibles in four weeks. . . ." Here was another independent living for Woman, and she seems to have taken it up widely, to judge from contemporary complaints about female book agents using tears and hard-luck stories to reinforce the sales talk. The elegant hero of John Hay's *The*

Breadwinners spoke feelingly of "the usual semi-mendicant, with sad-colored raiment and doleful whine, calling for a subscription for a new 'Centennial History. . . .' " [158] A very seductive one appeared in George Ade's "Fable of the Grass Widow." The book agents whom I remember from the Middle West just before World War I were almost always dreary, fast-talking women. But by then the industry had shifted from newly written or compiled items to library sets of standard novelists and historians or elaborate multivolumed anthologies of children's reading. Most of the subscription books of the Gilded Age were crudely compiled junk. But the fortune that the door-to-door method brought Mark Twain from *The Innocents Abroad* so impressed him that he used it for most of his early books—and all his best ones.

The American Publishing Company's lady book agents probably specialized in the works of Samantha Allen or, as she often called herself, Josiah Allen's Wife, a strong-minded and articulate upstate New York village matron created by a scribbling spinster, Marietta Holley. Borrowing tricks from the extremely popular Artemus Ward, she sent Samantha interviewing Horace Greeley, Victoria Woodhull and other newsworthy notables; speaking her mind in and out of season for Temperance and women's rights; pillorying sentimental old maids and soulful lecturers; reporting to her immense public on the Philadelphia Centennial and then, seventeen years later, on the Chicago Columbian Exposition; steering herself and her Josiah through the nonsense of Saratoga Springs. Josiah, a chin-tufted deacon old enough to know better, is always making a fool of himself over a pretty woman or a tourist snare or some half-witted new ambition to distinguish himself. Samantha, too, sometimes gets out of her country-bred depth as when she offers to swap home-knit mittens for yard goods at A. T. Stewart's department store in New York City, as she could have back home in Jonesville, New York. But compared to Josiah, she is all salt and gumption. The millions of these books giggled over by mother and the girls and read aloud in the evening to sheepishly grinning father and the boys must have put several finishing touches on the overweening belief of American women in the superiority of their sex—first more sensitive, then more righteous, now monopolizing common sense.

Miss Holley's good friends Susan B. Anthony and Frances Willard doubtless appreciated the way Samantha's books consistently implied that women's rights, as well as Temperance, had the Lord—or anyway Mrs. Grundy, often the same thing—on their side. For here was no bloomers-clad radical but a motherly soul in steel-rimmed specs and a tight little bonnet who had raised a family and was still running the Ladies Aid and proud of her hot biscuits. While she waits "to-home" for Josiah to return in the evening from a "trip to mill," she gloats over her kitchen's being

> slick as a pin. The painted floor was a shinin' like yellow glass . . . [the] braided mats was a layin' smooth and clean in front of the looking-glass, and before the stove . . . the wall . . . was papered with a light colored buff ground work with a red rose on it. . . . And Tirzah Ann had got a hangin' basket of ivy on the west winder. . . . The stove hearth shone like a silver dollar, and there was a bright fire, and in a minute the tea-kettle begun to sing. . . . I drawed out the table. . . . I had baked that day, and my bread was white as snow, and light as day . . . canned peaches, and some thin slices of ham as pink as a rose, and a strawberry pie. . . .[159]

Samantha's blend of the housewifely and the militant recalls the Women's Crusade and points to its successor movement, the Women's Christian Temperance Union. It was founded soon after the crusade by several of its leaders who had been prominent in the Sanitary Commission. But it became formidable only after 1879, when its helm was taken by Frances Willard, rapidly risen from corresponding secretary to president. She was wispy and red-haired and in spite of the frosty air of her pince-nez glasses, as intensely affectionate as she was capable. Only she had never married, confining herself to spasms of admiration for certain men eminent in good causes, such as Powderly and Henry Demarest Lloyd, while making it clear she was only being sisterly. Her closest relations, chaste, I am fairly sure, but almighty warm, were with her inner circle of lady collaborators, one also a spinster, two estranged from prominent husbands. The rank and file of her forces were married women, of course, the same small-town elite who had marched in the crusade, whose matronly dignity and local social leverage were indispensable to the WCTU's effectiveness. But the organization's view of what the relative situations of the sexes should be was made ruthlessly plain by one of its lady poets:

> "Husband and wife are one,"
>   Says the perfect law divine.
> "That one the man," says human law
>   With its distinctions fine.
> But in the W.C.T.U.,
>   New realm of law and life,
> Husband and wife are often one,
>   But that one is the wife.*

* This section is a condensation of Chapter XII of my *The Life and Times of the Late Demon Rum.*

Though an avowed feminist, Miss Willard fought shy of the single-minded Susan B. Anthony approach to women's rights, preferring what was called her "Do Everything" policy, the fostering of all things bright and beautiful. Fluttering their chaste badges of pure white ribbon, the ladies of the WCTU were not only to work for Temperance in its various ramifications but also to seek to set up a new basic moral and social climate, a wide hegemony of women in which prohibition, women's rights, the end of the "Social Evil" (prostitution)—and the rescue of Man from tobacco, drink and his widely deplored coarseness would come about more or less automatically, like the Marxist's withering away of the state. So among the forty-odd special departments of the WCTU were agencies assigning an individual member in each chapter to encourage labor organization, or kindergartens, or purity of thought and deed in boys, or the substitution of matrons for male turnkeys in jails containing women, or the raising of the legal age of consent from barbarically low levels. Some of those were undeniably good causes, but the ladies pursued with equal fervor the most fatuous ones, such as that of the flower mission branch which sent them into the jails on Sundays to take each prisoner a pretty posy with a written Bible text attached.

This variety of activities was good membership policy, for it left wide scope for individual tastes. If kindergartens did not appeal, you could specialize in setting up anti-Rum booth exhibits at county fairs and conventions. And for all its scatter-gun tactics, it was in the field of Temperance that the WCTU accomplished most—specifically in the schoolroom. That came about after Mrs. Mary Hannah Hunt of suburban Hyde Park, Massachusetts, got *The Temperance Lesson Book,* sponsored by the National Temperance Society, into the local schools as a textbook. Appreciating the brilliance of this stroke, Miss Willard created for Mrs. Hunt a national WCTU Department of Scientific Temperance Instruction, the purpose of which was similarly to infiltrate all American public school systems. By 1902 the deed was done. Thenceforward the bulk of American children were compulsorily and arbitrarily exposed to never-touch-the-stuff propaganda, often in the guise of physiology lessons, concentrating on them all the libels that zealot physicians had smeared over the Demon Rum for the last 100 years. That first drink bringing on alcoholic ruin; that hereditary taint passed on to offspring; the classing of alcohol as poison as dangerous as arsenic; the doctor finding the drunkard's blood so rich in alcohol that it will catch fire from a match—all rammed down the throats of the schoolroom captive audience as unimpeachable science.

Such propaganda among children had previously been limited to a few bits of hortatory prose in school readers and spellers and to the dragooning of Sunday School pupils into juvenile Temperance organizations such as Cold Water Armies and the WCTU's Loyal Temperance Legion. Now it reached a maximum audience because it coincided with the nation-wide spread, county by county or state by state, of laws making attendance compulsory in elementary schools. With so many communities either passing truancy laws or putting new teeth into old ones, millions of children previously inaccessible because not attending Sunday School became vulnerable. At the same time the spread of public high schools extended the number of years during which brighter or better-off youngsters were thus brainwashed at the taxpayers' expense. Most of the boys thus exposed to WCTU-sponsored doctrines in the period from 1882 to 1900 were of voting age after 1900—the period in which the Anti-Saloon League won its sweeping victories at the polls.

After Miss Willard died in 1898, the WCTU lost momentum. A revival of the women's suffrage movement was attracting the attention and energies of abler ladies with ideas. But it had plenty of laurels to rest on. It had put the fear of Rum in a whole rising generation and simultaneously deepened the typical dynamic female's belief that women's rising influence on affairs would necessarily improve their moral tone. It was fitting that Frances Willard, investing the WCTU's money in a grandiose office building in Chicago as monument to it—and herself—called it not the WCTU Building but the Women's Building. For men had no such record in the same decades. Their best effort had been to found a national Prohibition Party. It toyed with piety sometimes in planks calling for the abolition of prostitution and compulsory Bible reading in schools, and sometimes flirted with Populism, calling for the referendum and recall and the regulation of railroads. Every four years it nominated for President a man of some ability and public experience with the necessary good record as an officer in the Civil War, usually a well-whiskered general. But the only time the Prohibition Party affected anything but its own bank account was in 1884, when the Republicans had the bad judgment to snub Miss Willard.

Along with General John P. St. John, the superbly mustached, Dry-committed governor of Kansas, she had gone to the Republican convention to plead for a Dry plank in the platform. The platform committee, though presumably less anti-Dry than the notoriously sinful Democratic Party, scornfully refused. Both suppliants were furious. St. John offered himself and was accepted as the Prohibitionists' candidate for President. Miss Willard gave the word for the WCTU ladies to work their hardest to get their men to vote for him particularly in New York State, on which he concentrated because it carried the largest block of votes in the electoral college. The 25,000 votes that St. John received there—more than any previous Prohibition candidate had ever got from the whole nation—

swung the state to Grover Cleveland and kept James G. Blaine, the favored Republican, out of the White House.* Not only was it a brilliant revenge, but its implicit lesson in the use of Dry minorities was soon cleverly used by the Anti-Saloon League in achieving prohibition. St. John was an able campaigner of the spellbinding sort and doubtless contributed much to his own triumph. But as much or more credit goes to the WCTU ladies, who, for the first time, had gone all out to pester man into voting righteously.

Frances Willard prepared herself to be the Uncrowned Queen of American Womanhood, as her henchwomen called her, at a girls' academy in Milwaukee; then at a sort of superacademy, Chicago's Methodist-sponsored Northwestern Female College; then by teaching in other such schools for girls here and there in the Old Northwest. As she rose in that profession, she went on studying and had the advantage, unusual for her time and background, of two years in Europe paid for by the father of her traveling companion and former pupil. In 1873 she was chosen first president of Evanston College for Ladies, at Evanston, Illinois, the Methodists' tidily godly suburb on the lakeshore above Chicago. Its founders wished it to be a Western counterpart of Vassar, then stimulatingly new. Instead, it became the separate Women's College of the Methodists' recently founded Northwestern University. This roughly anticipated the relation of the 1880's between Harvard and the Annex (now Radcliffe) and Columbia and Barnard College and furnished the opening wedge for eventual outright coeducation at Northwestern.

Miss Willard stayed on as dean. Unfortunately for America, if not for her, Northwestern soon had a new president who happened to be a man whom she had woundingly jilted when both were younger. Friction between them, possibly reflecting old emotions, caused her to resign and seek other work worthy of her talents. That proved to be the corresponding secretaryship of the WCTU, her assignment to which was as critical for the Temperance movement as was Stalin's secretaryship of the Communist Party of the Soviet Union for world Communism. The point here is, however, that her earlier career exemplified many of the new things bubbling up in education for women after the Civil War.

As usual, the first hints went farther back. Long since a few imaginative or strong-minded teachers in New England's academy-seminaries for

* Historians usually consider that what lost New York State for Blaine was the tactlessness of the Reverend Dr. Samuel D. Burchard of the Houston Street Presbyterian Church in New York City who alienated the Irish vote, which Blaine had been specially cultivating, by calling the Democrats a party of "Rum, Romanism, and Rebellion." But even so, Blaine lost the state by fewer than 1,000 votes. And those 25,000 votes for St. John were almost unquestionably mostly from Republicans, few of whom had ever voted for the Prohibition Party before.

girls had experimented with giving their pupils the same higher academic culture that colleges afforded young men. The first such to attract significant attention was Mrs. Emma Willard of Berlin, Connecticut—otherwise noted as author of "Rocked in the Cradle of the Deep"—principal (until she married) of the Female Academy of Middlebury, Vermont. A cousin of her husband's attending Middlebury College boarded with them. The story is that dipping into his textbooks showed her the range of stimulus that girls were deprived of and determined her to open things up for them. After some experiment and much stubborn agitation she managed to found in 1821 at Troy, New York, a girls' school soon famous for taking its pupils through the subjects, such as philosophy and mathematics, then thought to supply intellectual muscle. Another such pioneer was the Reverend Joseph Emerson, a relative of the philosopher-poet, who concluded from reading Hannah More that women were susceptible of learning and, after some years as a tutor at Harvard and in the pulpit, tested the notion in his girls' school at Byfield, Massachusetts. Among the pupils on whom it worked stimulatingly well were Zilpah Polly Grant of Norfolk, Connecticut, who installed his extended curriculum in her seminary at Ipswich, Massachusetts, and Mary Lyon, her assistant and fellow pupil under Emerson, who expanded what was done at Ipswich into the germ of the first American women's college. Her Mount Holyoke Seminary at South Hadley, Massachusetts, followed the curriculum of the then-newish Amherst College with lady teachers supplemented by occasional men lecturers from Amherst and Williams; caused further comment by making the girls work at the housekeeping to reduce expenses, for Miss Lyon felt strongly that these new intellectual privileges should be available to daughters of families of modest means; and eventually, in the academy-into-college evolution already described, became Mount Holyoke College.

Its graduates, imbued with Miss Lyon's sense of Woman's capacities and her duty to bring moral and intellectual light to her sisters, fanned out over the nation to found scores of academies on the Mount Holyoke model. For instance, for $100 a year plus firewood and lighting costs, the Female Seminary founded in 1856 at Elizabethtown, Ohio, by a recent graduate of Mount Holyoke (who was my wife's grandmother) gave its pupils three years of not only "Composition, Reading and Calisthenics" and "to those who . . . can attend to them without serious detriment to their . . . regular studies" the "Vocal and Instrumental Music . . . Linear and Perspective Drawing, Painting and French" of the conventional seminary, but also Latin to the level of Cicero, algebra, geometry and trigonometry and some experience with chemistry and botany. The entrance age was fourteen. The school year, with two two-week vacations, ran ten months. Emphasis on religion was so heavy that Sunday amounted to temporary retirement from the world, and each girl had to bring from home a Bible and hymnbook, as well as a dictionary, an atlas, her own bed linen, napkins and towels, a tablespoon and teaspoon, an umbrella and a pair of overshoes. Scholastically the school, probably representative, offered what a good urban high school would c. 1900. But in the 1850's that was as much as or more than was available at many a church-founded institution calling itself a men's college and giving AB degrees. These girls came out knowing as much of cosine and deponent verb as did their cousins at Kenyon or Wabash.

Once Mrs. Willard and Miss Lyon had shown that their schools were viable and their pupils as nimble as boys in the world of logarithms and hendiadys, higher education for women gradually turned from feminist myth into recognizable fact. In supplementary support women occasionally cropped up as editors of several kinds of publication—Cornelia Walter managing the rising Boston *Transcript* for five years, Sarah Josepha Hale making *Godey's Lady's Book* into the first really influential women's magazine, Mrs. Anne Royall running her own gossip sheet in Washington —and intellectualizing contributors to papers aimed at men, notably Margaret Fuller in Greeley's New York *Tribune*. Obviously it would be worth society's while not to force the Margaret Fullers and Bethania Crockers to depend on eccentric fathers as tutors, but to use formal schooling to tap the potential supply of scholarship, scientific ability and public cultivation otherwise going largely to waste in women's brains. In the 1850's, however, specific encouragement for the notion came from overseas in the successive versions, each applauded, of Tennyson's *The Princess*. This long fantasy is remembered chiefly for its inclusion of some of the poet's best-known lyrics. Twenty years before Oxford University gingerly ventured into its first women's college, the poem enticingly outlined contemporary English hopes of planting a new section of the grove of Academe for the exclusive use of self-admiring Woman.

The heroine, a lovely, learned and majestic princess, has withdrawn herself, her lady intimates and their girl disciples into a semi-monastic, fortified university with a female faculty and a curriculum based on the parity of female brains and the purity of feminine values relative to masculine coarseness. The princess' affianced prince and his cronies sneak into the place in women's garb and are detected. After great clamor the upshot is a treaty granting men as a special favor not a jot more than half-right to the universe. The content—the verse itself is often elegant— is *Lysistrata* as Louisa May Alcott might have handled it. Here is the actual source of the phrase *sweet girl graduates*.

In the fifteen years after 1869 England's "Oxbridge" had opened four precedent-eroding colleges for women. That Tennyson was responsible was clear to W. S. Gilbert, whose *Princess Ida* of 1884, though almost too close to the original to be travesty, warned girl undergraduates that they had better get somebody to bowdlerize Anacreon and Ovid for them. In America *The Princess* may have particularly led to action because many, men as well as women, interested in women's rights were aware that Mount Holyoke had already proved the point in the New World. It had been proved again in the 1850's, when the all-girl student body of newly founded Elmira College in Elmira, New York, was given and successfully met the challenge of a standard men's college curriculum—and note that the place frankly called itself college not *seminary* the term to which Mount Holyoke clung for thirty years more. Then, in 1861, S. F. B. Morse, already converted to Mary Lyon-like ideas, and Milo P. Jewett, an imaginative educationist from Vermont, persuaded Matthew Vassar, a wealthy brewer of Poughkeepsie, New York, to put some $800,000 into a large-scale application of the same principle. Vassar College opened in 1865 in an elaborately mansarded main building reflecting its founder's admiration for the Tuileries. Morale was inculcated among the students by calisthenics and baths twice a week. There were courses in music and hygiene, as well as the liberal arts, but there was nothing liberal about the young ladies' lives. They were roused at 6 A.M., had prayers till breakfast at 7 and a silent time for further prayer and meditation until 9, when classes began. The college authorities read all the girls' outgoing letters.

In decorous succession came Smith, Wellesley, Mills (duly evolved from seminary to college in the San Francisco Bay area), Bryn Mawr (created by Philadelphia Quakers in 1885 to afford women the new Johns Hopkins approach to graduate study), proclaiming that women could learn as much as men; that they would emerge from learning equally well qualified to teach their junior sisters; and that a purely feminine environment had something serenely winsome and elevated about it. This serenity did not, however, preclude occasional foot-stamping temper. The passage setting the theme of *The Princess* has a charming girl struck by a tale of the heroism of the chatelaine of a medieval castle bursting out:

> There are thousands now
> Such women, but convention beats them down.
> It is but bringing up; no more than that.
> You men have done it—how I hate you all!
>   . . . O, I wish
> That I were some great princess, I would build
> Far off from men a college like a man's,
> And I would teach them all that men are taught;
> We are twice as quick! . . .

Thirty years after Wellesley was opened they took H. G. Wells to see the place, and he was puzzled, as he was wafted from classroom to boathouse to library, because "everybody told me I should be reminded of the Princess. . . . 'I say,' I said, 'I wish you wouldn't all be so allusive. *What* Princess?' It was, of course, that thing of Tennyson's . . . in which a chaste Victorian amorousness struggles with the early formulae of the feminist movement . . . in Boston they treat it as a living classic. . . ."[160]

Fortunately mortarboards proved more becoming to women than to most men. Within a generation a new kind of social prestige had gathered on these first-founded independent colleges for women. After one term Octave Thanet left Vassar because, she said, its intensive publicity to attract enrollees to break the ice had drawn so many vulgar daughters of Civil War-created millionaires. From birth in the 1880's Radcliffe and Barnard had access to libraries and faculties larger and more distinguished than those available to their independent elder sisters. But neither such affiliate of an important university gave quite as warm a sense of *nunc dimittis* to a well-to-do matron in Pittsburgh or St. Paul *c.* 1910 as what she felt when her daughter, properly prepared at the local Miss Littlefinger's School for Girls, was accepted at Vassar or Smith. In a short time the daisy chain was a symbol very widely valued, and the *Princess* motif survived vigorously enough to appear, with some further variations, in the late 1920's in the form of Bennington and Sarah Lawrence colleges.

Without Tennyson's gyneolatrous suggestions such enclaves might never have come to be, for America's native trend had been toward coeducation. Considerations of cost had gradually enforced the policy of boys and girls together both in the schoolrooms of New York and in the old log or little red schoolhouses—a marked contrast with Old World practice. Private schooling on the elementary and secondary levels usually remained segregated by sexes. But in the late 1700's a few New England academies had taken the risk of teaching boys and girls on the same footing in the same room, and no skies fell. Soon advanced educationists yearned to emulate the success of Pestalozzi and disciples in that direction. Thus it was easier for many literate Americans, even those in affluent circumstances, to contemplate coeducation on secondary and higher levels because they had such unalarming childhood memories of the girls' side and the boys' side in the same room and on the same playground. As public high schools came in with a rush after the Civil War, segregation by sexes seldom long survived the obvious economies of running one large school instead of two smaller ones. By 1900, 98 percent of American high schools, in a total of 6,000-odd, were coeducational.

On the next level upward, Oberlin College, new-born exponent of reforms in northern Ohio in the late 1830's, added to manual labor and admission of Negroes the further eccentricity of allowing women not only to study there but also to take degrees. (For a while the girls were not allowed to read their own compositions aloud in class; male students did it for them.) In 1853 new-fledged Antioch College, not far away at Yellow Springs, Ohio, another focus of reformers' approving hopes, admitted women to its first enrolled class. Even though in the 1850's the average age of sexual maturity was much later than it is now, this was adventuring well into the area of presumedly higher biological risks. Horace Mann, first president of Antioch, had fought hard for coeducation in normal schools, as well as in secondary schools, in Massachusetts. But when putting the principle into practice at Antioch, he sounded like a selectman uneasy about admitting both sexes to the academy in Fishcake Falls. He and she students were forbidden to walk together without a faculty chaperon. The wooded stream gorge near the campus was taboo to males one day, to females the next. Supervision of dormitories was strict, and penalties for even the appearance of misbehavior were severe. Great as the advantages were, Mann confessed to a correspondent, "the dangers of [coeducation] are *terrible*. I have seen enough of young men to satisfy me that . . . not any great majority . . . would not yield to the temptation of ruining a girl if he could. The girls are far more pure but are they safe?" The only reason why there had as yet been no "accident," he said, was the "constant, sleepless vigilance" [161] of the college authorities.

Nevertheless, the University of Iowa was coeducational from its start in 1855. Among other state universities admitting women from the beginning were Utah, Washington, Kansas, Minnesota and Nebraska, all before 1871. In the same period the state universities of Missouri, Michigan, California and Illinois, originally segregated, decided to admit women. Many originally all-male colleges under religious auspices intended primarily to train preachers came around to admitting Betty Coed's grandmother. It would all have been a sound triumph for intellectual opportunity and equalitarianism across the sex boundary had Miss Elizabeth Coed's motives continued to be those of Mary Lyon. But, as the impertinent social prestige attached to Vassar, Smith and Wellesley was strongly hinting, the function of going to college in America was by no means so simple for either sex.

Since human beings are social animals sensitive to herd values, their educational institutions tend to replace the academic with the social and often the frivolous. The Yankee Quality of the 1800's no longer sent their sons to Harvard and Yale to make ministers of them, though the pulpit remained a proper career for a gentleman wishing it. It was just that a degree from either place went with being named Saltonstall or Trumbull. Not to have it was eccentric, to have deprived oneself of spontaneous close acquaintance with one's peers. In England the same function was performed by the traditional public schools recently revivified by Dr. Thomas Arnold's reforms in curriculum and teaching at Rugby. Princeton and the University of Virginia were serving the same need in their areas. As colleges and state universities fanned out toward the Mississippi, the prestige a boy acquired from having been to college came to outweigh considerations of what he might have learned there. To have been able to send him there was the outward and visible sign of economic arrival. His instructors did what they could to keep up the pretext of training him in mathematics, classical languages and smatterings of science while hoping that at least a few among these annual influxes of incurious youths would take to research or learning or anyway cultivation. But the most marked effect was the number of their male progeny named after classical poets—Horace, Vergil, Homer, Ovid.

A similar erosion eventually came to the "agricultural and mechanical colleges" founded from the 1850's on. Their original purpose, still persisting among their current activities, reflected misgiving about the utility of all the Latin and moral philosophy taught in the nation's rapidly multiplying colleges. What would balance such intellectualized luxuries, said Horace Greeley, Jonathan Baldwin Turner (of Osage orange fame), *et al.*, was high-level instruction for likely young fellows in practical engineering and the new scientific farming of fertilizers, crop rotation and selective breeding still neglected by the much flattered but fumbly American farmer. In 1862, the same year in which free land was offered to homesteaders, a momentous federal act sponsored by Senator Justin S. Morrill of Vermont offered large grants of federal land to any state founding such an "A and M" college. In some cases an existing institution, such as New Jersey's Rutgers, was delegated to set up an affiliate A and M school with the resources that the Morrill Act made available. The usual result, however, was an altogether new college well away from the state's largest city concentrating on cows, practical chemistry and drainage engineering, while teaching only enough academic courses to make sure the boys had the tools of knowledge. One way or another the Morrill Act had a major hand in the University of Illinois (Turner's pet project), Ohio State, Purdue, Auburn, Cornell. . . .

The nation has had ample return for its 30,000 acres per state. Graduates of the land-grant colleges were soon acting as missionaries of sounder farming all over the country just as Turner and Greeley had hoped. The wealth of scientific-technical and agricultural research done ever since by such institutions as Cornell and Purdue would alone have made Morrill's scheme worthwhile. The quality of engineering training has usually been high and indispensably supplemented the scattered poly-technic institutes appearing at about the same time. But the very word *college* in the Morrill Act was a social trap. A boy sent to Pennsylvania State up in the hills in the middle of the state could be spoken of by his parents as going to college just as if it were the much more expensive University of Pennsylvania in Philadelphia. As motives for attending shifted toward prestige, the liberal arts segment of the curriculum expanded to match. Ohio State Agricultural and Mechanical College at Columbus, chartered in 1870, was significantly renamed Ohio State University in 1878. Illinois Industrial University, chartered in 1868, upgraded its name in 1885. Women students were presently admitted, sometimes infiltrating by way of a state normal school attached. Fraternities established chapters. Nowadays what one might call a generic Morrill University is distinguished from any other socially oriented State U only by its agricultural and technological faculties flourishing among its many other newer ones.

Academic dilution is clearest in those Greek-letter fraternities. Nominally they began with Phi Beta Kappa, a students' literary society borrowing some details from Masonic secrecy—grip, oath, initiatory ritual—at William and Mary in 1776, soon inspiring sister chapters at Yale and Harvard. Gradually membership became synonymous with recognition of scholastic prowess. It remains so today, actually with the fraternal aspect so faint that on large campuses an undergraduate member may not know even the faces of some of his "brothers." But the tingle of mystery in those esoteric Greek initials was imitated in the 1820's at Union College, Dr. Nott's influential institution at Schenectady, New York, by the formation of several heavily social, though ostensibly literary, student secret organizations called Kappa Alpha, Sigma Phi and so on. Formalized snobbery and campus politics soon ousted literary values, and an epidemic of fraternity founding came with the nationwide spread of colleges after the mid-century. Quaker campuses resisted it because of Friends' ban on secret societies. Systems of clubs prevailed over the Greek-letter tradition at Yale, Harvard and Princeton. But practically everywhere else the typical Greek-letter system flourished with the brothers leaving college dormitories to live as well as eat together in separate fraternity houses—an unwitting counterpart of the men's society of the preliterate village.

This fraternity tradition rigidly fixed social standing under the elms, discouraged any surviving hope of keeping the college primarily an institution of learning, and added to the expense of four years' residence. By the time presidents and deans perceived what a subversive camel they had let the boys stable under Alma Mater's tent, it was usually too late to get it out. Sporadic efforts to that end were usually fruitless. One formidable difficulty was pro-fraternity sentiment among the influential alumni on whom Alma Mater counted for endowments or leverage on the legislature. Most of them had been zealous members in their time and recalled the frat house as a splendid institution. Nor was this mere sentiment. To have belonged to a well-considered frat at State U was to have the right connections in law, banking and clubs all over the state. In 1909, when the National Interfraternity Council was formed to coordinate the "Greeks"—as opposed to the "barbs" (for barbarians), the students not invited to join fraternities—its first president was the incumbent president of Brown. By then thirty-odd specialized Greek-letter fraternities had also appeared, sometimes honorary but often merely exclusive, among students of dentistry, engineering, law, medicine, veterinary surgery, music, osteopathy, pharmacy, journalism, physical education and elocution. Emulous adolescents had even installed the system in big-city high schools, where it led a hole-and-corner existence under strong disapproval from irate principals.

When allowed to enroll at State U, the girls naturally followed the same course, using Greek-letter sororities to keep other girls in their place and organize contacts with the fraternity boys. The Betas on the State U campus, say, were thought traditionally to favor the kind of girls recruited by the Thetas. The pledging season during which fraternities winnowed and competed for the new crop of freshmen was excelled in backbiting and chicanery only by the simultaneous maneuverings of the rival sororities. Inevitably, college as the place to find a husband much impressed well-to-do mothers with eligible daughters. Whereas founders and legislators had intended coeducation on the college level to secure intellectual and professional advantages for the underprivileged sex, it soon became a four-year equivalent of sending the girl to the right dancing class. More broadly seen, it gave her an extension—only this time nearer meaning business—of the boy-and-girling that the participants had already been deep in during their last year of high school. College authorities so frowned on marriage that it usually meant immediate expulsion. But engagements of several degrees of seriousness signalized by Her wearing His fraternity pin were many, and marriage after commencement to a college classmate as soon as His economic position allowed was the typical goal of a girl's going to college in the first place. That was the consideration, reinforcing the general attitude of the day, that made Horace Mann's fears fairly pointless. A co-ed who did even a little too much spooning was likely to disqualify herself for the hymeneal sweep.

The founding of marriages and the training of young persons in the manners, catchwords and personal associations expected in their social stratum are functions useful to society. But to the extent that institutions of learning supplied them, learning suffered. They encroached on learning time and energy and led to a flood of youngsters matriculating in order to acquire polish and status, not the skills of knowledge. That may be one reason why American education remained watery in comparison with the Old World's, why though American scientists and scholars are equal to any, it still takes them longer to mature professionally. In 1892 Charles W. Eliot had plenty of reason to complain that "the expectation of attainment for the American child, or for the American college student, is much lower than the expectation for the European. This error has been very grave in its effects all along the line. . . ." [162] In our time the gap has narrowed but still persists.

Yet Dr. Eliot's strictures on failure to demand enough of pupils should have been tempered by the realization that in his day it was still a problem to get all potential pupils into the schoolroom. The New Englander's ideal of a place in school for every child and every child in school at public cost —for private schools tend to be anti-equalitarian in effect, if not always in purpose—was approaching but only piecemeal, jerkily and with many frictions. Some states, led by Massachusetts in 1852, had attained enough elementary-school capacity to pass laws making attendance compulsory a few months in the year between the ages of, say, six and ten years. The upper limits gradually rose until in Massachusetts c. 1890 twenty weeks' attendance to the age of fourteen was required. Such measures brought on the national scene several things previously only hinted at or hesitantly tried. The state's new obligation to expose all small fry to the three R's required the truant officer to enforce it and inspection—in effect, licensing—of private schools to make sure that they gave satisfactory equivalents of public schooling.

Inevitably opposition came from Roman Catholic elements unwilling to see a secular state pass judgment on parochial schools; and from German and Scandinavian Lutherans in the upper Midwest accustomed to maintaining their own elementary schools taught in German or Swedish. That issue is now dead among American Catholics but still occasionally revives among the severe Pennsylvania Dutch Protestant sects bent on running their own schools their own way in their Midwestern colonies. A hundred years ago it was complicated by strong resistance among the urban poor, mostly Irish, largely Catholic, in textile centers where child labor was thought indispensable in the mills and crucial to family income; and by the not uncommon inability of law-abiding poor families to supply school-age children clothes decent enough to wear to school. By 1890 it was still visionary of Edward Bellamy's disciples to advocate "making obligatory the education of children during the whole school year, up to seventeen years, forbidding their employment during the school year, and providing for the assistance, from public funds, of children whose parents are unable to support them during school attendance." [163] Not until c. 1900 was elementary compulsory education pretty much taken for granted except in the South. Not until 1918 did Mississippi, last of the then forty-eight states to do so, pass such a law. And even after state laws were fairly stiff, enforcement might not amount to much in the particularly needy or unenlightened neighborhoods of a given state. In the post-Civil War South, so plagued by underprivilege and underenlightenment, to lag behind the nation in that respect was only one corollary of the dismal thing called Reconstruction. Nobody came well out of that. And, as usual, the Negro came out worst of all.

The wishful legend, popular among those deploring Reconstruction, is that had Lincoln lived to "bind up the nation's wounds," he would have solved the oil-and-water problem of restoring the seceded states to the Union while clearing up the status of the freed slaves and securing them opportunity to adjust to freedom. This is dubious. That Lincoln's grasp of the Negro problem was faulty is shown by his clinging to the possibility of Colonization. Few white men of his day, least of all the single-minded abolitionists, comprehended all the potential difficulties implied by emancipation. It would have been impossible for him or anybody else to reconcile the former slaveowner to the Union's programs, under Army and church auspices, to protect and educate the former slave. Lincoln's attitude toward the returning states had been moderate; he had already been standing between the vindictive Radical Republicans and the vanquished; his successor followed the lines thus laid down and observed pledges to refrain from retaliation against disbanded Confederate soldiers. Yet the new Southern state governments could see no farther ahead than the collapse of their traditional labor supply as many Negroes dazzled by freedom went aimlessly wandering anywhere away from the old plantation or trooping after the Union armies—the officers of which sometimes put them to what amounted to forced labor. The measures with which the South hoped to get the Negro back to work restoring the creaky economy that the war had ruined varied from state to state but generally used the legal devices of vagrancy, apprenticeship and contract to make him virtually a bound-to-the-land serf. His only gains over his former status were that he could not be sold and his marriage could be recognized as legally binding.

Such Black Codes, as Northerners called these loose bundles of laws, quickly jammed the delicate process of picking up the pieces. They gave the probably correct impression that the former slaveowners, still in the saddle though defeated after invoking wager by battle, were unable to accept the verdict rendered by the deaths of half a million men—which was maybe predictable but certainly ominous. It played square into the hands of the Ben Wades and Thaddeus Stevenses. Their robust doctrine of *Dixie delenda est* already appealed strongly to their dominant Republican Party, the formative career of which had been closely bound up with hatred of the Chivalry and Simon Legree. These radicals' countermeasures, half-punitive, half-protective of the Negro, grew more severe and more sweeping as Southern resistance grew and gave new excuses for further cracking down. In the process Congress, which had given Lincoln plenty of peevish trouble during the war, badly squeezed the Presidency and half-cowed the judiciary. That Lincoln could have made better headway than Andrew Johnson against these usurpations, which reflected the Republicans' harsh determination to stay in power through control of the Southern seats in Congress, is conceivable but again doubtful.

When riding highest, Radical Reconstruction was military government of most of Dixie supporting the Army-operated Freedmen's Bureau, an agency to uphold the slave while he learned to be a free man, and support of civil regimes based on taking the vote from most former Confederates and giving it to their former slaves. The leaders organizing this electorate were mostly white. Some were "scalawags" from among the several kinds of Southerner who had disliked Colonel Bighouse. The rest were Northern interlopers, some sincerely hoping to help the Negro, others seeing in him a means to power and pickings, both classes lumped as "carpetbaggers." Negro-dominated legislators advised by whites passed measures authorizing large public works and school systems. Negroes were elected to Congress and seated where Jefferson Davis, Alexander Stephens, Robert Toombs and Judah P. Benjamin had defied the Union only ten years previously. The most intransigent Quality took their fire-eating heartbreak to Europe or Mexico, where Juárez needed fightingmen for his war against Maximilian. Benjamin, Davis' cleverest Cabinet member, made a brilliant new career at the English bar. But most of the Confederacy's political leaders and generals stayed as second-class citizens impenitently unable to adjust to this world turned upside down. General Wade Hampton of South Carolina, General Nathan B. Forrest of Mississippi and General John B. Gordon of Georgia took part, each in his own fashion, in the organized, sometimes paramilitary Southern resistance that eventually turned that world partly former side up again. Forrest's Ku Klux Klan and Hampton's Red Shirts were the most striking and overt agencies. But another factor in the victory was the talent that such as Gordon showed for shady deals and strange bedfellows in these reactionary struggles.

The Negro legislators were inexperienced and ignorant, for which slavery, not they, was responsible. The often corrupt scalawags and carpetbaggers advising them were less than no help. Looting and grotesque proceedings unquestionably ensued. Vast sums procured by sale of bonds stuck to greedy fingers. The public purse paid for many private luxuries. But the Gilded Age was a corrupt time, and nothing that went on in South Carolina was more flagrant than what white men of experience and ability were simultaneously guilty of in New York City's Tweed Ring or the national scandal of the Whiskey Ring. And much as they earned most of the opprobrium since heaped on them, these Reconstruction legislatures did one thing for the South that her previous rulers might never have got around to—they voted for and laid the foundations of Northern-style public school systems.

That came of the Northerners' folk belief that literacy was good for each and all and of the hope that schooling the Negro freedman would enable him to make something of his new status. Well before the end of the war teacher missionaries, many of them women, some Northern Negroes, were sent into areas taken over by Union troops to teach refugee slaves the three R's and the elements of religion (Northern-style) and sanitation. The perplexities encountered by these young enthusiasts in the South Carolina Sea Islands, where slavery had been most isolated, were on the order of Miss Ophelia's with Topsy. Within a few years after Appomattox scores of elementary schools, dozens of attempts at higher education for potential Negro preachers and teachers, all under alien Northern auspices, were scattered from New Orleans to Maryland, Georgia to Kentucky. In Nashville, Tennessee, for instance, General Clinton B. Fisk, a well-meaning veteran up from the ranks, now area chief of the Freedmen's Bureau, worked with the American Missionary Society, largely Congregationalist, to found what would become Fisk University. Its first textbooks—spellers, as well as Bibles, pathetically betokening its first students' meager preparation—were bought with money got by selling for scrap the fetters and leg irons from Nashville's municipal slavepens.

The South's Negroes were almost altogether illiterate. The colossal task could only be nibbled at with strenuous effort and good intentions. Above elementary level the results were often valuably permanent. At first the term *college* for any of these new institutions was manifestly absurd. But Fisk, solidly based on the funds from those Jubilee Singers' tours, gradually became an intellectual lighthouse for Negroes. Also in Nashville, the North's volunteer Freedmen's Aid Society set up a Central Tennessee College with a medical department that became Meharry Medical College, the nation's center for medical and dental training for Negroes. South Carolina's Negro legislators put the state's land-grant funds from the Morrill Act into what is now Claflin College. Mississippi's Alcorn College had a similar origin. Virginia's land-grant money was indispensable in developing Hampton Institute, which set lasting patterns in the vocational education of Negroes. Howard University in Washington, D.C., was created by the First Congregationalist Church of Washington with indispensable financing from the Freedmen's Bureau at the instance of its chief, General O. O. Howard. From 1862 on, the American Baptist Home Mission Society sent missionaries South to open schools and spread a recognizable Gospel among the freedmen. Their and their Methodist rivals' work brought about the establishment of thousands of Negro congregations under ill-prepared but earnestly eloquent Negro preachers —a development crucial to the Negroes' struggle for a life of their own.

It speaks well for their stamina and for the devotion of such men as Fisk that most of the Negro colleges survived the reactionary assault on the Southern Negro's new position that began when the North betrayed its new wards in the 1870's. Thirteen years after the Union victory, as part of a shady deal involving land grants to Southwestern railroads and the juggling of Democrat Samuel J. Tilden out of the White House, the Army, the Negroes' shield while they tried to find their feet, was withdrawn from Dixie. That was politically feasible because the North had tired of all the turmoil that came of trying to secure for the Negroes what Northern victory had presumably implied. The Chivalry were back in charge, owing reinstatement to the stubbornness with which they had worn down their conquerors.

Now observers called them "the Bourbons" not for their taste in whiskey but because they had "learned nothing and forgotten nothing," least of all that for a dozen years that seemed 100 they had been subordinated to their former slaves. Under their redeemer regimes the typical Dixie state, giving corrupt auspices and the need for economy as reasons, repudiated most of the bonds issued or guaranteed by its Reconstruction government. Of a face value of $140,000,000 outstanding, $112,000,000 thus became waste paper—a transaction as cool as the defaults of the 1830's that had so outraged Europe. Northerners who, like Henry Clews, the eminent British-born Wall Streeter, had gone heavily into the bonds of the Carpetbagger and Scalawag Railroad could do nothing about it; Clews tried to tell himself that it was all the fault not of high-principled Southern gentlemen but of that convenient scapegoat Andrew Johnson. New state constitutions or drastic amendment of old ones began the cynical disfranchisement of the Negro and the cultivation of Jim Crow restrictions, many of them new to the Southern subculture. Rapid growth of the sharecropper system, which kept the cotton-growing tenant, poor white or Negro, in debt to the landowner most of the time and perpetually in thrall to a single cash crop, gave the South a version of peonage that kept social strata gratifyingly distinct.

The Bourbons' parsimony, reflecting their resentment of heavy taxes on an economy still recovering from war damage, made them look askance at the Reconstruction-founded public schools, which, in any case, had the carpetbagger taint and sometimes taught Negroes. But such schools had also begun to undermine the traditional illiteracy of the poor whites, and little love as there was between them and Colonel Bighouse, he did not quite dare destroy this innovation and revert completely to the neglect of the antebellum days. The principle of tax-paid elementary schools persisted—largely for whites, of course, though Negro schools were not altogether extinguished. Nor, though religious activity among the Negroes had been widely frowned on during slavery and had been a strongly cohesive force during Reconstruction, did the Bourbons seriously seek to check it after resuming power. The former slaves' scrawny little churches and highly effervescent versions of camp meetings were let alone. It is possible but unlikely that the reason was understanding that hopeful faith in the hereafter and the social joys of church membership would tend to keep the Negroes' dissatisfaction with their post-Reconstruction lot below danger level. Or maybe it was just realistic perception that after the epidemic spread of Christian catchwords during Reconstruction, the fat was irrevocably in the fire.

The Bourbons' victory at home was presently matched by another in external public relations. The North's boredom with responsibility for the Negroes it had freed and the economy it had gutted did not mean it was bored with the South. As C. Vann Woodward has pointed out, a new fiction character, the "Confederate censor for Yankee morals," [164] the aristocratic viewer with disdain of Northern crassness, appeared soon after the Civil War in Melville's *Clarel* and Henry Adams' *Democracy*; in Henry James' *The Bostonians* in 1886; and, he might have added, in Howells' *A Hazard of New Fortunes* in 1890. All four used as lens an articulately drawling Southerner impoverished by defeat but unconquerably knightly and all the more aware of Northern bumptiousness and corruption because fell circumstance had drawn a veil of suffering between him and worldly considerations. Few read *Clarel,* but the other items were well known and widely circulated—fresh illustrations of the cultivated American's fondness for being scolded by strangers whose manners seem to him exotically superior.

Those writers were Northerners only secondarily interested in the South's image. It took Southern novelists to impose on the American public a sweeping improvement in the folk concept of the South that Madison Avenue would not attempt today for less than $10,000,000. The 1880's were an era of regional writing as America discovered the drama in the contrasts between her rising industrial society, pretty much the same whether in Wheeling, West Virginia, or Moline, Illinois, and the elder ways of her preindustrial backwaters—New England's upcountry; Appalachia; New Orleans, that fragment of the West Indies embedded in Dixie and so picturesquely exploited by George Washington Cable; and a generalized South with due emphasis on the virtues of its archaisms. As this last became the nation's most popular literary raw material—except possibly the Old West—the widest currency went to Joel Chandler Harris'

E. W. Kemble draws the Southern Negro, c. 1890,
for a Joel Chandler Harris book.

Uncle Remus. Brer Rabbit and the Tar Baby were as well known as the Jumping Frog, and it seems captious to hear jangling overtones as the gentle old Negro tells the little boy by the cabin fire about animal anthropomorphs more interesting than people. Yet in Uncle Remus, Harris gave the nation, however inadvertently, a source of generalizations, the more persuasive because wholly inexplicit, about the solicitously treated, well-fulfilled slave—the kind that Dixie wanted remembered. A few years later, with the stories of Thomas Nelson Page and F. Hopkinson Smith, another alcove was added to the national waxworks for meltingly lovely but high-spirited Cindy Lou; her white-goateed father, the colonel, combining Robert E. Lee with Athos; Major Beauregard Effingham, gay and slender but whalebone-tough; stately, severe and ever-loving Mammy

Juno . . . Page was from the FFV background, not Dixie. The world that he thought he was re-creating, the one that vanished in his early teens, certainly had been somewhat more civilized than that of Mississippi's cotton snobs. But as his imitators spread his affectionate nostalgia through the former slave country, they naturalized the above cast in every state of the Confederacy except Texas. They were still extant in *So Red the Rose* in 1934 and in the Georgia upcountry in *Gone with the Wind* in 1936.

No Polynesian youth memorizing his 1,000 years of pedigree ever had a sense of continuity with the *mana* of the past greater than Page's, and by 1898, after he had dropped the practice of law to follow his popular success with the pen, he knew pretty well what he was doing—rubbing the nation's nose in the crime it had committed in forcing the South to test her theory that one Southron could lick *x* Yankees. His preface to *Red Rock* praised the antebellum Southern Quality with reproachful reverence:

> If they shone in prosperity, much more they shone in adversity; if they bore themselves haughtily in their day of triumph, they have borne defeat with splendid fortitude . . . their entire system crumbled and fell about them in ruins—they remained unmoved. They were subjected to the greatest humiliation of modern times; their slaves were put over them— they reconquered their section and preserved the civilization of the Anglo-Saxon. . . . Do you, young lady, observe Miss Thomasia the next time she enters a room, or addresses a servant; and do you, good sir, polished by travel and contact with the most fashionable—second-class—society of two continents, watch General Legaie and Dr. Cary when they meet Miss Thomasia . . . or the wagoner on the road. What an air . . . of old courts and polished halls. . . . What an odor . . . of those gardens which Watteau painted, floats in as they enter! Do not you attempt it. . . . You are imitating the duchess you saw . . . in Hyde Park. The duchess would have imitated Miss Thomasia. . . . She belongs to the realm where sincerity dwells and the heart still rules—the realm of old-time courtesy and high breeding, and you are the real provincial. It is a wide realm, though; and some day, if Heaven be good to you, you may reach it. . . .[165]

That sort of thing serialized in the best-considered magazines and best-selling in the bookstores made the North aware that it had inflicted "the greatest humiliation of modern times"—and on Anglo-Saxons, too. Obviously the least it could do was avert its eyes while the humiliated repaired the damage and got those Negroes back into knowing their place again. The Negroes in these stories were of two sorts: dignified house servants, honest and loyal, and a rabble of field hands, congenitally sub-human, noisy as poultry, light-fingered as monkeys, irresponsible as children. Northerners had been prepared for this view of Negroes by their own chance observation of Northern Negro slums and the harping on chicken stealing and hullabaloo in the minstrel show. After the war the stage carried it further through the far-ranging, vastly popular dramatizations of *Uncle Tom's Cabin*—the last source from which the South would have anticipated help. But as Tom shows grew stagier and stagier, strengthening entertaining capers at the expense of the less flashy values of the original, not only did Uncle Tom, the quiet, powerful, responsible slave, turn into a white-haired, meek, quavering shuffler, but Topsy, the simian imp child, came to be as much a principal character as he or Little Eva, the angelic, golden-haired, white-child foil.

Except for that contribution to bad race relations, the American theater between the Civil War and the 1890's was prosperously inconsequential. Its playwrights were mere scriptsmiths. The liveliest was Charles H. Hoyt, expert in farce with songs, whose successes first brought Maude Adams to fame and put "After the Ball" and "The Bowery" in the American songbook. Acting style seems to have remained extravagant and kept the actors dominating their vehicles. The best of them were seen in Augustin Daly's celebrated stock company in New York City built around John Drew and Ada Rehan. Imported scripts from England and occasionally France helped keep the road companies' bookings fat and the ghosts walking. In the 1880's Gilbert and Sullivan's masterpieces had the tumultuous success that they deserved. But there was small presage of Shaw and Ibsen soon to come except that the performers who would first play them in America, Richard Mansfield and Mrs. Fiske, were getting well established.

Actually the first hint of a changing world given on the stage had come soon after the Civil War with the unblushing, wholesale exploitation of women's legs—in tights, true, but unskirted right up to the crotch—in the momentously notorious *The Black Crook*. The breeches part for soubrettes had long been an institution, of course. The august Charlotte Cushman's rather androgynous career had often put her into tights as Hamlet. The ballet was less groaned over as its bouffant uniform became an accepted convention. Adah Isaacs Menken and several imitators had recently prospered by donning all-over fleshings and a few stray drapings for the rapid dash across the stage on horseback that made *Mazeppa,* a staging of Byron's pretentious poem, synonymous with Menken's name. But *The Black Crook,* a musical extravaganza drawing on Offenbach for atmosphere and England's Christmas pantomimes for production tricks, put on stage, in scene after scene, dozens of beautifully buxom British girls singing, dancing or just standing there all legs and décolletage.

This—and *Ixion* and *The White Fawn* and other successors in this suddenly full-blown idiom—was the cynosure of the Gilded Age. George Templeton Strong called it "the *Feminine-Femoral* School of Dramatic Art. . . . Ballet, spectacle, machinery and pink legs. . . . House packed—men mostly—and enthusiastic." [166] One expects "men mostly." But the notable thing is that before the brilliant run of *The Black Crook* had finished, Strong's wife, a perfect lady of impeccable social standing, made up a party of equally impeccable friends, of both sexes, to go see it and come home to supper afterward. Her mother would have died first.

VIII

The Midway Age

MR. DOOLEY'S AMERICA

VIII

The antecedents of *The Black Crook* were British and French. Most of its voluptuously tapered attractions were imports from England. But further occasions of public prurience tended curiously to have Egypt as context. At the Philadelphia Centennial of 1876 a young stage singer, Bettina Ordway, secured useful publicity by buying at the Egyptian exhibit a highly diaphanous nightgown of Egyptian cotton and leaving it on display with her name on it. (Less than a century ago even so feeble a hint of carnal display could set the press smirking and the staid shaking their heads.) The other exhibit noted for indecorum was a full-size waxworks figure of Cleopatra tinted to look as lifelike as possible and wearing very little, *à l'Egyptienne*. Then, seventeen years later, at Chicago's great World's Columbian Exposition celebrating (a year late) the four hundredth anniversary of the discovery of the New World, certain other daughters of Egypt with the advantage of being alive and wiggly gave America a persisting symbol of the lascivious.

For the great feature of the Chicago Fair, as it was popularly designated, was the Streets of Cairo, an elaborate concession in the amusement area, the prototype of which had greatly prospered at the Paris Exhibition of 1889. It consisted of mock-ups of Near Eastern streets thronged with picturesque Moslems right out of the *Arabian Nights* and exotic souvenirs and donkey and camel rides that were great "sources of boisterous fun" [1] and revenue. But the prime reason why this was the fair's most profitable concession was the theater in which at frequent intervals a rather swarthy girl came on stage to slow, tootly music and sinuously introduced the American nation to what the fair's management called "the genuine native muscle dance" [1] fresh from the banks of the Nile—soon renowned nationwide as the hootchy-kootchy.

Other concessions did well, too. The great Ferris wheel, slowly raising streetcar-size loads of patrons 200 feet in the air for a bird's-eye view of the grounds and Lake Michigan drew so much attention that its share in the success of the fair was likened to that of the Eiffel Tower at Paris four years previously. Crowds paid to see the Hagenbeck wild animal show and admired "the largest picture ever painted" [1]—a cyclorama of the Swiss Alps lighted by the still-novel incandescent bulbs. The beer, savory dishes and lilting waltzes of Old Vienna were far more popular than the Wagner played by the bands spotted around the grounds under supervision by Theodore Thomas, who never missed an opportunity to raise public taste. Also gracing this "Midway area"—originally intended seriously to educate visitors in the ways-of-doing of exotic cultures— were groups of Laplanders, West Africans, South Sea Islanders and so on living in huts or tepees and carrying on their daily lives under the stares of persons named Jones, Hochheimer, Clancy, McIntyre and Christiansen. The drumming, capering, singing and general vociferation with which they drew attention to themselves were sometimes fairly unbridled. But for the women who came away blushing, as well as for their menfolk trying not to grin and blink, the most memorable single phenomenon on the Midway, indeed in the whole encyclopedic fair, was the eloquent behavior of a female pelvis demonstrating how to dance without the aid of human feet. Apparently few failed to risk pollution. Even Julia Ward Howe, seventy-four years old and the national image of moral responsibility, was in a position to report that "The Cairo dancing was simply horrid, no touch of grace in it, only a most deforming movement of the whole abdominal and lumbar region. We thought it indecent." [2]

Thus to have stood out in the national mind was all the greater achievement for the hootchy-kootchy because, even without the raucous glories of the Midway, the fair would have been the most impressive thing America had ever seen, leaving marks even deeper than those of the Philadelphia Centennial. Many had thought it senseless to hold the Columbian Exposition at Chicago, a city so young and so far from salt water. But she was already the focus of more railroads than any other center, supplying the nation with its meat and telling it what to pay for wheat and corn. Exponent of the importance of the central strip of the country, she was giving new momentum to the cultural feedbacks from the newer states now permeating the seaboard of the Founding Fathers. With all the vigor appropriate to her youth, Chicago had screamed for the privilege of holding the great fair and what she did with it acknowledgedly justified the nation's having given in to her.

The Electrical Building's lamps, stoves, fans and even dishwashers— crude but promising—showed what soon to expect of electricity. Unobtrusively but significantly most of the machinery on exhibit was powered by electricity from the coal-fired dynamos in the fair's own powerhouse. Ever hungry for significance—if he sought it from the hootchy-kootchy, he recorded nothing about the matter—Henry Adams came and "lingered long among the dynamos, for they . . . gave to history a new phase" [3] and presently led him into some of the most grandiosely ironic passages in his *Education*. The fair also showed both a full-scale cross section of a great ocean liner and full-scale reproductions of the tiny, top-heavy ships in which Columbus had made his voyage, floating there in Lake Michigan 600 feet above sea level. In Venetian gondolas, the lines of which suggested to Winslow Homer one of his most evocative paintings, it wafted visitors from huge building to huge building along canals full of Great Lakes freshwater. Not only did the Women's Building exceed Philadelphia's in size but its Italianate grandeurs had even been designed by a recent woman graduate of the Massachusetts Institute of Technology. The murals on its interior walls and the symbolic statues outside were done by women artists no more and no less pretentiously than they would have been done by men. The dedicatory ode of the opening ceremonies of the whole fair, written by Chicago's own Harriet Monroe, soon to be a great catalyst for American poetry as founder-editor of *Poetry* magazine, was just as windy as if Edmund Clarence Stedman or Thomas Bailey Aldrich had been asked to oblige. And with notable impact on the material future—the building-material future—it awed and dazzled the American eye with the arched, vaulted, domed, gilded, pinnacled, colonnaded, vistaed, statue-studded, water-reflected grandiloquence, white as the icing on a wedding cake against the blue prairie sky and the glistening blue lake, of architecture with a capital *A* as the times understood it.

It was by no means only the millions of county-seat schoolteachers and dry goods clerks come to the fair on one-cent-a-mile excursion trains whom all this brilliantly coordinated elegance bedazzled. Maud Howe Elliott, daughter of Samuel Gridley Howe and Julia Ward Howe and spokeswoman for her sex at the fair, wrote that though she had seen the Sphinx and the Acropolis, "neither of these superlative legacies of the past impressed me more than . . . this miraculous city . . . arisen as if by magic. . . . For the first time in the history of our nation . . . art has asserted itself and triumphs over its handmaidens, commerce and manufacture . . . the World's Fair must convince the most indifferent European-American that, whatever may have been the case at an earlier period, the country which has produced this great, harmonious whole is not entirely lacking in art atmosphere." [4] Thirty years later Theodore Dreiser was still breathless about "this vast and harmonious collection of perfectly constructed and snowy buildings . . . as though some brooding spirit of beauty, inherent possibly in some directing over-soul, had waved a magic wand . . . and lo, this fairyland." [5] Henry Adams allowed that

"As a scenic display, Paris had never approached it." [6] As for Samantha Allen, duly covering the fair with her Josiah in tow, she compared the focal Court of Honor with what she expected to see after death when "the streets of the New Jerusalem open before my vision . . . this White City of magic and splendor . . . these snowy palaces, vast and beautiful.

Samantha and Josiah Allen are exhilarated by the beauty of the Administration Building at the Chicago Fair.

. . ." [7] For some decades afterward that honorific title, the White City, was borrowed for new-built amusement parks, just as "the midway" has remained *the* generic term for the amusement areas of county and state fairs.

The White City's multiplicity of columns with classic capitals and allegorical statues with floating draperies and rapt facial expressions led to many admiring references to Greece and Rome. Actually there was little Greece about it, and its Rome was mostly that of the baroque 1600's. The principal buildings were designed by various architects, half of them Northeastern, half Midwestern, but the prevailing influence was that of the Beaux-Arts, the great school in Paris where students from all over the world then went to learn a twice-diluted and thrice-distorted pseudo-classic architecture. Some of the states' individual buildings retained the

elder eclecticism with French Gothic or Richardsonian intent. Massachusetts reproduced the cupolaed Georgian of the old Hancock mansion in
Boston. But the Illinois Building, largest and most expensive in this category as befitted the hostess state, had all the domed and porticoed air of
the typical State Capitol, and most of the rest looked like the Renaissance
palaces that Richard Morris Hunt, dominant spirit of the World's Fair
designers, had been building at Newport for millionaires.

Dreiser's "perfectly constructed" needs qualification. These peristyles
and pediments were merely a superlatively elaborate stage set appropriate
to an architecture owing so much to the Roman theater. The much extolled gleaming white was all "staff"—a mixture of plaster and fiber as
plastic as chewing gum and painted closely to resemble tombstone marble.
(To get it all painted in time, Francis D. Millet, artist and semiexpatriate
intimate of Henry James and John S. Sargent, who was in charge of the
decorating, had to invent the first successful powered paint sprayer.) In
the California Building, second largest among the states, designed closely
after the old Spanish missions, of course, the staff was seamed with imitation cracks for an effect of reverend antiquity. Once the show was over,
this sensible material for evanescent pomp was readily torn down and
carted away. Indeed as November neared, it was coming apart of itself.
What held its whiteness up to be admired was structural skeletons of wood
with metal where necessary—the Illinois Building, for instance, contained 3,000,000 board feet of lumber and 650 tons of iron. Fair buildings
catching fire that winter before demolition got around to them burned like
waste paper. But when their designers patronizingly told Henry Adams,
who knew most of them personally, how these Midwesterners took architecture as "a stage-decoration," he reminded them that "all trading cities
[like Chicago] had always shown traders' taste" and "possibly the architects of Paestum and Girgenti had talked the same way." Anyway, he
said, "If [Chicagoans] actually knew what was good when they saw it,
they would some day talk about Hunt and . . . St. Gaudens [the sculptor
of the stark naked "Diana" brought on to the Fair from Madison Square
Garden], Burnham [supervisor of architecture of the fair] and McKim
and Stanford White [eminent Eastern practitioners of the Beaux-Arts
idiom] when their politicians and millionaires were otherwise forgotten." [8]

One way or another, practically everybody found the White City culturally momentous. Politicians, members of school boards, leaders of
women's clubs, newspaper editors, aspiring young architects, well-to-do
alumni of colleges and millions of taxpaying, stiff-collared Americans and
their wives went home from Chicago beatifically convinced that they had
seen Beauty miraculously risen out of the swampy lakeshore; that every

civilized city should have a complex of buildings looking as much as possible like the Court of Honor; and that a newly art-minded America should insist on Beaux-Arts treatment of all future railroad depots, courthouses, libraries, lecture halls, clubhouses and comfort stations in public parks. It was the same sort of contagious enthusiasm that had previously applied the pseudo-Gothic to railroad cars. The consequences are now all around us in the Union Station at Washington, D.C., and the colonnaded stone desert of Constitution Avenue and in the genteelly different but all too recognizable beaux-arty (a useful term employed by architect Claude Bragdon) examples of the Widener Library at Harvard, the New York Public Library, the Indianapolis Public Library.

No more mansarded livery stables or Venetian Gothic hotels; but a great economic boom in the quarries around Bedford, Indiana, whence came the fine limestone preferred for facing these monuments to the Chicago-inspired fashion. Even at the time the lasting importance of it was proclaimed. But from his less elevated vantage point Mr. Dooley was not misled:

> They tell me that [the Chicago Fair] give an impetus, whativer that is, to archytecture that it hasn't raycovered from yet. Afther th' fair, ivrybody that was annybody had to go live in a Greek temple with an Eyetalian roof. . . . But thim that wasn't annybody has f'rgot all about th' . . . Court iv Honor, an' whin ye say annything to thim about th' fair, they say: "D'ye raymimber th' night I see ye on th' Midway? Oh, my!" 9

At least the creators of the White City had accomplished a good deal toward smothering the grotesqueries of scroll-saw fretwork and Ruskinian clumpiness. But to one of the fair's architects this substitution of a flashily derivative idiom too easily learned by rote came to seem a calamity. Apparently Henry Adams' acquaintance did not include Louis Sullivan of the Chicago firm of Adler & Sullivan. His Transportation Building, the grand arch of its main entrance carved in original symbolic designs and gleaming with gold, was much commended in spite of its relative lack of conventional beaux-artiness. As Sullivan looked back later on the national impact of Mrs. Elliott's "great, harmonious, artistic whole," he was moved to strong language:

> These crowds [at the Chicago Fair] . . . beheld what was for them an amazing revelation of the architectural art . . . [and were] permeated by the most subtle and slow-acting of poisons . . . unexposed, unprepared, they had not time nor [sic] occasion to become immune to forms of sophistication not their own . . . what they saw was . . . an imposition of the spurious . . . charlatanry . . . expert salesmanship of the mate-

*Louis Sullivan's powerfully ornate, gilded entrance to the
Transportation Building at the Chicago Columbian Exposi-
tion of 1893 was what first persuaded Europeans that
America had a fertile future in architecture.*

rials of decay. . . . [The U.S. Government Building] was of an incredible
vulgarity . . . [the Illinois Building] a lewd exhibit of drooling imbecility
and political debauchery . . . the Palace of Arts . . . the most impudently thievish. [In due time] the virus of the World's Fair, after a period
of incubation in the architectural profession and in the population at
large . . . [appeared in] a violent outbreak of the Classic and the
Renaissance in the East, which slowly spread westward, contaminating
all that it touched. . . . Thus Architecture died in the land of the free and
the home of the brave. . . . Thus did the virus of a culture, snobbish and
alien to the land, perform its work of disintegration. . . . The damage
wrought by the World's Fair will last for half a century . . . if not
longer. . . .[10]

Such indignation must reflect Sullivan's long-standing awareness that
the fair had diverted attention from the recent birth in that same Chicago
of a native American architecture based on engineering, not imitation. He
may have been the more sensitive because he had had an important hand
in it himself, partly in building design, partly in the influence of his famous
eventual dictum: "Form follows function." [11] New as it was to his ad-

mirers in the early 1900's, this principle had actually been clearly enunciated by other Americans before he was born. In 1843 Horatio Greenough, expatriate Yankee sculptor, had ideas far more vigorous than the statues he turned out. The uncompromising functional beauty of the sailing ship as American shipyards had stripped her down from the grotesque floating castles of the 1600's was his point of departure:

"Observe a ship at sea!" he wrote. ". . . what imitation of the Greeks produced this marvel of construction? . . . Could we carry into our civil architecture the responsibilities that weigh upon our shipbuilders, we should . . . have edifices as superior to the Parthenon . . . as the *Constitution* is to the galley of the Argonauts." And again in 1852: ". . . the redundant must be pared down, the superfluous dropped . . . and then we shall find that beauty was waiting for us. . . . By beauty I mean the promise of function." [12] Some think that he picked up the germ of such notions from Emerson; in any case the 1850's saw some measure of agreement among people like Dr. Joseph Henry of the Smithsonian Institution and James Jackson Jarves, the critic and collector who brought America its first sizable exhibit of important European paintings, who cited "clipperships, fire-engines, locomotives" as inadvertently achieving "that equilibrium of lines, proportions and masses which are among the fundamental causes of abstract beauty." [13] But such precocious doctrine was ahead of its time and had to be born again from the union of Chicago's economic necessities with the technological advances of the mid-1800's. Doubtless the peculiar energies of Chicago also had something to do with it. It was she, after all, who had already revolutionized American building with the balloon frame.

The first and still the most conspicuous manifestation of this architectural esthetics of engineering was to be the skyscraper office building. Its determining innovation was the steel skeleton making obsolete the solid masonry wall, hence immensely increasing the possible height of buildings. And as concentration of offices had vastly increased the value per square foot of downtown land in New York City, Chicago and so on, pressure for ever higher buildings, piling more paying tenants on a given hideously expensive site, had grown to match. Within the last generation the hydraulic elevator and the telephone had made multiple stories above the level of four or five practical enough. But the increasing massiveness of masonry necessary as walls climbed higher inhibited upward growth. John Wellborn Root's redoubtable Monadnock Building in Chicago, fifteen stories high, completed in 1891, was a masterpiece of masonry engineering. Sullivan called it "an amazing cliff of brickwork rising sheer and stark, with a subtlety of line and surface, a direct singleness of purpose, that gave one the thrill of romance." But it was also, as he said, necessarily "the last work of its kind." [14] Masonry could go no higher and still serve the economic purposes of office building, hotel, apartment house or warehouse.

The disputes over which architect first utilized steel to remove limitations on building height can be quelled by taking matters a step farther backward and pointing out that the first suggestions to that effect came not from architects but from the booming new steel industry. By the 1870's both the Kelly-Bessemer and the open-hearth methods were well established in America, turning steel from a metallurgical luxury into a workaday replacement for iron in the girders of bridges, for instance, and a skyscraper skeleton is essentially a steel-girder bridge set on end. By 1885 the *Bulletin of the American Iron and Steel Association* was applauding architects' new interest in using steel structural members in commercial buildings. By the late 1880's several buildings in Chicago designed by such engineering-minded local architects as William Le Baron Jenney and the firm of (William) Holabird & (Martin) Roche consisted of all-steel skeletons carrying the structural load while acting as scaffold for mere curtain walls to keep the weather out and warmth in. The handsomest example appearing before the Chicago Fair turned heads toward beaux-artiness was the Wainwright Building in St. Louis designed by Sullivan and his German-born, engineering-minded partner, Dankmar Adler. That same year the public borrowed the word *skyscraper*—previously a sailor's term for the topmost possible square-rig sail—as special label for the new thing and portent of its great soarings-to-come.

Sullivan's particular contribution was manipulation of window spacing, curtain-wall masonry and other exterior elements of the steel-skeleton building to emphasize its height. This "accentuation of the vertical" [15] was, as Lewis Mumford has pointed out, a denial of the horizontal elements of the skyscraper, structurally just as important as the verticals, and thus is inconsistent with "Form follows function."* But it was the element of height that had caught public fancy and appealed to Sullivan's own somewhat romantic temperament. By 1913 this error in application of his theory had soared up 792 feet in the pseudo-Gothic verticalisms of Cass Gilbert's Woolworth Building. Thus to clothe a tapered steel cage with Gothic detail was very like the Chicago Fair's clothing wood-and-metal balloon frames with columns and entablatures of insubstantial staff. It also recalls the impact of the great fair that neither in Chicago nor

* This remains true even after one has allowed for the contention of Peter Blake (*Frank Lloyd Wright*, 27) that this formula of Sullivan's "has been one of the most widely misunderstood statements of aesthetic principle of all time: what he meant was *not*—or not *only*—that form must grow out of function, but that form, *beautiful form*, could only be created after functional expression had been satisfied. . . . To Sullivan and to Wright, beauty was only '*resident*' in function and form . . . never the inevitable by-product of function and form."

in any of the other American cities that took up the skyscraper did its first twenty-five years see any falling off in the yearning to draw cultural reassurance from imitation of the look of Old World buildings. It was felt necessary to top off skyscrapers with beaux-arty cornices at such heights that none of their elegant detail could be appreciated from below. Their street entrances were adorned by classical porticoes. As the shaft-tower came in, particularly in New York City, it was crowned with cupolas and curlicues or the Italianate belfry of the Metropolitan Life Insurance tower to make it unmistakable that this was architecture and not just a building.

Sullivan had a second reputation as creator of tastefully ornate, rather Art Nouveauish carved detail for his buildings. This remained with him as his later career dwindled into occasional designing of jewel-box-like quarters for small-town Midwestern banks. Some of it, plus Sullivan's strong sense of the new engineering freedom that new materials were giving the architect, rubbed off on Frank Lloyd Wright, who served his architectural apprenticeship in the office of Adler & Sullivan in the early 1890's. Where Sullivan made his name with vertical elements—though he by no means adhered to them slavishly—Wright made his with horizontals inspired, he liked to maintain, by his creative sensitivity to the wide Midwestern flatlands. Historically the prairie-style dwellings of his pre-World War I phase ably exploited that Italianate-Queen Anne tradition of irregularly free floor plans and use of cubage which had already struck Europeans as a valuable American innovation. On the outside this same flexible informality translated into long, low, wide-eaved roof lines, deep verandas and heavy walls of brick or stone that had a generally Oriental look but were actually an original style of building suited to the climate of northern America better than anything ever seen before Wright's time. He was also imaginative about the new poured concrete as a freedom-encouraging material. And the office building that he designed for the Larkin Company of Buffalo, New York, in 1904 not only anticipated many minor devices that still sound modern in the 1960's but determinedly got so far from decoration for decoration's sake that it looked like one of the movie sets for Babylon in D. W. Griffith's *Intolerance*.

Sullivan's and Wright's ideas were taken home to Europe by visitors avid for distinctively American developments and had much to do with the so-called International architecture of the Continent of Europe that America borrowed back again after World War I. Indeed the two probably had greater esthetic effect on the rest of the world than any other Americans of their time except the loose and largely unidentifiable group of Negroes in New Orleans who developed jazz music at about the same time that Sullivan was dreaming up the carvings on the fair's Transportation Building and Wright was designing his blocky first dwellings. Here was cultural feedback to the Old World with a vengeance. Maybe the high articulateness of both men was partly responsible. Both wrote of the close relations between architecture and society with a rather French type of sententiousness and in a windy vein that qualifies them to be called America's first examples of that singular anomaly, the architect-as-prophet.

Though Sullivan came from Massachusetts and Wright from Wisconsin, both were as truly products of Chicago as the smell from the stockyards. Here was the sprawling new city by the lake indeed "making culture hum," as a loyally ambitious Chicagoan had predicted. Ironically, however, the visitor of 1914 seeking the most striking consequences of Chicago's invention of the steel-cage building found it not at the lower end of Lake Michigan but on Manhattan Island. The cluster of skyscrapers on the tip of the island was less numerous then. But it had no rival uptown group captained by the overtopping Empire State Building; it already dramatically—and, some thought, appropriately—dwarfed the Statue of Liberty; and, as seen from a ship coming up New York Bay, loomed up as a pinnacled fantasy promising, with an authority such as the first look at no other country has ever afforded, a great differentness in this new nation. In no time the skyscraper had spontaneously displaced the official bald eagle as the world's symbol of America. A similar displacement also occurred internally. In the previous generation a new courthouse was what Zenith City built to express civic pride. Now its tower was likely to be overtopped by a single skyscraper across the level prairie visible even farther than the grain elevator.

The impetus that the Chicago Fair gave to beaux-artiness in America generally was as real as Lake Michigan. But it already had a promising foothold in the plutocratic Northeast, thanks to those architects whom Henry Adams credited with the fair's special character, particularly Richard Morris Hunt, Charles Follen McKim and Stanford White. Hunt may be said to have been high priest of the movement. His brother, William Morris Hunt, became an eminent painter. Richard's early years in Paris were devoted primarily to painting and sculpture, as well as architecture, and his first practice of his future profession consisted of acting as a construction inspector for one of the architects of Napoleon III's grandiose additions to the Louvre and the Tuileries. Shortly before the Civil War he opened in New York City an architectural studio attracting several young disciples with prominent futures. After another few years of development in Europe in the 1860's, he began to make himself the outstanding instrument for expressing the competitive spasms of mansion-building megalomania among New York City's outstanding rich men— in some cases, their wives.

Goelet, Gerry, Astor, Belmont were among the names on the checks rewarding his diligence in splashing around the requisite colored marbles, gilded carvings, priceless tapestries and cataracts of stately stairs. His Vanderbilt commissions alone would have been a career. William K.'s mansion on Fifth Avenue, immediately one of the sights of New York City, was followed in 1892 by Marble House, a Newport "cottage" so lushly reflecting Mrs. William K.'s passion for opulent settings that she was made a fellow of the American Institute of Architects—of which Hunt was a founder. Three years later Cornelius Vanderbilt weighed in with The Breakers, Italian Renaissance instead of French Baroque, which makes it slightly more habitable than Marble House, though the interiors are equally gorgeous. Larger than either and within a hair as gaudy is Biltmore, the country palace, including an imitation of the open spiral stair of the Château de Blois, that Hunt built for George W. Vanderbilt among the astonished shaggy hills outside Asheville, North Carolina.

Marble House was so dedicated to unflawed Frenchness that the plan omitted clothes closets, compelling guests and family alike to place suits and dresses in the standing wardrobes still familiar in Europe. Connoisseurs of the incredible greatly value its dining room, in which a portrait of young Louis XIV in ermine, hung between pilasters of pink Numidian marble with gilt capitals, looks down on a platoon of solid bronze dining chairs covered with gold-and-scarlet velvet vying for notice with the hysterical carving of the largely marble walls. The generosity with which Hunt lavished on the Vanderbilts costly marbles and specially designed French furniture might have suggested thirty years sooner the description that the 1920's applied to New York City's Paramount Theater: "Cecil B. DeMille's idea of God's bathroom." How did anybody, Vanderbilt or guest, ever manage to eat or converse amid all that visual din? But then how could George W. ever sleep in the somber, hideously intricate Spanish bed so reverently preserved in his bedroom at Biltmore? It looks as though Count Dracula had carved it expressly for spiders to infest. Yet Biltmore, unlike the Newport palaces, has an honorable place in history. George W. wanted the surrounding vast landholdings to be worthy of the mansion. By hiring a European-trained, cultivated young forester, Gifford Pinchot, later founder of the U.S. Forest Service, to do right by the wooded hills, he in effect subsidized the birth of scientific forestry in America.

Hunt's talent was not confined to post-1500 elegance. When O. H. P. Belmont, August's sporty son, preferred the medieval for his entry in the Newport Ostentation Sweep, Hunt gave him a courtyard of brick, halftimber and dormered gables and a ballroom that, instead of such a mass of wriggly gilt as at Marble House, is as Gothic as pointed vaulting and stained glass can make it, just the place for the waltzes and two-steps danced by Belmont's guests. Originally the entrance was so designed that he could drive a tallyho coach right into the house. Yet the least credible detail in Newport is not Hunt's but the work of Horace Trumbauer, later creator of the insistently Gothic campus of Duke University. In The Elms, Newport "cottage" of E. J. Berwind, Pennsylvania coal magnate, Trumbauer housed the several dozen servants in adequate quarters on the roof of the two-story French Baroque palace duly set on balustraded terraces sweeping down to ample lawns and distant plantings and summer-houses. But the servants were not afforded any view of the grounds from their windows. The roof is completely walled in by a solid, elegantly ornamented ten-foot parapet carrying at each corner an allegorical statue instead of a tower with an armed sentry.

Others among the turn-of-the-century plutocracy built similar palaces of marble, Bedford stone or Tudoristic half timber all the way from Deering's example at Miami to Rockefeller's at Bar Harbor, to be used only a few weeks, or at best a couple of months, per year. Both sides of the lower Hudson, the midsection of Long Island and the area northwest of Newark, New Jersey, were particularly thus encumbered with a new generation of achingly stately pleasure homes making the earlier Italianate

The Elms, a top-echelon Newport "cottage," has become a great tourist attraction; but the tour does not include the concentration camp for servants on the roof.

and Gothic villas look frumpy. But Newport was focus of this costly game, even developing its own shingle style of "cottage" for those millionaires modestly requiring only fifteen or twenty rooms in wooden construction that would not seem to challenge Vanderbilts and Astors. Such gilt-edged shingles accentuating the masses of Queen Anne-ish designs were associated with the architectural firm of McKim, Mead & White—which brings us to Henry Adams' other architectural missionaries to the traders' tastes of Chicago.

They had begun it in 1879, when designing the wooden Newport Casino, allegedly projected by James Gordon Bennett to give the growing summer colony a social focus broad enough to admit him. It has deep gables with subtly varied details, charming use of the Japanese openwork then coming into fashion, a Richardsonian entrance arch of brick—McKim and White had both been pupils of Richardson's. The genuine style of the whole excepts it from the complaints of Antoinette F. Downing and Vincent J. Scully, Jr., architectural historians, that though Newport cottages differ in style, "All . . . seem of a piece. . . . Most . . . are huge . . . dry and uninteresting, if correct in detail. . . . Seen together [they] constitute an exaggerated example of the super-suburb, which put a premium upon exclusiveness, pretension, and conformity." [16] Yet the Newport Casino still deserves some reproach, for it and some other McKim, Mead & White designs inspired a nationwide epidemic of shingles —a notoriously persistent disease—applied not only to myriads of summer cottages but even to the outsides of wooden approximations of the candlesnuffer towers of Carcassonne.

This firm's contribution to the Chicago Fair consisted of McKim's support for Hunt in keeping it beaux-arty, plus the designs for the New York State Building (a highly appropriate version of the Villa Medici) and the Agricultural Building—a strange assignment for architects so oriented toward urban values. But they made it as staidly ornate as its sister buildings and went on, unaffected by alfalfa. Like the Short Hills (New Jersey) Country Club, a Newport palace for Mrs. Hermann Oelrichs and a Dutchess County estate accommodating the zealous athleticism of Mrs. John Jacob Astor, their principal role was to provide New York City with the wide variety of buildings, largely nonresidential, with which it expressed its versatile, opulent narcissism.

The range was wide in traditional styles employed, as well as in functions served. In 1914 a three-mile walk, starting in Washington Square, up the spine of Manhattan Island, would have summed up their cultural indispensability. First the Italianate Judson Memorial Church with insipid glass by John La Farge and a square tower much too Catholic in feel to have set well with the renowned Baptist missionary thus honored. Then the Washington Arch permanently replacing its temporary, staff-built predecessor much admired during the centenary of George Washington's

first inauguration. Then the decorative base of the statue of Admiral Far-
ragut at Madison Square. Then the Madison Square Presbyterian
Church,* an ingenious revision of Rome's Pantheon. Then Madison
Square Garden,* rather gimcracky, more or less Spanish, but with a
graciously soaring tower crowned by the smaller version of St.-Gaudens'
naked but virginal "Diana." Then the Pennsylvania Railroad Terminal*
based on the barrel-vaulted roominess of Roman baths but also pleasing
functionalists by the frankly bared steel arches of its train concourse.
Then back across town to the Renaissance again in the pseudo-Venetian
Tiffany jewelry store* on Fifth Avenue and J. P. Morgan's Renaissance
private library housing his learnedly assembled collections. Then midtown
men's clubs—the Harvard staidly Georgian red brick, the Century in a
somewhat frivolous Renaissance idiom, the University a tricked-up Gen-
oese palace. Then the massed Italianate palaces, requiring a complete city
block, built for Henry Villard, immigrant reporter turned railroad magnate. Farther uptown the Metropolitan Club, a personal concern of Mr.
Morgan's but pure Hunt-Vanderbilt-Newport. Three miles farther north
one can still see the Low Memorial Library, Pantheonish again, at Columbia University, and off to the northeast the Roman colonnade of the Hall
of Fame at New York University, where the permanent residents already
included so catholic a mixed party as Frances Willard, Edgar Allan Poe,
Harriet Beecher Stowe, Gilbert Stuart, Ralph Waldo Emerson, William T.
Sherman.

Here were McKim, Mead & White arranging for staid Protestantism;
honors for the mighty dead; luxury trains to Florida; theater and horse
shows; diamonds and wedding invitations; cultivated bibliophilia; sporting recreation; august universities; several kinds of club life—and White
also found time to fit out the inside of Bennett's yacht. Among the partners William Mead was the taciturn engineer and administrator responsible for the economic and physical frames on which the other two hung
their and their clients' notions. St.-Gaudens, a much-valued crony of the
firm, caricatured him as struggling with two kites at once. McKim was
the quieter of the two and rather less adventurously eclectic. It was easy
to be less conspicuous than Stanford White whose thick red hair and formidable red mustache made the scholarly say that Vercingetorix, the great
Gallic chieftain who almost held his own against Julius Caesar, must have
looked like that. He was "exuberant, jovial, kindly, discriminately fond of
of the table, and eminently companionable," [17] a trait appreciated by
women and girls, too. He knew everybody who counted, he went everywhere that counted, and he worked feverishly to accumulate the decora-

* The asterisk indicates that the building mentioned has been demolished.

tive materials to suit both his and his clients' notions of what belonged in the firm's buildings, a function comparable to what Delmonico's and Sherry's did for the same people's gastronomic ambitions.

Now that his work is being respectfully restudied, his high visibility encourages attribution to him alone work that was more likely collaboration within the firm. Thus the Century Association was analyzed by McKim's biographer as comprising a floor plan from him and a street front from White, with its remarkable details the work of Joseph M. Wells, who was their junior expert on Italian Renaissance, though he had never been in Italy until shortly before he died in 1890. Works most probably largely White's are the Washington Arch, the Judson Memorial, the Metropolitan Club and Madison Square Garden—in whose roof garden in 1906 he inadvertently became a principal in the rankest scandal of the early 1900's when Harry Thaw, wildly unstable son of a Pittsburgh coal baron, married to one of the ladies of the chorus whom White had once viewed with favor, shot and killed him. There, at the age of fifty-nine, still bursting with a purposeful activity that would have tired Theodore Roosevelt, went America's greatest architect of the decorative persuasion.

At the Chicago Fair they asked Opie Reed, a local writer, to comment on California's exhibition, the most elaborate of any state's, representing an outlay of $300,000. He said it was worth $20,000,000 to the state—a fine return on the investment and, considering the tenor of its exhibits, probably not overestimated. For it enticingly heightened for millions a new set of notions about California. Though the name still set tingling the notions of gold, big trees, vigilantes, the vibrations were now masked by sunshine, oranges, mission bells.

That is, Southern California was now upstaging the previously dominant area around San Francisco. The display at Chicago was not blatantly partisan. The single most talked-of item was Northern—a full-size knight in armor on a full-size horse both made of dried prunes from Santa Clara County. There was a piece of a huge sequoia tree and masses of gold ore. The wine industry, by then well established by earnest Germans, Swiss and Hungarians adapting traditional viticulture to Californian conditions, was largely a Northern affair. But Americans in general, as Europeans often protested, were not impressed by sound California wines, preferring poor French ones when they bought any. The Mission motif of the California Building could refer to San Jose and Carmel, as well as to missions farther south. But both *Ramona* and Charles F. Lummis' campaigns to restore the disintegrating churches had fixed sentimentalists' attention stickily on *Southern* mission bells, those of Santa Barbara, San Juan Capistrano, San Gabriel. And the citrus-growing counties' exhibits did a great deal to strengthen the impression that oranges and lemons no longer rhymed with the bells of St. Clement's but with California—*sunny* California, not the foggy Northern part.

In the fair's Horticultural and Agricultural buildings, as well as in the California Building, visitors from Paducah or Menominee had the association between California and citrus reemphasized by a great tower or pyramid or 12-foot globe of oranges set in a sea of lemons renewed every few days by special rail shipments of fruit fresh from Los Angeles County. On Admission Day, marking the anniversary of California's becoming a state, the ceremonies climaxed in a largess of California fruit free to one and all present. Of the 200,000 eager applicants, some women fainted in the crush and presumably got nothing, but for all the rest, supplies were adequate, principally citrus, eked out by grapes and dried fruit. The master stroke was the successful transplantation to a protected courtyard of the Horticultural Building of twenty lemon and thirty orange trees. All through the fair they flourished, blooming and bearing fruit to the delight of the millions of visitors. Such touches admirably dramatized the supine balminess of Southern California's climate, always the chief argument for her existence. Then, to lend exotic elegance in a day when ladies' hats sported ostrich plumes, the Southern California ostrich ranchers' display of their huge and nasty-tempered birds received a great deal of attention from the crowds on the Midway.

Experiments in the 1860's, based on previous ones involving colonies of Germans and of Mormons, had shown that the wide valleys south of the Tehachapis, the traditional cattle country, would grow a great many things in profusion, if intelligently irrigated. Eastern capital raised by far-seeing promoters paid for the dams, flumes, canals, ditches and legal knot cuttings that enabled water from the distant mountains to nourish date palms, orange and lemon trees, year-round flowers and the incomes of real estate agents in new settlements called Riverside, Redlands, Pasadena, where two generations previously Don José Ranchero's herdsmen and wild-eyed cow beasts had reigned. Ever since then Southern California has based its exuberant existence on irrigation to a degree recalling ancient Mesopotamia, or as John L. Stoddard, king of the travel lecturers of the 1890's, said: ". . . all the fertile portion of this region has been as truly wrested from the wilderness, as Holland from the sea." [18] The navel type of orange proved particularly well suited to local conditions, and by the mid-1870's some 5,000,000 a year were shipped northward to San Francisco and profits of $1,000 an acre of orange grove were not unknown. Soon, as the promoters had foreseen, railroads were built to connect Los Angeles and San Diego directly with the East—the Southern Pacific, sister of the Central Pacific, first along its Sunset Route into connection with Texas, then the Santa Fe angling southwestward from Chicago.

The new rails not only took the ever heavier citrus crops eastward to market but also fetched people westward to see where these luscious things came from. The state government, the railroads and local real estate speculators all joined in a nationwide come-hither campaign on a scale previously known only among manufacturers of patent medicines. Easterners already settled in the region were systematically organized to write Back East to friends and relatives about flowers in January, oranges in the backyard, and what the climate would do for Uncle Henry. Journalists were subsidized to visit Sunny California, and gratifying rhapsodies in the Eastern press usually resulted. The indicated idiom was already well established. Even in pre-citrus days a parson henchman of Leland Stanford's had got it gurgling nicely:

"Our young queen [California] sitting by the sunset sea, bathing her feet in its pacific waters, her flowing hair touching our golden hills, her fairy fingers plucking the peach and the lily the year round. . . . No land so favored; none so promising." [19] A spellbinding lawyer brought out from New York City to break a California millionaire's will charged no fee to apostrophize the state as "Land of sunshine, eternal perfume and flowers, land of grave men and beautiful women, land which the Almighty has crystallized with a smile; the Elysium of the national domain. . . ."[20] Stoddard had his look at the national Elysium in 1890:

> At a time when many cities of the North and East are held in the tenacious grip of winter, their gray skies thick with soot, their pavements deep in slush . . . the cities of Southern California celebrate their floral carnival. . . . We . . . love [Southern California] as the dreamland of the Spanish Missions . . . a home for the invalid and the winter tourist . . . one of the few spots on this continent where the great faults of our American civilization—worry and incessant work—are not conspicuous . . . where flowers fill the air with fragrance, where fruits are so abundant that starvation is impossible, and where the nerves are not constantly whipped up by atmospheric changes, men live more calmly. . . . Meanwhile the northern millionaire breaks down from overwork and leaves his money to be squandered by his relatives.[21]

In the late 1800's the rival railroads' rate wars sometimes had the day-coach fare from Kansas City to Los Angeles down to $2, even $1. Those taking advantage of these economic puerilities found the climate just as attractive for the coach as the Pullman passenger. Many never went home again or else soon returned, counting on the periodically prosperous local economy for livelihood—and with no coal to buy. What the Cham-

bers of Commerce and railroad advertising were really fishing for, however, was the class prevalent among Stoddard's lecture audiences—families with some or much capital. Railroad-built or -encouraged resort hotels,
colossal wooden extravaganzas like the Coronado at San Diego, waited at
the end of the transcontinental trip that such people made in Pullman
sleepers. Even when they came only as vacationing tourists lured by guaranteed sunshine and a yearning to see where Ramona lived, they took
home memories of flowers and fruit and many persons of their own stripe
taking it congenially easy. As the growing inconveniences of age made it
seem advisable to try a milder climate, they might well return to look for
a place to buy and settle down on, maybe with a few acres of income-pro-
ducing citrus attached. Other likely prospects were invalids or semi-
invalids persuaded that Southern California's relatively dry air and lack
of blustery winter—the sunbathing cult was far in the future—were good
not only for rheumatics but also for respiratory ailments such as tuberculosis, asthma, catarrh (sinusitis) at all ages. New Mexico, Arizona, Colorado (particularly recommended for tuberculosis because altitude was
then thought positively beneficial) also shared in the economic tonic thus
created by ecological medicine.

The ensuing "Pullman migration" into Southern California may have
been somewhat overstressed by historians. Much young energy from
Northern California, some of it already Californian-born, some originating Back East but with talents—and talons—sharpened in the speculative
free-for-alls of San Francisco, came southward in the new rush for gold
growing on trees and in the pockets of sanguine newcomers. As early as
1868 a San Francisco syndicate cleared $2,000,000 in a sort of dress re-
hearsal for later real estate booms by buying Don Abel Stearns' 200,000-
acre ranch and using high-pressure advertising to sell it off in 40-acre
plots. Yet the self-selection of settlers implied by emphasis on undemanding climate was bound to have important consequences. This steady inflow of bank credits and respectability cleaned Los Angeles up, changing
it from a sluggish little Port of Missing Men into a churchgoing center
of, among other things, Temperance propaganda that caused great trouble
with the wine-growing industry. The only member of the U.S. House of
Representatives that the Prohibition Party ever elected came from Los
Angeles in 1914. Worse, it was inevitable that these thronging newcomers,
whether affluent or not, included an unusually high admixture of middle
age gone sluggish, of wishful gullibility, of hopeful hypochondria. Among
those deploring this phenomenon is R. L. Duffus, who spent part of his
early career on the ground: "Los Angeles has got . . . too much of what
it asked for. . . . Nobody can make a strong, secure community out of
a new population . . . running away from something, whether it is the

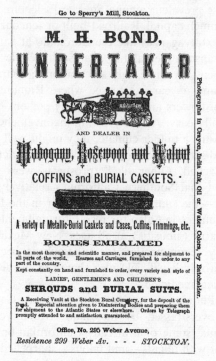

A California undertaker advertises in the local town directory.

police, a pestilence or bad weather. What Southern California needed was people . . . running *toward* something." [22]

Doubtless that shrewd formulation accounts for many of the marked differences between the two halves of the Golden State. The temperaments naturally drawn into the gold rush, whether those of actual gold seekers or of their suppliers and parasites, tended not only to youth— that alone contrasts sharply with the paunchy Pullman migration—but also often to adventurousness, imaginative enterprise and egocentricity. The forty-niners were crass but dynamic and had plenty of scope because even outside the traditions of mining and merchandising, the Bay Area offered other ways to the wealth that one came West for. For instance, Hugh Glenn, MD, a young forty-niner, never bothered either to prospect or to practice his profession but got immediately into the freighting business, made money, and devoted it to showing that growing wheat in the Sacramento Valley produced gold more consistently than any known diggings. Within fifteen years he owned 50,000 acres, had harvested more than 1,000,000 bushels of wheat in a single year, and employed more than 1,000 men. In the San Joaquin Valley in the middle of the state even larger wheat ranches were soon making fortunes for those who had known how to secure huge land grants early in the game of grab, shipping the consequent rivers of grain out the Golden Gate into the world market. This was no subsistence-plus-cash-crop farming of the Back East, family sort. It was an industry based on hired, seasonal mass labor, heavy capital investment in ever more numerous and larger planting and harvesting machines, and marketing on such a scale that the larger ranchers were as much grain speculators as they were boss farmers. When Frank Norris planned his trilogy of novels about wheat, he used as setting for the first the struggles between the wheat men of the San Joaquin and the Southern Pacific—which was, of course, another example of the portentous giants that came to birth in the same part of the state that produced the big trees.

Southern California did not wholly lack imaginative initiative. In the 1870's some of its residents banded together to introduce the eucalyptus —an Australian forest tree attaining great size and making valuable timber—to correct the gaunt treelessness of much of the landscape of paradise. Eucalyptus liked the region as much as any Pullman migrant, seeding itself prolifically and growing like Jack's beanstalk at a rate, some enthusiasts swore, of 15 feet a season. The vision of valuable forests vanished as something in the California climate made the wood shattery. But the other objective—impressive vegetation that would care for itself—was attained. Paradise has looked much better ever since. Other thoughtful Southern Californians, recognizing that the citrus industry had problems of marketing standards and of overproduction, developed the great California Fruit Growers' Exchange, a monopolistic cooperative that handled California's oranges and lemons so skillfully that it made Florida look amateurish. As electric traction cars came in, Los Angeles as well as San Francisco acquired them under the auspices of Henry E. Huntington, nephew protégé of Collis P. Huntington of the Big Four. Los Angeles streetcars and interurbans made him an area-straddling economic potentate in his own right, much to the stimulus of the whole region. Little is left of the Huntington kingdom now except the invaluable Huntington Art Gallery and Library at San Marino, the latter a researcher's and bibliophile's heaven, the former glistening with Gainsborough, Reynolds and Company—the Huntington mansion, of course, just as beaux-arty but considerably more elegant than any of the palaces that even greater fortunes built in the same period at Newport. It also compares well with much then being built in the Bay Area by the sort of people deplored by Harry Leon Wilson's Ma Pettengill:

". . . pretty soon they got into this darned swell little suburb out from

San Francisco, through knowing one of the old families that had lived there man and boy upwards of four years. . . . So . . . they set to work building their present marble palace bigger than the state insane asylum and very tasty and expensive with hand-painted ceilings and pergolas. . . ." [23]

It remains true, however, that until Southern California struck oil, the principal economic prop of paradise, barring citrus, was the sale of real estate in parcels to suit all unwary appetites. The brokers thereof usually showed more impudence than judgment. Once the genuinely enterprising founders of places like Riverside and Pasadena, mostly Back Easterners, had the movement under way, the prospect arriving by train with money in his hands was as easy to exploit as the legendary little pig running round squealing "Eat me! Eat me!" in the Land of Cockaigne. Barefaced swindles succeeded as handsomely as subtle ones. The spirit of it survives in the old-timers' tales of how so-and-so stuck ripe oranges on the spines of the giant cacti infesting a tract of downright desert and sold it in parcels as orange groves in production. Hence came the razzle-dazzle methods used ever since to fleece the gullible in land booms in Florida, Arizona, Long Island—the free excursion by train, bus or plane, the free dinner, the Potemkin-village model house, the exhilarating band music, the now-or-never closing crackdown. But one cannot justly accuse Southern California of having invented the elaborate land swindle as such. That was already full blown Back East in the 1830's when Zephaniah Scadder showed Martin Chuzzlewit the map of the thriving city of Eden—which proved to be a swamp with a few log cabins sheltering miserable victims of fevernager and sharp practice.

The cultural cleavages between San Francisco's and Los Angeles' spheres of influence, still marked today though less so, were evident in their repercussions on the elder states. Ideas—the single tax, the Yellow Peril, Isadora Duncan's subjectively barefooted innovations in dancing—usually came from San Francisco, not Los Angeles. Within fifteen years of the gold rush San Francisco was incubating writers, such as Bret Harte and Mark Twain, soon to command attention from the nation. The process continued with Joaquin Miller, Ambrose Bierce, Frank Norris, Jack London, Edwin ("The Man with the Hoe") Markham, Gertrude Atherton. The journalistic freebooting that William Randolph Hearst taught the nation came from San Francisco's Market Street. But long after recurring booms had made Southern California a going concern of great scale, even well into the 1900's, its contributions to American life went little beyond the inclusion of fruit in salads; the cafeteria system of self-service; and the cults of Mission architecture and the California bungalow. Soon there were also Mission-style tables and chairs of glum fumed oak with which to furnish the hundreds of thousands of those bungalows that still survive coast to coast.

The popularity of these insistently wooden dwelling boxes came of simple design, hence lower building cost, plus what struck the women's magazines as a fashionable new style. *Bungalow* was soon so much part of the language that by 1912 Meredith Nicholson wrote confidently in a novel about a college town in Indiana of "the new bungalow addition across the Monon tracks." [24] The word came from India, probably by way of Kipling. The style deserved some gratitude from society for doing its share to discourage the jigsaw-and-turret school of architecture. But in itself it was a clumsy affair with its ungainly, wide-eaved roof sweeping forward, often owlishly dormered, to be propped up by squatty wooden pillars—or they might be faced with cobblestones—set on a planked or shingled bulwark to make a deep, shady front porch. The porch furniture was a settee-like swing hung on chains and several rattan chairs with limp, faded cushions. Some of the early bungalows in California filled much of the upper half story with a water tank to absorb the heat of the persistent sun. When the half story was used for bedrooms, the heat engendered up there in Midwestern and Northeastern summers was better suited to sala-manders than to human beings.

Presently the compact boxiness of the bungalow fused with the wide roofs and pyramid-topped towers of Spanish Mission into a style in which wooden sheathing painted or stained a lugubrious brown or green replaced stucco. The resulting all-wooden churches, schoolhouses and such added to a super-Richardsonian gloom a rickety effect never before approached in public buildings. The associated Mission furniture had Back Eastern

The confused, sweltering Eastern version of the California bungalow.

affinities with the late-blooming artsy-craftiness represented in the Roy-crofter movement—or private cult industry—of that well-staged eccentric Elbert Hubbard, who had met and admired William Morris after making a stake as a soap salesman. One must be fair to Southern California. The outstanding mass eccentricities of the generation before World War I—Christian Science and its sister New Thought, chewing gum, the Keeley cure for alcoholism—originated Back East. The one conspicuous crankishness out of California in that period was Fletcherism, the cult of attaining the Good Life by way of the alimentary canal, specifically by chewing one's food to nothing—and Horace Fletcher, its prophet, was no Los Angeleno but a Yankee-born importer of Oriental goods so closely identified with San Francisco that he was one of the founders of its famous Bohemian Club. Nor can one blame Southern California's cultural delusions altogether for the tendency of turn-of-the-century architecture toward castles in Spain. Much of the onus of that lies on Florida in a context that, by striking coincidence, consists of oranges, invalids, railroads and real estate booms.

Florida's building at the Chicago World's Fair was modeled after the sturdiest secular vestige of Spain in America—the old star-shaped fort at St. Augustine built of the local coquina (shell limestone) in the mid-1700's with such costly care that the King of Spain is said to have complained that its walls must be of solid silver. It does not look specifically Spanish, however, being merely a typical example of the international style of fortification built in the 1700's wherever Europeans applied the teachings of the great French military engineer, the Marquis de Vauban. Nor was there much Spanishness about the 400-mile peninsula with 200 miles of Gulf Coast attached to its northwestern corner that America hustled Spain into handing over in 1819. Spain had done little with it. St. Augustine in the northeast was a permanent settlement, but its harbor was poor. The potentially better one formed 30 miles north by the estuary of the St. Johns River, where Americans created Jacksonville, was neglected. Tenuous communications spread westward 350 miles to another settlement at Pensacola on the Gulf. But the flavor there was less Spanish than frontier English—arising from gamy British and American frontiersmen and Indian half-breeds. The rest of the new Territory of Florida consisted of two neglected seaboards sprawling southward; a swampy southern third then about as accessible as the sources of the Nile; and a variously forested interior into which the northward-flowing St. Johns would have afforded good transport had Spain only bothered to develop it.

The birdlife was rich; indeed ornithologists had been the first to make Florida generally known to the outside world. Other flourishing wildlife included bear, deer, raccoon, wildcat; several venomous snakes; and, as local specialties, the alligator and the walrus-size manatee (or sea cow) chomping aquatic vegetation in the coastal waters and thought, in spite of its innocent hideousness, to have inspired some of the sailors' tales about mermaids. In this balmily favorable environment with little molestation the fauna, particularly the alligators and rattlesnakes, achieved enormous size. The mosquitoes were probably no larger or more savage than those of adjacent swampy regions. Nor were the itchings set up by the practically invisible red bugs (the same entomological villains known farther north as chiggers*) more excruciating in Florida than elsewhere. Cognate animal nuisances had not kept whites out of the Gulf Coast, and the north-central uplands of Florida were promisingly fertile and well watered. But the standing menace of the Seminole Indians long damped the infiltration of permanent white settlers.

Originally seceders from the relatively advanced Creek Indians of Alabama and Georgia—in the Creek tongue Seminole means come-outer—they had drifted southward into Spanish territory, learned the ways of subtropical swamp and hammock extremely well, welcomed and absorbed numbers of runaway Negro slaves and a few white renegades, and become striking examples of what geneticists call hybrid vigor. Their Creek forebears had been tough. These were super-Creeks. It took the U.S. Army, up to the waist in muck, eyes blinded by sweat, mosquitoes and Indian cunning, twenty years to break the Seminoles and keep them broken. Most of them were removed to new lands in the Southwest; a minority withdrew into the unexplored Everglades, where they still persist as a minor tourist attraction.

Their downfall made way for a marked expansion of the Dixie-style economy of slaves, cotton and some sugar developing around Tallahassee, the territorial capital, and for admission to the Union as a state in 1845. Poor whites drifted across the border bringing their usual hand-to-mouth culture. It gave them a better living here, where growing seasons were longer and game and fish more plentiful. But they retained the generic name, crackers,† of their Georgian heritage. From such beginnings Florida might never have been more than a minor Alabama. But tokens of a special future soon appeared. One was a trickle of health seekers—Ralph Waldo Emerson among them—wintering in St. Augustine even before the

* Not to be confused with the jigger (also often pronounced *chigger*) of the West Indies, an exotic from West Africa that bores under the toenail to lay a sac of eggs that creates itching and often infection.

† Usually taken to be short for corncracker, signifying the prevalence of corn in the Georgian poor white's diet. The American Guide *Florida* (128) derives it from the sound of the ox driver's whip in the Florida lumber industry. In view of the provenance of Florida's poor whites, this seems needlessly elaborate.

Seminoles were overcome. After the Seminole War regular steamers came down from Charleston, South Carolina, and Savannah, Georgia, to Jacksonville, whence St. Augustine was accessible. Or visitors went by river steamboat up the St. Johns to boardinghouses in riverside hamlets away from the sometimes chill seacoast winds. Southernmost was Palatka, born as an Indian trading post, then a base for the Army, soon a thriving resort with some substantial buildings. On the return trip in season the steamboats were loaded with the second token of today's Florida—boxed oranges from groves already vigorous thereabouts. Wild orange trees, descended from those long since imported by Spaniards, were plentiful. They were ragged from neglect, and their fruit was unsalably bitter. But in the 1830's enterprising newcomers learned to graft sweet orange buds on them with good results. After a disastrous freeze-up in 1835 this new upriver industry sent a growing stream of fruit to Jacksonville and transshipment for Northern ports.

The Civil War broke off the southward flow of invalids—mingled with healthy tourists—and the northward one of oranges. Both revived soon after Appomattox. It was good long-term publicity that the sick lists of the Union regiments holding St. Augustine and Jacksonville were notably shorter than those of comparable units elsewhere. The thousands of Northern men constituting those garrisons took home enticing accounts of June in January, good fishing and lack of colds in the head. When civilian transport resumed, Northern capital began to look into orange groves as investments and to expand facilities for winter visitors at St. Augustine and the upriver landings. Harriet Beecher Stowe put some of her literary gains into a house and land at Mandarin on the river and wintered comfortably there, though Florida, as slavery-minded as any other of King Cotton's fiefs, might not have been expected to tolerate the author of *Uncle Tom's Cabin*. Thus began that sun seekers' invasion, leapfrogging over the whole of intervening Dixie, that has made peninsular Florida's ways and values by now half Northern. A journalist visiting St. Augustine in 1871 reported a good thousand paying customers per season in spite of primitive accommodations, horrible food and almost complete lack of livery-stable facilities. Three years later another was noticing in Jacksonville that half the resident population was Northern, settled there since the war.

Yet so long as steamers remained the best available transport, modern Florida could not really come into being. The St. Johns River was usefully navigable only a third of the way down the peninsula. On the east coast hundreds of miles of sandy keys backed by shallow lagoons kept deepwater ships from putting in between Jacksonville and Key West. On the Gulf side Tampa Bay, the only prime natural port below Pensacola, had little land access to the rest of the state and no *raison d'être* except one sugar plantation and some cattle grazing between it and the Everglades. What cured this torpor was a massive application of railroad track. Until the 1880's the state's experience with railroads had consisted largely of odd lines across the northern segment connecting Jacksonville with the Gulf and serving the plantation economy. In that decade, however, princess Florida, as yet merely stirring coyly in her sleep, was kissed wide awake by two puissant princes—Henry M. Flagler of Cleveland, Ohio, and Henry B. Plant, another Yankee, born in Branford, Connecticut.

Flagler was not only handsomer than most princes, he was also richer. This commandingly good-looking, heavily mustached man of fifty-odd had been one of John D. Rockefeller's first partners in what became the Standard Oil Company. Not only was he thus in on the ground floor of the classic example of fabulously profitable monopoly, he was also probably the most capable of Rockefeller's associates. He first saw Florida when spending some weeks in Jacksonville with his ailing first wife. In 1883 he brought his newlywed second wife also to Jacksonville for their honeymoon and on to St. Augustine on a new-built but wheezy little railroad that, for lack of a bridge across the St. Johns, could not get their private car to its destination. St. Augustine delighted him as much as its lack of up-to-date accommodations irked him. Returning the next year, he found two smallish but modern hotels under construction, which stirred him into devoting the rest of his life, his many, many millions and his superb organizing skill to make Florida live up to her charming possibilities.

He bought and rebuilt that little railroad and its fragmentary lines south, combining, building and rebuilding ever southward until his Florida East Coast Railway, as it was eventually known, had done over the eastern half of the peninsula. In effect he was an imaginative hobbyist, dealing in millions of dollars and millions of acres, who must take the chief praise or blame for everything, high-rise or honky-tonk, between Anastasia Island and Key West, except the installations at Cape Kennedy —a truly awesome responsibility.

Some think a passion for hotels was the core of his schemes. Emulating the Southern Pacific's Del Monte Hotel at Monterey, California, he marked each successive leap of his right-of-way by a huge, luxurious hotel, the patrons of which would help make the trackage pay. The most glorious was his first, at St. Augustine. He closely supervised its creation by Thomas Hastings and John M. Carrère, American-born young architects, Beaux-Arts-trained in grandiloquent pseudo-classicisms. Their work in that idiom is best seen in the New York Public Library and the Memorial Theater at Arlington, Virginia. But Flagler wanted Spanishness to match the historical past of St. Augustine; the larger of the two hotels projected was to be named after Ponce de León, the Spanish Colonial leader who first explored Florida in the early 1500's and finally died of a wound received while fighting the local Indians. Neither Hastings nor Carrère had ever visited Spain, but from drawings and photographs they gave Flagler for his money what a handbook of 1892 guaranteed to be "the best school of Spanish art . . . not a copy of any existing examples [but] the result of conscientious study of principles that have made famous the cathedrals, universities and palaces of classic Spain." [25]

The scale is indicated by the dining hall, which could seat 800. Rich with arched galleries, wrought-iron balconies, a dome, towers, red-tiled roofs, its interior stiff with sculpture and carvings and awash with allegorical murals of Adventure, Discovery, Conquest and the four elements (Hastings himself painted some of them), it covers a site larger than five football fields and had—and still has—the air of a single-unit world's fair. But this was no insubstantial dream of four-by-fours and staff soon to be dismantled. The architects adopted a recently developed local method of mixing crushed shells into concrete to make it highly durable —something like the tabby of the Colonial Carolinas—and made the Ponce de Leon a monolithic mass that, other things being equal, might well outlast the peninsula of Florida. Knowledge of synthetic Spanishness thus gained stood the firm in good stead in 1901, when they were supervising planners and part designers of Buffalo's great Pan-American Exposition—a sort of world's fair for the Western Hemisphere that, it was thought, required architectural deference to Latin America's tradition of elaborate Spanish Baroque. Thus it came about that the western tip of New York State, land of smothering snowstorms, blossomed with arabesqued arcades and porticoes reminiscent of Lima and the roses of Seville. And inevitably one building was an Old Spanish mission very like the famous one at Santa Barbara, California, its staff-and-wood exterior stained with artificial age, its tiled roof green with moss, its architect dutifully babbling about Ramona.

Here was reinforcement for America's new leaning toward red tiles, stucco, curlicued wrought iron and the not-too-well-understood term *patio*. For the next two decades New England and the Midwest, as well as Florida and California, were likely to build banks, schools and post offices in a Spanish vein that, though anomalous, was a gratifying shift toward simplicity of outline and ornament after the delirium of Queen Anne. After one fling at rampant Hispanisterics, however, Flagler took in architectural sail. The other hotels that he built or remodeled as his railroad crept southward—the Ormond at Ormond, merely an enlargement of a resort hotel already in being, the Royal Poinciana and the original Breakers at

Palm Beach, the Royal Palm at Miami, the Casa Marina at Key West, each opened as the railroad arrived, each painted yellow and white to match the colors of the Florida East Coast stations—were, though huge and luxurious, mere elaborations on the dormered or mansarded or verandaed great wooden resort hotels of Northern seasides. The Ponce de Leon remained queen of the chain architecturally, if not in social prestige, and St. Augustine was the line's headquarters whence this mass eviction of water moccasins and great white herons, trappers and moon-shiners was planned and directed. Also crucial to the development of the scheme was the rebuilding of rail lines down from the Virginia line to standard gauge (track width) so that by 1888 winter visitors and eco-nomic explorers could come all the way to Flagler country without changing trains.

The logistics involved in thus putting the east coast to use were as unwieldy as those of Seabees creating air bases on tropical islands in World War II. It is difficult now to realize how recently southern Florida was far out of touch with the great world. A few affluent climate fanciers, notably one of the Chicago McCormicks of the farm-machinery dynasty, had built winter places on Lake Worth (in the environs of what is now glittering Palm Beach), but they were accessible only by steamer down the Indian River, already the backbone of the orange country, connecting with a rattly 8-mile railroad to the head of the lake. Thence a miniature steamer took one to Lake Worth village, where three small hotels charged $10 a week for room and meals at the height of the season; then half a mile beyond to Palm Beach, which had one hotel and the botanical charms of a large royal poinciana tree (a showy-blooming native of Madagascar) and a lush grove of coco palms. They, too, were exotics, offspring of 20,000 coconuts that had washed ashore after the wreck of a Spanish vessel carrying them as cargo. Beyond the southern end of Lake Worth was no habitable building, except for a few houses of refuge for cast-aways, all the 50-odd miles to the precarious settlement at the mouth of the Miami River on Biscayne Bay. In 1867, says Sidney Walter Mar-tin's able biography of Flagler, the only human inhabitants of the Lake Worth area had been two deserters from the Confederate Army still un-aware that the war had been over for two years.

Though Miami now had a post office, the mails arrived at best once a week in a pouch carried by a man walking along the beaches from Lake Worth and crossing the intervening creeks by canoe. He was seldom weighed down, for Miami then consisted largely of a general store on the south side of the river, catering to Seminoles bartering alligator hides and surplus game and fish for gaudy calicoes and fishhooks, and an aban-doned U.S. Army post on the north side, repaired and inhabited by a widow from Cleveland, Ohio, Mrs. Julia Tuttle, who owned and was grimly determined to make a fortune out of the 640-acre section of land including it. At nearby Cocoanut Grove a boardinghouse lodged hunters and fishermen eager enough after the teeming local fauna to come all that way in the occasional sailing vessel from Key West that was the only practical means of access.

In 1893 Lake Worth had become Flagler's objective. Using a farsighted charter from the state allowing him to build all the way to Miami if he chose, he was now pushing rails southward where none had been before. He bought a tract of land on Lake Worth from McCormick and set out to create from practically nothing but sand and climate a hedonistic-minded resort city centered on a Flagler hotel served by a Flagler railroad, just as Peter the Great created an imperial capital from nothing but swamps and geographical situation. Both men were highly personal about it; Flagler had a finger in every detail of street planning, waterworks and landscaping. The difficulties were of similar order. While the new railroad inched southward, all construction material for the hotel and the ancillary aspects of the scheme had to be fetched down by the rickety steamer-and-rail Indian River route. And in size the Royal Poinciana was his capsheaf —its dining room seated 1,600; its standard of one waiter for every four guests meant that the staff totaled 1,400; after enlargement to six stories it accommodated 1,200 guests. Further to show that Palm Beach was the place he delighted to honor, he built there for his third wife—the second had gone hopelessly psychotic and been divorced—a Newport-style palace on which Carrère and Hastings exhausted their talents and 2,500,000 of Flagler's dollars. Its ballroom was 91 by 37 feet.

All the while Mrs. Tuttle had been prodding at Flagler in letters exhorting him to bring his railroad down to develop the Biscayne Bay area as he had Palm Beach. In 1893 she had personally gone to see him at St. Augustine. But he was not interested—until in the winter of 1894–95 the worst freeze-ups since 1835 destroyed orange trees and coco palms as far south as Palm Beach. While Flagler was supervising financial relief measures for the hard-hit settlers in his personally created kingdom, Mrs. Tuttle wrote again to point out that Miami had had no killing frost, and didn't that make the area worth attention? One of Flagler's aides visited her, brought back to his employer a carefully packed sample of undamaged flowers—and within a few days a mule-drawn cart, the only transport available below the launch-landing at Fort Lauderdale, appeared at Mrs. Tuttle's door bearing Flagler and his chiefs of construction and development. She made Flagler a well-calculated present of 100 acres for a hotel and railroad terminal at the junction of river and bay, reserved what is now the heart of downtown Miami for herself and divided the rest of her land into strips shared alternately between Flagler and herself. The same indefatigable magic wand that had created Palm Beach had an equally extraordinary effect 70 miles farther south, though by then the magician was well into his sixties. His Miami was a going concern well before development of Miami Beach began just before World War I. Presently, however, because it proved a disappointing deepwater port, he made the grand gesture of building causeways and bridges between the large and small bits of land that make up the Florida Keys and took his railroad 100-odd miles out to sea to end at Key West with a railroad-car ferry to Havana.

After that he died, in 1913. A man of imagination in the most authentic American tradition, except that his pouring huge sums into Florida—well over $30,000,000 by the time Miami was launched—was not entirely inspired by gain. Economically his Model Land Company's sales of the state subsidy lands that went with his acquisitions of minor railroads were probably what profited him most as his tracklaying made them desirable purchases. For though his railroads and hotels usually made profits, they were nothing like what the same capital would have brought in from many other opportunities, of which the second-ablest founder of Standard Oil was certainly well aware. It was an original solution to the old problem of how a plutocrat can enjoy his wealth without playing the aimless spendthrift.

Throughout the growth of his 500-mile hobby his solicitude for the economic well-being of the settlers whom his scheme attracted was as marked as it was well advised. But on occasion he could play high-handed monarch of all he surveyed as bluntly as any of the Southern Pacific's Big Four. The instance that understandably caused the most comment was his single-handed revision of the Florida divorce law to suit his personal needs. In 1901, after four years of increasingly severe paranoia, it became clear that the second Mrs. Flagler could never be allowed to leave custody. Flagler decided on divorce. In New York State, his legal residence, insanity was not grounds for divorce. He shifted his legal residence to Florida, of which the same was true—up to then. Exerting his well-established leverage on Florida's politicians, he had introduced into the legislature, passed and signed by the governor within eight days an act making insanity grounds for divorce in Florida, provided the trouble had lasted for four years or more and the discarded spouse's interests were taken care of. Within six weeks Flagler sued for his divorce in a Florida court, obtained it, appointed proper guardians for the lady, and endowed her with securities paying some $120,000 a year for her maintenance.

Within the next two years he also gave $20,000 to the University of Florida. The new statute naturally was called the Flagler Law.*

Flagler's success in creating the American Riviera, as his promotion men called it, in the late 1880's need not obscure the only slightly smaller achievement of his counterpart, Henry B. Plant, in simultaneously glorifying the lower Gulf Coast of Florida. Here too a health-seeking wife was involved. Plant was a self-made Yankee risen rapidly high in the great Adams Express Company of the mid-1800's. In 1853, on doctor's advice, he took his wife to Jacksonville for some months, came back Southern-minded, and soon arranged to take over management of the Adams interests south of the Potomac, with headquarters at Augusta, Georgia. As war approached in 1861 and the Adams Company feared confiscation of its business in Dixie, Plant created a new Southern Express Company to replace Adams. With either marked realism or a strong sense of his duty as a Northerner naturalized in Dixie, he acted as an agent of the Confederate government in important matters and remained in the South after the war.

That put him in a position to keep his eyes open for war-crippled railroads going cheap. By the early 1880's his Plant Investment Company dominated the lines westward from Jacksonville and southward into western Florida. Among his backers, able men who knew another when they saw him, were William T. Walters, organizer of what became the Atlantic Coast Line and a renowned art collector; Morris K. Jesup, New York City banker who godfathered the American Museum of Natural History and Peary's expedition to the North Pole; and Flagler, whose faith in Florida was not limited to the east coast. Presently Plant's intricate interests included several lines of river steamers in Florida; a railroad consolidation aimed at making Tampa an important port; a steamer line thence to Key West and Cuba; and, as token of his intention to make the most of the lovely Gulf Coast climate, the Plant-built Tampa Bay Hotel. This was fancier than any of Flagler's, a sweeping pageant of Moorish arches and balconies and onion-topped pinnacles such as the nation had not seen since P. T. Barnum's Iranistan had burned down.

A few years later the same freeze-ups that gave Mrs. Tuttle her chance with Flagler struck the orange groves north of Tampa Bay and scuttled the Orange Belt Line railroad serving the St. Petersburg side of the bay. It fell into Plant's waiting hands—an acquisition celebrated by the building of the huge Belleview Hotel on the Gulf north of St. Petersburg. He did not live to see the land boom of 1911 set St. Petersburg on its curious

* The foregoing owes a good deal to Professor Sidney Walter Martin's thorough *Florida's Flagler*.

future as the Sunshine City of the retired elderly; or the vigorous, rail-based development of the Gulf Coast all the way down to Fort Myers. But it was his astuteness as collector of stray railroads and promoter of land values that had made it all possible. Though he was more the promoter and less the builder than Flagler, he unquestionably bulked as large in the future of his chosen third of the state as the younger man had in his.

By pushing rails into the southernmost parts of the state, both these men enabled thousands to grow citrus and off-season garden truck for Northern markets in the latitude least liable to freeze-ups. Florida also had an economic future in lumbering, cattle and the mining of phosphates for fertilizer, all facilitated by the presence of railroads and the sale of state land-grant-subsidy tracts to build up populations. The similarity to what the iron horse did for California is striking. But the two cases are not altogether alike. Florida was spared California's abject and costly dependence on irrigation. Nor have cultural feedbacks from Florida reached the rest of the nation. Nobody thinks of her as a source of strange cults and folkways and economic eccentricities ranging from the movie industry to the Townsend Plan. Her principal role in American culture was to make the winter vacation an institution.

What originally sent the affluent, the ailing and the elderly for a few weeks away from Northern chill was doctor's orders. But by 1874 a visitor to Jacksonville was already reporting that only one-fourth of the annual visitors were in pursuit of health. Gradually social were replacing therapeutic considerations. The same process had recently converted the French Riviera from a vast tuberculosis sanitarium into a smart winter resort. As happens when standards of living are rising, new fashions of behavior gradually leached down into lower strata. The very rich built mansions for their annual season in Florida, like Flagler's at Palm Beach. Thus James Deering, son of a great farm-machinery fortune, put seven years and $15,000,000 into a pseudo-Spanish architectural explosion just below Miami. The very well-off could afford the Royal Poinciana and then The Breakers as those houses successively took over from the Ponce de Leon as focuses of prestige. And as investors following the lead of Flagler and Plant expanded accommodations to fit all but very lean purses, many successful businessmen could afford the rail fare and a few weeks of hotel bills in Miami or Bradenton or Winter Park, fishing and golfing while their wives played cards and embroidered and struck up acquaintances with their counterparts from Utica or Fort Wayne.

For most Americans California was markedly farther away than Florida, more expensive to get to, hence thought of more as a place to retire to. There was also much retiring to Florida, which was what made the fortune of St. Petersburg. But to live in Florida the year round in those times before air conditioning exposed one to summer temperatures even higher than those that the prosperous of Fort Wayne and Utica went to the lakes or the mountains to avoid, whereas in Southern California July and August are more temperate. So, in spite of her growing importance in horticulture and extractive industry, Americans, well into our time, kept Florida as seasonal pet. Ability to have a month or so there in the depths of February became a token of socio-economic success long before the automobile and the plane opened up the winter vacation to the younger and less affluent. For the wife of a small-town banker *c.* 1910 going to Florida regularly was as gratifying as having her own electric runabout and both son and daughter at college and in the best fraternities.

Note that in both California and Florida the railroad went in ahead of the settler—a new sequence. The early turnpikes, canals and railroads east of the Mississippi had usually been built to connect elder settlements, say, New York City with Albany, or elder ones with younger ones that were already going concerns, say, Pittsburgh with Cleveland. (The Erie Canal was an exception; most of the region it served was rather undeveloped; it did for upper New York State what the later Western railroads did for the plains states.) After the Civil War, however, the new-building railroad was likely to resemble the grin without the cat, pushing into lands that had never known a plow, through forests that had never felt the ax, across swamps innocent of ditches since the creation.

The theory was that farmer, lumberjack, miner and real estate salesman would adventure along the new railroad to give it a *raison d'être.* It had worked well when first tried on the Illinois Central Railroad, from Chicago to the Ohio, begun in 1850. Congress empowered Illinois to grant six alternate sections of public land to the railroad company per mile of line built, a subsidy without which rails might never have got into the discouragingly sluggish area it was to serve. A similar arrangement encouraged the building of the connecting Mobile and Ohio line from Mobile into Kentucky, giving the nation its first Great Lakes to the Gulf route. That eventually doomed the steamboats on the Western waters, but the immediate result was rapid settlement of the potentially rich interior of Illinois as the railroad encouraged land-hungry Americans and immigrant aliens to buy subsidy lands. Thenceforth it was settled policy to use generous land grants to stimulate railroad building, particularly west of the Mississippi. Eventually land grants built some 10 percent of America's total trackage. The scheme of alternate sections was always retained, making the affected areas checkerboards of mile-squares of railroad and government land.

Such an arrangement, supplemented by large loans of U.S. bonds, financed the Union Pacific as it crept westward in the mid-1860's to connect the upper Missouri with the similarly subsidized Central Pacific gnawing eastward through the Sierra Nevada. The immediate purpose of the federal subsidy was at least partly military—to enable the West Coast to keep in touch with the nation in such wartime crises as the Civil War. A European government might well have built and operated such a line itself. In America in the 1860's such a possibility was not considered. Besides, the long-range purpose was to get the trans-Missouri country stabilized, maybe settled and possibly producing, for the success of settlement in eastern Kansas and Nebraska was undermining the daunting old legend of the aridly useless Great American Desert. It was no coincidence—though both measures also had political aspects, of course —that the Homestead Bill of 1862, offering land free to anybody undertaking to establish himself on it, became law only a few weeks before the act subsidizing the Union-Central Pacific. And the existing example of the Illinois Central led people to assume that land grants to private enterprise were the method of choice to open up a country with railroads. In confirmation the Civil War was hardly over when, as first dividend, the subsidized Kansas Pacific, supplementing the Union Pacific scheme, strikingly boomed the cattle industry and set up the Great American Ranch. Soon too the subsidized Northern Pacific was creating in the Dakotas the bonanza-style wheat farming that sowed and planted huge holdings with mechanized equipment.

One condition of the subsidies required the beneficiary railroads always to carry federal personnel and goods at sharply reduced rates. Up to 1946, when this clause was abrogated, Uncle Sam had saved more than $1 billion in transportation costs in return for land grants totaling some 130,000,000 acres considered at the time worth less than $1 an acre. The railroads did their best to squirm out of paying the loans of U.S. bonds included in some early subsidies. But Uncle Sam was firm and in the late 1890's collected $167,000,000 in principal and accumulated interest on an original outlay of $64,000,000. Both transactions made the old gentleman look a better businessman than he often is. The winding-ups had been long in coming, however, and meanwhile, persons exasperated by the railroads—often with good reason—had made devastating use of the subsidies as horrible examples of how overgrown, soulless corporations could fatten on corrupt government. From the 1880's on, school textbooks, as well as political propaganda, might feature maps showing the extent of railroad land grants up to four times as large as they really were and almost always failing to make it clear that the alternate-section arrangement gave the railroads only half of what even an accurate map showed. In 1945 a railroad man checking school texts on this point found few mentioning that the bonds had been repaid, and several flatly denied that repayment had ever occurred.

By cynical sharp practices and heedless public relations the railroads—particularly the land grant roads—had brought such hostility on themselves. The backers of the Union Pacific and the Central Pacific seem to have realized that revenue from the disposal of subsidy lands for

A Union Pacific locomotive of the 1870's at Sherman, Wyoming. Note the horse-drawn vehicle waiting for passengers and the conspicuousness of the hotel barroom.

farms and townsites would be slow because of the competing availability of those alternate sections free to homesteaders; and that the revenue-producing growth of the wheat, cattle and other industries of the trans-Missouri West would be, though often vigorous, necessarily gradual. They had also had to anticipate the opening of the Suez Canal spoiling their original dream of shuttling goods between Europe and the Far East across America. Unwilling to wait too long for returns on their investments of time, energy and a certain amount of their own money, they made themselves handsome fortunes by—among other devices—hiring and heavily overpaying themselves as construction contractors. Oakes and Oliver Ames, shovel manufacturers of Massachusetts, conducted the Union Pacific version of this lucrative sleight of hand with subsidy funds. The heir to Oakes Ames' share of the proceeds used some of them for those model municipal buildings that he employed Richardson to design for North Easton, Massachusetts.

The Ames' counterparts in the Central Pacific were, of course, the redoubtable Big Four, who further built the Southern Pacific into Southern California and across the Southwest to the Gulf. Their thimblerigging practices in land sales and wheat transport in the San

Joaquin Valley in the 1800's brought on something like civil war and put the Southern Pacific into literature as *The Octopus* of Frank Norris' projected trilogy on wheat. Its literary qualities are undistinguished, but as an index of Californians' hatred for the SP it is significant history. For the Big Four's high-handedness was indeed flagrant. Their political leverage matched the economic leverage of their monopoly of long-distance transport within the state. When their abuse of the two brought about a state railroad commission to regulate them, their remedy was cynically handy—they arranged to have the new commission packed with the SP's henchmen. The device has been reverently imitated ever since by American industries coming under public regulation.

Not that railroad hating was a Californian specialty. Well before completion of the Central Pacific founded the Big Four's power, farmers in Midwestern areas that owed their opening up to rails were already boiling with wrath. Grains, particularly wheat, were the chief cash crops in Illinois, Iowa, Minnesota, the new fringes of Kansas, Nebraska and the Dakotas. The primary grain market, where case-hardened speculators juggled the basic prices of wheat and corn—that was the way the wheat farmer saw it—was in Chicago. That was what ambitious young Mr. Norris wrote the second novel of his trilogy, *The Pit,* about. Out in the wheat country distances were great, and water transport was seldom available. The only logistic link between wheat field and market was the railroad, which had enticed the farmer out there to begin with—or, again, that was the way he saw it—and now had him at the mercy of whatever freight charges on wheat the traffic would bear. Since there was probably only one railroad within feasible wagon haul of a given farm, competition among rival lines seldom affected rates, which stayed pretty much at Civil War levels when, after the war, grain prices naturally slacked off.

Besides, between the farmer's wagon and the railroad car stood the grain elevator, the great expansion of Oliver Evans' mechanized, fed-from-the-top gristmill that grades, cleans and stores his grain to await loading into cars—all at a further percentage cost kept high by the elevator operator's virtual monopoly on handling the produce of the area. Even where monopoly did not obtain, the farmer had good reason to suspect collusion among rivals, and railroad and elevator were often hand in glove in arranging supply of cars to suit mutual interests. Indeed all too often the railroad admittedly owned the elevator. Eventually students of American architecture would be taught to admire these grouped Brobdingnagian cylinders of wood (later concrete) as examples of clean, functional design. In any case, as the largest things of man's making for hundreds of miles around, they were as imposing as they were important. Chicago's eclipsing of St. Louis as transport hub of the Middle West has been attributed to the latter city's lack of grain elevators. But to the Nebraska farmer seeing them picked out on the far horizon by the first rays of sunrise, they were neither vehicles of beauty nor symbols of progress, but instruments of economic oppression, looming up as sinister to his eyes as the castle towers of the toll-greedy barons of the Rhine were to those of the medieval trader. He was certainly in no mood to deduce from them the principle, of which West Indian and Hawaiian planters had long been painfully aware, that it is not so much the primary producer as the middleman taking a straight percentage off the top who makes the money out of the crop.

Well before the end of the Civil War, farmers in Iowa felt so strongly about being gouged by railroads that they agitated for a new canal— long after the great days of towpath and low bridge—from the Rock Island area to Chicago to force lower rates on the railroads. Soon a new approach was opened up by the Grangers—formally the Patrons of Husbandry, whose popular name comes of their calling their lodges granges, an archaic terms for barns.* The purpose of their founder, Oliver H. Kelley, who had been reared among farmers' troubles in Minnesota and then been a field investigator for the U.S. Bureau of Agriculture (precursor of today's department), was largely educational and social— to organize farm people, shrewdly including wives and daughters as officers as well as members, to better themselves culturally and technologically. The initiations and rituals had an earnest flavor of Masonry. The leaders thus installed provided constructive or inspirational talks and demonstrations about fertilizer at this meeting, righteous citizenship the next; the suppers that the ladies provided were usually the finest country eating and vastly enjoyed by all. But Kelley's scheme appeared just when the first antirailroad storm was reaching gale proportions west and north of Chicago. This first widely organized farmers' movement, being a natural vent for grass-roots pressures, spread rapidly with a momentum attributable largely to antirailroad ferment. Specifically and effectively in most of the states where the grain-transport bind was tightest the massed Granges demanded—and after bitter pulling and hauling usually secured from their legislators—state regulation of the rates charged by railroads and elevators.

The basic tenet was that by securing charters of special privilege, including the sovereign's right of eminent domain, the railroads had re-

---

* Note, however, that the numerous American towns and villages called La Grange represent an indirect compliment to the Marquis de Lafayette, whose triumphal visit to the United States in 1824-25 caused many Americans to be aware of the name of his French countryseat—La Grange.

linquished the status of normal private enterprise and could be required to observe public interests to an extent not required of the tanner or the hog buyer. The railroads fought such "Granger laws" up to the U.S. Supreme Court and lost in 1877. This farmers' victory was undercut later by a supplementary decision confining state regulation to intrastate traffic—that is, exempting the immense volume crossing state lines. The principle remained intact, however. Thenceforward, hindsight now makes it clear, either the railroads would mend their ways or federal power to regulate interstate traffic would eventually be created.

In trying to cope with overgrown economic power, the Grangers also picked up notions already stirring in Europe and organized their own retail cooperatives, creameries and grain elevators. They went into manufacturing their own farm machinery to avoid paying tribute to the dominant International Harvester trust. They sold their own line of sewing machines to protect the farmwife from the inferior workmanship and unscrupulous sales methods infesting the industry after the old-line companies' basic patents expired. But soon, as was inevitable, energies spread so thin began to flag. The Grange lost ground in its stronghold in the upper Mississippi Valley and retreated into its original sphere of social and educational work, in which it is vigorous today in the Northeastern states. In many rural areas the local Granges' exhibits at the country fair are still cause for strong rivalries, and the Grange hall, drawing members from two or three contiguous townships, still sees regular meetings opened by the prescribed lodge officials, women included. In the last generation Grange-sponsored cooperatives and Grange-influenced politics have regained some weight. But the greatest significance was attained 100 years ago, when the Grange conjured up public regulation as a likely weapon against private monopoly. The Granger laws foreshadowed not only such federal and state regulatory agencies as the Interstate Commerce Commission of 1887 but also the Sherman and Clayton Antitrust acts and the Wagner Act of the New Deal.

Since the practicality of nagging government into trying to bell the private-enterprise cat was first demonstrated by organized farmers, the rising American radicalism of the Populists and Bryan's free silver campaign had marked dustings of hayseed that was not always liberal. Populism exploited the countryman's sulky fear of the wickedly scheming big city, den of silk hats, sin and slums, that so readily verged into anti-Semitism and nativism, as Ignatius Donnelly's books showed. Some of its aspirations retained the self-improving innocence of Kelley's original Granges. But in the economic guerrilla war of the 1880's and 1890's its dominant emotions preferred the self-pitying hatred behind Bryan's vision of mankind tortured on the plutocrats' cross of gold.

New bad odors had welled up from the ballast in 1881, when Henry Demarest Lloyd made it so clear that the Standard Oil monopoly, prototype trust, was founded on the willingness of the railroads, particularly those of Vanderbilt's empire, to be blackmailed into secret, discriminatory rate cutting. This put the iron horse into the black books of the many small-town oil dealers whom the Standard had squeezed out and of most persons in the wild economics of the spreading oilfields; and damagingly associated railroads with the suspicion among users of kerosene lamps that the Standard's oil would come cheaper if it had some competition. Creation of the Federal Interstate Commerce Commission was promising. But at first it had no enforcement powers of its own, and the courts to which it took its rulings were the preferred habitat of railroad lawyers skilled in delays and pressures behind the scenes of just the sort further to exasperate. All the while, to judge from contemporary complaints, the railroads' conductors, trainmen and station agents, their representatives in direct contact with the farmers and small-town citizens who used the day coaches, were going out of their way to be haughtily unpleasant. Maybe it was the effect of the long and irregular hours that then went with railroading, long before the overcorrections of featherbedding. In any case, it sharpened the tendency to snarl when railroads were mentioned. Other smelly associations came with the conspicuousness of railroad securities in the predatory capers of Wall Street.

Enthusiastic empire builders like Flagler and James J. Hill of the Great Northern doubtless softened the public attitude toward railroads by their solicitude in helping settlers along their new-built lines secure the best seed-grains, planting stock and agricultural and engineering advice. Such self-interest was as enlightened as it was candid. Railroad money founded Leland Stanford Junior University, opened in 1891 and highly approved by righteous persons, such as Samantha Allen, who called it "that noble school . . . finest . . . in the world for poor boys and poor girls, as well as rich ones . . . a-takin' the youth of this country out into a new realm. . . ." [26] Henry Villard, the German-reared opportunist whom journalism took into gigantic rule-or-ruin games with the Northern Pacific, also put substantial railroad money into higher education as angel of the University of Oregon. The name of Vanderbilt University celebrates the commodore's sizable contributions to its founding. But such sporadic side benefits from swollen power did little more to damp hostility than John D. Rockefeller's princely endowment of the University of Chicago did to make Standard Oil popular. It might well be true that, as Earl Pomeroy says of the Far Western lines: ". . . in the long run the companies' interests were in the country's favor . . . materially the railroads built more than they smothered or destroyed." [27]

But the typical railroad president or principal stockholder of *c*. 1890 was inescapably and conspicuously too big for his breeches.

This was inherent in the railroads' situation. They had pretty much smothered competition from canals. Where they could not kill coastwise shipping by moving many kinds of goods faster at competitive rates, they could and did buy up shipping companies. The internal-combustion engine had not yet begun to undermine them with trucks and buses and private automobiles. The opprobrium that their ill-mannered dominance then drew on them has proved disastrous in our time. Therein lies much of the explanation for the stepchild's status of American railroads relative to that of highway, plane and even inland waterway when government is making regulations and awards. Here the principle of the sins of the fathers damages the whole community. It now keeps America from the potential benefits of optimum use of a great and long-standing national investment. The antirailroad tradition was useful around the turn of the century, however. It gave the average American a habit of mistrusting great corporations that prepared him well for the era of muckraking and trust-busting.

The boom of 1911 that made a lively resort out of sleepy St. Petersburg, Florida, was set off by the building of an electric streetcar line extending the main street westward to the waters of the Gulf and providing access to thousands of new building sites. The first American electric car had gone into service in Richmond, Virginia, in 1887. For the generation thus bracketed this new form of wheels on rails greatly stimulated American life. Horsecar, cable car and elevated railroad had already bulked large, of course—and incidentally created noisome stenches not only of horse dung and coal smoke but moral ones as financiers made huge private fortunes out of corruptly obtained use of public streets. But propulsion by electricity fed through an overhead wire and trolley or a protected third-rail-and-shoe relieved street-railway systems of several major and minor shortcomings all at once. Electricity was markedly cleaner. It dropped no excrement and puffed no cindery smoke into tenement windows. It accelerated faster than the El's steam locomotive, was simpler to maintain, and needed no fireman. Under icy winter conditions it was slightly nearer weatherproof than the cable car, much more so than the horsecar with its miserable beasts slipping and falling and struggling in terror. As electric motors gained power, streetcars could be enlarged to handle three or four times the passenger load practical in a horsecar. And since most of these changes implied not only better service—not too important for management of a monopoly—but also lower operating cost per passenger-mile, the changeover was rapid.

The electric trolley car—the term replacing *streetcar* in most towns —brought to American life the explosive *pop!* of the circuit breaker when the motorman gave her too much juice; the clash and grind of steel on steel as she took curves; and a newly impatient note in the gong borrowed from the horsecar to warn persons and wagons out of her way. The motorman, replacing the handler of the reins, was never such a small boy's hero as the engineer of the steam locomotive. But he contributed to popular speech: "Tastes like the inside of a motorman's glove," and the "motorman's friend," meaning a rubber urinal strapped to the leg under the trousers, was a token of the long hours that he usually worked. The users of horsecars were accustomed to hanging in clumps on the steps of front and rear platforms at rush hours. Electricity permitted still more of that, an overload that could keep even a heavy-duty motor down to a few miles an hour. A youth failing to reach the street-corner stop in time could sprint after the car, overtake it in motion, and climb aboard—always room for one more on that rear platform. With a light load among the vacant lots in the outskirts of town, however, a trolley car could work up a very skittish speed, the wooden body yawing and cantering on its fastenings till it was a wonder it didn't jump the track.

This was especially exhilarating in a "summer car"—airily designed with transverse seats, no side walls and a full-length, fore-and-aft step on which the conductor clambered sidewise to collect the fares. As the step filled up with passengers clutching the handles they were supposed to use, his job called for the combined talents of a squirrel and a sloth, but there was no National Safety Council then. Summer cars saw charter use for such picnics as the one Booth Tarkington immortalized in the closing pages of *Seventeen*. Their objective was usually the amusement park or wooded picnic grounds maintained by the streetcar company, following the tactics of the hotel-building railroad, at or beyond the city limits on the local river. The roller coaster cost a nickel a ride, the picnic grounds with a band concert twice on Saturdays were free to all trolley patrons. Real estate promoters soon set up developments along the overextended track and the city pushed a tentacle of sewers and curbed streets into the shrinking countryside. The entrepreneur might name the new cross streets after his womenfolk, Cora Drive, Mabel Avenue . . .

The trolley had barely begun to replace the horsecar when, in the early 1890's, electricity was competing with steam for fast light freight and short-range passengers. On new trackage, self-propelled interurbans followed overhead-trolley wires fanning out from major centers in the Northeast, the Midwest and the West Coast. They were heavier than streetcars, with elephantine foreheads, locomotive-style cowcatchers and sizable freight compartments for milk cans, crates of eggs, bundles of the city newspapers and spare parts for farm machinery. Since they did without crushingly heavy locomotives, their rights-of-way could be far more cheaply built, hence their passenger fares and freight rates undercut those possible with steam. Part of the financing came of selling shares to farmers and local bankers told that milk would reach the city creamery in better condition if shipped daily from the interurban platform at Stop Seven and that business trips to the city would be easier when one merely stepped aboard a streak of bridled lightning instead of taking the accommodation to Prairieville and waiting for the express. Wherever available, interurbans made striking changes. In the Massachusetts Berkshires, Edith Wharton saw them easing communication "between the scattered villages and the bigger towns in the valleys . . . [which] had libraries, theatres and Y.M.C.A. halls to which the youth of the hills could descend for recreation." [28] In 1906 Waterbury, Vermont, celebrated its new electric railroad link to the outside world with a parade of sleighs and "everybody hooting and hollering . . . and tooting on horns. A person would have thought that America had just been discovered." [29] Arthur M. Schlesinger, Sr., has ranked the interurban with the rural telephone among the technological changes that, by de-isolating the farmer, cooled his Populistic wrath at the big city.

Use of the word *interurban* as a substantive to mean a thing looking like a strayed Pullman sleeper streaking across the landscape all by itself is said to have originated with a politician from Anderson, Indiana. That is fitting because Indiana was a notable center of interurban services centering in Indianapolis, where a million-dollar traction terminal built in 1904 had the same function as today's bus terminals. There more than 7,000,000 passengers a year boarded the slick-speeding Muncie Meteor or Marion Flyer to one or another of Indiana's subsidiary towns or to ride the local that stopped at a wooden trackside shelter every few miles all the way to Brazil or Shelbyville. Around Los Angeles, Huntington's Pacific Electric system served forty-two incorporated cities within 35 miles "and others beyond," says Pomeroy. "Life came to a focus where the tracks intersected in enormous terminals on Main Street." [30] Schedule time from Los Angeles to Redondo was forty-five minutes less than half today's expectation in congested traffic.[31] Nor did interurbans add to the smog that now plagues Paradise.

But shortsightedness, mass-mindedness and pressures from the automobile and construction industries enabled the internal-combustion engine to smother the self-propelled electric wheels on rails in most cities. In Boston, San Francisco, New Orleans, Philadelphia and Pittsburgh some partial relics survive. Elsewhere the trolley car has been so long dead that trolley museums exist to preserve and demonstrate summer cars and interurbans and Toonerville trolleys—a generic name drawn from the one-truck, single-track, one-man-crew Toonerville service that met all the trains in Fontaine Fox's cartoons of the 1920's. For railroads the trolley-fed electric locomotive looked most promising in the early 1900's. As the electric mule it was assigned to tow ships through the locks of the new Panama Canal. The Pennsylvania Railroad found it handy to eliminate the smoke nuisance in the new tunnels giving the line direct access to New York City. With it the Chicago, Milwaukee, St. Paul and Pacific electrified its new transcontinental line to the Pacific Northwest. But in our own time the diesel-electric eliminated both the coal-fired locomotive and the problem of maintaining overhead wires. The one lasting aspect of electric propulsion on rails has been the big city subway which Europeans and Americans considered impractical so long as it required the smoke-belching steam propulsion of London's original underground railroad system. With electric underground trains Boston was first in America in 1897; New York City second seven years later; other American cities waited until World War I. But nobody ever romanticized the subway, even in Boston, where it retains some slight vestiges of civilization, whereas forty years ago there were persons so fond of trolley cars that they collected timetables and worked out ways to travel from Philadelphia to Buffalo, say, using only electric streetcars and interurbans all the way.

Subways sound contemporary and certainly are so. Yet so striking a technological advance as electrical propulsion did not mean annihilation of archaisms in a country so large and culturally complex as America. In the same pre-World War I decade when passengers were whisking from Indianapolis to Evansville, Indiana, in interurbans, a steamboat wheezing up the Green River, which enters the Ohio a few miles above Evansville, was the only way mails could penetrate a sizable area of Kentucky. And steamboats were still the most convenient transportation from river towns on the Indiana shore downstream to Louisville or upstream to Cincinnati. In the hills north of the river oxcarts persisted, while in Louisville, only a few miles away, prosperous matrons were long since used to sleeking about town in their own electric automobiles.

People sometimes objected to the stealthiness of trolley cars and electric automobiles—no hoofbeats or snorting exhaust to warn of their approach. There was some of the same unostentatious quiet about the penetration of our forebears' lives by electricity. Not that this technological revolution exactly went unheeded. Electricity was a magic word with quacks recommending costly electric belts for all ills. The elec-

tric shock machine—grasp the handles and get a shivery jolt for a nickel
—was popular in amusement arcades. But the data surviving from the
1890's show a striking lack of excitement about electrical innovations.
The 1840's had been all openmouthed about the steam railroad and
Morse's telegraph. In 1879 Cleveland and San Francisco installed
Charles F. Brush's carbon arc lights as street lighting. A year later a mile
of them started New York City's Broadway on its career as the eventual
Great White Way. By the early 1880's the system had spread to such

The primitive electric arc light
on watch at the end of a wharf.

minor centers as Norfolk, Virginia, and San Antonio, Texas. But even
in New York City it seems to have caused much less talk than the opening of the Croton waterworks had in 1842 or the completion of the
Brooklyn Bridge in 1883. Children paid more heed to arc lights because
the burned-down sticks of carbon discarded after replacement were
good for marking hopscotch diagrams on pavements.

Edison's rise to national hero of subscientific ingenuity, the archetype of the strive-and-succeed tinkerer, came as much from work on
phonograph and moving picture as from successful search for an efficient
incandescent bulb. Though the arc lights and incandescents at the

Chicago Fair were the first such artificial brilliance that many of its country visitors had ever seen, they were not much mentioned. It took showmanship to focus the national fancy on electric lighting—at the Pan-American Exposition in Buffalo, where the main building was crowned with a floodlit Goddess of Light and every evening rheostats brought the incandescents outlining the buildings up from a mere glow to a blaze of glory like permanent fireworks. The City of Light was the adulatory label applied by, among others, Richard Watson Gilder, civic-minded bard and editor of the august *Century Magazine,* in verses such as:

> We who have seen, when the blue darkness falls,
> Leap into lines of light its domes and walls,
>   Pylons and colonnades and towers
>   All garlanded with starry flowers. . . .[32]

But what seemed to impress the public about it all was less the scenic effect than the source of all the lavishly expended current—not the prosaic boilers of the Chicago Fair but the thundering energy of nearby Niagara recently harnessed to make artificial lightning.

The tricks to be played with rheostats and varicolored incandescents and spots potentially revolutionized stage lighting but had small actual effect on plays or stage sets till after World War I. It became usual to wire new dwellings. In older ones, wiring gradually superseded gas lines, often with the old gas fixtures cautiously left in place. But within a few weeks the members of a household thus aligned with the new century took it for granted that pushing a button was far better than fumbling for matches to light the gas. Nor did many users of the telephone really understand that the croaky little voice in the receiver depended on the same thing that propelled the interurban and made sparks jump from your finger ends in carpeted, hot rooms on cold, dry days.

The telephone, too, had been rather slack about taking on. The first exchange to service a number of subscribers appeared in New Haven, Connecticut, only five years after the device had caused much comment at the Philadelphia Centennial of 1876. By the late 1880's it was well enough utilized in the business practice of, among other cities, San Francisco, to be used in novels set there. But the annual accretion of new subscribers dawdled along at some 13,000 for the whole country to the end of the century. Only after 1900 did reform of the charge basis bring hundreds of thousands of private households, as well as business offices, on the line. The social and cultural impact was heavy. Firemen and policemen and the doctor were newly immediate. The phone gave Tin Pan Alley topical song material and added Central, the hello girl, to the gallery of America's sweethearts; enabled playwrights to convey in-

formation to the audience with only one actor on stage, killing the clumsy old soliloquy; usually, not always, simplified love affairs; suggested practical jokes to idle children; lightened the isolation of heedlessly garrulous farmwives on party lines—indeed so sober an observer as Burton J. Hendrick suggested that the telephone was greatly reducing the previously high incidence of insanity among farmers' womenfolk, as well as giving them their first effective protection against vicious tramps. It also ruined privacy. One of the first to protest was Robert Louis Stevenson, who, finding an American-installed telephone system in Honolulu in 1889, wrote to a local newspaper his doubts about the advisability of thus admitting "this interesting instrument . . . into our bed and board, into our business and bosoms . . . bleating like a deserted infant." [33] To the amazement of Europeans, however, just before World War I the number of telephones in use in America was pushing toward 10,000,000—almost 1 per 10 persons.

Except for the telephone's insistent ring, the very simplicity and silence of electricity made it inconspicuous. Mrs. J. Lucius Quality in her electric brougham with the French gray upholstery and the single rosebud in the slim crystal vase needed to know only that the thing went when you squeezed the button with your elegantly gloved thumb, turned right when you pulled on the tiller, and stopped when you put your foot on that thing down there. It could not go fast enough to get her into serious trouble and would never bolt in terror of a windblown newspaper, which made her relatively independent of menfolk, whether husband or servant, and it cost so much that relatively few could have it, which was pleasant. Though Henry Adams might brood about the dynamo in a cultivated fashion, by 1910 his native land was well into the electrical age; the sole emphatic token of it was the multiplicity of overhead wires downtown in cities—trolley wires, telephone wires, power wires, telegraph wires carried on or slung from multiple crossarms that made the supporting wooden poles, a linear forest of them, look like the Cross of Lorraine seen in the fourth dimension.

Until the eve of World War I the electric road vehicle was considered to have a thriving future. Mrs. Quality's electric brougham had been joined by electric taxicabs and electric delivery wagons. The speed and cruising radius of all were limited by the inefficient storage batteries of the day, on which Edison had done important work but not got far. In a society used to horse-drawn speeds, however, 10 miles an hour sufficed, particularly in town. The sanguine assumed that batteries, like all else that one put one's mind to, would improve until the electric runabout would do everything that the Tom Swift books for boys promised. People envisaged electric automobiles cruising all over and refueling—turning low batteries in for freshly charged ones—at highway-side depots like our filling stations. The electric had many advantages over the internal-combustion vehicle appearing from Europe at about the same time. It was far quieter, needed no cranking, was more reliable in cold weather, simpler to maintain and less likely to get out of order in use. Compared to its other rival, the steam automobile that to many at the time seemed superior to the internal-combustion kind, the electric was simpler to operate and needed no long delay for getting up steam.

But batteries did not improve enough. Even suppose they had done so, the electric was so undemanding as to be a bore, as dull as a large and well-oiled roller skate, whereas the internal-combustion engine over-heated, bucked and banged, spewed smoke and bad smells—and then, when understandingly coddled by the right man, would, like a temper-amental mistress, delight him with a sudden access of angelic behavior. Without reference to such values it is hard to understand why the Dur-yeas, Elwood Haynes, Henry Ford, *et al.* were so obsessed in the 1890's with horseless carriages making such hideous noises. Note that these Americans struggling toward the successful gasoline buggy were all, like Edison, the Wright brothers and the arc light's Charles F. Brush, Mid-westerners. In fact, all were born and reared in the 200- by 400-mile area north of the National Road between Canton, Illinois, and Cleveland, Ohio. The central strip of the nation was ably keeping up the traditions of Oliver Evans and the several developers of the steamboat. The other point to their Midwestern origin is that in the East the typical automobile buff was a millionaire who had imported from the Old World both the vehicle and the chauffeur to operate and repair it, whereas these were woodshed experimenters of sharply limited resources.

In that day, however, the Midwesterner tinkerers, not the million-aires, were the anomalies. For the automobile, now chief mass tyrant over our ways-of-doing, began as and long remained a gilded exotic. In 1904 a hospitable plutocrat showing Westchester County to H. G. Wells did so in a motorcar as he would today—only at that time, fifteen years after the motorcar had become recognizable, England had more of them on the road than all America could show. Their European flavor combined with their high cost to make most people consider them play-things for the rich. Popular fiction was full of willowy Newport heiresses wooed and won by level-browed, spade-chinned young scions of wealth mistaken for chauffeurs because first glimpsed lying under a car and covered with grease. The comic papers were always picturing encoun-ters between farmers and beefy plutocrats whose cars, topped off with expensive-looking women in veils and dusters, had got stuck in the mud. Resentment of the automobile as ostentatious symbol of wealth had as much as dislike of noise and bolting horses to do with the many ordinances hampering or forbidding the use of such vehicles in town—and with the popular taunt of "Git a hoss, mister, git a hoss!" whenever a car was disabled.

At the same time, however, between the undaunted tinkerers and the affluent buffs, it was growing clear that the automobile—anyway the presumably improved versions soon to come—might be a practical contribution to daily life. In 1904 the two-year-old American Automobile Association began to demonstrate that the gasoline buggy was anything but town-bound by holding annual reliability runs named the Glidden Tours after Charles J. Glidden, self-made telephone magnate and addict of balloons as well as motorcars, who gave the winner's trophy. Each year a greater proportion of entries managed to finish the prescribed city to city course over the atrocious roads of the day. Average miles per hour also crept up. At the same time the stamina to be expected of specially built automobiles, presumably anticipating the average-to-be, was being excitingly—and expensively—tested in the Vanderbilt Cup road races on Long Island and, after 1911, the man- and machine-killing 500-mile races on the closed track at Indianapolis, then rather more of an automobile town than Detroit. By 1910 Hiram Johnson, campaigning for the governorship of California after gaining fame for jailing grafters in San Francisco, stumped the state in an automobile. It began to occur to others than inconvenienced millionaires that, given navigable roads, the gasoline buggy could carry enough fuel and develop enough reliability to be useful as well as striking evidence of high solvency.

In that same year of 1910 America produced 187,000 automobiles—forty-seven times the 1900 figure. And the flood was just beginning, for only the year before Henry Ford had launched the Model T, the necessary complement to the inchoate good roads movement.

Some of Ford's rivals in the gas-buggy business—most notably the Duryeas and Scottish-born Alexander Winton—were making or repairing bicycles when they became addicted to the odor of burning hydrocarbons. This is notable because it had familiarized them with mass assembly of machines from interchangeable parts—the technique that Eli Whitney applied to firearms, that American makers of locomotives and farm machinery had carried to momentous lengths, and that, as Ford used it in converging assembly lines, turned the Tin Lizzie loose on America for good or ill. During the bicycle craze of the 1890's, as Mark

Sullivan has pointed out, much that was said about the effect of the new machine on the population, particularly young persons, anticipated what the 1920's said about the social consequences of the automobile. The bicycle further anticipated it in creating a demand for at least better if not good roads. For a third strong association, the British invention of the pneumatic rubber tire was originally meant to reduce road shocks not for the automobilist, who did not yet exist, but for the behindside and forearms of the bicyclist of 1888. Yet the eventual popularity of the automobile depended abjectly on this improvement over the solid rubber tire, even though it was disastrously prone to blowouts, punctures and slow leaks. For at automotive speed over any but the smoothest track, the relative nonresiliency of solid rubber meant merciless jostling and jarring.

The bicycle had first enjoyed extended American notice at the Philadelphia Centennial. But it was then solid-tired and grotesquely composed of one five-foot wheel and one tiny one, which made it difficult to mount and hazardous to manage when under way. Late in the 1880's a Briton adapted it to mass use—accomplishing what the self-starter did for the automobile—by making both wheels of reasonable size. The new triangular frame could be modified for the timid sex by strengthening the bottom angle and omitting the top bar so they would not have to ride astride. These "safety" models were quickly brought to America, exuding the prestige of the latest English sport for ladies and gentlemen. To keep floppy skirts out of the chain-and-sprocket drive remained difficult, however. A daring few women adopted the loose, just-below-the-knee breeches—the English called them knickerbockers because they were like those worn in Cruikshank's engravings for Washington Irving's *Knickerbocker's History*—that British gentlemen had been donning for country sport and that now proved admirable for bicycling. The eventual solution for women not daring enough to confess bifurcation was a metal-and-wire housing to keep skirts away from mechanism and rear wheel. Gentlemen unable to bring themselves to knickerbockers secured their trousers at the ankle with spring clips.

One of the sights of Garden City, Long Island, in the early 1890's was the elegant Mrs. Burke-Roche in her gray-and-white cycling costume on her silver-plated bicycle. The flashier one that Lillian Russell rode in Central Park had gold trim. During a temporary remission of the second Mrs. Flagler's psychosis in 1896 her husband hired an instructor to teach him and her to bicycle for hygienic purposes; she tiny and redheaded, he already in his stately, gray-mustached sixties, solemnly rode six or seven miles a day around their estate at Mamaroneck, New York. But rapid Americanization of "the wheel" (as its users called this miracle of equilibrium) soon diluted its prestige while immensely widening its use. Mass production manufacturers of sewing machines and firearms—Singer, Iver-Johnson, *et al.*—took it up as a promising sideline, and the price came down until even Wilbur and Orville Wright, very small bicycle

Charles Dana Gibson draws the results of a doctor's advising bicycling for elderly men.

makers in Dayton, Ohio, could sell their cheaper model for $18, about what the average suit of ready-made clothes cost. As skiing has done in our time, bicycling widened from a specialty of the fashionable-leisured into a popular craze. In 1896 the Hearst newspapers staged a bicycle relay, a sort of pony express on wheels, carrying a pouch of mail from San Francisco to New York City in the respectable time of eleven days —about the same average miles per hour as the Union Pacific's early transcontinental trains. Its finish was celebrated with a Bicycle Carnival along Central Park West of riders in fancy dress carrying Japanese lanterns, shooting off fireworks, supporting enormous floats, the whole climaxed by the music of Professor Bilbo's Olympic Mounted Bicycle Band braying, tooting and banging as they rode. Tandems for holidaying couples became popular, and we still sing about them as Daisy's bicycle built for two. "Scorching" in excess of hastily imposed speed limits added to the risks among the throngs of cyclists on paths reserved for the sport in municipal parks.

It looked for a while as if the bicycle might become a good-weather substitute for the streetcar in getting to the job in America, as it did in Europe. The sharp rise of the automobile in America checked that, not only by making the man on the bicycle look humble but also by making the streets dangerous at rush hours. Soon after World War I the American bicycle reverted to the status of plaything and occasional economic tool for juveniles. The telegraph messenger boy and the corner druggist's delivery boy continued to use it. The boy with a suburban afternoon-paper route learned to twist the *Daily Bugle* into a compact projectile that, riding one-handed, he could hurl onto successive front porches without even ceasing to pedal. Meanwhile, however, the bicycle had done the nation the service of persuading so many adults of both sexes to enjoy using their muscles.

It had been preceded by other slower-fused examples of an outdoor sport newly popular in Britain being imported by affluent Americans for snobbish reasons but eventually taking on among the less gilded strata. A Dutch form of golf had been played in New Netherland, apparently in the streets, to judge from complaints about consequent broken windows. Scattered references to golf clubs and balls in advertisements or inventories hint at awareness of the game in the Colonies in the 1700's. Scottish immigrants established the modern version of the game at least temporarily near West Virginia's famous White Sulphur Springs in 1884. A couple of years later it was played in embryonic Sarasota, Florida, and in Foxburg, Pennsylvania, in 1887. But the conspicuous and infectious transplantation came when, reflecting the spread of Scotland's game among the English Quality in mid-Victorian times, the St. Andrew's Golf Club was opened in 1888 in Yonkers, New York, to give the expensive squires of Westchester County a context in which to wear knickerbockers and feel tweedy. The prevailing tone is evident in the locations of the five golf clubs forming the United States Golf Association in 1894: Yonkers as above, Shinnecock Hills on Long Island, Newport, Brookline, Massachusetts, and Chicago. Press and public naturally jeered at cow-pasture pool. William H. Taft's liking for the game presently earned him the honor of being the first U.S. President criticized for spending much time on the links, whereas Theodore Roosevelt's tennis was considered admirable. By 1900, however, the nation had 400-odd golf clubs, and by the time Sarajevo was in the headlines *fore* and *stymie* were so much in the national language that Mr. Dooley took cognizance:

"With th' exciption maybe iv th' theery iv infant damnation, Scotland has given nawthin' more cheerful to th' worruld thin th' game iv golf. . . . How's it played, says ye? I don't exactly know. I niver

studied law. But ye can get th' rules . . . in siven volumes edited be
th' Lord Chief Justice o' Scotland. . . . Th' next pleasantest feelin' . . .
to bein' perfectly happy is bein' perfectly cross. That's why it's took up
be middle-aged gintlemen. They want a chanst to go into a towerin' rage
in th' open and undher th' blue sky." [34] Already, however, the image of
the golfer as prosperous and in his forties, created by doctors' habit
of recommending the game to plethoric patients, was eroding. Teen-age
caddies, observing their elders and assuming correctly that youth
could do better at what looked like fun, took up the sport, gradually
producing a class of American-developed pros and a presumption
that young fellows, too, could enjoy golf. Also gradually the country-
club member's younger womenfolk discovered that, though their collar-
bones were unsuited for ball throwing, they could swing a brassie as
smoothly as their brothers at Yale.

Young women of the gilded strata were already much at home in
lawn tennis. Indeed it was Mary Ewing Outerbridge of a highly placed
family who first brought the newly invented British game from Bermuda
in 1874, setting it up on the grounds of the Staten Island Cricket Club,
now site of the Staten Island ferry terminal. The inventor's original
purpose had been to create a sport for summer afternoons not too
active for ladies in toe-length skirts. Perfect for the wholesome fiancée of
Edith Wharton's *The Age of Innocence,* conducive to mixed doubles,
soon leading to tournaments for ladies, as well as for gentlemen, the
game duly spread among the best people of Philadelphia, Boston and
Newport. Grass tennis courts were the core of the new Newport Casino *c.*
1880. By then the court had lost its original hourglass shape and the net
was lowered and tautened to develop something like the game we now
know. For a generation, however, tennis remained rather a patty-cake
affair compared to what it became after redheaded Maurice McLoughlin
transformed service into an aggressive weapon. This already growing
vigor of play was inevitably leading to the same social erosion that had
occurred in golf. Clay courts, economical to maintain, were appearing
for plebeian use in public parks. But strenuous though it became, tennis never got rid of women. Their physical emancipation was proceeding
more than adequately in step.

This can be taken as part of a growing sports-mindedness that
built for Buffalo's Pan-American Exposition a stadium seating 12,000
with a daily athletic program including baseball, track-and-field events
and such rising new team sports as basketball, lacrosse (both American
inventions) and the American colleges' version of rugby football. The
trend was international, too, of course, leading to polyglot Olympic Games
in the 1890's and ever since. By the time Theodore Roosevelt was in the

White House the American public was ready to applaud him for sending paunchy generals on grueling horseback rides and personally taking a strenuous ax to the woods on his estate on Long Island. The general effect on the national lymphatic system was as beneficial as bicycling had certainly been for the aging Mr. Flagler. Even the golfer, however agonized his soul, was walking some three miles in short stretches amidst quantities of the fresh air that doctors had taken to recommending. Note in passing the architectural side effect of the fresh-air cult, as the houses of the prosperous and the apartment buildings multiplying for them in larger cities west of Pittsburgh sprouted screened sleeping porches —sensible for summer but also doughtily used in winter by many families able to persuade themselves that natural refrigeration was just what they and their children needed.

The new cult of sports not only embedded the dubious ethics of baseball in the American habit of mind, but also severely damaged secondary- and college-level education by fixing the attention of students, alumni and general public on football. In the 1880's the ill-starred example of elder Northeastern colleges—Princeton, Columbia, Rutgers, Yale, Harvard—in fielding teams in intercollegiate contests had proved irresistible to most younger institutions. When Rockefeller money revivified the University of Chicago in the early 1890's, it was taken for granted that for all the Baptist-flavored decorum of the new campus, it would have eleven shockheaded young giants in moleskin uniforms in butting matches with other Midwestern college teams and trained by a member of a new academic profession—that of football coach. Chicago's Amos Alonzo Stagg, a product of Yale, eventually became the grand old man of the sport. The same assumptions were made at the new Leland Stanford Junior University and the University of California across the bay. The game was even more bone-crushing than the modern, more open version. In spite of periodic outcry against many permanent injuries and some deaths, it swelled into the American's analogue to the Iberian's bullfight—soon so swathed in ritual acceptance that its basic visceral brutality was little considered. The prize ring had no such social luck, probably because it came out of the lower strata, not, like football, from the highest. This American rugby had moral advantages over bullfighting. Neither side had a superiority of weapons or numbers; both were there voluntarily. But the players' equivocal status as both gladiators and students came to threaten the typical American campus, not too learning-minded to begin with, with domination by football abetted by the rah-rah alumni who also doted on the fraternity system. Suppose that the bull were studying at and

representing the prestige of Salamanca, the matador and his team that of
Valladolid. . . .

Football had thus joined baseball in diverting the new taste for sports
into the absurdity of passive mass sitting to watch others play team
games. As World War I neared, ice hockey in the Northeast and basketball in the Midwest drew rising attention of the same sort for winter
competition; among high schools particularly, rivalry was growing so keen
that every other barn in Indiana displayed a basketball hoop for home
practice. Single-player sport, however, had a constructive effect, at least
physically—markedly among men whose father had lived slackly sedentary lives, more so among women whose mothers had talked about
carriage exercise. Horseback riding, ladylike enough since it was done
sidesaddle, was too costly for any but fairly wealthy men's daughters.
But when the most eligible young women of Newport took up bicycling, tennis and golf, which cost less, ladylike languor began to dwindle
among small-town bankers' womenfolk. Dressmakers soon felt the effects.
One could play croquet in grass-sweeping skirts, could even manage the
gentle early tennis by holding them up with one hand while skittering
after the ball to pop it back over the net. But the greasy bicycle
sprocket and the rough along the fairways forced a lifting of hemlines
leading to longer strides and frequent glimpses of the region of the
anklebone. In the lower strata the roller skate, a flourishing novelty from
the 1880's on among adults patronizing rinks at amusement parks and
elsewhere, had the same influence. (Eventually the spread of concrete
sidewalks made the steel-rollered skate the particular joy of city children.)
All this encouraged experiments with the rainy-daisy skirt c. 1900—short
enough not to trail on wet sidewalks in rainy weather.

Horsiness, whether mere hacking in the park, polo or fox hunting,
was guarded by the dollar sign from the mass popularity that successively overcame baseball, bicycling, golf and tennis. Hence it was fitting
that the new institution of the country club, where the Quality could in-
dulge in outdoor sports without the lower orders breathing down their
necks, was associated with the importation of polo from England and
the Anglophile revival of fox hunting in the Northeast in the 1880's. The
Country Club of Brookline, Massachusetts, one of the first, originally
had no facilities for games except a curling rink and was largely devoted to keeping horses and hounds for Boston Brahmin members,
no women allowed. Equally horsey was the polo- and coaching-mad
Meadow Brook Hunt Club set up on Long Island in the early 1890's by
August Belmont, Jr., Colonel William Jay and certain other of their peers
on a site that had been part of the Hempstead Plains—where the first for-

mal American horse races were run in the 1660's. New York City's gilded youth had taken up coaching ahead of Boston's. But soon enough members of the Myopia Hunt Club—so named, they say, because the four Brahmin brothers who founded it were all nearsighted and bespectacled—added coaching to the fox hunting, and their four-in-hands

Peck's Bad Boy's Pa comes to grief trying to take part in the roller-skating craze of the 1880's.

came tooling along Beacon Street on the way to the Country Club with top-hatted gentlemen coachmen just as proudly fanatical as any New Yorkers about the proper way to hold the reins. As golf and tennis came to intrude on the original horsiness, so did women—and the country club spread rapidly southward and westward until, in the 1890's, the phrase had come to mean, as in the Cincinnati exemplar, "a very comfortable place . . . with a convenient clubhouse and large grounds

. . . [providing] any sport . . . a pleasant drive for the members and their friends. . . ." [35] Presently came the weekly dance, then the custom of holding at the club such social events as anniversaries and debuts. By the time most of the members owned their own motorcars to make that pleasant drive in, F. Scott Fitzgerald would have felt right at home. Indeed the white-flanneled sniffiness permeating his first stories has embalmed for posterity the essence of the Midwestern version of the country club *c.* 1913.

The site of the Meadow Brook Hunt Club was leased from the executors of the estate of A. T. Stewart, the department-store king of New York City in the mid-1800's, who had unsuccessfully tried to dedicate the tract to the good of the common man. By 1869 Stewart was reputedly the richest man in America. His holdings in textile mills and real estate, particularly hotels and theaters, cross-braced the earnings of his great white iron-and-marble palace of retailing at Broadway and Ninth Street, next to fashionable Grace Church, and of his great wholesale dry goods operation farther downtown. He was also reputedly a cheeseparing employer, paying his sales clerks just as little as the traffic would possibly bear, and a social climber, disappointed because his residential palace of white marble on Fifth Avenue had not brought him recognition by the best society. In any case Stewart could certainly well afford to pay out $400,000 for 7,000 acres of the Hempstead Plains on which to create a Garden City for commuters of moderate income. He had already made altruistic gestures with a checkbook. Scotch-Irish born himself, he had chartered a ship outbound with provisions for famine-stricken Ireland in 1847, homeward bound with immigrants for many of whom he found jobs as they landed. He had competed with Commodore Vanderbilt in giving six-figured sums to the U.S. Sanitary Commission during the Civil War—which was fair enough, for the $2,000,000 a year he was clearing on his contracts for war supplies was probably even more than Vanderbilt was making out of the shipping aspect of the war. Doubtless he had no intention of altruistically losing money on Garden City. But like Flagler, he did put into it large sums that would have brought far larger returns in other investments.

The notion of the garden city came from a paternalistic English textile magnate, Sir Titus Salt, who created for his mill hands a model residential environment called Saltair based on space, quiet and greenery in sharp contrast with the bleak squalor of the typical British mill town. Stewart's community was to supply white-collar families with those same amenities, plus low rentals and the requisite trimmings of a gas plant, waterworks, hotel, shops, churches and a specially built spur railroad connecting with the Long Island Railroad for husbands to get to the job on. But the building went slowly, and the response from potential tenants with the stipulated modest income was slower still. In terms of the time Garden City was far from town, and maybe many were put off by the notion of having skinflint Stewart as landlord. When he died in 1876, the scheme was already spoken of as Stewart's Folly, and his wife could find nothing better to do about it than to build a memorial to him there in the shape of a new cathedral and administrative center for the Episcopal diocese of Long Island. Not until the 1890's did final settlement of the estate enable a new Garden City Company to salvage the place by raising its tone. McKim, Mead & White, the fashionable architects of the day—Stanford White was on the board of the new company—remodeled the hotel to attract gilded patrons. The regrettable odors of modest self-respect were further exorcised by supplementing Meadow Brook's polo and coaching with golf and a gun club where the original version of trapshooting—live pigeons released one by one—amused sporting types. Not until our own time did the growing congestion of Long Island drive these facilities for conspicuous consumption farther afield.

In 1906 Russell Sage, a chilled-steel Wall Streeter with $70,000,000 acquired chiefly from moneylending and the manipulation of railroads, died and left it all to his widow. Conscientiously she funneled important sums into higher education; set up the great Russell Sage Foundation, which has financed much sociological research; and, with the same purpose as Stewart's, turned a 175-acre farm in the then-rural back parts of Queens Borough into Forest Hills—a complex of curving, quiet streets, small, open parks and sturdily built dwellings intended for worthy folk of modest means. Frustration occurred here, too. Standards of design and construction were too high. The smallest houses were beyond the reach of the intended class. The suburbanites who bought them were several cuts above the sort Mrs. Sage had had in mind, and soon Forest Hills was best known for the stadium in which the most important American tennis tournaments were played.

It should already have been clear that schemes for single-stratum communities were likelier to succeed when the prospective population was very prosperous to wealthy. The pattern had been sketched before the Civil War—picturesquely, too—by Alexander Jackson Davis in planning the landscaping and layout of Llewellyn Park, New Jersey, the first scheme of deliberate colonization of the rich. Its site in the hills northwest of Newark, New Jersey, suited Davis' taste for "rushing brooks, woodland dells, and sweeping meadows . . . with rustic bridges, arbors, gatehouses and lookouts . . . ample privacy and restrictions

. . . the first attempt," says Robert Hale Newton, authority on Davis, "at creating an exclusive residential area combining rural solitude with suburban comfort and all the advantages of an estate upon a smallish lot." [36] The colonists, including Lowell Mason and Thomas A. Edison, lived there the year round in houses stiff with mid-century eclecticism —Oriental, Baronial Gothic, Swiss, French Mansard. Commuting to New York City, 15 miles away, was made convenient at Llewellyn Park's own station on the Erie Railroad.

In the same period the creation of New York City's Central Park, influential masterpiece of F. L. Olmsted, was drawing national attention to the virtues of informally tailored vegetation and artificially enhanced vistas. Hence a powerful nationwide movement toward large municipal parks where all classes could enjoy what had previously been reserved largely for noblemen and millionaires. But there was a contrary trend —toward combining all this green luxury with private enjoyment. "It has always seemed to me," confessed Charles Nordhoff, "that it would be the summit of human felicity, to have a handsome house in the Central Park," and went on to praise the moneymen who had recently bought a tract on the Des Plaines River near Chicago, named it Riverside, installed "Central Park roads and drives . . . gas and water . . . a hotel . . . all the comforts and advantages of the city and the country. . . ." [37] Meanwhile, New Rochelle, New York, had acquired its Huguenot Park "to be held in common by the owners of the adjacent property . . . laid out in English landscape style. . . ." [38] A notably elaborate version of the notion was the private clublike Tuxedo Park created in the 1880's by wealthy Pierre Lorillard in the Ramapo Mountains of New York only 40 miles from New York City—and contrasting strongly with the Jackson Whites' squalid fastnesses practically next door.

From these toploftical schemes—adapted to lower strata as the bicycle and the Florida vacation had been—evolved the exclusive addition, the high-class development still familiar in American real estate promotion. The great residential park to be bought into and collectively maintained by men of similar views and large substance lost momentum after the graduated income tax came into effect in 1913. But the speculator with an eye on the merely well-to-do was soon borrowing atmosphere and stage properties from that glittering tradition. With things like Llewellyn Park in mind he embellished the entrances to his tract with gateways of cobblestone or iron-garlanded brick and planned the streets in confusing but artistic curves. He named them Woodland Drive and Sylvan Lane. The need to keep up with the Joneses could be trusted to maintain lawns, trees and dwellings properly, particularly since he had laid down protective conditions against untidy elements. Purchasers could be forbidden to reduce the size of lots, build houses of unacceptable style or unimposing size, resell to those disapproved by the neighbors, which, in practice, usually banned Irish and Jews, as well as Negroes. Some such tracts were set up as small municipalities managed

Outside Holyoke, Massachusetts, cobblestone pretentiousness still advertises a "park"-style subdivision.

among gentlemen owners and paying the nearby city for police and fire services.

Thus Booth Tarkington's Major Amberson bought "two hundred acres . . . at the end of National Avenue . . . built broad streets and cross-streets; paved them with cedar-block . . . set up fountains where the streets intersected, and at symmetrical intervals placed cast-iron statues, painted white, with their titles clear upon their pedestals: Minerva, Mercury, Hercules, Venus, Gladiator, Emperor Augustus, Fisher Boy . . . Wounded Doe, and Wounded Lion. . . . All this Art showed a profit from the start . . . there was something like a rush to build in the new Addition . . . at the juncture of the new Boulevard and the Avenue, Major Amberson reserved four acres for himself, and built his new house—the Amberson Mansion, of course." [39] On a livelier basis Ellis Parker Butler's Perkins of Portland, an irrepressible promoter of the generation after the major's, turned his dairy farm into Cloverdale, "Paradise Within Twenty Minutes of the Chicago Post-Office," and borrowed California-style methods to exploit it:

People would open their morning mail and a circular would tell them that Cloverdale had an ennobling religious atmosphere. Their morning paper thrust a view of the Cloverdale Club-House on them. As they rode down-town in the street-cars, they read that Cloverdale was refined and exclusive. The bill-boards announced that Cloverdale lots were sold on the easy payment plan. . . . Round-trip tickets from Chicago to Cloverdale were furnished any one who wanted a look. . . . Occasionally, we had a free open-air vaudeville entertainment . . . a few visitors kicked because we did not serve beer with the free lunches . . . but Perkins was unyielding. . . . Cloverdale was to be a temperance town.[40]

Major Amberson was out of line in giving his scheme so unpretentious a name as the Amberson Addition. It should have been at least Amberson Park, though there was little park about it. Appropriateness soon ceased to matter much to the speculative developer or, to judge by his successes, to his potential buyers. Llewellyn Park was named for its founder, one Llewellyn P. Haskell; Huguenot Park for the French Calvinist founders of New Rochelle; and Riverside, Illinois, is at least on a sort of river. But Ravenswood, an early park-style development on Long Island, is a long way from the range of either species of American raven. And by the time I was personally observing things before World War I in the Midwest it seemed to puzzle nobody but me that the addition out north of town, still mostly vacant lots, was called Meridian Heights though it was as flat as the Dead Sea in a calm. (Tramps used its grandiloquently arched stone gatehouse as a latrine.) As cities spread and these techniques were applied to wider segments of the house-building population, nothing was too incongruous, provided it sounded high-toned—which often meant Walter Scott-British. Prairie subdivisions not yet scarred by drainage ditches were launched as Glendale Manor. Those completely lacking woody vegetation as well as profile were advertised as Woodridge Hills. Even after such tracts were built up and absorbed into the neighboring municipalities, the name often remained, its pointlessness a memorial to the long-forgotten promoter and doubtless a grievous intellectual hazard for the archeologist of the future. Today's maps of Cook County and western Long Island are full of downgoing areas called something like Ivanhoe Park.

Many visitors to the Chicago Fair still unsated with sight-seeing let curiosity attract them a few miles south of the city to see Pullman, Illinois, the nation's best-known example of a model town for industrial employees. It was named for its creator, primly chin-bearded George M. Pullman, inventor and operator of the dominant line of American sleeping cars and builder of railroad cars generally, including much of the rest of the highly varnished rolling stock—dining, parlor, observation cars—in which the well-to-do traveled. Chicago being America's key railroad hub and focus of the mid-continent, it made sense for the Pullman Company's large new manufacture-and-repair shop to be near it—specifically on 4,000 acres near the main line of the Illinois Central and the edge of shallow Lake Calumet. There, beginning in 1879, had been built a large plant soon to employ 2,700 men and a company town to house them and theirs and show how beneficial that widely decried kind of community could be. Fifteen years later, only months after the last visitor to the fair had departed, Pullman was destructively conspicuous as a planned community gone sour.

Its planners had been the architect and landscapist who designed Pullman's elegant summer mansion and grounds at fashionable Elberon, New Jersey. The building material was mostly handsome cream-colored brick burned on the spot from clay dredged out of the lake. They laid out a modified-gridiron town with a central square, an arcaded block of shops, a 1,000-seat theater with a blindingly lavish, allegedly Moorish interior, a Queen Anne-style hotel of seventy rooms named for Pullman's daughter Florence, a savings bank, a tax-financed school of eight grades presently prefaced by a free kindergarten and followed up by night high school courses, a church to serve all denominations. In two parks, one on an artificial island in the lake, a company-sponsored athletic association encouraged boating, ice skating, bicycling, baseball and cricket in deference to the several hundred English immigrants on the payroll. The bulk of the place was dwellings, of course—on Florence Boulevard or Arcade Park, nine-room, city-style houses for top-echelon employees; in the side streets for lower ranks row houses of smaller size, each with a small front yard, and a few apartment houses with two- to four-room units. The prevailing architectural style, described as "advanced secular Gothic," [41] facilitated keeping even the small houses from looking too depressingly alike.

Things were well thought out at Pullman. The company, landlord of the whole thing, also operated the gas plant, the ice plant, the 100-cow dairy supplying nice clean milk and the large vegetable farm fertilized by the local sewage, duly processed. The sewer system, like the houses, was built to high standards—doubtless one reason why Pullman's annual death rates ran 7 to 15 per 1,000 of population while those of American cities then averaged 22.5. (Another may have been relative scarcity of the retired elderly among this newly formed population of men of active working age.) Forbidding private stabling and concentrating all local horses in a community stable minimized the horse-dung problem.

Keeping such other smelly animals as pigs and chickens was also forbidden. The only bar allowed was that of the hotel, and its high prices kept the workman drinker away. Experts on community planning, sanitation and so on had been consulted, and Pullman was widely acknowledged to be a commendable showplace. It was certainly unlike the usual company town with its bleak board cottages and barracks and primitive sanitation, the company store bleeding the employees because it alone accepted the company scrip in which they were paid. Pullman had no company store. Instead, the company took its share off the top of the employees' local purchases by leasing store space to storekeepers at rates so high they could barely stay in business.

By 1893 the value of the whole settlement was some $8,000,000—an eighth of the company's net worth, rolling stock included—and George Pullman was nothing if not businesslike about so large an investment. Nor, being proud of his brainchild, which he liked to display to his fellow captains of industry, was he about to let the factory rank and file mess up those fine new houses and streets or get the notion they should have a hand in running things. His objective was paternalism with a profit. Between those two notions life in Pullman resembled life in a coeducational boarding school that permits marriage. A resident employee could not drive a nail in the wall or plant a bed of sweet peas in the front yard without written permission, for it was the company that took the responsibility for all repairs and sprinkled and mowed all the lawns and cultivated all the plantings that visitors so admired. His lease required him not to enter his house with muddy feet or play musical instruments after bedtime, to avoid loitering on the apartment-house stairs. . . . Nor would the company ever sell him a house to do what he liked with. For that he had to buy outside the wide Pullman holdings, and it was known that on the whole, particularly after hard times began in 1893, the company gave preferential status to workmen who were also tenants. His lease was cancelable on ten days' notice from either side, however, and until a state law forbade the practice in 1891, the rent came out of his pay before he ever saw it.

It was a large bite, too, for rents in Pullman ran 20 to 25 percent above those for similar accommodations in nearby Chicago. The reason was that these high-standard houses were unusually expensive to build and were meticulously maintained—and George Pullman felt that the company should get 6 percent on its outlay. The dairy and farm paid good profits. The company's charge for use of the church was so high that only one congregation could afford to use it. So the company thought it consistent to add up not only interest on investment and annual cost of maintenance but also the expenses of all that hand-tailored shrubbery, athletic programs, crack fire department and the famous Pullman Band and charge the total pro rata in the tenant employee's rent. Actually net return never rose above 4 percent. But even so the employee had reason to wonder whether the privilege of living in an advanced-secular Gothic cottage was worth the surcharge—and the frank pressure to keep the nose clean and vote Republican that went with it. Not all outside observers were as pleased with the social overtones of Pullman as they were with its clean streets and esthetic integrity. Richard T. Ely, a rising young economist at Johns Hopkins who later took up Christian Socialism, reported to *Harper's Magazine* that "Pullman is un-American . . . benevolent, well-wishing feudalism," [42] with a smell of Bismarck's Germany about it.

The summer of the Chicago Fair had been preceded by the Wall Street slump and the spreading bank failures of the panic of 1893. As winter came on, the company felt the repercussions in a sharp falling off of orders for new cars, though receipts from operation of Pullman rolling stock held up pretty well. George Pullman's response was to cut new-car prices far below cost to attract orders to keep the plant going, lay off some help, and cut the wages of the rest to match the prospective manufacturing loss. It might have sounded slightly less unfair to his rank and file had he also cut his own and his chief lieutenants' salaries and passed or reduced dividends to the stockholders. But full dividends were kept up out of the company's ample surplus and full salaries paid to the top echelon. With further exquisite tactlessness the landlord branch of the company went on charging full rents regardless of layoffs and wage cuts. It was explained that real estate management was a function completely separate from manufacturing. But such organizational metaphysics did not prevent something grimmer than exasperation in the carshop sweeper-outer as his family had to choose between paying the rent and eating. And, as it happened, Pullman's whipsawed employees could turn for help to a source come into being only the previous June —Eugene Debs' American Railway Union.

Partial efforts to organize among Pullman employees had been firmly suppressed by management in the 1880's. Among railroaders unions had previously consisted largely of the brotherhoods of train-operating personnel whose leaders were shy of strikes and could be played off against one another in a fashion with which Debs, long editor of the firemen's house organ, was very familiar. His ARU was meant to organize the remaining majority of railroad personnel—switchmen, towermen, section hands, yard clerks, roundhouse help and so on—nationwide, with cooperation from the brotherhoods, to match the railroads' own powerful combinations, such as the General Managers' Association that included all twenty-four railroad lines coming into Chicago. Soon strong in the trans-Mississippi region, the ARU won its first battle handsomely. In a swift, short masterpiece of a strike it forced James J. Hill's Great Northern to arbitration and consequent rescindment of a heavy wage cut while yet refraining from violence and observing the public interest by letting mail trains go through. Anybody working in any capacity for a company that ran a railroad was eligible. The Pullman Company necessarily had a few miles of its own railroad to handle its cars. The success of the Great Northern strike had electrified labor everywhere, and by May Day, 1894, some 4,000 Pullman employees had joined semiautonomous ARU locals organized at meetings held in halls outside the company boundaries.

The ARU's national leaders advised them against striking. But refusal of management to treat with them at all embittered them beyond caution. Out they went, and Debs, dismayed but loyal, led the ARU in support, denouncing George Pullman in a shrilly savage tirade calling him "a greater felon than a poor thief . . . a self-confessed robber" and likening his paternalism to "the interest of a slave owner in his human chattels. You are striking to avert slavery and degradation." [43] He sought help from the brotherhoods and the American Federation of Labor, already fairly strong, but got none. Food supplies for the strikers at Pullman came from individual contributions raised in the Chicago area. The ARU, strong among switchmen, instructed its members to boycott Pullman cars—that is, refuse to handle switches for trains containing them, which did not affect freight or commuting trains but would greatly reduce the Pullman Company's revenues. The General Managers' Association, which seems to have meant war from the beginning because it offered an opportunity to catch the ARU in a highly unfavorable situation, made no effort to get its member lines to set up all-mail trains without Pullmans, which would have kept the mails moving without defying the boycott. Indeed it was strongly suspected of advising including Pullmans in previously nonmail trains to make the tie-up worse. The purpose—to force the federal government to send U.S. Army units to maintain movement of the mails—was achieved.

Debs professed to believe that "The first shot fired by the regular soldiers at the mobs here will be the signal for a civil war." [44] The matter did not come to the test because, of the thirteen killed and fifty-three seriously wounded before things simmered down, none had stopped a U.S. Army bullet. The lead involved came from state militia and probably from hoodlums or casually recruited U.S. marshals. But the presence of federal troops—whether justifiable or not is debatable—certainly did heat up the situation. The mobs Debs referred to took over freightyards and burned hundreds of boxcars, disregarded the ARU's pleas for peaceful procedures and prevented trains from entering or leaving, and defied federal injunctions against interfering with mail movements. This use of the federal injunction was the second trial of a potent antistrike weapon destined to overgenerous use during the next several decades. It had been first applied earlier in the year when the Commonwealers, the movement set off by Coxey's Army of unemployed demonstrators, had stolen trains to take themselves to Washington, D.C., to expostulate against hard times.

One of the railroads' strengths was the willingness of numbers of experienced Eastern switchmen and such to act as strikebreakers in the Chicago area. Some of these told the press that they had been ousted from the Gould railroads of the Southwest during the Knights of Labor strike in the preceding decade by the very men they were now replacing and did not mind getting some of their own back. In any case, as the ARU had foreboded in warning its Pullman locals, times were hard everywhere, tempers ragged, pockets emptying—it was a poor time to strike. The same story of federal troops protecting strikebreakers, a gradual rise in violence, sharply rising public dismay, unions looking unnecessarily bad, was occurring elsewhere, notably in the Southwest. But Chicago was the focus, just as it had been for the Fair of the preceding year.

Bullet for bullet, mob for mob, stubbornness for stubbornness, the nation had already seen worse strikes and would again. But this one had especially versatile consequences. In spite of widespread public mistrust of railroads, the implied threats to the mails and to supply of food to so great a city's people deepened the already strong impression of a great majority of Americans that, in Ely's regretful phrase, strikes were the "chief of social sins." By corollary it made Grover Cleveland, who had ordered in the Army, a hero in the eyes of most of the nation, though not in those of Governor John P. Altgeld of Illinois, who kept asking— and never getting an intelligible answer—why Washington had acted before the Chicago authorities had asked for state troops, which Altgeld had readily used to quell strike disorders in the past—and eventually did more to protect Chicago than the regulars accomplished. But then Altgeld had been tagged as a suspicious radical ever since he had pardoned the three surviving Haymarket anarchists to redress the error of their conviction. The Pullman strike also showed up the lack of solidarity among the growing segments of American labor and tended to discredit the industrywide union. For it utterly smashed the American Railway Union, drawn reluctantly into a battle that looked hopeless—a result serving only the interests of railroad management. The ensuing frustrations attacking Debs' impressionable temperament as he sat in jail six months for contempt of a federal injunction completed his conversion into a class-struggle-minded, root-and-branch Socialist. That gave American Socialism the most effective leader it ever had. Eighteen years later Debs got more than 900,000 votes for President in the Wilson-Roosevelt-Taft election of 1913—some 6 percent of the popular vote, better than any third-party candidate, except La Follette in 1924, has done since.

George Pullman's insistence on doing things his own way had been remarkably catalytic even though he had not been personally on the ground. Leaving the blow-by-blow tactics to his well-chosen aides, he spent the first part of that grisly summer at his seaside place in New Jersey, the rest at his other summer retreat in the Thousand Islands. In the same Chicago *Evening Post* that denounced the strike mobs as "BENT ON DEATH AND DESTRUCTION," Mr. Dooley remarked:

> This here Pullman makes th' sleepin'-ca-ars an' th' constitootion looks afther Pullman. . . . He don't need to look afther himself. . . . Whin he has trouble ivry wan on earth excipt thim that rides in smokin'-ca-ars . . . runs to fight f'r him. He calls out George Washin'ton an' Abraham Lincoln and Gin'ral Miles . . . an' thin he puts on his hat an' . . . "Gintlemin," he says, "I must be off," he says. "Go an' kill each other," he says. "Fight it out," he says. "Difind th' constitootion," he says. "Me own is not iv th' best," he says, "an' I think I'll help it be spindin' th' summer," he says, "piously," he says, "on th' shores iv th' Atlantic ocean." [45]

In 1896, after the ARU was dead and Pullman's shops were back at work with the personnel men keeping the blacklists tidy, an International Hygienic and Pharmaceutical Exposition held at Prague awarded Pullman, Illinois, first prize as the world's prime example of ideal town.* George Pullman died the next year probably unaware that there was anything ironical about the two medals and elaborate diploma that documented the award.

Those seeing the Pullman strike as lurid evidence of immigrant subversion—and it was true that most of the strikers and the most violent mob members were aliens—would have been startled to be told that actually the union thus smashed had made America's only original contribution to the labor movement—the principle of the industrial union. Old World unions typically limited membership and field of fire to par-

---

* This account of the Pullman troubles is very deeply indebted to that admirable recent work, Almont Lindsey's *The Pullman Strike*; to Ray Ginger's biography of Debs, *The Bending Cross*; and to Harry Barnard's biography of Altgeld, *"Eagle Forgotten."*

ticular crafts or trades. So did the American railroad brotherhoods and the growing number of craft unions—machinists, cigar makers—affiliated with the upcoming American Federation of Labor led by the able English-reared, Dutch-Jewish Samuel Gompers. In contrast the rapidly disintegrating Knights of Labor had sought to enlist all who worked for pay with their hands, skilled and unskilled, in a single nationwide comradeship of mutual support against all employers. Unwieldiness and a tendency to bite off more than they could chew broke up the Knights. But Debs had cannily revived the principle on a smaller scale in his scheme to get all wage earners connected with all American railroads to stand together in his American Railway Union against all railroad managements.

It was an essentially radical approach and sharpened class consciousness. The very form of such an industrial union preached the identity of interests among all categories of wage earners as opposed to the bosses'. Some see this development as inevitable reaction matching the scale of combination represented by the many overt or clandestine trusts formed among employers in the 1880's. That is, the industrywide union was the logical response to industrywide collusion. It also sought to rescue the unskilled and semiskilled, mostly recent immigrants, with whose interests the AF of L was insufficiently concerned. True, in the German-dominated brewery workers and the United Mine Workers of the coalfields the AF of L included what amounted to industrial unions. But to the class-conscious, Gompers' craft-minded tactics were seen as widening a dismaying split between the machinist, say, and the loom tender on the same payroll.

Practically the only remaining vestige of the American Railway Union was the notorious and possibly but not probably legendary swan with a broken neck. After the Pullman strike the railroads by no means blacklisted all who had participated. Many were allowed to return to the job. But managements did cooperate informally in refusing work to those known to have been active in strike agitation and issued to employees leaving the payroll a service letter to be shown to any prospective railroad employer stating length of service and reason for leaving. The paper on which this was written, railroad labor insists, was watermarked with a swan—in good shape if the applicant carrying it had no militant union record, but if he were a known bad actor, the watermark swan's neck was broken. Real or not, the allegation shows that the rout of industrial unionism had left seething emotions behind it. In 1905 a veteran group of militants met in Chicago to revive it and colored it frankly red with the first sentence of their manifesto: "The working class and the employing class have nothing in common." [46] Their immediate objective was to undermine and discredit the AF of L, which they despised with the bitterness characteristic of schismatics and doctrinaires. Their long-range objective was so thoroughly to organize industrial wageworkers, industry by industry, that they could "take possession of and operate successfully" [47] the whole economic system, much as in Bellamy's vision of the payrolls taking over capitalistic monopolies as they came ripe. Historically they were crossing the industrywide ambition of the dead ARU with the nationwide aims of the old Knights of Labor, for the scheme envisaged an economywide union of industrywide unions with local affiliates blanketing each separate plant.

Hopefully they christened their project the Industrial Workers of the World, a grandiose title, but they were headily aware that they had 20,000,000 potential converts among as yet unorganized American workers, a promising start on collectivizing the Western world. This courted anticlimax, of course. At their height, *c.* 1912, they probably had only 100,000 members. Their only worldwide aspect was an international reputation for militancy—feedback again as this American innovation of the industrial union drew the notice of European far leftists such as Lenin. But they also trained in agitation and the cultivation of class hatred such figures as William Z. Foster and Elizabeth Gurley Flynn, who were to be very tough leaders of American Communism after World War I. Some of their tactics were effectively used by the CIO of the 1930's to impose industrial unions on employers. And set it down also to their account that they probably did more than even the Mollie Maguires in their time to keep the average American viewing organized labor with alarm.

Eugene Debs, by then the perennial standard-bearer of the Socialists in national elections, was among their founders but bowed out within a few years because he found the IWW's flavor too anarcho-syndicalist— which was evident in its stated ambitions from the beginning. In spite of this Old World ideology, however, the IWW was largely as American as it was militant. Its chiefs, Vincent St. John and William D. "Big Bill" Haywood, were born and reared in Kentucky and Utah respectively. The core of its first phase was the Western Federation of Miners, union of the successors of the hard-bitten wageworkers, mostly American-reared, who had manned the early mechanized mines of Virginia City and Deadwood. From the 1890's on their localized struggles to impose the eight-hour day on the mineowners of Idaho or Colorado or Nevada kept the West scarred with strikes, gunplay and occasional dynamitings in much the same tradition of violence as that of the cattlemen's wars against sheepmen and nesters. The WFM lost oftener than it won, for the owners were close to the state governments and could readily whistle up the militia, as well as their own private guards, to protect strike-breakers, disperse meetings, run strike leaders out of the state, shoot up camps of evicted families. According to the WFM, it was always the owners who grew violent first, always their secret agents who blew up or set fire to mine property to make the union look bad when tension was highest. One can agree that the owners were ruthlessly and consistently quick on the trigger without having to believe that the WFM's rough-and-ready members were always innocent lambs, even though juries trying them for the felonies of which the owners accused them almost always acquitted.

The newborn IWW's purpose to organize everything naturally led to some waste motion at first. Haywood even formed a Broncho Busters' and Range Riders' Division for the West's cowhands. It aborted, along with the Chicago Window Washers' Division. But the experience and momentum of the WFM took the organization to its early peak in 1907, when a foray into the mining center of Goldfield, Nevada, put the miners on top in a fashion unknown since the great old days of Virginia City. Most jobholders in the booming community—waiters, messenger boys, ostlers, as well as miners—were gathered into the IWW fold and everywhere in town, as St. John wrote with nostalgic joy years later, "the eight hour day was universal. . . . The unions adopted the wage scales and regulated hours. The secretary posted the same on a bulletin board outside the union hall, and it was the LAW. The employers were forced to come and see the union committees." [48] But this taste of the union man's millennium was obviously too far out of phase with the times to last. The repercussions of the Wall Street panic of 1907 upset it. The WFM had to retreat from Goldfield, and IWW locals fell apart in many other places. Presently the crippled WFM withdrew to go it alone. The one-big-union cause had never looked less promising.

Actually all this cleared the decks for the IWW's best or anyway liveliest years. With doubters and trimmers gone, it could openly renounce collective bargaining, government-led mediation, wage contracts with time clauses and all the other devices for masking what its leaders considered the tooth-and-claw, class-warfare realities of strike, boycott, lockout and—though it was consistently denied for public purposes, of course—sabotage. That is, says Paul F. Brissenden, early historian of the IWW, it now "combined the indigenous doctrine of industrial unionism with the ideology and practices of [European] syndicalism." [49] And its leaders soon were ably exploiting fresh opportunities—among the migratory workers who handled the lumber and harvested the wheat and fruit of the trans-Missouri West; among the recent immigrants who manned the textile and steel mills of the industrial Northeast; among the loggers of Louisiana and Arkansas with Negroes and whites in the same locals. For to the IWW's everlasting credit it was the first sizable American labor organization except the Knights of Labor consistently to breach the color line. Not even Debs' American Railway Union had done that. And the AF of L's idea of how to handle the problem when it insisted on not going away was to set up separate Jim Crow locals.

Lumbering and harvesting had long been mainstays of the hobo stratum of boxcar-riding migrants, those most work-minded and nearest stability. Without them seasonally supplementing local hands the lumber barons and the wheat and fruit ranches between the Mexican and Canadian borders could not operate. Typically they were young, unmarried, hence footloose, never in one spot long enough to qualify for voting, cynically disgruntled about bosses, policemen, lawyers, preachers, authority in general—perfect recruits for the IWW organizer's talk about the one big union to sweep away all the bosses and their sycophantic henchmen. Though almost half of them were immigrants—Finns, Swedes, assorted Slavs—their shifting lives had forced them to learn English better than the Pole or Italian of the Eastern city who never got outside his own ethnic enclave. From among them developed the Wobbly* of American labor folklore, the hobo hero with a revolutionary star in his eye and in his pocket the little red card of IWW membership that train crews often accepted as evidence that the hobo in the boxcar was a good Joe and should be allowed to ride. His favorite way to harass the bosses was to single out a town that had roughed up an IWW street-corner agitator, summon all the Wobblies in the region to swarm into town, and hold interminable, shrilly defiant street meetings to force mass arrests, clogging of local jails and courts—and restoration of free speech. Police usually responded with ill-advised harshness. But the really outrageous attacks on the IWW did not occur until after the intensifications consequent on World War I had built up.

"I Won't Work" was the popular interpretation of the initials that were soon very much alive in public consciousness. Patrick Renshaw, a sympathetic student of the IWW, thinks it was unfortunate for the union's public relations that its best-known song, "Hallelujah, I'm a Bum," summoned up all the connotations of the blear-eyed chronic mission stiff. In his view these Wobbly migrants were not "work-shy tramps . . . [instead] usually decent working-men, more perceptive and spirited than most . . . using the only weapons they had at hand to assert the dignity of their labor." [50] That may well be a tenable as well as comradely generality. But after the IWW became what Wallace Stegner calls

* The origin of this name for an IWW man is hopelessly lost. For summary see Patrick Renshaw's *Wobblies*, 21-22. I am much indebted to this book.

"a singing union,"[51] its deliberate specialization in parodies of revival hymns implies a considerable admixture of men fecklessly resentful of disinfectant-perfumed mission quarters and the Salvation Army approach of sing-for-your-supper. The outstanding item, to the tune of "Revive Us Again"

> Hallelujah, I'm a bum, bum,
> Hallelujah, bum again!
> Hallelujah, give us a handout,
> Revive us again![52]

is, in fact, omitted from the current editions of the IWW's famous *Little Red Songbook*. But the atmosphere is just as self-evident in several others almost equally well known:

> Longhaired preachers come out every night.
> Try to tell you what's wrong and what's right;
> But when asked how 'bout something to eat?
> They will answer with voices so sweet:
>
> You will eat, bye and bye,
> In that glorious land above the sky;
> Work and pray, live on hay,
> You'll get pie in the sky when you die.[53]

That devastating use of the tune of "In the Sweet By and By" and several other well-known Wobbly songs is credited to Joe Hill, the Swedish-born IWW songsmith who became a potent martyr figure when Nevada executed him after conviction for what even Renshaw calls "a sordid murder"[54] that was not, so far as anybody ever found, connected with IWW affairs. Wallace Stegner's careful study of the case from a point of view sympathetic to the Wobblies led him to believe that, though the state failed adequately to prove it, Hill was probably at least occasionally a stickup man and guilty as charged. But then the rank and file of hard-pressed causes are seldom choosy about their martyrs. And in "pie in the sky" Hill did contribute to the American idiom a metaphor that one hopes will never drop out of usage.

While the IWW was prospering among the Western migrants, it was also learning to capitalize on the woes of unorganized factory workers. It plunged uninvited into a struggle at McKees Rocks, Pennsylvania, between a subsidiary of the U.S. Steel Corporation and a largely unorganized work force exasperated by a puzzling change in wage basis. The strikers were mostly recent immigrants of such diverse ethnic origins that the eulogy of one of them killed in a clash with the police was given in fifteen languages. In spite of this legacy from the Tower of Babel, IWW leaders managed to concentrate their bitterness effectively enough to win their fight for them. In 1912, two years later, the IWW applied the lesson again in Lawrence, Massachusetts, where it already had a miniature organization and the textile millowners were embroiled over wage cuts for women and child workers with another highly mixed work force. Only 8 percent were American-born. Italians, Germans, French Canadians, Poles, Lithuanians, Belgians, Letts, Greeks, Syrians had now replaced the Yankees and the Irish at the looms and spinning machines of New England. Police and militia obligingly cast themselves as heavy-handed bullies, it was a severe winter, and when the authorities prevented strikers' wives from sending a consignment of hungry children out of town to be cared for by sympathizers, the public-relations fat was in the fire. Protests roared in from not only predictable publicists such as William Dean Howells and William Allen White, nationally influential editor of the Emporia (Kansas) *Gazette,* but also from the Solicitor General of the United States and Senator William E. Borah, who had once been chief prosecutor of IWW leaders in a dynamite-murder case in Idaho in the old WFM days. By spring the millowners had given in. Again the IWW had won the game for a mass of badly treated workers about whom nobody else was bothering.

In 1913 they tried it again in Paterson, New Jersey, a silk town chronically full of sharp-edged labor troubles with a work force of anarchistically inclined Italians, plus Irish, Germans, Poles, French Canadians. . . . This time, in spite of normally heavy-handed law and order, the magic failed to work. The strikers eventually had to accept the very same conditions that had moved them to go out in the first place. And once the tension relaxed, the IWW organization in Paterson fell apart— as it already had in Lawrence in spite of victory. Haywood's task forces, though able whippers-up of emotion, did not know how to keep permanent tactical units together. Even in the relatively homogeneous West their membership turnover had always been over 100 percent a year. But Paterson was not all loss. It was near New York City where an ineffable heiress from Buffalo, Mrs. Mabel Dodge, had recently appointed herself focus of a really-truly salon attracting Manhattan's intellectuals to her apartment on lower Fifth Avenue in Greenwich Village. During the strike the Paterson police had temporarily jailed John Reed, a romantic-minded radical journalist who much admired Haywood. At a Greenwich Village gathering Reed and Haywood were introduced to Mrs. Dodge. Haywood spoke fervently for the strikers' cause. Chronically susceptible, the lady not only sympathized with them—and their troubles were hard to exaggerate—but also, studying Reed's ram-like good looks, fell in love with him.

The upshot of the evening was a great pageant, highly effective by all accounts, at Madison Square Garden written by Reed, underwritten by Mrs. Dodge, sets by Robert Edmond Jones, soon to be America's most renowned stage designer, acted by 1,000-odd genuine strikers fetched from Paterson to sing their own songs, display their own hunger-bitten faces—the whole staged by the IWW. Though 15,000 persons paid admission to feel themselves in tune with the struggling masses, the thing lost money. But all evening IWW in fiery red letters over the stage had imposed itself on the mass consciousness as symbol and synonym of righteous social instincts. Thenceforward the Wobblies were unimpeachable sacred cows among the many literate Americans lavishing fashionably warm collective emotions on radical causes.

Such people badly needed revived prestige for militancy because the year before the strange McNamara case had proved highly disconcerting. Late in 1910 an explosion had set off a fire that killed 20 persons in the building of the Los Angeles *Times,* which had been vehement against a local union campaign to impose the closed shop. It was widely assumed that the IWW was involved. But the men arrested for the crime and taken (illegally) to Los Angeles for arraignment were John J. McNamara, an official of the Structural Iron-Workers' Union, and his brother, James B. Their union was an affiliate of the AF of L, which called the case a frame-up and procured them the best available counsel, Clarence Darrow, liberal lawyer, renowned champion of underdogs and foe of capital punishment. The IWW tried to glean some attention by denouncing the AF of L for not helping the McNamaras, when it actually had done its best; asserting that the explosion had come from a defective boiler; and labeling the case a shameful example of the bosses' persecution of union leaders. All over the country people were taking the affair as a potential equivalent of the Haymarket case—a legal lynching of scapegoats.

The one trouble was that the case against the McNamaras was so strong that even Darrow could assemble no promising defense. Helped by Lincoln Steffens, the best known of the magazine reporters of the muckraker school, he arranged for his clients to make surprise pleas of guilty—which they unquestionably were—in return for minimal sentences instead of the death penalty. Their doing so rocked the world of labor and its sympathizers more violently than the bomb had rocked the *Times* building. The streets of Los Angeles, where a Socialist candidate had been given a good chance to win a pending election for mayor, were, Steffens recalled, "strewn with the socialist party buttons which voters had thrown away when the news came." [55] Those Easterners who had sunk so much emotional capital in the frame-up theory on the word of the leaders of both the AF of L and the IWW had reason to be grateful to Reed's pageant as restorative of their confident equilibrium. But the average man had been convinced once again—by no means unwillingly, of course—that labor and irresponsible violence were synonymous. That impression was one of the bitterest and most destructive of the legacies that pre-World War I America passed on to succeeding generations.

Bill Haywood was proud of the IWW's success in getting Paterson strikers of twenty-odd different nationalities to sing the same songs in unison. Doubtless one of the selections was "Solidarity Forever," polysyllabic exploitation of the incomparable tune of "John Brown's Body":

It is we who plowed the prairies, built the cities where they trade;
Dug the mines and built the workshops; endless miles of railroad laid.
Now we stand outcast and starving, 'mid the wonders we have made
But the union makes us strong.
Solidarity forever! . . .[56]

That more or less fitted many of the Americans, Scandinavians, Welsh, Irish and Germans in the WFM and the IWW branches among lumberjacks and migrant labor in the West. But most persons Haywood had been working on in Paterson had never seen a plow since leaving the Old Country; knew nothing of mining or building up the new country with transport or bricks and mortar; had merely replaced in Paterson's grimily run-down silk mills previous immigrant groups most of whom had managed to get away, sometimes into better lives. For the pool of unskilled labor on which mills and factories drew c. 1900 was rapidly changing its composition and becoming even more of an ethnic crazy quilt than the nation had previously known.

That began about halfway between the Civil and the Spanish-American wars. In the rising flood of newcomers the Germans, Irish, Scandinavians and French Canadians appeared in important numbers. A large trickle of English as well as Welsh persisted. But beginning with the Eastern Jews, even greater numbers now came from Eastern Europe and the northern and eastern shores of the Mediterranean. The Italians were conspicuous first, soon joined by throngs from the unwieldy Austro-Hungarian Empire and the Balkans—Bohemians, Slovaks, Hungarians, Croats, Serbians. Presently the impulse struck the Greeks, Syrians and Armenians. The Portuguese, first as fishermen, later as industrial

workers, were an old story in New England. The Poles were quitting
Russia's Little Father, the czar, almost as eagerly as the Finns and the
Jews . . .

Most of this New Emigration had the same old reasons for self-exile.
The first tremors of industrialization and liberalization of social classes
were shaking up Poland and Hungary as they previously had Sweden
and Germany. Centuries of cumulative neglect and wrongheadedness—a
case can be made for its going back to Roman times—had southern Italy
and Sicily in stagnation as despairing as that of Ireland c. 1840. The
effects of faltering Turkish rule in the Balkans and the Levant had been
almost as bad. Replacement of sail by steam and subsequent brisk competition among shipping lines into the Mediterranean as well as Northern
Europe had made it far easier and cheaper for the Central European
to reach America. (And Latin America; the same causes sent many
Italians, Syrians and others to South America, but the bulk of the movement naturally went to North America, where a vast growth of industry
offered the best chance of employment.) Except among Jews a specific
thirst for freedom is not implied beyond the young men's wish to evade
conscription. But then freedom-mindedness as such had never dominated
those emigrating to America.

Other aspects were familiar despite the change of idiom from Teutonic to Slavic. There was a high proportion of unaccompanied men hoping
soon to save enough to pay the passages of their families, not only wives
and children but often parents or married younger brothers hoping to do
the same in turn. Many letters went home to urge one's relatives to scrape
up steerage fare and follow, for—a point that Americans of conscience
and goodwill often failed to grasp—squalid as were the stinking, ratty
tenements of New York City's East Side, the slums of Naples were even
worse, and a peasant hovel in Galicia or Macedonia made the shacks of
a mining-company town in western Pennsylvania look good. The Irish
had made the same sort of discovery in their time.

Also like the Irish these new emigrants usually clung together in urban
enclaves, still persisting among, say, the Poles of Detroit and Buffalo.
Consider the parents of Leon Czolgosz (the psychotic who killed President McKinley in 1901): They had come straight from Poland to Detroit; soon moved to a small farm, working it with their sons' labor; sub-
sequently lived in four small towns, three in northern Michigan, one
near Pittsburgh, all practically solid Polish, one so much so that the
women still wore Old Country peasant garb. No wonder that after thirty
years in America the father knew hardly any English. The enclaves of
New York City's Italians were less than national, actually provincial
—Southern Italians concentrated here, Sicilians a few streets away, the

small proportion of Northern Italians the other side of town. The failure of the New Emigrants to go to farming, though most of them were of peasant background, probably reflected lack of resources, as well as clannishness. Relatively few landed with even the meager cash needed to begin homesteading. Nor did railroads and state immigration bureaus bother much with land-sales propaganda among Balkan and Mediterranean peoples. Only after a couple of decades could Italians and Poles use savings accumulated from industrial employment to buy up abandoned farms in Connecticut and New Jersey and try their Old World patience and peasant skills on tobacco, poultry and other intensive husbandry. Basically it was not land-hunger but livelihood-hunger, the prospect of a wage-earning industrial job, that brought them overseas—one reason why they were often in bad odor with union men as strikebreakers in mines and steel mills. They knew nothing of labor's struggles, had merely gone where the often predatory but helpful big-city labor agency had set up paying jobs.

Yet this New Emigration—say, from 1885 to World War I—was no repetition of the old. Its being almost altogether non-Protestant lowered the general social acceptability of the immigrant. Nor was this entirely the fault of nativist dislike of Popery, hot as it was again under the stoking of organized bigotry like that of the American Protective Association. The Catholic or Greek Orthodox priest also had a tactical interest in keeping his flock culturally insulated, hence loyal. His purpose was aided by rapid development of native-language newspapers. Uneasy observers developed an impression that many New Emigrants, particularly Italians and Levantines, considered the New World not as their potential new country but as only a place to save money on which to retire back home in Calabria or Arcadia. Norman Douglas' *Old Calabria* contains some of the evidence that there was much in this. Most villages that he visited in the foot of the Italian boot *c.* 1900 contained Americanos talking good Brooklynese and contemptuous of the archaic ways in which their countrymen persisted.

Nativists irked by such light regard for the privilege of becoming American knew nothing of the already long-standing custom of Italian men going to Northern Europe to work for a few years and then returning to their families with substantial savings and were probably unaware that many Old Emigrants, too, such as the Scandinavians, had long been thus retiring to the Old Country on resources acquired in America. The reason for recent increase in that sort of thing was technological. Cheap steamer fares and shorter, hence less hazardous, passages encouraged many New Emigrants, particularly those so shut away in enclaves that they learned little about America, to do what would have been out of economic reach in the days of sail. What the nativist most flagrantly ignored, however, was that the savings with which such returnees departed were the best evidence that before leaving they had done a great, great deal of hard, dirty, necessary work that Americans disliked doing for themselves.

The standing charge that labor organizers, anarchists, Socialists and such disruptives were usually alien-born actually applied largely to Old Emigrants, particularly English, Irish and Germans. In spite of fermenting Italian anarchists in Paterson and the conspicuousness of Eastern Jewish organizers like Emma Goldman and Morris Hillquit, this distinction largely held good until World War I. The New Emigrant's numbness about unions and the staggering number of languages required for collective communication with him help explain some of the neglect with which American unionism treated him. Historians of labor point out that the principle of the industrial union could not triumph until the 1930's—after the immigration quotas of 1924 had largely halted the New Emigration and the children of those already here had had time to learn enough English to understand what the organizer was saying. Yet it is not easy to work out a clear old-new pattern in the varying behavior of the ethnic groups in the Lawrence strike of 1912, for instance. The Italians were thought of as the backbone of the strike, but the bulk of the first members of the IWW local involved had been Franco-Belgians. The French Canadians came in strongly halfway through the trouble. Most of the Germans remained sluggish. The Irish, largest ethnic group in town and reputedly fond of a fight, largely stayed out of this one. Several Syrians were militant leaders. The one thing evident is that ethnic influences were deeper than class feeling.

In 1892 the rush of immigrants into New York City, focus of transatlantic shipping, moved the federal government to take the processing of them out of the hands of New York State and handle it directly. The old reception center in Castle Garden at the tip of Manhattan Island was replaced by new federal buildings on Ellis Island out in the harbor. This isolation, resembling quarantine measures against a plague, tended unfortunately to symbolize and bolster a growing revulsion among established Americans against unrestricted immigration. "As a pilgrim father that missed th' first boats," said Irish-born Mr. Dooley at the height of one of the peaks of such feeling, "I must raise me claryon voice again' th' invasion iv this fair land be th' paupers an' arnychists iv effete Europe. Ye bet I must—because I'm here first . . . if ye wud like . . . to discuss th' immygration question, I'll send out . . . f'r Schwartzmeister an' Mulcahy an' Ignacio Sbarbaro an' Nels Larsen an' Petrus Gooldvink an' we'll gather to-night at Fanneilnovski Hall at th' corner iv Sheridan an' Sigel sthreets. All th' pilgrim fathers is rayquested f'r to bring interpreters." [57]

Skilled labor was uneasily aware that the proportion of skilled men among the New Emigrants was almost as high as it had been among the old—and this influx was greater. General viewers with alarm maintained the opposite—that the country was flooded with nothing but low-grade, illiterate misfits unable even to make a living by swinging a pick in the Old Country. There was indignant and not ill-founded suspicion that some European countries were exporting their minor felons to America, and it was seldom recalled that much the same process had had a great deal to do with peopling Colonial America. Truant officers learned that resistance to sending children to school instead of to the factory or into the street to shine shoes or sell newspapers was strongest in New Emigrant families—because the breadwinner was not paid enough to feed his dependents or, in less desperate cases, because of what John Spargo, most cogent crusader against child labor, saw as "the senseless, feverish, natural ambition of the immigrant to save money, to be rich . . . to barter the manhood of their sons and the womanhood of their daughters for gold." [58] For either reason parents were likely to swear that the boy was any indicated number of years older than he really was to circumvent state laws about working age. (There seems to have been less of this among the Jews, who, however slummy their own lives, felt strongly the traditional prestige of schooling and longed for their sons to escape the slums as rabbis, schoolteachers, lawyers, doctors.)

Many sociologists, some of liberal bent, finding the slums seething with New Emigrants, made a natural, if dubious, *post hoc* correlation between dirt, overcrowding and the New Emigration, unaware of what the Five Points had been like in their grandfathers' time. Henry George, the crusader for the hopes of humanity in the single tax, applied the phrase "human garbage" [59] to the immigration of the late 1880's. Particularly noisy was the Reverend Josiah Strong, eminent champion of home missions and civic reform, who also managed to combine whiteman's-burden imperialism with denunciation of immigrants as subversive paupers. "A social and ideological gulf," says John Higham's discerning study of American nativism, "yawned between the well-established groups afire with visions of change and the uprooted folk who had already experienced more change than they could comprehend." [60] Even among men of goodwill the viscera may have been obscurely involved in alarm over unchecked immigration. The tendency of most new emigrants to be swarthy and undersized must also have stirred up latent xenophobia.

A more civilized reaction was the American version of the "social settlement." This English innovation had developed in the slums of London to bring cultural decency to the native urban proletariat. Brought to America in the late 1880's by Stanton Coit and Charles B. Stover in New York and the famous Jane Addams in Chicago, it was soon seeking to bridge the gap between the slum-bound New Emigrant and his new country. It coaxed him—or even more important, his wife and children—into a building right in his own slum that not only was clean, orderly and cost nothing to frequent but was also full of persons eager to teach him English, listen to his troubles, steer him to sources of further help, furnish stimulating activities and generally give him a sense of belonging and being taken seriously. Settlement-house influence was confined to large cities and even there never reached a scale proportionate to the need. But it often did achieve a sense of neighborliness, help thousands on thousands to get the hang of their bewildering situation—and at the lowest reckoning improved the nation's scenery with this spectacle of so many devoted citizens of obviously marked ability, a good half of them women, working harder for others than most people did for themselves.

They did little to reduce mistrust of aliens, however. In 1910 resurgent nativist feelings were wrapped up in the messy forty-two-volume report of a commission assigned in 1907 to furnish an intelligible basis for legislation to control immigration. A searching recent analysis by Oscar Handlin, authority on immigrants, shows that most of the experts employed on this Dillingham Report already favored restrictions; that their two-volume summary, on which legislators largely relied, often disregarded serious conflicts within the commission's own data and ignored important materials available in U.S. Census reports; and that in consequence it was "neither impartial nor scientific." [61] Its findings were nevertheless one of the principal bases on which the post-World War I quota system, sharply restricting the new emigration, was founded. And at the time it helped to confirm among responsible persons the popular distaste for the generic Immigrant—a term become sweepingly pejorative, implying a slum-creating, soap-shy, illiterate, jargon-speaking, standoffish interloper, innocent of civilized values, indeed hardly human, labeled variously dago, wop, hunky, bohunk, polack, yid . . . Harry Leon Wilson was soon depicting the German barber in Red Gap, Washington, complaining that "the country was getting overrun by foreigners, with an Italian barber shop just opened in the same block. . . ." [62]

The Italian supplied the commonest specific image. He cranked a music box, employed a bedizened monkey on a chain to collect the pennies, and used a knife instead of his fists in fighting. (The knife was really there; never forget Nathan Glazer's remark about "the . . . degree of truth that most stereotypes have, that is, a good deal." [63]) He also did as much as the vaudeville tenor to make "Santa Lucia" part of American life. Otherwise, thanks to mutual mistrust hardened by purveyors of new nationalisms and old prejudices, America's general ways-of-doing have had little enrichment from the New Emigration, nothing like what came from the Irish or Germans of the previous inflow. The major exceptions consist of the special intimacy between New Yorkers and Jewish cuisine, entertainment and folkways and the nationwide eagerness for Italian cooking, the south-of-Rome sort based on pasta, tomatoes, garlic, peppers and olive oil. An anomaly even more striking developed in the strange bedfellows created by the question whether the New Emigration should be checked. It was not just that much of organized labor and many leaders of reform, doughty fighters against privilege, took what we now would consider the illiberal side. On the liberal side—or what now seems so—opposing any barriers at all, presently turned up the National Association of Manufacturers and many a candidly reactionary individual industrialist.

Part of the reformers' error came of overreliance on wrongheaded experts' faulty theories about hereditary disabilities, backed by distorted statistics. The reactionaries' position was not, for their purposes, an error. Their spokesmen proclaimed open-armed refuge for the oppressed, but what they really had in mind was a steady supply of ignorant, unskilled, cheap labor to man mills and factories, where machinery was making skill less and less necessary. The New Emigrants not only would work for less than the sons of the Old, but were less likely to organize in their own interests. Their immunity to organizers' efforts could be prolonged by deliberate adoption of a policy of balanced nationalities —getting as many ethnic groups as possible on the payroll, keeping each relatively small, none large enough to overbalance the others. Thus the language barriers exerted optimum usefulness as preventers of fellow feeling. Against that background the IWW's adventures in Lawrence and Paterson gain dramatic force. It was trying to break through the employers' clever exploitation of the relative failure of the melting pot—a phrase coined by British-Jewish Israel Zangwill in 1908 as title for his play about Jews in New York City—to perform as advertised even after being allowed generations to work on urban enclaves of Germans and Irish.

Sixty years later it looks as if the restrictionists had been right for the wrong reasons, the National Association of Manufacturers too clever by half. The genetic arguments had little merit. The average inborn potential quality of the new emigrants was probably as high as that of the indentured servants dominating the human raw material of most of the Colonies, or as high as that of the Irish and Germans of the early 1800's. Probably the real trouble was numerical. Volume of influx very likely was outrunning capacity to assimilate. Though it was not much higher proportionate to existing population than it had been before the Civil War, the situation had changed internally. Free land had ceased to be available with the famous closing of the frontier in the early 1890's. Industrial employment was increasingly the economic prospect for all inhabitants of America, native or immigrant. Labor was correct in feeling that the annual flooding-in of the ignorant and unskilled hampered its struggles toward power and leverage equal to the boss'. Standards of social decency were rising along with the standard of living, and it was clear that they would continue to be threatened by erosion, that there was small prospect of getting rid of slums and slummy ways of life, so long as millions of the abjectly poor and underprivileged kept coming in to fill the old slums and often create new ones. (The consequences of the mass migration of the Southern Negro into the North is today's miserable parallel.) H. G. Wells, high priest of cultivated radicalism, visited American slums in 1904 and came away doubting that "these huge masses" could be adapted to "the requirements of an ideal modern civilization" and suspecting that Americans were "biting off more than they can chaw." [64]

True, the quota system imposed in 1924 and continuing until very recently was unfairly weighted against Eastern and Southern Europeans because the experts' false teachings had felt welcome in the viscera of many persons of goodwill. But had all the immigrants streaming through Ellis Island between 1900 and 1914 been Scotch-Irish and Protestant Dutch laborers, the difficulties they posed the society they were joining would probably have been of the same order. It was the nation's bad taste but good luck to have immigration curbed for reasons not merely wrong but also unworthy.

To see boys in their earliest teens acting as uniformed messengers late at night in New York City also struck H. G. Wells hard. He laid it down that "Nocturnal child employment is a social abomination" and called "the childish newsboys who sold me papers . . . the little bootblacks at the street corners . . . the weakest spot in America's fine front of national well being." [65] Of the three occupations the messenger boy's may have been most destructive to judge by the high rates of venereal disease and commitments to reformatories among them in Philadelphia as well as New York City. New York State had laws against sending minor messengers on errands for patrons or inmates of brothels, but nobody bothered to enforce them, and the boys preferred such assignments because of the fat tips often entailed. Doubtless it could be almost as destructive, however, to be an Italian or Greek urchin dodging about the streets cajoling passersby into letting him shine their boots in order to take home enough day's gains to avoid being skinned alive by the *padrone*—the enterprising Neapolitan who bought such boys from their parents in Italy and brought them through Ellis Island as his sons or cousins. And in spite of the monument to the generic newsboy presented to Great Barrington, Massachusetts, in 1895 by the owner of the New York *Daily News,* in spite of the newsboy's standing as minor folk hero created partly by Horatio Alger, Jr., partly by the Chimmie Fadden stories by Edward W. Townsend that were making the nation aware of New York City's dese-and-dem dialect, it did society little good and him less to have him hawking extras at all hours, misrepresenting the headlines when necessary, fighting rivals for rights to street corners, doing odd errands for shady characters as occasion served, and, when he lacked a family to absorb his earnings, living in loose colonies of other such derelicts in flophouses or patched-together shanties.

These juvenile street operators were the highly visible aspect of the scandal, duly pilloried by Wells, shown in the U.S. Census of 1900—when more than 4 of every 100 nonagricultural American jobs were held by persons between the ages of ten and fifteen years, an array of almost 700,000. In the Pennsylvania coal mines they breathed coal dust ten hours a day as they crouched over moving expanses of new-broken coal to pick out bits of slate and other adulterants. Now and again a boy lost his balance, fell into the rushing coal, and failed to survive. In the Midwestern glassworks rushed into operation wherever newly discovered natural-gas fields supplied the necessary fuel cheap, boys fetched and carried for the glassblowers on night as well as day shifts. Automatic machinery to do their work was available, but the management preferred paying wages, which did not tie up capital. Boys and girls both worked in nonunion shops rolling cigars for a third of the pay exacted by Gompers' Cigar Makers' Union. In textile mills most child labor consisted of girls tending spinning machines as the sprightly young ladies of Lowell had done two generations before. Only these were no apple-cheeked farmers' daughters saving up for a hope chest but scrawny little examples of malnutrition, whose earnings were necessary to eke out family income for new emigrants. In the South they were sharp-jawed little poor whites whose folks had been tempted down from the hills or out of the piney woods by the prospect of cash wages and hired out to the mill as a whole family—mammy, pappy and all the younguns out of bed before sunup to tend machinery all day long in the mill, back at sundown to the company-owned weatherboarded

shack, living largely on corn and fatback procured at the company store
with the company scrip issued in lieu of cash for at least part of the family
earnings. Delivery boys of ten and twelve vibrated between customer and
drugstore, printer, milliner, grocery. Preadolescent girls scampered to
the call of "Cash girl!" in department stores.

Historically this was nothing new in either the Old or the New Country.
"Until modern times," wrote Raymond G. Fuller, studying the psychology
of child labor, "income had always taken the form of a family income
. . . children were accustomed to contribute . . . by . . . agricultural
work and by spinning and weaving cloth." [66] Orphans were customarily
bound out to earn their keep at a pretty tender age, performing any odd
chores they could stagger in town as well as farm households. It developed
naturally that many early English textile mills used large job lots of pauper
children and that English-trained Samuel Slater should hire children of
ages between seven and twelve for his pioneer American cotton mill, then
soon adopt the British practice of hiring whole families.

In Northeastern America there was also a vague presumption grown
out of imperfectly administered laws that children of tender ages were
best-off learning the three R's. That could be squared with early-morning
and late-afternoon domestic or farm chores in the less active months. It
could not square, however, with a sunup to sundown mill job. One of the
factors in the gradual rescue of American children from industrial employment was the competition for the child's time represented in the rise of
compulsory school attendance. The first legal curb on child labor was
Massachusetts' rule that after 1836 children under fifteen years could not
do manufacturing work unless they got three months' schooling a year. In
the next decade New England states began to limit hours to ten a day in
certain occupations for children. But enforcement was lax at best, hard-
pressed parents likely to connive with management in faking age data, and
the increasing trend away from skills and toward mere machine tending
steadily enhanced demand for children's services—at a bargain. The
money saving so gratifyingly evident on payday was the core of the whole
miserable situation.

So the child's relative numbers in nonagricultural occupations kept
rising after the Civil War, keeping pace with industrialization. Some of
this reflected the shift of cotton textile manufacturing from New England
to the South to take advantage of the cheaper labor afforded by poor white
families. The differential in labor costs thus attracting new industry was,
of course, the reason why it proved notably difficult to get anti-child-
labor laws or their complements—compulsory school-attendance laws—
passed in Dixie. South of the Mason and Dixon-Ohio River Line governors and legislators had small intention of discouraging that trend, which

eventually resulted in today's impressive belt of textile towns in the Piedmont of North and South Carolina. It was soon clear that, as in so many other matters, federal legislation was the best way to prevent this contest in callousness among states. The battle for that, begun by 1900, was never completely won, though the Fair Labor Standards Act of 1938, barring the products of industrial child labor from interstate commerce, has accomplished most of what the still unratified Child Labor Amendment of 1924 sought. Of the twenty-eight states ratifying it before it was dropped in 1938, none was in Dixie proper, and only four were even marginally Southern.

A minor novelist from Tennessee, John Trotwood Moore, contributed to the battle against child labor *The Bishop of Cottontown,* portraying a cotton-mill community in the Tennessee Valley with what Donald Davidson, an eminent Southern critic of the agrarian persuasion, calls "a social consciousness in advance of his time . . . perhaps the first Southern novel to treat industrial forces that were changing Southern life." [67] Sandwiched in among its horseplay and claptrap is lively indignation against what millwork did to children and to the adults that they turned into:

> Years in the factory had made them dead, listless, soulless and ambitionless creatures. To look into their faces was like looking into the cracked and muddy bottom of a stream which once ran. Their children . . . little tots . . . worked in the factory because no man or woman in all the State cared enough for them to make a fight for their childhood. They were children only in age . . . little, solemn pygmy peoples, whom poverty had canned up and compressed into concentrated extracts of humanity . . . the juices of childhood had been pressed out . . . no talking inside the mill. . . . No singing—for songs come from the happy heart of childhood, unshackled. No noise of childhood, though the children were there. They were flung into an arena for a long day's fight against a thing of steam and steel. . . . They were more dead than alive when, at seven o'clock, the Steam Beast uttered the last volcanic howl which said they might go home . . . a speechless, haggard, over-worked procession.[68]

It was a *national* shame in 1900, however. ". . . less than a dozen states were seriously attempting to limit the labor of children in mills, mines, factories or stores, in sweatshops or street trades. . . . Such laws as existed were chiefly unenforced . . . all . . . lamentably meagre. . . . In most states it was not illegal to send children as young as 10 or 8 or 7 years into a mill, and keep them at work unlimited hours." [69] Soon national pressures were being applied. Organized labor, however split up on other subjects, was united and strong on this one, nor can it be assumed that this came solely of the elementary consideration that every child employed at bargain wages meant lower average income for men. The National Consumers' League, created in the 1890's by reform-minded women of New York City and Chicago to discourage sweatshops and filthy processing of food, came to see child labor as a particularly vicious form of sweating and set to work on the national conscience about it. By 1904 a National Child Labor Committee was in effective action, and John Spargo was writing *The Bitter Cry of the Children,* which ably combined scandalous sociological findings with an eager hand on the *vox humana* stop: ". . . the price we pay for the altogether unnecessary and uneconomic services of children would . . . stagger humanity if it could be comprehended. . . . Statistics cannot express the withering of child lips in the poisoned air of factories; the tired, strained look of child eyes that never dance to the glad music of souls tuned to Nature's symphonies. . . ." [70]* By 1907 federal legislation against the products of child labor in interstate commerce was being powerfully backed by Senator Albert J. Beveridge of Indiana, the most eloquent spokesman for Progressive causes in the U.S. Congress.

Meanwhile, passage of child labor and compulsory school-attendance laws in numerous states was being added to stronger enforcement of existing laws, and the Census of 1910 showed the child's share in the non-agricultural labor force cut almost in half. By 1915 thirty-three states required children to attend school to the age of sixteen. The Beveridge-style federal law passed in 1916 was struck down by the U.S. Supreme Court. But the social point had been well and truly made. Though the matter of children in agricultural work has never been properly looked after, the small-fry factory worker was on the way out fifty years ago, except in the South. Henry Pelling, British historian of American labor, calls this "A good example of . . . action taken as a result of information and public concern" and, like the simultaneous advances in legislation requiring labor-safety measures and workmen's compensation for accidents, "the result of the advance of public knowledge and the general social conscience, rather than the work of particular pressure groups." [72]

Large as industrial child labor bulked among new emigrants and Southern poor whites, it seldom involved a third group of underprivileged

* The other most effective literary blow against child labor was struck ten years later by what Sarah Cleghorn, a Quaker spinster-poetess zealous in many causes, called her "burning" quatrain in reaction to the sight of a child-employing textile mill overlooking a nice green golf course:

The golf links lie so near the mill
That nearly every day
The laboring children can look out
And see the men at play. [71]

Americans, the Negroes. Most particularly in the South a millowner trying to mingle Negro workers of any age with his white machine-tending
employees would have found the building deserted in five minutes. Industrialization by way of textile plants and the great post-Civil War coal-
and-iron development in northern Alabama was in some sense creating

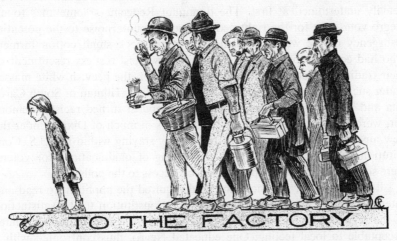

"AND A LITTLE CHILD SHALL LEAD THEM"

Attacks on child labor were a specialty of the humorous weekly
Life, just before World War I.

the New South celebrated in a famous speech in 1886 by Henry W. Grady,
editor (with Northern backing) of the Atlanta *Constitution*. But little of
the economic or social result was dripping on the Southern Negro. In some
important ways, in fact, his position was deteriorating.

One of the measures of Reconstruction most resented by white Southerners had been a federal statute requiring public places of resort and
means of transportation to accord "full and equal enjoyment . . . to
citizens of every race and color, regardless of any previous condition of
servitude." The U.S. Supreme Court invalidated that in 1883. Consequently the Redeemers—the old-line Southern leaders who were jockey-
ing Uncle Sam into scuttling Reconstruction—passed and enforced a
haphazard network of state, county and municipal legislation gradually
turning Jim Crow from a semiprivate into a rigid public institution. It was
not only hazardous, it was now illegal for a Negro to seek equal footing in
the South's public schools (which had been created largely for his benefit), railroad cars or stations, restaurants, hotels, theaters . . . And much
of this was new. As C. Vann Woodward, shrewd student of the South, has

shown in *The Strange Career of Jim Crow,* in some respects the pre-Civil War South had been considerably more lenient. Indeed it was often more so than many Northern states, where the habit of Negro-despising was also strong and yet there was no slavery system automatically to keep the Negro in his place.

The Negro citizen's exercise of his right to vote in the South was not so heavily undermined at first. The dominant Redeemers sometimes found Negro votes cast for the right people a good counterpoise to the potential insurgency of the wool-hat element—the red-neck small cotton farmers who had come around to sharing the poor whites' restless resentment of their traditional betters. By the 1880's, however, the peevish white masses under such leaders as the raucous "Pitchfork Ben" Tillman of South Carolina and Thomas E. Watson of Georgia, Populist turned racist hatemonger, were getting the better of the Redeemers in much of Dixie. Under the new auspices various legal tricks technically staying within the U.S. Constitution, which left to the states the setting of qualifications for voters, were soon effectually denying the Negro's access to the polls.

Literacy tests, for instance; one kind required the applicant to read and interpret a chosen passage from that very Constitution to the satisfaction of the registrar—who, of course, failed all Negroes and passed all whites acceptable to local feeling. One educated Negro, thus confronted with a turgid slab of Constitution, gravely read it, legend says, and replied: "I interpret this as saying no Negro can vote in Mississippi." In Louisiana a "grandfather clause" exempted from literacy tests and property requirements all those who had been eligible to vote before 1867 (the effective beginning of Reconstruction) together with all their male descendants. The poll tax—a dollar or two paid well in advance of the election, void if the receipt was not preserved and shown at the polls, cumulative over the years—discouraged Negroes who seldom saw much cash, while still permitting interested parties to pay the poll tax for any white whose vote was needed. Sometimes the method was forthright—the law looked the other way while individual whites roughed up Negroes attempting to register or vote. Within a short while in most of Dixie the Negro voter was almost as unthinkable as the Negro juror. Add the reluctance of Southern courts to convict whites accused of crimes against Negroes and Southerners' readiness to lynch Negroes transgressing against whites, and the term *second-class citizen* flatters the situation of the Southern Negro *c.* 1900.

Until near our own time, of course, lynching as national bad habit left over from Colonial improvisations was no Southern monopoly. One of its sustaining elements, often unjustifiably invoked, was the tradition of vigilance committees. They had ranged in quality from the more or less responsible ones of early San Francisco to the one in New Orleans in 1891 that executed eleven Italian gangsters after a flagrant and probably corrupt miscarriage of justice acquitted them of murdering an anti-Mafia chief of police. But lynching in its distinctive sense—"a vengeful torture and execution of individuals without trial and regardless of the existence of regular courts of law" [73]—was more and more becoming a particularly Southern institution and applied primarily to Negroes. That is, though the national total of lynchings per decade was declining *c.* 1900, the South's proportionate share of them was rising, and at the same time the proportion of Negroes among the victims was rising past a 4 to 1 majority. In 1901 Mr. Dooley was quoting an imaginary Southern editor as writing: "We threat the Negro right. He has plenty to do and nawthin' to bother him an' if he isn't satisfied he be hanged. . . . Th' black has many fine qualities. He is joyous, light-hearted, an' aisily lynched." [74]

This persistent taste for sadistic, collective race-vengeance does seem to have associations with the rise of the red-necks at the expense of the Quality. Yet the Quality, though retaining considerable social leverage, did little to discourage lynching and sometimes stood by approvingly. The emotional purpose of both strata so far as it was rational was so violently to manifest whites' intolerance of Negro insubordination that the Negro racial caste would stay timidly docile—the same as that of the previous Ku Klux Klan. That comes out in the analyses of the alleged offenses for which Negroes were lynched. (None of this implies that the charges were always or even usually false—authoritative estimates show that the victim was falsely accused in only one-third of Southern lynchings, and the liberal novelist's assumption that the white woman's tale of criminal molestation is invariably sheer hysteria or hate is necessarily gratuitous.) The traditional crime—rape or attempted rape of a white woman—appears in only 23 percent of cases; homicide in 38 percent. The balance among some 4,500 cases studied represents transgressions that have not been capital crimes anywhere in America for generations. Among the 24 percent of "miscellaneous offense or no offense at all . . . are . . . testifying in court against a white man or bringing suit against him, refusal to pay a note, seeking employment out of place, offensive language or boastful remarks." [75] From such petty stimuli can come the grisliness that until so recently frequently blackened the land of the free—the ears and fingers taken home as souvenirs, the small white boy saying to his mother as she brings him home from the lynching: "I've seen a man hanged; now I wish I could see one burned." [76]

Consider too that the Southern lynch mob never had the vigilantes' or Western cattlemen's excuse that a corrupt or prejudiced court would turn the accused loose to prey on society again if the unofficial public did not take the law into its own hands. Dixie judges and juries were all too likely to disregard the doctrine of "innocent until proved guilty" when Negroes were concerned. After proper allowance for such often explored subtleties as the dullness of life in obscure Southern settlements and the erotic tensions of poor whites juxtaposed with Negroes, it probably remains crudely true that straight caste-vengeance is the basic factor—that the typical Southern lynch mob was still punishing the Negro for having been partial cause and greatest beneficiary of the overthrow of white supremacy in the defeat of the Lost Cause. In that light the wool-hatted red-neck was not too unlike the New York City Irish who shot, hanged, burned and otherwise killed nearly 1,000 Negroes in the Draft Riots of 1863. He was merely extending the thing, making it a recurring institution, a sort of irregular festival of exasperated caste-savagery.

By 1910 a quickening flow of Negroes northward had somewhat raised the low proportion of them in the old free states and begun the nuclei of black ghettos in such neighborhoods as Indianapolis' Indiana Avenue and Chicago's South Side. Why the flow was no larger—it lacked important scale until World War I drew heavily on the South for casual labor—has puzzled many, not least Gunnar Myrdal, the Swedish sociologist whose monumental study *An American Dilemma* probably had more than any other single thing to do with the U.S. Supreme Court's school decision of 1954. In another form this may be the same problem as why more Border State slaves did not run away when they knew freedom was so near. In any case a promising basis on which many postslavery Southern Negroes could stay where they were appeared in the 1880's, centered on Booker T. Washington and the Tuskegee Institute that he created in central Alabama.

Its local founders were in themselves propitious omens. One was Lewis Adams, trained as a slave in tinsmithing and shoe and harness making, who had used his freedom to become a successful dealer in hardware and leather goods—the epitome of the responsible, locally respected Negro good citizen. The other was Colonel W. F. Foster, former slaveholder, who had an eye for Negro votes and recommended to the state legislature a scheme of Adams' for a school that would teach Negroes ways to prosper in addition to conventional schooling. The result was an annual $2,000 for teachers' salaries and creation of a supervisory board. One of the outstanding successes of Reconstruction had been the Hampton Institute at Hampton, Virginia, developed by a keen young Yankee, General Samuel C. Armstrong, to train young adult Negroes of both sexes not only in academic subjects but also—according to sex—in sound farming, housework and other domestic skills, and the elementary hygiene of which Negroes had learned so little as slaves. The purpose was to produce teachers to pass these new acquisitions—and the self-respect assumed to go with them—on to other Negroes far and wide or at least to send students back where they came from trained to prosper in their own exemplary right. The Tuskegee board asked Armstrong for somebody from Hampton, presumably white, to get their school going. Instead, he so strongly recommended a half-Negro assistant of his that the board accepted him sight unseen. The Booker of his name was what he had been called as a ragged child slave in southwestern Virginia. He added the Washington when, on first enrolling in a school, he was required to have a surname. The T. was for Taliaferro, the highly FFV name that his mother gave him at birth. That may be a clue—though he never said so— to the white man who begot him.

His frantic wish to learn secured him admission to Hampton penniless but gamely capable of scrambling and struggling to make both ends meet. The place immersed him in absorbing matters—Puritan moral standards, building construction, orderly method, agriculture, Bible-based religion, meticulous cleanliness, public speaking. Before and during his studies there he had worked in the West Virginia salt mines, as houseman for a demon housekeeper, as handyman in a restaurant, as teacher in a Negro school—versatile and by no means cloistered additions to academic experience. As he matured at Hampton, he was entrusted with organizing and teaching six dozen Red Indian youths whom Uncle Sam wanted educated to cope with the white man's world. (His success with them led to the famous Indian School at Carlisle Barracks, Pennsylvania, famous then for unmatchable football teams, now for having had Marianne Moore, the poetess, on its teaching staff.) After that he had organized the Institute's work-your-way-through night classes.

At Tuskegee he had to begin with no enrollment and for buildings the loan of an abandoned church and a tumbledown outbuilding. Within fifteen years the Tuskegee Institute had 800-odd students, a staff of 55, property worth $200,000 including a several-hundred-acre farm worked by the students and 165 graduates already out in the Southern world spreading what they had learned. Essentially it was another Hampton worthy of its parent. But there was one crucial difference. Hampton was the Northern white man's creation for uplifting the benighted Negro. Tuskegee was the Negro's own creation, symbolically built brick by brick burned on the place by Negroes, a hard-earned instrument of self-uplift. The white man's contribution had only been much of the money—not all, for local Negroes gave the little they could, and the farm, brickyard, sawmill, printshop and such were profitable—and those mounting contributions from well-wishers, including many eminent Northern plutocrats, were the direct result of Washington's being as good at fund raising and public relations as he was at teaching, poultry raising, administration and thinking out race problems.

As striking examples of strive-and-succeed, which was still the nation's favorite story line, both Tuskegee and Washington greatly took Americans' fancy. He and it were as widely known as Franklin and his kite, and his autobiography, *Up from Slavery* (1900), was a best seller. His long-boned figure and alertly handsome head—markedly Negro in structure in spite of that white father—were familiar to millions on the lecture platform. In his view both his and his school's striving-and-success went far to prove the point that he had been consciously trying to make for Negroes and whites, particularly Southern ones—that the Southern Negro could solve the race problem by staying in the South and, with God's help and his own intelligence and persistence, demonstrating that he was entitled to full acceptance. In a recent study Samuel R. Spencer, Jr., has summed up Washington's approach in today's terms: The Negro had to "destroy the stereotype which years of slavery had fixed in the minds of even his friends and eliminate each of the negative slave characteristics which still clung to him . . . substitute efficiency for the slipshod work of slavery days, accepted moral standards for the amorality of the slave quarters . . . the Negro needed much more than academic training. . . . Washington . . . proposed to take the young men and women from the farm, educate them in agriculture and send them back as the backbone of a solid and prosperous [Negro] citizenry." [77]

He recommended that while this gradual rise was occurring, Negroes should abandon their visions of personal equality with whites. Their immediate business was to make themselves the white man's equal in productivity, skill and stability. In a speech before the National Education Association in 1884 he was already saying that passing laws "cannot make one citizen respect another. These results will come . . . by beginning at the bottom and working up." [78] In 1895 responsible Southerners' impressions of what he was doing at Tuskegee were so favorable that he was invited to make one of the opening day addresses at the Cotton States Exposition in Atlanta. His speech made about as much of a sensation as Bryan's "Cross of Gold" did the next year at Chicago, because it told the South and the heavily prejudiced nation in general that the Negro should no longer grope after social equality. To agitate that question, he said, was "the extremest folly . . . progress in the enjoyment of all the privileges that will come to us must be the result of severe and constant struggle rather than of artificial forcing." Showing the audience his big, capable right hand, he spread the fingers: "In all things that are purely social we can be as separate as the fingers, yet"—balling them into a fist —"one has the hand in all things essential to mutual progress." [79]

He was actually saying to Negroes: Build an abler Negro, and recognition of him as social equal, as well as economic partner, will come in due time; and to whites: Give Negroes a fair opportunity to show what they can do. But the South and the nation took it as a self-respecting permanent capitulation to a two-stratum Southern society, and, as Spencer points out, the next year the U.S. Supreme Court handed down the opinion that allowed Southern public schools to segregate white and Negro children on the separate-but-equal basis. Thus Washington's strategy of patience encouraged the permanent legal installation of Jim Crow at every important crossroads of race relations. Washington seems not to have questioned the separate-but-equal doctrine himself. That would have flawed his position as the cool-headed counsel for his people, aware that he was negotiating from weakness on some fronts and all the more determined to make the most of the cards he held in the shape of the Negro's potential capabilities. Also, the psychological considerations enabling the Court to destroy that doctrine in 1954 hardly existed in his day. But the South was incapable of keeping its end of the implied bargain. Schools, drinking fountains, park and hospital facilities, railroad cars and waiting rooms were signally separate but never equal in quality, often inadequate for Negroes in quantity, sometimes nonexistent. Employment for Negroes remained largely mere drudgery or somehow menial. The practice of the Negro physician or lawyer was confined to Negroes. The Negro scholar or teacher could find a post only in Negro institutions. Even the Negro athlete was barred from any kind of whites' playing field. In most of these respects the North was little better than the South, partly from indigenous prejudice, partly because of the destructive weight of the Southern example. The truth was that Washington's self-reliant confidence, assuming proudly that demonstrated worth would eventually get spontaneous recognition, was an unjustified compliment to the human race, a shameful failure of its white division.

In 1901, only the year after *Up from Slavery* had candidly spread his hopes before the nation, their lack of substance was shown by the violent reaction when it leaked out that President Roosevelt had had him to dinner at the White House. Or was it lunch? The uproar was so great that nobody was ever quite sure. The Southern press foamed at the mouth, showing how unlikely it would be in foreseeable history that solid, valuable Negro citizens—of whom Washington was the deliberate prototype in the very terms likeliest to command respect from whites—could be accorded a commensurate social footing in Dixie. The President had been guilty of "the most damnable outrage ever committed by a citizen of the United States." He was "willing that negroes shall mingle freely with whites in the social circle . . . white women . . . receive attentions from negro men . . . that . . . whites and blacks may . . . marry and intermarry . . . the Anglo-Saxon mix negro blood with his blood." And those comments are not from obscure weeklies upcountry in darkest Arkansas but from important papers in Richmond, Virginia, and Memphis, Tennessee. Senator Tillman was quoted: "The action of President Roosevelt in entertaining that nigger will necessitate our killing a thousand niggers in the South before they will learn their place again." [80] The Atlanta *Constitution* ran a cartoon showing Roosevelt cuddled up with a pop-eyed Negro wearing the traditional minstrel-show costume of huge collar, gaudy shirt, speckled spats.

Washington's work at Tuskegee had eventually cured the parents of his students of mistrusting his emphasis on industrial education because they regarded schooling as a magical way to the white man's broadcloth and leisure. But with the 1900's came a different kind of restlessness among certain cultivated Negroes of militant temperament who thought his policies lamentably unaggressive. Chief among them was W. E. B. Du Bois, born in western Massachusetts, where anti-Negro prejudice was relatively very light, product of graduate study at Harvard and in Germany, a brilliant mind, and a good hater of whites. He wanted Negroes to congregate in cities and struggle with all the energy of the unjustly deprived against denial of the right to vote, the deleterious effects of caste distinction and discrimination in access to education. Persistent Southern recalcitrance in such matters received supplementary support in 1905 in the publication of *The Clansman* by the Reverend Thomas Dixon, Jr., a Carolina-born Baptist once ornamenting Northern pulpits but a classic example of the racist-minded Southern parson. This best-selling novel, following his anti-Reconstruction fiction called *The Leopard's Spots* (1902), went far beyond Page in glorifying the Ku Klux Klan and depicting the Negro as a bestial menace. Northern Negroes' bitter protests against a dramatized version of *The Clansman* were supported by such respected figures as Jane Addams of Hull House. But that did not keep D. W. Griffith, great technical innovator of the movies, from gloatingly screening it in 1914 as *The Birth of a Nation,* thereby fathering the so-called revival of the Ku Klux Klan in the 1920's.

Meanwhile, the sickening Atlanta race riot of 1906 and the persisting savagery of lynchings had been making Du Bois' approaches feel more pertinent to impatient Negroes than Washington's admitted temporizings possibly could. Within a few years Northern Negroes and their white sympathizers had formed the National Association for the Advancement of Colored People, and Du Bois was editing their magazine, the *Crisis*. This organization, now under fire from the Black-Power-minded for lack of aggressiveness, then represented a new militancy. The *Crisis* cogently deplored the Tuskegee approach, and understandably Washington preferred to cooperate with the National Urban League, founded in 1911 to look after Negroes migrating into cities, particularly to bring them together with employers offering appropriate jobs.

For the nation at large Booker T. Washington remained Mr. Negro, giving the well-meaning white man a living stereotype as foil for the subhuman, gaudy creature of the comic papers. He died secure in that role in 1915. But the future lay with the NAACP and their agitation for integration that is still going on. Today's articulate Negroes regard him as an outstanding Uncle Tom, of course. That he was, in their sense of the phrase, though not the truckler that the epithet usually implies. It also fits well, however, when one considers not the current distorted notion of the original Uncle Tom but the powerful Christian actually shown in Mrs. Stowe's book who deplored slavery primarily because it so warped the souls of both slaves and masters. Washington once said that "hating the white man did him no harm and . . . was narrowing up my soul and making me a good bit less of a human being. I . . . quit hating the white man." [81] His thoughts were often as broad as his own shoulders, though the psychological idiom and economic range of his ideas was patently narrow. John Spencer Bassett, a great Southerner, as well as an authority on the history of North Carolina, told Dixie in 1903 that this Negro was "the greatest man, save General Lee, born in the South in a hundred years." [82] Du Bois, bitter contemner of all Washington stood for, nevertheless summed him up well: "He instilled into the Negroes a new respect for labor and impressed upon the whites the value of the Negro as a worker. His earnestness, shrewd common sense and statesmanlike finesse in interracial contacts mark his greatness; and Tuskegee Institute stands as his magnificent monument." [83]

As it happened, in the same years when Washington was trying to make Negroes count as potential staid good citizens, other Negroes of distinctly unstaid habits were endowing the nation with its second kind of Negro music—ragtime. It first came to general notice as a novelty adding its bit to the many-layered cacophony of the ever-memorable Midway at the Chicago Fair. But it had been developing for years in Mississippi River towns. The basic device was "a highly syncopated air played [on the piano with the right hand] against a regularly accented beat in the bass."[84] Some ascribe its origin to honky-tonk pianists' efforts to make a piano sound like a banjo—the Negroes' own instrument long conspicuous on the minstrels' stage. Its background remains misty in spite of devoted experts' efforts to piece it together. It probably shared some ancestors with jazz, particularly the syncopated treatment of march tunes in the New Orleans

Negroes' marching bands. But jazz, like the tradition of the blues, remained latent so far as the general white public was concerned until the eve of World War I, whereas ragtime was coming up the river by 1890. The ensuing decade saw it well established in the night places of St. Louis, a river town of wide-open habits. In Sedalia, Missouri, in the center of the state, site of the annual state fair, certain Negro pianists, most notably Tom Turpin and his disciple, Scott Joplin, were working out the first classic ragtime compositions, such as Joplin's "Maple Leaf Rag."

Why the term *rag* is no clearer than the early history of the style. It was essentially a piano creation, the left hand bumping away in steady march time, the right performing miracles of syncopation, a sort of exultant stumble, in exhilarating contrast. Its aggressive lightheartedness was far from the cathartic sadness of spirituals, and an expert ragtime player could, as Cousin Egbert Floud said of the quondam Klondike dance-hall girl in *Ruggles of Red Gap,* "make a piano simply stutter itself to death." [85] It had the get-up-and-*dance* feeling of an Irish reel. It had penetrated to New York City's cabaret world by 1897 and was pumped thence all over the country by the song publishers concentrated on Tin Pan Alley. In 1904 Louis C. Elson's grave *The History of American Music* was indignant about ragtime as a "false vein . . . derived from the negro music of the South. . . . The plantation music sometimes employs syncopation, but it certainly does not suffer from such a St. Vitus's dance. . . . This rubbish must be cleared away before a true use can be made of the plantation music as a folk-song foundation." [86] When the turkey trot, grizzly bear, bunny hug and other zoologically hyperkinetic diversions invaded the American dance floor after 1910, they were collectively known as the ragtime dances. By then, of course, the style was being done to death and was approaching extinction in merger with jazz, its more elaborate cousin, already about to follow ragtime's path up the river to Chicago and then eastward. Not that jazz was likely to make Mr. Elson feel any better.

On an August morning in 1897 Julia Ward Howe, a devout as well as witty and important woman, thought that the unsatisfactory state of her soul required her to pray for some "direct and definite service which I might render" to some worthy cause. By noon she had what she took to be an answer—a call from a reporter for the New York *Journal* asking her to "write something to help the young Cuban girl who is in danger of being sent to the Spanish Penal Colony [Ceuta] in Africa."[87] Mrs. Howe obliged by writing an appeal to the Pope for intervention in the case, and the reporter cabled it off. She was not personally acquainted with the Pope but seems to have assumed that, as may have been the case, he had heard of her. Nor did she know much about the "young Cuban girl," a certain Evangelina Cosio y Cisneros. Had she ascertained the actual facts, she would have learned that she was being used as tool in the most flagrant example yet known of what was coming to be called Yellow

Journalism. For the last two years the New York *Journal* had been the property, expensive pride and joy and journalistic laboratory of William Randolph Hearst, a rich young man from San Francisco with abilities far greater than his emotional balance, and the Cisneros case was his master-piece, the finest deliberate publicity buildup since Barnum had sent the nation off its head about a stolid Swedish singer named Jenny Lind.

Señorita Cosio y Cisneros was the pretty daughter of a zealot in the current Cuban rebellion against Spain who had been sentenced to a prison on the Isle of Pines off the southern coast of Cuba. Daughter went there and, presumably with a view to forcing release of her father, used herself as bait to enable her rebel friends to kidnap the commandant of the prison. The plot was broken up, and she was imprisoned in Havana to await trial. A *Journal* correspondent interviewed her and filed a story saying that her only crime had been resisting the commandant's dishonorable advances, that she now had to share noisome quarters with the worst prostitutes in Havana, and that she had been sentenced to twenty years in Ceuta. Actually, according to the American consul at Havana, a warm sympathizer with the rebels, she had decent quarters with other political prisoners, not prostitutes, and had not yet been tried, let alone sentenced. But Hearst, long bent on securing American intervention in the Cuban troubles, blew the episode up into a nationwide crusade in defense of an innocent girl and enlisted American womanhood under the leadership of not only Mrs. Howe but also the mother of President McKinley, the widows of U. S. Grant and Jefferson Davis, and the wife of Senator Marcus A. Hanna, quarterback of the Republican Party. The caper culminated in a comic-opera rescue of the girl with the connivance of bribed guards—a detail omitted from the *Journal*'s accounts making its correspondent a dashing hero—and a great parade in New York City followed by a reception for the Flower of Cuba at Delmonico's and a mass meeting in Madison Square with the principal speech praising the *Journal*'s gallantry made by . . . Henry George, once a newspaperman himself, now the focus of single tax radicalism for the common man.

His presence countenancing such faking, the motive of which was to involve the United States in an unnecessary, empire-building war, is significant. For Yellow Journalism was only the circulation-building aspect of what should be called the New Journalism, which, between 1885 and World War I, was thoroughly remodeling that extremely important institution the American periodical press. The newspaper phase of it was based on championing the cause of Henry George's client, the common man—or anyway the urban immigrant-wageworker aspect of him—by Hearst, Joseph Pulitzer and E. W. Scripps. The scale on which those giants operated would have been impossible without several timely technological improvements open to all papers but most ably exploited by Pulitzer and Hearst. Once they had shown the way, many of their technology-encouraged methods were eagerly imitated. Between them they achieved the first circulations of modern scale, the first institutional promotions of newspapers, the first modern-style display advertising, the first cult of the reporter as romantic leading man.

It began rather sluggishly when, in 1866, a German process for making white paper out of chemically digested wood pulp began to create stenches near Stockbridge, Massachusetts. Wood-pulp paper takes printer's ink well enough, is far cheaper than the waste-rags paper on which printers had always depended, and the supply is not limited by the rag supply. Its first American newspaper user was, appropriately, the German language *Staats-Zeitung,* a leader in the flourishing German-American press. But wide acceptance waited until the 1880's, when the new journalism was about to need it. Meanwhile, photo-engraving had become practical. That enabled ambitious publishers to dress up their papers with pictures for those a bit awkward about reading English or otherwise susceptible to curiosity appeal unobtainable when the page was solid reading matter. Now an artist's line-drawing could be made quickly into a line-cut exactly reproducing it on the page, instead of waiting for a highly skilled crafts-man to cut it into printing shape on a wooden block—a process fast enough for weekly or monthly publications but not for daily papers. Soon it also meant the halftone—a photographic trick that made a photograph into a metal plate furred with dots in varying densities that printed off on paper a recognizable version of the original.

At once the political cartoon, long the monopoly of the weeklies, was at home in the dailies, even on the front page—an innovation that made much talk when Pulitzer's New York *World* was pillorying James G. Blaine during the Presidential campaign of 1884. The daily-paper adver-tiser, long confined to straight typography, could now incorporate in his advertisements pictures of his face—as W. L. Douglas did for his mail-order shoes and Mrs. Lydia Pinkham for her medicine for female com-plaints—or, if he liked, of his factory belching smoke as it turned out

Towers and battlements romantically ornament a huge watch factory of the 1880's.

cookstoves, or even of the particular corset, steamboat, gates-ajar collar or bicycle that he was recommending. As pictures broke up the previously uniform-gray newspaper page, makeup became a skill in its own right, an element that could make or break circulation. As photographic films and cameras became faster, the news photographer, impudently confronting the world with camera in one hand and flashgun in the other, was added to the newspaper payroll with frequently curious consequences on the practice of journalism.

Principal source of the New Journalism was not Hearst, who was rather a Johnny-come-lately, but Joseph Pulitzer, a strange figure. His family had been prosperous half-Jewish Hungarian bourgeois. When they fell on hard times, the tall, slender boy sought a career in European armies, but his weak eyes ruled him out. Like so many other Central Europeans at loose ends in the early 1860's, he seized the opportunity to secure a free passage to America by enlisting in the Union Army. When the ship reached Boston, he swam ashore ahead of his fellow recruits in order to collect his own enlistment bounty instead of seeing it go to the shipping agent. He had some hard service in the Union cavalry in the last year of the war, then drifted to the large German colony in St. Louis. After much odd-jobbing, free-lancing, becoming a crack reporter for the local German language press, learning political ins and outs, studying law, and being admitted to the bar, he raked together the resources to merge two English language dailies into the St. Louis *Post-Dispatch.* It flourished under his imaginative management. Within five years he was in New York City taking over at the asking price the New York *World,* a conservative daily consistently losing money for its bored owner, Jay Gould, the glum but gaudy manipulator of railroads. The Brooklyn Bridge, then the greatest feat of American engineering—albeit designed by German-reared John A. Roebling—was about to open. When it did, a three-column cut of it was in the middle of the new *World*'s front page—an unprecedented bit of flash betokening that after Pulitzer was through with the American daily press, it would never be the same again.

Four years of brilliant toil to revolutionize his new paper so overworked his eyes and nerves that he had to retire from active management. He spent the remaining twenty-three years of his life, much of it on his yacht, directing the *World* by remote control, having the papers and a vast number of other things read to him and dictating voluminous but always keen-edged instructions to his executive officers. By 1900 he had invented or made first major use of not only daily newspaper illustrations but also the magazine-style Sunday supplement, the comics, the sports page and outsize type for headlines. That he created for use during the Spanish-American War. He soon came to hate it and tried to revert to more conservative methods, but Hearst's *Journal,* the *World*'s aggressive rival, had taken it up, and there was no turning back.

The other side of the coin was a deliberate policy of covering and printing what would please the underprivileged and championing their interests as against those of the powerful and prosperous. Pulitzer's youth

among liberal-minded Germans in St. Louis had combined with the back-
stairs disillusionment so common among newspapermen to make him a
lifelong enemy of entrenched privilege even after he became a multimillionaire yacht owner from the profits of helping the underdog. Allan Nevins credits him and his staff with perfecting, "if they did not invent,
the use of the news columns to support . . . exposure . . . of municipal graft, state corruption and business abuses," and points out that his
original program in 1883 included "a federal income tax, inheritance
taxes, thorough civil reform, a revenue tariff and relentless prosecution of
corruption" [88]—all without rigidly aligning the paper with either of the
principal political parties. Pulitzer's sincerity in caring about the weak
and exploited is unquestionable, yet it was convenient that one hand
washed the other. There were so many underdogs that to create a paper they wanted to buy every day was highly profitable.

   In New York City at the time most of the underdogs were Irish, German and Scandinavian, so the doings and special ethnic points of view of
those groups were most cordially handled—a pleasing novelty. Pulitzer
imposed on both the *World* and the *Evening World* (later teamed with it)
strict rules against hurting the feelings of the foreign-born by attributing
broken English or dialect to individuals. (It is ironical that it was the
World that in the mid-1920's, when Pulitzer was ten years dead, delighted
its readers with Milt Gross' Nize Baby sketches in East Side Jewish dialect.) As the Italians began to bulk large in New York City, they received
similar courtesies and coverage. But he seems never to have required
equal regard for Negroes. This may have been tactful recognition that
they were quite as unwelcome among Germans, Irish and Italians as
among any other whites. Or, as George Juergens, a recent student of the
early *World,* suggests, it may have come of his early life in a semi-South-
ern city and his marriage to a girl distantly related to Jefferson Davis. For
its battles for genuinely good causes did not imply that the *World* was a
journalistic angel. Its artificial news-making stunts were often cheap. It
would not truckle to large advertisers, but it accepted advertising from
prostitutes and the keepers of houses of assignation as freely as did the
notorious New York *Herald* and got its share from the advertising of
quack medicines then so important to the American press. As circulation
attracters, sex and juicy details of crimes played up like the end of the
world were even more important in its tactics than the pursuit of crooked
aldermen and presidents of life insurance companies. And the part it
took in getting the dogs of war loosed on the dismayed Spaniards in 1898
was, thanks to greed after circulation, almost as grotesque as William
Randolph Hearst's.

   Hearst's father, one of the ablest mining men in the West, had made millions out of heavy interests in the fabulous Ophir, Homestake and other claims. In 1880 he acquired the San Francisco *Daily Examiner,* a steady money loser but useful in politics. In 1887 he allowed to take charge of it his tall, high-voiced and notably egocentric son recently expelled from Harvard for one crude practical joke too many. The boy's avowed purpose was to make the *Examiner* "imitate the New York *World* . . . the best paper of that class which appeals to the people and depends for its success upon enterprise, energy and a certain startling originality. . . ." [89] The formula would be, as one of his editors told a new reporter, to keep in mind "a gripman on the Powell Street [cable car] line [who] takes his car out at three in the morning, and while he's waiting for the signals, he opens the morning paper. . . . Don't write a single line he can't understand and wouldn't read." [90] His editorial and news-creating stunts were soon outshrieking his model. His paper's battle against the Southern Pacific's effort to avoid repaying its huge construction loan from the federal government was quite Pulitzer-style. The *Examiner*'s circulation rose steadily. In 1895 Hearst secured from his recently widowed mother a war chest of $7,500,000, bought the ailing New York *Journal* for two-thirds of what Pulitzer had originally paid for the *World,* and set out to out-Pulitzer him in his own territory.

He made sweeping use of not only the money but also of his own journalistic genius and ability to hire able lieutenants. He created expensive but attention-demanding promotional stunts like that coast-to-coast bicycle relay. He hired away the *World*'s best cartoonist, T. E. Powers. He hired away most of the staff of the *World*'s extremely successful Sunday supplement including Richard F. Outcault, who drew its pioneering comic "Shantytown," the star of which was a dese-and-dem slum waif in a yellow nightgown widely popular as the Yellow Kid. The *World* continued "Shantytown," drawn thenceforth by George Luks, later an eminent member of the Ashcan school of painters, while Hearst put Outcault on a rival Yellow Kid feature. From the exploitation war between the two came the phrase *yellow journalism.* In general policy for the news and editorial columns, says W. A. Swanberg's recent biography of Hearst, "if the *World* was the organ of the underdog, the *Journal* fought for the *under* underdog." [91] And not long after the battle was joined, the lively American interest in the chronic guerrilla rebellion against Spanish rule in Cuba tempted Hearst into a megalomaniac conviction that the United States should go to war over it and that the *Journal* was the destined instrument to bring that about, incidentally gaining an immense prestige and popularity that would smother the *World.*

He did not succeed in smothering the *World,* which fought back with methods about as raucous and irresponsible as Hearst's own. Pulitzer's competing shrieks against Spain seem not to have been altogether Hearst-inspired. He "once confessed that he had rather liked the idea of a war—not a big one—but one that would arouse interest and give him a chance to gauge the reflex in . . . circulation . . ." [92]—a strangely coldblooded attitude in a man who had seen fighting and thought it miserable. Only after he had set the cost in money and energy against the evanescent circulation gains did he conclude that he "never wanted another." There is no evidence that even that kind of uneasiness ever assailed Hearst. The Cisneros case was representative of the way he cooked up his war. Another crudely cynical, sexy fake involved Richard Harding Davis, the most renowned reporter of the day, and Frederic Remington, outstanding depicter of the cowboy West, both sent to Cuba by Hearst to keep the propaganda spewing. They sent in and the *Journal* made a great splash with a story and drawing showing how Spanish police had boarded an American ship just before she sailed for New York City and publicly stripped and searched three Cuban girls as suspected carriers of insurgent dispatches. Actually neither Davis nor Remington had been there, and the search had been conducted by police matrons in a stateroom. Daily the *Journal*'s (and the *World*'s) headlines screamed and sobbed about Spanish atrocities and gallant Cuban heroes (who were brave enough but needed no lessons from Spaniards in the atrocity line), and Hearst fretted because, no matter how thick he and his rival laid it on with their circulations approaching the magic million mark, war would not come. Remington, bored in Havana, cabled Hearst: "Everything is quiet . . . no war. I wish to return." Hearst's reply is the most famous wire in journalistic history: "Please remain. You furnish the pictures and I'll furnish the war." [93]

With the help of whoever blew up the U.S. battleship *Maine* in Havana Harbor, whether Spanish zealot or Cuban crisis-provoker, Hearst kept his word. He had American opinion so overheated that even when Spain virtually capitulated to all American demands about Cuba, President McKinley did not dare let the fact keep war from being declared. It is widely accepted among historians that the ensuing Spanish-American War was primarily of Hearst's making through what Swanberg admirably sums up as "the orgasmic acme of ruthless, truthless newspaper jingoism" [94]— a startling demonstration of what the New Journalism could do. In the past a paper with national circulation and high prestige such as Horace Greeley's New York *Tribune* could make life miserable for the administration during the Civil War—indeed get credited with forcing the premature advance that led to disaster at Bull Run. In the 1890's it was already lamentably well established that industrial power concentrated on government by bankers and collusive captains of industry could make Washington dance to its tunes. But there was no precedent for a big press playing the same scale of game with different pieces but the same success. Such power in the hands of an irresponsible, obviously megalomaniac temperament like Hearst's could be a social calamity of the same order as the Standard Oil trust.

A probably accidental but striking reminder came in 1901. Governor William Goebel of Kentucky had been shot and killed early in 1900. Ambrose Bierce, a longtime fixture in Hearst's papers who combined high writing skill with the disposition of a molting rattlesnake, presently contributed to Hearst's current war on President McKinley some grimly tasteless verses:

> The bullet that pierced Goebel's breast
> Can not be found in all the West;
> Good reason, it is speeding here
> To stretch McKinley on his bier.[95]

That spring the prospect of McKinley as Republican candidate to succeed himself in the Presidency roused Hearst to mountingly violent attacks on him, during which a staff member on his *Journal* concluded an anti-McKinley editorial with "If bad institutions and bad men can be got rid of only by killing them, then the killing must be done." [96] Hearst had the sentence dropped in late editions, but many remembered both it and the Bierce verses when, six months after McKinley's inauguration for his second term, a dim-witted psychotic who considered himself an anarchist shot and killed him. That the assassin had seen either item in print was never established. The point, however, is that Hearst's own emotional warping made it all too conceivable that some of his henchmen would put such a thing into print. And Bierce, it appeared, was never rebuked.

Lincoln Steffens interviewed Hearst in 1906 while writing a magazine piece about him and a generation later recalled this so widely reprehended figure as "a remarkable man . . . with patience . . . superb tolerance . . . so far ahead of his staffs that they can hardly see him . . . [proposing] to give the people democracy as others of his sort gave charity or an art museum." [97] This sounds strange to those recalling the reactionary Hearst of the post-World War I era. But back when the new journalism was new, Hearst several times sought public office as a radical, though within the regular two-party pattern, and seems to have considered himself some kind of Socialist. Thus to the raucousness of his methods as cause for the well-placed to dislike him was added their natural antagonism to a self-proclaimed friend of the downtrodden and enemy of the interests. And most appropriately it had been a Hearst paper that gave

America of the late 1890's its most evocative symbol of social oppression, "The Man with the Hoe."

The occasion was a painting by the Barbizon-school artist Jean François Millet, showing a simianlike peasant leaning in exhaustion on a hoe handle. A literary-minded California schoolteacher, Edwin Markham, was greatly impressed by the brutalized hardships that it expressed when he saw a reproduction of it in a magazine in the 1880's. When, twelve years later, he saw the original on exhibit in San Francisco, it overwhelmed him. He wrote a blank-verse poem about it and read it to a private gathering that happened to include the editor of Hearst's San Francisco *Examiner,* who was impressed in turn. Published in the Sunday *Examiner,* it swept the nation like *Uncle Tom's Cabin* and *Looking Backward,* universally reprinted, with sermons and lectures based on it and parodies written of it. Markham's name was suddenly as well known as that of Admiral George Dewey, hero of Manila Bay. Indeed one reason for its explosive success may have been its catching the public on the rebound from the brassy exultations of the Spanish-American War. It was all rumbling gloom and social self-accusation, calling to account "masters, lords and rulers in all lands" for the bestialization of the painter's hulking subject, "The emptiness of ages in his face. . . . Stolid and stunned, a brother to the ox. . . .":

> Who loosened and let down this brutal jaw?
> Whose was the hand that slanted back this brow?
> Whose breath blew out the light within this brain?
> Is this the Thing the Lord God made and gave
> To have dominion over sea and land . . . ?

They called it "the battle cry of the next thousand years" and would have set it to music if its lumbering form had not precluded the possibility.

The shoe did not fit too well on the clay feet that America certainly was showing *c.* 1899. The subject was from the Old World to begin with, a peasant thus searing the conscience of one of the few Western nations then lacking a peasantry, a victim of agricultural backwardness, not of the industrial brutalities and neglects that really were stultifying children in cotton mills and slag shovelers in steel mills and should have been uppermost in American minds. Markham's anthropological assumptions about the origin and significance of the creature's head shape reflected pseudo scientific notions of the day that were then under heavy attack. But apparently the public was newly eager to hear the economic powers denounced. "The Man with the Hoe" doubtless did much to loosen up the soil which the muckrakers would begin so successfully and on the whole constructively to cultivate within three years. Doubtless also the national furor created by this journalistic shot in the dark helped confirm Hearst in his policy of ostentatiously backing the common man against the interests.

He was, of course, one of the interests himself, between the family mining and landholding empire and the chain of newspapers that he was soon piecing together coast to coast, with his editors in key cities like Chicago, Pittsburgh, San Francisco and so on taking their lead and much of their copy from his *Journal* or his syndicates. The chain newspaper had long since been invented, however, by Edward Wyllis Scripps, third genius of the new journalism dedicated to the masses. They make a striking trio —the lank, Mephistophelian-bearded, cosmopolitan but self-made Hungarian; the hulking Californian mama's boy born with a spoon of Comstock silver in his mouth; and the half-schooled country lad from Rushville, Illinois, whose newspaperman half-brother, James, infected both his sister and young E. W. with newsprint itch. About all these great journalists had in common was that they were tall and paid no heed to what others thought of the way they lived.

In 1875 James and E. W. founded what was probably the first tabloid daily, the Detroit *Evening News,* a foot wide; then another tabloid, the Cleveland *Penny Press;* then E. W. alone made a going concern of the Cincinnati *Post;* and so on up to a fortune of millions and management by remote control from either a yacht or a hideaway ranch in Southern California. The only city in which Scripps failed to make a paper stick once he started it was St. Louis, where, he later admitted, Pulitzer beat him at his own game. For even before the *World* went upside down for the common people, Scripps' papers were so committed to them that his staffmen spoke habitually of "the C.P." His Cleveland paper, Scripps' intimate aide wrote, "was always on the side of the working man, boosting . . . union labor . . . always on the side of the striker . . . persistent in printing news no matter . . . who or what was hit." [98] In the 1880's such consideration for organized labor in the daily press was extremely scarce. Wealth did little to modify E. W.'s views on labor, which seem to have been as much emotional bias as circulation-building judgment. He was nearing his seventieth year and luxuriously rich when Steffens found him about the only important newspaper owner in America on the side of the McNamaras in their scrape over bombing the Los Angeles *Times.* He seemed to enjoy going out of his way to annoy large advertisers and in 1914 had a tabloid without advertising, the Chicago *Day Book,* actually turning a small profit; World War I sent the price of paper too high for it to survive. But then he treated himself no better than advertisers. When his personal affairs got into court—once when he was arrested for riding an improperly shod horse; once when a former mistress tried to blackmail him—he told his editors to go right ahead and print all about it.

In fact, one scents a somewhat nihilistic imp in Scripps. He grieved conventional minds by maintaining that the secret of his strive-and-succeed story was "Never to do today what by any means can be put off till tomorrow and never to do himself what he could get anyone else to do half as well as he could do it." [99] In a sort of creed that he formulated when founding the Newspaper Enterprise Association in 1902, he declared that "thrift is not the greatest of the virtues . . . life insurance . . . [is] one of the greatest and most costly modern vices." The rest of it was an able summary of many of the assumptions of the muckraking movement: ". . . capital is a danger; large capital is never got by perfectly fair means; capitalists should be kept alert defending what they have and not be left . . . secure behind obsolete and corruptly obtained laws . . . we should use and guard natural resources with an eye to the future of the American people. . . ." [100]

The battle in the Sunday papers between Pulitzer's and Hearst's rival Yellow Kids was so bitter because they were powerful circulation-bait. Soon multiplication and syndication of such storytelling cartoon panels humorous at least in intent, dialogue issuing from the characters' mouths in balloons, gave America a whole new tradition in popular entertainment and a new phrase for it—*the funny papers*. Sunday after Sunday in crude but sometimes highly stylized drawing and cruder color Hans und Fritz and der Captain and Mama and der Inspector, and the Newlyweds and Old Doc Yak with his automobile and Buster Brown and his dog Tige (Outcault's successor to the Yellow Kid) and Foxy Grandpa always outpractical-joking his grandsons returned to the family living room. Bud and sis wheedling mom or pop into "reading us the funnies" became as much a Sunday institution as overeating.

Each funny-paper episode was self-contained—no story line lasting weeks as in today's comics, no cliff-hanging finales. The artist used a full page of four to eight panels, sometimes two pages' worth, and his end product was more like a movie short. Indeed the funnies were obvious ancestors first of slapstick one-reelers and then of animated cartoons. The circulation-building continuity of interest lay in the characters themselves. Their catchwords, foibles and appearance never varied whether they fell through the ice or got snatched away by the trailing grapnel of a balloon. Children, always conservative, knew they could count on Maud the Mule's kicking somebody, usually her farmer owner, half a mile in the last panel. In great contrast with today's fashion in daily comic strips, the universal purpose was to be funny. Not until the late 1920's did infusions of melodrama and sentimentality begin to make the term *comic* meaningless. Appeal to adults, as well as to children, was so profitably strong that F. (for Frederick) Opper, Hearst's leading political cartoonist, consistently devoted much time and energy to the chunkily drawn chronicles of Maud the Mule, and Happy Hooligan with his triplet nephews, all wearing tin cans for hats, and Alphonse and Gaston, forever stuck in their *après vous, monsieur* routine like the figures on Keats' Grecian urn.

In time the dailies began to borrow this surefire circulation builder from the Sunday papers, and the term *comic strip* came in because the daily versions consisted of only a single strip of a few horizontally joined panels. Early in the field was the San Francisco *Chronicle* with Bud Fisher's gangly character named A. Mutt, soon joined by a stubby, silk-hatted crony, Little Jeff. In both Sundays and dailies the episodes were usually barbaric in tone with emphasis on ethnic clichés—German in "The Katzenjammer Kids," Irish in "Bringing Up Father," Negro wherever an imbecile comic butt as waiter or watermelon addict was needed—did much to perpetuate stereotypes. But the funnies also had a cohesive effect. They gave all the polyglot consumers of the new journalism a common set of references much as churchgoing people used to have in common familiarity with Bible stories.

The New Journalism's exposures of corruption and social abuses were not a new idiom. The New York *Times,* for instance, had had a large hand in tearing down New York City's Tweed Ring. The savage anti-Tammany cartoons drawn for *Harper's Weekly* by German-born Thomas Nast did even more. Henry Demarest Lloyd's scathing descriptions of the unholy alliance between the railroads and Standard Oil had found wide readership in Howells' *Atlantic Monthly.* But Pulitzer had made such material a steady circulation-building institution like the Sunday funnies. The Pulitzer papers thus filled, Juergens suggests, "a function not unlike that which brought fame to muck-rakers like Upton Sinclair and Lincoln Steffens; indeed, in many ways, [Pulitzer] qualified as first of the breed." [101] Lloyd had the better title to that. Nevertheless, there is a clear apostolic succession between the New York *World*'s reliance on exposure stories and the magazines' elaborate expansion of the technique soon after 1900.

The journalistic tool for the purpose came into being in the 1890's in the shape of the monthly ten-cent magazine with wide national circulation. The first was Frank A. Munsey's lavishly illustrated *Munsey's Magazine.* The new halftone method of reproducing photographs and artists' contributions was as important in developing its vast number of readers as in making the Sunday newspaper so successful. Soon after competitors, particularly the *Cosmopolitan* and *McClure's,* came into the field, the public's intense interest in the Spanish-American War took these circulations to new heights. Editorial enterprise, serializing the most conspicuous novelists of the day and splashing pictures around more freely than ever, kept them climbing. Tremors premonitory of what would be known as muckraking were felt in an antitrust piece in *Munsey's* in 1900 and in an anti-steel-trust piece in the *Cosmopolitan* in 1901. Not only the Pulitzer and Hearst papers but also the humorous weeklies—*Puck, Judge, Life,* a field born of German-Americans' skills,— had long been sniping at the trusts. But the main storm was brewing up in the research on the Standard Oil Company being done by Ida M. Tarbell, a formidably able lady writer reared in the early Pennsylvania oilfields who had already created much of the success of *McClure's* with her scholarly but readable serial biographies of Napoleon and Lincoln.

Her monumental findings, impressively expanding on Lloyd's work of 1881, began to appear in the magazine late in 1902. At the same time Lincoln Steffens, an extremely canny newspaperman also working for *McClure's,* had grown fascinated by the stenches developed in large cities by the triangular alliances of plutocrats, politicians and the underworld. He launched on a series of spot exposures not of New York City or San Francisco as usual but of St. Louis, Minneapolis, Pittsburgh, Philadelphia, rubbing the nation's nose in the dismaying fact that vice and corruption were no monopolies of the Tenderloin and the Barbary Coast. Still another former newspaperman on *McClure's* payroll, Ray Stannard Baker, was simultaneously getting cogent copy out of the high-handedness and occasional underhandedness of labor leaders. In handling such subjects, the monthly magazine had advantages over newspapers. Its less demanding deadlines and ability to use longer articles enabled it to pull together and get national attention for accumulated data about bosses, boodle, collusion, lobbying and monopoly that newspapers could handle only in confusing bits and pieces—and for at best a regional audience.

Shocked but titillated by the scale and flagrancy of what it thus learned of, already sensitized by previous attacks on trusts and news of local corruptions, the public swarmed to buy and read *McClure's,* and rival magazines swarmed to emulate it. At least half-inadvertently S. S. McClure, the volubly flighty Scotch-Irishman whom Robert Louis Stevenson had tried to portray in *The Wrecker,* had created the highest expression of the New Journalism by recruiting a superbly able staff at a time when social uneasiness was on the rise. Soon *Collier's* dropped its price to ten cents and joined the game. In the next few years not only were trusts and high-placed chiselers raked over the coals by magazine reporters, but the chicaneries of Wall Street, the iniquities of child labor, white slavery, life insurance companies, patent medicines were also well and truly exposed. Hearst bought the *Cosmopolitan* for the string of magazines that he was assembling and sent it crusading against big business' relations to the legislatures that then elected U.S. Senators. David Graham Phillips, the newspaperman-novelist on the assignment, swung so wildly that he drew a public rebuke from President Theodore Roosevelt. Though sympathetic with much that *McClure's, Collier's* and the rest had been printing, Roosevelt put the permanent label of "muckraking" on the movement by likening editors going on and on with repetitive exposures to the character in *The Pilgrim's Progress* who kept his eyes on the filth he was raking together when all the while an angel above him was offering to trade a celestial crown for his muckrake. That same year, however, muckraking resumed its upward curve when most of *McClure's* editorial team went into business for themselves as purchasers of the *American Magazine.* Further enlisting William Allen White and Finley Peter Dunne, whose Mr. Dooley had previously been ornamenting *Collier's,* they added another big gun to the battery that had already been shelling Roosevelt's malefactors of great wealth so mercilessly.

By 1912, in the judgment of Frank Luther Mott, historian of American journalism, muckraking was dead. Some of the reforms it had sought, such as direct election of U.S. Senators and curbing of child labor, had been wholly or partly achieved. The edge of public interest in many of its other topics had worn dull. Yet it left a huge residue of cultural effect. The emotional net of it was a lasting uneasiness about corporations tending to the monopolistic—not from hostility to size as such, not from labor-oriented dislike of the capitalist as employer, but because it had been so well demonstrated that disproportionate concentrations of economic power almost inevitably led to corruption of government on all levels. And the magazines themselves were institutions. Observing them at the height of the uproar in 1904, H. G. Wells thought them a unique and valuable medium of "grave national discussion" [102] read not merely by a governing elite but by concerned millions. Until television chipped away their importance in advertising, they never quite lost that function, part of what made Americans the most magazine-reading people in the world. The rest was the result of George Horace Lorimer's extraordinary five-cent weekly, the *Saturday Evening Post,* and of the triumphant women's magazines, usually launched as media for advertising paper dress patterns, then mingling popular fiction with household, medical and culinary advice. And both the *Post* and its sister in the Curtis Publishing Company, Edward Bok's *Ladies' Home Journal,* had been dabbling in muckraking at the right time.

The soberness of the muckrakers' factual reporting enhanced its social usefulness. But one of the chief monuments of the tradition, as conspicuous as Miss Tarbell on Standard Oil and Steffens' *The Shame of the Cities,* was a hard-breathing piece of fiction, *The Jungle,* which disconcerted its author and backers by doing much good in an unanticipated quarter but very little in the expected one. Its author, Upton Sinclair, a zealous young Socialist with literary urges, was planning a great, grim depiction of what capitalism did to the immigrant workers. On $500 supplied by a Socialist periodical, he lived for seven weeks in the stockyards-meat packing district of Chicago gathering data among the welter of new emigrant nationalities there struggling to adjust to the New World. Breathing in the combined stenches of the plants of the Big Five meatpackers was in itself an alarming experience. ". . . you could literally taste it, as well as smell it . . . take hold of it . . . an elemental odor, raw and crude . . . almost rancid, sensual and strong." [103] Out of it he shaped the story of a family of Lithuanians harassed by real estate swindlers, venal foremen, speedups, blacklistings, death overtaking some by accident or in childbed, prostitution lying in wait for the girls . . . The hero eventually turns to Socialism, and it all ends with a Socialist leader exhorting a crowd of the exploited to "Organize! Organize! . . . We shall bear down the opposition . . . sweep it before us—and Chicago will be ours! *Chicago will be ours!* CHICAGO WILL BE OURS!" [104]

It was pellucidly earnest, as Sinclair always has been, and approached literary merit rather closer than his many, many other books. He dedicated it to "The Workingmen of America" and procured it a preface by his fellow Socialist novelist Jack London, predicting that "It will open countless ears that have been deaf to Socialism! . . . It depicts what our country really is, the home of oppression and injustice, a nightmare of misery, an inferno of suffering, a human hell, a jungle of wild beasts. . . . What 'Uncle Tom's Cabin' did for the black slaves, 'The Jungle' has a large chance to do for the white slaves of to-day." He also warned that the capitalists would encourage "a conspiracy of silence . . . the deadliest danger this book has to face." [105] Silence did not ensue. Serialized in the Socialist press, *The Jungle* caused a promising intraparty stir. The first five regular trade publishers to whom the book rights were offered thought it too hot to handle. But Doubleday, Page and Company agreed to consider it if its content stood investigation. A responsible checkup indicated that, as Mark Sullivan later wrote, it was "a not too greatly exaggerated bit of truth about American industrial life as it was at that time—a 'Jungle' could have been written about the coal mines, the steel-mills. . . ." [106] The firm published it and immediately had a roaring best seller on their hands as word leaped from horrified reader to horrified reader.

Socialism did not benefit much, however. Public attention concentrated not on the scandalous miseries of the proletariat that Socialism would sweep away but on the luridly nauseating incidental details of Chicago's handling of the meats that the whole nation had been eating. The Big Five packers had long asserted the efficiency with which they utilized every scrap of the animal, hair, bones and all, by boasting that they made money out of "everything but the squeal" of the pig. Now it appeared that the economics of by-products was being carried to dismaying lengths. The packers' deviled ham was minced tripe dyed red. Much of their lamb and mutton was goat. They kept down the rats in the noisome packing plants by putting out poisoned bread, and then dead rats, bread and all went into the hoppers of oddments used for human consumption in sausages and such. And—this was the bit that no reader ever managed to forget—now and again an employee slipped on a wet floor, fell into a vat of boiling oddments, and "was overlooked for days, till all but [his] bones . . . had gone out to the world as Durham's Pure Leaf Lard." [107] No wonder that, as a packers' spokesman told a committee of the U.S. House of Representatives, the sale of meat and meat products fell more than half.

Instead of making his countrymen Socialists, Sinclair had only made them self-convicted involuntary cannibals. It dismayed him and disappointed his backers. His luck was also bad with Helicon Hall, the radical cooperative community in New Jersey into which he put much of his royalties. But he had given President Roosevelt the final increment of public indignation against the food processors needed to force through a reluctant Senate both a sweeping reform in federal inspection of meat handling and the Pure Food and Drugs bill that federal agencies and women's clubs had been demanding for years. The latter is usually associated—and justly—with the name of Dr. Harvey W. Wiley, the devoted chief chemist of the U.S. Department of Agriculture, who was its father and doughtiest champion. But that little blue-ink U.S. inspection stamp on a cut of meat at the supermarket represents an inadvertent great service done you by Upton Sinclair—who leaned toward vegetarianism himself and for a while there had made vegetarians of a large number of Americans.

His literary purpose probably had been to use on an American subject the intense consciousness of social issues and the dogged documentation that ambitious American writers had long been admiring in the novels of certain Frenchmen and Russians. That is, tardily they were following the lead of painting and women's fashions in turning to the Continent. They usually began by reading Balzac, probably in translation; then Tolstoy, certainly in translation; presently Dostoevsky and Turgenev; eventually Maupassant and Zola so far as their works could be obtained in a culture that censored "September Morn" at the behest of Anthony Comstock and ran Maxim Gorky out of the country because he was not married to the lady he was traveling with. Since translation bulked so large in such seminal reading, whatever stylistic merits the originals had were largely lost. Content and organization were the whole appeal. That led to enduring consequences. Between the mid-1890's and 1950 the basic orientation of serious American novelists was, like that of their British counterparts, Continental.

Howells' development was well along when he encountered these influences. He wrote perspicaciously and admiringly about some of them, but their effect on his work was minor. His juniors with promising talent, however—Stephen Crane, Hamlin Garland, Frank Norris, for instance—fell bleakly in love with fiction as artificial documentation. Garland's *Main-Traveled Roads* (1891), stories doing numb justice to the sordid emptiness of trans-Mississippi farm life, could have been a translation from some grim Scandinavian of his own generation, say Knut Hamsun. Crane's *Maggie: A Girl of the Street* (1892), duly recognized at the time as a milestone in American fiction, was a creditable text for an unwritten sermon on social compassion. His renowned *The Red Badge of Courage* showed what a promising young man who had read Tolstoy might have felt about being under fire had he ever been there.* Norris' trilogy, *The Epic of the Wheat,* of which only the first two books were completed (*The Octopus* in 1901, *The Pit* in 1903), smelled of the magazine serial and the high-strung Broadway play, but the intention was homage to Balzac from a young man who had lived in Paris and read him in the original. The authority of the trend is clear in the case of Theodore Dreiser after 1900. In various degrees Garland, Crane and Norris had most of the basic abilities of the writer as such. Dreiser had chiefly the ability to organize a text, gained in competent newspaper reporting, and the ineradicable conviction, gained from fellow reporters admiring the great Frenchmen, that he had the makings of a novelist. Between

* Thirty years earlier Major John W. De Forest, who had been frequently under Confederate fire, had written about it far better and got himself something of a reputation for inquisitive realism in a competent novel, *Miss Ravenel's Conversion from Secession to Loyalty;* but he was ahead of his time, or anyway of American literary fashion.

his persistence and the prestige of the kind of novel he had in mind, he succeeded in being taken as one.

The basic difficulty was that even the best of these hard-driving young fellows was skewed by literary hero worship of august exotic models. Their imitativeness had something in common with the Anglophilia of the son of a natural-gas fortune tooling his English-built four-in-hand up Fifth Avenue on the way to his half-timbered Tudor manor house in Westchester. Yet their sedulous apery continued to find favor among the socially conscious and knowingly cultivated. Early doubts of its validity were hinted at in the Chicago *Record* by a young newspaperman, George Ade, summarizing the prevalent kinds of novels. Type Ten was "The dull, gray Book of the Simple Annals of John Gardensass. In Chapter I he walks along the Lane, stepping first on one Foot and then on the Other, enters a House by the Door, and sits in a four-legged wooden Chair, looking out through a Window with Glass in it. Book denotes careful observation. Nothing happens until Page 150. Then John decides to sell the Cow. In the Final Chapter he sits on a fence and Whittles. True Story, but What's the Use?" [108] Yet this was not Philistinism. Ade was also as dubious as any budding prairie Zola about Type Eight, "The Book that gets away with one Man asking another: 'By Jove, who is that Dazzling Beauty in the Box?'" and Type Nine, "The Book that tells all about Society and how Tough it is. Even the Women drink Brandy and Soda, smoke Cigarettes, and Gamble. . . ." [109]

Within a few years another Chicago newspaperman, young Joseph Medill Patterson, published a novel that managed memorably to combine Types Eight and Nine with an aching social conscience. The author, as his full name showed, was an heir of the eminent family prosperously publishing the Chicago *Tribune,* who were allied with the great McCormick farm-machinery fortune. He probably found it simple to get a job on the *Tribune* when he left Yale. His undergraduate observations of the lives rich people led, particularly in the effete Northeast, seem to have revolted him to the point of considering himself a Socialist. Out of these strains came *A Little Brother of the Rich,* the story of a handsome young Midwesterner, penniless but ambitious, who starts to work his way through Yale—at least the book was not autobiographical—makes rich friends and, discarding his fiancée at home, rises toward the top of the Fifth Avenue-Newport world at the price of his own soul.

What made this a conspicuous item was, of course, the notion of a young plutocrat with a famous name turning radical and exposing the ways of his kind. In its unintentional travesty of the Type Eight idiom it was, however, also notable. For instance, the hero, enmeshed by a lissome, married plutocratess on a yacht, says to her: "Surely this is an iron and unlovely code which forbids one to observe and perhaps inhale the fragrance of beautiful flowers which now and again border the path which one takes along his walk of life, even though one knows that the garden where those flowers grow belongs to another man." [110] *A Little Brother* belongs in history for other reasons. Writing such things so purged him that he doffed his Socialism and became one of the nation's most effective mass-circulation publishers as founder of the tabloid New York *Daily News*. And in 1906, when F. Scott Fitzgerald was still in knickerbockers, *A Little Brother* casually tossed in an episode strangely prophetic of the novel of the 1920's. A melancholy adulteress, wearing heavy lipstick and smoking cigarettes, dines with her millionaire lover in a conveniently dubious roadhouse. Between them they drink four cocktails, three pints of champagne and three brandies, then drive away in his long, low, powerful automobile, and get killed trying to beat a train to a crossing.

Most of the successful novels with which *A Little Brother* had to compete were more professional but had few other virtues. Edith Wharton and Ellen Glasgow had been feeling their way into their work for more or less a decade with great profit to literature and some to their publishers. But the really moneymaking woman writers attracted hundreds of thousands of women and girls with slightly varying versions of the Cinderella story: Small girl alone in the world, not attractive in the blue-eyes-and-golden-hair way but plucky and alert; is handed over to bleakly severe adults; after 300 pages of alternating comic and teary episodes is taken to adults' bosoms all softened up by her winsomeness; after thus establishing *Rebecca of Sunnybrook Farm* (the prototype of this highly lucrative convention), do a sequel of Rebecca's young womanhood a few years later. The appeal to the large number of girls and women not qualified to look like magazine covers was irresistible.

The equivalent for men was likely to be red-blooded and outdoorsy with a strong-chinned young engineer, say, in high-laced boots and a flannel shirt and a tall, lissome girl with gray eyes falling in and out of his violently active life until completion of the dam, in spite of bandits or unions, gives them time to fall into each other's arms. Or it could be all crusty but lovable millionaires and made and broken fortunes with a strong-chinned young man finally routing the swindlers and convincing a tall, lissome, gray-eyed girl that it was not he who had bankrupted her father with the big deal in Amalgamated Pitchfork. Or the setting could be historical with a similar young couple working it out from opposite sides of the Revolution or the Civil War with George Washington or Robert E. Lee stepping out of the wings at one point. The young people looked so much alike not only because of the author's descriptions but also because they were probably drawn by the same illustrator in a day when who did the illustrations for popular fiction was almost as important as who wrote it. Whether among the Kentucky mountains with John Fox, Jr., or out in the great open spaces with Zane Grey and Harold Bell Wright, their clean young healthiness had to be stylishly spelled out for the reader in line drawings done at considerable expense. When the illustrator was Howard Chandler Christy or E. W. Kemble, the expense was even greater, but then their work would almost sell the book by itself.

Despair over the poor quality of the most popular novels of a given decade has been endemic among us for 100 years, usually with justification. But not since World War I have things been quite as bad as when Gene Stratton Porter's idylls of the Indiana swamps were competing for attention with Eleanor H. Coburn's *Mollie Make-Believe* in 1911. By then Jack London was following his egocentric bent into sadistic radicalism, and Owen Wister's best was behind him. Of the other six writers then listed by a knowing editor as commanding at least twenty cents a word from the mass-circulation magazines—a sound enough criterion of popular appeal—only young Booth Tarkington had the real writer's wrist, and he would never quite do with it all that it could have accomplished.

Those standard young couples with whom Robert W. Chambers and George Barr McCutcheon provided the illustrators had another striking family resemblance. Until the last few pages they never laid a finger on each other unless he had to rescue her from some fearful animal or mineral threat or she found him bleeding after a dire mishap and had to bandage him up with a strip torn from her petticoat. It was a world openly given to jokes about spooning on buggy rides and secretly fond of jokes about shotgun marriages and salesmen and farmers' daughters, but in the rarefied circles frequented by these romantic waxworks standards of proper behavior were as high as the heroine's boned net collar, which rose to her earlobes. Persistent efforts toward a Continental realism occasionally flawed this convention but seldom penetrated the mass market of magazine serials and well-established popular novelists.

In 1907, however, the year after *The Jungle,* the veil of the temple of decorum had been rent from top to bottom by a novel of equal notoriety. Its author was slim, red-haired, blue-eyed, beautiful—the authority is Mark Twain, on whom she called seeking support for some newspaper publicity—an Englishwoman wafted across the Atlantic by the furor caused by her having written a juicily romantic tale about an aristocratic Briton's affair with an even more aristocratic woman of mystery of swooningly perfect beauty, cultivation and taste in bedroom arrangements. For *Three Weeks*—the immediately notorious title of the book —in a mountain hideaway of more than Occidental luxury they explore each other's talents for elegant and *almost* explicitly described carnalities; then at the lady's insistent instance, they part. Eventually the hero learns that she is the previously childless queen or grand duchess of Weissnichtwo and has reason to believe himself father of the newborn crown prince. But they will never meet again . . . Mark Twain described the literary workmanship of *Three Weeks* as excellent. He was usually a better judge of others' works. But then few authors had an exquisite complexion to go with red hair and a dainty figure.

In the 1920's Mrs. or, as she preferred to be called, Madam Glyn became Hollywood's empress of hard-breathing scenarios and must also be held responsible for the use of *It* as synonym for sex appeal. In 1907 her significance was less crude. Even while the queen was voluptuously pulling the young fellow down on the fur rug with her, she was unmistakably the dominant female. It is she who chooses him, gets all possible sentimental and physical use out of him, and then turns him away to yearn the rest of his life. The many, many women who surreptitiously read *Three Weeks* were likely to conclude not just that the erotic impulse is so glorious that society has no business restricting it— which is what Madam Glyn said she meant—but that woman is essentially and rightly sovereign and man the born vassal.

George Ade, Theodore Dreiser—both Indiana-born and Chicago-trained, after which likeness ceases—and young Patterson were only some of the variegated, spontaneous bloomings of the Midwestern newspaper press. It also gave to the world Artemus Ward; Eugene Field, creator of the newspaper column, as well as of the calamitously sentimental elegy for "Little Boy Blue"; William Allen White; Brand Whitlock, for whom newspaper experience was a springboard into Progressive reformist politics and diplomacy. Like so many things, this Midwestern press tradition centered on Chicago, and its finest manifestation was wholly Chicagoan—Finley Peter Dunne, a phenomenon of the first order. Born into the second-generation, lace-curtain stratum of Chicago's large Irish population, he had no more college than Howells or Mark Twain, only a book-minded mother and a career in newspapering so precocious that at the age of twenty-one he was city editor of the Chicago *Times*. For the Chicago *Evening Post* in 1893—the fateful year of the Chicago Fair, the completion of Henry Ford's first automobile and the founding of the Anti-Saloon League—he began to create Mr. Martin Dooley, Irish-born saloonkeeper who once a week swabbed off the bar, leaned on his elbows, and, addressing a faithful customer on his way home from shoveling slag in a steel mill, began: "I see be th' pa-a-pers, Hinnissy. . . ."

None of the several illustrators who tried ever drew a credible likeness of Mr. Dooley, though he was soon as real a presence as Huckleberry Finn. One knows only the slow, clear, warbly Irish voice and the easy slide of the shrewdest humor that America has ever produced. With it came a nimble wit and a tart skepticism appropriate in a man whose creator's favorite reading was Montaigne. Sometimes Mr. Dooley was aphoristic. A fanatic "does what he thinks th' Lord wud do if He knew the facts iv th' case." "No man that bears a gredge again' himsilf'll iver be governor iv a state." [111] Oftener he solicitously coaxed a leisurely idea to perfect itself in an arabesque of exquisite exaggerations. In either case the language was as sleekly fitted to content as a leopard's skin is to the muscle and bone beneath—a virtue now obscured for many by Dunne's use of spelling and punctuation to convey Irish brogue, a thing that in that time of rampant ethnic humor, people did not find irksome. The same skill glitters in the nondialect pieces that he wrote for a department called "The Interpreter's House" in the *American Magazine* as foil for its vigorous muckraking. For instance, on Theodore Roosevelt's departure for Africa to shoot big game just after a second Presidential term of heavy conflict with his favorite antagonists, the malefactors of great wealth:

> In a few days he will carry his little guns to the jungle to shoot . . . the vested interests that abound there. Some of them he will cripple and some put out of business for a time. He won't change the jungle much. It will continue to be the jungle. . . . Let us hope that he will not be hooked by the elephant or the rhinoceros, or chewed up by the lion or the tiger or stung into somnolency by the fly that causes the sleeping sickness. Of this last contingency I have small fear. There is more danger that the flies which bite him will spread St. Vitus's dance among the population of Africa.[112]

But "The Interpreter's House" had a shifting cast of characters, whereas Mr. Dooley remained the same, yesterday, today and forever. The scope of acceptance for the Dooley newspaper pieces and the immense popularity they enjoyed collected in successive books over twenty years, covering a far wider spectrum of ideas, events and things than Mark Twain ever touched on, rouse the suspicion that as between the two, Dunne better fitted the notion of a national humorist.

*   *   *

Among the pictures singled out by Samantha Allen in the Palace of Art at the Chicago Fair were Whistlers, Sargents, Innesses—and the originals of Elihu Vedder's illustrations for *The Rubáiyát of Omar Khayyám,* which, she said, gave her "from eighty to a hundred emotions right along." [113] Among them could have been amazement at the rapidly mounting popularity in America of Edward FitzGerald's trans= lation of Omar since the James R. Osgood Company of Boston had brought it out in 1882. The effects on religious and moral attitudes would, though gradual, be eventually cataclysmic. Thanks to the zealous admiration of the Pre-Raphaelite poets, FitzGerald's Omar had also been sweeping literate England. John Hay assured the Omar Khayyám Club of London in 1898 that Americans as cultivated as he were sharing England's enthusiasm; *The Rubáiyát* was, he averred, "one of the most thoroughly used books in every [American club] library. . . . [But] Omar can never be numbered among the great popular writers . . . [instead] will hold a place forever among that limited number who look deep into the tangled mysteries of things. . . ." [114]

It was poor prophecy. After 1900 the cult of Omar became another example of an import from the British upper strata going epidemic in America. One or another of the many fast-selling illustrated editions "was a favorite birthday remembrance," Mark Sullivan recalled, "especially among young folks. . . . By 1910, millions lay on parlor tables upon which, incongruously, the only other book was the Bible. Tens of millions of individual quatrains were 'pyrographed'* on leather sofa-cushions; hand-painted as ornaments for walls . . . [along with] quotations from Emerson and 'God Bless Our Home.' "[115] And wall mottoes, unlike the contents of giftbooks in artsy-craftsy limp leather bindings, are sure to get read and embedded in the mind all the more firmly for the reading being often half-unconscious.

The favorite quatrain was, of course, "A Book of Verses underneath the Bough. . . ." But "The Moving Finger writes; and, having writ, / Moves on . . ." was also popular. So was "Ah, take the Cash and let the Credit go, / Nor heed the rumble of a distant Drum. . . ." Humorous weeklies were studded with parodies of Fitz-Geraldian quatrains by conspicuous names like Oliver Herford, Carolyn Wells and James Whitcomb Riley. On Broadway Persia, as a scene designer conceived it, made *Omar the Tentmaker* a box-office success.

---

* Pyrography was the fine art of branding lettering or designs of cattails, water lilies or some other flora associated with Art Nouveau or William Morris, on wood or leather with a red-hot iron. Young women took courses in it, and parlors *c.* 1890 were full of it.

No poem, particularly 400-odd lines long, could deeply affect a vast number of admirers today, when few read poetry at all except in academic situations and fewer still buy books of verse. In those days there were Browning Clubs, and Tennyson and Longfellow were still in many a bookcase and often taken out of it. But though Omar began his American conquests with that promising audience, he was soon far beyond the regular, usually female, public accustomed to valuing verse. He got into the fraternity house and the discussion around the stove in the country store. Mediocre-looking men downing one too many in bars were likely to start mumbling: "Ah, make the most of what we yet may spend, / Before we too into the Dust descend; . . ." The frankly hedonistic, ironically agnostic content impressed many emotionally ready for such attitudes, whether or not they had the cultivation or sensibility to appreciate the magnificence of the verse. The contribution of those deliberately glowing monosyllables and the doom-filled rhyme scheme was to make the key quatrains as easily remembered as the best of Mother Goose. Mark Sullivan's summary of the consequences on the rising generation *c.* 1900 is from a shrewd member of it:

> . . . not many American youths really believed Omar, or embraced him as a practicable philosophy of life . . . any more than they took the Sermon on the Mount as a practicable rule of business. But the young American was made aware for the first time . . . that there is more than one philosophy of life . . . started . . . upon an intellectual path . . . that took away authority from all dogma. . . . The spirit of Omar Khayyam . . . seeping into the minds of . . . American youth from about 1895 on, had an effect of sapping and undermining . . . characteristic American . . . standards of conduct.[116]

The long-dead Persian sage may have had the way prepared for him among the boys around the cracker barrel by a regally handsome Illinois country lawyer-politician-spellbinder, Colonel Robert G. Ingersoll— his title meritoriously acquired in two years' able command of a regiment of Union cavalry. Such a record was a good start both at the bar and in politics. Ingersoll's high point in politics was his speech at the Republican national convention of 1876 nominating James G. Blaine for the Presidency as a "plumed knight"—a *nom de guerre* that stuck to Blaine the rest of his rather tarnished career. In court Ingersoll's high point was his securing acquittal for the unquestionably guilty defendants in the Star Route cases of fraud on the U.S. Post Office. But he was no simple career-seeker. He knowingly risked grave difficulties by not only having but expressing shocking ideas bound to be unpopular. Though his father had been a Presbyterian minister, Ingersoll was presently prominent in the work of the National Liberal League to repeal laws requiring Sunday observance, Bible teaching in public schools and government sponsorship of religious festivals and to repeal or modify intelligently the newish federal statute against obscene matter in the mails that was Anthony Comstock's offspring, pride, joy and chief weapon against the lust of the eye. Worse, he had come to doubt the existence of any God and the divine authenticity of the Bible—a misgiving then rising in the Western world in consequence of the higher criticism and Darwin's momentous theories.

America, like other countries, had long known and preferred to shun the odd atheist if he tried to be articulate. Ingersoll now proceeded to use his imposing, ingratiating person, archangelic eloquence —Mark Twain spoke of how he "poured the molten silver from his lips" [117]—courtroom footwork and pitchman's wit to make a prosperous career of lectures promoting an irreverent agnosticism through the town halls of America. There was scandalized opposition. The Young Men's Christian Association worked ahead of his tours to flood towns in which he was booked with leaflets warning church members to avoid him at the peril of their immortal souls. But once curiosity got the heedless into the hall, what he was saying about the old-time religion and its documentary and theological bases seemed to many well worth hearing —in any case, highly entertaining, for in repartee, written or spoken, he was often a cross between Mark Twain and John Randolph of Roanoke with his spurs on. A manufacturer of refrigerators wrote to him on his business stationery challenging him to debate the existence of hell. Ingersoll noted what the man manufactured and suggested in reply that he obviously "did not want hell abolished but hoped to carry on business in the next world!" He jeered at the YMCA for its faith in a God who had once struck its building in Washington, D.C., with lightning while leaving unscathed the law office of Bob Ingersoll, notorious atheist, only a few blocks away. When the clergy of Hoboken, New Jersey, threatened him with an archaic state law against blasphemy, he accused them from the platform of being so virtuous because "they haven't got the physical constitution to be wicked. You can't blame 'em for their views. They get 'em in sectarian colleges . . . the storm centers of ignorance. They come out like the lands of the upper Potomac as described by John Rogers—almost worthless by nature and rendered wholly so by cultivation. . . . I do not know why these clergymen should wish to throw me into the penitentiary when they know what I shall have to endure in the next world. That ought to satisfy them, I should think." [118]

Presently a man who had never heard Bob Ingersoll discuss "The

Mistakes of Moses" felt as badly deprived as one who had never seen Joe Jefferson in *Rip Van Winkle* or Frank Mayo in *Davy Crockett*. Ingersoll moved his law office to New York City, where he specialized in cases against the telegraph and elevated railroad monopolies and entertained lavishly in a good house well uptown on Fifth Avenue. His godlessness did not alienate a curious mixture of prominent friends—big business giants like John Mackay and Chauncey Depew, front man for the New York Central Railroad; radicals like Henry George and Elizabeth Cady Stanton; professional politicians like Thomas B. "Czar" Reed, Speaker of the U.S. House of Representatives, and Charles W. Fairbanks, Republican U.S. Senator who would be Theodore Roosevelt's Vice President; artists like George Grey Barnard and Gutzon Borglum; and the topmost stratum of Broadway actors, all hobnobbing round the huge punch bowl. As a salon it was more versatile, though less intellectual, than the one Mabel Dodge would so preen herself about fifteen years later at the Greenwich Village end of the avenue—and probably more enjoyable. But Ingersoll seems to have enjoyed himself most during occasional evenings with his particular crony Andrew Carnegie, emptying a bottle of Scotch between them as appropriate accompaniment to reading aloud from the works of Robert Burns. Doubtless "Holy Willie's Prayer" was Ingersoll's favorite.* America was indeed changing when that career was possible in the same atmosphere as Comstock, the Anti-Saloon League and President McKinley's explaining to the nation that he had annexed the Philippines because God told him to.

In some ways, however, the greatest portent of erosion of traditional American attitudes *c.* 1900 was a prophet little honored in his own country until well after World War I—Thorstein Veblen. Like Dunne, he came of well-established immigrant parents. But his were Norwegians prosperously farming in a tight Norwegian enclave in Wisconsin—a fitting matrix for such an intellectual troll as he turned out to be. At a succession of universities—Johns Hopkins, the pioneer in transplanting German standards of graduate study to America; Yale; Cornell; the new University of Chicago—he was sometimes recognized as crossgrainedly brilliant in philosophy or economics. But he had a thorny personality and presently a habit of getting into trouble over women, neither of which traits made university administrators of the 1890's eager to see him stay. He was still fairly new at Chicago when he published his basic work, *The Theory of the Leisure Class,* in 1899, the year of Ingersoll's death.

Economists do not seem to have taken in its importance at the time.

---

* This account of Ingersoll owes most of its data to Orvin Larson's recent *American Infidel: Robert G. Ingersoll.*

Actually in their sense it was hardly economics at all, reflecting rather the fact that those most influencing Veblen are thought to have been William James, psychologist-philosopher, and at Chicago John Dewey, educationist-philosopher; Jacques Loeb, physiologist; and Franz Boas, anthropologist. Veblen was no man's disciple, however, signally doing his own thinking and, even more to the present point, his own feeling. What he produced was a psychology of the culture of private property in America. It lacked Marx's oversimplified notions of class motivation but offered instead a hatred of plutocratic values as passionate as that of a flaming anarchist. To thoughtful minds Marx's denunciations of capitalists had always been flawed by the consideration that in his deterministic world capitalists did only what the evolving economic system, the holy dialectic, made it inevitable they should do. It was, therefore, pointless to scold them. But Veblen put free will back into the situation and replaced the economic man of the 1800's with the emotional man with whom the 1900's are all too familiar. In these terms the plutocrat glorying in conspicuous leisure, conspicuous waste and conspicuous consumption because of his positive lust after prestige and self-esteem was displaying a sort of economic original sin originating when man fell from the state of his first innocency by ceasing to be a savage living communistically hand to mouth.

His anthropology was as poor as Marx's. His advantage was that he dwelt on the plutocrat's most vulnerable aspect—not his ruthlessness or thirst for power, which can be the materials of tragedy, but his vulgarity. Allow him to arrogate to himself outrageously disproportionate purchasing power and what will he do with it? Build a Newport "cottage"—delusions of royal grandeur set off by useless lawns pampered by uselessly expended labor and fitted out with luxurious borrowings from earlier cultures become fashionable because raided by many previous self-glorifiers. After Veblen had so gloatingly shown the way, cultivated radicals who had been merely exasperated with the plutocrat as an insensate brute and feared him as a menace to social and economic decency now had the visceral pleasure of despising him as a vulgarian. Cartoonists and some novelists had long been using that approach for their own purposes. But here was a brilliant presentation of such vulgarity as the very core of the society of private property, the touchstone with which to explain the whole world of the successful man and his toadies and imitators, clear down to the hod carrier who keeps one white shirt to wear on Sunday. Gradually he gained wide readership among the thoughtful from William Dean Howells on and, as Arthur K. Davis has recently observed, many of Veblen's doctrines and attitudes have "become part of our culture, familiar to many who have never heard of [their] author." [119]

His style admirably reinforced his teaching. No radical American publication since Thomas Paine "displays such growling pith, such undershot determination to rend and destroy. . . . Its polemic effect would be graceful if the final effect were not that of being muscle-bound. Reading Veblen is like seeing a bulging giant juggling a grand piano with the same skill that a skinny Japanese used on a paper lantern—an appropriate figure because, at a certain point, after a brilliant display of skill, the giant wantonly lets the piano fall and smash into a heap of tangled wires and splinters with the black and white keys still handsome among the ruins but somehow vulgar in their handsomeness . . . in spite of Veblen's . . . pomposity and false front of dispassionate inquiry, his meaning swims in his freshets of superfluous verbiage as lustily and venomously as a water-moccasin. . . . [Read him and] from that moment on [see] the whole bourgeois world through the yellow-tinted spectacles of contempt." [120] He also had the tactical shrewdness, or maybe pessimism, to eschew constructive suggestions, the area where social criticism is always weakest. He was, as economist Douglas Dowd says in a recent, highly respectful study, "basically indifferent, even scornful, toward attempts to translate his ideas into political programs. He seemed content to probe and to report, as though his aim were *merely to discharge irritating matter from his system* [italics mine]." [121]

Certainly the man gives the impression of being first and last a self-tortured temperament seeking relief in elaborately expressed scorn of a world that nauseated him—a small Swift trying to be scientific, actually achieving some acute intuitions. He need not be suspected of anarchism. Most of his life he took no stock in the good time coming after the cancer of authority relaxes its hold. Rather, he was an almost unflawed nihilist. His descriptive aspect made him a chief creator of the emotional climate of the New Deal of Tugwell, Arnold and Ickes. But since the nihilist tends to appeal to the romantic-minded as an exhilarating anti-Prometheus, a brother to Milton's Satan, a Samson gloriously pulling the whole contemptible society down on his tormentors, Veblen's implicit gospel of hate and black destructiveness became eventual preparation for the New Left of the 1960's. For our purposes it is a striking token of America's growing cultural independence—it was a homegrown radicalism that, like the industrial union, proved more important to following generations than to its own.

Veblen seems to have felt small moral difference between the prodigal American man and the greedy woman he married. Both were foul with conspicuous consumption, he as self-impressed bill payer, she as self-admiring, bedizened show window. Actually, as the 1880's merged into the 1890's, the superiority that the American woman felt as chief patron of the arts, promoter of good causes such as Temperance, and exponent of carnal virtue was widening its scope. Whereas the standard heroine of the novels of the mid-century was small-made and kittenishly or wistfully pretty, the trend was now toward Tennyson's "divinely tall, and most divinely fair" sort of thing. The Pre-Raphaelite painters' statuesque ideal women were part of this, and George du Maurier had borrowed from them for the towering but winsome girls in his elaborate drawings for *Punch,* highly familiar to Anglophile Americans. Late in the 1880's his well-bred giantess emigrated to America, took

Recurring examples of the tubular contour.

From pp. 14–16 *Recurring Cycles of Fashion* by Agnes Brooks Young. Copyright 1937 by Harper & Row, Publishers, Incorporated. By permission of the publishers.

on a more voluptuous depth of bosom and roundness of arm and bottom, and appeared as the Gibson Girl, trademark of Charles Dana Gibson, a rising young artist specializing in drawings gently satirizing affluent society in *Life,* the rising young humorous weekly.

The Gibson Girl had cloudy masses of hair piled high on a patricianly small head, a neck like an antelope's, broad shoulders allowing vast expanses of décolletage, the carriage of a West Point cadet and long legs invisible under sweeping skirts but so far out of proportion that between them and the small head she looked as if Gibson had groveled on the floor while drawing her. Her favorite garb was elaborate evening gowns or the newly popular shirtwaist (a boxy exaggeration of the man's shirt, often worn with collar and cravat) tucked into a statuesquely tubular straight skirt, the belted waistband of which showed how exquisitely small her waist was. She unquestionably had a wholesome influence on girls of normal dimensions keeping their shoulders back and their heads high in hope of looking like her; indeed wholesomeness, a glow of decorously vigorous well-being, was one of her chief traits. Mark Sullivan credited her presence in Gibson's drawings, soon reproduced by the millions as she mushroomed into a national cult, with crowding the painfully garish chromos off American walls. But her effect on relations between the sexes was probably deplorable. For some while the American man had been acceding to woman's claim that she belonged on a pedestal. Now she looked as if she had always been there, all goddessy and immaculate and utterly self-contained with no more need of men than St.-Gaudens' "Diana" felt high on the tower of Madison Square Garden.

Gibson's favorite theme was an unequal yoking of this graciously elegant divinity with a crass, foolish or elderly husband or fiancé. Even when he showed a well-bred and handsome suitor—it is said that his model for these exceptions was either himself or Richard Harding Davis, the famous reporter-fictioneer whose style of good looks put chins into fashion in collar advertisements—the man was seldom in command of the situation. One of Gibson's best series, "Leap Year," had serenely divine beauties getting carriages for their escorts after the theater, staying in the dining room for port and cigarettes while the men of the party went up to the drawing room. He also liked to show the small henpecked husband and father dominated physically, as well as morally, by the splendid wife and daughter who spent his money. Thomas Craven calls it "a crafty stroke" for him to have made the Gibson Girl "the commander of men, the herald of the emancipated woman." [122] Indeed it was, for the new century would see a new aggressiveness in the feminist movement.

*Charles Dana Gibson's dominant girl and subordinate male
on the beach.*

In 1890 the two separate camps of workers for women's rights had rejoined forces and begun systematic agitation for votes for women in the separate states. Their few successes were limited to the trans-Missouri West. In the South, usually last to adopt any reform, it was feared that letting women vote would reopen the whole potentially dangerous issue of the Negro as voter. In vain the few militant Southern feminists bitterly complained that in most Southern states the law gave the despised Negro man the privilege—if only theoretically and nominally—of voting where a white lady could not. In the rest of the nation professional politicians stoutly resisted votes for women in the belief, confirmed by the suffragists' own propaganda, that women would be likelier than men to vote for reform and against machines. The brewing and distilling interests took the same side for fear women's votes would be cast for local option or statewide prohibition, which the persisting size and activity of the WCTU made all too probable. By 1896 only Wyoming, Utah, Colorado and Idaho had been chivalrous—or logical—about it. There had never been anything wrong with the basic logic of the women's case, but there the movement stuck. Ten years later in none of those four states had the great benefits that women predicted would follow if they got the vote—a wholesale throwing out of political rascals, an increased quality of social responsibility—come strikingly to pass. But nobody brought up that negative evidence. The dominant interests in the remaining states continued to counter prosuffrage propaganda with nonsense about how voting women would be defeminized

—that was the mainstay of the comic weekly magazines. The minority of women determined on equality with men in every respect in which they did not claim superiority continued to promise the remaining states, persuasively here, fumblingly there, miracles that were unlikely to come to pass.

In 1903 Emmeline, Christabel and Sylvia Pankhurst, widow and daughters of a founder of the British Labour Party, organized their strong-minded sisters among both English factory women and upper-class ladies for votes for women with new propaganda methods. They employed highly modern-style campaigns of mass demonstration in defiance of police rules with stone-throwing, name-calling—anything to get the lady demonstrators arrested and made martyrs of. Often enough the authorities obliged. "It is by going to prison rather than by any arguments . . . that we will eventually win all over England," Mrs. Pankhurst told a heroine-worshiping audience of American feminists in New York City in 1909. "Much has been said about our throwing stones . . . stone-throwing is a time-honored British political argument." [123] Living in England at the time was Elizabeth Cady Stanton's daughter, Harriot Stanton Blatch, widow of an Englishman through whom she had come to know conspicuous Fabian Socialists and other English radicals sympathetic to the Pankhursts' cause and methods. Returning to America in 1907, she found the American suffrage movement, her late mother's prime concern, merely repeating itself like a broken record.

Borrowing from the Pankhursts, she added to the cause's task forces organizations of workingwomen, particularly from New York City's garment trades and, a Vassar graduate herself, from college women, of whom by then the nation had many, particularly from the noncoeducational campuses. A very heavy whiff of the The Princess arises, in fact, from Mrs. Blatch's complaint after a few years of watching the New York State legislature take evasive action in response to her forces' well delivered attacks: "We are up against a hard proposition in the American man . . . in England . . . they take us seriously. They deny us our rights, but they don't put us away as if we were spoiled children . . . the police put us off the streets; they send us to jail! . . . in America, they blandly admit us before the legislative committees, listen to all we have to say, treat us with perfect courtesy . . . and never so much as bother to answer our arguments. As for voting on our measures, they simply pocket them without a word. . . . They won't so much as put us in jail. It's . . . highly insulting!" [124] That is, she was discovering that a pedestal is a poor position to fight from.

In 1907 she got down and invaded the roof garden of New York's elegantly worldly Hoffman House, demanding service as an unescorted woman seated alone. Rebuffed, she sued the hotel; but the jury refused her redress. In 1910 she and her sisters organized a parade down Fifth Avenue—3,000 suffrage-minded women, including the Woman's Suffrage League of New York in sixty-three automobiles; the Collegiate Equal Suffrage League in caps and gowns; the Equality League of Self-Supporting Women carrying a banner inscribed "New York State Denies the Vote to Idiots, Lunatics, Criminals and Women." All wore sashes and waved flags of the movement's chosen color, yellow. They attracted a huge crowd—and all the police did about it was to provide a strong and courteous mounted escort to see that nobody was rude to the embattled marchers. Nevertheless, the suffragists' Fifth Avenue parade became an annual institution, larger each year, soon with bands, floats and a Men's League for Woman Suffrage with such distinguished marchers as John Dewey; Witter Bynner, the poet; George Harvey, editor of *Harper's Weekly,* and Oswald Garrison Villard, owner-editor of the highly respected New York *Evening Post.*

There was also Mrs. O. H. P. Belmont, her zeal for suffrage finally overcoming her ladylike scruples against public participation. Few of the spectators can have realized that what looked to them like just another suffragist in a well-made tailored suit marching on the same footing as the girls from the East Side sweatshops was actually one of the most striking products of plutocracy—born high in Knickerbocker Quality, married first to a Vanderbilt fortune, then to a Belmont fortune, thus presiding as mistress of two of the most astounding Newport "cottages" in majestic succession. The crowd's eyes were probably on the "suffrage cavalry" clattering along smartly, mostly mounted sidesaddle but some daring troopers astride in the divided skirt that eased the way to ladies' riding breeches. Chief horsewoman of suffrage was Inez Milholland, a beautiful recent graduate of Vassar, who had held suffrage meetings in a cemetery near the campus while still in college and died of overwork for the cause within a few years. Veteran suffragists reminiscing about the great days of struggle always brought in Inez Milholland, booted, sombreroed, divided-skirted, sitting her great black horse like a she-centaur at the head of the parade of 1913.

Other large cities began to hold such parades with growing success. But the results of nibbling at legislatures were so slow as to frustrate Mrs. Blatch to a pitiable degree. In 1911 Washington State capitulated, in 1912 California. At the rate of a state a year it would be the mid-1950's before votes for women were nationwide. But things began to look brighter —or anyway livelier—in 1912, when darkly intense young Alice Paul, Swarthmore 1905, and statuesque, red-haired Lucy Burns, Vassar 1902, came back from several years each in Europe. Both had been marching with the Pankhursts, getting jailed, going on hunger strikes, and learning the value of militancy as a propaganda tool. Observing American suffragism, they felt even more strongly than Mrs. Blatch that its bloodstream needed adrenalin. At their own instance they were sent to Washington to revive the votes for women amendment to the Federal Constitution that had been dormant for twenty years.

In 1913 their first parade of thousands of marching women devotedly filling Pennsylvania Avenue in a cold spring rain—Miss Milholland's horse was white this time—drew enough obscene heckling and minor violence to cause the Secretary of War to send in troops. After 1916 picketing of the Capitol and White House, dishearteningly peaceful at first, finally produced arrests, sentences to the District of Columbia workhouse, charges of police brutality, hunger strikes. At last men in authority were taking women's resentment of their inferior status seriously enough to get nasty—and create public sympathy. The momentum thus secured combined with the emotional shakings up of the coming war to secure Congressional passage and the states' ratification of the Nineteenth Amendment in 1920. Never had direct imitation of the British worked out better—except in the appearance in the 1890's at the best clubs of the Scotch and soda, which, as it spread down into lower strata, did much to wean American drinkers away from the slug of straight whiskey.

Charles Dickens' second visit to America came at the height of the Gilded Age in 1868, but he professed himself charmed with the country about which he had been so harsh in the 1840's, and all went well. New York City's official dinner for him was attended by all with any claim to cultivation—except women, none of whom was invited. The manners of the day gave them no right to expect to be included. Yet it annoyed a prominent lady journalist, Jennie June (Mrs. Jane Cunningham Croly), who, though the mother of five and wife of a well-known newspaperman, had long been mainstay of the Demorests' women's magazines. She knew many women whose attainments were equal to those of many men thought eligible to help dine Dickens. Her exasperation led her to call together the cream of the neglected ladies to organize a women's club named Sorosis to meet regularly for dinner or luncheon, edify one another in sisterly harmony, and occasionally hear speakers on matters of public concern or particular interest to women. At about the same time a strong-minded Boston lady, Mrs. Caroline Severance, was persuading her cultivated lady acquaintances in and around the city that they needed a centrally located clubhouse where, when shopping or coming in for a concert or good-cause meeting, they could recuperate and enjoy feminine comradeship. That resulted in the New England Women's Club, at first admitting a few men of such quality as Emerson but presently following Sorosis into a women-only policy. Julia Ward Howe soon succeeded Mrs. Severance as president and, with two small interregna, guided it—and the ensuing women's club movement —till she died in 1910.

The Boston version was very like a men's private club with clubhouse and convenient facilities. Sorosis was more like today's service club. But as the two examples spread and fused with the already strong conviction that woman was the vehicle of civilization, they led to what Mrs. Howe's daughters called "the great network of clubs which, like a beneficent railway system of thought and good-will, penetrates every nook and corner of this country." [125] Large cities, say, San Francisco, might persist in the clubhouse feature, but many a flourishing women's club called the Clio or the Wednesday Afternoon got along nicely meeting at one another's houses in succession. Octave Thanet attributed the rapid spread of the movement in the Midwest to women's finding post-Civil War life "a little tame when there were no more sanitary fairs" and founding in her middle-size town in Iowa "the Ladies' Literary Club and the Spinsters' Alliance . . . [tackling] the same great themes of ethics and art . . . [allotting] a winter to the literature of a nation, except in the case of Greek and Roman literatures, which were not considered able to occupy a whole winter apiece, so they were studied in company." [126]

Meetings, almost invariably in the afternoon, consisted of an opening business session with the secretary reading last week's minutes and Madam President in her most impressive hat skillfully entertaining motions in accordance with *Robert's Rules of Order;* then a member's paper on "The Place of the Sublime in Romantic Poetry" followed by discussion from the floor; then tea and ladyfingers and gossip ad lib. Membership being largely a matter of local social standing, not cultural attainments as such, the gossip was a valued by-product. So, to the local librarian, were the fees she received for writing papers for some of the less intellectually given members. A few times a year a paid lecturer, often male, was booked for the evening with tickets sold and husbands invited and the profits, if any, going to the local soup kitchen. The cultural basis of the whole tradition was that of the lyceum lecture, the assumption that to hear about a thing in congenial company and surroundings is more rewarding than to explore it for yourself. But its real function was to give the typical member—the clubwoman, a new but soon instantly recognizable figure in the American landscape—the equivalent of what her daughter was getting from a good sorority at State U; only here there was no question of husband hunting.

Mrs. Howe's daughters saw the movement as partly occupational therapy for underemployed, prospering wives. "To thousands of elder women . . . [clubs] came like a new gospel of activity and service. They had . . . seen [their] children take to flight . . . had learned to work with and beside men [in Civil War activities]. . . . How could they go back to the chimney-corner life? In . . . an answer from Heaven . . . came the women's clubs with their opportunities for self-culture and service." [127] At first the General Federation of Women's Clubs, formed in 1889, admitted only those advancing "literary, artistic or scientific culture." [128] But as women's interest in civic matters and social issues grew and clubs began to appoint committees to chivy the city fathers into cleaning up the park or suppressing public drinking cups, the bars came down. Eventually the federation had departments of education, home economics, industrial conditions for women and children, civic improvement. Here the thousands of women's clubs paralleled the "Do Everything" policy of the WCTU. Indeed many a club member also belonged to the WCTU. But by and large the club tradition was slightly more urban and considerably more urbane than that of Frances Willard's adoring disciples, and as the 1900's came on, its higher prestige combined with the new dynamism of the suffrage movement to entice away from the WCTU, also damaged by Miss Willard's death, many of its potentially ablest prospective members. Women's clubs had relatively small place, however, in the lives of the wives and daughters of the Newport-Lenox-Bar Harbor stratum of Northeastern established society. Its most intelligent product, Edith Wharton, curled her lip at "ladies who pursue Culture in bands, as though it were dangerous to meet it alone." [129]

Looking back on the Waterbury, Vermont, of *c.* 1890, R. L. Duffus wondered why women had cultural clubs but men didn't. "Did they consider culture, under that name, effeminate? Maybe . . . [also] they were expected to be at their place of business . . . ten hours or so a day and couldn't conveniently hold meetings at each other's houses to talk of the latest novel or study the situation in Hungary." [130] Their wives, thanks to the servants then still available and paid for by the husbands' ten-hour stints, had plenty of time for such topics. Thus a major consequence of women's clubs, increasing their number and widening their scope steadily after 1900, was further to deepen the breach between masculine intelligence and cultivated leisure, or rather, to tighten the exclusive grip that Woman was assumed to have on it. American women, the author-character told the inquiring traveler from Altruria in 1894, "are as a rule better schooled, if not better educated. . . . They certainly go in for . . . art and music . . . and the drama . . . and psychology . . . heaven knows what all. They have more leisure for it . . . all the leisure there is, in fact; our young men have to go into business. . . . [Women] are the great readers among us. . . . American literature exists because American women appreciate and love it." [131] For his radical lectures on thorny social problems Henry Demarest Lloyd preferred audiences of ministers—or women's club members. When among like-minded cronies speculating about the specific details of the millennium, he would laugh and say: "We will all be women some day," [132] as if that were by definition a forward step toward the good time coming.

The progression that had begun with American men's accepting the early Victorian convention of Woman as the fragile and more sensitive object of deference was getting out of hand. The Women's Crusade had shown to women's own satisfaction that when they put their minds to it, they could accomplish things that men wouldn't even try. With help from their mothers the WCTU had expanded that into the doctrine that man was coarse, weak and insensitive to higher things and that his only hope of civilization was for Woman to try to raise him nearer her level. Such women as Susan A. King of New York City, creator of her own fortune by real estate speculation, then successful tea importer making her own deals in person in the Far East, and Hetty Green, grimly adept manipulator of the millions her father left her, had shown that their sex could be as able in business as the other—and not in simple Colonial terms but in those of the complicated, high-stakes late-1800's.

It was fitting that the women's club movement culminated in the formation of a militantly feminist club in New York City just before World War I. Its members—Charlotte Perkins Gilman, Inez Haynes Irwin, Fola La Follette, et al.—were the picked shock troops of the founder, Marie Jenney (Howe), a former lady Unitarian minister and admirer of George Sand, so firm against conventional arrangements between the sexes that she was furious when Mabel Dodge treacherously married Maurice Sterne, the painter she had been living with for some years. The functions of the club—its name was Heterodoxy—appear to have been mutual congratulations among members on being women and the cultivation of condescending hatred for men—the sort of thing that presently founded Alice Paul's Woman's Party and has recently flared up again among the disciples of Betty Friedan. But the Gibson Girl was the superb symbol of it all. With consistent ominousness she had always been a touch reminiscent of the large she-spider that can eat the small he-spider whenever she is so inclined. The eve of World War I, when feminism was all self-aggrandizing promises with no need yet to fulfill them, was the high-water mark of Woman's dominance over Man in America.

The Gibson Girl presently acquired rivals, however. With the turn of the century began a heretical schism hankering after something just as supple but less generous. The heroine of Norris' *The Pit* (1900) was tall and had beautiful shoulders, but "Her almost extreme slenderness was her characteristic . . . the swell of hip and breast [was] . . . low; from head to foot one could discover no pronounced salience. Yet there was no trace . . . of angularity . . . She was slender as a willow shoot. . . ." [133] Edith Wharton's Lily Bart (1905) was of the same school, so costumed in a "living picture" affair got up for a plutocratic country weekend that elderly voluptuaries noted "there isn't a break in the lines anywhere," [134] an effect requiring subtle corseting as it grew stylish. By 1908 *Life* was asking:

> We don't wish to insinuate
> That they were not real before;
> But where, oh where, are the hips that we
> Don't notice any more? [135]

And an inchoate cult of slenderness necessarily encouraged relish for the adolescent. Stanford White, Evelyn Nesbit testified at the trial of his murderer (her husband), told her that "only very young girls were nice, and the thinner they were, the prettier they were. . . ." [136] J. G. Huneker, a high priest of cosmopolitanism in the arts, gloatingly described the naked girl who rose out of the colossal pie at a famous stag dinner as "A shining child of exquisite beauty. . . . Her breasts were lilliputian, tender, rose-colored. Her evasive hips proclaimed precocious puberty. . . ." [137] In the color reproductions of Maxfield Parrish's blue-flushed paintings that sold almost as widely in the early 1900's as the Gibson Girl had in the 1890's, pagan young persons, innocently naked, disported themselves among scenery taken straight from theatrical backdrops—and the nymphs were hardly distinguishable from the adolescent boys. Here was the germ of the boyish form of the 1920's, of the flapper who, as Ogden Nash said, wanted to look like her little brother. And she represented an important step down from the Gibson Girl's pedestal, being neither a goddess nor a lady.

Among the flapper's tribal attributes were cigarettes and alcohol—both duly coeval with her slenderized ancestresses of twenty years earlier. The cigarette-smoking woman in America is traceable back to fast theatrical circles of the mid-1800's. But her entrance under sponsorship from elegant society may have waited until the 1880's, when Mrs. Burton Harrison, well placed among the best people, mentioned in a novel, *The Anglomaniacs,* how smoking after-dinner cigarettes had "swept like a prairie fire over certain circles" of ladies after being "introduced by a Russian lady of rank in Washington." [138] The Princess Eulalie, representing the Spanish Crown at the Chicago Fair, the first female royalty ever to visit America, caused a sensation by freely smoking cigarettes, which again associated the habit with unimpeachable and enticingly exotic aristocracy.

Soon Uncle Peter Bines, self-made but unspoiled millionaire miner in Harry Leon Wilson's *The Spenders,* observed that the New York City women he had seen smoking gold-monogrammed cigarettes out of silver boxes "was some of the reg'ler original Vanvans." [139] "Now that women have taken to tobacco," says a sagacious clubman of the Newport-Tuxedo world in *The House of Mirth,* ". . . study the effect of cigarettes on the relation of the sexes. Smoke is almost as great a solvent as divorce; both tend to obscure the moral issue." [140] Cigarettes attacked next on the left-bohemian flank, creeping uptown from Greenwich Village, as well as downtown from tall Bedford stone mansions fronting on Central Park. Headwaiters and city councils were strongly agitated about them because they were unladylike and, besides, associated with either monocled dudes or pimply youths on street corners and objects of attack as viciously unhealthy "coffin nails." (At the time the attackers had no intelligible scientific basis for the last; once more cranks were right for the wrong reasons.) But when Newport took up the cigarette, the wall was breached. Thenceforth only delaying actions were tactically possible.

Alcohol took the same routes. Edith Wharton's elegant women not only kept pace with the wines as course succeeded course at gilded dinners but also drank a brandy and soda late in the evening as freely as their great-great-grandmothers in Colonial times had taken rum-and-water nightcaps. In San Francisco in the mid-1890's a young man-about-town in Norris' *Vandover and the Brute* noted with relish but also some disapproval that a fair number of girls at the best-considered private dances "like their champagne pretty well now, and don't you forget it," [141] and that young men crowded to dance with any of them who got detectably tiddly. There had always been some of that sort of thing in American social circles too sophisticated to adopt Temperance notions. But at the tea dancings that came over from Britain as World War I neared, He and She tangoing among potted palms at the smartest hotel, sherry or cocktails began to replace literal tea for Her, as well as for Him. A highly significant *Life* cartoon of this ragtime era of 1912 shows a slender, pretty girl sitting on the edge of a table swapping back-chat with an elegant young man. In one hand she has a cigarette; in the other a cocktail glass. The attitude and stage props could come right out of a John Held, Jr., drawing of the 1920's. Only two details are anomalous. Though she shows a good bit of ankle, her skirt is long. And there is no reason to believe that she has left off her corset.

The protoflapper's display of ankle—probably in a silk stocking by then—was accompanied by certain relaxations in what men wore. The boater-style hard straw hat (Americans often called it a sailor) with a fancy band, in some cases carrying club or college colors, had come to dominate from Decoration Day to Labor Day—when ritual required scaling it onto the diamond after the last out of a baseball game. By 1912 the white shirt with attached, turnover soft collar was creeping in for daily wear among young men who had gone to the right Northeastern colleges. Both were Anglicisms adapted to town from sport—the boater from the turnout in which the Briton took a lady sculling; the shirt from the proper garb for polo or tennis. Both made minor sense in terms of comfort. The great breakthrough in that respect, however, consisted of a new type of men's underwear—a sleeveless, knee-length, loose "union suit" of a cotton fabric called nainsook. Usually referred to as BVD's after the brand name of the original manufacturer, this garment looked ungainly even as worn by elegant young men in the advertisements. But it was an immense improvement over the close-fitting knit woolen underwear, ribbed at ankle and wrist for maximum stuffiness, either long-sleeve shirts and ankle-length drawers, or the two combined into a union suit with drop seat, that had replaced flannels for most men and children and some women toward the end of the 1800's.

They suited well enough for outdoor work in cold weather. But civilization was turning indoors, and under most circumstances the things were miserably itchy and sweaty, as well as stuffy. R. L. Duffus recently recalled with a shudder "the dreadful squalor of the . . . [Pullman] dressing room . . . [fellow passengers'] suspenders hanging down their backs and their heavy underwear and the heavy smell of them, and how I loathed them, and they me. . . ." [142] Much of the blame for it lies at the door of a monomaniac German physician, Dr. Gustav Jaeger. In the 1870's he developed the notion that to wear vegetable fibers is practically poisonous, since they do not absorb the body's exhalations as well as wool does, and that conversely one's health requires wool in contact with the body. After his hobby got really galloping, he advised women, for instance, to wear not only woolen chemise, drawers, stockings, petticoat, corset, dress and shoes but even to use woolen handkerchiefs and sleep in woolen sheets. For men a complete Jaeger suit, tight-fitting to allow the least possible movement of air along the skin, was available. (Such suits appear in early pictures of George Bernard Shaw.) The same hygienically naïve kinds of people as those who had reverently accepted Priessnitz's hydropathy a generation earlier now bought Jaeger outfits from the shops springing up to supply them in England and America, and the same kinds of doctors assured their patients of the validity of the Jaeger Sanitary Woolen System.

Wool flannel fitted the general theory. But since knit woolens clung more tightly, they were particularly favored. The general public never really took up Jaegerism. But the less ardent among his devotees compromised on Jaeger-inspired knit woolen underwear beneath conventional clothing, whence seems to have sprung a vague conviction permeating England and America that to replace flannel with knit wool was essential to well-being. Britons, still largely committed to small coal fireplaces for winter heating, probably did not suffer. For Americans, overheated by stoves or furnaces, it was calamitous. There was eventually some merciful substitution of cotton yarn, which insanely retained the close-fitting design while rejecting Jaeger's wool—the original basis of the whole misbegotten cult. But millions sticking to the long-johns woolens had no relief. For the less frivolous sex, underwear suited to American conditions was rare until those BVD's began infiltrating society, down from the higher rungs as usual. At first they were recommended for coolness in summer, but the daring soon found that no harm—and far greater comfort—came of wearing them the year round.

Over the long-johns, wool or cotton, small boys and small girls alike had long black cotton stockings. For everyday wear shoes were ankle-high, buttoned or laced. Small boys were likely to wear a blouse-and-knickerbockers Russian suit, so called for its high collar buttoning under the ear. As they gained size, knickerbocker suits took over and, for state and festive occasions, called for the Buster Brown collar with a Windsor scarf tied in a great drooping bow. Little girls' dresses dutifully followed the shifting juvenile fashions shown by the women's magazines and their pattern-selling subsidiaries. But they were consistently short enough for high activity. Among children of affluence both sexes were much better off than their grandparents had been when girl children wore fragile pantalets and billowy skirts and boys were kept in skirted dresses hardly distinguishable from those for girls until the age of at least three or four. For their parents, especially in summer, there was no such improvement. Aside from the question of lingerie, the prevalent full corset, boned, tight-laced and impermeable, was torture in hot weather no matter how cool the lady's voile or dotted swiss looked. All summer, even when relaxing on the resort hotel's veranda, men of standing wore high stiff collars and buttoned-up vests. The most anomalous hot-weather costume ever shown in a portrait is that of Anson Phelps Stokes (with Mrs. Stokes) by Sargent, the client in immaculate white ducks including an elegantly tailored white

Charles Dana Gibson records the impact of knee-length bathing suits on the values of his time. Note also the vest as necessary part of the middle-aged gentleman's summer resort apparel.

duck vest. Doubtless beneath it was some version of wrist-to-ankle knit underwear. Even on sweltering summer evenings on Broadway it was *de rigueur* for the gay young fellows in straw hats to carry light summer overcoats.

Over the years since the Civil War the outdoor worker, whether on the farm or clambering around on a scaffold, had acquired what amounted to a dim blue uniform in the shape of overalls—often not illogically pronounced *overhauls*—consisting of loose denim trousers made all of a piece with a high-rise bib secured by shoulder suspenders. The strategically placed pockets hinted that carpenters or masons had been the originators; as farmers learned of the garment's virtues—it would slip over warm pants and underwear in winter, yet enable a man to wear very little in the hot sun of the harvest field—farmwives stitched up their own variations on the theme. In the 1870's a former salesman of Singer sewing machines, James A. Orr of Wappingers Falls, New York, experimenting with better modulation of sizes in work clothing, set six girls turning out a standardized bib overall in hard-wearing blue denim—alias jean—to see if it would sell at 75 cents. It sold like lemonade on the Fourth of July. The resulting Sweet-Orr company made him and two partners rich and also made labor history by being one of the first American manufacturing firms to welcome union organization of its employees and peacefully to set up procedures for collective bargaining. But quite as important was the universality of the product whether made by Sweet-Orr or the competitors who soon put out bib overalls. In the stereotype of the American farmer—wide straw hat, chin beard, spear of grass in the mouth, tendency to say, "Dern my skin" and "I swan"—overalls to hook the thumbs into were invariable. As early as the 1880's *bluejeans* had become one word, and its implications of honest toil were so widely understood that Joseph Arthur, popular playwright, used it as the title for a by-gosh drama of heartbreak on the old farm.

The great West's folk equivalent was, of course, "Levis,"—the low-slung, slim-legged work pants with copper-riveted pockets created for miners, cowhands, lumberjacks and gandy-dancers by Levi Strauss and Company of San Francisco. When Strauss first made them in 1850, he used tent canvas from a supply he had fetched with him around the Horn. The heavy blue denim used later was woven to his own specifications for durability, and his trademark, showing two horses straining in vain to tear a pair of Levis apart, was—and still is—as well known west of the Missouri

The manufacturers' label on "Levis," as widely known in Western bunkhouses as the wording on Borden's condensed milk.

as the Union Pacific Railroad. Indeed it has become a national institution, for an apotheosis of Levis occurred in the 1930's, when Eastern girls met them on dude ranches and brought them back to show off slim figures.

The sweltering consequences of Dr. Jaeger's ideas lasted for only a generation or so. The gastronomic consequences of Dr. John H. Kellogg's equally crankish notions of what to eat, developing in the same period, are with us yet as dry, cold breakfast cereals. In the mid-1850's vegetarianism became part of the righteous life as conceived by the Seventh-Day Adventists, successor cult to the Millerites, whose plans to fly to heaven had gone awry in the 1840's. Under a lady prophet, Ellen Gould White, who had once visited heaven in a trance, they founded at Battle Creek, Michigan, a Western Health Reform Institute combining some accepted medical methods with hydropathy and vegetarian diet. By 1876 management of the place was in the hands of Kellogg, a young physician whose conventional medical training had not set him against vegetarian doctrine. For the patients at Battle Creek he developed, among other hygienic comestibles, the first peanut butter; a flaky-dried, precooked preparation of wheat that, though meant for eating alone as a vegetable snack, became popular among the patients as a breakfast dish with milk and often sweetening; and, taking a leaf from the famous vegetarian sanitarium of Dr. James Caleb Jackson at Dansville, New York, a baked and ground-up sort of super zwieback that he called Granola, eaten similarly. Soon manufacture and distribution of these items in paper cartons became a flourishing business. At much the same time a prim rolling stone, Henry D. Perky of Denver, Colorado, was working out the process for making Shredded Wheat—and a fortune.

Between them the two would revolutionize American breakfasts. Presently they had much, if undesired, help from Dr. Kellogg's brother Will K., who took over and made a world institution of flakes made of corn, and Charles W. Post, a hypochondriac promoter who did equally well with an imitation of Granola called Grape Nuts, an imitation of cornflakes called Post Toasties, and a coffee substitute based on bran, wheat and molasses called Postum. Neither cornflakes nor most of its dry-cereal rivals, which were many as the profits began to show, have ever contained much substance per serving. But the accompanying sugar and milk were of more nutritional value, and dry cereals require no preparation, whereas the oats or wheat porridges that, under one brand name or another, came in toward the 1890's needed overnight simmering. It also proved that children liked cold dry cereals better than hot gluey ones. The advertising of Grape Nuts or Force (wheat flakes) or Shredded Wheat strongly hinted that each in itself was an adequate breakfast, no supplementary items needed. This ran counter to the ideal breakfast of the time as described by Ma Pettengill recalling the Union Pacific's breakfast stop at North Platte, Nebraska, before the transcontinental trains had dining cars: "ham and eggs and fried oysters and fried chicken and sausage and fried potatoes and hot biscuits and corn bread and hot cakes and regular coffee . . . and first thing you knew you had your plate loaded . . . and yes, thank you, another cup of coffee and please pass the sirup. . . ." [143] But soon enough convenience and the dwindling appetites of sedentary workers won the dry cereals' game for them. The creation of strawberry shortcake, which seems to have had definite form by the late 1870's, was a finer contribution to gastronomy than all cold cereals put together. But it is undeniable that by taking breakfast off the list of meals at which America overate, the Kelloggs' vegetarianism did the nation a service.

Note that Ma Pettengill listed no fruit. In her time there was already a presumption, however, probably also the work of the vegetarian mind, that fruit in some form was hygienically indicated at breakfast. Fresh in season was best, and beginning breakfast with a half cantaloupe or ripe sliced peaches with cream is pleasant. But most of the year in households of moderate means the burden was put on stewed prunes, which not only could technically be regarded as fruit but also alleviated the national curse, also suspected of coming from overeating, of constipation. Gradually as Florida and, even more, California organized citrus distribution, the orange acquired a dominance over the American breakfast table never since challenged, grapefruit being a mere also-ran. The awkward task of peeling was avoided by cutting it in half and scooping out the pulp with a sharp, slender "orange spoon." But the triumph of the juice orange, crucial to Florida's citrus industry, and advertising symphonies on the theme of vitamin C could not begin until well after Dr. Elmer V. McCollum of the University of Wisconsin revolutionized the science of nutrition in 1913 by identifying the first vitamin.

Nutritionists were highly articulate long before that, however, primitive though their theories were. Between them and printed recipes in the periodical press the American table was shifting away from sheer number of dishes and a generally quantitative approach—the folk attitude of the farm household—toward delicacy, which in America necessarily meant the ladylike. Urban cooking schools, of which the best known was the Boston Cooking School, source of the Fanny Farmer cookbooks, were attended not by servants honing up their culinary skills but by affluent ladies hoping to learn how to refine their dinner tables. Women's magazines probably did even more than schools and cookbooks to encourage the housewife to avoid overcooking, too much starch and too much frying and to seek the savory and the succulent. Sometimes for the wrong reasons, sometimes by accident, these trends were hygienically sound.

The ensuing vicissitudes can be studied in the rise of salads after, say, 1880. Coleslaw had been a rural staple wherever cabbage and Pennsylvania Dutch influence penetrated—that is, in most of the nation. Lettuce was grown in the same garden patch to be eaten with sugar and vinegar (acceptable) or wilted with sugar, vinegar and hot bacon fat (superb). But the European salad of greens with oil, vinegar, salt and pepper was known only to the well-traveled and insistently French city restaurants. The most knowledgeable cookbooks strove to inculcate sound principles for salad and did at least succeed in conveying the notion that the word was synonymous with elegance. But it was difficult for the American lady to believe that it could be so simple. Considering vinegar coarse, she inclined to substitute lemon juice. On encountering mayonnaise sauce, she used it to dress lettuce probably because the ingredients sounded daintier, possibly also because she could buy it ready-made. Durkee's mayonnaise soon flanked the ketchup bottle. Fretting about the untidy appearance of leaf lettuce tossed in a bowl, she turned to the cabbage-stiff head or iceberg kind that could be neatly quartered and covered with pink Russian dressing made by spiking mayonnaise with bottled chili sauce. Aware of the high repute of fruit, she created fruit salads—sliced oranges, sliced bananas, grapes, bits of raw apple, bits of canned pineapple and such—mixed together and topped with mayonnaise or, as audacity grew, whipped cream buoying up a maraschino cherry. Sometimes the results of this ingenuity—Waldorf salad, for instance, and some other manipulations of fruit—were quite palatable. All, however, signified reluctance to let a good thing alone. And before she had finished fussing, she had convinced her husband and millions like him that any and all salads belonged to the world of hen bridge-parties and ladylike tearooms and were no fit part of a man's world.

Apropos, by the time of the votes-for-women parades in New York City one section of marchers, coequal with the units of trained nurses, garmentworkers and the like, consisted of lady operators of tearooms clothed all in white and bearing a banner with the device of a mammoth teapot. It should have shown an order of creamed chicken and waffles quartered with a pineapple salad—typical items in the tearooms then springing up in prosperous parts of large cities and in summer resorts. The refined atmosphere of such enterprises made them eligible livelihoods for women owners and managers. The good ones did well because they offered inexpensive and quiet places where women infiltrating the professions or with enough leisure to have a cordially long gossip with a woman friend could meet for lunch.

The menu seldom included many items that could not be eaten with a fork alone. This subtly reflected the ladylike attitude toward the table knife until recently fixed in American manners to the bewilderment of the alien visitor. The heinousness of using the knife to transfer something from plate to mouth—a technique all too common among us in the early 1800's—was so decried in the etiquette manuals of the mid-century that a sort of half taboo gathered over any use of the knife at all. The well-mannered took to using the fork to fragment not only vegetables but fish and meats whenever it was possible. Americans thus became a nation of right-handed fork wielders, marvelously skilled in making the tool do things for which it was never designed. On those unusual occasions when skill was baffled and resort to the knife was necessary—say, in eating steak or broiled chicken—the foreigner observed with mounting astonishment how the fork shifted to the left hand, the knife was used with the right, then the knife was laid on the plate, and the fork returned to the right hand to convey the resulting morsel to the mouth—all with the unconscious ease of lifetime habit. Two-handed eating, as in Britain or on the Continent, was deplored as vulgar where it survived among farming households or recent immigrants. By association, tenderness and ease of fragmentation, as if the knife had yet to be invented, became tokens of a successfully refined cuisine. To see a guest give up and reach for the knife would send a tiny pang of dismay through the conscientious hostess. It will be a pity when this national trait—so cleanly observable, so significant culturally—disappears, as it probably soon will, under the general erosion of manners and the growth of cosmopolitanism.

The triumphs of brand-named breakfast foods would never have occurred without vast advertising campaigns on billboards and in newspapers and magazines. W. K. Kellogg's pretty girl advertisements promising "Genuine Joy, Genuine Appetite, Genuine Health and therefore Genuine Complexion" [144] from eating cornflakes eventually settled down into a winsome trademark portrait of the Sweetheart of the Corn to impress name and the wholesomeness of the product on a malleable public. Jingles about a character named Sunny Jim made sunny and egregiously energetic by the health-giving qualities of Force were the talk of the nation. Mr. Dooley's friend Mr. Joyce was an addict of:

Guff . . . ye've seen th' advertismint: "Out iv th' house wint Lucky Joe; Guff was th' stuff that made him go." Mother prefers Almostfood, a scientific prepartion iv burlap. I used to take Sawd Ust . . . later I had a peeryod iv Hungareen, a chimically pure dish, made iv th' exterryor iv bath towels. We all have our little tastes an' enthusyasms in th' matther iv breakfast foods, depindin' on what pa-a-pers we read an' what billboords we've seen iv late. . . . I take gr-reat pains to see that nawthin' is sarved f'r breakfast that ain't well advertised an' guaranteed pure fr'm th' facthry, an' put up in blue or green pa-aper boxes.[145]

With that alliance of extravagantly advertised brand names and factory-filled packages, modern merchandising of foods and many other things had come of age. Today's consumer buying crackers, prunes, flour, sugar, oatmeal, butter, coffee, rice and other such staples would have been dismayed in the grocery of 1880 where all those things, plus vinegar, molasses, kerosene—you brought your own can—and salt fish were measured or weighed out from bulk containers, such as barrels, kegs and firkins, under rather unappetizing conditions. The persistence of Peck's Bad Boy in accusing the grocer of letting the cat sleep in the box of dried apples signified not so much morbid imagination as quite possible fact. Separate packaging by the pint or pound adds to the cost of the product but, granting reasonable inspection at the factory, is more hygienic than was the butter scooped up with a seldom-washed wooden paddle and passed across the counter in a piece of newspaper in a quaint, old-time country store. Brand-name packaging also enabled the food processor to break through the anonymity of just another barrel of sugar and exploit the possibilities of national advertising. The canners of pork and beans, tomatoes, corn, corned beef and such were playing the same game at about the same time. The cereal manufacturers "transferred patent-medicine hyperbole to the field of grocery advertising," [146] as is pointed out in Gerald Carson's invaluable *Cornflake Crusade*. And at just that time the enterprising ingenuity of the patent-medicine industry was clambering near its amazing peak of impudence.

Its first stage had been bitters—the mixtures of alcoholic spirits, odd, pungent-tasting herbs from the folk-medicine tradition and sometimes quinine that malaria-ridden America took before breakfast to ward off the shakes. The quinine had therapeutic point. In any case the alcohol made the subject feel robust. By the 1840's numerous proprietary-brand bitters were advertising widely in the press, led by Hostetter's Stomach Bitters, "harmless as water from the mountain spring," based on "vegetable curatives," which contained 44 percent alcohol and made its manufacturer, Colonel David Hostetter, a multimillionaire. Its claims as panacea gradually widened until by 1867 it would not only ward off the shakes but also:

Dyspepsia's pangs that rack and grind
The body and depress the mind; . . .
Colics and dysenteric pains,
'Neath which the strong man's vigor wanes;
Bilious complaints,—those tedious ills,
Ne'er conquered yet by drastic pills; . . .
Nervous prostration, mental gloom,
Heralds of madness or the tomb. . . .[147]

As the panacea business gained momentum, quite as well known as Hostetter's Bitters was Dr. Ayer's Sarsaparilla (26 percent alcohol, though the label said nothing about that) to be taken particularly in the spring to invigorate the blood and prevent "That Tired Feeling, Indigestion, Headache, Pains in the Back and Limbs, Feverishness. . . ." [147] It and other patent medicines made a multimillionaire out of Dr. Ayer, whose title was at least more genuine than those of his competitors—the University of Pennsylvania had given it to him for inventing an efficient pill-rolling machine. Presently Dr. Buckland's Scotch Oats Essence "WILL POSITIVELY CURE SLEEPLESSNESS, PARALYSIS, OPIUM HABIT, DRUNKENNESS, HYSTERIA, NEURALGIA, SICK HEADACHE, SCIATICA, NERVOUS DYSPEPSIA, LOCOMOTOR ATAXIA, HEADACHE, OVARIAN NEURALGIA, NERVOUS EXHAUSTION, ST. VITUS' DANCE, NEURASTHENIA, &c." [147]

Toward the end of the century the most renowned panacea was Dr. S. B. Hartman's Pe-Ru-Na, which, with about the same alcoholic content as a Manhattan cocktail, vaunted itself as good for catarrh—and then so defined catarrh that it included practically every ailment known to man. Special-purpose items also reaped golden harvests. The remedies for female complaints were led by Lydia Pinkham's Vegetable Compound, "The Greatest Medical Discovery Since the Dawn of History," impressively applying black cohosh, liferoot plant, fenugreek seed and other esoteric herbs from the old eclectic doctor's pharmacopoeia—dissolved in 21 percent alcohol. The public's kidneys, lungs and sexual powers were variously appealed to. Granted, the alcohol perked up the ailing, even though they did not realize it was there, and the herbs did no harm. But the $60,000,000 that Americans are known to have spent for proprietary medicines in the sample year of 1900 had several grave sides. Advertising products heavily laced with alcohol as cures for chronic drunkenness probably resulted in many an alcoholic's losing his struggle with himself. Use of bottled quackery for suspected diseases as serious as cancer, kidney disease and tuberculosis amounted to prolonged neglect and must often have led to unnecessary deaths. And the ingredients themselves were not always harmless. Mrs. Winslow's Soothing Syrup, for instance, very widely given to children, had morphine in it. Opium and cocaine accounted for the apparent good effects of other freely sold proprietary medicines.

Though there was obviously room for many rivals in the depth and breadth of public gullibility, competition made it necessary for such patent medicines to run like mad to stay in the same place, like the Red Queen. Hence an unprecedented flood of advertising in old and new techniques. A farmer with a barn visible from a railroad right-of-way could get it painted free if he didn't mind CASTORIA or PE-RU-NA in letters 10 feet high on its broadside. Itinerant sign painters put ST. JACOB'S OINTMENT on every accessible rock face in the country. The same was painted in huge letters on a bright red steamboat running up and down the Mississippi. Distribution of free almanacs sandwiching the incredible virtues of such-and-such pills or elixir among the phases of the moon and clusters of bad jokes was a widely used device. *Hostetter's Almanac* was a national institution. Dr. Ayer's print order for his was already 5,500,000 in 1868. It was notorious that without patent-medicine advertising most of the smaller newspapers in the United States would shut down, so it was unlikely that the editors would refuse any patent-medicine copy, however extravagant its claims. It usually went in for testimonials, often from Mrs. G. H. of Farmbelt, Illinois, who had been one foot in the grave with fits and consumption, but two bottles of Dr. William Hall's Balsam for the Lungs made a new woman of her. Now and again, however, celebrities who should have known better, like the Reverend Dr. Henry Ward Beecher or Horace Greeley or Senator Joseph Wheeler, Confederate hero, allowed use of a signed endorsement of Bristol's Sarsaparilla or Dr. Townsend's Remedy for Catarrh. The Pinkham company invited any and all women to write for medical advice to Mrs. Pinkham, whose high-necked, middle-aged picture appeared on every bottle of compound and in most of the advertising; the prompt replies were signed "Yours for Health, Lydia E. Pinkham." Legend says that when Queen Victoria died in 1901, minor papers lacking a picture of her ran instead the cut from the Pinkham advertisement, which was available in every newspaper printshop in the land.

Bottled quackery was even more of a bonanza because, as the 1900's neared, between Temperance propaganda damning drinking as sin and local option and state prohibition laws, procuring liquor was either inadvisable or inconvenient. Those aware of the high alcoholic content of Paine's Celery Tonic could buy it at the local drugstore without the social onus risked by buying a pint of bourbon. George Ade recalled "all those deacons who never drank anything stronger than Hostetter's Bitters." A

Midwestern friend of mine tells how his doctor father found a huge heap of Pe-Ru-Na bottles in the barn of an eminent local Temperance leader, dead of what had to be diagnosed as acute alcoholism. Those unaware of how many millions of gallons of potable alcohol flowed into the patent-medicine industry annually might become indignant when reproached with getting tiddly on Kilmer's Swamp Root. But none of William Lloyd Garrison's acquaintances ever told him why people sometimes smiled curiously when he, a great foe of Rum, recommended Dr. Church's Anti-Scrofulous Panacea as "permeating the whole system in a most delightful manner."

When Edward Bok's *Ladies' Home Journal* opened the muckraking attack on the quack bottlers and pill-rollers in 1904, it published a photograph of Lydia Pinkham's tombstone showing that the motherly old soul to whom so many women had been writing about the ills that Eve is heir to had been dead for more than twenty years. The next year came a rousing series of exposure articles expertly done by Samuel Hopkins Adams in *Collier's.* Thanks to the two magazines, to strong pressure from the American Medical Association and women's clubs and to the explosion set off by *The Jungle,* the federal Food and Drug Act of 1906 was passed and soon effectively curbed the worst of the patent-medicine trade. Its most dangerous claims could no longer be made; its labels had to state what went into the bottles, alcohol and all. Lydia Pinkham's Vegetable Compound and Pe-Ru-Na can still be bought. But the alcohol content is much lower these days, and those who knew both well in their great days say that the flavors are much altered for the worse. It is even unlikely that undergraduates still sing of how:

> Mrs. X had bosom trouble,
>   She was flat across the bow;
> Then she took three bottles of Compound,
>   Now they milk her like a cow!
> Oh we sing, we sing, we sing
>   Of Lydia Pinkham, Pinkham, Pinkham
> And her love for the human race! *

Even in eclipse, however, the old lady shares in what glory may attach to having played an outstanding role in the first great blooming of American brand-name advertising. The job that she and Dr. Ayer and the others did could hardly have been improved on by today's Madison Avenue with full use of television and radio.

*   *   *

* Data in the above section otherwise unattributed, like this version of the Pinkham song, are from my *The Life and Times of the Late Demon Rum.*

The chief purpose of sealed packaging, whether of foods or of nostrums, was to prevent substitution under the advertiser's brand. (Inadvertently it encouraged the development of the self-service store and then the supermarket in the decades after World War I.) Nevertheless, the greater cleanliness of Mr. Dooley's "blue or green pa-aper boxes" was also part of the new sanitation-mindedness sweeping America as the implications of the germ theory of disease gained currency. From the findings of the new microbiology the New Journalism created constructive, if sensational, ballyhoo about microbes, germs and the ubiquity of disease-bearing filth. The Sunday papers had horrendous pictures of flies enlarged to the size of frogs, all fearsome eyes and bristly legs, and texts explaining how diligently they carried germs from privy to table. Hence "Swat the Fly!" campaigns and widespread—and long overdue —installation of window screens and screen doors. Equally horrendous enlarged pictures of germs also helped. The garbage dump, paradise of rats, as well as flies, began its long retreat in 1885 when the U.S. Army demonstrated incinerators on Governors Island in New York Harbor in a day when nobody had reason to consider the ensuing rise in air pollution anything important.

Chlorination of water supplies was a crude but effective response to the menace of polluted streams. Local boards of health began to look askance at the public drinking cup chained to the fountain in the park. Adoption of the disposable paper cup in a dispenser near the ice-water tap in the railroad car was duly celebrated by the Lackawanna's Phoebe Snow:

> On railroad trips no other lips
> Have touched the cup that Phoebe sips.
> Each cup of white makes drinking quite
> A treat on the Road of Anthracite.

Pasteurization of milk greatly reduced the "summer complaint" that annually killed more babies than Pharaoh or Herod ever dreamed of. Laws barring sale of unpasteurized milk came in, despite the opposition of the dairy industry and of well-meaning persons who thought it unnatural. Other new laws required the proper washing of milk containers and of the udders and hinder parts of cows—measures now so taken for granted that it is strange to think that they were once radical innovations resented by both farmers and cows.

Europeans had made the first great discoveries in microbiology leading to modern epidemiology. Americans made a solid contribution when, during the occupation of Cuba after the Spanish-American War, Colonel Walter Reed of the U.S. Army Medical Corps and a group of heroic human guinea pigs, mostly enlisted men, demonstrated the previous theory of Dr. Carlos Finlay, a Cuban physician, that the virus of yellow fever was transmitted by the bite of a certain kind of mosquito. Not long before, a British doctor in India, Ronald Ross, had found certain other mosquitoes transmitting malaria. Thenceforward health authorities could make complete sense of the half sense of traditional notions about malaria being caused by miasma rising from swamps and of yellow fever coming from rotting refuse—which often supplies the small accumulations of water that the guilty mosquito needs to breed in. Now that the *why* was known, swamp drainage and municipal cleanups to eliminate breeding sites could be far more effectively applied. Experience gained in Havana enabled Americans to build the Panama Canal that yellow jack had forced the French to abandon and to lift from American coastal cities the standing menace of yellow fever that had struck them heavily, though only occasionally, for the last 100 years. Drainage, cleanups and screening gradually forced malaria, the old fevernager devil, the settler's worst enemy, the scourge that explained the advertisements of quinine-bearing patent medicines on farm fences over half the nation, into the slow retreat that has now largely eliminated it in America.

The South, where milder climate and less drainage made malaria most at home, benefited most. Then, late in 1902, an American type of hookworm, the other parasite perpetuating the caste of Southern poor whites, was found epidemic in areas where casual defecation, mild climate and lack of shoes—the new-hatched worms usually enter through the soles of the feet—had made it welcome. This discovery was the work of Dr. Charles Wardell Stiles of the U.S. Public Health Service based on previous location of such a parasite in Puerto Rico by Colonel Bailey K. Ashford of the U.S. Army Medical Corps. (Foolish as it was, the Spanish-American War had some valuable consequences; it brought Mr. Dooley to national notice and gave Reed and Ashford their opportunities.) Hookworm infesting the intestines leads to severe and debilitating anemia, often gives the victim an irresistible craving to eat earth— hence the poor white clay-eaters of the South—and usually so poisons him with the tiny worms' effluvia that he would be chronically listless even without the anemia. Dr. Stiles' announcement of his devotedly long-sought proof that so many underprivileged—hence shoeless— Southerners got their notorious sluggishness from hookworm inspired the national press to a volley of fair to poor jokes about the germ of laziness. This outraged Southerners and probably had something to do with the federal government's apathy about utilizing Dr. Stiles' findings. But he got his story to the chiefs of the Rockefeller Institute for Medical

Research, who granted him $1,000,000 for wholesale diagnosing and dosing of poor whites. The striking results led into wider programs until, twenty-five years after the furor about the germ of laziness, the South was, for the first time since William Byrd found the ne'er-do-wells of North Carolina so amusing, practically clear of its second most debilitating handicap. If there was to be a genuinely New South, this was a *sine qua non.*

Medicine was becoming socially important in America, as well as elsewhere, because the new epidemiology based on the germ theory could remove from whole populations the lethal pressures of many germ-based diseases. Our ancestors of 100 years ago could hardly have conceived of getting under strict control, often to the point of annihilation, not only smallpox but the great scourges of yellow fever, cholera, bubonic plague and the standard childhood diseases. Luckily for America, improvements in the quality of her medical profession now came along to give her full advantage. It was high time anyway. Americans had made important contributions to anesthesia and major surgery. American dentistry was acknowledged best in the world. But by European standards the regular medical schools that had gradually replaced the apprentice system during the 1800's ranged from mediocre at the eminent universities to discouragingly poor, and below them was a squirm of homeopathic, Thomsonian and eclectic institutions little better than diploma mills, though chartered by state legislatures and handing out degrees recognized by law.

Likely American aspirants to medicine who had the resources usually preferred to study abroad, probably in France or Scotland in the pre-Civil War era. They might well return highly qualified in terms of the time, like Dr. Oliver Wendell Holmes, early pointing out the obvious, if then ill-understood, connection between lack of cleanliness in the delivery room and childbed fever. But there were too few of Holmes' sort to accomplish much toward raising home levels of teaching and practice. After the Civil War, as German medical schools led the way in adding the test tube and the microscope to the dissecting table and the pharmacopoeia, young Americans followed the crowd to Germany and profited greatly. A crucial result was the foundation in 1893 of the great hospital and medical school at the new Johns Hopkins University in Baltimore which injected into students' bloodstreams German standards of research and scientific responsibility. After that the trend curved slowly upward. One of the brightest omens was the birth of the Rockefeller Institute putting to use generous funds administered by brilliant men like Hopkins- and German-trained Dr. Simon Flexner.

But the lag of generations of neglect was not easily overcome, and many of the best young Americans continued to flock to Europe.

An unmistakable turning point came in 1910 with the publication by Simon Flexner's also brilliant and also Hopkins- and German-trained brother, Abraham, of a Carnegie financed report that mercilessly analyzed the shortcomings of American and Canadian medical education. In direct consequence the next ten years saw most of the fringe-cult medical schools closed down. Almost as directly the legitimate ones were stimulated into stiffened standards—and American medicine was on its way to becoming, by World War II, scientifically and clinically the strongest in the world. Borrowing German medicine had proved an even better notion than borrowing German beer. In close parallel the application of German standards of study and research in the liberal arts was making genuine universities out of many American institutions that had previously been only intensified academies with law and medical schools attached. There again Johns Hopkins had led the way with the first European-style school of graduate studies in 1876. The improvement was worth the clotty pedantry that often came with the apparatus. It was even worth the cultural arrogance of the large, self-conscious segment of the German-American community, which on one level provided Harvard with a Germanic Museum and on another forced optional classes in German on completely tax-supported public schools in certain Midwestern cities with large German colonies.

Those crucially effective enlargements of photographs of houseflies were, of course, an additional cultural credit to the invention of photo-engraving—that is, linecuts and halftones. There was a large mixture of debit, however, in another conspicuous use of the halftone. Combining it with the steady improvement in cameras, well-meaning persons began reverently to photograph great works of art, reproducing the photographs in very fine-screen halftones and printing them off for the culturally ambitious to buy, frame and hang on the wall. True, they did help the Gibson Girl suppress chromos, as chromos had suppressed lithographs and engravings. But they had overtones much more pretentious than storytelling and penetrated more cultivated strata. "Photogravures" was one name for them. Boston, when H. G. Wells visited there in 1904, was so full of them that he said he would never see one again without thinking of the place. He recalled Botticelli's "Spring" and the "Victory of Samothrace" as prevalent subjects, but he must also have often encountered Murillo's and Raphael's best-known Madonnas, Gainsborough's "The Blue Boy," Böcklin's stagy "The Island of the Dead,"

Burne-Jones' shiny-armored "Sir Galahad" and the clustered rumps of Rosa Bonheur's "Horse Fair." Conspicuous in the affluent bachelor dilettante's apartment in San Francisco in Norris' *Vandover and the Brute* were photogravures of Rembrandt's "Night Watch" and a Velásquez portrait. Instead of buying original pictures and statues, Suzanne La Follette observes, Americans *c.* 1900 "usually contented themselves with the photographs of famous masterpieces. . . . The great majority who remained at home found . . . their aesthetic interests in reading about art, and seeing it only in . . . engravings (and . . . photographic reproductions) that accompanied the texts of books and magazine articles." [148]

The salient fact about the photogravure was the insistent brownness of the ink used, varying in subtle gradations from the lightest cream to Pittsburgh-stogy dark, a brownness so pervasive that it stained the soul. It did best with sculpture, where color values were not involved. With painting the results were, though honest as far as they went, dismal. Edith Wharton professed to believe that a good photograph of a painting was better than the usual copy in oils or watercolor. That must have been revulsion from encountering too many incompetent copies. The photogravure could do well only what able copying could—give an accurate notion of the relative elements of composition—while lacking the copyist's other opportunity, to have at least a stagger at the coloring. Further, the photogravure was usually reduced far below the scale of the original, and there was none of the sense of craftsmanship often valuable in a good engraving of the sort given out by the former art unions. Old World households were similarly infested; indeed the most acceptable photogravures were of European making for a European market. But Old World tastes still had far more opportunity to form themselves on actual sound paintings in museums than had Americans growing up outside a few great cities—New York City, Boston, Philadelphia, Chicago. Perversely, the reproduction of stimulatingly fine drawings—which photogravure could have done so much better—was seldom attempted. As it was, many an American child born into a household that hung the best-accepted photogravures in the right places grew up with the unconscious impression that great art was composed of various shades of maple syrup. Its presence in the home in this guise made it certain that he would instantly identify Frans Hals' "Laughing Cavalier" if he ever encountered the original, but appreciating it on its own merits would be almost impossible.

Further to bemuse the young, after 1890 Art Nouveau crossed the Atlantic to wash over America. This heavily influenced the design of books and minor household adjuncts—vases, bookends, ornamental ironwork—with the advantage of simplifying them, even though in what a recent writer defines as "a long sensitive sinuous line that reminds us of seaweed or of creeping plants[149] that left an oozily morbid flavor. It is a problem whether to deplore or applaud the effect of Art Nouveau on the career of Louis Comfort Tiffany, son of the wealthy proprietor of New York City's most conspicuous jewelry store. He began as a painter of very solid promise, European-trained, but with a personal directness in using his considerable skill that, as Dr. Robert Koch recently wrote for the Museum of Contemporary Crafts, was comparable to Winslow Homer's. But work in glass and the esthetics of William Morris and Ruskin attracted him and since he could afford any amount of trial and error, he had presently become exponent of an American variant of Art Nouveau regarded most favorably overseas, as well as at home. Under his intense supervision the designers and craftsmen of his various workshops made Tiffany glass shimmeringly famous. Those now collecting Art Nouveau—a field very lively since 1960—particularly value the jugs and bowls and goblets of colors as voluptuous as their shapes, and the leaded-glass lampshades, many with floral or fruit designs, in mushroom shapes that would have been impractical before electricity took over from gas and kerosene. Tiffany's work was unique, had its own fascination, and was moving away from the clutter of the esthetic notions that he began with. But it is a thorough pity that the man who painted his "Duane Street"—a study of a slum organized like a Vermeer, self-sufficient as a tree—did not go on painting.

Koch calls "Duane Street" "a forceful prefiguration of those New York painters of the early twentieth century known as the 'Ash Can School.' "[150] That was the critics' testy name for the group of maturing artists centering around Robert Henri, a spirited portraitist and gifted teacher, specializing after 1900 in painting Manhattan's lower orders and their environment. Among them John Sloan, George Luks, Everett Shinn and William Glackens had been staff artists on big-city newspapers. In a sense they remained journalists. But they soon grew out of the illustrator's leaning on anecdotes—the curse of the painting of the 1800's. Their adept enjoyment of Greenwich Village rooftops, the foreshortenings of elevated tracks, the set and huddle of city crowds, bubbles out of their paintings in a most exhilarating fashion. This concentration on urban materials was rather new, too. Previous generations of American artists had only picked sentimentally at such things. The most significant work outside portraits had gone to the woods or the seashore or the farm for data. John Canaday, summing up American painting since the Revolution, has dismissed the Ashcan school as "American subject matter presented in a passé European technique." [151] Technically there was a good deal of the Parisian art-school idiom in the way its members painted. But sweeping technical innovation is not a *sine qua non* in art. These men were using French methods as a golfer uses his clubs, not in order to design different ones but as tools enabling him to achieve a desired end.

Actually several of the group, including Sloan, probably the strongest, had not formed themselves on study abroad. Neither had George Bellows, much the Ashcan men's junior, markedly intensifying their idiom. He gives that feeling immanent in Copley, Eakins and Winslow Homer of being the born artist as some are born athletes. But by now transatlantic currents were running high as warning of tidal waves to come. At about the same time Bellows was coming into his own, an exhibit of the watercolors of the much older John Marin, who had been working abroad, attracted the discerning to Alfred Stieglitz's growingly renowned little gallery in New York City. Half-expatriate Maurice Prendergast's idiosyncratic version of European Impressionism was gaining acceptance, partly, no doubt, because no matter what the stuffy might think of its radical techniques, his work had an irresistible gaiety and integrity.

In 1908 some of the Ashcan men and a few others, including Prendergast, had informally organized as the Eight in order to arrange their own exhibits in defiance of public reluctance to accept them. Five years later it was the Eight who revolutionized American painting with their cataclysmic Armory Show that brought from Europe, principally France, hundreds of examples of the most radical canvases of the day—the innovations, including Cubism, that had been influencing them directly or indirectly but of which Americans in general knew nothing. The press particularly singled out Marcel Duchamps' "Nude Descending a Staircase" and made it as much a public byword as the germ of laziness. But the impact on the young from among whom American painters and critics would come after World War I was deep. Bellows would go on painting and lithographing his own way until his untimely death in 1925. Marin widened and sharpened his own idiom. But generally for the next generation American painting would be, as Canaday has said, "second-rate Europeanism as practiced by American-born artists." [152] The Eight were distinctly valuable figures. But the results of their Armory Show remind one of the sorcerer's apprentice.

The assumption that the sex that did not shave also did not drink had probably reached its peak in the 1890's. Of those then rejecting it one group was very small—the more sophisticated segment of the plutocracy —and one very large and at the other end of the economic scale, mostly New Emigrants. Neither had much more contact or sympathy with the suffrage than with the Temperance movement. The context in which foes

"Mystery"

"Brancusi's Pogany"

"As it is to-day"

Ballad
of
Dead Masters

AT THE INTERNATIONAL ART EXHIBITION

WHERE are the Masters we used to know—
    Titian and Rembrandt and Raphael?
Holbein and Michael Angelo?
    Luini, Da Vinci, Van Dyck as well?
Were we blinded beneath their spell,
That we thought they had come to stay—
    Titian and Rembrandt and Raphael?
Where is the Art of Yesterday?

Mystery dwells with us still, God wot!
    To Duchamp's canvases where's the clue?
Form they may have, and may be not.
    What is that to the Cubist's view?
Beauty? Color and line? Go to!
Does Picabia paint that way?
    False ideals with which we're through!
Where is the Art of Yesterday?

Could Velasquez a Matisse paint?
    Rubens, a fair Picasso dame?
Where is the della Robbia saint
    Brancusi's Pogany would not shame?
Donatello is lost to fame;
Archipanko now wears the bay;
    Somehow nothing is quite the same—
Where is the Art of Yesterday?

Nay, disturb not the Ancients' Swoon!
    Slumber is sweet to such as they.
Oh, that our dreams were like theirs, immune—
    Safe from Art as it is To-day!

M. M. Lyall.

"What is that to the Cubist's view?"

"Archipanko now wears the bay"

"A fair Picasso dame"

In verse and travesty-drawings the humorous weekly, Life, *expresses America's bewilderment over its first acquaintance with avant-garde art in 1913.*

of the Demon Rum hoped that votes for women would eventually win great victories for them was outside the big cities. Some of the suffragists' elder stateswomen, such as Susan B. Anthony, thought this implicit alliance unwise and strove to keep the two issues in watertight compartments. But most rank-and-file workers for votes for women probably deplored the Demon and specifically resented the saloon as men's womanless world. High on their list of what the triumph of suffragism would bring was the annihilation of the saloon. Jack London, no feminist but a fragilely reformed alcoholic well aware of the dangers of bars for those like himself, told his astonished wife that for that reason he voted yes in a votes-for-women referendum in California in 1912.

But for all the parallels between their separate routes to victory, the Prohibition (Eighteenth) Amendment was ratified months before the

Votes for Women (Nineteenth) Amendment. So Woman at the polls had very little to do with leading the nation into the promised land of nationwide drought. Here was a foretaste of higher frustrations to come as it proved that women enfranchised could not after all clean up politics, wipe out prostitution, or suffuse American life, as per invoice, with the bright light of womanly purity and idealism. Other federal amendments ratified just before World War I in the same atmosphere of hopeful reform all had substantial results one way or the other. The Sixteenth (making graduated income taxes legal) had wide social as well as fiscal consequences. The Seventeenth (requiring U.S. Senators to be elected by popular vote) made it more difficult for the vested interests to dominate the Senate. The Eighteenth broke down the presumption that nice girls never touched the stuff and also entrenched organized crime deep in the national economy in a fashion that old-style moonshiners had never dreamed of. But when the suffragists' dust had settled—as it did quickly—politics were seen to be going on much as usual. Apparently most women voting did so not so much as women with a special mission but as adult Americans acting as such without regard to sexual caste—just as men did. Their citizens' right to do so had always been the only valid reason for according them the franchise. It was all highly anticlimactic.

The geographical loci of votes for women and prohibition differed significantly. Suffrage won its sporadic preliminary victories in the Far West. In spite of occasional local meteors like Juliette Gordon Low in Georgia (she founded the Girl Scouts) and Mary Elizabeth Lease in Kansas (she came to fame by telling the Populists that Kansas should raise less corn and more hell), its guidance came principally from college women and organized women industrial workers in the Northeast. The WCTU, the Prohibition Party and the Anti-Saloon League, though each was active on a national scale at one time or another, were all basically Midwestern in outlook and had less impact in the Northeast than anywhere else. Their secondary stamping ground was the South.

Here this book's taboo on politics must be temporarily lifted. Into the 1890's the Prohibition Party had been regularly putting up candidates for federal and sometimes state office outside the two-party system and endorsing a Populist-flavored cluster of good causes along with a standing demand for a federal constitutional amendment outlawing alcoholic drink. The WCTU had been supporting them, usually informally by praising their objectives and creating a moral climate favorable to their cause. In 1893, however, the Ohio Anti-Saloon League was founded. Soon linked with other such statewide organizations into a national Anti-Saloon League, this was the agency that actually brought federal prohibition to pass by first undermining the Prohibition party and then stealing its thunder at the right moment.

The League was born in a church in righteous-minded Oberlin, Ohio, midwifed by a hot-gospel evangelist and home missionary Congregationalist parson, Howard Hyde Russell, whose previous career had taken him into Iowa, Missouri and a slum mission in Chicago. Like a virus invading a cell, the League remained parasitical on churches—sometimes Presbyterian or Congregationalist but usually of the more numerous and lively Methodist and Baptist persuasions. Indeed Virginius Dabney, distinguished editor of the Richmond (Virginia) *Times-Dispatch,* has called the League's Southern manifestation "Virtually a branch of the Methodist and Baptist churches." Its motto became "The Saloon Must Go!"—a shrewd appeal to public disapproval of the smelly institution on the street corner controlled by alien interests, teeming with corrupt politics and frequented by frowsy ne'er-do-wells. Its basic feelings were peevishly aggressive. It appealed to the country against the immoral big city; to the native against the immigrant, for the stereotype barkeeper was Irish or German, and his customers were alien-born industrial workers; and in the South to the white against the Negro on the theory that the less liquor was available, the less dangerous Negroes would be. There was also a tinge of Protestant against Catholic, for though the Roman Catholic hierarchy deplored drunkenness and sometimes developed its own Temperance activities, it was hardly conceivable that the small-town Methodists and Baptists of the League would approach Father Ryan about creating a branch of it among his parishioners—or that he would consent if approached.

The method was to set up in a given state within as many Protestant congregations as possible League branches, the members of which were kept inflamed with anti-Demon propaganda and pledged to vote as state headquarters directed. The current objective might be a statewide prohibition statute or a state local-option or no-license law enabling voters to dry up the state county by county. In any case, notice was served on legislators at county or state level—later federal, too—that thenceforth their getting reelected might well depend on whether they voted *right* as the Anti-Saloon League saw it. And that actually was the situation in many places. For the League had renounced not only the Prohibition Party's scatter-minded running after distracting good causes but also its candid policy of playing its own game outside the major two parties. That had never secured more than a few hundred thousand votes from the entire nation. The League had a better notion of what to do with those proportionately small numbers—use them to exploit one of the great flaws in democratic representative government, the disproportionate power of any organized bloc of voters able to keep the bulk of its members obeying orders in the voting booth.

Say the xth District of Ohio usually elected a Republican to the legislature with 10,000 votes to his Democratic opponent's 9,500. The League would move in and pledge, say, 1,000 local church members, probably prevalently Republican but including a sizable minority of Democrats, to vote as it directed. Then it demanded of both candidates in the next election pledges to support League-endorsed bills at the next session. If both submitted, the League let its members vote as they liked. If the Republican refused and the Democrat submitted, the members were told to vote for the latter. If most of them obeyed—as they usually did—they carried the day for the Democrat, though they actually made up only 5 percent of the electorate. The next time the Republican was likely to do what the League wanted, particularly since it notoriously paid little heed to its protégés' personal habits. It would turn out the anti-Rum vote for a renowned tosspot so long as he voted right on the League's measures.

The technique was not new, as the Prohibitionists had shown James G. Blaine in New York State in 1884. It would not have worked for the league's purposes in the tightly organized, heavily Catholic big cities. But it was ruthlessly and widely used elsewhere in a nation where a majority of people still lived outside large cities. The most renowned wielder of this political blackjack was Wayne B. Wheeler, a product of Ohio farms and Oberlin College, who enlisted with the League as soon as he had earned his way to a degree. Within fifteen years he was one of the most feared political manipulators in American history. About as handy with the device was James Cannon, Jr., a Methodist bishop from Virginia, who managed the League's gradual take-over of Southern legislatures and went on to become its brilliant chief tactician in Washington. Others shared the glory, of course. The rise of workmen's compensation laws, which made it expensive for employers whose drunken or drink-jittery employees had accidents on the job, brought the anti-Rum cause money, as well as encouragement, from many railroad managements and industrialists such as Rockefeller and Carnegie. Piously inclined kings of retailing, like John Wanamaker of Philadelphia and J. L. Hudson of Detroit, were already generous.

After 1900 rising general sentiment against the Demon made it advisable for most mass-circulation magazines to bar liquor advertising. The anti-Rum lecture was always on the program of the annual visit of the chautauqua that gave the typical small town several days of mingled entertainment, instruction and uplift. In such an atmosphere it was not surprising that the American Medical Association and the General Federation of Women's Clubs should come out against the saloon. Social workers in settlement houses, often admirably capable women, were seeing so much of the evils of drink among their clienteles of slum-dwelling new emigrants that they came around to agreeing that maybe alcohol should be outlawed, that certainly the saloon had to go. The Reverend John G. Woolley, last of the great reformed-alcoholic orators, told a conclave of Temperance campaigners in 1908: "The enemy has read the writing on the wall, and . . . is all but panicstricken. . . . The [liquor] trade runs like a scared wolf, ears low, tail between its legs. Local option presses hard upon it, and the deep sea of National Prohibition roars in front. . . ."

Presently the League took its blackjack to Washington and by 1913 had secured passage of the Webb-Kenyon Act, a federal ban on shipping liquor across the boundaries of dry states, which dried up an immense leakage previously created by express companies delivering "original package" liquor to mail-order customers. That was the League's first important victory on the federal level. It was probably what prompted its leaders to drop the pretense of the saloon's being the prime target and plump for a federal amendment forbidding manufacture and sale of alcoholic beverages. That, of course, was the very thing that the League had long been telling the Prohibition Party was a wrongheaded objective, and to add treachery to injury, it soon admitted that its strategists had had an eventual amendment in mind all along. The WCTU eagerly and the Prohibition Party dazedly joined it in a National Temperance Council to coordinate a new nationwide crusade to put prohibition into the Constitution.

At any other time this wrenching change of course might well have been a mistake. It was likely to cool off many who considered the saloon and not John Barleycorn himself the prime villain. And Woman's vote, which might well be crucially helpful in many areas, was still in the future in the more important states. The League's arm-twisting skill had its work cut out for it this time. But . . . the next year came World War I and the same dislocations and confusions that so aided the campaign for the Nineteenth Amendment. The League exploited the repercussions of the war so adroitly that by late 1917 it had the Eighteenth Amendment on its way to ratification, completed in 1920. It actually had Congress so bewildered and tame that a bill imposing national prohibition presented as a war-emergency measure was passed ten days after the war was over.

Several waves of experience with prohibition in a number of states over the previous eighty years had left small grounds for believing that national prohibition would accomplish what its proponents hoped. But to many persons of goodwill, ability and position—William Allen White, Dr. Harvey W. Wiley, David Starr Jordan—including many who also believed in the socially cleansing effects of votes for women, it seemed a great step toward a happier world. So did it also to the moonshiners and bootleggers who, having learned their business well in the successive dry spells in various states, now had only to apply them profitably coast to coast.*

The Anti-Saloon League was no democratic institution. Its leaders were a self-perpetuating oligarchy. But its great shift of objective to outright prohibition did finally make the anti-Rum movement wholly equalitarian in tone. Until then, some elements in the Temperance cause had consciously or unconsciously been seeking to protect the lower orders from their baser selves by wiping out the saloon that tempted them to tipple, while the better element could still drink like gentlemen at their clubs or at home with bottled stuff from the state liquor store or shipped in by express on mail order. Suppose the Eighteenth Amendment well enforced, however, and private stocks exhausted, mansion and club would have no more drinking privileges than Joe's place on the corner. The preamble of this Declaration of Independence from alcohol might have had a line about all men being equally unfree. The gentlemanly drinker was to do without for the sake of his weaker brethren. As the League saw it, that was no great deprivation, for good Methodist or Baptist men had no business wanting to drink anyway.

This equality of abstinence was fitting in a nation where caste feeling probably was lower than anywhere else outside the English-speaking world in 1914, and lower than in England, too. To make that statement one must, of course, ignore the caste aspect of the Negro problem, but until all too recently, ignoring all its aspects was customary. One must also except the South, where the caste of poor whites persisted more distinctly than any such group of Old American whites elsewhere, their position remaining much like that of England's Cockneys, who are as much Englishmen as any peer of the realm, yet categorically despised. One must disregard Northern nativist uneasiness about and contempt for the Jews, the Catholic old emigrants and pretty much the entire New Emigration; and also except the gringo Southwesterner's scorn for the distinct and rapidly growing caste of Mexican-Americans. Qualifications so numerous and broad sound ironic. Yet it remains true that in general within the American white community of people named Smith, Jones, McIntyre and Wagner—call it Norman Rockwell's America—Americans as of the Fourth of July, 1914, were nearer than most human beings to treating one another as equals. They were also much nearer it than their forebears had been on that date in 1770.

Non-Americans certainly saw them as highly equalitarian. They had

* The preceding section is largely a condensation from Chapter XIII of my *The Life and Times of the Late Demon Rum.*

less than other Western peoples of one kind of politeness for A and another for B because he was on a different social footing; indeed to the European it often looked as if they had no politenesses at all. They valued informality in their leaders. They called all women ladies and treated them much alike, usually with intentions of deference so marked that Europeans thought them grotesque. They gloried in strive-and-succeed and regarded America's relative incidence of economic opportunity, still higher than anything in the Old World though eroding, with particular pride. In the student's working his way through college in jobs traditionally considered menial, jerking sodas or firing furnaces during the academic year to cover living expenses, waiting table in summer resorts to cover tuition and clothes, they had a unique innovation. They sometimes even felt misgivings about the humble-origins story. Ruggles of Red Gap, the English gentleman's gentleman in process of Americanization, is struck by an inspirational list of great men who had come far: "Demosthenes was the son of a cutler. Horace was the son of a shopkeeper. . . ." But Cousin Egbert, born to and adept in American values, is annoyed: "I don't see what right they got to rake up all that stuff. . . . Who cares what their folks was? Horace was the son of a shopkeeper—Horace who?" [153] Part of that may have been residue from the great Western tradition that it was not only discourteous, it might even be unsafe to show interest in a man's origins. But another element is equalitarianism uneasy about the ostentation of the self-made man.

Proof of the validity or, anyway, vigor of such American feeling lay in the quickness with which newcomers picked up its shibboleths and often much of its spirit. Nothing so shocked the visiting upper-class Briton as free-and-easy treatment from an Americanized fellow countryman from the lower classes at home. The four major nonpolitical phenomena in America between the Revolution and World War I might be set down as: the spread across the continent; the industrialization of the economy with concomitant mass immigrations and partial shift of native population off the land; the rise of American women to an importance unknown elsewhere; and the growing application to social as well as political relations of the belief that "all men are created equal."

That is the view from outside, nor was it illusive. It was true, as the established peasant immigrant so often wrote back to the Old Country, still gloating over it, that the only persons to whom he was supposed to take off his hat were women. This was not just leveling either. It was leveling *up* as Thomas Jefferson Wertenbaker sagely noted in *The Middle Colonies*: "The vital phenomenon in American history has been the lifting of millions . . . from the lower class into the middle class. The destitute, the unfortunate, the oppressed trooped across the Atlantic . . . and

America has turned them into prosperous farmers, traders, manufacturers, doctors, lawyers, skilled artisans." [154] The second-generation Irish hung lace curtains; the Russian or Polish Jew bent over the sewing machine would see his son in law or medical school. The process is continuing today in the large and growing number of American professional men, many high in their professions, with Italian, Polish, Syrian names.

But thoughtful and candid persons born inside Norman Rockwell's America as WASPishly as Cousin Egbert have often come to see that the view from within has curious ripples, flaws and broken patterns, some so subtle as to be discernible only by peripheral vision, disappearing when looked at directly. They promise to stay a good while too. *Over in the project* means pretty much what *the wrong side of the tracks* used to.

Howells, possibly slightly idealizing the boys of his generation in Hamilton, Ohio, in the middle of the 1800's, thought that he had seen valid equality only in their "rude republic, where one fellow was as good as another, and the lowest-down boy in town could make himself master if he was bold and strong enough." [155] By the time he was in Columbus, Ohio, as a young man just before the Civil War, he found the superficial wide equality of the many, many people he mingled with flawed by the realization that it neglected to include "people who worked for a living with their hands." He thought it "strange and sad" that "if I had still been a compositor at the printer's case I could not have been received at any of the houses that welcomed me as a journalist." [156] In the next generation R. L. Duffus found in Waterbury, Vermont, cliques tenuously associated with which religious denomination one belonged to. There was "a lot of good will in the atmosphere but it also had about as much diversity as to who called on whom as could be found in a much bigger community." [157]

The great West was well started on the same sortings out and siftings into layers. ". . . one man has been as good as another in [only] three places," Owen Wister said in noting a persistent friendship between a rolling-stone cowhand and a territorial governor, "Paradise before the Fall; the Rocky Mountains before the wire fence [a moral and also nostalgic equivalent of Howells' boys' republic]; and the Declaration of Independence." [158] Harry Leon Wilson made the mining magnate's mansion in Montana City "a landmark in the most fashionable part . . . such distinctions are made in Western towns as soon as the first two shanties are built." [159] An early governor of Colorado found it necessary to break out: "I don't want to hear any more about First Families in this State . . . may I remind you that our First Families were miners married to whores?" [160] By 1890 Howells made the uneasy hero of *A Hazard of New Fortunes* say it was no use pretending that America had no nobility.

". . . we might as well pretend we haven't first-class cars in the presence of a vestibuled Pullman . . . if the plutocracy that now owns this country ever sees fit to take on the outward signs of an aristocracy . . . it won't falter from any inherent question of its worth. Money prizes and honors itself, and if there is anything it hasn't got, it believes it can buy it." [161] It is understandable that Howells was one of the first to applaud Veblen's skill in detecting the gleam of dollars in social data.

Vestiges of medieval attitudes complicated these subtleties without improving them. The contrast between blue and white collar was as powerful as considerations of income in Howells' Columbus. Even today the dollar of the skilled craftsman cannot always buy the same amount of prestige as that of his white-collar cousin making no more money selling life insurance. And among the uppermost social strata of large communities, inherited prestige, not necessarily matched by money of the same order, soon played a part. Mrs. Van So-and-so's income might dwindle, but she retained her social standing, and a young man from the West with raw millions felt that he did well by his future in marrying her daughter. The roles of the sexes were reversed, though the ethics were the same, in the many real-life instances, causing paroxysms of gossip and gloating newspaper stories, of the British duke or the French marquis marrying $10,000,000 in railroad securities with a pretty and ambitious American girl thrown in. That was another of Gibson's favorite subjects for drawings.

In one crosslight all this bears a strong resemblance to *Animal Farm,* where, though all animals were equal, some were more equal than others. But there is a clue to the antidote in Duffus' further reflections about the cliques of Waterbury: "At the same time, anybody who tried to divide us into upper, middle and lower classes, in so many words, would have found himself a lower class all by himself. We didn't quite practice equality, but we did believe in it." [157] One result was that equality *was* practiced more frequently, though inconsistently, in such a community than in a counterpart little town in Devonshire or Franconia.

Note, too, that America was (except in the South after the full development of sharecropping) a plutoaristocracy without a countervailing peasantry. Farmers, their number still large though dwindling, usually shared in a gradual increase of standards of rural living and rural expectation of town-style things. The farmer's daughter was likely to have a piano in the parlor; his son was planning to go to the Ag School at State U. In 1904 a cartoon by John McCutcheon is already showing a novelist going to the country for local color where farmers say, "I'll jest swan to Guiney," and finding his first specimen driving an automobile and planning to attend a chautauqua meeting that evening. In the background of the drawing stands the windmill that has exempted human muscle from the water-pumping chores, and behind it should have loomed the silo, revolutionizer of stock feeding, that was now making American barns look like French medieval castles. The lonely squalor of the frontier farm persisted in patches, waiting for the good roads movement set off by the automobile to come to the rescue where railroads and interurbans had not yet penetrated. But even those underprivileged farmers were not what Europe thought of as peasants. And the genuine immigrant peasants who got beyond the port cities and took up and worked land, such as the Scandinavians and Bohemians of the Plains states, tended to lose the knack of being peasants in one generation.

Nor was the essential leveling-up which encouraged the antidote a matter purely of economics, of the crude almighty dollar, as had looked likely in the Gilded Age. An unchecked plutocracy, such as Howells came to postulate, should have taken for its symbol some self-made man of righteousness such as John Wanamaker or maybe the more imaginative as well as public-spirited kind of great fortune-founder, enjoying his millions by employing them in constructive adventures, like Andrew Carnegie or Henry Flagler. All three were classic cases of strive-and-succeed; all had a great deal of adulation. But toward 1900 it was unmistakable that the national hero replacing Washington in the hearts, if not the minds, of his countrymen was no plutocrat, however well-meaning, however consonant with the national cult of Mammon, but Abraham Lincoln. His was also a strive-and-succeed story. But it had little to do with dollars and much with equalitarian values.

Lincoln's assumption of the role had been a gradual process. His personality did not have as wide an opportunity to be appreciated as it would have had today. The rail-splitter reference in the campaign of 1860 had been useful but meant little more than the log cabin motif that elected Harrison in 1840. Few Americans outside Illinois and Washington had seen any more of him than campaign pictures badly drawn from photographs. It was the drama of assassination that started him immediately on the way to apotheosis. But that was no unfailing formula. Though President James A. Garfield, a famously charming man, met the same sort of death in 1881, sizable efforts to make a significant martyr of him came to little, even though his life story was almost as poor boy-to-White House as Jackson's or Lincoln's. Besides it took time for the North's large minority of Democrats to lose the habit, acquired during the backbitings of the Civil War, of mistrusting Old Abe, martyr or not. What may have made the difference for Lincoln was an accumulation of widely read biographies so marshaling the data about a prepossessing character that a folklore figure gradually formed from their emanations and went floating over America as the ideal for the nation to love and trust—not a father image, but rather a favorite-uncle image.

There was little false about it in the earlier stages. Lincoln was markedly honest but also a politician able to turn keen horse trader; bent on justice but readily distracted into mercy; capably wielding power but never confusing his personal attributes with those of his office; intensely humorous but little given to the sting of wit; intensely religious but relying on no particular sect; a prose stylist employing with ingratiating clarity and pith the widely familiar words and music of the King James Bible and *The Pilgrim's Progress.* And though he had striven and succeeded to the highest office in the land, he could never be got to prefer pomp and ceremony to the ways of a self-educated backwoods lawyer yarning with the boys on the store porch with his cowhide boots on the railing higher than his head.

But *c.* 1900 this posthumous hero worship began to get out of hand, skirting blasphemy. Consider *The Crisis* by Winston Churchill, a widely esteemed novelist then far better known in America than his dashing young English namesake. The hero, a young Easterner beginning life in St. Louis just before the Civil War, is sent to see Lincoln by his legal mentor, who later, on his deathbed, says: "I sent you to see Abraham Lincoln—that you might be born again. . . . You were born again. . . . I saw it in your face. O God, would that . . . Abraham Lincoln's hands might be laid upon all who complain and cavil and criticise and think of the little things in life!" The Southern heroine is asking President Lincoln for a military pardon for a Confederate: "Oh . . . the sorrow in those eyes, the sorrow of a heavy cross borne meekly. . . . The pain of a crown of thorns worn for a world that did not understand. . . . 'Virginia,' said Mr. Lincoln, 'I have suffered with the South . . . your pain has been my pain. What you have lost, I have lost. And what you have gained,' he added sublimely, 'I have gained,' . . . With his long arm he pointed across the [Potomac] to the southeast, and as if by a miracle a shaft of sunlight fell on the white houses of Alexandria." [162]

One would give a good deal to hear the forks-of-the-crick monosyllables in which Abraham Lincoln would have expressed his opinion of that passage. But overdoing things is an American trait. This example does not vitiate the reassuring implications of the mass impulse that led the nation of trusts and Newport "cottages" and lynch mobs and yellow journalism to choose Lincoln as national archetype. Veblen could readily have accounted for France's cult of Napoleon I or the destructive emotions involved in the cartoonists' abstractions of Uncle Sam and John Bull. He could never have explained how the society that inspired his corrosive notions could settle on Lincoln as its persisting ideal.

Fashions in ideas change. The distribution of certain temperaments among Western peoples changes much less. By 1900 the same kinds of people—not the same individuals but their emotional counterparts—who had taken up Grahamist vegetarianism had taken up Dr. Fletcher's cult of chewing everything into nothing or Dr. James Henry Salisbury's doctrine that chopped beef three times a day was the road to health. At least that was how Salisbury's thousands of adherents interpreted his teachings; remember him next time you see "Salisbury steak" lingering on a bill of fare. After 1909, when Dr. Sigmund Freud came to Clark University to expound his startling new psychiatry, already much talked of in medical circles, the same kinds of people who had admired phrenology—many distinguished minds among them in both cases—were deeply impressed with psychoanalysis and the patter of the well-informed broke out in a rash of *complex, sublimation* and *subconscious.* Don Marquis, the brilliant custodian of the "Sun Dial" column in the New York *Sun,* had a character named Hermione who, with her Little Group of Serious Thinkers, eagerly followed the intellectual gleams of the day—the Russian ballet, Bergson, Gertrude Stein. Presently she was announcing that "There is the real Ego, and there is the Alter Ego. And besides these, I have so many moods which do not come from either of my Egos! they come from my Subliminal Consciousness. Isn't the Subliminal Consciousness wonderful; simply *won*derful! . . ." Later they took up "the Exotic. . . . Quite different from the Erotic, you know, and from the Esoteric, though they're all mixed up with it sometimes. . . ." [163]

Greenwich Village, already for two generations a refuge for money-shy artists and writers, now became a nationwide concept, and its denizens were complaining that prosperous hangers-on of bohemia were moving in and raising the rents and the prices at the Italian table d'hôtes. Ibsen and Shaw had been showing the American theater that dramatized ideas could attract audiences. Those seeking occasion to feel optimistic about the future of education and the American child were all agog over the imaginative and charming kindergarten methods developed by an Italian theorist, Dr. Maria Montessori; their counterparts had felt thus about Pestalozzi. (Interest in the Montessori method has revived in the last few years.) There was talk about a new, low-down Negro music called jazz. How much of this sounds familiar, as if of a fairly recent past instead of the practically prehistoric period before World War I! For a strikingly contemporary touch, the press c. 1900 was deploring the spread of hashish or hemp cigarettes; only the smokers were not self-conscious rebels against conformity but rah-rah college boys given to mandolins and peg-top trousers.

Between 1900 and 1914 American consumption of conventional cigarettes had risen 500 percent. City gutters were dotted with discarded empty packs of Sweet Caporals, Omars and Fatimas, brands less expensive than the all-Egyptian Melachrinos and Egyptian Deities. Later it was thought to have been the war that set America smoking cigarettes, but the acceleration was actually well under way before fighting began. Indeed it has been clear in the last hundred pages that the Jazz Age and maybe the lost generation too were well into the pilot-plant stage ready to unfold like a parachute when World War I should come along. In view of the momentum already acquired by iconoclastic ideas and practices before 1914, doubtless much of the 1920's-to-be would probably have come to pass had the war never occurred.

For the further purposes of this book consider how many of these important innovations were of Old World origin: Freud; the Ibsen-Shaw approach to theater; the naturalistic (as in Zola) and the prophetic (as in Tolstoy) approaches to the novel; Omar; Madam Glyn, for that matter; the imported tactics of the English suffrage movement; the automobile; the cigarette; the Montessori method; bicycles, golf, tennis. In spite of growing lend-lease in the arts, America's chances of weaning herself from cultural colonialism had never been high. Indigenous hints, such as Mark Twain, the skyscraper, the interurban, ragtime, industrial unions, antitrust laws and inscrutable caste system, had usually been overshadowed by the borrowings of snobbishness or, in worthier instances, by sensible realization that America had always been part of the general Western tradition and that German music, say, was much better than anything America was likely to produce for generations. Not for fifty years, however, had the westward flow been so pronounced, so insistent that America should remain a cultural province of the West as a sort of collective Mother Country. On the eve of Europe's first really serious effort to commit suicide, she was pouring out striking and fertile things with a richly heightened vigor. The Niagara River markedly quickens its pace and turns all slick and brilliant before reaching the brink of the fall.

The deeper cultural involvement of the Old and New Worlds could have been an omen of the thickening political and emotional involvement inevitable after Wilhelm II's army crossed into Belgium. Both political and cultural relations have continued to deepen through two universally disastrous wars and half a century. Neither isolationism among many Americans nor puerile resentments of American power have sufficed to slow that intermingling. Since World War II, of course, the balance of intercontinental relations has been shifting to match technological shifts.

Accounts are still in the Old World's favor in many matters. No Old World press habitually employs New World critics, whereas Old World critics are often conspicuous on the staffs of the best American newspapers and magazines. The presumption maintained so long by Old World experience and skills continues to dominate. But it may mean something about the future—good? bad?—that it was the New World's movies, airplanes and economic innovations that have established *le Dry* (the martini cocktail) and *le drugstore* in the heart of Paris.

The martini is one result of the imaginativeness that, it was surmised, often distinguished the emigrants who founded America from those who stayed at home. That choice of Abraham Lincoln was another.

The analytical candor with which many aspects of America are treated in the foregoing is not likely to distress Americans of common sense and balance. But it may unduly gratify certain Old Worldlings accustomed to dine out on their impatience with Americans' alleged crudities and confusions. To them let me apply what Robert Louis Stevenson wrote when his little book about his dearly beloved Edinburgh occasioned too much chuckling in the rival city of Glasgow: "To the Glasgow people, I would say only one word, but that is of gold: *I have not yet written a book about Glasgow.*"

Notes

Notes

Full titles for the following references are given in the subsequent list of quoted sources.

PRELUDE

1. Van Buren, "Wiltwyck Under the Dutch."

SECTION I

1. Hanna, *Wilderness Trail*, I, 272.
2. Welby, *Visit*, 200.
3. John Smith, *Travels*, I, 57.
4. Beverley, *History*, 139.
5. John Smith, *Travels*, I, 120-121.
6. Hakluyt, *Voyages*, VI, 169-76.
7. E. M. Andrews, *Colonial Period*, I, 300
8. John Smith, *Travels*, II, 726-27.
9. John Winthrop, *History*, I, 26.
10. *Narratives of Early Maryland*, 296.
11. Drayton, *Minor Poems*, n.p.
12. Personal communication from Indianapolis *News*.
13. Beverley, *History*, 125, 244.
14. *Ibid.*, 230.
15. Wertenbaker, *Old South*, 146.
16. Van Wagenen, *Golden Age*, 155.
17. Fithian, *Journal*, 118.
18. Hanna, *Wilderness Trail*, I, 370.
19. Crane, *Southern Frontier*, 111.
20. *Ibid.*, 117.
21. Weeden, *Economic and Social History*, I, 129.
22. Dunbar, *History of Travel*, 431-36.
23. *Narratives of Early Pennsylvania*, 411.
24. Franklin, *Works* (Bigelow ed.), II, 467.
25. *Ibid.*, III, 78.
26. Hanna, *Wilderness Trail*, I, 2.
27. Crane, *Southern Frontier*, 124-25.
28. J. P. Hale, *Trans-Allegheny Pioneers*, 171.
29. Crane, *Southern Frontier*, 124-25.
30. Flexner, *Mohawk Baronet*, 393-94.
31. Johnson, *Wonder-Working Providence*, 257.
32. Gordon, *Journal*, 483.

SECTION II

1. R. L. Stevenson, *Scotland to Silverado*, 34, 11.
2. Willison, *Saints and Strangers*, 197.
3. John Smith, *Travels*, II, 953.
4. W. B. Smith, *White Servitude*, 83.
5. Trevelyan, *English Social History*, 164-65.
6. Byrd, *Histories*, 2.
7. John Smith, *Travels*, II, 444, 486, 929.
8. C. M. Andrews, *Our Earliest Colonial Settlements*, 3.
9. *Ibid.*, 19.

10. Hakluyt, *Voyages*, VI, 140.
11. C. M. Andrews, *Colonial Period*, I, 55.
12. Drayton, *Minor Poems*, n.p.
13. C. M. Andrews, *Colonial Period*, I, 80.
14. John Smith, *Travels*, II, 499.
15. Byrd, *Histories*, 122.
16. Atkinson, *History of Spain and Portugal*, 135.
17. Byrd, *Histories*, 3-4, 120-22.
18. *Narratives of New Netherland*, 50.
19. John Smith, *Travels*, II, 193.
20. Bradford, *Plymouth Plantation*, 72.
21. Johnson, *Wonder-Working Providence*, 40-41.
22. Bradford, *Plymouth Plantation*, 178.
23. *Ibid.*, 120-21.
24. John Smith, *Travels*, II, 516.
25. C. M. Andrews, *Colonial Period*, I, 372.
26. Weeden, *Economic and Social History*, I, 54-56.
27. *Ibid.*, I, 272-73.
28. *Ibid.*, I, 364.
29. R. C. Winthrop, *John Winthrop*, I, 309.
30. Parkes, "Morals and Law Enforcement," *New England Quarterly* (July, 1932).
31. Wertenbaker, *First Americans*, 75.
32. Lodge, *Short History*, 473.
33. Johnson, *Wonder-Working Providence*, 22.
34. C. M. Andrews, *Colonial Period*, II, 119.
35. Wertenbaker, *Puritan Oligarchy*, 33, 214-15.
36. Fox, *Yankees and Yorkers*, 3.
37. Angoff, *Literary History*, 132.
38. John Winthrop, *History*, II, 53.
39. *Ibid.*, II, 73n.
40. *Ibid.*, II, 73.
41. *New England Primer*.
42. Bill of Lading in Warner House, Portsmouth, New Hampshire.
43. R. C. Winthrop, *John Winthrop*, II, 152.
44. *Narratives of New Netherland*, 204.
45. Fox, *Yankees and Yorkers*, 3-4.
46. Johnson, *Wonder-Working Providence*, 5.
47. Morison, *Builders*, 232.
48. Miller, *Colonial Image*, 191-92.
49. E. D. Andrews, *Shakers*, 21.
50. Bridenbaugh, *Cities in the Wilderness*, 101.
51. Putnam, "Dutch Element," 207.
52. Fox, *Yankees and Yorkers*, 38-39.
53. Dobrée, *William Penn*, 237.
54. Willison, *Saints and Strangers*, 376.
55. Jefferson, *Basic Writings*, 156.
56. Lodge, *Short History*, 238.
57. Bridenbaugh, *Cities in the Wilderness*, 57, 169.
58. Hanna, *Scotch-Irish*, II, 46-47.
59. Sheffield, *Address*, 28.
60. *Ibid.*, 8-9.
61. Downing and Scully, *Architectural Heritage*, 39.
62. Dankers and Sluyter, *Journal*, xxiv-v.
63. *Narratives of Early Pennsylvania*, 395n.
64. Dobrée, *William Penn*, 409.
65. Singleton, *Social New York*, 25.

66. Franklin, *Works* (Sparks ed.), VII, 66.
67. *Ibid.*, 66ff.
68. Franklin, *Autobiographical Writings,* 719.
69. Burke, *Works,* IX, 347-48.
70. Hanna, *Wilderness Trail,* II, 162n.
71. C. M. Andrews, *Colonial Folkways,* 234-35.
72. Cuming, *Sketches,* 42-43.
73. Downing and Scully, *Architectural Heritage,* 38.
74. Franklin, *Autobiography,* 236.
75. Dexter, *Colonial Women,* 114.
76. Beverley, *History,* 286.
77. A. E. Smith, *Colonists in Bondage,* 5-7.
78. Bradford, *Plymouth Plantation,* 316.
79. Sollers, "Transported Convict Laborers," *Maryland Historical Magazine,* II.
80. Lamont, *Brief Account,* 3.
81. C. M. Andrews, *Colonial Folkways,* 183.
82. Boucher, "Letters," *Maryland Historical Magazine,* VII-X, 253.
83. *Narratives of New Netherland,* 196.
84. Ebenezer Cook, *Sot-Weed Factor,* 21.
85. W. B. Smith, *White Servitude,* 49.
86. *Narratives of Early Maryland,* 293.
87. Hanna, *Wilderness Trail,* I, 523; II, 2.
88. Beverley, *History,* 68-69.
89. C. M. Andrews, *Colonial Period,* I, 65n.
90. Donne, *Sermons,* IV, 272.
91. A. E. Smith, *Colonists in Bondage,* 133.
92. Sollers, "Transported Convict Laborers," *Maryland Historical Magazine,* II.
93. Southey, *Chronological History,* 146.
94. Franklin, *Works* (Federal ed.), V, 87.
95. Behn, *Widow Ranter,* 115.
96. Boswell, *Samuel Johnson,* 299.
97. A. E. Smith, *Colonists in Bondage,* 107.
98. Sollers, "Transported Convict Laborers," *Maryland Historical Magazine,* II.
99. Franklin, *Works* (Federal ed.), V, 87.
100. Franklin, *Autobiography,* IV, 35-37.
101. Boucher, *View,* 183-84.
102. Footner, *Eastern Shore,* 9.
103. Bridenbaugh, *Myths,* 16.
104. Owen Wister, *Virginian,* 147.
105. J. T. Adams, *Epic of America,* 241.
106. John Smith, *Travels,* II, 541.
107. John Winthrop, *History,* I, 149.
108. Boyd, Smith and Griffin, *Here They Once Stood,* 94.
109. Johnson, *Wonder-Working Providence,* 262.
110. Hill, *Yankee Kingdom,* 85.
111. Giles, *Singing Valleys,* 85.
112. Samuel Sewall, *Diary,* 179.
113. Knight, *Journal,* 38.
114. Byrd, "Letters," 88-90.

SECTION III

1. C. M. Andrews, *Colonial Folkways,* 2-3.
2. Gordon, *Journal,* 405.
3. Dexter, *Colonial Women,* 31-32.
4. Marckwardt, *American English,* 106.
5. H. L. Wilson, *Ruggles of Red Gap,* 198.

6. Hanna, *Scotch-Irish*, II, 66.
7. Weeden, *Economic and Social History*, II, 537-38.
8. Eggleston, *Circuit Rider*, 54-55.
9. Wertenbaker, *Puritan Oligarchy*, 166-67.
10. Weeden, *Economic and Social History*, I, 227.
11. Colonial Williamsburg, *Leatherworker*, 27.
12. Parkman, *Oregon Trail*, 290.
13. Howells, *Years of My Youth*, 53.
14. C. F. Adams, *Three Episodes*, II, 806.
15. Lancaster, *Homes, Sweet Homes*, 12.
16. C. F. Adams, *Three Episodes*, II, 806.
17. *Ibid.*, 807.
18. Cecil Drinker, *Not So Long Ago*, 29.
19. Wildes, *Lonely Midas*, 334.
20. C. F. Adams, *Three Episodes*, 802-3.
21. Byrd, *Histories*, 96.
22. Bridenbaugh, *Cities in the Wilderness*, 17.
23. Harrower, *Journal*, 73.
24. Quincy, "Journal," 465.
25. Pound, *Penns*, 238-39.
26. Beverley, *History*, 120.
27. Wertenbaker, *Old South*, 8.
28. Byrd, *Histories*, 114.
29. C. M. Andrews, *Colonial Self-Government*, 297.
30. *Travels in American Colonies*, 590.
31. Moreau de St.-Méry, *Journey*, 100-1.
32. Basil Hall, *Travels*, I, 71.
33. Personal communication.
34. Cuming, *Sketches*, 320.
35. Dankers and Sluyter, *Journal*, 394-95.
36. Knight, *Journal*, 52-53.
37. Beverley, *History*, 289.
38. Boucher, *View*, 40.
39. Cecil Drinker, *Not So Long Ago*, 32.
40. Joseph Kirkland, *Zury*, 148.
41. Forbes, *Paul Revere*, 70.
42. Bridenbaughs, *Rebels and Gentlemen*, 228-29.
43. Ebenezer Cook, *Sot-Weed Factor*, n.p.
44. W. R. Bliss, *Colonial Times*, 50.
45. Byrd, *Histories*, 55.
46. Beverley, *History*, 318.
47. *Ibid.*, 312.
48. Byrd, *Histories*, 197.
49. Thomas Morris, *Journal*, 311.
50. Dankers and Sluyter, *Journal*, 122-24.
51. Beverley, *History*, 309.
52. *Ibid.*, 314.
53. Dankers and Sluyter, *Journal*, 139.
54. *Travels in American Colonies*, 74.
55. Beverley, *History*, 132.
56. Bridenbaugh, *Cities in the Wilderness*, 88.
57. Hamilton, *Gentleman's Progress*, 79.

SECTION IV

1. Sally Wister, *Journal*, 92.
2. Toulmin, *Western Country*, 135.

3. J. P. Martin, *Private Yankee Doodle,* 105.
4. Quincy, "Journal," 477.
5. Nelson, *American Tory,* 67.
6. Quincy, "Journal," 455-65.
7. Burnaby, *Travels,* 4-5.
8. Gordon, *Journal,* 403.
9. Morison, note p. 188 to Bradford, *Of Plymouth Plantation.*
10. Fithian, *Journal,* 180-81, 220-21, 262.
11. Bridenbaugh, *Myths,* 30-2.
12. Lodge, *Short History,* 61.
13. Boucher, "Letters," 171-72.
14. Lodge, *Short History,* 123.
15. Weeden, *Economic and Social History,* I, 295.
16. Maclean, *Historical Account,* 58.
17. Kennedy, *Swallow Barn,* 168-69.
18. Lodge, *Short History,* 84-85.
19. Byrd, *London Diary, passim.*
20. Guess, *South Carolina,* 94.
21. Jefferson, *Crusade Against Ignorance,* 107-9.
22. Van Doren, *Benjamin Franklin,* 263.
23. Bridenbaugh, *Cities in the Wilderness,* 253.
24. Harrower, *Journal,* 54-58.
25. Durand de Dauphiné, *Un Français en Virginie,* 87.
26. Dexter, *Colonial Women,* 9.
27. Franklin, *Education,* 99.
28. Wertenbaker, *Old South,* 60.
29. Wright, *Cultural Life,* 184.
30. Bridenbaugh, *Cities in the Wilderness,* 432.
31. Fithian, *Journal,* 212.
32. *Narratives of Early Pennsylvania,* 321.
33. Bridenbaugh, "Baths and Watering Places," *William and Mary Quarterly* (April, 1946).
34. Flexner, *Steamboats Come True,* II, 53.
35. Bridenbaugh, "Baths and Watering Places," *William and Mary Quarterly* (April, 1946).
36. Bridenbaugh, *Cities in the Wilderness,* 263.
37. Boucher, "Letters," 184.
38. Gordon, *Journal,* 410-12.
39. Quincy, "Journal," 472-77.
40. Guess, *South Carolina,* 90.
41. Drinker, *Journal,* 273.
42. S. J. Hale, *Northwood,* 60.
43. *Larousse Encyclopedia of Modern Art,* 419.
44. Frankenstein, Introduction.
45. Bridenbaugh, *Cities in the Wilderness,* 458.
46. *New York Historical Society Quarterly Bulletin*
47. Flexner, *Light of Distant Stars,* 21.
48. Prown, *Copley,* I, 48.
49. Harlow, *Old Postbags,* 228-29.
50. Dunbar, *History of Travel,* 173.
51. Samuel Sewall, *Diary,* 41.
52. Gordon, *Journal,* 405.
53. *New England Primer.*
54. Fithian, *Journal,* 39.
55. Nelson, *American Tory,* 148.
56. Birkit, *Remarks,* 65.

57. Trevelyan, *English Social History,* 387.
58. Weeden, *Economic and Social History,* II, 536.
59. Morison, *Builders,* 224.
60. Fithian, *Journal,* 84.
61. Nelson, *American Tory,* 156.
62. Howard, *Our American Music,* 122.
63. Bridenbaugh, *Cities in the Wilderness,* 224.
64. Cecil Drinker, *Not So Long Ago,* 48.
65. J. T. Adams, *History of the Town of Southampton,* 60-61.
66. Watson, *Men and Times,* 137-40.
67. Angoff, *Literary History,* I, 187.
68. John Winthrop, *History,* II, 265-66.
69. Bridenbaugh, *Rebels and Gentlemen,* 125.
70. Burnaby, *Travels,* 26-27.
71. Jefferson, *Crusade Against Ignorance,* 152.
72. Elizabeth Drinker, *Journal,* 81.
73. Hamilton, *Gentleman's Progress,* 177.
74. Bridenbaugh, *Cities in the Wilderness,* 435n.
75. Swiggett, *Extraordinary Mr. Morris,* 142-44.
76. Hamilton, *Gentleman's Progress,* 151.
77. Gordon, *Journal,* 405.
78. Prown, *John Singleton Copley,* I, 9.
79. W. R. Bliss, *Colonial Times,* 29.
80. R. C. Winthrop, *John Winthrop,* II, 228
81. Eggleston, *End of the World,* 60.
82. Drake, *Pioneer Life,* 8.
83. Bridenbaugh, *Rebels and Gentlemen,* 70-71.
84. *Dictionary of American Biography,* "John Peter Zenger."
85. Jefferson, *Basic Writings,* 550.
86. C. M. Andrews, *Colonial Folkways,* 231.

SECTION V

1. Nelson, *American Tory,* 61.
2. Crèvecoeur, *Letters,* 159.
3. Angoff, *Literary History,* II, 312.
4. Crèvecoeur, *Letters,* 43.
5. Saugrain, *Odyssée,* 19.
6. *Library of American Literature,* IV, 150.
7. *Representative American Plays,* 71.
8. Shepard, *Pedlar's Progress,* 248-49.
9. Knight, *Journal,* 41-42.
10. Hamilton, *Gentleman's Progress,* 38.
11. C. M. S. Kirkland, *New Home,* 89.
12. Melville, *Mardi,* 426.
13. Howe, *Historical Collections of Ohio,* III, 207.
14. Eggleston, *Circuit Rider,* 214-15.
15. Crockett, *Life,* 154-55.
16. Paulding, *Letters,* 33-34.
17. Hawthorne, "Mr. Higginbotham's Catastrophe," 128.
18. Irving, "Legend of Sleepy Hollow."
19. Hansen, *Atlantic Migration,* 91.
20. Thomas Wilson, "The Arkansas Traveler," 297.
21. Hanna, *Scotch-Irish,* II, 84-85.
22. Bacon, "Journal," *Indiana Magazine of History* (December, 1944), 374.
23. Cox, *Recollections,* 14.
24. Niemcewicz, *Under Their Vine and Fig Tree,* 242.

25. Dickens, *American Notes*, 397-98.
26. Eggleston, *Hoosier Schoolmaster*, 24.
27. Eggleston, *Roxy*, 183.
28. Eggleston, *Graysons*, 133-34.
29. Nicholson, *Hoosiers*, 8-9.
30. Wildes, *Lonely Midas*, 290.
31. B. R. Hall, *New Purchase*, 306.
32. Joseph Kirkland, *McVeys*, 111-13.
33. *Ibid.*, 119.
34. Eggleston, *Circuit Rider*, 68-69.
35. Eggleston, *Graysons*, 18-19.
36. C. M. S. Kirkland, *New Home*, 156
37. Cox, *Recollections*, 18.
38. C. M. S. Kirkland, *New Home*, 42-43.
39. Burchard and Bush-Brown, *Architecture*, 162.
40. Howells, *Impressions*, 6.
41. Buley, *Old Northwest*, I, 394.
42. Malin, "The Grasslands of North America," 356-57.
43. Buley, *Old Northwest*, I, 13.
44. Cuming, *Sketches*, 218-19.
45. Kennedy, *Swallow Barn*, 18.
46. Buley, *Old Northwest*, I, 232n.
47. Kennedy, *Quodlibet*, 44-46.
48. Hamlin, *Greek Revival*, 299-300.
49. Newton, *Town & Davis*, 801.
50. Van Wagenen, *Golden Age*, 116.
51. McMaster, *History*, IV, 221n.
52. J. T. Smith, *Journal*, 14.
53. Niemcewicz, *Under Their Vine and Fig Tree*, 75.
54. Martineau, *Retrospect*, I, 224.
55. Welby, *Visit*, 213-14.
56. David Stevenson, *Sketch*, 132.
57. Howe, *Historical Collections of Ohio*, II, 453.
58. Lowenthal, *George Perkins Marsh*, 134.
59. David Stevenson, *Sketch*, 131-32.
60. Congdon, *Covered Bridge*, 22.
61. Chevalier, *Society*, 257.
62. Dunbar, *History of Travel*, 772.
63. Dickens, *Martin Chuzzlewit*, 134.
64. Rubin, "Canal or Railroad?"
65. Westcott, *David Harum*.
66. Finley, *Lady of Godey's*, 163.
67. Greeley, *Recollections*, 64.
68. E. E. Hale, *New England Boyhood*, 90-91.
69. Howells, *Boy's Town*, 738-39.
70. Combe, *Notes*, II, 296-97.
71. Martineau, *Retrospect of Western Travel*, I, 77-79.
72. Dunbar, *History of Travel*, 354.
73. Strong, *Diary*, I, 144.
74. Dickens, *American Notes*, 276.
75. David Stevenson, *Sketch*, 82-83.
76. James Hall, *West*, 147.
77. Reniers, *Springs of Virginia*, 91.
78. Fulton and Thomson, *Benjamin Silliman*, 198.
79. Mirsky and Nevins, *Eli Whitney*, 192.
80. Evans, *Pedestrious Tour*, 248-49.

81. Hulme, *Journal,* 79.
82. Buckingham, *America,* I, 243-44.
83. Paine, *Ships and Sailors,* 404.
84. Marvin, *American Merchant Marine,* 268.
85. Jewett, *Country of the Pointed Firs,* 25.
86. Cameron, *Samuel Slater,* 93.
87. Furnas, *Late Demon Rum,* 51.
88. Mirsky and Nevins, *Eli Whitney,* 3-4.
89. Paulding, *Chronicles,* 128.
90. Furnas, *Late Demon Rum,* 50.
91. Weeden, *Economic and Social History,* I, 84.
92. Kennedy, *Swallow Barn,* 49.
93. Kimball, *Jefferson,* 293, 295.
94. *Letters of Theodore Dwight Weld,* I, 369.
95. Wendell, *Literary History,* 74-75.
96. B. R. Hall, *New Purchase,* 166-67.
97. Fithian, *Journal,* 96.
98. Hanna, *Scotch-Irish,* 80.
99. B. R. Hall, *New Purchase,* 344, 347.
100. Twain, *Mark Twain's San Francisco,* 231.
101. Joseph Kirkland, *Zury,* 204.
102. R. L. Stevenson, *Scotland to Silverado,* 154.
103. Joseph Kirkland, *Zury,* 151.
104. *Ibid.,* 175.
105. Twain, *Autobiography,* 11-12.
106. Drake, *Malaria,* xviii.
107. Howells, *Boy's Town,* 872.
108. Nicholson, *Hoosier Chronicle,* 44.
109. Twain and Warner, *Gilded Age,* I, 161-62.
110. Cecil Drinker, *Not So Long Ago,* 143.
111. Flexner, *Doctors on Horseback,* 109-10.
112. Cecil Drinker, *Not So Long Ago,* 159.

SECTION VI

1. Thoreau, *Walden,* 134-36.
2. Haliburton, *Clockmaker,* 39.
3. Alexander, *Pennsylvania Railroad,* 9.
4. Mencken, *Railroad Passenger Car,* 101.
5. Strong, *Diary,* I, 243.
6. Faust, *German Element,* II, 341.
7. R. L. Stevenson, *Scotland to Silverado,* 121.
8. Stover, *American Railroads,* 17.
9. Weld, *Vacation Tour,* 222.
10. Mencken, *Railroad Passenger Car,* 172.
11. Alexander, *Pennsylvania Railroad,* 94-95.
12. Dreiser, *Book About Myself,* 300-1.
13. H. L. Wilson, *Merton of the Movies,* 14-15.
14. *Treasury of Railroad Folklore,* 68-69.
15. *Ibid.,* 437.
16. Dunbar, *History of Travel,* 1092.
17. M. A. Holley, *Texas,* 129-31.
18. W. W. Sewall, *Bill Sewall's Story,* 15-16.
19. Elliott, *Imperial Spain,* 64.
20. Berger, *Franciscan Missions,* 16-17.
21. Elliott, *Imperial Spain,* 70.
22. Duncan, *Reluctant General,* 30.

23. Pomeroy, *Pacific Slope*, 6.
24. Ramsdell, *San Antonio*, 46.
25. Atherton, *Doomswoman*, 235, 274.
26. Duffus, *Queen Calafia's Island*, 153.
27. Twain, *Roughing It*, 309-10.
28. Brewer, *Up and Down California*, 14.
29. Eggleston, *Circuit Rider*, 253.
30. Simons, *Social Forces*, 243.
31. Dickens, *American Notes*, 430.
32. Chevalier, *Society*, 97-98.
33. Broehl, *Mollie Maguires*, 83-85.
34. Rynning, *Account*, 246.
35. Larcom, *New England Girlhood*, 118-19, 165.
36. Faust, *German Element*, II, 351-52.
37. Hansen, *Atlantic Migration*, 149.
38. Faust, *German Element*, I, 440.
39. *Ibid.*, 442-45.
40. *Ibid.*, II, 184-86.
41. Mathews, *American English*, 143.
42. Howells, *Years of My Youth*, 43.
43. Flexner, *That Wilder Image*, 124.
44. Gronlund, *Cooperative Commonwealth*, ix.
45. William Cooper, *Guide in the Wilderness*, vi.
46. Levinger, *History of the Jews*, 152-53.
47. Niemcewicz, *Under Their Vine and Fig Tree*, 110-11.
48. Jefferson, *Basic Writings*, 160.
49. Craven, *Coming of the Civil War*, 1.
50. Jefferson, *Basic Writings*, 161.
51. Twain, *Life on the Mississippi*, 416.
52. *Southern Reader*, 273.
53. McCabe, *Centennial Exhibition*, 895.
54. Moreau de St.-Méry, *Journey*, 65, 69.
55. *Culture in the South*, 147.
56. Strong, *Diary*, II, 275.
57. Duffus, *Nostalgia, U.S.A.*, 65.
58. Hawthorne, *Scarlet Letter*.
59. J. F. Cooper, letter, *Spirit of the Fair*.
60. Newton, *Town & Davis*, 83.
61. Dickens, *American Notes*, 287.
62. A. J. Downing, *Architecture*, 202-6.
63. Mitchell, *Rural Studies*, 292.
64. Theodore Winthrop, *Cecil Dreeme*, 101.
65. Newton, *Town & Davis*, 217.
66. Twain, *Tramp Abroad*, 323.
67. Wharton, *Age of Innocence*, 128.
68. Giedion, *Space*, 363.
69. Hone, *Diary*, 550.
70. Wharton, *Age of Innocence*, 69.
71. Van Wyck, *Recollections*, 53.
72. Solon Robinson, *How to Live*, 298-99.
73. *Practical Housekeeper*, 17.
74. Rothschild, *Casual View of America*, 23.
75. Van Wyck, *Recollections*, 124.
76. Beecher and Stowe, *American Woman's Home*, 49-55.
77. *McGuffey's Fifth Eclectic Reader*, 305.
78. *Narratives of Early Pennsylvania*, 321.

79. T. M. Harris, *Journal*, 346.
80. *Story of Phoebe Snow*, n.p.
81. Beecher, *Treatise on Domestic Economy*, 112-15.
82. Howells, *Boy's Town*, 165.
83. Westcott, *David Harum*, 189.
84. Beecher, *Treatise on Domestic Economy*, 95.
85. Holmes, *Medical Essays*, xiv.
86. Furnas, "Sermon in Skulls," *Virginia Quarterly* (January, 1932).
87. Ade, *Fables in Slang*, 1.
88. Strong, *Diary*, III, 1-2.
89. Hone, *Diary*, 199.
90. *Ibid.*, 211-13.
91. Tharp, *Until Victory*, 117.
92. Hone, *Diary*, 522.
93. Stuart, *Three Years in North America*, I, 28.
94. Combe, *Notes*, II, 13.
95. Vaux, *Villas and Cottages*, 48.
96. Dickens, *American Notes*, 290-91.
97. Strong, *Diary*, II, 104.
98. Howells, *Traveler from Altruria*, 189.
99. Drinker, *Not So Long Ago*, 17.
100. Dana, *Two Years Before the Mast*, 286.
101. Welby, *Visit*, 172.
102. Rabb, *Tour*, 14.
103. Van Wyck, *Recollections*, 124-25.
104. Trollope, *North America*, 490-91.
105. Theodore Winthrop, *Cecil Dreeme*, 31.
106. Chevalier, *Society*, 290.
107. Menu in display in Casino Museums, Saratoga Springs, New York.
108. Weld, *Vacation Tour*, 33.
109. Stuart, *Three Years in North America*, I, 193, 128.
110. D. W. Bliss, "The Centennial of Justin Morgan," *Eleventh Vermont Agricultural Report* (1889-90).
111. Buckingham, *America*, III, 203.
112. Mirsky and Nevins, *Eli Whitney*, 160-61.
113. *Men and Manners in America*, 146.
114. Hulme, *Journal*, 71.
115. Basil Hall, *Travels*, 287.
116. Dickens, *American Notes*, 268-72.
117. Weld, *Vacation Tour*, 51.
118. Larcom, *New England Girlhood*, 223.
119. *Ibid.*, 199.
120. *Lowell Offering*, I, 2.
121. Chevalier, *Society*, 138.
122. Robinson, *Loom and Spindle*, 76.
123. Fite, *Social and Industrial Conditions*, 186-88.
124. C. M. S. Kirkland, *New Home*, 66-67.
125. *Narratives of Early Pennsylvania*, 325.
126. Bremer, *Homes of the New World*, I, 111, 120.
127. Maass, *Gingerbread Age*, 12-13.
128. Niemcewicz, *Under Their Vine and Fig Tree*, 286.
129. Chevalier, *Society*, 72-73.
130. Dickens, *American Notes*, 305-19.
131. Buckingham, *America*, I, 56.
132. Strong, *Diary*, II, 209.

133. Beecher, *Treatise on Domestic Economy*, 37.
134. Furnas, *Late Demon Rum*, 315.
135. Grund, *Aristocracy in America*, 155.
136. Jones, *Woman's Dress*, 9.
137. Elizabeth Drinker, *Journal*, April 27, 1796.
138. Blackwell, *Lucy Stone*, 24-25.
139. *Ibid.*, 122.
140. Parker, *Yankee Saint*, 169-70.
141. Jones, *Woman's Dress*, 21-22.
142. Blackwell, *Lucy Stone*, 103-10.
143. Tharp, *Until Victory*, 290.
144. Bremer, *Homes of the New World*, I, 80.
145. Weld, *Vacation Tour*, 48.
146. E. D. Andrews, *Shakers*, 21-23.
147. Dickens, *American Notes*, 432.
148. E. D. Andrews, *Shakers*, 236-37.
149. Nordhoff, *Communistic Societies*, 229, 231.
150. Parker, *Yankee Saint*, 243.
151. Donovan, *Assassins*, 38-39, 40-42.
152. Furnas, *Road to Harpers Ferry*, 356.
153. *Harper's Encyclopaedia of American History*, "John Cleves Symmes."
154. Strong, *Diary*, II, 165.
155. Perkins and Wolfson, *Frances Wright*, 255-56.
156. Howard, *Our American Music*, 185.
157. Twain, *Autobiography*, 366.
158. Mackay, *Life and Liberty in America*, II, 41.
159. Litwack, *North of Slavery*, 127.
160. *Ibid.*, 73.
161. Eggleston, *End of the World*, 294.
162. Gustavus Myers, *History of Bigotry*, 132.
163. Sigourney, *Scenes in My Native Land*, 125.
164. Hone, *Diary*, 209, 880.
165. Angoff, *Literary History*, II, 80.
166. Forrest Wilson, *Crusader in Crinoline*, 89.
167. Strong, *Diary*, 228-240.
168. Paulding, *Letters*, 370-71.
169. Weld, *Vacation Tour*, 62-63.
170. Mott, *American Journalism*, 147.
171. Andrews, *Colonial Background*, 211-12.
172. Tharp, *Until Victory*, 5.
173. W. W. Sewall, *Bill Sewall's Story*, 27.
174. Thoreau, *Maine Woods*, 169.
175. Howe, *Historical Collections of Ohio*, II, 96-98.
176. Rothschild, *Casual View of America*, 81.
177. Jefferson, *Basic Writings*, 151.
178. Shepard, *Pedlar's Progress*, 97.
179. Fennelly, *Town Schooling*, 28.
180. Buley, *Old Northwest*, II, 371.
181. *Ibid.*, 358.
182. Cox, *Recollections*, 61.
183. Eggleston, *Hoosier Schoolmaster*, 1.
184. Cuming, *Sketches*, 184-85.
185. Newton, *Town & Davis*, 49.
186. Schmidt, *Old Time College President*, 102.
187. *Ibid.*, 88-89.

188. E. E. Hale, *New England Boyhood*, 19.
189. Shilling, "Pioneer Schools and Schoolmasters," *Ohio Archeological and Historical Publications*, XXV.
190. Pestalozzi, *Leonard and Gertrude*, ix-x.
191. *McGuffey's Sixth Eclectic Reader*, xiv.
192. *The Republic and the School*, 60.
193. Tarkington, *Penrod*, 45.
194. *Edinburgh Review* (January, 1820).
195. Larcom, *New England Girlhood*, 99.
196. Rabb, *Tour*, 169-75.
197. *Female Poets of America*, 44.
198. Duncan, *Reluctant General*, 109-10.
199. Grund, *Aristocracy in America*, 193.
200. Strong, *Diary*, IV, 430n.
201. Mackay, *Life and Liberty*, II, 138.
202. Browne, *Artemus Ward*, 37-38.
203. Buckingham, *America*, III, 164.
204. Howells, *Modern Instance*, 137.
205. Buckingham, *America*, I, 47-48.
206. Eggleston, *Roxy*, 250-51.
207. Angoff, *Literary History*, II, 180.
208. Furnas, *Late Demon Rum*, 144.
209. Taubman, *American Theatre*, 78.
210. Fulton and Thomson, *Benjamin Silliman*, 59.
211. Mabee, *American Leonardo*, 111.
212. Twain, *Tramp Abroad*, 95.
213. Bernard, *Retrospections*, 256.
214. Paulding, *Letters*, 443.
215. Kimmel, *Mad Booths*, 157.
216. Browne, *Artemus Ward*, 67-68.
217. Flexner, *Light of Distant Stars*, 146.
218. Stein, *John Ruskin*, 7.
219. John Durand, *A. B. Durand*, 70-72.
220. Wharton, *House of Mirth*, 30.
221. Steegmuller, *James Jackson Jarves*, 188.
222. Bakeless, *Eyes of Discovery*, 376.
223. Mabee, *American Leonardo*, 97.
224. Mackay, *Life and Liberty*, II, 141-42.
225. Thomas Wilson, "The Arkansas Traveler," 306.
226. Furnas, *Late Demon Rum*, 216.
227. D. W. Bliss, *Colonial Times*, 166.
228. Charles Francis Adams, *Three Episodes*, 907.
229. Rich, *Lowell Mason*, 9.
230. Jameson, *American Revolution*, 59.
231. Schmidt, *Old Time College President*, 138.
232. Rich, *Lowell Mason*, 60.
233. *Ibid.*, title page.
234. Schlesinger, *Paths to the Present*, 184.
235. Niemcewicz, *Under Their Vine and Fig Tree*, 8-9.
236. Faux, *Memorable Days*, 130-31, 164.

SECTION VII

1. Murdock, *Patriotism Limited*, 5.
2. *Dutchess County and Poughkeepsie Sanitary Fair*, 21-22.
3. Ingram, *Centennial Exposition*, 608-10.
4. *Ibid.*, 706.

5. Jewett, *Country of the Pointed Firs*, 196.
6. Clarence Cook, *House Beautiful*, 161-63, 187.
7. *Ibid.*, 59-60.
8. Howells, *Rise of Silas Lapham*, 198-99.
9. Clarence Cook, *House Beautiful*, 187.
10. Henry Adams, *Democracy*, 12-13.
11. Eastlake, *Hints on Household Taste*, 165.
12. Downing and Scully, *Architectural Heritage*, 144.
13. Thanet, *Stories of a Western Town*, 208.
14. Strong, *Diary*, II, 418.
15. Gardner, *Winslow Homer*, 102.
16. Paulding, *Bulls and the Jonathans*, 142-43.
17. Strong, *Diary*, I, 260.
18. Devens, *Our First Century*, 758.
19. Fawcett, *Gentleman of Leisure*, 158-59.
20. Wharton, *House of Mirth*, 94, 135.
21. Howells, *Rise of Silas Lapham*, 215.
22. Howells, *Impressions and Experiences*, 240.
23. Mackay, *Life and Liberty*, I, 186.
24. Hosmer, *Short History*, 344.
25. Ziff, *American 1890s*, 54-55.
26. Hosmer, *Short History*, 351-53.
27. Dunne, *Mr. Dooley in Peace and in War*, 54-55.
28. Dunne, *Mr. Dooley in the Hearts of His Countrymen*, 19-21.
29. Furnas, *Anatomy of Paradise*, 253-54.
30. McCabe, *Centennial Exhibition*, 82-84.
31. T. H. White, *America at Last*, 45.
32. Newton, *Town & Davis*, 106.
33. Butler, *Pigs Is Pigs*, 42.
34. Trevelyan, *English Social History*, 305-6.
35. Howells, *Impressions and Experiences*, 267-68.
36. Cook, *House Beautiful*, 147.
37. Schuyler, *American Architecture*, 34-47, 64.
38. Tarkington, *Magnificent Ambersons*, 17-18.
39. Morison, *Oxford History*, II, 373.
40. Schuyler, *American Architecture*, 158-60.
41. La Follette, *Art in America*, 256.
42. Maass, *Gingerbread Age*, 39, 64.
43. Orton, *Famous Rogers Groups*.
44. Lloyd Morris, *Incredible New York*, 169.
45. Louis Prang & Company Catalogue (1876).
46. Gronlund, *Cooperative Commonwealth*, viii-ix.
47. Goodrich, *Winslow Homer*, 203-4.
48. Gardner, *Winslow Homer*, 59.
49. Goodrich, *Winslow Homer*, 168-69.
50. Gardner, *Winslow Homer*, 34.
51. Mumford, *Brown Decades*, 213.
52. *Larousse Encyclopedia of Modern Art*, 240.
53. Gardner, *Winslow Homer*, 134.
54. Phelps, *Silent Partner*, 118.
55. Ingram, *Centennial Exposition*, 705-6.
56. McCabe, *Centennial Exhibition*, 654-56.
57. Broun and Leech, *Anthony Comstock*, 15.
58. Howells, *Traveler from Altruria*, 138-39.
59. Irving, "The Creole Village," in *Wolfert's Roost*.
60. Strong, *Diary*, III, 567.

61. Fawcett, *Gentleman of Leisure*, 295-98.
62. Julia A. Moore, *Sweet Singer of Michigan*, 59-60.
63. Hone, *Diary*, 619-20.
64. Devens, *Our First Century*, 844-47.
65. Elson, *History of American Music*, 86.
66. Strong, *Diary*, II, 332-33.
67. Russell, *Theodore Thomas*, 307.
68. Morison, *Oxford History*, I, 375.
69. Duffus, *Nostalgia, U.S.A.*, 23.
70. Browne, *Artemus Ward*, 109.
71. Eliot, "The New Education," *Atlantic Monthly* (March, 1869).
72. Strong, *Diary*, II, 553.
73. Howells, *Suburban Sketches*, 112-4.
74. Howells, *Hazard of New Fortunes*, 61.
75. Stevenson, *Wrecker* (South Seas edition), 123.
76. Howells, *Impressions and Experiences*, 258-59.
77. Howells, *Suburban Sketches*, 86.
78. Gronlund, *Cooperative Commonwealth*, 104.
79. Flynt, *Tramping with Tramps*, 302-3.
80. London, *Road*, 128.
81. Flynt, *Tramping with Tramps*, 307.
82. Barnard, "Eagle Forgotten," 81.
83. *Ibid.*, 54.
84. Fanny Kemble Wister, *Owen Wister Out West*, 258.
85. Twain, *Roughing It*, 141.
86. Holbrook, *Machines of Plenty*, 142-7.
87. Owen Wister, *Virginian*, x.
88. Fanny Kemble Wister, *Owen Wister Out West*, 20.
89. Owen Wister, *Virginian*, 50.
90. "Dame Shirley" (Louise Amelia Knapp Smith Clappe), *Letters*, 212 ff.
91. Twain, *Tramp Abroad*, 572-75.
92. Norris, *McTeague*, 5.
93. *Anthropology A to Z*, 113.
94. *Spirit of the Fair*.
95. Rynning, "Account," *Minnesota History Bulletin* (1917-18).
96. Howells, *Suburban Sketches*, 62-70.
97. E. B. Andrews, *History*, I, 356.
98. Dreiser, *Book About Myself*, 160-1.
99. Norris, "Thoroughbred," *Collected Writings*, X, 204-5.
100. Dunne, *Mr. Dooley in the Hearts of His Countrymen*, 86-87.
101. Strong, *Diary*, IV, 371, 432.
102. *Ibid.*, III, 40.
103. Fawcett, *Gentleman of Leisure*, 302.
104. Birmingham, *Our Crowd*, 146.
105. Gronlund, *Cooperative Commonwealth*, 44.
106. Levinger, *History of the Jews*, 268-69.
107. Hillquit, *History of Socialism*, 234.
108. Cahan, *Rise of David Levinsky*, 93.
109. Collier, *America and the Americans*, 4-7.
110. Eliot, "Wherein Popular Education Has Failed," *Forum* (December, 1892).
111. Howells, *Son of Royal Langbrith*, 178.
112. Howells, *Rise of Silas Lapham*, 181.
113. Hillquit, *History of Socialism*, 139.
114. Caro Lloyd, *Henry Demarest Lloyd*, I, 136.
115. *Ibid.*, I, 304.
116. Nordhoff, *Communistic Societies*, 12-15.

117. Korngold, *Two Friends of Man,* 367-68.
118. Barnard, *"Eagle Forgotten,"* 97.
119. Joll, *Anarchists,* 141-42.
120. Bellamy, *Looking Backward,* 282 and n.
121. Broehl, *Mollie Maguires,* 346-47.
122. E. B. Andrews, *History,* II, 238.
123. Eliot, "Wherein Popular Education Has Failed," *Forum* (December, 1892).
124. Hay, *Breadwinners,* 89-90.
125. Howells, *Traveler from Altruria,* 46-47.
126. McMichael, *Journey to Obscurity,* 126.
127. Gronlund, *Cooperative Commonwealth,* 32.
128. *Dictionary of American Biography,* "Henry George."
129. Gronlund, *Cooperative Commonwealth,* 76.
130. *Encyclopaedia of the Social Sciences,* "Henry Demarest Lloyd."
131. Caro Lloyd, *Henry Demarest Lloyd,* v.
132. *Ibid.;* I, 155.
133. H. D. Lloyd, "The Story of a Great Monopoly," *Atlantic Monthly* (March, 1881).
134. Caro Lloyd, *Henry Demarest Lloyd,* 171.
135. *Ibid.,* I, 298-300.
136. *Ibid.,* II, 114.
137. *Ibid.,* II, 26.
138. Gronlund, *Cooperative Commonwealth,* 4.
139. Beards, *Rise of American Civilization,* II, 253.
140. Bowman, *et al., Edward Bellamy Abroad,* 93.
141. Bellamy, *Looking Backward,* 62.
142. *Ibid.,* 78.
143. Bellamy, *Edward Bellamy Speaks Again!,* 78.
144. *Ibid.,* p. 78.
145. *Ibid.,* 188.
146. Bowman, *et al., Edward Bellamy Abroad,* 31.
147. Bellamy, *Edward Bellamy Speaks Again!,* 236.
148. Bowman, *et al., Edward Bellamy Abroad,* 86-7.
149. *Ibid.,* 75.
150. *Ibid.,* 253.
151. Bellamy, *Edward Bellamy Speaks Again!,* 224-30.
152. Dunne, *Dissertations by Mr. Dooley,* 267.
153. Hofstadter, *Age of Reform,* 69.
154. Howells, *Years of My Youth,* 17-8.
155. Howells, *Traveler from Altruria,* 42-3.
156. Howells, *Hazard of New Fortunes,* 289.
157. Frank, *Our America,* 38-40.
158. Hay, *Breadwinners,* 10.
159. Marietta Holley, *My Opinions and Betsey Bobbet's,* 426-27.
160. Wells, *Future in America,* 231.
161. Tharp, *Until Victory,* 280-81.
162. Eliot, "Shortening and Enrichening the Grammar School Course," 52.
163. Bellamy, *Edward Bellamy Speaks Again!,* 117.
164. Woodward, *Burden of Southern History,* 134.
165. Page, *Red Rock,* vii-x.
166. Strong, *Diary,* IV, 164.

SECTION VIII

1. World's Columbian Exposition, *Memorial Volume,* 41-42.
2. Richards and Elliott, *Julia Ward Howe,* II, 182.
3. Henry Adams, *Education,* 342.

4. World's Columbian Exposition, *Art and Handicraft*, 24-25.
5. Dreiser, *Book About Myself*, II, 207-9.
6. Henry Adams, *Education*, 334.
7. Marietta Holley, *Samantha at the World's Fair*, 235-37.
8. Henry Adams, *Education*, 341.
9. Dunne, *Mr. Dooley's Opinions*, 141.
10. L. H. Sullivan, *Autobiography of an Idea*, 320-25.
11. *Ibid.*, 258.
12. Wynne and Newhall, "Horatio Greenough," *Magazine of Art* (January, 1939).
13. Steegmuller, *James Jackson Jarves*, 242-43.
14. L. H. Sullivan, *Autobiography of an Idea*, 309.
15. Mumford, *Brown Decades*, 152-55.
16. Downing and Scully, *Architectural Heritage*, 150.
17. *Dictionary of American Biography*, "Stanford White."
18. Stoddard, *Lectures*, X, 9.
19. Cleland, *Cattle*, 217.
20. Lewis, *Silver Kings*, 196-97.
21. Stoddard, *Lectures*, X, 21-23.
22. Duffus, *Queen Calafia's Island*, 93.
23. H. L. Wilson, *Somewhere in Red Gap*, 146.
24. Nicholson, *Otherwise Phyllis*, 259.
25. Norton, *Handbook of Florida*, 168.
26. Marietta Holley, *Samantha at the World's Fair*, 670.
27. Pomeroy, *Pacific Slope*, 101.
28. Wharton, *Ethan Frome*, 4, 7.
29. Duffus, *Waterbury Record*, 178.
30. Pomeroy, *Pacific Slope*, 144.
31. Duffus, *Queen Calafia's Island*, 94.
32. Pan-American Exposition, *Art Hand-Book*, 6.
33. Furnas, *Voyage to Windward*, 531-32.
34. Dunne, *Mr. Dooley on Making a Will*, 145-51.
35. Howe, *Historical Collections of Ohio*, II, 79.
36. Newton, *Town & Davis*, 107-8.
37. Nordhoff, *California*, 22.
38. Colt, *Tourist's Guide*, 43.
39. Tarkington, *Magnificent Ambersons*, 16-17.
40. Butler, *Pigs Is Pigs*, 42-4.
41. Ely, "Pullman," *Harper's Magazine*, LXX (1885), 452.
42. *Ibid.*, 465.
43. Lindsey, *Pullman Strike*, 124.
44. *Ibid.*, 175.
45. Ginger, *Bending Cross*, 142-43.
46. Haywood, *Bill Haywood's Book*, 185.
47. *Ibid.*, 174-75.
48. Renshaw, *Wobblies*, 112-13.
49. *Encyclopaedia of the Social Sciences*, "Industrial Workers of the World."
50. Renshaw, *Wobblies*, 128-29.
51. Stegner, "Joe Hill, the Wobbies' Troubadour," *New Republic* (January 5, 1948).
52. Lomax, *American Folk Songs*, 129.
53. Industrial Workers of the World, *Songs of the Workers*, 9.
54. Renshaw, *Wobblies*, 187.
55. Steffens, *Autobiography*, 688.
56. Industrial Workers of the World, *Songs of the Workers*, 10.
57. Dunne, *Observations by Mr. Dooley*, 50, 53-54.
58. Spargo, *Bitter Cry*, 214.

59. Higham, *Strangers in the Land*, 42.
60. *Ibid.*, 118.
61. Handlin, *Race and Nationality*, 80.
62. H. L. Wilson, *Somewhere in Red Gap*, 232.
63. Glazer and Moynihan, *Beyond the Melting Pot*, 33.
64. Wells, *Future in America*, 138.
65. *Ibid.*, 109-15.
66. *Encyclopaedia of the Social Sciences*, "Child Labor."
67. *Dictionary of American Biography*, "John Trotwood Moore."
68. J. T. Moore, *Bishop of Cottontown*, 209-10, 262-72.
69. *Encyclopaedia of the Social Sciences*, "Child Labor."
70. Spargo, *Bitter Cry*, 180.
71. Cleghorn, *Portraits and Protests*, 49.
72. Pelling, *American Labor*, 123.
73. *Encyclopaedia of the Social Sciences*, "Lynching."
74. Dunne, *Mr. Dooley's Opinions*, 210.
75. Myrdal, *American Dilemma*, 561.
76. Spencer, *Booker T. Washington*, 130.
77. *Ibid.*, 51-52.
78. *Ibid.*, 94.
79. *Ibid.*, 101.
80. All foregoing quotations from Mark Sullivan, *Our Times*, III, 133-36.
81. Spencer, *Booker T. Washington*, 153.
82. Mott, *History of American Magazines*, IV, 213.
83. *Encyclopaedia of the Social Sciences*, "Booker T. Washington."
84. Rex Harris, *Jazz*, 69.
85. H. L. Wilson, *Ruggles of Red Gap*, 285.
86. Elson, *History of American Music*, 134-35.
87. Richards and Elliott, *Julia Ward Howe*, II, 234-35.
88. *Encyclopaedia of the Social Sciences*, "Joseph Pulitzer."
89. Swanberg, *Citizen Hearst*, 30.
90. *Ibid.*, 59.
91. *Ibid.*, 102.
92. Seitz, *Joseph Pulitzer*, 238.
93. Swanberg, *Citizen Hearst*, 108.
94. *Ibid.*, 137.
95. Mark Sullivan, *Our Times*, III, 281.
96. Swanberg, *Citizen Hearst*, 191.
97. Steffens, *Autobiography*, 543.
98. Gilson Gardner, *Lusty Scripps*, 65-66.
99. *Ibid.*, 86.
100. *Ibid.*, 175.
101. Juergens, *Pulitzer*, 283.
102. Wells, *Future in America*, 205.
103. Upton Sinclair, *Jungle*, 30.
104. *Ibid.*, 341.
105. Mark Sullivan, *Our Times*, II, 472.
106. *Ibid.*, II, 475.
107. Upton Sinclair, *Jungle*, 102.
108. Ade, *Fables in Slang*, 91.
109. *Ibid.*, 92.
110. Patterson, *A Little Brother of the Rich*, 40.
111. Dunne, *Mr. Dooley's Philosophy*, 258, 18.
112. Dunne, *The World of Mr. Dooley*, 202.
113. Marietta Holley, *Samantha at the World's Fair*, 437.
114. Hay, *In Praise of Omar*, 7, 9-10.

115. Mark Sullivan, *Our Times*, IV, 278.
116. *Ibid.*, IV, 182.
117. Larson, *American Infidel*, 235-36.
118. *Ibid.*, 200-1, 253.
119. *American Radicals*, 289.
120. Furnas, *Many People Prize It*, 84-85.
121. Dowd, *Thorstein Veblen*, 1.
122. *Cartoon Cavalcade*, 15.
123. Blatch, *Challenging Years*, 114.
124. Andrew Sinclair, *Better Half*, 285-86.
125. Richards and Elliott, *Julia Ward Howe*, I, 291-96.
126. Thanet, *Man of the Hour*, 58-60.
127. Richards and Elliott, *Julia Ward Howe*, I, 296.
128. *Encyclopaedia of the Social Sciences*, "Women's Organizations."
129. Mott, *Golden Multitudes*, 184.
130. Duffus, *Waterbury Record*, 249.
131. Howells, *Traveler from Altruria*, 26-28.
132. Caro Lloyd, *Henry Demarest Lloyd*, I, 306.
133. Norris, *Pit*, 4.
134. Wharton, *House of Mirth*, 135.
135. *Life* (November 19, 1908).
136. Langford, *Murder of Stanford White*, 111-12.
137. *Ibid.*, 45.
138. Harrison, *Anglomaniacs*, 49.
139. H. L. Wilson, *Spenders*, 132.
140. Wharton, *House of Mirth*, 159.
141. Norris, *Vandover and the Brute*, 96-102.
142. Duffus, *Nostalgia, U.S.A.*, 28.
143. H. L. Wilson, *Somewhere in Red Gap*, 130-31.
144. Mark Sullivan, *Our Times*, IV, 97.
145. Dunne, *Dissertations by Mr. Dooley*, 170-71.
146. Carson, *Cornflake Crusade*, 146.
147. Reeves, "Come All . . . ," *Harvard Library Bulletin* (July, 1967).
148. La Follette, *Art in America*, 166.
149. *New York Times Book Review* (August 23, 1964).
150. Koch, catalogue of exhibition of work of Louis Comfort Tiffany, Museum of Contemporary Crafts, January 24, 1958.
151. *New York Times*, December 3, 1967.
152. *Ibid*.
153. H. L. Wilson, *Ruggles of Red Gap*, 198.
154. Wertenbaker, *Middle Colonies*, 2.
155. Howells, *Boy's Town*, 790.
156. Howells, *Years of My Youth*, 173.
157. Duffus, *Waterbury Record*, 240.
158. Owen Wister, *Lin McLean*, 127.
159. H. L. Wilson, *Spenders*, 125-26.
160. Amory, *Who Killed Society?*, 49.
161. Howells, *Hazard of New Fortunes*, 236-37.
162. Churchill, *Crisis*, 397, 431.
163. Marquis, *Hermione*, 21, 120.

Quoted Sources

Quoted Sources

The following alphabetical list identifies where necessary the sources directly quoted and distinguished by a number in the foregoing text. In addition to substantiating the data thus cited, it serves as small but probably representative sampling of the formal materials, absorbed over the last forty years, on which much of the book is based. A proper bibliography would obviously be impossibly bulky. It must not be assumed that because a given work or authority is not cited here, the author is not acquainted with it.

ADAMS, CHARLES FRANCIS, *Three Episodes of Massachusetts History: The Settlement of Boston Bay. The Antinomian Controversy. A Study of Church and Town Government.* Boston, Houghton Mifflin Company, 1892.

ADAMS, HENRY, *Democracy: An American Novel.* New York, Henry Holt and Company, 1933.

———, *The Education of Henry Adams: An Autobiography.* The Riverside Library. Boston, Houghton Mifflin Company, 1918.

ADAMS, JAMES TRUSLOW, *The Epic of America.* New York, Triangle Books, 1931.

———, *History of the Town of Southampton* (East of Canoe Place). Bridgehampton, L.I., Hampton Press, 1918.

ADE, GEORGE, *Fables in Slang and More Fables in Slang,* illustrations by Clyde J. Newman, with an introduction by E. F. Bleiler. New York, Dover Publications, 1960.

ALEXANDER, EDWARD P., *The Pennsylvania Railroad: A Pictorial History.* New York, Bonanza Books, 1947.

American Radicals: Some Problems and Personalities, Harvey Goldberg, ed. New York, Monthly Review Press, 1957.

AMORY, CLEVELAND, *Who Killed Society?* New York, Harper and Brothers, 1960.

ANDREWS, CHARLES M., *The Colonial Background of the American Revolution: Four Essays in American Colonial History.* New Haven, Yale University Press, 1924.

———, *Colonial Folkways.* New Haven, Yale University Press, 1919.

———, *The Colonial Period of American History.* New Haven, Yale University Press, 1934.

———, *Colonial Self-Government; 1652–1689.* The American Nation: A History, Vol. 5. New York, Harper and Brothers, 1904.

———, *Our Earliest Colonial Settlements: Their Diversities of Origin and Later Characteristics.* New York, New York University Press, 1933.

ANDREWS, E. BENJAMIN, *The History of the Last Quarter Century in the United States, 1870-1895.* New York, Charles Scribner's Sons, 1896.

ANDREWS, EDWARD DEMING, *The People Called Shakers: A Search for the Perfect Society,* new enlarged ed. New York, Dover Publications, 1963.

ANGOFF, CHARLES, *A Literary History of the American People.* Two Volumes in One . . . New York, Tudor Publishing Co., 1935.

Anthropology A to Z. Carleton S. Coon and Edward E. Hunt, Jr., eds. New York, Grosset & Dunlap, 1963.

ATHERTON, GERTRUDE, *Before the Gringo Came.* ("Rezánov" and "The Doomswoman".) New York, Frederick A. Stokes Company, 1915.

ATKINSON, WILLIAM C., *A History of Spain and Portugal.* N.P., Penguin Books, 1960.

BAKELESS, JOHN, *The Eyes of Discovery: The Pageant of North America as Seen by the First Explorers.* New York, J. B. Lippincott Company, 1950.

BARNARD, HARRY, *"Eagle Forgotten": The Life of John Peter Altgeld.* Indianapolis, Bobbs-Merrill Company, 1938.

BEARD, CHARLES A., and MARY R. BEARD, *The Rise of American Civilization,* new ed., two vol. in one, revised and enlarged. New York, Macmillan Company, 1936.

BEECHER, CATHARINE E., *A Treatise on Domestic Economy, for the Use of Young Ladies at Home, and at School.* New York, Harper and Brothers, 1847.

BEECHER, CATHARINE E., and HARRIET BEECHER STOWE, *The American Woman's Home.* New York, J. B. Ford and Company, 1869.

BEHN, APHRA, *The Widow Ranter, or, The History of Bacon in Virginia,* in *Plays Written by the Late Ingenious Mrs. Behn.* London, 1724; reprinted London, John Pearson, 1871.

BELLAMY, EDWARD, *Looking Backward: 2000–1887.* The Riverside Library. Boston, Houghton Mifflin Company, 1929.

———, *Edward Bellamy Speaks Again! Articles—Public Addresses—Letters.* Chicago, Peerage Press, 1937.

BERGER, JOHN A., *The Franciscan Missions of California.* New York, G. P. Putnam's Sons, 1941.

BERNARD, JOHN, *Retrospections of America: 1797–1811,* edited from the manuscript by Mrs. Bayle Bernard with an introduction, notes and index by Laurence Hutton and Brander Matthews. New York, Harper and Brothers, 1887.

BEVERLEY, ROBERT, *The History and Present State of Virginia,* edited with an introduction by Louis B. Wright. Chapel Hill, University of North Carolina Press, 1947.

BIRKIT, JAMES, *Some Cursory Remarks Made By James Birkit in His Voyage to North America: 1750–1751.* New Haven, Yale University Press, 1916.

BIRMINGHAM, STEPHEN, *Our Crowd: The Great Jewish Families of New York.* New York, Harper & Row, 1967.

BLACKWELL, ALICE STONE, *Lucy Stone: Pioneer of Woman's Rights.* Boston, Little, Brown and Company, 1930.

BLAKE, PETER, *Frank Lloyd Wright.* Architecture and Space. Penguin Books, 1964.

BLATCH, HARRIOT STANTON, and ALMA LUTZ, *Challenging Years: The Memoirs of Harriot Stanton Blatch*. New York, G. P. Putnam's Sons, 1940.

BLISS, D. W., "The Centennial of Justin Morgan." *Eleventh Vermont Agricultural Report* (1889–90).

BLISS, WILLIAM ROOT, *Colonial Times on Buzzards Bay*. Boston, Houghton Mifflin Company, 1888.

BOSWELL, JAMES, *The Life of Samuel Johnson*. London, Collins Clear-Type Press, n.d.

BOUCHER, JONATHAN, *A View of the Causes and Consequences of the American Revolution in Thirteen Discourses Preached in North America Between the Years 1763 and 1775* . . . London, G. G. and J. Robinson, 1797.

BOWMAN, SYLVIA, *et al., Edward Bellamy Abroad: An American Prophet's Influence*. New York, Twayne Publishers, 1962.

BOYD, MARK F.; HALE G. SMITH; and JOHN W. GRIFFIN. *Here They Once Stood: The Tragic End of the Apalachee Missions*. Gainesville, University of Florida Press, 1951.

BRADFORD, WILLIAM, *Of Plymouth Plantation: 1620–1647*, new ed., the complete text, with notes and an introduction by Samuel Eliot Morison. New York, Alfred A. Knopf, 1952.

BREMER, FREDRIKA, *The Homes of the New World: Impressions of America*. New York, Harper and Brothers, 1853.

BREWER, WILLIAM H., *Up and Down California in 1860–1864: The Journal of . . . Professor of Agriculture in the Sheffield Scientific School from 1864 to 1903*, Francis P. Farquahar, ed. New Haven, Yale University Press, 1930.

BRIDENBAUGH, CARL, "Baths and Watering Places of Colonial America." *William and Mary Quarterly*, Third Series, Vol. III (April, 1946).

————, *Cities in the Wilderness: The First Century of Urban Life in America 1625–1742*. New York, Alfred A. Knopf, 1955.

————, *Myths and Realities: Societies of the Colonial South*. Baton Rouge, Louisiana State University Press, 1952.

BRIDENBAUGH, CARL and JESSICA, *Rebels and Gentlemen: Philadelphia in the Age of Franklin*. New York, Oxford University Press, 1962.

BROEHL, WAYNE G., JR., *The Molly Maguires*. Cambridge, Harvard University Press, 1964.

BROUN, HEYWOOD, and MARGARET LEECH, *Anthony Comstock, Roundsman of the Lord*. New York, Albert & Charles Boni, 1927.

BROWN, CHARLES FARRAR, *The Complete Works of Artemus Ward*, new ed. London, Chatto & Windus, 1898.

BUCKINGHAM, J. S., *America: Historical, Statistic, and Descriptive*. London, Fisher, Son & Co., 1840.

BULEY, R. CARLYLE, *The Old Northwest: Pioneer Period 1815–1840*. Bloomington, Indiana University Press, 1950.

BURCHARD, JOHN, and ALBERT BUSH-BROWN, *The Architecture of America: A Social and Cultural History*. Boston, Little, Brown and Company, 1961.

BURKE, EDMUND, *Works*. Boston, C. C. Little & J. Brown, 1839.

BURNABY, ANDREW, *Travels Through the Middle Settlements in North-America: In the Years 1759 and 1760. With Observations upon the State of the Colonies,* 2d ed. Ithaca, N.Y., Cornell University Press, 1960.

BUTLER, ELLIS PARKER, *Pigs Is Pigs and Other Favorites.* New York, Dover Publications, 1966.

BYRD, WILLIAM, II, "Letters to the First Earl of Egmont." *American Historical Review* I.

———, *William Byrd II's Histories of the Dividing Line Betwixt Virginia and North Carolina,* with introduction and notes by William K. Boyd. Raleigh, North Carolina Historical Commission, 1929.

———, *The London Diary (1717–1721) and Other Writings,* Louis B. Wright and Marion Tinling, eds. New York, Oxford University Press, 1958.

CAHAN, ABRAHAM, *The Rise of David Levinsky.* New York, Harper and Brothers, 1917.

CAMERON, E. H., *Samuel Slater: Father of American Manufactures.* N.P., Bond Wheelwright Company, 1960.

CARLTON, ROBERT. *See* Hall, Baynard Rush.

CARSON, GERALD, *Cornflake Crusade.* New York, Rinehart & Company, 1957.

Cartoon Cavalcade, Thomas Craven, ed. New York, Simon and Schuster, 1943.

CHANNING, EDWARD, "The Narragansett Planters . . ." *Johns Hopkins University Studies in Historical and Political Science,* Fourth Series, Vol. III (March, 1886).

Charles W. Eliot and Popular Education, edited with an introduction and notes by Edward A. Krug. Classics in Education, No. 8. New York, Teachers College Press, 1961.

CHEVALIER, MICHAEL, *Society, Manners and Politics in the United States: Letters on North America,* ed. and with an introduction by John William Ward, translated after the T. G. Bradford ed. New York, Anchor Books, 1961.

CHURCHILL, WINSTON, *The Crisis,* introduction by Joseph Mersand. New York, Washington Square Press, 1962.

CLAPPE, LOUISE AMELIA KNAPP SMITH, *The Shirley Letters from the California Mines 1851–1852,* with an introduction and notes by Carl L. Wheat. New York, Alfred A. Knopf, 1949.

CLEGHORN, SARAH, *Portraits and Protests.* New York, H. Holt & Co., 1917.

CLELAND, ROBERT GLASS, *The Cattle on a Thousand Hills.* San Marino, Calif., Huntington Library, 1951.

CLEMENS, SAMUEL LANGHORNE. See Twain, Mark.

COLLIER, PRICE, *America and the Americans from a French Point of View,* 6th ed. New York, Charles Scribner's Sons, 1897.

COLONIAL WILLIAMSBURG, *The Leatherworker in 18th Century Williamsburg.* 1967.

COLT, MRS. S. S., *The Tourist's Guide Through the Empire State Embracing All Cities, Towns and Watering Places by Hudson River and New York Central Route.* . . . Albany, N.Y., edited and published by the author, 1871.

COMBE, GEORGE, *Notes on the United States of North America During a Phrenological Visit in 1838-9-40*. Philadelphia, Carey & Hart, 1841.

COMMAGER, HENRY STEELE, "Foreword" to *McGuffey's Sixth Eclectic Reader* 1879 ed. A Signet Classic. New York, New American Library, 1963.

CONGDON, HERBERT WHEATON, *The Covered Bridge: An Old American Landmark*. New York, Alfred A. Knopf, 1946.

COOK, CLARENCE, *The House Beautiful*. New York, Charles Scribner's Sons, 1881.

COOK, EBENEZER, *The Sot-Weed Factor, or a Voyage to Maryland*. London, D. Bragg, 1708.

COOPER, JAMES FENIMORE, "Letter" in *Spirit of the Fair* (April 6, 1864).

COOPER, WILLIAM, *A Guide in the Wilderness, or the History of the First Settlements in the Western Counties of New York with Useful Instructions to Future Settlers, in a Series of Letters Addressed by Judge William Cooper of Cooperstown, to William Sampson, Barrister, of New York*. Dublin, Gilbert & Hodges, 1810.

COX, SANDFORD C., *Recollections of the Early Settlement of the Wabash Valley*. Lafayette, Courier Steam Book and Job Printing House, 1860.

CRANE, VERNER W., *The Southern Frontier: 1670-1732*. Durham, Duke University Press, 1928.

CRAVEN, AVERY, *The Coming of the Civil War*, 2d ed. rev. University of Chicago Press, 1957.

CRÈVECOEUR, MICHEL-GUILLAUME-JEAN DE, *Letters from an American Farmer*. Everyman Edition. New York, E. P. Dutton & Co., n.d.

CROCKETT, DAVY, *The Life of Davy Crockett*. A Signet Book. New York, New American Library, 1955.

Culture in the South, W. T. Couch, ed. Chapel Hill, University of North Carolina Press, 1935.

CUMING, F., *Sketches of a Tour to the Western Country . . . Commenced at Philadelphia in the Winter of 1807, and Concluded in 1809 . . .*, in Thwaites, *Early Western Travels*, IV.

DANA, R. H., JR., *Two Years Before the Mast: A Personal Narrative of Life at Sea*. New York, F. M. Lupton Publishing Company, n.d.

DANKERS, JASPAR, and PETER SLUYTER, *Journal of a Voyage to New York and a Tour in Several of the American Colonies in 1679-80, by Jaspar Dankers and Peter Sluyter of Wiewerd in Friesland*, trans. from the original manuscript in Dutch for the Long Island Historical Society, and ed. by Henry C. Murphy, foreign corresponding secretary of the society. *Memoirs of the Long Island Historical Society*, Vol. I. Brooklyn, N.Y., published by the society, 1867.

DEVENS, R. M., *Our First Century: Being a Popular Descriptive Portraiture of the One Hundred Great and Memorable Events of Perpetual Interest in the History of Our Country, Political, Military, Mechanical, Social, Scientific and Commercial . . .* Springfield, Mass., C. A. Nichols & Co., 1878.

DEXTER, ELISABETH ANTHONY, *Colonial Women of Affairs: A Study of Women in Business and the Professions in America before 1776.* Boston, Houghton Mifflin Company, 1924.

DICKENS, CHARLES, *American Notes.* New York, Thomas Y. Crowell Company, n.d.

————, *Martin Chuzzlewit.* New York, Thomas Y. Crowell Company, n.d.

DOBRÉE, BONAMY, *William Penn: Quaker and Pioneer.* London, Constable & Co., 1932.

DONNE, JOHN, *The Sermons of John Donne,* George R. Potter and Evelyn M. Simpson, eds. Berkeley, University of California Press, 1959.

DONOVAN, ROBERT J., *The Assassins.* New York, Popular Library, 1964.

DOWD, DOUGLAS, *Thorstein Veblen.* Great American Thinkers Series. New York, Washington Square Press, 1964.

DOWNING, ANTOINETTE F., and VINCENT J. SCULLY, JR., *The Architectural Heritage of Newport Rhode Island: 1640–1915.* Cambridge, Harvard University Press, 1952.

DOWNING, A. J., *The Architecture of Country Houses.* New York, D. Appleton and Company, 1850.

DRAKE, DANIEL, *Malaria in the Interior Valley of North America.* A Selection by Norman D. Levine from a Systematic Treatise . . . on the Principal Diseases of the Interior Valley of North America . . . Cincinnati, Ohio, 1850. Urbana, University of Illinois Press, 1964.

————, *Pioneer Life in Kentucky: 1785–1800,* edited, from the original manuscript, with introductory comments and a biographical sketch by Emmet Field Horine, MD. New York, Henry Schuman, 1948.

DRAYTON, MICHAEL, *Minor Poems of Michael Drayton,* Cyril Brett, ed. Oxford, Clarendon Press, 1907.

DREISER, THEODORE, *A Book About Myself.* Greenwich, Conn., Fawcett Publications, n.d.

DRINKER, CECIL, *Not So Long Ago: A Chronicle of Medicine and Doctors in Colonial Philadelphia.* New York, Oxford University Press, 1937.

DRINKER, ELIZABETH, *Extracts from the Journal of Elizabeth Drinker. From 1759 to 1807* A.D., Henry D. Biddle, ed. Philadelphia, J. B. Lippincott Company, 1889.

DUFFUS, R. L., *Nostalgia, U.S.A.: or, If You Don't Like the 1960's, Why Don't You Go Back Where You Came From?* New York, W. W. Norton & Company, 1963.

————, *Queen Calafia's Island: Facts and Myths about the Golden State.* New York, W. W. Norton & Company, 1965.

————, *The Waterbury Record.* New York, W. W. Norton & Company, 1959.

DUNBAR, SEYMOUR, *History of Travel in America* . . . New York, Tudor Publishing Co., 1937.

DUNCAN, ROBERT LIPSCOMB, *Reluctant General: The Life and Times of Albert Pike.* New York, E. P. Dutton Co., 1961.

DUNNE, FINLEY PETER, *Dissertations by Mr. Dooley.* New York, Harper and Company, 1919.

————, *Mr. Dooley in Peace and in War.* Boston, Small, Maynard and Company, 1919.

————, *Mr. Dooley in the Hearts of His Countrymen.* Boston, Small, Maynard and Company, 1899.

————, *Mr. Dooley on Making a Will and Other Necessary Evils.* New York, Charles Scribner's Sons, 1919.

————, *Mr. Dooley's Opinions.* New York, Harper and Brothers, 1906.

————, *Mr. Dooley's Philosophy.* New York, Harper and Brothers, n.d.

————, *Observations by Mr. Dooley.* New York, Harper and Brothers, 1906.

————, *The World of Mr. Dooley,* edited with an introduction by Louis Filler. New York, Collier Books, 1962.

DURAND, JOHN, *The Life and Times of A. B. Durand.* New York, Charles Scribner's Sons, 1894.

DURAND DE DAUPHINÉ, *Un Français en Virginie: Voyages d'un Français Exilé pour la Religion avec une Description de la Virgine & Marilan dans l'Amérique.* D'après l'édition originale de 1687. Avec une introduction et des notes par Gilbert Chinard . . . Baltimore, Johns Hopkins Press, 1932.

Dutchess County and Poughkeepsie Sanitary Fair. Poughkeepsie, 1864.

EASTLAKE, CHARLES L., *Hints on Household Taste in Furniture, Upholstery, and Other Details,* edited, with notes, by Charles C. Perkins. First American, from the revised London, ed. Boston, James R. Osgood and Company, 1872.

EGGLESTON, EDWARD, *The Circuit Rider: A Tale of the Heroic Age.* New York, J. B. Ford and Company, 1874.

————, *The End of the World.* New York, O. Judd & Co., 1892.

————, *The Graysons: A Story of Illinois.* New York, Century Co., 1887.

————, *The Hoosier Schoolmaster.* New York, Grosset & Dunlap, 1892.

————, *Roxy.* New York, Charles Scribner's Sons, 1878.

ELIOT, CHARLES W., "Shortening and Enrichening the Grammar School Course." *Addresses and Proceedings,* National Education Association (1892).

ELLIOTT, J. H., *Imperial Spain: 1469–1716.* New York, New American Library, 1963.

ELSON, LOUIS C., *The History of American Music.* The History of American Art, John C. Van Dyke, ed. New York, Macmillan Company, 1904.

EVANS, ESTWICK, *A Pedestrious Tour, of Four Thousand Miles, Through the Western States . . . 1818 . . .* Concord, N.H., Printed by Joseph C. Spear, 1819. (In Thwaites, *Early Western Travels,* VIII.)

FAUST, ALBERT BERNHARDT, *The German Element in the United States: with Special Reference to Its Political, Moral, Social, and Educational Influence.* Boston, Houghton Mifflin Company, 1909.

FAUX, WILLIAM, *Memorable Days in America . . . ,* in Thwaites, *Early Western Travels,* X.

FAWCETT, EDGAR, *A Gentleman of Leisure.* Boston, Houghton Mifflin Company, 1881.

Female Poets of America, Rufus Griswold, ed. Philadelphia, Moss, 1860.

FENNELLY, CATHERINE, *Town Schooling in Early New England: 1790-1840.* Old Sturbridge Village, Sturbridge, Mass., Old Sturbridge Booklet Series, 1962.

FINLEY, RUTH E., *The Lady of Godey's: Sarah Josepha Hale.* Philadelphia, J. B. Lippincott Company, 1931.

FITE, EMERSON DAVID, *Social and Industrial Conditions in the North During the Civil War.* New York, Macmillan Company, 1910.

FITHIAN, PHILIP VICKERS, *Journal and Letters of Philip Vickers Fithian, 1773–1774: A Plantation Tutor of the Old Dominion,* edited, with an introduction, by Hunter Dickinson Farish. Williamsburg, Va., Colonial Williamsburg, 1943.

FLEXNER, JAMES THOMAS, *Doctors on Horseback: Pioneers of American Medicine.* New York, Garden City Publishing Co., 1939.

———, *The Light of Distant Stars.* [American Painting]: 1760–1825. New York, Harcourt, Brace and Company, 1954.

———, *Mohawk Baronet: Sir William Johnson of New York.* New York, Harper and Brothers, 1959.

———, *Steamboats Come True: American Inventors in Action.* New York, Viking Press, 1954.

———, *That Wilder Image: The Painting of America's Native School from Thomas Cole to Winslow Homer.* Boston, Little, Brown and Company, 1962.

Florida: A Guide to the Southernmost State . . . American Guide Series. New York, Oxford University Press, 1939.

FLYNT, JOSIAH, *Tramping with Tramps: Studies and Sketches of Vagabond Life,* with Prefatory Note by Hon. Andrew D. White. New York, Century Co., 1907.

FOOTNER, HULBERT, *Rivers of the Eastern Shore: Seventeen Maryland Rivers.* New York, Farrar & Rinehart, 1944.

FORBES, ESTHER, *Paul Revere and the World He Lived In.* Boston, Houghton Mifflin Company, 1942.

FOX, DIXON RYAN, *Yankees and Yorkers.* New York, New York University Press, 1940.

FRANK, WALDO, *Our America.* New York, Boni and Liveright, 1919.

FRANKENSTEIN, ALFRED V., Introduction to Catalogue of Exhibit at Everson Museum, Syracuse, N.Y., December 3, 1965.

FRANKLIN, BENJAMIN, *The Autobiography of Benjamin Franklin,* Leonard W. Labaree, Ralph L. Ketcham, Helen C. Boatfield and Helene H. Fineman, eds. New Haven, Yale University Press, 1964.

———, *Benjamin Franklin on Education,* edited, with an introduction and notes, by John Hardin Best. Classics in Education, No. 14. New York, Bureau of Publications, Teachers College, 1962.

———, *Benjamin Franklin's Autobiographical Writings,* Carl Van Doren, ed. New York, Viking Press, 1945.

———, "Dialogue Between X, Y, and Z, Concerning the Present State of Affairs in Pennsylvania," 1755, in *Works,* Federal ed., III, 102–17.

FULTON, JOHN F., and ELIZABETH H. THOMSON, *Benjamin Silliman: 1779–1864. Pathfinder in American Science.* New York, Henry Schuman, 1947.

FURNAS, J. C., *The Life and Times of the Late Demon Rum.* New York, G. P. Putnam's Sons, 1965.

————, *Many People Prize It.* New York, William Morrow and Company, 1937.

————, *The Road to Harpers Ferry.* New York, William Sloane Associates, 1959.

————, *Voyage to Windward: The Life of Robert Louis Stevenson.* New York, William Sloane Associates, 1951.

GARDNER, ALBERT TEN EYCK, *Winslow Homer, American Artist: His World and His Work.* New York, Bramhall House, 1961.

GARDNER, GILSON, *Lusty Scripps: The Life of E. W. Scripps.* New York, Vanguard Press, 1932.

GIEDION, SIEGFRIED, *Space, Time and Architecture.* Cambridge, Harvard University Press, 1939.

GILES, DOROTHY, *Singing Valleys.* New York, Random House, 1940.

GINGER, RAY, *The Bending Cross: A Biography of Eugene Victor Debs.* New Brunswick, N.J., Rutgers University Press, 1949.

GLAZER, NATHAN, *American Judaism.* Chicago, University of Chicago Press, 1957.

GLAZER, NATHAN, and DANIEL PATRICK MOYNIHAN, *Beyond the Melting Pot: The Negroes, Puerto Ricans, Jews, Italians, and Irish of New York City.* Cambridge, Mass., M.I.T. Press, 1963.

GOODRICH, LLOYD, *Winslow Homer.* New York, Macmillan Company, 1944.

GORDON, LORD ADAM, *Journal . . .*, in Mereness, *Travels in the American Colonies.* New York, Macmillan Company, 1960.

GREELEY, HORACE, *Recollections of a Busy Life.* New York, J. B. Ford and Company, 1868.

GRONLUND, LAURENCE, *The Cooperative Commonwealth*, Stow Persons, ed. The John Harvard Library. Cambridge, Belknap Press of Harvard University, 1965.

GRUND, FRANCIS J., *Aristocracy in America: From the Sketch-Book of a German Nobleman*, with an Introduction by George E. Probst. Harper Torchbooks. The Academy Library. New York, Harper and Brothers, 1959.

GUESS, WILLIAM FRANCIS, *South Carolina: Annals of Pride and Protest.* A Regions of America Book. New York, Harper and Brothers, 1960.

HADLEY, HENRY H., *The Blue Badge of Courage.* Akron, Ohio, Saalfield Publishing Co., 1902.

HAKLUYT, RICHARD, *The Principal Navigations Voyages Traffiques & Discoveries of the English Nation. Made by Sea or Overland to the Remote & Farthest Distant Quarters of the Earth at Any Time Within the Compasse of These 1600 Yeares.* Everyman Series. London, J. M. Dent & Co., n.d.

HALE, EDWARD EVERETT, *A New England Boyhood*, with a new introduction by Nancy Hale. Boston, Little, Brown and Company, 1964.

HALE, JOHN P., *Trans-Allegheny Pioneers: Historical Sketches of the First White Settlements West of the Alleghenies.* Cincinnati, Samuel C. Cox & Co., 1886.

HALE, SARAH JOSEPHA, *Northwood: or, Life North and South,* 2d ed. New York, H. Long & Brother, 1852.

HALIBURTON, THOMAS CHANDLER, *The Clockmaker: Sayings and Doings of Samuel Slick of Slicksville.* Boston, Houghton Mifflin Company, 1871.

HALL, BASIL, *Travels in North America in the Years 1827 and 1828.* Philadelphia, Carey, Lea & Carey, 1829.

HALL, BAYNARD RUSH (Robert Carlton, pseud.), *The New Purchase; or, Early Years in the Far West,* 2d rev. ed. New Albany, Ind., Jno. R. Nunemacher, 1855.

HALL, JAMES, *The West* . . . Cincinnati, H. W. Derby & Co., 1848.

HAMILTON, ALEXANDER, *Gentleman's Progress: The Itinerarium of Dr. Alexander Hamilton 1744,* edited with an introduction by Carl Bridenbaugh. Published for the Institute of Early American History and Culture at Williamsburg, Va. Chapel Hill, University of North Carolina Press, 1948.

HAMLIN, TALBOT FAULKNER, *Greek Revival Architecture in America: Being an Account of Important Trends in American Architecture and American Life Prior to the War Between the States* . . . New York, Oxford University Press, 1945.

HANDLIN, OSCAR, *Race and Nationality in American Life.* Garden City, Doubleday Anchor Books, 1957.

HANNA, CHARLES A., *The Scotch-Irish* . . . New York, G. P. Putnam's Sons, 1902.

————, *The Wilderness Trail: or, The Ventures and Adventures of the Pennsylvania Traders on the Allegheny Path* . . . New York, G. P. Putnam's Sons, 1911.

HANSEN, MARCUS LEE, *The Atlantic Migration, 1607–1860: A History of the Continuing Settlement of the United States,* edited with a foreword by Arthur M. Schlesinger; with an introduction to the Torchbook Edition by Oscar Handlin. New York, Harper and Brothers, 1961.

HARLOW, ALVIN F., *Old Postbags.* Introduction by Joseph Stewart. New York, D. Appleton and Company, 1928.

————, *Old Towpaths: The Story of the American Canal Era.* New York, D. Appleton and Company, 1926.

HARRIS, REX, *Jazz.* N.P., Penguin Books, 1952.

HARRIS, THADDEUS MASON, *The Journal of a Tour into the Territory Northwest of the Alleghany Mountains* . . . , in Thwaites, *Early Western Travels,* III.

HARRISON, CONSTANCE CARY, *The Anglomaniacs.* New York, Cassell Publishing Company, 1890.

HARROWER, JOHN, *The Journal of John Harrower, an Indentured Servant in the Colony of Virginia, 1773–1776,* edited, with an introduction, by Edward Miles Riley. Williamsburg, Va., Colonial Williamsburg, 1963.

HAWTHORNE, NATHANIEL, "Mr. Higginbotham's Catastrophe," in *Twice Told Tales,* Vol. I. Boston, Ticknor, Reed, and Fields, 1861.

HAY, JOHN, *The Breadwinners: A Social Study*. New York, Harper and Brothers, 1905.

——, *In Praise of Omar: An Address Before the Omar Khayyám Club*, Portland, Me., printed for Thomas B. Mosher, 1898.

HAYWOOD, WILLIAM D., *Bill Haywood's Book: The Autobiography of William D. Haywood*. New York, International Publishers, 1966.

HIGHAM, JOHN, *Strangers in the Land: Patterns of American Nativism 1860–1925*, corrected and with a new Preface. New York, Atheneum, 1963.

HILL, RALPH NADING, *Yankee Kingdom: Vermont and New Hampshire*. A Regions of America Book. New York, Harper and Brothers, 1960.

HILLQUIT, MORRIS, *History of Socialism in the United States*, 5th rev. and enlarged edition. New York, Funk and Wagnalls Company, 1910.

HOFSTADTER, RICHARD, *The Age of Reform from Bryan to F.D.R.* New York, Vintage Books, 1960.

HOLBROOK, STEWART H., *Machines of Plenty: Pioneering in American Agriculture*. New York, Macmillan Company, 1955.

HOLLEY, MARIETTA, *My Opinions and Betsy Bobbet's . . .* By Josiah Allen's Wife. Hartford, American Publishing Company, 1890.

——, *Samantha at the World's Fair*. New York, Funk & Wagnalls Company, 1893.

HOLLEY, MARY AUSTIN, *Texas*. Lexington, Ky., J. Clarke & Co., 1836.

HOLMES, OLIVER WENDELL, *Works,* Vol. IX. Boston, Riverside Press, 1892.

HONE, PHILIP, *The Diary of Philip Hone, 1828–1851*, edited with an introduction by Allan Nevins, new and enlarged ed. New York, Dodd, Mead & Company, 1936.

HOSMER, JAMES K., *A Short History of Anglo-Saxon Freedom: The Polity of the English-Speaking Race . . .* New York, Charles Scribner's Sons, 1890.

HOWARD, JOHN TASKER, *Our American Music: Three Hundred Years of It*. New York, Thomas Y. Crowell Company, 1930.

HOWE, HENRY, *Historical Collections of Ohio . . .* Ohio Centennial ed. Columbus, Henry Howe & Son, 1891.

HOWELLS, WILLIAM DEAN, *A Boy's Town,* in *Selected Writings of William Dean Howells,* Henry Steele Commager, ed. New York, Random House, 1950.

——, *A Hazard of New Fortunes,* with an introduction by Van Wyck Brooks. New York, Bantam Books, 1960.

——, *Impressions and Experiences.* New York, Harper and Brothers, 1890.

——, *A Modern Instance,* with an afterword by Wallace Brockway. A Signet Classic. New York, New American Library, 1964.

——, *The Rise of Silas Lapham,* with an introduction by Harry T. Moore. New York, New American Library, 1963.

——, *The Son of Royal Langbrith.* New York, Harper and Brothers, 1904.

——, *Suburban Sketches,* 12th ed. Boston, Houghton Mifflin Company, 1888.

————, *A Traveler from Altruria,* introduction by Howard Mumford Jones. American Century Series. New York, Sagamore Press, 1957.

————, *Years of My Youth.* New York, Harper and Brothers, 1916.

HULME, THOMAS, *A Journal Made During a Tour of the Western Countries of America . . . 1818–1819,* in Thwaites, *Early Western Travels,* X.

HUTCHINSON, THOMAS, *The History of the Colony and Province of Massachusetts.* Cambridge, Harvard University Press, 1936.

Industrial Workers of the World, *Songs of the Workers to Fan the Flames of Discontent,* 31st ed. Chicago, Industrial Workers of the World, 1964.

INGRAM, J. S., *The Centennial Exposition.* Philadelphia, Hubbard Bros., 1876.

JAMESON, J. FRANKLIN, *The American Revolution Considered as a Social Movement.* New York, Peter Smith, 1950.

JEFFERSON, THOMAS, *Basic Writings of Thomas Jefferson,* Philip S. Foner, ed. Garden City, Halcyon House, 1944.

————, *Crusade Against Ignorance: Thomas Jefferson on Education,* edited, with an introduction and notes, by Gordon C. Lee. New York, Bureau of Publications, Teachers College, 1961.

JEWETT, SARAH ORNE, *The Country of the Pointed Firs and Other Stories,* selected and arranged with a preface by Willa Cather. Anchor Books. Garden City, Doubleday & Company, n.d.

JOHNSON, EDWARD, *Johnson's Wonder-Working Providence: 1628–1651,* J. Franklin Jameson, ed. New York, Charles Scribner's Sons, 1910.

JOLL, JAMES, *The Anarchists.* Boston, Little, Brown and Company, 1964.

JONES, MRS. M. M., *Woman's Dress: Its Moral and Physical Relations.* Essay delivered before the World's Health Convention, New York City, November, 1864.

JUERGENS, GEORGE, *Joseph Pulitzer and the New York World.* Princeton, Princeton University Press, 1966.

KENNEDY, JOHN PENDLETON, *Quodlibet: Containing Some Annals Thereof, with an Authentic Account of the Origin and Growth of the Borough,* edited by Solomon Secondthoughts, Schoolmaster. Philadelphia, Lea & Blanchard, 1840.

————, *Swallow Barn, or A Sojourn in the Old Dominion,* rev. ed., with twenty illustrations by Strother. New York, G. P. Putnam & Company, 1854.

KIMBALL, MARIE, *Jefferson: War and Peace.* New York, Coward-McCann, 1947.

KIMMEL, STANLEY, *The Mad Booths of Maryland.* Indianapolis, Bobbs-Merrill Company, 1940.

KIRKLAND, CAROLINE MATILDA STANSBURY, *A New Home: or, Life in the Clearings,* edited and with an introduction by John Nerber. New York, G. P. Putnam's Sons, 1953.

KIRKLAND, JOSEPH, *The McVeys.* Boston, Houghton Mifflin Company, 1888.

————, *Zury: The Meanest Man in Spring County: A Novel of Western Life,* facsimile reprint with an introduction by John T. Flanagan. Urbana, University of Illinois Press, 1956.

KNIGHT, SARAH KEMBLE, *The Journal of Madam Knight*, with an introductory note by George Parker Winship. Boston, Small, Maynard and Company, 1920.

KORNGOLD, RALPH, *Two Friends of Man: The Story of William Lloyd Garrison and Wendell Phillips*. Boston, Little, Brown and Company, 1950.

LA FOLLETTE, SUZANNE, *Art in America*. New York, Harper and Brothers, 1929.

LAMONT, THOMAS, *A Brief Account of the Life at Charlottesville of Thomas William Lamont and of His Family Together with a Record of Their Ancestors*. New York, Duffield & Company, 1915.

LANCASTER, OSBERT, *Homes, Sweet Homes*. London, John Murray, 1939.

LANGFORD, GERALD, *The Murder of Stanford White*. Indianapolis, Bobbs-Merrill Company, 1962.

LARCOM, LUCY, *A New England Girlhood: Outlined from Memory*. Boston, Houghton Mifflin Company, 1892.

LARSON, ORVIN, *American Infidel: Robert G. Ingersoll*. New York, Citadel Press, 1962.

Letters of Theodore Dwight Weld, Angelina Grimké Weld and Sarah Grimké: 1822–1844, Gilbert Hobbs Barnes and Dwight L. Dumond, eds. New York, D. Appleton-Century Company, 1934.

LEVINGER, LEE J., *A History of the Jews in the United States*. Cincinnati, Union of American Hebrew Congregations, 1930.

LEWIS, OSCAR, *Silver Kings: The Lives and Times of Mackay, Fair, Flood and O'Brien, Lords of the Nevada Comstock Lode*. New York, Alfred A. Knopf, 1947.

A Library of American Literature: From the Earliest Settlement to the Present Time, Edmund Clarence Stedman and Ellen Mackay Hutchinson, eds. New York, Charles L. Webster & Company, 1889.

LINDSEY, ALMONT, *The Pullman Strike: The Story of a Unique Experiment and of a Great Labor Upheaval*. Chicago, University of Chicago Press, 1964.

LITWACK, LEON F., *North of Slavery: The Negro in the Free States, 1790–1860*. Chicago, University of Chicago Press, 1961.

LLOYD, CARO, *Henry Demarest Lloyd, 1847–1903: A Biography*, with an introduction by Charles Edward Russell. New York, G. P. Putnam's Sons, 1912.

LODGE, HENRY CABOT, *A Short History of the English Colonies in America*, rev. ed. New York, Harper and Brothers, 1886.

LOMAX, ALAN, *The Penguin Book of American Folk Songs*. Baltimore, Penguin Books, n.d.

LONDON, JACK, *The Road*. New York, Macmillan Company, 1907.

The Lowell Offering: A Repertory of Original Articles, Written Exclusively by Females Actively Employed in the Mills. Lowell, Mass., Powers & Bagley, n.d.

LOWENTHAL, DAVID, *George Perkins Marsh: Versatile Vermonter*. New York, Columbia University Press, 1958.

McCabe, James D., *The Illustrated History of the Centennial Exhibition . . . to Which Is Added a Complete Description of the City of Philadelphia . . .* Philadelphia, National Publishing Company, 1876.

McGuffey's Fifth Eclectic Reader, 1879 ed., with a foreword by Henry Steele Commager. A Signet Classic. New York, New American Library, 1962.

Mackay, Charles, *Life and Liberty in America: or, Sketches of a Tour in the United States and Canada, in 1857–8.* London, Smith, Elder and Co., 1859.

Maclean, J. P., *Historical Account of the Settlements of Scotch Highlanders in America Prior to the Peace of 1783 . . .* Cleveland, Helman-Taylor Company, 1900.

McMaster, John Bach, *A History of the People of the United States, from the Revolution to the Civil War.* New York, D. Appleton and Company, 1904.

McMichael, George, *Journey to Obscurity: The Life of Octave Thanet.* Lincoln, University of Nebraska Press, 1965.

Maass, John, *The Gingerbread Age: A View of Victorian America.* New York, Bramhall House, n.d.

Mabee, Carleton, *The American Leonardo: A Life of Samuel F. B. Morse,* with an introduction by Allan Nevins. New York, Alfred A. Knopf, 1943.

Malin, James C., "The Grasslands of North America . . . ," in *Man's Role in Changing the Face of the Earth,* William L. Thomas, Jr., ed. Chicago, University of Chicago Press, 1956.

Marckwardt, Albert H., *American English.* New York, Oxford University Press, 1958.

Marquis, Don, *Hermione and Her Little Group of Serious Thinkers.* New York, D. Appleton and Company, 1920.

Martin, Joseph Plumb, *Private Yankee Doodle: Being a Narrative of Some of the Adventures, Dangers and Sufferings of a Revolutionary Soldier,* George F. Scheer, ed. New York, Popular Library, 1963.

Martin, Sidney Walter, *Florida's Flagler.* Athens, University of Georgia Press, 1949.

Martineau, Harriet, *Retrospect of Western Travel.* New York, Harper and Brothers, 1838.

Marvin, Winthrop L., *The American Merchant Marine: Its History and Romance from 1620 to 1902.* London, Sampson Low, Marston and Company, 1902.

Mathews, M. M., *The Beginnings of American English: Essays and Comments.* Chicago, University of Chicago Press, 1931.

Melville, Herman, *Mardi and a Voyage Thither,* edited with an introduction by Raymond M. Weaver. New York, Albert and Charles Boni, 1925.

Men and Manners in America One Hundred Years Ago, H. E. Scudder, ed. New York, Scribner, Armstrong, and Company, 1876.

Mencken, August, *The Railroad Passenger Car: An Illustrated History of the First Hundred Years with Accounts by Contemporary Passengers.* Baltimore, Johns Hopkins Press, 1957.

MEYER, DUANE, *The Highland Scots of North Carolina: 1732–1776.* Chapel Hill, University of North Carolina Press, 1957.

MILLER, JOHN C., *The Colonial Image: Origins of American Culture.* New York, George Braziller, 1962.

———, *The First Frontier: Life in Colonial America.* New York, Dell Publishing Company, 1966.

MIRSKY, JEANNETTE, and ALLAN NEVINS, *The World of Eli Whitney.* New York, Macmillan Company, 1952.

MITCHELL, DONALD, *Rural Studies, with Hints for Country Places.* New York, Charles Scribner & Company, 1867.

MOORE, JOHN TROTWOOD, *The Bishop of Cottontown: A Story of the Southern Cotton Mills.* Philadelphia, John C. Winston Company, 1906.

MOORE, JULIA A., *The Sweet Singer of Michigan: Poems by Julia A. Moore,* edited and with an introduction by Walter Blair. Chicago, Pascal Covici, 1928.

MOREAU DE ST.-MÉRY, MÉDÉRIC LOUIS ÉLIE, *Moreau de St.-Méry's American Journey,* trans. and edited by Kenneth Roberts, Anna M. Roberts . . . ; introduction by Stewart L. Mims. Garden City, Doubleday & Company, 1947.

MORISON, SAMUEL ELIOT, *Builders of the Bay Colony.* Boston, Houghton Mifflin Company, 1930.

———, *The Oxford History of the United States.* London, Oxford University Press, 1927.

MORRIS, LLOYD, *Incredible New York: High Life and Low Life of the Last Hundred Years.* New York, Random House, 1951.

MORRIS, THOMAS, *Journal of Captain Thomas Morris,* in Thwaites, *Early Western Travels,* I.

MOTT, FRANK LUTHER, *American Journalism: A History of Newspapers in the United States through 250 Years, 1690 to 1940.* New York, Macmillan Company, 1947.

———, *Golden Multitudes: The Story of Best Sellers in the United States.* New York, Macmillan Company, 1947.

———, *A History of American Magazines: 1885–1905.* Cambridge, Harvard University Press, 1957.

MUMFORD, LEWIS, *The Brown Decades: A Study of the Arts in America 1865–1895.* New York, Dover Publications, 1955.

MURDOCK, EUGENE CONVERSE, *Patriotism Limited, 1862–1865: The Civil War Draft and the Bounty System.* N.P., Kent University Press, 1967.

MYERS, GUSTAVUS, *History of Bigotry in the United States.* New York, Random House, 1943.

MYRDAL, GUNNAR, *An American Dilemma: The Negro Problem and Modern Democracy* . . . , with the assistance of Richard Sterner and Arnold Rose. New York, Harper and Brothers, 1944.

Narratives of Early Maryland: 1633-1684, Clayton Colman Hall, ed. With a map and two facsimiles. New York, Charles Scribner's Sons, 1910.

Narratives of Early Pennsylvania, West New Jersey and Delaware: 1630–1707, Albert Cook Myers, ed. Original Narratives of Early American History. New York, Charles Scribner's Sons, 1912.

Narratives of New Netherland: 1609–1664, J. Franklin Jameson, ed. Original Narratives of Early American History. New York, Charles Scribner's Sons, 1909.

NELSON, WILLIAM H., *The American Tory.* Boston, Beacon Press, 1864.

The New England Primer. Twentieth Century Reprint. Boston, Ginn & Company, n.d.

NEWTON, ROBERT HALE, *Town & Davis Architects: Pioneers in American Revivalist Architecture 1812–1870, Including a Glimpse of Their Times and Their Contemporaries.* New York, Columbia University Press, 1942.

NICHOLSON, MEREDITH, *A Hoosier Chronicle.* Boston, Houghton Mifflin Company, 1912.

———, *The Hoosiers.* New York, Macmillan Company, 1916.

———, *Otherwise Phyllis.* Boston, Houghton Mifflin Company, 1913.

NIEMCEWICZ, JULIAN URSYN, *Under Their Vine and Fig Tree: Travels Through America in 1797–99, 1805* . . . , translated and edited with an introduction and notes by Metchie J. E. Budka. Collections of the New Jersey Historical Society, Vol. XIV. Elizabeth, N.J., Grassmann Publishing Company, 1965.

NORDHOFF, CHARLES, *California: For Health, Pleasure and Residence.* New York, Harper and Brothers, 1873.

———, *The Communistic Societies of the United States.* New York, Hilary House, 1962.

NORRIS, FRANK, *Collected Writings,* with an introduction by Charles G. Norris. Garden City, Doubleday, Doran & Company, 1928.

———, *McTeague: A Story of San Francisco,* edited with an introduction by Carvel Collins. New York, Rinehart & Company, 1950.

———, *The Pit: A Story of Chicago. The Epic of the Wheat.* New York, Doubleday, Page & Company, 1903.

———, *Vandover and the Brute.* New York, Grove Press, n.d.

NORTON, CHARLES LEDYARD, *A Handbook of Florida,* 3d rev. ed. New York, Longmans, Green, and Co., 1892.

ORTON, VREST, *The Famous Rogers Groups: A Complete Check-list and Collectors' Manual* . . . , Weston, Vt., Privately Printed, Vrest Orton, 1960.

PAGE, THOMAS NELSON, *Red Rock: A Chronicle of Reconstruction.* New York, Charles Scribner's Sons, 1898.

PAINE, RALPH D., *The Ships and Sailors of Old Salem: The Record of a Brilliant Era of American Achievement.* New York, Outing Publishing Company, 1909.

Pan-American Exposition, *Art Hand-Book* . . . *Official Handbook of Architecture and Sculpture and Art Catalogue to the Pan-American Exposition.* Buffalo, David Gray, 1901.

PARKER, ROBERT ALLERTON, *A Yankee Saint: John Humphrey Noyes and the Oneida Community.* New York, G. P. Putnam's Sons, 1935.

PARKMAN, FRANCIS, *The Oregon Trail*, with an introduction by James D. Hart. New York, Washington Square Press, 1963.

PATTERSON, JOSEPH MEDILL, *A Little Brother of the Rich*. New York, Grosset & Dunlap, n.d.

PAULDING, JAMES KIRKE, *The Bulls and the Jonathans: Comprising John Bull and Brother Jonathan and John Bull in America*, William I. Paulding, ed. New York, Charles Scribner & Company, 1867.

———, *Chronicles of the City of Gotham, from the Papers of a Retired Common Councilman, Containing the Azure Rose, the Politician, The Dumb Girl . . .* New York, G. & C. & H. Carvil, 1830.

———, *The Letters of James Kirke Paulding*, Ralph M. Aderman, ed. Madison, University of Wisconsin Press, 1962.

PELLING, HENRY, *American Labor*. Chicago, University of Chicago Press, 1960.

PERKINS, A. J. G., and THERESA WOLFSON, *Frances Wright, Free Enquirer: The Study of a Temperament*. New York, Harper and Brothers, 1939.

PESTALOZZI, JOHANN HEINRICH, *Pestalozzi's Leonard and Gertrude*, trans. and abridged by Eva Channing. Boston, D. C. Heath & Co., 1906.

PHELPS, ELIZABETH STUART, *The Silent Partner*. Boston, James R. Osgood and Company, 1871.

POMEROY, EARL, *The Pacific Slope: A History of California, Oregon, Washington, Idaho, Utah, and Nevada*. New York, Alfred A. Knopf, 1965.

POUND, ARTHUR, *The Penns of Pennsylvania and England*. New York, Macmillan Company, 1932.

The Practical Housekeeper, Mrs. Ellet, ed. New York, Stringer and Townsend, 1857.

PROWN, JULES DAVID, *John Singleton Copley*. Cambridge, Harvard University Press, 1966.

PUTNAM, RUTH, "The Dutch Element in the United States." *Annual Report of the American Historical Association for the Year 1909*. Washington, 1911.

QUINCY, JOSIAH, JR., "Journal of Josiah Quincy, Jr." *Proceedings of the Massachusetts Historical Society*, XLIX (June, 1916).

RABB, KATE MILNER, *A Tour Through Indiana in 1840: The Diary of John Parsons of Petersburg, Virginia*. New York, Robert M. McBride & Co., 1920.

RAMSDELL, CHARLES, *San Antonio: A Historical and Pictorial Guide*. Austin, University of Texas Press, 1959.

RENIERS, LERCEVAL, *The Springs of Virginia: Life, Love and Death at the Waters, 1775–1900*. Chapel Hill, University of North Carolina Press, 1951.

RENSHAW, PATRICK, *The Wobblies: The Story of Syndicalism in the United States*. New York, Doubleday & Company, 1967.

Representative American Plays, Arthur Hobson Quinn, ed. New York, Century Co., 1919.

The Republic and the School: Horace Mann on the Education of Free Men,

Lawrence A. Cremin, ed. Classics in Education No. 1. New York, Bureau of Publications, Teachers College, 1957.

RICH, ARTHUR LOWNDES, *Lowell Mason: "The Father of Singing Among the Children."* Chapel Hill, University of North Carolina Press, 1946.

RICHARDS, LAURA E., and MAUD HOWE ELLIOTT, assisted by Florence Howe Hall, *Julia Ward Howe.* Boston, Houghton Mifflin Company, 1915.

ROBINSON, HARRIET J. HANSON, *Loom and Spindle or Life Among the Early Mill Girls.* New York, Thomas Y. Crowell & Company, 1895.

ROBINSON, SOLON, *How to Live* . . . New York, Fowler and Wells, 1860.

ROTHSCHILD, SALOMON DE, *A Casual View of America: The Home Letters of Salomon de Rothschild, 1859–61,* trans. and edited by Sigmund Diamond. Stanford, Stanford University Press, 1961.

RUBIN, JULIUS, "Canal or Railroad? Imitation and Innovation in the Response to the Erie Canal in Philadelphia, Baltimore, and Boston." *Proceedings of the American Philosophical Society,* New Series, Vol. 51, Part 7 (November, 1961).

RUSSELL, CHARLES EDWARD, *The American Orchestra and Theodore Thomas.* Garden City, Doubleday, Page & Company, 1927.

RYNNING, OLE, "Ole Rynning's Account of America," trans. and edited with introduction and notes by Theodore C. Belegen. *Minnesota History Bulletin,* II (1917).

SAUGRAIN, ANTOINE, *L'Odyssée Américaine d'une Famille Française.* Baltimore, Johns Hopkins Press, 1936.

SCHLESINGER, ARTHUR M., SR., *Paths to the Present.* New York, Macmillan Company, 1949.

SCHMIDT, GEORGE P., *The Old Time College President.* Studies in History, Economics and Public Law . . . Number 317. New York, Columbia University Press, 1930.

SCHUYLER, MONTGOMERY, *American Architecture.* New York, Harper & Brothers, 1892.

SEITZ, DON C., *Joseph Pulitzer: His Life and Letters.* New York, Simon and Schuster, 1924.

SEWALL, SAMUEL, *Samuel Sewall's Diary,* Mark Van Doren, ed. N.P., Macy-Masius, 1927.

SEWALL, WILLIAM WINGATE, *Bill Sewall's Story of T.R.* . . . New York, Harper and Brothers, 1919.

SHEFFIELD, WILLIAM P., *An Address Delivered by William P. Sheffield Before the Rhode Island Historical Society in Providence, February 7, A.D. 1882, with Notes.* Newport, R.I., John P. Sanborn, 1883.

SHEPARD, ODELL, *Pedlar's Progress: The Life of Bronson Alcott.* Boston, Little, Brown and Company, 1937.

SHILLING, D. C., "Pioneer Schools and Schoolmasters." *Ohio Archeological and Historical Publications,* 1916.

SHURTLEFF, HAROLD R., *The Log Cabin Myth: A Study of the Early Dwellings of the English Colonists in North America.* Cambridge, Harvard University Press, 1939.

SIGOURNEY, MRS. L. H., *Scenes in My Native Land*. Boston, James Munroe & Co., 1845.

SIMONS, A. M., *Social Forces in American History*. New York, Macmillan Company, 1911.

SINCLAIR, ANDREW, *The Better Half: The Emancipation of the American Woman*. New York, Harper and Brothers, 1965.

SINCLAIR, UPTON, *The Jungle*. A Signet Classic. New York, New American Library, 1960.

SINGLETON, ESTHER, *Social New York Under the Georges 1714–1776* . . . New York, D. Appleton and Company, 1902.

SMITH, ABBOT EMERSON, *Colonists in Bondage: White Servitude and Convict Labor in America, 1607–1776*. Chapel Hill, University of North Carolina Press, 1947.

SMITH, JOHN, *Travels and Works of Captain John Smith*, Edward Arber, ed., new ed. with a biographical and critical introduction by A. G. Bradley. Edinburgh, John Grant, 1910.

SMITH, JOSHUA TOULMIN, *Journal in America: 1837–1838*, edited with introduction and notes by Floyd Benjamin Streeter . . . Metuchen, N.J., printed for Charles F. Heartman, 1925.

SMITH, WARREN B., *White Servitude in Colonial South Carolina*. Columbia, University of South Carolina Press, 1961.

A Southern Reader, Willard Thorp, ed. New York, Alfred A. Knopf, 1955.

SOUTHEY, THOMAS, *Chronological History of the West Indies*. London, Longman, Rees, Brown and Green, 1827.

SPARGO, JOHN, *The Bitter Cry of the Children*, with an introduction by Robert Hunter. New York, Macmillan Company, 1906.

SPENCER, SAMUEL R., JR., *Booker T. Washington and the Negro's Place in American Life*, Oscar Handlin, ed. The Library of American Biography. Boston, Little, Brown and Company, 1955.

Spirit of the Fair. October 5, 1864.

STEEGMULLER, FRANCIS, *The Two Lives of James Jackson Jarves*. New Haven, Yale University Press, 1951.

STEFFENS, LINCOLN, *The Autobiography of Lincoln Steffens*. New York, Harcourt, Brace and Company, 1931.

STEIN, ROGER B., *John Ruskin and Aesthetic Thought in America, 1840–1900*. Cambridge, Harvard University Press, 1967.

STEVENSON, DAVID, *Sketch of the Civil Engineering of North America*, 2d ed. London, John Weale, 1859.

STEVENSON, ROBERT LOUIS, *From Scotland to Silverado* . . . , James D. Hart, ed. Cambridge, Harvard University Press, 1966.

———, *The Wrecker*, South Seas Edition. New York, Charles Scribner's Sons, 1925.

STODDARD, JOHN L., *John L. Stoddard's Lectures*. Boston, Balch Brothers Co., 1909.

STOVER, JOHN F., *American Railroads*. The Chicago History of American Civilization. Chicago, University of Chicago Press, 1961.

STRONG, GEORGE TEMPLETON, *The Diary of George Templeton Strong,* Allan Nevins and Milton Halsey Thomas, eds. New York, Macmillan Company, 1952.

STUART, JAMES, *Three Years in North America.* Edinburgh, printed for Robert Cadell, 1833.

SULLIVAN, LOUIS H., *The Autobiography of an Idea,* foreword by Claude Bragdon; with a new introduction by Ralph Marlowe Line . . . New York, Dover Publications, n.d.

SULLIVAN, MARK, *Our Times.* New York, Charles Scribner's Sons, 1930.

SWANBERG, W. A., *Citizen Hearst: A Biography of William Randolph Hearst.* New York, Bantam Books, 1963.

SWIGGETT, HOWARD, *The Extraordinary Mr. Morris,* Garden City, Doubleday & Company, 1952.

TARKINGTON, BOOTH, *The Magnificent Ambersons.* Garden City, Doubleday, Page & Company, 1921.

———, *Penrod: His Complete Story: Penrod. Penrod and Sam. Penrod Jashber.* Garden City, Doubleday & Company, n.d.

TAUBMAN, HOWARD, *The Making of the American Theatre.* New York, Coward-McCann, 1965.

THANET, OCTAVE (Alice French), *The Man of the Hour.* New York, Grosset and Dunlap, 1905.

———, *Stories of a Western Town.* New York, Charles Scribner's Sons, 1893.

THARP, LOUISE HALL, *Until Victory: Horace Mann and Mary Peabody.* Boston, Little, Brown and Company, 1953.

THOMSON, SAMUEL, *Narrative of the Life and Medical Discoveries of Samuel Thomson: Containing an Account of His System of Practice . . . ,* 2d ed. Boston, printed for the author, 1825.

THOREAU, HENRY DAVID, *The Maine Woods,* arranged with notes by Dudley C. Lunt. New York, Bramhall House, 1950.

———, *Walden,* introduction by Basil Willey. New York, Bramhall House, 1951.

TOULMIN, HARRY, *The Western Country in 1793: Reports on Kentucky and Virginia,* Marion Tinling and Godfrey Davies, eds. San Marino, Calif., Henry E. Huntington Library and Art Gallery, 1948.

Travels in the American Colonies, Newton D. Mereness, ed. Edited under the Auspices of the National Society of the Colonial Dames of America. New York, Macmillan Company, 1916.

A Treasury of Railroad Folklore: The Stories, Tall Tales, Traditions, Ballads and Songs of the American Railroad Man, B. A. Botkin and Alvin F. Harlow, eds. New York, Crown Publishers, 1953.

TREVELYAN, G. M., *English Social History: A Survey of Six Centuries Chaucer to Queen Victoria.* London, Longmans, 1961.

TROLLOPE, ANTHONY, *North America.* New York, Alfred A. Knopf, 1951.

TWAIN, MARK (Samuel Langhorne Clemens), *The Autobiography of Mark Twain,* as arranged and edited, with an introduction and notes, by Charles Neider. New York, Harper and Brothers, n.d.

————, *Life on the Mississippi*. Boston, James R. Osgood and Company, 1883.

————, *Mark Twain's San Francisco*, Bernard Taper, ed. New York, McGraw-Hill Book Company, 1963.

————, *Roughing It*, with a foreword by Leonard Kriegel. A Signet Classic. New York, New American Library, 1962.

————, *A Tramp Abroad*. Hartford, Conn., American Publishing Company, 1894.

TWAIN, MARK, with CHARLES DUDLEY WARNER, *The Gilded Age: A Tale of Today*. New York, Harper and Brothers, n.d.

VAN BUREN, AUGUSTUS H., "Wiltwyck Under the Dutch." *Proceedings of the New York Historical Society*, XI (1912).

VAN DOREN, CARL, *Benjamin Franklin*. New York, Viking Press, 1938.

VAN WAGENEN, JARED, JR., *The Golden Age of Homespun*. American Century Series. New York, Hill and Wang, 1963.

VAN WYCK, FREDERICK, *Recollections of an Old New Yorker*. New York, Liveright, 1932.

VAUX, CALVERT, *Villas and Cottages: A Series of Designs Prepared for Execution in the United States*. New York, Harper and Brothers, 1857.

WATSON, ELKANAH, *Men and Times of the Revolution; or Memories of Elkanah Watson*, Winslow C. Watson, ed., 2d ed. New York, Dana and Company, 1857.

WEEDEN, WILLIAM B., *Economic and Social History of New England*. Boston, Houghton Mifflin Company, 1890.

WELBY, ADGARD, *A Visit to North America . . .* , in Thwaites, *Early American Travels*, XII.

WELD, CHARLES RICHARD, *A Vacation Tour in the United States and Canada*. London, Longman, Brown, Green, and Longmans, 1855.

WELLS, H. G., *The Future in America: A Search After Realities*. New York, Harper and Brothers, 1906.

WENDELL, BARRETT, *A Literary History of America*. New York, Charles Scribner's Sons, 1901.

WERTENBAKER, THOMAS JEFFERSON, *The First Americans*. A History of American Life. New York, Macmillan Company, 1927.

————, *The Middle Colonies*. The Founding of American Civilization. New York, Charles Scribner's Sons, 1938.

————, *The Old South*. The Founding of American Civilization. New York, Charles Scribner's Sons, 1942.

————, *The Puritan Oligarchy*. The Founding of American Civilization. New York, Charles Scribner's Sons, 1947.

WESTCOTT, EDWARD NOYES, *David Harum: A Story of American Life*. New York, D. Appleton and Company, 1898.

WHARTON, EDITH, *The Age of Innocence*. New York, Modern Library, n.d.

————, *Ethan Frome*. New York, Charles Scribner's Sons, 1939.

————, *The House of Mirth*. New York, Charles Scribner's Sons, n.d.

WHITE, T. H., *America At Last: The American Journal of T. H. White*, with an introduction by David Garnett. New York, G. P. Putnam's Sons, 1965.

WILDES, HARRY EMERSON, *Lonely Midas: The Story of Stephen Girard.* New York, Farrar & Rinehart, 1943.

WILLISON, GEORGE F., *Saints and Strangers: Being the Lives of the Pilgrim Fathers & Their Families* . . . New York, Reynal & Hitchcock, 1945.

WILSON, FORREST, *Crusader in Crinoline: The Life of Harriet Beecher Stowe.* Philadelphia, J. B. Lippincott Company, 1941.

WILSON, HARRY LEON, *Ruggles, Bunker & Merton: Three Masterpieces of Humor. Ruggles of Red Gap. Bunker Bean. Merton of the Movies.* Garden City, Doubleday, Doran & Company, 1935.

———, *Somewhere in Red Gap.* New York, Doubleday, Page & Company, 1916.

———, *The Spenders: A Tale of the Third Generation.* New York, Grosset & Dunlap, 1902.

WILSON, THOMAS, "The Arkansas Traveler." *Ohio Archeological and Historical Publications,* VIII.

WINTHROP, JOHN, *The History of New England from 1630 to 1649.* James Savage, ed. Boston, Little, Brown and Company, 1853.

WINTHROP, ROBERT C., *Life and Letters of John Winthrop* . . . Boston, Ticknor, and Fields, 1864–1867.

WINTHROP, THEODORE, *Cecil Dreeme,* with biographical sketch of the author by George William Curtis. Edinburgh, William Paterson, 1883.

WISTER, FANNY KEMBLE, *Owen Wister Out West: His Journals and Letters.* Chicago, University of Chicago Press, 1958.

WISTER, OWEN, *The Virginian: A Horseman of the Plains.* New York, Macmillan Company, 1929.

———, *Lin McLean.* The Writings of Owen Wister. New York, Macmillan Company, 1928.

WISTER, SALLY, *Sally Wister's Journal: A True Narrative, Being a Quaker Maiden's Account of Her Experiences with Officers of the Continental Army, 1777–1778,* Albert Cook Myers, ed. Philadelphia, Ferris & Leach, 1902.

WOODWARD, C. VANN, *The Burden of Southern History.* New York, Vintage Books, 1960.

World's Columbian Exposition, *Art and Handicraft in the Woman's Building of the World's Columbian Exposition,* Maud Howe Elliott, ed. Chicago, 1893. New York, Goupil & Co., 1893.

———, *Memorial Volume.* Dedicatory and Opening Ceremonies of the . . . Historical and Descriptive as Authorized by Board of Control . . . Chicago, A. L. Stone, 1893.

WRIGHT, LOUIS B., *The Cultural Life of the American Colonies: 1607–1763.* The New American Nation Series, Henry Steele Commager and Richard B. Morris, eds. Harper Torchbooks. New York, Harper and Brothers, 1957.

ZIFF, LARZER, *The American 1890s: Life and Times of a Lost Generation.* New York, Viking Press, 1966.

Index

INDEX

Figures in italics refer to page on which illustrations occur.

Insects and pests, 22, 140, 141, 163, 202–3, 259, 278, 333, 334–35, 348, 785, 908–9
Instrumental music, 581 ff.
Intellectuals and professionals, immigrant, 381–82, 387 ff., 392, 394
Internal-combustion engine, 808
International Art Union, 579
International Harvester, 799
International Hygienic and Pharmaceutical Exposition, 827
International Workingmen's Association, 645
"Interpreter's House, The" (Dunne), 878
Interstate Commerce Commission, 799, 800
Interurban transit, 802–4
Intolerance, 71–72, 393–94, 521 ff., 820.
  See also Segregation and discrimination; specific aspects
  among immigrant groups, 91, 93, 97, 216, 382, 533, 698, 700–1, 703
  class hatred, 453
  ethnic stereotypes, 381, 386, 700, 709–10, 840–41
  political and social, 313–14
  racial. See specific aspects
  religious, 61, 64 ff., 75 ff., 91, 522 ff.
  xenophobic, 390–91, 452–53, 481, 524, 698–99, 837 ff.
Iowa, 248, 252, 257, 529, 797, 798. See also specific names, places, subjects
Iowa, University of, 745
Ipswich, Mass., 741
Iranistan, Bridgeport, Conn., 425
Ireland, 91–92, 103, 189, 382, 384, 385, 642, 694, 817
Irish, 287, 288, 381 ff., 394, 452, 480, 481, 520–21, 533, 659, 695, 698–99, 701–5, 713, 749, 820, 833, 835, 838, 861.
  See also Ulster Irish
Iron and iron industry, 29, 32–33, 318, 432
Iron frame construction, 624
Iron mining, 397
Iron smelting, 623
Ironwork, ornamental, 623–24
Ironworking, 103, 397
Irrigation, 777
Irving, Washington, 247, 260, 322, 323, 647
Irwin, Inez Haynes, 893
Isaacs, Abraham, 706
Italianate villas, 422–25
Italians, 29, 381, 654, 715, 833, 835 ff.
Italy, 836, 837
Ives, James Merritt, 576

Jackson, Andrew, 265–66, 527, 531, 542, 751
Jackson, Helen Hunt, 371
Jackson, James Caleb, 443, 900
Jackson, Thomas J., 381
Jackson Whites, 109, 819
Jacksonville, Fla., 792, 793
Jaeger, Gustav, 896–97

Jaeger Sanitary Woolen System, 897
James, Henry, 322, 361, 595, 608, 611, 635, 722, 730, 732, 754, 765
James, William, 595, 730, 883
James River, 285, 293
James River and Kanawha Canal, 287, 345
Jameson, John Franklin, 586
Jamestown, 30, 49–53, 57, 97, 147–48, 165, 457
Jarves, James Jackson, 575, 576, 580, 768
Jarvis, William, 473
Jay, John, 77, 321
Jay, William, 815
Jazz, 355, 585, 855
Jed the Poorhouse Boy (Alger), 654
Jefferson, Joseph, 395
Jefferson, Joseph, III, 569, 595
Jefferson, Thomas, 79–80, 192, 201, 202, 222, 227, 235, 241, 267–68, 272, 313, 317, 321, 406, 407, 464, 470, 476, 535, 543
Jefferson Market Courthouse, New York City, 614–15
Jenney (Howe), Marie, 893
Jenney, William Le Baron, 769
Jerome, Jerome K., 730
Jesup, Morris K., 792
Jewett, John, 510
Jewett, Milo P., 743
Jewett, Sarah Orne, 600, 732
Jew's rafts, 95
Jews, 74, 95, 392–95, 670–71, 705 ff., 713, 835, 836, 838, 839. See also Anti-Semitism
Jim Crow, 516
Jocker, 681
Jockey Club, Fredericksburg, Va., 190
Johnny Appleseed (John Chapman), 502, 503
Johns Hopkins University, 910, 911
Johnson, Andrew, 753
Johnson, Eastman, 628, 630
Johnson, Hiram, 809
Johnson, Samuel, 106
Johnson, Sir William, 193, 200, 266
Jones, John Paul, 197, 233
Jones, Maldwyn Allen, 394 n.
Jones, Mrs. M. M., 438, 488, 493
Jones, Robert Edmond, 834
Joplin, Scott, 856
Jordan, David Starr, 372, 918
Josiah Allen's Wife. See Holley, Marietta
Journalism, 491, 556 ff., 856 ff. See also Newspapers; specific names
Judah, Theodore D., 373
Judges, 256–57
Judson, Edward Zone Carroll (Ned Buntline), 524
Judson Memorial Church, 774, 776
Juergens, George, 861, 868
June, Jennie (Jane Cunningham Croly), 890
Jungle, The (Sinclair), 871–72

Red Stockings, Cincinnati, 656, 658
Redeemers, 847, 848
Redemptioners, 85, 385, 695
Redpath, James, 610
Redwood, Abraham, Jr., 198
Reed, John, 833–34, 835
Reed, Opie, 776
Reed, Thomas B. "Czar," 882
Reed, Walter, 908–9
Reeve, Tapping, 542
Reform movements, 316–21, 449 ff. *See
  also* specific subjects
Refrigeration, 163, 457, 458, 692
Regional differences and dissensions, 181 ff.,
  254
Rehan, Ada, 757
Religion, 27, 41, 57, 61 ff., 195, 323 ff.,
  496 ff., 501 ff. *See also* specific de-
  nominations
  agnosticism, 880–82
  communities, 496 ff., 501–2
  Great Awakening, 127, 324 ff., 326, 327,
    331
  higher criticism, 881
  intolerance, 61, 64 ff., 75 ff.
  Jewish, 708
  Negroes, 754
  religious divergences, 183–85
  women, 218
  writings and publications, religious, 235,
    236
Religious Society of Friends. *See* Quakers
Remington, Frederic, 684, 690, 863
Renshaw, Patrick, 831
Resorts, 604, 779
  campgrounds, 329–31
  hydros, 443
  spas, 193–95, 412–13
"Respectability," 314
Restaurants, 463–65, 692–93. *See also*
  Taverns and inns
Retailing. *See* Merchandising; Peddlers
Revere, Paul, 207, 523, 572
Reynolds, Sir Joshua, 206
Rhode Island, 66, 81, 119, 120, 156, 195,
  196, 210, 218, 326. *See also* specific
  names, places, subjects
Rice, 41, 111, 116, 147, 318
Rice, Thomas D. "Daddy," 516
Richardson, Albert D., 734
Richardson, Henry Hobson, 424, 595,
  620–22, 623, 774, 796
Richmond, Va., 267–68, 397, 399, 400,
  529, 686, 801
Richmond, Fredericksburg and Potomac
  Railroad, 346
Riley, Ashbel, 292
Riley, James Whitcomb, 437, 682, 728,
  879
Riley, Terence, 694
Riots and violence, 412, 521–22, 526, 527,
  701–2, 703, 711, 715–16, 825–26, 850,
  854. *See also* Terrorism
Rivermen, 298

Rivers, exploration of, 24–25
Riverside, Ill., 819, 821
Road kid, 681
Roads, 144, 208, 245, 274–77, 278–79,
  674
  automobiles and, 908
  right, driving on, 249 n.
  turnpikes, 274–76
Roanoke colony, 24, 25, 27–28, 50
Robinson, John, 75
Robinson, Solon, 246, 449, 458
Rochambeau, Comte de, 223, 224
Rochester, N.Y., 644
Rockefeller, John D., 540, 596, 654, 658,
  672, 699, 787, 800
Rockefeller, William, 442
Rockefeller Institute for Medical Re-
  search, 909–10
Rocking chair, 305
Roebling, John A., 860
Rogers, John, 625–28
Rogers, Moses, 302
Rolfe, John, 35, 60
Roller skating, 815, *816*
Rollo series (Abbott), 552, *553*
Rölvaag, Ole Edvart, 696
Romanticism, 409–11, 415–16
Rome, N.Y., 285
Roofs, thatch, 155–56
Roosevelt, Theodore, 531, 612, 688, 718,
  721, 812, 813–14, 853, 854, 870, 872,
  878
Root, James Wellborn, 768
Ross, John, 269–70
Ross, Ronald, 909
Rothschild, Salomon de, 427–28, 535, 705
Row houses, 425–26
Rowdyism, 215–16, 533
Rowing, 468, 658
Royal Palm Hotel, Miami, Fla., 789
Royal Poinciana Hotel, Palm Beach, Fla.,
  788, 790, 793
Royalists, 110
Royall, Anne, 742
Roycrofter movement, 784
Rubáiyát of Omar Khayyám, The (Fitz-
  Gerald), 879–80
Rugby, 658, 746
Ruggles of Red Gap (Wilson), 222
Rugs and carpets, 139
Rum, 94, 143
Rumsey, James, 304
Running water, 162
Runyon, Damon, 689
Rural Studies (Mitchell), 420
Rush, Benjamin, 143, 194, 313, 315, 325,
  333, 335, 337, 393, 483, 504
Ruskin, John, 615, 619
Russell, Bertrand, 725
Russell, Charles Edward, 663, 721
Russell, Charles M., 690
Russell, Howard Hyde, 917
Russell, Lillian, 810
Russell Sage Foundation, 818

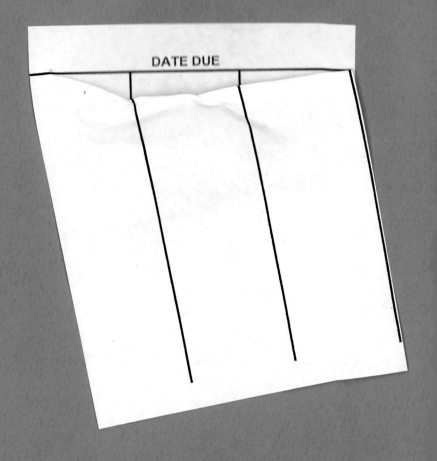

DATE DUE